Dedicated to
Peter Lemesurier
1936 – 2016

Authors' Foreword

Welcome to the second volume of Outremer. In volume 1 a lot of information was included to set the stage and foundations as well as establish some of the main characters. Some of it was difficult to absorb as there was so much being imparted from a wide range of sources, but within this volume, I believe you will find the information a lot easier to digest. Several major new characters enter into the story as revelations about mankind's past are detailed, as well as more esoteric teachings.

The story starts to become far more adult as Alisha and Pauls lives move forwards, but also more other worldly as the magic of an enchanted history starts to unfold through the revelations of mysterious individuals they encounter...but also the brutal consequences and reality of others determined to eradicate both of their family lines. As they both become politically aware, they have to question everything and try to judge who is genuine and who plots against them. But they must also face up to the path they have chosen and the great responsibility that falls upon their shoulders alone...one that still echoes across the pages of history to our times now.

Outremer II

'Revelation Cometh'

D N Carter

Clink
Street

London | New York

Published by Clink Street Publishing 2018

ISBN: 978-1-912262-11-3 paperback
978-1-912262-13-7 hardback
978-1-912262-12-0 ebook

Acknowledgements

Within Outremer I have had cause to refer to factual research for both religious and historical accuracy, as well as many documents, abstracts and books on a wide range of subjects, and where I have used that information, I have inserted bibliographic references, all of which are listed at the rear of this volume. However I wanted to make special mention of a few authors and their books who years of dedicated and diligent research made my work a lot easier to cross reference and check the validity of what I have written. They include John Michell for his book 'The New View over Atlatis' with all its esoteric and mathematical revelations connected to Gematria, ancient sacred sites across our world, cathedrals to so-called ley lines. 'The Old straight track' by Alfred Watkins, which many claim spawned countless other books and research into so-called ley lines and paths of the Dragon. A very insightful and forward thinking author ahead of his time when published. To Alan Alford and his interpretation and presentation of ancient Sumerian and Babylonian creation myths within his book, 'Gods of the New Millennium'.

I cannot express enough my gratitude to the works by Dr Helen Nicholson and Dr David Nicolle and their many books on the Crusades, from Castles to Saracens to the Knights Templar as well as the most comprehensive and detailed accounts of life and the main characters who shaped the Middle East during the Middle Ages. Their work was an invaluable asset for time lines, people, the political situation and equipment used by all sides in the region...especially their joint publication 'Gods Warriors' published by Osprey Ltd.

And finally to Peter Lemesurier. A true guiding light for many with several highly acclaimed and international bestselling books on Pyramids and world acknowledged authority on Nostradamus. Your work was, and remains so, as we once laughed when I said it and you lectured me on using three words that mean the same, 'incalculable, immeasurable, and invaluable'.

Characters

Philip Plantavalu

Stewart Plantavalu

Thomas

Percival

Count Raymond III

Countess Eschiva

Balian d'Iblin, Lord of Rama (Ramlah)

Master Roger des Moulins

Umar Turansha

Ashashin Grand Master
Rashid al-din Sinan

Ishmael the Tall

Muzaffar al Din Gokbori
(Known as the Blue Wolf)

Contents

Acknowledgements   v
Characters   vii

PART V   1

Chapter 25: Cathars   3
Chapter 26: Thomas   31
Chapter 27: Honesty and Good Deceit!   59
Chapter 28: Rashid and the Ashashin   97
Chapter 29: Crac de l'Ospital   126
Chapter 30: Sacrament of Tears   157

PART VI   183

Chapter 31: Where Shadows Cannot Reach   185
Chapter 32: Jerusalem. The Gateway   212
Chapter 33: My Dark Rose   241
Chapter 34: Messengers of the Light   274
Chapter 35: Guardians of the Gateways   293
Chapter 36: Pistis Sophia and the Book of John   315

Part VII   339

Chapter 37: Turansha   341
Chapter 38: Ishmael – The fight!   365
Chapter 39: Between Worlds   383
Chapter 40: A Journey of Study   406
Chapter 41: Alexandria & the Emerald Tablet   433
Chapter 42: Kratos, Staffs & Bees   456

PART VIII   499

Chapter 43: Dark Sun & the Celtic Cross   501
Chapter 44: Emissaries and Final Farewells   531
Chapter 45: Twin Churches, Meditation and the Atbash Cipher   561
Chapter 46: The Holy Grail & The Keepers of the Faith   581
Chapter 47: Darkest of Ages & the Solace of Stewart & Taqi   629
Chapter 48: The Halls of Amenti   649

PART IX

Chapter 49: Cairo. The Path is Followed Again
Chapter 50: A Queen, Camelot & a Land of Dolmens
Chapter 51: Not all you Fight are your Enemy
Chapter 52: Living Legends
Chapter 53: Queen of Kings & the Chains that Bind Us
Chapter 54: Baptism of Fire and Water

PART X

Chapter 55: The Hearts Code
Chapter 56: Home of the Brotherhood
Chapter 57: Prophecy & the Seeds of a Promise
Chapter 58: Beyond the Veil, Revelation Cometh
Chapter 59: Altar of Stone.
Chapter 60: Once and Future King – Arthur

PART XI

Chapter 61: A Darkness Falls
Chapter 62: Hymn of the Risen
Chapter 63: Quiet before the Storm
Chapter 64: Storm Fall
Chapter 65: The Deepest Wound.
Chapter 66: Betrayed & Broken – A Hearts Memory

PART XII

Chapter 67: Wilderness of the Soul
Chapter 68: Vows, Oaths and the Nine
Chapter 69: Fists of Iron & Godspeed
Chapter 70: Crossing Destiny
Chapter 71: Tears of War
Chapter 72: End to All That Was

PART XIII

Chapter 73: Annihilation of the Soul.
Chapter 74: Fortress of Solitude.
Chapter 75: Cresson – Clash of the Wolves
Chapter 76: The Candle is Lit
Chapter 77: The Sacredness of Tears
Chapter 78: Hattin – Lost unto Dust

PART XIV

Chapter 79: The Deepest Wound Unseen that Does Not Heal.
Chapter 80: Jerusalem – The Candle Burns Down
Chapter 81: Walls of Men and Shields
Chapter 82: Everything to Live For, All to Die For
Chapter 83: The Cave of Despair
Chapter 84: The Final Hour

PART XV

Chapter 85: The Long Shadow of Rome
Chapter 86: The Impossible
Chapter 87: An End, but the Voice Within Remains
Epilogue:

Appendix:

Bibliography:
Index:
List of illustrations:

"Revelation Cometh'"

PART V

Chapter 25
Cathars

Paul and Theodoric walked out into the castle's main courtyard to be greeted by several Frankish Knights and several Templar sergeants manhandling a caravan twice the size of Paul's, with four large wheels up against the side of the main Keep wall. Despite the late hour, the courtyard was still a frenzy of activity. Paul breathed in the salty sea air and looked up to see many stars sparkling brightly, the nearly full moon directly above him. He looked ahead as he heard women laughing. To his front, he saw Princess Stephanie and Sister Lucy along with two of her maids walking towards the large caravan, Brother Teric leading them.

"Looks like you will have your privacy back tonight now her new caravan has arrived," Theodoric said quietly, patted him on his arm and walked away giving a slight backhand wave. "See you in the morning."

Paul's ears began to ring with a high pitched whine and he sensed a humming vibration. His first thought was that another earthquake was about to happen. Quickly he went to move but found he could not. He felt frozen. His heart began to race as everything turned to silence. His vision began to blur. 'What is happening?' he asked himself, alarmed. He could sense his sword as if it was pulsing. Suddenly he was bathed in a brilliant white light that cut out all his vision. As he blinked and tried to see properly, he started to see what looked like the huge stone lintels from his dreams. Images of people slowly walking through the stones, formed like a doorway, and vanishing. A tall white haired man stood next to the stones and turned his gaze to look at him. Images of the Kizkalesi castle merged at times with the stones like an overlay. Paul instinctively knew he was seeing the same place but at a different time.

"Remember me?" the white haired man said without moving his lips.

Paul fought to move but was completely paralysed. Was he having some kind of seizure? Had he eaten something bad that Balian had given him? Was Alisha okay? As soon as he thought that, he saw her step into view. She was wearing the same cream and white dress as he had seen the woman wear in his dreams. Her dark hair blew back across her shoulders as she looked at him. She smiled and slightly raised her eyebrows to acknowledge him. He tried to call her name but nothing came out. She looked at the white haired man, who gestured she should walk through the stone gateway. She smiled once more at Paul and slowly turned her back on him and walked through. The white haired man then waved, smiled and followed her and vanished. Suddenly and without warning, a massive roar filled Paul's head as a black wall of water and debris hit the stones obliterating them instantly.

Paul recoiled in panic, drew a deep breath, his eyes wide as the bright white light just vanished instantly leaving him standing alone on tip toes, rigid. He gasped

3

for breath then coughed out as he tried to stand up properly, feeling dizzy. As the vision in his eyes returned, the courtyard was silent apart from someone snoring loudly off in the distance. A lone Templar stood watch at the open entrance to the castle. The small campfires that had been burning when he came out were now just smouldering embers. Adrastos snorted nearby drawing his attention. Paul looked around, confused. He looked up. The moon was now almost setting behind the castle wall. He looked at his hands, and then felt for his sword. It was still there. 'Ali' he thought, alarmed, and began to walk as fast as he could towards his caravan. His feet feeling heavy.

Inside the caravan, he found Alisha safely tucked up in the main bunk bed asleep with Arri wrapped up in swaddling next to her. The moon shone as if sitting on the castle wall, directly into the caravan. He sighed heavily with relief but still confused. He shook his head. He had not drunk anything but water. If he had passed out or fallen asleep, surely someone would have woken him or checked he was okay. His mind raced as he fought to remain rational. He had seen for real, or so it seemed, what he had so often dreamt of. However, this time, the woman was without any doubt Alisha. He looked at her as she slept. He slumped back exhausted onto the wide bench seat, rested his head back and closed his eyes. Quickly he opened them again fearful of another experience...but eventually tiredness enveloped him completely.

Port of La Rochelle, France, Melissae Inn, spring 1191

"Oh my...that is horrible that people would want to kill Alisha. 'Tis an awful thing," Ayleth remarked.

"Believe me, you try explaining that to some people, from both sides, Christian and Muslim alike, and you are banging your head against a wall...trust me, I have tried. And when you do try to correct them or show them the error of their ways...well," the Templar explained.

"That is sadly true. An old saying is well suited to many in Outremer. 'Do not correct a fool, for he will hate you. Correct a wise man and he will appreciate you.' Sadly too many of the wise ones get themselves killed too early," the old man explained.

"What I do not understand is all this need for symbols...you mentioned spirals. I have seen them carved upon stone in almost every land I have been in. How does just a symbol evoke so much feeling in a person?" the Hospitaller asked.

"Perhaps you should ask your brother that for he should know of a few," the old man answered.

"Hey...we only got taught the basic meanings behind some of our symbols. Only those of higher rank truly learnt the rest. We just accepted it that we would in time understand as we progressed within the order," the Templar replied.

"Then let me quickly explain the importance of symbolism...for nearly all of human history the world was once an enchanted place. And myths emerged as an attempt to explain unknowable mysteries. But as material and rationalist ideas gain in value and importance, spiritual values decline in direct proportion. Once uprooted from the world of symbols, the art that created them is lost and separated from its links with myth and sacramental vision.

The kind of sacramental vision I am referring to is not that of routine church-going or religious dogma as such, but a mode of perception that converges on the power of the divine. 'Tis 'the Old Gnosis', a visionary style of knowledge as distinct from the theological or a factual one, that is able to see the divine in the human, the infinite in the finite, the spiritual in the material. This sacramental vision, which underlies our perception of the Absolute, can never be completely uprooted...despite the dogged persistence of kings and church to try and do so who attempt to debase it all as something evil and pagan. But however much we ignore, camouflage, or degrade that art's sacred elements, rendered as simple and beautiful symbols, they still survive in the unconscious. 'Tis why so many tattoo themselves without really grasping what it is they do...Indeed, the recalling and setting up of sacred signs is even more urgent a task for an artist in times estranged from symbol and sacrament. 'Tis what Paul's father, Firgany and Theodoric tried to do where ever they went." He paused. "But know this also, that when the usefulness of a myth or legend has exhausted itself, it dies...and then any artificial means to keep it alive only serves to make those very actions and symbols of that myth, counterproductive. It becomes outdated with the present times, so has to be completely changed and written anew." He sighed.

"Ah...just like the new Grail myths...yes?" Simon stated.

1 – 16

"Indeed, Simon. See, you learn fast. So imagine our great Church's' myths that have served the papacy well these past eleven hundred years...what would we have but for the virgin birth, the Resurrection of the body and the Ascension? They are supposedly unarguable dogma to all Christians...so imagine the problems faced when trying to demystify the spiritual mysteries when maintenance of those very same myths becomes counterproductive and destructive as is happening now...and that will steadily worsen unless measures are taken now."

"I have heard that the same principle applies to poems and allegorical sayings...is this true? And what of magic with all its many symbols and practices?" Gabirol asked.

"I explained what magic stands for and where the root word for magic comes from... from the Magi as detailed in the Bible...but magic is essentially the higher understanding of nature herself. 'Tis that simple," the old man answered.

"And poems and allegorical sayings?" Gabirol asked again.

"Aye...absolutely yes, 'tis true. Most of you here would have heard of so many without even realising it. Simple statements, words or poems that touch you deeply without you noticing. Even a statement like 'Jesus acts as the key to heaven, as does Mohammed, but faith unlocks the door' will sit within your mind and soul, but symbols, they are images and our minds love images. 'Tis why it is easier to remember a sigil, motif or coat of arms than it is to recognise a string of words and letters," the old man answered.

"So this Kizkalesi castle location...it was once a part of an ancient sacred site...that Paul knew of or had once been before...in a previous time, yes. Have I understood that correct?" the wealthy tailor asked. "And is why he saw it as before...in the light."

"Yes. That is why he collapsed as they approached the place, as the last time, if we are to believe such things; the area had a traumatic effect upon him and his very soul. To feel it again in this lifetime was overwhelming. 'Tis why some people can sense past events held within the very fabric of a place, especially in the land and stone around them. It is as if the land records and remembers events," the old man recounted as he caught the eye of the Templar looking at him intently.

"Old man...I feel wrong calling you that...but as you will not tell us your name yet, I am afraid I have to. I am eager to learn all that you tell us. 'Tis now Saturday and the morrow is Easter Sunday. 'Tis good that Stephan has closed this place to afford us your hospitality... but I am fearful that this tale will take more than this day to complete and we shall miss its conclusion," the Templar remarked.

"My friend...I know that you and your Order prepare to depart for Sicily to join with King Richard the First...but I assure you, we have time. He will not be leaving Sicily just yet," the old man replied. "Besides, after I have concluded my tale...then you must open the letter I gave you earlier."

Miriam looked at the Templar, placed her hands upon his right forearm, and gently squeezed. He feigned a smile but was clearly saddened.

"Brother...we plan to follow an English King...one who cannot even speak English...and our French King plays second fiddle to him...what say you and I seriously reconsider our positions?" the Hospitaller asked as all looked at them.

"We took vows, my brother," the Templar replied, surprise written across his face.

"Hey...you already broke them so break some more," Simon interjected loudly.

Miriam bowed her head embarrassed as the Templar looked at him puzzled, not angered, which the old man was quick to see. He smiled.

The Genoese sailor sat up straight and part raised his hand to get their attention.

"Well, I and our ship are due to leave to join King Richard on the Monday high tide. I have no choice but to go. But I hear this King Richard makes wise plans for all of our ships to cope well with all the natural challenges of the sea as we sail east. Storms, fog, currents, rocks and other dangers. 'Tis rare for a landlubber to be a good leader upon the seas too. With a massive fleet like the one Richard is gathering, ships being separated from the main group could cause delays or worse. We hear that he is having set upon his ship a great candle in a lantern that will be lit at night and will burn all through the night to show others the way. We were told that the fleet would not leave Sicily until the tenth of April at the earliest. There are to be some fifty-two ships in all...so, my Templar friend, we have until at least Sunday eve to hear the end of this tale," he explained.

"What...King Richard cannot speak English?" Simon asked, puzzled.

"No he cannot. He was born in Oxford but came to France almost immediately. 'Tis why Philip often gets concerned that he will attempt to take his crown of France. Egos...," the old man answered and shook his head.

"So did Paul ever discover how he lost what appears to have been several hours after he left Theodoric that evening?" Simon asked.

"In truth...yes, but not for many years," the old man answered.

"And....you will explain later...?" Simon smirked as the old man simply nodded.

"So did they leave for Tarsus as Teric...was it Teric? Yes it was...that he said they had to go to and wait?" the farrier asked.

"They did indeed. All the women, especially Alisha and Princess Stephanie, looked forward to being able to take a proper bath once they arrived. But Tarsus would also be the place where Paul encountered for the first time what most people call the Cathars. His father and Niccolas had spoken of them many times but he had yet to actually meet one. It was fifty-two miles from Kizkalesi to Tarsus and the first day travelling had been uneventful and the evening only served to demonstrate that the new caravan Princess Stephanie had acquired already had several guests infesting it. She was not happy...but Brother Matthew sorted her a spacious and well provisioned tent for the night as she refused to sleep in it," the old man explained.

"I have heard much of Tarsus but never been. I was aware that many Cathars reside there as they make a good living from the many passing pilgrims. Is that correct?" Gabirol asked.

"'Tis true indeed. It also acts as a staging post for many of the Orders and knights heading to and from Outremer...especially the mercenaries under the employ of the Hospitallers," the old man explained.

"Mercenaries! How are they employed by the Hospitallers?" Simon asked immediately and looked at the Hospitaller. The old man looked at the Hospitaller.

"'Tis well known that mercenaries play an important role within the Holy Land. The Hospitallers were amongst the first to employ knights to protect the pilgrim routes. They were and are in the main of European origin...but some come from the Orient and some are even Muslims themselves. It is not uncommon either for Muslims to hire and pay Frankish knights to protect their interests in the region. Conflict is a profitable business, my friends..." the Hospitaller explained.

"This shocks you?" the old man asked Simon, seeing the look of horror on his face.

"Well yes...actually it does," he replied and folded his arms, shaking his head.

"Let me explain a few things about Tarsus for you then." The old man coughed and cleared his throat. "This may sound like a bit of a history lesson, but it may help you understand the place better. You see Tarsus is the capital of Cilicia, situated on the banks of the River Cydnus and commands the roads from the Mediterranean Sea to Central Anatolia through the Cilician Gate. It is why so many pilgrims and knights pass through it. Hittite texts from the fifteenth century BC referred to it as 'Tarša'. One of the city's main gates is the stunning and beautifully made so-called 'Gate of Cleopatra'. According to local tradition, this was the site of Marc Antony's meeting with Cleopatra in 41 BC. It is made from the finest cut stone and has the old Roman road still running through it. Theodoric pointed this out as they passed through it. In 333 BC Alexander the Great occupied the city, and stayed there while recuperating from an illness, but after the death of the Macedonian conqueror, Tarsus became part of the Seleucid Empire under the new name of Antioch on the Cydnus. Becoming Hellenised, Tarsus began to claim it had been founded by Perseus. In 171 BC the city unsuccessfully revolted because King Antiochus IV Epiphanes had given it as a present to his concubine, Antiochis. When the Seleucids went down in a series of dynastic conflicts, Tarsus was the capital of the northern part of the empire, until the Roman general Pompey the Great added Cilicia to the Roman Empire in 66 BC when the city got its old name back again, although after the death of Julius Caesar it was briefly called Juliopolis. It played a role in the civil wars and at one stage all inhabitants were awarded Roman citizenship. This was the age of Tarsus's greatest prosperity, and it was often called the greatest of all towns in Cilicia. It still has beautifully paved Roman streets with an unusual drainage system. Some of you may have heard of Apollonius. He found the atmosphere of the city harsh and strange and not conducive to the philosophic life, 'for nowhere are men more addicted than here to luxury; jesters and full of insolence are they all; and they attend more to their fine linen than the Athenians did to wisdom; and a stream called the Cydnus runs through their city, along the banks of which they sit like so many water-fowl', is how he described the place. During the Empire, the city was an important centre of the cults of Mithras and the emperor, but it also appears to have been open to cult reformers like Apollonius of Tyana himself. But Tarsus's most famous son was of course...the apostle Paul, a Pharisaic Jew who converted to Christianity and spread the Gospel to the pagans. The well that is nowadays shown to Pilgrims as 'Paul's Well' is of course fake, I can assure you of that," the old man smiled. "There is still a great Byzantine bridge that spans the river commissioned by the Byzantine

Emperor Justinian. They even re-directed the actual river. The town was briefly captured by Muslim forces, and, for that reason, there are still many Muslims who live and work there."

"And you say Cathars mainly nowadays?" Simon asked.

"Yes...many Cathars, though that is not a name they would like to hear you call them."

"Why...is that not their name? For I have heard them called that in London even," Ayleth stated.

"'Tis but a slang word for them only. And Paul was eager to meet them. That is why as soon as they arrived, whilst the Templars and Hospitallers set up their tents next to the main Templar chapter building within the town, next to its stabling and training field, he was off with Taqi, Theodoric and Tenno to one of the many Cathar pilgrim hostels...they are like a huge inn where pilgrims could rest, eat, bathe and generally secure items required for their journeys," the old man explained. [27]

Boni Homines Inn, city of Tarsus, Cilician Armenia, 1179

Paul listened as Theodoric and Taqi were discussing a myth about the 'Seven Sleepers of Ephesus' as they all walked downhill slowly toward an inn Brother Teric had recommended. He vaguely recalled that Niccolas had mentioned the 'Seven Sleepers' before but he could not recall exactly. What he could remember was that the legend had been attributed to several locations including Jordan, Tarsus itself, Ephesus, even Glastonbury in Britain and to places in northern Europe.

"Listen Taqi...the 'Seven Sleepers' are one and the same as your Qur'an details. In Arabic they are known as 'Ashab al Kahf', which simply means 'companions of the cave'. But here in this region the tale specifically refers to a group of Christian youths who hid inside a cave outside the city of Ephesus, supposedly around AD 250, to escape persecution of Christians during the reign of the Roman emperor Decius. Another version is that Decius ordered them imprisoned in a closed cave to die there as punishment for being Christians. Having fallen asleep inside the cave, they supposedly awoke approximately one hundred and eighty years later during the reign of Theodosius I, after which they were reportedly seen by the people of the now-Christian city before dying. The earliest version of this story comes from the Syrian bishop Jacob of Sarug around AD 450–521, which is itself derived from an earlier Greek source, now lost. An outline of this tale appears in Gregory of Tours and in Paul the Deacon's *History of the Lombards*. The best known Western version of the story appears in Jacobus da Varagine's *The Golden Legend*. The Roman Martyrology mentions the Seven Sleepers of Ephesus under the date of 27 July, as follows: 'Commemoration of the seven Holy Sleepers of Ephesus, who, it is recounted, after undergoing martyrdom, rest in peace, awaiting the day of resurrection'. The Byzantine calendar commemorates them with feasts on the 4th August and 22nd October. But you are correct, young Taqi, when you say that the story has its highest prominence in the Muslim world; it is told in the Qur'an (Surah 18, verse 9-26). The Qur'anic rendering of this story doesn't state exactly the number of sleepers (Surah 18, verse 22). Unlike the Christian story, the Islamic version includes mention of a dog who accompanied the youths into the cave, and was also asleep, but when people passed by the cave it looked as if the dog was just keeping watch at the entrance, making them afraid of seeing what is in there once they saw the dog. In Islam, these youths are referred to as 'The People of the Cave'. Some of our more esoteric friends connect the dog as symbolic of the ancient Egyptian dog headed god Anubis.

"If my memory serves me right, Niccolas said that the story alleged that after hundreds of years, as you said but apparently during the reign of Theodosius II (AD 408–450), the landowner decided to open up the sealed mouth of the cave, thinking to use it as a cattle pen. He opened it and found the sleepers inside. They awoke, imagining that they had slept but one day, and sent one of their number to Ephesus to buy food, with instructions to be careful lest the pagans recognise and seize him. Upon arriving in the city, this person was astounded to find buildings with crosses attached; the townspeople for their part were astounded to find a man trying to spend old coins from the reign of Decius. The bishop was summoned to interview the sleepers; they told him their miracle story, and died a short while later but praising God," Paul explained as Tenno listened intently.

"Look, this legend of 'Seven Sleepers' is recounted in many manuscripts from across the known world, both Christian and Muslim, and all with considerable variations to the actual numbers and names. What appears to be the important aspect here, is that they fell asleep, for what in their minds seemed like one night, but in fact was many years. So many other legends detail similar aspects of a person falling asleep and awaking after many years has passed. That is the true mystery here," Theodoric explained.

Paul thought upon Theodoric's last comments as his mind ran over the events of when he fell asleep in the caravan for what only seemed like a moment to him, only to wake a day later in Princess Stephanie's caravan. That he could put down to exhaustion...but what of the night when he left the Keep, saw what he believed was an image of a time from antiquity, only to then see the moon had moved considerably in just a few minutes, the camp fires burnt out almost and many hours having actually elapsed. He shook his head, bemused.

"Even in the farthest boundaries of Germany toward the west-north-west, on the shore of the ocean itself, there is supposedly a cave under a projecting rock, where for an unknown time seven men reposed wrapped in a long sleep. Their dress identified them as Romans, according to chroniclers and none of the local barbarians dared to touch them. During the last Crusade, bones from the sepulchres near Ephesus supposedly identified as relics of the Seven Sleepers, were transported to Marseille, France in a large stone coffin, which remained a trophy of the Abbey of Saint Victor, Marseille. The Seven Sleepers were included in the *Golden Legend* compilation, presently one of the most popular books of our time no less, which fixes a precise date for their resurrection, AD 378, in the reign of Theodosius," Theodoric continued to explain as the group turned down a wide corbelled street towards several column fronted buildings surrounded by a bustle of people, knights and many pilgrims.

"My father once told me that there is a greater mystery that can be opened by fully understanding the values and numbers within the Qur'anic version. He said if I studied the verse 18:22 I would have part of a key to unlocking the location of a great hidden mystery as set down by Allah himself. He said the very fact that it highlights a dog in the story is very significant and that it represents a connection the Dog Star, Canis Major...Sirius, I think," Taqi recounted as they made their way further down towards the main area where several hospices and inns were now clearly sign posted.

"Yes...I am aware of that passage and others. According to Muslim scholars, God revealed those verses because the people of Mecca challenged the Prophet Muhammad with questions that were passed on to them from the Jews of Medina in an effort to test his authenticity. They asked him about young men who disappeared in the past, about a man who travelled the earth from east to west, Zulqurnain, and about the soul. The story parallels the Christian version, recounting the story of a group of young believers who resisted the pressure from their people to worship others beside God, and took refuge in a cave, following which they fell asleep for a long time. When they woke up they thought that they had slept for only a day or so, and they sent one of them back to the city to buy food. His use of old silver coins revealed the presence of these youths to the town. Soon after their discovery, the People of the Cave, as the Qur'an calls them, yes, died and the people of their town built a place of worship at the site of their burial, the cave! The Qur'an does not give their exact number. It mentions that some people would say that they were three, others would say five and some would say seven, in addition to one dog, and that they slept for 300 years, plus 9, which could mean 300 solar years or 309 lunar years, 300 solar years are equal to 309 lunar years. The Qur'an emphasised that their number and the length of their stay is known only to God and a few people, and that these issues are not the important part of the story, but rather the lessons that can be learned from it," Theodoric explained.

"We have a similar myth...as does China," Tenno suddenly chipped in.

"Really?" Theodoric asked and waited for Tenno to say more, but he did not, so continued. "Well Muslims firmly believe in the story as it is mentioned in the Qur'an; however, some aspects of the story are not covered in its account, including the exact location of the cave. Some allege that it is in Ephesus, Turkey; others cite a place near Amman, Jordan. Uyghur Muslims even suggest Tuyukhojam, Turpan is the location of the cave, because they believe that place matches the Qur'an's description. The exact dates of their alleged sleep are also not given in the Qur'an; some allege that they entered the cave at the time of Decius, AD 250, and they woke up at the time of Theodosius I (378–395) or Theodosius II (408–450), as you said, Paul...but neither of these dates can be reconciled with the Qur'an's account of sleeping 300 or 309 years. Some Islamic scholars, assert that the 300 or 309 years mentioned in the Qur'an refers to periods of time alleged by those telling the tale, rather than a definitive statement by Allah as to how long they were actually there or this difference can be of solar and lunar years. But another interpretation is based on the earlier legend of Joseph of Arimathea having gone to Glastonbury, and the cave has been identified as the Chalice Well," he explained further then stopped to look up at the sign of the large stone fronted inn before him. [28]

"Shall we eat here?" Taqi asked as he looked at several major meals being served to some knights sat around a nearby wooden table sheltered beneath a large open canopy that hung out from the main wall shielding them from the sun.

"Sister Lucy will not be impressed if we eat here without informing her," Paul remarked, looking at Theodoric.

"You may be correct. I do not wish to wear a meal upon my head this eve. Perhaps we can just share a drink and a little bite now," Theodoric replied as he bent low to read the badly written menu board.

Paul sat himself down upon a bench at a table set end on next to the knights table, all of whom were clearly filthy and covered in dust and grime from several days of hard travelling. One of the knights looked at Paul briefly. With long blonde hair and matching beard, his blue eyes looked tired yet he smiled, acknowledging him. He looked up at Tenno as he stepped closer and studied him for a few moments. He nodded at Tenno and carried on eating his meal. Theodoric vanished inside to order as Taqi sat opposite Paul, looking at the dirty knights next to him quizically. Theodoric soon reappeared with a large grin carrying a tray and four drinks. He placed it down hard and ushered Taqi to move along so he could sit nearest the table with the knights on.

"Fear not...'tis not beer. Well mine is but yours are all girly drinks," Theodoric joked as he handed them out.

The blonde knight stopped eating and looked at Theodoric quizzically.

"Were you a Templar?" the knight asked politely.

"Me...No, not I. I am assuming you think me such because of this habit I wear... yes?" Theodoric replied and pulled the patch that once had a badge on.

"Partly...but you have the manner of a man who has seen much," the knight remarked and smiled and nodded. Tenno looked across, concerned.

"Oh...alas I have seen much and enough indeed that is true...as you clearly have. Tell me...are you on your way or, as is more likely, returning home?" Theodoric asked, which made the other knights look his way.

"Homeward bound. Been fourteen years at best...so a somewhat overdue return," the blonde knight answered and then looked at Paul. "I see you are a mixed bunch of travelling companions. Do you travel alone or escorted?"

"Yes, you could say that. We are heading for Alexandria...the long way," Theodoric replied and smiled as the other knights listened.

"You are certainly a long way off that place. A great city though and well worth the effort," one of the other knights interjected, smiling as he leaned forwards into view.

"You have been there?" Paul asked.

"Yes. We all served there for four years," the knight answered.

Paul frowned puzzled and leaned over to look back at all the other knights sat at the table.

"How did you serve there...'tis under Muslim rule is it not...or do we have a force there we know not of?" Paul asked.

"My friend...I fear you have much to learn. I would advise you learn it fast," the blonde knight smiled and winked at Theodoric.

"Paul...these men are not Affiliated nor Confrere Knights. They serve both Christian and Muslim commanders alike," Theodoric said quietly.

"He speaks the truth. We protect pilgrim routes, towns and wherever else we are required...to whomever pays us." The blonde knight smiled again turning his gaze to Paul.

"You mean you are hired hands to the highest bidder?" Paul shot back, surprised.

"Paul...'tis not that basic a principle," Theodoric started to explain before the blonde knight waved his hand.

"Yes it is that basic...worry not yourself, friend, we are not offended he does not understand. Young man...we have served both good and bad, from all religious persuasions and all sides. At least we got to choose which masters to serve. As free men!" the blonde knight explained and winked again at Theodoric.

"I did not mean to sound rude or appear judgemental," Paul remarked.

Tenno sat up straighter as Taqi looked at the knights, bemused and fascinated.

"You are not sounding rude, young man...trust me on that score. You will see and learn much that will surprise and shock you where you are all going. We may appear brash and loud, and some would say we are but a scourge...just another bunch of mercenaries returning to the West, but we have served well our masters, and, yes, as said, that includes Muslim commanders. We know of their Islamic methods and we respect them accordingly. We would all do well to learn from them...before they outwit us all," the knight explained and paused. Paul was astonished to learn these facts and that they had actually served Muslims directly as soldiers. "And I would wager it is good fortune you have a man like him with you...is he perhaps the new legendary Bull's Head Slayer we hear so much of on this trip?" the blonde knight asked and nodded toward Tenno. All looked at Tenno as he scowled indignantly.

"No...We can certainly answer that one straight away," Theodoric replied and tried not to give anything away. Taqi chuckled but soon dropped the smile when Theodoric glanced at him seriously.

"Well your friend certainly looks big and strong enough to have dealt with him," the blonde knight explained, looking at Tenno.

"You knew of this Bull's Head bandit then?" Paul asked.

"Sadly...yes we do. Correctly...did."

"How so?" Tenno asked bluntly.

"He was one of us for years," the drunken knight shouted out followed by a grunt as the knight nearest to him kicked him hard to be silent.

Theodoric and Tenno both looked at the blonde knight suspiciously.

"Fear not...he chose a different path to us. He was truly a great knight...with much honour," the blonde knight remarked then hesitated as he looked at his drink clasped in his dirty hands. "But he became mad. Mad with anger...mad with greed... mad with lust...and mad with power. Was a great shame...he was not the same man we once knew, for sure. Whoever ended his misery did him a great service. We just pray the good Lord in his heavens forgives him for what he did and remembers his far greater earlier deeds," the blonde knight explained and sighed as several of his knights nodded silently in agreement.

"Gentleman knights, I would bid you all a safe journey home then," Theodoric said and bowed slightly to them.

"Thank you and may your journey be as boring and as uneventful as possible," the blonde knight replied and raised his tankard of mead beer high. "There were seventy-two of us when we went to Outremer and Egypt. This is all that remains of us," he explained and looked at his fellow brother knights.

"And this is a big number of us to return still alive," the drunken knight at the far end shouted and laughed.

Theodoric nodded and pulled his own drink close and then looked at Tenno. After a brief awkward silence, the knights returned to their own conversation as Tenno studied them and the other people milling about, as ever watchful. Taqi smirked and indicated toward Tenno. Theodoric coughed and looked at Paul and Taqi and decided to change the subject.

"Hey, you do realise that this place is also reputed to contain the tombs of the prophet Daniel of the Bible, and the caliph Al-Ma'mun? Saint Paul was, as you should know, a resident of Tarsus. He was born and lived here as a Jew, but his name was Saul then and only became Paul after converting. You all know the story of Paul, well, the official version anyway, and how he made a number of missionary journeys after which he was arrested and beheaded by the emperor Nero of the Roman Empire in AD 64 or 67 on the 29th of June. There is also a mosque said to be the burial place of the Prophet Daniel," Theodoric explained then took a very large mouthful of mead beer.

⚔   3 – 7

"Niccolas told me that the mythical Pegasus is connected to Tarsus. Is that true?" Paul asked.

"Ah the ancient story of Pegasus, the winged horse!" Theodoric replied and smiled broadly as if a hundred images and stories had filled his head. "Because of Pegasus's faithful service to the god Zeus, he was honoured with a constellation. On the last day of his life, Zeus transformed him into a constellation, then a single feather fell to the earth upon this city. Tarsus is also but one of a number of cities that claim to be the burial place of Bilal ibn Rabah, the first muezzin, or caller to prayer, in Islam. This whole coast was part of a greater Cilicia and Armenia named after a Phoenician, though some argue he was an Assyrian prince that had settled here. As I just said, Tarsus was the hometown of the apostle Paul (Acts 9:11), a city of great importance (21:39) as a learning centre of the ancient world, alongside Alexandria and Athens. Notably, Jewish citizens of Tarsus were granted Roman citizenship. As a child, Paul was raised in Jerusalem and properly educated under the tutelage of Gamaliel, a member of the Sanhedrin. Paul's trade, tent making, fits well with this, a city which is well known for making a certain type of felt cloth from the wool of shaggy black goats. But then he became a tax collector... Legend says that St Paul often drank from a well said to have special curative properties, but I can tell you now, 'tis but a pilgrim gimmick," Theodoric explained as he looked into his tankard.

The blonde knight, having heard Theodoric's comments, leaned across and tapped his forearm.

"Sorry to intrude again...but please be careful how loud you speak, friend. This inn is run by a Cathar and there are many of them in this part of Tarsus. I fear they would not be best pleased to hear of what you speak," he whispered and sat back up.

"Thank you...and I am indeed aware of their strong presence here. Though I know they hate being referred to as Cathars...," Theodoric replied as the drunken knight at the end of the table fell off the bench clearly more drunk.

"Ignore him...he is actually our moral advisor on all matters...," the blonde knight smiled.

"Huh...someone has needed to keep you heathens on the straight and narrow," the drunken knight blurted out as he stumbled back to his feet and sat down hard again on the bench. He looked at Theodoric and then Paul and waved his finger at them. "Let me tell you lot, for I have heard so many so-called scholars claim they know all about the past, what the Bible, the Qur'an and the Torah says...but 'tis a simple thing to understand and follow. Many of you scholar types need to take a history course along with Christian Anthropology. God works through the doings of man. The ancient fertility rites of ancient paganism involved cultic prostitution and human sacrifice...murder. Judaism replaced human sacrifice with sacred animal sacrifice, but when the Temple was destroyed, that ended also. Christ replaced all sacrifice once and for all with his own sacrifice by travelling to Jerusalem to take up his kingship, and so, died on the cross as the Romans would not allow another king. People of faith need to keep their history straight and not be confused by all the faithless mumbo jumbo. Jesus was sacrificed on the cross, and there were numerous witnesses to his resurrection at the time and down through the centuries, many more have experienced visions of the Lord. And he did so... so that no more ridiculous murders under the guise of religious sacrifice would ever again be required...That, my friends, is all you need to know," the drunk concluded, gulped down the last of his beer...belched loudly and then fell backwards and simply laid on his back motionless having passed out. His friends roared with laughter.

"Apologies for my friend's outburst. He drowns his sorrows and frustrations all too often in his drink, and he cannot ever reconcile the opinions and faith of Cathars," the blonde knight explained.

"Why, what is so different about Cathars?" Taqi asked, puzzled, as Paul nodded in agreement.

"Cathars.... they believe in a deity known as Rex Mundi, the king of the world. But in actual fact they believe in two gods, one good and one evil, who both ride the same horse, like Pegasus almost...," Theodoric started to explain.

"Sounds like the image of two knights upon a single horse the Templars use as a symbol," Paul remarked.

"'Tis not that far off the mark, Paul...Catharism...what can I tell you? I can tell you that the actual name comes from the Greek 'kæθərɪzəm', which in turn comes from the Greek καθαροί, katharoi...it means 'the pure ones'," Theodoric explained and quickly pulled out a small notepad of velum sheets and wrote out the words in Greek letters and showed Paul and Taqi. "In essence it is a Christian dualist movement that thrives and is growing in some areas of Southern Europe, particularly northern Italy and Southern France, and their numbers grow fast. Their beliefs vary considerably between communities because what they teach and preach is presently taught by ascetic priests who have set few guidelines...some argue they pose a direct threat and challenge to the Catholic Church. Some have even petitioned the Pope already, denouncing its practices and dismissing it outright as the Church of Satan," Theodoric explained.

"I see you are a learned man...perchance a true scholar no less?" the blonde knight remarked.

"Oh he is that for sure," Paul interjected quickly as Tenno frowned and shook his head.

"I try to be," Theodoric replied before continuing. "Believe it or not but Catharism had its roots in the Paulician movement in this region, mainly the Armenian areas and the Bogomils, who took influences from the Paulicians. Though the term Cathar has been used for a while now to identify their movement, they do not like the term themselves. In Cathar texts, the terms 'Good Men' or Bons Hommes or 'Good Christians' are the common terms of self-identification they prefer. The idea of two gods or principles, one being good the other evil, is central to their beliefs."

"The Yin and Yang then? Light and Dark, Good and Evil. This is a concept well known in China and my lands," Tenno interrupted.

Theodoric looked at him briefly then continued.

"The good god was the God of the New Testament and the creator of the spiritual realm, as opposed to the bad god, whom many Cathars identify as Satan, creator of the physical world of the Old Testament. All visible matter, including the human body, was created by Satan; it was therefore tainted with sin. This is the antithesis to the monotheistic Catholic Church, whose fundamental principle was that there was only one god, who created all things visible and invisible. Cathars think that human spirits are the genderless spirits of angels trapped within the physical creation of Satan, cursed to be reincarnated until the Cathar faithful achieve salvation through a ritual called the Consolamentum. They have many troubles ahead of them I fear! Cathar is a slang word for them so keep that word low if you must mention them," Theodoric outlined quietly, the blonde knight nodding in agreement.

"They hate sex too!" the drunken knight on the floor shouted out, but not moving.

"My friend is clearly drunk. You say you are going to Alexandria...perhaps whilst you are there, if ever you get the chance, you can try and learn all you can about the Caliphs who rule from Cairo...and especially the upcoming Saladin. He alone knows that the best way to win security in the region of Outremer for us would be to oust the Caliphs in Cairo. He understands that if we realise this, we could oust them all. And as for all the fund-raising taxes for the crusades, many of us now know this is simply systematic establishment fraud, for the Saracens are still there in peace and I think may sleep on undisturbed and brutality and destruction are still the only reality behind so-called chivalry," the blonde knight explained solemnly.

"I see you have clearly been in the region too long, my friend," Theodoric remarked.

"Yes...far too long. But mark my words...unless you un-seat the Caliphs in Cairo, we shall never win," the blonde knight sighed. "And Saladin is the key. All Arabs and Turks are mutually hostile towards each other, but they both hate the Kurds. But both grudgingly admit respect for Saladin despite being a Kurd himself. To Christian perceptions, Islam is still a new religion. You probably know that it was in the seventh century that the armies of Islam exploded in lightning conquest of the jihad, meaning holy war, after the death of Muhammad in AD 632 under the supreme command of Caliphs, the successors of Muhammad the prophet just like the Pope's 'commanders of the faithful'. The first Christian crusade was undoubtedly a military success recovering much of the former Holy Lands of Outremer. Numbers of men never before seen, some two hundred thousand, marched three thousand miles to war. Do you know these facts?" the knight asked, looking at Paul and Taqi in turn.

"They do," Theodoric answered for them as Tenno listened intently. Loud laughter went up from another table opposite as several Hospitallers joked with the innkeeper.

"Then you will know that 'jihad' originally meant 'striving' and denoted the effort to advance Islam in one's own life by striving for religious virtue; but it soon came to mean, even during Muhammad's life, striving by warfare to defend or to extend the territory of the faith in Arabic called Dar al-Islam. The battlefield zone or territory was known as Dar al-Harb. Pope Urban only initiated the first crusade as an excuse and camouflage to allow Bohemond to attack Byzantium and so redirect the energies of the military elite caste thus combining warfare with a sense of righteousness. Jerusalem had been Islamic since AD 638 when Caliph Omar received the surrender from the Christian patriarch of the city. 'Tis funny... or perhaps not, that St Helena, the Roman Emperor Constantine's mother, found the supposed true cross of Christ in Jerusalem in AD 327; what a joke...," the blonde knight trailed off and shook his head and paused for several moments. "Do you know that Muhammad was a business manager for a wealthy merchant's widow, Khadija, and when you meet your Muslim friends, just pronounce Qur'an as Qur'an properly for they will respect you more for that alone."

"We know that already," Taqi said and leant forward resting his elbows upon the table.

"Then perhaps you will also know that by the time of Muhammad's death the warring tribes of Arabia had been united into the 'Zone of Truth', a community of the faithful called Umma. Fatimid rulers claimed descent from Fatima, daughter of Muhammad of Egypt, of the Shiite branch of Islam. Shiites are viewed as heretics by Sunnite rulers in Baghdad. The sixth Fatimid Caliph, Hakim, called 'The Mad', abandoned tradition of tolerance and destroyed the Church of the Holy Sepulchre in Jerusalem and also announced himself the reincarnation of God. In AD 1021 he disappeared courtesy of the Ashashin," the blonde knight recounted. Taqi raising his eyebrows at Paul at the mention of the Ashashin. "Muhammad made a mystical ascent into heaven on the site of the rock of Solomon's temple and Muslims only venerate Jesus Christ and fully expect his second coming in the last days...but only to confirm that Islam is the only way. There were many Muslims who believed those end times were sometime between AD 1106 and 1107, the 500th year AH (Arabic History), when Jesus Christ would return, destroy the cross and call all peoples of the world to submit to Islam but it had still not happened then...and I suspect will still not happen in the future." The blonde knight sighed heavily. "Hate...It has caused a lot of problems in this world but has not resolved one yet."

Paul looked up as he saw Percival walking towards them alone. He waved as soon as he saw them all sitting at the table and began to run over to them.

Tenno looked up at a group of pilgrims walking by virtually all dressed the same with large wide brimmed hats, with scallop shells affixed to their chests and hats, and shook his head puzzled.

"I hear what you speak of...but as has been the case since the beginning of Christianity, all sides use accusations of denial of Christ, sodomy and idolatry...standard accusations against heretics for centuries, most recently against the Cathars, whom I strongly suggest will one day bear the brunt of the might of the Church against them. They will of course in turn accuse all their rivals of such crimes and accuse them of heresy in equal measure," the blonde knight explained and moved to sit at the end of his table and rested his arm upon the table next to Paul.

"How can you be so sure of that?" Paul asked.

"Simple," the blonde knight replied instantly and sat up straight. "You see, orthodox Christian belief and faith is deemed essential for the health of society and to ensure God's favour. Heresy is seen as a disease which must be eradicated before it overcomes the whole Christian body. Powerful political rivals could use, will use and do already use the charge of heresy with devastating effect against their opponents...we have seen this often, and within Islam, mark my words. That is why I fear that within a short period of time, most of the Cathars, especially those in Southern France, who received most of their Gnostic teachings from the Bogomils, which means 'beloved of God', will be persecuted as fiercely as Islam is now."

"At least Islam does not tear itself apart like Christians," Taqi commented.

"You think that so...then you have much to learn also," the blonde knight replied as Theodoric nodded in acknowledgement. "Sunni and Shiites will do more harm to their religion from within than any outside force ever will do!"

"But why...what makes these Cathars so different and such a threat then?" Paul asked puzzled as Taqi rubbed his hands through his hair pondering the knight's words carefully.

"Because at the heart of Cathar doctrine is the notion that true Christianity, as they preach only and received via a secret line of apostolic succession from St John, is a life lived, not simply a doctrine believed. For them the life of Jesus was a model the 'Good Christian' must strive to emulate, not a vicarious sacrifice to be blindly accepted on trust. The existence of the Cathars challenges the legitimacy of the Roman Church directly...and that will not be allowed to continue. The Cathars declare they are the true heirs of a tradition that was older than that held by the Church of Rome and, by implication, both less contaminated and near in spirit to the apostolic tradition. They claim to be the only persons who keep and cherish the Holy Spirit which Christ had bestowed upon His Church; and it looks as though this claim was at least partially justified...," the blonde knight explained further as Tenno just looked around at the various people coming and going.

"My master, I mean my tutor, taught me none of this," Percival interrupted.

"Not surprising," the blonde knight shrugged. "Like the earlier Bogomils and the followers of the Eastern Gnostic Prophet Mani, the Cathars believe in a cosmic battle between the principles of Light and Darkness on whose meetings and encounters everything in the Lord's universe is based. Darkness was for them dark matter, the unperfected, the transient. They identified all clerical and secular rulers, principally the Roman Church, as the personification of the Darkness. That is why they claim, with an elitist arrogance at times, that they merely follow a tradition more ancient than that of the Church herself and why they charge, not totally unfounded I must confess, but that is my view, that it is Rome who is the party guilty of 'heresy' through her falling out from the original purity which had characterised the Church of the Apostles." The blonde knight paused as he looked at his tankard for a few moments, his brother knights listening now to what he was saying.

"Paul, this man clearly knows his facts. You should pay attention to what he says...and you also, Taqi. We know that the Church sees the Cathars as a great threat for it is spreading with extraordinary speed...especially in Southern France as he said," Theodoric advised quietly.

"Well if it spreads so quickly, how will the Church be able to stop it...and perhaps it spreads as it is true. Is that the reason?" Paul asked.

"My young friend...It is an almost radiant kind of cult of the pure spirit which takes possession of men's souls, and it seriously endangers the materialistic Church of the Pope believe you me...and note I say materialistic. We know from their sacred books, primarily the Book of the Two Principles and The Questions of John, which relates a discussion between Jesus and the apostle John, that the Cathars believe they are the only true Christians faithful to a secret tradition stretching back to St John himself and rejecting most of the Old Testament, whose deity they identified with Satan, the Cathars hold the Gospel of John in highest esteem and made use of it in their rituals. It is for that reason alone, 'tis but a short while before the Church will come down upon them hard before it overwhelms them," the blonde knight explained and shook his head again.

"'Tis a ridiculous thing...religion. And this Christ I hear so much of...'tis truly a contradictory concept that makes no sense," Tenno suddenly interrupted, some passing pilgrims looking at him fiercely upon hearing his comment.

"Really...how so and explain yourself, good sire," the blonde knight requested.

Theodoric looked across at Tenno interested to hear his response and raised his eyebrows.

"I can explain it...and even so that my good friend Theo there can understand it simply too," Tenno stated and leaned forwards and nodded at Theodoric. "This Christianity of yours states as a matter of faith and fact that this Jesus person, a God made flesh, deliberately died upon the cross, supposedly, to stop all and any further sacrifices...but the church argues loudly that he died for our sins to God...he died on the cross for the world's sins, and you all shout and say 'I believe in you...Jesus saves' yes?" Tenno pointed out.

"I think we would agree upon that...yes," the blonde knight replied as his friends nodded in agreement.

"Then that is absurd, unless I have totally misunderstood your Christianity. Absurd because why would a god need to sacrifice himself...to himself to allow himself to change a set of rules he himself made anyway?" Tenno asked and looked at Theodoric and the blonde knight with a fixed stare.

Theodoric smiled broadly, secretly impressed with Tenno's question and logic.

"Perhaps you can answer that?" Theodoric said looking up at the blonde haired knight.

"He won't answer that...'cos your strange companion speaks the truth!" the drunken knight shouted out from his position lying on the floor still.

The blonde knight laughed and shook his head as Paul and Taqi looked at each other, confused. Percival shrugged his shoulders as he moved to sit nearer.

"I like his answer...but there are few who would ever raise it in public. He is clearly brave...or foolish," the blonde knight remarked looking at Tenno. "The Cathars would probably agree with you on your comments. I shall simply say that as far as I am personally aware, the Christ we have thrust down our throats is not the same one the Cathars believe in. They are the legitimate heirs of the early Gnostic Christians and through them of the first apostles, their central tenets of veneration being the prominence of Mary Magdalene and St John...which to me confirms they are a manifestation of an underground stream of secret teachings called by the prophet Mani, the universal 'Religion of Light'. The persecution and massacres that will undoubtedly be unleashed by the Roman Church upon them will simply force the Gnostics underground to re-emerge at a later time in fulfilment of the Great Plan," the blonde knight revealed.

"Now you can see why our number are so few, just don't start him on the Johannite Church or we shall never leave this place," the knight sat nearest to Theodoric suddenly spoke up and feigned a smile of sorts.

"You are most clearly a well informed man, Sir Knight. Much respect to you," Theodoric said and bowed his head slightly at the blonde knight.

"'Tis why I ended up in the Holy Lands...my unquenchable thirst for the truth," he replied.

"And did you find it?"

"No...'Tis why we now return to our homes...if they even still stand," he sighed.

"You mentioned a prophet...Mani. Who is he for I have never heard of him," Paul asked.

"I have," Taqi said pleased by the fact that he knew someone Paul didn't.

"Mani, Mani," Theodoric coughed out. "He was a man who lived from AD 216 to 274 and was of Iranian origin. He is known for being a so-called prophet and founder of Manichaeism, a Gnostic religion once widespread but now extinct. Mani was born in or near Seleucia-Ctesiphon in Parthian Babylon, which was then still part of the Parthian Empire. Six of his major works were written in Syriac Aramaic, and the seventh, dedicated to the king of the empire, Shapur I, was written in Middle Persian, his native language. He died in Gundeshapur, under the Sassanid Empire. Much of his Gnostic teachings and writings have been destroyed, on purpose by the church, or hidden away. If they could, they would eradicate him from history completely."

"I am surprised to hear you know much of this man too. We had assumed we were but the last of a few who remember and know of him," the blonde knight said as he studied Theodoric closely.

"Mani, as I just said, was born near Seleucia-Ctesiphon, perhaps in the town Mardinu in the Babylonian district of Nahr Kutha, but according to other accounts in the town Abrumya. Mani's father, Pātik, a native of Ecbatana (modern Hamadan, Iran), was a member of the Jewish-Christian sect of the Elcesaites. They were a smaller group of the larger Gnostic Ebionites. His mother was of Parthian descent, as in from the Armenian Arsacid family of Kamsarakan. Funnily enough her name is reported variously, among others as Mariam, or Miriam. Between the ages of twelve and twenty-four, Mani had visionary experiences of a heavenly twin of his, calling him to leave his father's sect and teach the true message of Christ. In AD 240–41 Mani, after being banished from Persia, travelled to India to the Sakhas region (in modern-day Afghanistan), where he studied Hinduism and was influenced by Greco-Buddhism. But he returned in AD 242 and joined the court of Shapur I, to whom he dedicated his only work written in Persian, known as the *Shabuhragan*. Shapur, however, was not converted to Manichaeanism and remained Zoroastrian. Shapur's successor, Hormizd I, who reigned only for one year, patronised Mani, but his successor Bahram I, a follower of the Zoroastrian reformer Kartir, began to persecute the Manichaeans. He incarcerated Mani, who died in prison within a month, in AD 274. Mani's followers depicted Mani's death as a crucifixion in a deliberate conscious analogy to the death of Christ. Bahram ordered the execution of Mani. Then at the order of the emperor, Mani's skin was flayed and filled with grass, and hung at the gate of Gundishpur. Bahram also ordered the killing of many Manicheans."

"That doesn't sound too good," Paul remarked.

"No...But his works survived," Theodoric replied instantly. "They included 'The Canon of Mani', six works originally written in Syriac, and one in Persian, the *Shapuragan* as I have said already. While none of his books have survived in complete form, there are many fragments and quotations of them, including a long Syriac quotation from one of his works, as well as a large amount of material in Middle Persian, Coptic and numerous other languages. Examples of surviving portions of his works include: the *Shapuragan*, the 'Book of Giants'...a favourite of Abi's by the way."

"No surprise or guesses why?" Taqi laughed. Tenno shot him a disapproving look.

"Then there is the 'Fundamental Epistle', which was quoted at length by Saint Augustine, a number of fragments of his Living Gospel, or 'Great Gospel', a Syriac excerpt. Mani also wrote the book *Arzhang*, a holy book of Manichaeism unique in that it contained many drawings and paintings to express and explain the Manichaeist creation and history of the world. You see, Mani's teachings were designed as succeeding and surpassing the teachings of Christianity, Zoroastrianism and Buddhism all together. It is based on a rigid dualism of good and evil, locked in eternal struggle. In his mid-twenties, Mani decided that salvation was possible through education, self-denial, fasting and chastity. Mani claimed to be the Paraclete promised in the New Testament, and his theology had much to say on Christianity."

"Sorry, but what does Paraclete mean?" Percy asked awkwardly, embarrassed.

"Paraclete...in simple terms it means 'one who consoles, comforts or encourages'. Or even 'refreshes and intercedes' on our behalf as an advocate court, or on behalf of man! The active form of the word, parakletor, is not found in the New Testament but is found in Septuagint in Job 16:2 in the plural, and means 'comforters', in the saying of Job regarding the 'miserable comforters' who failed to rekindle his spirit in his time of distress. It was Philo who spoke several times of 'paraclete' advocates, primarily in the sense of human intercessors. The word later went from Hellenistic Jewish writing into rabbinical Hebrew writing. In the Greek New Testament the word is most prominent in the Johannite writings, 'tis why I explain this word now in detail...Let us see if you remember it still by the time we get to Alexandria," Theodoric said and looked at Taqi and Paul in turn. "It appears in the Gospel of John (14:16, 14:26, 15:26, 16:7), where it may be translated into English as 'counsellor', 'helper', encourager', 'advocate' or 'comforter'. The Church simply identifies the Paraclete as the Holy Spirit (Acts 1:5, 1:8, 2:4, 2:38) and Christians continue to use Paraclete as a title for the Spirit of God. In the Gospel of Matthew, chapter 5 v. 4, Jesus Christ uses the verb παρακληθήσονται, paraclethesontai, traditionally interpreted to signify 'to be refreshed, encouraged, or comforted'. In 1 John 2:1 'Paraclete' is used to describe the intercessory role of Jesus Christ, who pleads to The

Father on our behalf. And in John 14:16 Jesus says 'another Paraclete' will come to help his disciples, implying Jesus is the first and primary Paraclete, but that another will come. Many assumed that was Mani."

"See...this Jesus logic makes no sense for again you have your God manifest as flesh now talking to himself in this role...," Tenno commented, bemused.

"Well...perhaps in the literal sense that may appear so...but to continue. In Matt 3:10–12 and Luke 3:9–17 John the Baptist says that a more powerful one is coming after him and 'will baptise you with the Holy Spirit and with fire. His winnowing fork is in his hand, and he will clear his threshing floor, gathering his wheat into the barn and burning up the chaff with unquenchable fire'. Now verses like that are often used by Christians in Trinitarian theology to describe how God is revealed to the world and God's role in salvation. According to Trinitarian doctrine, the Paraclete or Holy Spirit is the third person of the Trinity, who among other things provides guidance, consolation, strength and support to people. Other titles for the Holy Spirit include 'Spirit of Truth', 'Lightful Spirit of God Almighty', 'Holy Breath', 'Almighty Breath', 'Giver of Life', 'Lord of Grace', 'Helper', 'Comforter', 'Counsellor' and 'Supporter'. And yet another Paraclete is termed as the invisible presence of Jesus. More correctly that the 'another Paraclete' of John 14:16 is in many ways 'another Jesus'; the Paraclete is the presence of Jesus after Jesus ascends to his Father."

"But this is all Christian orientated...so how come you knew what this word means?" Paul asked Taqi.

"We have this term in Islam," he replied and shrugged his shoulders.

"That is true," Theodoric remarked. "Many Muslim writers have argued that 'another Paraclete' (John 14:16), the first being Jesus, refers to Muhammad. Islamic tradition states he was the grandson of a Christian. Others who interpreted the Paraclete as a reference to Muhammad and a few Muslim commentators argue that the original Greek word used was periklytos, meaning famed, illustrious or praise-worthy, rendered in Arabic as Ahmad, and that this was substituted by Christians with parakletos. I hope that answers what Paraclete means," Theodoric asked, looking at Percy. He simply nodded yes. "Good...so getting back to Mani then... while his religion was not strictly a movement of Christian Gnosticism in the ear-lier mode, Mani did declare himself to be an apostle of Jesus Christ and extant Manichaean poetry frequently extols Jesus Christ and his mother Mary with the highest reverence. Manichaean tradition is also noted to have claimed that Mani was the reincarnation of different religious figures from Buddha, Lord Krishna, Zoroaster and Jesus."

"Phew...claiming such today is almost guaranteed to get your head cut off," the blonde knight remarked and raised his eyebrows.

"Yes...very true indeed. But by the time those claims were made, Mani's follow-ers were organised into a church structure, divided into a class of 'elects' or 'electi' and 'auditors' (auditores). Only the electi are required to follow the laws strictly, while the auditores care for them, hoping to become electi in their turn after rein-carnation. The Christian tradition of Mani is based on Socrates of Constantinople, the historian who wrote in the fifth century AD. According to his account, one Scythianos, a Saracen, husband of an Egyptian woman, introduced the doctrine of Empedocles and Pythagoras into Christianity and he had a disciple, Buddas, formerly named Terebinthus, who travelled in Persia, where he alleged that he had been born of a virgin, and afterwards wrote four books, one of Mysteries, a second *The Gospel*, a third *The Treasure*, and a fourth *Heads*. While performing some mystic rites, he was hurled down a precipice by a daemon, and killed. A woman at whose house he lodged buried him, took over his property, and bought a boy of seven, named Cubricus. This boy she freed and educated, leaving him the property and books of Buddas-Terebinthus. Cubricus then travelled into Persia, where he took the name of Manes and gave forth the doctrines of Buddas Terebinthus as his own. The king of Persia, hearing that he worked miracles, sent for him to heal his sick son, and on the child's dying put Manes in prison. Thence he escaped, fleeing into Mesopotamia, but was traced, captured, and flayed alive on the Persian king's orders, the skin being then stuffed with chaff and hung up before the gate of the city. For this narrative, Socrates gives as his authority 'The Disputation with Manes of Archelaus bishop of Caschar', a work either unknown to or disregarded by Eusebius, who in his *History* (vii.31) briefly vilifies Manes without giving any of the above details. In the *Chronicon of Eusebius* the origin of the sect is placed in the second year of Probus, AD 277. According to Jerome, Archelaus wrote his account of his disputation with 'Manichæus' in Syriac, whence it was translated into Greek. The Greek is lost, and the work, apart from extracts, subsists only in a Latin translation from the Greek, of doubtful age and fidelity, probably made after the fifth century. By Photius it is stated that Heraclean, bishop of Chalcedon, in his book against the Manichæans, said the 'Disputation of Archelaus' was written by one Hegemonius, an author not otherwise traceable, and of unknown date. In the Latin narrative, 'Manes', or Mani, is said to have come, after his flight from court, from Arabion, a frontier fortress, to Caschar or Carchar, a town said to be in Roman Mesopotamia, in the hope of converting an eminent Christian there, named Marcellus, to whom he had sent a letter beginning: 'Manichæus apostle of Jesus Christ, and all the saints and virgins with me, send peace to Marcellus'. In his train he brought twenty-two, or twelve, youths and virgins. At the request of Marcellus, he debated on religion with bishop Archelaus, by whom he was vanquished; whereupon he set out to return to Persia. On his way he proposed to debate with a priest at the town of Diodorides; but Archelaus came to take the priest's place, and again defeated him; whereupon, fearing to be given up to the Persians by the Christians, he returned to Arabion. At this stage Archelaus introduces in a discourse to the people his history of 'this Manes' very much to the effect of the recapitulation in Socrates. Among the further details are these: that Scythianus lived 'in the time of the Apostles', that Terebinthus said the name of Buddas had been imposed on him; that in the mountains he had been brought up by an angel; that he had been convicted of imposture by a Persian prophet named Parcus, and by Labdacus, son of Mithra; that in the disputation, he taught concerning the sphere, the two luminaries, the transmigration of souls, and the war of the Principia against God; that 'Corbicius' or Corbicus, about the age of sixty, translated the books of Terebinthus; that he made three chief disciples, Thomas, Addas and Hermas, of whom he sent the first to Egypt, and the second to Scythia, keeping the third with him; that the two former returned when he was in prison, and that he sent them to procure for him the books of the Christians, which he then studied. According to the Latin narrative, finally, Manes on his return to Arabion was seized and taken to the Persian king, by whose orders he was flayed, his body being left to the birds, and his skin, filled with air, hung at the city gate."

"He does not have much luck keeping his skin in any of the accounts," the drunken knight shouted out half laughing as he did.

"As Taqi can probably confirm, in the Islamic tradition, Mani is described as a painter who set up a sectarian movement in opposition to Zoroastrianism. He was persecuted by Shapur I and fled to Central Asia, where he made disciples and embellished with paintings a Tchighil, or picturarum domus Chinensis, and another temple called Ghalbita. Provisioning in advance a cave which had a spring, he told his disciples he was going to heaven, and would not return for a year, after which time they were to seek him in the cave in question. They then and there found him, whereupon he showed them an illustrated book, called *Ergenk*, or *Estenk*, which he said he had brought from heaven: whereafter he had many followers, with whom he returned to Persia at the death of Shapur. The new king, Hormisdas, joined and protected the sect; and built Mani a castle. The next king, Bahram or Varanes, at first favoured Mani but, after getting him to debate with certain Zoroastrian teachers, caused him to be flayed alive, and the skin to be stuffed and hung up. Thereupon most of his followers fled to India, and some even to China, those remaining being reduced to slavery. In yet another Muslim account we have the details that Mani's mother was named Meis or Utachin, or Mar Marjam, as in Sancta Maria no less, and that he was supernaturally born. At the behest of an angel he began his public career, with two companions, at the age of twenty-four, on a Sunday, the first day of Nisan, when the sun was in Aries. He travelled for about forty years; wrote six books, and was raised to Paradise after being slain under Bahram 'son of Shapur'. Some say he was crucified in two halves and so hung up at two gates, afterwards called High-Mani and Low-Mani; others that he was imprisoned by Shapur and freed by Bahram; others that he died in prison." Theodoric paused. "But he was certainly crucified either way." [29]

"Why have you told us all of this? Could you not have simply said he was a prophet known to both Christians and Muslims?" Tenno asked bluntly.

"I could have...but I wished to recount the details...for one day Paul...and Taqi... may need to know all about Mani and Paraclete...and I hope they recognise and note the very similar attributes to Jesus, but also the symbolism within all the accounts and the numbers and values," Theodoric answered.

The blonde knight sat up, coughed and placed his hands upon the table and looked at Theodoric for several long minutes.

"'Tis a bizarre day for sure. Tell me...all of you. The journey ahead you wish to travel is long and arduous...full of many dangers. Would you like an escort?" he asked, his drunken friend spitting out a mouthful of beer and looking up fast.

"I am afraid...we do not have sufficient coinage to afford just one of you for the service let alone a full escort. Besides, we will be travelling most of the way with a Templar and Hospitaller escort. But thank you," Theodoric replied.

"No one mentioned payment in coinage my friend. You have spoken more knowledgeably in the brief time it has taken to drink one flagon of mead than I have heard in fourteen years," the blonde knight replied.

"Does this mean we do not have to return to our piss pot infested homes?" the drunken knight asked with a huge exaggerated grin.

"Before I answer that request and most generous offer, I would need to speak with our travelling companions and their agreement. But for now, may I ask of you if you are aware of the Greek Levitikon?" Theodoric asked, Paul immediately recognising this word from his previous studies.

"Of course...anyone seeking the truth would have, or should have come across it in their quest. I know our brother Templar Knights have imbibed many Gnostic ideas while in the Holy Land. The Levitikon contains a version of the Gospel of John though we are told it was only compiled in the last century," the blonde knight recounted.

"What is the Levitikon?" Taqi asked as Tenno listened in closely.

Theodoric coughed just as the blonde knight indicated to him that he should explain. Theodoric nodded and cleared his throat before continuing.

"It is an ancient text, though some copies are obviously new, that reveals the truth about the Church of John and the secret history of true Christianity. In the Levitikon the orthodox presentation of Christ has been excised in favour of a version which eliminated the miracles and the Resurrection, and presents Christ as an initiate of the higher mysteries, trained in Egypt. This is not new to Paul... anyway, God is understood as existence, action and mind, and morality as rational and benevolent conduct. The cosmos, in the ancient Gnostic tradition, is viewed as a hierarchy of intelligences. The part played by privileged initiation in the transmission of divine knowledge is central. Christ conferred the essential knowledge of this Gospel on John as the best loved apostle, and it was transmitted thence through the Patriarchs of Jerusalem until the arrival of the Templars in 1118, after which the secret teaching was kept by the Templar Grand Masters. The esoteric doctrine has been passed down through the official Order ever since," he explained.

Paul sat back and pondered thinking upon the many books, parchments and items he had seen in his father's study back in La Rochelle, all of which not only had his name on, but 'John' inscribed or written next to it.

"You know much too, my new learned friend. 'Tis a pity our paths had not crossed earlier," the blonde knight remarked.

"Thank you...I think! Well, you probably know then that the mysterious Levitikon inspired the formation, or correctly re-formation, of the hidden 'Johannite Church', much of which is hidden in Southern France, where as we know the Cathars are growing and Mary Magdalene is revered in very high esteem. Cathars secretly teach that Jesus was married to Mary Magdalene but only to its highest initiates. Plus they practise other rites of a sacrificial nature, apparently enabling those who perform them to receive the merits of 'redemption', and to participate in the preparation for the coming of the Paraclete whom they are still waiting for. The belief in the efficacy of a specific rite in freeing man from the fetters of matter and bringing him nearer to the spiritual redemption which would announce the Third Reign is very near to that of most Gnostic sects, for whom the method of redemption consisted not so much in the profession of certain opinions or virtues as in the practice of certain rites. In other words, the wish to escape the physical bounds of flesh and move on to higher realms of existence," Theodoric explained and sipped some of his drink. "The ancient Gnostics even included both men and women in the priesthood for women were permitted into the priesthood of the rite, in fact they held a very important place, for it was through Woman that salvation was to come. And in the attitude towards the Virgin Mary they, and even our Templar brothers, found a conception of her as 'Created Wisdom', the invariable reflection of 'Uncreated Wisdom', a Gnostic belief in which Sophia, or Wisdom, a divine principle which had fallen from the realm of light into the realm of matter, was conceived as being a double figure. The higher Sophia remained in the sphere of light, the lower Sophia had sunk into darkness. Through this duality Sophia became the fallen divinity through whom the mingling of light and dark, of spirit and matter, in the world, had been achieved; she was also seen as the intermediary between the lower and higher worlds and an instrument of redemption," Theodoric explained as the knights at the table all listened more intently.

"Why does the Lord cause this meeting today of all days?" the blonde knight asked aloud and crossed his arms.

"What do you mean?" Theodoric asked puzzled.

"You know much...and long have we sought a teacher of truths and clear insight and wisdom."

Tenno coughed very loudly and pretended to clear his throat. Both Paul and Taqi had to laugh.

"I am sorry, but you mentioned a word...consol something...what does that mean?" Taqi asked as a large pilgrim bumped into him by accident as he pushed past behind him.

"Perhaps your friend can answer that better than I," the blonde knight replied.

"Huh...Consolamentum, or as Christian opponents call it, the heretication. 'Tis but a unique sacrament of the Cathars. In common with Christianity, Cathars believe in original sin, and, like Gnostics, believe temporal pleasure to be sinful or unwise. The process of living thus inevitably incurred 'regret' that requires 'consolation' to move nearer to God or to approach heaven. It occurs only twice in a lifetime: upon confirmation in the faith and upon impending death. It was available to both men and women who made a commitment to the faith. Following the ceremony the consoled individual becomes a 'Cathar Perfect'. Some, though not all, Cathars, the consolamentum is a full immersion baptism in the Holy Spirit. It implied reception of all spiritual gifts including absolution from sin, spiritual regeneration, and the power to preach and elevation to a higher plane of perfection. Reference to the trinity was systematically replaced with the name of Christ since the doctrine of the Cathars professed a single unified deity. The ritual took various forms; some used the entire New Testament scripture whilst others relied on extracts such as the Gospel attributed to John while administering consolation. There are some remote cases where holy water is used as a cleansing agent during consolamentum, being profusely poured over the recipient's head until he or she was completely wet. In contrast to mainstream Christian ceremonies the form used by the majority of Cathars only requires verbal blessings and scriptures administered to the person to be consoled, and does not involve tokens such as consecrated bread or wine because these would pass through the body and become befouled. Dying persons might abstain from food in order that their bodies be as pure as possible as they passed into eternity. According to a few known cases the terminally ill would voluntarily undertake a complete fast known as the endura. It is only undertaken when death is clearly inevitable. It was a form of purification and separation from the material world which was controlled by the evil one. They believed that this final sacrifice ensured their reunification with the Good God. Laying on of hands is always part of the ceremony. Some claim that incidences of ecstatic utterances during consolamentum were actually glossolalia, or 'speaking in tongues', which demanded that the rite be even more secretly guarded since this phenomenon occurring outside of the Church was considered witchcraft and was punishable by death. Once consoled, Parfaits were required to be vegetarian, to be celibate, and to dedicate their lives to travelling and teaching Cathar doctrines. These Parfaits were the leaders of the Cathar communities. The vast majority of Cathars do not receive consolamentum until on the verge of death. Once given the consolamentum, the same rules applied to them, though they were obviously not expected to travel or preach from their deathbed. This allowed most believers to live somewhat normal lives and receive consolamentum shortly before passing away."

"A bit of a last minute insurance guarantee then?" Taqi stated.

"Look...Gnosis," Theodoric started to explain but hesitated as the inn's keeper walked by carrying a large tray of food. "Gnosis is the complete and definitive synthesis of all beliefs and all ideas of which humanity has need of again to realise its origin, its past, its end, its nature, the contradictions of existence and the problems of life....Gnosis is the very essence of Christianity. But, by Christianity, we do not only mean the doctrine taught since the arrival of the divine Saviour, but also the one taught before Jesus's arrival, in the old temples, the doctrine of Eternal Truth. The Gnostic church is the antinomy of that of Rome. The name of that one is Force; the name of the Gnostic church, the Cathars and the original Druids, is Love. The Sovereign Patriarch is not Peter, the impulsive, who denied three times his master and took up the sword, but John, the Saviour's friend, the apostle who relied on his heart and in it knew best the immortal sentiment, the oracle of light, the author of the Eternal Gospel, who took up only Speech and Love. The main aim of the Universal Gnostic Church is to restore the original religious unity that is to establish and spread a Christian Religion true to the universal religious tradition. It is not hostile towards any Church. It respects the customs and laws of all peoples. It is essentially large and tolerant, which permits it to admit all men without distinction of nationality, language or race."

"How does your head hold all this knowledge?" one of the other knights asked out loud leaning forwards to look at Theodoric better.

"I could tell you that I learnt it all as I knew people who have vowed to re-establish and one day bring to the world a form of a Pre-Nicene Gnosto-Catholic Church, its single intention of restoring the Gnosis, that Divine Wisdom, to the Christian Church, and to teach the Path of Holiness which leads to God and the Inner Illumination and Interior Communion with the Soul through the mortal body of man," Theodoric explained and winked at the blonde knight. Tenno frowned, a little puzzled. "Plus the hidden teachings, the Gnosis of the Soul, which exposes the false vestiges of truth that have been foisted upon all of us. In simple terms, the true Gnostic or Christian makes no claim that he alone is right or that his teaching is the only one required or necessary for salvation. He demands that no one accept the statements of himself or anyone else on faith, but insists that everyone should prove these things for himself."

Paul thought upon Theodoric's last statement as it reminded him soundly of comments both his father and Niccolas had repeatedly kept telling him, about always checking his sources and never accept anything on blind faith alone.

The blonde knight sat up straighter and looked at Theodoric intently for a few moments in silence before speaking again.

"I was led to understand that the first followers of Jesus the Christ did not see his teachings as merely intellectual fodder meant for endless debate, nor as a mere set of humanitarian principles and moral pronouncements. The teachings of Jesus were meant to be lived so that the individual person may awake to 'Christ in you, the hope of glory'. The 'Secret Church' still exists in this world and that Gnostic Christians are united not by a rigid set of beliefs, but by a mysterious bond of brotherhood derived from a shared vision and experience of the living Christ. Gnostic Christianity is experiential...it is about transformation, about a higher consciousness, not about dry words or external forms. Theologies and commandments are the formulations of men. No matter how sublime or noble, rational or logical, they are all man-made," he explained quietly.

"See...he agrees with me," Tenno interrupted.

"Gnosis is the experience of the divine. Words along with all theological and philosophical discourses are insufficient to explain it. You must taste it, as the Psalmist declares; 'O taste and see that the Lord is good' (Psalm 34:8). The goal of the Gnostic Christian is nothing short of Awakening, of Christ Consciousness. Following the Way of the Christ, as revealed in the Gospels, we are called to 'Let this mind be in you, which was also in Christ Jesus', is that not the case?" the blonde knight then asked.

"Almost the entire history of Christendom is a protest against the words of Jesus the Christ," Theodoric replied. "Hatred and persecution, hypocrisy and ignorance, intolerance of one's neighbours...all in the name of him who gave the commandment to love your enemies...in the name of him who said 'My kingdom is not of this world'! Institutional Christianity, with its religious dogmatism and obsession with commandments, is a contemporary example of the same force that confronted and sought to kill Jesus in his own time. But behind worldly Christianity is the interior Church of John, the universal Gnostic Church where the Living Christ continues to impart spiritual knowledge. This is the other tradition of Christianity, the hidden one, but it is always accessible to seeking souls," Theodoric revealed, just loud enough to be heard. [30]

Paul looked at Tenno as he saw him deep in thought actually listening to Theodoric and the blonde knight.

"Today will truly go down as a strange day indeed. On the cusp of me and my men leaving the lands of the Levant and Outremer for good, the Lord places you next to us and like some fisherman playing with a fish hooked on a line, you reel us in with revelations of meanings we have sought nigh on fourteen years past!" the blonde knight exclaimed as he looked at his brother knights all nodding in agreement. "Many of us died not only from our enemies and robbers, but as many from malnutrition on our long journeys, the parasites that infect our water and foods did many of the Crusaders in...and our brothers. In fact, fifteen to twenty per cent of all Crusaders die of either malnutrition or infectious disease while on expeditions, aided by an abundance of intestinal creepy-crawlies, so I would urge you pray vigilance on what you eat and drink as you travel for I would hate to see you fail in your aims...for I suspect there is more you aim to achieve in your journey, unlike us, for I fear we seem to have lost our way utterly."

"Well, before you leave us, I take it you are all aware that Cathars teach secretly that Jesus was married to Magdalene but only to its highest initiates, as I mentioned earlier...Is this something you agree with?" Theodoric asked.

"Of course...we knew that when we started our adventures. But we have found no trace in all of our travels of any bloodlines and surviving family."

"Perhaps they are nearer than you suspect," Theodoric remarked as Tenno frowned at him.

"We have tried, despite the many contradictions we have witnessed, to maintain a distinction between the Jesus of history and the Christ of faith, for as long as distinction was acknowledged, faith remained tenable. If the distinction is not acknowledged faith would inevitably find itself eroded and embarrassed by the ineluctable facts of history," the blonde knight replied.

"How do you mean?" Paul asked.

"Well, the most obvious being the simple fact that the gospels were written sixty to a hundred years after Jesus. The myth of Christ has since served the church well...as the Qur'an and Islam maintain that Jesus survived the cross. Other Christians will of course say this is heresy and that Muslims lie, but from what we know, 'tis not exactly a lie," the blonde knight explained and studied all their faces in turn to see their reactions.

"You have learned much of what is truth," Theodoric remarked and looked at the blonde knight for several minutes.

 2 – 11

"Do not misunderstand me...us...we understand the real concept and meaning of what a Messiah was and still is...a true king, a priest and prophet...not Divine but acknowledged as an anointed one by God. At the time of Christ's birth it was into a world that was supposedly to be at the cursed end of days. Herod was an usurper on the throne and many believed Jesus would overthrow him and the yoke of Rome. Even if Jesus was not Divine his legitimacy to kingship was still genuine by bloodline to the House of David and was why Herod felt threatened by him. Jesus's legal claim could be recognised by Rome to keep peace and Herod simply booted out. Most Christians do not even question how it was that Jesus came from a wealthy background as he was literate, could quote law and Judaic gospels. So if all else about Jesus was fake and not God manifest in flesh, he was still a genuine good and worthy cause to fight for. We also learnt about a prophecy for the real end days when an antichrist would be born of a Royal Christian bloodline and Islamic line...though antichrist would be wrong!"

Theodoric looked at Tenno immediately, then Paul. The fact that Paul was Christian and Alisha Muslim and both apparently of an ancient bloodline was not lost on Tenno.

"I think you would understand then why Constantine's influence on the early Christian world and powers he passed on to the Church to anoint kings etcetera. And remember so much else was also deliberately changed," Theodoric stated.

"Such as? I fear I am so out of this conversation by way of understanding that I feel somewhat stupid," Taqi exclaimed.

"You and me both," Percival said and shook his head.

"Well such as Christianity originally held Saturdays, the Jewish Sabbath, as holy but an edict in AD 321 by Constantine ordered law courts closed on Sundays declaring it day of rest in honour of Sol Invictus as Christianity basically coalesced from Mithraism and the Sol Invictus cult under Constantine. Constantine's religion had from the outset lowered the Jesus Christ as we know him to a lower degree role than that played by Constantine's role as a more effectual Messiah than Jesus Christ himself. Muhammad was a military commander and fought, and Jesus as a Messiah was expected, as a king, priest, prophet and warrior, to fight and lead his people, not so the meek lamb as later presented at Nicea and agreed upon at the Council of AD 325. You simply need only read in the New Testament where Jesus tells his disciples to buy swords and states that he does not bring peace but a two edged long sword. Also his acts of turning the money lenders' tables over violently cannot exactly be viewed as the actions of the image we are led to believe, for human nature being what it is, they would have resulted in riots as coins rolled everywhere."

"So the arguments we have been told that Jesus was in fact a later Roman fabrication to pacify the Jews who had or were becoming militant Christians may not be as farfetched as some may claim?" Paul commented.

"Okay, let me ask you this. Who is the biggest and most recognised bad man within the New Testament?" Theodoric asked.

"Judas!" the drunken knight called out and tried to pull himself up.

"Yes...yes indeed. Judas Iscariot, the Sicarius or zealot. Yet without his pivotal and vitally critical role, the whole Jesus initiative would never have even started. He was actually the hero of the Passover plot for without his actions the whole saga could not be played out. And why was Jesus crucified with two other zealots, not criminals, and why did the Romans crucify him as a revolutionary and not simply just let the Jewish Sanhedrin execute him by stoning, as was customary? These are the questions all Christians should ask themselves. And why and how come in the Garden of Gethsemane when Jesus was arrested did it take an entire cohort of nearly six hundred Roman soldiers, not just a few as is often mistakenly assumed?

"I am half tempted to follow you on your path to learn more from you," the blonde knight commented.

"Yes...let's do that as I for one do not wish to return home to a sedate and boring lifestyle," the drunken knight shouted out and raised his beer high!

"When we served in Cairo, we learnt many different aspects of Jesus, and not only from the Islamic point of view either, his crucifixion and resurrection being of identical symbolism to ancient Egyptian myths," the blonde knight began to explain.

"Yes, we have certainly been taught the same," Paul interrupted and looked at Theodoric.

"Then I envy you. You are privileged to learn much whilst still so young. So tell me," the blonde knight said, looking back at Theodoric, "Jesus we are told was an Essene but also taught in Pharisaic thought. Essenes were not celibate as we are oft told nowadays but married and were also excellent warfare specialists... not pacifists as claimed. At twenty they could marry and at thirty were considered mature, just as Jesus started his ministry at that age. We were also told by several Sufi mystics we happened per chance to meet, that Jesus was also a Nazarean...Essenes, Zadokites, Zealots and Nazareans all being one and same group but known under different metaphors. We were also taught that the Maccabeans were the last dynasty of Judaic kings that ruled Israel from the second century BC before Herodian times, and that is why Herod tried to legitimise his kingship by marrying a Maccabean princess...but then murdered her and her sons thus ending that bloodline. Is that all true?"

"From what I have learnt and understand myself, then you have learnt the truth well," Theodoric answered and part bowed his head. "You will probably be aware then that Jesus's brother Jacob, known as James the Just and St James, resulted in the foundation of the order of St James of Altopaso but also that the Nazarean party and consequently Jesus had no intention of starting a new religion and would be horrified to start a new one as they were, in the main, Jews. Imagine how they would feel now, mortified to learn their new religion, started after them, has become their main persecutor." [31]

"We were also told that Muhammad's father was raised in Nazarean tradition and that one of his wives was Nazarean and the treatment of Jesus in the Qur'an is essentially Nazarean in orientation...but until this day, we have never met a clearly gifted and talented scholar of Christian origin to confirm or deny this... most just refusing to enter into a conversation on the whole matter," the blonde knight explained.

Paul laughed quietly seeing the expression on Tenno's face being one of pained embarrassment almost.

"I think we should wind this conversation up or we shall be here all eve and I shall indeed get a severe speaking to by Lucy," Theodoric remarked and sat up straight.

"Then think on what I have offered. We would be honoured to escort you all to where you need to be. I sense our Lord has plans for us to be of assistance. 'Tis after all what we have lived for these past years...and now it appears to us a real reason to do what we do best...protect people," the blonde knight said and stood up and outstretched his hand for Theodoric to shake.

Tenno stood up slowly and looked at the knights, suspicion written all across his face.

"Do you not seek to find peace after all you have been through?" Tenno asked the knight.

"Peace...As I said, there were seventy-two of us when we set out...and peace... we all, we all have learnt that peace does not mean to be in a place where there is no noise, trouble or hard work or war...It means to be in the midst of those things and still be calm in heart," the blonde knight replied.

Tenno looked at him. He was suspicious yet the knight's words resonated with him. He would reserve judgement upon the knight and his fellow brethren, clearly a seasoned and battle hardened group.

"We shall stay a while longer in Tarsus...in case you decide to take us up on our offer," the blonde knight said and stood up and bowed towards Tenno, Theodoric and then Taqi and Paul. He quickly acknowledged Percy with a nod.

Chapter 26
Thomas

Port of La Rochelle, France, Melissae Inn, spring 1191

The old man sat back and paused as he shook his head clearly recalling details from years past.

"I just know you are going to go mad...Sarah...but telling us all about the Seven Sleepers, the Cathars and that Mani fellow...was that all necessary?" Simon asked the old man but looking cautiously at Sarah.

"I am afraid yes...'twas indeed necessary. It was that conversation that prompted the returning knights to listen to what Theodoric was saying...and consequently volunteer their services," the old man answered. "As well as stay in Paul's mind."

"So am I correct in assuming that what was said, in regard to Jesus being crucified, was in fact a way of stopping and negating all reasons and manner of sacrifices?" Gabirol asked as he waved his quill.

"Yes...that is but just one of the reasons Jesus had to be seen to be crucified and then resurrected. But as per the Cathars' beliefs and as Jesus himself even taught, true initiates do not need to attend a church to follow God. He is even quoted within the New Testament saying that you can look under a stone and find the Kingdom of Heaven, just as Cathars would tell you and according to Gnostic beliefs, especially as written in the Gospel of Thomas."

"Really...how so? I mean, does that mean none of us here need attend church tomorrow, even though it be Easter?" Simon asked enthusiastically.

"In truth...no, you do not need too! But if we all stopped attending church, that would be the end of Christendom," the old man answered. "There are many secret teachings that the living Jesus spoke and Didymos Judas Thomas recorded them...but sadly it will be a very long time before the mother church admits to them...but she will...eventually."

"I would like to know of these secret teachings," the farrier asked politely.

"Well there is much, far too much for me to recount now. But I can quote several notable teachings to give you an idea of what was being imparted," the old man replied and looked inside his main leather satchel. After a short while, he removed a leather bound booklet, untied its fastenings and opened it. "Here...let me read these details." He paused then began to read from the booklet. "And he said, 'Whoever discovers the interpretation of these sayings will not taste death.' Now is that the actual figurative death, or spiritual death?" the old man asked and looked at the group. None answered. "Jesus said, 'Those who seek should not stop seeking until they find. When they find, they will be disturbed. When they are disturbed, they will marvel, and will reign over all. And after they have reigned they will rest.'" He paused again. "That passage I suppose we could aptly apply to the mercenary knights... but as for attending a church, Jesus also said 'If your leaders say to you, "Look, the Father's kingdom is in the sky", then the birds of the sky will precede you. If they say to you, "It is

31

in the sea", then the fish will precede you. Rather, the Father's kingdom is within you and it is outside you'. An important quote that Paul took literally was the one that said 'for there is nothing hidden that will not be revealed. And there is nothing buried that will not be raised….and also as Jesus said, 'Don't lie, and don't do what you hate, because all things are disclosed before heaven. After all, there is nothing hidden that will not be revealed, and there is nothing covered up that will remain undisclosed.' Simon Peter said to Jesus, 'You are like a just messenger'. And Matthew said to him, 'You are like a wise philosopher'. And Thomas said to him, 'Teacher, my mouth is utterly unable to say what you are like'. Jesus said, 'When you see one who was not born of woman, fall on your faces and worship. That one is your Father'. Jesus said, 'Perhaps people think that I have come to cast peace upon the world. They do not know that I have come to cast conflicts upon the earth: fire, sword, war. For there will be five in a house: there'll be three against two and two against three, father against son and son against father, and they will stand alone.' The disciples said to Jesus, 'Tell us, how will our end come?' Jesus said, 'Have you found the beginning, then, that you are looking for the end? You see, the end will be where the beginning is. Congratulations to the one who stands at the beginning: that one will know the end and will not taste death.'" He paused. "Jesus also said 'If you become my disciples and pay attention to my sayings, these stones will serve you. For there are five trees in Paradise for you; they do not change, summer or winter, and their leaves do not fall. Whoever knows them will not taste death.' The disciples said to Jesus, 'Tell us what Heaven's kingdom is like.' He said to them, 'It's like a mustard seed, the smallest of all seeds, but when it falls on prepared soil, it produces a large plant and becomes a shelter for birds of the sky.' I would urge you all to make a special note of the mustard seed…for it plays an important part in the codes that Paul was to discover," the old man said quietly.

"I feel so utterly inadequate to understand what you tell us," Ayleth said, embarrassed.

"That is why 'tis people like you who will in time understand…trust me on that point," the old man said looking at her intently. "One very perplexing though delightful saying he gave related to two souls joining as one in order to enter the Kingdom of Heaven. I am sure you must have heard of 'Soul mates'?" the old man asked looking at them all.

The Templar and Miriam looked at each other and smiled unable to hide their affection for each other. Sarah smiled at Stephan briefly.

"I have never heard of any mention by Jesus of soul mates…," the wealthy tailor stated.

"Then I shall read it to you…here…Jesus said to them, 'When you make the two into one, and when you make the inner like the outer and the outer like the inner, and the upper like the lower, and when you make male and female into a single one, so that the male will not be male nor the female be female, when you make eyes in place of an eye, a hand in place of a hand, a foot in place of a foot, an image in place of an image, then you will enter.' Jesus also said 'Whoever blasphemes against the Father will be forgiven, and whoever blasphemes against the Son will be forgiven, but whoever blasphemes against the Holy Spirit will not be forgiven, either on earth or in heaven.'"

"Ah…so Gerard will be forgiven for swearing and blaspheming when Alisha kneed him in the groin…," Simon commented.

"In truth again…yes. Here is another saying you should make particular note of. Jesus said, 'From Adam to John the Baptist, among those born of women, no one is so much greater than John the Baptist that his eyes should not be averted. But I have said that whoever among you becomes a child will recognise the Father's kingdom and will become greater than John.' Jesus said, 'Show me the stone that the builders rejected: that is the keystone.'" The old man stopped abruptly, paused in silence for a few moments then continued. "But back

to attending church...Jesus said 'Split a piece of wood; I am there. Lift up the stone, and you will find me there.'"

"I am not sure I follow that...but I shall accept what you say," the Genoese sailor remarked.

"So these mercenary knights...did they travel onwards with Paul and his group?" the Hospitaller asked.

"Yes...they did indeed. And by the most curious of coincidences, and the leaders name just happened to be Thomas too. 'Tis one of the reasons he listened in when Theodoric mentioned his name."

"You mentioned that without Judas, the whole history of Jesus would be different. How so?" Gabirol asked.

"The short answer to that is during the last supper Jesus gave instructions to Judas to comply with in order to fulfil the prophecies as given by Zechariah. If he had not complied, we would not have had Jesus arrested, crucified and subsequently resurrected," the old man answered.

"But we were often told when out there, that the Qur'an claims the body on the cross was a substitute of Jesus. Was that true?" the Templar asked.

"If I told you that the man was indeed Jesus, but he did not die, but was revived later, and that subsequent renderings and re-telling of the story is what fuelled the confusion...would you believe me?"

"But if he did not die...then that means the whole sacrifice issue is a lie," Gabirol stated, puzzled.

"But what if it was a necessary one to stop and negate all the sacrifice practices...for good?" the old man posed the question. "Things were not helped by the knowledge at that time, that Jesus had a twin brother, who was also known as Thomas. You see, there are Essene, who were one and the same Zadokites whose texts speak of two Messiahs, twin pillars etcetera, also connected back through antiquity to the Upper and Lower Pillars of Egypt...But in the biblical sense, there was one, a Priest Messiah of Aaron descended from Israel's first high priest in the Old Testament and would be an interpreter of the law presiding over a nation's spiritual life. The Second Royal Messiah would be from the Davidic line presiding over secular admin of a new kingdom as a royal figure using his military prowess. Mandean and Johannite sects in the Tigris-Euphrates region who honoured John the Baptist believed Jesus to be a rebel, a heretic who led men astray and betrayed secret doctrines. Before I forget, know that in Hebrew, Thomas actually means 'twin'. But on top of that, Jesus's family survived and continued. Only obvious really. His bloodline remained intact and one branch became the 'House of Edessa' now Urfa. They were and still are known as the 'Master's People' or the 'Desposyni', surviving members of whom journeyed to see the Pope requesting revocation of Pauline Church bishops in the Kingdom of Jerusalem and to be returned to them. The Pope threw it out and that was the last official meeting of the Desposyni and Roman church in AD 300...roughly! In AD 200 the Bishop of Lyon, Irenaeus, issued an attack on prevalent heresies of the time, especially against a group called the Ebionites, the later name of Nazareans, al-nasara in Arabic, meaning poor, who believed Jesus was a man not of virgin birth, who became a Messiah only after being anointed by John the Baptist, adhered to Judaic law and called St Paul an apostate from the law. The Nazarean sect still exists, though its numbers dwindle. The Templars use an ancient Nazarean Atbash code...but that need not concern us now," the old man explained.

"We all know that Christianity did not just pop up overnight...but all this that you tell us...no wonder the church does not want it common knowledge," Gabirol remarked.

"You are correct, it did not just pop up overnight. Both David and Solomon were Messiahs, as was Jesus, who tried to remove the Maccabeans, who had previously usurped the Davidic line.

"But what of this Palacate or person Mani mentioned who would show up in the end times, the comforter or whatever he was called?" Simon asked.

"Hmm, it would perhaps be easier for me to simply say that in the end times, though not an end to the world literally, but to the present way and order of things, a man would come who would navigate the peoples of this world...'tis one of the reasons why the Prior de Sion call their master a 'Nautonier' who guides...a navigator. Just like Jean de Gisors, an obscure knight who led to Merovingian dynasty. He is related to Hugues de Payens, the first Grand Master of Knights Templar. But here is a secret I can tell you that perhaps even our Templar friend does not know himself....that the Prior de Sion actually founded the Templars in 1099 in Jerusalem. Members from the secret order of the Triple tau started it....so you see the Templars were actually formed before 1118 and known as 'La malice du Christ'. In 1114 the Count of Champagne was about to go to Jerusalem, but the Bishop of Chartres cathedral urged him not to as he had bigger plans for him later. The city of Troyes became the Templars' strategic centre for the Order, and it is no coincidence that the majority of Grail Romances originate from there. Make a note of the Abbey of Notre Dame du Mont de Sion. It was a self contained building on a high hill south of Jerusalem. It was the headquarters of the Prior de Sion and known by the highest initiates as the 'mother of all churches'. That is where the Prior de Sion took its name from. And you may recall that previously I explained that the nine original founding Templar Knights were actually aided by another thirty knights...this is why."

"No...I was not aware of those details," the Templar remarked uneasily.

"You have all probably heard of Peter the hermit...well he was a personal tutor to Godfroi de Bouillon and also the main protagonist for calling Pope Urban the Second to instigate the first crusade. And it was monks from Calabria in southern Italy, where Paul and Alisha just happened to stop over on their way to Outremer, who all went to Orval in Belgium, and set up a major monastery. Peter the hermit came from this group. This same group then went on to set up the actual Abbey of Notre Dame du Mont de Sion, in Jerusalem. And Theodoric... remember he was heading for Jerusalem to join the Knights of St Lazarus...well their headquarters is still in Orleans in France. And I know I have mentioned already the connection of Paul's mother to Gisors in France and, as I have just mentioned, Jean de Gizors that led to the Merovingians...well they claimed descent from Noah, whom they regarded, even more than Moses, as the source of all Biblical wisdom. They also claimed descent from ancient Troy, hence the explanation of why the French use Trojan names such as Troyes and Paris. Plus we can trace Merovingians to ancient Greece, specifically to a region known as Arcadia. Ancestors of Merovingians are connected to Arcadia's Royal House. And just in case I am not being clear on this, the third hidden secret order behind both the Templars and Cistercians was also established and led by none other than Bernard of Clairvaux. The Prior de Sion being the admin order that originated from the far older Order of the Sword, also known as the Order of the Triple tau," the old man explained at length without stopping.

Gabirol looked up when he stopped talking and recharged the ink in his quill.

"All that I tell you is connected. The headquarters of the Prior de Sion now resides at Gisors, in Normandy. It is also connected to Giza in Egypt or as it is also known, Jeezah, which is almost identical linguistically to the name of Jesus himself...and I shall have much more to explain on that matter...for that all most certainly does relate and apply to this sword," the old man said and looked at the sword upon the table.

"I had heard that one of the original founding Templar Knights, Godfrei de Bouillon, who captured Jerusalem, was descended from Dagobert II and his son Segisbert, who were both of Merovingian bloodlines and were known as Fisher Kings...that much I do know," the Templar commented as Miriam held his hand tightly.

"That is indeed correct. It was his brother who accepted the crown of Jerusalem upon the death of King Baldwin, who some call Baudouin I of the Holy Land. The Order of Sion, as the Prior de Sion, was, as I have stated, founded in 1099 but its conception was started in 1090 by Godfrei himself at Mount Sion the famous high hill south of the city. It was then that a mysterious conclave led by a tall distinguished white haired man, whose name was never listed, unanimously elected Godfrei ruler. The mysterious conclave I can tell you was in fact none other than those same monks from Orval, including Peter the hermit, who by that date had just en masse disappeared from Orval at the same time as Godfrei headed to the Holy Land. It was those monks who set up Notre Dame du Mont de Sion etc. Orval in Belgium was known to have been founded by these mysterious monks in 1070 from Calabria in southern Italy as already explained."

"But...but if that is the case, then why did they do this and how did they get their information and knowledge to send Godfrei and his knights to go and recover further artefacts as you have explained from beneath the Temple? It does not make sense!" Simon asked, confused.

"All I can tell you at this stage in this tale is that there are those, some call them angels, some call them messengers of the Lord...others know them as watchers or bird men...but in short, and to describe them as best I am able...they were assisted, shall we say, by individuals of a race of man long since lost to the mists of time...and just a faded memory to man...tall, wise and often mistaken for being what became known as Druids," the old man explained.

Ayleth shuddered in her seat and pulled her shawl around her shoulders tighter.

"Are you cold Ayleth?" Stephan asked as all looked at her.

"No...Not cold...just a quick shiver passed over me...that is all. I am fine...honestly," she answered, but looking pale.

"Sorry to throw this one at you then...but I can see why someone who leads people would be called a navigator...and I am guessing here that Paul is obviously, or will become, the navigator...but why expressly use a maritime analogy? Is it because water is equal to Aqua which in turn is equal to spirit?" Simon asked.

"My friend...that is twice you have surprised me now. 'Tis a great and valid question," Gabirol remarked.

"Why navigator? In simple terms, because it all relates back to ancient symbolism regarding the ancient Egyptian solar barge, the Magan Boat that sailed across the heavens...known as the Stella Maris, just as the boat that brought the family of Christ to these shores was also named the Stella Maris. A rudder- and oar-less boat," the old man explained as Simon shook his head and Gabirol wrote quickly.

"That is of course if all of what you state is truth...that the Magdalene did indeed come to these shores," the wealthy tailor remarked, shaking his head.

"Let me quickly state something to you now, of which I shall remind you later to recall. All symbolism relating to Jesus's family and bloodline is represented by way of vines, viticulture as lineage etcetera and water symbolism, such as having disciples who were fishermen, and recall the Merovingians were known as Fisher Kings, and water equals spirit symbolically. Jesus was initially symbolised by the fish, the Vesica Pisces. Much of this you will learn if you stay to hear me out to the end. And the Vesica Pisces sets out the entire Giza pyramid

complex in Egypt as you shall also learn...if you stay until the end...," the old man said quietly and seriously. "And please try to keep in mind, that the wholly unholy slander of labelling Mary Magdalene a prostitute is probably one of the greatest untruths our world has ever had thrust upon it for not at any point in any of the gospels was she ever called a prostitute...but was once described as a woman out of whom went seven devils. But that is just a symbolic representation of the dictates of the original cult of Astarte, or Ishtar, she was once part of that involved a seven stage initiation ceremony. Prior to Jesus's new ministry Mary was part of this cult so Jesus had to drive out those original practices, symbolically of course. Note carefully too that Lazarus was termed as the 'favoured confidant' of Jesus just as Mary was also referred but Lazarus was in fact Mary's actual brother hence why other disciples were envious of him. The Gospel of John never mentions who actually wrote it. Not once is the name John mentioned. But the author claims he is the beloved whom Jesus referred to as the beloved disciple. Only Lazarus was called this. And it was Lazarus who would eventually land in France with Mary Magdalene, also known as Mary of Bethany, and Martha her sister, and Joseph of Arimathea, though he went on to Glastonbury...but Lazarus and Mary stayed in France having landed in Roussillon, not Marseilles as often quoted and claimed," the old man detailed.

"Am I correct in saying that the town of Nazareth did not exist during Jesus's time?" Gabirol asked. "Sorry to change the subject matter."

"No need to apologise...and yes, there was no such town recorded as Nazareth when Jesus was born. Now before I forget, let me just quickly say that Jesus was, as most scholars agree, from the line of David from the tribe of Judah who usurped the house of Saul, first king of the Jews, from the tribe of Benjamin. Mary was from the tribe of Benjamin and Saul so by both marrying, a full legitimate king of the Jews was made. Now the Sanhedrin could stone Jesus to death without Roman permission. So keep it clear in your minds that it is the Romans who are wholly responsible for his crucifixion. And Jesus was not crucified at Golgotha, the hill of the skull, but in a private garden opposite Joseph of Arimathea's house and it was his tomb they used. This alone shows that Jesus and his family, as Joseph was his uncle after all, were well connected and wealthy. Not just everyone has a tomb! Jesus in short was by the very definition also an aristocrat, and remember where the root word for that comes from...Ari?... as well as being a wealthy and rightful priest king. Islam even goes as far as to say that after his fake crucifixion, or the substitute one, that he went to Kashmir where he lived to a ripe old age then died. And as you know the Cathars teach secretly that Jesus was married to Mary Magdalene, but it is only taught to its highest initiates. The actual new religion of Jesus the Christ as we now have it is in fact a religion based upon the 'faith of Jesus' and his divine status to compete with Roman, Egyptian and Babylonian gods. It is not based upon the actual real Messiah Priest King he actually was," the old man explained and looked at each in turn to gauge their reactions.

"Okay...let us say we accept what you are telling as truth...I feel that we are somehow being prepared or educated for something more than just being told a story about a sword. Am I correct that there is something else being played out here?" the Hospitaller asked quizzically, almost suspiciously.

"Perhaps...but 'tis only costing you your time to sit and listen. And as I said, at the end of this tale, I may perhaps ask you all to do something...but after that, 'tis totally your choice and free will to either accept what I ask or not to...and nothing more will be asked or desired or expected of you. Upon that you have my most solemn vow and promise."

"So these other knights whom Paul met at the Cathar inn...am I correct in believing that *they perhaps have a part to play in this tale that is perhaps not as obvious as we assume?"* the Hospitaller asked.

"My friend...you are indeed perceptive. Yes they will indeed play a part...and I shall come to that."

"The sword...did any priests ever carry out the Vexillum Sancti Petri upon it?" the Templar asked.

"The what?" Miriam asked, perplexed.

"He means the holy banner militia Christi, a priest's blessing of a knight's sword. And no it never was...ever," the old man stated.

"Can I ask, these mercenary knights...how come they served in the area for what...fourteen years was it?" the farrier asked.

"I shall, I promise, come to that in good time. But unlike Templars and Hospitallers, or knights of the land who serve four months at the frontiers, four at a garrison, and four at home etcetera, and can serve until sixty-one, mercenaries were free to choose where, when and whom they served."

"Is that not a bad thing then? Just paid and hired murderers?" Ayleth asked.

"Some were like that...others just sought adventure and some who could not be confined by the strict rules of the Orders but wished to serve the Lord and be granted salvation, as promised by the Pope, so took up arms to protect pilgrims and serve where fate took them."

"And these knights...they are of good character?" the Templar asked.

"Let me just say, they had been searching for a long time...and in Theodoric and Paul they would find what had eluded them for so long," the old man revealed.

"Then please...the suspense of this is getting to me...tell us what happened next," Sarah asked.

"Okay...then let me explain that Paul and Alisha did not stay long in Tarsus, just a few days, by which time Theodoric had spoken with both Guy and Balian and permission had been granted for the blonde knight, Thomas, and his men to accompany them. Balian saw it as a distinct advantage having them along. It transpired that they both knew of and held each other in high regard and respect. Tenno kept a very close eye on them all for both reason of caution of their motives and also a fascination of their experience and skill."

Tarsus, Cilician Armenia, June 1st 1179

The hour was still very early, but the entire column of Templars, Hospitallers, wagons, caravans and other assorted Confrere Knights and Thomas's knights, were already in position and ready to move off. The morning air was still refreshingly cool when Taqi jumped up next to Tenno on the caravan. Theodoric was coughing loudly near the rear of the caravan as Sister Lucy patted his back. Paul was inside with Alisha and Arri, who was asleep securely wrapped up and placed inside a large drawer Alisha had started to use as a crib. Paul looked at Alisha. She still looked tired despite having managed to get four hours' sleep undisturbed. Paul went to stand when she suddenly grabbed his hand quickly and beckoned he sit next to her.

"What is it?" Paul asked.

"Nothing...I just need to hold you...for a moment. Please," she replied softly.

Without hesitation Paul wrapped his arms around her and held her close, her head resting upon his chest, her eyes shut. After a few minutes Paul went to move but she pulled him back closer and tighter.

"Ali...come on. What is the matter?"

"Nothing," she paused. "But...I have this feeling I cannot shake. Part of me wants to turn back now and stay in La Rochelle...or perhaps even go to Britain," she said softly, her eyes still closed.

"Ali...why have you not said this before?"

"Sorry Paul. I am just being silly. I just sense that so much has changed...and is changing...fast. Please just tell me everything will be okay."

Paul kissed the top of her head and held her tightly. He could tell she was feeling uncharacteristically unsettled.

"All will be well...I promise," he told her and looked upwards and raised his eyebrows.

∞ ∞

Paul stepped down from the rear of the caravan, letting go of Alisha's hand just as she moved aside so Sister Lucy could step up and inside. Theodoric nodded at Paul as he straightened out his robe and adjusted the rope tied around his waist keeping his sword in place.

"You need to get yourself sorted with a new scabbard for that," Theodoric said as Thomas walked up alongside guiding his large war horse in full armour.

"'Tis a fine day to return to Outremer," Thomas said politely and bowed.

"'Tis my first time," Paul replied looking at the armour upon both Thomas and his horse.

"I see you have a marvellous Turcoman. Truly a magnificent horse. They are worth what....nearly two hundred camels where as an ordinary horse is worth just three," Thomas commented just as Balian rode past, nodded at them all and carried on towards the front to check the Templars acting as the vanguard of the column.

"Really?" Paul asked and looked at Theodoric.

"Did you not know this?" Theodoric asked, a little surprised.

"No...No I did not," Paul answered and thought of his father. Not only had he entrusted the sword to him, but also an incredibly expensive and valuable horse. It had never occurred to him, the value of Adrastos. He smiled to himself and shook his head. "Theo...What was it you said once...about never mentioning camels to Sister Lucy?"

"Do not ever ask," Theodoric laughed and began to walk towards the front of the caravan to join Taqi and Tenno. "And is that wise in this heat...an equus armigerus et ccoperus?" he shouted as he walked away.

Paul returned his gaze to Thomas and his horse. It was fully armoured, which surprised him as he knew the heat would affect them, and Theodoric was pointing out the obvious. All of Thomas's knights had their horses wearing chamfrons, testieres as some called them (head armour), crupieres for the rear and flanchiers for the front and sides of their horses. Paul noted they were also wearing padded covers, caparisons that were gamboises or pourpointe and quilted. Some, including Thomas's horse, had couvertures de fer, which were mail. Thomas and his knights had clearly spent several hours cleaning themselves up since he saw them last. It was only now that he could see they had no markings of any political allegiance. They also had full face covering helmets all with their own particular coat of arms being applied to their pennons, shields and surcoats and smaller versions upon their horse harnesses and even weaponry.

"He means fully armoured of course!" Thomas remarked as he watched Theodoric walk away. "Our horses are well suited to heat. my friend. 'Tis why we have our own water wagon. We keep them watered often. On these routes you have to be ready at all times I am afraid to say. The Orders may travel in light order when it suits, but we know that there are those out there who will seize upon a convoy knowing that fact...so let them just try it against us. And Paul...just so you know, my men and I are honoured to be able to escort you and your family to Alexandria. Your tall dark friend up front is most clearly a warrior...an unusual one but still a warrior...but where we are going, if trouble starts, you will need all the swords and good men you can get," Thomas explained as he stroked his horse.

"It is greatly appreciated. I just pray you still hold the same views by the time we get there...for I have no doubt that we shall get there. I do not see what is in this venture for you?" Paul asked.

"'Tis refreshing to speak with one who says as he thinks. I am confident we shall get there also...and our reward is nothing that you can pay us or give. Just accept we will receive just exactly what is deserved for us from him up there." Thomas smiled and pointed upwards just as Percival pulled up alongside on his horse. It looked tiny compared with Thomas's.

"We are off," Percival stated and smiled.

Port of La Rochelle, France, Melissae Inn, spring 1191

"And so perhaps the toughest part of their journey was about to start. If Paul had thought it tough going before, it was about to get a whole lot harder," the old man explained and shuffled on his chair as if uncomfortable.

"I thought it would have got easier surely?" Simon remarked puzzled.

"Trust me, brother, once in the principality of Antioch and Tripoli, the harshness of the terrain and the criminals becomes a very real and ever present danger," the Templar pointed out. "'Tis why we were forever going up and down that land patrolling. Always patrolling!"

"Let me explain fully then," the old man responded looking at Simon. "After several days of hard travel through spectacular but mainly dry countryside, their column passed the outskirts of Antakya, in the principality of Antioch, stopping briefly to pick up fresh supplies, sealed letters and deliver others to the Templar Marshal garrisoned there. Paul wanted to stay longer at the Templar fortress, which had the biggest circular water cistern he had ever seen. The views from its commanding position were stunning but despite the women's insistence they stay longer to hopefully bathe, they were soon on their way. They also picked up many fine silk items as it was still a major part of the silk trade routes. Paul recalled what he had been told about the place, that it was acknowledged as the very first place where Christians had actually started to be called Christians, but to him the city did not look much at all, and more the size of a town than a city as he looked down the hill from their position overlooking the valley it was nestled in. A totally unassuming place he thought. He could see

the remains of several massive Roman walls and other fortifications snake up the side of the nearest hill as they skirted the town travelling along a well preserved Roman road. He would have liked to visit the town properly...for there was far more to see than he realised. Antioch-on-the-Orontes, the city once called 'the fair crown of the Orient', was a city of great religious importance. It was the home of several Roman temples and its suburb, Daphne, was held to be the very place where Daphne was turned into a laurel tree to escape the affections of Apollo. Antioch had also been the home of a large Jewish community since the city's founding in 300 BC. Antioch played a truly important role in Christian history for it was indeed the base for St Paul's missionary journeys, where Jesus's followers were first called 'Christians' (Acts 11:26) and where the Gospel of Matthew was probably written. Antioch hosted a number of church councils, developed its own characteristic school of biblical interpretation, and produced such influential Christian figures as the martyr-bishop Ignatius of Antioch, the pillar-saint Simeon and the 'golden-mouthed' preacher John Chrysostom," the old man explained shaking his head, smiling. "How many of you here know that we get the name Catholic from Ignatius? For he alone is responsible for the first known use of the Greek word katholikos (καθολικός), meaning 'universal', 'complete' and 'whole' to describe the Church. It is from the word katholikos that the word catholic comes." He paused again as they all shook their heads no. "Well you do now...so I shall continue. The women were still all wishing for a bath as they had not managed to have one in Tarsus due to water supply problems after the aqueducts had been damaged in the storms and an earthquake. Flies seemed to increase in number daily, which, coupled with the ever increasing heat, only added to their discomfort. Paul had noticed that when they had struck or set camp each day, Percival remained quite solitary and seemed awkward when sorting his horse and equipment. Something in Paul's mind about him did not quite ring true. Tenno and Theodoric teased Taqi constantly when showing him ways to use a sword and crossbow as well as bow and arrow and clean his equipment, much to the merriment of Thomas and his men. Tenno, despite his earlier reservations over Thomas, fitted in only too well with them. They were fighting men just like him whom he could relate to, and they to him." He paused. "But travelling overland was difficult as Paul was rapidly finding out daily. As you must all know, undertaking a long distance journey to the Holy Land is a decision not taken lightly but Paul had not even considered any aspect of it and just trusted it to his father and Firgany... and only now was he realising the sheer amount of planning they had obviously put into their trip, as well as funding."

"Tell them about all the pilgrims who follow the routes because they have to...the criminals and those who had the pilgrimage imposed by a priest or a court of law to seek redemption and forgiveness of their sins. So many criminals made the trip having been forced to do so," the Hospitaller stated.

"Yes...there were many of that type, and numbers only increase yearly. And so many chose lesser places to visit than Jerusalem as their pilgrimage site as new ones were acquired...or in most cases, invented, or a new relic or perhaps a new saint had been created (canonised), the most significant canonisation in recent times being that of Thomas Becket at Canterbury. You see many Churches compete to attract pilgrims by using a range of different 'advertising' techniques. The first important practical consideration was cost. If a pilgrim wanted to undertake a long distance pilgrimage and expected to travel comfortably, they had to expect a very big bill. Many rich pilgrims needed a year's income and were forced to sell their land to the Church. Although the religious authorities recommended that a true pilgrimage should be undertaken in poverty and on foot, many richer pilgrims did not do that. German *pilgrims in particular were notorious for travelling in style, as many thieves noted. Poorer pilgrims would have to live on the charity of people who provided alms."*

"Yes...many times we had to rescue them...but often as not we would end up having to bury them instead as the criminals would always attack when we were the furthest away," the Templar explained.

"As I am sure most of you here must know, before leaving home, a pilgrim has to clear up all their unsettled business, pay all debts, make a will, settle arguments and apologise to everyone he or she might have offended. Finally, the pilgrim has to make an appointment to see his priest. In front of the priest the pilgrim makes a vow to complete his journey. In return the priest gives the pilgrim his blessing. Having made the vow the pilgrim has to make the journey or face being excommunicated. But only after having made the vow can he or she put on the uniform of the pilgrim. The pilgrim's uniform fascinated Tenno and he found it difficult to understand their motives no matter how much Theodoric tried to explain it," the old man explained as the wealthy tailor raised his hand.

"I do a good trade in their attire. I must tell you that we only make and sell the finest and toughest pilgrim's uniform around. For practical considerations of course," he commented.

"Well...a good pilgrim needs to distinguish themself clearly as a pilgrim. The staff and scrip are perhaps the earliest and most obvious parts of the uniform, and both are very practical. The staff has to be made of strong wood, preferably with a metal tip. Apart from its obvious use to someone walking hundreds of miles, the staff can be an important means of self defence against wolves or human attackers. The scrip is a soft pouch, usually made of leather and tied to the pilgrim's waist. The scrip was used to store all the essential belongings: food, money, documents etc. The long tunic or sclavein has now become part of the pilgrim uniform," the old man detailed, when the wealthy tailor interrupted.

"Yes, that is precisely what we sell the most of...the sclavein...and mainly in blue nowadays," he explained excitedly.

⚜   2 – 15

"Well, we now have priests bless the pilgrim's actual clothes...for a fee of course usually. Most robes serve as coats and sleeping bags and most pilgrims now wear a wide-brimmed hat. They also carry some form of bag or sack, often a book bag, carrying with them some sort of religious book. In the religious ceremony, which very much resembles the 'dubbing' of a knight, the pilgrims are presented with the staff from the altar. This ceremony began in imitation of the blessing of the first Crusaders. In time, the staff, scrip and sclavein have taken on their own religious symbolism: the staff is used to ward off wolves, which symbolise the Devil, the scrip is small, symbolising the poverty of the pilgrim and the sclavein's complete covering represents Christ's love for mankind."

"Sounds like one big money making system to me," the Genoese sailor commented and sat back and crossed his arms looking at the wealthy tailor.

"Hey, if they did not require them, we would not make and supply them...," the wealthy tailor shot back defensively.

"You may have seen pilgrims pass here on their way back. Have you noticed how they wear a lead badge to show where they have been and to prove they have fulfilled their vow? From the Holy Land a pilgrim wears a palm, from Rome a set of keys and from Santiago de Compostella on the up-turned brim of the hat they pin a shell from the St James' scallop, which has now become the symbol most often associated with pilgrims," the old man said.

"We always come across stalls that sell souvenir badges which usually represent a famous miracle associated with the patron saint. We have seen many pilgrims apparently very well travelled wearing hats covered in the badges of many shrines they have visited," the Hospitaller stated, shaking his head dismissively.

"Can I ask why the need for pilgrims to be so distinctive...surely that would only attract criminals and robbers to you?" Simon asked keeping an eye on Sarah as he did so.

"It was distinctive and was important because it entitled the wearer to be treated as a pilgrim. This was supposed to guarantee their safety along the road and to give them admission to the many shelters and hospices that have sprung up along the bigger roads. As we all here know, long distance travel whether overland or by sea is very difficult and very often dangerous. If travelling overland you face the problem of very poor quality paths that are badly signposted, if at all. Where roads are well maintained, the chances are you will be expected to pay a fee or toll for their use. Even an experienced rider on horseback can only expect to cover thirty miles a day. The pilgrim also faces thick forests, mosquito infested marshes, wild animals, impassable rivers and undrinkable water. Supplies of water and drink are a constant problem and pilgrims are advised not to travel at certain times of year. Although punishments for attacking pilgrims are very harsh, that does not stop them being attacked by robbers and bandits. In northern Italy the problem is with German robbers, in northern Spain on the routes to Santiago, the bandits tend to be English," the old man explained, when he was interrupted by Ayleth.

"English...surely never?" she exclaimed, astonished at the old man's revelation.

"Yes, English. Criminals come from all nations...now by far the most dangerous route is without any doubt the pilgrimage to the Holy Land. The overland route from Joppa to Jerusalem is notorious. Many criminals and robbers, as well as soldiers from both Muslim and Christian armies, lay hidden in caves and crevices, waiting day and night for people travelling in small groups or straggling behind their groups. Not a good route. Of course, as Alisha and Taqi had done many times already, the alternative to the overland route was to travel by sea. Travelling long distances by boat for most is not an easy option though. As with the overland route, it is also dangerous, extremely uncomfortable and has the additional inconvenience of being very boring. The journey from Venice to the Holy Land takes six weeks or more. In addition to the obvious threat of shipwreck, there is also the problem of piracy. Accommodation is very basic. Pilgrims are crammed into small boats where they hardly have room enough to turn over in their sleep. The ships are rat and flea infested and the animals stored as the only fresh food sometimes break out and trample on paying guests. If you have a choice of where to sleep, you will be well advised to take a place as close to the deck as possible. Fortunately Alisha and Taqi had always travelled in the best available ships...at great financial cost no less. The food is very poor and the water stale. Experienced pilgrims advise others to take their own food, including laxatives and restoratives such as ginger, figs and cloves."

"Do you hear that part...for when you make your pilgrimage!" the Templar joked looking at Simon.

"In addition to the problems of hunger and sleeplessness, there is also the boredom. The only organised activity is the daily sermon. Otherwise pilgrims are left to their own devices. Some pilgrims gamble and drink while others play chess and try to keep fit. But most people just sit about looking blankly, passing their eyes from one group to another, and thence to the open sea. But whether the pilgrim travels by land or by sea, there are certain experiences common to both...language...it is always a major obstacle to be overcome. The guidebooks *offer some help with common phrases but even the educated pilgrims can only speak a few words of any language apart from their own or Latin. Attitudes to the host people along the way reflect at best ignorance but often hostility," the old man explained in detail.*

"Why do you explain all that?" Simon asked.

"So that those of you here who have never experienced the journey will hopefully grasp just a fraction of the conditions that Paul, Alisha and the others had to endure," the old man answered. "And on top of that, the ever increasing raiding parties by all sides and tensions being raised only added to the problems that were rapidly unfolding in Outremer...and Paul and Alisha were in the very heart of that whirlwind."

ഇരു

Ruins of San Simeon Monastery, Principality of Antioch, 6th June 1179

Balian approached Paul as he stepped down from his caravan. The day had been a long one and the sun was still scorching down upon them. Paul looked on as the Templar's Gonfanier placed the Order's standard where they would site camp for the night a short way off the main track. Balian had used the site of the ruined monastery previously as it had commanding views all around as well several walls that could be defended should the need arise. The air was also cooler as they were higher, which made it a lot more comfortable. Paul was fascinated by the ruins all around them.

"Make camp, Lord Brothers, on God's behalf!" the Gonfanier called out.

Paul wondered what his brother Stewart was doing at that moment.

"Rule, section 148...," Balian stated as he removed his riding gloves.

"Pardon? "Paul asked, puzzled.

"'Tis their rule, section 148...to set camp. Your brother as a Gonfanier will certainly know the rule. Should you ever decide to become a Templar, 'tis one of many you shall learn," Balian explained as the Templars immediately started to set their camp.

"Vespers follows I believe...but I am afraid I shall not be taking up the calling to become a Templar," Paul remarked.

"Never say never, young Paul...for who knows what the Lord has planned for you...or any of us."

Both Balian and Paul looked to the end of the convoy as it began to spread out to form up for the evening just as a Templar courier came galloping into view in a cloud of dust. Hurriedly the knight dismounted clearly exhausted, blood upon his mantle and out of breath. Brother Matthew came over walking quickly.

"Brother...what urgency is this?" he asked the Templar, who was still out of breath.

"Brother Matthew...'tis good to see you. I come directly from Master Odo. He is calling all brothers, including Hospitallers and any knight who will answer the call," the Templar explained quickly and bent forwards as he tried to catch his breath still.

"Why...what has happened?" Brother Matthew asked, concerned.

"Saladin...he moves from Damascus for Jacobs Ford, he intends to besiege and take the new castle at Chastellet Odo has been constructing. 'Tis vital all knights answer the call to reinforce him," the Templar explained and fell to his knees utterly exhausted.

"Brother Matthew...I shall leave immediately. We have but a few hours before darkness. But we cannot leave these people unprotected," Balian said as he waved for one of his own knights to come over.

"Sires, I am at your service in whatever capacity I am able," he stated and bowed slightly as he looked at the kneeling knight.

"Good...in that case you can stay here and help protect this column," Balian remarked. Percival saw what was happening and rushed over.

The Hospitaller's master approached with several of his knights.

"What occurs?" he asked bluntly.

"Our master has sent out a call to all knights to assist as Saladin plans to attack the castle at Chastellet," Balian explained.

"But that is at least two to three days' travel away," he remarked.

"Not if we leave now. We can be there by nightfall on the eighth," Balian explained.

"Sires...," the kneeling Templar said and stood himself up slowly. "Master, your Grand Master Brother Roger requests all available Hospitallers to likewise come," he explained, still out of breath.

"Good man...you must stay and rest. Percy here will assist you...but we must leave soonest," Balian said as Guy approached, smiling. "Sorry Guy...you must remain with this column. I shall return as soon as I am able, and I shall leave you most of your brothers at service," Balian commented. Guy immediately outstretched his hands disappointedly.

Paul looked around as he heard the caravan's door swing open. Alisha looked at him concerned just as Thomas walked up brushing dust from his surcoat.

"See...I told you we would come in handy to escort you," Thomas said politely and confidently to Paul and nodded at Alisha and smiled.

"'Tis a good thing indeed," Balian remarked.

඗ ⌘

As word spread down the column, people started to talk frantically. Brother Teric assured Princess Stephanie that he would remain with a small escort of four Templars for her. Sister Lucy and Theodoric shook their heads clearly concerned but smiled broadly as soon as Alisha came close carrying Arri. Within less than fifteen minutes Paul found himself stood with Taqi, Tenno and Theodoric alongside Percy and Thomas watching the bulk of the Knights Templar and Hospitallers and other assorted knights form Balian's group rapidly head off out across the open plain that stretched away before them. Balian turned briefly and waved at Paul.

When Tenno and Paul turned to return to the caravans, they looked on bemused as several new pilgrims that had joined their column ate and laughed as if oblivious to the seriousness of the unfolding drama. They were certainly different. Paul and Tenno went and joined Theodoric and Sister Lucy as she cooked up some food, Alisha feeding Arri in the privacy of the caravan. By the time the meal was ready it was rapidly getting dark and most of the talk had been about the urgency and call to arms issued by Odo de St Armand.

"My lord, have you seen those new pilgrims?" Sister Lucy asked as she stirred in some seasoning. Theodoric shook his head no. "Not only are they badly dressed, but they eat and drink in the most disgusting way…they eat with their hands, slobbering over their food like a pig or dog. To hear them speaking, you would think they were a pack of hounds barking, for their language is absolutely barbarous sounding…They have dark, evil, ugly faces…They are like fierce savages, dishonest and untrustworthy, impious, common, cruel and quarrelsome looking…They will kill you for a penny I am sure…and have you seen the way both men and women alike warm themselves by their fires, revealing those parts which are better hidden," she explained.

"My, my Lucy…'tis not like you to pass such observations, or comments," Theodoric remarked, surprised at her comments.

"Oh ignore me. I am just tired and well overdue bathing…and this heat!" she replied and feigned a smile. "Well so long as they don't expect us to feed them all for free. Like yesterday."

Port of La Rochelle, France, Melissae Inn, spring 1191

"I know where this tale is taking us next," the Templar remarked.

"Really, how so?" Simon asked.

"The dates given…'tis too near the date of the battle at Banjas and Marj Ayun later…am I correct?" the Templar asked.

"Yes…but let me get to that save you spoil the story," the old man smiled.

"You know of this event?" Gabirol asked.

"He should do…he was there," the Hospitaller stated and winked as Miriam held the Templar's hand tightly.

"I was…but I shall cease my tongue so you may continue this tale," he commented.

"Thank you…"

"Sorry…this may sound like a silly question…but why were they all set up out in the fields…or wherever they were. Why not in one of the many hospices along the route?" Simon asked.

"Because they were aware of the many assaults and pillaging that was being orchestrated by Saladin's forces to weaken the Crusader forces' grip and control of the region, especially at the River Jordan crossing where Odo de St Amand had been building the new fortress… that would in effect control it completely. With all the tensions, many pilgrims decided to remain in the locations they had reached, thus filling up further the already overcrowded inns and hospices. Besides, with a full escort, it had been deemed safer to set up where they could easily defend themselves. They had not expected to have that escort reduced to a minimum… so it was indeed providential that they had run into Thomas and his men," the old man explained.

"Is it true that pilgrims are entitled to free food, as you mentioned Sister Lucy complained they did…?" Ayleth asked quietly.

"I can answer that…if you wish?" the Hospitaller said aloud. The old man proffered

his right hand as if to say continue. "You see according to custom, pilgrims are entitled to free food and a roof over their head. Providing that service was the responsibility of the Church and, in particular, the monasteries. On the busy pilgrimage routes it has become impossible to accommodate everyone in the monasteries, so smaller hospices were built and now run by small groups of monks. Now, so many hospices have been built that one hospice is rarely more than a day's travel from the next. The quality of the hospices do vary considerably and nowadays, as is becoming more commonplace, not all hospices provide food and usually only the very poorest receive alms as you already said," he remarked looking at the old man. "And beds are a rarity and most pilgrims have to make do with a straw covered floor...so as Sister Lucy commented, some do look pretty wretched by the time they get to Outremer. But for the richer pilgrim, there is always the possibility of staying at an inn. However, the standard of comfort is usually much lower than a rich pilgrim would be used to. No one has a bed to themselves and is expected to share the room with a number of other paying guests. The innkeepers do not have a good reputation these days. They are often accused of cheating the pilgrims with high prices for poor quality food and flea infested beds. Many German pilgrims and rich ones who travelled in style are often attacked as a consequence, as mentioned already also. So staying out in the field is by contrast actually preferable," he explained.

"Hey, before anyone says it, we run a clean and tidy inn here...no fleas or rats and anyone who complains about the food, they can join the pigs for dinner...," Sarah stated as Stephan nodded in agreement, smiling.

"'Tis perhaps the finest inn I have ever stayed at," Gabirol commented and smiled.

Sarah mouthed him a silent thank you and smiled back. Simon pretended to scratch himself but soon stopped as she glared at him, the old man smiling before continuing.

"Yes...our Hospitaller friend is correct and that is why Brother Matthew set up the caravans in a tight formation and posted what few Templars and Hospitallers he had left as watchmen for the night. Princess Stephanie felt particularly uneasy and did not want to spend the evening alone and practically begged Sister Lucy to invite Alisha, Paul, Taqi, Theodoric and Tenno to her caravan to pass away the time. Theodoric tried to teach Tenno the game of chess but with no luck. Princess Stephanie eventually asked Tenno questions about his origins and travels, which resulted in Tenno fetching his maps and displaying them out across the table. Alisha saw the excitement in Paul's eyes as he viewed the maps. Guy came in and joined them at this point of the evening.

"Are Tenno's maps authentic then?" Gabirol asked.

"Oh yes...'tis a real pity lesser informed people did not view them as such. Most dismissed them out of hand...yet they reveal a truth of our world that is still being challenged now," the old man sighed.

"'Tis a pity then that you do not have them," the farrier remarked.

"But I do!" the old man answered simply.

"You do?" Gabirol shot back, surprised.

The old man leaned down and reached beneath the table and lifted into view a leather bound scroll tube. Gently he offered it towards the farrier. Hesitantly almost, the farrier took the tube and began to open it. Slowly he removed several linen and silk sheets and parchments clearly showing maps of extremely high quality and intricate detail. Gabirol leaned over to view them in awe.

"Tenno's maps. Now note the Chinese and Japanese characters around them. That main one you see there," the old man explained and pointed to a large circular map on silk. "That *one goes with the parchment...which I have written upon as the 'Sung' document. Tenno explained that this was made during that ruler's reign."*

"What does it all say?" Gabirol asked as he moved closer to study the large circular map.

"The document details the discovery of a place they named 'Mu Lan Pi'. There are many Muslim sailors who also claim to have been there...across the other side of the world where Tenno said he first landed before walking across the land to return home as I explained previously. Those who know of this land oft call it Mulan. Tenno wrote down all the details whilst staying with Paul's father in La Rochelle in 1178. In this very room in fact," the old man explained and sighed.

"I have heard of this name," the Genoese sailor interrupted. "But we were told it was but a tale by Muslim mariners who had in fact simply landed in a southern part of Spain."

"'Twas not Spain, friend. Just look at the maps. They are drawn just as Tenno said, after he travelled east from mainland China and landed on the shores of the unknown lands. But those same lands are identical to even far older maps from antiquity that Paul would happen to fall upon...in time," the old man explained as the maps and parchments were looked at closely, Gabirol trying to make a quick drawing of the main circular map.

"I know many argue that Arabic ships could not have been able to withstand a return journey across the great Atlantic ocean without knowledge of prevailing winds and currents...so how did they...if this is real?" Gabirol asked, perplexed.

"Because they sailed east and landed on the western shores of the great landmass. That is how. In time this truth will be revealed...just as many more," the old man answered.

"I note this Tenno fellow has drawn his homelands at the centre of these maps," Peter commented whilst studying them.

"No...Not his homeland, but that of China," the old man corrected.

"My friends...if these are genuine, then we are all party to a great secret revealed this day. We are indeed privileged," Gabirol remarked and sat back in his chair looking at the old man curiously.

County of Tripoli, river crossing, 13ᵗʰ June 1179

Brother Matthew and Brother Teric had navigated the column and caravans to a secure and safe river crossing without incident. They had all seen fires on the horizon to the east but clearly miles away. The sun was beating down and Brother Teric had agreed they would all wait awhile so that Princess Stephanie and the other ladies could wash themselves properly in the clear waters of the river. In the morning they would decide on whether to travel to Crac de l'Ospital or Tortosa. Most in the convoy wished to go via Tortosa but the remaining Hospitallers wanted to head directly to their main headquarters at Crac de l'Ospital. Taqi would leave for Castle Blanc and eventually onwards to meet up with Rashid as arranged. Paul and Taqi left Tenno and Theodoric with the women at the caravans, who were preparing themselves to bathe, and led Adrastos and their other horse to the water's edge to drink. They looked on as another caravan approached through the trees from the northeast. Thomas immediately recognised the lead knight, clearly of Frankish origin, and beckoned him over as the small caravan column pulled up alongside theirs. Several other Arabic knights appeared with the convoy. Taqi immediately looked at Paul, concerned. They both watched closely as Thomas greeted all the men with smiles. Though puzzled, Paul felt reassured. Within minutes the knights had all dismounted and were talking amongst themselves.

Brother Teric positioned Alisha and Paul's caravan directly beside Princess Stephanie's far larger caravan just inside the tree line for shade as Thomas guided one of the large caravans from the column that had just arrived on the other side. Feeling reassured, Paul removed the harness from Adrastos, and his covers, laid them out across a broken tree branch that angled towards the river, and let him drink and stand freely. Taqi followed his example with the other horse. As Paul sat down, placing his sandalled feet into the cool river, Taqi just stood looking around. Paul moved and untied the rope around his waist so he could remove his sword. He stretched up and hung it on the tree and relaxed back upon his elbows.

"What troubles you, my friend?" Paul asked as he closed his eyes and looked up.

"Not sure...just anxious I guess," Taqi replied, unclasped his sword and hung it next to Paul's and sat down beside him placing his feet in the river.

"I am eager to get to Alexandria...and out of this mad land, for that is how it feels...but I am also sad too," Paul commented as he continued looking upwards letting the sun fall upon his face.

"Why sad?"

"Sad...because the sooner we get to Alexandria, then even sooner we shall have to bid our farewells to you...we have but days left together, my friend, after which we shall not see each other for who knows how long?" Paul answered and sighed.

Taqi lowered his head and looked at the clear water gently flowing around his feet.

"I did not think of that...you will look after Ali wont you?"

Paul punched Taqi hard on the arm and looked at him shaking his head for asking such a stupid question.

Both heard a loud pop sound from the tree line where the caravans were still being moved into position. At first they ignored it, but then a woman screamed hysterically. They jumped to their feet and turned around, just in time to see one of the caravans near the end of the column, next to the blacksmith's three wagons, erupt in a vicious red and yellow gout of flame from a naphtha grenade thrown inside, a woman fully alight screaming in agony as she jumped down in flames. Paul's eyes widened, his heart exploding with panic as he looked towards his caravan, several black robed men rushing towards it. He just saw Tenno take out his main sword whilst pushing both Alisha and Princess Stephanie down behind him. More attackers rushed into view from within the tree line. Several horses came galloping into view to Paul's right, lances lowered at full charge as Brother Teric and Brother Matthew tried to mount their Destriers; panic and confusion was everywhere as more people began to run and scream and more grenades popped. Taqi blinked several times as his mind fought to make sense of the sudden chaos he was witnessing. Paul slapped his hand across Taqi's chest for him to follow him.

Quickly Paul mounted Adrastos, leaned towards the tree, grabbed the handle of the sword and raised it high immediately, and with no saddle and using his left hand to hold the mouth bit strap, he geed Adrastos forwards. He did not even hear Taqi shout behind him as he shot off at full gallop towards Tenno, Alisha and Princess Stephanie with just one thought in his mind...to get to Alisha and Arri. He wielded the sword high and charged, ignoring the riders coming in from his right.

Alisha pulled Arri close and turned over onto her knees to shield him as Princess Stephanie instinctively lay over them both protectively just as Tenno thrust his sword in a wide arch slashing across the chest of the man nearest to him. Another dark robed man aimed a crossbow at him almost point blank and fired, the bolt deflecting off his sword, which Tenno immediately raised and slashed down upon the man's right arm severing it instantly, the man falling away to the left screaming, Alisha shielding her ears cowering over Arri. A mounted knight rushed through the tree line with a lance pointed directly at Tenno. Just as he was upon him, Tenno turned and saw the lance flash into view. Instantly he dropped his sword, clasped his hands together as the lance came his way, gripped tighter and thrust his arms and hands upwards, then grabbing the lance completely, pulled it sideways as the knight rode almost over him. As the horse jumped, Tenno yanked the lance and pulled the knight off the horse. As Tenno leaned forwards to push the knight down and away from Princess Stephanie and Alisha another man appeared running towards them about to bring his sword down upon Princess Stephanie. Tenno could only look up briefly as he struggled to hold the other knight down whilst trying to grab his sword back. As the other knight's sword was about to contact across Princess Stephanie's back, Paul made Adrastos jump over all of them, jumping off mid flight throwing himself at the swordsman.

As Adrastos landed and steadied himself, immediately turning about, Tenno finally grabbed his sword as Paul crashed into the other knight throwing him backwards away from Princess Stephanie and Alisha. Alisha looked up, her heart pounding so fast she thought she would be sick. Arri was crying but she could not hear him. She could see Paul jump to his feet, kick the knight backwards hard so he could not get back up, then she saw another man in a black surcoat step in front of her, his sword ready to thrust into her face. She saw the tip of the sword draw back, then start to come for her. Paul looked to his right seeing the man thrust forwards...without hesitation he raised his sword up high, and in one almighty shout, he yelled and swung his sword down as hard as he could against the right shoulder of the man, his sword continuing its downward motion through the man's collar bone, shoulder blade, chain mail surcoat and only stopping when it reached the man's belt midway. Wide eyed and shocked...the man looked at Paul. His eyes were green. Alisha looked at Paul, her eyes wide and full of terror as Princess Stephanie wrapped her arms around her protectively. Paul stood up straight, pulled the sword out of the man and stepped back. The man just stood for what seemed an age before the right side of him fell away, his right arm and side just hanging revealing his internal organs as blood spurted everywhere, he rolled his eyes and fell backwards dead. Alisha gulped as she was nearly sick, Tenno still pushing the knight's head into the dirt. Paul's eyes fell upon the man's black surcoat...it had a Templar red cross on the top left breast area. As that realisation hit him, the sword covered in blood, Paul's head was suddenly filled with noise again of people screaming and shouting. He knelt to check Alisha as he heard Brother

Teric shouting loudly to stand down. Confused, Paul looked up to see Taqi run up as Brother Matthew was pushing away other Templars angrily, slapping one as they all started to realise a terrible mistake. Alisha struggled to her knees holding Arri as Paul wrapped his left arm around her, Princess Stephanie on all fours, just kneeling on her hands and knees, staring at him in awe and surprise. Black smoke wafted across the area from the burning caravan and naphtha grenades as Brother Teric shouted more orders. Paul looked to his left as Thomas stepped into view physically restraining another Templar and looking at the dead knight almost cut in two.

"You did that?" Thomas asked.

Paul stood up and helped Alisha to stand as Princess Stephanie shook her head.

"'Tis okay...I am only pregnant after all...I can stand," she exclaimed as she tried to get to her feet. Tenno grabbed her arm and lifted her up as Brother Matthew ran over.

Paul looked at the dead knight he had killed and then the knight Tenno had dealt with, who was still alive. Blood was pumping out of his severed arm near his shoulder. A Hospitaller started to pack the wound with a compound and a powder.

"What in the fucking hell's breath of the devil are you doing?" Brother Teric uncharacteristically yelled out as several other Templars approached on horseback slowly lowering their lances.

The Muslim knights that had come in with the new caravans were being manhandled and pushed and pulled between the newly arrived Templars and some of Thomas's men shielding them.

Paul saw movement to his left. Three men were hiding beneath the front wheels of Princess Stephanie's caravan. Wearing large Burnash helmets, it was clear they were Muslim noblemen from the big caravan that Thomas had greeted just minutes before the assault.

"Well, well, well...look who we meet yet again," Gerard suddenly said, drawing Paul's attention back.

Paul let go of Alisha and stepped past Princess Stephanie and walked towards Gerard, who was sat upon his horse. Adrastos snorted loudly from behind the caravans. Brother Teric was shaking his head in utter dismay at the assault as Paul began to walk towards Gerard, his sword still dripping blood.

"You reckless stupid fool," Paul blurted out uncontrollably to Gerard. "Are you blind...are you all blind!" Paul then shouted looking around at all the knights.

"Brother...'twas a great error, that is all," Stewart said as he rode into view from behind Gerard. "We are travelling light, to reach Odo. Hence why we are dressed as such. We saw this was a Muslim caravan...and..."

"And what...what! You thought you would just attack it for no good reason. That is murder by any measure," Paul shouted back, his voice deeper and full of authority that surprised Stewart.

Gerard smiled and sat back in his saddle and rubbed his beard.

"Murder you say! Hmmm. That was an accident," Gerard smirked, pointing without looking at the burnt out caravan and smouldering body of a dead woman as her family tried to cover her remains. "But that...that is murder of one of my knights," he stated and pointed to the man Paul had killed. Paul walked nearer to Gerard, who backed up his horse hesitantly unsure what Paul was about to do. "And I see you use that sword of yours again with remarkable force. Lucky for you, you have such a weapon."

Paul looked at the sword and only then realised it was in fact Taqi's sword... not his own. He looked up hard at Gerard. Gerard frowned. Paul looked past him at his brother.

"You have no standard for where is your Beauseant? You do not wear your white mantels but black in this heat...you clearly set out to deceive this day," Paul exclaimed, his face full of anger but controlled. Stewart was surprised by the look upon his brother's face.

"Brother...do you honestly think I would be party to an attack knowing full well you and Alisha are within?" Stewart asked.

Gerard smirked, folded his arms and sat back in his saddle and looked at Paul as if to ask 'Well?'

"I never thought you would be party to the death of Firgany...but you are... so I do not know what to make of you any more...brother," Paul replied, but staring at Gerard all the while.

"Careful, young Paul. You have this day murdered one of my men...whilst we were in the genuine pursuit of Saladin's brother himself no less. You hamper the king's orders too!" Gerard stated smugly.

Paul raised Taqi's sword and looked at it closely, then past it at Gerard.

"There will be no such charge of murder or hindering the king's orders...," Stephanie called out as she stepped forwards and approached Paul and Gerard. "This man saved my life. If he had not cut your man down, following your orders...not the king's I suspect, you would now be party to my murder. And it would be interesting to see and hear how you would have explained that one to your good friend...and my husband...and soon to be father of my child," Stephanie said loudly so all could hear.

"We had our orders...," Gerard snapped back as Stephanie just smiled at him and pulled her clothing straight.

Alisha approached Paul slowly and stood behind him holding Arri close followed by Tenno, then Taqi and then Thomas along with all of his knights to form a semicircle behind him. Taqi gently took his sword from Paul and handed him his own sword.

"So the great Bull's Head Slayer we hear so much of has friends now," Gerard exclaimed patronisingly as Stewart looked down at Alisha.

Thomas frowned briefly in surprise upon hearing Gerard's comments and looked at Paul, then at his men, who all nodded they had heard, several of them smiling and impressed.

"And just what are your orders pray tell?" Brother Teric asked and moved to stand with Paul's group.

"We have orders to proceed with all of God's speed to meet up with Balian and Odo de St Amand and defend the new fortifications at Chastellet whatever the cost...but should we come across the whereabouts of Saladin's brother Turansha, known to be in this area...to hunt him down as a priority...to use as a bargaining tool should Chastellet fall," Gerard explained and dismounted. "So when our spies told us he was in this area, we saw his caravan and so attacked. 'Tis but unfortunate that somehow it became mixed with yours...would you not agree?"

Two riders came galloping into view and splashed across the river crossing towards them. Everyone looked as they rapidly approached and pulled up hard in a cloud of dust. They were both Templar fast couriers. One dismounted quickly and walked up to Gerard.

"Master, have you not heard?" he asked breathless almost. Gerard shook his head no and raised his hands almost dismissively as if irritated even. "Saladin went to attack Chastellet castle, but Master Odo went out to engage him direct before he could get there. He met up with Balian and his men," the courier explained.

"What of Balian?" Guy called out as he approached from the midst of his own men accompanied by Percy.

"'Tis sad and grave news indeed...the Lord Toron was sadly slain on the field of battle at Banias, just two days past on June the tenth. He died gloriously saving the very life of King Baldwin the Fourth."

Princess Stephanie let out a slight gasp but quickly composed herself.

"Say that again...," she said, her throat dry.

"Lord of Toron...he has been slain, My Lady...Oh my Lord, my sincere apologies My Lady. He was once your father-in-law...I...I did not know you were here," the courier apologised and bowed.

Alisha put her left arm around Princess Stephanie as she held her hands to her mouth. Paul noticed Gerard appeared to smirk upon hearing the news.

"And what of Master Odo?" Gerard asked.

"Master...I am afraid to report that Master Odo has been taken prisoner by Saladin."

"What of Balian?" Guy shouted.

"Balian...he also," the courier answered and bowed his head slightly.

Paul shot a look of concern at Brother Teric, who simply shook his head.

"How did this happen?" Stephanie asked, her voice slightly broken with emotion.

"My Lady...Saladin had invaded from the direction of Damascus and based his army at Banias...from there he sent out raiding forces to despoil villages and crops near Sidon and the coastal areas. He then came to attack the new castle at Jacobs Ford...but Master Odo defended it well, then went in pursuit...that is when your father-in-law was sadly killed," the courier explained.

Paul tied his own sword back around his waist and turned his back on Gerard and began to usher Alisha away.

"You dare turn your back on me," Gerard shouted at Paul.

Paul stopped, hesitated for a moment, turned and walked back up to Gerard stopping just feet in front of him.

"We have nothing further to say...and I am not one of your Order. Death seems to accompany you wherever you go...so I am kindly...and respectfully... asking you to keep away from me and my family," Paul stated.

"How can I when your brother at least has the good sense to be on the right side?" Gerard shot back sarcastically, thumbing towards Stewart behind him. Brother Teric shook his head in despair at Gerard's gesture. "Besides, you really would be as wise to start being a little more respectful towards me...for if Master Odo is no more...it will not be long before I am the Grand Master himself," Gerard said loudly.

"Then God help us all...and Stewart...is he my family?" Paul replied and again turned around and started to walk away immediately wishing he had not said that last remark.

Stewart looked at Alisha as she stared at him. She could see Paul's words had touched him. He feigned a brave smile but then lowered his head sadly.

"And what of your Muslim friends here this day?" Gerard called out. Tenno immediately stood beside Taqi and clasped his hand over his sword clearly obvious for Gerard to see.

"All and any persons in this caravan fall under my protection...is that clear? No one here today, Christian, Muslim or Jew, will be harmed...and I can have that order sent and confirmed to my husband within the day if needs be...do I make myself clear?" Stephanie called out so all could hear.

"The Bull's Head Slayer himself no less," Thomas said to himself quietly as Paul led Alisha back to their caravan.

ℴ≋

Two Templars were lifting the dead Templar onto a flat wooden stretcher. As they manhandled him upon it, more of his insides fell out. The nearest Templar used his own hands to quickly push it all onto the board, the stench of blood mixed heavily with the stench of the man's open bowels. The two Templars quickly lifted the stretcher to take away the body when Paul raised his hand for them to stop. Briefly he looked at the man's face. Alisha turned her gaze away feeling nauseous at the smell. The two Templars looked at Paul.

"You were not to know...besides, you saved the Princess who we were supposed to protect...you did well. He would understand and tell you himself if he could," the Templar nearest Paul explained.

Paul was surprised to hear him say this.

"None of us hold you responsible for this...," the other Templar stated and looked over towards Gerard as if to indicate they did him. They both bowed their heads and struggled to carry the dead Templar away. Paul thought he recognised the dead knight but he could not recall from where. Must have seen him previously he assumed.

Paul slowly opened the small door to the caravan and was about to help Alisha up the steps when he saw three men, clearly wealthy by their rich attire, sitting quietly inside upon the left bench. They were the same three he had seen earlier hiding beneath Princess Stephanie's caravan. One was praying with his eyes closed, the elder of the three looked wide eyed at Paul, in terror he thought. The third man, in his mid thirties wearing what looked like a gold silk gown, smiled at Paul disarmingly. He had a kind face and he just sighed resigned to whatever fate was about to befall him. He raised his hands as if in surrender. Paul looked to his right towards Gerard who was by now consulting with Brother Teric and

53

Brother Matthew. Tenno and Taqi were walking back towards them, Tenno with his arm around Taqi's shoulders protectively.

"You just heard what Stephanie said," Theodoric suddenly said making both Paul and Alisha jump as he appeared beside them from between the tight space separating their caravan from Stephanie's. He indicated towards the three men inside with his head. "No one gets harmed!"

Paul climbed up inside the caravan. He knew without a shadow of a doubt that one of these men was Saladin's brother as Gerard had spoken of. Thomas clearly knew them as he had greeted them when they arrived. The man praying started praying even harder. Paul raised his hand at Alisha to wait before coming inside.

"Just answer me this...do you wish us any harm?" he asked the three men.

"Us...harm you...should it not be us asking you that question?" the man with the kind face asked politely and indicated to Paul to look at himself.

Paul looked down at himself. He was covered in blood and dust. Quickly he untied the rope around his waist and took his sword off and laid it upon the bench beside him and beckoned for Alisha to enter.

"Ali...'tis all right...these men are noblemen...I sense that," Paul said quietly.

The man praying stopped and opened his eyes to look at Paul as Tenno and Taqi stood at the doorway alongside Theodoric. As Alisha sat herself down with Arri held in her arms, Thomas peered in.

✳ 2 – 3

"I see you have now met. Not the best of introductions," he remarked smiling.

"Was it you who put them in here...to hide?" Alisha asked as she studied the men sat in front of her. They were all sweating heavily as the temperature inside the caravan rose.

The three men all shook their heads no then pointed at Theodoric, who was leaning looking in on the opposite side of Thomas. He just shrugged his shoulders and smiled.

"Well...I could not just leave them cowering beneath Stephanie's caravan now could I?" he finally said.

"I prefer hiding than cowering," the man with the kind face said and smiled nervously.

"You know what will happen to you if Gerard finds you here don't you?" Alisha asked as Arri started to cry.

"Baby's crying...I'm off," Theodoric joked and stood up and began to back away.

Tenno shook his head at him and leaned in outstretching his arms for Alisha to pass him Arri. The three men looked on puzzled as she handed him Arri and he started to gently rock him back to sleep almost at once.

"Fear not...You must stay here as long as needs be until Gerard has gone... besides, Princess Stephanie has given her word no one will be harmed," Paul explained.

"Of that I have no doubt...but taking us prisoner for ransom is another thing," the kind faced man said quietly and looked at his friends in turn who both nodded in agreement.

"Then I pray none of you snore too loudly this eve," Paul smiled. "So please, what are your names?"

They all looked at each other briefly before the kind looking man finally nudged the man next to him to speak.

"I am Soleim Al-Razi, I am a physician and I treat the wounded on both sides...your friend Thomas can vouch for that I am certain," the elder of the three answered.

"I can indeed for he has fixed me up on more than one occasion," Thomas replied as he leant against the door frame looking in.

"And I am just Ahmid...I look after both of these two," the youngest of the three said and shook his head and laughed nervously and starting to shake with relief.

Alisha leant over and placed her hand upon his hand.

"You are safe...trust me...I am Muslim too," she said softly and smiled.

The three men looked at her and Paul in surprise.

"And you also?" the kind looking man asked Paul directly.

"No...But we are married...with special dispensation," Paul quickly answered seeing the surprise upon their faces.

"Truly it must be special. Perhaps you would explain how so at some stage as your being married has surely saved us this day...But no matter...and yes...I am indeed the brother of whom you name Saladin, for I am Turansha...and it is my pleasure to be blessed this day in meeting you," Turansha said softly and bowed his head slightly.

Port of La Rochelle, France, Melissae Inn, spring 1191

"So...let me just get this right...Paul waded into the melee and almost cut a man in two... and with an ordinary sword...not his own?" the Templar asked, amazed.

"Yes, that is correct," the old man answered.

"I know it is possible for I myself have see it so...but for a young inexperienced man to wield such a force and with no training...well, 'tis truly amazing," the Templar continued.

"So what exactly happened at Banias and the castle? I do not recall hearing much about that event here," Simon asked.

"Are you sure you want another history lesson?" the old man asked.

"Yes I most certainly do," the farrier agreed.

"Okay, let me start by explaining then that Gerard and Reynald had a network of spies in their employ. They passed on information to Reynald and Gerard that Saladin was hoping farmers and townspeople impoverished by continued Saracen raids would be unable to pay rent to their overlords and it would weaken the Crusader kingdom. So in response, Baldwin moved his army to Tiberias on the Sea of Galilee. From there he marched north-northwest to the stronghold of Safed. Continuing in the same direction, he reached Toron castle, about thirteen miles east-southeast of Tyre. Together with the

Knights Templar led by Odo de St Amand and a force from the county of Tripoli led by Count Raymond III, Baldwin then moved northeast. But earlier, in March of 1179, Odo de St Amand oversaw the construction of the Chastellet fortress. Its position and impregnability made it a thorn in Saladin's side and he offered considerable amounts of money to have it destroyed. It was so effective that Saladin's May assaults were defeated. His forces broke on the fortress's thick walls, and the fierce fighting of the Templars stationed there scored heavy losses on the Muslims. Trying to capitalise on the victory, an assault on the Islamic forces was organised, which resulted in the Battle of Marj Uyun as Saladin was able to deploy his forces from nearby Banias. It was spearheaded by King Baldwin the Fourth, Raymond the Third of Tripoli, Odo de St Amand and Roger des Moulins. However, Saladin had regrouped and then decimated the Christian forces. Baldwin the Fourth escaped the carnage, taking with him the so-called True Cross, but St Amand was captured and taken hostage," the old man explained.

"When I was there, we were told that the construction of the Templar fortress at Jacobs Ford on the upper Jordan is what led to the fresh Saracen invasion and the disastrous Battle of Marj Uyun in the first place. The young king Baldwin the Fourth and the True Cross escaped as you say but only with extreme difficulty, while Odo de St Amand, the Grand Master, was carried away captive and never returned. He was succeeded as Grand Master by Arnaud de Toroge and thankfully not Gerard at that time," the Templar remarked and sighed as he thought back on that period.

"Well, even though the attack from Banias in the region of Sidon in the spring of 1179 turned out to be yet another raid with the intention of weakening the kingdom, the Battle of Marj Uyun, or as some call it 'Ayyun', in June did present Saladin with the opportunity to press his attack southwards after the Frankish field army was decimated. However, Saladin's actions were limited to the destruction of the stronghold of Chastellet that the Franks were building at Jacobs Ford, thus discouraging the Franks from any offensive actions and further raids on Damascus. At this time he could not afford the risk of taking the bulk of his army that far south, while internal rivalry among the emirs in Syria and the constant danger from Aleppo and Mawsil threatened his rule. Sadly Humphrey the Second of Toron, Stephanie's former father-in-law, was indeed injured during this battle. He had helped negotiate a truce between the Knights Hospitaller and Knights Templar just months previously before accompanying Baldwin the Fourth in the attack on what they thought was just a small Muslim force near Banias...but, although he saved Baldwin the Fourth's life, he suffered mortal wounds and soon died. He was succeeded in Toron by his grandson Humphrey the Fourth, son of Humphrey the Third and Stephanie of Milly...Princess Stephanie of course! Humphrey the Third was his son by his unknown first wife." The old man paused. "You see, this all happened as from the eastern side of the coastal range, the Crusaders saw Saladin's tents in the distance. Baldwin and his nobles decided to descend to the plain and attack at once. As the Frankish army moved downhill, the mounted troops soon outstripped the foot soldiers. After a few hours' delay, the Crusader army reassembled, then encountered and easily defeated the Saracen raiding forces, who were returning from their forays. But believing the battle won, the Franks let their guard down. Raymond's knights and Odo de St Amand's Templars moved onto some high ground between the Marj Uyun and the Litani River. The Crusader infantry rested from their hurried march earlier in the day. Suddenly, Saladin's main army attacked the unprepared Crusaders, defeating them badly. Observers of the time blamed the defeat on Odo of St Amand, who was as *you now know captured in the battle. King Baldwin barely escaped capture...Unable to mount a horse because of his crippling disease, he was carried to safety by a knight as his bodyguard cut a path through the Saracens. Many Frankish survivors of the struggle fled to shelter at Beaufort Castle about five miles southwest of the battlefield,"* the old man explained and sat back and looked directly at the Templar and raised an eyebrow. [32]

"What?" he asked, puzzled.

"You know what...you should not be so embarrassed," the old man said, smiling, and folded his arms.

Miriam looked at him puzzled and squeezed his arm.

"Please....do not embarrass me. I was only doing my duty," the Templar remarked.

"What...what did you do?" Miriam asked.

"He was the knight who carried the king to safety...aren't you?" Gabirol stated.

The Templar shook his head, looking down, clearly embarrassed.

"Brother...you should be proud. You have hidden your story for too long. Being humble is one thing, but do not hide what should not be hidden!" the Hospitaller said and nudged his brother gently as Miriam looked at him proudly.

The Templar shook his head, still visibly embarrassed.

"That, my friend, is why you have that letter to read once I have finished this tale," the old man smiled.

"Well done, you...well done, you," the wealthy tailor said.

"Can I ask how did Princess Stephanie dealt with the news of the death of her father-in-law then...and having Saladin's brother in her immediate presence...or did she not find out?" Ayleth asked trying to draw attention away from the Templar, who was looking even more embarrassed at the revelation.

"The Princess...oh yes she became very much aware of the presence of Turansha, besides she had met him previously. And she was acutely aware of what Gerard would do with him, but more concerned with what her husband would do to them. As for the death of her father-in-law, it was not that great a shock as she always knew he was a professional soldier, much respected and she took some small measure of solace in the fact that he had died in a manner befitting his character...helping save the king. But more worryingly, it meant that her son would now become the new Lord of Toron with immediate effect from the day Humphrey the Second was killed on the tenth of June. He was just twelve years old, not quite thirteen. It would be people like Turansha that her son would have to deal with in the future...and so using the efficient heliograph network that ran the length of the King's Highway, she was able to signal ahead and receive a response as to what paths on the King's Highway were safe to travel on...more correctly, times *when it would be safe,"* the old man explained.

"So what happened with Gerard...did he not find the three men inside Paul's caravan then?" Simon asked.

"Well of course he could not have...or this story would be over...am I right?" Sarah said aloud.

"No...he did not discover them and the following morning, Gerard left heading for Tortosa and to start negotiations for the ransom and release of Odo de St Amand... though Odo refused to be ransomed," the old man explained and shook his head briefly. *"And Thomas...well, unbeknown to Paul, he and his men had actually averted a greater tragedy unfolding by stopping and blocking off Gerard's main charge. Paul had not*

even witnessed it...just one in a long line of similar incidents Thomas and his men would do all unnoticed. And like Theodoric...he too had a tattoo placed upon him that he did not choose," the old man said very quietly.

"Really...such as?" Peter asked.

"'Twas but a small few words...of a sword and the numbers from a Psalm in the Bible...Psalm 144:1," the old man revealed.

"Psalm 144:1....I know that one," the Templar said and sat up straight clasping Miriam's hands. "It reads 'Praise be to the Lord my rock, who trains my hands for war and my fingers for battle' I think..."

Chapter 27
Honesty and Good Deceit!

County of Tripoli, river crossing, June 13ᵗʰ 1179

It was dark when Theodoric and Thomas managed to sneak Turansha and his two friends across to Princess Stephanie's larger caravan for the night. Stephanie had spent a few hours with the family of the woman who had been killed trying to make amends for she knew it would ultimately fall at her husband's feet, any blame for the attack in error. She had agreed the three men should stay in her caravan as it was far larger and no one would dare enter without her permission. She informed Brother Matthew that she would retire early and that she did not wish to be disturbed, not even by her maids, until the morning. Feeling unsettled and alone, she asked Alisha if she could once more impose upon them and sleep upon the bench in their caravan. Alisha agreed and Paul said he would sleep outside with Tenno and Taqi anyway, himself feeling very unsettled. Gerard and his men set up camp without tents a short distance away and argued over who of the two Orders would take the Muslim escort as prisoners. Gerard was highly suspicious of their claim that they were just protecting the other Muslim pilgrims in their charge and that the wealthy silk trader who owned the caravan had obviously run into the woods at the first sign of the assault earlier.

After kissing Alisha and Arri good night, Paul made himself comfortable near to a small open fire that had burnt out near to a fallen tree. Theodoric had damped it down before darkness as it would have been seen for miles around giving away their position. It surprised him to see that Gerard and his knights still had several camp fires burning, confident no one would attack during the night. Brother Teric did not share his views and set himself up next to Paul for the night. Brother Matthew took first watch within the woods behind the caravans where Thomas and his men had set themselves up further into the tree line. Taqi sat down next to Tenno upon another fallen tree trunk opposite and looked up at the moon just breaking upon the horizon, shining across the open plain and running a white line of light vertically across the river. Paul felt slightly apprehensive that Stephanie was hiding Turansha and his men inside her caravan. Gerard would probably not contain himself if he found them. He was puzzled why she was helping them but also privately pleased.

"Brothers, may I sit with you awhile?" Thomas asked quietly as he stepped into view.

Tenno immediately moved along the trunk to make room for him to join them.

"And I also?" Percy suddenly asked coming in from the other side of the caravans.

"Of course...'tis a warm night and I doubt we shall sleep that well so the company will be welcome," Theodoric replied and motioned Percy to sit on one of the other fallen trees nearby.

"You do not sit upon your saddles then?" Percy asked as he made himself comfortable looking at several horse saddles slung high on the caravan's side boarding panels.

"No...not unless you wish to have every god forbidden flea and louse in the field jump on attracted by the horse's sweat...I am surprised you do not know this, young knight!" Theodoric said and looked at Percy.

Paul noted this instantly and tried not to look at Percy suspiciously...but something was still ringing untrue about him in his mind.

All looked up at Paul's caravan as they heard the women all laugh quietly inside.

"Stephanie will give her presence away if she speaks too loudly," Taqi said before Tenno quickly elbowed him to be silent.

₭ℂ

Inside the caravan Princess Stephanie and Alisha were laughing as they tried to contain Arri on the table as he weed upwards and wriggled all at once. Sister Lucy was trying to place a dirty shawl over him to stop the wee from going everywhere and all over his clean shawl and swaddling.

"Ssssh! Brother Matthew will hear you," Sister Lucy whispered as Arri cried out a cross between a laugh and a cry.

Alisha quickly wiped Arri down with a damp cloth and wrapped him up. She sat down and began to rock him slowly as Princess Stephanie and Sister Lucy cleared up the mess and table. One of the two candles flickered as it reached its last point of burning. Alisha kissed Arri on his forehead as Princess Stephanie sat opposite her and just stared for a few moments.

"That will be you soon enough," Sister Lucy whispered to her and then nodded at Alisha.

Princess Stephanie placed her hands upon her tummy and smiled then sighed with tiredness.

"To bring a child into this world when there is so much madness...I have to question is it right to do so?" Stephanie remarked quietly.

"Tell me...these wars, all these truces broken and all the killing...is it always so?" Alisha asked as she hugged Arri closer.

"Sadly...it would appear so," Sister Lucy answered and sat down next to Alisha.

"Then I will do all and everything to protect this one," Alisha said and pulled out her three pronged dagger and placed it upon the table. "Anyone who threatens my son will have that through them...that I swear."

"Ali...you surprise me," Stephanie said as she leaned forwards and picked up the dagger, unsheathed the blades and looked at it closely. "My Lord...'twas a very long time ago when I last saw this," she remarked and studied the dagger near to the single candle. "Did Paul's father, Philip, present you with this?"

"No...and when did you see this...or was it just another one of similar make?" Alisha asked, perplexed.

"No...'tis the same one. For there is this only this one...and last time I saw it, a very wizened old soul placed three special acorns within the sheath's pocket...

here," Stephanie explained and opened the little side pocket and quickly tipped out two acorns. She shook it again then ran her finger inside the pouch. "Oh...there appears to be only two now. So pray tell how did it come to be in your possession?"

"A tall woman, whom I now know is called Abi, she threw it to me as I left Tortosa harbour last spring. 'Twas she who also saved Arri's life when he was born," Alisha explained. "And why did you ask if Philip had given it to me?"

"I ask as the last time I saw this very dagger, 'twas the last day I ever saw Philip and the old man. But what has happened to the third acorn?...It is important," Stephanie explained and asked looking confused then looked at Sister Lucy.

"I...I planted it at the Dolmen stones...back in France where we met Theo," Alisha replied quietly as Arri started to close his eyes. Princess Stephanie and Sister Lucy looked at each other for a few moments in total silence. "What have I done wrong?"

"Nothing...absolutely nothing," Stephanie answered and smiled and tilted her head to one side as she looked at her and Arri.

"See...I told you. Everything still continues," Sister Lucy remarked.

"What do you mean?" Alisha asked.

"Oh nothing really...just a promise an old man made us once. We did not believe him at the time, but it would appear that what he said is coming to pass," Sister Lucy answered and smiled again as Princess Stephanie nodded in acknowledgment with her.

"Just tell me we shall get to Alexandria safely then, for that is all I need to hear and know," Alisha said and kissed Arri again.

"That is in the hands of God...but I think his hands wrap around you quite well," Stephanie said and smiled broadly.

"Well I hope you are right...I also hope you will explain to me how it is you know Saladin's brother and why you are risking your very life to hide him?" Alisha asked and looked at Princess Stephanie intently.

"That, my dear lady, is a very long story...suffice it to say Philip acquainted us all. As I understand it, Philip was working jointly on several manuscripts with Turansha in Aleppo, about courtly love and codes of chivalric conduct," Stephanie replied and covered her mouth with the back of her hand as she yawned.

"Yes indeed...but 'twas no ordinary manuscript was it?" Sister Lucy commented, her face looking stern in the candle light. "Mystery of the Rose wasn't it?"

"What is that?" Alisha asked as she moved Arri to get comfortable.

"Let me explain as briefly as I can then," Sister Lucy said as she picked up the dagger from the table and looked it over. "Mystery glows in the rose bed; the secret is hidden in the rose, that was the title of the book Philip was working upon with help from Turansha and some other types...a Sufi mystic in fact but I cannot recall his name. Philip's book, the *Roman de la Rose* (French: ʁɔmɑ̃ də la ʁoz) 'Romance of the Rose', was originally a French poem styled as an allegorical dream vision of courtly literature written to both entertain and teach others about the Art of Love," she explained and winked at Stephanie.

"But at various times in the poem, the 'Rose' of the title is seen as the name of the lady, and as a symbol of female sexuality in general. Likewise, the other characters' names function both as regular names and as allegorical symbols for the various factors that are involved in a love affair. Its emphasis on sensual language and imagery provoked some hostility when Philip tried to have it released. The last I saw of it, he was using another name as a cover. 'Tis why I loved that man so...," Stephanie explained and looked down sadly.

"You loved Paul's father?" Alisha asked surprised.

"Oh yes...very much so, and I make no apology for it," Stephanie replied quietly and started to wrap her hair around her fingers as she clearly thought back to a time with Philip. "Men should think twice before making widowhood women's only path to power," she sighed.

"I do not claim to understand what you just said, but I do know that as my father taught us, there is no such thing as coincidence, so our meeting as we did has some purpose...I am just not sure what yet," Alisha said looking at Princess Stephanie with many questions running through her mind.

℘ℭ℞

Brother Teric was making himself comfortable when several Templars from Gerard's force approached silhouetted by the light from the ever rising moon.

"Brother Teric...Master Gerard requests to know why you remain here instead of with the rest of the brothers?" Stewart asked as he stopped just in front of the whole group.

Paul immediately looked up but only knew it was Stewart from his voice.

"Tell him because someone needs to watch upon you lot with your fires that burn away like a beacon to any forces of Saladin for miles around," Brother Teric replied and rested back upon the caravan's front wheel. "Besides I am assisting Brother Matthew keep an eye upon Princess Stephanie."

Stewart stood silently for several moments, his mantle blowing in the breeze that came up off of the plain.

"Well I shall bed down here," Percival said breaking the awkward silence and began to unfasten his chausses and unclipped his spurs.

"Percy...I advise against that. Do as we Templars do here...you keep your shoes on and sleep ready to fight if needs be," Brother Teric said and pulled his mantle around himself tighter, his sword by his side still worn. "Is that all, Brother Stewart?"

"Huh...obviously," Stewart replied but remained standing for several more minutes.

"Brother, if you have something to say, say your piece for you are spoiling my view of the moon's reflection upon the river," Thomas commented.

Stewart stepped nearer and leaned lower to see Paul.

"Paul...you say you have no desire to be a knight, ever...and that you prefer peace always...how so is it then that I am the knight of us two, yet it is you who has already killed two persons?" Stewart asked, his tone terse. Paul moved to sit up higher against the fallen tree trunk. "And are you aware that the good man you killed this day was in fact Brother Lawrence Monteacute whom you spied upon during our initiation ceremony back home?"

"That is unfair, Brother Stewart...," Theodoric interrupted quickly and stood up directly in front of Stewart. "If Paul had not done as he did, Princess Stephanie would now be dead. 'Twas a matter of bad error and decision by your master...so go tell him that, if you must report anything, for what you say is truly unworthy a statement for a knight to make. I expected better of you."

"I do not remember you and I only know of you by what scant rumour I have heard. 'Tis only out of respect for your former friendship with my father that I do not correct you in your manners when addressing a knight," Stewart replied.

"'Tis only out of respect for your father I do not put you across my knee and slap your wee backside, young man, for clearly you have many manners to learn first before I would deem you a knight," Theodoric shot back.

"I am a knight and I am even the Gonfanier already," Stewart replied, anger rising in his voice.

"Yes, and don't we all know it...and we all wonder just how so quickly too," Theodoric mussed and rubbed his chin.

"Gerard obviously has an eye for him! I would cover your arse, young knight!" Thomas said aloud. Taqi sniggered as Tenno watched Stewart and the other three knights behind him carefully.

Paul jumped up to his feet.

"Thomas, please no...this is my actual brother," Paul remarked quietly and then stepped closer toward Stewart. He could not see his face properly in the darkness. "Stewart. I did not ask nor wish to kill anyone. I would rather that fell upon you to do than me...but I did what needed doing...and it was Alisha your brother knight would have killed...and may the Lord forgive me, but I would have done it a thousand times over to save her," Paul explained and shook his head at Stewart.

Stewart stared at him for several moments. Eventually one of the Templars pulled his arm to usher him backwards. Stewart flounced his arm away hard. The Templar behind him shook his head and started to back away with the other Templars.

"Stewart...I was there the day you were born. I respectfully ask you curb that temper rising within you and just walk away," Theodoric stated calmly but squaring up to him.

For several long minutes Stewart just stood staring at them all. Eventually he turned around and walked away back towards Gerard's group nearer the river.

"And he is your actual brother, yes?" Thomas asked quietly and looked over toward Princess Stephanie's caravan as Brother Matthew moved to stand near the main side door and listened.

"Yes...yes he is," Paul answered and looked where Thomas was looking.

Brother Matthew became aware that he was being watched and stepped away from the caravan and slowly walked past their group, nodded good evening and continued walking towards the other caravans further along.

Paul sat back down next to Taqi and Tenno and pulled his knees up to his chest. Stewart's words had certainly hit their mark and he felt sick. He shook his head just as Taqi rubbed his shoulder supportively.

"Paul," Thomas said to get his attention. "Try to ignore what he said. Tomorrow they will head for Tortosa with the prisoners captured today whilst we shall head for Castle Blanc then on to Crac de l'Ospital. We can all rest there awhile and see how things progress with Saladin, for who knows, by then another truce will be in force anyway."

"They came with mischief in mind...for where are their sergeant turcopoles and other horses?" Tenno stated looking towards Gerard's position. "And how was it that they used Muslim naphtha grenades?"

"Good question," Theodoric remarked.

"That Gerard has the devil walk beside him," Thomas stated and shook his head.

"Devil you say. No I think you will find it is Reynald who holds that dishonour," Theodoric remarked quietly and paused. "Now as for the real Devil...there is a subject that is greatly misunderstood too, especially the significance of the mark of the beast...it being 666," Theodoric continued and pulled on a heavy padded leather cape. "The nights turn cold here so I advise you go and get yourselves one of these too. Niccolas placed several in the bottom external panniers."

"I shall wait until I start to feel cold," Paul replied.

"What say you of this Devil and numbers?" Tenno asked, bemused, and made himself comfortable upon his thick blanket and propped himself up against the fallen tree trunk.

"I think I should leave the 666 aspect to another time...suffice it to say it has nothing to do with any evil forces...just but part of a key that unlocks much wisdom," Theodoric answered.

"Please, pray tell for I am keen to learn of such things," Thomas asked.

"Let us just say I will need to show you in the light of day, details about 666, and Jesus's connection to it...and this very earth we stand upon."

"This Jesus...I have heard much on him, but in China and my country they know not of him, then they will not have redemption or salvation? Yet this God who supposedly created the entire world...he excludes them...yes?" Tenno asked.

Paul immediately thought back to what Niccolas had shown him on his map and the little circle drawn around certain areas within Outremer, it being the sum total area where everything that had ever occurred within the pages of the Bible, the Torah and the Qur'an had taken place. Tenno's question was a good one.

"Maybe they are not left out as Jesus did state after he was resurrected, that he had other sheep that he must tend too. In time the whole world will hear of him," Theodoric answered.

"But what of Christian and Islamic theology that both hold the Devil is a being who tries to lead people into sin and, ultimately, into hell fire? Christians refer to the Devil as Satan or Lucifer, while Muslims refer to him as Shaytan or Shaitan or even Iblis...is this not correct?" Tenno asked.

"Satan is but a fallen angel...No?" Thomas commented.

"Well, let me explain that most Christians believe the Devil, or Satan, is a fallen angel. In Christianity, a fallen angel is an angel who has been banished from heaven for rebellious or disobedient behaviour. Henceforth, they are known as arch-angels, satans, or devils. Satan is believed to be the most powerful among them. But contrary to what most believe, while the Bible does make reference to the fact that Satan was cast out from heaven, there is no verse in the Bible which specifically labels him either an angel or a fallen angel...," Theodoric explained.

"Satan is a jinnee and not an angel in Islam," Taqi remarked.

"That is true," Theodoric commented. "In Islamic teaching there is no such thing as a fallen angel, because angels don't possess free will and are incapable of disobedience to their creator. Although Iblis was originally in Heaven in the company of angels, he was a jinnee, a different kind of being than angels. You see angels are created from light, while jinn are created from smokeless fire. Unlike angels, jinn do have free will and can commit sins. As for Satan, the same Iblis in the Qur'an, the Bible offers no account of why Satan, Iblis, or Shaytan was thrown out of heaven, but the Qur'an explains that his fall from grace was due to his refusal to obey Allah and prostrate to Adam. According to the Qur'an, Allah said, 'What prevented you O Iblis that you did not prostrate yourself when I commanded you?' Iblis said: 'I am better than him Adam. You created me from fire, and him you created from clay.' Allah said: 'O Iblis get down from this Paradise, it is not for you to be arrogant here. Get out, for you are of those humiliated and disgraced.' (Qur'an 7:12–13) Muslims believe that for his punishment, Allah sentenced Satan to eternity in Hell. However, at Satan's request, Allah permitted him to roam the earth and misguide man until the Day of Judgement. According to the Qur'an, Iblis said, 'Allow me respite till the Day they are raised up, (the Day of Resurrection) Allah said: 'You are one of those respited.' Iblis said, 'Because You have sent me astray, surely I will sit in wait against them...as in us human beings, on Your Straight Path. Then I will come to them from before them and behind them, from their right and from their left, and you will not find most them as thankful ones, they will not be dutiful to you.' Allah said to Iblis, 'Get out from this Paradise, disgraced and expelled. Whoever of them mankind will follow you, then surely I will fill Hell with you all.' (Qur'an 7:14-18)."

"So this Christianity shares the belief with Islam that Satan will attempt to lead men astray?" Tenno asked.

"Well yes...despite the different natures of Satan in Islam and Satan in Christianity, both theologies agree that the Devil is a powerful entity who was disobedient to God and wishes mankind to be sinful as well," Theodoric replied.

"I do not understand this Muslim concept enough," Tenno remarked and looked at Taqi.

"Tenno, 'tis simple really," Taqi began to answer and quickly looked at Thomas before continuing. "Islam is a monotheistic religion with six articles of faith: belief in one God, belief in the angels, belief in the prophets, belief in the scriptures, belief in the Day of Judgement, and belief in divine decree."

"But what is this one God?" Tenno asked, still puzzled.

"I can answer that," Taqi said as he sat himself up. "Muslims believe that God, Allah the Creator has no partners, only he should be worshipped. Allah is the same God of the Jews and Christians. However, the Qur'an rejects the idea of the trinity, indeed, they disbelieve who say, 'God is the third of three', when there is no god but one God (Qur'an 5:73). Muslims believe in angels, special beings created by Allah to worship and serve him. They include Jibreel, or Gabriel, who delivered God's revelation to Muhammad, peace be upon him, Israfil or Rafael, who will blow the trumpet on the Day of Judgement, 'Izra'il, the angel of death, the angels who guard Heaven and Hell, and the angels assigned to every person to record their deeds. Angels are mentioned numerous times in the Qur'an, including: 'Praise be to Allah, the Originator of the heavens and earth, who made the angels messengers, with wings, two, three or four' (Qur'an 35:1). Then there is the belief in the prophets for Muslims believe that Muhammad, peace be upon him, is the last in a line of prophets and messengers who called people to true monotheism. In the Qur'an, God says, 'He has ordained for you the same religion which He ordained for Noah, and that which we have revealed to you Muhammad and that which we ordained for Abraham, Moses, and Jesus, saying that you should establish religion and make no divisions in it (Qur'an 42:13). And Muhammad is not the father of any one of your men, but he is the Messenger of God and the last of the prophets' (Qur'an 33:40). Muslims believe in the revealed books of God, the Qur'an, the Torah, the Psalms and the Gospel. The Qur'an receives precedence because Muslims believe earlier scriptures were altered over time, while God promises to preserve the Qur'an's original revelation for it states 'Indeed, We have sent down the Qur'an, and surely We will guard it from corruption' (Qur'an 15:9)." Taqi paused as he was surprised to realise that they were all listening to him.

"Continue," Tenno stated bluntly.

"Then we have a belief in the Day of Judgement and Afterlife when all souls will be held accountable for their sins and be assigned to either Heaven or Hell. God says, 'We shall set up scales of justice for the Day of Judgement, so that not a soul will be dealt with unjustly in the least' (Qur'an 21:47). God created everything, and everything happens with His Will and Knowledge. Although people do have free will, God knows what choices they will make. What will happen has already been predetermined and recorded in a book called *Al-Lawl Al-Mahfud* (the 'Book of Decree'). God says, 'With Him are the keys of the Unseen. None but He knows them. And He knows what is in the land and the sea. Not a leaf falls but he knows it; not a grain amid the darkness of the soil, nothing of wet or dry, but it is in a Manifest Book' (Qur'an 6:59). Tenno, you see Islam is a faith in both doctrine and action and these six doctrines are among the teachings of Islam. Muslims demonstrate belief in them by submitting to God and by performing Islam's pillars of faith, including daily prayer, fasting, giving charity and making a pilgrimage to Mecca (hajj)," Taqi finished and sat back. [33]

"Taqi...you know your Islamic Qur'an well indeed. I am impressed," Theodoric commented as Paul and Thomas nodded their heads in agreement.

"Thank you, Taqi. I shall have to ponder your words. I think it sad that your faith shares so much with Christianity, yet you tear each other apart," Tenno commented and looked up as stars twinkled brightly above.

"Both Christians and Muslims tear themselves apart from within let alone against each other," Theodoric stated and followed Tenno's gaze upwards to the stars. "That is Orion," he remarked pointing to the constellation Tenno was looking directly at.

Paul looked at the constellation.

"My father says that Orion holds a great key to antiquity. That the belt stars hold the sword of Damocles, that is now called Excalibur...but that it also leads the way to where all souls are created. Is that true?" he asked Theodoric.

"Aye...it does indeed...but again, I shall need light and a good table to show you and explain to you those mysteries," Theodoric answered quietly but still looking at the constellation.

"I hope we stay with you long enough for you to share that knowledge with us also," Thomas commented. "My father once told me that I should never judge a person by what faith they follow, or from where they come nor the colour of their skin, but by their present actions and what is their hearts."

"Your father sounds like a wise man," Theodoric commented.

"He was...the best," Thomas sighed as he clearly reflected upon thoughts of his father.

Tenno sighed heavily then looked back at the group sat huddled close in the dark. All looked around as Alisha stepped down from the caravan and silently walked over. She made out Paul as he moved to sit up and she immediately sat beside him handing him a large thick fur cover.

"I was worried you would be cold," she whispered.

"What about me then?" Taqi protested jokingly.

"You are a Muslim remember...we supposedly have cold blood, and not much of it," Alisha replied and moved in closer to Paul pulling the fur cover over both of them.

"What are you doing?" Paul asked.

"I just want to spend what time I can with you. Arri is asleep soundly...and I could not help but hear your conversation," she answered.

"Surely our discourse would bore you?" Theodoric remarked.

"No not at all...I may be a woman but I do have a brain."

"Then pray tell us what you make of all this killing and religious fanaticism we see raise its ugly head all too often?" Thomas asked.

"All I can say is that it is truly sad that so many of you, from all sides, joyfully march to the sound of the drums in your masses unquestioningly. 'Tis like you have all been given a large brain by mistake, whereas just the spinal cord would surely suffice. This disgrace to civilisation should be done away with at once. Heroism at command, senseless brutality, deplorable love-of-country stance and all the loathsome nonsense that goes by the name of patriotism and religious fervour...how violently I hate all this, how despicable and ignoble war is...I would rather be torn to shreds than be part of so base an action! It is my conviction that killing under the cloak of war, worse, in the name God or Allah, is nothing but an act of murder. None of us are born cruel and mean...but it is something we learn and are taught," she sounded out confidently.

"'Tis a pity all woman think not like that, for surely if they did, they would convince all men of that same sound simple logic and peace would win," Thomas stated as he looked at Alisha.

Paul looked at her in the moonlight. He smiled, proud at her words, and pulled her closer to him.

"'Tis not simple logic...just the logic of women of all ages and races," Alisha replied.

"Exactly, simple!" Taqi joked.

"No...there is much insight and wisdom in her words," Tenno remarked.

"And do you know what the mad thing is about it?" Theodoric asked. "It is from the Bible that man has learned cruelty, rape, and murder, for the belief of a cruel god makes a cruel man."

"Woo...comments like that will cost you your head in unguarded company," Thomas pointed out.

"It does not stop the simple fact of that being true nevertheless...and are we not in guarded company?" Theodoric replied.

"Do not get me wrong...I fully agree with you, we are a murderous race. In Genesis, it took fewer than four people to make the planet too crowded to stand,

and the first murder was a fratricide. Genesis says that in a fit of jealous rage, the first child born to mortal parents, Cain, snapped and murdered another human being. The attack was a bloody, brutal, violent, reprehensible killing. Cain's brother, Abel, probably never saw it coming," Thomas remarked and moved to sit up straighter.

⚜   3 – 55

"Look now," Theodoric interrupted. "In all of history men have been taught that killing of men is an evil thing not to be countenanced. Any man who kills must be destroyed because this is a great sin, maybe the worst we know. And then we make him a soldier and put murder in his hands and we say to him, 'use it well, use it wisely'. We put no checks on him. Go out and kill as many of a certain kind or classification of your brothers as you can. And we will reward you for it even though it is a violation of your early training, that is why we have men like Gerard and his friend Reynald free to do as they will."

Tenno coughed slightly and shook his head.

"If there is a deity, this single God or Allah or whatever, then it is that deity, the creator of all things, who is then solely and wholly responsible for the diseases and wars that kill and maim and cause much suffering to millions…for the mass killings of people in floods and earthquakes and too great a mountain of other natural evils to list besides. This deity would also be the creator of human nature, so again ultimately responsible for the unbeatable human lengths and depths for hatred, malice, greed, and all other sources of the cruelty and murder people inflict on each other hourly."

"Then I am too a party to that," Paul commented quietly.

"NO! Your intentions were not to kill…you had no choice. Your heart does not desire it. It is 'intention' that matters," Tenno suddenly replied back, his tone clipped.

Port of La Rochelle, France, Melissae Inn, spring 1191

"Strong words from that Tenno. I bet he will cause some trouble," the farrier remarked.

"That was Tenno for you," the old man smiled in response.

"I apologise right now…but I am still having trouble grasping what I hear, especially in regard to Jesus. Is Islam right then in stating that Jesus was and is a fraud, that he did not die on the cross…was not even born of a virgin birth?" Simon asked and leaned away from Sarah.

"My dear Simon, 'tis good that you question and not follow blindly as I have already said before," the old man answered and nodded yes slowly. "Let me try and proffer some facts that may help…. you see…the early Church fathers, for its very survival, needed to change it into a force that would unite and strengthen what was the Roman Empire complete with its values, politics and social as well as military order. They chose to glorify certain gospels that would strengthen their version of Christianity. In Jesus's life time, he did not have thousands of followers and nor were there many thousands of documents written about him…for very

few were even literate. But Constantine at the council of Nicaea selected which few gospels to include within the Bible and in what order. Consequently the new state Church systematically started to eradicate Gnostic and other perceived heretical influences including those that were closer to the original teachings of the true Jesus...for as said, he was a genuine figure. They chose those teachings that best served the new empire! And so they were able to establish a standardised hierarchical powerful Church with two clear paths...one for the mystical where ecstatic experiences could be had and a belief in the divine, but also one that has strong Popes, strong rules and laws, and all set to a backdrop of Heaven and Hell. They kept it simple, and they kept it so they were in control."

"But how could ordinary men and woman all fall for that?" Simon asked, perplexed.

"'Tis so very easy. Most people are lazy and it is easier to accept what one is told, especially if it is by your own leaders who claim direct infallible guidance from God above...and you cannot read yourself to learn more, even if the information was made available," the old man answered.

"So, once this emperor Constantine converts to Christianity, he converts to an orthodox form only and so does the state...which starts immediately exerting its influence over Christianity with legislation set out against heretics and Gnostics...so it went from being a totally anti Christian state to one of total Christianisation but dictated on its terms?" Gabirol stated.

"Yes...and very well put. And most of it was down to the writings and guidance of some of Christianity's earliest and most influential writers like Tertullian, Irenaeus and Eusebius. Now here is the important point to keep in mind...these three people, unlike Jesus, were all well documented historical figures who are acknowledged as playing a pivotal role within the early Church. But despite playing a critical role, they were also responsible in selecting what would eventually make up the New Testament as well as destroying the intellectual, ideological and physical so-called Heretical Christian Church at the same time. Know however that these men lived in a time that was far more darker and fearful than we live in now. They were the editors of the Gospels as they understood them in their times. The Gnostic gospels were and are without doubt a more humanistic, more meaningful and certainly more feministic as well as a more spiritual path than the Church that ultimately triumphed," the old man paused. "Yet despite that, the feminine Church would have almost certainly died off and be supplanted or totally eradicated by other beliefs if the Church herself had not been so dominating and strong...by being so, it has inadvertently acted as a solid and strong vehicle that still carries the message of truth within itself without even realising it...to one day be revealed again.!

"You mean like the monasteries being built with all the hidden esoteric codes you spoke of being hidden but plain view all along?" Peter remarked.

"Aye yes indeed. In real terms, after Nicaea, you had one small pile of Gospel truths on one side and on the other, another greater pile of Gnostic and heretical documents. And the very word God instead became the word of man!" the old man explained and shook his head slightly. "The truly deep spiritual, mythical, poetic, romantic, almost goddess and sacred feminine roots of Christianity were ruthlessly stamped out. This was something that Paul's father tried so long and hard to correct and reset the balance. Some claim that Jesus was just another in a long line of so-called god-man figures that have occurred throughout all known history...and who all existed in harmony with the Goddess principle. That is why you will find so many sayings quoted as coming from

Jesus as being identical to earlier Goddess teachings, as Jesus had many words put into his mouth."

"I think I am confused now...," Sarah exclaimed and shot Simon a look. "Did Jesus exist or not? Simple answer...please."

"Sarah, simple answer...yes he did really exist," the old man answered.

Both Sarah and the wealthy tailor sighed with a clear sign of relief.

"But not born of a virgin?" Gabirol stated.

"Not in the sense we would all understand it. But let me continue before you make any final conclusions. You see, we are taught, as the Church teaches, that Jesus was a man of Jewish origins, wealthy origins I must add, though that is not explained, and Christianity developed from his teachings, Gnosticism being a later deviation from the true path. That is what we are taught. However...the reverse is in fact the case. And Gnosticism in its own turn was born of Judaism and the pagan mystery religions and that is what became the beginnings of the Jesus mystery initiative, much of which was placed upon the shoulders of a real man, Jesus, a Messiah...but a Messiah as understood in those times as I have already explained. A burden no mere ordinary man could be expected to carry...so on that basis alone, the real physical Jesus of history is worthy of honouring in his own right. As you may recall, I have explained how all across the ancient world, all mystery schools taught of the dying and resurrecting god-man, just like the Osiris myths...and all connected to constellations in the heavens..." He paused.

"Orion being the most obvious?" Gabirol asked.

"Yes," the old man nodded. "You see The real Jesus, a genuine Messiah, had his whole life orchestrated to fit into the prophecies of the Old Testament, which is why he had his disciples fetch palm leaves and lay them before him as he rode a donkey into Jerusalem...all to fit the prophecies. His life was not his own...it was all sacrifice and service to others. Some call it God, or gods, but some mechanism was behind the Jesus initiative that carefully and diligently crafted and encoded upon him spiritual teachings created by Jewish Gnostics, pagan mysteries that were inherited from a far greater time back in antiquity. This the founders of the Templars knew, still know and understand."

"Is that why they sought a fusion with Islam and Judaism?" Gabirol asked.

"Yes...and they still seek it," the old man answered and looked at the Templar to see what his reaction was. The Templar simply nodded as if to agree.

"The Jesus initiative is not just a myth, though many will argue that is the very case in the future as much about his true path is revealed. Though we do not believe the myths about Osiris, Dionysius, Adonis, Attis, Mithras and older pagan mystic saviours, with identical stories that recount being born of a virgin, walking on water, healing the sick etcetera, we nevertheless believe the very same story as told in a Jewish context of a carpenter from Bethlehem, though carpenter should say craftsman and Bethlehem did not exist in his time...But as I am trying to explain, the real Jesus of antiquity had his entire life set out to mirror and mimic the past Messiahs and fulfil the prophecies of the Old Testament...but more crucially...to continue the ancient codes from our ancient forefathers across time and remain intact. That is why the same reoccurring and identical themes and actions keep being repeated. And an even greater code using mathematics runs throughout all of them...identical!" the old man concluded and sat back looking tired.

"Mathematical you say?" Gabirol asked.

"Yes...and if we have time, I shall show you exactly how."

"I look forward to that, for mathematics is my strong point...'tis how and why I became a stonemason," Peter remarked and smiled broadly.

"'Tis the mathematics that will give away the great schism and machinations that have destroyed so many truths and replaced documents with forgeries...the history of accepted Christianity as bequeathed to us by the great Roman Church has become a great and grotesque distortion of the truth outwardly with its dogmatic religion enforced upon us...'tis perhaps one of the greatest cover ups in history, yet it serves a purpose," the old man explained as Ayleth bit her thumb nail clearly uncomfortable with what she was hearing.

"Are there but any proofs, real documents and people that prove this and what you say?" she asked hesitantly.

"Yes of course there are. Just one example I can detail is the man I mentioned earlier... Eusebius. For it was he who alone primarily compiled from legends and myths at the beginning of the fourth century his understanding of Jesus and, in some cases, complete fabrications based upon his fertile and active imagination alone. His is the only early history written down that exists today and upon which all subsequent histories, by the enforced power of the Roman Church, have to be based upon. Anyone saying or claiming otherwise was and is branded a heretic and all traces of information or documents claiming otherwise were systematically eradicated...forever. It was Eusebiius's so-called facts as written down then that have been handed down to us now as established and accepted unquestionable facts."

"And this Eusebius...he was employed by the Roman Emperor Constantine, the same Constantine who made Christianity the state religion?" Gabirol commented.

"Yes he was. You see, Constantine wanted one god, one religion that would consolidate his claim as Emperor of One Empire. It was he who created the Nicene Creed, the article of faith repeated every day and in every church to this day. All Christians who refused to accept his doctrine, were banished from the empire...the more vociferous simply being made to vanish," the old man sighed.

"So our entire faith is based upon a lie, and murderous beginnings?" Ayleth asked, clearly saddened.

"No. 'Tis not as simple as that," the old man answered.

"But I heard that this Constantine returned home after his meetings in Nicaea and promptly had his wife suffocated and his son murdered," Gabirol commented.

"Yes that is also true. He also refused to be baptised until his death bed so that in his mind, he could continue his atrocities and still receive forgiveness of sins upon his death bed and thus be guaranteed a place in Heaven by being baptised at the last moment."

"What a wicked and evil man...no wonder many Muslims condemn us. It makes you have to wonder. Is it true you could do that...commit all those sins knowingly and in the belief that you could be forgiven your sins at the last moment, even though it is deceit and planned?" Ayleth said and wiped a tear from her eye.

"That is the nature of salvation and forgiveness according to the New Testament... but no, in reality, it is all about intent. As Tenno snapped at Paul, he was more correct in his outburst than perhaps he realised. You see, it is all about intentions...what is in their heart, more correctly in the soul. If good men do not pick up the sword in defence of good people and good practices, then evil men will prevail," the old man explained and slowly pulled the sword closer across the table and rested his hand upon the rough leather scabbard. *"It was Eusebius who composed the biography of Constantine who was*

nothing more than a monster of violence, greed and power hungry just as the many emperors before him. That is why Paul and Taqi were constantly having it drummed into their heads to always check the validity and origination of anything they were told or learnt."

"So the whole edifice of the Holy Roman Church was in effect written up and created by a scribe, philosopher or whatever Eusebius was, in the service of a Roman Tyrant... and mainly a pack of lies which he hung upon the shoulders of a real Jesus character?" Gabirol stated and shook his head disbelievingly.

"You of all people, Gabirol, should know that history is indeed written by the victors. It has always been an accepted part of political expediency and policy that the creation of an appropriate history is used for just such manipulation...but what you have just said is, in essence, correct," the old man replied.

Ayleth burst into tears. Quickly Sarah moved nearer to her and placed her arm around her comfortingly.

"Sorry, Ayleth, if this news shocks you...but the continuing legacy we all must endure for heaven knows how much longer has caused and will continue to cause horrendous acts of murder and brutality on an unimaginable scale all in the name of God...and, dare I state the obvious, it will be the females of our kind that will undoubtedly then suffer the harshest extremes of all," the old man said looking at Ayleth and then waited until she looked at him.

"How so?" she asked sniffing and wiped her eyes as Sarah and Miriam both stared at him curiously.

"Simply by the rejection of the now wholly patriarchal Church position on the sacred feminine, which has damned women, damned sex and set up monastic institutions that would keep men and women apart...and flagellations in the misguided belief they should learn to suffer as Jesus had done. Yet almost all of Jesus's suffering was allegorical and metaphorical. You can understand why the early Church was so against woman as they blamed a woman for leading Adam astray, but also within the Gnostic system, it was women who wrote many of their gospels, their teachers were mainly women and many of their leaders were often women," the old man said and paused as he looked at the Templar and Hospitaller. "Perhaps you two could answer this simple example. On the field of battle...when men lay mortally wounded...what is it that most cry out for?"

The Templar looked at his brother and shook his head bemused. The Hospitaller sat up straight and thought for a moment.

"I can only answer as but from what I recall...I can say that many a man, when mortally wounded...oft call out for their mothers!" the Hospitaller replied and clasped his hands together and took a deep breath as he recalled many images from his past. He looked down at the table as his Templar brother reached over and touched his arm. He looked up at him and feigned a brave smile.

All sat in silence. Ayleth sobbed, the wealthy tailor shook his head and pondered upon the old man's words. Simon just sat in silence with his arms folded. The Genoese sailor watched Gabirol as he charged his quill and wrote more lines. Peter the stonemason rubbed his chin constantly as he thought. The farrier, Thomas, just closed his eyes and placed his hands together as if in prayer on the table. Miriam tucked herself in closer to the Templar and rested her head upon his shoulder. The Hospitaller just stared at the sword upon the table. Stephan stood behind Sarah and placed a reassuring hand upon her shoulder, which she quickly grasped. The silence was long until the old man finally spoke again.

"Yes...precisely...their mothers," the old man sighed. "Their mothers."

County of Tripoli, river crossing, June 13ᵗʰ 1179

Paul shivered slightly from the cold as he drifted in and out of sleep propped up
against the fallen tree. The night was silent, not even the sound of a breeze blowing in the trees or any wildlife or night insects. It was peaceful. Alisha was sound
asleep resting upon his chest. Tenno was sat cross legged but perfectly still facing
towards Gerard's camp where several Templars could be seen silhouetted against
the moon as it sat low on the horizon having traversed the night sky. Taqi was
sound asleep resting against Theodoric who was himself asleep, his head resting
against the tree trunk, his mouth wide open as if looking up at the stars. Thomas
was walking about and Paul saw him assist Sister Lucy down from the caravan.
Quietly but quickly she came over and knelt beside Paul.
"'Tis Arri. He is awake and needs his feed…that is one thing I am unable to do,"
she whispered to Paul, her smile visible in the moonlight.
Paul looked at Alisha sound asleep. He did not want to disturb her and the
warmth from her body was welcoming, but he knew she had to be woken. Gently
he shook her until she opened her eyes wearily. She blinked a few times as she
looked at Paul and then Sister Lucy. No sooner had Sister Lucy stood up straight
when Alisha quickly removed the fur blanket from over her, stood up, placed the
blanket back over Paul and without a word quickly followed Sister Lucy back into
the caravan as silently as possible. She never complained, just got on with things.
He loved her the more for it.
Paul shivered again and pulled the fur blanket closer. He could still smell Alisha's light perfume upon it and he pulled it even tighter. As he looked across the
open plain ahead of them, he could see the constellation of Orion as his father had
taught him so many times over the years. Below it and to the left he could see the
bluish coloured flickering star of Sirius, the Dog Star, perfectly sat on the line of
the horizon. It sparkled brilliantly in the cloudless clear night sky. He wondered
how Balian was being treated and said a silent prayer for his safety. Percy let out a
yell in his sleep, sat up briefly, looked around then lay back down again. Tenno just
turned his head very slightly but remained exactly how he had been all night. Paul's
mind began to ponder Princess Stephanie's comments about his father, but more
importantly, about his mother. Eventually he fell asleep.

෪෨

Guy tightened his sword belt as he walked towards Paul's group near the fallen
trees. He stopped and kicked the feet of Percival, who was still asleep. The sun
was casting a deep red hue on the eastern horizon creating massive crimson and
golden yellow beams of sunlight to reach out from the trees as they shone almost
horizontally through them. It was early still but Guy stood bolt upright smiling as
he looked towards Paul. Paul shuffled to sit himself up as Tenno stood up slowly
and stared at Guy. He kicked Percival's feet again. Percival flinched and pulled his
feet up, then jumped up alarmed before realising it was Guy.
"Did we all sleep well?" Guy asked aloud.
"Yes…until some noisy fool woke my beauty sleep!" Theodoric said as he
stretched his arms and yawned as Thomas smiled at him and nodded in agreement.

73

"Come come dear friends. Our Templar brothers have already left…'tis not too early for them," Guy announced and pointed towards Gerard's now empty location with his opened hand.

Paul jumped up to get a clearer view as Thomas stood to see for himself. Taqi pulled his blanket over his head and muttered some words.

"So much for their orders to protect the Princess?" Thomas exclaimed as he rubbed his hands.

"Their primary orders are to harass Saladin. 'Tis perhaps a good thing they have already left. Which way did they go?" Percival remarked as he stood up.

"They have set off west for Tortosa. They have taken the Muslim prisoners with them. And why is it a good thing?" Guy asked.

"Well, at least he won't find…," Percival started to say and indicated towards Princess Stephanie's caravan with his left thumb over his shoulder, when Theodoric went to stand and pretended to fall against him hard.

"Find what?" Guy asked suspiciously.

"Any…he won't find any trouble that way if that is what he is after…," Percival quickly replied and smiled as he helped Theodoric stand up straight.

"That is true…but he leaves us vulnerable for sure. We have but a small force now," Guy replied and looked around the caravans and few remaining Hospitallers and Thomas's men.

"We shall be fine…besides…we have Thomas and his men, Brothers Teric and Matthew as well as Tenno," Paul explained as he stepped forward still looking down towards where Gerard's camp had been, his first thought being one of concern for Stewart, but also anxious in case Gerard would use the excuse to set an ambush to yet again attack them.

"We shall head directly south for Castle Blanc…every Muslim raiding party will be stretched out along the King's Highway all the way to Tortosa for sure. If Gerard has gone that way, 'tis surely for reasons that he spoils for a fight…as usual," Brother Teric said as he approached from the direction of Princess Stephanie's caravan.

"Castle Blanc…why not go straight to Crac de l'Ospital?" Guy asked perplexed.

"Because from this position, we would have to use the King's Highway again. Besides Crac is further south and we pass Castle Blanc first. No…we need to circumvent those routes, go via Castle Blanc then on to Crac and enter via the northeastern route south," Brother Teric explained as Theodoric listened in, a little puzzled too.

"I shall go and speak with Brother Matthew on the matter. I disagree!" Guy exclaimed and flounced around and headed off to where Brother Matthew had rested the night.

Theodoric looked at Brother Teric hard and frowned questioningly as did Tenno. Paul approached him and raised his eyebrows as if to ask him to explain.

"Fear not, I have not gone mad. Besides, you have a valuable cargo in Stephanie's caravan that will assist us…do you think me that blind that I do not know what occurs beneath my very nose?" Brother Teric explained and winked indicating towards Pauls caravan. "And besides…I have orders…to entrust the care of that young man to one certain Rashid…the old man of the mountains himself," he explained further and nodded toward Taqi. "When we have done so, his men will guarantee our safety to Crac…now say no more of this, get yourselves breakfasted and we can be away," he finished and bowed his head slightly at Theodoric, Tenno and then Paul.

"Did he just mention who I think he did?" Taqi asked as he sat up quickly.

"Typical Firgany…leaves nothing to chance even when he is not around," Theodoric said quietly and smiled as Brother Teric stepped back and walked away. "But what of Brother Matthew?"

"Him…he protects the Princess well enough…but his loyalties lie with Gerard and Reynald. He has his orders…and I have mine," Brother Teric answered.

Brother Teric distracted Brother Matthew with a warm drink as the remaining Templars and Hospitallers broke camp. As he did, Princess Stephanie quickly stepped down from Paul's caravan and walked over pretending she had just left her own as one of her maids rushed over to ask if she required anything. Paul watched her closely as she started talking with Brother Matthew as cool and as calm as anything. He wondered why exactly she was helping Turansha and his men. More perplexing was why was Brother Teric helping them and who gave him the order to get Taqi to Rashid? He felt a hand gently clasp his right arm. It was Alisha.

"These are strange times are they not?" she said softly and rested her head against his arm.

"Strange days indeed…very strange," Paul replied. "How is Arri?"

"Typically…he now sleeps. Sister Lucy watches him," she said and yawned covering her mouth as she did. She sighed, exhausted.

2 – 8

Both looked behind them as they heard horses approach from the northeast coming through the small track that ran from the wooded area. Brothers Teric and Matthew immediately ran from Princess Stephanie and called their men to arms. Paul grabbed the handle of his sword as Alisha ran for the caravan and Arri just as Thomas and Tenno ran up to Paul. Paul squinted to see better as the lead element of a convoy of riders appeared galloping into the open area. Immediately Paul saw the standard of the Hospitallers flying. His entire body relaxed as the tension ran from him and he smiled with a large sigh of relief. Two Templars escorted Princess Stephanie as the other knights and men all formed in a protective defensive posture. Within moments the mounted Hospitallers pulled up. The Hospitaller at the front looked behind him at his men quickly to check they were all accounted for then looked towards Brother Teric as he approached.

"Brother Armengaud…you are late!" Brother Teric said with a broad smile and outstretched his hand, grabbed the knight's forearm and they greeted each other.

"My friend…we have ridden all night. It took a while to correctly work out your cryptic message sent via heliograph," Brother Armengaud explained as he looked at the people from the caravan now gathering to see and hear what was happening.

"I feared your Grand Master would refuse the request."

"My friend…there may be issues between our Orders, but thankfully Brother

Moulin's has the foresight to know we must work together. Besides, he knows you have important guests travelling with you."

"I am glad to learn that he was not captured or killed at the recent attack."

"No...he was fortunate enough to escape...my condolences for the present loss of your Grand Master Odo though. I am sure ransoms or exchanges can be secured for his release," Armengaud explained and dismounted.

"So, is it total war or just another breach of a truce?" Brother Matthew asked out loud as he moved forwards closely followed by Guy.

"It looks like it could be war...Saladin wants the castle at Jacobs Ford dismantled and the cross roads routes left open to all...he will not stop until the fort is dismantled by agreement or action," Brother Armengaud explained as Paul studied him.

"Can we win this war?" Guy asked bluntly.

Armengaud looked at Guy and frowned. He removed his riding gloves and shook his head.

"My friend...no one wins when war starts. The only way we can hope to win this war is to prevent it."

"What...you cannot say that surely?" Guy remarked surprised.

"I see you have not been in this region long for if you had, you would know what I say is true," Brother Armengaud replied, his eye then catching sight of Alisha carrying Arri toward Paul.

Paul noticed this and immediately put his arm around her protectively feeling uncomfortable with the look he was giving her. Armengaud approached them.

"Sorry...please excuse my ignorant manners...but am I correct in assuming you are per chance the lovely Lady in Blue?" he asked and bowed slightly.

Alisha and Paul looked at each other confused then at Alisha's dress, which was a dark blue, but more a greenish colour.

"No...I think you must have her mistaken for someone else," Paul answered.

"No...I think not. You wear a blue dress...and your beauty is beyond what we have been told," he remarked and paused for a few moments. "And you...you must be the Bull's Head Slayer we hear so much of?" he asked Paul, looking intently at him.

Tenno stepped forwards and put himself just on front of Alisha as Taqi watched curiously. Percival and Theodoric looked at each other and shrugged their shoulders.

"Please...everyone, this is Brother Armengaud d'Asp...he has come to escort us to Crac. It would appear stories of you two have gathered a whole life of their own," Brother Teric commented and smiled.

"It is our pleasure to assist and escort you. All of you. We shall water our horses, check our equipment and make haste to all be on our way soonest," Brother Armengaud said and bowed slightly and smiled at Alisha. "My master Roger des Moulins sends his best regards. He knew you were part of this convoy."

Princess Stephanie walked over and made her way next to Alisha.

"And I thought I was the important guest to be escorted," Stephanie joked.

"My Lady...I am led to believe you have a part escort...but we are here to escort all of you in. 'Tis a pleasure to meet again," Armengaud replied and bowed his head.

Paul looked up and became aware that most of the men in the column were talking amongst themselves and several looked at Alisha and Paul. He felt as though they were on display. Tenno, as ever aware, moved to stand in front of them. Princess Stephanie also noticed the interest they were generating.

"That is very reassuring to hear, then let us be on our way shall we?" she commented and beckoned Alisha to follow her.

Alisha grasped Paul's hand and pulled him to follow also as she held Arri close against her chest with her other arm. Brother Teric nodded at Brother Matthew indicating they start their preparations and then ushered Armengaud to follow Princess Stephanie to her caravan as Thomas took the reins of his horse and steadied it.

Outside Stephanie's caravan they all stopped.

"You do know who my guests are I assume before I open this?" Stephanie asked.

Both Brother Teric and Armengaud nodded yes upon which she opened the side door, pushed the netting aside and stepped up inside.

"Fear not My Lady, we have used our contacts to pass on the message to Saladin that his brother is in safe custody and will be safely handed over to Rashid to escort on from Castle Blanc, to his castle at Masyaf and then onwards. Gerard still believes him to be here, but, and with no disrespect intended, your husband believes him long since travelled through since April...'twas but a necessary rouse," Armengaud explained and followed her into the caravan.

Brother Teric stood aside and beckoned for Alisha and Paul to enter before entering himself.

℠℞

Inside the caravan it smelt from the three men having slept inside all night. Quickly Princess Stephanie opened the side windows slightly and looked for an incense candle to light. Alisha and Paul sat down on the large bench that ran opposite the bed, Turansha and his two colleagues looking on apprehensively, Brother Armengaud acknowledging him with a smile. They clearly already knew each other. Turansha stood up immediately alarmed as Brother Teric entered dressed in his Templar uniform so clearly different from Brother Armengaud's black mantle.

"Fear not gentlemen...I too have orders to secure you safely on your way," Brother Teric stated and part bowed his head.

A strong smell wafted up from a full chamber pot beneath the bed. All in the caravan could smell it as they all sat themselves down, Brother Teric closing the door behind him. Arri started to wriggle as he began to wake up.

"We are and shall be eternally indebted to you all," Turansha said quietly and bowed his head. "And you young sir...you saved us yet without not knowing us... that truly is the mark of a great man. We thank you," he remarked, looking at Paul.

"Officially you should already be in Alexandria two months past...I am not sure how you got delayed nor do we need to know, but thankfully we have you now," Armengaud said as Princess Stephanie sat down upon a single chair, her hands placed upon her knees. She exuded an elegance that was immediately obvious.

"We have much to discuss, as well as keep you out of sight in here I am afraid, but do as we ask, and you will soon be free to be on your way," Stephanie remarked and smiled and looked at each of them in turn.

"Why are we in here too?" Paul asked.

"Because this concerns you both...and you have saved both of our lives these past days," Stephanie answered and nodded at him.

Port of La Rochelle, France, Melissae Inn, Spring 1191.

"So why is the princess helping Saladin's brother...surely that is treason?" Simon asked, puzzled.

"Because she knew him well. They were friends. Besides, as the Templars' administrative arm knew only full well, if they were to ever have any kind of workable peace in the region, they needed people like Turansha alive who could influence his brother Saladin."

"But surely, her husband, Reynald would kill her for sure if he found out?" Ayleth asked.

"No...you see what many people do not realise here, is that the aim is not to necessarily kill the perceived enemy, but in the main, injure or weaken him. A dead man is buried. A wounded man takes two more to look after him as well as still feed him. But also, men such as Turansha could be ransomed for vast amounts of money...or in exchange for prisoners such as Odo de St Armand. Stephanie was astute, sadly more so than her husbands ever were, and she knew that if she wanted safety for her own children, long term, she would need to plan accordingly. Besides that, she was a woman of genuine honour and integrity with principles," the old man answered.

"Not towards Paul I think not!" Sarah stated loudly.

"She did feel strongly toward Paul yes, but she also had the emotional maturity to know she could not, nor would try to take it further. She adored little Arri and Alisha... but you cannot simply stop or switch off a set of feelings for someone, but she did keep them in check for that is the type of woman she is," the old man replied solemnly.

"Can you clarify something for me? This castle that Odo was building...why was it so significant and why did Saladin feel the need to destroy it?" Gabirol asked.

"Why? Because it was situated at a strategically positioned cross roads of both major trade and pilgrim routes. Reynald had continually broken truces and agreements, so you can imagine what he would do with a set up like that...and Saladin knew it. Saladin had many within his own ranks who constantly urged him to deal with Reynald before he became too powerful and so they demanded he take action to secure the free and safe movement of Muslim pilgrims. We cannot hide from the reality that in this instance, building the castle was of sound military strategic importance...but whether of moral right is one I am afraid we could argue about for a very long time," the old man explained.

"So you mean this Saladin did not have total authority over his armies then?" Ayleth asked, somewhat surprised.

"No...not at all. He was having to constantly justify and appease many within his own ranks and leaders. The whole edifice of his command was a constant one of changing loyalties and attitudes...and egos as well as fanatics. For keeping that under control alone deserves respect, let alone his military prowess," the old man replied.

"I have heard that it was more luck that he succeeded often," Peter remarked.

"And I bet you heard that from men who have never been there?" the Templar interrupted and looked at him and shook his head.

"In war, there is always an element of luck...always. And as our two knight friends here

will probably confirm and agree, no plan survives contact with the enemy," the old man said and looked at the Templar and Hospitaller, who both nodded in agreement.

"So how did they manage to hide Saladin's brother...especially with people like that Matthew guard always hanging about?" the Genoese sailor asked.

"'Twas not hard. Brother Matthew was informed that Princess Stephanie was in mourning for the death of her father-in-law, was feeling unwell also with a terrible stomach affliction so did not wish to be disturbed. Not even by her chamber maids. Getting enough food inside was perhaps the biggest problem, but Sister Lucy managed that."

"So she stayed in the caravan with three men?" Ayleth asked.

"No...no of course not. She stayed with Alisha in her caravan. Besides, it was only for a few short days of travel to Castle Blanc. Paul, Tenno and Taqi took it in turns doing watch through the nights alongside Thomas and his men. Theodoric and Sister Lucy concentrated on feeding them as well as constantly distracting Brother Matthew," the old man explained then laughed briefly. "In fact Brother Matthew became rather fond of the attention he received from Sister Lucy as she practically mothered him."

"So I assume they got to Castle Blanc without incident?" Gabirol asked.

"Yes...that they did," the old man answered and nodded.

Castle Blanc, County of Tripoli in the Levant, June 17th 1179

It was late in the evening when the column arrived at Castle Blanc having been deliberately delayed by Brother Teric. The sun sat low on the western horizon. Alisha sat up front on the caravan next to Tenno as he steered it through the main castle wall entrance. It had been a year since she was last there. Sister Lucy was in the back with Arri whilst Princess Stephanie, having managed to move across without being seen, was back in her own caravan, which pulled to a halt immediately opposite the main Keep's entrance steps. Alisha's heart was pounding as she watched concerned that at any moment someone would discover the three men still hiding inside. Princess Stephanie had assured her all would be okay as no one would be allowed to enter her caravan. Hidden in plain sight she had confidently stated, but that did not stop Alisha from feeling tense. She had to admire Stephanie's calmness. Paul, Taqi and Theodoric walked alongside with Thomas and Percival, who on foot led their own horses. Guy immediately dismounted, handed his reins to a Templar stood nearby and ran up the steps and inside the main Keep entrance hallway. Brother Armengaud pulled up near to Thomas and shook his head dismissively at Guy's behaviour.

"It will be a tight squeeze fitting all the caravans in here," Thomas commented as he looked around the internal forecourt as more caravans and carts pulled inside. Brother Armengaud nodded in agreement as he looked around.

No sooner had the caravans and carts all stopped, when other Hospitallers appeared and several Templars came down from the main Keep to greet Princess Stephanie. Some were carrying burning torches for light. Alisha saw Brother Nicholas step down and greet Princess Stephanie. Quickly she jumped down from her seat and rushed over towards him. Princess Stephanie saw her approach and stepped back a pace. Nicholas saw her and his eyes visibly widened and almost lit up as a large smile appeared upon his face. Brother Baldwin, who approached down the stairs behind him, shook his head and looked up as if in dismay but smiling.

"Ali...I mean Alisha...what, I mean how come you are here...right now?" Nicholas asked with excitement clear in his voice as he greeted her and outstretched his hands.

Alisha quickly stepped up onto the lower step and held his hands, looked at him for a moment as Brother Baldwin stood behind him with a burning torch flickering away. Princess Stephanie looked on bemused just as the Templar Turcopole in charge of the Keep started to walk down the steps. He waved at Brother Armengaud and headed straight for him assuming Princess Stephanie was being dealt with.

"And you. How come you are still here?" Alisha asked, smiling broadly.

"Er...after my run in with Master Gerard and Reynald, I am not exactly popular in their company. So I get to stay here and garrison this place most days," Nicholas answered, at which point Alisha just pulled him close and hugged him. He smiled then placed his arms around her as Princess Stephanie raised an eyebrow and then looked at Brother Baldwin.

"Brother Blancofort!" Brother Teric shouted out as he quickly approached leading his horse.

Paul and Taqi looked over at hearing Brother Teric call out someone's name. Paul's eyes immediately fell upon Alisha hugging Nicholas. Taqi slapped his arm and gestured they go over. A little more than puzzled Paul started to walk toward them. Brother Nicholas immediately let go of Alisha and stood back a pace from her as Brother Teric looked at him hard and handed him the reins of his horse, Brother Armengaud looking over also.

"You say my husband Reynald is responsible for you being stuck here...yes?" Stephanie asked Nicholas and looked at Alisha in turn just as Paul stood behind her.

"Sorry My Lady...I forget myself. Yes...I am not the most favoured with Master Gerard nor your husband I am afraid to say," Nicholas answered politely as the Templar Turcopole tood still a little confused waiting for Brother Armengaud to come over.

"Good...then that means I can probably trust you," Stephanie laughed back. "Alisha...please do not stay in your caravan tonight. Please bring Arri and come stay inside where it will be more comfortable," she said as she started to walk up the steps closely followed by the Templar Turcopole.

"And you...stable my horse if you would grace me with your service this eve?" Brother Teric said and immediately started to follow Princess Stephanie up the stairs.

"And who is Arri?" Nicholas asked as he held the reins of Brother Teric's horse tightly.

"My son," Alisha replied.

"Your son!" Nicholas coughed clearly surprised. "How...I mean, when...I mean the last time...ah, let me guess...of course...your Paul...yes?" Nicholas said trying to compose himself when it was obvious to all listening he was shocked. Brother Baldwin shook his head and frowned.

Paul stood silently behind Alisha with Taqi next to him as Tenno came over. Nicholas looked over Alisha's shoulder and saw Paul. Nicholas coughed to clear his dry throat just as Paul stepped forward and beside Alisha as she looked at him briefly then back at Nicholas. She could see the disappointment in Nicholas's eyes as he tried to hide his emotions. She sighed and forced a smile. Paul could sense the sudden awkwardness between them as Alisha started fiddling with her hands nervously as she often did when uncomfortable.

"Brother Nicholas isn't it?" Paul asked and outstretched his hand. "I have heard much about you and I understand I owe you a great deal?"

Nicholas looked at Paul's hand for a moment before grasping it and shaking his hand tightly. Paul looked into his eyes. Nicholas stared back as they shook hands.

"'Twas my honour...and I was only doing my duty. I am pleased to meet you," Nicholas replied.

"Bullshit!" Brother Baldwin half coughed quietly but still audible.

As Paul looked at Nicholas, both having heard Brother Baldwin's comments clearly, held their shake for a few moments. Paul had heard so much about him and Nicholas likewise about him. Nicholas knew Paul was still young yet he had an air about him that solicited respect. He smiled at him and bowed his head in recognition and acknowledgement, almost like an unspoken agreement had been reached. Paul bowed his head back and smiled too, Alisha letting out a sigh and a little nervous laugh. Paul and Nicholas both laughed and looked at Brother Baldwin and both shook their heads at him. Tenno looked at Taqi and they both frowned.

"I am forever indebted to you," Paul finally said as they broke their handshake.

"'Twas my privilege...truly. Now if you will excuse me...I have a horse to stable. Paul, it is nice," he paused as he smiled again and Paul smiled broadly both recognising the awkwardness of the situation. "Is nice to have finally met you."

"Likewise. I am sure we will see each other before we leave here," Paul replied as Alisha held onto his arm. Nicholas seeing this smiled again despite his heart feeling torn in two.

"Alisha, I am truly pleased for you. It would seem you have a good man here," Nicholas remarked. Brother Baldwin raised his eyebrows and shook his head mockingly and then pushed Nicholas to move.

They all smiled as Brother Baldwin led Nicholas and the horse away.

"Well...that was awkward," Taqi joked.

"Sorry, Paul, if I have done the wrong thing...I should not have hugged him like that," Alisha said softly.

"Ali...I fully understand. I am not the same childish fool I was back in La Rochelle last year. Besides...he seems like a genuine nice man...and why would he not like my beautiful wife, eh?" Paul remarked and put his arms around her.

As Nicholas walked away with Brother Baldwin, he looked back over his shoulder at Paul stood with his arms around Alisha.

"Upside...did you have to be so obvious?" he asked Brother Baldwin.

"Hey...you know me. Tell it as it is. If you had seen the look in your eyes when you saw her again, and then the look of utter crushed little heart feelings when she said she had a child..."

"Upside...there are times when I wonder if you really are actually my friend," Nicholas remarked as he started to tie up Brother Teric's horse.

"The best and only one you will ever have."

"Yes...such is my luck," Nicholas joked and looked once again back at Paul and Alisha. He sighed and his heart felt heavy. He wanted to dislike Paul and he knew he felt incredibly envious of him, but he also tried to keep that emotion in check. Begrudgingly he had to admit to himself he liked Paul. He shook his head and started to unbuckle the saddle on the horse.

ഇ൦ജ

Princess Stephanie stood in the third upper level corridor talking quietly with Alisha and Sister Lucy discussing how Brother Teric had managed to secure Turansha some food and water whilst Sister Lucy had kept Brother Matthew distracted. One single torch burned away set upon the wall. Guy could be heard talking loudly and moaning to Percival in one of the rooms. It was late and the Templars and Hospitallers had all finished their evening vespers whilst Paul and Theodoric were in a small bedroom chamber watching over Arri as he slept wrapped up in the shawl Taqi had stitched his pattern upon. Tucked beside him was Clip clop. Alisha had been offered the same bedroom where she had stayed previously but she declined it. Taqi and Tenno took that room as Taqi wished to be where Raja had last been alive. Alisha promised him she would take him to her grave in the morning. Thomas declined to stay in one of the billeted rooms preferring to sleep with his men and their horses inside one of the main covered stable blocks. Paul knelt down on the thick rug that covered the stone floor next to the bed and looked closely at Arri. He could not get over how much he felt for this little bundle in front of him. He could not believe it either that he had brought both him and Alisha all the way out here with all the now very apparent dangers. Theodoric looked at Paul and could see the love and concern in his eyes, his face lit up from the single flickering candle on the side.

   10 – 2

"Paul...things will be all right...I promise you, and I do not make promises lightly," he said quietly and leaned back against the wall next to the tall thin window.

"I never realised just how brutal and stupid people can be...," he replied and placed his hands on either side of Arri.

"You have seen nothing yet...trust me. 'Tis why you have to be so guarded."

"Yes tell me about it. I already hear ridiculous stories of the great Bull's Head Slayer...things I have never done and in places I have never been."

"That is why the sooner we get to Alexandria the better. People like to tell stories...that is how legends start and myths are born. Your father knows this fact well and it's why he has tried for so long and so hard to convey the utter folly of war and real truths within his writings," Theodoric explained and moved over to sit on the corner of the bed near to Paul.

"I think I am only just beginning to realise that. But why did we not just stay in La Rochelle then if he knew all of this?"

"In short...because your path, call it your destiny, is calling you there...that is why."

"You mean those damn parchments?"

"You may curse them, but if you learnt to understand them, you could use them for your benefits. Believe me, it does work. I have a bloody great tattoo on my back to prove it...and another on my arse which I shall not show you," Theodoric said quietly and laughed.

"You never did explain what your tattoo means…nor why Tenno and I should not ask about camels in relation to Sister Lucy," Paul replied and looked at him and raised his eyebrows as if to question him.

"Oh, have I not?" Theodoric answered knowing full well he had not. "Well I can tell you about the tattoo…but the camels, hmm! No!" Theodoric smiled and paused. "The tattoo was a gift…a gift I tell you. Lord I would hate to have gotten something that was meant not as a gift…but I can tell you that the trees that make up my tattoo symbolise, well more correctly its roots, symbolise and represent the very foundations upon which we all base our beliefs. The trunk represents the body, mind and spirit, and the ever changing leaves represent wisdom, for like wisdom leaves can be blown away and re-grown as new wisdom is learnt. And the tree trunks are drawn representing two females, which in turn represent the true sacred femininity of both mother nature and our Earth Goddess…in fact all of womankind. It is all shaped like a pair of wings to represent freedom on many levels."

"It sounds like a real positive image to carry upon your back."

"Yes…you would say that," Theodoric sighed and smiled sitting himself down on the end of the bed. The bed kept sinking lower and Paul had to support Arri to stop him rolling. Theodoric patted his stomach. "I think my Luce feeds me too well these days," he whispered.

A gentle rap on the door drew their attention. Quickly Theodoric stood up and approached the door. He looked through a small peep hole to see Brother Nicholas standing outside the door. He looked back at Paul and mouthed it was him.

"Let him in then," Paul said quietly.

Theodoric opened the door and put his finger to his lips to indicate silence and beckoned him inside. As Nicholas entered the room, Theodoric peered out and saw Alisha, Princess Stephanie and Sister Lucy still talking at the end of the corridor. Alisha looked his way and gave a quick wave and continued talking. Nicholas had clearly come up the western stairwell and not the wide steps on the eastern side. Paul looked up at Nicholas bemused as Theodoric closed the door quietly.

"Paul…please accept my apology for disturbing you this late hour…but as I saw you were all still awake, I felt compelled to seek your company to explain some things and clear the air between us," Nicholas said confidently as he stood upright.

Theodoric walked around him and over toward Paul and looked at him as puzzled as Paul was.

"Sorry…I do not think I understand. Have I missed something?" Paul asked and knelt up higher letting go of Arri.

"Your son. You must very proud?" Nicholas said quietly and paused as he just looked at Arri for a few moments. "Oh Lord listen to me…what a fool I can be. I came to apologise for my inappropriate behaviour earlier…you know…as in hugging Alisha when you arrived. Brother Teric and Brother Baldwin both chided me for doing so…'tis just that Ali…sorry, I mean Alisha, she erm…she just has that effect upon me. It troubles me that I have behaved thus and I have come to apologise as I have said and to promise you this eve, not to do it ever again. 'Twas truly wrong of me," Nicholas explained quietly and tried to clear his throat as it became dry.

Paul stood up and quickly poured a ceramic cup of clear water out and handed it toward Nicholas. He declined the drink so Paul placed it back down upon the small table dresser.

"Nicholas, if I may call you that. I did not expect or need an apology from you. 'Tis I who am indebted to you for saving Ali. And yes, she certainly has an effect upon all of us I am afraid. My father always said if I wished to remain happily married, I should marry an ugly woman...so I fear I shall have lots of unhappiness," Paul said and smiled.

"If the measure of unhappiness is thus proportional to the woman's beauty... then I am afraid my friend you are indeed in deep deep trouble," Nicholas replied and smiled back. "I am sorry...I am doing it again, being inappropriate in what I say. Can I just say what I wish to express once and for all and I shall never say it again?"

"Of course...I think," Paul replied and stood up straight.

"I have heard this eve that it is you who is known as the great Bull's Head Slayer... that is one accolade I would not wish upon anyone for every pumped up idiot fool who wishes to make his mark and reputation in this land will challenge you at the slightest excuse...and I know how that will impact upon Ali...Alisha sorry. I have but known you less than a few hours and the briefest of meetings...but I sense you are a good, decent and honourable man. I take some comfort in that fact for if you had been a right royal shit whom I could hate, then that would have been a different matter."

"I am not sure exactly what you are saying," Paul remarked, perplexed, and frowned.

"Sorry. Erm. Okay...this is probably, no...this is most definitely out of order, not least because I am supposed to be a knight who has renounced all claim to possessions and earthly desires...but when I met Alisha," Nicholas coughed.

"His wife!" Theodoric interrupted.

"I know that...I know that. But in this land I know you have to say what is on your mind when you can while you still can...so I need to explain my actions... more importantly my intentions. I cannot hide how I feel towards...your wife. 'Tis not a set of emotions I either wished for or asked for, they just happened, from the minute I first saw her. And I know I shall feel those emotions until the day I depart this world," Nicholas explained, his voice getting louder and more nervous as he explained himself, his face reddening. "But Paul, I swear by all that I am, in the eyes of the Lord Almighty and you both present here, I would die for her in a heartbeat, and knowing the love she has for you too, I also vow this eve to lay down my life in the service and protection of you also should you ever need it. There, I have said my piece and what needed to be said. I shall never repeat it again," Nicholas explained and bowed his head solemnly and placed his hands together across his sword belt.

"I do not want anyone dying for me...ever," Alisha suddenly said, her voice quiet and broken with emotion as she pushed the door open and slowly walked in. She stared at Nicholas and Paul in turn looking shocked.

"Alisha...forgive my words and intrusion into your world...I am so sorry. I am trying to do my best to resolve the turmoil in my heart and act according to what my head tells me I should do," Nicholas said quietly as Theodoric shook his head.

"I do not know whether to thank you, smack you or run from you," Paul said as he stepped closer to Nicholas. Alisha quickly put her arms up between him and Nicholas. "Ali...I have no intention of becoming hostile...you should know me better than that?" Paul frowned. Nicholas stepped back a pace toward the door as Sister Lucy and Princess Stephanie peered in.

"No one...no one dies for me. Do you understand...both of you?" Alisha demanded, her eyes wide and filled with an anger Paul had never seen before, not even when he had deeply hurt her back in La Rochelle.

"I have not come to cause trouble. But I know you are not stupid and clearly very wise for your age...that is why I know you would question my motives and be suspicious of Ali. That kind of suspicion festers and can turn into a poisonous venom that will eat away at you...I know this and you knowing already how I feel, or suspect it for I saw it in your eyes when you arrived, I knew I had to set this matter straight and proper. I am nothing if not honest...at all times," Nicholas explained to Paul, sensing Alisha looking at him puzzled.

"And you got all that from one hug?" Theodoric asked and folded his arms.

"I saw how Paul looked at me. He already knows of me that I am sure, am I correct, for he knew I had saved Ali?"

"Nicholas...as I have said, I do not know whether to thank you or slap you... but I have to say I admire your honesty. And you speak wise words for, yes, I know myself well enough to know I probably would, as I had done so once before, make all the wrong assumptions and let fear and paranoia eat away at me. At least your frank and open explanation puts everything out in the open," Paul commented.

"Oh Nicholas...you know Paul has always had my heart...but likewise, you shall always have a part of my heart too," Alisha remarked and placed her hand upon his forearm. She looked into his eyes.

"That is perhaps more than I deserve. I must go now and beg your pardons for I fear I have embarrassed us all enough this eve," Nicholas said and stepped back. He looked at Paul and bowed his head, Paul doing likewise in return. Nicholas looked at Paul for several moments, smiled and turned around, walked past Sister Lucy, nodded at Princess Stephanie and walked between them to leave the room.

As soon as Nicholas had left, Princess Stephanie closed the door quickly and quietly. Alisha grabbed Paul's hands and looked into his eyes intently searching for what he was thinking and feeling. He smiled and sighed at the same time.

"Oh my dear Paul...does this hurt you, what has been said?" she asked.

"No...no not at all. He has your best interests at heart and clearly is prepared to put them above his own. I know very few people like that. I do not fear his actions now. I have seen much honesty but also much deceit these past months from people. Even good deceit from a wife towards a husband for very good reason," Paul exclaimed and looked at Princess Stephanie. She smiled and shrugged her shoulders. "Should I now fear your actions?" he asked looking back at Alisha.

Alisha immediately screwed up her face in anger at his comment as Theodoric looked up to the ceiling and raised his hands.

"No...you...you," Alisha tried to say something but was lost for words. As she looked at Paul she could see the affection in his eyes for her and her anger just as quickly left her. She wrapped her arms around him tightly and pulled him close closing her eyes. Paul rested his face against the side of hers and closed his eyes and just held her.

"Time we were leaving," Princess Stephanie whispered beckoning both Theodoric and Sister Lucy to follow her out.

It was early morning when Alisha led Paul and Taqi to where Raja had been buried just outside the castle walls in the small cemetery. Paul carried Arri carefully as Theodoric and Sister Lucy followed accompanied by Tenno. Few people were up except several Knights Templar as their guard duties were coming to an end. Despite the early hour it was already hot. Sister Lucy wiped her forehead and sighed.

"I do hope they have some water at Crac so we can finally have a proper wash," she commented.

"There is a stream not far if that helps?" Alisha responded as she held Taqi's hand as they turned into the cemetery.

"No there isn't. Went there already. With this drought, the stream has dried up," Theodoric replied and put his arm around Sister Lucy. She stopped and held Theodoric back as Alisha, Paul and Taqi stopped just short of Raja's grave. Just a slight raised mound of earth remained and totally unmarked apart from a stone placed at the foot of the grave.

Alisha looked at Taqi as he knelt down. She went to step closer when he raised his hand rapidly to stop her.

"No Ali...'tis forbidden," he exclaimed emotionally and covered his eyes with is right hand.

Paul looked at Alisha puzzled.

"What is forbidden?" he asked quietly.

"Strictly speaking...women do not return to a grave, only the men may do so," she answered and looked down at Taqi. He was crying but trying his hardest to hide the fact.

Paul handed Arri to Alisha and knelt beside Taqi and placed a reassuring arm around his shoulders.

"Taqi...'tis fine to cry..."

Taqi just shook his head as he cried and began to sob even more screwing his eyes up shut tighter. He shook his head. Paul looked back at Alisha. She sighed and shook her head sadly. Taqi's outpouring of emotion was quite unexpected. Theodoric shrugged his shoulders, surprised. Tenno walked over as Paul looked back at Taqi.

"Raja, she is gone...she has been delivered into the hand of Allah," Taqi blurted out and cried more, tears streaming down his face and he shook uncontrollably. Alisha welled up with tears seeing the state of him. After a few minutes, Taqi, his face streaked from tears, his nose running, sniffed and stood up slowly and tried to compose himself. He stared at Raja's grave. "I...I think all that has happened of late, and losing father...I think it has finally caught up with me. I am sorry," he explained tearfully and wiped his face. He coughed and sighed a few times as Paul rested his hand upon his left shoulder and they all patiently waited whilst he regained his composure.

"Come with me," Tenno finally said quietly and with a gentleness he had not shown before. He pulled Taqi around to face him. Taqi took a deep breath as Tenno looked him in the eye then he ushered him away placing his arm around Taqi and leading him off back toward the main Keep.

Theodoric looked on bemused at Tenno's actions. Alisha quickly wiped away a single tear before Paul looked back at her. She rocked Arri gently and then handed him back to Paul. Quickly she located the small piece of cloth Raja had given her just before she had died. She opened it and read the names upon it again. She bit her bottom lip trying not to cry as she looked at the words and then the dry and dusty grave in front of her. Theodoric stepped closer.

"What is that, my dear girl?" he asked softly as Sister Lucy feigned a brave smile to Paul.

"Just a few words...my birth name. Raja gave it to me just before she died," Alisha explained and showed Theodoric the images and words.

"Ailia...," Theodoric said quietly and breathed out as if suddenly winded.

Sister Lucy's eyes widened in surprise hearing him speak her birth name. Paul saw the look upon her face and Theodoric's reaction.

"What is it...what causes you both to look so alarmed?" he demanded urgently.

"'Tis nothing to be alarmed by...I promise you that. 'Twas just a surprise to hear a name we have not heard of for so long...and surprised that Raja passed this on," Theodoric answered seeing the alarm registering upon Alisha's and Paul's faces.

"Ali...what did she say when she gave you this?" Sister Lucy asked.

"Only that it was my real birth name...and that I had to show Paul's father, Philip....but not my father...Why?" Alisha answered, clearly suspicious.

"I see," Theodoric replied and shook his head. "And did you show him...Philip, alone, that is?"

"Yes...of course. I do not know what it meant to him...but immediately after I had, that is when both my father and he changed their minds about Paul and I being together," Alisha explained, puzzled.

"Why...what does this mean?" Paul asked and studied Theodoric's reactions closely.

"Probably nothing...honestly," Theodoric answered awkwardly, which was unusual for him.

"I am sure it is nothing, and I guess we shall never know. Now come on...we have a long journey ahead of us today," Sister Lucy interjected quickly, seeing the look upon Theodoric's face and gently pulled Alisha to follow her.

Alisha looked at Paul quizzically before following alongside Sister Lucy. Paul took one last look back at Raja's grave before walking away with Theodoric.

"I know you know far more than you let on...I pray you at least inform me in good time...whatever it is," Paul whispered.

"Paul...that I swear I shall...all in good time...all in good time," Theodoric replied and patted Paul on the back.

Just as they were about to enter the main Keep's outer wall, Brothers Nicholas and Baldwin appeared. Alisha hesitated briefly, smiled at Nicholas and continued walking into the main courtyard with Sister Lucy.

"This could be awkward," Theodoric said quietly.

"Paul....if I may call you that?" Nicholas asked politely.

"'Tis my name so of course," Paul replied.

"I just wanted to show you something...if you would come with me?" Nicholas asked and beckoned he follow him as he started to walk down the hill towards a lemon and orange orchard. "Please. It will take but a moment."

Paul looked at Theodoric, who frowned, perplexed.

"You go with him. I shall stay here with this fine fellow," Theodoric remarked and looked Brother Baldwin up and down, who scowled at him.

એ ભ

Nicholas led the way further into the orchard, the ground dry and dusty. Paul was both curious and cautious as to why he wanted him to follow. After a few moments, the ground began to rise and they reached the very far edge of the orchard. A small wall separated the orchard from the land beyond. Nicholas beckoned him over and outstretched his arm to show him the rolling plain beneath that stretched out toward the sea on the far western horizon.

"'Tis a magnificent view yes?" Nicholas stated.

Paul stepped closer and looked. It was a stunning view. Both stood in silence for several moments just looking at the rolling hills to the north and the plain to the west. Paul placed his hand upon his sword handle.

"You will never have any need of that with me...that I can promise," Nicholas said aware of what Paul had just done.

"I do not believe you have simply brought me here to look at a view...and you said your piece last eve...so what brings us here now?"

"I meant every word of what I said last eve...but this place. This is my most favourite place in the whole world. When my time comes, this is where I wish to be laid for it holds special reverence for me," Nicholas explained then looked directly at Paul.

"Really?"

"Yes...really. 'Tis also a place Alisha sat often too...though not with me I must add!" he quickly explained and smiled. Paul looked at him curious as to his motives. He was older than Paul yet still looked boyish and he did have a kind face. "Look, after Alisha left here, I would oft visit...sad, right?"

"Sad...no," Paul replied seeing the genuine feeling in Nicholas's face and the tone of his voice. Part of him felt sorry for him...for obviously loving Alisha too. "I am the lucky one of us two...and I know I am blessed having Alisha as my wife."

"That you are indeed," he sighed and paused just looking at Paul. "I so wanted to hate you...that would have been easier for me then...but I see you are a good man. You will be a great man too."

"Great...no I doubt that," Paul smiled in answer partly embarrassed.

"Look...come. I have something else I wanted to show you," Nicholas said and walked over to the lemon tree nearest the wall. "Look," he said and pointed to the initials Alisha had carved deep into the tree trunk a year ago in both Latin and Arabic. "The day I saw that was the day your friend Raja died...but also a part inside of me...for that day was the day I first saw this...and knew she would never be mine," he explained sadly.

Paul knelt down to look at the carved initials. He ran his fingers over them softly and his heart almost ached. He looked up at Nicholas as he stood with the sun behind him, sweat forming upon his brow. He was wearing his full uniform and chain mail. But he still looked composed and confident. Paul stood up and faced him. He understood the gesture Nicholas was making.

"Thank you, Nicholas. I admire you and your honesty. It is refreshing and most welcome for I know not many whom I can trust these days. I would like to consider you a friend," Paul explained and offered his hand.

"I would be honoured to be considered such," Nicholas replied and bowed his head slightly, closed his eyes briefly then shook Paul's hand. Both smiled. "'Tis a bond I shall never break."

Port of La Rochelle, France, Melissae Inn, spring 1191

"I am not sure I trust this Nicholas...," Sarah remarked as she sat back in her chair.
"I think he is most honourable," Ayleth said, smiling.

>:X: 1 – 4

"Well I suspect he is either very devious or genuine. They say all is fair in love and war... but, well there are limits surely?" Gabirol asked.
"Not in Outremer there aren't," the Hospitaller remarked.
Miriam looked at the Templar. He shrugged his shoulders.
"I cannot say anything for fear of spoiling this tale, for I know of this Nicholas...and that is all I shall say," he stated and feigned a smile of knowing and winked at Miriam.
"I sense much cynicism here," the old man joked as he picked up his empty water jug. "Stephan...may I," he asked and passed the jug across the table. Stephan picked it up and without a word went to the kitchen to fetch fresh boiled water cooled within the larder. "All I shall say about Nicholas is that he may surprise you."
"So I take it he did not attack Paul in the orchard then?" the Genoese sailor asked as Simon nodded as if in agreement with him.
"No he did not," the old man answered, smiling.
"I want to know, what happened then with the three men in Princess Stephanie's caravan...?" the farrier asked and rested his elbows upon the table.
"Oh, they remained perfectly well hidden, in plain sight, within her caravan. Brother Teric saw to that. Within the hour of his visit to the orchard, Paul found himself standing next to his caravan preparing to leave along with the Hospitallers and Brothers Teric and Matthew and a smaller contingent of Templars. Brother Teric explained to Armengaud that their planned route would take them near to the monastery near to Crac where they would meet up with Rashid from the Ashashin fortress of Masyaf so they could hand over Taqi but also to receive intelligence gathered by his Ashashin members for Roger des Moulins. In turn the Ashashin would part escort Turansha past Crac de Moab in Kerak in the south, and safely on his way to Alexandria," the old man explained.
"I find it strange to hear that the feared Ashashin and Templars and Hospitallers all work together...truly strange," Simon commented, shaking his head.
"'Tis the way things worked out there. The Ashashin answered only to themselves. The last thing they wanted was for either side to become all too powerful and dominating...so in some respects it served them well that they all fought each other...until a time they would hopefully fuse and all join as one force. But that was a strategy that depended heavily upon all parties playing their respective roles and remaining principled and honourable," the old man explained and paused as Stephan handed him a fresh jug of water. "'Twas indeed a crime that certain individuals did not have the wisdom nor the foresight to see that."
"What...like Gerard?" Peter asked.
"No...Gerard was at times reckless and driven by ambition...but people like Reynald...a

truly troubled soul. A man torn emotionally on many levels...not that that excused his behaviour...but a complex man. Very complex," the old man said as he poured himself a drink.

"So did Saladin's brother escape then...please just tell us?" Sarah asked impatiently.

The old man laughed slightly, took a sip of water, placed his drink down and looked at her.

"Did Nicholas go with them?" Ayleth asked.

"No...no he did not. His place was at Castle Blanc. Paul offered to let him say goodbye to Alisha, but he declined saying it was best he just remained out of sight until they had gone."

"Did not Alisha want to say goodbye to him?" Sarah asked.

"Yes...and she asked where he was. In a way by not showing up to say goodbye made it easier...but also meant Alisha would think more on him...," the old man explained.

"Yes...that is rather sneaky if you ask me and too contrived...is that the correct word?" Simon asked, looking at Gabirol, who nodded yes.

"No...I think he was both embarrassed and also hurting. A broken heart, for that is what he was carrying, is a heavy burden to carry, especially unrequited love," the old man said in defence of Nicholas. "Though he did watch out from the Keep's roof as the convoy left... Alisha looking up at the last minute just in time to see him. She waved briefly before moving back inside the caravan feeling embarrassed and a little foolish. Nicholas stood with Brother Baldwin beside him and stared until the entire column had vanished from sight."

"And Taqi...did he leave them to join those Ashashin then?" Miriam asked.

"Well, the journey toward Crac was long, hot and dry with water being very limited as a drought persisted that year. Alisha, Paul and Taqi spent most of the journey in silence each in deep thought at the many changes that had already happened but also about the many coming changes rapidly approaching. Taqi had been hit hard by many realisations when he saw Raja's grave. It somehow signalled the end of his former days...his childhood... everything about who he was and the loss of his father...it all dawned upon him at that one moment," the old man explained.

"And Paul...was he changed inside?" Gabirol asked.

"Well...It was oft said that in many ways Paul was born old...but yes, he had already changed so much himself...he just didn't realise it at the time," the old man answered then paused briefly. "But let me tell you what happened to Turansha and his two friends, for it was late in the afternoon on the second day of the journey from Castle Blanc to Crac de l'Ospital that signalled the start of some major changes. In the caravan, Alisha sat feeding Arri as Princess Stephanie and Sister Lucy discussed her pregnancy. The caravan bumped occasionally hard as they travelled along the old major Roman road that passed through the fertile valleys that connected the coast to the west and the deserts to the east. Crac was strategically situated and was garrisoned by nearly two thousand Hospitallers. They all joked that as the castle had a huge artificial reservoir of fresh water, they would at last be able to bathe properly and in relatively safety. Paul rode up front with Tenno and Taqi discussing Taqi's very imminent departure. With the whole convoy stretched out along the main old Roman road, it was called to a halt just a few miles short of Crac at a nearby Christian monastery."

The monastery of St George of Al-Humaira, County of Tripoli, June 1179

One of Thomas's men came riding up fast from the rear of the column and pulled up alongside Brother Teric at the front of the convoy. Paul watched as words were exchanged between them. Brother Teric waved the convoy on to pull up next to the main entrance of the monastery. As Tenno steered the caravan forwards and around the bend in the road, they all saw the massive structure of the Crac de l'Ospital rise up upon the adjoining hillside across the lush green valley. It was constructed in brilliant white stone, but appeared almost pink in the fading rays of the early evening sun setting in the west. Brother Teric rode down the line of caravans and carts stopping next to Paul's.

"We have a slight problem," he exclaimed and leaned in nearer. "One of Thomas's men whilst out foraging and making sure no other forces were nearby in preparation for handover of young Taqi there, smelling death and hearing the flies, discovered the bodies of our guests' escort."

"What do you mean?" Paul asked, alarmed.

"The Muslim escort that Gerard took away. It would appear they did not head for Tortosa but Crac up yonder also...and on the way summarily dispatched the escort," Brother Teric explained.

"What do you mean dispatched?" Taqi asked concerned as Tenno shook his head in disgust at the news.

"Dispatched...as in they were all stripped and all have had their throats cut," Brother Teric explained quietly.

"And you believe Gerard did this?" Paul asked hesitantly, his mind running asking and wondering how he could do that, but also that his own brother, Stewart, would have been party to it. His mind also raced wondering why Gerard had not mentioned the parchments he had been after when they had met up again. Had he now in fact received them and was satisfied with their content after his men had seized them at Kizkalesi Castle, or had the parchments really only ever been an excuse to get Firgany all along?

"No other explanation for it. It means we will have to be especially cautious this eve if Gerard and his men are about," Brother Teric explained just as Guy, Percival and Brother Matthew rode up from the middle of the convoy accompanied by Brother Armengaud.

"Brother Teric, I shall take the vanguard ahead with Princess Stephanie to Crac immediately," Brother Matthew explained as he struggled to control his horse as it bucked.

Adrastos also suddenly bucked and momentarily reared up on his hind legs causing Tenno to pull the reins hard to control him as the whole caravan jolted forwards. The women in the rear let out a cry as they were thrown forwards, Princess Stephanie yelping. Paul jumped down and quickly held the mouth guard on Adrastos to calm him down as Brother Matthew looked over the caravan thinking he had heard the Princess. Brother Armengaud moved his horse nearer the caravan so Brother Matthew could not get closer.

"Brother Matthew...take just two fast riders and secure the final leg to the gates of Crac and return only when you are sure the path ahead is safe. Something has agitated the horses and I fear assault. If needs be, bring further reinforcements to us as we can defend ourselves better here within the monastery lest we get caught on the steep path," Brother Armengaud ordered.

Hesitantly Brother Matthew looked at him, then forwards to Princess Stephanie's larger caravan being surrounded by four Templars, one at each corner. He nodded acknowledgement to Brothers Armengaud and Teric and rode to the front of the column and picked out two other Templars to follow him. Brother Teric watched as he galloped off ahead and out of sight. Quickly he checked where Guy had gone.

"Tenno, I need you to follow me into the monastery's main court yard and position yourself between the exit and Princess Stephanie's caravan so I can get our guests out and into the building unseen. Are you okay with that?" Brother Teric asked Tenno and confirmed it with Brother Armengaud as a slight drizzle of rain started. He looked up. "Rain...now...really my Lord?" he asked and shook his head.

Tenno steered the caravan out and past Princess Stephanie's larger caravan as Paul followed alongside on foot. The four Templars then escorted the larger caravan behind and in through the narrow main entrance of the monastery. Thomas immediately had his knights file in behind blocking it off so the remainder of the convoy pulled up alongside the main monastery wall itself as Armengaud positioned the remainder of his men to protect the rear and vanguards. Guy moved his horse to try and enter but Thomas blocked his path and simply smiled at him. Paul walked around to the rear of his caravan just as Stephanie opened the small rear door and glimpsed out. Brother Teric ordered the four Templars guarding her caravan to move along and form up to the front to cover an open area of exposed courtyard. As soon as Princess Stephanie saw Paul, she smiled, looked over toward Brother Teric as he dismounted and quickly stepped down and moved over to the side door of her own caravan. She went to open the door when two monks dressed in brown habits, their hoods up, approached her carrying a large sack each. Brother Teric walked over fast checking that Guy could not see what was happening. He opened the door and ushered Princess Stephanie inside, the two monks throwing the two sacks inside after her. Paul looked on puzzled as Tenno and Taqi kept an eye out. It was clear Brother Teric had organised this somehow with the full cooperation of Brother Armengaud. He pointed at Taqi and gestured he come over and mouthed 'quickly'. Taqi frowned, hesitated for a moment and quickly jumped down and ran over to Brother Teric. He opened the door and practically pushed Taqi inside closing the door fast and standing upright with his hands behind his back. Paul and Tenno tried to not look too puzzled as he approached, one of the Templar guards looking back briefly.

"What falls here?" Tenno whispered.

"Rashid is already here...look, see his horses secured under cover yonder," Brother Teric whispered and indicated with a slight nod. "Taqi and our guests will be changing into some clothing to pass off as his men. Will take but a few moments. I fear Gerard may be smarter than we thought...that is why he probably tortured the escort trying to discover what is afoot this hour. They died for their silence clearly."

Paul looked toward Princess Stephanie's caravan with a sudden sense of dread. One, that his friend was now in immediate and real danger, but also that he would now be leaving him. He had not even been given the chance to say goodbye. A lump swelled in his throat. The side window slot on his caravan slid back as Alisha looked out to see what was happening. Paul looked up at her eyes. The drizzle was now turning to heavier rain. Alisha could see in his eyes something was worrying him. Within seconds she appeared at the rear of the caravan holding Arri and stepped down. Paul rushed to her side. She took one look at him, then Princess Stephanie's caravan and then Brother Teric's eyes. Without a word she rushed over, opened the door to Princess Stephanie's caravan and stepped up inside. Paul rushed after her just as Theodoric and the blacksmith walked into view.

₧ ₨

Inside, Alisha was greeted by the site of Taqi half laying across the main bed as he pulled up a pair of black and baggy chausses whilst Turansha and his two friends were just finishing affixing the black full face head covers. They all froze momentarily until Paul entered and closed the door behind him. Tears instantly welled in Alisha's eyes at the realisation her brother was about to leave as arranged. She had known this moment was coming, but now suddenly it was upon them it hit her like a punch to the stomach. Taqi stood up fast and placed his hands upon her shoulders and looked her in the eyes. Princess Stephanie beckoned her to let go of Arri as she gently took him from her. Alisha took a deep breath and went to speak, but she couldn't. Turansha stepped forwards as Taqi just looked at her.

"Young lady...we can never thank you enough, as we have explained to the Princess here. You and your honourable husband undoubtedly saved us. We hope one day you will explain to us how it was you managed to marry legally... but that aside, we are forever indebted to you. To all three of you. If there ever comes a time when we are able to help you, you need only ever call upon us, and we shall come," he explained quietly as he tied off the last section of his black face cover and pulled up the hood on his black mantel.

"Ali...'tis time, my beautiful sister, that I must go. My destiny lies elsewhere now. 'Tis what I wish so please do not be sad," Taqi explained softly as the door opened again and Tenno squeezed himself through the door.

He stood up tall and stepped forward. He looked around the room at all of them in turn. He nodded at Taqi and part bowed his head slightly.

"Sister, and you, Paul...my brother. I shall miss you both dearly, but I know I leave you in safe hands," Taqi said and smiled at Tenno as Paul moved closer to Alisha. "I shall miss you...and little Arri, who will most likely have outgrown his shawl I made him by the time I next see him...but...this is Allah's will. I just hope I make Father proud of me."

"Taqi no. You do not have to do this. You can come with us," Alisha said emotionally and struggled not to cry.

"Yes I do. We all saw and know what was written upon our charts. As your path has led you thus far, we know therefore my path leads this way," Taqi commented.

The door swung open again and Rashid appeared; he paused briefly to look at all the people now crowded inside the caravan. He smiled broadly and squeezed himself in and stood almost shoulder to shoulder with Tenno. Both looked each other up and down and then around the room. Both Rashid and Tenno smiled at the absurdity of the situation and Rashid suddenly laughed.

"Ah...young Taqi. Are you ready for adventure beyond your wildest dreams now?" Rashid asked.

Taqi looked Alisha in the eyes again, his hands still placed upon her shoulders.

"I am if my sister gives me her blessing," Taqi whispered. Alisha flung her arms around his neck and pulled him close and closed her eyes tightly. "And I guess I must start calling you Master?" he asked, looking at Rashid.

"I promised you adventure and a calling last year. I also promised your father we would train you well and look after you until you were ready...but yes, you will be treated exactly the same as the other noviciates to our Order...and calling me respectfully is but one task," Rashid said smiling. "And you...you look like the type of man who could teach us a thing or two, no?" he asked Tenno. "And you...," he said to Paul and stepped closer to look at him. "You I have heard much of."

"Well please...do not believe it for I hear it is all exaggerated and myth making lies," Paul answered as Alisha held Taqi tightly.

"You know who I am...yes?"

"Yes...Taqi would not shut up talking about you for at least a month in La Rochelle."

"Did he now...lesson two...discretion must be learnt, young Taqi," Rashid smiled, looking at Taqi briefly before returning his gaze to Paul.

"And despite all you hear of me, you are not afraid?"

"No...if what Taqi and his father have told me is true, and my father also, then I do not fear you...and besides we are inside a woman's caravan...it does not seem right to fight in here," Paul replied.

Turansha stepped forwards past Princess Stephanie.

"Master Rashid...It is a great risk you take in assisting us this hour. We thank you," he said and bowed his head.

"Thank me if and when we get you to Egypt safely...not before. Now come... we have four extra horses. No one will question who you are as they will assume you are my men. Do not say anything nor speak to each other unless I tell you too. Gerard is already at Crac. I met with him earlier. He supposes, correctly, that I am seeking you out to help you. It appears he has good spies too...but not as good as mine," Rashid laughed. "Now come," he said and beckoned Taqi to follow him.

"Ali...look after Paul for me for he is hopeless without me," Taqi joked and pushed her away gently as tears started to fall down her cheeks. "Say nothing. I shall write."

"No you won't. Third lesson, no writing or contact whilst you serve," Rashid stated but smiled as he said it.

"I knew that," Taqi smiled back and kissed Alisha on her forehead.

Alisha shook her head in silence not able to say anything, her throat feeling dry and a lump in it so big she thought surely everyone in the caravan must surely see it.

"Paul, my brother...the time is upon us. Until we meet again," Taqi said as he grabbed Paul's right hand tightly.

"In this life or the next eh?" Paul tried to joke but suddenly felt overwhelmed with emotion. He coughed and cleared his throat.

Taqi said nothing but stood in silence for a few moments. Rain started to fall hard upon the caravan roof noisily. Arri let out a brief cry as Princess Stephanie pulled his shawl up to shield his ears. The caravan door opened and Brother Teric leaned in and beckoned with is hand for them to come outside now. Quickly Turansha's two friends pulled up their hoods and moved to go outside as he himself grasped Paul's shoulder.

"You shall always be welcome in my home, young Paul...or should I say Bull's Head Slayer?" Turansha exclaimed quietly. He smiled at Paul and quickly followed his friends outside before Paul could reply.

"Ah so the rumours are true...the Bull's Head Slayer is young indeed," Rashid said as he looked at Paul intently then Alisha. "And so much rests upon you three!"

Alisha looked at him puzzled as Rashid indicated towards Arri. Paul placed his arm around her comfortingly as more tears ran down her face. Taqi smiled at her as Rashid indicated for him to leave. Taqi pulled Paul and hugged him quickly without saying a word. He then kissed Alisha on her tear streaked cheek quickly and then leaned over and kissed Arri on his forehead. As he stepped down from the caravan he stopped momentarily and looked back at Paul and Alisha. He smiled broadly, pulled his hood up over his face, nodded and then stepped out of sight and he was gone into the rain. Rashid stood in silence looking at them and Princess Stephanie as Tenno watched bemused.

"I promise you we shall take very good care of him. We do not spend years educating and training men like him only to throw their lives away recklessly...I cannot afford it," Rashid joked but his sentiment genuine. "And you, I am glad to see you have no arrogance or boastfulness. You are indeed like your father. You have made some powerful friends already."

"And some powerful enemies too it would seem," Tenno remarked.

"That is inevitable...now I must go, but we shall I am sure, if Allah wills it, meet again. Until then, may his blessings be upon you and be many," Rashid said and bowed. "And you...as I said, I have heard of you too and I am sure you could teach us much...if you wish to ever put your skills to good use once you have delivered your charges safely, my doors are open to you at Masyaf," he finished and without any further words, turned, pulled his hood up over his head and stepped out into the rain.

"Paul," Alisha said in a broken whisper and buried her face into his shirt and started to sob, "how many more tears is a woman supposed to cry?"

Paul sighed and feigned a brave smile at Tenno who despite trying his hardest could not hide his own sadness at Taqi leaving. Princess Stephanie rocked Arri and sat down upon the edge of the bed as Theodoric, soaking wet from the rain, popped his head inside and looked up at everyone. Princess Stephanie let out a sigh and took several deep breaths as Theodoric entered closing the door behind him. She closed her eyes and fought to remain calm and collected, but the sudden release of tension proved too much and she started to cry. Alisha looked at her in surprise and quickly moved to sit beside her and gently took Arri. Princess Stephanie clenched her hands tightly, placed them together in her lap and closed her eyes and part laughed and cried all at once. She had acted and remained utterly calm throughout everything, but now, as Turansha had left, she let herself relax and consequently the full enormity of the risk she had taken was now taking its toll.

"Oh dear...look at me. A silly woman," she remarked and wiped her face quickly and sat up straight and feigned a brave smile.

Chapter 28
Rashid and the Ashashin

Port of La Rochelle, France, Melissae Inn, spring 1191

"I think I am lost," Simon exclaimed looking utterly confused.

"That's not hard for you to do!" Sarah shot back instantly.

"Okay then...can you explain to me how this Teric Templar was able to organise a pick up of three valuable potential prisoners...Saladin's brother himself for goodness' sake, after hiding them for days on end by Reynald's very own wife...is she mad? But more confusingly...how the heck did Muslim Ashashin so easily walk into a Christian monastery, and then just as easily trot out? How come the Hospitallers and Templars there did not stop them when it was at the height of a war being waged? I do not understand," Simon explained, shaking his head.

   5 – 22

"Yes I have to admit it does all seem a little too convenient...was this Brother Teric a double spy or whatever he would be called?" Ayleth asked quietly.

"No, Brother Teric was no spy," the Templar shot back immediately but pleasantly.

"I can explain if you wish," the old man said softly and smiled at Ayleth and Simon. "You see, at that time, the Ashashin answered to no one...I think I explained that earlier. But they were also highly respected by all sides...even Saladin feared them...well, feared what they could do if Rashid set his mind to it. Reynald relied heavily upon Rashid's vast network of spies to further his own networks and as Rashid had made it clear to all sides he had no desires nor designs upon their lands and trade routes, Reynald would often have cause to meet with him in person. But also unbeknown to Reynald and subsequently Gerard, Rashid had greater plans in mind with the political masters of the Templars themselves, the Prior de Sion, but also other groups. There was far more to Rashid than most people are aware, and perhaps never will be aware," the old man explained and smiled.

"So why the need to meet at the monastery and not Crac itself?" Peter asked as Simon and the Genoese sailor both nodded their heads in agreement with his question.

"Why indeed? First off, it was darkening quickly, was easier to count his men out without four extra men being noticed as all persons entering and exiting Crac were logged in and out, and to hide the fact that three of the men came out of Princess Stephanie's caravan, which they would have undoubtedly been spotted doing within the walls of Crac itself."

"Good point...I think," the Genoese sailor remarked.

Gabirol wrote several lines and the old man waited for him to finish before continuing.

"After Princess Stephanie broke down with relief, Brother Teric returned informing her that as it was now almost dark, they would stay the night at the monastery. He knew full

well they would not be attacked and, besides, he preferred the monastery and explained that a fresh water spring would offer the women a chance of cleaning themselves undisturbed in the morning if they so wished."

"I know that monastery well," the Hospitaller said and nodded at the old man. "'Tis a truly beautiful monastery and surrounded by lush green all year. I did consider staying once..."

"It is that indeed. It is known as Wadi-An-Nadara, or the 'Valley of the Christians'. It lies on the ancient Roman road that joins the coastal cities with the east, between Homs and Tripoli. The history of the monastery goes back to the sixth century, the reign of Emperor Justinian, and was consecrated in honour of the Great Martyr George, called by non-Christians Al-Hodr al Abbas. The monastery is supposedly linked with an historical monument located nearby, and with an ancient village that was named after the pagan god of rain. Others say that the monastery was built upon the ruins of a pagan temple dedicated to the pagan god Humaira. This temple became the foundation of the St George Monastery, and is now the first floor. Some argue that the word Humaira is the Arab transcription of the Greek word 'homiros', which means 'spiritual brotherhood of common life'. The original monastery was a cave surrounded by the cells of pious monks."

Gabirol coughed and cleared his throat. He looked at his writings for a few moments before looking up at the old man.

"Hmm. I once heard of this cave, a long time ago...but I am concerned a little about why Taqi was so keen to join these Ashashin...or, as many are calling them now, Assassins," he said quietly and paused. The old man shrugged his shoulders. "Firgany...surely he wanted the safest and best life for his son, yes?" he asked, puzzled. The old man nodded yes. "Then why would he encourage and agree to his son joining such an organisation...for we hear nothing but vile stories of the cunning and evil measures this Rashid man does, upon both Christian and Muslims alike...and for what? Sneaking into someone's chambers in the dead of night to cut their throats whilst they sleep. There is no honour in that!" Gabirol remarked and put his quill down upon some blotting sheets.

"You pose a very good point...very relevant. I can answer if it pleases you all?" the old man replied.

"Yes...please do as I am also a little confused on that point," Simon said loudly.

"Just that point?" Sarah asked and raised an eyebrow quizzically.

"I shall explain about Rashid then, for sadly, much like the founding brothers of the Knights Templar, he too is much maligned and misunderstood...and I fear it will be a very long time until the day shines when people will again learn the truth...and remember the past," the old man explained and shook his head slowly before continuing. "Rashid al Dinan...or more correctly, Rashid al-din Sinan, the Grand Master of the Ashashin, or as you just said, the Assassins. He and his followers, for followers is what they are, operate from their main spiritual base at Masyaf Castle. They were such a force, despite their small size, to successfully alarm Saladin enough not to assault the realms of their sect. However, the real story of why Saladin eventually chose to leave Rashid alone I shall try and explain. You see Rashid, also known as 'The Old Man of the Mountains', was born in 530/1135, or 528/1133 and some even say 527/1132...He is the leader of the Isma'ili religious sect, the Nizari branch. Many Christian chroniclers call him Vetulus de Montanis, derived from the Arabic title Shaykh al Jabal, which means 'wise man or elder of the mountain', and, believe me, he was certainly wise as well as brave," the old man explained and smiled as he clearly recalled the man.

"But we know him only as a cut throat Assassin," Peter interrupted.

"That is because you only read or listen to what you are told as fact by the Church," the Templar answered before the old man could respond, who simply nodded in agreement before continuing.

"Just hear me out before you judge him," the old man said and paused briefly. *"Rashid was born in Basra and, as a youth, he went to Alamut, the centre of the Hashshashin, whom we call Ashashin and now it seems, Assassins. Just like Taqi he received the typical training but in 1162, the sect's leader, Hassan 'Ala Dhikrihi's Salam, sent him to Syria, where he proclaimed Qiyamah, which in Nizari terminology meant the time of the Qa'im and the removal of Islamic law. Based in the Nizari stronghold of Masyaf, he controlled the northern Syrian districts of Jabal as-Summaq, Maarrat Misrin and Sarmin. And so he found himself at odds with Saladin, whom by now was his chief enemy. But this is where the rumours start about him and Saladin. Saladin managed twice to elude assassination attempts ordered by Rashid and as he was marching against Aleppo, Saladin devastated the Nizari possessions. In 1176 Saladin laid siege to Masyaf but he lifted the siege after two notable events that reputedly transpired between him and the Old Man of the Mountain. According to one version, one night, Saladin's guards noticed a spark glowing down the hill of Masyaf and then vanishing among the Ayyubid tents. Saladin awoke from his sleep to find a figure leaving the tent. He then saw that the lamps were displaced and beside his bed lay hot stones of the shape peculiar to the Ashashin...Assassins, with a note at the top pinned by a poisoned dagger. The note threatened that he would be killed if he didn't withdraw from his assault. Saladin gave a loud cry, exclaiming that Rashid himself was the figure that left the tent. As such, Saladin told his guards to come to an agreement with Rashid. Realising he was unable to subdue Rashid, he sought to align himself with them, consequently depriving the Crusaders of aligning themselves against him."*

"What was the second notable event then?" Gabirol asked.

"Well, there were many actually. But one rumour had it that Saladin was approached by representatives, more correctly, a representative of the Templars and Rashid. That a strange light was seen at the castle Masyaf, just like the light that shone down upon Alisha on the boat journey...and that the same light was shone all around Saladin's tent, after which black and white stones were found." The old man paused as he rubbed his neatly trimmed white beard for a few moments. *"Saladin had an audience with two people inside his own tent whereby agreements were made. As the two people just vanished, part alarmed and in response to his bodyguards having seen the mysterious lights and a tall man just vanish... Saladin had no choice but to make up a story about what had just happened...but you can see how such an event can turn so quickly to one of legend?"*

"What...was it some kind of visitation by an angel then? Is that what you are saying?" Simon asked. The Genoese sailor frowned deeply as the wealthy tailor shook his head.

"All I shall say at this moment is that after that night Rashid enjoyed considerable independence from the Nizari centre in Alamut and some writings attribute him with a semi-divine status. The Isma'ili movement was the most dynamic and vigorous of the Shi'i movements in the known world. You see, and this is what attracted Taqi to them when he travelled in their company, but also after learning that his father himself had been a great friend of Rashid's, Isma'ilism presented an unexampled spiritual and political challenge to the dominance of Sunni orthodoxy and to the authority of contemporary Sunni rulers and dynasties, such as the Saljuq Sultans and Abbasid Caliphs. You must understand that the Isma'ilis of Alamut are somewhat different from those of Masyaf. Rashid was without

doubt, and even our orthodox brethren accord him the same respect, one of the greatest and most valiant of the Isma'ili da'is ever known. Reading through the literature on Alamut, one finds ample information about the activities of the Isma'ilis in Persia, but very little about Rashid and the Ashashin except short passages in Arabic chronicles and cursory allusions from the Western Crusader chronicles. There is some argument as to how old he was when he took over at Masyaf for it was a traditional Isma'ili rule that appointments to the 'higher grades' (Ar' maratib 'ulya) were preferably made from among those who were not less than forty years old. This customary rule was not based solely on the consideration that leaders ought to possess maturity and experience but also on the fact that the Isma'ili regard the numbers forty, twelve, seven, five and four as having certain symbolic meanings. Numbers Paul was already familiar with from teachings by his father and Niccolas...numbers which would have a major significant role for Paul later...but I digress. Rashid was a native of 'Aqr al-Sunden, a village between Wasit and Basra which is inhabited mostly by extreme Shi'i sects. It is believed that his parents were Twelver Shi'is. Isma'ili sources confirm that Rashid was in charge of the Isma'ili da'wa in Iraq up to the time of his appointments as deputy of the Imam of Alamut, but do not confirm that he was a Twelver Shi'i by origin. Some of these sources state that he had family connections with the Isma'ili Imams, whilst others go so far as to suggest that he was himself the real Imam. Before his first appointment as da'i in the district of Basra, Rashid is reported to have taken a full course on Isma'ili theology and philosophy at the madrasa, a centre for religious teaching, of the Imam Hasan Ibn Muhammad Ibn 'Ali, surnamed al-Qahir, the conqueror, at Alamut, so as you are hopefully learning, he was not this simple barbaric and ruthless cut throat you mistake him for," the old man said and looked at everyone in turn.

"Just because he is well read does not mean he is any less capable of murder and evil... surely?" Simon asked.

"No of course not. It is a fact that some of the cruellest people have been well read, educated and very intelligent men...and women!" the old man replied. "What Rashid did in Alamut besides studying Isma'ili doctrines, we do not know for certain, but during his stay in Alamut he met the future Imam Hasan the Second, 'Ala Dhikrihi al Salam', who later sent him to Masyaf to succeed the chief da'i Abu Muhammad. Rashid was transferred to Masyaf not long after his first appointment as da'i in the district of Basra, believed to have taken place around 556/1160. We know he travelled via Mawsil, where as you know Firgany lived for many years and with Raja, Alisha and Taqi, before arriving in Aleppo, which was, and still is, accessible to Isma'ili da'is, who enter the city often disguised as merchants. Firgany you must recall was a merchant...Rashid did not have any difficulty in finding his contacts in the capital of the Zangids, and if 558/1162 was actually the date of his arrival he probably had the good fortune to arrive when Nur al-Din was absent from the city warring against the Franks. Rashid arrived in Masyaf where he stayed for some time without revealing his real identity and then later went to Bastiryun, a village near al-Kahf, the castle which was the residence of the Isma'ili chief da'i, Abu Muhammad. Rashid had to wait seven years, at the end of which, while Abu Muhammad was on his death bed, he presented to him his credentials as the new leader. If Rashid's arrival at Masyaf and the incidents which preceded his ultimate assumption of the leadership are correct, it is then highly probable that he was sent to Masyaf by the father of Hasan the Second, 'Ala Dhikrihi al-Salam', and subsequently confirmed or appointed as chief da'i by his son. This would mean that Rashid in fact arrived earlier than 558/1161–2 and sometime around 552/1157, a date coinciding with an earthquake, during which Rashid was injured. A massive earthquake is recorded to have taken place around 551/1156 destroying the main cities. The fact that he did not report to Abu Muhammad on arrival of his visits to the Isma'ili groups is suspicious. During the last decade of Abu Muhammad's leadership, weakness, disorganisation and disunity manifested themselves in the northern Isma'ili community. Many Isma'ilis immigrated to the neighbouring cities of Hama, Homs and Aleppo, not only in order to strengthen their da'wa, but also to earn a living, for the Isma'ili territory was not fertile, and they lived mostly on their cattle. This situation was worsened when, around 546/1151, the Frankish Count of Tripoli, Raymond the Second, was murdered in consequence of which the Templars raided Isma'ili territory and compelled the inhabitants to pay a tribute. Another factor which weakened the Isma'ili da'wa was the personal disputes among the Isma'ilis which added to the complexity of the problem to be faced by the successor of Abu Muhammad. The most important events after Rashid took command arose from his efforts to consolidate the position of the Isma'ilis and to solve their manifold internal problems. The principal aim of his external policy was to defend Isma'ili territory against hostile Muslim and Frankish neighbours, as well as dealing within his own group, such as an episode involving a group of Isma'ili extremists in northern Syria called the Sufat, 'pure'. After becoming its leader Rashid found himself facing many serious and urgent problems. To protect his people was not so easy as to win their love and admiration during his early years, the pious Iraqi Shaykh, al-Shaykh al-'Iraq, of yesterday, the teacher of the children, the renderer of medical treatment for sufferers, and the austere and ascetic man of religion living by prayer and meditation, had now to concentrate on the practical needs of his people and save them from becoming an easy prey to their enemies. In order to meet the dangers from outside, he began reorganising his men and choosing the most eligible and devoted to form the core of fidais, devotees. Thanks to his strong personality and incisive intellect, he was able to smooth away the internal dissension which had been jeopardising Isma'ili unity. In almost all these objectives, and in securing his own position, he was successful; he had his fidais trained in various languages and in the art of collecting secret information from the courts of kings and princes. He organised an elaborate communication system, making full use of pigeons and coded messages by which the commanders of the various Isma'ili strongholds were kept informed about his plans about possible threats to any of the widely scattered Isma'ili fortresses."

"I am seeing this man in a totally different light. I had this image of this tall, dark haired brute of a man," Sarah interrupted.

"Not surprising. I am glad I have this opportunity to explain him better," the old man said, smiling back. "Besides organising and training the various groups of his fida'is, he also rebuilt two Isma'ili castles which had fallen into ruin, either through natural calamities or through assaults by enemies. These were at al-Rasafaj, which is less than four miles south of Masyaf, and al-Khawabi, which is about four miles south of al-Kahf. He also looked to the north and by a military stratagem captured al-'Ullayqa, which is less than eight miles northeast of the impregnable and well known Frankish castle al-Marqab. But the key strongholds which gave him an excellent strategic position were Masyaf, al-Kahf, al-Qadmus and al-'Uilayqa. Masyaf, being on the eastern fringes of Jabal Bahra', served as a window on the Muslim principalities of Hama and Homs. As for al-Kahf, the centre of the previous chief da'i, it became the fortress from which he was able to keep an eye on Tortosa, Tartos or Antartus as some call it, and other Frankish strongholds to the southwest of his territory. Al-Qadmus was his forward post in the west and al-Ullayqa that was in the northwest. Rashid still received direction from Alamut, an example being the case of Khawaja 'Ali, who tried to take over the leadership in succession to Abu Muhammad without having been designated by the Imam of Alamut, and the subsequent murder of Khawaja 'Ali at the instigation of two prominent members of the community, Abu Mansur Ibn Ahmad Ibn al-Shaykh Abu Muhammad, and al-Ra'is Fahd. Later Alamut sent instructions to Rashid to put the murderer to death and to release Fahd. Also Hasan the Second, 'Ala Dhikrihi at-Salam, instructed Rashid to abide by the rules of the Qiyama and to watch the activities of the Muslim princes. Many have argued that Alamut had lost control of Rashid, or that there was a serious separatist movement against Alamut on the part of the northern Isma'ilis but it can be equally argued that the authorities in Alamut had full trust in his ability to run the affairs of the northern Isma'ilis, and consequently have seen no need to intervene."

"But why then do we hear such stories that his followers almost worship him as a great holy warrior?" the wealthy tailor asked.

"As I have said before, many simple truths can be exaggerated and turn into a myth of their own, becoming legends...just like the stories that rapidly grew up about Paul killing the Bull's Head bandit. Many stories have grown up around Rashid whereby many chroniclers pour lavish praise on his heroism, telepathic powers even and wisdom. Some refer to him as the 'deputy', na'ib, of the Imam of Alamut and ascribe certain miraculous actions; this may be explained by the Isma'ili belief that a trusted servant of the Imam, who stands as his evidence, could become a recipient of al-ta'yid, spiritual help from the Imam, which would confer upon him some of the Imam's supernatural powers. It is a point worth noting that many Sufi terms and phraseology are widely used by the northern Isma'ilis, who claim that the Sufis should be recognised as wise men and recipients of the 'light' of the Prophet. But to answer the question why his followers thought of him as some great mystical and religious leader it is because he was considered by his followers to be an Imam, and even to be the 'Seventh Imam' of the series of Imams beginning with the Fatimid Imam ai-Mu'izz (AD 952–976). And do you also know that one of Rashid's best friends was a poet named Mazyad ai-Hilli al-Asadi?" the old man asked.

"So he is a great warrior, spiritual leader and loves poetry...a strange combination?" the Genoese sailor remarked.

"No different to Paul or Tenno!" Ayleth interrupted then blushed as everyone looked at her.

"Rashid possessed outstanding abilities as an organiser and leader, and was the hujja of the Imam of the Qiyama. He successfully transformed the northern da'wa from a weak one, depending mainly on the help of Alamut and the occasional patronage of a local ruler, into a powerful agency having its own fortresses and its own corps of fida'is, who were trained in a special centre situated in the renowned Isma'ili castle ai-Kahf. Rashid also had his own da'is to assist him and a large number of rafiqs who used to accompany him on his frequent visits to the various Isma'ili castles. The northern da'wa under his leadership was no longer just a branch. It could be classified as virtually autonomous da'wa, with its territory and headquarters and its own hierarchy of dignitaries headed by Rashid."

"What does da'wa mean?" Ayleth asked, confused.

"Da'wah...is a form of 'invitation', it basically means the preaching of Islam...more literally though it means 'issuing a summons' or 'making an invitation'," the old man answered.

"I understood it as simply meaning 'to summon' or 'to invite' as is done by a Muslim person or group either as a religious worker or as a community effort, and is called a dā'ī or the plural du'āh or du'āt...I think!" Gabirol explained then looked unsure.

"You are indeed well read, Gabirol. A dā'ī is thus a person who invites people to understand Islam through dialogue, not unlike the Islamic equivalent of a missionary inviting *people to the faith, prayer and manner of Islamic life. And Duat, 'tis a very ancient word... was identical to an ancient Egyptian, in fact pre-dynastic Egyptian language word...but that I shall leave for later," the old man smiled impressed with Gabirol's knowledge. "The term da'wah had other meanings too in the Qur'an. In sura (Chapter) 30:25, for example, it denotes the call to the dead to rise on the Day of Judgement. When used in the Qur'an, it generally refers to Allah's invitation to live according to His will. Thus, when used in the first centuries of Islam, it refers to that message and was sometimes used interchangeably with shari'a and dīn. Da'wah is also described as the duty to 'actively encourage fellow Muslims in the pursuance of greater piety in all aspects of their lives', a definition which has become central to contemporary Islamic thought. The purpose of da'wah is to invite people, both Muslims and non-Muslims, to understand the worship of Allah as expressed in the Qur'an and the sunnah of the Prophet Muhammad and to inform them about Muhammad. Da'wah as the 'Call towards Allah' is the means by which Muhammad began spreading the message of the Qur'an to mankind. After Muhammad, his followers and Ummah, the Muslim community, assumed responsibility for it. They convey the message of the Qur'an by providing information on why and how the Qur'an preaches monotheism," the old man continued until the wealthy tailor raised his hand.*

"I am sorry to interrupt you...but it almost sounds as if you are trying to convert us to become Muslims. Is this so?" he asked.

"No...that is not my intention. But I wish for you to have all the facts...and understand them for what they are," the old man replied softly. The wealthy tailor sighed and frowned and bit the inside of his lip as he thought about the old man's reply. After a brief pause the old man continued. "In the Hadith, which means 'sayings' of Muhammad, dawah is mentioned to emphasise importance and virtues, such as 'Whoever directs someone to do good will gain the same reward as the one who does good.' 'Whoever calls to guidance will receive the same reward as the one who follows him without any decrease in the reward of his follower.' 'For Allah to guide someone by your hand is better for you than having red camels.'"

"Having red camels!" Simon laughed out loud then coughed as Sarah shot him a pained look.

"Yes, Simon...In ancient Arabia, camels, especially of a reddish hue, were considered particularly valuable property," the old man answered and nearly laughed himself. "Now it is oft argued in regard to Muhammad's mild nature in preaching Islam that his ways have been usurped and misinterpreted. But to quote the Qur'an, it says, 'And by the mercy of Allah you dealt with them gently. If you were harsh and hard hearted, they would have fled from around you' (Qur'an 3:159). The Qur'an speaks about Moses and Aaron who preached to the Pharaoh, the claimant of God, 'So speak to him, both of you, mildly in order that he may reflect or fear God' (Qur'an 20:44). Now I mention this as it specifically names Moses and Aaron, whom you shall hear more of later...if you have not fallen asleep or run off prior."

"I for one am going nowhere until I have heard the end of this tale," the Templar remarked loudly and held onto Miriam's hand tightly.

"I am pleased to hear that...I was just about to say that Muhammad was reported by his wife, Aisha, to have said 'Whenever gentleness is in a thing it beautifies it and whenever it is withdrawn from something it defaces.' Muhammad was also quoted by Jareer as saying, 'One deprived of gentleness is deprived of all good.'"

"Okay...now I just know I am going to be in trouble for asking this...but what exactly does that word Hubba mean...was it Hubba?" Simon asked awkwardly.

"As I have said before Simon, if in doubt, always ask. Never stop asking. And the word

you are looking for was hujja. It is a term used in Shi'i terminology, and means 'proof' as implied by God, usually used to refer to a single individual in any given human era who represents God's 'proof' to humanity, just as we have the Pope as the Lord's infallible voice and proof of God. In Islam, the hujja is a prophet or an Imam who possess a relationship with God that is greater than anyone else's. The Imam who is the hujja of his time functions as the ultimate mediator between God and humanity, giving the Imam the greatest precedence for interpretation of the Qur'an, again identical to our Pope in regard to the Bible. As the mediator between God and humanity, the Imam is the only one who can properly resolve conflicting interpretations of the Qur'an's words, giving the Imam ultimate authority over divine knowledge. In Twelver Shi'ism the title 'hujja' is specifically applied to the Twelfth Imam who is currently in a period of hiding and is attributed with the tradition of using Shi'i Hadith to guide the religious community. It is important to note that the words Imam and hujja do not necessarily refer to the same person because an Imam may not be hujja but may keep the title of Imam. The Imam that is hujja is hujja for several different logical proofs that are supported by Shi'i Qur'an interpretation and Shi'i Hadith. The first proof of an Imam who is hujja is presented by the Imam's role as mediator between God and humanity. The divine appointment of the Imam, according to Shi'i belief, was passed down from the Prophet Muhammad to 'Ali and his sons al-Hasan and al-Husayn, who passed the divine knowledge on to their sons and so on. Therefore it is only those who are members of the Prophet's family line that possess the divine knowledge from God and therefore are hujja. The second proof an Imam is hujja is shown by the inner guidance the Imam provides for mankind for he is a channel of divine grace which comes to him inwardly from the suprasensible realm. The Imam, with his extensive knowledge of the different levels of human behaviour and spiritual faith, is able to influence others' thoughts and inner beings to help aid them in the refinement of their souls and inward journey. The Imam's divine guidance from God gives him the ability to lead and influence, which is why the Imam is hujja, proof of God."

"And many believe that Rashid is the same as this, yes?" the Genoese sailor asked.

The old man nodded yes and continued to explain more.

"The third proof an Imam is hujja is based on the Imam's immunity from the pollution of human sin. The Imam is such a divine spiritual figure he is free from committing human error or misinterpreting the Qur'an, which would otherwise lead to human error and sin. For a man who does commit sin is not fit to lead for he can spread sin and is therefore denied the rank of Imam and therefore cannot possess hujja. Only those who are free from error can be considered divinely touched and therefore are hujja and entitled to the Imamate. The fourth proof that the Imam is hujja is deducted by reason. God's grace keeps his creatures towards obedience and keeps them away from disobedience. However if God orders man to do something he knows man cannot do or will have difficulty doing, he would contradict his own aim. Therefore God gives humanity hujja to help lead man toward God and His spiritual greatness. The hujja sent here is filled with spiritual guidance and helps direct man towards God, which is also what the Imam does, which is why the Imam is hujja. The last justification of the hujja comes from the idea that without the hujja the world would not exist. The world cannot exist even for a moment without the imam who is the hujja of God. If the imam were to be taken away from the earth even for an hour, the earth would swallow up its inhabitants just as the sea swallows its people. The idea that the Imam, who is hujja, is always present helps support the fact that God is always present to mankind and it supports the fact that it is only through the Imam that God can be known."

3 – 2

"Are you serious that we need to know and understand all of this?" Peter asked scratching his head.

"Trust me when I say it is," the old man answered and nodded slightly. *"You see it is all linked to what both Islam and Christianity refer to as the Day of Judgement...and that is such a secret that has been so very badly understood, it pains me greatly."*

"How so, old man?" the Hospitaller asked and moved in his seat.

"The Day of Resurrection! This part may indeed send you to sleep, so I beg your indulgence a while longer...then perhaps some much needed food and drink, I suspect...," the old man stated and looked at Stephan. He nodded acknowledgement at his request. *"I mentioned the word Qiyamah when discussing Rashid. Yawm al-Qiyāmah, pronounced yome-ul-key-ah-mah, means 'the Day of Resurrection' or Yawm ad-Dīn, pronounced yome-ud-dean, 'the Day of Judgement'. This is believed to be the final assessment of humanity by Allah, or God if you are Christian, consisting of the annihilation of all life, resurrection and judgement. The time of the event is not specified, although there are major and minor signs which have been foretold to happen with Qiyamah at the end of time. Many verses of Qur'anic Sura contain the motif of the impending Day of Resurrection. And within the Bible, in Revelations especially, there are so many clues and signs we can look out for,"* the old man started to explain when he noticed Ayleth looking uncomfortable. He looked at her for a few moments until she looked up at him.

"I am sorry. Forgive me...I just get very nervous when I hear such matters discussed. All too often in my childhood I would hear such terrible stories about the end of days, judgement day...and I still feel uneasy to this day. But please...please continue," she explained nervously. Sarah leaned over and held her hand then nodded at the old man to continue.

"Fear is no way to teach a practice of so-called love," the old man sighed. *"But I shall continue as quickly as I am able...The seventy-fifth sura of the Qur'an, al-Qiyama, is mainly about the resurrection. Its tribulation is also described in the Hadith. The Day of Judgement is also known as the Day of Reckoning, the Last Day and al-sā'ah, or the Hour. The Hadith describe the end time in greater detail than the Qur'an, describing the events of al-Qiyamah through twelve major signs. I hope you are all taking note of the numbers I speak? Now at the time of judgement, terrible corruption and chaos will rule. The Mahdi will be sent and with the help of Isa will battle Masih ad-Dajjal. They will triumph, liberating Islam from cruelty, and this will be followed by a time of serenity with people living true to religious values. However, there is no mention of the advent of Mahdi and Isa in one era in any of the Hadith. Some Muslim scholars translate the Arabic word 'Imam' as 'Mahdi' to prove the advent of Mahdi and Isa in single era."*

"Sorry, but who is Isa?" the farrier asked abruptly.

"Isa is Jesus...yes?" Simon answered quickly and looked at the old man and Gabirol in turn for confirmation.

"In short yes...but not as you would fully understand as the Jesus you presently know as taught by the Church. Now what I tell you next should explain to you why so many Christian knights convert to Islam...but also why there are those who so desperately try and strive to fuse Christianity with Judaism and Islam, as Rashid and people like Philip and Firgany tried...for sadly too many people cannot see why they would try and do this...so let me explain. And we must start with Jesus's name, which in Arabic is 'Îsâ Ibn Maryam' or

simply *'Īsā', known as Jesus in the New Testament, who is considered to be a Messenger of God and al-Masih, the Messiah, in Islam who was sent to guide the Children of Israel with a new scripture, al-Injīl, the Gospel. The belief that Jesus is a prophet is required in Islam, as it is for all prophets named in the Qur'an."*

"What...then if they all believe in him...then what the....what the...why all the war and slaughter?" Sarah interrupted exasperated almost, her face turning red.

"I shall explain in time, but the simple answer to that it is man's interpretations of how they believe things should be understood. Jesus, as Isa, is clearly a significant figure in the Qur'an appearing in ninety-three ayaa,t or verses, though Noah, Adam and Moses appear with even greater frequency. It states that Jesus was born to Mary, Maryam in Arabic, and is where your name derives from," the old man explained and nodded toward Miriam briefly. *"And born as the result of a virginal conception, a miraculous event which occurred by the decree of God, Allah. To aid in his ministry to the Jewish people, Jesus was given the ability to perform miracles, such as healing the blind, bringing dead people back to life, etcetera, all by the permission of God rather than of his own power. According to the Qur'an, Jesus, although appearing to have been crucified, was not killed by crucifixion or by any other means, instead, 'God raised him unto Himself'. Like all prophets in Islam, Jesus is considered a Muslim, as in one who submits to the will of God or Allah, as he preached that his follow-ers should adopt the 'straight path' as commanded by God. But Islam rejects the Trinitarian Christian view that Jesus was God incarnate or the son of God, that he was ever crucified or resurrected, or that he ever atoned for the sins of mankind. The Qur'an says that Jesus himself never claimed any of these things, and it furthermore indicates that Jesus will deny having ever claimed divinity at the Last Judgement, whenever that time comes, and God will vindicate him. The Qur'an emphasises that Jesus was a mortal human being who, like all other prophets, had been divinely chosen to spread God's message. Islamic texts forbid the association of partners with God, emphasising a strict notion of monotheism or tawhīd. An alternative interpretation of this theology is held by Messianic Muslims. Numerous titles are given to Jesus in the Qur'an and in Islamic literature, the most common being al-Masī 'the Messiah'. Jesus is also, at times, called 'Seal of the Israelite Prophets', because, in general Muslim belief, Jesus was the last prophet sent by God to guide the Children of Israel. Jesus is seen in Islam as a precursor to Muhammad, and is believed by Muslims to have foretold the latter's coming. Muslims believe that Jesus will return to earth near the Day of Judgement to restore justice and to defeat al-Masih ad-Dajjal, who is 'the false messiah', also known as the Antichrist. Just like other Abrahamic religions, Islam teaches resurrection of the dead, a final tribulation and eternal division of the righteous and wicked. Islamic apocalyptic liter-ature describing Armageddon is often known as fitnah, malāhim, or ghaybah in Shīa Islam. Righteous are rewarded with pleasures of Jannah, while unrighteous are tortured in Jahan-nam. Islam also proclaims Jesus's lineage, going back to his great-grandfather. The Qur'anic account of Isa, as Jesus, begins with a prologue, which describes the birth of his mother, Maryam, or, as we call her, Mary, and her service in the Jerusalem temple, while under the care of the prophet and priest Zechariah, who was to be the father of John the Baptist. The Qur'an describes the conception of Isa. Mary, whom the Qur'an states was chosen by God over the women of all the worlds, conceives Isa while still a virgin. Maryam had withdrawn into the Temple, where she was visited by the angel Gabriel, or Jibrail in Arabic, who brought the glad tidings of a holy son. The Qur'an states that God sent the message through the angel Gabriel to Maryam, that God had honoured her among the women of all nations. The angel also told Maryam that she would give birth to a pure son, named Isa, who would be a great*

prophet, to whom God would give the Gospel. The angel further told Maryam that Isa would speak in infancy and maturity and be a companion to the most righteous. When this news was given to Maryam, she asked the angel how she could conceive and have a child when no man had touched her. The angel replied: 'Even so, Allah createth what He willeth, When He hath decreed a plan, He but saith to it, "Be", and it is!' The Qur'an, therefore, states that Isa was created from the act of God's will. The Qur'an compares this miraculous creation of Isa with the creation of Adam, where God created Adam by his act of will, kun-fa-yakun, meaning 'be and it is'. According to the Qur'an, the same answer was given to the question of Zechariah, when he asked how his wife, Elizabeth, could conceive a baby, as she was very old. The Qur'an narrates the virgin birth of Isa numerous times and states that Maryam was overcome by the pains of childbirth. During her agony and helplessness, God provided a stream of water under her feet from which she could drink. Furthermore, near a palm tree, Maryam was told to shake the trunk of the palm tree so that ripe dates would fall down and she could eat and be nourished. Maryam cried in pain and held onto the palm tree, at which point a voice came from 'beneath her', understood by some to refer to Isa, who was yet in her womb, which said, 'Grieve not! Your Lord has provided a water stream under you, and shake the trunk of the palm tree, it will let fall fresh ripe dates upon you. And eat and drink and calm thy mind.' That day, Maryam gave birth to her son Isa in the middle of the desert. Maryam carried baby Isa back to her people. The Qur'an describes that Maryam vowed not to speak to anyone that day, as God was to make Isa, who Muslims believe spoke in the cradle, perform his first miracle. The Qur'an narrates that Maryam brought Isa to the temple, where she was immediately ridiculed by all the temple elders. But Zachariah believed in the virgin birth and supported her. The elders accused Maryam of being a loose woman and having touched another man while unmarried. In response, Mary pointed to her son, telling them to talk to him. They were angered at this and thought she was mocking them, by asking them to speak with an infant. It was then that God made the infant Isa speak from the cradle and he spoke of his prophecy for the first time. He said, which are verses 19:30–33 in the chapter of Maryam in the Qur'an," the old man explained and paused as he quickly looked through his leather satchel and pulled out some written notes upon parchment. He cleared his throat and continued and read directly from it. *"He said, 'I am indeed a servant of Allah. He hath given me revelation and made me a prophet; And He hath made me blessed wheresoever I be, and hath enjoined on me Prayer and Charity as long as I live; He hath made me kind to my mother, and not overbearing or miserable; So peace is on me the day I was born, the day that I die, and the day that I shall be raised up to life again!'"*

"Now I am truly lost and confused. I always thought Islam rejected Jesus and are totally opposed to Christianity," the wealthy tailor said, utterly bemused, and shrugged his shoulders hard.

"Then let me explain a little more. You are all familiar with the meeting of Jesus with John the Baptist on the River Jordan?" the old man asked and waited as each in turn nodded yes they did. *"Well, some Muslim accounts narrate that Isa met with Yahya ibn Zakariyya, otherwise known to us as John the Baptist, on the River Jordan just as we believe, but also Islamic texts state Isa was divinely chosen to preach the message of monotheism and submission to the will of God to the Children of Israel. Muslims believe that God revealed to Isa a new scripture, al-Injīl, the Gospel, while also declaring the truth of the previous revelations such as the al-Tawrat, the Torah, and al-Zabur, the Psalms. The Qur'an speaks favourably of al-Injīl, which it describes as a scripture that fills the hearts of its followers with meekness and piety. The Qur'an says that the original biblical message has been distorted or corrupted,*

or tahrif, over time," the old man explained and again read from his parchment directly. "It is He Who sent down to thee, step by step, in truth, the Book, confirming what went before it; and He sent down the Law of Moses and the Gospel of Isa before this, as a guide to mankind, and He sent down the criterion of judgement between right and wrong."

The old man looked up at the puzzled faces before him.

"I think I am beginning to understand why the Church does not teach us these things openly...for I fear many Christians would be left confused," Peter remarked and shook his head perplexed.

"Let me read this from the Qur'an, sura 3. 'And in their footsteps We sent Isa the son of Maryam, confirming the Law that had come before him: We sent him the Gospel: therein was guidance and light, and confirmation of the Law that had come before him: a guidance and an admonition to those who fear Allah. Let the people of the Gospel judge by what Allah hath revealed therein. If any do fail to judge by the light of what Allah hath revealed, they are no better than those who rebel. The Qur'an states that Isa was aided by a group of disciples who believed in His message. While not naming the disciples, the Qur'an does give a few instances of Isa preaching the message to them. The Qur'an mentions in chapter 3, verses 52–53, that the disciples submitted in the faith of Islam: When Isa found Unbelief on their part He said: 'Who will be My helpers to the work of Allah?' Said the disciples: 'We are Allah's helpers: We believe in Allah, and do thou bear witness that we are Muslims. Our Lord! we believe in what Thou hast revealed, and we follow the Messenger; then write us down among those who bear witness. The longest narrative involving Isa's disciples is when they request a laden table to be sent from Heaven, for further proof that Isa is preaching the true message: Behold! the disciples, said: 'O Isa the son of Maryam! can thy Lord send down to us a table set with viands from heaven?' Said Isa: 'Fear Allah, if ye have faith.' They said: 'We only wish to eat thereof and satisfy our hearts, and to know that thou hast indeed told us the truth; and that we ourselves may be witnesses to the miracle.' Said Isa the son of Maryam: 'O Allah our Lord! Send us from heaven a table set with viands, that there may be for us for the first and the last of us a solemn festival and a sign from thee; and provide for our sustenance, for thou art the best Sustainer of our needs.' Allah said: 'I will send it down unto you: But if any of you after that resisteth faith, I will punish him with a penalty such as I have not inflicted on any one among all the peoples.'" The old man read aloud then sat up quietly for a few moments as they all pondered what he had explained and read out to them.

"But they do not believe he was crucified do they?" the Templar remarked questioningly.

"No...," the old man replied instantly. "Islamic texts categorically deny the idea of crucifixion or death attributed to Isa by the New Testament. The Qur'an states that the people, as in the Jews and Romans, sought to kill Jesus, but they did not crucify or kill him, although 'this was made to appear to them'. Muslims believe that Jesus was not crucified but, instead, he was raised up by God unto the heavens. This 'raising' is often understood to mean through bodily ascension. 'And they said we have killed the Messiah Isa son of Maryam, the Messenger of God. They did not kill him, nor did they crucify him, though it was made to appear like that to them; those that disagreed about him are full of doubt, with no knowledge to follow, only supposition: they certainly did not kill him. On the contrary, God raised him unto himself. God is almighty and wise.' The denial, furthermore, is in perfect agreement with the logic of the Qur'an. The Biblical stories reproduced in it of Job, Moses, Joseph, etcetera, and the episodes relating to the history of the beginning of Islam demonstrate that it is 'God's practice', sunnat Allah, to make faith triumph finally over the forces of evil and adversity. 'So truly with hardship comes ease' (XCIV, 5, 6). For Isa to die on the cross would have meant the triumph of his executioners; but the Qur'an asserts that they undoubtedly failed: 'Assuredly God will defend those who believe' (XXII, 49). He confounds the plots of the enemies of Christ (III, 54). So you see, contrary to Christian teachings, Islam teaches Jesus ascended to Heaven without being put on the cross, but that God transformed another person to appear exactly like Isa who was then crucified instead of Isa. Isa ascended bodily to Heaven, there to remain until his second coming in the end days."

"So they believe in a second coming of Jesus too...like us?" Simon asked, shaking his head.

"Yes...yes indeed. Islamic tradition describes this graphically, Isa's descent will be in the midst of wars fought by al-Mahdi, as in 'the rightly guided one', known in Islamic thought as the redeemer of Islam, against al-Masīh ad-Dajjāl, the Antichrist or 'false messiah', and his followers. Isa will descend at the point of a white arcade, east of Damascus, dressed in yellow robes, his head anointed. He will say prayer behind al-Mahdi then join him in his war against the Dajjal. Isa, considered as a Muslim, will abide by the Islamic teachings. Eventually, Isa will slay the Antichrist, and then everyone who is one of the People of the Book, ahl al-kitāb, referring to Jews and Christians, will believe in him. Thus, there will be one community, that of Islam. The Hour will not be established until the son of Maryam, Isa, descends amongst you as a just ruler, he will break the cross, kill the pigs, and abolish the Jizya tax. Money will be in abundance so that nobody will accept it as charitable gifts. After the death of al-Mahdi, Isa will assume leadership. This is a time associated in Islamic narrative with universal peace and justice. Islamic texts also allude to the appearance of Ya'juj and Ma'juj, known also as Gog and Magog...ancient tribes which will disperse and cause disturbance on earth. God, in response to Isa's prayers, will kill them by sending a type of worm in the napes of their necks. Isa's' rule is said to be around forty years, after which he will die. Muslims will then perform the funeral prayer for him and then bury him in the city of Medina in a grave left vacant beside Muhammad, Abu Bakr, and Umar, companions of Muhammad and the first and second Sunni caliphs Rashidun respectively. Islamic texts regard Jesus as a human being and a righteous messenger of God. Islam rejects the idea of him being God or the begotten Son of God. In blasphemy indeed are those that say that Allah is Christ the son of Mary. Say: 'Who then hath the least power against Allah, if His will were to destroy Christ the son of Mary, his mother, and all everyone that is on the earth? For to Allah belongeth the dominion of the heavens and the earth, and all that is between. He createth what He pleaseth. For Allah hath power over all things. The Christian doctrine of the Trinity is rejected in Islam. Such notions of the divinity of Jesus, Muslims state, resulted from human interpolations of God's revelation. Islam views Jesus as a human like all other prophets, who preached that salvation came through submission to God's will and worshipping God alone. Thus, Jesus is considered in Islam to have been a Muslim by the definition of the term...one who submits to God's will, as were all other prophets in Islam. But then we come back to Rashid and an alternative, more esoteric interpretation as expounded by Messianic Muslims in the Sufi and Isma'ili traditions so as to unite Islam, Christianity and Judaism into a single religious continuum. Other Messianic Muslims hold a similar theological view regarding Jesus, without attempting to unite the religions. Making use of the New Testament's distinguishing between Jesus, Son of Man, being the physical human Jesus, and Christ, Son of God, being The Holy Spirit of God residing in the body of Jesus, The Holy Spirit, being immortal and immaterial, is not subject to crucifixion, for it can never die, nor can it be touched by the earthly nails of the crucifixion, for it is a being of pure spirit. Thus while the spirit of Christ avoided crucifixion by ascending unto God, the body that was Jesus was sacrificed on the cross, thereby bringing the Old Testament to final fulfilment.

Thus Qur'anic passages on the death of Jesus affirm that while the Pharisees intended to destroy The Son of God completely, they, in fact, succeeded only in killing The Son of Man, being his nasut, material being. Meanwhile, The Son of God, being his lahut, spiritual being, remained alive and undying, because it is The Holy Spirit."

"I must be truly stupid...for I am lost. Is anyone else confused here?" Simon asked.

"I am a little...but I think I understand the basics here," Ayleth responded shyly.

"I am sorry if this confuses...but all that I say and explain is so very relevant and important...and I promise you this...as much as you think you do not understand now, I assure you, your heart and soul does...and you will remember all of this," the old man explained softly and looked at Ayleth and Simon for several minutes in silence before continuing. "In Islamic tradition there are six prominent prophets whom you as Christians will be familiar with. They are Adem, Adam...Nūḥ, Noah...Ibrāhīm, Abraham...Ismā'īl, Ishmael...Isḥāq, Isaac... Mūsa, Moses...Marīam, Mary...now please note that Islam has no problem in recognising Mary as a prophet! Then we have 'Īsā, Jesus...Abdul-Muttalib, Muhammad. Muslims believe that Jesus was a precursor to Muhammad, and that he announced the latter's coming. They base this on a verse of the Qur'an wherein Jesus speaks of a messenger to appear after him named Ahmad. Islam associates Ahmad with Muhammad, both words deriving from the h-m-d triconsonantal root which refers to praiseworthiness. Muslims also assert that evidence of Jesus's pronouncement is present in the New Testament, citing the mention of the Paraclete whose coming is foretold in the Gospel of John as I explained earlier. Muslim commentators claim that the original Greek word used was periklutos, meaning famed, illustrious, or praiseworthy, rendered in Arabic as Ahmad, and that this was replaced by Christians with parakletos. Jesus is widely venerated in Muslim ascetic and mystic literature. These works lay stress upon Jesus's poverty, his preoccupation with worship, his detachment from worldly life and his miracles. Such depictions also include advice and sermons which are attributed to him. Some Sufic commentaries adapted material from Christian gospels which were consistent with their ascetic portrayal."

"And do they see Jesus as we do or all dressed in black or similar?" Sarah asked.

"Well," the old man paused briefly. "Well, based upon several Hadith narrations of Muhammad, Jesus can be physically described thus, with any differences in Jesus's physical description being due to Muhammad describing him when seeing him at different occasions, such as in a dream, during his ascension to Heaven, or when describing Jesus during Jesus's second coming...A well-built man of medium, moderate or average height and stature with a broad chest. Straight, lank, slightly curly, long hair that fell between his shoulders. A moderate, fair complexion of red or finest brown."

"But what of this Day of Judgement stuff?" Ayleth asked.

"There are two main sources in Islamic scripture that discuss the Last Judgement, the Qur'an, which is viewed in Islam as infallible, and the Hadith, or sayings of the prophet. Hadith are viewed with more flexibility due to the late compilation of the traditions in written form, two hundred years after the death of Muhammad. The Qur'an describes the Last Judgement, with a number of interpretations of its verses. There are specific aspects such as The time is known only to Allah, Prophet Muhammad cannot bring it forward, Those who have been dead will believe that a short time has passed between birth and death, Nothing will remain except Allah, God will resurrect all, even if they have turned to stone or iron, Those that have accepted false deities will suffer in the afterlife. Then there is what is known as the Three periods before the Day of Judgement, also known as ashratu's-sa'ah or alamatu qiyami's-sa'ah, with some debate as to whether the periods could overlap. The first period began at the passing of Muhammad, and the second began with the passing of his companions and will end a thousand years later. Some Sufi mystics claim that during this period, not long from now, another force will descend upon Islam, not that of the Franks or Christianity, and they shall massacre millions of Muslims, and turn the water of the river Tigris red with blood. This is another reason why some within Islam seek a union now with Christianity to counter whatever savagery shall befall all of us. The Qur'an also foretells a fire at Madinah in the Hijaz near Busra, so many will be keeping eye out for that. We are currently in the start of the second period, with the end of days beginning with the appearance of Mahdi as I explained earlier."

"But this end of days, Armageddon or apocalypse...did you not say before that it simply means an end to the present way, a lifting of a veil, to reveal?" Gabirol asked.

"Yes it does...but that is why there is so much confusion and misunderstanding. People are fallible and gullible and so people's interpretations create a source of terror, which is totally opposite of what the plan is that was set out for mankind...a very long time ago," the old man explained and sighed. "You see, there are markers, pointers if you will, that can guide us and many have been carried over into all the major religions. There are a number of major and minor signs of the end of days in Islam. There is debate over whether they could occur concurrently or must be at different points in time, although Islamic scholars typically divide them into three major periods as said. But there will be signs following the second period, with the third being marked by twelve major signs known as alamatu's-sa'ah al- kubra, The major signs of the end. They are as follows. The False Messiah, Masih ad-Dajjal, shall appear with huge powers as a one eyed man with the other eye blind and deformed like a grape. He will claim to be God and to hold keys to Heaven and Hell and lead many astray, although believers will not be deceived. His Heaven is the believers' Hell, and his Hell is the believers' Heaven. The appearance of the Mahdi will be revealed. Medina will be deserted, with true believers going to follow the Mahdi and sinners following Dajjal. The return of Isa, from the second sky, to kill Dajjal and wipe out all falsehood and religions other than Islam. He will then rule the world until he dies. Ya'jooj and Ma'jooj, two tribes of vicious beings which had been imprisoned by Dhul-Qarnayn, will break out. They will ravage the earth, drink all the water of Lake Tiberias, and kill all believers in their way. Isa, Imam Al-Mahdi and the believers with them will go to the top of a mountain and pray for the destruction of Gog and Magog. Allah will eventually send disease and worms to wipe them out. Mecca will be attacked and the Kaaba will be destroyed...Reynald knew and understood this prophecy only too well having spent years as a captive in Aleppo. 'Tis why he vowed to descend upon Mecca like a great eagle and make this prophecy come to pass...A pleasant breeze will blow from the south that shall cause all believers to die peacefully. The Qur'an will be forgotten and no one will recall its verses and all Islamic knowledge will be lost to the extent where people will not say 'La Illaha Ila Allah', There is no god, but Allah, but instead old people will babble without understanding 'Allah, Allah'. Dabbat al-ard, or the Beast, will come out of the ground to talk to people. People will fornicate in the streets 'like donkeys'. A huge black smoke cloud will cover the earth, The sun will rise from the west...now mark that point well as it has happened before in mankind's past...Then there will be the first trumpet blow sounded by Israfil, and all that is in heaven and earth will be stunned and die except what God wills, silence envelops everything for forty, though an undetermined period of time of 40...could be forty days, forty years or more...The second trumpet blow will be sounded, the dead will return to life and a fire will start that shall gather all to Mahshar Al Qiy'amah, The Gathering for Judgement."

"*Trumpet sounds...like the noise heard at Kizkalesi Castle when the earthquake struck and as explained by Theodoric...yes?*" Simon asked quickly.

The old man nodded yes as Gabirol wrote a note.

"*There are of course many more minor signs, too many for me to speak of, but I have a list here you can read through at your leisure if you wish,*" the old man commented and gently pushed across the table a parchment sheet with details written upon it.

Gabirol took the parchment and turned it to view it closely as the Genoese sailor and Simon leaned in closer to see. The Templar let go of Miriam's hand and stood up. Quietly he moved around the table and stood beside Gabirol to view the list.

The parchment read:

Minor signs.

The 77 Minor Signs of Qiyamat:

Time will pass rapidly.

Good deeds will decrease.

People will become miserly.

There will be much killing and murder.

Power and authority will be given to wrong people.

Honesty will be lost.

The disappearance of knowledge and the appearance of ignorance.

A mountain of gold will be disclosed from beneath the River Euphrates, but we are not to take anything from it.

The appearance of 30 false messengers.

Two large groups, adhering to the same religious teaching, will fight each other with large numbers of casualties.

Earthquakes will increase.

Wealth will be in abundance, to the extent that it will be difficult to find someone in need of Zakat.

When people begin to compete with others in the construction of taller buildings.

A man will pass by a grave and wish that he was in their place.

The conquest of Constantinople by the Muslims.

Stones and trees will help the Muslims fight against the Jews.

The consumption of intoxicants will be widespread.

Adultery and fornication will be prevalent.

Women will outnumber men, eventually the ratio will be 50 women to 1 man.

People will strive for power about mosques.

People will cheat with goods.

Paying Zakat becomes a burden and miserliness becomes widespread; charity is given reluctantly.

Leaders will not rule according to the Commands of Allah.

Only the rich receive a share of any gains, and the poor do not.

The leader of a people will be the worst of them.

A trust is used to make a profit.

When a man obeys his wife and disobeys his mother; and treats his friend kindly while shunning his father.

When voices are raised in the mosques.

People will treat a man with respect out of fear for some evil he might do.

Men will begin to wear silk.

Female singers and musical instruments will become popular.

When the last ones of the Ummah begin to curse the first ones.

The nations of the Earth will gather against the Muslims like hungry people going to sit at a table full of food. This will occur when the Muslims are large in number, but like the foam of the sea.

The Muslim conquest of Jerusalem.

A great plague will spread over the land – may be in reference to the plague of Amwas during the Caliphate of Hazrat Umar ibn al-Khattab.

Wealth will increase so much so that if a man were given 10,000, he would not be content with it.

A trial will arise in Arabia which will not spare a single household.

A peace treaty will be made between the Muslims and Rûm – which they will breach.

Other signs mentioned in Hadith Sharif include:

Books and writing will be widespread and religious knowledge will be low.

People will beat others with whips like the tails of oxen – this may be in reference to the slave trade.

Children will be filled with rage.

Children will be foul.

Women will conspire.

Rain will be acidic or burning.

Children of fornication will become widespread or prevalent.

When a trust becomes a means of making a profit.

Episodes of sudden death will become widespread.

There will be people who will be brethren in public, but enemies in secret. When asked how that would come about, he replied, Because they will have ulterior motives in their mutual dealings, and at the same time they will fear one another.

People will walk in the marketplace with their thighs exposed.

Great distances will be traversed in short spans of time.

The people of Iraq will receive no food and no money due to oppression by the Romans.

People will hop between the clouds and the earth.

When singers become common.

People will dance late into the night.

People will claim to follow the Qur'an but will reject Hadith & Sunnah.

People will believe in the stars.

People will reject al-Qadr, the Divine Decree of Destiny.

Smog will appear over cities because of the evil that they are doing.

People will be carrying on with their trade, but there will only be a few trustworthy persons.

There will be attempts to make the deserts green.

Women will be naked in spite of being dressed, these women will be led astray & will lead others astray.

The conquest of India by the Muslims, just prior to the return of Prophet Jesus, son of Mary.

There will be a special greeting for the people of distinction.

Wild animals will be able to talk to humans.

A man will leave his home and his thigh or hip will tell him what is happening back at his home.

Years of deceit in which the truthful person will not be believed and the liar will be believed.

Bearing false witness will become widespread.

When men lie with men, and women lie with women.

Trade will become so widespread that a woman will be forced to help her husband in business.

A woman will enter the workforce out of love for this world.

Arrogance will increase in the earth.

Family ties will be cut.

There will be many women of child-bearing age who will no longer give birth.

There will be an abundance of food, much of which has no blessing in it.

People will refuse when offered food.

Men will begin to look like women and women will begin to look like men.

"I see a great many of these things already in the world...," the Templar remarked as he read through the list looking over Gabirol's shoulder. Both he and Gabirol looked closer at the diagram beneath it.

Fig. 28:

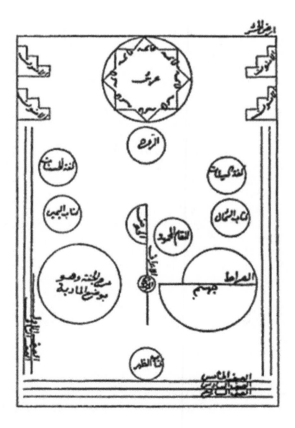

Shown are the 'Arsh, Throne of God, pulpits for the righteous, al-Aminun, seven rows of angels, Gabriel, al-Ruh, A'raf, the Barrier, the Hauzu'l-Kausar, Fountain of Abundance, al-Maqam al-Mahmud, the Praiseworthy Station; where the prophet Muhammad will stand to intercede for the faithful, Mizan, the Scale, As-Sirāt, the Bridge, Jahannam, Hell and Marj al-Jannat, Meadow of Paradise.

The old man waited until they had viewed it long enough and then continued.

"That diagram is familiar to most mystic Sufis though it is not widely known yet to the average layman. Now in the last days as I explained, the Mahdi, the 'guided one', much like the 'navigator' the Prior de Sion teaches of, his appearance will be the first sign of the third period. Hadith writings state that he will be a descendant of Muhammad through his daughter Fatimah and cousin Ali. The Mahdi will be looked upon to kill Al-Dajjal and end the prevalent disintegration of the Muslim community to prepare for the reign of Jesus, who will rule for a time after. The Mahdi will similarly kill all enemies of the Prophet and fulfil the prophetic mission as a vision of justice and peace before following Jesus's rule. The physical features of Mahdi are described in the Hadith...he will be of Arab complexion and average height with a large belly, large eyes and a sharp nose. He will have a mole on his cheek, the sign of the Prophet on his shoulder, and be recognised by the caliphate while he sits at his own home. The Mahdi will have a broad forehead and a pointed or prominent nose. He will fill the earth with justice as it is filled with injustice and tyranny. He will rule for seven years. Though the duration of his rule differs, Hadith are consistent in describing that Allah will perfect him in a single night with inspiration and wisdom, and his name will be announced from the sky. He will bring back worship of true Islamic values, and bring the Ark of the Covenant to light. He will conquer Constantinople and Mount Daylam. And will Eye Jerusalem and the Dome as his Home. His banner will be that of the prophet Muhammad, black and unstitched, with a halo. Unopened since the death of Muhammad, the banner will unfurl when the Mahdi appears. He will be helped by angels and others that will prepare the way for him. He will understand the secrets of abjad. Sunni and Shi'ite Islam have different beliefs on the identity of Mahdi for, historically, Sunni Islam has derived religious authority from the caliphate, who were in turn appointed by the companions of Muhammad at his death. The Sunnis view the Mahdi as the successor of Muhammad; the Mahdi is expected to arrive to rule the world and re-establish righteousness. Various Sunnis also share a parallel belief that though there may be no actual Mahdi, the existence of mujaddid will instead lead the Islamic revolution of a renewal in faith and avoidance of deviation from God's path. Such an intellectual and spiritual figure of Sunni tradition has been attributed to numerous Muslims at the end of each Muslim century from the origin of Islam through to our present day. This classical interpretation is favoured by Sunni scholars. Shi'a Islam, in distinction, followed the bloodline of Muhammad, favouring his cousin and son by marriage, Ali. Ali was appointed the first Imam, and following him there would be eleven more. Muhammad al-Mahdi, otherwise known as the twelfth imam, went into hiding in AD 873 at the age of four. His father was al-'Askari, and had been murdered, and so he was hidden from the authorities of the Abbasid Caliphate. He maintained contact with his followers until AD 940, when he was hidden. Twelver Shia Islam believes that al-Mahdi is the current Imam, and will emerge at the end of the current age. Some scholars say that, although unnoticed by others present, the Mahdi of Twelver Shi'a Islam continues to make an annual pilgrimage while he resides outside of Mecca. In distinction, Sunni Islam foresees him as a separate and new person. The Mahdi is not described in the Qur'an, *only in Hadith, with scholars suggesting he arose when Arabian tribes were settling in Syria under Muawiya. Throughout history, there have been multiple claimants to the role of Mahdi that had come into existence through their pious deeds and by subsequently acquiring their own following. One of these men, Muhammad al-Hanifiyya was said to have judgement and character over rival caliphs; and mysteries of his death arose in the eighth century. It was believed he had in fact not died and would one day return as the Mahdi. And as history carries on, I can assure you there will be many more claimed as being the Mahdi," the old man explained and shook his head.*

"I am more interested in what you say about Jesus and his connection with Islam, for it is all new to me," Peter remarked and looked at the others looking for their thoughts.

"I must confess I too would like to hear more...if there is more?" Ayleth remarked.

"Oh yes...there is indeed more. Let me explain...then we shall break for some food as my belly hungers, I am afraid," the old man replied and smiled, rubbing his stomach before continuing. "Jesus in Islam...As you now know, Isa is the Arabic name for Jesus of Nazareth, and his return is considered the third major sign of the last days, while the second is the appearance of Masih ad-Dajjal. Although Muhammad is the preeminent prophet in Islam, Jesus is the only prophet who is said not to have died but rather 'raised up' by Allah, other than Idris, whom you as Christians know as Enoch, mentioned in the Qur'an. Thus, in accordance with post-Qur'anic legend, he will conceivably return to earth as a just judge before the Day of Judgement as written in Hadith. Abū Hurayrah narrates that the Messenger of Allah said, 'By Him in whose hands my soul rests! It is definitely close in that time that Isa, Son of Maryam, descends amongst you as a just ruler. He will break the cross, kill the swine and abolish jaziya. And money will abound in such excess that no one will accept it."

"Sorry, but who is this Abu whoever?" the Hospitaller asked.

"Abd ar-Raḥmān ibn Ṣakhr al-Azdī, better known by the name kunyah Abu Hurairah or Abū Hurayrah. He was an actual companion of the Islamic prophet Muhammad and the narrator of Hadith most quoted in the isnad by Sunnis. Abū Hurairah spent three years in the company of the Prophet and went on expeditions and journeys with him. It is estimated that he narrated around 5,375 ahadith. Abū Hurayrah has been quoted as having a brilliant mind and that he could look at a parchment just once and be able to recall it from memory word for word...Now back to the Hadith, which reference both the Mahdi and Isa simultaneously, and that the return of the Mahdi will coincide with the return of Isa. He will descend from the heavens in al-Quds at dawn, al-Quds being the Arabic name for the city of Jerusalem. It is the short form of Arabic, Beit al-Quds and comes from the verb (سُدَق) qádusa, which means 'to be holy', 'to be pure'. The two will meet, and Mahdi will lead the people in fajr prayer. After the prayer, they will open a gate to the west and encounter Masih ad-Dajjal. After the defeat of ad-Dajjal, Isa will lead a peaceful forty-year reign until his death, though some say seven years. He will be buried in a tomb beside Muhammad in Medina. Though the two most certainly differ regarding their role and persona in Islamic terminology and meaning, the figures of the Mahdi and Isa are ultimately inseparable for according to the Prophet, though Isa is said to descend upon the world once again, the Mahdi will already be present."

"How do you recall all of this knowledge...are you sure you are not this Mahdi?" Simon asked the old man.

"No...of that I can assure you. I do have the ability to remember things very well. That is all," the old man replied.

"What of this so-called anti-Christ?" Ayleth asked looking concerned.

"Al-Dajjal or the Antichrist or False Messiah...he does not appear in the Qur'an but is a prominent figure in the Hadith and Islamic teachings as a whole. He appears gruesome and is blind in his right eye. His one eye is thought to be a symbol that correlates with how single minded he is in achieving his goal of converting Muslims to his side. Al-Dajjal has the intention of gaining followers through his miracle working abilities and apparent wealth and generosity. These abilities are a test for true believers of Islam, who have been warned about his power and must resist his material temptations. He is thought to appear prior to the Day of Judgement, where he will engage in an epic battle with and be killed by either Jesus, according to Sunni tradition, or the Mahdi, according to the Shia tradition. Al-Dajjal functions symbolically as a key cog in the overall Islamic picture, which emphasises the world coming to an end, of good finally triumphing over evil, and of the remarkable events that will prefigure the replacement of the mortal world with a more authentic form of existence in the afterlife. Various Muslim political movements use the concept of Al-Dajjal to comment on contemporary events, and often identify him with opposing regimes or other worldly forces that they consider as harmful to Islam."

"So in other words, it can be made to fit any given time and place that best suits?" Simon remarked cynically and shook his head then folded his arms.

"Yes, you could say that, just as Christianity does...that is why I must explain about Ya'juj and Ma'juj in Islam but to Christian and Jews known as Gog and Magog...You see, the fourth major sign of the end time will be that the wall which imprisons the nations of Ya'juj and Ma'juj will break, and they will surge forth. Some Islamic scholars believe the wall began to crack during the life of Muhammad. This is supported in the Hadith when the prophet mentions that 'a hole has been made in the wall containing the Ya'juj and Ma'juj', indicating the size of the hole with his thumb and index finger. Their release will occur forty years prior to the Last Judgement. But when Ya'jooj and Ma'jooj are let loose and they rush headlong down every hill and mountain (Qur'an 21:96) they will ravage the earth. Ultimately, Allah will send worms and insects to destroy them. Gog and Magog, now this I fear you will have difficulty in following, but stop me at any time if I do make myself clear," the old man explained and sat himself upright and cleared his throat. "Gog and Magog, Hebrew (גּוֹג וּמָגוֹג) Gog u-Magog, which in Arabic, is Ya'jūj wa-Ma'jūj and in Persian yagug va Magug, are names that appear in the Old Testament, and in numerous subsequent references in other works, notably the Book of Revelation, as well as in the Qur'an. They are sometimes individuals, sometimes peoples, and sometimes geographic regions. Their context can be either genealogical as Magog in Genesis 10:2, or eschatological and apocalyptic, as in the Book of Ezekiel and Revelation. The passages from Ezekiel and Revelation in particular have attracted attention due to their prophetic descriptions of conflicts said to occur near the 'end times'. But as I shall reveal later, Revelation has many secrets encoded within it in plain view." He paused and closed his eyes briefly. "Let me try to explain. The origins of both the names Gog and Magog remain uncertain...so many would have you believe. The ma- at the beginning of Magog indicates a land, as well as meaning 'from', so that Magog means 'of the land of Gog' or 'from Gog'. Gog originated as the Hebrew version of the name of Gyges of Lydia, who made his kingdom a great power in the early seventh century BC, but this explanation, although common, is not universally accepted. A different theory is that 'Magog' is a reference to Babylon, by turning BBL 'Babylon' in Hebrew script, which originally had no vowel-signs, into MGG Magog. Chapter 10 of the Book of Genesis, commonly called the 'Table of Nations', names

some seventy descendants of Noah from whom 'the nations spread out over the earth after the Deluge.' Noah has three sons, Shem, Ham and Japheth; Magog is the second son of Japheth. This is the account of Shem, Ham and Japheth, Noah's sons, who themselves had sons after the Flood. The sons of Japheth: Gomer, Magog, Madai, Javan, Tubal, Meshech and Tiras. 1 Chronicles begins with a list of genealogies repeating that in the Table of Nations but continuing well beyond. In Chapter 5, among the many descendants of Reuben, first of the twelve sons of the patriarch Jacob, it mentions an individual named Gog. The two names first appear together in Chapters 38 and 39 of the Book of Ezekiel, but here Magog is a place and not an individual. 'Son of man, direct your face towards Gog, of the land of Magog, the prince, leader of Meshech and Tubal, and prophesy concerning him. Say: Thus said the Lord: Behold, I am against you, Gog, the prince, leader of Meshech and Tubal. Ezekiel lived in the first half of the sixth century BC, and the earliest possible date for the prophecy is 585 BC. Scholars disagree, however, as to whether Ezekiel 38–39 was part of the original text. Its prophecy of a savage foe from the north is based on Jeremiah 1:3–16, where Jeremiah is talking about the Babylonians. Ezekiel turns this into an eschatological enemy who will come 'in the latter years', an apocalypse at the end of time. Gog's allies, Meshech and Tubal, Persia, Cush and Put, and 'Gomer with all its troops, and Beth Togarmah from the far north', are all, with the exception of Persia, taken from the Table of Nations. Meshech, Tubal, Gomer and Beth Togarmah can be identified with real eighth and seventh century peoples, kings or kingdoms of Anatolia, our Armenian Cilicia as Alisha and Paul travelled through. While Gomer probably refers to the Central Asian, though ethnically Indo-European horse nomads, Cimmerians. Why the Prophet's gaze should have focused on these particular nations is unclear, some argue, but their remoteness and reputation for violence and mystery 'made Gog and his confederates perfect symbols of the archetypal enemy, rising against God and his people'. Cush, in Sudan or Ethiopia, but there is also a Cush in the Persian plateau, the land of the Kassites, and Put, from Punt, are sons of Ham according to Genesis 10, while Persia is located to the east, and is not mentioned in Genesis 10 at all. Since Ezekiel insists on a northerly situation of Gog and his allies. Gog is to be defeated and buried in the Valley of Hamon-Gog, Israel. Around the middle of the second century BC, the Sibylline Oracles mention the 'land of Gog and Magog' as 'situated in the midst of Aethiopian rivers', but a second mention links it with the 'Marsians and Dacians', in eastern Europe; in both cases they are about to receive 'woe', and according to Boe, 'there can be little doubt about the direct use of Ezekiel's oracles' in their composition. The Book of Jubilees, known from about the same time, mentions Magog as a son of Japheth to whom land is allocated, while Gog is a region on Japheth's borders. 1 Enoch tells how God stirs up the Medes and Parthians, instead of Gog and Magog, to attack Jerusalem, where they are destroyed; an indebtedness to Ezekiel 38–39 has also been asserted. The first-century Liber Antiquitatum Biblicarum is notable for listing and naming seven of Magog's sons, and mentions his thousands of descendants. The Greek translation of the Hebrew Bible, made during this period, occasionally introduces the name of Gog where the Hebrew original has something else. Thus at Numbers 24:7 it replaces Agag, a mysterious but clearly powerful figure, with Gog, and at Amos 7:1 the Greek has Gog as the leader of a threatening locust-like army. The Greek translation of Ezekiel takes Gog and Magog to be synonyms for the same country, a step which paved the way for the Book of Revelation to turn 'Gog from Magog' into 'Gog and Magog.' By the end of the first century, Jewish tradition had long since changed Ezekiel's Gog from Magog into Gog and Magog, the ultimate enemies of God's people, to be destroyed in the final battle. The author of the Book of Revelation tells how he sees in a vision Satan rallying Gog and Magog, 'the nations in the four corners of the Earth', to a final battle with Christ and his saints: When the thousand years are over, Satan will be released from his prison and will go out to deceive the nations in the four corners of the Earth, Gog and Magog, and to gather them for battle. In number they are like the sand on the seashore. Ezekiel's Gog from Magog was a symbol of the evil darkness of the north and the powers hostile to God, but in Revelation, Gog and Magog have no geographic location, and instead represent the nations of the world, banded together for the final assault on Christ and those who follow him. Separate passages in the Jewish Antiquities and Jewish War of the first-century Jewish historian and scholar Josephus show that Jews of that time identified Gog and Magog with the Scythians: Alexander the Great, Josephus said, had locked these horse-riding barbarians of the far north behind the Caucasus mountains with iron gates. This gate is situated in Georgia, near the Caucasus mountains. Georgian kings were mentioned as guards of the Gog and Magog gate in various historical sources. Jordanes, a Goth himself, identified Magog as one of the ancestors of the Goths in his book Getica. The Goths, according to Isidore of Seville, were thought to be descended from Gog and Magog, and of the same race as the Getae. Some early Christian writers, like Eusebius whom I mentioned earlier, identified Gog and Magog with the Romans. After the Roman Empire became Christian, this was no longer possible, and attention switched to Rome's northern barbarian enemies. Ambrose identified them with the Goths, and Isidore of Seville confirmed that people in his day supposed that the Goths were descended from Magog because of the similarity of the last syllable. In the sixth century, the Byzantine historian Procopius of Caesarea saw Attila and the Huns as the nation locked out by Alexander, and a little later, other Christian writers identified them with the Saracens. Still later, Gog and Magog became identified with the Khazars, whose empire dominated Central Asia in the ninth and tenth centuries. In his ninth-century work Expositio in Matthaeum Evangelistam, the Benedictine monk Christian of Stavelot referred to them as descendants of Gog and Magog, and says they are 'Circumcised and observing all the laws of Judaism'. But understand this...that the Arabic words for Gog and Magog, Yājūj and Mājūj, derive from the root word ajja, to burn, blaze, hasten, which suggests that Gog and Magog will excel all nations in harnessing fire to their service and shall fight their battles with fire and those nations opposed to Islam that will ultimately be destroyed by the 'fire' of their own making. Jewish scholars associate no specific nation or territory with Magog, beyond locating it to the north but some believe Zechariah 14 refers to the war of Gog and Magog, when at the end of days Jerusalem will be the battle ground," the old man explained and then sat back in silence.

"What really does all that have to do with the end days exactly...and the sword?" Simon asked hesitantly.

The old man smiled.

"I am so glad you are with us Simon. You ask what must be asked...and so to answer, let me explain further, then Lord willing we shall eat," the old man remarked and looked at Stephan, who smiled back and nodded his acknowledgement. "Philip, as well as other architects and masons, used the symbols and images of Gog and Magog depicted as giants. This is despite their apparent negative aspects. According to tradition, the giants Gog and Magog are guardians of the City of London. The present account of Gog and Magog says that the Roman Emperor Diocletian had thirty-three wicked daughters. He found thirty-three husbands for them to curb their wicked ways; they chafed at this, and under the leadership of the eldest sister, Alba, they murdered their husbands. For this crime they were set adrift at sea; they washed ashore on a windswept island, which they named 'Albion' after Alba. Here they coupled with demons and gave birth to a race of giants, whose descendants included Gog and Magog. Note the numerical value of thirty-three, which I have previously explained. An even older British connection to Gog and Magog appears in Geoffrey of Monmouth's influential and recent Historia Regum Britanniae, which states that Goemagot was a giant slain by the Cornish hero Corin or Corineus. The tale figures in the folklore that has Britain settled by the Trojan soldier Brutus and other fleeing heroes from the Trojan Wars. Corineus supposedly slew the giant by throwing him into the sea near Plymouth, where there is the presence of chalk figures carved on Plymouth Hoe in his time. Wace (Roman de Brut), Layamon (Layamon's Brut), who calls the giant Goemagog, and other chroniclers retell the story, which was picked up by later poets and romanciers. The island, not yet Britain, but Albion, was in a manner desert and inhospitable, kept only by a remnant of Giants, whose excessive force and tyranny had consumed the rest. Then Brutus, having secured the land divides it amongst his people, which, with some reference to his own name, he thenceforth calls Britain. To Corineus, Cornwall, as now we call it, tales of Brutus wrestling with Goemagog, the hugest, in height twelve cubits, giant, broke three of his ribs. Nevertheless Corineus, enraged, heaving him up by sheer brute force, and on his shoulders bearing him to the next high rock, threw him headlong into the sea, and left his name on the cliff, called ever since Langoemagog, which is to say, the Giant's Leap. But from this period we have yet another connection to sacred oak trees and the acorn. Recall how Alisha had the dagger with three acorns? Well, two ancient oak trees near Glastonbury Tor in Somerset, southern England, are named Gog and Magog. There are also a pair of very old oak trees named Gog and Magog flanking a road near Glanvilles Wootton in Dorset, southern England. Now then...in Britain there is a place called the Gog Magog Downs that are about three miles south of Cambridge, said to be the metamorphosis of the giant after being rejected by the nymph Granta. There lies still hidden a group of three hidden chalk carvings in the Gogmagog Hills. Those who know, understand these carvings to represent 'Gog' and his consort 'Ma-Gog', which represent the sun and moon. There are also similarities between the name and nature of the purported 'Gog' and the Irish deity Ogma, or the Gaulish Ogmios. I have already explained about the connection with Ireland, when Philip, his wife and Theodoric travelled there...but let me explain further how Irish mythology, including the Lebor Gabála Érenn, the 'Book of Invasions', expands on the Genesis account of Magog as the son of Japheth and makes him the ancestor of the Irish through Partholón, leader of the first group to colonise Ireland after the Deluge, and a descendant of Magog, as also were the Milesians, the people of the fifth invasion of Ireland. Magog was also the progenitor of the Scythians, as well as of numerous other races across Europe and Central Asia. His three sons were Baath, Jobhath and Fathochta."

"I do not claim to take in all that you explain nor that I even understand it, but I am getting the point that all and everything is indeed connected, especially by way of name and their meanings," the farrier remarked.

※ 2 – 11

"Can we quickly go back to the major signs of the Qur'an...we only got to the fourth sign I think?" Gabirol said and looked over his notes.

"Yes...of course. You will have to forgive me if I stray...Now the fifth sign is that Medinah will be deserted, and all that remains in the city will be date palms and the just will have gone to join Mahdi, and the evil to Dajjal. Medinah will have been depopulated for forty years by the time of al-Qiyama. Now the sixth sign is that a thin ruler with short legs from Ethiopia will attack Mecca and destroy the Kabah. The seventh sign is written in the Ahadith, and is the appearance of the da'ba-tul-ard, or the Beast of the Earth, who will populate the entire world and judge the wicked. And when the Word is fulfilled against the unjust,it is said that we shall produce from the earth a Beast to face them. He will speak to them, for that mankind did not believe with assurance in our Signs. In the Qur'an 27:82, the entire world will be engulfed by dukhan or smoke, for forty days and there will be three huge earthquakes. The Qur'an will be taken to the heavens and even the huffaz will not recall its verses. Finally, a pleasant breeze will blow that shall cause all believers to die, but infidels and sinners will remain alive. A fire will start from Hadramawt in Yemen that shall gather all the people of the world in the land of Mahshar, and al-Qiyamah will commence. The eighth sign is a breeze bearing a pleasant scent will emanate from Yemen, causing the awliya, sulaha and the pious to die peacefully once they inhale it. After the believers die, there will be a period of 120 years during which the world will hold only kafirs, sinners, oppressors, liars and adulterers, and there would be a reversion to idolatry. The ninth sign is the rising of the sun from the West after a long night, which after midday will set again. According to Hadith: Abu Hurayrah states that the Messenger of Allah as said, 'The Hour will not be established until the sun rises from the West and when the people see it they will have faith. But that will be the time when believing of the soul, that will have not believed before that time, will not benefit it. The final signs will be nafkhatu'l-ula, when the trumpet will be sounded for the first time, as I explained earlier, which will result in the death of the remaining sinners. Then there will be a period of forty years. Then a second trumpet will sound to signal the resurrection. The eleventh sign is the second sounding of the trumpet, at which time the dead will be resurrected as ba'as ba'da'l-mawt. At divine judgement, each person's Book of Deeds will be read, in which 'every small and great thing is recorded', with actions before adolescence not written. Records shall be given in the right hand if they are good, and the left if they are evil. Even the smallest acts will not be ignored: Then shall anyone who has done an atom's weight of good, see it! And anyone who has done an atom's weight of evil, shall see it. This will be followed by perfect, divine and merciful justice. The age of the hereafter, or rest of eternity, is the final stage after the Day of Judgement, when all will receive their judgement from God. Those who believe in that which is revealed unto thee, Muhammad, and those who are Jews, and Christians, and Sabians, whoever believeth in Allah and the Last Day and doeth right, surely their reward is with their Lord, and there shall no fear come upon them neither shall they grieve. The dead will stand in a grand assembly, awaiting a scroll detailing their righteous deeds, sinful acts and ultimate judgement. Muhammad will be the first to be resurrected. If one did good deeds, one would go to Jannah, and if unrighteous would go to Jahannam. Punishments will include adhab, or severe pain, and khizy or shame. There will also be a punishment of the grave, for those who disbelieved, between death and the resurrection. While appearing similar to certain parts of the Bible Ezekiel, James, 1 Peter, Revelation, Catholics, however, cite James 2:24 as evidence that judgement is not based on faith alone."

"Now sorry to do this, as I know all wish for food, but can you quickly finish off what *you were explaining about Rashid and Saladin please...so we know," Gabirol asked and looked at everyone in turn.*

"I already know of those details, so I shall go and prepare some food now whilst he explains," Stephan said politely and stood up.

"You do?" Sarah said, surprised as Stephan nodded yes in reply and winked.

"Let me continue about Rashid and his relations with Saladin then, for it would have profound implications for Alisha and Paul later...As you now understand the importance of Jesus, Isa in Islam, you will hopefully understand the final words I shall explain on Rashid and his Ashashin. It all started during a siege of Ja'bar in 1146, after the Turkish ruler of Mawsil and Aleppo, 'Imad al-Din Zangi, had been murdered by his slave troops... the mamluks, succeeded by his son, 'Nur al-Din Mahmud Zangi, who maintained his father's efforts to defend Syria against the Crusaders. After the fall of Edessa to 'Imad al-Din Zangi in December 1144, the Crusaders launched their second Crusade of 1146–1149, which had ended in complete failure. This was the one both Philip and Firgany fought in. In March 1154, Nur al-Din captured Damascus, and from then onwards Egypt had been the decisive factor in his relations with the Crusaders. But in Egypt, the failing Fatimid regime had reached its final stage and with the death of the Fatimid Caliph al Fa'iz in 556 AH/AD 1160 there followed a disastrous struggle from the Wazirate during which the Fatimid commander Shawar sought help from Nur al-Din, who sent the Kurdish governor of Homs, Shirkuh, on his first Egyptian campaign. Shirkuh, who was the uncle of Saladin, restored Shawar to power in May 1164, but Shawar refused to pay the promised tribute, and appealed to the Franks for help. Shawar continued his duplicitous policy for a few years, but in 1167 Nur al-Din made a second intervention in the affairs of Egypt, followed by a third in 1168, and on this occasion the Fatimid territories had been overrun by Shirkuh, who died soon afterwards leaving his nephew Saladin, Salah al-Din Ibn Yusuf as the Wazir, or Vizier of Egypt. While Nur al-Din was alive, Saladin mainly occupied himself in establishing control over Egypt, eradicating the Fatimid power and planning continued war against the Crusaders. Although the relations between Rashid and Nur al-Din had been tense, both on account of Nur al-Din's suspicions that the Syrian Isma'ilis were collaborating with the Crusaders, and on account of their unfriendly activities in Aleppo and their ceaseless efforts to seize more strongholds, Nur al-Din had not undertaken any major offensive operation against the Isma'ilis, though there are reports that threatening letters were exchanged between him and Rashid, and rumours that he was planning, shortly before his death, to invade the Isma'ili territory. The death of Nur al-Din and the King of Jerusalem Amalric the First, son of Fuik, in 1174, gave Saladin his opportunity and on an urgent request from the commandant of Damascus, he entered that city on Tuesday, 27th November, 1174 claiming to have come to protect Nur al-Din's eleven year old son and successor, al-Malik al-Salih, against aggression from his cousins who ruled Mawsil. From Damascus Saladin marched northward to Homs, which he captured without its castle, and proceeded to Aleppo, which he besieged for the first time. It was during this siege that Rashid, in answer to an appeal from the Regent of Aleppo Sa'd al-Din Gumushtigin, sent his fida'is to kill Saladin. This attempt, which took place in December–January 1174/5 was foiled by an Amir named Nasih al-Din Khumartakin, whose castle of Abu Oubays was close to the Isma'ili territory and who recognised the Ashashin fida'is. The second attempt took place more than a year later on the 22nd May, 1176, when Saladin was besieging 'Azaz, north of Aleppo. Thanks to his armour of chain mail, Saladin escaped with only slight injuries."

"Why would Rashid want Saladin dead?" Peter asked.

"Many people have raised that question. Most Arabic sources state that Gumushtigin had implored Rashid to take action against Saladin. But, as we know, Rashid would never have acted merely as a protégé of the rulers of Aleppo, obeying their orders or accepting their bribes to commit an act which might have endangered the whole safety of his people. Even despite knowing Saladin's general policy, which from the time when he overthrew the Fatimid Caliphate was biased against all the Isma'ili, although the Nizari Isma'ilis to whom Rashid belonged considered the Fatimid Caliphs after al-Mustansir to be usurpers, Saladin's gross ill-treatment of the Fatimid family caused indignation and anger among all the Isma'ilis, whether Nizaris or Musta'lis. I believe I explained earlier, Saladin was not so wise in his early years but changed dramatically...too suddenly according to some. Saladin also embarked on a systematic campaign to suppress Isma'ilism in Egypt, destroying the rich Fatimid libraries, exterminating the Isma'ili system, and introducing Sunni institutions. Moreover, it was Saladin's manifest ambition to recreate a Syro-Egyptian state under his rule and the rise of a strong anti-Isma'ili ruler in Syria was bound to be a source of anxiety to the Syrian Isma'ilis. It is known that Rashid had earlier sent one of his fida'is, named Hasan al-'Ikrimi al-'Iraqi, to Egypt where he left a knife with a threatening letter near Saladin's bed. Such reports in the Isma'ili sources about fida'is being sent to threaten Saladin shed a light on a letter from Saladin to Nur al-Din drafted by al-Qadi al-Fadil concerning a pro-Fatimid plot against him in Egypt, in 1173. The letter also adds that the conspirators in this plot appealed to Rashid for help. Rashid could have had Saladin killed on several occasions yet he did not, even after Saladin's aggression against the Isma'ilis in 1174–5. In that year, a militant Sunni order called the Nabawiya raided the Isma'ili centres of al-Bab and Buza'a and Saladin took advantage of the resultant confusion to send a raiding party against the Isma'ili villages of Sarmin, Ma'arrat Masrin and Jabal al-Summaq, which were looted. No doubt they confirmed Rashid's belief that Saladin was a menace to Isma'ili existence in Syria, and they may have led to the second attempt on the 22nd May 1176, an attempt we understand to have been a deliberate one to warn him off for if they had a wish to kill him...he would indeed be dead. Besides, as Abu Firas mentions the raid of the Nabawiya on the Isma'ilis, they were soundly defeated. For all these reasons Rashid would have had strong motives to join hands with the rulers of Aleppo and Mawsil against Saladin...but he still did not. Having twice defeated the rulers of Mawsil and forced the rulers of Aleppo to seek a peace treaty, Saladin, after capturing 'Azaz on the 24th June 1176, marched against the Isma'ili territories. On his way to Masyaf, he encamped near Aleppo, where the daughter of Nur al-Din came out to see him and on her demand he presented her with the town of Azaz. Saladin entered Isma'ili territory during the summer, which was the best time to attack such inaccessible places. The actual siege of Masyaf took place in July 1176, but lasted no more than one week. Apparently Rashid was out of Masyaf during the siege, and his absence might have been expected to make the other's task easier, but surprisingly Saladin withdrew after only a few minor skirmishes with the Isma'ilis. The reasons for Saladin's withdrawal from Masyaf are explained differently by various sources. But practically all the chroniclers agree that the withdrawal was brought about through the good offices of the Prince of Hama, the maternal uncle of Saladin, Shihab al-Din Mahmud Ibn Takash. Though it is not clear whether Saladin or Rashid requested the mediation of the Prince of Hama. According to the Isma'ili author, Abu Firas, Saladin woke up suddenly to find on his bed a dagger with a threatening letter, and partly out of fear, partly out of gratitude

to Rashid for not having killed him when he could, and partly on the advice of his uncle Taqu al-Din, Saladin sought peace with Rashid. Among the other sources dealing with Saladin's withdrawal from the Isma'ili territories, Ibn Abi Tayy, quoted by Abu Shama, gives the most reasonable explanation of Saladin's withdrawal from Masyaf. He states that Frankish military movements in the south near Ba'iabak in the Biqa' valley convinced Saladin that the threat from the Franks was more urgent and important. At the same time, the prince Shihab al-Din al-Harimi of Hama must have had good reasons to avoid provoking the anger and enmity of his Isma'ili neighbours in the west and some sort of a settlement which might qualify to be called a peace treaty between Rashid and Saladin may have been arranged on Saladin's initiative. Whatever were the real reasons for the withdrawal, it is clear that Saladin, probably under the influence of his uncle Shihab al-Din, and as Ibn al-Athir says because of the weariness of his troops, did decide to reach some sort of an agreement or a settlement with the Isma'ilis. Although the sources have not recorded the terms of the settlement, it seems almost certain that the two leaders must have agreed to some form of 'peaceful-co-existence'. Although hostilities between Rashid and Saladin appear to have ceased after the latter's withdrawal from Masyaf, the relations between the Isma'ilis and the rulers of Aleppo entered a difficult period. A wazir of al-Malik al-Salih, called Shihab al-Din abu Salih Ibn al-'Ajami, was assassinated on August 31ˢᵗ 1177, and this murder was attributed to the Isma'ilis. Al-Malik al-Salih held an inquiry in which it was alleged that Sa'd ai-Din Gumushtigin had sent forged letters to the Isma'ilis urging them, in the name of al-Salih, to perpetrate the murder. Gumushtigin was found guilty and ultimately ruined by his enemies. The other main event affecting the relations between Rashid and the rulers of Aleppo was the burning of the markets at Aleppo in 1179–80. The fires broke out in several places and were attributed to arson by the Isma'ilis in revenge for seizure of their stronghold al-Hajirah by al-Malik al-Salih in 1179/80."

"But you said earlier that Saladin finally agreed to cease hostilities after Rashid himself had broken into his tent with another large person, and surrounded by lights...is that not still the case?" Gabirol asked looking confused.

"Yes...that is the case, but I have just recounted the most oft quoted version so you will know the truth of what I reveal in this tale later," the old man replied. Gabirol smiled and the old man continued. "Most of the strongholds which the Isma'ilis seized or bought in Jabal Bahra had previously been in the hands of the Crusaders and many of the most important Frankish castles were situated very close to the Isma'ili fortresses. In 1142 or 1145, the lord of Tripoli gave to the Hospitaller Order the fortress known in the medieval Arabic sources as Hisn al-Akrad or Qal'at al Hisn, as you know it Crac de l'Ospital, twenty-five miles south of Masyaf, and a few years later fighting between the Isma'ilis and the Franks over the fortress of Mayhaqa broke out. Some suggest that the Frankish raids on the Isma'ili territories were in reprisal for the murder of the Count of Tripoli in 1151 and that they ceased after the Isma'ilis had agreed to pay a yearly tribute to the Templar Order. It is quite possible that when Rashid succeeded Abu Muhammad, the Isma'ilis had been fighting with the Franks somewhere in the County of Tripoli. But there is far more to the story than that and it was not a tribute paid to the Templars to appease for the murder of the count...realising the danger of being nearly surrounded by both Muslim and Frankish hostile forces, Rashid attempted to reach a settlement with the Franks. His efforts were made difficult by the fact that the two Frankish Orders, and especially the Templars, more often than not conducted their affairs independently of the

Kingdom of Jerusalem so Rashid sought a rapproachment with the Frankish kingdom of Jerusalem hoping to be absolved from paying the yearly tributes to the Templars. The negotiations with the King of Jerusalem, Amalric I, son of Fuik, began some time in 1172 or 1173, and they were successful. Amalric agreed that the tribute to the Templars should be cancelled. But this did not please the Templars, who caused Rashid's ambassador to be murdered on his way back from Jerusalem. Again, the story is not that simple, for in truth the Templars were already working closely with Rashid and his Ashashin and the tributes paid by Rashid were to help towards researching and funding excavations within Egypt...more specifically, Cairo! I shall explain later why. The chronicler William of Tyre blamed the Templars for depriving the Franks of a strong ally, and claimed that Rashid's embassy proposed to embrace Christianity. It is highly probable that the Isma'ili embassy mentioned to the king something about the relationship between their religious views and Christian beliefs. They would have emphasised their high regard for Jesus, Isa, as being both a Prophet and a Natiq 'speaker or addresser'. For as will be seen later, the Isma'ilis believed that God had been sending, since the beginning of the human world, a succession of prophets for the guidance of human beings, who are always in need for such guidance. According to them, religions evolve from one another and each represents a certain stage in the chronic evolution. After the death of Amalric the First, in 1174, and the withdrawal of Saladin's army from their territories, the Syrian Isma'ilis threw their weight on the side of Saladin in his wars against the Franks. The reason for this was that the hostile attitude of the Templars, in the main down to Gerard de Rideffort and Reynald, as well as some within the Hospitaller towards the Isma'ilis in disregard of the official policy of Jerusalem, and the aggressiveness of the Hospitallers who in 1186 set up their military headquarters at al-Marqab, less than thirteen miles northwest of al-Qadmus, left Rashid with no alternative other than to ally himself with Saladin in later years. But as for Rashid himself..." The old man paused for a while. "The great Isma'ili leader Rashid al-din Sinan, whose nickname Shaykh 'al-Jabal used to be mentioned in frightened whispers at the courts of king and princes, was a man of knowledge, statecraft and skill in winning men's hearts. He was handsome, middling in height, having wide black eyes set in a ruddy face tending to brown, eloquent in expression, powerful in argument, sharp of vision, swift in improvisation, and unmatched in the principles of philosophy and in the sciences of allegorical interpretation, poetry and astronomy. In Jabal Mashhad, Rashid used to spend much of his time praying and practising astronomy."[34]

Stephan walked in carrying several large wooden platters covered with bread and cheese. He placed them down upon the table with a broad smile.

"There you all go. You have fed your souls, hearts and minds with new ideas and teachings, now fill your bellies too," he said with a huge smile. "Afterwards, we shall learn of what happened next...at Crac de l'Ospital".

Chapter 29
Crac de l'Ospital

The monastery of St George of Al-Humaira, County of Tripoli, June 1179

Paul leaned back against the side bench as he held Arri close. The first rays of daylight were just beginning to shine through the rear door window slot bathing the inside of the caravan in a warm orange glow. He looked at Alisha fast asleep on the bunk. It had been nice to have the caravan just to themselves for once. Alisha was tired and felt dirty, and the last feed had taken it out of her. He watched her as she lay on her side, her eyes closed, but her mouth open. He smiled at this. Then he looked down at Arri wrapped in his arms. His mind drifted back to the time he had spent with Niccolas and recalled his words about having three paths he could choose and what the parchment charts had revealed. He studied every little facet and feature of Arri's face and his heart ached almost. As he looked at Arri then at Alisha, he knew he had most definitely made the right choice. These were the most treasured moments that he relished...just him, Alisha and Arri together where he could protect them. His right hand moved to cover the handle of his sword laid next to him on the bench. He looked up and closed his eyes, tired. He could almost see Firgany as if he were standing in front of him. 'I swear, I shall protect them always...always,' he said in his mind. He wondered how Taqi was doing and then his father. 'But you have total freedom of choice. You will always have a choice,' he recalled Niccolas clearly. Paul started to fall asleep when he was jolted from his slumber by a rap on the door. He opened his eyes wearily to see Theodoric opening the door and peering in with a large smile upon his face.

"Bring some towels and a change of clothes...we are off to the spring to clean ourselves up....so come on....quickly," he beckoned Paul with his hand.

Paul sat up and looked across at Alisha still sound asleep. He did not want to wake her but he knew she would welcome the chance at getting washed properly.

⃝⃞

Paul stepped down from the caravan holding Arri in his right arm and helping Alisha follow him holding his left hand still half-asleep. In the daylight they could see the main entrance to the monastery from the southern side which was adorned with a Byzantine façade. The gates were not as wide as they had looked when they had first arrived. They were built surmounted with black stone. Next to the gates was a stone window used for distributing bread and other foods to the needy. One of the monks was already instructing several people and a couple of pilgrims in the Orthodox faith and morals through this window. The entrance to the actual

126

monastery itself was built of black stone tiles of the same size as those on the first floor, and faced west. Over the entrance was a sculptured image of a cross.

"The gates are called the 'horse gates' despite their narrowness, because they are the entrance through which horses pass. On the first floor is a church called 'the Old Church' as opposed to the new church on the third floor," Theodoric explained as he approached Paul and Alisha with Sister Lucy by his side. "Now follow me and I shall take you to the fresh water spring before the pilgrims swamp it."

Alisha held Paul's hand and simply followed him still with her eyes half closed. She was exhausted. Sister Lucy beckoned Paul to pass her Arri. Paul then placed his arm around Alisha and kissed the side of her head as he led her toward Theodoric, who was beckoning them to hurry up as he headed off down a small-corbelled pathway that cut through some trees. Paul took in the beautiful lush green scenery. Despite there being a drought across most of the region, this valley was fertile. Tenno appeared to his right following them as Thomas gave him a thumbs up that he too was watching them. This reassured Paul, knowing that they seemed to always be present. Paul smiled to himself as he realised that he had never actually seen Tenno asleep. Princess Stephanie came running after them carrying some clean dresses and washing items closely followed by Brother Matthew having to run in his full armour to catch up with her. She patted Tenno as she ran past him and stopped just short of Paul.

"My Lady, I have just this moment returned from Crac de L'Ospital with orders to bring you in as fast as possible...your husband awaits you there...impatiently I may add," Brother Matthew said out of breath.

"Does he now? Hmmm, then patience he must learn for I shall clean myself ready to present to him. Ah joy, a wash at last...you men will have to avert your eyes for I am going in naked," Stephanie commented with a smile as Alisha looked across at her. "And here, I have a new dress that will fit you perfectly. 'Tis light and comfortable," she said and handed across a cream coloured dress. "And do not let them bully you into wearing any silly head covers whilst inside Crac...'tis too hot in this climate to be doing so."

Sister Lucy winked at Alisha as she rocked Arri in her arms.

෨ ඐ

A crystal clear stream bubbled down a slight incline into a pool of water surrounded by plants and overhanging trees that sheltered the spring. It was secluded, private, and beautiful to behold. Sister Lucy sat down on a carefully placed tree trunk with Arri as Princess Stephanie immediately started to unlace her dress with her back towards Paul, Theodoric and Tenno. Brother Matthew stepped forwards quickly and coughed to get her attention.

"My Lady...," he said aloud.

"Oh...just look the other way for a moment. I need this more than I care for my modesty!" she replied and looked over her shoulder smiling as she let the dress drop from her shoulders to her waist. "Now turn around."

Alisha smiled at her behaviour and slowly stepped forwards to stand next to her. Tenno frowned at Paul, then turned his back and kept watch behind them as Alisha started to unlace her green dress, smiling. When her dress rested upon her waist like Princess Stephanie's, her arms across her breasts to cover them, they both started to giggle. Quickly she removed the three-pronged dagger from her waistband and passed it to Paul. He looked at it briefly bemused as Alisha dipped her toe in the water and quickly pulled it out.

"'Tis freezing," she exclaimed, laughing.

"Is it?" Stephanie replied and pushed her into the clear pool of water, then dropped her dress completely, stepped out of it and briefly looked back to see Paul looking at her.

Paul could not help but see her slender fully naked figure until Theodoric pulled him around quickly as Alisha shrieked out laughing at the cold water as she raised her head out just as Princess Stephanie jumped in beside her. As she came up, she laughed. Theodoric and Paul stood with their backs to the pool as Brother Matthew looked away awkwardly, embarrassed. Sister Lucy laughed as she watched both Alisha and Princess Stephanie lie back in the pool enjoying the fresh water. After several long minutes, Alisha stood up, her dress clinging to her soaking wet waist and legs as Princess Stephanie relaxed, her eyes shut just facing upwards resting back upon her elbows. Alisha picked up a towel and started to dry herself, smiling.

"Paul...I need your help please," she called out softly.

Theodoric nudged Paul in the side, winked at him, and indicated with a nod he should go over. Paul turned and saw Princess Stephanie still in the water, just her head and shoulders visible. Alisha beckoned him over to hold another towel up to shield her as she removed her wet dress. As he held the towel, Alisha smiled at him as she stood naked momentarily before pulling up the other towel and started wiping herself dry. Her eyes were clear and ablaze with life and beautiful. He could not help himself as he looked at her. She bit her lip playfully, winked at him, and smiled knowing he was looking at her intently. Slowly she stepped nearer to the towel he was holding until her body almost touched it. She stood still just staring into his eyes. Sister Lucy saw Princess Stephanie looking over at the two of them. She then became aware that Sister Lucy was looking at her and she feigned a smile.

"Your turn next...,"Alisha said, smiling, and stepped against the towel.

"Only if you follow me back in," Paul replied, wrapped the towel around her tightly, and pulled her close to him. She looked up at him and smiled as he just held her.

Princess Stephanie just watched them as they stood together.

"Get a room you two...," Theodoric joked loudly and stepped forwards and beckoned Sister Lucy to pass him Arri. "Your turn my dear," he said to her as Paul and Alisha laughed. "We shall keep our backs to you until you are finished and out," he said looking at Princess Stephanie. She nodded in acknowledgement then closed her eyes again and rested back.

Alisha quickly dried off and pulled on the new dress Princess Stephanie had brought down. As she tied off the middle waist cord, making sure her dagger was secured beneath the dresses waistband, she flicked her wet hair and pulled it back. Theodoric handed Arri to Paul and immediately shielded Sister Lucy as she part undressed and entered the water with gasps as the cold hit her. No sooner had she sat down next to Princess Stephanie, than Theodoric stepped back a few paces, then ran and jumped into the pool with a massive splash still fully clothed. All laughed as he came up shouting from the coldness.

Paul sat down with Arri and watched with amusement as Theodoric messed about in the water with Sister Lucy and even splashed Princess Stephanie several times. Alisha shielded Princess Stephanie with a towel when she finally stepped up and out of the water, Sister Lucy fighting playfully with Theodoric to cover his eyes, Brother Matthew watching their every move.

 4 – 54

"That dress suits you better than me," Stephanie remarked looking at Alisha as she wrapped the towel around herself tightly.

"Thank you. I shall return it of course. And I feel so much better after that."

"Yes so do I," Stephanie replied and looked over at Paul sitting with Arri. "I hope you men will likewise bathe whilst you can?"

Tenno looked round briefly but went back to keeping a watchful eye out for anyone else who may come down. Brother Matthew shook his head no and sat down on a natural stone platform.

The morning sun shone down on an exposed area of grass near the tree line where a fallen tree trunk lay outstretched as if reaching out for the water's edge. Alisha went and stood within the large sunbeams that streamed down at an angle. As she stepped into the beams of light, it immediately reminded Paul of their shared dream within the ruined cathedral. Alisha smiled at Paul as she sat down slowly upon the tree trunk and then outstretched her legs and leaned back upon her elbows and raised her head so her face caught the sunlight. She closed her eyes and smiled knowing Paul was watching her. As she raised her right leg, her dress fell slightly revealing her inner thighs partly. She just held the position and enjoyed the warmth of the sun upon her face and legs. Paul cradled Arri and just watched her. He wished he could capture that moment and image forever. She looked so beautiful. She was strong but kind. He knew this woman totally and utterly and vowed he would love her forever...had loved her forever he shrugged to himself. Brother Matthew studied Princess Stephanie as she was looking intently at Paul. He shook his head. Theodoric noticed this as he was helping Sister Lucy.

"Tenno!" Paul called out and stood up with Arri. Tenno turned to face him. "Can you hold Arri whilst I quickly get something?" he asked and handed Arri over to him. Tenno nodded and took Arri. Brother Matthew looked at him, puzzled. Tenno frowned back at him with a hard stare as he cradled Arri protectively.

Quickly Paul ran back to the caravan, located his drawing materials and some blank parchments in a bound folder and ran back to the stream and pool. Alisha sat up wondering what he was doing as Theodoric stripped off his wet clothes revealing the large blue winged symbol tattoo across his shoulders.

"No Ali...stay exactly as you were...please. 'Tis a vision I wish to capture forever," Paul explained and waved that she resume the position she had.

Alisha obliged and leaned back upon her elbows again and looked upwards as Princess Stephanie walked up behind Paul to see what he was doing. She watched patiently as he sketched Alisha using charcoal sticks. After ten minutes, Alisha looked over at him.

"Are you done yet?" she asked as her arms were getting tired.

"Nearly...just a few more minutes," Paul answered as Tenno stepped nearer and looked upon his work as he rocked Arri still. Princess Stephanie offered to take him but he shook his head no and kept hold of him. Princess Stephanie leaned down closer to view Paul's artwork. But she also studied Paul's face as he concentrated.

"What I would give for a man to love me as you love her," she whispered near to his head.

Paul stopped drawing and looked up at her. Her eyes were glazed, full of emotion, but not envy or malice, more the look of love. Her eyes were piercing. She smiled an enigmatic smile. She placed her left hand upon his right shoulder and gently squeezed. Their eyes locked for what seemed like an age before they were interrupted.

"Can I get up now?" Alisha called out.

Princess Stephanie stood up straight and just looked down at Paul for a few moments.

"He has finished. 'Tis a work of true art...and love," Stephanie replied aloud.

As Princess Stephanie turned and began to walk back up the pathway, Brother Matthew looked at Paul glaringly. Tenno stared back at him even harder. Brother Matthew then followed Princess Stephanie quickly. Alisha walked over to Paul to view his work. She knelt down beside him as he presented her the image he had drawn. She kissed him on the cheek.

"You make me look like a harlot with my legs showing like that," she remarked.

Fig. 29:

"No!...this is how I see you...my beautiful wife," Paul answered immediately and lifted up the image so Tenno could see it properly. As he raised the parchment folder, a single small white sheet fell from the pages onto Paul's lap. Surprised, he handed Alisha the parchment folder, picked up the sheet, and unfolded it. It had the symbol of a tiger drawn in Arabic calligraphic style. Immediately he knew it was the symbol that Rashid used.

"What is it...what does it say?" Alisha asked, puzzled, as Theodoric looked around from the side of the pool's edge.

"It reads...here, your Arabic is better than mine," Paul remarked and handed Alisha the parchment to read.

Alisha studied the words carefully before looking up at Paul then Theodoric in turn. She knelt down upon her knees next to Paul and began to read it out.

"We must remember that one determined person can make a significant difference, and that a small group of determined people can change the course of history. Rashid."

Paul looked at her and shook his head, puzzled. She raised her eyebrows questioningly. She was about to say something else when Brother Teric appeared walking down the path fast.

"Ah so here you all hide. Come...we must leave now for Crac," he said, his gaze falling upon Theodoric's large blue tattoo.

With that, Paul stood up, placed the note from Rashid back in his parchment folder, and closed it shut. Alisha held Paul's hand tightly and smiled reassuringly.

೩ Cಖ

It was midday almost by the time the small convoy arrived at Crac de L'Ospital. Alisha sat in the caravan feeding Arri as Tenno pulled it up to a halt just short of the main entrance behind Princess Stephanie's caravan. He looked briefly at Paul sat beside him. The main building material at Crac was limestone and the ashlar facing was so fine that the mortar was barely noticeable. Paul was impressed with the beauty of the castle as they paused the caravan within the walled suburb known as a burgus just in front of the entrance. A stone curtain wall studded with square towers, which projected slightly, defended the castle. The main entrance was set between two towers on the eastern side, and there was a postern gate in the northwest tower. At the centre was a courtyard surrounded by vaulted chambers. Several mounted Knights Hospitaller were leaving for a patrol as Brother Matthew pushed past them trying to enter. Brother Teric pulled up alongside Paul's caravan.

"Young Paul...you have met Gerard of course...but have you met Reynald before?" he asked quietly.

"Not yet...but I think I shall soon," Paul answered as he looked up at the great white castle walls before him.

"Several more Knights Hospitaller started to file past on horseback when one stopped opposite Tenno's side of the caravan.

"Paul...'tis indeed young master Paul is it not?" the knight called out looking across Tenno at Paul.

Paul looked at the knight dressed in his black mantel and chain mail surcoat and helmet bemused for a moment before he recognised him.

131

"Master Roger," Paul said and smiled.

"I see that scar has healed well upon thy face!"

"Yes…thanks to you…but where are you heading…will you be back?"

"Me…I have negotiations to make to secure the release of Balian and others."

"Balian…a good man. I pray you every success in the matter, and speedily so," Paul replied as he heard Alisha open the small window slot behind him.

"Paul, do not leave these walls until I have returned and reacquainted with you… if you would be so kind," Roger asked as he turned his horse slightly to face forwards.

"If that is in my power, I shall of course wait."

"Good…then let my men know you are to be afforded whatever you require whilst here…and make sure they let you use the main guest chamber next to mine for your duration…and no arguing about that," Roger explained and waved briefly with a large smile and started to pull away beckoning his knights to follow behind him. "Sergeant! Put these good people in chamber twelve…please!" he shouted out to an approaching sergeant on foot.

"And do I get the pleasure of this chamber too…so that I may keep a safe watch upon you?" Tenno asked clipped.

"Hey…why not…of course. That was Master Roger des Moulins's after all…and he is in charge here…or supposed to be," Paul replied just as the Hospitaller sergeant approached with a parchment record note board to mark them in.

No sooner had the sergeant taken their details and looked briefly in the rear of the caravan than Paul was looking at the brightly coloured depictions and frescoes painted upon the main internal walls of the steep and curved entrance passage way that led up to the central part of the castle. Paul's mind raced. If Gerard was still here, then so would Stewart be, he thought. Moreover, what should he say of the murder of Turansha's escort? In addition, what of this Reynald whom he had heard so much about? This could prove to be an interesting visit and he was glad to have Tenno by his side.

Tenno steered the caravan along a steep vaulted corridor that led uphill from the entrance that made a hairpin turn halfway along its length. Bent entrances were a Byzantine innovation, but this one was a complex route that ran for nearly 450 feet. Paul noticed that all along its length were murder-holes that allowed defenders to shower attackers with missiles. Anyone going straight ahead rather than following the hairpin turn would emerge in the area between the castle's two circuits of walls and be trapped. To access the inner ward, the passage had to be followed round into the main castle courtyard, where Tenno managed to pull up alongside Princess Stephanie's caravan. The inner courtyard, as seen from the south, caught Paul's eye with its beauty and ornate styling. Large gothic arches and windows fronted onto the courtyard. Adrastos neighed and snorted loudly so Paul quickly stepped down and stroked his head to calm him. Brother Matthew dismounted his horse and quickly tied him up next to several other horses just as Thomas and his men pulled into view with Guy and Percival in the middle of them, where Guy had asked to be positioned on the journey up. Brother Matthew quickly walked over to Princess Stephanie's caravan and knocked upon the door loudly. After a few minutes, she had still not answered the door and he knocked again. Inside, Princess Stephanie looked at herself in the mirror and rearranged the simple gold band around her forehead with a single pearl hanging down from it. She placed a part lace shawl over her head that hung down beside her ears. She sighed and then took in a deep breath, anxious. She placed her hand across her tummy and closed her eyes.

"Lord my God give me the strength to see this all through," she whispered to herself, opened her eyes and composed herself.

Brother Matthew banged on the door harder just as she turned the handle to open it. Gracefully she stepped down into the bright sunlit courtyard, her long sleeved full-length white and gold patterned dress sparkling in the sun. She looked more like a bride about to attend her wedding. She looked at Paul and nodded with a smile. Brother Matthew shot him a look of annoyance almost.

"Is she here...well is she?" Reynald shouted out from behind the caravans.

Tenno looked around to see who was shouting just as Paul leaned out from Adrastos in time to see Reynald walking towards Princess Stephanie's caravan fast, his arms swinging out from his big build, his chain mail surcoat and mantle almost trailing behind him blowing up. Princess Stephanie looked at Paul and feigned a nervous smile. Alisha appeared carrying Arri from the rear of their caravan just as Reynald reached them. He stopped and looked at her momentarily. Immediately Paul headed for Alisha, alarmed. She looked up at Reynald as he stared hard at her, his beard and hair as unkempt as the first time she had ever met him. Princess Stephanie walked towards him gracefully smiling and outstretched her hands for Reynald to take hold of.

"You...what are you doing here?" Reynald demanded to know, looking at Alisha and ignoring Princess Stephanie's open hands.

"She has travelled with me...my good husband," Stephanie said softly and grasped Reynald's large hands. "And before you demand more answers, simply know this... if it was not for her, and her husband, I would be dead, so please...be nice," she explained and smiled at him. Reynald looked at Alisha hard then at Princess Stephanie. He looked her up and down, which made Alisha shudder as she held Arri tightly. "Do I not please you My Lord?" Stephanie asked.

"Yes my woman...you are a fair sight for these tired eyes...and I look forward to seeing more of you later without all that on," he answered and looked her up and down again. "I am glad you live...Gerard has already informed me of the incident at the river crossing. So show me the man who saved you...this great Bull's Head Slayer we all hear so much of. Is it him?" Reynald asked pointing toward Tenno.

Paul stepped closer to Alisha and put his arm around her protectively as Reynald looked past him as if he did not exist.

"No My Lord...this is the man," Stephanie said gesturing towards Paul.

Reynald stood back from Princess Stephanie and looked at Paul. Paul looked back at him and did not break his stare despite Reynald's eyes narrowing. Reynald was certainly broad shouldered and powerfully built Paul noticed just as Alisha had told him. Reynald stepped closer. Tenno immediately jumped down from the caravan and started to walk over fast. Reynald raised his finger and pointed at Paul waving it several times, as he struggled to find whatever words he was looking for. Princess Stephanie pulled Reynald's hand down.

"I think a simple thank you would suffice...and I shall thank you later for we have much catching up to do, my husband," Stephanie said softly and stood closer to Reynald. His eyes flashed from her then back to Paul.

"Boy, we have much to discuss you and I…much," Reynald exclaimed and waved his finger at him again as Princess Stephanie tried to pull him to follow her.

"I look forward to that," Paul replied, Alisha elbowing him in the side as he said it.

Sister Lucy and Theodoric appeared from one of the blacksmith's wagons as it came to a halt behind them. As Theodoric walked over brushing himself down of dust, Reynald looked at him in amazement.

"And just what the fuck…is he doing here?" Reynald demanded to know, pointing at Theodoric.

Theodoric gestured with his hands to his own chest and smiled broadly.

"Who me, Sire…?" he replied.

"Yes, you. You are supposed to be dead. Why did Gerard not inform me of this?" Reynald asked, looking around to see where his own men were and Gerard.

"'Tis many years since last we met…and I see you stand well," Theodoric remarked.

"Aye 'tis that, you ugly bastard no good for nothing," Reynald bellowed out loudly and then laughed, pulled Theodoric close and hugged him. 'Tis truly great to see you, old man…come…I have many questions," Reynald exclaimed and placed his arm around Theodoric and started to walk him towards the main entrance of the castle.

Sister Lucy just shrugged her shoulders as they walked away laughing with each other. Paul looked at Sister Lucy, bemused. She shrugged her shoulders again then nodded toward Princess Stephanie. She stood motionless looking down, her right hand placed across her eyes clearly upset and anxious. She shook her head before taking in a deep breath and looking up again. Alisha stepped closer to her and held her left hand. Sadness and disappointment were evident in Princess Stephanie's eyes. She had not seen her husband in months, and now he just ignores her practically and walks away. She shook her head and sighed heavily.

"Are you okay, my dear?" Sister Lucy asked quietly.

"Yes…but I worry he may know things about who we helped. He has many spies…some too close," Stephanie replied and looked across at Brother Matthew. "But I am sure I will know by the end of this eve…for he is not a man to be immoderate and patient and he will demand an explanation if he is indeed aware," she sighed as Alisha rubbed her arm gently and reassuringly.

Paul could see the deep sadness and worry in Princess Stephanie's eyes. He felt sorry for her and part of him wished he could comfort her somehow, but he knew he could not. She was clearly worried and tense as well as hurt by his apparent lack of interest. Paul recalled a comment his father had once made that there is nothing sadder and lonelier that being in a loveless marriage. The Hospitaller sergeant approached Paul with his parchment record note board followed by two other Hospitallers.

"Sire, these men will take you to your chambers. 'Tis a fair walk…they will assist you to carry your belongings," the sergeant explained.

"I shall show them the way," Stephanie said and feigned a brave smile. "Heaven knows I have been here more times than my own home it feels."

"I will carry what needs carrying!" Tenno stated and made it clear no one else was to. The two Hospitaller knights looked at each other, shrugged their shoulders and simply smiled in agreement. "And do not forget Arri's Clip clop."

Sister Lucy looked back at Theodoric and Reynald as they vanished into darkness as they entered the main entrance doorway into the keep. She shuddered.

Port of La Rochelle, France, Melissae Inn, spring 1191

"That princess so wants that Paul," Sarah stated and shook her head disapprovingly.

"Can you blame her...with a husband like that Reynald?" Miriam replied.

"Paul was an easy man to love," the old man commented and smiled. *"But he was also an honourable man...and he loved Alisha totally..."*

"I have known men who love their wives more than life itself...but still have strayed," the wealthy tailor remarked.

"Yes...for that sadly appears to be the way with man...," the old man replied and sighed. *"But not all men."*

"Yes right. Men such as that old white haired man maybe...," the Genoese sailor stated and shook his head.

"Well you better not be like that," Sarah said and pointed at Stephan. He quickly put his hands up in protest but smiled at her. *"You are dead if you dip it elsewhere,"* she said and folded her arms.

"I feel for the Princess...but did her husband know she had helped that brother of Saladin?" Peter asked.

"I shall come to that. But let me explain that Reynald was staying at Crac de L'Ospital as a staging post only. Gerard was passing through as he and his knights were viewed with much suspicion still by the Hospitallers' Grand Master Roger des Moulins. But it was Roger's intention to secure better relations between the two Orders so had graciously offered them temporary residence and respite within the castle walls," the old man explained as he picked up his last piece of bread from the plate in front of him.

"I have heard this castle is the grandest and best in the whole of Christendom...is that true?" Simon asked.

"Perhaps you should ask our Hospitaller friend here that question," the old man replied and looked at the Hospitaller.

The Hospitaller sat up and coughed briefly before gulping down some rose water quickly.

"Aye 'tis indeed the finest castle I have ever personally seen...a wondrous and strangely beautiful castle. But that is about all I can tell you of it...oh and that I actually carved my initials in the outer curtain wall masonry when I helped build part of it...that is all," the Hospitaller explained.

"I can tell you if you wish more about the castle?" the old man commented.

"If we have time...yes please do tell," Simon remarked.

"We have time enough," the old man replied and finished the piece of bread. After a mouthful or rose water, he continued. *"The site of the castle was first inhabited in the earlier part of the last century by a settlement of Kurds, and recall Saladin is a Kurd...as a result it was known as Hisn al Akrad, meaning the 'Castle of the Kurds'. In 1142 it was given by Raymond the Second, Count of Tripoli, to the Knights Hospitaller...mainly because he could not afford its upkeep and to garrison the strategic site. The Hospitallers began rebuilding the castle in the early 1140s and finished it in its present state by 1170, when an earthquake damaged it, after which they rebuilt the chapel. The Order controlled a number of castles along*

the border of the County of Tripoli, and Crac de L'Ospital is amongst the most important and acts as a main centre for administration as well as a military staging base. That is another reason why and how both Reynald and Gerard were able to make use of it. At its peak, it can house a garrison of around two thousand. Such a large garrison allows the Hospitallers to extract tribute from a wide area. It was called by the Franks Le Crat, but then by a confusion with Karak fortress, Le Crac. Crat was originally the Frankish version of Akrād, the word for Kurds. After the Knights Hospitaller took control of the castle, it became known as Crac de l'Ospital. The castle sits atop a 2,130 foot high hill east of Tortosa, in the Homs Gap. On the other side of the gap, seventeen miles away, is Gibelacar Castle. The route through the strategically important Homs Gap connects the cities of Tripoli and Homs. To the north of the castle lies the Jebel Ansariyah, and to the south Lebanon. The surrounding area is fertile, benefiting from streams and abundant rainfall. Compared with the Kingdom of Jerusalem, the other Crusader states had less land suitable for farming, however, the limestone peaks of Tripoli are well suited to defensive sites. The Hospitallers effectively established a 'palatinate' within Tripoli. Their properties include castles with which the Hospitallers are expected to defend Tripoli. Along with Crac de L'Ospital the Hospitallers were given four other castles along the borders of the state which allows the Order to dominate the area. The Order's agreement with Raymond the Second states that if he did not accompany Knights of the Order on campaign, the spoils belonged entirely to the Order, and if he was present, it was split equally between the Count and the Order. Raymond the Second could further not make peace with the Muslims without the permission of the Hospitallers. The Hospitallers made Crac their main headquarters for all its administration for their new properties, undertaking work at the castle that would make it one of the most elaborate Crusader fortifications in the Levant...and Paul loved the place, which took him by surprise," the old man explained and sat himself back in his chair fully.

Crac de l'Ospital, Homs Gap, County of Tripoli, June 1179

Tenno stepped out of the small side room used as a maid's quarters that adjoined the main bedroom chamber Alisha and Paul had been given to use. Princess Stephanie had been taken to the larger guest chambers directly opposite their room. She had walked in a dignified silence all the way from the courtyard despite being clearly upset by Reynald's total lack of interest in her and concern for what he might know. Thomas had got some of his men to help carry up several of her large travelling trunks. She asked Sister Lucy to join her in her chambers, expressed her thanks to the men, and said she would see Alisha and Paul later over an evening meal.

 4 – 32

"'Tis a sufficient size and even has its own garderobe facility...I will be able to keep guard without invading your privacy," Tenno said as he pulled the door shut and pushed the latch down and stood with his hands behind his back as he looked around the large room.

Alisha was looking out of the arched window down into the inner courtyard as she gently rocked Arri in her arms. It was obvious the castle was a fully functioning military stronghold simply by the number of men and knights, some very brightly coloured with their various banners, about the place in stark contrast to the many black and dark brown clad Hospitallers. The few Templars stood out even more than the colourful Confrere Knights in the white mantels. She turned to look back in the room, which itself was basic but with a very large four-poster hung bed. Paul noted the sophisticated fabric canopy, a 'tester' suspended from the rafters, with ornate bed curtains hanging from it. The curtains hung on rings which ran on iron rods. The heavy draperies around the top edge could be pulled across to keep out the cold. Paul knew from his father that a canopy used over chairs, thrones or classic poster beds was a mark of privilege, and known as a 'canopy of state', but when it extended over the whole bed as this one did, it indicated high honour indeed to a guest. He felt honoured and a little embarrassed that Master Roger had put them up in such a chamber. The expensive draperies were embroidered with small flowers, plant forms and several heraldic devices. The stone floor had no mats or carpets but at least it felt clean and cool. Paul yawned and stretched, tired, and lay himself out upon the high bed, his feet still on the floor.

"I feel for Stephanie...," he stated quietly.

"Really...do you now?" Alisha asked and looked at him.

"Not that way...I just feel her pain and embarrassment. Reynald did not even ask how she was or pay his respects at the loss of her father-in-law."

"That is because he is a brute," Alisha remarked and moved to sit next to Paul on the bed.

"You two tire...I shall leave you in peace whilst I check this fortress out. I shall return when we are called to the dining halls...," Tenno said politely and moved toward the main door to the room. "I would advise sleep while you can."

"Thank you, Tenno," Paul said and raised his hand as Tenno left the room.

"My Lord...a proper bed at last," Alisha said quietly "And I bet with no little occupants already as these Hospitallers are fanatical about cleanliness and hygiene. We have not slept in a proper bed since La Rochelle," she commented, looking at Arri asleep in her arms.

As she spoke Paul's mind was flooded with images of La Rochelle and home... but it was no longer his home. He sighed heavily and for the first time since leaving, he actually felt homesick. He untied his sword belt and placed the sword up by his side and moved his arm around Alisha, rubbing the small of her back.

"You looked unbelievable in that dress at the stream earlier today," he said quietly as he watched her looking at Arri.

"Did I now? Well don't be getting any ideas just because we are in a proper bed tonight," she replied and looked directly at him. "'Tis too soon for such activities," she continued and smiled almost apologetically.

"I know that. I know...and I can wait as long as you need...so long as I have your love," Paul replied and sat up to face her.

"You have always had my heart...and you always shall," she said softly, placed her left hand upon his face, leaned in and gently kissed him upon the lips. "Never doubt that," she said as she pulled back and looked into his eyes. "Never, do you hear?"

Paul just looked back at her. There were times when he could not believe how lucky and blessed he was in having her and now Arri also. Alisha moved up and onto the bed fully and lay down upon her side placing Arri in the middle of the bed, then motioned for Paul to lay down opposite. After just a few minutes, his hand resting upon her hip, his arm across Arri, she was asleep herself. Eventually Paul fell asleep too and the three of them just lay together. None of them heard the light rap on the door as Sister Lucy knocked. After several raps, she opened the door quietly, saw that they were asleep and very gently closed the door again leaving them in peace. Two hours later Paul awoke as Arri made a noise. Alisha was still asleep and had not moved an inch. Being a new mother was taking its toll upon her. He checked Arri was okay and sat up and looked around the room. He felt fortunate he had run into Master Roger and grateful for his offer. Alisha started to mumble in her sleep and twitch her head slightly. Paul rubbed her arm gently but she still flinched. He could see that she was obviously dreaming.

„‟

In her dream, Alisha could not make out where she was, surrounded by nothing but white light. Then suddenly she could see herself lying on the floor of the church giving birth to Arri. She could see her own face screwed up in agony as she pushed. She could hear Sister Lucy and see Paul. She looked sideways and saw Tenno watching as she gave birth. She felt embarrassed. She then heard her father calling out her name. She looked all around but could not see him. 'Ali' she heard him call again. Frantically she looked around. It was as if she was actually standing back in the church seeing everything as it had happened for real again. Then she saw what looked like two figures walk towards her through the light. Suddenly Firgany appeared, smiling, his hands outstretched toward her. Then Raja appeared beside him. She smiled and tilted her head slightly. She looked incredibly well. Alisha gasped in shock and joy at the same time but utterly confused. 'I am dreaming aren't I?' she said to herself, but her father shook his head no. As he did, Alisha could see Paul look up towards him from the floor as if he could see them both. Alisha looked on as Firgany and Raja knelt down beside the Alisha she was watching give birth and was amazed when she saw them support her when she had fainted...or so it appeared. Alisha tried to focus her eyes and looked at her own hands to see if she could see them. She could. In awe she watched on as her father and Raja were behind her until Arri was delivered. She started to cry with emotion seeing the look of joy upon their faces and then the fear in Paul's eyes as Sister Lucy struggled to get Arri to breathe. Then Abi appeared and took him. Alisha followed her to the corner of the church and watched intently as Abi massaged his little chest, and breathed gently into his mouth and nose making his chest rise and fall. She cupped her mouth as she watched on, tears now streaming down her face, her hands shaking uncontrollably. Suddenly she felt the presence of her father and Raja on either side of her. 'He will live and he will be fine,' she heard her father say. 'And you will be a great mother...and we shall be with you always,' she heard Raja say softly without moving her lips. Arri started to breathe on his own and Abi closed her eyes in relief and drew a deep breath herself. Alisha could see her clearly and cried even more and turned to look at her father as Abi took Arri back to Alisha. 'This is no dream, my child...you are simply remembering what happened during the birth...and we were with you all the while. And we shall remain so...your mother and I, always,' she heard her father say. Alisha gulped hard and tried to speak but as she tried, Firgany and Raja started to vanish before her eyes and the bright light all around her started to close in fast. She gasped for air and reached out for them.

ം ൧

"Father!" Alisha called out loudly and sat up, startled, sweat beading down her forehead. "Paul...I saw!"

Paul held her hands quickly as she shook and looked utterly confused. Her eyes were wide and full of emotion. She clasped his hands tightly then looked at Arri still asleep.

"You were dreaming...vividly it would appear. But I am here...okay?" Paul said softly trying to reassure her.

"Paul...answer me this...when I gave birth...did you see anyone standing or kneeling behind me?" she asked hurriedly.

"No...why?"

"Paul...think again. Are you sure?"

"Yes I am pretty sure. Why?" he replied then hesitated as he thought back upon the birth. "But..." He paused again.

"But what?" Alisha snapped.

"Well...I was feeling pretty ill remember...but...I do recall I thought I could see two people holding you up from behind...just a whisper of a voice and the faintest of outlines...but I put it down to me hallucinating...but why?"

"Paul," she suddenly smiled broadly and knelt up on the bed and held both his hands. The pupils in her eyes were incredibly wide. "'Twas my father...and Raja. They were there, beside me all the while. I even saw you look at them...," she explained excitedly and half laughed and half cried at once. A single tear ran down her face. "Paul...don't you see. They are still watching over us," she smiled. "I do not know how...but they are."

Paul looked at her, puzzled, but knew in the back of his mind that he had thought he had seen two people behind Alisha as she gave birth, but he had never mentioned it to her. She pulled him near and wrapped her arms around his neck and hugged him tightly. He placed his arms around her waist and held her as she cried with relief. As she held him, her mind racing, she recalled her father's words from the dream, or whatever it was, that her mother and he would be with her always. She had seen her father and Raja but no one else. This puzzled her for a moment. She squeezed Paul tightly and for the first time in a long while she felt that everything would indeed be okay. She smiled broadly and kissed Paul on the side of his neck. She then sat back upon her heels and quickly pulled out the small linen cloth Raja had given her with her birth name written upon. She unfolded it and read her name...Aalia. She recalled how she had indeed done things her own way and not as her father had wanted her to do. She had followed Raja's advice and it had brought them all safely this far. She looked at Paul again and smiled and quickly kissed him. She held the kiss until a rap at the door drew their attention.

"Come in," Paul said.

"'Tis only I," Theodoric said as he entered the room. "Looking for my lady."

Alisha and Paul looked at each other and laughed. Bemused, Theodoric shook his head as Alisha kissed Paul again.

139

Theodoric closed the door and coughed to get Alisha and Paul's attention. Paul stood up still holding Alisha's hand.

"So Theo...you know Reynald as well!" he remarked.

"A horrid man," Alisha said and swung her legs off the bed to stand up.

"Hmmm. Horrid, perhaps...and yes I know him. Only too well," Theodoric answered and rubbed his chin.

"How so?" Alisha asked.

"'Twas a long time ago. I was party to organising his release from Aleppo. He had great potential back then...and we....huh, we!" Theodoric started to explain but then paused. "We had hoped that during his stay as a captive, he would have learnt much about the Muslim way. His charts, believe it or not, showed three paths he could take...just like yours...but he chose a darker route...sadly for all of us. That is really all I can tell you about him."

"I do not like him," Alisha commented and turned to look at Arri.

"You do not have to like him...but as the old saying goes, keep your friends close, but keep your enemies closer. That rule especially applies to him. Now then, Thomas was asking after you. He is in the Confrere Knight's quarters. I think him and Tenno have some concerns over Percival they wish to discuss. And steer clear of Guy if you can...he is doing nothing but moan at the moment."

"Do we need to worry about Reynald?" Alisha asked, concerned.

"No...not for now at least, but he trusts no one. 'Tis his greatest weakness. But we are all safe with him. But I would urge caution with Gerard...he is perhaps the one to watch closest as I suspect he has an unhealthy interest in both of you."

"And Stewart. Is he here?" Paul asked.

"Aye he is. I am sure you will run into him at some point soon enough."

ॐ ௰

Paul managed to find his way to where many knights not part of the Hospitallers' Order would billet for the duration of their stay at Crac. He had passed through the main chapel taking in its massive barrel vaulted ceiling and brightly coloured frescoes and been directed to a small room that Thomas had been allocated. He was about to knock on the door when Thomas opened it and ushered him inside. The room was small and dark with just one small window. Thomas was dressed in just his chausses and a white cotton shirt, the remainder of his kit and uniform laid out upon a single simple bed. Another bed was similarly laid out with another knight's uniform. Thomas noticed Paul looking at the other bed covered in kit and equipment.

"That all belongs to Percival. He will be here later. He is sucking up to Guy presently," Thomas remarked.

"And Tenno. Where is he?"

"He will be here presently. I left him helping the blacksmith unload some items."

"I hear you have some reservations about Percival. Is that correct?"

"Paul...look at his equipment. Closely."

Paul moved nearer to study Percival's equipment. After several minutes, he looked up at Thomas puzzled.

"What am I missing?"

Tenno knocked on the door and entered, quickly shutting the door behind him.

"Sorry I took my time. I was in discussions with the engineers; they are having problems with their mangonels and that great skien bow outside. 'Twas a simple error to correct," Tenno explained.

Paul looked at Thomas's equipment laid out upon his bed and then back at Percival's. They had what looked like identical items, only the colours of Percival's cloth items being green instead of the brown and black of Thomas's. Both had a segmented Spangenhelm (helmet) with a broad nasal section, mail coif with ventail with soft leather lining, a quilted gambeson, though again Percival's was a dark green, mittens of mail hauberk with slit leather palms, quilted mail-lined chausses and several pairs each of woollen hose and cotton breeches. Percival had an extra set of gilded prick spurs. Thomas lifted them up shaking his head dismissively as he was against using them personally on his horse. He then lifted up Percival's unmarked and free-of-any-decoration leather covered wooden shield with a simple fluted iron boss. Thomas pulled hard upon the shield's enarmes and guige straps.

"I am not sure what I am supposed to be looking for?" Paul explained, perplexed, as Thomas handed him Percival's shield.

"Do not misunderstand me. My men and I like Percival much indeed...and he certainly talks the talk...but something is amiss and we cannot fathom what. That is why I have asked you both here now. Do you have suspicions about him?" Thomas asked quietly.

Tenno looked at Paul blankly and shrugged his shoulders.

"I have noticed that he watches you all very closely. He studies you almost. And apart from one incident when he was about to undress in the field, when you all remained dressed and ready for battle, I see him as a good man. But yes, I too have had a suspicion that all is not what it appears to be with him. I do not know why or what, but something does not ring as totally true," Paul remarked and looked again at Percival's items on his bed.

"I have watched him closely these past days. He learns fast...too fast. But he has no banners, never talks about his past, his family and his equipment. It is as heavily pitted and used as mine. Even his sword! It is worn and has been worn many times in combat...yet Percival states he has yet to see any proper action. So I ask you... what plays out here?" Thomas explained and asked taking the shield from Paul.

"I know not. But I trust my instincts that he is a good man of good intention," Paul replied and looked at Tenno.

Thomas looked at Tenno too for several minutes in silence as he clearly pondered upon both Thomas's and Paul's comments.

"His intentions are good and honourable. We all have a past...some choose to hide it for many reasons. If his intentions are good, honourable and genuine, which I believe they are...then I have no problem with him," Tenno finally stated.

Paul looked again at all of Thomas and Percival's huge amount of equipment and shook his head.

"It beats me how you all wear that and fight at the same time," Paul commented.

"So do I. You should all wear what I wear...much better," Tenno remarked and patted his own lamellar armour upon his chest.

"Can we agree to be on our guard with Percival...please?" Thomas asked.

Paul and Tenno looked at each other and nodded yes in agreement.

Paul left Tenno with Thomas in his room. As he crossed the main chapel again on his way back to Alisha, he stopped to admire the large high vaulted room. It was cool inside. The tower itself served two purposes, as both a chapel and a fortress. Several Hospitallers walked across the room, their shoes echoing out, their black mantels flowing as they walked fast. 'Taqi would have loved this castle' he thought to himself. He laughed as he recalled how Taqi had often told him he had no fear entering a Christian church, despite it being against that of his teachings. If Allah can give me strength and courage by prayer alone to walk into hell itself, I am sure he is strong enough and understanding enough to give me the strength of my faith to enter a building of Christ. Paul shook his head with a little concern as the realisation suddenly hit him that Arri had actually been born within a church. That would be one aspect of his birth that perhaps he and Alisha should keep quiet about. Quickly he moved off and headed up the winding stairs that led to his room. He approached his chamber door and was about to open it when he heard Reynald approach from the other direction talking loudly with someone. Then he heard Gerard reply just as loudly and laugh as they stepped up into view. Paul quickly ducked back out of sight into a small alcove that cut into the wall of Princess Stephanie's chambers.

"I have my suspicions Turansha was helped, and I shall find out," Gerard said as he stopped outside Princess Stephanie's door.

"None of my contacts have heard anything...they simply keep stating that he is already in Alexandria and has been two months past now...," Reynald replied.

"'Tis bollocks...that escort was no escort for a mere merchant trader."

"And you dealt with them I take it?"

"What do you think? But the silly bastards cut their own damn throats before we had time to properly interrogate them," Gerard laughed.

Paul took a deep breath silently and pushed himself further back into the recess. Was Gerard speaking truthfully or had he murdered them himself? Was Stewart a party to it?

"Well my good friend, 'tis time I saw my wife...and relieve some of the tension that has built within me these past months apart from her," Reynald laughed and pulled at his groin.

"Lucky for some...," Gerard replied then looked toward the door of Paul's chamber with Alisha and Arri still inside. "'Tis a pity that Paul lives...for I would not mind a dip into that woman of his," Gerard sneered and wiped his hand across his face.

"Can be arranged most easily," Reynald commented.

Paul's heart started to beat faster. He grabbed the handle of his sword. Anger welled within him at Gerard's remark and concern over Reynald's. Should he confront them both now or bide his time he thought. 'I must get Alisha away from them,' he told himself. 'Use your head!'

"I shall see you at supper, my friend, when you are done with your silly vespers. Now behave yourself. If your loins need release also, you know where Stephanie's maids both reside this eve," Reynald said and winked.

"No...I have more pressing matters to resolve...such as one Turansha and just where the hell he is. You go and have your fun. I shall see you later," Gerard replied and started to walk back the way he had come.

Paul sighed and shook his head as he heard the latch upon Princess Stephanie's chamber door open. He waited and listened as it closed behind him.

"My Lord...finally you see fit to visit upon me," Stephanie said, her voice clear through the small open air vent above Paul's head. Her stomach knotted with tension and she clasped her hands together tightly across her tummy as she stood to greet Reynald.

"Outside, earlier, I could not speak as I feel in front of everyone. You know my feelings for you, I do not need to broadcast that fact aloud do I?" Reynald replied and unbuckled his leather sword belt, took his sword and scabbard and placed it upon a chair against the wall. "Now come here and let me show you how I feel," he grinned.

Princess Stephanie gulped, her throat dry.

"Before you do anything, are you not aware of the passing of my father-in-law for you have said nothing?" she asked and stepped back, the large four poster bed stopping her going any further.

"Woman...I was there...of course I know. And I know your son now has his titles...would you like it if I said meaningless words to you for you know exactly how I felt toward your father-in-law, great as he was, he showed me no respect ever for he did not approve of me," Reynald said and grabbed her left forearm. "Now come to me...for I have missed you and I know you have missed me. You can never resist me eh?" he laughed and pulled her close to him and looked directly down her white and gold dress at her chest. He licked his lips.

"My Lord...my man...," Stephanie coughed and placed her right hand upon his thick bearded face. "You have not washed...surely this can wait until you have and we have eaten?" she said softly.

"Bugger that...I have waited these past months for this for I have missed your body much...if I am filthy and my appearance offends thee, then 'tis good that you prefer it when I take thee from behind," Reynald laughed and quickly spun her around and wrapped his powerful arms around her and started to kiss her neck. "You are my wife...'tis my right."

Paul opened his eyes and shook his head hearing Reynald's comments. He stepped forwards about to leave feeling embarrassed for Princess Stephanie when he heard Reynald speak again.

"I know that somehow...Turansha was in that caravan Gerard rightly attacked... but what I do not know...is how he managed to evade us all...someone within the caravan must have helped him...and I resolve and swear to find out who," Reynald said quietly but laced with menace that was tangible. Princess Stephanie closed her eyes but forced a smile.

Paul's heart skipped a beat as he heard this. Princess Stephanie took a deep breath. She knew that if Reynald was aware that she had been involved, he would have already said so. She knew him well enough on that front. Her mind raced in concern for Alisha and Paul for she also knew he would not shirk from blaming them as a scapegoat and as excuse to get at Paul on Gerard's behalf. She had to play this very carefully. She held his strong muscular forearms and opened her eyes. She sighed and Reynald felt her body relax. He smiled broadly. He pushed her forwards forcing her to rest upon her elbows on the bed. Quickly he lifted up her dress and threw it forwards over her back and head. She gritted her teeth and pulled the dress back off of her head. Reynald eyed her legs and thighs up and down and rubbed his large hands over them and her hips.

"You have a fine arse My Lady…," he said loudly and quickly pulled down her undergarments and pushed them to her ankles. Princess Stephanie sighed and shook her head and leaned her head down between her elbows as Reynald manoeuvred himself directly behind her. Quickly he unbuckled his chausses, dropped them to his knees and pushed down his undergarments and thrust himself against her. "See…see how fast you make me hard…" Princess Stephanie winced as he pushed against her but he could not enter her. "Bloody hell fire woman…you are as dry as the desert…do I not arouse you?" he asked and looked down at her.

"Reynald…It was your sharp wit, humour and intelligence I fell for, not just lust for your body," she replied and moved her hand between her legs to open herself better for him resigned to the fact he wanted, and was going to have, his way with her whatever she said or felt. How much this man had changed, she thought. "I need mental and emotional stimulation from you as much as the physical!"

2 – 7

"Ha! And I always thought it was my massive cock! We can talk afterwards," he laughed then spat in his hand and wiped it between her inner thighs to moisten her. She shook her head as he quickly, almost instantly guided himself straight into her hard.

"Gently…," she moaned and winced in pain as he pushed inside her further.

"What…but you always prefer it this way? What is the problem with you now?" he demanded, his voice getting angry.

"I am with child, you fool," she snapped back and looked back at him.

Reynald hesitated for a moment. Smiled broadly then pulled her hips back against his and held the position for a few moments.

"My child I assume?"

Princess Stephanie swung her left arm around hard and hit his arm.

"Of course it damn well is," she yelled angrily at him and moved forwards away from him.

"No you don't, my woman…," he said quietly and pulled her back against himself and just held her for a few minutes.

Princess Stephanie buried her face into the bed covers and closed her eyes. She could feel him pushing back and forth very gently. Just hurry up she thought to herself. He started to push back and forth faster and harder. She felt his right hand move around the front of her belly and gently hold it there for a few moments. Then he moved it down to her groin and used his fingers to stimulate her. She shuddered as the sensations started to course through her body, even though she did not want them too. With every push forwards, he stroked her more vigorously at the same time. She consoled herself that at least he was not a totally selfish lover. She could feel herself start to climax and a rush overwhelmed her as she started to orgasm. She did not want to enjoy this but her body was reacting to him and she could not resist the sensations. She let out a moan and tried to remain quiet as

Reynald kept moving inside her and stimulating her. He started to moan the more she moaned. She bit the bed sheets in an effort to remain quiet but as she orgasmed again uncontrollably, she let out a long deep moan she simply could not hold in. She then laughed and outstretched her arms as Reynald jerked and pulled her against him as he came. He let out a loud moan and looked to the ceiling.

"God, my Constance, I needed that," he said loudly and just held her against himself not letting her move.

She shook her head sad upon hearing him call out his first wife's name. It was not the first time he had done so...and it would probably not be the last time, she suspected. Her thoughts turned to Paul. She closed her eyes and sighed again.

Paul backed away from the small enclave and walked quietly towards his own chamber door. As he grabbed the door latch, he looked across the corridor at the bigger door into Reynald and Stephanie's chamber. He had heard everything. He felt desperately sorry for her. His mind returned to Gerard's and Reynald's earlier comments regarding Alisha and him. He would need to leave as soon as possible even though Roger had asked him to wait until his return. It was simply too risky. He would never let his sword leave his side, he vowed, never!

℘☾☙

Alisha and Paul declined an evening meal in the main halls and had some food brought to them by Sister Lucy. Paul felt uneasy and Alisha sensed this even though he tried to reassure her all was well. As they were finishing the meal, Tenno entered with some boiled water that had been cooled. He was followed by Thomas, who asked to enter. Sister Lucy started to clear away the meal quickly and made a space at the small table so they could all sit around it.

"I am sorry to trouble you, my friend...but Tenno informs me you wish to leave by early morn at the latest. This is not a problem for my men are ready at a moment's notice...but I do fear the route you propose as it will take us well within Muslim lands," Thomas explained as he sat himself down.

"I am aware of that. But trust me when I say I know we will be protected," Paul replied and sat opposite him.

"Paul...no disrespect, but I have learnt that assurances like that seldom work out here. There are always bandits, profiteers, and raiding parties that constantly attack..."

"I am aware of that. But I fear we are at a greater danger whilst we remain here. Do not ask me how I know...but I do," Paul replied as Tenno frowned at him quizzically.

"Then let me and my men guide you a better route," Thomas said and looked at them both in turn.

"I am all ears," Paul replied and paused as he studied Thomas for a few moments.

"What?" Thomas asked bluntly.

"Why is a man like you not amongst the ranks of the Templars or Hospitallers?" Paul asked.

"Why? Many reasons. Too many that would bore you."

"Well I am interested to know why," Paul shot back.

"Paul...do not be so rude and ask such things," Alisha said softly as she picked Arri up.

"'Tis a good valid question...but my answer may bore you," Thomas replied and smiled at Alisha.

Tenno sat down at the head of the small table and looked at Thomas, waiting for him to speak.

"I am too also all ears," he remarked and pointed to his ears.

"Okay, but I have warned you...first of all, I am lousy at taking orders from people I do not hold much regard or respect for, but more importantly, I make my own destiny and I am not accountable or beholden to any organisation, especially those that commit all manner of grave sins in the name of our Lord...take for example the Templars. There are many good and noble men among them, but sadly men like Gerard are able to use the very system that controls them to bend it to his own personal base desires and ambitions. The Brothers are oft accused of a variety of crimes, which are said to be long-established in the Order such as serious abuses in the admission ceremony, where the Brothers deny their faith in Christ. The Order encourages homosexual activity between brothers and the worship of idols. Now I know this all to be hearsay and fabrication, but these are charges that will ultimately stain the Order and bring it down...they are victims of their own success and fame...whereas me and my men, we wish to remain in the shadows of history. Also Chapter meetings are held in secret. The brothers do not believe in the mass or other sacraments of the church and do not carry these out properly, defrauding patrons of the Order who had given money for masses to be said for their families' souls. What is more, the Templars do not make charitable gifts or give hospitality, as a religious Order should. At least the Hospitallers do, as we can see. The Order encourages brothers to acquire property fraudulently, and to win profit for the Order by any means possible. In Europe the members' lifestyle is much like that of ordinary monks. The Order's rule laid down a strict regime on clothing, diet, charitable giving and other living arrangements. In theory only men can join the Order, but in practice women are also admitted."

"Women!" Alisha said surprised. "I know there are women in the Hospitallers, but the Templars also?"

"Yes, there are. The Order of the Temple was the first military Order, but others soon followed. The Order of the Hospital of St John of Jerusalem was founded as a hospice for pilgrims, but by the 1130s the Hospital was employing mercenaries to protect pilgrims from bandits, that is how we come to be here now. The Hospitallers, as they became known, were soon involved in the defence of the frontiers of the Kingdom of Jerusalem alongside the Order of the Temple. Rather than taking up weapons for a short period to defend Christ's people, the members of the military Orders did so for life. In return, they expected to receive pardon for all their sins and immediate entry into Heaven if they died in action against the enemies of their faith. What shite that is eh, pardon my language," Thomas laughed then continued. "I can tell you now, and yet I am no seer of the future, that there will come a time when all the great courageous and noble acts that the men, women and knights of these Orders will be all but forgotten and only their last failings recounted...for that is the way of people in general. Much resentment is already directed toward the Templars and Hospitallers due to the many generous donations of money and privileges they both receive. But the Templars' and the Hospitallers' legal privileges are what are specially resented. Templars summon their legal opponents to courts in far-off places that they have no hope of reaching by the specified day, so that they are then fined for failing to appear. The brothers have also been taking annual payments from clergy and laity in return for allowing them to share their legal privileges…this is something we know Gerard has pushed particularly hard to fill their coffers. But my biggest fear, as I am constantly seeing getting worse yearly, is that they are now not only wealthy and privileged, but are becoming increasingly proud and treacherous."

"Treacherous I would agree with," Paul interrupted as he thought back upon what he had heard Gerard and Reynald talking about earlier.

"Pride, the first of the seven deadly sins, is already the military Orders' most infamous vice and has been since at least the 1160s. This has become perhaps the Orders' biggest complaint against them, as if it was 'their' sin. Pride has made the Orders jealous of each other and of other Christians, so that they fight each other instead of fighting the enemy."

"Yes…but just who is the real enemy?" Tenno asked bluntly.

"I wonder myself that same question often," Thomas replied. "The Templars' and Hospitallers' quarrels have became notorious and despite the great lengths men such as Roger des Moulins have gone to, to ensure a greater professional working relationship, I foresee a time when it will prove to be a major contributory factor in their final defeat in these Holy Lands…and I for one cannot subscribe to that any longer for I have been responsible for throwing away the lives of too many of my greatest men," Thomas commented and lowered his head, clearly saddened as he recalled the men he had lost. "I know that some people allege that the military Orders are unwilling to fight the Muslims because they are secretly in alliance with them. This seems to be common knowledge out here, but from what we have learnt, the military Orders make alliances with Muslim rulers on occasions, but these alliances are intended to promote the Christian cause, not to hinder it…and I fear they are all in vain and will be met with failure just as before."

"There will always be failures and we shall all pass many failures on our way to success, but when that happens, then we must all do as I was once taught by my father," Tenno said calmly with his arms folded.

"And what pray tell is that?" Thomas asked, his eyes heavy and tired looking.

"You look up, then you get up, and you never give up!" Tenno answered.

Thomas placed his hand upon Tenno's forearm and smiled at him.

"I do not know whence you came…but I know a wise man when I see one. I like what you speak," Thomas commented. Tenno stared at Thomas's hand upon his arm and frowned. Thomas laughed and quickly removed it.

ℴ⅋

Thomas left soon afterwards, helping Sister Lucy to carry away the meal plates and to find Theodoric wherever he had sneaked off too. Tenno took himself to his room that adjoined the main chambers leaving Alisha alone with Paul and Arri. Paul had hoped to relax and feel safer inside the castle but after hearing Gerard and Reynald he felt anxious. As soon as Alisha had fed Arri, cleaned him and wrapped him up again, placing Clip clop beside him in the small crib Sister Lucy had managed to find, she made herself ready for bed. Paul watched her undress slowly and felt aroused seeing her naked, if only briefly. He tried to avert his eyes as she faced him. She smiled seeing him look away awkwardly.

"Just because you cannot touch me yet, does not mean you cannot look at me... or am I all fat and out of shape now?" she joked and looked down at herself naked.

"My Lord no...you are more beautiful now than ever," Paul replied and stood up and walked over to her, immediately placing his arms around her. He ran his hands down between her naked shoulders, placed his palms across the middle of her back and pulled her close. Her skin was smooth and felt cool to touch. As he smelt her dark hair, she wrapped her arms around him and rested her face against his chest.

"I can feel your heart beating," she said quietly.

A thousand thoughts ran through Paul's mind. What was Percival hiding from them all...was Theodoric actually a real Druid himself? This made him laugh briefly. The fact that Princess Stephanie had known his mother, Alisha's vivid dream, Thomas and his men...what was their real motive in escorting him and Alisha. Could he trust anyone? He felt sad for Princess Stephanie and Reynald's disgusting treatment of her. It had felt wrong to listen as Reynald had taken what he desired, but he needed to hear what else he may have said regarding him and Alisha. He began to feel aroused so stood back slightly from Alisha. She looked up at him.

"My Paul...just because you cannot enter me does not mean I cannot pleasure you in other ways," she smiled mischievously and pulled him towards the bed.

"Really...how so?" Paul asked, his heart beating faster already.

Alisha waved her hands and smiled broadly and quickly checked Arri was asleep in the small crib. Paul stood closer, but just as Alisha went to untie his sword belt, a commotion of noise kicked up outside as many horses were heard entering the main courtyard amidst lots of shouting. Paul rushed to the window and looked down. The sky above was darkening but the horizon was still blue with a tint of yellow as the sun was setting. It cast long shadows from the castle walls across the courtyard obscuring most of the mounted knights from view. Several pilgrims, looking exhausted, pushed themselves to one side. Alisha came and stood beside Paul, and they were both able to make out Roger des Moulins enter the courtyard with several other Hospitallers and a knight on a horse covered in the banners of Balian. Several Templars on foot came into view including Guy and Gerard side by side. Paul looked at Alisha in surprise.

"That cannot be Balian surely...not this quick?" Paul exclaimed and started to tie the sword belt around his waist as he headed for the door.

"Paul...be careful," Alisha said quietly and kissed him on the cheek.

ഈ ഇ

By the time Paul reached the main courtyard, Thomas and his men were already there trying to see what all the commotion was about. Many pilgrims came walking in behind the mounted knights. Gerard pushed his way through the gathering crowd and approached Roger des Moulins.

"What is afoot here, Master Roger?" he demanded almost in tone.

"I return with Balian...plus quite a few much relieved pilgrims," Master Roger replied and leaned forwards upon his saddle's pommel and looked across just as Balian pulled his horse into view.

Balian looked tired but otherwise well. He raised his hand to acknowledge Gerard just as Reynald pushed his way through the crowd forcibly. He stopped in front of Roger and Balian looking surprised.

"You only left this very morn. How is this possible?" Reynald asked and shook his head perplexed and put his hands upon his hips.

Paul looked at Reynald. He could not push the image out of his mind of what the man had done to Princess Stephanie and how he had spoken to her. 'A man like him does not deserve a woman like her' he thought. Paul then noticed Gerard was staring at him directly with a look of disdain. Paul looked around to see if he could see Stewart anywhere but he could not.

"Lord Reynald...I see you have made yourself quite comfortable within my walls already," Master Roger said as he dismounted and handed the reins to a brother sergeant at arms. "The Lord works in mysterious ways. No sooner had we set out, than we were approached by representatives of Saladin's forces. They had many Christian pilgrims, as well as Lord Balian. They did not wish to keep them, so they simply handed them over as a gesture of good will."

"What...what horse shit is this? No ransoms demanded...no exchanges. 'Tis unheard of," Reynald said loudly and walked up to Balian.

"'Tis the truth. I am as much surprised as you...but much relieved," Balian said and started to dismount.

"What machinations have you set in motion to secure this? Pray tell what manner of agreements you have made?" Reynald demanded to know.

"Lord Reynald...may I remind you that you are presently here by the grace of God and my Order's hospitality. Please do not abuse that privilege and demand answers to questions we have no intention of responding to," Master Roger said calmly.

"Why...what have you got to hide? Or is it that Saladin is indeed good friends with Balian just as he is with Lord Raymond?" Gerard asked.

"I make no secret that I am well acquainted with Saladin both professionally and personally...so perhaps maybe indeed he has shown me leniency after our debacle at Banius...an action I did warn both of you and Odo not to enter into...but did any of you listen? No! And I am sure these pilgrims will not care this eve by whom or by what manner they were freed...just grateful to be here," Balian explained loudly for all to hear. "Now gentlemen...if you have said your piece...let me retire to clean myself up so that I may present myself properly in the morrow." He then looked across at Paul and nodded with a smile.

Several pilgrims started to clap him whilst others bowed in silence toward him. Master Roger raised a single eyebrow at Reynald and tilted his head slightly as if to ask if he had any further questions.

"Damn right, we shall discuss this further," Reynald said angrily and flounced around and pushed his way back through the pilgrims and Hospitaller knights and sergeants. As Paul watched him leave, Balian approached him and tapped him on the shoulder to get his attention.

"Paul...I must speak with you later...in private. 'Tis important," Balian said quietly.

"Yes, yes of course," Paul replied. "I am most pleased to see you return safe and uninjured."

"I am indeed most fortunate…thank you."

Without any further words, Balian walked off to join his own contingent of knights that had been released with him. Gerard was again looking at Paul with a hard stare, his arms folded. Stewart appeared behind him and whispered in his ear then looked up and saw Paul. Instinctively Paul smiled and waved at him, but Stewart just ignored him and turned his back as Gerard turned to follow him. Paul watched as they disappeared through the many pilgrims. Some were crying with relief. Some were praying. Several young children just stood holding their parents' hands utterly bewildered. Concerned for Alisha and Arri, Paul rushed back to his chambers. As he opened the door, Alisha was sat with Sister Lucy, Theodoric and Tenno as ever watchful near the door.

"We see Lord Balian is returned already," Theodoric commented as he held Sister Lucy's hand.

"Yes…but Reynald and Gerard do not seem best pleased for some reason," Paul answered as he moved to sit next to Alisha.

"No…because they will be expected to return the many prisoners they hold in return without any ransom…'tis all about wealth with them two," Theodoric explained.

"I suggest we all stay together this eve…and prepare to leave early in the morning," Paul said. Tenno nodded in agreement.

A rap at the door drew their attention to it. Tenno leaned across and opened it slightly looking out to see who it was. Balian raised his hand holding a small candle to light his face. Tenno opened the door fully so Paul could see it was him. Balian beckoned Paul to follow him outside. Quickly Paul stood up and left the room and followed him a short distance down the corridor now mainly in darkness save for the few burning night lights spaced out along its length. Tenno stood between the door frame so he could see Paul as well as into the main chamber room.

"Paul…I have a message for you…from Turansha. Do not worry, your secret, and that of Princess Stephanie, is safe with me I promise you that. Your deed in helping him has in turn helped me…It was he who demanded our immediate release and return. There are a lot of people downstairs who owe you and Stephanie a great deal. 'Tis a pity they will never know. Turansha says he shall wait for you past Kerak so that he may in turn help escort you the last leg of your journey to Alexandria in safety," Balian whispered and paused for a few moments as they both heard Reynald raising his voice to Princess Stephanie in their chambers. "And I thank you," he said with a slight bow of his head and held Paul's right hand with both of his. "'Tis a pity you will not be staying in these lands for we are in dire need of men of your calibre."

Both looked back down the corridor as they heard Princess Stephanie yelp! Reynald was shouting something at her they could not make out. Paul moved to walk toward her door but Balian pulled him back firmly and shook his head no.

"Why…you ask…God, you push me, woman!" Reynald was heard shouting. "Why…because you are not Constance…can I not make that any clearer for you! Those bastard Muslims stole away my life with her…and for that they will pay. I shall never rest until every last one of them is done away with. Do you understand that part?"

Balian looked at Paul and shook his head again. They listened as Princess

Stephanie spoke with him trying to placate him and calm him down though they could not hear what she was saying. Tenno stepped closer to her door and looked at Paul and raised his hands as if to ask if he should intervene. Both Paul and Balian shook their heads no.

"Come...release your tension and anger within me," Stephanie said a little too loudly.

Balian looked to the floor feeling embarrassed for her.

"On your back then this time...and make it worth my while," Reynald was heard saying, his voice laced with a meanness that shocked Paul.

Within moments both Princess Stephanie and Reynald were grunting and moaning as both Paul and Balian walked back down the corridor as quietly as they could. As Tenno opened the door wider for Paul to enter back into the room, Sister Lucy paced up and down. She looked through the open door at Princess Stephanie's door, concerned for her.

"That is not love...Lord so help me I would cut that man's balls off!" she said angrily.

Tenno's eyes widened in surprise as he heard her say this. Balian sniggered at her comment as Alisha looked on in astonishment at her remark.

"That's my girl," Theodoric laughed loudly.

Paul put his finger to his lips for them to be quiet.

"No I shan't be quiet. Perhaps if the arrogant bastard hears us, he will know that we know he is a complete shit," Sister Lucy said loudly.

"Sssssh...," Paul said as Balian raised his hand farewell and quickly and quietly walked away as Tenno rapidly closed the door as quietly as he could.

"That woman is a true princess and she deserves better than that," Sister Lucy said angrily and huffed with frustration.

"She will feel far worse if she knows we can all hear them," Theodoric remarked and rubbed his hand upon her shoulders.

Port of La Rochelle, France, Melissae Inn, spring 1191

"Oh my Lord above...," Sarah said resting her head forwards in her hands.

Ayleth blushed at hearing the old man explain in detail what had happened. Miriam shook her head as the Templar held her hand tightly.

"I will never treat you like that...I swear," he said to her in a gentle manner that made his brother look at him.

"Well...of course you will not for you are soon to leave," Miriam shot back, the hurt of acknowledging that fact clear in her eyes.

The Templar sat up straight and put his arm around her and pulled her closer.

"Miriam...I think it safe to say, I shall not be leaving your side any time soon," he explained and smiled at her.

"Do not tease me!" she snapped and slapped his arm.

"I am not teasing you. Ask him," the Templar stated and nodded towards the old man.

The old man smiled at her.

"The choice has been given to him should he wish it. That is all I shall say...but I suspect very strongly he has made his choice," the old man explained.

The Hospitaller looked back and forth at the pair of them, puzzled.

"Well...that Reynald...I do not care what excuses you make for him...he is one nasty piece of work," Simon remarked, shaking his head disapprovingly.

"As I said before...he was certainly a troubled soul...but Princess Stephanie did feel very strongly toward him," the old man explained.

"So this Balian knight...he was released as a direct consequence of Paul and the Princess helping Turansha to safety?" Gabirol asked.

"Yes. But also because Balian was indeed a good friend of Saladin. That was the way things were in Outremer at that time, and it would have been very easy for both Balian and Count Raymond to side with Saladin."

"The whole land sounds messed up to me!" the wealthy tailor remarked.

"So what happened? Did Gerard and Reynald start trouble the following day or did they manage to leave early enough?

"Not quite. Paul spent most of the night awake unable to settle. He felt desperately sad for Princess Stephanie and hoped she was okay. Twice more during the night they could all hear as Reynald had his way with her again," the old man explained.

"The poor woman. 'Tis no way to be treated...like a piece of meat no less...and pregnant," Sarah said shaking her head in dismay at his actions.

"I think that Sister Lucy had the best idea," Ayleth commented shyly.

"Hey, some women would love to have a man that could do that several times in one night...but not like that," Sarah replied and picked up a knife and waved it pretending to slice the air.

"Really my dear?" Stephan asked and frowned mockingly.

Sarah put the knife down and blushed. The old man laughed then continued.

"Neither Tenno nor Theodoric could sleep and both whispered about their many adventures from their past as they sat in the small side room, Paul eventually joining them in the early hours. Paul raised the question again about Theodoric's connection with camels and Sister Lucy, but again he refused to divulge what it all meant. They could still hear Princess Stephanie and Reynald talking until the early hours also. At one point Reynald did hold her and apologised and asked for her forgiveness. He explained that he had not meant what he had said about Constance, his first wife. Whom it must be admitted, he never once hid the fact that he had always loved her and always would even before Princess Stephanie married him and after they were betrothed. Reynald was a man filled with at times an uncontrollable anger and frustration. He simply did not know how to deal with his emotions. It was just the way he was made. But they all heard him when he cried and Princess Stephanie consoled him in the early hours just before dawn."

"She must be a saint that woman," Sarah said and looked at the old man.

"She certainly had the patience of one. Reynald vowed he would show her more attention...especially as she was going to give him a son or daughter, an heir no less...but only after he had finished business in the County of Tripoli and the Principality of Antioch," the old man explained.

"And like most women, she believed him I bet...," Sarah remarked sarcastically.

"What other options did she have?" Ayleth asked.

"Cut his balls off," Sarah stated. Stephan nearly choked upon hearing her words.

The old man smiled at her remark and smiled even more as she started to blush heavily with her face turning a bright red.

"I think I am in love with this Princess," Simon sighed and looked forward as if daydreaming. Gabirol and the Genoese sailor both looked at him.

"Well she clearly forgave him for his behaviour," Gabirol remarked.

"Forgiveness does not excuse his behaviour...but Princess Stephanie knew and understood that forgiveness prevented his behaviour from destroying her heart," the old man remarked quickly.

"So what happened come the morning?" the farrier asked.

Crac de l'Ospital, Homs Gap, County of Tripoli, June 1179

The main courtyard was still in shadow as the morning sun had still to breach the top of the ramparts and walls. Paul helped Alisha, carrying Arri, step up into their caravan as Tenno adjusted the straps around Adrastos and the harness that tethered him to the caravan. Theodoric was helping Sister Lucy climb up upon the second of the blacksmith's three carts when Balian approached them cleaned and dressed in a change of clothes. He looked a lot better than he had the night before. Thomas walked up leading his fully armoured horse alongside with his men following him.

"I have a route planned that will take us all the way to the coast and down to Darom past Gaza missing Jerusalem and the main King's Highway, with all its tolls. But it will take us some time," Thomas said to Paul just as Balian reached them.

"Before you go, I strongly urge you to take the eastern route direct to Kerak...all the way south. And take the princess with you. Trust me on this matter for I have been given assurances you will not be attacked. All the freed pilgrims yesterday were given guaranteed safe passage if they followed that path. It was part of my release agreement," Balian explained.

"How can an agreement be made when no ransoms were exchanged...surely you must consider it a possible trap and that they shall all be ambushed on the route?" Thomas said concerned.

"Thomas...I beg you trust me on this matter when I say I know that if you take this route, there will be those who will ensure your safe passage all the way...for it has been arranged and agreed," Balian explained.

Alisha held her position at the stop of the rear steps listening to what they were saying.

"Hmm. If you are wrong on this matter, it is our deaths you are signing us to," Thomas said, incredulous.

"I promise you...you will reach Crac de Moab in Kerak," Balian said assuredly.

"No! You cannot leave yet!" Stephanie called out as she ran across the courtyard still dressed in her night shawl and chamber robe. Out of breath she leaned against the caravan's rear wheel. "No...you cannot leave...I insist...please....I shall beg if I must!"

Alisha stepped down from the steps and placed her hand upon her reassuringly.

"What panics you so?" she asked softly.

"I must return to my home in Kerak...I have much to sort out for my son and his affairs as well as put in order any outstanding matters of my father...but I could not bear the journey south alone. Please...I beg of you wait until I leave," Stephanie pleaded.

Sister Lucy and Theodoric walked over seeing the look of concern upon her face.

"Oh no you don't!" Gerard shouted loudly as he walked down the steps of the main entrance to the hall. "None of you are going anywhere until we have all had a little chat...about a certain brother of Saladin..."

Thomas and Balian both turned to face him as he walked towards them flanked by Stewart, Brother Matthew and Brother Teric behind. Princess Stephanie drew a sharp intake of breath just as Reynald appeared at the smaller side door that led up to their chambers. Thomas nodded at his men to be ready as Tenno walked up and stood beside Alisha. Paul noticed Gerard had several scrolls rolled up tightly in his left hand. Several of the pilgrims who had remained outside sleeping on mats started to wake up and some stood up.

"Master Gerard...you have my scrolls I see. Have you come to return them to me?" Paul asked politely.

"Do not patronise me or show belligerence, boy!" Gerard said loudly, clearly angered, and stopped just a few feet in front of Paul.

"Surprised you know such words," Thomas commented calmly and with a smile whilst staring at Gerard.

"These...these charts....they show clearly where your sympathies lay...I have had them read and interpreted," Gerard snarled at Paul.

Paul looked past Gerard and at his brother. Stewart looked at him briefly then looked away shaking his head. Reynald sauntered over slowly as he adjusted his belt around his open white cotton shirt. Paul thought it strange to see him without his usual armour.

"Then, respectfully, your reader is a bad interpreter," Paul replied politely.

"Paul...do not anger the man," Alisha said quietly.

"Too late for that, young lady...These charts, they are not what I was after...but they show your connection to Muslims is all too clear and defined. It also has sigils of Saladin himself...so you tell me right here and now that you had nothing to do with helping to aid the escape of Turansha, for I know he was in that caravan," Gerard demanded as Reynald listened in, bemused.

"Hmm, Saladin's banner...or sigils did you say? That one is new to me I must confess...and tell me...as I know full well, you murdered the Muslim escort...under what pretence was that as it is not under the agreed terms and articles of war now is it?" Paul replied as Alisha squeezed his hand tight with apprehension.

"Articles of war! What horse shit do you spout, boy?" Gerard demanded angrily.

Tenno stepped forwards and looked at him, his eyes narrowing even more.

"Clearly you have read none of them then?" Paul replied calmly.

"Do you deliberately try to provoke me?" Gerard asked and waved the scrolls about near his face.

"No not at all...but I fear you do try me," Paul answered and pushed Alisha back gently behind him and placed his right hand over his sword handle.

Gerard's eyes immediately looked at his hand then back at Paul.

"You would not dare?" he snarled, his eyes widening in fury.

"Would I not?" Paul replied quietly but confidently. "And if you had taken your time to read those parchments properly, if they are to be believed, 'tis after all just words and symbols are they not, then you would also have seen that there are three paths of each. If it is my destiny that my path should cross Saladin's, then who knows that it does not mean that I am the one who will kill him...eh?" Paul commented and stepped forwards toward Gerard. In his stomach he felt sick to the core but he was not going to let Gerard see that.

"He has a good point, my friend," Reynald said with a smirk. He then motioned with his head for Princess Stephanie to come and stand beside him. Slowly she moved across to him looking at Paul intently as she went. "So, my woman...you wish to travel home with these people...yes?" he asked whilst looking at Paul directly.

"I know these people...very well and I have travelled far with them already. And what better protection could I have than the man and people who have already saved me twice thus far...?" Stephanie explained and held Reynald's hand. "My Lord...I will be safe with these people...and, look, Thomas there and his men are veterans of some fourteen years in these lands. What better escort could we ask for...to protect me and...and our soon to be child?" she explained further and looked into his eyes.

Reynald looked at Gerard and raised his eyebrows waiting for Gerard to reply. Gerard said nothing.

"My friend, she has a point." Reynald stated.

"This is utter bollocks...bollocks. I know he and perhaps even your good lady there mock us behind our backs having helped Turansha...you mark my words," Gerard said angrily, his tone deeper and laced with rage and menace.

"My friend, be careful of what you say and whom you accuse of such a treasonous matter...'tis also my wife you accuse," Reynald said looking at Gerard scornfully.

Gerard stared at Paul for several minutes. Theodoric coughed loudly.

"Well look, the sun comes up," he said with a broad smile and pointed to the first long beams of sunlight passing through the battlements as the sun broke fully on the far horizon.

Princess Stephanie looked pleadingly at Reynald and she rubbed her other hand over her stomach.

"Fine. 'Tis agreed then, you shall travel with them to Kerak. But you will need an escort of Templars too...you have no problem with that do you?" Reynald ordered and looked at Gerard. "And take that Guy fellow with you before I throttle him myself...wherever he is."

Gerard shook his head in defiant protest.

"As you wish...My Lord...on your head be it," Gerard finally replied and turned around and pushed Stewart and Brother Teric aside hard. After a few paces he stopped, looked at the scrolls still in his hands then threw them down upon the floor and carried on walking.

"Thank you...thank you so much," Stephanie said and leaned up and kissed Reynald on the lips quickly and then smiled at him.

Paul relaxed as the tension left his body. Theodoric patted him on the back as Alisha looked at him. She was proud of him and that he had again stood up to Gerard. She then realised that Stewart was staring at them. She smiled at him but as Paul looked across toward him, he quickly turned his back and followed off after Gerard. Brother Teric came over.

"I shall delegate a troop of Templars to escort My Lady," he said to Reynald.

"Good…and if your master agrees, I would like you to go with them…and take an entire squadron if you have to, to protect the mother of my unborn," Reynald ordered and placed his arm around Princess Stephanie's shoulders and pulled her against him.

"You should smile more often…it suits you greatly," Paul remarked.

"Does it now? You should speak less," Reynald shot back but still smiling. "And you, young lady…it would seem our Lord has plans that constantly cause our paths to cross. So in the nicest way, I hope this will be the last time we do so," he said to Alisha.

"Amen to that," Theodoric said all too loud as everyone heard him. He smiled quickly.

"We can be ready to leave within the hour," Brother Teric said and looked at Thomas and Tenno in turn to confirm.

"An hour…good, that gives us some time to say goodbye," Reynald commented and pulled Princess Stephanie around and ushered her towards the steps leading to their chambers. Princess Stephanie glanced round quickly smiling broadly at Alisha and Sister Lucy.

Paul walked over to the parchment scrolls, picked them up and gently rolled them. He caught a glimpse of Stewart as he disappeared through the main entrance doorway. 'Why is everything out here such a constant battle?' he asked himself as he looked at the scrolls in his left hand. He sighed just as Alisha came and stood beside him aware of his sadness because of Stewart.

Suddenly an old lady dressed all in black approached them. She tugged at Paul's cloak gently. Paul immediately recognised her as the old fisher woman who sat at the harbour in La Rochelle and who had also given him and Alisha a pressed lily flower on their wedding day. Both were surprised to see her as she bowed gracefully to them. The little girl from La Rochelle then ran up to them from amongst the other pilgrims. She had grown, but not much.

"How…how did you come to be here?" Paul asked, surprised at their presence.

"Same as you…by ship and by land. Then we got caught up with these pilgrims… but by the grace of our Lord and mercy upon us, we were released along with Lord Balian…and now we find ourselves here. I knew 'twas you the moment I saw you both…I told you once before, they watch you…and they watch you still," she smiled and just turned around and ushered the little girl to follow her. The little girl smiled, bowed at Alisha and then ran after the old woman.

"Hmmm…well that was certainly odd," Theodoric exclaimed as he watched the old woman and little girl walk away back into the crowd of pilgrims.

Chapter 30
Sacrament of Tears

Paul sat at the front of the caravan with Tenno waiting patiently having formed up on the wide section of road a short distance from the castle just past the village that overlooked the valley and castle itself below. Princess Stephanie had still to arrive along with the main troop of Templars before the convoy could move off. Theodoric was talking and laughing with the blacksmith beside his cart. It was good to see the blacksmith laugh again. The loss of Tara had naturally hit him and his wife very hard. Theodoric and Sister Lucy had spent many hours with him and his wife since she had been killed, becoming firm friends. They also gained exclusive use of the blacksmith's spare covered second cart. By midday, Tenno was impatient to get moving as was Thomas and his men unlike the many pilgrims sat beside the pathway resting waiting patiently. Brother Teric rode up and stopped alongside Tenno.

"She will be with us in about another half an hour. Reynald I am afraid is doing what he did last eve and making the most of her...but I shall tell the others they are changing horses," he explained quietly, being discreet, then moved along the column to inform the others of the delay.

Tenno released the main brake control lever and reapplied it again firmly as Paul pulled out his drawing folder and immediately started to sketch the castle as they looked down upon it.

Fig. 30: .

He was just putting the finishing touches on his drawing when Tenno pointed towards a large column of knights approaching from the south kicking up a lot of dust behind them as they crested the brow of the hill. Paul made out the banner of the Templars' black and white Beauseant fluttering at the front as the column drew nearer. Several pilgrims stood up alarmed thinking it was a Muslim fighting force until Brother Teric pulled up alongside the caravan again and reassured them. Within moments, the lead element of the convoy slowed to a trot and then pulled up just in front of Brother Teric. With dust swirling everywhere, Paul and Tenno had to cover their mouths briefly until it settled. The lead knight pulled the cloth cover down from over his face. His Destrier war horse was covered in white sweat lines. They all looked filthy from their hard ride and all were travelling in light fighting order with no coverings on their horses or armour at all. Paul noted they carried several variations of shields and patterns. Some had the top half black and lower section white, whilst others had the opposite and a little black cross upon the white. He had never seen this format before.

"Brother Teric...'tis good to see you," the lead knight said and smiled as he leaned forwards upon his saddle pommel.

"Brother Jakelin de Mailly no less...you must have travelled hard for I thought you were still many days' ride away," Brother Teric replied.

"We have. We were given urgent orders to proceed to meet Princess Maria Comnena to help her secure the release of her husband Lord Balian and also Baldwin of Ramla. 'Tis why we travel light."

"You need not worry about Lord Balian for he is already free. He resides this very hour in yonder Crac resting," Brother Teric explained and pointed toward Crac de l'Ospital.

"Really...how so? We were not informed of this," Brother Jakelin replied looking a little confused.

"'Twas only last eve he returned. Not exactly sure how or why yet," Brother Teric started to explain then looked at Paul directly. "But either way, he is one less person you need not worry about."

"'Tis good news. Princess Comnena will be most pleased," Brother Jakelin remarked and looked at Paul. He frowned and looked at him for a few moments. "Young Sire...do we know each other?"

"I...I do not think so, unless you have been to La Rochelle...," Paul replied.

"Hmm...You look indeed very familiar to me. I never forget a face," Brother Jakelin remarked looking at Paul intently then turned to look at Brother Teric again. "So we hear you have the Bull's Head Slayer travelling with you. Would be an honour to meet him...he has done us all a great service."

"You just have," Brother Teric replied and gestured towards Paul with his open hand.

"Really...and one so young. Pray tell what is your trade or occupation?...for your reputation travels well in advance of you."

"I...I do not have a trade or occupation yet...and it was just luck that saved me when I confronted the Bull's Head...whatever you all call him. Just luck," Paul answered.

"Luck...is that what you call it? That man had been a thorn in all our sides...I think that should you ever require an occupation...you may find your calling and profession within our ranks for we have sore need of men like you," Brother Jakelin explained as he drew his horse nearer. He took off his riding glove and outstretched his hand toward Paul. "I offer you my respects. You have the look about you of a professional soldier already. You ever wish to serve, just seek me out."

      5 – 10

Paul leaned across from the caravan seat and took Jakelin's sweaty hand and shook it firmly just as Alisha stepped into view carrying Arri. Both looked down at her.

"Thank you kind sir but he will not be taking up your offer. For one he is married and secondly, he has other priorities," Alisha said confidently.

"Ah...a woman who is not afraid to speak her mind openly. You must be the great Bull's Head Slayer's beautiful wife we have also heard so much of...the stories do not do you justice," Brother Jakelin said and part bowed his head and smiled. Several of the other Templar knights looked at her.

"Stories exactly," Paul said and looked at Brother Jakelin.

"This land, and these people...they need stories to keep them going...to give them hope and you two I am afraid are part of that system whether you wish it or not. Embrace it and use it to your advantage whilst you can, for it will soon vanish and become just another forgotten tale just as quickly," Brother Jakelin explained and smiled at Alisha. He paused for a moment as he looked at Paul again. "I do know you somehow...but until I remember, I shall bid you safe passage on your journey south, and you, good lady," he nodded at Alisha. "Now brother Teric, is Master Gerard here?"

"Yes...with Lord Reynald also."

"Oh marvellous...would you like to swap Orders?" Brother Jakelin joked as Brother Teric shook his head no. "'Twas an honour meeting you...both. I pray our paths shall cross again. And being married does not preclude you from joining us... for a term. Half my men behind me are still married," Brother Jakelin explained.

"But I thought you could not be...," Paul remarked, puzzled.

"Manpower shortages...and so long as a man has his wife's blessing, he can sign up for a term of service...perhaps you should consider it," Brother Jakelin replied then put his glove back on and raised his hand for his column to follow him. "Till we meet again," he said aloud and started to move off past Brother Teric, who bowed as he left.

"Do not even think about it as you will never get my blessing to join an Order," Alisha said quietly as she looked up at Paul. "We are you Order," she then smiled and raised Arri up so he could see him.

Paul looked back as the column of Templars set off for Crac and watched them as they had to move to one side as Princess Stephanie's large caravan came into view being pulled by two large Shire Horses closely followed by Guy sat upon his brightly coloured armoured horse and several other just as brightly coloured and armoured mounted knights from his entourage.

Port of La Rochelle, France, Melissae Inn, spring 1191

"So how come stories about Paul and Alisha were spreading so fast?" Simon asked.

"In Outremer there was always a sense of expectation of the arrival of some great knight or great king or a Messiah figure that would transform everything. The slightest character who showed any display of being different was seized upon and with fast couriers travelling the King's Highway and using heliographs, messages and stories of the death of the almost mythical Bull's Head bandit generated a massive amount of storytelling and in some cases great fabrications," the old man explained.

"That Reynald...utter brute," Ayleth remarked and bit her fingernail as she thought about what she had heard.

"Grief and loss can change a person utterly. With the loss of his true love, Constance, a part of Reynald died too. I am not condoning what he became or excusing his behaviour, but I have known far worse men...and women!" the old man sighed.

"Did it take them long to travel the eastern route then?" Gabirol asked.

"Well...as Balian had been assured, they would not be attacked by any of Saladin's forces...but that did not mean other bandit groups could be counted upon to keep the promise by Turansha. But the first few days of travelling was certainly hard for the many pilgrims on foot who accompanied them...and Theodoric was taken ill. The many scars and scabs upon his face had long since healed but something laid him low on the first day and he had to take himself away to rest in the back of the blacksmith's second covered cart. Sister Lucy had to wake him several times to take water, as he was sweating uncontrollably. He was too weak to even eat. The days had been long and drawn out and matters made worse by the searing high temperatures. Alisha and Princess Stephanie had spent most days together in her larger caravan with her two maids. The entire caravan and walking pilgrims eventually pulled up at a way station watchtower fort, part of an old Roman network. It was manned by a small contingent of Templars and other confrere land knights. It was thirty-five miles to the next fort so Brother Teric knew the next day would prove very hard going. Paul and Tenno had taken it in turns driving the caravan, Tenno always looking out for any signs of potential threat or danger, whilst Thomas and his men kept riding out ahead and to the sides constantly scouting the area. Brother Teric said that they had been a most welcome help," the old man explained. "But that night turned out to prove uneventful other than the worry about Theodoric's worsening condition. By the morning, despite Theodoric still sleeping, Sister Lucy agreed they should travel on and so they did starting off very early. Brother Teric pushed the column long and hard that day to reach the larger watchtower fort at Umm Quasi."

"Was Theodoric really ill then?" Sarah asked.

"Ill...I am not sure you could call it being ill. 'Twas a fever of sorts...but not one they could understand or seem able to treat. 'Tis why Brother Teric thought it best to reach Umm Quasi as several Hospitaller surgeons were garrisoned there."

"You mentioned helio staffs or graphs...what are they?" Ayleth asked.

"They are small pieces of mirrored glass used to reflect the sun in a sequence that spells out letters. Each day the sequence is changed so they have to be matched with the correct table. The King's Highway was a major road that entwined its way through mountains from Celician Armenia all the way in the north to Cairo in the south, but there was also the eastern route the Romans had built that Alisha and Paul were following. The weather could change fast up in mountains, even to snow and sleet. Kerak, Princess Stephanie's main home,

had grown wealthy charging road tolls to all that passed on the eastern route through their lands. The heliographs could send signals from the north to the south in under twelve hours and all the castles and outposts were set within a day's ride of each other and within line of sight for signalling so if needs be they could use flaming torches instead of the mirrors," the old man detailed as Ayleth listened intently.

"Is this Kerak the same Kerak as mentioned in the Bible?" Gabirol asked.

"Yes...yes it is," the old man replied.

Simon looked at Gabirol, puzzled, and shook his head and raised his hands as if to ask him a question. Gabirol looked at him and smiled.

"Simon...you should read your Bible properly," Gabirol remarked. "'Tis the same Kerak that Noah was sent to, to warn all those present that it would soon fall as per the prophecies foretold by Isaiah."

"Oh...so it's got some history behind it?" Simon replied just as Gabirol and the old man nodded yes in agreement.

"How long would it take them to get from Crac to Crac de Moab in Kerak then?" Peter the stonemason asked.

"Two weeks...as the roads are pretty good that way...so long as they did not run into any trouble," the Templar answered.

"Roughly two weeks, yes, especially as they had many pilgrims travelling on foot with them so they could only do the maximum of twenty miles per day. It took them just five days to reach Umm Quasi, again only because Brother Teric pushed them so hard on that last stretch travelling an extra fifteen miles...but the road they were travelling along was a very good one, well made and maintained. It enabled Reynald fast access up and down the entire region, as well as Saladin likewise...the ancient King's Highway itself," the old man explained.

"I thought the King's Highway was along the coast," Simon stated and moved in his seat.

"No, the main route, that many have and do confuse with the King's Highway, was the road named the Via Maris meaning the Sea Route. But the original King's Highway as mentioned within the Bible itself was an excellent piece of Roman engineering...though some argue they simply built over an older route that was once part of the ancient paths of the dragons..."

"I have travelled many roads in my time, and I can tell you that much of the King's High-way is indeed a great road to travel upon...'tis in the main nearly thirty feet wide most of the way and paved," the Templar stated as his brother nodded in agreement.

"Yes, the Romans were indeed experts at surveying and building roads," the old man continued. "They would plan out a strategic route and remove any obstacles in its path. Then they would dig a trench about three feet deep and ten to twenty-five feet wide, depending upon the importance of the road, and then build it in four layers...though if you dig deep enough on their oldest roads, you will find evidence of yet far older pathways...though no one knows who built them! The deepest portion of the trench was filled in with a layer of large stones tightly fitted together. This was strategic in preventing puddles and keeping the roads from freezing, which caused cracks. The second layer was filled with smaller stones compressed together and filled with opus caementicium (concrete). The third layer was filled with gravel and flattened out smoothly. The fourth and last layer was a pavement of large smooth stone slabs. It must be noted that every major road had kerbs and drainage ditches. The largest roads were in Rome and on its borders, to bring a sense of awe to anyone from the outside. They sometimes reached fifty feet wide."

"So do all roads lead to Rome?" Ayleth asked smiling beautifully.

"I guess you could say that," the old man answered. "It has oft been said, 'all roads lead to Rome' and this was certainly correct in the time of Jesus. Actually all roads led 'from' Rome because the Roman Forum (Romanium) marked the starting point and every road was measured from it, from a gilded pillar that Caesar Augustus had placed there. The roads were clearly marked with milestones from the 'Eternal City'. No pilgrim or merchant can ever forget that they journey upon an imperial road. The Roman mile was a thousand paces and it was marked with a milestone; mille is Latin for thousand. As for the Via Maris route you mention, it is still one of the most important trade routes in the Middle East, and especially so in far more ancient times, and the Latin term means 'Way of the Sea'. It is even referenced in Isaiah 8:23 in the Tanakh and in the Christian Old Testament it is Isaiah 9:1, as 'Derech HaYam' or 'Way of the Sea'. The Latin name comes from the Vulgate, the Latin translation of the New Testament, in Matthew 4:15. The term 'Via Maris' comes from the Romans and hence the terminology 'Via Maris' tends to be an exclusively Christian reference to the Sea Road. Other names for the Derech HaYam, Via Maris include 'Coastal Road' and 'Way of the Philistines'. From the coast to Damascus, the route is called the Trunk Road. The 'Way of the Sea' is one of three major trade routes in ancient Israel, the Via Maris, Ridge Route, and the King's Highway. It is situated from Galilee in the north to Samaria to the south, running through the Jezreel Valley. At the Philistine Plain, the Way broke into two branches, one on the coast and one inland, through the Jezreel Valley, the Sea of Galilee, and Dan, which unites at Megiddo, or as we know it 'Armageddon'. The location of Megiddo in relation to the Via Maris explains why Megiddo was a very important route for travel and a trading city in ancient Israel. The Way of the Sea connected the major routes from the Fertile Crescent to Mesopotamia, from Egypt to Celician Armenia. The road was the main thoroughfare running north to south from the Sinai along the coastal plain and, as said, through the Jezreel Valley, Beit Shean and on until Damascus. Throughout the centuries, once the Jews were exiled from Israel, the Jezreel Valley became abandoned and the area became an infested swamp. But the original eastern King's Highway was a very ancient trade route that was important in Biblical times. The Highway started in Egypt and went up through the Sinai Peninsula over to Aqaba and up the eastern side of the Jordan River to Damascus and the Euphrates River. The King's Highway is mentioned in the Bible in many places, such as Numbers 20:17–21 as an example. Numerous ancient states, including Edom, Moab, Ammon, and various Aramaean groups, depended largely on the King's Highway for trade. The Highway actually began in Heliopolis, Egypt and from there went eastward to Clysma, through the Mitla Pass and the Egyptian forts of Nekhl and Themed in the Sinai desert to Eilat and Aqaba. From there the Highway turned northward through the Arabah, past Petra and Ma'an to Udruh, Sela, and Shaubak. It passed through Kerak and the land of Moab to Madaba, Rabbah Ammon that is Philadelphia, Gerasa, Bosra, Damascus, and Tadmor, ending at Resafa on the upper Euphrates as I said...The Nabataeans used this road as a trade route for luxury goods such as frankincense and spices from southern Arabia. During the Roman period, the King's Highway was rebuilt by Trajan and called the 'Via Traiana Nova'. It was King Herod's goal to make Jerusalem the most impressive city in the world. He would go to any means to impress the world with his Hellenised buildings and magnificent Greek architecture. The Roman road was the bloodstream of the empire. Merchants paid taxes to Rome on all their transactions, and they needed the roads to carry their goods to an ever-widening market. Legionnaires marched upon them swiftly gaining efficient access to battle. In a sense, the roads were funding and facilitating Roman expansion. You know of *course that many priests talk of roads and paths within their sermons and preachings. Some argue that God had a higher purpose for the roads and that a new kind of merchant would soon traverse the entire Mediterranean area, not one who transports his treasure to the city marketplace, but one who is a treasure, and who carries true riches, not to sell, but to give away freely. The transforming good news of God's forgiveness through Jesus the Messiah was embedded into the hearts of the Apostles and early believers, and God prepared those roads for them to walk upon and lead others into His path. A new kind of soldier would be running these well built thoroughfares to fight, not flesh and blood, but a spiritual warfare that would liberate entire civilisations from the bondage of Satan's tyrannical oppression and coercion, to a kingdom ruled by love, service and willing devotion. That is how some argued the reasoning behind the great roads...Of course, throughout history 'the road' has provided an excellent metaphor for life's journey. We can all look back over the winding grades of difficulty, the narrow pass of opportunity, the choices between security or adventure, when our road divided and we had to make the call. But as both metaphorically and physically, some will always stray from the path and many would fall, and some would of course pay with their very lives," the old man sighed.* [35]

"Ha...I still have a parchment I was given years ago about being a pilgrim following the path...here look...read it yourselves," the Genoese sailor said and pulled out a small dirty rolled up parchment. As he laid it upon the table, the old man smiled at him.

"You have kept that upon yourself?" he asked.

"Yes...to remind me that perhaps I may be granted the chance of one day redeeming myself and undertaking the pilgrim's way...," the Genoese sailor replied. "Besides, it looked important..."

Gabirol pulled the parchment around so that he could read it properly. It was a page taken from the main pilgrim's guide. It had a beautiful stylised capital letter at the top left hand corner than ran down the left of the page.

"Ah this is the codex as presented by Calixstinus, yes? For all pilgrims to follow. And wear the scallop shell as St James started when he visited Spain. My friend, I am surprised to discover you carry this...pleasantly surprised," Gabirol commented as he read the parchment.

The parchment read:

'The pilgrim route is a very good thing, but it is narrow. For the road which leads us to life is narrow; on the other hand, the road which leads to death is broad and spacious. The pilgrim route is for those who are good: it is the lack of vices, the thwarting of the body, the increase of virtues, pardon for sins, sorrow for the penitent, the road of the righteous, love of the saints, faith in the resurrection and the reward of the blessed, a separation from hell, the protection of the heavens. It takes us away from luscious foods, it makes gluttonous fatness vanish, it restrains voluptuousness, constrains the appetites of the flesh which attack the fortress of the soul, cleanses the spirit, leads us to contemplation, humbles the haughty, raises up the lowly, loves poverty. It hates the reproach of those fuelled by greed. It loves, on the other hand, the person who gives to the poor. It rewards those who live simply and do good works; And, on the other hand, it does not pluck those who are stingy and wicked from the claws of sin.'

Codex Calixtinus

"But I heard that it was not actually the Pope Calixtinus who wrote that?" Simon interjected, much to the surprise of Gabirol and the old man.

"Simon, again you surprise us with your knowledge...," the old man smiled to him and shook his head.

"Hey...I may stink of fish and not have had any tutelage but I hear much on the market," he replied with a large grin as Sarah shook her head.

"Well let me explain briefly that The Codex Calixtinus is an illuminated manuscript... formerly attributed to Pope Callixtus II, though now believed to have been arranged by the French scholar named Aymeric Picaud. The actual author is given as 'Scriptor I'. It was intended to give background detail and advice for pilgrims following the 'Way of St. James' to the shrine of the apostle Saint James the Great, located in the cathedral of Santiago de Compostela, Galicia (Spain). The codex is also known as the Liber Sancti Jacobi, or the Book of Saint James. The collection includes sermons, reports of miracles and liturgical texts associated with Saint James, and a most interesting set of polyphonic musical pieces. In it are also found descriptions of the route, works of art to be seen along the way, and the customs of the local people. It has served as a great help to many pilgrims since it was first released....and some have died for it and a great many more fallen whilst following it."

"You say that many fall, and some die...does that include Theodoric?" Ayleth interrupted looking at the old man.

"No...don't tell us Theodoric dies?" Sarah interrupted alarmed.

"Well..." The old man paused as he thought for several minutes. *"His fever just got worse and..."*

Gadara, Umm Quais, King's Highway, Kingdom of Jerusalem border, June 1179

Sister Lucy sat next to Theodoric as he lay unconscious in the back of the black-smith's second cart. It was early evening and the Templar escort were busy setting up for the night. Brother Teric pulled the heavy cover back and looked in upon them just as Sister Lucy wiped Theodoric's forehead with a soaked cloth. She turned to look at him, her faced etched with concern and anxious.

"Sister Lucy...I am under instruction to bring Theodoric to Princess Stephanie's caravan...and she is not taking no for an answer. We have a Hospitaller surgeon from the watchtower fort who will check him over and see if we are missing something. So please, let Tenno and I carry him," Brother Teric explained and asked.

Before Sister Lucy had time to say anything, Tenno pulled aside the remainder of the rear curtain cover, leaned in and grabbed Theodoric's feet. Quickly he looked at Sister Lucy, simply nodded and pulled Theodoric back towards him. He grabbed his top and hauled him upwards so he was sitting up still unconscious. He pulled his arm up and over his shoulder and literally just scooped him up as if he weighed nothing. He again looked at Sister Lucy who just sat staring holding the wet cloth.

Within moments, Tenno was backing himself into Princess Stephanie's caravan despite the protestations of Brother Matthew and watched by a bemused Guy, who stood nearby surrounded by his constant entourage. Sister Lucy followed in behind him helped by Brother Teric. Princess Stephanie then ushered in the Hospitaller surgeon from the watchtower contingent. All watched and listened in silence as he checked Theodoric over thoroughly. He checked his pulse, looked into his eyes that had rolled appearing just white nearly. He had stopped sweating now and was very cold and pale. The Hospitaller surgeon stood up slowly and looked at Sister

Lucy, her eyes pleading almost with him. He shook his head no. Sister Lucy gasped and fell to her knees nearly, Princess Stephanie just managing to catch her and sit her down on the chair nearest to the bed. Tenno took a deep breath and sighed. He looked at the Hospitaller hard.

"I am sorry...his heart beats too weak...his temperature has broken but I fear that is because his body succumbs to whatever ailment has befallen him. I am surprised he still lives now...but I strongly suspect he does not have much longer. He may have stood a chance if we had gotten him to the Cave de Sueth for we are better equipped there...but no," the Hospitaller surgeon explained softly and shook his head.

Sister Lucy started to cry and moved nearer to the bed and held Theodoric's hand tightly then kissed it. Princess Stephanie tried to calm herself and took a deep breath as she fought not to cry.

"Theo...Theo," Sister Lucy said in a whisper, her voice broken with emotion. "You bastard...you cannot leave me now...not after I have only just found you again...," she cried and held his hand to her face.

ωα

Alisha and Paul were getting ready for the night in their caravan with just one candle illuminating the inside. Paul was holding Arri's feet in his hands rubbing his thumbs over his toes making him smile as he lay out upon the shawl Taqi had given him. Alisha was preparing his night time wear as a knock at the rear door drew their attention. Paul picked up Arri, who was naked and kicking his legs playfully, and handed him to Alisha. Quickly he opened the door to see Tenno stood bolt upright; instantly Paul knew something was wrong by the look upon his face.

"Tenno...what is it?" he asked alarmed.

"'Tis Theo...he will not survive this night," Tenno answered bluntly.

"What?" Paul shot back and opened the small door completely and looked at Tenno puzzled. "But...but I thought he was recovering. Sister Lucy said...she said," Paul shook his head, looked across at the blacksmith's second cart and stepped down.

"He is in the Princess's caravan now," Tenno replied.

Alisha stepped down behind Paul carrying Arri. She went to speak when Paul ran off toward Princess Stephanie's caravan.

"Tenno...please, would you?" Alisha asked and offered Arri up for him to take.

Tenno looked at her for a moment, and then took Arri. As Alisha gathered up her dress and ran after Paul, Tenno noticed an old woman, the same one who had approached Paul in Crac, looking at him. She smiled, almost menacingly Tenno thought, as she slowly walked towards him as if she was stalking her prey and tip toeing as silently as she could. Tenno pulled Arri close to his chest protectively.

"What do you want of me, old woman?" Tenno asked coldly as she stood silently before him.

"Nothing...nothing at all...but the babe, he is bonded to you, yes?" she asked in a deep almost gravelly voice and smiled a wide smile that made Tenno feel uncomfortable.

"You...you are not of normal countenance...what are you?" Tenno asked perplexed and part turned away so Arri was further from her.

165

"Ah you have the sense indeed. Thought you did...it surrounds you," the old woman remarked as she lightly stepped around Tenno to see Arri again closer.

"State your intentions, old woman, for you unnerve my skin...," Tenno stated and turned Arri away again.

"Tenno...for that is your name yes? You need not fear me...I am here to give life back to your friend," the old woman exclaimed and looked across toward Princess Stephanie's caravan.

"How so...are you a witch or sorceress?" Tenno asked.

"I am many things to many people, but 'tis you I need to get me beside your friend, for if you do not, he will die within this hour."

"And what reason do you have for wanting to help him and what payment will ye demand?"

"Who said anything about payment?"

"Old woman, I learnt a long time ago to trust my instincts...and something does not ring true with you. What are you?"

"Me...I am the only thing on God's earth this night that will save your friend... despite your refusal to admit he is your friend...so trust your instincts...Tenno," the old woman said and stood a pace nearer and looked at him directly in the eyes as the sun finally disappeared behind the horizon. Tenno stared back into her eyes. For just a moment, as she smiled, she appeared youthful, beautiful even. Tenno shook his head and blinked convinced the changing light was playing tricks upon him. But again, as she smiled, she seemed beautiful. Arri made a noise, as if he was calling out a name, and outstretched his little arm from his shawl towards the old woman. She just smiled back at him then Tenno again.

ଈୠ

Sister Lucy had her face buried in the sheet covers as she held Theodoric's right hand. She fought not to cry but the tears kept on flowing. Alisha knelt beside her and put her arms around her as Paul slowly moved to the other side of the bed just looking down upon Theodoric. He looked white he was so pale. Paul clasped Theodoric's left hand with both of his and was struck at how cold his hand was. Princess Stephanie cupped her mouth and shook her head sadly as Brother Teric showed the Hospitaller surgeon out of the caravan. Just as he was about to pull the door shut, Brother Matthew, who was guarding the door outside, stepped aside as Tenno appeared and placed his free arm across the path of Brother Matthew whilst still holding Arri in his other arm.

"I pray you let this woman in. She will help Theo...," Tenno stated as Brother Teric looked down, puzzled.

Brother Teric's eyes widened slightly as he saw the old woman step into view. Tenno nodded he should let her in. As Brother Teric held the door open for her and she stepped up inside the caravan, he sniffed the air as she passed him for she stank. Sister Lucy looked up, her face streaked with tears as Tenno followed the old woman in. All looked at her and Tenno, puzzled. The old woman smiled broadly and silently stepped closer to Theodoric and stopped beside Paul, who drew in a sharp breath as the smell of her hit him. She just smiled even more.

"Please, excuse my stench, but alas, it has been too long since my clothes and body have seen clean water and soaps...but it will not stop nor detract me from doing what I have come to do," she said almost in a whisper.

Paul looked at Alisha, puzzled, as Sister Lucy looked at the old woman, confused. The old woman sat on the edge of the bed beside Theodoric and gently pulled his arms up, forcing Sister Lucy to let go of his hand. Very gently she held Theodoric's hands and in the dim light studied his palms for several minutes.

"What...what are you doing?" Sister Lucy finally asked and sat up straight and wiped her face.

Princess Stephanie watched on as Alisha stared at Paul, her eyes wide. Tenno held Arri and just shook his head as the old woman ran her fingers across the lines upon Theodoric's palms, checking first his right hand, then his left. She then placed them together and pulled them against her chest. Sister Lucy looked on almost shocked until Alisha placed her left hand upon her shoulder reassuringly

"We know this woman...from La Rochelle," Alisha coughed, her throat dry.

The old woman closed her eyes and held Theodoric's hands tightly as she started to whisper something. After a few minutes, she opened her eyes; her pupils appeared enlarged as she looked at Sister Lucy only.

"He stands at the threshold between this world and the next. Do you answer for him?" she asked Sister Lucy quietly.

"What...what are you asking me...?" she replied emotionally and looked at every one in turn to see what their reactions were and any hint of guidance.

"Do you answer for him...yes or no?" she asked again.

"Then yes...damn it yes whatever that may entail YES!" Sister Lucy snapped back.

"Then answer me this...do you wish him to move on or stay in this world?"

"What...you cannot ask that of me....I...I...I am too selfish to let him go...I want, I want," Sister Lucy answered, then paused as she shook her head confused and emotional. "I need him here," she finally blurted out as tears fell again.

Alisha gulped hard as Princess Stephanie quickly wiped a tear away. Brother Teric moved in closer to see exactly what the old woman was doing. The old woman leaned over and gently placed her hand upon Sister Lucy's right hand and moved it to rest upon Theodoric's chest. She held her hand over Sister Lucy's and pushed it down firmly much to her surprise. Tenno shook his head as he refused to get emotional in front of everyone. He had developed a begrudging liking for Theodoric. Taqi had now gone and now he feared he was losing Theodoric.

"'Tis written in his hand that he has a choice now to leave should he wish...but 'tis also written that he has another path he can follow...with another who answers for him...so it is written," the old woman explained as she looked at Sister Lucy intently. "Now do not interrupt anything I do, no matter how long this takes...do you understand me?"

Sister Lucy nodded her head yes emotionally. The old woman then moved up closer to Theodoric and pushed both of her hands down upon Sister Lucy's hand over his chest, closed her eyes and took in a very long and deep breath. She then put her head upon her own hands and started to breathe out very slowly. Paul looked at everyone in the room in turn as they all stared at the old woman.

"My hand...it feels hot...too hot," Sister Lucy remarked alarmed.

"Ssssh...just let it pass....sssshh!" the old woman said very quietly.

The old woman held the same position for many minutes in total silence. Arri made a slight sound but Tenno gently rocked him and he soon fell asleep in his arms. The old woman seemed to fall into a deep sleep and not move, Sister Lucy's hand still pushed beneath hers upon Theodoric's chest.

৪১ ৫২

Theodoric was drowning. He could not breathe and his chest felt like it was about to explode. He could hear Sister Lucy in the distance but could not see her. He opened his eyes and they stung. Sunlight flickered through the cloudy water that surrounded him, the desire to breathe becoming overwhelming. He felt annoyed that he could not spend more time with Sister Lucy...his Lucy. He felt confused why he was in water. Had the cart fallen into a river, he thought...was Lucy okay?

"Theo...do you remember me?" a woman's voice gently called out, very soft and comforting. "Theo...come on, remember me," the voice said again.

Overwhelmed by the desire to breathe, he took in a deep breath knowing it would be his last, a burst of twinkling bright light spinning up above him. But as he drew in, he discovered he could breathe.

"Who are you?" he called out with the realisation he could breathe and speak. "Where am I? Am I dead...is this it...truly it, this time?"

"Theo...I promised we would meet again, and we have. 'Tis not your time...you still have much work to finish as you promised me you would," the female voice said softly.

Theodoric's mind raced, the voice becoming more familiar now. The moment he recalled the promise he had made back in Ireland many years previous in the sweat hut, a beautiful woman suddenly appeared before him smiling gracefully, her eyes sparkling, her skin a pure flawless white. All at once he felt warm, secure, loved and protected and happy. The woman smiled at him again and outstretched her hands for him to take. He quickly clasped her hands and nearly cried as emotions filled him as if streaming from her into him. They both stood facing each other for what felt like an age. She then lifted his right hand and indicated toward it. Without speaking, he still heard her inside his head as she explained his hand still had a path that had to be followed if he so wished it. A large part of him wished to stay exactly where he was. Just as he was about to ask if he was dead again, he saw another woman approach from behind her.

"The last time we were all together was in Glendalough, the Valley of the Two Lakes in the Emerald Isle...," the approaching woman said softly and also smiled.

Theodoric let out a gasp as he realised he was looking at both the old woman from Glendalough but also Paul's mother now standing beside her. She stood still and bowed her head slightly.

"I am dead aren't I?"

"No...but very nearly. You can stay and come with us...well, go with her, or come back with me and finish what you started. You have free will and the choice is yours," the old woman said softly but looking many years younger.

Theodoric looked at Paul's mother. She smiled at him uncontrollably, almost laughing, her hands placed together across her tummy. Her face shone with a radiance he could hardly believe. As he looked at her, he could feel a pressure pushing into his chest that felt uncomfortable. He then heard what he thought was Sister Lucy calling his name.

"Protect the crimson line, hide the line and then hide the sword when it is done... remember your promise," Paul's mother spoke without moving her lips.

"Hurry...you must decide quickly as the silver cord is almost severed...," the old woman said, her features rapidly aging again.

Alarmed, Theodoric looked at Paul's mother again as she urged him to make a decision. He looked over his shoulder as he thought he heard Sister Lucy again. 'You bastard...you cannot leave me now' he heard her say clearly. He laughed briefly.

"That's my girl...that's where I belong right now," Theodoric said and thumbed to indicate behind him.

As soon as he had made the gesture, Paul's mother smiled and simply vanished into light, the old woman looking at him intently.

"Do not forget again," she said and vanished.

He looked at his hands as his vision was filled with an ever increasing bright light until he could no longer see anything.

₧₧

The old woman suddenly let out a loud gasp as she drew in a large breath, her eyes closed as if in pain. She raised her head, arched her back and pulled her hands away fast from over Sister Lucy's causing her hand to jump up from Theodoric's chest. Quickly Sister Lucy held her hand in pain as Theodoric let out a sigh and relaxed.

"He is dead now...no?" Brother Teric asked as Theodoric slumped and lay perfectly still not breathing.

Sister Lucy started to shake as Princess Stephanie held her hand to her mouth. Paul shook his head and looked at the old lady still sat beside Theodoric. She suddenly opened both her eyes and breathed in again and faced Sister Lucy.

"'Tis done," she remarked as she got up from the bed, straightened her black dirty dress. "He will sleep now...but he will live," she explained and looked at Theodoric. She smiled, shook her head and turned to walk for the door. Tenno was in her way still holding Arri. He looked down at her suspiciously.

Theodoric coughed slightly, licked his dry lips, and blinked his eyes open very briefly. Sister Lucy immediately grabbed his right hand. Alisha could feel her eyes welling up with tears but quickly gulped and tried to remain calm. Sister Lucy looked over at Paul and smiled, then looked at the old woman. She looked up at Tenno still blocking her way.

"I do not know what you did...but I thank you," he stated bluntly and stepped aside.

The old woman smiled at him, bowed her head, opened the door, and stepped out. As the door shut, all looked back at Theodoric. Sister Lucy buried her head in the sheet next to him and sobbed with relief. Princess Stephanie looked at Alisha then Paul just as another single tear fell from her eye.

Port of La Rochelle, France, Melissae Inn, spring 1191

"So he died...but did not die?" Ayleth asked puzzled.

"He was very near to death...some will argue that as his brain was low on breath, his mind played tricks upon him...as often happens, but the silver cord was not severed and he returned to us," the old man explained.

"Silver cord...what is that?" the farrier asked.

"'Tis a statement within the Bible that states a person is not dead and cannot pass over from this world to the next until the silver cord that connects the spiritual body to the flesh is severed," the old man answered. "The term is derived from Ecclesiastes 12:6–7 in the Old Testament, where it states..." The old man paused as he removed his small leather-bound Bible from his larger satchel and flicked through the pages until he found what he was looking for. "Here, it reads, 'Remember him, before the silver cord is severed, or the golden bowl is broken; before the pitcher is shattered at the spring, or the wheel broken at the well, and the dust returns to the ground it came from, and the spirit returns to God who gave it.'"

"I have heard it said the book Ecclesiastes is a very unusual book...is that true?" Gabirol asked.

"Many in the Bible are unusual for all manner of reasons...but yes, Ecclesiastes is a very unusual book mainly because the phrase 'under the sun' in reference to life on this earth occurs twenty-seven times in this book, more times than in any other book of the Bible. In sharp contrast, the phrase 'under heaven' occurs only three times. This reveals that the book describes what life is like for the person who rejects God. The opening statement is, 'Vanity of vanity. All is vanity'. Another way to say it is 'Empty of empties. All is empty'. Life without God is empty. The first two chapters of the book remind us that life is repetitive and there is no lasting eternal advantage with wealth, fame, possessions, pleasure or worldly wisdom. The rest of the book tells us that life is unfair, foolish things occur, and work is hard. The last chapter, twelve, focuses on the death of a man. It describes how we age, the aches, pains, and the eventual failure of parts of the body. Ecclesiastes 12:6–7 describes the final end of man and is the verse we are speaking of that mentions the silver cord...but this cord is mentioned in all major religious texts and pre-dates the Bible," the old man explained.

"That is what I heard. But like you said previously, all within the Bible is also allegorical and symbolic. Is it true therefore that the phrase you mention is likewise symbolic. Does it have other meanings?" Gabirol asked.

"Yes it does. The verse accurately translates the Hebrew by giving us the various ways a man can die. Some believe the golden bowl is the head, head injury, the pitcher is the lungs, lung disease, and the wheel is the heart and circulatory system, heart failure. But the most interesting one is the silver cord. This is the only place in the Bible this term is used. The Hebrew word for 'loosed' has the idea of being removed far away. Since it is difficult to understand how the spinal cord, that some claim is what the silver cord is, could be removed, it appears best to understand this phrase as referring to the departure of the spirit of a man, natural death. When a man dies his spirit departs."

"And is that what happened to Theodoric?" Sarah asked.

"Almost...as he recounted it to everyone later anyway."

"Slightly off from this phrase, I have also been told that there is a great mystery that can be understood if you can understand what 1 Corinthians, 15:51 says in the Bible," Gabirol remarked.

The old man flicked through his Bible until he came to the page and phrase.

"Behold, I shew you a mystery; We shall not all sleep..."

"Yes, that is the one. Can you explain what that means?" Gabirol asked and sat back.

"Well, by 'sleep' St Paul means that not everyone remains conscious after physical death. If the consciousness and spiritual aspects of an individual have evolved and developed enough in the mental body, a state of consciousness is retained, a sense of self, after death. It is believed that this is a more blissful experience because thoughts instantly manifest. It is possible that this is a heavenly experience. The Bible expressly informs us of different levels of Heaven just as Islam does as I explained earlier...such as seventh heaven remember? Even the Apostle Paul said he was taken up to the 'third heaven'. Doesn't it make more sense that there can be different degrees of both Heaven and likewise Hell?" the old man explained as they all listened intently.

"So what happens if you have not developed or evolved enough when you die?" Ayleth asked, looking a little nervous.

"Some say your very essence is immediately reborn, to learn again and develop further until eventually you reach that point whereby you can evolve. To grow...the apotheosis of man as I mentioned before. Remember...know ye not that ye are gods?" the old man answered.

"No...I think you must have explained that before I arrived," Ayleth replied.

"I wish to know what the old woman was talking about with hands...I did not know it says in the Bible about your hands. I was told that palm readers are doing the Devil's work," Sarah commented and looked at everyone.

"Yes, good point. I have had enough old nags read my hands...and all said something different," the Genoese sailor remarked.

"Do you wish me to explain about the hands and the markings within that each of us carry?" the old man asked.

"Aye, I am interested," the Templar replied instantly as he studied his own hands carefully.

"I can give you but the briefest of explanations...such as," he paused. "Well I could state that our hands are the creation of God, full of symbolic meaning and each hand has its very own unique identity. No two hands are ever the same. Each hand has five fingers, five being the number for grace. Four fingers are weak, but the addition of the thumb provides strength, which is an illustration of grace, just as the Lord rules over the four seasons. There are two hands, one to help the other. With two hands there are ten fingers, the number for the Laws of Establishment. There are Ten Commandments in the Bible. There are fifteen finger joints in each hand, the number for a covering. The hands cover objects which they grasp. The hands are used for manual work. The fingers are used for writing, pointing, feeling, and touching. Now if you look at your own hands carefully, you will note the many lines in the palm, which are similar in everyone, and yet with subtle variations. There are a multitude of marks in the palm. Some appear to be symbols of crosses, pits, mounds, spots, and circles. These, if you believe in this, are not simply random. Our hands are full of meaning that can be readily understood," the old man explained as everyone around the table looked carefully at their own hands. This made the old man smile.

"But palm reading and divination is expressly prohibited by the Word of God. Palm readers name the parts of the hand after demons like Venus, Saturn, and Apollo. Satan did the same thing with the planets and constellations. When the Devil invents a system of lies about something, he's obviously trying to hide something important," the wealthy tailor commented, looking concerned.

"The stars aren't evil and the hands aren't evil. God never intended for Christians to be prohibited from looking at their own hands or understanding the signs of the Zodiac. However, Christians who have been brainwashed with what many would call the Devil's lies don't have a clue about the real meaning of the hands. The only way to know who is right and who is wrong is to go back to the Bible and dig out the truth as so many place so much value and credence upon it. Unfortunately too many people see Bible doctrine as the only vocabulary for understanding the truth. The Bible contains the truth about hands, which will be demonstrated. But it turns out that the hands have their own unique vocabulary and system of explanation. The rules of interpretation of scripture can be applied to the hands in order to establish an understanding for Christians that is true and not based upon the Devil's lies as some claim. But in simple terms, God's gifts, or special talents for an individual, are recorded in your hands. The hands are an excellent record of the past, but the future belongs to God. Definitions of personality and mental problems will be given through the hands." The old man paused for a moment as he watched them all looking at their own hands still. "The study of hands is as old as history. Hands were understood in Job, which is the oldest book in the Bible. Elihu, the Judge, discussed the analysis of hands with Job during his illness. When Job got sick, the hands were one of the first things consulted. The insight into hands offered by Elihu was obviously common knowledge shared by Job and the other four men who came to try to help Job. No one tried to refute Elihu's observations. This indicates that Job's helpers were pursuing a spiritual solution to Job's illness. They, therefore, consulted the hands as a part of their diagnosis. Elihu said 'He sets a seal on the hand of every man, that all Right Men may come to knowledge of His creative work' (Job 37:7). God sets His seal on the hand of every man. The word for setting a seal is the Hebrew 'chatham', which means to seal, to affix one's seal in attestation of a covenant. I can tell you that even the layout of Jerusalem is mainly based upon the hand...the Lord's hand...and in Isaiah he states this: 'Behold, I have inscribed you on the palms of my hands; your walls are in my view continuously' (Isaiah 49:16). The walls of Jerusalem form the outline of a palm...but that is another mystery we simply do not have time to cover today," the old man explained.

"I see...I think," Simon finally said as he studied his hands closely.

"So Theodoric recovered from this, yes?" Gabirol asked.

"He did...Princess Stephanie insisted he remain in her caravan with Sister Lucy to help him. Alisha and Paul took her to their caravan despite her maid's and Brother Matthew's protestations that she should at least stay with them in their separate caravan. Paul stayed outside with Tenno lest anyone complained of inappropriateness."

"This place they are staying at...is it not the same place that Jesus drove out pigs...," Simon asked. Sarah shot him a look of bewilderment almost as Ayleth laughed.

"Simon speaks the truth for, yes, 'tis the very place mentioned in the Bible," the old man replied.

"Pigs?" Ayleth stated questioningly.

"Yes pigs. You see, Umm Quais, as it is more frequently named these days, but once known as Gadara, was once a very strategic and important town," the old man said, smiling as he looked at Ayleth and Sarah clearly surprised that Simon knew this.

"Both I and my brother have been to Umm Quais...'tis right on the border, in fact the main King's Highway I believe separates the Kingdom of Jerusalem from Muslim lands to the east. 'Tis truly a fine place to behold. I made a prayer there once to a goddess statue to help find me a good woman," the Templar explained and looked at Miriam. "Seems she must have heard my prayers," he smiled and kissed her hand quickly.

"Umm Quais is the site of the ancient Greco-Roman town of Gadara, and, according to the Bible, the place where Jesus cast out the Devil from two men into a herd of pigs (Matthew 8: 28–34). It is located upon one of the highest peaks in the region with stunning views of Lake Tiberias, which is the Biblical Sea of Galilee and the Yarmuk gorge...there is no better vantage point in the whole region. Gadara was renowned for its cosmopolitan atmosphere, attracting an array of writers, artists, philosophers and poets. It also served as a resort for Romans vacationing in the nearby al-Hemma hot springs. It is blessed with fertile soil, abundant water, and a location astride a number of key trading routes connecting Asia and Europe. The city was founded by the Greeks during the fourth century BC. Gadara was overrun by the Seleucid ruler Antiochus the Third in 218 BC. When the Romans, under Pompey, conquered the East and formed the Decapolis, the fortunes of Gadara, taken in 63 BC, improved rapidly and building was undertaken on a large scale. During the early part of Roman rule, the Nabateans, with their capital at Petra, controlled the trade routes as far north as Damascus. Aiming to put an end to this competition, Mark Antony sent King Herod the Great to weaken the Nabateans, who finally gave up their northern interests in 31 BC. In appreciation of his efforts, Rome rewarded Herod with Gadara. The city remained under Herod's rule until his death, and then reverted to semi-autonomy as part of the Roman province of Syria. The Byzantine era witnessed the decline of Gadara into relative obscurity. Earthquakes destroyed many buildings, and by the dawn of the Islamic era Gadara became just another village. The town became known by the Arabic name Umm Quais only recently. Today, a considerable portion of the original Roman amphitheatre survives. The seats face west, and are brought to life at sunset. Covered passageways stand in the back," the old man detailed, when he was interrupted by the Templar.

"Yes...that is where I saw the goddess statue I mentioned. It still had a head then, but upon my return a year later, its head had gone," he explained enthusiastically.

"Yes, a six-foot white marble goddess sat at the foot of one of the amphitheatre's internal staircases. 'Twas thought to be of Tyche, the patron goddess of Gadara. Next to the theatre is a colonnaded street that was once the town's commercial centre. Also near the black basalt theatre are the columns of the great Basilica of Gadara. Further west along the colonnaded street are a mausoleum and public baths. There are still a few remains you can just make out of what once was a hippodrome. Believe it or not it was once called Antiochia or Antiochia Semiramis, or Seleucia. That similarity to Antioch once caused Paul's father and Firgany great confusion and nearly cost them their very lives...but that is another story," the old man said and sighed heavily, paused for a few short moments and then smiled again.

"Sounds truly romantic almost. Beautiful," Miriam said softly and looked at the Templar.

"'Tis that indeed. The place has a certain strange feel to it that is for sure," the Templar replied.

"Brother Teric knew the place well and said he would take Princess Stephanie and Alisha to the nearby al-Hemma hot springs in order to bathe properly. He had agreed with Brother Matthew that they would stay a day to let the walking pilgrims rest before continuing south after their great effort the previous day...plus he hoped the so-called healing springs would help Theodoric."

3 – 40

"As you know, I study philosophy...am I correct in saying that this place was the birth-place of the satirist Menippos, a slave who became a Cynic philosopher and satirised the follies of mankind in a mixture of prose and verse as detailed and imitated by Varro and Lucian?" Gabirol asked.

All looked at him, puzzled, the Genoese sailor shaking his head.

"We are in exalted presence...I feel rather inadequate," he exclaimed and smiled mocking himself.

"You are correct, Gabirol...and as our sailor here states, we are clearly in learned company. It would be a pleasure to spend more time with you than I fear the good Lord will afford us," the old man said.

"I would love to visit these places you speak of...I feel like I am travelling a great journey through the pages of history," Sarah remarked and looked at Stephan.

"Well the history of the place was not as romantic as the present ruins may fool you into thinking. Despite the Greek historian Polybius describing Gadara as being in 218 BC the 'strongest of all places in the region' it nevertheless capitulated shortly afterwards when besieged by the Seleucid king Antiochus the Third of Syria. The region passed in and out of the control of the Seleucid kings of Syria and the Ptolemys of Egypt and in 167 BC the Jews of Jerusalem rebelled against the Seleucids, and in the ensuing conflict in the region Gadara and other cities suffered severe damage. In the early first century BC Gadara gave birth to its most famous son, Meleager. He was one of the most admired Hellenistic Greek poets, not only for his own works but also for his anthology of other poets, which formed the basis of the large collection known as the Greek Anthology. In 63 BC, when the Roman general Pompey placed the region under Roman control, he rebuilt Gadara and made it one of the semi-autonomous cities of the Roman Decapolis, and a bulwark against Nabatean expansion. But in 30 BC the Roman emperor Augustus placed it under the control of the Jewish king Herod as I have already mentioned. The historian Josephus relates that after King Herod's death in 4 BC Gadara was made part of the Roman province of Syria. Then in the first century AD, that is when Jesus drove demons out of a man into swine 'in the country of the Gadarenes' according to the Gospel of Matthew, though the Gospels according to Mark and Luke read 'country of the Gerasenes'. Josephus states that in AD 66 at the beginning of the Jewish revolt against the Romans the country around Gadara was laid waste. So Vespasian marched to the city of Gadara. He came into it and slew all the youth, the Romans having no mercy on any age whatsoever. He set fire to the city and all the villas around it. The Gadarenes captured some of the boldest of the Jews, of whom several were put to death and others imprisoned. Some in the town surrendered to Emperor Vespasian, who placed a garrison there. The second century AD Roman aqueduct to Gadara supplied drinking water through a qanat a hundred and five miles long. Its longest underground section, running for fifty-eight miles, is the longest known tunnel from ancient times. Now Gadara did continue to be an important town within the Eastern Roman Empire, and was long the seat of a Christian bishop but with the conquest of the Arabs, following the Battle of Yarmouk in AD 636, it came under Muslim rule. Around AD 747 it was largely destroyed by an earthquake, and was abandoned. But you can still see the ancient walls which may be traced for their entire circuit of over a mile. One of the Roman roads runs eastward to D̲er'ah; and the aqueduct has been traced to the pool of K̲hab, about twenty miles to the north of D̲er'ah. The ruins include those of two theatres, a temple, a basilica and other buildings. A paved street, with double colonnade, ran from east to west. The ruts worn in the paved road by the chariot wheels are still to be seen," the old man detailed fondly as if recounting a personal visit.

"I am interested in the biblical pigs story," Simon remarked.

"That figures," Sarah laughed.

"Well in truth, Simon," the old man started to explain, "no town of Gadara is named in the Gospels, but a territory is described as (χώρα τῶν Γαδαρηνῶν), chō˙ra tō˙n Gadarēnō˙n, 'country of the Gadarenes' (Matthew 8:28). In the parallel passages of Mark 5:1; Luke 8:26, 37 is written (χώρα τῶν Γερασηνῶν), chō˙ra tō˙n Gerasēnō˙n 'country of the Gerasenes'. Greek manuscripts show variant readings or harmonisations in all three Gospels of Gadarenes, Gerasenes and Gergesenes, but scholars agree that the original Greek text at Matthew 8 was 'chora ton Gadarenon', as in 'the country of the Gadarenes', and the original text at Mark 5 and Luke 8 was 'chora ton Gerasenon', as in 'the country of the Gerasenes'. In fact these two Gospel place-names probably refer to the same region. The Greek city of Gadara was considered to belong to the larger region of Gerasa. Neither Gadara nor Gerasa is on the shore of the Sea of Galilee. But that Gadara's territory extended to the Sea of Galilee is clearly indicated by the fact that a ship is frequently an emblem on its coins. Josephus, too, makes reference to the territory of Gadara 'which lay on the frontiers of Tiberias and formed the eastern boundary of Galilee', thus placing the region of Gadara along the coast of the Sea of Galilee. And so it is here that the Exorcism of the Gerasene demoniac where Jesus healed him casting out the demons into a herd of swine which ran into the Sea of Galilee took place. The three Synoptic Gospels indicate that it was a site where, when Jesus and his disciples stepped ashore, there met Him 'out of the tombs' a man possessed by demons (Mark 5:9) whom Jesus sent into a nearby herd of 'many swine feeding there on the mountain' (Luke 8:32), swine which ran 'down the steep place into the sea'; at which point those who kept them fled 'and went away into the city' (Matthew 8:32–33). Thus the three Gospel accounts indicate that the location was near a port, near tombs, for the men to live in, near an area for pigs to graze, near a town, to which the men could flee, and most importantly, near a steep bank, for the herd to rush down. Umm Quais has high ridges and steep slopes, down which pigs could have run 'violently down into the sea' (Matthew 8:32). Above the port are hills, which match the Biblical account. Other features of this site match the Gospel accounts. In addition, there is a nearby site where swine would have grazed and 'the groves of oak trees on the plateau above would have provided the acorns they favoured'. Thus the site of Gadara we can safely attribute to that being one and the same as recounted within the Bible, which just proves the validity and authenticity of just another story within the Bible as being based upon fact," the old man explained. [36]

"I note your comment about oak trees again...And Alisha and Paul stayed at this very place?" Ayleth asked.

"Yes...walking almost in the footsteps of our Lord Jesus himself, in a fashion."

Gadara, Umm Quais, King's Highway, Kingdom of Jerusalem border, June 1179

Paul placed his hand upon Sister Lucy's shoulder reassuringly. She looked up at him. She looked utterly broken. She feigned a brave smile as she held Theodoric's hand tightly.

"He will be okay...he will," he said softly.

Alisha indicated with her head that they all leave and quietly and quickly they all left the caravan to give them some much needed privacy.

Paul helped Alisha to their caravan as Brother Teric escorted Princess Stephanie as she followed carrying a large blanket. She walked looking downward sadly. Tenno, still carrying Arri, looked back at Princess Stephanie's caravan and in the rapidly dimming evening light, it looked as though he smiled with relief. When he noticed Paul looking at him, he quickly wiped the smile from his face.

"Here, take. I shall sort us our sleeping mats," Tenno stated and handed Arri to him.

Paul could not help but smile. Alisha stepped up into the caravan and beckoned Princess Stephanie to follow her and gave her hand to help her up. She stopped half way up and looked back at Paul.

"Paul, are you sure I can stay again?" Stephanie asked quietly.

"Of course...I am sure Alisha welcomes the extra room in the bed and that Tenno and I remain outside keeping watch...well, Tenno does," Paul answered.

"Thank you...both of you. I have asked Brother Teric to arrange to take us in the morning on just a short little trip to the al-Hemma hot springs. It is truly worth the visit," she said and stepped up into the caravan, Alisha looking out.

"You better take Arri though," Paul laughed as he passed him up.

Alisha took Arri and smiled at Paul. 'I love you' she mouthed silently quickly looking behind at Princess Stephanie as she sat down upon the wide bench. Paul smiled and replied the same in silence and within moments Paul was standing alone with Tenno and Brother Teric listening to the pilgrims who were all talking quietly as they prepared for the night. The stars were just beginning to sparkle above their heads as the very last hues of orange and yellow faded upon the horizon.

"I best go and check the night watch. 'Tis a great miracle I sense we saw this eve...I must speak with the old woman in the morrow, before we visit the hot springs," Brother Teric said as he looked up and down the caravan, the old Roman columns looming in silhouette like tall guardians along the length of the road.

"Do you think it wise and safe to spend a day resting here and visiting the spring?" Tenno asked.

"Yes. The road is good all the way to Kerak direct, and I think the spring will not only do the women some good, but also Theodoric if we can get him there. They are reputed to be quite therapeutic and healing...though that could all be a load of nonsense. Besides, we have been given assurances...," Brother Teric answered, looked at Tenno and winked.

෯ ෬

After a surprisingly cold and uncomfortable night, Paul removed the blanket he was lying beneath and stood up. The sun was just breaking on the horizon. Only now as the camp slept, save for the Templars still stood guarding the party, could he see the view that stretched out all around him. 'No wonder I was cold...this high up' he thought to himself. Two knights stood guard at the entrance to a small white tent Guy had got his men to set up. Paul smiled as he thought it made for the most obvious target to hit first if attacked. Guy had clearly not listened to advice given by Brother Teric. Tenno stepped beside him having obviously been up some time. Both looked over toward Princess Stephanie's caravan as the side door swung open and Theodoric peered out looking exhausted. Sister Lucy was directly behind him clearly trying to get him to stay inside. Paul and Tenno immediately walked across to him.

"Where is she...where is the old woman? I must speak with her...now!" Theodoric exclaimed and looked around fast.

"Theo, you must rest...please," Sister Lucy pleaded.

"I must find that old woman. I know her of old...I knew I recognised her at Crac. I must speak with her," he exclaimed getting more agitated as Sister Lucy tried to pull him back.

Brother Teric and Matthew appeared with Thomas and Percival. They looked at Theodoric, puzzled.

"We shall find her. She will be somewhere in the convoy," Tenno said and placed his hand upon Theodoric's arm and indicated with his head to go back into the caravan with Sister Lucy. Theodoric looked at him, shook his head tiredly but then nodded he would. "Good."

"Who are we looking for?" Thomas asked.

"The old woman dressed in black...and carries a bit of a smell with her," Paul answered.

"Oh her...yes, she could do with a visit to the springs. We can easily find her... just follow the smell," Brother Matthew remarked.

As Sister Lucy took Theodoric back into the caravan, Brother Teric immediately started to organise several of his Templars and some of Thomas's men to help look for the old woman. Guy's men simply refused to assist saying that had to guard him at all times as they feared an assault by the Ashashin. Paul was about to help when Alisha appeared at the rear of their caravan.

"Paul," she called out quietly and beckoned him over. He approached her as she stepped down from the caravan and pulled her dress taut. "Paul...Arri and Stephanie still sleep...so I shall prepare us some breakfast," she explained and put her arms around him. As she held him, she looked at the stunning view all around them. She took a deep breath and sighed as Paul held her. "We are blessed aren't we?" she whispered.

"Yes...so long as you do not now poison me with breakfast," Paul joked in reply.

Alisha hit him on the chest and pulled a face at him playfully.

"I have not had the proper opportunity to show you just how well I cook," she laughed. Adrastos snorted loudly from where he had been tied for the night. "And I think your horse is jealous of me," she laughed again.

Within half an hour it became apparent that the old woman and the young girl who accompanied her were nowhere to be found despite none of the knights on guard during the night seeing anyone leave.

Port of La Rochelle, France, Melissae Inn, spring 1191

"So the old woman just vanished?" Simon asked.

"She must have walked away during the night with the young girl...The Confrere Knights based at the watchtower built nearby and the dwellings and hospice had not seen them neither. The King's Highway stretched off in both directions for miles and from the view point

they were at, they could not see anyone. They did note a caravan following some distance north that had stayed overnight at the previous watchtower location. They would be with them soon enough and Brother Teric promised Theodoric, who was utterly confused by that stage, that they would check that caravan as it passed through. When Theodoric heard that they were all heading for the hot springs, he told them all in not too uncertain terms that he was going also," the old man explained and smiled.

"Why would he do that after such a near death experience?" Ayleth asked, perplexed.

"Theodoric had visited the springs many times before. It was he who had initially suggested the visit. It was just four miles away and in his opinion well worth the trip. Plus he wanted Sister Lucy to experience the springs as he had always promised her that, one day, he would take her to the healing springs there."

"Healing?" the Genoese sailor asked.

"Yes...healing springs. They were famed for it. 'Twas a peculiar thing too that both sides, Christian and Muslim, agreed not to war there...such is the strangeness of the times," the old man confirmed. "There is also a tiny village named Al Hemma. The hot springs was a favourite of Roman dignitaries and holidaymakers who held its therapeutic abilities in high esteem. Some pilgrims still make the journey despite the obvious risk of attack as the springs have a very high content of minerals as they bubble up at high temperature, but then cool as they filter into a second pool. Brother Teric organised a troop of Templars and some of Thomas's men to escort Princess Stephanie, Sister Lucy, Theodoric, Alisha and Paul as well as several other pilgrims and Princess Stephanie's two maids to the springs. Guy was asked but he declined preferring to relax within his cool tent for the day. They took only horses leaving Brother Matthew at the main watchtower fort with the rest of the pilgrims much to his annoyance as he had to answer to Guy for the duration. The route down to the springs is a spectacular winding mountain road that descends steeply. Water falling in the mountains filters down through the rock to emerge from a series of hot and cold springs that cascade in waterfalls over the cliffs of a tight wadi. Just like the Dead Sea, which is renowned for its healing properties with its mineral rich water, the springs are curative, being particularly good for people with skin problems or in pain. So you can see why Theodoric was insistent upon going."

"Yes, we had cause often to detour to the springs for our wealthier patrons as they travelled to and from Kerak castle...though we called it Crac de Moab as you have explained also. 'Tis indeed a beautiful sight to behold," the Templar remarked.

"When they did arrive, the springs were deserted, even the small village, probably due to the rumours of war and the recent worsening barbarity by which the conflict was being prosecuted by both sides, despite their agreements not to engage in war at the springs. Alisha loved the place instantly and within minutes was already in her undergarments and in the warm pool sitting beneath a cascading waterfall. Sister Lucy helped Theodoric ease himself in, and once in, remove his wet overshirt revealing the full brilliant blue colour of his winged tattoo plus the small red Castellan shield at the base of his neck."

"Did Paul not enter?" Sarah asked.

"No...not straight away. He held on to Arri whilst Tenno stood as ever watchful with Brother Teric, Thomas and his men...just in case."

"Sounds idyllic?" the wealthy tailor remarked and smiled as he looked upwards trying to imagine what it was like.

"It is indeed. Eventually Alisha got out leaving Princess Stephanie resting near the waterfall and told Paul he must try it. Only after Theodoric beckoned him did he take off his robe and sword and stepped in wearing just his undergarments. He went to sit near to Theodoric but he motioned he sit next to Princess Stephanie. She lay back with her eyes shut, the water from the fall just catching the back of her head and hair."

"What...they all got in just wearing their undergarments?" Ayleth asked, looking shocked.

"My young woman...in the heat and conditions, no one stands on ceremony or modesty when one can steal the chance to clean oneself and cool off," the Hospitaller explained and nodded at her with a smile and winked. Ayleth blushed.

"Sitting next to Princess Stephanie though, Paul could not help but glance at her," the old man started to explain but was interrupted by Sarah.

"See, I knew it...the silly sod could not keep his eye off of her. Told you he would."

"No Sarah, he glanced at her, for what man in his right mind would not, unless he was blind. You must understand, Princess Stephanie is a very alluring and beautiful woman. It would, I think you would agree, be unnatural for him not to have looked. She lay with water cascading over her shoulders, her face looking up, her eyes closed and her wet top clinging to her figure revealing more than it should. Paul, even if out of curiosity looked at her."

"And what was Alisha doing at this point?" Sarah asked.

"She was actually sorting Arri out to wash him. But Sister Lucy saw him looking at her and reached across Theodoric and slapped his right arm hard. Paul looked at her feigning indignation but he knew what she meant just as Princess Stephanie did likewise and smiled to herself."

"Hmm. This princess seems like a contradiction in terms. She values Alisha's friendship and yet covets her husband...clearly," Sarah commented and shrugged her shoulders.

"Princess Stephanie was nevertheless a moral and principled woman, believe me," the old man said in her defence. Gabirol looked at him for several moments then wrote some personal observational notes. "I can tell you that day was one of the most relaxing and memorable days for Alisha and Paul. Tenno even spent an hour with Theodoric alone...just the two of them as Theodoric went through his grounding practice."

"Grounding practice...what is that?" Gabirol asked.

"Theodoric had a theory, from several sources he had studied over the years, that we all are a part of this earth we live upon. He also believed that to keep one's balance and harmony with it, to regulate our bodies to the natural forces that surround us, we must all ground ourselves by standing barefoot upon the earth itself...no shoes, no blankets, just the earth. Tenno had a similar belief so when he saw Theodoric doing this, it intrigued him...and from that moment on, that marked the start of a deeper understanding between them. Sister Lucy nearly cried when she watched them both together."

"I am sorry, how does this grounding work? What is it for and how do I do it?" Simon asked shaking his head.

"Any of us can do it, especially if you are feeling anxious or stressed. Grounding techniques are easy to learn and easy to do. You do not really need any special training, just a basic understanding of the purpose of grounding and a few ideas on how to kick it into action if you feel anxious or stressed. It is a way and means to get back in touch with yourself in the present moment, to feel safe in your surroundings and calm and in control of your breath and your body...and it works," the old man answered.

"Then pray tell me for I think I need grounding." Sarah laughed as Stephan agreed with a nod, smiling at her.

"'Tis simple enough. By practising awareness of your posture and breath in certain situations you can quickly master the art of stopping anxiety before it takes control by using *a simple grounding technique, the simplest way being to just look up. When we are feeling stressed and anxious we tend to look down, this puts us in an internally looking state where any stress or negative feelings are easily built up and can quickly grow and manifest. So the first key step in any situation of uncertainty, overwhelming feelings or anxiety is to look up. Move your eyes up toward the sky and take a deep breath in. Then feel your connection with the earth. When we are un-grounded we feel disconnected and out of sorts. To feel grounded again you need to concentrate on your connection with the ground. Feel your feet on the floor, move them about and feel the sensation of the ground against your feet. Start walking about or stamp them against the floor and really think upon the solid feel of the earth beneath you. Then feel your body, bend your knees slightly and push your hands down onto your thighs, feel how solid your body is. Pat up and down your arms and legs and relax... and you will feel better almost instantly," the old man explained and smiled broadly as he looked at the wealthy tailor rubbing his hands down his thighs with his eyes shut.*

"Sounds a bit weird to me," the Genoese sailor remarked almost dismissively and also looked at the wealthy tailor.

"But can I ask, did our Princess try anything 'inappropriate' with Paul or did she behave?" Sarah asked sarcastically.

"She behaved...just as she always had before. After a brief snack of dates, olives, for there were many olive trees scattered about, they set off to rejoin the main caravan. They actually arrived back at Umm Quasi just as the other larger caravan they had seen in the morning pass through heading south also did. There were many children and several silk traders and wealthy merchants. They were escorted by a mix of both Frankish and Muslim mercenaries. Thomas acknowledged one of the knights having served with him previously. Theodoric checked through all of their wagons and caravans before they finally pulled away in order to get to the next watchtower fort ten miles further on before sunset."

"Why did he do that?" Simon asked.

"Looking to see if the old woman and young girl were with them. People do not just walk off and leave an escorted caravan convoy in peace time, let alone with hostilities flaring up everywhere," the old man explained.

"But Brother Teric had them all stay a whole day to rest...why?" Gabirol asked suspiciously.

"Why?...because he had pushed them so hard and made them cover nearly twice the distance the previous day remember...and also because he knew that other groups were at large in the area, but also that Princess Stephanie needed some time to get her head straight. He may have been a Templar, but he was still a man first...and he had always admired Princess Stephanie...perhaps more than admired...and so they stayed and rested."

Gadara, Umm Quais, King's Highway, Kingdom of Jerusalem border, June 1179.

A chill wind blew up from the eastern side of the mountain as Paul wrapped a thick shawl around Alisha and helped her step down into the top tier of the old Roman amphitheatre. The sun was an almost blood red circle as it sat upon the horizon, the many remaining Roman columns looking black behind them. Sister Lucy was looking after Arri as well as keeping a close eye upon Theodoric as he slept soundly upon Princess Stephanie's bed. Brother Teric escorted Princess Stephanie towards the amphitheatre as they both followed Alisha and Paul just as loud laughter echoed from Guy's tent. Little fires grew brighter as pilgrims and the blacksmith set their fires for the night. Paul stood behind Alisha and wrapped his arms around her, gently kissing and caressing the side of her neck and then looked out to the horizon, their faces pressed together. Princess Stephanie stopped and just watched them, as Brother Teric took a deep silent breath as he watched her closely. Alisha and Paul just stared at the stunning view that stretched out in a wondrous panorama of colours and shadows, Lake Tiberius glistening almost black as it sat in shadow far off below. Paul smelt Alisha's hair and closed his eyes as he held her. She moved slightly to look at him and kissed the side of his face, as he again kissed her neck and she laughed lightly. Princess Stephanie sighed.

"You like him don't you?" Brother Teric whispered.

1 – 8

"Lord forgive me...but yes I do...and I hate myself for it," she whispered back. "And Alisha...she is by far a greater and better woman than I."

"I would beg to differ, My Lady."

"Huh. Do you know that all I have done of late is cry. When I am alone in that big empty caravan, I cry...for I feel so alone. 'Tis perhaps just a womanly thing, being pregnant, as it does that to a woman...but the vastness and emptiness of that caravan accurately conveys and portrays just how I feel," she explained and turned her head to look at him.

"I may speak out of turn...but a woman like you should never feel alone...and you are not alone."

"Thank you, Brother Teric...but I fear my strength has abandoned me these past months. As I said, all I do it would seem, is cry. I am a 'sacrament to tears' only. I am not as strong as I thought I was and I am certainly not ready for this child," she said quietly and placed her hands upon her belly and sighed.

"My Lady...you are here, you are strong and you can cope. And as I have learnt, in life, none of us is ever ready...for we are never ready, there is no such thing as ready, there is only now!" Brother Teric stated then looked at her intently. "My mother always told my sisters, a woman's strength isn't just about how much she can handle before she breaks, it's also about how much she must handle after she has broken."

Princess Stephanie looked Brother Teric in the eye for several moments.

"But why cannot I shake this deep fear that resides within me for I am constantly afraid...always afraid?" she asked.

"My Lady...when I feel like that, I simply remind myself of one simple fact," he said and paused briefly. "The phrase 'Do not be afraid' is written within the Bible 365 times...that is a daily reminder from God to live every day fearlessly."

"You are more insightful and wiser than I gave you credit for, Brother Teric," Stephanie replied sadly. "My mother likewise told me that in most cases, 'tis the strongest amongst us, the ones who smile through silent pains unseen, who cry behind closed doors, who fight the hardest battles that nobody else knows about who fall and break the hardest."

"My Lady...if you fall...I shall catch you," Brother Teric said reassuringly.

Princess Stephanie did not know how to reply to his last statement. She simply

181

smiled at him then looked back towards Alisha and Paul, their bodies embraced forming just one silhouette against the bright red setting sun. Brother Teric continued to look at Princess Stephanie as her words ran through his mind. He shook his head slightly. 'Sacrament of tears' he heard her say again in his mind. Here was a woman whom he would give everything up for, yet he knew it would never happen in this life time.

PART VI

Chapter 31
Where Shadows Cannot Reach

When Paul awoke, he breathed in deeply the cool fresh morning air. As he sat up and removed the thick heavy blanket, he noticed Tenno looking south to the horizon with Brother Teric and Thomas. The western horizon still appeared black but the sky lightened as it arched to the east into a light blue sky tinted a light yellow as the sun rose. Several people were coughing and a baby cried further down the column. Paul stood up and approached Tenno, looking to where they were pointing. On the far horizon, a single large column of black smoke was spiralling upwards and flattening out as it spread westward. The main road vanished off toward it almost like an arrow pointing at the smoke. Brother Teric looked at Paul, his face etched with concern.

"Not good?" Paul asked.

"Not good," he replied and headed straight for Guy's tent.

"Look," Tenno said and nodded toward the column of smoke on the horizon. "Can you make out the gathering vultures circling above? Means only one thing... there is death there."

Paul instinctively clasped his hand over the pommel of his sword as Percival came and stood beside him looking puzzled.

"Have everyone stand to, and prepare to move within the hour...and place all children under cover in the caravans and carts. I fear what lay ahead will not be pleasant," Brother Teric shouted back as he pulled Guy's tent ropes up causing it to fold in upon itself. Muffled protestations by Guy inside could be heard, but not understood. Thomas laughed as the tent collapsed.

಄ ಐ

After a two-hour march, the road started to incline downwards and pass between two natural high mounds on either side. The column of smoke was now just a whisper of pale grey gently rising, the fires having mainly burnt themselves out. Several Egyptian vultures and other birds circled above. Thomas and his men rode close to Alisha and Paul's caravan as Brother Matthew, Guy and his men surrounded Princess Stephanie's caravan. Brother Teric rode at the front of the column with the vanguard of Templars, the remaining knights at the rear. Tenno looked across from his driving seat at Paul as they crested the brow of the road. Brother Teric halted the column as he studied the scene that lay ahead of them where the road opened into a wide plateau, a perfect ambush position where attackers could rush down from either side of the two raised mounds and assault any caravan from behind. The smell of smoke and burnt flesh started to waft past them. Paul wasn't sure what the smell was at first. Brother Teric ordered two of his vanguard knights to proceed forwards carefully with their lances forward. Paul tried to lean out and see forwards but Princess Stephanie's caravan was blocking his view.

"I shall go and have a look," he said and went to step down.

"No you don't. You stay with us," Alisha called out through the small window from behind him. Tenno nodded he should stay.

Guy pulled his horse out from his position and moved toward Brother Teric. They exchanged words before Brother Teric turned and rode back along the column. He stopped next to Tenno.

"'Tis not a pretty sight to behold. Make sure the women and children remain under cover. 'Tis the caravan that came through Umm Quasi yesterday," he explained and then looked back toward the rising smoke. "But I am troubled. There is something highly unusual about this attack."

"How so?" Tenno asked as Brother Thomas moved closer upon his horse to listen.

"Not sure yet...but when a caravan is assaulted, the attackers usually take captive the civilians and any soldiers and knights not killed for ransom. They usually take all the spoils they can carry," Brother Teric explained and paused as he kept his eyes upon the two knights probing their way through the burnt wreckage of the destroyed convoy. "All the knights, from what I can see, are slaughtered as are all the other men, women and children...'tis not normal...for it looks like whoever did this has not even taken any of their goods."

"And they must have been well trained to have taken the knights out so effectively," Thomas commented and scanned the two sides of the gorge they were in. "I would say whoever they were, they have gone...but I would advise we move from this place now as we are exposed to ambush all too easy here."

"I agree," Brother Teric replied. "We shall have to send a bigger fighting column back later to bury the dead and recover what can be salvaged...'tis too obvious a trap in my opinion."

Guy came riding back and pulled up alongside Brother Teric.

"Looks like the handiwork of the Ashashin," he remarked, his yellow horse armour coverings reflecting the sun making him stand out incredibly brightly.

"No, 'tis not their way at all...and I would advise you to remove and pack away your banners and colours...for if we are being targeted or set up, 'tis the likes of you any assailant will go for first," Brother Teric stated looking at Guy shaking his head.

One of the vanguard knights checking the destroyed caravan trotted back and pulled up opposite Brother Teric.

"Brother Teric...all are slain. We cannot see or find any survivors...even babies. 'Tis not a pleasant sight indeed, so I would recommend closure of all windows as we pass through...so as not to upset the ladies and children as you advise. 'Tis truly a brutal sight," the Templar explained.

Paul looked behind him as Alisha opened the small window looking at him concerned.

"We shall stay inside...but I do not like this being stuck here feeling trapped... especially with the smell of smoke entering so thickly," she exclaimed.

"I have it under control here!" Theodoric called out from his position on the blacksmith's second cart further back.

Paul went to reply, when Brother Teric motioned the entire column to start moving. All he could do was look on as Tenno slowly steered the caravan through the burnt out shells of various caravans and carts. Several dead camels blocked the main route, but were quickly pulled aside by several of the Templar sergeants on foot using ropes. Several beasts of burden and sumpter horses stood motionless until two of Thomas's men rounded them up and began tying them to the rear of Guy's personal cart containing all of his tentage and supplies. The air became filled with the pungent smell of burnt bodies, several of which hung over the sides of the destroyed carts with grotesque burnt faces that revealed their teeth in bright contrast as if smiling. Paul noted several small children's corpses so badly burnt their arms and legs were almost burnt away. Several other children lay ahead as if asleep with no visible signs of any injury. Several more yoked horses and camels secured by rope halters were pulled aside by two Templars to join the end of the convoy. Tenno nodded towards several mules loaded with spices of different kinds, and clearly of great value as one of Thomas's men lifted gold and silver purses high. Cloaks of silk, purple and scarlet robes, and variously-ornamented apparel, besides arms and weapons of many different forms including coats of mail, commonly called gasiganz, costly cushions, pavilions, tents, biscuits, bread, barley, grain, meal, and a large quantity of conserves and medicines. Basins, bladders, chessboards, silver dishes and candlesticks, pepper, cinnamon, sugar, wax and other valuables of choice and various kinds and clearly an immense sum of money, and an incalculable quantity of goods, were simply strewn across the road. One of Thomas's men quickly dismounted and picked up one of the chessboards and chess box sets, placed it within his side satchel and remounted. He rode over to Paul's side of the caravan.

"I have secured this shatranj set as it is marked with its owner's name. There is far too much here to recover now but this is no ordinary ambush. This is pure wanton murder for no obvious reason, and by the lack of other evidence, I would wager 'twas a small highly trained group that did this," the knight explained then took out the chessboard and box of pieces and leaned across to hand it to Paul. "Here...take this and present it when we arrive at Kerak lest I am accused of theft."

Paul took the set without even thinking. Tenno looked at him and then the ornate and clearly expensive gold edged and gilded chessboard.

"The game of Kings and Princesses," Tenno commented.

Paul nodded his head as he placed it upon his lap and continued to look at the carnage as they moved slowly through the wreckage. Thomas stopped his horse next to the body of the knight whom he knew and had waved through only the previous day. He had several arrows in him, several deep slashes and many stab wounds. He had clearly put up an epic fight against whoever attacked him. He lay half-prostrated across a young woman dressed in expensive silks, half of her face and jaw cutaway by a sword stroke revealing her tongue and side teeth. To their side lay two Muslim mercenaries, one with his arm missing, the other with his head almost severed but still connected to his torso by the tendons and muscle of his neck, his spinal column bones above his shoulders sticking out a brilliant white in the sun. Paul's stomach started to retch as he felt nauseous. However, it was the many children, their little bodies crumpled and twisted, that burnt into his memory the most. Finally, after what seemed an age, they passed out the other side of the carnage. Paul took a deep breath and sat back against the seat's backboard. Paul looked across just in time to see Brother Teric reach down from his horse and pull out a small arming dagger from the throat of a dead Frankish knight. He held it up as he studied it before wiping away the blood. Paul's attention was drawn towards Princess Stephanie's caravan as Guy leaned over from his horse vomiting uncontrollably.

Port of La Rochelle, France, Melissae Inn, spring 1191

"That is truly terrible," Ayleth commented and held her hand to her mouth, shocked.

"Why would anyone do that...for no obvious reason? Those poor little babes," Sarah said, clearly saddened.

"It may not have seemed obvious then...but in time they would all find out why and by whom!" the old man stated.

"Really, then pray tell you inform us now!" Simon almost demanded.

"No...but I shall by the close of this tale," the old man replied.

"Why did the knight take the shatranj...that is a chess set right?" Peter asked.

"Because it was marked with the owner's name. So many pilgrims, and especially wealthy merchants who were murdered and simply left, were often under obligations or fiefs to the Orders and to keep an accurate record of dealings, as in some cases vast sums of money and material wealth was involved. If a person was known to have been killed, then appropriate action could be taken. No point in chasing a dead man is there or having someone else cash in their credit praesciptiones(cheques)," the old man explained.

"Did they all get to Kerak without incident?" Sarah asked hesitantly.

"Yes...yes they did. In fact, they made good progress, probably spurred on by what they had seen. Normally pilgrims on foot can take what seems like forever and of course the escorts were under obligation to protect them, but the pilgrims with them did not need telling nor encouragement to move," the old man answered.

"I am not surprised," the wealthy tailor remarked and shook his head, dismayed at what he had just heard.

"It was certainly a relief for all when they eventually saw Crac de Moab in Kerak. Princess Stephanie had stayed with Alisha and Sister Lucy almost every waking hour. Theodoric had made what can best be described as nothing short of a miraculous recovery and was soon back to his normal ways. Princess Stephanie became very quiet and almost withdrawn as they drew near to Kerak," the old man explained, when Ayleth politely interrupted him.

"Why would she be like that?"

"In truth...because she knew that she would again have to revert to being the Countess and Princess she was, with all its obligations and expectations placed upon her that her status entails and requires. She would again have to fall back into the strict and rigid practices of courtly behaviour. She had loved the semi autonomous freedom she had enjoyed over the past few months...and she would miss her friends whom she knew must move on with their own lives in vastly different directions."

"More like Paul you mean?" Sarah remarked.

"Perhaps that too...but her pain and sadness was nevertheless just as real. The only consolation she took from arriving back at Kerak was that her children were there. It was common practice to send children away to other households to be tutored, but she had argued her cause and refused to allow them to be sent elsewhere, much to the insecurities of Reynald..."

"Well as I have said, he sounds like a total brute...an animal," Ayleth remarked.

"As I have said, there is far more to him than that. There was a time when Theodoric and others saw great potential in him...but as oft is the case, sometimes when you give too much power to an individual, it corrupts and ruins them," the old man explained.

"Did that Stephanie Princess love him then...Reynald, that is?" Sarah asked.

"There was a time when she thought he was the answer to all her prayers, desires and needs...When they first met she had heard much about him, and his charm certainly told her all that she wanted...more importantly needed...to hear...and Reynald knew that," the old man revealed.

"Can I ask a question...about all the children in the caravan that were slaughtered...how come there were so many for surely they cannot be pilgrims too?" Simon asked and looked across to Sarah.

"No they were not. But many families travelled the King's Highway and other routes as they moved to either better themselves in a new location, leave a bad situation or simply to meet family...most were merchants of sorts who took their families like the nomads and Bedouins of the deserts..."

"Would not catch me doing it," Simon replied.

"So you mean to say you shan't be doing a pilgrimage after all?" the Templar joked.

"It all sounds so distant and removed from us here doesn't it?" Ayleth commented and strung her long hair around her finger as she pondered all of what she was hearing.

"I thought Theodoric was supposed to go to Jerusalem to join those Lazarus knights...or did I miss something?" the Genoese sailor asked.

"Oh he was intending to resolve that matter. It would mean travelling west then north from Kerak, but only after he had fully rested and knew that Alisha and Paul were on the last road to Alexandria...well that had been his initial intention! Going to Jerusalem was an obligation he did not wish to fulfil, but it was one he had taken on so had to make suitable agreements with the Order if he were to remove himself from it..."

 1 – 24

"And did he?" Gabirol asked.

"You should know by now...I shall of course answer that in due course. But as for Crac de Moab and Kerak itself, that was to be a place where Paul would start to see that life was not all as straightforward, nor black and white and that every person has a story to reveal...and that you cannot choose or help how you feel...things change," the old man sighed.

"He better not fall for that Stephanie!" Sarah stated and frowned hard.

The old man looked at her and smiled.

"Then let me explain, for even as they approached Kerak, Paul sensed a knowing for the place. Kerak Castle by the way got its name of Crac de Moab as it is built upon land of the former Biblical Moab. The city of Kerak was the ancient capital of Moab. During Roman times it was known as Characmoba. Most in the region simply refer to it as Le Crac which did cause some confusion with the other Crac...Crac de l'Ospital."

Crac de Moab, Oultrajordain, Kingdom of Jerusalem, June 1179

Tenno steered the caravan following closely behind Princess Stephanie's as the column reached the summit of the hill and then began to descend slightly towards the northern entrance of Crac de Moab that loomed like some great ship stranded upon the top of the hill. As the road curved slightly to the left, Paul could see the Templar vanguard form up into a tighter formation just as Guy trotted past him to his right to move to the front. Tenno shook his head. Paul had thought that Crac de l'Ospital had looked impressive but this castle appeared twice the size. 'Not as appealing to the eye,' he thought, but it was still massive in its presence, its sloping outer walls at its base adding to the sense of solidity. Many houses formed a sizable town around the castle and valley in front of it. As the column pulled to the right Paul saw several knights at the main entrance formed up as a welcoming party. They were all brightly coloured in stark contrast to the Templars and stood out against the mud coloured stonework with their banners and horse covers. Princess Stephanie's caravan stopped just short of the main entrance on the right side of the northern wall. Brother Matthew dismounted and quickly lowered the extendable steps out and secured them just as Princess Stephanie opened the side door. She looked up at the castle walls and shielded her eyes from the bright sunlight. She looked back towards Paul, smiled and gave a quick wave before stepping down. One of the welcoming party knights rode forwards and stopped a few paces from her. He bowed and they started talking just as Theodoric appeared standing next to Tenno.

"Bit odd...that is Raymond, the Count of Tripoli she's talking to. I wonder what brings him this far south?" he commented and squinted from the sun.

Sister Lucy appeared beside him carrying a wide brimmed hat and tried to place it upon his head.

"You are still not well enough to be standing out in the full sunlight...now put this on," she demanded and placed the hat upon his head.

"What are they doing?" Paul asked.

"Raymond is probably asking permission to enter her castle, as is custom. And I bet he will refuse all questions regarding his health," Theodoric answered.

"Questions?" Paul remarked questioningly.

"Yes...'tis a policy they have here. Anyone entering the castle must answer questions on their health and if needs be, prove it. Do you have leprosy...got worms, you name it, and they will ask it. And if you have anything nasty, they send you to the external hospice further on. 'Tis but a precaution. Too many pilgrims turn up here with many ailments and diseases after their long journeys. Many die," Theodoric stated.

Thomas rode up to Paul's side of the caravan and stopped.

"Do you think they will allow me and my men to enter?" he asked.

"Why would they not?" Paul answered, somewhat confused by his question.

"Hmmm, we shall see. Last time we were here, they refused us entry."

As soon as Paul heard this, he jumped down from his seat and started to walk over towards Princess Stephanie.

"Paul," Theodoric called out.

Paul raised his hand briefly back to Theodoric and continued to approach

Princess Stephanie. Brother Matthew immediately stepped in front of him stopping his progress. Paul frowned at him as Raymond sat up straight in his saddle and looked across at them both. Princess Stephanie looked over.

"This is Kerak. Here things are different and you will do well to remember that. Here they have rules and protocols of court to follow...so your days of over familiarity with the Princess ends the moment you walk through those gates...is that understood?" Brother Matthew stated, his teeth almost gritted together as he spoke quietly.

"I do not care where we are...she is my friend and I shall talk with her as I see fit...is that understood?" Paul shot back as Princess Stephanie started to walk towards them closely followed by Raymond on his horse.

"Really? You show your youth and ignorance in these matters. I offer you sound advice yet you choose to ignore me and become defensive," Brother Matthew replied quickly.

"Then perhaps you should check the manner and tone in which you give it," Paul replied just as Princess Stephanie reached them.

"Brother Matthew...Paul. Is there a problem here?" she asked seeing the strained looks upon their faces.

Paul looked at Brother Matthew for a moment, their eyes locked.

"No...there is no problem here," Paul answered. "I simply wish to know if Thomas and his men are to be allowed to enter, for I am informed they were barred last time," Paul explained as Count Raymond dismounted his horse and stood beside Princess Stephanie.

"I see no reason why not. 'Tis my castle and home after all," she answered puzzled.

Paul became aware of Raymond looking at him. He stood tall and wore a bright red surcoat and mantle over his chain mail.

"Lord Raymond...please let me introduce you to the man who has saved my life twice already. Paul Plantavalu," Stephanie said softly and smiled as she gestured toward him with her hand. "And Paul, this is Raymond, the Count of Tripoli."

Paul shook Raymond's hand firmly as Brother Matthew looked at him sneering.

"Paul...I knew your father well. A very learned man. I miss his presence in my court," Raymond said politely, his voice confident but pleasant.

"You knew my father?" Paul asked as Raymond held the handshake. Paul had only ever known his father in La Rochelle as a writer and map maker. He was now constantly learning so much more about him from his time in the Holy Land.

"Yes. Very well. How is he?"

"Last I saw, he was very well," Paul replied and Raymond broke the shake.

"Sire...you reply by saying Sire or Lord. 'Tis only good manners," Brother Matthew interrupted.

Paul looked at him puzzled then back at Princess Stephanie and Raymond, who smiled.

"'Tis not necessary. He is clearly new to these parts. I am sure Princess Stephanie will teach him the strange and oft mysterious ways of court whilst here," Raymond said and laughed.

Brother Matthew stepped back and shook his head clearly displeased with Paul. Brother Teric rode up from the rear guard and stopped behind Paul.

"Ah another friendly face. 'Tis good to see you, Brother Teric. We have much to discuss I believe?" Raymond said as Brother Teric dismounted.

"Aye My Lord...that we do indeed. That we do," Brother Teric said and shook his hand.

Port of La Rochelle, France, Melissae Inn, spring 1191

"Why is that Matthew so against Paul?" Ayleth asked.

"Jealous I bet," Simon remarked as Sarah shook her head in agreement.

"Perhaps," the old man commented.

"You say Raymond of Tripoli...we both know him," the Templar said as he looked at his brother, who nodded.

"Was he like Reynald then?" Gabirol asked as he waved his quill between his fingers.

"No...totally the opposite...and as he said, he knew Paul's father, Philip, well enough indeed," the old man replied in answer with a smile as if recalling fond memories.

"Seems like everyone knew everyone," the farrier remarked.

"That is because most did...within the ruling families at least. Even Reynald was connected by family all the way back to the Counts of Champagne...'tis one of the reasons why he had access to certain secrets," the old man explained and sat up straight.

"Probably explains how he managed to worm his way up the social ladder," Peter interrupted.

"As I keep saying, there is more to Reynald. But as for Raymond, 'tis a great pity there were not more like him and Balian. If there was, the story would certainly be a different one," the old man sighed.

"How so?" Sarah asked softly and leaned forwards.

"Let me tell you a little about Raymond, whom you know as Raymond the Third then, for I feel it necessary if only for the accuracy of later generations...should you remember this of course," the old man laughed lightly. "He was the great-great-grandson of Raymond the Fourth of Toulouse, also known as Raymond the First of Tripoli, who was succeeded by his father Raymond the Second, who was killed by the Ashashin in 1152, when he was just twelve. His mother, Princess Hodierna of Jerusalem, daughter of King Baldwin the Second, ruled as regent until he came of age three years later. He was also known as Raymond the Younger to distinguish him from his father. In 1160, the Byzantine emperor Manuel I Komnenos was seeking a wife from the Crusader states. The two candidates presented to him were Raymond's sister Melisende, and Princess Maria of Antioch, whom I have already spoken of. At first, Melisende was chosen, and Raymond collected an enormous dowry, while negotiations continued for over a year. During this time he prepared a fleet of twelve galleys to escort Melisende. However, Manuel's ambassadors heard rumours that both Melisende and Raymond himself might have been fathered by someone other than Raymond the Second, and the marriage was called off."

"Fathered by someone else! Who?" Sarah asked puzzled and intrigued.

"That, Sarah, is truly a tale for another time. But whatever the truth of the matter, Manuel married Maria instead. Raymond, feeling slighted for both himself and his sister, responded by converting the galleys into men-of-war, to plunder the Byzantine island of Cyprus. Sadly Melisende entered a convent, where she died fairly young. Then in 1164 Raymond and Bohemund the Third of Antioch marched out to relieve Harim, which was under siege by Nur ad-Din Zengi. The Crusader army was defeated in the ensuing battle

on August 12th, and Raymond, Bohemund, Joscelin the Third of Edessa, Hugh the Eighth of Lusignan, and others were taken captive and imprisoned in Aleppo. Raymond remained in prison until 1173, when he was ransomed for eighty thousand pieces of gold. During his captivity, King Amalric the First of Jerusalem ruled as regent of the county, and dutifully returned it to Raymond once he was released."

"So how come he got released but Reynald did not?" Gabirol asked.

"Simply because a bigger ransom for Raymond was raised and paid. But unlike Reynald, Raymond used his time in captivity to learn to read and write and study."

"Really. I thought that if they were in a prison, they were tied up in chains and hung from dungeon walls etcetera...is that not so then?" Ayleth asked.

"For men of high rank, no that is not so. In fact in some instances they were afforded more comfort and luxury than they got at home," the old man explained.

"By the Lords I never knew that. So Reynald spends sixteen years in pampered luxury and he still comes back hell bent on war," Simon said and shook his head surprised at what he had heard.

"Well, In 1174 Amalric died and was succeeded by his son Baldwin the Fourth, who was still too young to rule on his own and furthermore was suffering from leprosy as most of you now know. Miles of Plancy, the then 'seneschal of the kingdom', claimed the regency. But Raymond soon arrived and, as first cousin and closest male relative of King Amalric, demanded to be named bailli, which also means 'bailiff' or 'regent'. He was supported by the major barons of the kingdom, including Humphrey the Second of Toron, Balian of Ibelin, and Reginald of Sidon. But mysteriously Miles was assassinated in Acre and Raymond was duly and rapidly invested as bailli."

"I thought you said this Raymond was a good man?" Ayleth asked.

"He is. He had no dealings in the machinations that led to Miles's assassination. Besides, sometimes bad things have to be done in order for a greater good to be achieved. That is a point I would ask you all to remember...," the old man answered and paused to give them all time to think upon his words. "Raymond married Eschiva of Bures, the Princess of Galilee and the widow of Walter of Saint-Omer of Tiberias. This then allowed him to gain control over much of the northern part of the Kingdom of Jerusalem, especially the fortress at Tiberias on the Sea of Galilee. As regent, he appointed William of Tyre chancellor of Jerusalem in 1174 and archbishop of Tyre in 1175. He retired as bailli when Baldwin the Fourth came of age in 1176, having arranged for Baldwin the Fourth's sister Sibylla of Jerusalem to marry William Longsword of Montferrat though he soon died in 1177 while Sibylla was pregnant with the future Baldwin the Fifth."

"My Lord, they all seem to die pretty frequently and marry fast," Sarah joked.

"Yes they do don't they," the old man acknowledged and smiled at her before continuing. "Amalric the First had married twice, to Agnes of Courtenay, now married to Reginald of Sidon, and to Maria Comnena, the dowager Queen, who had married Balian of Ibelin in 1177. His daughter by Agnes, Sibylla, was already of age, the mother of a son, and was clearly in a strong position to succeed her brother, but Maria's daughter Isabella had the support of her stepfather's family, the Ibelins. Raymond's own position amid these tensions was difficult and controversial. As the king's nearest relative in the male line, he had a strong claim to the throne himself. However, although his wife had had several children by her first husband, he had no children of his own to succeed him...and this seems to have held him back from advancing himself as king. Instead, he acted as a power-broker, working closely with the Ibelins and attempting to influence the marriages of the princesses. The king, meanwhile, relied considerably on his mother and her brother, Joscelin the Third of Edessa, who had no claims of their own to advance. It was during this period, now 1179, that Baldwin began planning to marry Sibylla to Hugh the Third of Burgundy. It was one of the main reasons he was visiting Kerak when Paul arrived. But by spring the following year in 1180 this would still prove to be unresolved and Raymond attempted a coup. He would march on Jerusalem with Bohemund the Third, to force the king to marry his sister to a local candidate of his own choosing, Baldwin of Ibelin, Balian's older brother. To counter this, the king hastily arranged her marriage to Guy de Lusignan, younger brother of Amalric, the constable of the kingdom. A foreign match was also essential to bring the possibility of external military aid to the kingdom. With the new French king Philip the Second a minor, Guy's status as a vassal of the King and Sibylla's first cousin Henry the Second of England, who owed the Pope a penitential pilgrimage, was useful. Raymond consequently returned home without entering the kingdom."

"What...so that is how that idiot Guy climbed the ladder and became king," the Templar remarked, shaking his head in surprise.

"Basically...yes! But we are again running ahead of ourselves in this story, so let me just quickly explain further that Raymond would later have great cause to despise Reynald for he would be the man, the main protagonist in fact, that would use his marriage to Princess Stephanie and of being Humphrey of Torons...Stephanie's son remember...and his position as his stepfather to swing things in favour of Guy. He would ultimately use Gerard himself to back him militarily with the Templars' full might to instigate his will. Reynald saw Guy as easily manipulated and believed he could get him to do his will and bidding later," the old man explained. He noticed the Templar shaking his head, saddened.

"What naivety I and my men so blindly followed," he said shaking his head further. "We were all just pawns in a big game of chess weren't we?" he remarked and looked up. Miriam clasped his hand and rubbed his shoulder.

"My good Templar...we are all but pawns upon God's great board...but it was because of all of these dealings and machinations that Raymond tried to make peace with Saladin and, like Balian, became friends with him. Raymond was astute and intelligent enough to have the foresight to see the long-term potential of Reynald and ultimately Guy as becoming a bigger enemy than Saladin himself. But that I shall cover later when our tale reaches that time. But as I mentioned William of Tyre, I should perhaps tell you how he viewed Raymond for he wrote much about him. He said that Raymond was a man of slender build, extremely spare, of medium height and swarthy complexion. His hair was straight and rather dark in colour. He had piercing eyes and carried his shoulders very erect. He was prompt and vigorous in action, gifted with equanimity and foresight, and temperate in his use of both food and drink, far more than the average man. He showed munificence towards strangers, but towards his own people he was not so lavish. He was fairly well-lettered, an accomplishment which he had acquired while a prisoner among the enemy, at the expense of much effort, aided greatly, however, by his natural keenness of mind. Like King Amalric the First, he eagerly sought the knowledge contained in written works. He was indefatigable in asking questions if there happened to be anyone present who in his opinion was capable of answering..." The old man paused. "And that is why he relished his time with Paul's father previously, but also Theodoric's and in time Paul's." [37]

"How could he enjoy time with Paul if he was leaving for Alexandria?" Simon asked, impatient in tone.

"Let me continue and I shall explain then," the old man answered and smiled broadly at him.

Crac de Moab, Oultrajordain, Kingdom of Jerusalem, June 1179

Raymond politely bowed his head at Paul and ushered Princess Stephanie towards the main entrance on foot, crossing the large wooden draw bridge that spanned a specially dug moat. Brother Teric started to wave the column to follow inside slowly. As Brother Matthew flounced off and led Princess Stephanie's caravan across the bridge and through the main gates into Crac de Moab Paul climbed up onto the seat next to Tenno. Tenno solicited some strange looks from the men and sergeants manning the actual entrance. He ignored them. Paul looked up as they passed beneath the great northern walls. Theodoric had already explained the castle in detail and how it was laid out on a roughly trapezoidal plan which followed the contours of the ridge on the western and eastern sides, while on the northern and southern fronts it was protected by deep dry moats. Placed beneath the southeastern battlement, a massive glacis of a paved steep slope was placed to secure that direction. The castle had been commissioned by Payen Le Bouteiller (Pagan the Butler), 1139 and was completed in 1142 and it looked pristine. The plan was based on that of an upper and a lower enceinte (court). The upper enceinte comprised the bulk of the castle's surface area and a church, olive and grape presses, bakeries and a palace keep. The lower enceinte occupied the western side of the ridge complete with a subterranean level containing two large halls running north to south and joined by a large central chamber; it also contained two additional halls at the northern end of the compound. The northern battlements had immense arched halls on two levels built into them. Paul would later learn that these were used for living quarters and stables, but also served as a fighting gallery overlooking the castle approach and as shelter against missiles from siege engines. Once inside, Paul looked across the vast courtyard as Princess Stephanie's son Humphrey appeared with a Cistercian monk beside him closely followed by her very young daughter Isabella sucking her thumb. The monk pulled her hand away from her mouth hard. She scowled at him. Hesitantly Humphrey looked at his mother before realising it was her. As soon as he did, he ran over to her, flung his arms around her waist, and buried his face in her chest as Isabella ran over to her. Princess Stephanie smiled and stroked his long blonde hair and rubbed her other hand over Isabella's head playfully as she hugged her leg. The monk approached shaking his head disapprovingly at Humphrey and Isabella's display but Princess Stephanie raised her right hand slightly toward him to keep back and then hugged her son and daughter tightly. Paul noticed that for a boy of thirteen Humphrey was tall. He smiled seeing the obvious delight and happiness she had at seeing her children again. Brother Teric approached as Tenno applied the main brake lever.

"Paul, Tenno, I shall see to it you get a decent abode for your stay...and suitable quarters for Thomas and his men. I am afraid it will be Brother Matthew whom you will have to deal with in my absence," Brother Teric explained looking up at them both.

"How so?" Tenno asked bluntly.

"I have to return to the scene of the caravan assault I am afraid. But I shall return here just as soon as is possible," he answered and looked across at Princess Stephanie still hugging her children and laughing with them.

Tenno nudged Paul after a few minutes as they watched Brother Teric stood in silence just staring at Princess Stephanie. Eventually Tenno coughed loudly on purpose to get his attention again.

1 – 8

∞ ∞

After Paul and Tenno had untethered Adrastos from the caravan and made him comfortable in the covered stables, they both helped carry Sister Lucy's and Theodoric's trunk, which had gained in weight somewhat, to the second floor of the main Keep. They looked at the massive vaulted passages almost in awe at their size as they walked along them; the walls brightly covered in frescos and white plaster and hung banners. Alisha and Paul were taken to a small room on the same level by one of Stephanie's resident chambermaids. She was a slight wisp of a girl who spoke very little. Sister Lucy and Theodoric were placed in a larger room near to Princess Stephanie's master chambers. Paul joked how they were obviously getting preferential treatment, but Theodoric joked back it was because Brother Matthew had secured their accommodation and they were lucky not to be in the stables with Adrastos. No sooner had Paul helped Alisha into their room than Theodoric was beckoning Paul to follow him. Sister Lucy took Arri from Alisha so she could unpack the few items they had and pushed Paul out of the room almost. Paul followed Theodoric up a set of steep winding stairs of the furthest tower. Paul had to pull on the rope side rail supports as Theodoric seemed to race off.

"Thought you were supposed to still be recovering?" Paul called out as Theodoric was out of sight as he climbed the spiral staircase faster.

"Nope...whatever the old woman did, I feel twenty years younger...but do not tell Luce that as she'll stop being so nice," he answered laughing.

"First lesson in castle warfare," Theodoric called back. "Why do the staircases spiral right handed?"

Paul looked up puzzled at his question then looked out of the small slit window to his left as he passed it. He looked at the stairs as he stepped up each one wondering indeed why the stairs spiralled upwards to the right.

"No idea," he called up.

"Tut tut...'tis so that any attacking knights have to wield their swords in their left hands whilst the defending knights can hack downwards with their right hands still. These are basics, Paul, you need to learn," Theodoric called back down as he stepped out and onto the main course of the battlements' northern wall.

"But I am not a soldier nor to become a knight...unless there is something you are not telling me?" Paul replied as he caught him up and stepped outside into the brilliant sunlight.

"Now just look at that view eh," Theodoric said and outstretched his hands.

"That has to be one of the most amazing views I have ever seen," Paul remarked as he stood against the balustrades, then looked down at the sheer drop beneath him. His head momentarily spun and he felt slightly dizzy. Quickly he stood back a pace and took a deep breath.

Theodoric laughed seeing his reaction at the near 300 foot drop. A Muslim call to prayer echoed out below and Paul looked to see where it was coming from amongst the various buildings on the other side of the main road that led up to the castle. He frowned puzzled at hearing the call to prayer.

"'Tis a mixed area...you will hear that five times a day without fail. 'Tis a good sign as it shows tolerance is exercised here," Theodoric explained and laughed at the look of apprehension on Paul's face at the height they were at. "Like me, you don't have a head for heights," Theodoric said and patted Paul on the back and then pointed north. "Look...see that, that is the Dead Sea...and just before you get there, there is a wonderful wadi. Truly beautiful. 'Twas the place I first laid hands upon my Luce...though just a passionate kiss," he explained and just stared with a broad smile in the direction he had pointed.

"Would not Sister Lucy be embarrassed you tell me such things?" Paul asked, bemused.

"No...of course not...not much anyway. Besides, you will not exactly tell her now will you...for this is man's talk," Theodoric replied smiling broadly. "I shall take you there if we are able...but regards talking and what we tell our women, Paul, 'tis not a light subject. There will be times when you simply cannot tell Alisha things you know, experience or discover."

Paul looked at him.

"No, I promised Alisha I would always tell her everything...everything," Paul replied, surprised at Theodoric's remarks.

"Paul, do not take this as an insult...but that is the response of a young man... for it shows you have much to learn still...and it does not, I repeat, does not mean you are being dishonest with Alisha...for there will come a time when you must lie, even bare faced, in order to protect her. I wish it were not so, but as life will teach you, some things must remain private and secret."

"No...Ali and I have an understanding...a connection I cannot understand," Paul shot back.

Theodoric turned to face Paul properly and sighed. He placed his hands upon his hips as he looked at him for several minutes.

"Paul...when the time comes and you find yourself having to bend the facts, for her own safety or sanity, you will recall this conversation...and when you do, you must not chastise yourself. Him upstairs will understand."

"Is that why you still have not mentioned anything further about that old woman...whoever or whatever she was, since she saved you. Is there a dark secret you hide from Sister Lucy?" Paul asked, his tone raised.

"My friend...you see much and you learn fast. But not all that you see is what you think you perceive or understand...and no, for the record, 'tis not a dark secret, for not all secrets are dark. Some secrets have to remain hidden...out of sight from where shadows never reach...," Theodoric explained and feigned a smile of sorts.

"Then what do you know of that old woman for she was always in the harbour back home. She gave Ali and me a lily flower, and...and she keeps telling me they, whoever they are, watch me...so what is that all about?" Paul asked and looked Theodoric in the eyes intently.

"Lord, you are your father's son all right. You have that same look when you ask questions..."

"You know that woman and I know she is not normal. I need you to be honest with me and explain what she wants."

"Yes...yes I know that woman," Theodoric started to explain when a sudden up draught blew up the side of the castle hard and pushed them both back slightly. Quickly Paul grabbed the side of the battlements with his right hand and grabbed Theodoric with is left hand to steady him. "Huh, see, even the bloody elements that woman controls," he laughed as he steadied himself. Paul frowned at him quizzically. "Paul...I know the old woman...and all I can tell you at this moment is that I have known her a long time. A very long time in fact! But you must trust me when I say she is not bad, neither is she as old as she presents herself."

"What? What do you mean?" Paul asked confused.

"I would have to show you as no amount of explaining will help you understand," Theodoric replied and paused. "I have to go to Jerusalem...so come with me and I will show you."

"Jerusalem!" Paul exclaimed. "I cannot...not without Alisha and Arri."

"They will be perfectly safe here...especially if we leave Tenno with them."

"No...no I cannot," Paul replied shaking his head and looked out across the valley and towards the Dead Sea on the far horizon just visible as it shimmered.

"No such thing as cannot...and check your parchment...for it is marked on all three of your paths you will visit Jerusalem."

"No it is not," Paul shot back with alarm in his voice.

"Paul...I will not speak of this again or ask again...but check your paths again," Theodoric said and gently held Paul's forearm. "Just check again."

Theodoric looked Paul in the eyes, nodded, let go of his arm and immediately headed back into the doorway of the spiral stairway of the tower. Within seconds he was gone and out of sight leaving Paul to stand alone looking out across the vast landscape that stretched from horizon to horizon on all sides. It then struck Paul that there were no guards or look outs in the watchtowers. He placed his hands upon the battlements and looked over the edge again carefully. It was a dizziness inducing height and he slowly pulled himself back, took a deep breath and thought upon Theodoric's words.

෴

Paul and Alisha sat quietly upon the bed as Arri smiled and wriggled between them. The room was a welcoming cool. Paul's mind raced with a thousand questions as he recalled all the events of the past year and a half. All that he had learnt and seen. He looked at the parchments placed upon their travelling chest still rolled up and with dirt upon them where Gerard had thrown them to the ground. Alisha could see him looking at the scrolls several times and sensed something was clearly playing upon his mind. She placed her hand upon his hand and looked at him in silence but as if to ask what was he thinking. He clasped her hand gently then quickly kissed it. She smiled but frowned questioningly at him.

"Come on...what troubles you, Paul?" she asked softly.

"I am not sure really," he replied and paused as he looked at Arri kicking his legs. "I asked Theo about that old woman...and, and he said he could not answer but could show me if I went to Jerusalem with him," Paul explained quietly.

"Then go to Jerusalem," Alisha replied simply and smiled as she clasped his hand in hers.

"What?" Paul asked surprised.

"Paul…Stephanie has asked, actually begged more like, for Sister Lucy to stay here as her midwife until her baby is born. Sister Lucy has said she must stay with me and Arri…and so Stephanie has asked if I would likewise stay the period," Alisha explained.

"But I cannot leave you and Arri. No way, I would miss you too much…besides, 'tis far too dangerous at the moment."

"Paul…listen to me, my man. I have travelled much already in my life…you have not had the chance to travel and enjoy the lands…for you worry too much about us. Besides, look where we are. 'Tis perhaps the most heavily defended castle in all of the kingdoms…and it has never been breached yet," she explained to reassure him.

"Yet…and what happens when Reynald returns?"

"He will not return until the winter begins…so Stephanie said…as that is when the pilgrims and caravans almost cease and you will be back by then. And if Reynald did return early, he will not hurt me," Alisha explained looking Paul in the eyes. "Arri and I would and will be far safer here whilst the troubles continue. Do you not agree?"

"And what of us meeting Turansha as arranged?" he whispered.

"As Stephanie explained…she can have word with him by tomorrow."

"What…you have discussed this already…?"

"Of course…what else do we women have to do?" Alisha joked and smiled but she could see the concern in Paul's face.

"But I do not wish to be apart from you and Arri. Not ever…not for a single day," Paul replied looking confused.

"Nor I you…but I think we need some answers if we are to ever have a normal life. Do you not agree and is it not better we find out now…whilst we are here and before it can impact upon Arri?" Alisha said softly and pulled Paul's face gently so he looked at her. "There are things happening we have no understanding of and no way of controlling…and I have already said to Stephanie I would stay with Sister Lucy."

"What?" Paul said aloud and stood up fast.

"Paul…do not get angry. Do you think I do not read those damn things over there?" she said and stood up and took hold of his hands again whilst indicating with her eyes towards the scrolls. "'Tis far better and wiser we tick off that Jerusalem visit now. It will save you having to make the journey at a later date when you will have to travel further and be away from us longer."

Paul looked at the scrolls then back at Alisha. He knew what she said made sense but it cut into him almost like knife. Arri made a noisy squeal laugh and was looking at them. Paul looked back at his smiling face and then Alisha. He felt sick but knew that what she said made sense…if the parchment scrolls were to be trusted or were somehow genuine. A part of him wanted to throw them away and never refer to them again, but his mind was curious to find out all he could about the old woman and just how she had saved Theodoric's life in the manner she had. And who the people were she said were watching him and Alisha. He sighed heavily and pulled Alisha close and hugged her tightly.

"I am not so sure. I will have to think upon it," Paul finally remarked.

When Arri started to get agitated, as he was hungry, Alisha pulled away from

Paul and picked him up. As she started to feed him, Paul opened the scrolls and rolled them out flat and studied them. 'Look again.' He recalled Theodoric's comments. Should he pay any attention to them or throw them away? he thought. But Niccolas had spent a long time working upon them and he felt it would be an insult to his memory to dismiss them out of hand. He followed the lines until he located a link that had the image of what appeared to be a knight but without a knight's symbol. It was illustrated in green on all three lines. Next to them was a symbol of a circle with a dot, which he knew represented God, and a symbol for a city and beneath that, a symbol for a sacred doorway. He had never paid much attention to these symbols among the many. His heart sank and he felt sad that he would have to be apart from Alisha and Arri but he also knew she was right, as she usually was, that it would be better to go now whilst they were near. He looked across at Alisha feeding Arri. She smiled beautifully at Arri and Paul felt the tug inside his heart for them both. He looked back at the scrolls just as Alisha looked up at him. Not for one moment did she want him to leave them and though she was smiling outwardly, she felt part terrified at the prospect of him leaving. She laughed to herself seeing his sword still simply tied to his waist by a piece of rope. She would have to sort him a proper scabbard before he left.

Port of La Rochelle, France, Melissae Inn, spring 1191

"Ah, well she must have as the sword now has a scabbard," the Genoese sailor remarked pointing toward the sword.

"In time...but not then," the old man replied looking down at the sword and running his finger along the pattern on the simple leather scabbard.

"I am confused," Gabirol stated and re-read a section of his notes before looking up at the old man. "Theo said he helped in the negotiations to ransom Reynald...but that was a long time ago he said. How can that be as the time you speak of was only...what, three years maximum since his release?"

"No, Theodoric had been one of the original delegation that sought to have Raymond and Reynald released soon after their captivity begun...and at the time it was Raymond who was the priority...due to his true lineage," the old man explained.

"Ah! So there is some question over his bloodline?" Simon interjected quickly and nodded with a smug grin as if he had just cracked some code. He folded his arms again, proud of himself.

"Good, Simon...very good," the old man remarked.

"So are you going to tell us about Raymond's true lineage then?" the wealthy tailor asked.

"No...not at this moment. Perhaps I shall, depending upon how you take everything else that I tell you...," the old man smiled.

"What about this old woman then? Is she some kind of sorceress...or witch thing they call them now?" Sarah asked.

"And what about the Noah prophecies? Did you not mention them earlier at Kerak?" Peter asked.

"Let me start by answering Sarah's question first. I will explain in full about the old woman once our story gets us to Jerusalem, for it is there, as Theodoric stated, that the

explanation and answer could be seen...and more importantly, understood," the old man answered and paused as he studied their reactions. "And in answer to Peter's question...the Noah prophecies dealt with things that would come to pass as written within the Bible and attributed to Noah. People can read prophecies from an ancient book or attributed to a past prophet...yet you get a living person, who can prophecy just as accurately, or use astronomical calculations like the three wise men, the Magi, did and nowadays they will accuse you of heresy, Devil worship or worse. But sometimes that can work in your favour," the old man explained.

"How so?" Ayleth asked quietly.

"Remember that Gerard had Paul and Alisha's scrolls? Well, his interpreter read several of their symbols and noted them as referring to the Despesini and Elohim...He understood it as meaning that Paul and Alisha were both Elohim...of course Gerard did not believe that... at first...but it made him stop and think."

"Oh I see. So are we saying that Paul is as we thought some kind of new Messiah?" Simon asked.

"No...though some would claim that and it was possible to see why they thought such a thing. But as for the Noah prophecies...you must understand that near to Kerak was a tomb claimed to be that of Noah himself. Princess Stephanie had promised to show Paul and Alisha the site as Theodoric had spoken often of it, especially in regard to the original Noah being symbolically identical with a guide...as a navigator," the old man explained.

"Yes...I can see the connection there," Gabirol stated and wrote some notes quickly.

"I think I can confidently say that this is something that we all know about...Noah and the Flood. For 120 years, Noah predicted according to God's instruction that there would be a flood upon the earth. It is written in Genesis, Chapter 6 where it says, 'The Lord saw the wickedness of man was great on the earth and that every intent of the thoughts of his heart was only evil continually. So the Lord said, "I will destroy man whom I have created from the face of the earth"' (Genesis: 6:5–8). And so, for a hundred and twenty years, Noah built the ark and he also preached a message of repentance. Of course many disbelieve the account but what is important is the moral tale it teaches but also the mathematical values within it as well as the size and dimensions of things mentioned. I will, if we have time, explain them to you later. Of course many discount much of this story as just a very, very ancient fable and myth but I can tell you it is all based upon a much earlier tale that in turn was based upon real events in mankind's past. But let me bring you to the New Testament, and another biblical period that we all believe in, where we find Jesus Christ talking about Noah. In Chapter 24 of Matthew, he states in verses 37 to 39, 'As it was in the days of Noah, so shall it be in the days of the coming of the Son of Man' (Matthew: 24:37–39). Jesus was speaking of the prophecy of His second coming, more specifically, about the conditions of the end time prior to His coming being very similar to the conditions of the time of Noah and the Flood."

"Such as?" Simon interrupted bluntly.

"Such as people turning away from God, adultery being accepted, many of the signs I mentioned previously that even the Qur'an details. But sadly many turn to the story of Noah and the Flood as a way to teach on the end times, and consequently they do serious damage to the text of scripture by insisting it purely relates to its first-century context. That Jesus used the story to describe what was going to happen to Jerusalem, the temple, and the nation of Israel within a generation...but it was not exclusively about that period. It also carried codes and symbolism that would be required, more importantly, to be understood in the real last days...which are still many hundreds of years away," the old man explained.

"*Really? Well that is okay then. I need not worry for now,*" Simon joked loudly.

"*But it does concern you...for what if I told you that you will be around in those days... that all of you will be. Perhaps not in the bodies you presently have, but still present nevertheless,*" the old man asked.

1 – 20

"*You mean as in reborn, resurrected for the last judgement?*" Ayleth asked nervously.

"*In a fashion...I suppose you could say yes.*"

"*But what does Kerak have to do with Noah?*" Sarah asked.

"*There is a tomb, supposedly of Noah himself, in Kerak. But there are several in the region, another notable one being at Karak. Noah was the tenth prophet and last antediluvian patriarch. Noah was apparently aged 950 years and was extremely tall,*" the old man explained when Simon interrupted.

"*Just like that Abi...,*"

"*Yes, just like Abi. As I explained earlier, the story of Noah and the Flood is found in a number of different passages in the Qur'an as well as the Bible. Muslim exegetes say that the Ark came to rest on Mount Judi and that Noah was buried nearby. Some claim that Noah founded a city called al-Thamanin, meaning 'the Eighty' because there were eighty people on the Ark. Many exegetes say that the first city founded by Noah, and where he was buried, was called 'Karak'. This may account for the fact that there are tombs of Noah in several different cities named Kerak and Karak. But in and around Kerak other shrines of significance to Islam are located. That is why so many Muslims live there. Reynald wanted them all removed but by the grace of Princess Stephanie's persuasive nature, and to keep the peace, he let them remain. Besides, you can actually visit the Prophet Nuh 'Noah' shrine in the city of Kerak. God sent Noah to his people in Kerak to warn them of divine punishment if they continued to worship idols. As stated in the Holy Qur'an in a sura entitled Noah (Sura 71, verses 1–3) 'We sent Noah to his People, with the Command, do thou warn thy People before there comes to them a grievous Chastisement. He said, O my People! I am to you a Warner, clear and open: That ye should worship Allah, fear Him and obey me'.*"

"*I find it amazing that we actually have so much in common with our prophets and beliefs with Islam. I never knew this,*" Peter remarked.

"*Well that is not all at Kerak. Credited with great wisdom and piety, the King of Israel, 'Solomon', known as Sulayman in Islam, also has a shrine in Sarfah very near to Kerak. Solomon had great powers that included control over the winds, over the jinn and understanding the language of birds and other animals. Islam regards Solomon as impeccable like his father King Dawud or David and is mentioned in sixteen verses in the Holy Qur'an. Plus there is the shrine of Zaid ibn Ali ibn Al-Hussein. He was the great, great, grandson of the Prophet Muhammad himself and a religious leader known for his righteous, majestic and knowledgeable ways. When describing Zaid May, Al-Imam Ja'far Al-Sadiq said: 'Among us he was the best read in the Holy Qur'an, and the most knowledgeable about religion, and the most caring towards family and relatives'. So you can see, Crac de Moab in Kerak was not simply a Crusader castle within a city. It is a living part of both Biblical and Qur'anic history,*" the old man said and nodded.

"*Sounds more important than Jerusalem to me. So why do they all fight so fiercely over Jerusalem rather than places like Kerak?*" Gabirol asked.

"*Because of what still lies beneath Jerusalem...what still waits,*" the old man smiled in reply. *"But before I explain that, I have to tell you about Paul and his visit to Wadi Al Karak near to Kerak accompanied by Princess Stephanie."*

"Why would he go to a wadi with the princess?" Simon asked.

"Because she wished to show him its beauty and as Theodoric had mentioned it. He and Sister Lucy would stay with Alisha, who was originally going to go with them but after a fretful night with Arri, she insisted he go alone with the princess still, especially as they had to leave so early in the morning. They had been at Crac de Moab for several days by this time and she could see Paul was eager to explore and visit the shrine of Noah on the way back if time permitted. So they set off alone, well, they were not quite alone as she had a full escort of her own knights."

"And Brother Matthew no less I bet?" Peter stated.

"No...no knights from either the Templars nor the Hospitallers went. Just her own Confrere Knights and of course Tenno."

"Sounds too convenient to me," Sarah remarked and huffed.

"Perhaps. But the day taught Paul a valuable lesson if nothing else."

"Just one quick question...this Reynald, at this time in the story...he was fifty-three years old already yes?" Sarah asked. The old man nodded yes. *"Hmm. No wonder the princess took a fancy to Paul."*

Wadi Al Karak, Oultrajordain, Kingdom of Jerusalem, July 1179

Paul pulled Adrastos up as the small group of knights at the front stopped briefly to check the route ahead was clear. The early morning sun was already beating down and Paul was glad he was not dressed and fully suited in armour like the knights. His one piece full length cotton robe and wearing just sandals was practical and cool, though he did not take any headwear for protection against the sun, which he was now regretting. Princess Stephanie was in front of him sat side saddle. She wore a pale purple dress and a white lace covered wide brimmed hat. Tenno pulled up beside Paul as several other knights stopped behind them. It all seemed like a lot of knights and a lot of effort for one visit to a wadi but he understood the need for protection whilst hostilities continued. Tenno constantly checked his surroundings and despite wearing his full armour, he looked remarkably cool compared with the other knights. Princess Stephanie looked over her shoulder at Paul and smiled. The wide brimmed hat with white lace down the sides shaded her face. Ahead, the path curved to the left and followed the contours of the start of the wadi as it cut into the rock. The path followed its contours steeply descending. Paul could see the Dead Sea in the distance. It looked silver from the sunlight reflecting off of it. After several more minutes of travel, they entered the wadi properly and the air became cooler almost instantly. The sides of the wadi became much steeper and greener from the various vegetation that grew and clung to the sides. The rocks were a multitude of brilliant hues of orange, browns and yellows. A few palm trees grew from flat areas and beside the ever widening stream that flowed gently along the length of the wadi. Several black goats stood their ground and seemed to stare at them as they all passed on their horses in single file. The further they travelled, the deeper they went and the higher the sheer cliff walls on either side appeared, 'like a natural cathedral', Paul thought to himself. Princess Stephanie looked awkward as she rode side saddle. She had said it was not how she wished to ride but court protocols for a Lady dictated so. Eventually the wadi opened out in a wide flood plain area with shingle banks on either side of the crystal clear waters that were flowing by gently. The knights stopped and dismounted, their horses quickly drinking the fresh water. Tenno looked up and all around checking the area. As Paul dismounted, he only then noticed Percival was with them at the rear. He waved in acknowledgment. Tenno remained upon his horse as the others all dismounted. Princess Stephanie stepped down onto a small wooden step one of her knights quickly placed beside her horse. She shook her head feigning embarrassment as Paul looked over smiling. She certainly appeared different from the woman he had come to know over the past few months. She was now formal and clipped in her words and controlled in her behaviour and mannerisms. For that, he felt sorry for her. She unbuckled a small satchel from her horse and started to walk towards what looked like a large crack in the high rock wall ahead of them. But as Paul looked at her, he could see the wadi cut through the rock and curved off to the left. Like a secret door almost. She stopped and looked at him for a few moments. Paul shrugged his shoulders not sure what he was supposed to do as the other knights tended to their horses. Paul felt like they were being deliberately discreet almost. She feigned a look of confusion at him then smiled and indicated with a slight nod of her head he should follow.

"Go on, Paul. We shall keep watch here," Percival suddenly said behind him. "I have been told this is the only way in and it is blocked at the end with a waterfall. The other way leads down to the sea. So I have been told."

"I cannot go alone," Paul replied quietly.

"Why not? Afraid she may lure you into doing something inappropriate? I think not. We all know she is with child," Percival said, Paul surprised at his frankness.

"Go!" Tenno suddenly said as he finally dismounted. "There is no one else here but us. I shall follow at a distance. 'Tis why we came here is it not? So that she may show you where Theodoric speaks of?"

"Well yes...but...but," Paul protested just as Princess Stephanie shook her head.

"Then here. Take this and do one of your drawings. But we shall not be visiting any shrine as that is on the other side of Kerak," Tenno stated and passed Paul his leather satchel containing his drawing folder. "Alisha said you would forget this."

Paul smiled as he took the satchel. Two of Princess Stephanie's knights smiled at him as he passed them and looked at Tenno curiously. He just stared at them hard. When Paul reached Princess Stephanie, she silently turned and walked towards the cut through the rock face. As the stream ran through it, the sides of the walls drew closer leaving no shingle or sand to walk along. She stopped and pulled off her sandals, lifted her dress up and held it at her knees and walked through the water and carried on. Paul quickly removed his sandals and followed, his feet partly sinking into the soft sand of the stream bed. Tenno kept his boots on and just followed straight into the water. The sides arched upwards, the sun shining directly through the gap. Eventually the stream opened again into a wider area almost like a natural arena. A large boulder hung above their heads wedged between the two sides of the wadi. As they stepped beneath it, Paul saw a beautiful waterfall ahead emptying into a clear blue pool. A slight raised rock plateau was just off to the left side of the waterfall. Princess Stephanie immediately stepped up onto it and sat down putting her feet in the water again. She looked at Paul and beckoned him to come and sit beside her. Paul looked back at Tenno. He shrugged his shoulders. Shook his head and turned around. Paul looked at him as he walked over to an area of bright green grass in the shade and promptly sat himself down. He nodded at Paul. As Paul looked around, he told himself he must bring Alisha here. It was indeed beautiful. As he turned, his eyes caught Princess Stephanie's as she looked at him. She patted the stone beside her. Paul hesitated for a moment wondering what her intentions were but then stepped up upon the rock and sat beside her, placing his feet in the cool waters. They sat in total silence for several minutes, an awkward silence almost until Princess Stephanie laughed and pulled off her hat and shook her head so her hair hung loose.

"Lord help me. You can see now why I long to escape the confines of the castle can't you?" she exclaimed and looked upwards, the rays of the sun lighting up her features in stark contrast. "I come here where the shadows of my past cannot reach."

"That is twice I have heard that saying this week," Paul replied.

Princess Stephanie opened her eyes and looked at him intently. She did not look away when Paul looked back at her. There was a familiarity about her that shook Paul. He loved Alisha totally but something about her struck a chord within him. Paul finally broke away his stare and placed his leather satchel upon his knees and looked into the water. Princess Stephanie smiled as she studied his face in profile. She could not understand the feelings that were running through her. Paul laughed sensing that she was staring at him. She looked away and into the water.

"Is it my husband that concerns you, being alone with me?" she asked without looking him.

Paul shook his head no as he looked at the gently flowing water. It felt cool as it ran past his feet. Princess Stephanie then sat in silence just staring into the water. After what seemed an age Paul looked at her directly again.

"Look, I know about your husband and his past. There are unfortunately too many people eager to tell me all about him."

"That does not surprise me. Tell me, what does Theo say of him?"

"He is perhaps the fairest and most grounded in comment. Obviously he and Reynald go back many years...it was he who told me just how controversial he was...still is. That he was born in France in 1125, but that his origins are vague. Some say deliberately so...who knows? I know that just like me, he too was a man of middle class ranking in French society and his father was said to be a Lord of Châtillon. However, Theo seems unsure if Reynald came from Châtillon Sur on Marne or Châtillon on Loing but each Châtillon is on a river. He said that was important. I am not sure why."

"Yes...he told me that too. I do know that as a young man he was incredibly reckless and rebellious and was sent away on the Second Crusade at the age of just twenty-two years. That was back in 1147. That is when he entered the service of Constance of Antioch, a noble born lady who had been widowed in 1149. That woman is but the bane of my life at times," Stephanie sighed and moved her feet about in the water, her foot catching Paul's briefly. She smiled broadly and then laughed gently. "When Reynald moved here to Kerak he brought with him a sealed trunk. I ignored it for a while but then I opened it...it was full of letters from her to him. He certainly made an impression upon her that was clear," she part laughed again but shook her head.

"Doesn't he on everyone?" Paul asked and looked at her directly. Her eyes were full of emotion.

"Constance was certainly impressed by the 'brash young chancer' as she wrote; the element of danger about him fascinated her and made her feel alive. I was wrong to read her letters, but I could not help myself. But I pitied her as I know now just how she was manipulated by him from the outset, just as I have been. However, Constance, was used as a commodity of power from a young age. Her mother, Alice of Antioch, tried to marry her off to a Muslim prince to gain control over Antioch as a regent. This was when Constance was still an infant. For that, Alice of Antioch was banished and when she was allowed to return, she tried to broker a marriage alliance for herself with a Christian Crusader called Raymond of Poitiers. Through this marriage they could both rule Antioch, by her young daughter, as regents. Again Alice was foiled by Raymond of Poitiers himself for he married her nine year old daughter in secret and Alice was forced into a humiliated exile. The nine year old wife, Constance, could hardly have known what was going on. This was in 1136 I think," Stephanie explained still looking directly into Paul's eyes. [38]

"My father did speak of Reynald and tried to explain the differences out here. Ali and I were initially going to live in Antioch...my father had connections there... plus children of mixed religious origin are not looked down upon. Poulions I think they are called? I know that in Outremer, lower ranked individuals can rise in social standing, far easier than in Europe. Here, areas are being colonised by Christians and small vassal kingdoms are being set up in various surrounding cities. My father did say that Reynald, once he had married Constance, that Antioch then became one such place for him through his devious means...from low beginnings as a low ranking knight, he had won control of a small kingdom state within the Crusader Kingdom of Jerusalem," Paul said then paused. "I am sorry...I speak ill of your husband. I should not."

"'Tis not ill if it is the truth...and besides, he wishes to do the very same here. But I have other priorities...such as my children." Stephanie smiled at him. She still looked at him intently and did not turn her gaze.

"'Twas Theo though who has explained to me, on more than one occasion I can tell you," Paul laughed and looked away from her fearing it impolite to keep looking back at her. Paul heard Adrastos snort loudly in the distance as it echoed through the gap in the rock walls as if to confirm his very thought.

"'Tis a great shame that here, the situation has developed where wealthy men can pedal religion...Christianity and Islam...as a material business. Anyone can jump on the band wagon...and we all delude ourselves if we think for one moment that we are doing God's work." She sighed and paused looking back at the flowing water. "Some may believe this, but many are intelligent enough and astute enough to grasp the situation of ambition and acquisition whereby they can easily manipulate the more pious and devoted men, of lower rank, to naively support hidden and unscrupulous causes. Reynald does this exceedingly well...," she explained and closed her eyes and held her left hand upon her stomach.

"You must have been smitten with him once?" Paul asked hesitantly.

"Yes...yes very much so. He is many years older than I am, but he had a certain confidence I found attractive...but he knew that and used it to his advantage. Huh, I can even now understand why Constance having been married at nine herself to such an older man did, by the time she was twenty, see Reynald as this bright fresh faced knight arrive from France come into her service, under the command of her husband and literally able to sweep her off of her feet. Her letters state she loved his rebellious streak." She paused and sat in silence for several moments. "You know, he did explain to me once...back when he used to actually talk to me and not simply use me as his personal gratification lump of meat," she stated matter of factly.

Paul coughed and tried to clear his throat, surprised at her comment. Princess Stephanie laughed at his reaction and saw that he blushed.

"I think you tell me too much...," Paul said awkwardly.

"You need never feel embarrassed with me, Paul...besides, I am with child so you are safe," she remarked and placed her hand upon his hand. Paul quickly removed his hand away and she feigned a smile and sighed. "Paul...Reynald is as tall as you, broad of shoulder and strong...proven in combat. Yet I do not feel safe with him," she paused. "But I do when I am with you."

Paul's mind raced and he thought back to when Alisha was pregnant and they had still made love. Why had she brought him here alone? Was she going to try and seduce him? Surely not, he thought, with Tenno so close.

"Stephanie...I do not think I can find the words to answer that," Paul replied and forced an awkward smile.

"As I was saying," she smiled and continued. "Reynald told me how he had witnessed Muslims and Hebrews being subjugated to Christian rulers, who were all basically immigrants who believed their prophet Jesus Christ should have Christian people rule the area. He may have been indifferent to them and probably the lower ranks of his own kind but he did say that he initially struggled and found it hard to put himself in the minds of such men when they could do underhand things and peddle forgiveness and penance so easily through their Church...Imagine, suddenly here he was in this so-called land of milk and honey to plunder and presented with a God-given right to do whatever he wanted, provided he ruled as a believer of the Christian religion...or as he said, say you do, if you are of an unscrupulous and cunning mind."

"He has come a long way. I did not realise he was so much older than you," Paul remarked.

"Yes, you have to give him that. He certainly looks and behaves far younger than his age."

"So how did he marry Constance if he was employed by her husband?"

"I can tell you that easily for I have been told so many times by Reynald. It was in 1149, just two years after he had arrived in Antioch, that his lord and master was killed at the Battle of Inab. Raymond of Poitiers, her husband, who had tricked her into marriage at the age of nine as I explained, was beheaded by his Muslim foe after being captured. His head was sent to the Caliph of Baghdad as a gift...and by the Grace of God, Reynald was not in attendance at that battle...just exactly why not no one dared to ask for he was in the service of both Constance and Raymond, the co-rulers of Antioch, so he should have been. Then four years later in 1153, she secretly married Reynald. How this secret marriage came about is not well known, but I know, as he told me so, that Theodoric had some involvement, but it was not approved by King Baldwin the Third of Jerusalem."

"Theo did? He has never mentioned that before," Paul remarked, surprised.

"I believe...though I could be wrong, that Theo saw Reynald as a potential protégée whom he could school and help build a greater kingdom here in Outremer...but Reynald's uncontrollability negated that from going any further. So please, my Paul, be careful in just how much to trust Theo for I fear he has other plans for you that are designed to better suit his own plans," Stephanie explained and again looked at Paul.

Paul's mind ran and he did not even notice her comment when she referred to him as her Paul. Paul knew Theodoric had had some kind of falling out and disagreement a long time ago with his father, but was it down to foul play on Theodoric's part? Suddenly he felt unsure of his absolute confidence in him. It made him feel decidedly unsettled.

"You know Reynald and Constance have two daughters, one named Agnes and the other he never speaks of," she said with a tinge of sadness in her voice and looked up, the sun lighting up her face again.

 0 – 0

"I thought you were having his first child?"

"No...though he never sees Agnes. She grew up without him ever being present as he was held captive in Aleppo and besides, her mother's marriage to a man of such low birth was not permitted, but this was the Holy Land where men could better themselves in the service of God. Reynald had got his foot on the ladder of ambition and climbed up a few steps. Being his usual reckless self he was captured by the Muslims in November 1160 and was confined in Aleppo for the next fifteen years, nearer sixteen actually."

"Why do you say reckless?"

"Because it was but a stupid rampage in the anti Taurus against Madsch-ed-Din, the Governor of Aleppo. Whilst he was held there, Constance then claimed her independent rule over Antioch. The popular party supported her son from her first marriage, the fifteen-year-old Bohemond. However, Constance being just as stubborn and ambitious as Reynald did not wish to hand over the principality to her son, who was now legally old enough to rule. However, King Baldwin stepped in and had Bohemond made Prince and appointed an old opponent of Reynald's, the rich and worldly Patriarch Aimery of Limoges, as regent. Constance protested against this decision to the Court of Constantinople. When word reached Reynald he was more than furious, he told me to the point of nearly losing his mind he thought for a while. Perhaps he did. It was then that he vowed he would never let anyone ever again outsmart him...obviously that did not work," Stephanie laughed and shook her head. "Constance also had a daughter, Maria, from her first marriage to Raymond. In 1159 Bertha of Sulzbach, wife of Manuel the First died, and the following year the Emperor married Maria, which served to strengthen the position of Constance, who now held the Regency of Antioch. After many internal troubles, in 1163, Constance asked the Armenian Kingdom of Cilicia for aid in order to maintain her rule but the citizens of Antioch rioted and exiled her. She died later that year, allowing Bohemond to take full control. That I am afraid was the final straw for Reynald. He had been bad enough before, but from that point onwards he even drove his captors mad and he became very angry and resentful towards everyone it would appear...and as you know, he was not released until 1176. Huh!" Stephanie sighed, shook her head again, and turned to look at Paul.

Paul could sense her sadness. A large part of him wanted to hold her and comfort her. No one else was about apart from Tenno, and he was confident he would say nothing and Alisha would never know. As soon as he thought that, he instantly felt uncomfortable with that feeling. Gently he placed his hand upon her right hand and placed his fingers between hers. He recalled how harsh and stupid he had been when accusing Alisha of having feelings for Brother Nicholas, yet now he found himself sat beside Princess Stephanie, holding her hand and with feelings growing he knew he should not have.

"Stephanie...," he said softly looking at their hands entwined.

"Do you know...," she interrupted before he could say anything further. "Even after his years of confinement, he immediately returned to his old habit of attacking Muslim caravans, and we have seen what carnage such things leave behind. Even signed truces do not deter him...'tis though he is possessed at times. I had hoped that my love and his age would have mellowed him...but no...and that is despite all the trouble his impulsive and disorderly conduct has brought upon him in the past. He even makes threats upon the Islamic Holy Temple of Mecca and this concerns me greatly...for ultimately that kind of talk will bring death to the doors of Kerak that will make Noah's prophecies seem mild in comparison...and I cannot allow that, so I must somehow get him to heel...," Stephanie explained, pained. She raised his hand and placed it upon the side of her face and closed her eyes. "That is why the Muslims call him the Mad Red Wolf of Kerak," she sighed and kissed the side of his hand.

"And that wolf would kill us both where we sit if he saw you do that," Paul commented.

Princess Stephanie just held his hand against her face and sighed. A single tear rolled down her cheek. Paul turned to face her properly and instinctively placed his other hand upon her cheek cupping her face in his hands. She opened her eyes and looked deeply into his. Her mind raced as she struggled with her emotions. She could talk to Paul like no other man, save Theodoric. She could not tell whether the feelings pouring from her uncontrollably were down to being exceptionally emotional caused by the pregnancy or just a rekindling of the intense love she once held for his father, Philip. She had been a very young girl then but now, she felt almost helpless. Guilt flooded through her as she thought of Alisha...but right there, right now, she needed to feel wanted and loved. She felt angry that Reynald was away and showed her scant attention other than to use her body as if it were his to do with as he wished. She shuddered and moved nearer to Paul. She wanted to kiss him and the urge was overwhelming. Paul's heart beat faster as he looked into her eyes. Her lips were moist and inviting and the emotion in her eyes was intense. He thought of Alisha and Arri...quickly he pulled her close placing her face against his chest, then quickly placed his arms around her and held her so he could not look directly at her nor kiss her. She wrapped her arms around him tightly and pulled him close. He could sense her shaking gently clearly sobbing. She felt delicate almost in his arms as they hugged, their legs and feet almost entwined still in the gently flowing waters.

Port of La Rochelle, France, Melissae Inn, spring 1191

"The dirty unfaithful bastard!" Sarah exclaimed angrily.

The old man laughed at her outburst.

"Sarah!" Stephan said, surprised at her language.

"Well...honestly," she replied and shook her head.

"I can tell you that after that hug...Tenno walked over and stood beside them and coughed...loudly. He later told Paul that he could see he was feeling awkward so came to his aid...in a fashion...ever the diplomat," the old man explained.

"Hey...I certainly would. A real princess giving you the biggest hint possible...though the pregnant aspect is a bit strange to deal with," the Genoese sailor commented and waved his hand from side to side. He feigned a mock grimace as Simon thought upon his words.

"So did the castle have the best toilets?" Simon asked, which made Gabirol laugh.

"Yes...yes they did, Simon. Not only that but they also burnt off the excrement in large deeply dug holes just outside the castle walls...to reduce the smell and risk of disease. It is a practice they should consider here rather than just letting it run free in the streets and into rivers," the old man explained and wiped his beard as he laughed to himself at Simon's question.

"So what happened when Tenno interrupted?" Ayleth asked quietly.

"Paul released Princess Stephanie and she quickly wiped her tears away. Paul then sat with her whilst he drew the wadi, writing down notes of the various birds and wildlife that were abundant. If you look through Paul's folder, I am sure the picture he drew is still inside (Fig. 31: Wadi Al Karak). They had a light snack and then returned to Crac de Moab with the promise that they would visit the shrine of Noah the following day. When Paul went to his room, he found Alisha fast asleep with Arri on the bed with Sister Lucy keeping an eye on them. Paul's heart felt heavy and he was glad that Tenno had been at the wadi. He could have so easily kissed Princess Stephanie and he felt guilty for it. Theodoric's words came rushing back to him about how there would come a time when he would have to lie. He just did not realise it would be so soon. His heart had jumped as he thought that perhaps this is how Alisha had felt when she kissed Nicholas. He shook his head and quietly sat beside Sister Lucy, who raised her finger to her lips for him to remain quiet."

"So did Paul decide to go to Jerusalem or stay with Alisha after that?" Gabirol asked.

"After the wadi visit, Paul knew he had to go with Theodoric, not only to put some distance between him and Princess Stephanie, but also so that he may get to learn and understand more about Theodoric. He declined the offer of visiting the shrine of Noah for fear of where that may lead if left alone again with Princess Stephanie and her words of caution about Theodoric had sat heavy within him...and so all too soon, Paul found himself saddling up Adrastos, looking at Alisha holding Arri as he was about to depart for Jerusalem. She had made him a lightweight scabbard. At first she was embarrassed to give it to him as she felt it was not well made enough by her hand," the old man explained and ran his fingers along the scabbard of the sword. "Paul felt assured knowing that Tenno would be with them, who part bowed his head, his hands behind his back, stood bolt upright as ever. Alisha appeared very calm outwardly, but all she wanted to do was rush up to Paul and beg him not to leave... but she knew it would deeply upset him. She had to look strong. Paul likewise did not want

to leave and he felt truly sad, the saddest he had felt since La Rochelle when he thought he would never have Alisha. Count Raymond offered Paul and Theodoric passage with him most of the way north, as he was travelling back that way to Tiberias and had to escort Guy to the gates of Jerusalem, much to Guy's disappointment as he had hoped to stay in Kerak. Thomas and his men would all accompany Paul and Theodoric, which made Alisha feel slightly better at ease."

"And what of Stephanie?" Sarah asked, clipped.

"She had more immediate issues to deal with, mainly her son and his new position. He was also upset at the loss of his grandfather and was more than a little vociferous in his condemnation of Reynald, whom he held responsible for his death. He made it very clear he wished it had been Reynald who had been killed instead...and made comments that his mother preferred Paul as he had heard her speak to Sister Lucy in confidence about her confused feelings...and Brother Matthew was only too keen to make a written note of it all," the old man explained.

Fig. 31:

Chapter 32
Jerusalem. The Gateway

Crac de Moab, Oultrajordain, Kingdom of Jerusalem, July 1179

It was early morning and the main courtyard was full of people waiting around for the convoy of knights to leave. No pilgrims would be accompanying them and all would be travelling on horse except the single cart belonging to Guy with all of his supplies. Count Raymond was finishing off signing papers and expense chits with the castle's quartermaster. Sister Lucy fought to control her emotions and playfully slapped Theodoric as he stood beside her holding the reins of the horse he had been loaned by Princess Stephanie for the duration of the trip. Jerusalem was just fifty-four miles away but it would still take them two days to travel the distance. Alisha held Arri forward so Paul could kiss him on his forehead. He was asleep. Alisha had vowed not to cry and she stood looking outwardly calm...yet inside felt as if she was falling apart. She only wanted Paul to leave seeing a smile upon her face and to be confident that she was all right. Tenno stood directly behind her.

"'Tis not a fighting patrol we are leaving on," Theodoric said aloud and wiped Sister Lucy's face. She slapped his arm hard again and sniffed.

"Make sure he does not enter into trouble...," Tenno stated, looking at Theodoric.

"I shall keep an eye upon him at all times," he replied and looked across at Paul and winked.

"No...I think it should be Paul who must keep an eye on this old bag of bones and bring him back to me quickly," Sister Lucy exclaimed emotionally and tried to laugh.

Paul looked in silence at Alisha. Tenno leaned across and handed her a small leather wallet tied up which she then passed to Paul.

"You nearly forgot your small travelling pack. I do not want you returning with a dirty thick beard upon that face of yours," Alisha explained softly.

Paul took the small leather packet and placed it inside the satchel upon Adrastos. As he did, his eye caught sight of Princess Stephanie walking towards the stairs that led to the cross arched main balcony that overlooked the courtyard. Her two children followed closely by her side. Theodoric slapped Paul's back hard when he looked at her for too long. He turned to face Alisha again. Her eyes were wide and her pupils large despite the glaring sun above already burning down fiercely. She cradled Arri against her chest rocking him gently. As they looked at each other in silence, Percival walked up close with his horse. Both Paul and Theodoric looked at him, puzzled.

"I am to come with you...Brother Teric said I may as I am supposed to be travelling with Guy after all," he explained with a large grin and indicated with his head towards Guy saddling up, his horse still covered in bright yellow and his banners.

"Green!" Alisha whispered to Paul noting Percival's dark green surcoat and chausses.

Paul knew immediately what she was referring to. The green knight symbol on his parchment. Brother Teric rode over slowly and leaned down to pass Paul a small dagger.

"'Tis the dagger I took at the ambush site. 'Tis similar to an Ashashin blade...but it is different enough to distinguish it as not being one of theirs. When we reach Jerusalem, I shall not have time to investigate it properly...so can I ask that you and Theodoric do so? I feel it is important," he explained as Paul studied the small black all metal dagger.

Paul nodded yes and placed the small blade into his side satchel.

"Are we actually leaving today?" Guy called out loudly as he turned his horse to face the northern wall entrance gates.

Brother Teric shook his head, unimpressed. Paul quickly looked at Alisha, his heart pounding and feeling quite sick. He had no real idea how long it would be before he would see her and Arri again. He held the reins to Adrastos in his left hand as he pulled Alisha close and kissed her on the lips. She gulped with emotion and broke the kiss just for a moment refusing to let herself cry. She kissed him again on the lips harder and longer. She then stepped back as Paul looked at her. She smiled and indicated with a slight flick of her head to leave. Paul acknowledged Tenno, who part bowed his head goodbye in silence then placed his right foot in the stirrup and pulled himself up onto Adrastos. He watched in amusement as Theodoric struggled to pull himself up into the saddle of his horse, Sister Lucy shaking her head. She laughed as he tried several times before finally sitting himself properly. He let out a laugh.

Within less than a minute, the vanguard of Templars were leading out the convoy in pairs, followed by Guy and his knights with his cart in tow. Percival hung back to travel alongside Paul. Thomas pulled up with his men behind Theodoric and before Paul had the chance to say anything else, he was guiding Adrastos towards the main gates to leave. Alisha simply smiled, Sister Lucy wiping away tears half laughing and crying at Theodoric's riding ability as he fought to guide his horse erratically. Paul looked back once more at Alisha and Arri as he was about to pass beneath the balcony over the exit. She gave a simple wave. He looked forwards and upwards just in time to see Princess Stephanie looking directly down upon him. She looked solemn and pale, the white headdress she was wearing looking very formal. Both her son Humphrey and daughter Isabella looked down at him too. In that instant as her eyes locked with his, he recalled Theodoric's comments about her when they had first met. 'That is one woman you do not want to get tangled up with. Don't get me wrong...she is beautiful and smart, but she has a habit of turning people's lives upside down.' Theodoric's words seemed to echo in his head. He tried not to look up or wave for fear of upsetting Alisha. But then why would she mind if he did, he thought. It was only his guilt that made him think that way. She nodded slightly at him as he passed beneath her. She looked sad. Paul led Adrastos around the turn in the bridge that crossed a dry moat. This led from the elbow-shaped entrance in the western flank of the eastern salient in the north wall.

Every part of Paul wanted to turn around and return to Alisha and Arri and Theodoric could see the pain in him as they rode side by side, Percival having eased back to ride beside Thomas. Theodoric handed him a wide kefieh scarf. Paul looked at it quizzically.

"You will need that wrapped around your mouth...the dust further down becomes very fine and all those horses up front will kick a shit load of it into your face that will stick in your throat...trust me," Theodoric smiled.

Percival immediately started checking through his various pockets and satchels upon his horse. He looked at Paul almost alarmed. Paul remembered that Taqi had given him a large linen kefieh scarf with the embroidered image he had done as a gift.

"Can I give this to Percy for I have a kefieh already?" Paul asked.

Theodoric looked back at Percival who feigned a smile and he nodded of course. He was surprised that Percival did not have such a face cover as an experienced horseman should have. Paul threw the kefieh scarf and Percival just caught it. He raised his hand in thanks and began to tie it around his neck. Paul leaned down and took out the linen kefieh Taqi had given him from the bottom of his satchel. As he opened it up to fold into shape, he suddenly saw the pattern embroidered upon it Taqi said his father had told him to put on it. As he unfurled it further, he looked closely at the embroidered image. He gasped nearly at the realisation it was identical to the winged tree motif Theodoric had tattooed across his back and shoulders. How could he have not remembered this? He looked across at Theodoric and opened the image towards him. Theodoric pulled his horse closer so he could see. He looked at the image and simply shrugged his shoulders and smiled.

"We shall discuss that when we are in Jerusalem," Theodoric smiled and carried on riding looking straight ahead. "After I have sorted my obligations to the Order of St Lazarus..."

ℂℂ

After several stops for water and a very light lunch midday, Paul found himself looking at the knights as they travelled. Some remained bolt upright whilst others clearly suffered in the intense heat whilst wearing their full armour. Guy to his credit remained sat upright and appeared composed. Paul found that his own saddle started to slide slightly from side to side. Adrastos was sweating heavily as were all the other horses. Paul could not believe the knights kept the armour and covers upon their horses except for Thomas and his men who removed all but the horse's saddle, bridle and reins to travel. Percival copied Thomas and did likewise. Theodoric looked at Paul and quickly pulled alongside him closer.

"Paul, you will need to adjust the girdle straps or you risk creating sores for Adrastos," he explained pointing to the main strap around Adrastos's middle. "You must constantly check and adjust your saddle when riding for long periods. Did your father not teach you these basics?"

✱   3 – 31

"He tried...but I never paid much attention to be honest," Paul answered and looked down at the main girdle straps rubbing against sweat.

Raymond heard Paul's reply and raised his arm and called out for the column to stop. Guy looked back at him puzzled as Raymond moved and pulled up alongside Paul's right side.

"Quickly sort your horse. It will do neither of you any good out here if he gets sore and lame!" Raymond commented and stood up upon his stirrups to look ahead. "We have but a few more miles to our rendezvous point with Henry," he explained and sat back upon his saddle and looked at Paul. He frowned momentarily as if to ask what was Paul waiting for.

Paul quickly dismounted and pulled the main girdle strap tighter around Adrastos, pulled in the front buckling and quickly remounted.

"Thank you," Paul said politely as Raymond nodded in acknowledgement.

"You still have much to learn out here. Men are plentiful, but good horses, especially ones like the Turcoman you have there, are expensive and valued," Raymond explained and waved his hand forward. The lead knight nodded acknowledgement and moved the column off again. "We shall be meeting Count Henry this eve. He knew your father well as he does Theodoric so I am sure he will have much to say to you. And do not worry about Thomas and his men…I have paid for their stay at Kerak and Henry will do likewise in Jerusalem."

"Paid for them! What do you mean?" Paul asked, puzzled, as he rode between Raymond and Theodoric.

Raymond looked at Paul and smiled.

"I shall let Theo explain that," he stated and pulled his horse up to stop and smiled again even broader as he then looked back for Thomas, who was riding near to the rear with Percival.

Paul looked at Theodoric, confused.

"Do not look so concerned Paul. You don't think knights and men at arms simply get free lodgings and food do you? They are not pilgrims after all," Theodoric laughed. Paul shook his head, still puzzled. "Raymond knew your father well. He had Thomas and his men work with his own knights to train them hard whilst they stayed at Kerak. In return he paid for all their expenses. Did you not see him pay the quartermaster as we were leaving?"

"No…I mean yes…but," Paul replied and paused as he looked back at Thomas now talking with Raymond and both laughing. "It never crossed my mind they would have to pay for their lodgings!"

"No…But you know now."

"But why then do they insist on taking us all the way to Alexandria knowing I cannot pay them?"

"Paul…not all payments in this life are by way of coinage, gold or property," Theodoric replied and raised his eyebrows at him. "Thomas and his men have their reasons…noble ones, so just be grateful of that."

Brother Teric looked back at Paul and nodded as if to confirm Theodoric's remarks. Paul shook his head, perplexed, and as the column started to head downhill slightly, the stunning views stretched out ahead of them only added to his sense of being overwhelmed with all that was rapidly happening all around him. It had only been a matter of hours yet he already missed Alisha and Arri. He would not be there during the night to check on Arri as he always did. He wondered how his father was and if Taqi was okay. And why were Thomas and his men so keen to help him? He was rapidly developing a new found respect for his father he never knew he was capable of. He loved his father but with all that he was learning about him, he was seeing him in a totally different light. And Theodoric...he looked across at him just as he smiled at him disarmingly.

Western path at Masada, water station, Kingdom of Jerusalem, July 1179

Paul removed his saddle from Adrastos as the Templars set camp and Thomas and his men scouted the immediate area. Theodoric painfully dismounted rubbing his aching back as Guy barked orders for his cart to be unloaded and his personal tent to be erected before nightfall. From their high position he could see down towards a plain that led to the shores of the bright blue waters of the Dead Sea. It looked bluer than he anticipated by the white marl shoreline. They had already ridden through many miles of white marl salt deposits which he had found fascinating to see. Theodoric had taken great pleasure in telling him all about the nearby ruined fortress, one of many of the Biblical King Herod's, they would be staying near to for the night that the Romans had besieged and where the Jews who had held out there had been utterly defeated. As Theodoric explained, the siege of Masada was among the final accords of the Great Jewish Revolt, occurring from AD 73 to 74 on a large hilltop (current-day Israel). According to Josephus the long siege by the troops of the Roman Empire led to the mass suicide of the Sicarii rebels and resident Jewish families of the Masada fortress. The siege was chronicled by Flavius Josephus, a Jewish rebel leader captured by the Romans, in whose service he became a historian. Masada has become a controversial event in Jewish history, with some regarding it as a place of reverence, commemorating fallen ancestors and their heroic struggle against oppression, and others regarding it as a warning against extremism and the refusal to compromise. Theodoric also wanted to travel via an ancient site that reputedly had an ancient oak tree growing that was known as Abraham's Oak but Raymond and Brother Teric said it was too far west of the main route they would be taking. Paul thought about Theodoric's comments regarding the sacred oak tree and the winged tree tattoo upon his back, plus the acorns hidden within the Alisha's dagger scabbard. Was there a connection? he wondered. The Oak of Mamre. also called the Oak of Sibta, at Hirbet es-Sibte, 1.2 miles southwest of Mamre near Hebron, is also known as the 'The Oak of Abraham' and is an ancient tree which, according to tradition, is said to mark the place where Abraham entertained the three angels or where Abraham pitched his tent. It is said the oak is approximately 4,000 years old and was venerated by Jews and Christians for hundreds of years, until Constantine in the fourth century stopped the practice by building a church there. There is a long-standing tradition that the Oak of Abraham will die before the appearance of the Antichrist. The main oak trunk is still just alive Theodoric explained...but only just! Paul looked around as he heard many horses approach through a pass in the rock face nearby. He placed his saddle down just as the column of Knights Templar and several other knights slowed to a canter then pulled up just feet away. Immediately Raymond approached the group of almost sixty knights and sergeants all on horseback. Jakelin de Mailly was at the front of the Templars. He leaned down and outstretched his hand to shake Raymond's as another knight wearing a black mantel similar to the Knights Hospitaller but without the white crosses upon it pulled up beside Raymond, dismounted and they shook hands vigorously. They exchanged a few words before Raymond pointed directly at Paul. Paul frowned for a moment and looked on puzzled as the man rapidly walked towards him removing his riding gloves and smiling very broadly. He walked straight up to Paul, stopped and proffered his hand to shake.

"By the Lord himself...indeed it is true. You are the absolute double of your father. Young Paul isn't it?" the man said with an enthusiastic tone in his voice.

Paul studied the man briefly. He had a symbol similar to the fleur de lys upon his chest and helmet. The scabbard of his sword was made from an intricate patterned leatherwood format with gold leaf inlay motifs. Theodoric coughed loudly from behind him. Quickly Paul shook the man's hand firmly as he kept smiling and just looking at Paul intently. Raymond approached slowly.

"Sorry. Forgive me my manners...but," Paul finally spoke.

"No no never mind, young man. 'Tis but unbelievable how identical to your father you look. It is as if he were standing before me again...and forgive me for I am remiss with my manners for I have not introduced myself. I am Count Henry... and I have heard much about you already," he explained. Paul turned to look back at Theodoric briefly. "And by the Lord again...is that really you, Theo?"

Theodoric smiled and nodded yes and stepped closer.

"Aye 'tis indeed my Lord," Theodoric answered and part bowed his head.

"This is indeed an auspicious eve. We shall have much to talk about...you must join with me for dinner after Brother Jakelin has concluded vespers for all...I insist," Count Henry stated.

Brother Jakelin walked over looking at Paul intently and pointing his finger at him.

"Of course...I told you I never forget a face," he remarked.

Paul felt awkward and as if he was some kind of show piece. He felt partly embarrassed but also secretly proud of his father's reputation. Is this how Stewart had managed to become the Gonfanier standard-bearer with Reynald so quickly? he thought. Paul looked at Theodoric and then over at Thomas and simply nodded. Paul shook his head bemused.

Port of La Rochelle, France, Melissae Inn, spring 1191

"Sounds to me like Theodoric and Paul's father knew everyone...," Sarah interrupted.

The old man looked at her and nodded in agreement.

"This Henry, Count Henry. Is he the same as Count Henry of Champagne?" the Templar asked.

"Yes, the very same man...and just like Raymond he was perhaps years ahead of his time. Paul's father, Firgany and Theodoric all played significant parts in each of these men's lives...as well as Reynald and Gerard's...but that I am afraid I simply do not have time to explain," the old man said and sighed. He paused for a few moments before continuing. "I can

tell you, though many will argue it is not truth I speak of now, but it is, that Count Henry of Champagne, also known as John, which I shall explain later before you ask, Simon, was not only a Count, but also the Grand Master of the Prieure Sion, the political and administrative leaders who were the main force behind the formation and control of the Knights Templar. He would teach Paul much about the Order and many esoteric mysteries, as well as political awareness in the region. He would also ultimately educate Paul to what his father was and did...as well as his grandfather before him. You see, Count Henry thought he could bring Paul's family tree back in line with the Order of Sion and be part of its future. Something his father had broken away from. Count Henry was also a man who loved Isabella, the sister of Queen Sibylla, for many years...but she was married."

"You mean to tell us that Paul's family is indeed linked to the Order then...is that what you are saying?" Gabirol asked.

"I think I feel a long and confusing part coming up," Simon joked.

"And what of this Jakelin fellow then?" Peter asked.

"Oh Jakelin," the old man said softly and pulled the sword closer and swung it around so the pommel roundel was nearest to him. He ran his finger across it to where a slight nick was cut into it. "But for him, this sword would be in the hands of another now."

"But you won't tell us now though!" Simon joked loudly as Sarah looked at him and shook her head again at him.

"Not just yet...but I shall. As for Jakelin though, he was an utterly reliable and honourable Knight and the local Templar Marshal for many years. He was often openly in disagreement with Gerard de Ridefort...but he never the less honoured his orders."

"I knew Master Jakelin...I also know he was rather fond of females...," the Templar remarked with a smile.

"Yes...he was indeed known for that, despite his best efforts at being discreet. However, I can and will explain that aspect of his nature lest you think ill of him and his sworn oath as a Templar. He was charming, dark haired and good looking, he made no secret of his love of women and was often in their company and quite the flirt. And like Count Raymond, Balian and Count Henry, he too was a good personal friend of Saladin himself," the old man explained.

"Why...if all are such good friends, did and do we have this continuing bloody war then?" the wealthy tailor blurted out suddenly.

"Because of all the other political demands and machinations placed upon them by others...," the old man answered.

"Like Reynald you mean?" the farrier remarked.

"Yes...but also from members from within Saladin's own ruling elite who demanded action against the Christians. Now I would suggest we rest briefly, eat something and prepare yourselves indeed for what will be a lengthy and perhaps confusing account of what happened to Paul when he finally reached Jerusalem."

"I want to know about this symbol on Theodoric's back and that Taqi had done upon Paul's face cloth kefiea whatever you called it...plus the old woman. Surely there is more to her than you have told us?" Peter commented.

"Kefieh...and yes there is indeed much more about the old woman to tell and it is whilst in Jerusalem that Paul was to find out firsthand what she was about...so let me explain if you are all ready?" the old man said and asked looking at each of them in turn.

Ayleth looked at the old man, smiled softly, and nodded yes to continue as if answering for all of them present in the room.

City of Jerusalem, Kingdom of Jerusalem, July 1179

As the troop of Templars at the vanguard of the convoy left the shade of the tree-lined road, they immediately shielded their eyes from the bright sun. The road opened out from the fertile greener hillsides onto a wide and flat plateau. The midday sun blazed fiercely upon Paul's back and shoulders as he steadied Adrastos and drew up alongside Count Henry and Theodoric with Percival following closely behind him. Theodoric pulled a large sun hat up over his head. It looked ridiculous but was effective. Paul felt tired having spent many hours with Count Henry and Count Raymond talking until the early hours about his father and listening to many tales as recounted by them and Theodoric in Raymond's tent. He noticed on many occasions during the conversation, little comments and jokes between them that he was simply not privy to understand. Guy initially sat and ate with them but afterwards as Count Henry and Theodoric started to talk about their previous experiences, he left the small tent and retired to his own tent early. Paul wiped his face using the ends of the large kefieh that hung from his head around his neck, as a hot wind blew sand into mini whirlwinds ahead of them. The major walls of Jerusalem shimmered in the heat haze ahead, at that distance giving the impression of the city being surrounded by water.

"Well young man, there she is in all her glory!" shouted Count Henry above the wind as he held his hand to his face, shielding it from the sand.

Theodoric pulled up further alongside Count Henry's Gonfanier and squinted to view the city. He sat upright and stared momentarily before looking across at Paul.

"It has been many years since I was last here. I just hope they have sorted the food out!" Theodoric shouted.

Paul and Percival both looked at him quizzically as the remainder of their escort pulled into a tighter formation behind them. Several pilgrims walked past heading for the city across the open plain. Thomas rode up, stopped beside Paul, looked toward Jerusalem, and simply shook his head.

"The street of bad food, my friend," Thomas answered for Theodoric. "In the Malquissinat quarter. It is where food for pilgrims is produced and sold. It's all crap!" he further explained loudly with a large smile.

Paul smiled back then looked towards the city, the city he had heard so much about. In anticipation and expectant excitement, he held his position as Count Henry motioned his escort forward. Brother Teric waved his Templar vanguard on and Paul just looked as they all began to move forwards. After all this time he was finally about to enter the great city itself. Paul waited as he savoured the moment. When Count Henry, Theodoric, Percival and Thomas's men, along with a very tired looking Guy and his escort cantered ahead, he had to jerk himself alert and with trepidation rushed after them. As the troop passed through David's Gate, or also known as Bab al Khalil, on the west curtain wall of the city, Paul gazed up viewing its construction, made of immense pale white and sandy coloured solid stone blocks, many bigger than a man.

"Impressively large eh? That's why it's called the Citadel," Theodoric explained noting Paul's wonder as people bustled about them on foot, Confrere and other knights coming and going.

As they moved further in, Paul looked up to his right at the Tower of David, just as a contingent of Knights Templar greeted Count Henry. Brother Jakelin saw Paul brushing himself down and immediately beckoned him and Theodoric to follow him. Paul in turn beckoned Thomas and his men to follow. Percival watched as Guy and his escort continued to follow Count Henry being led off one way as Paul, Theodoric and Thomas's men followed Brother Jakelin and two other Knights Templar. Quickly he hurried after them and joined up behind Thomas's men.

"My friends it is good to see you both safely here at last, in the city of Jerusalem herself," Brother Jakelin said riding alongside Paul.

"Very much", was all Paul replied as he took in all the busy chaos of people and horses about him.

Brother Jakelin pointed towards a large domed building to their left.

"This city is divided into various quarters, my friend; over there, the northwest is the Patriarch Amalric's' quarter centred upon the Church of the Holy Sepulchre. It's a Byzantine replacement for the building destroyed by the Sultan al Hakim...and just over there is the Patriarch's nearby palace. That is all subject to the administrative jurisdiction of his court, the curia patriarchae. So we keep out," he informed him and then laughed.

Paul stared at the Holy Sepulchre, the sun shining brightly off its dome as Theodoric just nodded.

"Don't worry; I shall take you to visit it when the Pilgrims are not thronged about it later, but if you look just south, over there; that's our good friends the Hospitallers' quarter. At its heart, they have a great hospice and infirmary. Catch anything nasty whilst here, I recommend you go there immediately," Brother Jakelin joked.

Paul looked towards it and saw what he immediately considered perhaps the most beautiful building so far. He pulled up his horse momentarily.

"Now that is truly a marvel to view," he announced.

Brother Jakelin came over, his horse rearing for a moment as a child ran across his path. He quickly steadied it.

"That is indeed...the hospital of St John of Jerusalem. It can house two thousand sick and infirm in abundantly supplied and provisioned rooms. You ever need a really good night's sleep, go there. They have large beds each fitted with their own coverlets and sheets; and staffed by professional doctors no less."

As Paul looked his ears were filled with the many different dialects of the people that passed him; Greek, Arabic, French and many others but he was surprised to note they all dressed almost identically with Christians undifferentiated from their Muslim colleagues.

"Not much has changed I see," Theodoric remarked as he looked about the place.

"It has been a while since you were last here, but much has changed even if not outwardly," Brother Jakelin replied and ushered for them to again follow him.

They slowly made their way through the streets heading east across the city, and Paul noted an open baker's oven where a blonde haired Christian was laughing as he made bread alongside an Arabic man who was stoking a furnace that heated not only the oven but also a large water boiler that supplied a public bath. Just beyond that, were a mixed group of Christians and Muslims making and packing soap underneath the protection from the sun of a roofed handsome stone vaulted covered market. High windows allowed light to pour in. Further in Brother Jakelin stopped them and pointed towards an area known as the Malquissinat.

"We know," Theodoric intoned with a wry smile.

"Don't eat in there that's all I'll say," Brother Jakelin laughed.

"We know...Thomas already explained," Paul replied and looked back at Thomas, who followed in silence with his men.

Paul looked on, seeing the vaulted ceilings of the market pierced with holes allowing smoke and cooking smells to escape, the market was thronged with many people and pilgrims. Brother Jakelin led onwards to a large walled enclosure.

"Beyond that wall, through that gate is 'Haram al-Sharif', our main headquarters," Brother Jakelin announced.

Paul had longed for this important moment, getting to the very heart of the Templars themselves. He was now going where Stewart had longed to visit and spoken of so many times over the past few years, yet it was he who was about to see it first. Most of all though, he wanted to visit the large underground stables where the original nine founding knights had carried out their secret excavations and found something as his father and Theodoric had explained many times to him. He felt saddened that Alisha was not with him to share the experience. As they passed through the gate into the enclosure Paul was surprised to see how large and open it was, the huge Temple of the Lord, the Dome of the Rock, stood to his left, a massive construction far bigger than he had imagined. He was eager to explore and take in the whole experience but as they pulled up at the former Al Aqsa Mosque, now the Templar Headquarters, and dismounted, other Templars greeted them and immediately took their horses away to be stabled. Adrastos snorted and kicked up and Paul had to calm him before the Templar could gently coax him to follow him down a wide incline path that led down into the stable area. Paul watched as Adrastos was led away. Paul shook his head as his ears started to ring and he felt dizzy. Theodoric noticed this and immediately grabbed his arm to steady him. Paul raised his hand to indicate he was all right.

"Thomas. You and your knights are more than welcome to stable with us whilst here. We have heard much about you. I shall send a sergeant to assist you and accommodate you if that is acceptable?" Brother Jakelin said as Thomas dismounted.

"'Tis greatly appreciated...and accepted," Thomas replied and part bowed his head to Brother Jakelin.

"Don't worry, you'll have plenty of time to muck out in the stables," Theodoric joked.

"Where...where do I go?" Percival asked sheepishly still sat upon his horse as Brother Teric followed him into the courtyard with several other Templars.

"Were you not supposed to follow Guy to the palace?" Jakelin asked.

"No...No one said anything, to be honest," Percival answered.

"He can stay with us if that is all right with you...as part of our troop if he wishes," Thomas said and smiled at Percival. "Though Lord help you as my men will run you ragged," he then laughed.

Percival looked at Thomas's rugged looking men, who all looked at him.

"Well...as I am so young compared to you all, running ragged around you old men will be no problem," Percival joked, which solicited some comments and laughs from the men.

"I am happy with that if you are?" Brother Jakelin replied.

"My cock will need cleaning first thing in the morning," one of Thomas's men called out, laughing.

"Okay...that won't be a problem...as it's so small it won't take long...if I can find it," Percival shot back. The men all laughed as Brother Jakelin shook his head silently but amused.

"You will fit in just fine, young Percy," Thomas remarked smiling.

Percival looked at Paul and winked. Percival's earlier concerns about not fitting in anywhere may just have been resolved he thought.

Paul turned to look upon the grand frontage of the Al Aqsa mosque, with seven vaulted Gothic archways ending with a larger eighth archway at the far right side of the building that covered the entrance with a large dome on top of its tower above. It was a large and beautiful off-white stone building. As Thomas, his men and Percival were led off with Brother Teric and the other Templars exchanging friendly insults, Paul followed Brother Jakelin and Theodoric up a wide, open flight of steps and entered the cool Al Aqsa Mosque, their footsteps echoing in the large open entrance hall. Paul gazed in awe at the beautiful yet simple high vaulted white ceiling.

"I can't believe I am actually within the Al Aqsa Mosque itself," he whispered, but not quiet enough.

"You are inside the Temple of Solomon," a stern voice bellowed out from a side alcove where an Augustinian and a Cistercian monk both stood.

Paul swung his gaze to look at them as Brother Jakelin ushered Paul and Theodoric onwards and into a separate large room, the Templars' main reception and induction room, before he could respond.

"Fear not what they say as they just get a little too possessive over this place and its name," Brother Jakelin explained.

The reception room was Spartan with just a minimal amount of furniture; two chairs, one table in the centre and two large black and white banners displaying the Knights Templar cross, hung on each side of the room. A large wall mural greeted them depicting the crucifixion of Christ but it puzzled Paul immediately as it only showed the bottom half of the cross, a black sun in the background and the Virgin Mary and other assorted people at the foot of the cross. One individual had his face turned away from the cross whilst another had his finger pointing upwards, whilst in the background a carob tree was visible and a bush also. On the lower part of the cross, a green leaf shoot sprang out. A man was also depicted with a large lance that dripped three drops of blood. This clearly puzzled Paul as he approached the image. He stood in silence looking at it until Theodoric came and stood beside him.

"This puzzles you?" he asked as Brother Jakelin approached and stood the other side.

Paul looked on studying all the details on the mural and silently nodded.

"Come, there is much you have to learn," Brother Jakelin announced and placed his arm around Paul and ushered him towards the main stairway that led to the upper rooms of the building.

Theodoric sensed Paul's unease at the depiction, shook his head gently, and followed them upstairs. They were led into another large open room with a balcony that faced north overlooking the city and as they made themselves comfortable, Brother Jakelin showed them a garderobe washroom where they could freshen up.

"Hey, in this climate and environment we have to maintain health by cleanliness, whatever the orders," Brother Jakelin explained with a wry smile as he passed them both a large simple white towel each.

"So what do we do now?" Paul asked.

"Freshen up and rest. As soon as Count John is back, we shall dine," Brother Jakelin answered, shrugged his shoulders and immediately closed the door behind him.

"John. Who is John?" Paul asked even before the echo from the door shutting had gone. Theodoric approached him and looked at him in silence for a moment. "You are doing that look again," Paul remarked.

Theodoric sighed and placed a hand upon Paul's shoulder.

"My dear good friend. There truly is much you must learn; and you don't have the luxury of time to learn it either. John is the symbolic spiritual name of Count Henry," he explained and paused. "But it is neither for me nor my place to explain why. You will have to allow him to do so in his own time; if and when he thinks and sees fit," he continued almost solemnly.

Paul's curiosity was now aroused. A knock at the door interrupted before he could respond and a casually dressed man wearing just a single long light brown robe entered the room with some cold fresh water to drink and a small snack of unleavened bread strips, roasted vegetables and a herb and olive oil mix dip. After he left, they freshened themselves up, ate the snack and relaxed to the sound of other Templars in the nearby chapel singing out their vespers for the dead. As the afternoon wore on, Paul continually pressed Theodoric for more information about Count Henry and the strange mural in the reception and induction room but Theodoric constantly waved his finger back at him 'no' mockingly trying to make light of it. Paul knew Theodoric clearly understood and knew far more than he was letting on. He started to fall asleep as a cool breeze gently blew across him. Several times he shook his head as his ears kept ringing and he heard what he thought was a woman whispering close by.

As evening approached, Paul awoke from a light sleep to the sound of Muslims being called to prayer. The sun was setting when he walked out onto the balcony and looked down into the inner courtyard of the Al Aqsa Mosque. Theodoric stretched his arms and yawned joining him as many Muslims knelt facing south towards Mecca and started their prayers; many were positioned next to a single porch they had been allowed to use. Suddenly a loud clang of metal rang out and their gaze immediately fell upon a large fully armoured Latin knight who had just thrown his helmet in disgust.

"Get away you filthy heathen infidels. Away with practising your abominable creed here!" fumed the knight loudly, his face red with rage as he approached the nearest Muslim.

Two Templars rushed out towards him as he grabbed the Muslim and pulled him around shouting "this is the way thou shouldst pray!" Quickly and efficiently the two Templars ushered him away. No sooner had they let go and left the knight after handing him back his helmet than he again rushed towards the praying Muslims determined that he would make at least one Muslim pray the right way as he saw things. The two now highly embarrassed and apologetic Templars grappled the knight to the floor this time and sat on him until four other Templars arrived and physically escorted him out of the building as he continued to shout that they all had to "be wary of contamination of the faith".

"Obviously new to the city," Theodoric commented with a frown and making a gesticulating hand gesture, which made Paul laugh.

"Is it always like this?" he asked.

"Sadly, it is; and nothing has changed despite what Jakelin said earlier," Theodoric answered quietly as he looked upon the other Muslims still praying.

"Sad because they still pray?" Paul enquired quizzically.

"Oh no not for that reason. Sad because idiot knights like him still act like that," Theodoric immediately replied. "For too many pilgrims, it is a culture shock. Even for those who take the long slow overland route as we have, you would think they would have grown used to the idea of foreign customs in a foreign land. What do they honestly expect for God's sake? Nothing changes! At Nablus, when I was last there at the well where Jesus supposedly conversed with the Samaritan...I saw Latins murder Muslims for daring to visit it...and just twenty-five miles from here is the pit, according to Muslim tradition, where Joseph's brothers threw him after stripping him of his multicoloured coat, where Christians still try to lord it over Muslims. You should go to Damascus. There they have an image that supposedly heals Jews, Christians and Muslims indiscriminately, while all together they make their devotions at a spring where Mary supposedly washed the infant Jesus's clothes and where the palm trees bent to shield her from the sun and bring her dates. It is plain to see that in a country where the Divine appears so ecumenical, sectarian purity lingers dangerously close. How little they all really know; and how so futile and wrong," he continued, his disappointment evident and sadness etched across his usually smiling face. Paul's expectations of Jerusalem had been high, and despite not feeling any great overwhelming sense as he had hoped for, he could see that the visit was affecting Theodoric on a wholly different level. Maybe he would feel better once he had sorted his obligation to the Knights of Lazarus he thought. "All this is such folly," Theodoric sighed heavily and stood still staring at the Muslims praying.

"Why?" Paul enquired.

"The heart of Jerusalem. This noble sanctuary of Al Haram al Sharif...all thirty-five acres of it and all regarded by Muslims as a mosque. Jerusalem is known to them as 'Al Quds', the Holy. This was the place, where the Dome of the Rock stands, that Muhammad was brought by night from Makkah (Mecca) and from which he then ascended to the heavens to our Lord," Theodoric explained.

"So who has rightful claim over this site?" Paul asked.

Theodoric shook his head and paused before answering.

"No one, in reality. I mean all this...these buildings were all designed and built by Arabs. It was the Umayyad Khalif, 'Abdul Malik ibn Marwan', who commenced work on the Dome of the Rock in AD 685. I do not think many would argue that it is a truly beautiful architectural treasure. This huge mosque we now stand in was commissioned after that and could accommodate a vast congregation of more than five thousand worshippers. Although it too was started by 'Abdul Malik ibn Marwan', it was actually completed by his son Al-Walid in AD 705 and became known as Masjid al-Aqsa, Al-Aqsa Mosque. Every Friday prayers, this building would have overflowed with thousands of worshippers, who must now make their prayers outside in the courtyards of the vast open expanse of the Noble Sanctuary. Our Christ was resurrected in the tomb, now covered by the Holy Sepulchre, so I ask you then, who has rightful claim? Neither and both," Theodoric said, his voice tinged with sadness.

Before Paul could press or discuss the matter further, Brother Jakelin's squire informed them they were both called upon to join Count Henry that evening. Brother Jakelin shortly arrived after having completed his nightly chore of checking his horses, equipment and men, and then escorted Paul and Theodoric on foot a short walk to an extravagant and opulent local merchant's house.

୨୦ ଓଈ

"The Count has much to discuss tonight...more so with you, Paul, and as it's going to be a long night, we cannot hold the meeting at the Temple...so it'll be in here," Brother Jakelin stated looking directly at Paul, then pulled a cord to the side of the double door, which rang a bell deep within the house.

Puzzled, Paul frowned as Theodoric shrugged his shoulders, as much in the dark as Paul.

"Oh don't worry. Contrary to what you may have heard, there will be no homosexual activities and weird practices behind these doors tonight," Brother Jakelin joked.

"Not tonight maybe, but what about tomorrow night?" Paul joked back.

"A sense of humour at last. I'm sure Theo here has enlightened you...if not did your father not explain much about us?" Brother Jakelin asked.

"He said very little...certainly nothing much about the Templars," Paul replied.

The ornate double hardwood doors swung open held aside by two house servants who bowed as Brother Jakelin led them inside.

"You should speak much with Theo then. After all he served with your father as a brother Templar," Brother Jakelin matter of factly remarked.

Paul's mind fired up as he heard this. He knew Theodoric and his father had been close friends before their fall out, and he knew his father had been a Templar once...but Theodoric had always maintained he had not been one. Surprised he mentally wrestled with Brother Jakelin's statement as he looked hard and quizzically at Theodoric, who looked away sheepishly as they moved forwards.

"Theo, what is he on about?" Paul asked quietly.

"We'll talk later, later okay," he answered.

Sweet smells of incense filled the entrance room and Paul saw Count Henry standing at the head of a large table set up in the middle of a courtyard, the centrepiece of the large house. As Paul headed towards him, another man appeared wearing a very large, almost outlandish burnous turban and greeted him effusively.

"Assalamu aliekum," he said and beckoned them closer as Brother Jakelin and Theodoric followed.

"Wa allakam assalam," Brother Jakelin replied as all took up positions around the table.

After a few initial pleasantries and introductions, Paul learnt that the man was named Usamah, who was a prince in his own right, a diplomat and traveller. A few claps of his hands later and the table was immediately covered in exotic foods

and drink. As Paul looked about the large house, he noted the heavy Italian presence mixed with Arabic traditional furniture complete with ornate decorative
inlays. The walls and floors were covered in mosaics and marble lending to the
coolness inside compared with the torrid heat outside. Many expensive carpets
overlaid large areas of the floor whilst rich damask hangings adorned the walls.
Upon the table, expensive 'Port of Symeon' tableware and glazed polychrome
pottery sat alongside Jewish manufactured vases, goblets and beakers. The food
was all served upon silver with gold edged plates. Paul looked at a very well made
fork quizzically.

"You like? Our best cutlery. A new fangled eating fork," Usamah commented,
noticing Paul's interest, who half embarrassed looked up as they all laughed.

Paul's mind ran as he pondered what Count Henry wanted to talk with him
about alone, but more importantly Brother Jakelin's comment that Theodoric
had served with his father as a Templar. This more than a little disturbed him as
why, during all their time together, had he never once mentioned it? He found
himself getting increasingly agitated and impatient as the night wore on, the
discussion primarily between Usamah and Count Henry relating to setting up
a joint Muslim and Christian village as up until then the rural population had
always remained segregated. A lot of aggravation had been caused over the years
as Muslim villages had to hand over a substantial part of their crops each harvest
as payment for pasture rights as well as pay a tithe or dime to the Church. Paul
listened intently, Stephanie's earlier words on the same subject being recalled as
she had explained to him previously though he had not really paid much attention then. Templars received tithes also but Count Henry wanted to start a more
dynamic and inter-related system. This he intended by way of setting up an entire
new Villeneuve (village) where the settlers were not just serfs but liber homo,
meaning 'freeman'. Paul liked this idea. The main problem Count Henry faced
was the simple fact that the Church of the Holy Sepulchre held the majority of
properties and plots about Jerusalem. Usamah acted as the intermediary whereby
either party could agree to rent those plots by way of a land tax. What all this had
to do with Paul he could not figure out. Count Henry believed that a joint new
village would foster a greater understanding and tolerance of faiths as well as
be mutually beneficial. Using a new layout for the set up of the village as per his
designs would enable easy partitioning of plots as well as make it more defend-
able. The crops produced would all be sugar cane, which was rapidly becoming a major trade in the region. The cultivation and refining of the crop had
opened a completely new unlimited export trade to Europe. Both Usamah and
Count Henry agreed that it was trade and trade alone that brought Christian and
Muslim together like nothing else could. Theodoric remained for the main very
reserved and quiet.

"Are you all right?" Paul eventually asked him.

"Me. Yes of course. I find the food a little too rich," he answered and raised his
glass again.

Theodoric's response drew Usamah and Count Henry back to them.

"I have something that will settle your stomach and scintillate your tongue,"
Usamah smiled and nodded to one of the servants nearby who soon returned with
a large platter.

As Usamah removed a silver conical mould, he revealed a sugarloaf shaped dessert, and, using tongs, placed it into a Fatimid, an Egyptian imported high quality glazed, vessel ornate with blue and black motifs. The whole thing looked very delicate as Paul took it and viewed the sweet inside quizzically.

✳〼✳   1 – 8

"It is sweet and almost divine," Usamah explained with a large smile.

Paul tasted the sweet and momentarily shuddered as his tongue tingled with the new taste.

"Very good," he responded as all in the room laughed except Theodoric.

Usamah rinsed his hands in a bowl of fresh, hot water then stood up.

"My friends. It is time that I must leave for it is late. Please stay and accept my hospitality further," he announced. Paul stood up to shake his hand.

"Thank you kindly for your hospitality. You have a lovely house here," Paul commented.

The room fell silent before Brother Jakelin, Count Henry and Usamah all laughed.

"You are indeed new to this city," Usamah replied and bid his farewells.

As Count Henry and Brother Jakelin saw him to the door, Paul sat down next to Theodoric.

"Did I miss something?" he asked. Theodoric tilted his head towards him almost mockingly.

"Muslims and Jews can still visit daily and stay overnight, but they can't reside here or own property here. This is officially not his house, though in reality it is," Theodoric explained.

Paul sat silently for a moment.

"Theo, I have to press a matter with you as I need to know. I trust you totally but I must ask and get this straight in my mind. What did Jakelin mean? That you served with my father as a Templar?" Paul quizzed.

As Brother Jakelin and Count Henry returned, the two house servants left the room leaving them alone.

"Servants can stay. Stupid rule eh?" Theodoric said as if trying to change the subject and avoid Paul's question.

Count Henry sat opposite Paul and coughed to get his attention as Brother Jakelin fetched more wine.

"Gentleman; now the official formal business has been concluded with Usamah, we have much to talk about this night," Count Henry announced almost officiously and clasped his hands together.

Brother Jakelin sat down to Paul's left as Theodoric on his right turned to face Paul directly. Hesitantly Paul looked at each in turn, a little concerned and somewhat bemused at what was going on.

"What is this? What's going on?" he asked them.

"We could not hold this meeting at the Headquarters as too many brother knights with sharp eyes and eager ears would overhear, so Usamah has kindly allowed us to hold this meeting here, for as long as it takes," Brother Jakelin explained and started to pour them each a large goblet of wine.

Paul looked at Theodoric questionably as he placed his left hand upon Paul's shoulder.

"Paul, you have many questions, and we have much we need to know of you. I confess it now that yes, I did once serve alongside him as a Templar...but that was a long long time ago. If people know you were a Templar, they start asking all manner of questions and place burdens and expectations upon you...that I learnt the hard way. You know me as...for me and who I really am," he explained quietly.

"I don't understand. Why, I mean how, how, was our meeting genuine or contrived then? I don't understand why you have not told me this before," Paul replied, confused, a sense of betrayal overwhelming him almost with emotion.

Theodoric sighed heavily and drew a deep breath.

"I was genuinely just passing through Rochefort, picking up some old items from my former home before moving on. Our meeting was not contrived...maybe ordained by Him upstairs, but I did know you were your father's son the moment I saw you in the square...you are the double of him when he was your age." he explained looking Paul in the eye. "Do you remember how I was, how I acted?" he asked.

Paul hesitated as he thought as all looked at him in silence.

"Yes, I remember thinking you were a little strange. Overly friendly considering you had only just met me," Paul answered. Theodoric nodded silently.

"You see he recognised you," Count Henry interjected.

"But, but why then did you not, have you not, said anything about being a former Templar yourself until now?" Paul shot back.

"I tried to; many times. I almost blurted everything out. Think back to when I was delirious with fever. Did I not rave on about John the Baptist, Mary Magdalene and that everyone was an idiot?" Theodoric answered. Paul recalled the event and simply nodded. "To see you, the double of your father and in such circumstances was truly a shock to me. It was more than a coincidence, more than synchronicity, it was, almost Divine intervention; that's how I saw it, and as I have explained, people place expectations upon you if they know you were once something more than you are now," he detailed further as Paul drank more wine in two large gulps. The room fell silent as Paul stared ahead. "I loved your father like a brother. He and I learnt much together and endured many things," Theodoric explained softly.

"But my father, he never once ever mentioned you by name that I can recall. And only once did he tell us that he was once a Templar, but only for a brief period. It was only last year that he and Firgany told Taqi and I about their past, how they met and connections with the Templars and Ashashin...but that is all," he paused. "So what was so bad or went so wrong about you all that he could never be compelled to speak of you?" Paul asked.

Theodoric looked across at Count Henry.

"Theodoric and your father were truly great knights, but, also both were very impetuous and eager to learn. I don't think I need point out Theodoric's talents and knowledge do I?" Count Henry stated. Paul looked at Theodoric.

"Let me continue," Theodoric asked and Count Henry nodded. "I got your father into many scrapes and a lot of trouble. On top of that I convinced him that we could unravel all the mysteries that we, as Templars, were the guardians of," he started to explain as Paul stood up and turned his back to them, arms by his sides and fists clenched and sweating, his emotions confused. Theodoric stood up beside him. "Your father spoke much wisdom, but I chose to ignore his advice. We had secrets and doctrines and were on the verge of answering some of the enigmas we have been entrusted to safeguard, but that was where I made the mistake. Those secrets were entrusted into our hands for future generations' sakes and benefits; yet I, and I alone, chose to consider that I knew best and wanted them revealed in my lifetime. Your father and I fell out as a consequence, but every time we patched up our differences and our friendship continued as we served together."

Count Henry walked over and stood in front of Paul, who was now clearly more confused and placed his hands upon his shoulders.

"Sit back down, Paul. As I said, there is much we need to discuss tonight," he said as he ushered him to retake his seat. "There is more than what Theo has told you. Your father had a destiny, some say it was not the case and ultimately that is what your father chose to believe," Count Henry started to explain, as Paul looked at him and shook his head disbelievingly.

"It is true Paul. Hear him out," Brother Jakelin interrupted. "Your father and Theo here felt it wise and prudent, in their own fashion, to start divulging certain of our esoteric secrets by way of poems and writings composed into Holy Grail romances they both concocted. They assumed they knew better and that all should have the right to the knowledge and secrets. Powerful secrets that are not meant for men of our times. Naturally we could not allow that to continue. But nor could we physically stop them short of killing the pair," he continued.

"Perhaps you should have," Theodoric, stated almost sarcastically.

"Not our way. Besides we did the one thing we knew would be more effectual, more lasting," Count Henry said almost coldly. Paul looked at him hard. "We excommunicated the pair of them, for life ...though we did eventually overturn that verdict," he announced.

Paul looked sideways at Theodoric, who nodded in acknowledgement.

"Your father never forgave me for that. He left immediately for France, swore he would have nothing more to do with any of us and did indeed continue to write many more poems as you are aware," Theodoric explained solemnly, his voice tinged with sadness as he reflected upon the past.

"Tell him the rest," Brother Jakelin spoke loudly.

"Your father was also a member of the Prieure de Sion, of which I now hold the honour of being its Grand Master. Your father was in line to be the next one after my grandfather passed away. He had eighty-one days to decide to accept it. If he had, he would now be the Grand Master, and you would be the next hereditary heir in line to continue after him. Your father claimed he could not keep the secrets as Theo here had convinced him that all had the right to know," Count Henry outlined as Paul looked at Theodoric again, who shrugged his shoulders.

"You see, now you probably hate me as your father does. That is why I said nothing. But after you found me, I saw it as God's way of giving me another chance to put right that great mistake that I alone had done. Do you see that? Do you understand?" Theodoric almost pleaded.

Brother Jakelin coughed loudly.

"Tell him all of it," he demanded almost.

"There is more?" Paul asked, bemused.

"Much more, and you must trust us and learn, and hopefully not make the same errors as your father," Count Henry replied.

"Be careful; do not insult my father for in his absence I will defend his honour," Paul responded snappishly.

"Calm down, Paul, you misunderstand us and our motives. Your father's honour is now impeccable. We learnt much ourselves at the time from his and Theo's actions back then. I am Grand Master by hereditary right of my father and his father before; but your father, and you, yours is the right by blood. From a bloodline that stretches far back into antiquity, further than you can imagine. My father was only elected as at that time, the order could not trace your father as he had disappeared in combat, presumed dead. It was years before we discovered he had been held as a prisoner in Aleppo," Count Henry informed Paul.

Confused, Paul shook his head.

"My father was a prisoner in Aleppo? He has never told us this...," Paul replied visibly shocked. Paul's mind ran as he made connections linking Reynald and Raymond, who were also once prisoners in Aleppo. Had they been captive together? Why had his father never told him this major event in his life?

"It will take time but you will learn all there is to know, but tonight, especially tonight, we need to know of your intentions long term. Do you intend to divulge secrets of your true origins and past as your father tried to?" Count Henry asked.

"I don't understand what you are asking. My true origins? My intentions?" Paul answered, even more puzzled.

Theodoric stood up and placed his hands upon Paul in a comforting gesture.

"Count Henry has no heir. Your brother, who is the natural true bloodline heir to take his place, is, dare I say it without offending you, not as bright, intelligent or as wise as you...and that is the criterion the position requires. As your father renounced his claim by default of not giving his answer to take his position up within the eighty-one days' notice required, it now falls to Count Henry to find his successor. You arriving as you did was not just coincidental as I have tried to tell you already on many occasions," Theodoric explained sympathetically.

Paul looked at Count Henry as he acknowledged Theodoric's comments as being correct. Paul drank another large mouthful of wine.

"I must explain what this is all about so you fully appreciate what it is we ask of you and why. Will you listen to what we tell you or are we wasting our time?" Count Henry asked solemnly but succinctly.

Paul simply nodded, his head swimming with emotions and questions.

"I will listen, and also promise not to divulge anything you tell me this night; but answer me this, what in Heaven do you mean about my right by my bloodline?" he asked emphatically.

Brother Jakelin, Count Henry and Theodoric all looked at each other for a moment.

"I will come to that, but first I need to explain some other points so that when I tell you about your bloodline, you will understand. Are you agreed upon that?" Count Henry asked.

Paul simply nodded again in agreement then looked at Theodoric.

"Don't tell me later that you never said anything as your astrology charts told you not to," Paul remarked, his comment laced with a sarcastic tone.

"Please, just hear the Count out before you make any final judgement upon me," Theodoric asked.

"Paul, you have been made aware, almost since your first arrival at Crac de l'Os- pital I am sure and subsequently at Crac de Moab that we are not exactly what we outwardly appear to be. You are also aware that there is another more secretive arm, which is the governing, political as well as administrative Order behind both the Knights Templar and the Cistercians. Both were presided over by Bernard of Clairvaux, yes?" Count Henry asked Paul.

"Partly," Paul answered.

"We, that is the Prieure de Sion, are that hidden political and administrative Order, yet we in turn originated from the much older 'Order of the Triple Tau'. Your destiny, should you choose to accept it, is ultimately connected with them. Look at your sword. You see the emblem there, the stylised version barely visible upon the blade ...and maybe Theodoric has explained some of its symbolic and esoteric meanings, but I bet not all of it," he further stated as Theodoric shook his head 'no' indicating that he had not told Paul.

Paul looked at his sword pommel, the triple Tau symbol upon it he had had engraved by the blacksmith not even aware a stylised version was actually upon the blade as well as the rose and cross emblem.

"Before the Knights Templar were formed, as a military wing to our existing Order, a monastery was set up in Jerusalem founded by members from the 'Order of the Sword'. They were also known as the 'Order of the Tau' whose origins go back to Altopascio in Italy, from where they moved to a monastery in Orval in Belgium, founded by mysterious monks in 1070 from Calabria Southern Italy. From there they went directly on to Jerusalem, finally becoming the 'Order of Sion' or 'Prieure de Sion' as we are known today," Count Henry detailed as Paul sat down silently.

"Perhaps Theo can explain more," Brother Jakelin interjected.

"Yes right, like what?" Theo asked.

"How about explaining the 'Order of the Sword'?" Brother Jakelin responded as he poured himself another wine.

Theodoric sat up and looked at Paul.

"Okay if you insist," Theodoric coughed to clear his throat and continued. "The 'Order of the Sword' well, it was named and based upon the allegorical allusion to the two edged long sword that Jesus proclaimed in the New Testament as well as the Sword of Orion, or the sword of Damocles...in fact by many names. All that sword symbology has now been updated, in part by me and your father, into some of the Grail poems and romances we wrote, but already doing the rounds as recounted and updated into other Grail romances as Excalibur. The sword represents knowledge and wisdom being drawn from the stone. You write Excalibur in Greek, or Hebrew, its Gematria or mathematical value is exactly the same as that of the 'two edged long- sword' of Jesus; it being 755. The Great Pyramid in Egypt is exactly 755 feet long on each of its sides. Our measurements are identical to the Egyptian Sacred foot as the modern measure was taken directly from there. As you are aware, no matter how strong the person, if he is not pure of heart and the rightful heir, he can never pull the sword from the stone, that's because it is knowledge and wisdom that only the wisest adept will understand how to draw from the stone," Theodoric explained, cautiously checking for Paul's reaction. "Do I continue?" he asked looking at Count Henry.

"Yes for you know far more than I ultimately," Count Henry answered.

Paul looked up at Theodoric and also nodded for him to continue.

"Well, the original group, as you are aware from our previous discussions on this matter, was known as the 'Order of the Triple Tau' based in Calabria, Southern Italy but," he paused, "it originally came from earlier origins in Palestine having fled from there after the first fall of Acre. They became widely known during the ninth and tenth centuries as 'The Order of St James of Altopascio'. As for the 'Triple Tau', well that signifies among other occult things, 'Templum Hierosolyma', meaning 'The Temple of Jerusalem'," Theodoric detailed as Paul looked up intently. "It also means 'Clavis ad Theosaurum', which in turn means," as Brother Jakelin also spoke in unison, "a key to a treasure."

Both looked at each other and laughed before Theodoric continued.

"And 'Theca ubi res pretiosa deponitur', which means 'a place where a precious thing is concealed'. It also means 'Res ipsa preiosa', which stands for 'the precious thing itself' but the actual Triple Tau symbol itself is also a modern pictogram for an H with a T set on top for Hermes Tresmigestis, which in turn means Hermes thrice greatest."

All three sat in silence looking at Paul waiting for a reaction.

"So, all your history and rituals all link to something that is hidden, that only the purest of heart adepts of the occult can learn of its whereabouts and secrets, but not in our times; is that what you are saying? Is that what all of this is for? No wonder my father walked away from it all," Paul finally blurted out.

"You are your father's son all right," Theodoric shot back. "But no, that is not all that it is for. I know that in time your father came to fully understand the enormity of responsibility that came with knowing these secrets and that they were meant for later generations' benefits. I learnt that, perhaps a little too late, but I learnt it. The hardest thing ever was having to learn patience and not ruin it for those that will need it the most when, and only when, the time is right."

 3 – 35

After a few more minutes in silence, Brother Jakelin leaned nearer to Paul.

"Ever wondered why we wear white robes in our best dress order?" he asked Paul quietly.

"No not really. Just assumed it was to signify purity. Why?" Paul asked back.

"In our inner circle temples," Brother Jakelin started to answer then paused and looked at Count Henry for approval before continuing. He nodded he could. "We have what we call the Royal Arch Degree, symbolically and diagrammatically set out as a double triangle. It is called the 'Seal of Solomon' (see Fig. 32) and is placed within a circle of gold. Below it is placed a scroll with the words, 'Nil nisi clavis deest'. This means, 'Nothing is wanting but the key'. Your mother's maiden name was Keys...did you know that?"

Fig. 32:

Paul frowned and nodded his head yes in silence as Brother Jakelin continued.

"On the circle are the words 'Si tatlia jungere possis sit tibi scire posse', meaning, 'If thou canst comprehend these things, thou knowest enough'. We inherited these sayings directly from our original order, via Palestine, that ultimately came in its turn directly from the Essenes, who in their turn took it from much further back in antiquity. From this group, knowledge regarding hidden secrets eventually resulted in Godfrei de Bouillon relinquishing all his rights in France, and heading for Jerusalem and ultimately the first crusade. Pope Urban II and St Bernard of Clairvaux were instrumental in this as you will learn in the fullness of time if you are prepared to listen and learn", he informed Paul.

Paul's mind struggled to take on board and memorise all that he was hearing and a large part of him felt betrayed by Theodoric, but his emotions were confused as he nevertheless still respected him immensely. He wished his father had been with them to answer the many questions now running through his head. As he sat and pondered he recalled his father's parting comments about truth being an elusive goal. He could hear his father's words clearly and only now did it make sense and not just the emotional ramblings of an old man he had so lightly dismissed out of hand when he had left. 'Truth can be an elusive goal, yet it can be the greatest reward when understood for what it is. It is in some respects the Grail of life itself. It is well known that you value something far more when you have to work hard for it, possibly fight for it, sacrifice for it or journey far to acquire it. How diluted the elusive prize is when given to us all too easily; something very profound and deep is lost in the very act of just getting it for nothing. The value of the truth is greatly magnified by the very act of the sacrifice, the journey, the years of searching, and the joy of discovery; so look, listen, search and find. And remember, there is a concerted effort being made to raise our awareness and educate us. The only limits to your understanding will be the self-imposed barriers that you put in the way, as there are none so blind as those who will not see.' As Paul recalled those words, he welled up with emotion. He was only now really beginning to understand another side of his father.

Theodoric placed an arm across Paul's back reassuringly, sensing his sadness. Paul looked at him and feigned a brave smile.

"I'm fine, honestly, I'm fine now. It is, believe me or not, all becoming a lot clearer to me now," he stated. "So please, I would like to know more, if you will continue."

Count Henry sat up, took some wine, ate some sugar loaf, cringed momentarily as the sweetness tingled his teeth and spoke.

"Paul, all you hear tonight is not for other ears. I pray that our faith in you is justified and you will not divulge it to any others unless permission and authority is given. You are not a sworn member, nor have you taken any vows, so you are under no oath to keep it privy other than your word of honour. How say you?" he asked Paul.

"You have my word, on my honour I swear it so," he answered solemnly.

"Good, very good, then know that the distinctive white robes of the Knights Templar warriors are naturally their most easily recognisable feature. This too was adopted from the dress of the Essene Nazarenes, though the name is grossly mis-understood nowadays. Jesus was part of this sect, which was really just another name that covered a whole band of sects living around the same time as Jesus. You know Jesus himself was always described in scripture as wearing white robes. Jesus was claimed to be Jewish it must be remembered and used the symbol of the Star of David as used by all Jews, though in fact he was not a practising Jew as we will shall instruct you. Does that not shock you?" Count Henry asked. Paul shook his head no. "Even better, for what we tell you now caused many potential members a crisis of faith. Theo, can you explain about the Merkaba as I know you can inform upon it better than I?"

Theodoric sat up quickly and Brother Jakelin nodded with a smile as Paul relaxed a little and even forced a smile.

"Right, well okay, the Merkaba. Well, it's Solid Gold and pronounced Mer Ka Ba and is more commonly known as the 'Star of David'. Erm, well...one solid gold Merkaba once stood on top of the Great Pyramid in Egypt for hundreds of years, as did many others upon the oldest Pyramids of ancient Egypt. You have to under-stand that no burials or bodies have ever been found inside the ancient Pyramids. When the Merkaba is viewed from below, the Sun creates a shadow of both dark and light...and," he paused, "and this is where the Knights Templar Cross symbol is derived from." He paused again longer this time as Paul just sat quietly listening. "Remember all that I explained previously about how many esoteric and mystical teachings were carried over from antiquity by use of symbols and mathematical codes; mathematics being the only truly universal language that can span time intact. Well, whilst names and even languages have changed throughout history the common beliefs are fundamentally the same. The Merkaba star was derived from the ancient Egyptian heretic Pharaoh Akhenaton and his monotheistic reli-gion; his belief in 'One God'. It was he who created, more correctly, reinstated, the Mer-Ka-Ba symbol originally. Very few initiates and even those of the higher cir-cles within the Templars know the full facts or even the name of this Akhenaton, the language of ancient Egypt and how to read its writings now being systemati-cally eradicated by the Church. But he was the first to believe that all men are equal in the love of 'One God'. Now, if this is not too much for you to handle, the most potent symbol of the Jewish faith is the 'Star of David'. The earliest examples of this symbol date back to 600–700 BC yet as you now know this most Jewish of icons comes directly out of ancient Egypt. Its use started as a three dimensional shape that rose to prominence during the reign of Akhenaton as recovered documents on plates of brass and gold found by the founding Templars proves (18th Dynasty 1372–1354 BC). The Star of David is an accurate two-dimensional representation of the original Merkaba," Theodoric explained quietly then paused as he took some wine. (See Fig. 33).

Fig. 33:

All looked up suddenly when a loud bang at the front door echoed throughout the building. As Brother Jakelin stood to answer, one of the servants rushed from an upstairs room, down the stairs and opened one of the main front doors.

"Is he here? Is he still here?" a voice shouted out as a man entered the building.

It was the Patriarch, Amalric of Jerusalem himself demanding to know where Usamah was. Count Henry stood to face him.

"No our very good friend is not here," he replied coldly.

"Friend! Good friend you say! Ptuh! Have you not heard how he mocks you behind your backs? He states in his many writings that all Franks possess none of the virtues of men except courage, yet he espouses admiration for the Mongols and those heathens of the Orient. What say ye to that?" Amalric demanded to know, angrily banging his staff hard on the marble floor.

Paul noted how lavish and richly dressed Amalric was. His short white hair and clean shaven image solicited an air of authority, but his eyes were cold and hard. Count Henry walked over and stood face to face very closely to him.

"As I said, he is our very good friend. He is not here and we are having a private meeting. I would therefore kindly ask you to leave us to continue in peace," Henry answered sternly but quietly.

Amalric looked condescendingly at him, then Brother Jakelin, Theodoric and finally Paul, pausing to stare at him. Paul stood up slowly, his sword pommel showing in the light of a candle.

"Your Holiness," Paul politely said.

Amalric looked back at Count Henry then back to Paul, his gaze fixing upon the emblem on his sword pommel.

"I am pleased to see there is at least one person here who still knows how to show reverential respect. Even though I see he wears a sword with that damned emblem. I would advise you part with that sword, young man, before it leads you wildly astray," he bombastically sounded off.

Paul looked down at the emblem and paused before looking back without saying a word.

"We are explaining that very aspect with him...if you would let us continue," Count Henry remarked and frowned at Amalric.

"And let me guess...you will fill his head with utter nonsense about the sacred feminine, the rose symbol and sex rituals. Will you also explain to him about 'The Good Fight' and female symbolism of she who stands as the representation of the mother church? I suspect not," he said in a tone laced with annoyance. "So before they utterly poison your mind, young man, let me first tell you that 'The Good

Fight' is a reference to St Paul, at the end of his life, where he is stating that he has fought the good fight in defence of truth and the true faith. As for the sacred feminine, along with so much spiritual confusion in the world now, is a matter that deeply grieves me. The woman, who rightly should be depicted within our religious art and is an everlasting and endearing symbol that the Lord uses towards his Church, should only be 'The Bride of Christ'. That includes not only women but men and children, the entire body of Christ, it is a picture of his deep and abiding love for his children. So ask yourself before they start this eve...what really is the so-called sacred feminine?"

"We have not even begun to explain those details," Count Henry interrupted.

"Good...then my arrival was perhaps providential after all for I shall tell this young man the real answer to that question...the answer is simple for all to see, in plain and open sight, for the 'sacred feminine' these men will tell you of is but purely a religious movement that emphasises femininity as being closer to divinity than masculinity. Those of the sacred feminine tradition worship feminine beauty and the power of sexual reproduction. The sacred feminine assumes that women, through the ability to bear children, are more 'sacred' than men. Men can only experience the sacred feminine, spiritually, through sexual intercourse. Just ask him," Amalric said and pointed at Brother Jakelin shaking his head disapprovingly. "Advocates of the sacred feminine viewpoint range from pseudo-Christians to Goddess worshippers, and Wicca witches. Hints of the sacred feminine viewpoint can be seen in the Bible with the examples of ritual prostitution in Genesis 38:21–22; Hosea 4:14, and Goddess worship in Jeremiah 44:17–25; 2 Kings 23:7. Other examples can be seen in the Easter fertility rituals and some aspects of Mariology. All this sacred feminine rubbish is based upon the unfounded and baseless theory that Jesus's mission was to father children through Mary Magdalene, thereby producing a 'royal' bloodline, and that Mary Magdalene was the 'Holy Grail' that carried Jesus's blood, and Mary Magdalene was Jesus's intended leader of the Christian Church. It was the patriarchal disciples and early Church that demoted Mary, denied the sacred feminine, and instituted a patriarchal caricature of Jesus's intention for Christianity. But that is all utter heretical nonsense!" He paused as Paul just looked up at him. "The fanciful imaginations of the Orders' upper rites and teachings are purely the work of the Devil himself for the sacred feminine has no, I repeat NO basis in the Bible. Jesus chose twelve male disciples, hardly the move of a man seeking to establish the sacred feminine. The New Testament is replete with examples of male leadership in the Church such as 1 Timothy 2:11–14. Biblical Christianity has lifted women to equality and oneness in the 'Body of Christ' as stated in Galatians 3:28, while maintaining a distinction in roles. Yes, a woman receives glory through childbirth as mentioned in 1 Timothy 2:15, but the role and value of women is no more nor no less sacred than that of men. The 'sacred feminine' is not sacred, nor does it accurately represent what the Bible describes as true femininity...so I shall be watching you, young man, mark my words," Amalric warned, his tone almost seething with tempered anger before flouncing round, immediately leaving the building slamming the door behind him hard before Paul could even reply. [39]

"And that is why this place is still, and will remain, such a melting pot of religious bigotry and blind arrogance," Theodoric said aloud and clapped his hands towards the door, shaking his head.

Count Henry hesitated then turned back to Paul.

"Do you wish to continue this tonight?" he asked him.

"Yes, if you all are willing to continue."

They all took their seats again as Brother Jakelin poured yet more wine for them.

"Okay, where was I?" Theodoric mused. "Oh yes, the star stuff...Paul, understand this, the Star of David, it being the Merkaba star, was brought out of Egypt by Moses himself, at the time of the Exodus. Even the Bible categorically states that Moses was 'versed in all the ways of the Egyptians'. In addition, Moses was himself of the Egyptian Royal Family, and he too taught monotheism to the Hebrews. You have to accept now, on faith I guess, and listen to your own heart and instincts, pray upon it if necessary to ask if what I say is true now as I know that the spirit runs deep and strong within you," Theodoric said as he eyed all in the room. He paused as he struggled to find the correct words and a way to explain what he wished to impart next.

Brother Jakelin leaned forward.

"Paul, what he's trying to explain is that Moses, as most people understand his character, was Akhenaton! Okay do you get that?" he simply stated. "And try to take what our great Patriarch Amalric has said with an open mind."

Paul looked at him intently, and then Theodoric before finally staring at Count Henry.

"It is true," Count Henry acknowledged.

Paul sat motionless and silent for a while, closed his eyes and thought.

"Okay, I take on board what you are stating; maybe it is the truth, I have no way of knowing. But who is this Pharaoh and why have I never heard of him before?" Paul asked as he opened his eyes again.

Count Henry sat down opposite him and leaned closer.

"Paul, we have the proofs of this and much more. Moses and his 'exodus' and Akhenaton's sudden 'disappearance' describe the same event from two different viewpoints. But all records in Egypt of Akhenaton were brutally and systematically erased from the face of history by his priesthood after he left his city of Tel al Armana with those that would follow his new monotheistic beliefs. But we also have the proofs of why this man suddenly changed his whole religious viewpoint," Count Henry explained.

"So all that we are taught from the Old Testament is nothing but lies and all based upon pagan rituals?" Paul replied.

"No, not at all. It is the same historical facts just different names, complete with mathematical codes, as I believe Theo here has elucidated upon many times already with you," he answered.

Paul stood up straight and ran his fingers through his hair.

"Paul, please sit," Theodoric calmly asked.

After a while Paul sat again as Theodoric passed him a small gold pendant.

"Here, I want you to have this. I was given it by your father. It is the three dimensional Merkaba talisman. When viewed in specific light conditions it produces a series of shadows that clearly form a 'cross', our Templar Cross. The angle of view needed in order to see this cross is exactly the same as the angle is when looking up if the Merkaba star was situated on top of the Great Pyramid at Giza in Egypt," he explained as Paul looked over the small object.

"What does all this mean?" Paul asked sadly, his shoulders hunched now.

"Erm, well in its literal sense it means we got our cross emblem directly from this. What it means linguistically if you are interested is that, er, the Mer part means 'Ascending Place', the Ka part means 'True Spirit' and Ba means 'Soul' in ancient Egyptian. Mer-Ka-Ba therefore means 'Ascending Place of True Spiritual Souls'," he replied then paused. "But it is also known as something you are perhaps far more familiar with, 'The Ark of the Covenant' the communication device with God or 'Temple'."

Paul looked up, emotion and confusion etched across his face.

"You made me promise months ago to always keep an open mind and heart to all possibilities, but this, all of this, this apparent knowledge; these secrets that you, no, now we, us, that we hide from all; can that be right?" he asked, impassioned.

"When you learn and understand the rest, then yes it is right and you will fully understand why. We have had years to learn this and take it all on board. You alas have to take it all in very fast I am sorry to say," Count Henry informed him.

"Here, you need some more wine, and plenty of it," Jakelin said as he passed a new full bottle of wine across the table.

"I think I need it more," Theodoric joked as, taking the wine, he refilled his goblet and then Paul's. Paul let out a nervous laugh and sat back again still examining the small Merkaba star.

"So, let me see if I understand this correctly. If then there was a solid gold Mer-Ka-Ba symbol on top of the Great Pyramid, and with all the other connections you have informed me of these past months, then it infers that the Great Pyramid is, if perhaps not physically, then certainly symbolically 'The Ark of the Covenant'? Moses is said to possess the Ark, and if Moses and Akhenaton were one and the same person, then that would make a lot of sense," Paul mused aloud.

"You are your father's son all right as you learn fast as he did. But know this also, the Merkaba was only placed as a temporary symbol, the original cap stone itself being a major secret and hidden away until a time a long way off in the future when it would once again be found. Moses, being aware of all the hidden secrets as he learnt from the Emerald Tablets of Hermes, managed to locate it, buried and surrounded by twelve other chambers. What he discovered and learnt changed him profoundly. That is why he started the first ever monotheistic belief system and religion base upon the pre-Deluge worldwide civilisation that hid the knowledge and wisdom as their world came to end," Count Henry explained.

Paul immediately looked up as his mind ran through all the images from his dreams about an ancient civilisation that he saw burying large stone constructions. His mind flashed back to Kizkalesi Castle and the images he saw there and the loss of time he experienced.

"That I can understand," Paul whispered.

"Good," Count Henry remarked hearing him. "But he also knew that it was for mankind's benefit in the future so he had to seal it all away again. In time you will learn all there is to know on this matter."

"Paul, look at me," Theodoric said pulling him slightly. "Think about this too. The Knights Templar use meditation daily; meditation is said to lead to a higher consciousness as used by Buddhists, those Orientals I told you about before. Christianity does not mention meditation anywhere. The Templar religious traditions and practices came from a different source not of Roman Catholicism," he explained.

"So where did the Order's traditions come from; Egypt as well?" Paul retorted.

"Sort of," Theodoric answered and paused briefly. "In a roundabout way, via the Nazarenes. The Nazarenes practised meditation too. This is why the Roman Catholic Church destroyed most of them. You will find many Merkaba and numerous examples of Templar crosses on temples in Egypt along with ankh symbols on Templar tombs here and in Europe if you care to check."

"I myself have seen genuine Knights Templar symbols of a Templar cross within a circle engraved deeply upon the ancient Egyptian Kom Ombo Temple on the banks of the River Nile in Egypt," Brother Jakelin interrupted.

2 – 13

Theodoric nodded in agreement and continued.

"The symbol is said to represent 'city', yet the use of the circle always represented the sun in Egypt as well as a god as Niccolas explained to you. This Knights Templar symbol was depicted within the sun and that has another meaning, 'Ra', often called the Sun God but also meaning God of Light. Emen-Ra, another word for God in ancient Egypt, where Emen means 'hidden' and 'Ra' light, therefore means hidden light. Atum-Ra, where 'Atum' means end and beginning, therefore means the beginning and end of Light. Identical to God's quote in Genesis 'I am the Alpha and Omega the beginning and the end' so that's just another piece of the jigsaw."

Paul shook his head.

"How am I supposed to take this all in and learn it?" he asked.

"Slowly and repetitively," answered Brother Jakelin.

"I'm sorry but you say I must trust my instincts, or pray on the matter, but, but I just can't buy into this Great Pyramid connection," Paul responded.

Theodoric looked at Count Henry and Jakelin in turn.

"Never accept at face value first time anything as fact. I told you before always question everything," Theodoric said as Paul stood up slowly.

"Yes and look how that nearly got you killed many times as I am learning," he replied.

"Paul, listen please. Once before I mentioned the saying from the Bible about the chief corner stone being rejected. Remember in Matthew 21:42, Jesus appears to apply the very same words to himself, 'The Stone, which the builders rejected, has become the chief corner-stone'. In the Grail legends as recounted in the epic of Parsifal many allusions are made to the stone and the one in which Excalibur is stuck firm. Jesus's statement is a clear indication that he is associating himself with the Great Pyramid, more specifically with the missing capstone, the ultimate and highest corner stone of all," Theodoric explained.

Paul turned and faced him.

"Really...how can you make such an assumption and be so sure?" he asked.

Theodoric cleared his throat and stood up also.

"We can be sure of this as not just any building has a chief corner stone that differentiates it from the others, apart from the apex corner of a pyramid as it is set above all the others. Again this certainly represents Jesus as symbolically different.

239

In addition, corner stone can be, and often is, translated as 'headstone', which fits perfectly the purpose and function of the capstone. This stone that the builders rejected is also directly connected with the black Kaaba stone venerated by Muslims in Mecca, but that I will explain shortly. In the passage from Matthew the reference is clearly and specifically related to a building, one that has its chief corner, or should say headstone, missing, the only building of which is the Great Pyramid with the temporary Merkaba star on its apex. Whether you accept it or not, both Matthew and Jesus directly refer to it and deliberately point out its missing capstone," Theodoric said and sat himself back down.

Count Henry moved around the table and sat beside Paul and handed him a length of black and yellow coloured entwined cord from under his surcoat.

"Paul, you have often asked Theodoric, I am led to believe, what this cord and those as worn by other Templars are for. You also asked why we have symbolism relating to nets, yes?" he asked Paul.

"Yes, I did," Paul answered quietly.

"Well, again it is all related and connected to Egyptian symbology carried directly over into Christian symbology. In Egyptian magic, and don't be afraid or put off by the word magic as it comes from the root word 'Magi', the three wise men," he started to explain as Paul interrupted him.

"I know about the Magi. Theodoric, Niccolas and my father have explained that much already." Paul cupped his hands over his mouth as he thought about what he was being told. He realised now why his father had so many items in his studio with the name John written upon them. So much about his father was a secret and unknown to him. "Can I just have a few moments to think before we continue?" he asked and looked at the three of them in turn…his own three wise men he laughed to himself inside as they looked back at him. Paul drew a deep breath and simply looked to the floor for several minutes. Eventually he looked up again, smiled and nodded. "Okay…I am ready to continue."

Chapter 33
My Dark Rose

Count Henry paused as Theodoric nodded in confirmation he should continue to explain further.

"You may know then that one of the most important symbols is that of the net. It represents many different things to us on several levels. From representing the net of natural lines that encircle our world, the paths of the dragon that flow with the earth's energy, to representing the nets cast by the goddess of love, who weaves her web with the lives of man to even the colour, being yellow and black representing the bee. In Greek traditions this same net is represented by the 'net of Hephaestus' with which the vengeful Olympian God ensnared his beautiful wife Aphrodite and her lover Ares. Always in net symbology, two deities or persons are linked to it, as are special knots for undoing them. In Egyptian myths, these two deities are Neith, known as Net, and Thoth. Thoth is called 'Great God in Het Abtit', or the 'Temple of Abtit', which was one of the chief sanctuaries of the God at Hermopolis. Thoth is the same as the Greek, Hermes, the god of wisdom and knowledge who sealed away items in sealed vaults so that one day mankind would be able to recover hidden artefacts intact. It is where we get our root word for hermetically sealed. Hermes symbol is also the 'Triple Tau'. The hieroglyphs with which the name 'Het Abtit' are written actually means, 'House of the Net', or more precisely as 'A Temple wherein a net was preserved and venerated'."

Paul looked down at the pommel of his sword and placed his hand over it knowing it too had the symbol of the Triple Tau upon it.

"Please, continue," he asked quietly.

Count Henry smiled, sat forwards and continued.

"Now according to the Egyptian 'Book of the Dead', a dreaded net was thought to exist in the underworld, which was greatly feared by the dead. The departed dead or dying were required to know the name of every single part of it, including ropes, weights, cords, hooks and so forth. In the mythical battle between Marduk and Tiamat in the Babylonian epic, Marduk also ensnared Taimat with his net before cutting her open," he detailed enthusiastically but again Paul stopped him.

"Marduk, Tiamat; who or what is that all about?" he asked almost incredulously.

"Sorry, I have not detailed that," Theodoric said quickly. "I'll simply say for now that it's a mythical story that actually relates to our very world we exist upon being smashed almost in half resulting in the world we now live upon."

"Sorry this is all so confusing, Paul. Perhaps we should stop for now?" Count Henry asked him.

Paul shook his head no silently and looked at Brother Jakelin as he moved to speak.

"Paul, all of this that Henry and Theo state is true, my friend. We have many ancient Egyptian, Persian, Babylonian and Sumerian scripts translated; scripts that we cannot ever reveal publicly," Brother Jakelin confirmed as Paul interrupted him.

"Yes I am getting the picture, mainly that you cannot reveal them as they are for future generations."

Brother Jakelin hesitated.

"You have read in the Bible where Jesus told his disciples to cast their nets to the right and catch 153 fish. That is just a symbolic and allegorical continuation of ancient esoteric wisdom that connects the Great Pyramid with him including important mathematical values. Peter written in Greek has a Gematria value of 153 also, as does the word 'Rock'; Peter was to become the rock and foundation of the Christian Church. The ordinary twelve disciples didn't know or understand Jesus's hidden messages, as they were not supposed to just as you've stated yourself, as they were meant for later generations' benefit," Brother Jakelin expanded upon.

Count Henry coughed slightly to clear his throat before speaking again.

"We mentioned Essenes earlier. They used a system, as we do now, of cryptography, called 'the Atbash cipher'. This code is used to conceal certain names in Essene, Zadokite and Nasorean texts. We apply this code to some of the exoteric names we outwardly use. You are familiar with the name 'Baphomet', the severed head we all supposedly worship; well it translates into the name 'Sophia' (ShVPIA), which for us represents female wisdom. Sophia is just another form and name of the ancient Egyptian Goddess Isis, which in turn represents the shining blue star Sirius. Isis's magic was allied to the wisdom of the Egyptian god Thoth, known, as you now know, as Hermes in Greek. His wife or consort, Nehemaut, was known to the Gnostics as 'Sophia' also," he divulged in a slower manner of tone.

Paul looked bemused and faced Theodoric.

"Understand from this, Paul, that when others charge us, or I should say them," Theodoric remarked pointing to Brother Jakelin and Count Henry in turn, "Templars, as they often do with worshipping Baphomet, what they are really doing is quite simply worshipping the principle of 'Wisdom'. But, as you will learn if your heart so desires it and you trust us, there is still far more to the mystery than that. Isis is symbolic for knowledge and Typhon to ignorance, obscuring the light of the sacred doctrine whose blaze lights the soul of the initiate. No gift from God is so precious as the knowledge of 'Truth', and that of the nature of the gods, so far as our limited capacities allow us to rise toward them. But know this, knowledge is always symbolised by the apple as detailed in Genesis, yes?" Theodoric asked.

"Yes, that I know from the Bible; when Eve tempted Adam with the apple, the forbidden fruit which after they ate they became aware of themselves", Paul answered quietly. "Plus Niccolas went to great lengths and spent many hours explaining all about the apple and rose symbolism."

"Good, well the star that represents Isis is Sirius that in turn is depicted as a five pointed star. All the stars of Egypt, except the Merkaba, are five pointed. Even Muhammad made sure the value of five was important as he received revelation from God on his visit to Heaven that he should pray five times a day when he went on his famous journey of the night from outside there on the Rock. Well, the blossom flower of the apple has five petals and five points also and is why it is used symbolically to represent knowledge. You may have noticed on our journey here that we passed many churches dedicated to Mary Magdalene. Inside they had black Madonnas all black in colour or dressed in blue. This does not represent that she was black in reality as they are symbolic icons just as those depicting Isis as a black woman, just as Osiris her husband was frequently depicted as green. Green is often associated with the Virgin Mary and Black Madonnas in one form or another. We three here all recognise the symbolic importance of being handed a black rose… This indicates that the colours are of symbolic significance, not their actual skin colour. Isis was also always dressed in blue as the actual star appears blue when looked at. Remember also when I pointed out the Virgin Marys and Black Madonnas both carried oddly shaped sceptres, well they are the same as the ancient Egyptian looped crosses, 'the Ankh', as carried by Isis, Sirius as a supreme initiatrix," Theodoric summarised and then sat back in silence.

"Put simply, the Black Madonnas and Virgin Mary symbolism is Isis, Sirius and we call her 'Notre Dame de Lumieres'," Brother Jakelin continued as Paul remained perfectly still, his mind racing.

"I thought the black Madonnas and Virgin Marys were black as they were darkened by smoke and fumes from votive candles," he stated quizzically.

"Not at all," Brother Jakelin interrupted. "Most are constructed of a dark wood like ebony, or pear, or deliberately darkened through periodic treatment with oil or wine. Understand also that black represents the colour of earth, the source of fertility and life, or divine flesh, or sorrow. Many Christian effigies of goddesses are black including Diana and Cyble. Have you never wondered why the churches for the Virgin Mary actually often have the name of Mary Magdalene?" he continued explaining and sipped upon his wine.

Count Henry looked at Paul patiently waiting for him to say anything.

"I am trying to remember all of this, but one thing. What does Notre-Dame de Lumieres symbolise then?" Paul asked.

"The black Madonna cult, for lack of a better word, is central to Templars, but more important to the Prieure de Sion…and we often use a black rose to symbolise her, though your father argued we should use a red rose, especially for Britain. But the one we singled out the most is the church at Goult, near Avignon, for special veneration for she is known as 'Our Lady of the Lights', which represents The Black Virgin as well as The Black Madonna and Isis," Count Henry outlined as Paul sighed heavily.

"Why she is important to us I fear we shall have to leave for another time once all that we have said tonight is accepted by you, but keep in mind the symbol of the black rose, for those of us who have a woman, it is she who becomes our very own manifestation of the pure black rose," Brother Jakelin stated seeing how weary Paul was getting.

"No, I wish to know as much as I can now. There are decisions I have to make and I cannot make them without all the facts," Paul eventually responded after a long silence his mind racing as he thought about Alisha and how she would obviously be his black rose. A woman of vision and wisdom.

"I am afraid, in this life time, you will never have all the facts. It was that driving ambition that caused your father and Theodoric so much hardship, and dare I say, suffering…and he still persists in getting Britain to adopt the rose as its national symbol," Count Henry replied as Theodoric agreed.

"Well I think I get the underlying message so far that all this symbolism is high-lighting the colours blue, black and green as well as yellow and all point towards Isis, or more correctly the star Sirius; but why?" Paul asked.

Brother Jakelin laughed before he continued to explain further details.

"Hey, you summed it up almost in one, but as to the why, that part we are still looking into. As we have said, all we do know for an absolute, is that over time, different people will be born who will in their turn understand and unlock another part of the key that will lead to its conclusion. We also know it is connected with numbers, importantly those of 72, 22, 7 and 12 and they are just the indicator num-bers that point the way. Isis as Sirius is linked to the 72 Dog Days in Egyptian, connected to the rising and falling of the star Sirius when the Nile floods, again connected to fertility but also to the supposed seventy-two disciples who went to France with Mary Magdalene and Joseph of Arimathea."

"And they think you are one of those said people; so Countess Stephanie's state-ment that you are wise beyond your years and obviously God sent struck a chord, not least because you saved her life twice," Theodoric revealed as Count Henry simply nodded he agreed with his remarks.

Paul looked again at the rose emblem and Triple Tau symbol on his sword.

"That explains Chartres Cathedral having twelve circles about its rose window, twelve disciples, twelve months of the year, twelve knights of the round table, and Mary Magdalene's feast day being the twenty-second of July. Twenty-second day and seventh month. That's obviously why your order accords so much unusual rev-erence to her," Paul shrugged.

"Yes…and as you shall learn, those values are connected to the sacred twin pillars of the Temple of Solomon of Joachim and Boaz. The main pillars being twenty-two feet tall each with a lintel seven feet wide," Theodoric remarked and smiled at Paul.

"Partly, but we also, or we at least in the higher circles of both orders, understand that the symbolism and allegorical information is what's important. We are aware that in the future, the names are likely to change again but the story will always be the same, as will the colours and numerical values. We revere Mary Magdalene, and it must be understood that she is the only woman mentioned in all Canonical Gospels. She is also always listed first, which in Jewish traditions indicates her seniority over those named after her. She also had the unusual title the 'first apos-tle', apostola apostolorum, and acknowledged as second only to Jesus in Gnostic Gospels of Egypt," Count Henry detailed further.

"No wonder the Church is suspicious of you and why Amalric has strained rela-tions with your Orders," Paul exclaimed.

"Oh no, that's not the reason. The Church and Amalric are more than aware of all these facts. Why do you think they try to hold the status quo by allowing only priests to read the Bible and keep it all in Latin?" Theodoric said.

"In that case what is the meaning behind Count Henry being called John? And is the Church also aware of that too?" Paul asked.

Count Henry shifted his position slightly.

"The Church knows. All Grand Masters of the Prieure de Sion are known as John starting at John the Second, the original John the First representing both John the Baptist and Jesus. It's a duality thing. Both were also represented symbolically as the lamb. It is just another reason why we use the twin riders upon a single horse as our sign and seal", Count Henry explained. "There are those who argue that Jesus and John were in fact twins...but that we can discuss at a later time. But know there are many other hidden reasons and esoteric meanings behind the seal of the lamb, which you will learn in due course," he stated then paused as he took some wine. "Our headquarters are at Troyes where all the Counts of Champagne hold their courts, but it is also where the Knights Templar have their first preceptory, and, from where the first nine knights, including Godfrei de Bouillon, came from. They were actually vassals of my father. The now famous church there is dedicated to Mary Magdalene also. As for the name John, it is used out of respect for John the Baptist. You may recall that he had his head cut off by Herod. Many have accused us of worshipping a head, but again that symbolism is complicated, but which you will come to learn. But for now, in its simplest form, John's head severed from his body represents the missing head stone or pyramidian of the Great Pyramid. John is also patron saint of both the Knights Templar and Prieure de Sion," he continued.

"You may also recall that some of the Grail stories talk of a severed head upon a platter, with no mention of a cup or with any connection to the last supper," Brother Jakelin interrupted as he took out a weather beaten piece of vellum parchment and unfolded it gently before passing it across to Paul. "Read it, please. It is mainly allegorical and symbolic and written by one of our more learned scholars; his name being Chretien whom Theo here more than knows," he said aloud.

"Yes I do. I er, sort of helped him on his early scholastic journey, shall we say," Theodoric answered almost apologetically.

Paul unwrapped the vellum sheet that had been written upon. He pulled a candle near and began to read it.

1 – 7

'Well I know that many brave knights dwell with the Grail at Munsalvaesche. Always when they ride out, as they often do, it is to seek adventure. They do so for their sins, these Templars, whether their reward be defeat or victory. A valiant host lives there, and I will tell you how they are sustained. They live from a stone of purest kind. If you do not know it, it shall here be named to you. It is called Lapsit Exillis. By the power of that stone the Phoenix burns to ashes, but the ashes give him life again. Thus does the Phoenix moult and change its plumage, which afterwards is bright and shining and as lovely as before. There never was a human so ill but that, if he one day sees that stone, he cannot die within the week that follows. And in looks he will not fade. His appearance will stay the same, be it maid or man, as on the day he saw the stone, the same as when the best years of his life began, and though he should see the stone for two hundred years, it will never change, save that his hair might perhaps turn grey. Such power does the stone give a man that flesh and bones are at once made young again. The stone is also called the Grail'.

Paul looked up again and looked at the three men staring at him as Brother Jakelin spoke further.

"As you can read, that alone shows that what we are trying to convey to future generations through Chretien's works, is the definite connection of the Knights Templar with the Grail itself, but also an account that relates the Grail to actually being a stone. The phrase 'Lapsit Exillis' those with eyes to see will know stands for 'Lapsit ex Caelis', which means it fell from Heaven. We have many ancient texts that use this exact same phrase that state that 'It fell from Heaven', the thing being a sacred stone known as a 'benben' stone; specifically a corner stone that was in fact the headstone of a pyramid. We have also encoded references to the Phoenix. The Phoenix is purely an Egyptian mythical bird so future readers will immediately see a deliberate symbolic clue that the Grail is in some way connected to Egypt. The Phoenix myths tell us that four ages of man have existed; we are in that fourth age, but it too will end and the mythical long awaited 'Fifth Flight of The Phoenix' will take flight after which the fifth age of man, a spiritually enlightened man, will commence. In short, Lapsit Exillis means stone, meaning a capstone...and for the record, John the Baptist's head was buried under Herod's Temple, symbolic for a buried headstone representing the capstone of the Great Pyramid. Throughout antiquity, even the ancient Egyptians themselves within their own writings always acknowledged that the Great Pyramid's capstone was always missing, as it was never set in place from its foundation, the chief corner stone the builders rejected. So we know that the true Grail is something very real that is buried, especially when we consider all the earlier Celtic and so-called pagan myths that all relate to severed heads, and how they were instrumental in maintaining the health and fertility of the lands and people they watched over, such as the head of Bran in England. In all the Grail and Celtic myths, the quest is all to do with asking the severed head the correct question. We now have the recovered head of John the Baptist," Brother Jakelin stated matter of factly and paused. "Munsalvaesche by the way is the castle of Montsegur in France in case you were wondering," he explained further as he studied Paul's reactions carefully.

"I have heard that Templars are both Christian and pagan at the same time," Paul finally said quietly as he continued to re-read the vellum document.

Theodoric looked at Paul and grasped his forearm tightly, leaning close towards him.

"Wine is strong, the king is stronger, women are strongest, but truth conquers all,' Theodoric said quietly. "It is an enigma 'for those with eyes to see' and I believe you indeed have eyes to see and will understand in time," he stated softly.

Paul again shrugged his shoulders.

"Sorry, I still cannot quite get my head around Jesus being connected with the Egyptians and some Great Pyramid," he replied.

"Okay, Paul, we have an eleventh century Gnostic Gospel of John. It describes categorically that Jesus is an initiate of the Egyptian Osiris cult. Also that he taught John the Baptist, but none of his other disciples, all of its secret teachings. This is what we know. At Nicaea in AD 325, the Gnostic version was excluded from the New Testament because of these revelations. We also know that Osiris's birthday was celebrated on the twenty-fifth December; that he was killed on a Friday just as Jesus and rose three days later just like Jesus," Count Henry explained.

Paul shook his head.

"What you are all saying is indeed heretical," he stated.

"Heretical in whose view, and from which perspective?" Count Henry asked immediately.

"If this information is all true, then, everything we are told is false. Wrong! How can the Church do this? The dishonesty of it all is in itself totally evil surely?" Paul exclaimed.

"So it seems. But appearances can be deceptive. It may appear the Church is doing wrong, and it is sad that as time progresses it will appear even more so. But there is even purpose in what they do. It is a very sad but real fact that the majority of people are still somewhat ignorant and easily led and impressionable. Some people, even the most intelligent, will still choose to believe what they want to, especially if they are comfortable with their ideas and beliefs no matter what hard and irrefutable facts and proofs you otherwise put in front of them. The Church knows this. It also knows and is aware that a great secret awaits us all, but a long way off in the future in the time of the great awakening," Count Henry continued.

"Great awakening?" Paul quizzed.

"Yes, of spiritual awakening. The age of Aquarius, the spiritual age; the time of the fifth flight of the Phoenix," he answered.

Paul looked immediately at Theodoric.

"I just knew it...it would have to do with something astrological wouldn't it," Paul remarked.

Theodoric shuffled on his seat before replying.

"Paul, you know how many times I have been correct. At times that skill, that knowledge has been more of a curse than a good thing. Nevertheless, as Henry says, most people are, sadly, putting it bluntly, easily led. Mob mentality, as we have both experienced, when faced with knowledge that is above their comprehension and understanding. Imagine therefore, if all the secrets became available to all, and that which has been hidden, but only to be recovered when mankind is again mentally, emotionally and spiritually advanced, and mature enough to handle what it would then posses, picture it being found now whilst we are still so ignorant and spiritually backward. The abuse of such knowledge would destroy us all," Theodoric explained solemnly as both Count Henry and Brother Jakelin agreed.

"I can understand that. But this Holy Grail, this great self quest for enlightenment and knowledge. This Gnosis whatever, what is this thing that fell from Heaven that is hidden, what is it?" Paul asked almost exasperated in tone.

"All we know at this stage is that sometime before the great flood that is recounted in the Noah story within the Bible, but also in all the ancient myths and legends, a great worldwide civilisation existed upon the whole world. With a unified religion that was based upon self-awareness and knowledge of God derived from a personal level and experience. Not channelled exclusively through a priesthood. As a worldwide cataclysm was predicted, as it is a reoccurring natural phenomenon, that world organisation buried a record of all its sum knowledge, our true origins and history plus tools of unimaginable power. They sealed them away and encoded their positions using mathematics, and sound by way of harmonics, within what became myths and rituals to guarantee they were carried across the millennia of time intact," Count Henry continued.

"They did, and the Church knows this too, so although its modus operandi is different to ours, and at times diametrically opposed to what we believe, it nevertheless also guarantees that those ancient codes are still carried forward to the correct time in the future intact," Brother Jakelin said as he moved to get some more food from the middle of the table.

"It is why the Church so utterly and ruthlessly guards these secrets; it sees itself as the guardians of that knowledge and as the sole vehicle that will carry the information forward. But human minds that we have, we are all fallible and mistakes and delusions happen. That is why Hermeticism and Gnosticism have resulted in Cathariscism as it now stands today based upon developments of both cosmological ideas coalesced from both streams. They believe, which we understand similarly, that the world we exist in, is but the lowest realm of nine spheres, planes if you will, with God being the highest. Man was a once-divine being too now trapped in this material world and body, but still retains some of that divine spark. 'Know ye not that ye are gods' is taught in both ideals, and it is possible, indeed it is our duty to try and reunite with the divine. A lot of this philosophy came out of Egypt, mainly the city of Alexandria in the first and second centuries BC, which then was a melting pot of religious ideas drawn from Greek, Persian, Jewish, Ancient Egyptian and Far Eastern religions. The results of which those ideas now totally underpin our whole culture," Count Henry expounded.

"What we do that is so different, is that we know we have more to learn and that we are simply acting as guardians of a code. We also, like our Gnostic and Hermetic predecessors, take personal responsibility for our own actions. This is why we keep our teachings strictly secret only revealed to those in the upper circles of our nine levels of initiation. This attitude is totally at odds with the Church at present. We do not believe that we should, or need to, grovel before our God unlike Catholics who do not think themselves worthy but as lowly and evil creatures destined for purgatory. By recognising we have the divine spark of God within ourselves bestows a confidence and self esteem that enables us to fulfil our true potentials without all the emotional hang ups and baggage of guilt thrust upon us," Brother Jakelin explained, his tone more enthusiastic now.

"But why should the Church see this attitude as so bad then?" Paul asked as he leaned forward to take more food.

"Why, huh, because by its very implication, this notion that all individuals have the potential for Godhood implies that women are as good as men, at least spiritually. It would also mean giving women a voice just as they had always had in the past. Without women we would be nothing," Theodoric answered.

"It also means that our beliefs do not accord with those of the Church regarding the idea of 'original sin', that all men and women are born sinful because of the 'Fall of Adam and Eve', especially Eve for tempting Adam with the forbidden fruit...the apple, which resulted in a vengeful God; but as you are now beginning to learn, all the Biblical stories were allegorical and symbolic. We emphasise the importance of exploring both outer and inner worlds for oneself, experiencing gnosis-self knowledge of the divine. The Church however sees this as totally heretical and evil with its insistence that only priests are the conduits through which God speaks. Imagine if the church had no priestly hold over its flock what chance it would have of maintaining its control, and by default, keeping the codes of antiquity in place and carried forward. So from that point one can almost understand the double sided sword it wields and the almost impossible position it finds itself in, for she cannot reveal all the hidden symbolism either just as we cannot. That is another reason why we can serve the Church as we do whilst pledging to Mary Magdalene and St John the Baptist at the same time. I hope that makes sense to you, Paul?" Count Henry detailed and asked.

Paul remained quiet for a moment as he thought upon what he had just been told, then stood up straight and walked across the room silently as he contemplated. After a few minutes Theodoric stood and approached him.

"Paul. Are you okay, my friend?" he asked softly.

Paul shook his head, took a deep breath and looked at Theodoric directly.

"I know what you mean now when you say it is as much a curse as a gift this knowledge. Please, I wish to learn more but, but I need just a short while to myself; a few moments. Is that okay?" Paul replied, and asked, as he faced Count Henry and Brother Jakelin.

"We have all night. Take as much time as you need," Count Henry answered.

Paul feigned a smile, nodded and slowly walked towards a stairway that led to a high veranda. Paul could hear Theodoric say something to Brother Jakelin and Count Henry as he made his way to a secluded section of the veranda that allowed him to look out towards the Holy Sepulchre, the moon reflecting brightly off its dome. In the distance he could hear people talking and laughing as a dog barked in an alleyway. He leant against the parapet, clasped his hands and closed his eyes. Thoughts of Alisha ran through his mind. He could see her face again as he remembered how he had made love to her.

"Alisha...where are you my life? For that is what you are. Where are you and Arri at this moment?" he whispered to himself. He sighed heavily. "It was not evil, nor in my heart can I feel it to have been a sin that I have loved you and made love to you. Not a sin...and that we have created a beautiful little boy," he again whispered as he mulled over what he had been told. "Know this, my Alisha, my love, I know in my heart for you is pure. I know I shall always love you for you are a part of me and wherever God wills that we now go, I carry you and Arri in me always."

Paul quickly returned to the table, his manner Brother Jakelin noted, more upbeat.

"That little break obviously did you good. Has it cleared your head some?" he asked.

"Not at all, for my head is still full and swimming with ideas, thoughts and questions; but the air did me well. Please, I would like to know more. But first, I should say thank you for what you entrust me with. I feel I am not worthy of your trust and what you tell me," he answered.

"Ha, see, that's the Catholic in you speaking. You won't think or feel like that for long," Theodoric joked, which raised smiles all round.

"In that case we shall hand you a copy of the Levitikon. You will need time to read and memorise it as it comes in two parts. The first details the religious doctrines and rituals concerning the nine grades of the Templar order. It describes in detail our 'Church of John' and why we call ourselves 'Johannites' or original Christians though that name is not really correct as you will learn," Count Henry explained.

Brother Jakelin passed Paul a small leather bound book.

"This is priceless, my friend, but you will need it. It is the second part. It reads pretty much the same as the standard Canonical Gospel of John, apart from Chapters 20 and 21 having been removed. Those are the last two chapters but also the miraculous story of Jesus turning water to wine, the loaves and fishes and the raising of Lazarus as well as certain references to St Peter, especially the part about

Jesus saying "Upon this rock I will build my church", have all been edited out," Brother Jakelin explained further.

"Be warned though. Don't be too shocked as Jesus is presented as an initiate of the Osiris mysteries," Theodoric warned.

"But what has all this Osiris mythology got to do in regard to our times? Okay I can understand that if it's all allegorical and symbolic to carry a message across time, fine, but what else?" Paul asked.

"In simple terms, Jesus was an Osirian initiate and understood all the esoteric secret teachings relating to Isis, and he passed on that knowledge to his beloved disciple John. But know this also, Lazarus was also known as his beloved disciple. For they were one and the same person. The Christian Church as it is today was founded by Paul and other Apostles but without any knowledge of Jesus's true teachings, as they were not part of his inner circle. It is John's teachings that we know and carry forwards still," Count Henry stated looking at Paul quizzically for any hint of a reaction.

Brother Jakelin interrupted with a slight wave of his hand and a smile.

"It was realised very early on that to ensure various esoteric secrets, including those from the Cabala, would have to be carried forwards in total secret from the mainstream populace as already explained. Especially as the Church grew and more pagan beliefs were adopted and added to the Gospels to win over more converts, such as making Jesus the son of God, born of a virgin etcetera, when in fact he was a man born of a woman. We also recognise that the title Christos merely means anointed one. We also formed our top inner circles into an underground movement, symbolised by an underground stream, as water is symbolic of 'spirit', which was taken from an earlier Greek underground stream symbolism as its myths are directly related. We would be the sole repository of the secrets placed openly in the face of kings and pontiffs but exoterically presented without them understanding the esoteric hidden true meanings behind them. The secrets would not in their true forms then be exposed to the corruption of power or subject to the vagaries and uncertainties of political and social changes over the centuries. Godfrei de Bouillon and Hugues de Payens along with all the other founding Knights Templar knew all of this and were what you could call 'Johannite initiates'. They were aware of the dual symbolism of John the Baptist and Jesus being represented by the lamb as well as John being one and the same person as Lazarus, and so they updated a new symbol, that of the twin riders upon a single horse. There is much more to learn symbolically regarding that image but it suffices to say there is a multitude of interpretations you must learn and understand fully. But one important element of it is to remind us that one of our patron saints is St John the Evangelist whom Rome has no problem recognising, but we hold him there as symbolic and in public representation of John the Baptist esoterically. The two riders, both on the same horse travelling in the same direction representing the staff of John the Evangelist and also the staff of John the Baptist," he explained.

Count Henry then continued.

"Know this too that the designation of John I reserved for Jesus as we have previously explained, as it was Jesus who taught the secret teachings to him. This confuses many but it is simple really; for John the Baptist knew he had to be symbolically remembered as important. He knew before his death he would, nay had to, be beheaded to recreate the esoteric image of the head being separated from the body. He took on this role bravely and willingly. As Lazarus, he wrote the majority of the Gospel of John prior to his arrest and execution. After the crucifixion it was Jesus himself that completed the gospel and why some in the Church hide the facts and obfuscate the details, with some claiming that Jesus wrote the entire Gospel."

"So you see John I is symbolically reserved for Jesus. The confusion that we revere John the Evangelist is a deliberate ploy. The Cathars share much in common with our closely guarded secrets but, again, they only have part of the knowledge; but here again it's just another root that carries the hidden codes intact. Our secrets run through all the heresies and cults, and because ours is the least known, it affords us a lot of protection and conceals us very well from the eyes of the world," Brother Jakelin explained and ate a date.

"But, how with such knowledge at your finger tips, with the full understanding that truth is an absolute must, how can you justify your actions of suppressing the real truths, but also in actions opposite to your vows of celibacy?" Paul asked looking directly at Brother Jakelin.

"In what context?" he asked.

"You know in what context, as in where I have heard you are often seen late at night; dare I say but clearly betraying your vows," Paul explained awkwardly.

Brother Jakelin smiled broadly.

"Oh you mean when I have been seen leaving the female quarters at Crac de Moab and de l'Ospital?" he responded with an even larger smile.

Count Henry looked at Paul intently and nodded at him.

"It is understood, Paul, within the top circles of our Orders, that we elevate the principle of the female. Granted our lay brothers swear an oath of celibacy as did we; but imagine if we all did all the time. Our bloodlines would end with us if we had not already sired children. As young or new initiates we keep to our vows of celibacy and demonstrate we are masters of our own desires, then we progress to the inner circles where it is learnt the true sacred sacrament, that being the acknowledgement of the equal rights of women and that sex is a sacred sacrament. Don't look too shocked at this revelation for Jesus himself fully understood this principle and was no celibate," he explained as Paul looked suddenly visibly moved.

He looked up in almost shock.

"I, I can tell you now then that I am not who you think I am then", Paul retorted.

"Why? Explain yourself," Count Henry demanded.

"I have already demonstrated that I cannot control myself then, for I gave in to temptation. I have failed in that respect already so as de Ridefort correctly pointed out way back in France, I am indeed not worthy to be a turcopole let alone a knight of any standing or Order," Paul blurted out.

"Paul, look at me. We are already aware of Alisha. As for Ridefort, just because he holds a high office as a Templar, it does not follow that he naturally assumes the mantel of initiate into our inner circles of the mysteries we hold," Count Henry explained as Paul shook his head. "Female wisdom has long been sought both in a philosophical sense, and as that which can heighten both partners in the sex act that bestows a divine, some say magical, element to the individual and pair as a whole. This search for female wisdom is new to you but in time, all will be revealed. You must not feel bad, guilty or that you have done wrong where Alisha is concerned for as you'll also learn, love such as you two share is something special and goes beyond the simple act of sex. You are nearer to the principle we search for as in female wisdom to balance that of the male, for without balance, all is wrong. That search we also name, Sophia," he said almost reverentially in tone, his voice indicating his genuine belief.

"It is an oversimplification to say that sex, or some might even call it sex magic, is the key that opens all the secrets as it is far more subtle and complex than that," Theodoric added. "Do you recall as we travelled through France just before Frejus, I explained about a Gospel text, the Pistis Sophia? Well it linked Sophia to being representative of Mary Magdalene, and Sophia is another modern representative in her own right as that of Isis. It is the connections between Mary Magdalene and John the Baptist, represented outwardly as John the Evangelist, that you must focus your mind and studies upon over the next months," he explained further.

"When you hear from the uninitiated, charges against our orders of homosexual acts, with worshipping a head called Baphomet, which represents both Sophia and John, you will know exactly what it is you are being charged with," Brother Jakelin pronounced as he emptied his wine goblet. "And for the record, Cybil, whom people see me visit...she is my wife, and through her I have found and understood the mysteries of the widow," he stated with a large smile.

Paul looked at him confused as to the comment about a widow.

"Rest your mind, Paul, for that is another secret for another time," Count Henry interjected as he passed more wine across to Brother Jakelin.

"In that case do you not also have a woman?" Paul asked Count Henry bluntly, which made him laugh, then shook his head slowly indicating no but then turned with a far off look in his eyes, as he clearly thought about someone dear to him.

"It would be indiscreet of me to say whom, suffice to say my heart does belong to a woman...but alas as cruel fate would have it, she is already married," he said quietly then looked at Theodoric and nodded that he should speak again.

"In France I taught you just a little about Mary Magdalene but I did not tell you that when she arrived, she actually landed, not at Camargue as many believe but the coast of Roussillon where she went on to live out her life in the Languedoc, not Provence as many also believe. Many have searched for her body so it is important that any real clues that would lead people to her final resting place are hidden," Theodoric explained as he ate then continued. "You asked me once about my family tree, well as we are telling you all this evening it makes no difference now that I tell you that my family originated from there...our family name was in fact Roussillon and our coat of arms depicted a cross that was still growing with a fresh shoot sprouting from it."

Paul looked at him immediately.

"That is the same as the image on the wall of the headquarters is it not?" Paul asked hurriedly.

"It is," Count Henry answered for Theodoric.

Paul looked at Theodoric for a long time.

"So all of this...it is as much all connected with you then?" Paul asked directly.

"No, no, no. My family were purely guardians of part of the secret where Mary Magdalene was really buried; of which before you ask I have no idea as my elder brother took that secret with him when he was killed," Theodoric informed them.

"I am sorry. I did not even know you had a brother either," Paul responded.

"Truly, there is much that you learn about me tonight," Theodoric replied looking at Paul as if waiting to be chastised.

Brother Jakelin passed across some more bread as both Paul and Theodoric sat in silence for a while.

   2 – 12

"You may consider our views and associated connections of John the Baptist with that of Mary Magdalene as heretical for nothing alludes to it in any of the four canonical gospels of Matthew, Mark, Luke and John, apart from that is, their apparent devotion to Jesus," Brother Jakelin started to explain. "You are aware of the wholly incorrect misrepresentation of Mary being viewed as a prostitute. The traditional story is that Jesus drove out seven devils from her...she reformed and spent the rest of her life as a penitent. Well that version couldn't be further from the truth and is a horrendous untruth that does her an injustice," he continued. "It is argued that Mary did not know John personally, but we know they were in fact related. John was Lazarus, Mary of Bethany's brother no less, and she in turn we know is one and the same Mary Magdalene. It was John who started and symbolically represents Jesus's ministry when he baptised him, and it was Mary who symbolically represented Jesus's death and an end to his ministry, being the first witness to his resurrection and whole point of Christianity. Both officiated at a set time of anointing Jesus with oils," Brother Jakelin explained and looked at Count Henry to continue.

"Others greatly misunderstand the connection between Mary and John, and argue they were rivals or that John was spiritually superior to Jesus, or that Jesus was an impostor, a liar or an usurper or former disciple of John's who then took over his group, but that is just scratching at some of the more obvious outwardly acknowledged facts so prone to being misinterpreted...hence the need for such an esoteric Order as ours again to keep the real facts alive," Count Henry added.

"I find it hard to rationalise or understand why so many great men of the Church, if it is true that they know these facts, still hide the truth or deny other Gospels which are just as valid," Paul commented.

"Hey, if you want an example, just look at the Gospel of Mark. It was rewritten and re-edited many times until the Church was happy with it. But as we said earlier, the Church had to likewise maintain its authority as it saw wise in order to guarantee the messages within were carried forward. Problem was as more and more was hidden, the further from the truth and more elusive to recognise became the codes. Even revered holy men such as St Clement were prepared to lie in order to prevent material, such as other gospels that correctly portrayed Jesus, from becoming widely known. He admitted one such Gospel, known as the 'Secret Gospel of Mark' existed, but as it taught sexual rites, he argued that followers of it had misinterpreted it, and he advised his other clerics to deny it to the populace at large. But then again we could understand that, as we in our orders do likewise with the rank and file, there being two levels of teaching, one exoteric for all believers and one, esoteric, purely for inner circle initiates," Brother Jakelin explained.

"You said you find it hard to accept Jesus's and I suppose Mary Magdalene's connection with Egypt and that of the symbolism to Isis. Then know that she was born and came from a town called Magdolum, in the northeast of Egypt near the border with Judea. Her name has nothing to do with the town of el Mejdel in Galilee as mentioned in the New Testament. Magdalen does mean 'of Magdala' always known as the town of el Mejdel, but during Jesus's time that town was known as Tarichea. But Magdala also means 'place of the dove', 'place of the tower' and 'temple-tower'. In Hebrew it actually means 'tower' or 'elevated, great magnificent'. As Magdal-eder it means 'tower of the flock'. This may seem nonsensical, however the implication is of a guardian watching over her flock, but more importantly it relates to the Old Testament prophecy as given by Micah," Theodoric outlined as he fumbled for his copy of the Old Testament from under his tunic. "Sorry, I can never remember this in full," he said as he flicked through the old pages. "Ah here it is. 'And thou. O tower of the flock, the strong hold of the daughter of Zion, unto thee shall it come, even the first dominion; the kingdom shall come to the daughter of Jerusalem'. There, see what it is saying?" Theodoric asked Paul.

"All I can deduce from that, if I trust my first gut instinct, and from what you have told me thus far, is that Mary obviously symbolises some form of tower, or she in turn represents and symbolises something that through her, or that thing, be it a tower or whatever, will open the way to the Kingdom of Heaven I assume will come. She's the key," Paul answered.

Count Henry paused as Theodoric looked at him and Brother Jakelin in turn.

"See, our faith and conviction in you is justly warranted. You have already put a new slant and understanding upon something we knew but still did not fully understand; but now you have stated it, it seems blindingly obvious," Count Henry said.

"Has Theodoric explained Hieros gamos to you?" Brother Jakelin asked.

Paul simply shook his head indicating no as Theodoric did likewise.

"It is the word meaning 'sacred marriage of a priestess to sexually anoint a true king'. The rituals behind it go all the way back to ancient Egyptian rituals again. You know that Jesus was in reality married, and to Mary Magdalene. Alas the guilt associated with sex is so deeply ingrained within our culture that any suggestion that Jesus had a sexual partner, even within a monogamous and loving relationship, is still viewed by almost all as sacrilegious and disgusting. To state that Jesus was married is considered the ramblings and work of the Devil himself. The fact is that the Jews regarded celibacy as improper at best, and as almost murderous in some sections as it showed an unwillingness to further the generations of God's chosen people. As the Jews have always been essentially a dynastic race, marriage was always central to their way of life. If Jesus had been celibate, that very fact alone would have been noted and written down as unique and heretical alone. But it never was mentioned because they knew he was married. Anything less for a charismatic leader of the time would have been scandalous. Jesus himself never once advocated celibacy nor did his lifestyle suggest it either. You may hear stories that Jesus married Miriam of Bethany who also fled to France where she bore a daughter, but remember this Miriam is the same Mary Magdalene. As for Mary being a prostitute; that only came about as the Jews of the time considered her a sinner, as she was, in fact, a practising priestess whom the Jews saw as abhorrent; sinner became mistranslated as prostitute. She was detailed and written in Greek, as a 'harmartolos', meaning one who has transgressed and placed themself outside the law. But she was only outside the law in the opinion of the prevailing Jews of her time because she did not adhere to the Jewish law or rituals, and she wore her hair loose, which was considered sexually inappropriate. In reality, as we have proof, it was the simple fact that she was just not a Jew; nor was she poor. Remember in the Biblical accounts she anointed Jesus's feet with spikenard, which came from very rare and prized Indian plants and was incredibly expensive at the time. She also lived with her sister Martha and brother Lazarus, whom we know was one and the same John the Baptist. If she had been a woman of bad reputation there is no way she would have been living with them in Bethany in the same house. Also, Christ comes from the Greek word Christos, which simply meant when translated back to Hebrew, Messiah, which in turn purely meant anointed one. The term Messiah in its original context should not be confused with the divinity implications it now carries, as it is no such thing. The idea of a divine Christ was a later Christian addition, whereas the Jewish Christ was expected to be a great military and political commander. It is for that real reason that the Romans crucified him as a threat, not the Jews. Christ simply meant anointed and the only person to have anointed him was Mary Magdalene with the spikenard. The symbolism is identical to the early Egyptian God making anointing ceremony whereby it was Isis who anointed the new king. So there you have the facts that the one person who Christ-ened Jesus was a woman. It was not when John the Baptist symbolically baptised him, as that would mean all the people he baptised that day in the River Jordan would likewise be termed Christos."

Paul sighed heavily and drank a large mouthful of wine and shook his head.

"Is this too much for you?" Count Henry asked him.

"Not at all, I am just trying to take it all in," he replied.

"So you see, Paul, there are just two people who during Jesus's life officiated at major rites; John at his baptism at the beginning of his ministry and Mary who anointed him at the end of his ministry. But both these people were deliberately marginalised by the early Church on purpose, and why is simple; because by acknowledging them they have to recognise that the baptism and anointing by them implied authority on the part of those who officiated for though, as baptiser and anointer, they bestow authority, they themselves must have authority to do so in the first place. It is after the anointing of Jesus by Mary that Judas became the betrayer. Though in reality if Judas had not accepted the heavy burden and task of doing as his master requested, the whole process, which led to Jesus being crucified, and the birth of Christianity would never have begun; remember that fact. The only other identical ritual practised at the time was the Egyptian sacred anointing of the king, whereby only a true king or priest could receive his full divine power through the authority and anointing by a high priestess. This tradition was continued in order to carry the symbolism across time intact. This act was known as the 'hieros gamos' itself. I hope you are following me still?" Theodoric asked Paul, as his mind seemed elsewhere. Paul simply nodded his response. "Okay, well understand then that this ritual must not be confused with just having sex. It is about the fusion of two people and it is only in the sacred marriage of hieros gamos that the man and woman actually become the gods; symbolically that is. The woman becomes the Goddess herself first who is then able to bestow the ultimate blessing of regeneration on the man who embodies the God. This act was viewed and believed to infuse both themselves and the world around them with regenerative balm and echo the creative impulse of the birth of the planet. You may recall when I explained about the King Arthur myth symbolism when his heart is broken and he falls ill, how the land becomes desolate and starts to die, but how once he is again risen, the land regenerates," Theodoric asked as Paul still sat in silence.

"I do not think I actually recall you explaining that part. But what you are saying in effect is that Mary Magdalene was a wealthy woman in her own right, was able to look after the disciples and was a priestess of the Isis cult?" Paul answered quietly.

"Paul, hieros gamos was the ultimate expression of what used to be called 'temple prostitution'. Like the vestal virgins in Rome, where a man visited a priestess in order to receive gnosis and to experience the divine for himself through the act of lovemaking. Such priestesses were called hierodules, which meant 'sacred servant' who was in total control of her body and the situation with the man receiving benefits in terms of physical, spiritual and magical empowerment," Brother Jakelin expanded upon.

"I see...so the body of the priestess literally and metaphorically becomes a gateway to heaven," Paul laughed out but his gaze firmly fixed forward staring at the far wall.

"You could say that," Theodoric replied.

"I fear the wine may be going to your head, Paul," Count Henry stated, as Paul shook his head no.

"It may sound sordid and shocking to you now, Paul, as it is new to you, and goes against everything you have learnt and thought so far. Men without this carnal knowledge, or this hieros gamos by the act with the priestess, called 'horasis', where the word 'whore' is derived, will remain spiritually unfulfilled. Alone or, worse, celibate, he has little hope of ecstatic contact with God, or that God essence force. But women have no need of such ceremony. This is why St Peter was so envious of Mary Magdalene and why he was so anti women in general. He knew this and that women are naturally in touch with the divine. All the ancient mystery rituals such as those of Osiris, Tammuz, Dionysus, Attis, all had their rituals acted out by human stand-ins where the God was anointed by the Goddess prior to his actual or symbolic death which would make the land fertile again. After three days the God would be resurrected thanks to the magical intervention of the priestess or Goddess. He would rise again. The mystery plays re enacted have the Goddess saying, 'they have removed my Lord and I do not know where to find him'," Theodoric continued to outline.

"Notice, Paul, it is the same words Mary Magdalene said when she went to the empty tomb of Jesus in the garden on the third day after he was crucified," Brother Jakelin added.

"So the entire crucifixion story is just that; a story concocted and re-enacted from ancient rituals?" Paul asked sadly.

"Don't be despondent, Paul, for although it was enacted per se, it was done to carry those codes forward into a new era, as our world passes into that time of Pisces, the fish," Count Henry answered.

Paul thought back upon the entire mystical and esoteric lesson he had already learnt from Theodoric. In part, it all seemed very plausible and believable but his heart felt heavy nonetheless. Everything he had believed in and thought he knew and understood was all being systematically turned upon its head. He could not help but think of Alisha.

"Do not be alarmed or sad, Paul. Even the Catholic Church, as well as so-called heretics, are in agreement and know and acknowledge that Mary of Bethany and Mary Magdalene are one and the same person. She was Jesus's own hierodule in simple terms. It was she who anointed and initiated him and inaugurated the Last Supper, for without her and the rituals that followed, we would not now be sitting here this night telling you all of this. For that reason we venerate her totally. In the patriarchal Judaic world of her time as she was so, she was indeed viewed and seen as a moral outcast," Brother Jakelin explained as he poured Paul yet another wine.

"The Prieure de Sion and Knights Templar are devotees of the Goddess, in the form of the black Madonna, as Mary Magdalene as Isis herself. It is that system that is our entire raison d'être," Count Henry stated very solemnly, studying Paul's reaction.

"She wasn't called the 'Apostle of Apostles and woman who knew all' for nothing in the Bible," Theodoric said loudly. "Read the 'Song of Songs', which is a sacred marriage liturgy for it has always been associated with Mary Magdalene. Mary was Jesus's partner in a sacred marriage though this is anathema to the Church of Rome that never wants its flock to know about the true relationship between Jesus and Mary and why the Gnostic gospels were deliberately excluded from the New Testament, and why the majority don't even know they exist."

"I hear what you are saying and recall earlier you said that the Church has its hands tied as it tries to maintain its position to guarantee the hidden codes it contains for the future, but why the censorship when they had no mandate to execute such a policy? It is such a major act of censorship," Paul asked and stated.

"Partly self preservation. When the council at Nicaea voted upon which gospels to include and those to exclude in AD 325, the power of the Magdalene and her followers was widespread and far too popular for the patriarchy to cope with or control. One set of material deliberately rejected was that Jesus gave Magdalene the title of Apostle of Apostles as you know, but that he also said she would be raised above all the other disciples and, more importantly, rule the forthcoming 'Kingdom of Light' just as you guessed earlier, giving her the name 'Mary Lucifer'. Mary the Light Bringer. There is much evidence, especially in the Gnostic gospel of Philip, that shows how Peter hated Mary very much. It went deeper than mere jealousy and he even stated 'Let Mary leave us, for women are not worthy of life'. But this was meant in the context of spiritual life, as you had to be spiritually raised from the dead, not physically raised. But this early statement, prior to the Nicaea agreement, took his words literally and many of the new clergy likewise turned against women as a consequence. From that stemmed the later additional practice of celibacy. It demonstrates how dangerous misinterpreting the meanings of the Gospels can be for it set the tone of the grim battle that would follow between the Church of Rome founded by Peter and the so-called heretical underground Church of Mary. It would be wrong to say that it all stemmed from a personal clash of two people but what is clear is that Peter and the other disciples were not privy to all the deeper hidden mysteries and secrets. The only bonus we have is that at least, by whichever system prevails, the message from antiquity still gets through. That is why we still work with the Church, for if we wished it, we have more than the military might to take over control totally," Brother Jakelin detailed as Paul was clearly analysing the information.

"Perhaps that would be a good thing," Theodoric stated.

"Not so, for none of us know which system will prevail, and it is the message and codes that take precedence, not personal control or what we wish to see happen," Count Henry responded sharply.

"The Gnostic gospel of Philip is specific when it described Mary as Jesus's sexual partner as well as many allusions between men and women and the symbolism of the union between the bride and bridegroom, where Jesus is that bridegroom, with Mary being his bride Sophia. Even in the Canonical Gospels Jesus refers to himself as the bridegroom," Brother Jakelin added.

"Much of the Jesus story you must understand was deliberately contrived, not simply to mimic the older religions of the era point for point in order to gain a stronghold, but in order to establish it and carry the codes in a new format that would be understood by later generations," Theodoric said before Paul interrupted him.

"Maybe, but it smacks at just being deceit, that we have all been deceived and misled."

Theodoric looked at him hard as Count Henry spoke up again.

"Paul, on the surface that may appear so but as you are surely learning, there was, shall we say, a method to the madness. It is not simply paganism repackaged as Christianity. All the old religions had their leaders or gods suffer and die only to be raised again. From Mithraism Jesus used the symbolism of the keys of Heaven and assumed the same function of the virgin born Saoshayant. The image of the child god Dionysus was in swaddling clothes in a basket manger and was born in a stable like Horus, the stable temple of the virgin goddess Isis, queen of Heaven. Dionysus also turned water into wine, like Aesculapius he raised men from the dead and gave sight to the blind; their resurrections took place from tombs attended only by women. In short there is nothing associated with Jesus that is not already common to some or all of the saviour cults of antiquity. Even Jesus's birth is not as it seems as it really states the earlier nativity God birth myths again and Jesus was not even born in Bethlehem. The Gospel of John even tells us that in 7:42, where it explicitly states, he was not born there. But astronomical codes that again relate to Sirius are encoded within the Jesus nativity with much symbolism as shepherds watching their flocks by night representing the passing era of Aries, the Ram, the period during which time all the parables were linked to goats and sacrificing lambs, and another reason why John was symbolised as a lamb. But Jesus was inaugurating a new era as our world passed into the astrological and zodiac stellar background of the sign of Pisces the fish, hence all new parables would be likened to fishing, nets and disciples being in the main fishermen. Jesus's teaching in Matthew 13–47 likens the coming Kingdom of God to the lowering of a net into the sea, after which the good fish are put into pails and the net thrown away. To us this does not detract or undermine things; it actually reinforces the fact that the codes are genuine and valid and stretch far further back in time, each in its turn being adapted to guarantee its continuation," Count Henry detailed.

"And as Theodoric once said, is that why both your Orders seek a fusion between Judaism, Christianity and Islam?" Paul asked.

"Yes. Our counterparts, especially within the inner circles of the Isma'ilis and Sufism groups understand our common ground, goals and the codes. Naturally it's impossible to educate and inform the layman as already explained; and that's the real tragedy here, that we are yet again faced with the prospect of confrontation with Islam when we should be working side by side," Count Henry continued. "When al Mamoon entered the Great Pyramid in Egypt, it was not simply to recover treasure or gold; it was to recover what he believed was a great secret and Ark of the Covenant. He was part of a Sufi inner circle and understood that the great secrets of antiquity were directly related to the Pyramid at Giza and Jesus and Muhammad. He also knew that its properties were somehow magical and that its inherent shape connected with reflective spheres and the pyramid generated images of a man, a sacred image, the face of God as one believed but alas that is way out of our present understanding to fathom at this time. It did however lead to the form and layout of our cross along with the Merkaba star. It is the shapes we can form from our cross that we use to make a symbolic code in conjunction with a cipher. It is the 52 (51.827) degree angle slope of the sides of the Great Pyramid in Egypt that embodies the Golden Mean, which is the ratio that is used in n nature to generate growth patterns in our world that cast the shadows exactly. Sacred geometry studies the relationships between numbers geometrically. The Vesica Pisces, the symbol of the fish, is one of the most fundamental geometrical forms of this ancient discipline, and it reveals the relationship between the Great Pyramid and the two dimensional expansion of a circle of one unit radius. It was the knowledge that a great mystery related to spheres which started the practice of crystal ball gazing, but more relevant to us was the symbology that it also represented the sacred geometrical ideal man in all its correct proportions, but with its head, the capstone, missing."

"In Mecca, they have the Black Stone of Kaaba, which incidentally can be called Lapsit Exillis as it too fell from heaven. But its origin is still an enigma to most Muslims, but we have proofs that it is actually part of the missing capstone itself. The rest being hidden until the time is correct, but I think Theo should explain more as he actually went there once," Brother Jakelin explained. All looked at Theodoric as he drained his wine goblet.

"Yes I went, a long time ago. I had to fake it as a Muslim," he explained.

"I don't know whether that was brave or plain stupid for if found you would have been killed immediately," Count Henry remarked.

"True, but I had to see for myself. Your father was with me but remained outside," Theodoric said as he looked at Paul then continued. "Well, The Black Stone of Kaaba or Mecca is called, in Arabic, Al-hajar Al-aswad. The word Kaaba, or Ka'ba or Ka'bah actually means 'cube'. Its symbolism is linked with metaphors for 'In the Box', Qabbalah or Kabbalah, the Tree of Life, Creation, Consciousness etcetera and spiritually evolving out of the box. But you will have to deal with a Sufi mystic to get all the details as I was unable to get all of the secrets relating to it, due to your father, I might add," Theodoric outlined and smiled broadly.

 5 – 4

"How due to my father?" Paul asked.

"Your father asked someone about the stone's origin. We were discovered and had to make a very fast exit, and then cross a hostile desert with quite a few angry Muslims in hot pursuit. But it was interesting," Theodoric explained with a nostalgic look upon his face. Paul could see the admiration in Theodoric's eyes he still obviously had for his father. "As for the Black Stone's origin, there are many various opinions as to what the Black Stone actually is. Muslims say it was found by Abraham (Ibrahim) and his son Ishmael (Ismail) when they were searching for stones with which to build the Kaaba. They recognised its worth and made it one of the building's corner stones. But we know that it is part of the pyramidian stone from the Great Pyramid, symbolically taken and placed as the corner stone to again keep alive and further the esoteric codes in Arabia. As you see, we are all part of God's great plan and all have the same information. As for it being Lapsit Exillis, this has made some argue that it is just a meteorite as often worshipped in Arabia at the time. The stone pre-dates the revelation of the Holy Qur'an and Muhammad's prophethood, as he even kissed it, so it must stem from the time of Abraham since the Hajj traditions are traceable to the patriarch of monotheism. The Ka'bah at Mecca describes the shape of the Black Stone structure on a marble base, which stands in the centre court of the Great Mosque, Masjidul Haram, at the centre of Mecca. It stands about fifty feet high by about thirty-five feet wide. Set into the eastern corner is the sacred stone. This Ka'ba is a cubed shaped temple rebuilt by Abraham and his son Ishmael. Reverently draped in black cloth throughout the year, it beckons to every Muslim of the world to come to its sacred ground. The Maqam Ibrahim, which means the place where Abraham was in the habit of standing, is opposite the Multazam, the only door of the Ka'bah. The Ka'bah, or Kaaba, is the canonical centre of the Islamic world just as Rome is now the Christian centre, and every pious act, particularly prayer, is directed toward it. Once a year it plays host to the greatest convention of religious believers and stands ready to sanctify the Umrah traveller through the rest of the year as they walk around it. The official starting point of the walk around the Kaaba, which forms the core of the holy pilgrimage, is called the Hajj. During the Tawaf pilgrims kiss or touch the Black Stone as they circumambulate the Ka'bah. Some Muslims believe the stone itself has some supernatural powers. They believe that this stone fell from the sky during the time of Adam and Eve, and that it has the power to cleanse worshippers of their sins by absorbing them into itself. They say that the Black Stone was once a pure and dazzling white and it has turned black because of the sins it has absorbed over the years," Theodoric explained as the others listened intently. He took some wine and continued. "It is remarkable, however, that even though the temple contained 360 idols worshipped before Muhammad's prophethood, the Black Stone was never kissed or made an idol of worship. In fact, the Ka'bah was never worshipped prior to Muhammad's prophethood. The building contained idols of worship but the building itself was never an object of worship. The fact that the Ka'bah was rebuilt by Abraham is a historical fact. Since the stone has been there ever since, it stands to reason that Abraham placed the stone in the Ka'ba. The Black Stone is in fact the cornerstone of the Ka'ba and is placed there as an emblem of the progeny of Abraham which was rejected by the Israelites and became the corner stone of the Kingdom of God. The Psalms contain a clear reference to it: 'The stone which the builders refused is become the head-stone of the corner'. Ishmael was looked on as being rejected by God, or so the Israelites believed. Yet it was a progeny of Ishmael that the Last Prophet, the 'head-stone of the corner', was to arise. While David referred to it as the stone which the builders refused, Jesus spoke of it more plainly in the parable of the husbandman, telling the Israelites that the vineyard, which in the parable stands for the Kingdom of God, would be taken away from them and given to other husbandmen. That the rejected stone in the prophecy (21:42) symbolised a rejected nation (21:43) is made clear by Jesus Christ. That this rejected nation was none other than the Ishmaelites has been borne out by history. Another reason why we, with the knowledge that we possess, have both a spiritual and moral obligation, as the Sufi mystics know and the inner circles of the Isma'ilis, to fuse all of our beliefs as one. It is symbolised by the reuniting of the staff of Ephraim with the Staff of Judah. That is why it is so important, as we approach a crossroads in our history, that we stop this coming war with Saladin." He paused. "Also this Black Stone passes for the Mithaq, the primordial covenant between the Creator and His created. And in the whole world there is only this unhewn stone, the stone, cut out of the mountains without hands (Daniel 2:45), and that is the corner-stone of a building, which in point of importance, stands unique in the world. Touching or kissing the stone has a profound impact on the faithful as it is supposed to count in their favour on Judgement Day. Judgement Day is a metaphor for the return to balance with the duality of our reality, but that aspect I am afraid must wait for another time when my head is totally clear," Theodoric joked, shaking his head. "It suffices to say that the Prophet Muhammad said that it is the Right Hand of God on Earth. The single most important reason for kissing the stone is that the Prophet Muhammad did so. No other devotional significance whatsoever is attached to the stone. Kissing or touching the Black Stone is a reverential act of acknowledgment that God's hand directed its placement and construction for some otherwise unknown reason other than that Abraham and Muhammad had touched and kissed the stone, and an acknowledgment that God had entrusted the 'corner stone' of His religious central focus for man upon that hollowed and sacred place. Furthermore, and what the majority of Muslims don't even realise, is that the Ka'bah is accurately aligned on two heavenly phenomena, the cycles of the moon and the rising of Canopus, the brightest star after Sirius, and as I shall teach you, Canopus is directly related to the Stellar boats of ancient Egypt, the Magan boats and Jason and the Argonaut symbolism," Theodoric explained, his speech beginning to slur a little from the wine. [40]

"Whatever you do, Paul, please don't do as Theodoric and your father did here in order to gain enlightenment," Brother Jakelin smiled, as Theodoric looked up quizzically, trying to focus his eyes and pouring himself more wine.

"Oh, and what was that?" Paul enquired as Theodoric waved his hand aside.

"They thought they would sleep the night upon the rock of the dome thinking they would experience some kind of mystical vision, or even ascend to the heavens as Muhammad had," Brother Jakelin laughed.

"Well, it stood to reason I thought," Theodoric waved as he spilt some wine.

"What did?" Paul pressed.

"Well, in the ninth year of Muhammad's mission, about AD 620 I think it was, yeah, yes it was, anyway, he rose in the middle of the night to visit the Sacred

Mosque in Mecca. After a time of worship he fell asleep near the Ka'bah and the angel Gabriel came to him and woke him and led him to the edge of the mosque. Awaiting them was al-Buraq, a white winged beast whose every stride stretched as far as the eye could see, and he mounted it and sped northwards with Gabriel to here and that rock outside. When they reached Jerusalem Muhammad dismounted and prayed near the Rock. Abraham, Moses, Jesus and other prophets, supposedly gathered together to pray behind him. Muhammad was presented with a vessel of wine and a vessel of milk. The Prophet chose the milk and Gabriel said, 'You have chosen the true religion'. Muhammad then embarked on the ascension, what all good Muslims call the 'Miraj' though don't ever confuse it with mirage for heaven's sake. Anyway, once there he received the command to pray five times a day, as we told you earlier, and the revelation encapsulating the beliefs of Islam. So, your father and I thought, as we thought we were worthy, we would see if anything would happen to us," Theodoric explained and poured the last of the wine.

"And did anything happen?" Paul asked. Theodoric looked up at Paul and stared momentarily in silence.

"Yes, we upset everyone, got chased out in the morning and had to leave the city fast for showing such disrespect...but your father did have a dream. One he refused to ever reveal other than that he saw something buried and that he knew where, and that it would unite Islam with all other religions all standing shoulder to shoulder," Theodoric answered.

"Muslims claim that each one believes in Allah and His angels and in His books and His messengers and make no division between any one of His messengers. And they say: We hear and we obey. Oh Lord, grant us Thy forgiveness; unto Thee we return (Qur'an II/285). But would they accept the teachings of another prophet if one came to them now, or in the future. Would Christians for that matter?" Brother Jakelin pondered aloud.

"Well, from my father's dream and all you know regarding something that is hidden then why have you not sought its location?" Paul asked incredulously.

"As I have said, because it is not for our times now," Count Henry answered. "Moses found it when he was a Pharaoh, but he likewise realised it was not for his time, but what he did learn from it set him on his path which led him to leave Egypt with his followers and that led to the birth of the Old Testament. He had to instruct his brother Aaron to re-seal the one part of the hidden complex he had entered. I can show you the actual paragraphs if you wish when we return to Kerak if you need proofs of this. Paul, do not fear the knowledge you are learning. It may sound heretical and to be delving into occult matters or worse in the Pope's eyes, learning aspects about Islam, but again, occult simply means 'hidden'."

All sat in silence simply looking at Paul as he ate some bread, cut some cheese and then poured some water over his hands. Count Henry watched Paul as he poured the water.

"Baptism. Why is baptism by water so significant then? If everything else is to symbolise some aspect then what does this mean?" Paul asked as the water sparkled as he poured it past the candle.

"Baptism by immersion was a feature of many of the mystery cults of antiquity," Count Henry answered immediately. "As water was symbolic for spirit, but it was most definitely not a ritual of Judaism, but came from the rituals of the Isis temple on the River Nile. John the Baptist learnt many of his secrets from Egypt when he lived there when his family too had fled from the wrath of Herod. Plus the dove, symbolic for the spirit of the Lord, seen when Jesus was baptised, is symbolic of the dove that also represented Isis as 'queen of heaven', 'star of the sea', the Stella Maris, and 'mother of god' centuries before the Virgin Mary was even born, though she is called exactly the same within the Catholic Church."

"Stella Maris...that is the name of the path that runs near to my home...former home," Paul interrupted, a sadness suddenly hitting him as he realised again it was no longer his home. He sighed heavily before Count Henry then continued.

"The dove has no parallel or precedent in Judaism but it does in the practices of Egypt. Isis was portrayed as suckling the baby Horus, the offspring of herself and her dead but resurrected husband Osiris. It was his annual festival, our modern Easter, that marked his death and three days later his resurrection, that, just as in the Bible, the sun turned black when he died and entered the underworld," he explained as Paul immediately thought back upon the wall mural in the Templars' headquarters that depicted a black sun. "But ask yourself this if your doubts still eat at you. If Jesus was the son of God and without sin, then why would he need to be baptised by John to wash away sins and seek redemption, which is what the Church tells its flock it is for?" Count Henry pointed out and posed the question.

"So in effect, the whole of Christianity then is in fact based upon the ancient Egyptian goddess Isis?" Paul replied quizzically after reflecting upon the question.

"Well, in a fashion. Chrestos also means 'gentile one' and is by the way a direct appellation of Isis but also an epithet to Osiris. But the Christian sacred meal of wine and bread, Mass, is not unique either for it was already a common practice of all the major dying and resurrection God mystery schools, and not something inaugurated for the first time at the last supper as representing his sacrificial body and blood. In our Gospel of John, we omit this to point out its significance and obviousness to later generations. The symbolism of this sacred meal is also in the image of the bread. The Egyptian hieroglyph for bread is a raised loaf shaped boss; it is identical to the shape of the boss in the Great Pyramid. It is the only marking, as no others are found present anywhere within the monument, or its immediate neighbours. It is somehow a key, but again a key we do not yet understand. We can assume that it represents that the Great Pyramid is identified as the 'Body' by the boss, and why we can say the missing builder's stone that was rejected, the capstone, is symbolised by a head. We do know from documents and proofs that we have, that the Giza pyramids were built many thousands of years before we credit them. The Egyptians themselves tell us this in their own words despite the dates not agreeing with Biblical chronology; another reason why we keep that knowledge secret, and why the Church in Alexandria was so keen to destroy all and any under-standing of the ancient writings and hieroglyphs. Also the Giza pyramids are built upon a plateau that has always been known as Jeezah; this is linguistically identical to Jesus as we know that is where his name derived from. You may also be aware of the connection of 58 as related to Giza from Baphomet and our esoteric code of 'Caput LVIIIM' meaning 'Head 58m'," Count Henry said.

"I am sorry but I have only heard briefly those details before...but I am afraid I cannot recall them fully," Paul said apologetically.

"Then let me quickly explain again to refresh your memory for I am sure I explained this previously," Theodoric said with a mocking frown, then smiled. "Throughout the ancient world, sunrise and its conjunction with other celestial events were always looked upon as very important. On the spring equinox of 10,500 BC a particularly spectacular conjunction occurred when the sunrise, the constellation of Leo and the meridian transit of the three belt stars all aligned to the Giza site for the first time exactly. This conjunction just happened to mark the beginning of the age of Leo, as in the Zep Tepi, meaning 'first time' of Leo. It is why the whole complex is set with the Guardian, the Sphinx with the lion's head. Of course it weathered badly so its head had to be re-carved but it still indicates clearly a lion's body. But the most important star, Sirius, is hidden from view set behind the horizon, its presence felt by its obvious omission. In 10,500 BC, the constellation of Orion was at its lowest point with Sirius hidden from view. This is the astrological clue because during this period the declination of Sirius was exactly 58 degrees and 43 minutes. I don't think I need explain the importance of the figure 58 all over again and how this very specific value has been carried across time to our present day. Not only that, but when the constellation of Orion reaches the highest point of its processional cycle in the years between AD 2,000 and 2,018, it will be exactly 58 degrees and 6 minutes above the horizon. This is, I fear, the time of the fifth flight of the Phoenix when the seasons will not be in their proper times, when animals will wander and get lost, when the birds shall lose their way also." Theodoric sighed deeply. "And I have already demonstrated how the entire Giza complex is set out within a 5:8 square so I need not repeat myself; unless of course you have forgotten it all?" he asked Paul with a wry smile and quizzical look. "If I have not, then we must cover that aspect in detail later."

"Paul," Count Henry said to get his attention. "Remember that Jesus was called a non Jewish Egyptian magician in the Holy Jewish Talmud. Many of Jesus's words and parables are word for word taken from the Egyptian 'Book of the Dead' and strictly Osirian. Jesus's words 'In my father's house are many mansion' (John 14:2) is but one. Many people do not believe, and certainly the Qur'an states it as fact, that Jesus did not die on the cross. We know the truth about this but that we cannot tell tonight…for that mystery we need to see how you adjust and deal with what we have already told you. All I will say at this point is that the death of the Osiris god is traditionally represented as a black sun, the forsaking of the light, and that Jesus's actual last words were in fact 'Helios! Helios!', which meant 'O sun! O sun! Why has thou forsaken me?' and that the crucifixion and resurrection are enactments of the Osiris and Isis ritual, but also that Jesus was actually sentenced and crucified by the Romans, not the Jews, for which they have suffered greatly as a consequence. You will learn much on this too if you stay with us," he explained then rested back in his chair.

Brother Jakelin coughed and leaned onto his elbows at the table.

"Thousands of years before Christ, there was a temple of Isis at Sais in Egypt where an inscription states 'I am all that was, that is, and that is yet to come', which later became Yahweh's, as in God's words in the Book of Revelation (1:8). Also word for word 'come to me all of you who are heavy laden and I will refresh you', which was lifted entirely from the sayings of Isis as inscribed at the temple of Dendera. But know too that in early Judaism, the worship of the female Asherah, who was the consort of Yahweh, was an integral and essential element of religious life in ancient Israel prior to reforms introduced by their King Josiah in 621 BC, and that both King David and Solomon, Sulyman to Muslims, were Goddess worshippers. And the Lord's Prayer," Brother Jakelin explained and paused as if in anticipation.

Paul looked at him.

"Let me guess...that too is of Egyptian origin?" he half sarcastically intoned.

"Yes, you guessed correctly, brother," Theodoric replied almost as sarcastically with a wry smile.

"It is taken directly from a prayer to Osiris-Amon and pre-dates the Lord's Prayer as we have it now by many centuries. We still conclude all our Christian prayers with the Egyptian 'Amen'," Brother Jakelin replied.

"The early Gospels, especially the Canonical ones were, for those very reasons subject to some serious re-writing and editing," Count Henry interjected. "They did likewise with much of the details surrounding John the Baptist. He was equal to Jesus...that is another reason why we have two riders travelling the same way upon a single horse to symbolically represent this fact too. I warned you it was multi-levelled. However, the early Church knew this so they re-wrote John into a new version as being subservient to Jesus. However much of what John taught many of his disciples carried on with their own traditions regardless for many years after his execution. Most of Jesus's disciples were taken from John's own followers. As John was the elder of the two he also baptised Jesus and chose him as his second in command. It was this familiarity that caused John to question his own judgement when asked whilst in prison if Jesus was the prophesied Messiah. Logical and understandable when you consider John had just deliberately put himself in the position to be beheaded in order to guarantee the symbolic continuation of a hidden code, and doubts would enter anyone's heart at the last minute," he outlined.

"If that is so, where did John's followers all go then?" Paul asked.

"I can answer that," Theodoric jumped in, "for I spent time with them. When I was in southern Persia (modern day Iraq) I spent many months with the secretive Mandeans. They claim to be followers of John the Baptist still, though having lost much of the esoteric hidden meanings and codes; they actually despise and hate Jesus, as they do not fully understand what went on between the two. They have a book named the Ginza, which means 'the treasure', also known as 'the book of Adam'. The 'sidra d'Yahya' which means 'book of John' as well as the book of kings. Manda in their name by the way means gnosis and their priests are called Nazareans. Mandeans share and state the same view as Jews do in their Talmud that Jesus was a sorcerer and liar, again because they had lost the true hidden meanings behind what went on between him and John. They also appear in the Qur'an under the name of Sabians and known as 'the people of the book'. Yahya is the Arabic name of John the Baptist in the Qur'an. One thing they do claim is that John is called the fisher of souls and the good shepherd, the former being used for both Mary Magdalene and Isis. Simon Peter as well as Jesus were both termed 'fisher of men'. In Syria, there is a highly secretive sect that still exists...they are the Nusairiyeh, also called Nosairi but also as Alawites from where they live in the mountains. They are outwardly Islamic but have adopted the trappings of its religion to protect themselves from persecution but they still retain their true religion as a sacred secret teaching. I learnt that their greatest secret is that the Grail is just a symbol that stands for a doctrine that Jesus taught John. We know that it deals with the head of a body being missing and buried as well as the principles of the feminine. Much of their secret teachings have been absorbed into Isma'ilis' secret teachings, especially amongst their inner initiate circles and some of the inner circles within Sufism," Theodoric divulged.

"Paul, if this is all too much you'd better tell us now," Count Henry remarked, concerned by the look upon Paul's face.

Paul moved his sword to rest more comfortably. He became aware of the rose emblem.

"I was told by a blacksmith who engraved this for me and by Theodoric that this rose symbol means much but neither would elucidate further. Is that still the case tonight?" Paul asked looking at them each in turn.

Theodoric looked at Henry for permission to speak.

"Yes, I think you should know at least some of its significance tonight," Count Henry answered.

Theodoric and Brother Jakelin looked at each other.

"You or me?" Theodoric asked him.

"I will if it helps," Brother Jakelin answered and sat himself more comfortably. "I'll try and explain this as simply as I can without shocking you I hope. The rose emblem was adopted to represent Mary Magdalene and her family tree as well as many other esoteric meanings. It is connected with the roots of the vine and Tree of Life and the flowering at the top, and symbolically represents love, as in both French and English the word rose is an anagram of Eros, the god of erotic love. You already know all the stuff about the sacred marriage etcetera now, so it should not come as a surprise to know that it is also connected with the Virgin Mary's flower, the lily. But the great cathedrals that we are now building have great rose windows, each with twelve sections, but they always face west, the traditional direction sacred to female deities. Always near the rose windows is a shrine to the black Madonnas. The entire cathedral's layout is symbolic of the feminine divine principle, its huge gothic entrance ways represent the most intimate part of the goddess, drawing the worshipper into the womb-like interior of the mother church through highly carved funnelling, ridged gothic vaulted doorways, topped off at the arch with the representation of the clitoris-like rosebud. The female is the only one that has this unique physical attribute designed purely for pleasure alone, whereas men have to double up their urinary system. This is why women did not need a man when it came to the sacred sexual experience to fuse with the God, and one of the reasons why Peter was jealous of them, for men could only achieve that union by way of a woman. In the cathedrals and churches, once through the arched door, you stop at the stoup of holy water, often represented as a giant shell, another symbol of the Goddess nativity of birth." Brother Jakelin laughed. "And I reckon many a good Christian I know would have a heart attack at these revelations on the spot."

 21 – 15

"Only because they have all been brainwashed into viewing it as something disgusting and abhorrent by the Church itself," Count Henry replied before Brother Jakelin continued.

"You know that all Christian pilgrims wear the cowrie shell as an emblem and sign that they are pilgrims, and all know that it represents symbolically the female vulva. These are all symbols of the feminine principle that communicate at a subliminal level and affect the unconscious mind. This principle was carnal, mystical and religious at the same time, its energy and power coming from its sexuality and its wisdom, known as 'whore wisdom', came from a knowledge of the rose, eros. This is something your father knew much about. As do Theo and I," Jakelin said with a smile. "But, I must remain reverential. Knowledge is power, and secrets like we hold wield power unlike any other, and this is why it poses such a threat ultimately to the Church of Rome. That is another reason why we seek a fusion of Judaic, Christian and Islamic thought as quickly as we practically can, before such a time comes that the Church turns upon us once it does realise what is openly being revealed for those who have eyes to see. Theo here reckons his charts already predict this in the future but as we have learnt, there are always different paths that can be followed, for the future is not set on one route only. Nevertheless, to the Church of Rome, sex is deemed only acceptable between those where union is likely to lead to procreation only. There is no concept of sex for joy let alone the fact that it can bring a heightened awareness that can lead to spiritual enlightenment. In fact the Church positively sets prohibitive rules on sex whereby you must learn to view sex with apprehension and as a joyless marital duty only. To feel and think otherwise is considered a sin. But we know that this is all about control over women. They have placed a belief and idea that sex is inherently dirty and shameful. The result of which is an attitude of repressed desire and guilt that inevitably gives rise to crimes against women. The puritanical background and its hatred and fear of sex bring a terrible legacy in the form of wife battering, paedophilia and rape. For wherever sex is distrusted, childbirth and children are seen as intrinsically dirty and both child and mother fall prey to violence; yet we as men are supposed to acknowledge our role as the physically stronger to protect always the women and young. But that can only be done when harmony and balance are complete with the full acceptance and understanding of sex," Brother Jakelin commented with a pickup of tone and volume.

Paul smiled as he thought about Alisha. To hear this from Brother Jakelin was like a light in the darkness of his heart. From just moments before where he had stood feeling guilty and ashamed to hearing his words of wisdom, he felt joyful and uplifted, the smile difficult to hide, and despite being told not to feel ashamed about sex, he still blushed regardless.

"All this sex talk aside, the main areas of learning you must concentrate upon for now, if you so desire to learn our teachings of course, are related to the Gospel of John. There may be confusion amongst the lay Christian and clerics themselves as to who exactly the author is, whether it be John the Evangelist or John the Baptist or as we know, in fact, Lazarus as John but completed by Jesus some twelve years after his resurrection. Some say Paul himself was in fact the resurrected Jesus continuing his own work under a new guise...it is why he was accepted and recognised when he arrived in Jerusalem, but I digress. It is the contents of that gospel that contain hidden values that will help one day lead us to the key that is buried as we know and as Moses found, to that which fell from heaven," Count Henry stated solemnly.

"It won't take long I fear for some intelligent cleric or scholar to piece the evidence together though and work out that Lazarus was in fact the 'beloved disciple' who was in reality John the Baptist, his cousin, not John the Evangelist...but then again perhaps it will confuse them for years to come," Theodoric laughed.

"Paul, you may have difficulty accepting that we, in our Orders, hold John the Baptist in such high esteem, but I hope that you are grasping the realities of the facts as they are. You must also realise that Jesus was in his true sense a Messiah as well as an initiate adept of the Egyptian mystery school of Osiris, the secrets of which he also taught John the Baptist being those of the Osirian inner circle," Count Henry said quietly and looked at Paul for several moments trying to gauge his reaction. When Paul feigned a smile, he continued. "Understand also that when Jesus gave bread in his miracle of feeding the five thousand, again using the symbols of bread and fishes, as the Bible states, they were all men. No children nor women and they sat in organised ranks; because they were all members of the various factions and the gathering was in fact his moment when he acted as their overall leader after John the Baptist had been beheaded. After this miracle of loaves and fishes, they all acknowledged and wanted Jesus to take up his rightful position as king. John had previously been the main force behind the various groups as the most charismatic leader of the time, and as a consequence was seen by Herod as a direct threat. In Herod's court was a female whom Herod promised anything if she would dance for him. The dance of the seven veils. She was named Salome...but she was also a female disciple of Jesus. Some argue that she betrayed John the Baptist to get him out of the way as the natural leader, thus clearing the way for Jesus to take over as leader, but as you now know, it was all part of a deliberate plot that Herod would arrest John and behead him. So it was that Salome, following orders to ensure the execution and that the symbolism would be carried forward, demanded the head of John on a platter, thus ensuring his execution to symbolically represent the severed head required to carry the message across time. Later gospel editors simplified the story in the mistaken belief they were drawing away any bad aspects from Jesus as they were not privy to the hidden agenda and symbolism. For John's clear bravery and for being such a major sacrificial lamb is why we use the symbol of a lamb again, to represent him. We venerate him so much, for without him, and later Judas as well, the Jesus initiative as we shall call it would never have even started. John is the beginning, just as Mary is the end as explained earlier." Count Henry stood up slowly as he dipped his hands in some fresh water to clean them. "I fear we have said more than enough for one night. You know our standing orders, to bed when dark and rise when light; but I think we have abused that this night. I knew this would be a late session and why I asked Usamah to allow us the privacy of his house. We have two rooms ready for us. I will take one with Jakelin, the other is across the hall for you two. I would advise sleep as tomorrow will be a long day," he advised as he dried his hands.

Paul stared at him for a few moments in silence.

"What?" Count Henry asked.

"But you still have not answered my original question from earlier; what has all this got to do with my bloodline?" Paul asked almost exasperated in tone.

Count Henry looked at Brother Jakelin, Theodoric and back at Paul in turn.

"Does not your name give it away?" Count Henry asked him.

Perplexed Paul shook his head no.

"Your father probably never mentioned his involvement with us or your true bloodline in order to protect you I am guessing, but in short, your ancestral tree is linked by blood to that of Jesus and in turn by your mother to the house of Judah also. But those details only you can discover for yourself," Count Henry replied seriously, his stare fixed upon Paul.

Open mouthed almost in shock Paul sat back hard as Brother Jakelin and Theodoric nodded in agreement.

"So gentlemen, I believe that is enough for one night. To bed," Count Henry finished.

ഔ ൏

After just a few short pleasantries and no further explanation, Paul found himself lying restless upon a large comfortable bed, the sheets made of silk and cotton. At least an hour had passed since retiring to bed but he could not settle. Theodoric, in the bed next to him, slept soundly, so Paul thought, as he gazed up at the window, a single candle burning away in one corner of the room brightly, as was customary for Templars at night, except when in the field.

"Don't stand on ceremony on my part about keeping the candle on all night," Theodoric suddenly muttered from under his sheets as if he had read Paul's mind.

Paul could not settle and sat up, many thoughts about what he had been told that evening running through his mind. He picked up his sword and looked at the emblem of the rose, still unsure exactly what it meant in relation to him personally. He moved nearer the solitary candle as Theodoric sat up too.

"What troubles you, my friend, or is that a stupid question?" he asked.

Paul slowly turned to face him, sword across his knees.

"I am still unsure and confused by all that I have learnt this night. I am happy that my heart no longer feels heavy and guilty for what I have done with Alisha, as my own selfish desires and love for her certainly made me ignore all the advice of our fathers...but I am trying to put everything into some sort of simple pattern that I can understand," Paul whispered back.

Theodoric ran his hands through his hair.

"Paul, what the emblem upon the sword means will reveal itself to you in due course. Your father understood this and hence he gave it to you and not your brother. As for the rest, I can simplify it if you wish?"

"No...My father meant it for Stewart...but he did not take it."

"I am aware of that...Tenno explained so, but I know your father and I bet he knew full well Stewart would not pick it up all along...and the sword chose you," Theodoric replied and winked. Paul just nodded silently. "Right, let's see if I can simplify what you heard this eve. Well, it's like this, Mary Magdalene was a priestess who followed the cult of Isis, symbolically represented by the blue star Sirius, and was Jesus's partner in the sacred marriage. Jesus's twelve disciples were not privy to the super secrets behind the plan. It was Mary Magdalene who rallied the despondent and almost panicking disciples after his crucifixion. Mary Magdalene, after the apparent death of Jesus, and another reason why we use the black rose to esoterically represent her, even according to standard orthodox accounts, went to Europe and formed her own Church, not based on Christianity, but the old religion of Egypt 'Isis and Osiris', believed to be the same beliefs of the Magi. She was accompanied by disciples of the faith known as 'keepers of the faith', the exact same terminology applied to the Knights Templar, to guard her. It is this Order, which led to the Order of Tau, its emblem being that second one beneath the rose on your sword and as you had put upon the pommel, which ultimately derived from ancient Egyptian symbols and the god of wisdom and knowledge, Thoth, as in Hermes. That Order led ultimately to the Knights Templar having taken the true faith from the Magi of Egypt, the same faith that Jesus practised. It is the significance of Mary Magdalene being blue and black and connected with Isis and Sirius that's important. She was first to see Jesus after he was resurrected. Is this making any sense?" Theodoric asked. Paul nodded again in silence. "Right, well many people believe the term 'Jesus the Nazarene' means the same as 'Jesus of Nazareth'. However, the town or city of Nazareth did not even exist in any form until some decades after his lifetime. The term 'Jesus of Nazareth' was planted in the Bible in a clumsy attempt to disguise its Egyptian and Persian origins of the 'Sect of the Nazarenes'. The Nazarene sect had three main centres and one of them was just outside Alexandria in Egypt! Coincidentally, the name 'Nazarean' is a form of the word 'Nazrani', which means both 'little fishes' and 'Christians' in Arabic exactly as it did in Aramaic a thousand years ago. The Nazarenes taught homeopathy, herbalism, alchemy and practised vegetarianism. They were the fore-runners of the medicine men or doctors, caring for the sick and diseased, a doctrine followed by the Knights Templar Order and Hospitallers. Justin Martyr, writing in AD 160, reported a discussion with a Jew, Trypho, who called Jesus a 'Galilean magician'. The philosopher Celsus, writing about AD 175, stated that, although Jesus grew up in Galilee, he worked for a time as a hired labourer in Egypt, where he learned the techniques of magic. In Arab countries to this day, the word used to describe Jesus and his followers is not Christians but 'Nazara'. This is confirmed in the Islamic Qur'an and the word means 'keepers' or 'guardians'. Knights are also known as protectors, and the Knights Templars' role was that of 'Guardians of the Holy Grail'. The full definition is Nazara ha-Brit, which means 'Keepers of the Covenant'. In fact, the 'Brit' aspect of that is the very root of the country name of Britain originally Britannia. Brit-ain actually means 'Covenant-land'. Remember too the account in the Bible about the 'Three Wise Men'? They were more accurately called 'The Three Magi' known for their knowledge and magic. What is less well known however is that they were also known as 'Nazars'. Also, there was an ancient city in Egypt called 'Nazara'. Sufi mystics knew that the Magi came from Nazara and were known as Nazarenes. The 'Three Wise Men' became the teachers of Jesus, 'Keepers of the Knowledge' the sacred knowledge taught to initiates of the Nazara and that 'baptism' performed by John the Baptist was the initiation ceremony, on graduation of that knowledge. Godfrei de Bouillon who captured Jerusalem was descended from Dagobert the Second and his son was Segisbert and of the Merovingian bloodline. Godfrei would not accept the Crown of Jerusalem but was king in all but name and considered as its rightful legitimate heir by his bloodline from Segisbert. It was Godfrei's brother who accepted the Crown of Jerusalem upon his death and became known as King Baldwin or Baudouin the First of the Holy Land. The Order of Sion, or as Count Henry prefers, the Prieure de Sion, had been founded by Godfrei at Mount Sion, the famous high hill south of Jerusalem. But it had been a mysterious conclave that had elected Godfrei ruler who were, in fact, the elusive monks from Orval, including Peter the Hermit, who just en masse had disappeared from Orval at the same time as Godfrei had headed for the Holy Land, the monks then setting up Notre Dame du Mont de Sion. Also all of this has been encoded with specific mathematical values that will one day lead some clever soul to locate and recover some great complex hidden by God, the true Ark of the Covenant, which at its centre has a pyramidian, the missing capstone symbolised by John the Baptist's head, a lump of which is the Kaaba stone in Mecca, and is surrounded by twelve chambers, that contains details and proofs of mankind's divine origins and history. It was buried ten thousand years ago just prior to the worldwide cataclysmic flood as recounted in all myths and religions across the world, as I did explain on our journey here. Finally, the headquarters of the Prieure de Sion is also at Gisors, in Normandy as a reminder of Giza in Egypt. As for your bloodline, don't ask me to explain that tonight as I'll get it all wrong. Just accept you have some genuine royal blood in you...Right, tomorrow I have to argue my case to be released from my obligation to the Knights of Lazarus...if I cannot, then the task of explaining to Lucy falls to you, young man...so can I get some sleep now?" Theodoric concluded and wrapped the sheets around himself, turning his back on Paul. [41]

"If that was a summary, then I must be stupid as I am just as confused. And I am certain I shall return to Kerak with you, and tomorrow perhaps you will explain further about my father being a prisoner in Aleppo and also about the old woman... but goodnight Theo...and I am glad that you brought me here," Paul said as he got out of bed and blew out the candle. Once back in bed he lay awake thinking about Alisha and Arri. Thoughts and images of a black rose ran through his mind. If all that he had heard about was true, then symbolically she was his sacred rose. "My Black Rose," he whispered and closed his eyes.

Port of La Rochelle, France, Melissae Inn, spring 1191.

"So what happened then?" Simon asked eagerly.

The old man sat forward and took some food and a small sip of fresh rose water Sarah had just placed upon the table.

"In the morning Paul awoke after a fitful and sleepless night to calls to prayers outside by Muslims. Theodoric had to be dragged from his bed, his head pounding from all the wine he had drunk. After a quick wash, and Theodoric promising to take Paul to visit the Dome of the Rock later, and after some breakfast served by one of the house servants, Count Henry joined them and explained that he and Brother Jakelin would accompany them back to Kerak if they could wait and travel in three days' time. Paul's heart sank; he wanted to get back to Alisha and Arri as fast as he could, as he explained.

"To Kerak? Yes right. But that Stephanie...she so wants Paul and I see trouble there," Sarah remarked.

"Of course. He wants to get into that gateway to heaven of hers!" Simon laughed aloud, which made the farrier and Genoese sailor laugh aloud also.

"Show some respect!" Stephan said loudly to be heard above the laughter seeing Ayleth and Miriam both blush.

Simon and the Genoese sailor kept on laughing as tears rolled down their faces. A sudden bang echoed throughout the room as the Hospitaller Knight slammed down his sheathed sword hard upon the table making the women jump.

"Silence!" he bellowed as he leaned up and glared at Simon and the Genoese sailor. "This may all sound like a joke to you, but to people like us who put our lives into such matters, this counts," he said, his voice laced with menace.

The old man looked at him surprised at his sudden outburst. Simon and the Genoese sailor started to calm down but still chuckling.

"It is okay, it is good to laugh. It will help him remember today if for no other reason," the old man said quietly as he looked at those about him.

"Oh dear, excuse me I'm sorry. Just couldn't resist. That was about the only part I can remember from all the stuff you have said," Simon explained wiping his eyes.

"Just goes to prove the pull and strength of the feminine principle," the old man remarked.

"'Tis that. 'Tis no doubt why men seek power, wealth and position...simply to succeed with women, for subliminally they seek out that feminine principle to take them nearer to God without even realising," the Knight Templar remarked quietly in a philosophical tone, then looked up directly at Miriam beside him and clasped her hand gently.

"If you are not Paul, who I guess you are way too old to be anyway, then you must be Theodoric," the Genoese sailor stated quizzically.

The old man shook his head silently no as Gabirol looked at him directly.

"Then you must be making most of this all up surely?" the Genoese sailor continued to press.

The old man looked across at him slowly with a wry smile of inner knowledge, calm and wisdom radiating from his deeply etched face.

"Let me finish, and then decide. It is only truth that I proffer as I have explained several times already...and what harm can truth do to you?" he stated and asked with a gentle smile.

All sat and looked at each in silence waiting for someone to speak first.

"Then continue; and I'll try to refrain from filthy comments. Try I said," Simon finally spoke up and laughed. All nodded in agreement.

"Then I shall continue," the old man said and sat himself upright. "But for your own peace of mind on whether I speak the truth or untruths, let me read you something I was given a long time ago," the old man said and gently pulled out a vellum sheet from his leather folder and rolled it out flat. He studied it for a few moments then began to read directly from it. "The goal of the Darkside is to drive a wedge between you and God, so how do you prevent this from happening? By closing the gap between you and God! Be Mindful of these three things. One. Distancing from God is done unconsciously. You become preoccupied, self-centred or overcommitted. Distancing is a subtle drift, not a sudden dash. Two. Distancing from God is dangerous. The Darkside's intention and aim is to separate you from God's blessing. Like a soldier in enemy territory who is cut off, you become an easy target. Three. Distancing from God is a choice...but it is your choice, never God's! Whatever your circumstances, God remains faithful and loves you. Choose to keep your dialogue with God going throughout your day. Remember to quieten your mind chatter so that you can hear what God is saying to you!" He then looked up and paused briefly. "And can you guess who wrote this?"

All around the table looked at each other puzzled shaking their heads until Ayleth spoke.

"Was it Paul?" she answered softly.

The old man shook his head no and began to gently roll up the vellum sheet.

"It was in fact Reynald de Châtillon...when he was a captive in Aleppo. He passed this to Philip when they were in prison together," the old man explained and raised his eyebrows as if to question them all.

"Reynald!" the Templar exclaimed surprised.

"Yes...Reynald. Like I said, he was not always the Mad Red Wolf of Kerak. And I shall explain why this is important...for Paul."

Chapter 34
Messengers of the Light

The Templar shook his head.

"Please do explain more about Reynald for he was certainly responsible for the loss of many of my friends," he remarked.

"And mine also...," the Hospitaller said still looking at Simon and the Genoese sailor.

"Okay, and at the risk of repeating myself, though Ayleth would not have heard these facts, I shall again briefly explain Reynald...," the old man replied and took a deep breath before continuing. "You others may recall this is exactly what Abi explained to Paul when he first met Princess Stephanie so apologies if I repeat it again word for word almost," he paused. "Now Reynaud de Châtillon was his proper name, though we all know him as Reynald de Chatillon. He was a minor nobleman who came to the Levant during the Second Crusade but stayed on in Outremer rather than return to France, where, as a younger brother from a small fief in the Loire Valley, he would not have expected advancement. Tall and handsome man with reddish hair and an impressive bearing, he turned the head of Princess Constance of Antioch, the widow of Raymond of Poitiers, the Christian king of the Outremer fief of Antioch. As already explained, this courtship shocked Outremer. She was one of the grandest ladies of the land, and by rights should have considered only the highest born of men as potential mates. But like him, Constance was strong-willed and married her apparent low-born lover in 1153. A real story of rags to riches. It was scandalous...but what most people do not realise, and perhaps never will, is that both Constance and Reynald were aware of his real bloodline and that despite appearances, he was probably more entitled to marry Constance that any one other high status suitor at the time."

"How so?" Gabirol asked immediately.

"Because, as history will one day testify, Reynald's lineage and background is open to debate and much speculation...but in reality his true origins had to be hidden and remain secret for his own safety as he had grown up. His family tree stretched far back into antiquity...and it was even connected to that of Alisha herself, but that I shall explain later. But him knowing this fostered an air of arrogance and entitlement within him. It was Theodoric who tried to steer him with wise counsel...and for a time it worked. But his self confidence and belief in his preordained destiny, helped along by some of Theodoric's teachings as well as Niccolas's, Lord rest his soul, meant he felt invincible and consequently, as the new prince of Antioch, wasted no time in making his mark. Disregarding the claims of its suzerain, the basileus, that means king or emperor, Manuel Comnenus, he decided to seize peaceable and prosperous Byzantine Cyprus. To finance this adventure, he demanded money from the Latin patriarch of Antioch, who had opposed Constance's love match in the first place and made no secret of his contempt for the parvenu prince. Predictably, the prelate refused to back or fund the scheme. By way of reply, Reynald had him stripped, beaten to a pulp almost, covered with honey, and exposed to the midday sun to be tormented by insects. Very

shortly afterwards, as you can imagine, the patriarch opened his treasury, and Reynald sailed to Cyprus. Once there he demonstrated that he was a crusader of the old style and his army pillaged, raped, and murdered at will, unmindful of the awkward fact that the islanders were Christian. He also rounded up all the Orthodox priests and cut off their noses, and sent the mutilated men to Constantinople as a signal of defiance to the basileus. So in no time, he had offended the Latins, by torturing the patriarch of Antioch, and outraged the Byzantines by laying waste to Cyprus."

"He sounds like a truly awful brute...makes me feel sick what that Princess Stephanie had to do with him," Ayleth shuddered.

"Both Theodoric and Philip realised that Reynald, despite his intellect and sheer physical presence, had in fact been seduced by the darker side of our own natures...which we all possess. They tried to rein him in but the more Reynald learnt the more superior he felt. That was one of the main reasons he was not allowed to climb the ranks of the inner circles of any of the Orders at the time. Reynald also believed that Islam was the making of the Devil's handiwork. When he learnt that many Muslim families allow and encourage marriage between first cousins to keep their bloodlines pure as they believed, he learnt that without the extra bloodlines of other diverse families, in time, all Muslim families would start to become more backward and unintelligent and brutish so had to be wiped out or converted to Christianity," the old man sighed.

 5 – 40

"Is that true...about families becoming more backward if they keep their family circles close...I mean is that not what most royal families do now already?" Simon asked.

"Ah, I bet your family is very close if you are the result," Sarah joked and patted Simon's arm.

"I mentioned earlier about bloods, that different types of blood exist within us between families. It is what was learnt from some of the artefacts recovered in Jerusalem, but exactly how the machinations work, we do not yet fully understand. But the ancient plates state that diversity must be maintained and not kept within families alone. It states that any defects or ailments will be reduced with the infusion of new blood from new families to a family, but if it is kept within a family only, those same defects will in fact increase and multiply. 'Tis why so many of the ancient Egyptian and later Roman families suffered both physical and mental problems due to their close inbreeding. 'Tis why it states a sister cannot lay with her brother or father," the old man explained.

"Err...but in the Bible they did," Simon interrupted. "You know, when Lot left Sodom and Gomorrah and set up home in a cave with his daughters. There were no other men so they slept with him."

"That is sick," Sarah said and slapped his arm hard.

"No, what he says is correct. But that story was from the Old Testament. The old ways that were replaced by the New Testament. The Old Testament speaks about an eye for an eye does it not, yet the New Testament speaks about turning the other cheek. But as far as Reynald was convinced, and as Constance believed, together they could bring in a new era for Christianity. But their plans all fell flat when in 1160, while out in the hinterland of Antioch rustling livestock from Syrian Christians, he was captured by an armed detachment of Nur al-Din's men. He was thrown into a cell in Aleppo's great citadel, to languish for sixteen years as you know, as no one offered to pay his ransom. Philip tried to rescue him *and that is how he was subsequently captured and spent a short period in Aleppo with him. That was another reason why Theodoric went to try and secure their release...which he was successful in doing for Philip as Philip was able to trade much knowledge with his captors, and they trusted him. Reynald was released during the unsettled period when the Zengids of Aleppo, following the death of Nur al-Din, sought allies among the Latins to deflect the ambitions of Saladin. They wrongly assumed that Reynald would side with them against Saladin, but Reynald simply saw all Muslims as the enemy. But his wife, Princess Constance, had died two years after his capture, leaving Antioch to a son from her previous marriage. He therefore had to seek a position elsewhere and as explained earlier, that is how and why he wooed and won Princess Stephanie de Milly as already explained ...heiress to Hebron and the Oultrajordain, the Latin marchland south of the Dead Sea known in the Bible as Moab. It was but a distant corner of Outremer, but nonetheless was of crucial significance as the main caravan routes from Syria to Egypt passed directly through Oultrajordain, as did, every year, thousands of pilgrims making the hajj to Mecca. Its two castles, Crac de Moab at Kerak and one at Montreal, rivalled those of Crac de l'Ospital and Marqab for massive impregnability. Now he became master of these fortresses, perched high above a valley frequented by treasure-laden travellers. As I also said previously, even for someone possessing scruples, the temptation would have been great and he intended to make his domain more important and bigger than any other principality answerable only to himself as he still believed his destiny foretold."*

"Do you mean he had parchments like Paul and Taqi had?" Gabirol asked.

"Niccolas had indeed drawn up one for him. 'Tis how and why Philip sought him out and later with Theodoric too. But they learnt the lesson well, that one must never place too much belief in what is written as absolute fact..."

"I do not like him nevertheless," Ayleth remarked, shaking her head.

"Changing the subject...you mentioned before, just briefly, about Masada. We oft used the water station near the base of the fortress, 'twas near the old Roman ramp constructed by them, but we were never allowed to visit the actual site as several Jews still remained there but I have always wanted to know more about the place," the Hospitaller commented.

"Good change of subject..." The old man smiled and turned in his seat to look at the Hospitaller better. "I can explain briefly if you want?" he asked as the Hospitaller quickly nodded yes in response. "The 'Siege of Masada'....The actual siege of Masada was among the final events of the Great Jewish Revolt, that occurred from 73 to 74 BC on a large hilltop in the Kingdom of Jerusalem near the shores of the Dead Sea. According to Josephus, the Jewish chronicler who accompanied the Roman forces, the long siege by the troops of the Roman Empire led to the mass suicide of the Sicarii rebels and resident Jewish families of the Masada fortress."

"Why was a Jew accompanying the Romans?" Simon asked, puzzled, and scratched his head.

"The siege was chronicled by Flavius Josephus to give him his full name. He was once a Jewish rebel leader captured by the Romans, but in whose service he became a historian. Masada became a controversial event in Jewish history, with some regarding it as a place of reverence, commemorating fallen ancestors and their heroic struggle against oppression, and others regarding it as a warning against extremism and the refusal to compromise," the old man answered.

"And they all committed suicide?" Ayleth asked quietly.

"Well...let me explain. Masada is a lozenge-shaped table-mountain that is very high

and isolated, and to all appearance impregnable. The terrain made it difficult to reach the top of the mountain because there was only one narrow pathway, not even wide enough for two people to climb together. This pathway is known as 'the Snake' because it worms its way to the summit with many ingenious zigzags. The fortress of Masada has been referred to as the place where David rested, after he had fled from his father-in-law, King Saul, so you can see, the place has historical value. Flavius Josephus, a Jew born and raised in Jerusalem, is the only historian to provide a detailed account of the Great Jewish Revolt and the only person who recorded what happened on Masada itself. After being captured during the Siege of Yodfat and then freed by Vespasian, Josephus chronicled the Roman campaign. Josephus, it is believed, based his narration on the field commentaries of the Roman commanders themselves. According to Josephus, Masada was first constructed by the Hasmoneans sometime between 37 and 31 BC and then Herod the Great fortified it as a refuge for himself in the event of a revolt. In AD 66, at the beginning of the Great Jewish Revolt against the Roman Empire, a group of Jewish extremists called the Sicarii over-came the Roman garrison of Masada and settled there. The Sicarii were commanded by Eleazar ben Ya'ir, and in AD 70 they were joined by additional Sicarii and their families expelled from Jerusalem by the Jewish population with whom the Sicarii were in conflict. Shortly thereafter, following the Roman siege of Jerusalem and subsequent destruction of the Second Temple, additional members of the Sicarii and many Jewish families fled Jerusalem and settled on the mountaintop, with the Sicarii using it as a refuge and base for raiding the surrounding countryside. The Sicarii were an extremist splinter group of the Zealots and were equally antagonistic to both Romans and other Jewish groups. It was the Zealots, in contrast to the Sicarii, who carried the main burden of the rebellion, which opposed the Roman rule of Judea, known as the Roman province of Iudaea, its Latinised name. Now according to Josephus, on Passover, the Sicarii raided Ein-Gedi, a nearby Jewish settlement, and killed seven hundred of its inhabitants. They then modified some of the structures they found there which included a building that was modified to function as a synagogue facing Jerusalem, though it may in fact have been a synagogue to begin with, although it did not contain a mikvah or the benches found in other early synagogues. It is one of the oldest synagogues in the region. In AD 72, the Roman governor of Iudaea, Lucius Flavius Silva, led Roman legion X Fretensis, a number of auxiliary units and Jewish prisoners of war, totalling some fifteen thousand troops, to lay siege to the nine hundred and sixty people in Masada. The Roman legion surrounded Masada and built a circumvallation wall, before commencing construction of a siege ramp against the western face of the plateau," the old man explained.

"Yes...that is near to where the water station is now and where I have been many times," the Hospitaller interrupted, excitement in his voice.

The old man smiled before continuing.

"The Romans moved thousands of tons of stones and beaten earth to make the siege ramp yet not once did the Sicarii attempt to counterattack the besiegers during this process, which is highly unusual from accounts of other sieges of the revolt. When the ramp was completed in the spring of AD 73, nearly three months into the siege, a giant siege tower with a batter-ing ram was constructed and moved laboriously up the completed ramp, while the Romans assaulted the wall, discharging a volley of blazing torches against one of the walls made of timber. This finally allowed the Romans to breach the fortress on April the sixteenth, AD 73," the old man detailed then paused. "But when the Romans entered the fortress, they found it to be a citadel of death for all of the Jewish rebels had set the buildings on fire, except the food storerooms, and had committed mass suicide, declaring a glorious death ...preferable to a life of infamy."

"That is madness...I thought 'twas a sin to commit suicide?" Ayleth remarked.

"It is...but they got around that. But as to why they did it...well, some argue that they hoped that all of their nation beyond the Euphrates would join together with them to raise an insurrection, but in the end there were only nine hundred and sixty Jewish Zealots who fought the Roman army at Masada. When these Zealots were trapped on top of Masada with nowhere to run, Josephus tells us that the Zealots believed 'it was by the will of God, and by necessity, that they are to die.' Some say that two women, who survived the suicide by hiding inside a cistern along with five children, repeated Eleazar ben Ya'ir's exhortations to his followers, prior to the mass suicide, verbatim to the Romans. Though to recall such a thing word for word is debatable and most probably a later addition. But they are quoted as saying something like this. 'Since we long ago resolved never to be servants to the Romans, nor to any other than to God Himself, Who alone is the true and just Lord of mankind, the time is now come that obliges us to make that resolution true in practice. We were the very first that revolted, and we are the last to fight against them; and I cannot but esteem it as a favour that God has granted us, that it is still in our power to die bravely, and in a state of freedom'. But as you say, Ayleth, because Judaism prohibits suicide, Josephus reported that the defenders had drawn lots and killed each other in turn, down to the last man, who would be the only one to actually take his own life. Josephus says that Eleazar ordered his men to destroy everything except the foodstuffs to show that the defenders retained the ability to live, and so had chosen death over slavery. Josephus only writes of only one palace, yet I can tell you that there were in fact two palaces on the site. Some still argue that the whole suicide event is fictitious and that they fought hard to the last man, and that is why the grain stores were still intact. But whatever the truth, the siege of Masada is often revered by Jews as a symbol of Jewish heroism for a heroic 'last stand'. It symbolises the courage of the warriors of Masada, the strength they showed when they were able to hold out for almost three years, and their choice of death over slavery in their struggle against an aggressive empire. Others, however, see it as a case of Jewish radicals refusing to compromise, resorting instead to suicide and the murder of their families, both prohibited by Rabbinic Judaism. There is also some discussion of Masada's defenders, and whether they were the heroic hard core of the great Jewish revolt against Rome, or just a gang of killers who became victims of a last Roman mopping-up operation. This is why it is so important to establish facts, so that later generations will know and understand the truth."[42]

"Can I ask a question, not about Masada, please?" Ayleth asked.

"Of course," the old man replied.

"If Reynald knew and believed in those parchments, is it possible that Gerard did likewise, and that is why he was so intent on retrieving whatever parchments he was really after...and did he believe in the bloodline thing and knew of Paul's, so consequently his brother Stewart's too?"

"A very good question, Ayleth...and yes, Gerard was more than aware of the parchments and others he wished to obtain. He was also more than aware of Reynald's supposed true bloodline and was in part one of the reasons why he was so prepared to follow him, despite his apparent low status...it is also why he rushed Stewart to his position as the Gonfanier standard bearer so quickly."

"And what happened to Stewart all the while Paul was in Jerusalem?" Ayleth asked as her face went red.

"Stewart...he spent most of his time either training, doing vespers, repairing his equipment and more training. He could not help but question Gerard's motives at times and he
felt very uncomfortable when they went out on several unauthorised raiding missions. Don't
get me wrong, Stewart did not just follow blindly and he did question Gerard on more than
one occasion, but as he viewed Stewart as more than just another Templar, he accepted his
comments and often answered them, usually with much more tact than he afforded his other
subordinates...but that is the power of belief and suggestion," the old man explained.

"What do you mean?" Simon asked.

"If Gerard did not believe for one moment in the validity of either Reynald's claims about
his true origins or the information as written and depicted within the parchments he had
seen, he would not have given Stewart a second look. But Gerard did believe in them. He did
not fully understand them, but he believed in them."

"And what of Taqi then? Is that him gone then from this tale?" the wealthy tailor asked.

"Taqi...no he has not gone from this tale. He did very much the same as Stewart. His
days, and nights, being spent in prayer, meditation and training...both physical and mental
training!"

"And Theodoric...did he manage to get out of his obligations to the Knights of Lazarus?"
Gabirol asked.

"And the stables beneath the mosque...I wish to know about them too," the farrier interjected abruptly.

"And what about Paul meeting up with Saladin's brother...what happened there then?"
Simon asked.

The old man smiled at them all.

"I shall explain all," he said softly and interlocked his fingers together and rested his
hands upon the table.

Jerusalem, Kingdom of Jerusalem, July 1179

Paul went to open the large double doors, but the house squire quickly rushed past
him and opened the door fully. He smiled and bowed as Paul stepped past him and
out into the bright blue morning sun. The street was empty of people. Theodoric
followed him putting his face inside his large hat to hide his tired and hung over
eyes. He tripped slightly on the large stone step as Count Henry grabbed him from
behind to steady him. He laughed seeing how ill Theodoric looked. Brother Jakelin
followed them out tying his sword belt up, pulling it in as hard as he could.

"Too much rich food...I am getting fat!" he joked as he struggled to engage the
pin in his belt.

"No...just getting old," Theodoric said in a dry voice rubbing his hat into his face.

"Gentlemen, I trust you slept well? I have duties to attend with our King and
Queen this hour but I am free again this eve if you are willing to continue our
discussions?" Count Henry asked just as several carts stacked with fresh bread
wheeled past them.

"If I have been relieved of my obligations...I shall be free this eve...if not, I shall
see you in another life," Theodoric half moaned as he waved his hand and started to
walk away following the carts. He stumbled but continued walking. "Paul...Come!"

Count Henry and Brother Jakelin both laughed at the sight of Theodoric walking away clearly still worse for wear after drinking too much.

"If you will excuse me...I think he may just need me for assistance," Paul remarked, gave a quick wave of his right hand, and ran off toward Theodoric. Once he had caught up, he placed his arm around him to steady him. "Theo...do you know where it is we are heading?"

Theodoric with his eyes half closed pointed with his finger down the road and just kept walking.

"Just keep an eye out for a large green sign that says 'The Military and Hospitaller Order of Saint Lazarus of Jerusalem'...or was it 'Ordo Militaris et Hospitalis Sancti Lazari Hierosolymitani'? Oh dear...I cannot remember...but we shall find it," he replied, his voice still dry.

"So what exactly is this Order and how come you volunteered to serve with them?" Paul asked as they stepped down a flight of wide stone steps that led to a long path.

"Like I said before, when I fell ill, I believed I had leprosy...and all knights who catch the disease from any Order may serve their time within the ranks of the Knights of Lazarus...'tis an order of chivalry originally founded as a leper hospital just after 1098 by the Crusaders of this Kingdom of Jerusalem. It was established purely to treat leprosy, its knights originally all being lepers themselves. Even King Baldwin the Fourth himself is a knight of this Order, well, he is certainly assisted by it," Theodoric started to explain, his voice beginning to clear. "They have a slight financial issue...as in not enough funds and that is why they wish to secure my services, which I agreed to. And as you know, being a former Templar myself, and sorry for keeping that from you by the way, I am entitled to join them." He paused as he looked around to get his bearings. He saw the large outer wall of the city a short distance away, pointed toward it, and started walking again. "Just keep your eyes out for knights wearing bright green habits with white mantles and a green Maltese Cross upon it...then we shall be close."

Paul helped steady Theodoric as they walked down hill towards a building adorned with two large white flags with green Maltese Crosses upon them.

"I think I can see where we need to go," Paul commented and ushered Theodoric towards the building.

"You do know, Paul, that one day, anything medicinal will have a ruddy great green cross on it...I know this for I have seen it," Theodoric stated as if fact. "And no not in a drunken stupor as I don't touch the stuff these days...except for last night."

"That probably explains why you feel so bad today."

"Most definitely...but if I walk away from here today, do not tell Lucy I was like this or my life is over," Theodoric joked and cracked a smile almost painfully. "You know, these knights...they dedicate themselves to two ideals, to aid those suffering from leprosy and the defence of the Christian faith. The order was initially founded as a leper hospital outside the city walls but hospitals dependent on the Jerusalem hospital have now been established all across the Holy Land, notably in Acre, and also Europe. It became militarised due to the large numbers of Templars and Hospitallers sent to the leper hospitals for treatment. They have four classes of members...brothers, knights, clerics and donors. Well I certainly won't be a donor," Theodoric laughed as they approached the main entrance doors. He stood still with his hands placed upon his hips and looked toward the doors just as one slowly opened up. Unlike the other Orders, there were no guards outside this building. "If I am not out within the hour...you will be travelling back to Kerak without me," he then said in all seriousness.

"Of course you will be out...won't you?" Paul asked suddenly feeling alarmed.

Without any further words, Theodoric just walked forwards, stepped up the single stone slab at the entrance and entered the building, his figure disappearing into the blackness of the building as if being swallowed. Utterly surprised, Paul just froze and looked on as the door shut closed. After a few minutes, Paul looked around. The street was empty apart from the lone figure of what looked like a very old woman hunched over sat some distance away. Paul suddenly felt concerned that he would not see Theodoric again. He had kept things from him, which had caused him to doubt his integrity, but he could not help but admire and respect him. Then he felt a shiver of cold pass over him momentarily and just for a brief moment he felt as if Firgany was beside him. That thought alone jogged his memory back to La Rochelle when both his father and Firgany had taken him and Taqi inside the small chapel to explain about their planned move to Alexandria but also the parchments Niccolas had compiled. He instantly recalled Firgany's comments about a good friend they had let down whom he now knew to be Theodoric. 'We once had a good friend who understood how the charts work. A brilliant man; a friend we let down and to our eternal shame, did not understand him nor pay heed to what he showed us. We shall not make that same mistake again.' Firgany's words echoed in his mind. If he did not come out after an hour, Paul resolved to enter the building and, if needs be, drag him out himself. He could not and would not lose Theodoric to the Order, he vowed. He looked around the deserted street, saw a circular wooden bench that surrounded a lone tree in the shade so made his way to sit upon it. As he sat down and rested his head back against the trunk of the tree, he glimpsed the old woman further down the street look his way and begin to stand up. He closed his eyes with the intention of feigning being asleep in case she started to talk to him or beg. He had nothing he could give her. He then felt guilty for feeling so selfish and opened his eyes again, but she was already gone from view. He looked up and down the street and at the small pathway that intersected it, but he could not see where she had gone. Bemused, he rested his head back against the tree and closed his eyes still tired from the previous late night.

ဆာ ၶ

"Paul...Paul," a woman's voice whispered softly. He blinked and tried to open his eyes. At first he thought it was the brightness of the sun but the light all around him did not hurt his eyes. A beautiful dark haired woman stood before him crouching forwards, her hands resting upon her knees. She smiled at him, her eyes wide and glistening. She looked serene and her skin almost white. Confused, Paul tried to sit up but she quickly rested her right hand upon his chest and shook her head no. "You wanted to know who I am...so here I stand before you," she said very softly, her voice gentle. Paul frowned. The beautiful woman smiled again and stood up straight and looked down at him. "I can but only show myself like this for a short time...and then only to a very few people. You and Theodoric being such persons."

"Theo!" Paul called out alarmed wondering how long he had been gone.

"Relax...he will be out soon," she smiled and looked at Paul with such a feminine and gentle manner, he felt almost beguiled by her presence. "His obligations are revoked. And you need not ask of him about me any more. But tell him not you have seen me as I am...for it will do him much harm."

 3 – 26

"Then why...why do you present yourself to me now?" Paul asked and tried to look around but could only see whiteness. He frowned, puzzled, which made the woman laugh softly.

"Because we need you to safeguard that which cannot fall into man's hands...at this time. We will show you some things...to inspire you and guide you, but you, as the navigator, must steer a ship of many souls. But it is a ship like no other for she is mother earth herself. You will understand in time, but for now, you must take Percival and find the place beneath and beyond the well of souls. Then you will see and glimpse but a fraction of what you must do,' she smiled and then began to change before his very eyes.

As she started to change before his eyes, images flashed up of what looked like a map. Directions being burnt into the image. He saw a Temple beautifully lit up by the setting sun. He knew it was the Temple of Solomon as he looked down upon it and travelled around it like a bird flying. Then he felt his head rush with a falling sensation as he felt himself dive beneath the temple. He saw a large rock, images of what appeared to be a man being led by tall beings of light into a large wheel-less chariot made of burnished silver and steel with copper lines, the top and bottom appearing a matt black. The whole image coalesced into a ball of light and shot up vertically and vanished in a flash. A carved symbol of a circle in the manner of a Celtic pattern beneath dirt and sand flashed brilliantly as if lit up by glowing molten gold made him jerk his head backwards. The woman's white flowing robes and bright blue shawl started to fade, darker and older, just as her skin aged rapidly, horribly almost. The air about them started to warm up and Paul felt sick and dizzy. His eyes blurred and as they refocused, the old woman from La Rochelle stood before him smiling with a crazed look upon her face. She was bent over and frail looking. She smiled revealing blackened and broken teeth just as the young girl who accompanied her ran up beside her and looked at Paul.

"I told you...they watch you...always," she said in her deep gravelly voice.

Paul went to stand but his legs were numb. It was only then that he noticed many people in the street going about their business, children stood nearby looking at Paul quizzically, the sun now high in the midday sky.

"Hey, why...why do you do this? How do you do this...is this magic?" Paul demanded and again tried to stand.

"Sit, for you will not walk until we are gone. Remember, magic is just but the higher understanding of nature and, like you, I too am just a guide. I appear like this as no one gives me a second look. Do not tell Theodoric of what I have shown you...but simply say you no longer have questions about me...and mention my name, Aethyr, and tell him I have restarted that which we did not finish. He will understand, but not how you saw me young." The young girl beside the old woman outstretched her hand and touched Paul's leg. Instantly he felt a sharp pain shoot through both his legs and up his spine. The little girl just smiled and stood back. He could move his toes. As he looked at the old woman again, she nodded, turned and walked away. "When the light returns to the dome, that marks the beginning...," she said raising her hand pointing a single finger upwards and slowly walked away with the little girl holding her other hand.

Paul tried to stand again, but his feet hurt, now that he could feel them, but his legs were still numb. He sat and watched as the old woman and young girl disappeared amongst the crowd of people and carts that now filled the street. As he strained to see them, Theodoric placed his hand upon his shoulder hard, making him jump. Paul looked up at him, Theodoric immediately seeing the clear expression upon his face being one of confusion.

"You all right?" Theodoric asked.

"Theo...huh...yes," he replied and looked away back towards the direction the old woman had taken. "I think so," he answered and then felt his legs come back again. He smiled and stood up slowly. "I...I must have fallen asleep."

"Truly, for I did not expect you to still be here. I said an hour and go if I was not out by then. 'Twas five hours past," Theodoric explained and looked at Paul carefully seeing that he was clearly dazed. "Come...I think you have been in the sun too long."

Paul rapidly placed his left hand over the left side of his face as a bolt of pain shot through his ear and he winced in agony. He looked at Theodoric alarmed. The intense pain that shot through his head was unbearable and he collapsed to his knees with his hands over both of his ears. Theodoric knelt down beside him to support him.

"Do you need a hand there?" Thomas asked as he suddenly appeared beside them with his men and Percival, who formed a circle around them against the crowd as they pushed by.

Paul tried to look up but the pain was intense. Theodoric nodded yes. As Thomas and Percival went to help lift him Paul raised his hand to keep away, his teeth gritted, his ears ringing. He took a deep breath as Thomas looked at Theodoric, concerned.

"We must get him out of the sun," Theodoric explained.

"Alisha!" Paul called out, his eyes rolling and then collapsed unconscious.

Crac de Moab, Oultrajordain, Kingdom of Jerusalem, July 1179

Alisha walked slowly carrying Arri with Princess Stephanie beside her. The walls of the inner courtyard reflected the sun in bright contrast to the clear blue sky. Tenno followed them at a discreet distance. Alisha took in a deep sudden breath, her eyes widening as if in shock. She started to lose her balance. Princess Stephanie quickly grabbed Arri as Alisha collapsed to the floor clutching her chest, breathless.

Tenno rushed over, knelt behind her and supported her back. Alisha fought to catch her breath. She looked up at Princess Stephanie.

"Paul," she said weakly, then fainted into Tenno's arms.

Tenno lifted her up and looked at Princess Stephanie as she cradled Arri.

"Quickly...take her to the infirmary," Princess Stephanie said pointing with her head where he should go.

ℬ ℭ

Alisha found herself surrounded by oak trees. She was wearing just a short white dress and the bee necklace around her neck. The trees seemed to form a long pathway as they stretched over, their branches meeting to make an arched over pathway. The path was almost white and felt soft to walk upon. She knew that Paul was up ahead somewhere and needed her. She started to run confused as to where she was. Beams of sunlight filtered down through the massive oak trees as she ran more frantically. Then in the distance she saw him lying on his side, his sword stuck in the ground beside him. She froze momentarily as she looked around, a sense of panic beginning to overtake her. She ran for Paul, reaching him within moments. Her eyes wide in panic she looked him all over to see if he was injured but she could not see any wounds. A single black rose lay upon the ground beside him, he wore just a single one-piece white robe and was barefoot. Quickly she knelt down beside him and lifted his head to rest upon her lap as she positioned her legs so his back rested upon her in a comfortable position. She stroked his face and brushed his hair back. He looked peaceful and asleep, but she could not wake him. She looked up and all around trying to understand where they were. "'Tis a dream... that is all,' she told herself as the branches upon the large oak trees swayed gently in the breeze. As she looked at them, only then did she see that the undersides of the leaves were a soft white colour. She had never seen such beautiful trees in all her life, she thought. Some reflected hues of yellow from the sun shining through the branches. A set of standing stones started to come into focus a short distance away within a circular enclosure. A sense of peace and calm washed over her as she tried to make sense of what was happening. She knew she had handed Arri to Princess Stephanie, but that was the last thing she could remember.

"Fear not, child...you are perfectly safe," a gentle but authoritative voice spoke.

Alisha looked around her frantically but could not see anyone except the oak trees that seemed to almost glow in a yellow and gold aura the longer she looked. She stroked Paul's forehead hoping he would wake up.

"Who are you? Where are we...are you God?" she called out loudly.

"You need not speak loudly...and no, I am not God, though many have supposed I was a god," the voice answered.

"Then where are we? Are we dead?" she asked looking about herself still. "Is this a trick?"

"My child. There are many forms of existence and many forms of life beyond your world as you understand it. Some have called us angels...some have called us watchers...some even call us devils. But we are simply people, like you from a long long time ago, who managed to overcome the physical bounds of this realm. We are your forefathers."

"What?" Alisha asked utterly puzzled and frowned hard. She looked down at Paul and saw the black rose. "And this," she exclaimed as she lifted the rose up and held it high to show. "A black rose...that is for death."

"Again, my child...a black rose does not mean death at all. Quite the opposite."

"This is trickery!"

"Ailia...you know in your heart this is not trickery. Why should miracles and angels appearing to people be exclusively confined to a history long since past?"

"You know my real name?" Alisha asked bemused.

"Of course. We know of what you are...and that is why we meet with you here, now, in this manner and form."

"What form for I see only trees?"

"Ask Paul when you next meet for he knows the sacred meanings and symbolism of trees," the voice answered but then paused. "We have called you here to offer you some guidance and advice, should you choose to listen, and understand. Do not simply listen in order to reply...listen to understand. Can you do that?"

Alisha looked around as the trees seemed to lean in closer. She felt very calm and at peace now.

"Is my father here...am I able to see him?"

"As I said, there are many realms of existence...he is not of this one, but he waits for you and watches over you just as he promised."

Alisha felt a lump swell in her throat and she could feel the tears well in her eyes. She rested her head lower and kissed Paul on the forehead.

"Why does Paul not wake?"

"He is presently poorly...but he will be fine. His presence ventures near to that which he once knew previously. But in the realm you inhabit, his physical senses cannot perceive it but his soul tries to. It is but a safety mechanism. He shall awake and remember none of this, but you shall."

"And can I tell of this? And just why exactly am I here?"

"You both experienced the vision of the ruined cathedral...and you saw it rebuild itself. As you sit here with Paul surrounded by beauty and peace, he sees another set of things that will come to pass. A long way in the future...terrible things that man can avoid...or bring upon himself."

"But if you can foresee these things, why can you not intervene and stop them?"

"Young child...we tried that and instead many of us became ensnared within your realms again. Some called us fallen angels...but if we forced you to be good, that negates entirely your individual right to free choice and freedom of will, the right of free agency. Your kind must choose to be good and love by your own choice...not forced to do so, which some of our kind tried to do. You know of them collectively as a single entity...as Shayton, Satan or Lucifer."

"But why us...why not someone else better suited?" Alisha pleaded.

"Because as spirit, you both chose, voluntarily, to undertake this life and this path. It is how and why you both recognised each other and love each other as you do. But there will come a time when you have to make some hard decisions and choices, and when that time comes...you must remember this day."

"Why can you not come down and tell people this...yourselves?"

"We have tried that before also. But can you imagine if we were to come down and walk openly amongst you again, those that would resent us would try to kill us,

285

those that envied us would try and take our tools and misuse them for destructive purposes instead. Imagine if we gave someone like Reynald a power tool that could wipe out an entire army in a single blinding flash, he would use it at once without hesitation. That is why we keep our distance and will do so until enough people decide they want a different and more peaceful and meaningful existence together. Only then will we again walk openly amongst you...for you are all but children of us and from us."

"I am surely dreaming this?"

Paul heard Alisha say this and he tried to move his head to look at her but he simply could not move nor open his eyes. He sensed that he was lying upon her but the images flashing across his mind were intense. The images and emotions that flashed across his vision were unlike the dreams he had so often had before. These images showed cities unlike anything he could imagine. Tall buildings that appeared as if they were made of glass stood hundreds of feet tall. Horseless chariots with people inside sped by in a blur. He looked on as darkness enveloped the city as many large fireballs streaked slowly across the dark reddish sky. People around him just looked up bewildered as the sun appeared to darken. As it did, another sun like disc loomed into view in the sky. Suddenly Percival stood beside him but dressed in a strange robe. "We failed!" he said above the rising noise and increasing wind. Alisha stroked Paul's forehead again and kissed him gently, sensing he was having a bad dream as he tried to move his head.

"What is wrong with him?" she asked and looked up again.

"He sees a glimpse of the future. That is all we can tell you."

"Is that what this black rose is for?"

"No...the black rose is symbolic within a code. To most people it signifies death, or hatred. They also believe it means farewell but does in fact represent rejuvenation or rebirth. Ask the one you know as Theodoric...he can explain."

Paul tried to turn again as he heard Alisha speak but he could also hear Thomas and one of his men arguing about something off in the distance. As the ringing in his ears intensified, he suddenly found himself looking down upon what he knew to be the Temple of Solomon shortly after it had been completed. He could see the bright colours painted upon it and the Tabernacle where the so-called Ark of the Covenant was held. He tried to look closer but he felt as if an invisible cord was holding him back. He blinked briefly and the entire image changed to that of an even older and grander yet more simple looking building. He shook his head as he somehow recalled the building as familiar. Without warning he found himself being drawn towards it fast. He braced himself as he thought he was about to hit the floor hard, but instead passed straight through it. He shot past what looked like an ornate wooden box with four gold angels at each corner. Three men stood nearby dressed in long white robes and bright blue sashes. Each wore an elaborate apron and breast plate that had twelve segments each of a different material. Two had pure white hair whilst the third had what looked like red hair. They reminded him of the tall old man who had saved him and Taqi in La Rochelle. They wore round metal rimmed glass lenses upon their faces and were all putting on some heavy looking sheepskin coloured overgarments. As Paul fell beneath the ground they stood upon, he found himself in a cave with a large rock inside. His mind raced as he saw what looked like a large white caravan appear to hover above it with no horses. The harder he looked, the more like a large egg it appeared. He tried to rub his eyes and focus but could not move just as two very tall individuals stepped into view. They wore an all in one body suit the like of which he had never seen before. Their heads were covered in the same material and their eyes were covered in what looked like a wrap around black reflective headband. Then a third, shorter, man, dressed in a single goat skin robe, stepped out and directly onto the rock. He fell to his knees as if in prayer. He then stood up smiling but as he looked toward Paul, the two far larger men looked his way. Paul suddenly fell downward again into an even bigger underground area that was cavernous. He jumped with a fright as a hand touched his shoulder. He swung around to see Percival stood there smiling. 'Well of Souls' he said without actually speaking. Confused Paul looked around the large underground room they were standing in. He wanted to ask Percival what he was doing there but he could not speak.

"Learn the secrets of this place and its connection with the sacred secrets hidden within what you know as the 'Book of Revelation'...for as a navigator of people, it will show you the secrets of the entire world you exist upon...and a gateway!" Paul and Alisha both heard the voice speak.

Suddenly Paul was no longer resting upon Alisha but was standing between two rough stone columns with another stone lintel across the top. All around the stone doorway was white light. Inside the stone doorway a light bluish, almost green light emanated softly but it looked like water. Paul looked back at Alisha, smiled at her, raised his right hand in a slight wave then stepped through the doorway and vanished.

ᴓ ᴓ

Alisha sat up fast and gasped, clutching her chest.

"Paul!" she yelled out in panic as confusion registered across her face.

Sister Lucy quickly sat on the bed beside her and clasped her free hand reassuringly as Princess Stephanie sat in a chair near to the large ornate stone window. She was gently rocking Arri. Tenno stepped into view looking at her, concerned.

"'Tis okay, dear child. You are safe. You simply fainted in the heat," Sister Lucy said softly.

Alisha looked around the large room she was in. It was Stephanie's bedroom chamber. She ran her fingers through her hair, which felt matted and greasy.

"Paul...I must go and see Paul...he is not well," she explained emotionally.

"My young lady, you are in no fit state to go anywhere. You are exhausted. We brought you here directly from the infirmary as we could not wake you. You have been asleep now for some five hours straight," Sister Lucy explained and gently pushed her shoulder to get her to lie down.

"No...you do not understand. The black rose...and the doorway, 'tis a gateway and he passes through it already," Alisha exclaimed alarmed and shaking. She paused as she rested back upon her elbows and looked down the bed. She was soaked in sweat but felt cold. "Five hours...that cannot be?" she remarked shaking her head, puzzled.

"Five hours. And we had to get Arri to feed off of one of the wet nurses I am afraid for we did not know how long you would be asleep," Stephanie explained.

287

"You were dreaming...that is all," Sister Lucy remarked and wiped her forehead with a cool damp cloth.

"No, 'twas not just a dream. Paul needs me...I must go to Jerusalem. I must!"

"Listen to me...we can have a message to Jerusalem and back within hours using the heliographs. Wait until we have a response. But either way, you are in no fit state to be travelling anywhere," Princess Stephanie explained rocking Arri gently. She looked across towards the large arched windows as sounds of trumpets echoed throughout the castle forecourt. "Do not be alarmed...'tis just the trumpets announcing the yearly tournament."

Alisha lay back into the pillows, sighed heavily and bit her thumbnail nervously as she thought of Paul. She looked at Sister Lucy hoping for some sign of reassurance. She simply feigned a brave smile and wiped her head again. Tenno looked at her.

"I would listen to what they tell you...and I must leave these chambers now that you are awoken lest we upset the likes of Brother Matthew...and if needs be, I shall depart for Jerusalem upon the content of any reply from there later this day," he explained, bowed his head and left the room.

Port of La Rochelle, France, Melissae Inn, spring 1191

"I just wish somebody would tell me exactly why a patch of land, land that could be any-where in this world, is so special. Can you tell us why and what is so special about the place and the holy shrines?" Peter asked.

"What is so special about Jerusalem...and the main area of the holy shrines? That is a big question so let me begin by saying that despite its appearance, the dome, called Qubbat as-Sakhrah in Arabic, was not a mosque but a shrine built over the rock from which the Prophet Muhammad is said to have ascended into Heaven."

2 – 4

"Ah like the image Paul saw in his dream of that man in the wingless flying chariot thing you mentioned?" Simon interrupted enthusiastically.

The old man nodded yes.

"You see, that is where I have a problem. A flying wingless chariot...and a voice speaking to both Alisha and Paul in a dream," the wealthy tailor remarked.

"Why...you are all too accepting when you read the Bible about such events as a matter of fact and history, yet when it happens in these times, you dismiss them as being delusions, hallucinations or the imaginings of a mad person. Do you think that a god's actions and miracles are exclusively consigned to the past only?" the old man asked patiently.

"Does seem a bit too farfetched though you have to admit," the Genoese sailor commented as he looked at the others around the table.

"I have said it before, and I shall keep saying it...all that happened previously as recounted within all the major religious books is based upon factual events...but simplified and con-densed into a format that we can comprehend and understand. And what seems like magic, or a miracle, will one day be shown to be that of the making of greater minds, the Elohim, the gods as written about," the old man replied.

"I believe it," Ayleth said softly. *"So please continue."*

"Then in that case, if just one person believes, that is all that is required," the old man smiled before continuing. *"There is a chamber located under the destroyed Jewish temple that still remains beneath a bedrock outcropping and is of the utmost significance to all the three major monotheistic religions. It is like a secret chamber! Some of you may have heard of it as mentioned within the Bible as the 'The Well of Souls'? It is known to Jews as the Temple Mount and to Muslims as the Noble Sanctuary, reputed to contain the fabled and elusive Ark of the Covenant. This is the sacred vessel that, according to biblical account, contained the original Ten Commandment tablets that God gave to Moses at Mount Sinai, though as you shall learn, it was in fact Jabal al Lawz, as the ancient Israelites wandered the desert where Moses saw and spoke with God, but God as he was simply understood and recounted during that period of time. The Well of Souls, located below the natural cave under the rock upon which Jewish tradition says Abraham prepared to sacrifice his son Isaac, purely to mark out its importance, but in Islamic tradition where Muhammad ascended to heaven. If you ever manage to visit the cave beneath the rock, and stamp your feet, it elicits a resounding hollow echo...but no one has ever been recorded seeing or entering this alleged chamber."*

"Let me guess...Paul does," Simon interjected, smiling broadly.

"Perhaps this tale is becoming too predictable for you?" the Templar shot back with a look that made Simon feel awkward.

"No...but...but I bet he does, doesn't he?" Simon replied defensively.

"He does indeed, young Simon," the old man answered. *"And yes I shall explain that shortly."*

"Alisha said something about a gateway. What did she mean?" Ayleth asked.

"That I shall also explain shortly, but for now, understand that there are many cases and incidents whereby sacred doors and pools of water open that lead to other realms...you will find stories and myths about them wherever you travel. And beneath Jerusalem, especially Temple Mount itself, it is rife with a network of some forty-five cisterns, chambers, tunnels, and caves. Historic references to the Ark of the Covenant were rare following the establishment of the First Temple, and it disappeared entirely from the record by the time of King Herod around 40 BC. Some argue that the Ark was possibly demolished during the Babylonian destruction of the First Temple in 586 BC or was spirited away and hidden during the invasion. It might also have been destroyed or stolen when the Roman legions invaded Jerusalem in AD 70. According to biblical accounts, the Ark was constructed of wood and coated with sheets of gold. There is a general agreement that, at least at one point, it was indeed hidden in a chamber under the Temple Mount, perhaps in the Well of Souls. But there are also accounts of identical Well of Souls being in Egypt and many various types of Arks. For each Ark was in fact a powerful tool and communications device. And in time, people will remember this..." [43]

"You said that Moses spoke with God in Jabal al laws or something...what do you mean?" Gabirol asked.

"Jabal al Lawz...'tis a high mountain with a plateau...and when man finally gets around to studying the place properly, they will see all the evidence as detailed within the Bible."

"I heard that Jerusalem is the very place where God himself took the dust to make man, that is why it is so important a place," the Hospitaller commented.

"That is true...for Jewish tradition holds that it is the site where God gathered the dust to create Adam and where Abraham nearly sacrificed his son Isaac to prove his faith. But as you will learn, that story is but symbolic and allegorical too. King Solomon, according

to the Bible, built the First Temple of the Jews on this mountaintop around 1000 BC only to have it torn down four hundred years later by the Babylonian king Nebuchadnezzar, who sent many Jews into exile. In the first century BC Herod expanded and refurbished a Second Temple built by Jews who had returned after their banishment. It is here that, according to the Gospel of John, Jesus Christ lashed out against the money changers. The Roman general Titus exacted revenge against Jewish rebels, sacking and burning the Temple in AD 70. But among Muslims, the Temple Mount is called Haram al-Sharif, the Noble Sanctuary, as I have already said. They believe it was here that the Prophet Muhammad ascended to the 'Divine Presence' on the back of a winged horse, some equate it with the mythical Pegasus winged horse. The Miraculous Night Journey, commemorated by one of Islam's architectural triumphs, the Dome of the Rock shrine. A territorial prize occupied or conquered by a long succession of people from Jebusites, Israelites, Babylonians, Greeks, Persians, Romans, Byzantines, early Muslims, and now Crusaders. Temple Mount has seen more momentous historical events than perhaps any other thirty-five acres in the world. Today the Temple Mount, a walled compound within the City of Jerusalem, is the site of two magnificent structures...the Dome of the Rock to the north and the Al-Aqsa Mosque to the south. In the southwest stands the Western Wall, a remnant of the Second Temple and the holiest site in Judaism. Some three hundred feet from the Al-Aqsa Mosque, in the southeast corner of the compound, a wide plaza leads to underground vaulted archways that have been known for centuries as Solomon's Stables, where the Templars now keep their horses. It is thirty feet tall and can hold a thousand horses." [44]

"But how does the place have such an effect upon Paul to make him feel ill and pass out... and Alisha many miles away?" Gabirol asked.

"As I said before...we are all connected to the earth we live upon, some more sensitive to it than others. And in Jerusalem, there lays a Gateway...a sort of spiritual doorway is the only way I can explain it. It was also once a great place of learning and healing, but that was before what we call history even began."

"And Paul and Alisha's blood somehow makes them sensitive to those forces in the area?" Simon asked, his face strained as he looked at Sarah, expecting her to comment.

"Yes Simon...yes indeed. But Alisha and Paul had a deep connection that was increased through their act of love making. The very essence of the pure energy that makes their souls can interlink during such times. It is why you should choose your partner wisely, for you can exchange emotions and feelings that can change the other person," the old man explained.

"Poor Princess Stephanie is all I can say then," Sarah remarked shaking her head.

"Yes," the old man said and paused briefly. "But, like a mother's deep knowing of her children, who can sense when something is wrong...a mother's instinct, Alisha and Paul were so closely linked, as the dreams demonstrated, that they could sense when the other was ill or in harm's way, though they did not fully understand or accept that then and it was the image of the black rose that so alarmed Alisha."

"Yeah, I don't think I understood that part. Can you tell me again...please?" Simon asked as Sarah shook her head.

"Of course. A black rose means overcoming a long hardship, war or on a journey from which one does not expect to return. In essence it means 'pure devotion' since a true black rose is impossible to produce. People use what you call the tarot card of death, yet it is depicted as a white rose symbolising purity, reverence and humility. The number XIII of the Tarot Cards is the card of Death and its banner contains a white rose, symbolising a long-standing symbol of purity, promise, and beauty. In the case of the Death card, this rose represents the promise of new beginnings. We must also take the thorns into consideration with the promise of new hope, we may have to endure a few stinging thorns that symbolise painful ordeals along the way. Such is the way of life. Now, the opposite of a white rose is a black rose. This may mean the opposite of what the white rose signifies, meaning impurity or immorality, revenge, and ugliness. Unlike the promise of new beginnings, the black rose may say otherwise, as signifying no return, or no hope. Of course, no black rose is actually featured in the tarot cards but Alisha in her exhausted state feared the latter aspects only."

"So I take it Paul recovered?" the farrier asked.

"Yes, of course. Though to be awoken to the sounds of Thomas arguing with one of his men, and to discover that he was in fact lying upon a bed within a house of ill repute," the old man explained when Ayleth put her hand up.

"House of ill repute. Does that mean what I think it means?" she asked softly and part embarrassed.

"A whore house!" Simon interjected loudly almost laughing.

"Yes...it does for it was the nearest place Theodoric and Thomas could take Paul out of the sun. Besides, most of Thomas's men were, how shall we say, enjoying the women's company within the house."

"But they are knights...surely not?" Sarah asked shocked.

"Yes, they were knights, but not ones that had sworn any oaths of celibacy...and besides, it was a common practice. In fact there were many women in the Holy Land who went with the express purpose of being what they saw as 'Holy Prostitutes' to ease the woes of the men. They saw it as a form of pilgrimage and an obligation just like knights who saw killing in the name of the Church...so you tell me what is worse, right or wrong?"

"Beating the wool," the Templar commented. "That is the term they used, beating the wool... and I know most men visited the places at least once, even if out of curiosity."

"What...did you then?" Miriam asked looking alarmed.

"No...that I can honestly answer," he replied and took both her hands and quickly kissed them.

"And Percival, he went also...and why was Thomas arguing with one of his men?" Peter asked.

"Yes Percival went with them. He had not known the ways of a woman, but inside, he declined to partake and simply waited. It was as they left, that they saw Theodoric over Paul. As for Thomas, he was arguing with one of his men over payments. One had paid for the company of the prettiest woman, but she had insulted him saying he stank of death and would not let him near her. She part ran the house and was very selective shall we say...and Thomas had to argue with his friend he should not offer all the money he had left but he was adamant."

"My Lord...I know we have a whore house in the town...but...but women who do it as a holy duty...and women who dress and fight as knights. How come we never knew these things?" Sarah asked puzzled.

"'Tis not the sort of thing a priest would shout from the pulpit is it?" Simon remarked.

"And how long did Paul stay there?" Gabirol asked.

"As soon as he was awake, Paul was given some food by the lady of the house, a very beautiful and yes, certainly seductive, woman...and then part carried from the building by Thomas and Theodoric and put upon a horse Percival had fetched. They left the house with Thomas's friend still arguing with the lady and that one day he would have her."

"And did Theodoric get out of his obligation to the Knights of Lazarus?" Ayleth asked.

"Yes he did. But as a goodwill gesture he did agree that from now on he would promise to eat his vegetables properly as having not done so, that was the main reason why he had fallen ill, so perhaps meeting Sister Lucy was literally a life saver for him. You see, there is truth in the Arab proverb, a table without vegetables is like an old man without wisdom... But he agreed he would go to the Port of Acre on their behalf and collect a shipment of horses they had ordered and for the correct fee. He wished to visit Lady Eschiva whom he knew well...she is the wife of Count Raymond of Antioch and she lived there. He would also oversee some orders for sugar from the Templars' sugar mill at Da'uk on the Nahr Kurdaneh, the River Belus south of Acre, and to collect wheat ground there. There were many fields of sugar cane in the region. Paul witnessed many Latin women arrive in Jerusalem via Acre eager to serve their Lord by giving sexual favours to Crusaders...and as our Templar friend here pointed out, they used the term 'beating' or 'working the wool', which is how the crusaders referred to the act of having sex with these women. As Paul was lifted upon the horse to take him back to his room at the Templars' headquarters, he was very surprised to see other horse mounted women ride past ready and eager for battle dressed in full combat armour. He thought he had dreamt them up as the next thing he remembered was when he awoke in bed in the small room he and Theodoric shared," the old man explained.

"Women knights eager for battle...'tis not right," Sarah remarked.

"Trust me...I have seen women fight harder and endure more than most men," the Hospitaller said smiling and looking at Ayleth briefly.

"Did Paul go with Theodoric then or return to Kerak?" Gabirol asked.

"He was exhausted. Brother Jakelin confirmed receipt of a message from Kerak via the heliographs and replied saying Paul was well but would return in several days' time. So whilst Theodoric went to Acre using Paul's horse, Adrastos, Paul remained within the city mainly accompanied by Percival. Count Henry put back their arranged meeting to continue their discussions until a time when Paul felt well enough and Theodoric had returned. But the longer Paul remained there, the stronger the pull to investigate further as the days passed into August, whilst Alisha sensed this as a very real danger.

Chapter 35
Guardians of the Gateways

Jerusalem, Kingdom of Jerusalem, August 1179

Paul looked down upon the small table positioned next to the window. He had drawn several images of what he believed Solomon's temple looked like as seen in his vivid dreams. Outside the evening sky darkened quickly as the last calls to prayer for Muslims echoed out across the nearby compound. He still felt weary and the dizziness in his head never seemed to leave him and the swollen lump behind his left ear remained despite the best efforts of the local Hospitallers. Count Henry and Brother Jakelin visited him several times but only briefly to check upon him whilst Thomas and his men were paid to help with training alongside the Knights Templars acting as opposing forces in tournament style contests. But it was Percival who visited every day and made sure he was okay and had everything he required. He missed Alisha and Arri intensely and vowed that once he had them back in his arms, he would never leave their sides again. He felt as though he had been away from them for an age, far longer than the actual fourteen days he had been absent. He sat himself down and looked out across the city. Feeling sorry for himself almost, he looked at the pictures he had drawn.

Fig. 34:

He pulled the largest one and started to draw in extra details that he recalled from his mind as if standing in front of him it was so clear. He then pulled the image he had drawn of the city walls from across the valley. Percival had tried to talk him out of riding out but Paul needed the change of scenery and he also wanted to be able to show Alisha Jerusalem.

Fig. 35:

Music seemed to float across the evening sky on the gentle breeze that blew. Indistinct music but it sounded soft and harmonious. He looked at the white robe he was wearing as given to him. His sword hung over the head bed post. As he closed his eyes to imagine Alisha, images of the layout and underground system beneath Jerusalem kept flashing in his mind as if to invade his every thought. A passageway entrance at the deepest section of the stables kept on repeating itself. Frustrated at not being able to dismiss the imaging, he stood up fast, surprised at how he did. A smile etched across his face. That was the first time he had been able to move like that since passing out several days earlier. His strength was returning. 'I shall go and see this place,' he told himself as he thought about the passageway images flashing through his mind.

⊗⊂⊗

First Vespers by the Templars had not even been called when Paul stepped out from the main entrance of the Templars' headquarters. Two knights briefly acknowledged him as he walked directly towards the wide sloping paved entrance to the stables. The sky was a dark blue, the sun having not risen fully yet on the horizon. Dressed in the white robe and a brown mantel Brother Jakelin had given him, his sword tied firmly around his waist and carrying a small shoulder satchel containing candles, he walked briskly breathing in the cool morning air. Whatever the images were that kept constantly entering his mind, he determined that he would find out this morning.

Paul waved at two sergeants sat inside a small sentry station, just a wooden box with a bench inside. One stood to challenge him but recognised him and simply waved him through the vaulted entrance. Paul smiled and nodded in acknowledgement as he followed the wide paved pathway that sloped ever deeper underground. He looked at the many horses stabled inside that seemed to stretch away into the distance. It was the largest vaulted building he had ever seen. Large mirrors and polished copper sheets had been placed at various positions that reflected the sun inside the stables but as he walked ever deeper, and with the sun still to rise fully, the darkness grew. He saw another two Templar sergeants and three farriers stood around a wooden boarded off area used as a makeshift blacksmith's. Pails of water were placed everywhere in case of an accidental fire. He removed a small lanthorn, opened it and lit it using a lighting stick from the small furnace fire the blacksmiths were using and closed it again safely. The men barely acknowledged him as he walked past them. When he reached the farthest point he could walk, the darkness was now almost complete, the light from the lanthorn casting long shadows about him. He heard the bellows of the furnace behind him being squeezed and a rattle from the copper piping used to funnel away the smoke to the outside as it started to warm up. The temperature within the large vaulted stables was constant and remained cool whatever the weather outside. Having a blacksmith's furnace inside seemed insane at first, but better than working with heat outside in the fierce summer sun. Plus it was safer having a furnace inside a stone built construction than an exterior wooden one. Paul started to feel around the end wall with his right hand as he held the lanthorn close to the wall looking for any hint of an opening. He knew from what his father and Theodoric had told him that somewhere nearby there was a small opening that led down to where the original nine knights had made their discoveries. That, coupled with his vivid dreams, he knew he was close. But half an hour later he had still not found any opening or markings indicating one, the candle in the lanthorn now almost burnt down. Behind in the distance he could hear more men entering to check upon their horses and saddle up. He knelt down and fumbled as he looked for another candle quickly before his other one burnt out. Suddenly a hand landed upon his shoulder making him jump. Quickly he turned around on his knees to look up.

"Tut tut...need I ask where you are going?" Percival asked, his hands upon his hips looking down at him in silhouette.

"Percy...you nearly gave me heart failure. What are you doing here?" Paul asked and stood up.

"Well, I saw you heading this way...and I knew, just knew you would be trying to follow in the footsteps of those original knights and as your father and Theo did," he replied and paused. "And I knew you would need these," he stated and lifted up three rings of rolled up rope and smiled, his teeth flashed white in the dimming candlelight.

"Thank you...I think," Paul replied, a little puzzled. He had not even considered taking any ropes. "But you do realise that all unauthorised searches are banned?"

"Of course...but what can they do to me? They cannot exactly kick me out of any Order now can they? Besides, you are not the only one who is cursed with strange dreams."

Paul looked at him, bemused.

"Then you will know what I am looking for?"

"No idea...unless it's the entrance, which if I am correct is in the northeastern corner, twenty-one stones in, and three high...or out, but I could be wrong as it was only a dream. I think it was anyway but it is something I have always just known. Does that make sense to you?" Percival explained and asked quietly.

⚔ 4 – 32

"Well...in my world right now, that makes total sense. We may as well start there as it sounds as good a place as any, and it is not here for sure," Paul replied.

Quickly Percival helped Paul light another candle just as the first one flickered out almost. They made their way to the furthest northeastern part of the vault where it was pitch black. No horses were stabled this far in. They had tried lighting the area before but the horses never settled. Both began to try and count the stones but as they were of different sizes and did not follow a straight and level pattern, it proved harder than either had imagined. After using two more candles and more than an hour of searching, they stopped and rested against the wall. Nothing in the stonework gave away any hint of an entrance way. Paul closed his eyes and tried to run through the images from his dreams and what he had drawn. Percival opened a small water bladder and drank a mouthful then offered it to Paul. As he took it, he dropped it, the water immediately spilling out across the hewn cut stone floor slabs. Quickly Paul picked it up and replaced the bung cap. They stood in silence for a moment to listen out and see if anyone had heard the water bladder hit the floor. As they stood in silence, they both distinctly heard drips as the water seeped away and obviously into a space big enough to make a splash sound that echoed as the water hit it beneath them.

"It's beneath us!" Paul whispered excitedly.

"Of course. It did not say it was the stones on a wall...'tis the floor stones! And why are we whispering?" Percival asked.

Both dropped to their knees and started to feel around the edges of the two wet stone tiles. Paul tapped the first one and then the second slab. He tapped the first one again that was three slabs away from the wall.

"That definitely sounds hollow doesn't it?" he said as he tapped it again.

Percival simply nodded yes, his face lit up by the single lanthorn candle. Within moments they had their fingers pushing into the dirt around the stone slab and started to ease it upwards. As soon as Paul managed to get his fingers beneath it, Percival forced his entire hand between the gap and heaved the slab upwards and backwards until it stood vertical. A rush of air blew past them as a small tunnel opened into view beneath them. Paul's heart raced with excitement just as the high pitched whine in his ears increased.

"You first," Percival said motioning with his head to go down whilst holding the slab up.

"No, 'twas your idea to check here, so you go first," Paul replied.

"No...I hate the dark and I am terrified of small spaces. You go," Percival replied.

"You will follow me, yes?" Paul asked as he swung his legs around and into the black hole.

296

"We have no idea of what is down there…but…but if you go first, I shall follow…so long as you have more candles?"

"I do. You can have this and I shall light another," Paul said as he gently eased himself down slowly, expecting to drop into a large tunnel, but his feet touched the bottom enabling him to stand with his head and shoulders above the entrance hole.

"Oh Lord…a small tunnel," Percival remarked, grimacing.

"You do not have to come if you are fearful. I cannot ask that of you."

"Hey…I am terrified…but I shall come with you, you may need me down there," Percival replied in all seriousness, his throat dry.

Paul immediately knelt down carefully and moved on his hands and knees a short way into the small tunnel. He held out the lanthorn to see ahead but all he could see was the stone tunnel curve away into the darkness. Percival climbed down behind him and nudged him he was now ready. Paul could hear Percival breathing heavily behind him and clearly struggling with his fear of confined spaces and he thought he would burst into tears at any moment. Paul was surprised at the total lack of spiders' webs or any sign of life. He was sure he would run into a snake or worse at any moment, but the tunnel had clearly been devoid of any life for many years. The floor of the tunnel was also laid stone with just a trace of fine sand. Scuff marks showed that, at some point, someone else had also crawled along this tunnel. Both began to sweat as the physical exertion began to take its toll and their knees began to hurt. They came to a junction that had another identical tunnel intersect and cross it. Paul looked at the dusting of sand and looked as best he could at which tunnel sections had the sand undisturbed. The tunnel that cut off to his right showed signs of being disturbed. As he moved the lanthorn inside for a closer look, he discovered the wooden remains of what was once a set of bellows. With sweat now dripping down his face, he turned to look at Percival. Percival had his eyes closed tightly grimacing, his elbows shaking. Only then did Paul realise just how terrified he really was.

"Percy…Percy," he said softly. "We can go back if you wish."

"Stuff that…I have come this far…just keep moving and I will be okay," he replied, tension clear in his shaking voice.

Paul looked at Percival thankful he was with him and honoured that, despite his terror, he had followed him in regardless. Percival was wearing his chain mail armour so the effort must have been far greater for him he thought. Slowly Paul squeezed himself around the corner and began to follow the tunnel as it started to descend steeply. Little red dots became visible painted upon the right side at regular intervals. Paul's candle began to burn out. Quickly he opened the lanthorn, replaced the candle and lit it from the last gasps of the previous one. Percival looking on, his eyes now open wide and his face one of almost total terror. Despite the orange glow from the candle he held near, his face looked ashen white. He indicated with his head for Paul to move, quickly. Paul continued to crawl onwards. After fifteen minutes, he saw ahead of them a small opening. As he crawled ever nearer, it became apparent there must be a room behind from the blackness of the square hole. Remnants of a piece of rope lay beside the wall. Just as Paul reached the dark opening, his ears started to ring louder to the point of almost hurting. He looked back at Percival. He shook his head puzzled.

"'Tis a room I think," Paul remarked.

"Good...I need to stand up...and I think I have messed myself," Percival replied.

Paul laughed then tried to cover his mouth and looked at Percival apologetically. Percival let out a nervous laugh then sniffed the air.

"Yes...I have," he remarked then laughed more, his arms shaking uncontrollably as he leant forwards upon them.

Paul laughed but was silently even more impressed and proud of Percival for following him. He had not truly appreciated just how terrified he was, yet had still pushed on regardless.

"Why did you agree to this?" he asked him.

"Why...ask me that again if we get out alive," he laughed back nervously and wiped his hand and forearm across his running nose quickly. "But I have dreamt of this place...so there must be a reason I need be here...other than protect you."

"Protect me?"

"Yes...believe it or not," Percival laughed again. "Though you probably can't believe that right now."

"Any man who can face his fear as you do, then I can believe it. We shall see what is here and then return...I promise," Paul explained and turned to look back into the darkness.

Slowly Paul leant into the darkness holding the side stonework and pushing the lanthorn out with his other hand. He looked down as the light barely reached the floor some eighteen feet below. He moved the candle around to see what else he could see, but the light simply did not stretch that far. To his left he saw what looked like a wooden ladder positioned a few feet away upright. Quickly he lay upon his stomach and reached around outstretching his arm to grab it. It was just out of reach. He leaned further and shuffled forwards, Percival just grabbing his legs as he nearly toppled forwards. As he steadied himself, he reached across again and this time managed to grab the ladder. He pulled it across but it was heavy. Slowly but surely he inched it across until it was in front of him. Percival looked past him at the ends of the thick wooden ladder.

"That is one heavy duty ladder, but do you think it rotten or still usable?" he asked.

"They must have made that down here...the knights who first came here. I shall try it," Paul commented as he tried to turn himself around in the cramped confines of the tunnel.

Slowly he eased himself backwards and onto the ladder keeping his weight upon his arms and chest as he let the ladder take his weight. It creaked but sounded solid still. Cautiously and slowly Paul edged his way step by step down the ladder, Percival crawling to the edge to watch him descend.

"Anything roars or spits fire and I am afraid I will be out of here," Percival remarked joking, his voice still trembling giving away his genuine fear.

After eighteen steps, Paul placed his foot upon solid stone. He swung the lanthorn around to view the room. Piled besides a single empty black granite box were several old reed torches unused. He picked one up. He smelt it and could smell the soaked reed as if it was new. Quickly he opened the lanthorn, took out the burning candle and used it to light the reed torch. Within seconds it burst into a large orange and yellow gout of flame filling the large vaulted room with light. Percival let out a sigh of relief, looked behind himself back down the darkened tunnel, then quickly edged himself onto the ladder and rapidly climbed down it and rushed to stand by Paul.

"My Lord...so the stories are true, they did find the Ark of the Covenant," Percival said as he looked around the empty room save the single black granite box and torches.

Paul began to move around the room. It was empty. He checked the floor and the marks in the thin film of white sand. In the far corner his eye caught the glimpse of light reflecting off of something. He walked over and knelt down to see what it was. It was a small bee-like pendant made out of a white polished stone. It immediately reminded him of the bee necklace Alisha wore. He studied it, puzzled. Why would the entire room be cleared of all objects except this tiny object that appeared to have been placed deliberately? He stood up again and moved the torch across the walls to see if there was anything. Percival came and stood beside him looking very nervous looking back over his shoulder.

"What is it?" Paul asked seeing the look upon his face.

"I...I think we are not alone down here," he replied nervously and gulped hard.

Just as he said that, their ears began to whine as a loud high pitched noise pierced the silence. It started to increase in intensity to the point it began to become painful. Percival rushed over to the ladder and started to climb it again. He only reached the fourth rung when it suddenly collapsed. As he fell backwards, the entire ladder just fell apart into many pieces. Paul rushed to his aid lifting him up quickly with one hand. As Percival brushed himself down, picked up his still burning candle, they both stared at the remnants of the ladder.

"Okay...now the Lord is messing with us," Percival exclaimed, alarmed, and took a deep breath.

Paul looked up at the small opening above them, now completely out of reach. Nor had they secured one of the three ropes prior to entering. Both looked at each other as they realised this at the same time.

"Percy...we shall not die down here," Paul remarked seeing the fear in his eyes.

"Really...how do you know that?" he asked, his voice deep and fearful.

"Why else would we have the dreams...just to lead us here to our deaths? I think not. There must be another way out," Paul answered and immediately started to walk around the walls.

"It could all have been a trick of the Devil...and we fell for it...for there is a presence here...can you not feel it?" Percival asked and looked around himself cautiously. "We are trapped like rats."

"No we are not...," Paul replied but praying secretly that Percival was wrong. "Besides, if we are unable to get out, eventually others will come looking for us and find the uncovered stone slab in the stables...so worry not, we just need to keep a single candle alight until they do..."

"Err...I pulled the slab back over...in case you meant to keep this a secret," Percival explained sheepishly as his shoulders drooped. "I have killed us both."

"No...no you have not...I have."

The high pitched whine suddenly went higher; Paul placed his hands over his ears in pain and fell to his knees. Percival fought to control the pain bursting through his head. He looked down at Paul, the burning torch dropped on the ground beside him, the lanthorn flickering away near to his left knee. The pain hit him too but clearly not as bad as it was Paul. Percival knelt beside him and put his arm around him whilst looking about frantically as he was sure someone else was nearby. Both heard a distant voice of a woman, yet despite being distant, sounded as though it was being spoken directly inside their heads.

"Do you remember Psalm 82:6?" the woman's voice said clearly.

Then Paul heard Niccolas speaking as if he stood beside him. In pain Paul opened his eyes but no one else was with them.

"Know that a key does exist hidden here, where the square meets the corner, the corner of which is the top," Niccolas's voice spoke.

Paul and Percival looked at each other, their eyes wide in pain and confusion and then the woman's voice spoke again.

"Know there is a dark side, a duality within man, but a side that can be mastered and controlled, and when the world is ready to change, some call it the end days when even the very light you see daily will change, then will a great many remember these sayings and beliefs. They may be revealed set within stories, or songs, but they will be remembered and revealed again for the truth touches all and many will recognise those truths."

Paul's mind raced as the words seemed to burn deeply into his mind in a manner he had never experienced before. The words that Reynald had written down about the dark side flooded his mind again as if he was reading them word for word with perfect clarity. A bright light filled the room and he looked up. Suddenly before him stood several very tall men wearing elaborate white robes. They immediately struck Paul as looking like the old white haired man that had saved him and Taqi in La Rochelle. He looked up at them in almost total disbelief as they spoke a strange soft sounding language he could not understand. One walked towards him. As he sat up straighter, the man just walked through him. Paul instantly realised he was seeing some kind of hallucination or vivid dream. He looked down at the burning torch. It was still alight but the flames were not moving. It was as if it was frozen in time. He looked back up at the men before him. One turned slightly, his gaze falling upon Paul as if he could see him.

"This gate is sealed. It is not for your time. You must leave it well alone," the man spoke without moving his lips, yet Paul heard it and understood him perfectly. "If you wish to ever see your wife and son again, leave and never return here because for you, the Legacy can be recovered. We are but the Guardians of the Gateways."

Paul's heart jumped and his neck tensed. He gasped as the man just turned away his gaze and carried on talking with the other tall men as if he did not exist.

"What gate...and how do I leave here?" Paul shouted, his throat hurting and dry. He looked down as he felt Percival's right hand touch his leg as he was reaching out for him. Quickly Paul tried to lift Percival up so he could witness what he was seeing, but he felt as though he weighed ten times his normal weight.

"I...I cannot see them...but I can hear them," Percival blurted out and fought to open his eyes but he could not.

Paul looked back at the tall men, all three of them now looking down at him, each holding a staff with a strange crescent symbol affixed to the top of a round metallic looking ball. All three balls started to light up and shine intensely, the light wiping out all other images as it seemed to envelope everything. The pain coursing through Paul's head forced him downwards, his face pushing into the white sand in agony as Percival took in deep breaths, his eyes still shut. Paul turned his head in time to see Percival raise himself upwards and sit upon his legs upright, his hands placed across his lap. As Percival drew in a deep controlled breath, Paul's vision started to fade to darkness rapidly and he passed out.

ॐ ॐ

When Paul came to, he was being dragged by Percival towards a stone cut stairwell. Light from a single candle lit the cave like room they were in. Confused and feeling sick and dizzy, Paul tried to turn upon his side. This was not the room they had been in. He raised his arm at Percival and grabbed his arm that was pulling him. Percival stopped and collapsed to his knees exhausted and out of breath.

"Oh thank the Lord...I was sure you were dead...you were not breathing," Percival explained as he tried to catch his breath.

"Where are we...how did you get us out of the room?" Paul asked as he tried to sit up and look around.

"I am not sure...you passed out...and I recall pulling you and a person beckoned me to pass them, and as I did, still pulling you, I found ourselves in a long straight and well made stone tunnel. So I kept dragging you until we got here...then I think I fell asleep. I am not sure," Percival replied puzzled.

Paul looked at the single lanthorn flickering away on the floor beside them. Nearby he saw three 'V' shapes carved next to each other into the limestone floor about two inches deep and twenty inches long. A faint sound of running water could be heard.

"Do you think that is the city's only natural water source, the Gihon spring? If it is, we can follow it out," he remarked as he strained to listen.

"I have no idea. Do you think those markings are pointers or something similar?" Percival asked as he ran his fingers inside one.

"Maybe...but I fear that we are the first people in a very long time to be down here...look the straight lines of the walls and level floors. That is very advanced and careful engineering,

"I think we should get moving. Can you walk?"

"I think so...yes," Paul answered as he tried to stand, his sword dragging across the stonework as he stood wearily. "I keep hearing references to Virgo...seeing the image of the symbol for it...but also about Nebuchadnezzar and gateways and Babylon...do you hear it too, like someone whispering close by?"

"No...I do not hear it now, sorry. But I am sure I did hear something about a gateway when we were in the other chamber."

Both held onto each other as Percival picked up the lanthorn and they began to follow the straight tunnel, the darkness stretching out before them. They stepped over several more 'V' shaped carvings in the floor. They were all set out in sets of threes. Eventually the tunnel opened up into a large spherical shaped cavern. As Percival lifted the lanthorn, they could just make out they were inside what felt like an underground dome, but more like a ball as the walls curved in towards the bottom finishing in a small circular platform that they were now standing upon. As they moved across it slowly, they could make out the outline of what appeared to be a stone relief carving of a large doorway.

It reminded Paul of the carvings and drawings he had seen of the Stonehenge upright stones capped with a lintel.

"'Tis a door," Percival remarked as he half pulled Paul towards it.

As they approached it, the solid stone wall within the shape of the doorway appeared to glisten as if covered in quartz or millions of tiny sparkling stars as it reflected the light from the lanthorn. But as Paul touched the surface, it was indeed solid rock.

"'Tis a dead end," he sighed, feeling exhausted. He raised his hand to his left ear as the swelling behind it started to throb and bolts of pain shot through his head again. He winced and buckled to his knees as the pain increased overwhelming his senses.

"Paul...Paul," Percival said alarmed and dropped the lanthorn.

As it hit the stone floor, it broke and the candle went out. They were in pitch blackness. Percival fought to control his fear and placed his arms around Paul. They would have no way of relighting the candle now.

 1 – 2

"If you know the words, you can pass through," a female voice said gently in the darkness.

Paul tried to raise his head but the pain was just too intense. Percival held onto Paul even tighter. Suddenly the pain stopped. Paul could hardly believe it had completely gone so quickly. As he turned around and rested his back against the solid stone wall, Percival sat beside him clutching Paul's arm tightly just as an intense and bright light flooded the circular domed cave with such brilliance they had to shield their eyes. The light was so white they could not see anything else, but the light did not hurt their eyes as they feared. Both looked at each other in astonishment.

"You do not have the words nor the song and language of the birds yet...you cannot enter or pass," the woman's voice spoke softly.

"What words...and what language?" Paul asked out loudly.

"You come too soon. Fear not...we know of you both. You shall not be harmed."

"Who are you? Where are we?" Percival called out.

An image of a female floating with what at first looked like wings flowing behind her, but was in fact white light swirling in strands like flowing silk sheets behind her appeared. But she was part of the light, her features almost indistinct from the light. Her face seemed to draw near and her crystal clear, almost translucent bluish green eyes looked intently at Paul first, then at Percival.

"You...you lie much, you hide much...but your soul and heart and intention are pure. You can leave," the woman said close to Percival's face. His eyes widened. He looked at Paul puzzled as the woman turned her gaze back to Paul. She seemed to study him closer and far longer. Paul sensed feelings coming from her like soft waves of warm water washing over him in rhythmic harmony similar to his vivid dreams when he had seen the old man asking him to remember him. "You do not remember me do you?" she asked without moving her lips. "You know not the words but you may pass and join with us if you wish for you are of us already though the veil of this world covers you," she explained.

Paul's heart raced. Pass to where. Would he die? Was he dead already? What did she mean that Percival lies but his soul is pure? Would he see Alisha again if he went? he asked himself. That last thought hit him like a punch to his chest.

"No...I must stay here...wherever here is," Paul blurted out, Percival letting out a laugh of relief.

"Yes...I see it in you now. What you seek is no longer here. Only the Gateway remains. Do not waste your time upon it, for it is blocked until Mother Earth herself once again enters the ring of light...and even then the Gateway may remain locked and blocked to mankind if it has not learnt," the woman said softly and placed what felt like a hand upon the scar on his face. He felt it tingle as her hand rested upon it and many vivid images flashed through his mind showing what he knew to be the Hanging Gardens of Babylon and many references to Nebuchadnezzar. "Do not repeat his mistakes with the Gateway, and do not return here ever again, for next time, you will not awake from this state," she said and pulled her hand away. "Now sleep again."

℠  ℞

Paul could hear Percival panting out of breath. Disoriented Paul opened his eyes to see a small hole above him with light entering in a bright beam downwards. He then became aware that Percival was trying to pull him across the floor of a smaller cavern. Quickly he grabbed Percival's arm, swung over onto his stomach and looked up at Percival who was straining, tears falling down his cheeks.

"Percy!" Paul shouted but he kept dragging him. "Percy!" he shouted again louder.

Percival froze, looked at Paul and gasped releasing his grip on his arms. He staggered backwards blinking from the dust in his eyes.

"You are alive?" he exclaimed perplexed. "But you were dead...truly dead this time."

Paul sat up and tried to stand but his legs were too weak. His mind raced again as he tried to recall all the images and what the female voice had said to him. He reached up and rubbed his fingers over the thick scar upon his face, but he could not feel it. He rubbed his fingers again where the scar should have been, but he could barely feel any mark at all.

"Are we dead?" he asked.

Percival shrugged his shoulders and leant back against a wooden door and started to laugh. As he continued to laugh, Paul looked around the hewn out cave. It was twenty-one feet across with a hole in the ceiling just over a foot wide. Suddenly the wooden door burst open and a Templar sergeant pushed his way in forcibly knocking Percival to the floor next to Paul. As dust followed the sergeant in swirling all around him, his sword drawn, two more Templars rushed into the chamber. Percival laughed even more and pointed at them.

"How did you enter here?" the sergeant demanded.

"Just exactly where is here?" Paul asked, his throat dry.

Percival fell backwards against Paul laughing out loudly part hysterical almost.

"You are beneath the Rock of the Dome...and there is no other way in so say how so ye entered," the sergeant demanded as he waved his sword nearer.

Paul suddenly felt overwhelmed with fatigue and nausea just as Theodoric pushed his way past the two Templars at the door.

"By the Lords, you are okay," he said and rushed over to Paul pushing the Templar sergeant's sword aside. "Where have you been?"

"You are back," Paul replied, his vision beginning to fade fast.

"Been back three days, you bloody fool. You were last seen in the stables so how did you get here?" Theodoric asked.

Paul and Percival looked at each other confused.

"Three days?" Percival asked.

"Yes, and you went into the stables two days before that, so tell me, where have you been these past five days?" Theodoric demanded as he knelt behind Paul and tried to lift him. He beckoned the two other Templars over to help him.

Paul and Percival just looked at each other utterly bewildered. Paul then looked around the cave and then back to Percival, who simply shrugged his shoulders, confused.

"How come you knew we would be here?" Paul asked as his voice became weaker and he slumped in Theodoric's arms.

"Planning a way to get in to search for you. I just happened to be checking an old route your father and I once discovered around here...but long since filled in I suspect," Theodoric explained as the two Templars grabbed Paul's arms and started to lift him.

Percival laughed even more. As the two Templars lifted Paul to his feet, he felt dizzy, his eyes rolled and he passed out cold, his head drooping forwards.

Port of La Rochelle, France, Melissae Inn, spring 1191

"So how on earth did they get beneath the rock if it is sealed and guarded?" Sarah asked.

"And take five days?" Gabirol remarked as he shook his head.

"How on earth indeed. I know it must sound impossible, but I swear to you, that is what happened," the old man replied seeing the looks of disbelief upon their faces, the wealthy tailor scratching his head hard.

"I want to know what all the gateway stuff means and that Nebe chad king," Simon said waving his hand.

The old man laughed at his comment.

"Gateway. I do not think we have time to fully cover that aspect, suffice to say, that according to myth and legend, and as written within holy books, so called Gateways exist whereupon, if you have the knowledge and understanding, you can travel through them to the realms and homes of the gods, the watchers or fallen angels depending upon what you believe."

"You mean there is a gateway beneath Jerusalem?" Ayleth asked, surprised.

"Perhaps...most likely in fact," the old man replied.

"What kind of gateway...and what did the woman of light say about it can only be opened when Mother Earth enters the ring of light herself?" Gabirol asked, perplexed.

"You see, this is a subject that is too involved and I suspect way beyond our own reasoning and comprehension at this time," the old man explained.

"Bet it's the same kind of gateway, doorway, that Paul saw in his dreams...isn't it?" Simon stated, smiling broadly again.

The old man simply nodded yes in agreement just as the wealthy tailor folded his arms and sat back still shaking his head.

"So what is the significance of Nebuchadnezzar being mentioned then? Does he somehow play a part?" Ayleth asked.

"Again, perhaps. But I cannot tell all of what his connection is as I do not know fully myself," the old man replied.

"But you know something of it?" Gabirol shot back immediately, his quill wavering over a piece of new parchment ready to write more.

"I know a little," the old man said and paused briefly. "I can tell you that around 600 BC King Nebuchadnezzar, the King of Babylon, conquered Jerusalem and flattened its walls, stripped its Temple of all its treasure including the Language of the Birds documents and the Ark of the Covenant. But as you are learning, the Ark of the Covenant is but just one piece of many items and many arks. The King set Jerusalem ablaze, and returned home to Babylon with the treasure of the Temple plus a fair few royal prisoners of war. Included among the captives were three wise men from the Temple, a young man and 'master magician' named Daniel, and another prominent prophet, Ezekiel, whom I am sure all of you must have heard of?" the old man asked and looked at them all in turn. "You have probably read his revelations about flying winged discs with several faces upon them? 'Twas Ezekiel who had visions of 'the kingdom of Heaven on Earth' while imprisoned in Babylon."

"Just like Paul's visions?" Ayleth remarked.

"Almost," the old man replied with a smile. "Now King Nebuchadnezzar is probably best known as the builder of the Hanging Gardens of Babylon. One of the seven wonders of the ancient world. They were built upon the seven stages of the fantastic ziggurat of Marduk, the well known Tower of Babel, which Nebuchadnezzar restored. Babel originates from the word Bab-li, which in the Babylonian language meant 'Gate of God'. This is a hidden clue to the fact that Nebuchadnezzar attempted to construct a means, a gateway, to transcend earth life and travel to the realms of the Elohim, the watchers themselves."

"Why? I mean why would he?" Gabirol asked.

"Nebuchadnezzar was driven to build the Hanging Gardens because of his belief that he was to emulate Sargon, from 2,300 BC, the great king of Akkad (now northern Iraq), a name from which is derived the term 'Akka', the name of the Creator goddess Akka and the first Semitic language. Akka comes from the primitive linguistic root ak, meaning great or mighty. The ak is persistently present in words which relate to our Languedoc, or Language of Ak. Note carefully that in Egypt, akh was the Pharaonic word for all aspects of light, particularly the 'transcendental' light of the transfiguration."

"Just where exactly is Babylon, for I thought it was just a mythical place from the Bible?" Peter asked.

"The ruins of Babylon are found buried beneath the sands of northern Persia (Iraq) about twenty miles from Baghdad. In its glory the city of Babylon was the greatest city in Mesopotamia, the centre of the new world order. It was a veritable playground for the gods. The ziggurat or temple of Marduk which formed its centre and the Tower of Babel were awesome structures by any standard. The Marduk temple housed the golden image of Bel and a strange golden table, with a combined weight of nearly fifty thousand pounds of solid gold! Nebuchadnezzar's Hanging Gardens were a spectacular, and almost unbelievable, sight to Daniel and the rest of the Jewish captives. Growing upon a huge artificial mountain, the Hanging Gardens could be seen for fifty miles across the flat desert. The seven terraces held trees, vines and flowers and were watered by a system of wells and fountains. King

Nebuchadnezzar had this wonder built for his queen who longed to return to her mountain homeland. People entered Babylon through the Processional Way, which led to the famed Ishtar Gate. This enormous entranceway was covered with brilliant blue glazed tiles on which were depicted lions, bulls and dragons in bas-relief. These animals represented the gods of the city, Marduk the dragon king was the most potent. Isis was the lion. Make special note of that fact," the old man explained.

"What fact?" Simon asked immediately.

"About Isis is the lion," the old man answered.

"I am guessing there will be a connection between Isis and a lion later then?" Gabirol commented as he wrote down some details.

"There has already been reference made to this fact...but mark it well for it does have relevance," the old man replied and waited whilst Gabirol finished writing. "As king, Nebuchadnezzar expanded Babylon's fortifications, paved her streets, and dug canals, and contrary to popular belief by many nowadays, Nebuchadnezzar was revered in his homeland as more than just a great temple builder. He was also revered as a wise man that surrounded himself with astrologers, architects, magicians, sorcerers and anyone who could help him decode his dreams and visions, some of which were deeply troubling to him. This made it perfectly natural for Daniel and the wise men from Solomon's Temple in Jerusalem to be mixed in with the sages of Babylon. Surprisingly, the Jews discovered that the Babylonians possessed long sought answers concerning their past because the Jewish and Babylonian histories emerged from the same original source...in Sumeria."

"What? Sumeria...really?" the wealthy tailor asked.

"Yes, as I have touched upon previously. From the Sumerian stories the Hebrews found missing pieces to their own Flood story and story of Creation. With a few name changes here and there the two traditions match. Most learned scholars now believe it was here in Babylon during the captivity of Nebuchadnezzar that the first five books of the Old Testament, including Daniel and Ezekiel, were constructed...and with a lot help from the original Sumerian stories. The epic of Gilgamesh and his flood story is identical and pre-dates the Biblical version by centuries. Most Christians are shocked to learn that the stories that form the foundation of their religion are but copies of original stories belonging to another time, place and people. That is why it is important to realise and understand the context in which these books were assembled and the captivity of their authors. But it is far more important to understand and accept that they are a compilation of actual history, mythology, literary devices and fond memories of a past that never was Hebrew, but Sumerian. Separating Hebrew from Sumerian is crucial. Why deal with second-hand copies when the originals are more valuable and accurate?"

"So everything we think we know and understand from the Bible is but copied...and useless?" the Hospitaller asked, disheartened.

"I like to say inherited...not copied. And it is far from useless for as we attempt now, all the codes and symbolism for future generations benefits are still all accurately encoded within the newer and, dare I say it, updated versions within the Bible," the old man explained. "Understand that the marriage between the Sumerian and Hebrew mythologies was a match made in Heaven. It was as if each carried the missing half to the other's message. This situation required that one side had to make a deal with the Devil to get what they wanted...and both sides wanted knowledge and access to the Gateways."

"I find this very hard to deal with and accept...forgive me for that," the wealthy tailor remarked looking saddened as he shook his head staring at the table and fumbling with his hands. "And I profess my ignorance for I have never even heard such matters as the language of the birds," he then sighed.

"Most best kept secrets you would not know of. But I shall try and explain them as best as I am able."

"But what happened to Paul and Percy?" Sarah interrupted abruptly.

"They took them both back to the Templar headquarters and put them to bed...separately."

"But what of Alisha...she had sensed great danger all along. What did she do?" Ayleth asked.

"When word came through to Kerak that he had gone missing via the heliograph, as the message was so short, she of course feared the worse. Wild horses could not stop her...not even Tenno," the old man began to explain and smiled to himself.

"What do you mean?" Sarah asked.

"Alisha knew something was not right...she could feel it. Princess Stephanie received word about Paul's disappearance and at first tried to hide the fact for fear of upsetting Alisha...but as Alisha grew wearier, and her own genuine concern for Paul overwhelmed her, Princess Stephanie informed Alisha...and that was that. Alisha grabbed Arri, got their belongings and was already harnessing their spare horse to their caravan when Tenno stepped in...initially trying to convince her to stay put where they were safe. He argued it was dangerous to travel alone, especially along a route she had never done before. When she took the caravan to the castle gates, Sister Lucy and Princess Stephanie both begging her to stay...only then did Tenno agree he would go with her. He knew there was no stopping her."

"Can I ask...is this Paul some kind of prophet then, as he has visions and things?" Ayleth asked cautiously.

"My dear young lady...if only you all but knew that you are all prophets and visionaries in your own rights...for we all have the ability," the old man answered and paused for several moments, poured himself a drink and continued. "That is why the truth is so brutally suppressed and hidden from you all."

"But this language of the birds. What is that all about? Does it mean we have to sing bird song?" Simon asked and laughed and tried to whistle but could not as he laughed.

"I shall come to that very shortly. But let me continue explaining about Nebuchadnezzar's Gateway which began after he acknowledged that Daniel had immense prophetic gifts, including the ability to interpret dreams. In Chapter four of Daniel, he is asked to interpret a dream in which Nebuchadnezzar saw 'a tree in the midst of the Earth, and the height thereof was great. The tree grew, and was strong, and the height thereof reached into heaven, and the sight thereof to the end of the Earth'. There was great fruit in this tree and the birds of Heaven lived in its branches. From this tree the king saw a 'watcher' and a 'Holy one' from Heaven emerge. They told him to destroy the tree, and leave its 'stump' in the earth. This was a confusing dream to the king, but not to us, those of us who know that 'the watcher' is the Egyptian name for 'divine being' or 'god' or ntr, or Neter, which means 'one who watches'. Neter-neter land is the name of the place in the stars where these beings dwell, along with the Green Man or Gardener. In Sumeria, this is known as another earthly land of the An-unnaki, the land of 'ones who watch'."

"So that old woman who follows Paul is a watcher...the same person that Theodoric met in the Emerald Isle...she is a divine being, yes?" Gabirol asked.

"The evidence would suggest that is so," the old man replied.

"But how did Pau and Percy get into the room, cave thing, beneath the Dome of the Rock though. I want to know that," the Genoese sailor demanded.

"I am sorry...but sometimes we do not get answers and I cannot give you details how they got there, for I do not know. Nor do they recall how either. Nor did they know or discover how, to them, they had been gone less than one day, when in fact five days had elapsed," the old man explained.

"Like those Christian men who slept in a cave and reappeared three hundred years later as you explained earlier," Gabirol remarked quietly and strummed his fingers quizzically upon the table in front of him. "Why didn't the watchers want Nebuchadnezzar to join them in Neter-neter land? Could it be that he was not one of them, but Daniel was, which explains why he could interpret their symbols? What did they mean by leaving the 'stump' of the 'tree' in the ground?"

"Nebuchadnezzar wanted to know if his dream foretold disaster of a project represented by the tree and if so, what is the specific project that is in danger? The story is told of what happened when Nebuchadnezzar set up an image of gold in Babylon. This wasn't some ancient status symbol the king kept on his desk for it was the image of a massive three score, that is sixty, cubits high and six cubits wide. A cubit is eighteen inches, making the image 540 inches high and three score or thirty times eighteen inches high. Five hundred and forty inches is forty-five feet high. This massive structure could be seen from miles around. In Revelation 13:11–15, the one who speaks like a dragon, 'the first beast, whose deadly wound was healed', does great wonders. He makes fire come down from heaven. And he tells the people to construct 'an image to the beast, which had been wounded by the sword, but did live'. The person who 'speaks like a dragon' has the power to give life to this image, in other words to make it speak. Any 'who would not worship the image of the beast should be killed', says Revelation. Nebuchadnezzar, on the other hand, could not make this gleaming Golden Head speak. This was a major failure. Like the tribal leader David, who ruled Jerusalem five hundred years before him, the king had planned to unify his kingdom, the golden image was the unifying force. He tried using music to get it to work. He demanded that when the people heard the music play they were to fall down and worship the golden image as if this act would impress the lifeless heap. If they didn't they would be tossed into a burning fiery furnace. Then three wise Jews from Babylon, friends of Daniel and Abednego, who worked at the Temple of Solomon, refuse to worship the hulking image or the god of the Babylonian king. What is more, the three insult Nebuchadnezzar by betting the king that their god will save them from the fiery furnace. Clearly, the three wise men from the Temple of Solomon possess crucial knowledge that Nebuchadnezzar needs to make this golden device work. Though he had limited success in firing up the fiery furnace component of the image. But beyond that he was stuck. He needed some magical other means, or words..."

"What is this device, this golden image of which you speak?" the wealthy tailor asked.

"While conquering Jerusalem, Nebuchadnezzar was known to have pillaged the Temple of Solomon and removed the holy objects. Some claim he retrieved the Ark of the Covenant and the ultimate Secret of the Temple...the Golden Head of God...or at least a device that showed a head that spoke as if from God."

"What...I have never heard of this before," Sarah interjected, puzzled.

"'Tis but all within the Old Testament for all to read," the old man replied. "Also references to a Golden Pillar with the forty-five foot 'tree' of Nebuchadnezzar's dream, and the Ark with the 'stump'...and so it now makes perfect sense why Nebuchadnezzar wanted to involve Daniel in this project. It was the sons of D'Anu, the people of Daniel, who had originally brought this device to earth. The angel who appeared to the king was related to Daniel. As for the watchers, the very same Neter gods, no one enters their realm uninvited," the old man explained.

"I am lost again," Simon laughed.

"Here, look at this as it is a depiction of the golden Pillar of Osiris as drawn by Paul," the old man said as he pulled out a drawing from Paul's folder and gently pushed it across the table towards Simon. (Fig. 36: Osiris Tree of Life.)

Fig. 36:

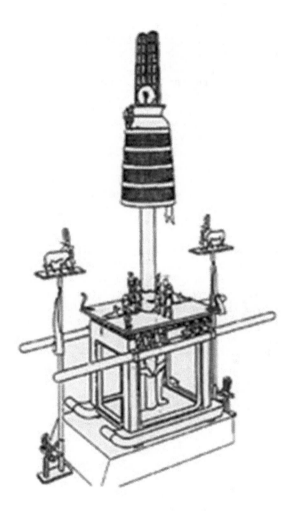

"Look carefully and you can see Osiris's ladder into the heavens is a pillar atop a platform or 'stump' that resembles the Ark of the Covenant, which the ancients said was made of gold. If this is the tree atop the stump of Nebuchadnezzar's dream, and if this is his golden image of the beast, then what these stories relate is his attempt to open a gateway! Osiris is the Serpent-soul who can utter the 'open sesame' or whatever the real words or sounds were to make this device work and initiate the opening of the gateway," the old man explained then looked at the reaction upon their faces as they listened and took it in turn to view the drawing. *"We've*

all been trained to believe the Devil is the Lord of Death who will imprison and torture our souls for eternity. However, the original Lord of Death was something completely different. He was the gatherer of souls or 'gardener of souls'. He shared with his wife a magnificent Underworld called 'the Abysmal Womb', the Land of Death. He holds the key to Heaven and Hell, also known as the Key of Life. And it is no coincidence that Jesus identifies himself as this figure in the Book of Revelation where he says 'I am he that liveth, and was dead; and behold, I am alive for evermore, Amen; and have the keys of hell and heaven.' This womb was believed to be a place of regeneration, an 'egg', if you please, where humans transformed themselves into higher beings of light, capable of going through the Gateways."

"What does this all have to do with ancient Egyptians and what happened to Paul and Percy?" the farrier asked.

"Because as I have been explaining, even Moses as you know him, was of Egyptian origin and much of their myth and legend is carried over into Christianity and again also connected with so-called sacred Gateways. You see Osiris is frequently shown sitting amidst a lake. In the Papyrus of Ani, this is called his Lake of Fire. The Egyptian Book of the Dead makes clear that it is an intermediate place between earth and Heaven that was guarded by none other than Thoth, known in Greek as Hermes. Therefore, it is likely it was located at or near the Egg of Creation, with its Great Pyramid and Sphinx, and is related to the Tree of Life. The pyramids of Giza by the way were once surrounded by water. It also warns impure souls that attempting to cross the Lake of Fire will result in disaster. The Lake of Fire 'cuts away' like a knife, or sword, all that is impure in a soul. From the wavy lines in the depiction in the Papyrus of Ani one gets the impression that the Lake of Fire emits or is a frequency or vibration of sound...or words...which leads to inner transformation and the purification of the soul. From the ancient stories it becomes abundantly clear, to transcend earth life one has to cross the Lake of Fire, which may appear as a fiery furnace. In order to ascend into the heavens one had to undergo a transformation. Preparing to effect this transformation through the 'cleansing mysteries', as Jesus proclaimed in the Pistis Sophia, was the purpose in life."

"The Pistis what?" Simon asked laughing.

"'Tis a secret Gnostic gospel. I can explain further after I have explained the Gateway details," the old man replied.

"That would be helpful," Gabirol said as if answering for all in the room.

"Then let me get back to Daniel and Nebuchadnezzar and the three wise men who refuse to worship what Nebuchadnezzar demands or tell him the secrets that will gain him access through the Gateways. Furious, the king ordered the three wise men be cast into the 'fiery furnace'. This is known as the trial of the three wise men that reject the image of Bel or as we know him, Baal, a head atop a pillar. The men seemed eager to partake of this experience! As Daniel said, 'they put on their coats, their hats and their other garments, and were cast in the midst of the burning fiery furnace' (Daniel 3:21). This is an immensely meaningful statement for why put on any clothes at all if your body is about to be consumed by the fiery furnace? Well, these garments turn out to be more than just ordinary robes worn at the Temple of Solomon or the simple clothing of hostages in Babylon. They are identical to the hat and the other garments the goddess Inanna wore at her Goddess temple in Mari. Inanna is often shown wearing the Shugurra helmet, 'a hat' that makes her go far into the universe. It is also the same as the 'helmet of salvation' described in Ephesians 6:17. Inanna also wears a heavy full-length coat and other garments. This coat is called the PALA garment. It works in conjunction with the palladium, lined Pillar of Love. This entire outfit is almost identical in all aspects in description to that described in Chapter 6 of Ephesians. There, in addition to the 'helmet of salvation', spiritual seekers are encouraged to 'put on the whole armour of God, that ye may be able to stand against the wiles of the Devil. For we wrestle not against flesh and blood, but against principalities, against powers, against the rulers of darkness of this world, against spiritual wickedness in high places'."

"Never heard of Inanna!" Simon stated as the others looked at each other.

"I thought I had mentioned her previously?" the old man remarked and thought to himself for a few moments. "Let me explain then that the principalities and powers are the angelic spiritual forces who work as heavenly governors and messengers in the heavenly realms. This is exactly the angelic level of the An-un-naki. Apparently, some of these are harmful creatures that seek to attach themselves to human souls. At Armageddon Jesus promises to send his angels to sever the wicked from among the just. And then shall cast them into the fire. You see, the 'armour of God' uniform described, including the Shugurra Helmet of Salvation and the PALA coat, simultaneously helps to sever or protect us from harmful spirits, and make the connection with a Gateway safely. We know this for Ephesians describes a person standing in front of the Ark of Covenant, the soul-transportation device that opens the fiery furnace! We know this because the person is wearing the Breastplate of Righteousness. Their feet are 'shod with preparation for the Gospel of Peace'."

"Truly lost now," Simon said flouncing his arms in a dramatic fashion. "How does one have their feet 'shod' in preparation for the Gospel of Peace?" he asked.

"In answer, a clue is given in the story of Solomon and Saba, Sheba as most call her now, when she lifts up her dress to reveal big, hairy feet. They are so ugly Solomon comments on them. The usual interpretation is that Saba did not shave her feet. However, we may add another explanation to this observation by remembering that hair-y is also a reference to the hare or the heron. In the case of the latter, the Queen of Saba would have had the feet of a bird. Indeed, once we know the Bird Language, which I shall explain in a moment, we acquire our 'bird feet' we are prepared to know the Gospel of Peace. And above all they take the shield of faith, the Helmet of Salvation and the (S)word of the Spirit, which is the word of God. All of these appear to be necessary for soul travel through the Gateways to higher realms of existence."

"So Paul and Percy could not have travelled through any Gateway for they did not have those items," Ayleth remarked.

"Very observant, Ayleth, but yes they could...but only one way as they would have had to shed their earthly bodies," the old man replied.

"So they would be killed in effect?" Gabirol commented.

"Physically, yes. But the three wise men suitably dressed, entered the fiery furnace, as Nebuchadnezzar and all the king's men cautiously approached the lethal furnace. He asked that the three men appear to him. When they do, the king stands utterly astonished. He's expecting nasty scorched and burnt corpses. Instead, he sees the men are in perfect condition! 'Did we not cast three men bound into the midst of the fire?' he asked, baffled. But to add to the high strangeness of this event, a fourth person accompanied them! However, this is not just any man for Nebuchadnezzar believed this fourth man was an angel...and not just any angel either."

"So tell us then," the Templar asked.

"The fourth man is like the Son of God! 'Is this Jesus, the Son of God?' Nebuchadnezzar asked...which really tells us that the three wise men returned from their Gateway travels with Jesus. By this point Nebuchadnezzar was convinced the god of the three wise Jews is the true only God. He proclaims that if anyone speaks against this God, he shall cut them to pieces, and their houses will be made into dunghills. Then he promoted the three wise men." [45]

"And the Language of the Birds?" Gabirol remarked questioningly.

"Yes...well you can hopefully appreciate that Paul and Percival were subjected to some kind of extra normal event and experience...and one connected with a Gateway, a watcher of sorts and the loss of time...and the language of the birds is likewise directly connected with Gateways."

"I have heard often of the 'watchers' for are they not also known as 'birdmen' and depicted as feathered?" Peter suddenly asked. All looked at him.

"Yes they are indeed. Tenno in his wanderings across the great lands of the west encountered many peoples who all worshipped various forms of winged and feathered gods. Many wore feathers in their heads. But as for the actual language, let me explain that it is connected closely to the 'Green Language'. In mythology, and occultism, the 'Language of the Birds' is given as a mystical, perfect divine language, a green language, an Adamic language, as well as the language of the angels. But also as the mythical language used by birds to communicate with the initiated. In Indo-European religions, the behaviour of birds has long been used for the purposes of divination by augurs. Birdsong has been the inspiration for some magical engineered languages, in particular musical languages. Whistled languages based on spoken natural languages are also sometimes referred to as the Language of the Birds. In Norse mythology, the power to understand the language of the birds was a sign of great wisdom. The God Odin had two ravens, called Hugin and Munin, who flew around the world and told Odin what was happening among mortal men. The legendary king of Sweden 'Dag the Wise' was so wise that he could understand what birds said. He had a tame house sparrow which flew around and brought back news to him. It is said the ability could also be acquired by tasting dragon blood. According to the Poetic Edda and the Völsunga saga, Sigurd accidentally tasted dragon blood while roasting the heart of Fafnir. This gave him the ability to understand the language of birds, and his life was saved as the birds were discussing Regin's plans to kill Sigurd. Through the same ability Áslaug, Sigurd's daughter, found out the betrothment of her husband Ragnar Lodbrok, to another woman. But in Greek mythology, according to Apollonius Rhodius, the figurehead of Jason's ship, the Argo, was built of oak from the sacred grove at Dodona and could speak the language of birds. Those aspects I would also urge you to remember for in time Paul would learn all about Jason, the Argo and Dodona as well as other sacred and connected places and the Egyptian Magan boats," the old man explained and paused as Gabirol wrote frantically to keep up. "Tiresias was also said to have been given the ability to understand the Language of the Birds by Athena. The language of birds in Greek mythology may be attained by magical means. Democritus, Anaximander, Apollonius of Tyana, Melampus and Aesopus, were all said to have understood the birds. In Sufism, the language of birds is a mystical language of angels. 'The Conference of the Birds' is a mystical poem of 4647 verses by the Persian poet Farid al-Din Attar."

"What...you know of this manuscript already?" Gabirol said excitedly, the first time he had shown such an outburst of uncontrollable delight upon his face.

"Yes, yes of course. I know the manuscript is fairly new...in fact it was compiled and completed in 1177...you are obviously aware of this book," the old man replied.

"Aware of it...oh yes. More than just aware for I have a copy myself...at great expense and much trouble," Gabirol explained excitedly and quickly rummaged near to his feet and quickly removed a dark blue, more dark green looking leather bound book and gently placed it upon the table. On the front, a gold edged and gilded picture showing a large oak tree and many birds, with three white heron type birds clearly visible was illustrated. "This is what has set me upon the path I now follow...'tis why I am passing through La Rochelle for I have only this past week secured it," he explained as they all leaned in closer to look at the beautiful book.

"Then let me explain the remainder so when you do come to read the book, you will have a better understanding of its content. You see, 'The Conference of the Birds' or 'Speech of the Birds', in Persian 'Manṭiq-uṭ-Ṭayr', also known as' Maqāmāt-uṭ-Ṭuyūr', is a long poem of approximately 4500 lines written in Persian by the poet Farid ud-Din Attar, who is commonly known as Attar of Nishapur. In the poem, the birds of the world gather to decide who is to be their king, as they have none. The hoopoe, the wisest of them all, suggests that they should find the legendary Simorgh, a mythical Persian bird roughly equivalent to the western Phoenix. The hoopoe leads the birds, each of whom symbolically represents a human fault which prevents man from attaining enlightenment or access through the Gateways. When the group of thirty birds finally reach the dwelling place of the Simorgh, all they find is a lake in which they see their own reflection. This book relies on a clever word play between the words Simorgh, a mysterious bird in Iranian mythology, which is a symbol often found in Sufi literature, and similar to the Phoenix bird and 'si morgh', which means 'thirty birds' in Persian. Even Tenno, though do not ask me how, had a copy of a poem about the Simorgh. It read...'It was in China, late one moonless night, The Simorgh first appeared to mortal sight. He let a feather float down through the air, and rumours of its fame spread everywhere'." The old man paused and sipped some rose water. "The story recounts the longing of a group of birds who desire to know the great Simorgh, and who, under the guidance of a leader bird, start their journey toward the land of Simorgh. One by one, they drop out of the journey, each offering an excuse and unable to endure the journey. Each bird has a special significance, and a corresponding human type fault. The guiding bird is the hoopoe, while the nightingale symbolises the lover. The parrot is seeking the fountain of immortality, not God, and the peacock symbolises the 'fallen soul' who is in alliance with Satan. The birds must cross seven valleys in order to find the Simorgh. Talab for Yearning, Eshq for Love, Marifat for Gnosis, Istighnah for Detachment, Tawheed for Unity of God, Hayrat for Bewilderment and, finally, Fuqur and Fana for Selflessness and Oblivion in God. These represent the stations that a Sufi or any individual must pass through to realise the true nature of God. Within the larger context of the story of the journey of the birds, Attar masterfully tells the reader many short, sweet stories in captivating poetic style. Eventually only thirty birds remain as they finally arrive in the land of Simorgh, but all they see there is each other and the reflection of the thirty birds in a lake, not the mythical Simorgh. It is the Sufi doctrine that God is not external or separate from the universe, rather is reflected in the totality of existence. The thirty birds seeking the Simorgh realise that Simorgh is nothing more than their transcendent totality. The idea of God within is an idea intrinsic to most interpretations of Sufism. As the birds realise the truth, they now reach the station of Baqa meaning Subsistence, which sits atop the Mountain Qaf. It basically is saying that Simorgh, God, is within each and all of us as a whole."

"Do Jews have this belief in the Language of the Birds then?" Peter asked.

"Yes. In the Talmud Solomon's proverbial wisdom was due to his being granted understanding of the language of birds by God. And we know the direct connections that lead back to ancient Egypt so it should come as no surprise to learn that in Egyptian Arabic, hieroglyphic writing is called 'the alphabet of the birds'. In Ancient Egyptian itself, the hiero-glyphic form of writing was given the name *medu-netjer* meaning 'words of the gods' or 'divine language'. The concept of speaking with the birds is also known from many folk tales where usually the protagonist is granted the gift of understanding the Language of the Birds either by some magical transformation, or as a boon by the king of birds. The birds then inform or warn the hero about some danger or hidden treasure. In Kabbalah, magic, and alchemy, the Language of the Birds was considered a secret and perfect language and the key to perfect knowledge, sometimes also called the *langue verte*, or Green Language."

"Hey I just realised...Percival, he wears green and did not Paul's parchment depict a knight in green connected with Jerusalem?" Simon asked.

"He does..."

"And he lies and hides things. That's what that woman of light said. So is he not what he seems?" Simon asked.

"Yes, Simon, he lies and hides things...but his intentions and doing so are for good. That is all I shall say upon him for now." The old man paused. "Now here in France, the Language of the Birds, *la langue des oiseaux*, is a secret language of the Troubadours, connected with the tarot, purely based upon puns and symbolism drawn from homophony, as in an inn called *au lion d'or* 'the Golden Lion' which is 'code' for 'au lit on dort' meaning 'in the bed one sleeps' though as yet the final t is not yet commonly used or pronounced but it shall be in time."

"You know so much, old man, that I struggle to keep up," Gabirol said and recharged his quill.

"I don't even try to keep up...I just go with it," Sarah said quietly.

"Then please let me explain again so we are all clear on this matter of the Language of the Birds, for it is all allegorical and symbolic. The Language of the Birds is also known as the Green Language or the Language of the Gods. It embraces Kabbalah, astrology, alchemy and tarot. Its grammar is symbolism, more to the point, physical dimensional symbolism, when properly understood. Birds symbolise in various forms the ascension of human conscious-ness in the alchemy of time, such as winged gods from the sky, bird-headed beings, Thoth in particular, linked to creation of this reality. Thoth the Scribe is the ancient Egyptian god who scripted the languages of our reality, to be viewed as symbolic messages through the ages, and finally brought to light at the end of the cycles of time, especially relevant in regard to the 'fifth and final flight of the Phoenix' and the reality of true 'consciousness'. If you do not or cannot remember anything of the Language of the Birds as I have explained, then please just simply remember the final aspect of the fifth flight of the Phoenix...that is all," the old man finished and sighed. [46]

"Sorry, old man, for you look tired, but what of that Pistis secret gospel you spoke of?" Gabirol asked politely.

"Are you sure, for it will take longer to explain?" the old man asked.

"We have time do we not?...and I wish to learn and hear of what the legacy is that Paul will recover...or was it a legacy uncovered...and just who these Guardians of the Gateways are," Gabirol replied and smiled.

Chapter 36
Pistis Sophia and the Book of John

The old man sat back in his chair and pulled back his hood to reveal his face a lot clearer. For almost two days he had recalled the tale in detail with his features, in the main, hidden by the hood. Gabirol looked at him to see if he could see any trace of a scar upon his face, just in case it was Paul himself. The Hospitaller looked at the old man intently too. He was too old to be Paul and his eyes gave away years of hardship. But his hair was pure white.

"'Tis good to see more of you," the Templar said.

"I chill easily...so please pardon the fact that I remain cloaked. Plus I keep myself hidden lest anyone decides they wish to report me...which has happened before, believe you me. But as you have sat and listened these past two days, I feel more than comfortable to reveal more of myself to you all. So please, I hope you will humour me just a while longer until I have finished this tale," the old man explained and clasped his hands together.

"So please pray tell us about this Pistis Sophia and the Book of John you mentioned."

"I thought we were going to eat?" Simon exclaimed loudly.

"Trust you...I see your stomach must be nourished before your soul...," Sarah remarked.

"'Tis not a problem. I know this man already and I know of this tale. I shall prepare a meal whilst he continues," Stephan remarked and stood up smiling at the old man.

"Thank you, Stephan. I am sure it will be most welcome," the old man said as Simon folded his arms, looking happy, Sarah giving him a cold hard look and shaking her head.

"Was Paul all right after they took him out of the cave?" Ayleth asked quietly.

"He was exhausted. Poor Percival was in a mild state of shock having experienced his worst nightmare scenario," the old man replied.

"Why his worst?" Peter asked.

"In his youth, well childhood, Percival spent many hours and even days locked beneath ground in a darkened cell by his adoptive parents for being wilful...though in reality he was not wilful at all." The old man paused as he thought for several minutes. "But Percival I shall leave until later to explain. But his trip had taught him that he could face and overcome his fears..."

"That is true courage," the Templar commented.

 1 – 36

"Indeed it is. But it was his sense of duty toward Paul that drove him to go with him. Thomas and his men joked and taunted him about the fact that he had messed himself with fear, but they respected enormously what he had done. Plus from their own experiences, some of them had done exactly the same. You see, being brave and having courage is not being fearless...it is being terrified yet standing your ground and facing that fear and controlling it. They were also thankful he had somehow pulled Paul out from wherever they

had been for five days with no food or water. And when Paul finally woke up, he was greeted by the sight of Percival, Theodoric, Count Henry, Brother Jakelin and all of Thomas's men standing around his bed looking at him, which surprised him greatly."

"Why?" the Genoese sailor asked bluntly.

"To wake up surrounded by them all, would you not be surprised?" the Genoese sailor remarked smiling broadly.

"No, I meant why about Thomas and his men," Gabirol replied.

"Why...because they were both concerned but also curious. Thomas's men had all agreed and taken it upon themselves to escort Paul and Alisha all the way to Alexandria, without ever really explaining their motivation fully, and now the very reason for their 'quest' or vow had almost been lost. They had questions they wished to ask and they wanted to make sure they had not failed in what they had set out to do," the old man answered.

"Hmm, I did wonder why this Thomas knight and his men were so keen to help. Do they have ulterior motives, as in after payment or something?" Gabirol asked.

"No, there was nothing sinister about Thomas and his men. Some of them were certainly rough diamonds and maybe one or two had some strange ideas on what constituted moral conduct and behaviour, but they were driven men. The scar upon Paul's face having all but vanished had not been lost on any of them. They were dedicated men who lived and breathed whatever it was they were tasked to do. It gave them a purpose, a direction and an explainable reason to do what they loved doing. I shall explain more about Thomas and his men as they would prove most valuable in time...especially as there was a greater evil that was to soon fall upon them all."

"A greater evil! Oh no. Do I want to know...and we do not know their names neither. Is that on purpose?" Ayleth asked.

"That was one thing Paul did redress and make amends for when he finally woke for it only dawned upon him then that he did not even know all their names or really appreciated their company. He had simply taken them almost for granted. That realisation hit him hard and touched him as he lay on his bed looking at them each in turn. He actually felt somewhat ashamed at his lack of attention and appreciation. Thomas had joked many times that his men were his own private army of kings, but Paul had simply and wrongly understood this as Thomas being boastful."

"Well at least he realised it...some never appreciate what they have or what others do for them without thanks or recognition," the Hospitaller remarked.

"Sorry to change the subject, but this Pistis Sophia...I am sure I have heard of this before, but I cannot recall from where and when. And I have never heard of the Book of John of Jerusalem, unless that is the book of Revelation supposedly written by John?" Gabirol interrupted.

"No, the Book of John of Jerusalem is a totally different piece of work. As for the Pistis Sophia, let me explain as best I am able for I have dropped its name in already in this tale," the old man answered. "It is just one document of many that the Church and scholars claim is fake, just like Book of John of Jerusalem written by one of the founding knights of the Temple because it has many prophecies within it...but first off, let me explain that the Pistis Sophia is an important Gnostic text written between the third and fourth centuries AD. It is so potentially damaging to the Church's present position and authority that the few manuscript copies of it are closely guarded and protected. Several have already been hidden away...one in particular by Philip and Theodoric themselves," the old man began to explain.

"How is it so damaging?" Peter asked.

"*Because it relates the Gnostic teachings of the resurrected Jesus, to his assembled disciples...including his mother Mary, Mary Magdalene, and Martha, when he continued teaching and speaking with them. The book details complex structures and hierarchies of Heaven familiar in other Gnostic teachings and proclaims that Jesus remained on earth after the resurrection for a further eleven years, teaching his disciples up to the first beginner's level of the great mysteries. It starts with an allegory paralleling the death and resurrection of Jesus, and describing the descent and ascent of the soul. It then proceeds to describe important figures within the Gnostic cosmology, and then finally lists thirty-two carnal desires to overcome before salvation is possible. Just like the Language of the Birds almost. The female divinity of Gnosticism is Sophia, a being with many aspects and names. She is sometimes identified with the Holy Spirit itself but, according to her various capacities, is also the Universal Mother, the Mother of the Living or Resplendent Mother, the Power on High, She-of-the-Left-Hand, as opposed to Christ, understood as her husband and He of the Right Hand, as the Luxurious One, the Womb, the Virgin, the Wife of the Male, the Revealer of Perfect Mysteries, the Holy Dove of the Spirit, the Heavenly Mother, the Wandering One, or Elena that is, Selene, the Moon. She was envisaged as the Psyche of the world and the female.*"

"*Do you think we should stop and continue after a rest for I sense this could be quite tough,*" Sarah interrupted.

"*Food would be good and as soon as Stephan brings in the meal...after I have explained this, then indeed we shall rest. Take a proper break. Are we agreed?*" the old man asked.

"*Food...I say yes,*" Simon smiled.

All in the room looked at each other and all agreed.

ᔅᦔ

"*Then let me continue by explaining the very title 'Pistis Sophia' (Πίστις Σοφία) for nowhere is it given as the title of the whole work. It was called this in error by misunderstanding the title. We have corrected this error, but it will again be misunderstood. It should really be titled 'Books of the Saviour' instead. The term 'Pistis Sophia' is often translated as faith, wisdom or simply 'faith in wisdom'. But a more accurate translation, taking into account its Gnostic context, is 'The Faith of Sophia', as Sophia to the Gnostics was a Divine double of Christ, rather than simply a word meaning wisdom.*"

"*So just like the Templars' worship of Baphomet, meaning Sophia for wisdom, the two are the same...yes?*" Gabirol asked.

"*In essence yes. But in an earlier, simpler version of Sophia, the transfigured Christ explains Pistis in a rather strange and cryptic manner when his disciples asked, 'tell us clearly how they came down from the invisibilities, from the immortal to the world that dies'. In reply he said 'Son of Man consented with Sophia, his consort, and revealed a great androgynous light. Its male name is designated "Saviour, begetter of all things". Its female name is designated "All-begettress Sophia". Some call her "Pistis"'.*"

"*Does this make sense to you?*" Simon asked Gabirol quietly.

Gabirol looked at him and smiled as he nodded yes.

"*Simon, I am trying to make this as easy as possible to follow and understand,*" the old man said. Simon smiled back and nodded quickly. "*The secret gospel itself is in four parts.*

The first three books make frequent reference to what is related in the fourth, and complete its descriptions. The gospel details at some length various descriptions of various realms and levels such as the Kingdom of Light, the rulers and beings who dwell in them."

317

"Like that woman of light?" Ayleth asked.

"Yes, I guess you could say that," the old man answered.

"If it was not all just a dream or hallucination of course!" the wealthy tailor interjected.

"Of course...The Pistis Sophia reveals details about absolute knowledge and wisdom and that the first mysterium, the greatest mystery in other words, is the supreme principle of all forgiveness of sin. From it proceeds the 'primum (unicum) mysterium primi mysterii', and from these two proceed a further three, five, and twelve other mysteries. The upper world, the kingdom of light, finds its completion in the twenty-fourth or last mystery, which again itself produces twelve subordinate mysteries and emanations. It explains about divisions into five which is further divided into seven further mysteries," the old man explained as Gabirol wrote as fast as he could.

"I note all the values and numbers are made clear and obvious," the Templar interrupted and nodded he understood the values.

"Yes, the numbers are all values of importance," the old man replied then continued. "Plus details on the twenty-four different mysteries and the various realms and regions inhabited by an infinite multitude of spirits are explained as well as their names given. It talks of a further five trees of light and twenty-four mysteries."

"Trees again...see even I can see that," Simon stated proud of his insight.

"Yes, trees again," the old man smiled at Simon. "Besides these are named 24,000 hymneutai, amenytoi, asemantoi, anennoetoi, asaleutoi, akinetoi, with taxeis corresponding. There is an upper realm of light, but is placed below the three choremata of the upper world, and stands at the head of the kerasmos or region of mixed light. The thesauros luminis, or terra lucis (topos probolon) is then, according to the explanation, the place whence the light, which has its source in the upper world, is brought down into the lower world, and whereby it is again transmitted upwards from the one world to the other. In this thesauros luminis are found twelve gathering-points of lights (taxeis taxeon), the seven phonai or amen, which, according to the fourth book, are the seven highest spirits of the world of light after the Pater paternitatis, as in father and five trees of light."

"Is that where we get the saying seventh heaven?" Simon asked.

"In part yes," the old man answered as Gabirol looked at Simon and grinned. "But beside the seven phonai and the five trees of light in this region are found three amen, the Gemini soteres, and nine phylakes, who are charged with the office of guarding the light. From the above named gathering points of light there are a further twelve soteres, each of whom again is set over twelve taxeis. The mixture of hyle with the thesauros, or treasury of light, or the already existing combination of purer and impurer elements wherein is produced the material out of which the lower regions of the kerasmos were formed."

"Lost...I am lost!" Simon laughed out loud, confused.

"Fear not, Simon, for it will make sense and even if you do not understand it now, you shall in time, believe me," the old man explained. Simon shook his head no but smiled regardless. "The Pistis Sophia also details the great 'Sabaoth', Father of the soul of Jesus."

"But that was God was it not?" the farrier asked.

"God as taught to us, yes," the old man answered. "These rulers are charged with forming and developing all lower spheres of existence by bringing down the light out of its treasury, and then conducting it back again, and so accomplishing the salvation of such souls as are capable of reception into the higher world."

"What, like that woman of light who said Paul could pass...or enter?" Simon asked.

"Well yes I suppose, if she was of that realm for there are many," the old man answered and waited for Simon to respond. He said nothing more so he continued. *"Now next, after the region of the right, comes that of the middle, the topos meson, where spirits are specially entrusted with the guardianship of human souls. Some believe these beings of light to be what we call our guardian angels who watch over us. Some Sufi mystics believe that these are the angels that watch and make notes upon all of our actions! Among them the fourth book names the great 'Iao the Good', and the little 'Sabaoth the Good', to which the first book adds the little Iao. In this place the light-maiden parthenos lucis has her seat, and is the judge of souls, who either discloses for them the gates of the light-realm, or sends them back into earthly existence. Perhaps it was she who Paul and Percival saw...or experienced would be a better understanding. Under her are placed seven other light-maidens with their fifteen helpers, all very similar to the female of light, and maybe even the old woman, the watcher...I guess we shall never know for certain. They are known as 'parastatai'. In the topos Parthenou, the sun, diskos solis, and moon, diskos lunae, also have their seats and transmit their light, obscured by many veils, katapetasmata, into the lower realms of creation. Basically meaning that real physical influences of these spheres affect us physical beings upon the earth. The moon we know seems to regulate women's cycles every month."*

"Ha, you do not need to tell us that...a curse you mean?" Sarah said loudly.

"A curse for us men you mean?" the wealthy tailor remarked and raised his eyebrows.

"'Tis but a necessary aspect of womanhood," the old man interrupted and then continued. *"The diskos solis is described in the fourth book as a great dragon carrying his tail in his mouth, and drawn by four great powers in the form of four white horses. Many Celtic and other ancient belief systems have images and symbols depicting a serpent in a circle swallowing its own tail. The moon is depicted in the form of a ship drawn by two white cattle and steered from the stern by a boy, a navigator no less! A male and a female dragon form the rudder. Beneath the place of the mid-region is that of the left, the place of righteousness, the lowest portion of the kerasmos, towards which penitent soul's head. It is here that the conflict between the light and the material physical world of our realm takes its beginning. Here dwell and exist, according to the fourth book, the aoratos deus and his magna dynamis the Barbelo, whence is derived the blood or corporeity of Jesus, and also the three dii tridynamoi, of which the two uppermost are called Ipsantachounchainchouchooch and Chainchooooch or Bainchooooch."*

"Ipsancochaninhooch a what?" Simon laughed.

"I apologise...that is a bit of a mouthful. You should try remembering it," the old man replied and winked at Simon. *"Know that these spirits belong to the thirteenth Aeon reckoned from below. Underneath this Aeon are the twelve Aeons, of which six are ruled by Sabaoth Adamas, and six by Jabraoth. These produce, by the exercise of the mysterion synousias, ever fresh ministering spirits, in order to extend the circuit of their power. These efforts are, however, opposed by Jeu, the Father of the Father of Jesus."*

"What? So God has a father?" Peter stated and shook his head.

"As I said, there are many levels of existence," the old man answered politely and paused as Peter scratched his head. *"Jabraoth, with his archontes, undergoes a conversion, and becomes a believer in the mysteries of light, in reward for which he is brought to a higher place, into an aera purum, and before the sunlight, ad meson and intra topous aoratou Dei. Sabaoth Adamas, on the other hand, because he will not abstain from the mysterion synousias, is confined along with his Archontes in the sphaira, or the eirmarmene sphairas, the visible star-heaven in which the twelve spirits of the zodiac have their seat. In other words, mankind, which is still influenced by the very stars and planets."*

"Ah...and why people like Niccolas and Theodoric relied and placed much value upon star charts...yes?" Gabirol interrupted.

"In part, yes. But know that over the sphaira Jeu seats five great Archontes, formed out of the light-powers of the right. These are the five planetary spirits...Kronos, Ares, Hermes, Aphrodite, Zeus. Under it he sets three hundred and sixty other Aeons. The present fixed order of the star courses is, therefore, originally a punishment inflicted on the Archontes for the misuse of their liberty. Three hundred and sixty Archontes then of the Adamas, having refused to believe in the mystery of light, are assigned a dwelling-place in an even lower region, that of the air 'topos aerinos', beneath the sphaira, or on the way of the mid-region, in via medii. Over these are likewise set five Archontes, Paraplex, Ariouth or Aethiopica, Ekate, Paredron Typhon, and Iachthanabas. Their occupation is to snatch away souls, to entice them to sin, and after death to torment them. Here, the description in the first three books is somewhat different. In these the thirteenth Aeon stands uppermost in the place of the left region, or that of righteousness. This Aeon is an image of the upper world, and like it contains innumerable spirits. The uppermost one is the 'magnus aoratos', or magnus propator, with his great dynamis the Barbelo, then follow the three tridynamoi, the third of which indicates by his very name, Authades, the intrusion at this stage of finite narrow-mindedness, the desire to exist for itself alone, which is characteristic of finite existence. As in service to self, not service to others. That is an important fact I urge you to always remember... service to self or service to others," the old man said looking at them all in turn slowly.

"I already guessed that," Simon said with a large smile.

"That is good, Simon. Very good," the old man said then continued. "From the great propator and the two upper tridynamoi proceed twenty-four other probolai aoratoi, which are thought of as syzygies, or pairs of Aeons. The last and lowest of these is the female Aeon, only occasionally mentioned in the fourth book, Pistis Sophia, whose audacious longing after the thesauros lucis has brought about her separation from her masculine Syzygos, and her Fall out of the World of Light. Below the thirteenth, stand the twelve other Aeons, which again are inhabited by innumerable spirits, with their ambitious rule-loving Archontes, among whom is specially named the Adamas magnus tyrannus, known to us from the fourth book, and again below them the Archontes of the eimarmene, the second sphaira and the sphaira, the prima sphaira, as in the first, reckoning from below. Further and finally beneath these are the Archontes of the way of the midst, with whom the moira has her seat, and through who according to the fourth book punishments are executed on such souls as are condemned to a second earthly life."

"So reincarnation you mean?" Sarah interrupted.

"If you accept the literal word, then yes as a second earthly life would imply that. But the books also speak of the formation of souls. In order to bring back the rebellious Archontes to a lasting obedience, Melchizedek came down to them from the place of the right, deprived them of light-power, and all finer elements, the breath of their mouth, the tears of their eyes, and the exhalations of their bodies, and restored to the thesauros luminis all the purer elements, of light contained in these. Out of the coarser remnant these Archontes then proceeded to form the souls of men and animals, and, urged on by their innate love of rule, found themselves compelled to continue in this occupation until they are completely emptied of even the less pure elements of light. In this creative work concur also the paralemptores solis et lunae, who, collecting the scattered elements of pure light on the one hand, and, on the other, the still relatively finer sediments of these, form out of them on their own account, also the souls of men and animals. And of the world it says, underneath the Way of the

Midst is the World or kosmos, which consists of the stereoma, or firmament, with the innumerable spirits, the earth, or kosmos hominum and the underworld. This last is divided into three places of punishment, Orcus, Chaos, or Orcus Chai, and the Outer Darkness, Caligo externa, into which are cast the souls incapable of redemption. Over Orcus rules the archon erinaios, Ariel; over Chaos, the lion-headed Ialdabaoth, along with whom are mentioned in the fourth book Persephone, and as it seems also Adonis. Caligo externa, the place of weeping and gnashing of teeth, is in the third book described as a great dragon which encircles the earth and carries its tail in its mouth, while the sunlight is obscured by the smoke and mist which issue from its darkness. In this dragon are twelve chambers of punishment, tamieia kolaseos, in which are housed all sorts of brute-shaped Archontes. The upper approaches to these receptacles are under the guardianship of the good angels, whereas souls thrust down into the outer darkness are made to enter them by means of the opening and closing of the dragon's tail. In Orcus, souls are tormented with flames of fire; in Chaos, with added darkness and smoke; in Caligo externa, with further additions, of ice, hail, snow, and cruel cold."

"Oh Lord...not what I wish to hear and learn as this sort of information simply terrifies me," Ayleth said nervously.

"Fear not, Ayleth...I think it safe to say you will not be visiting the lower realms any time soon," the Hospitaller said reassuringly at her.

"I think he speaks truthfully," the old man said softly and winked at the Hospitaller.

"I want to know what Archontes means or are," Simon said, bemused.

"Simon, it is just another name for someone who rules, mainly in reference to foreign rulers, that is all. I can strip away all the Latin names if it helps?" the old man explained.

"No...I require them," Gabirol shot back quickly and waved his quill.

The old man laughed lightly seeing him do this then continued with his explanation.

"The origination of human souls is described in the third book. They are of a different kind, according to the matter, more or less pure, out of which they are formed. In this formation each of the five rulers or planetary spirits contributes his part, that is why some argue that the actual planets' position at birth has a direct effect upon each of us...Anyway, after a human soul is formed, a Lethe-potion is offered them, e spermati kakias, and full of stimulant to evil lusts. This forms itself into their evil enemy, a spiritual substance surrounding the soul, antimimon pneumatos. This is done to teach us and test us on purpose. By the provident care of the sun and moon spirit, every soul has a spark of light intermingled with it, thence migma. The soul is then brought down from above by the Archontes, Ruler of the Way of the Midst, and by them associated with its moira, or Genius of Death or as we would understand it, fate, whereupon follows its investiture with the soma hylikon archonton. As soon as the various psychical elements of the future human being, which exist apart in man and wife, have been united in conception, the three hundred and sixty-five ministers of the Archontes proceed to fashion in the metra, the future body consisting of three hundred and sixty-five parts, impressing on it the sphragides of the days, which prove most significant in the formation of the man and the length of life assigned to him. These sphragides are then made known to the archontes erinaioi, and a child is born, which, apart from the indwelling spark of light, is a mere creature and formation of the Archontes, and stands wholly under their power. All future life-fortunes befall the man thus formed with absolute necessity, and in consequence of the moira by which he is accompanied. Even the sin into which the soul falls under the influence of the antimimon pneuma is an inevitable fate, a consequence per ananken eimarmenes, but every single act of sin is put on record in order to be punished. After the man's death his indwelling spark of light goes back to the light-maiden, while his

soul is laid hold of by the *paralemptores of the archontes erinaioi*, and after being led about for three days in all the *topoi kosmou.*"

"Like Jesus and raised three days later?" the farrier remarked.

"I suppose so. But after death, the soul is finally brought into the *Orcus Chai*. If not then condemned to eternal torment, the soul is, on the expiry of its term of penance, brought up out of chaos and placed before the *archontes viae medii* and there questioned concerning the mysteries of the *moira*, and if ignorant of them, is again condemned to yet more terrible punishments. When these have been endured, the soul is brought before the light-maiden, and again by her, on account of past sins, brought back into the *sphaira archonton*, and from thence into a second earthly life. Imbued once more with her old light-power, the soul is again born in the same way as before; and these *metabolai* or *metangismoi* repeat themselves till the soul has completed the number of *kykloi* assigned it in accordance with the extent of its guilt. Some eastern traditions call this Karma. Should the soul now having passed through all these cycles and trials without having found the mysteries of light, or if, having received the highest mysteries, has made no repentance, it will then be cast for ever into the outer darkness. Yet many souls can be delivered out of this outer darkness if they know the mystery of one of the twelve chambers of punishment in the dragon. In such cases they will be led upwards by the watch-keeping angels of *Jeu*, and being no longer capable of returning in new bodies to this world, will receive baptism from the seven light-maidens, be set free from all punishments, and be translated into the lowermost *taxa* of the treasury of light. The necessity of sinning is not, however, universal. The apostles, for instance, were exempt from it, their souls having been formed out of pure elements of light. The possibility, moreover, of a soul keeping itself free from sin is elsewhere occasionally assumed. A soul initiated into the higher mysteries, and yet sinning, will be more severely punished than one which has only received the lower mysteries. These lower mysteries, on the other hand, lose through persistence in sin their power of atonement, till at length only the highest mystery of all is able to absolve from sin. In this way the work seeks to combine a strictly ethical position with that Gnostic esteem for pure knowledge without which no one can attain to the upper world of light. It represents the mysteries whose knowledge is required for any entrance into the treasury of light, as, on the one hand, a free gift vouchsafed to man, and, on the other, an object of striving and spiritual warfare. Much like what Paul's father, Philip, explained in his written note for Paul if you recall? The absolving power attributed to them may be compared to the similar operation attributed to the sacraments of the Church. The fourth book describes the fates of souls after death, the punishments which await them for their sins, as well as the circumstances of their regeneration and the condition under which they may obtain forgiveness. The five Archontes of the *via medii*, and their subordinate *archidaimonia*, are first the tempters of the souls to sin, and afterwards the most terrible tormentors. The demons of the Paraplex, an Archon, with woman's hair flowing down to her feet, lead souls astray to wrath, evil-speaking, and slandering; the demons of Ariouth Aethiopica, who is also a female Archon, lead on, in like manner, to murder and bloodshed; and those of the three-headed Hecate to false-swearing, lying, and deceit; those of Paredron Typhon to uncleanness and adultery and, finally, those of Iachthanabas, to unrighteous judgement and oppression of the upright and the poor. Souls that have been carried off by these demons are tormented by them, according to the nature of their transgressions, for one hundred years, or longer, and only after a corresponding favourable conjunction of the planets can they be rescued from their tormentors by the five Archontes of the Aeons as in the planetary dynasts themselves, assisted by the higher spirits of the right and of the *midst. Such souls, as on account of sin have to undergo regeneration, are, after death, first tormented in orcus by Ariel, then in chaos by Ialdabaoth, then again by the Archontes of the way of the midst, and so, finally, are led before the light-maiden, who pronounces her judgement upon them. They are then brought back into the sphaira, and after being purified by the leitourgoi sphairas through the instrumentality of fire, smoke, and water, they receive from Jaluham the paralemptes of Sabaoth-Adamas, the drink of forgetfulness, and are then invested with a new body, the nature of which will be such as to put hindrance in the way of repetition of former sins."*

"Why drink to forget...surely it would be better and easier if you could remember so as not to repeat the same error again?" Peter asked.

"'Tis but a veil for this world. Can you imagine if you were able to recall all the events in your past life...or even lives? All the pain and suffering...though in reality many of us do carry them over without realising it, hence an irrational fear about something for no obvious reason. Plus if you were to recall that you were a murderer previously, how would you be able to forgive yourself, be tested again to see if you would do the same etcetera?"

2 – 18

"That makes sense," Simon stated, nodding in agreement.

"Those, on the other hand, who have been guilty of greater sins, like murder, blasphemy, sins against nature, or have performed the impure mysteries of the Borborites, who were another extreme Gnostic sect by the way, are not again invested with new bodies, but cast into the outer darkness where, along with the dragon, they will be destroyed at the last judgement. Good souls, on the other hand, who, without having committed grievous sins, have failed to find the mysteries of light, will according to the consentient representations of the third and fourth books, so soon as the favourable conjunction of the planets has taken place, be, after death, led about during three days in all topoi of the universe, and likewise in chaos, and made acquainted with all the forms of punishment there; the punitive spirits of those regions will have but little power over them, and being rescued from these and safely conducted past the Archontes, Rulers of the way of the midst, they will then be led before the light-maiden, and by her be signed with a sphragis praestans. They will then remain with the little Sabaoth till the favourable time has come for their renewed descent to earth. Each soul, being then supplied with a wisdom and watchfulness inspiring potion, and a soma dikaion, will set herself to seek the mysteries of the upper world, the Gnosis of which will render her worthy of a share in the Kingdom of Light. But, not these only, sinning souls also, who after they have found the mysteries of light, leave off sinning, may yet attain to the treasury of light. Such souls, when the favourable conjunction of the planets has come, will be once more sent back as righteous souls into the world. From all this it would seem that the fates of men after death will indeed depend on their moral conduct on the one hand, but also, on the other hand, on the conjunctions of the stars and the influence they exercise on the mysteries of light. Souls born under unfavourable constellations become bad, and will be unable to find the mysteries."

"But it is not their fault they were born under those circumstances surely," Ayleth exclaimed.

"No it is not...but some do so in order to instigate evils to test others. The redemption of human souls is, according to this, accomplished chiefly by initiation into the sin absolving mysteries. Into this Jesus first initiates his own disciples, and then commissions them to impart the knowledge of the same to others. In this impartation of absolving mysteries consist, *according to the fourth book, the work of Jesus upon earth. For which end he brings down water and fire from the topos luminis luminum, wine and blood from the topos of the Barbelo. His Father sends him the Holy Ghost in the form of a dove; fire, water, and wine, serve for the cleansing of all the sins of the whole world; while the blood serves him as a token propter soma generis humani, as of his own corporeity. The word of Jesus, I have come to send fire upon the earth, points to the purification of the sins of the whole world by fire; in like manner, the saying to the woman of Samaria about the water of life (John 4:10–14), the issuing of water and blood from the pierced side of Jesus, and the consecration of the Eucharistic cup as the blood of the covenant; all three refer to the forgiveness of sins accomplished by these mysteries of light. Of special energy and power for this end is the mystery of the Eucharist, consisting of oblations and special prayers. Jesus himself celebrates it, in the first instance, for the cleansing of his disciples, and bids them henceforth repeat it for the like cleansing of all future believers. The particular description here given of this celebration, the offering of water, wine, and bread, with solemn mystic forms of prayer, is of special importance as characteristic of the ritual and worship of the Gnostic party, among whom this work originated. Beside the mystery of the Eucharist, which is also designated as that of the true baptism, we find mentioned a baptisma fumi, abaptisma pneumatos sancti luminis, an unctio pneumatike, and as the highest mystery, that of the seven phonai, and their forty-nine dynameis and psephoi. These mysteries disclose to the souls of men the entrance to the Kingdom of Light, and the thus initiated have only to leave the soma hyles, and then restrained no longer by any hostile or subordinate power, they mount up freely through all those regions to the treasury of light. The Christology and Soteriology of the three first books is also much more developed and detailed than that of the fourth book. Jesus is represented as the universal Redeemer, whose historical manifestation and redeeming work on earth accomplishes at the same time a cosmical redemption. The prophets, patriarchs, and other righteous ones of the Old Testament, must wait in patience till Jesus has brought his disciples into the Kingdom of Light. Three only, Abraham, Isaac, and Jacob, are at once, at the time of our Lord's ascension, received with him into that kingdom; the rest have to return once more into earthly existence, and there receive the mysteries of light. Jesus, who proceeds from the first mystery, as in from his Father, bears himself the name of primum mysterium. The end of his mission to the earth is the revelation of the upper higher mysteries. As, on the one hand, even before his earthly manifestation, he had begun to work through the instruction of Enoch, as given in paradise; so, on the other hand, he makes the perfect communication of Gnosis and the accomplishment of his redeeming work coincident with the ascension. The deliverance of the Pistis Sophia is a prelude and fore type of the redemption of humanity. In her, indeed, is typically represented the original descent and implanting in the lower world of the spark of divine light. But Pistis Sophia herself obtains her full deliverance only at the ascension. The process of the work of redemption is as follows. The Soter rises from his seat in the twenty-fourth mystery, leaves there his endyma lucis behind, and descends unrecognised by the Archons who take him for the angel Gabriel into the lower regions. From the thesauros lucis he carries with him twelve powers of light, out of which the souls of the apostles are formed in the sphaira; from the little Jao, in the place of the midst, he takes another power of light, with which he combines the soul of Elias, and out of this the soul of John, the forerunner, is formed. Thereupon he announces, and once more in the form of Gabriel, to Mary, that she is to become the mother of the Soter, and brings down to her a psyche and a soma. The former is a vis luminis, from the great Sabaoth, in the place of the right; the latter is a robe of light from the Barbelo in the thirteenth Aeon, which, though a hyle needing some measure of purification, is yet no earthly or material corporeity. From these two constituents*

Jesus is formed. With him in his very childhood a pneuma is associated, called the simile Jesu or frater Jesu, which keeps him free from all hylic influences, and impels him to receive the baptism of John. The Soter himself descends at the baptism, in the form of a dove, upon Jesus. The work of redemption upon earth, or the imparting of the mysteries of the upper world, is now proceeded with, partly in the way of instruction given concerning thetopoi aletheias in general, partly in that of revelations concerning the remission of sins as mediated by various sacred actions and formulae. During his life on earth Jesus imparts the mysteries to his disciples, in the first instance, in allegorical and symbolic language, as in the numerous parables and discourses of our canonical gospels, the deeper significance of which is not disclosed to them until after his ascension. His death is described as an actual crucifixion. After the resurrection, as I said earlier, he remains for a further eleven years with his disciples, and then being reclothed with his heavenly endyma lucis, on which are inscribed the secret names of all celestial and supercelestial beings. He mounts upwards through all the middle regions to the higher world of light. On his way he overcomes the opposing world-rulers of the twelfth Aeon, and the Authades, the ruler of the thirteenth Aeon, depriving them of their power of light, and compelling them to yield up again the souls which they have devoured, so that the arithmos psychon teleion may be completed. After this he brings the Pistis Sophia with him into the upper realm of light. Thence, adorned with a triple crown of beams, the triple beams of light being a very ancient and even Druidic symbol, he descends again to earth in the glory of world-redeemer, and initiates his disciples into all mysteries, ab internis usque ad externa et ab externis usque ad interna. The personal work of redemption by individual souls is then proceeded with, through the mediation of the mysteries of light. After these, men must seek day and night, and render themselves worthy to receive them, by renouncing the world and the hyle, and all their cares, and sins, and occupations. These mysteries are again, in their turn, numerous and manifold. The 'mystery of baptism' imparts, by water and fire, the cleansing from sin and the soul's deliverance from the antimimon pneuma, the moira and the soma. But in order fully to accomplish this deliverance, further mysteries are also required from the primum chorema, a parte externa, the lowest region of the realm of light upwards to the highest mystery, that of the Ineffabilis. These mysteries are imparted to penitent souls in a regular series, one after the other, because, as has been already observed the lower mysteries lose their power after fresh relapses into sin, till at last the Mysterium Ineffabilis alone is of any help. The higher the mysteries that have been received, the severer is the punishment for relapses into sin. He who, after receiving the Mysterium Ineffabilis, falls again into sin and departs impenitent out of this life, will be cast into the outer darkness. But even out of the Caligo external deliverance is possible, through the mediation of others, who pronounce the Mysterium Ineffabilis. A soul thus delivered is brought before the light-maiden, and she sends it back once more to earth, clothed in a righteous body, soma dikaion. And even when it is no longer possible for a soul to return to earth in a new body, yet the possibility of deliverance is not fully excluded. The same series of mysteries, rising step by step up to the highest, serves also for the initiation of the dikaioi and agathoi. Those who have died penitent need not, after receiving the mysteries, submit again to a fresh metempsychosis. Souls perfectly pure, who have been partakers of the highest mysteries, ascend upwards robed in glorious light, and without encountering any hindrance, through all the intermediate realms up to the place of the inheritance. Others who have received only the lower mysteries, and have not lived perfectly free from sin, are required to produce at every stage their apologia 'apophasis', symbola, and are then taken up, step by step, by paralemptores from the realms of light, examined by the light-maiden, and finally transmitted by Melchizedek into the ultima taxis luminis. Of human souls, however, in comparison with all other spiritual existence, the saying is especially true 'the last shall be first' for though once the mere dregs and last deposit of the light of the middle regions, they will, after passing through conflicts and sufferings, be raised above all the world-rulers Archontes, and introduced into the realm of light."

"I am afraid to say I am confused," the wealthy tailor said, perplexed.

"You have been spending too much time next to Simon," Sarah laughed.

"Then let me finish explaining this quickly before I detail the Book of John," the old man said softly. "Understand that beneath these are placed the other souls of men in various ranks, according to the mysteries of which they have been made partakers. Among the Aeons, also, finally admitted into the realm of light, a corresponding order of ranks will be found, according to the places occupied by them in the times before their perfecting. Each one finally reaches the place pre-ordained for him (topos taxeos) from the beginning, and enjoys henceforth that measure of knowledge which has been procured for him by the corresponding mysteries. The basis of the whole system, namely, that spiritual purification and gradual deliverance from hylic elements is essentially dependent on a moral process, and this forms a distinguishing peculiarity of human souls in comparison with all other spiritual beings. Again, and this is specially to be observed, the fundamental conception of the whole system that the development of the universe is nothing else but the return of the light-power from the realm of the ἄρχοντες to the heavenly world. In both systems the light-power is arbitrarily misused by the world-rulers for the production of angeli, potestates, and dominationes. In both the creation of man is the means of depriving them of this power. In both Christ draws by degrees to himself the light-power confined in the earthly sphere, and the complete restoration of these elements of light to the upper world is the final close of the whole development. One other main point of doctrine in our system, that namely of the distinction made between souls, Mary Magdalene does actually play a distinguished part in the Pistis Sophia among the female disciples of Jesus, and is remarkable among all, both male and female, for her thirst for knowledge and her unwearied activity in asking questions. The continual progress and changes of use in regard to names, figures, and symbols among the Gnostic sects need not puzzle us any more than the circumstance, that these names are continually occurring in different connections and significations and belong to the conceptions of a light-maiden, a world of light, trees of light, and light saviours, soteres thesaurou luminis."

"Like the trees both Alisha and Paul saw in their shared dream...yes?" Ayleth asked.

"Yes...Now beside male disciples, females also appear, as you know...Mary Magdalene, Mary the Mother of Jesus secundum soma hyles, Martha and Salome. The instructions which Jesus imparted to them are for the most part elicited by questions they put to him, Mary Magdalene distinguishing herself as the chief questioner. Also, beside the canonical scriptures of the Old and New Testaments various apocryphal writings are made use of, all probably being of Gnostic origin. To these must be added the book Jeu, which Jesus is supposed to have dictated to Enoch in Paradise. It is cited as an authority for the knowledge of the mysteries of the three kleroi luminis, and appears to have been the main source of the fully developed Gnostic doctrine of the three first books. We find also some allusions to an apocryphal gospel of the childhood and, perhaps to the gospel of Philip." [47]

"All wars and conflicts are about land, resources, power and wealth. Religion and political ideologies are simply tools used to incite the masses into hysteria, subdue them, pacify them and make them malleable enough to follow orders," the Hospitaller said out of the blue as if his mind was thinking upon other issues.

"Please, I too, like Simon find all of what you have explained a little confusing," Ayleth said apologetically and twisted her hair in her fingers, embarrassed.

"All of what I have said is indeed confusing, but believe me when I say that even if you cannot understand it or it sounded boring and needless, your higher mind will remember it all. I can also tell you that all of what I have just explained is also but just a guide, like a spiritual map almost for people to learn and follow as best they can until a time when what it says can really and truly be understood. It is all allegorical and symbolic...yet still carries the values and truths required for later generations to understand," the old man replied.

"So what do you believe...how do you interpret what you have learnt?" Peter asked.

"Me?" the old man answered and paused for several minutes before answering. "I believe that we all come from the light of love, wherein lies the 'Seat of The Soul'. Here upon this earthly realm, our journey is from Love to Love and in between is what we call our life. We must all learn to stay in that Love...be the Love and when we physically die, return to that Love. That is why we must all first learn to love ourselves and then love others. Feel loved. We generate Love from inside of ourselves. From there great Love flows out to the world. And we can connect to that universal flow of Love too. Feel the Love today. Even of you feel disconnected from someone you love, feel the Love flow through you anyway. If you grieve, recognise that the grief comes only from Love and the loss of it. Drop down through the grief and recognise its very foundation is Love. Remember the Love. Reconnect with it. Stay connected to the reality of that. Perhaps no one is ever truly lost as we are eternal beings. Only a fragment of our soul is within our physical body, which is why I say your higher self will remember even if you cannot...so wrap the energy of love around you like a comforting cloak. And stay connected to source energy, call it what you will, it is Love. Life can be... is...tough. But it is always beckoning us forward into Love. Choose Love. Stay in the Light."

"But if we came from love, why is there so much death and evil in this world?" Sarah asked.

"Because we are masters of our own destinies. We have the right to free will and choice. As I have explained before, this world is but a school for our souls to learn and experience things. We would not appreciate the warmth of the summer sun if we had never experienced the cold of winter. We are all always being tested and fashioned in the fires and forge of life's great furnace."

"You mentioned something about man and woman being of one soul and then separated. Like soul partners. What did you mean by that?" Ayleth asked.

"Yes, as many of the religions and great belief systems of antiquity testify and claim...we were split at our creation. By doing so, there was balance and both parts could experience and learn things twice as fast. That is why we all strive and long for that other person...our soul mate, to reconnect and to reunite. Also, everything that a man and woman experience up to the point of creation of a new physical body for a new baby is recorded and remembered within the very building blocks of the new physical being. It is almost like a short cut to gaining new information, emotions and knowledge which is passed down from generation to generation so the new child learns so much more. And in the future, there will come a time when man will again understand what mechanism makes this happen...a time when man will act like gods themselves...but that I shall explain when I detail the Book of John of Jerusalem."

"Is that why the Bible says the sins of the fathers shall be visited upon the sons etcetera?" the Templar asked. The old man nodded yes. "Well that explains all the grief we have had thanks to Father," he half joked looking at his brother.

"But the Bible says that God took the rib from Adam to make woman," Gabirol stated.

"It does. But it was a simplified and allegorical version of the story taken from even older Sumerian and Babylonian myths. When translated properly the term for rib actually means 'Spirit' so in effect God took a part of man's spirit to make a female. But again, the scriptures actually state that the Elohim, which is plural for god, made man after his own image and then made woman as his equal. And I have a saying I always try to pass on about woman being made from man."

"What is it...perhaps Stephan will learn something," Sarah joked.

"I think Stephan knows this all too well...and I am confident he could recall it word for word if you ask him for I have told him oft its words," the old man smiled as Stephan approached the table carrying several balanced plates of food.

"What?" he asked, puzzled, noticing everyone was looking at him as he put the plates down.

"Stephan...would you be so good as to recall the words of the 'rib and woman' as you have learnt," the old man asked as Sarah looked at him quizzically.

"Er...yes I can recall the words if you wish," Stephan replied and rubbed his hands, puzzled at the request. He looked at Sarah and smiled. He coughed to clear his throat. "Woman came out of man's rib. Not from his feet to be walked upon...not from his head to be superior, but from his side to stand with him, under the arm to be protected, and next to the heart to be loved."

"My Lord...why have you never told me these things?" Sarah asked, her voice choked with emotion and surprised at his words.

"Sarah...I think there is far more to learn of your husband than you suspect," the old man remarked and winked. "Now I suggest we eat...then I shall explain about the Book of Jerusalem."

"But what about Paul and Alisha...did she get to him?" Ayleth asked.

"I shall explain that now then whilst you eat," the old man replied.

Jerusalem, Kingdom of Jerusalem, August 1179

"Gentlemen...I am somewhat at a loss what to say. But please pray tell for I am in grave error for my ignorance of not even knowing most of your names," Paul said as he tried to sit up.

"Don't worry, lad, for most people bother not with our names," the knight who had been so drunk when they had all first met in Tarsus said smiling broadly and wiped his beard.

"I do worry, for it was pure ignorance on my behalf. Please, I would like to know all of your names," Paul replied.

"Let me introduce you then to this rabble that tries to pass itself off as knights," Thomas joked as Brother Jakelin and Count Henry stood aside. "This ugly specimen is John," he said as he outstretched his hand toward the knight who told him not to worry. "He is rather too fond of beer...but that is but a minor vice." John nodded at Paul in acknowledgement. "And this is Mark," Thomas said as he pulled another of his men forward. He nodded likewise in acknowledgement before pulling the next man before Paul. As he reeled off their names, he was struck by how fierce they actually looked. Their hair long and unkempt, their beards uncut and rough, but they each had a sparkle in their eyes.

"I am most grateful to you all...and I am just glad you are on our side," Paul commented as Theodoric stepped closer.

"Here...whilst you rest, perhaps you will read this...tis the book I mentioned. Count Raymond's wife Princess Eschiva has held it in safe keeping for many years. 'Tis the book of John of Jerusalem...and my second copy is safely entrusted with Thomas here," Theodoric explained and handed him a leather bound book tied up inside a leather case. As Paul took the book, he noticed that Count Henry and Brother Jakelin were laughing and whispering.

"What is it? Why are you laughing and whispering?" Paul asked.

"You did not notice nor realise anything peculiar about Thomas and his men's names?" Count Henry asked as they all looked at each other smirking.

"No...is there some joke I have missed?" Paul asked.

"Paul...work it out," Theodoric said and patted him on the shoulder.

Paul felt embarrassed as he looked at them all in turn as they chuckled amongst themselves. Percival stepped forwards seeing how awkward he looked.

"Their names...Thomas...Mark, Matthew, Luke, Peter, John, Judas, Philip," Percival said and raised his eyebrows.

"Huh...all names of the disciples! Are they not then your real names?" Paul asked, bemused.

"My friend," Thomas said smiling as he stepped forwards. "They are indeed our real names...'tis but a coincidence that is all."

"Some coincidence," Paul replied and felt his face go red as he felt embarrassed as they all just stared at him in silence. "So what...why do you all smile so?"

"Paul...there are twelve of them, all named after disciples. And they all follow you...work it out," Percival said.

Paul sat up straight in the bed and shook his head fast.

"Absolutely no way. I am no Jesus...I am too full of sin and desires...my Lord... if you are here for you think that of me, then I am afraid to say you have all wasted your time," Paul explained feeling more embarrassed. All the men just stared at Paul, wide eyed almost and smiling. "No...I am not."

Suddenly the room erupted in full laughter from all of them including Count Henry and Theodoric. Thomas knelt beside the bed and looked Paul in the eye close trying to stifle his own laughter.

"My dear young and brave knight, for a knight you surely are...we tease you, but these are our names. Laughter is good for the soul. But in reality, and I speak for all of us here, there is something different about you and of course your very strange friend here," Thomas said and gestured towards Theodoric.

"Strange I will accept...just don't ever call me fat!" Theodoric joked back.

"And me and my men, though my men is incorrect for they are each here of their own free will and masters only unto themselves, but we shall serve you until we have discovered why the Lord, whatever you wish to call him, has placed us at your service," Thomas explained.

"But...but I have no means of paying you or thanking you enough," Paul replied.

"As we said from the start, 'tis not material wealth we seek. We understand that our journey now lies here with you wherever that shall take us. For how long." He paused. "Who knows."

"I am at a loss what to say," Paul answered wearily, his head feeling light.

Suddenly the large heavy wooden door to the room burst open as Alisha entered. Looking distraught, tired, her face covered in dirt from the road, she pushed past Count Henry and Brother Jakelin to stand beside Paul. Out of breath and her eyes were wide as she looked down at him, Thomas still kneeling beside him. Slowly Thomas stood up and took a step back. Alisha flung herself to her knees beside him and grabbed his left hand with both of her hands searching his eyes intently.

"Ali," Paul said, his voice breaking with emotion at her surprise entrance. "You are here...how...and where is Arri?"

As Paul asked that, Tenno stepped into view carrying Arri in his arms, his large figure filling the entire doorway frame. All looked at him then at Arri. Tenno raised a single eyebrow as he looked briefly down at Arri then back at all of them in turn as he stepped into the room. Alisha just stared at Paul without speaking. Paul could see her bottom lip begin the quiver. She was shocked at how pale he looked. Puzzled she raised her finger and ran it down his cheek where just the very faint line of the scar remained. She wanted to ask how come the scar had almost vanished, but her stomach was in knots and her throat felt as if it was swelled so much that she dare not speak. She knew if she said anything, her voice would give away the flood of emotion sweeping over her and she would burst into tears. She looked up at all the men stood around the bed. Count Henry coughed and motioned with his head they should all leave. Thomas acknowledged with a slight nod and beckoned his men follow him. He bowed his head slightly at Paul and then Alisha and without any further words, he left the room. Each of his men filed past simply nodding in silence as they left one by one until Count Henry, Brother Jakelin and Theodoric remained beside Tenno.

 8 – 21

"We shall leave you a while, but we shall need to talk further about what happened. Percival remembers very little himself," Count Henry said as he walked for the door.

"And you need to explain, if you can recall, whereabouts you found that," Brother Jakelin said pointing to the set of drawers to Paul's left side.

Paul looked across to see the small white bee type figurine pendant he had found inside the main vaulted room he had climbed into first. Alisha sat up onto the bed, looked Paul in the eyes. He could see the emotion in her face as she fought to control her tears from falling. Quickly she put her arms around him and hugged him tightly closing her eyes. He had been changed and bathed but he still stank of a sweet sickly sweat smell, but she did not care and she pulled him tighter. Gently he placed his arms around her, kissed the side of her head, her hair full of dust, and felt her breathing as she just held him. He looked up at Tenno gently rocking Arri.

"Thank you," Paul said quietly. Tenno simply nodded and looked at Theodoric.

"Time we were leaving," Theodoric said just as Brother Teric stepped into the room looking hot and covered from head to toe with dirt having ridden hard to Jerusalem.

"Thank the Lord I have found you. My Lord," Brother Teric exclaimed fast and stepped forwards briefly looking at Paul and Alisha. "'Tis Jacobs Ford...the castle has been destroyed and all knights either killed or taken captive this very day by Saladin."

"What?" Count Henry asked alarmed.

Alisha swung her gaze round to look at Brother Teric.

"'Tis true. All our forces have been utterly decimated to the last man and the castle brought down. Lord Balian is already making plans to negotiate a ransom but as Master Odo has already made clear, he forbids it..."

Count Henry stood thinking for a few minutes before he walked across to Brother Teric.

"This bodes very badly...very badly. We were but due to leave this very day to reinforce the castle," he remarked and walked out of the room.

"Paul, I must leave you. Alisha, 'tis good as always to see you and by the grace of our Lord it would seem you have arrived just in time. I shall be back later to discuss other matters," brother Jakelin said then bowed his head and patted brother Teric on the shoulder as he walked past him and left the room.

"What occurs here?" Brother Teric asked.

"Let me explain," Theodoric said and started to usher him back toward the door. He winked at Tenno as he went. "And you can tell me all about what has happened with Odo...for I am sure someone has indeed fouled up mightily so... for why so late in responding the call for reinforcements? Count Raymond was already prepared to go two days past."

Paul just watched as they left and Alisha rested against his chest. Paul looked at the small bee pendant again, a million questions running through his mind. He then looked at the leather book Theodoric had left. He sighed feeling exhausted but happy he had Alisha and Arri back by his side, especially now as open hostilities had started between Saladin and the Kingdom of Jerusalem. He pulled Alisha close and kissed her again. He would speak with Percival later he promised himself and he would make sure he got to know Thomas and his men better. Tenno carried on rocking Arri gently.

Port of La Rochelle, France, Melissae Inn, spring 1191

"Ah so it was Theodoric again who brings to Paul more knowledge," Gabirol remarked as he checked over the words he had just written.

"Yes...the Book of John. But Paul would not get to read it for some time," the old man replied and sighed. He looked at the plate of food Stephan had placed before him. He did not feel at all hungry but knew he should eat. He picked up a piece of bread and dipped it into the small dish of oil and took a mouthful, ate it and then continued. "Paul was shocked but also part relieved Alisha had taken the risk to get to him, but made her promise never to do so again even with Tenno escorting her. She refused to promise such a thing."

"Good on her, for I would not promise such a thing," Miriam interrupted.

"Sorry to push the matter, but what is this Book of John of Jerusalem then?" Gabirol asked.

"Here, look for yourself," the old man answered and pulled out a leather bound book wrapped inside a silk cloth. Gently he pushed it across the table toward Gabirol. "Open it and read it. In fact, keep it as a gift for I have others safely secured away."

"No, I cannot possibly take such a gift," Gabirol replied as he started to untie the string fastenings around the silk cover. Gently he unwrapped the leather book and very carefully opened it fully and turned the first page. All sat in silence as Gabirol flicked carefully through several pages reading parts from within it. After a while he looked up puzzled but smiling. "This, this details prophecies...yes?"

"Yes indeed it does. All the way to the next era of Aquarius and beyond that for another thousand years," the old man answered.

"So Armageddon is not coming any time soon?" Ayleth asked hesitantly.

"No, not in our life time," the old man answered.

"No, but perhaps our next life time," Simon remarked and winked at Ayleth.

"That could very well be true. But as I have said, the end days does not necessarily mean the end of man...just the end of a period of time," the old man explained.

"So what did Paul and Alisha do now that hostilities had started?" Ayleth asked.

"Yes, did they stay in Jerusalem or head for Alexandria?" Sarah then asked.

"They stayed a short while in Jerusalem so Paul could recover his strength. Alisha would not let him out of her sight. She told Theodoric off for not keeping a closer eye upon him and she would not accept his protestations that Paul took himself off when he should have been resting. Besides that, they needed to wait and find out what exactly had led to the failure at Jacobs Ford. A lot of questions were being asked and accusations thrown why the relief reinforcements took so long to respond. But they were internal matters beyond Paul. So whilst they waited, he read parts of the Book of John, but as often was the case, every time he tried to read, he would feel tired and fall asleep and often dream...those strange dreams he had so often. In fact, he dreamt several times about a New Jerusalem and how it related to the New Jerusalem as detailed with the Book of Revelation. In order to express his dreams he did what he always did," the old man explained and started to look through the leather bound folder of items.

"What is that then?" the farrier asked.

"Drew that which he could not fully understand," the old man answered just as he pulled out two parchment drawings and gently pushed them across the table toward him.

Fig. 37:

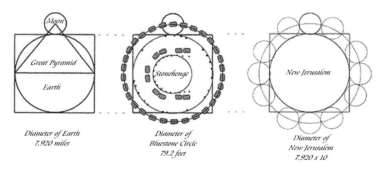

| Diameter of Earth 7,920 miles | Diameter of Bluestone Circle 79.2 feet | Diameter of New Jerusalem 7,920 x 10 |

""I hope you will explain these?" Gabirol said as he stood and leaned over the table to see the two images.

"I shall indeed. But you must promise to accept my gift of that book," the old man said as Gabirol sat back down and picked up the book again and looked at it. He nodded yes he would silently. "As you will all learn, just as all the great philosophers and artists know, there are three classes of people...Those who see, those who see when they are shown and those who do not see at all."

"So what prophecies does that book foretell?" the wealthy tailor asked as he looked at the bright coloured opening page as Gabirol turned to it. Two people were depicted standing beside a three turreted castle.

"Many, too many to explain in detail...but I can tell you there are forty prophecies in total. It foretells of a time when man will destroy much upon this earth, will be able to speak to each other no matter where they are in the world, they will be able to master the skies and build cities in the clouds, travel in horseless carriages and make man and animals in whatever fashion he chooses, like the gods of old. But it tells that after a great chaos, if man has chosen wisely, he will again restore order and balance...here, you just need only read the last few prophecies to get the idea. If you wish to read it in full, I suggest you share the book around before Gabirol departs us," the old man explained and then pushed another small vellum sheet forwards with several verses written upon it. "I always just keep these three last passages upon me...just in case."

38

In the heart of the Year Thousand that comes after Year Thousand
Each person will be like a measured footstep
They will know everything about the world and about their bodies
They will cure illness before it appears
Each person will be healer of himself and of the others.

They will have understood that you have to help to be able to maintain
And man, after the times of narrow-mindedness and of avarice,
Will open his heart and his purse to the poorest
He will feel himself to be a knight of the human order
And in this way a new time will at last begin.

39

In the heart of the Year Thousand that comes after Year Thousand
Man will have learnt to give and to share
The bitter days of solitude will be gone
He will believe once more in the spirit
And the Barbarians will have acquired recognition.

But that will come after the war and the fires
That will spring up from the blackened ruins of the towers of Babel
And it will have taken an iron fist
For the disorder to be put in order
And for man to find again the right path.

40

In the heart of the Year Thousand that comes after Year Thousand
Man will know that all living things are bearers of light
And that they are creatures to be respected
He will have built the new cities
In the sky, on the earth and on the sea.

He will have the memory of what was
And he will know what will be
He will no longer be afraid of his own death
For in his life he will have lived several lives
And the light, he will understand, will never go out.

ℰℭ

"So who are the Barbarians that will again be recognised?" Simon asked after reading the passages.

"Simon, I have said it already and I shall say it again...you are wasted as a fishmonger for you clearly see what must be asked," the old man smiled. "Well, if you consider that it was John, one of the first founding Templars, who wrote these prophecies in 1099, after experiencing a similar event as befell Paul and Percival beneath Jerusalem, it can be argued that the Barbarians in question refers to the Templars, the Ashashin and others whom history has already forgotten but viewed as being barbaric by their new standards."

"Is that not what you said from the very start of this tale...when the knights first entered the vault? Remember, you said that one of them said about not being remembered in their own life times, but that one day they would be...," Gabirol explained.

"That is what I said yes. So perhaps that is what the passage refers to."

"I am beginning to think that this Paul is perhaps a Messiah figure himself," Peter commented as he looked up thinking.

"You are not alone in thinking that...as I shall reveal," the old man stated. "Paul did instinctively know things. He knew that the New Jerusalem details related to our actual physical world, as in its size and place in the cosmos. But as more and more revelations opened up to him, so too did the sense and overwhelming feelings of responsibility weigh upon his shoulders."

"And what of Master Odo and Jacobs Ford?" the Genoese sailor asked.

"He refused to be ransomed and that is how Gerard became the new Master of the Order," the Templar answered and shook his head slowly, disapprovingly, as a thousand memories flooded his every thought. Miriam rested her head against his arm and rubbed his hand with hers reassuringly.

"Perhaps I should explain further as the battle at Jacobs Ford was a pivotal moment in our recent history...and it will give you time to finish your food before I tell of more unpleasant matters," the old man said quietly.

Ayleth placed her eating utensil down slowly, looking concerned.

"If Alisha or Paul are to be slaughtered then I wish not to hear of it," she said sadly.

"My dear child...you cannot ignore or bury your head and hope the reality of this world will not affect you for it has a habit of seeking you out wherever you go...but please hear me out," the old man replied. After a few minutes in silence, other than the chomping sounds of Simon eating noisily, Ayleth nodded yes reluctantly and took a deep breath. Sarah clasped her hand over hers reassuringly. "The Battle of Jacobs Ford," he started and looked at the Templar, who nodded back in silence. "It was a massive victory for Saladin against the King of Jerusalem, Baldwin the Fourth. As I have mentioned before, it occurred in August 1179 at Jacobs Ford in Syria, also known by the Latin name of Vadum Iacob and in modern Hebrew as Ateret. Many now believe that the Islamic takeover of Jerusalem in 1187 can be directly linked back to this earlier victory. After seizing power in Syria, Saladin vowed to forge an Islamic empire with the ultimate goal of recapturing the holy city of Jerusalem from the Crusaders, a significant stride towards an end to the jihad. As you know, King Baldwin the Fourth took control over the Kingdom of Jerusalem at the age of thirteen after the death of his father Amalric the First in 1174, the same year that Saladin came to power. Although Baldwin was a rich and powerful leader, he was stricken with leprosy at a very young age. After approximately three years on the throne he was faced with his very first military challenge. Saladin invaded the Christian kingdom in 1177 to rout the Crusaders. Although Saladin was almost twenty years older and more experienced than Baldwin, the youthful king did not flounder in stressful situations. Baldwin and his Crusaders outwitted the Muslims at Mont Gisard on 25 November 1177 as we spoke about earlier. It was the only defeat in pitched battle that Saladin suffered and by the end of it, Saladin was forced to flee back to Egypt after narrowly escaping death. Although the victory resulted in tremendous losses for Baldwin's armies, his image throughout the kingdom gained in strength. Jacobs Ford was situated approximately one hundred miles north of Jerusalem at the Jordan River and was a key river crossing on one of the main roads between Acre, Israel and Damascus. It was also one of the safest crossings of the Jordan and, because of its location and importance, was utilised by Christian Palestine and Muslim Syria as a major intersection between the two civilisations. Baldwin and Saladin continually contested over the area and as a bold strategic move and as a result of his military victory at Mont Gisard, Baldwin decided to march to Jacobs Ford and build a defensive fortress on its territory. The king and his Crusaders theorised that such a fortification could protect Jerusalem from a northern invasion and put pressure on Saladin's stronghold at Damascus. Between October 1178 and April 1179, Baldwin began the first stages of constructing his new line of defence, a fortification called Chastellet, at Jacobs Ford. While construction was in progress, Saladin became fully aware of the task he would have to overcome at Jacobs Ford if he were to protect Syria and conquer Jerusalem. At that time, he was unable to stop the erection of Chastellet by military force because a large portion of his troops were stationed in northern Syria, putting down Muslim rebellions. Saladin was always at pains to portray himself as the champion of Islam against the European intruders, but in reality he spent just as much of his career involved in a war against...other Muslims. Consequently, he turned to bribery and offered Baldwin sixty thousand dinars to halt construction. Baldwin declined, but Saladin made a counter-offer of a hundred thousand dinars...but again Baldwin refused and continued to build Chastellet. By the summer of 1179, Baldwin's forces had constructed a stone wall of massive proportions. The castle now had a formidable thirty foot high wall, an almost impregnable rampart of stone and iron and a single tower, but it was still a work in progress."

"And this was all overseen by Master Odo?" Gabirol asked.

"Yes, yes it was and he took on the task with much vigour. Especially after Baldwin refused both bribes and Saladin turned his attention away from the uprisings in northern Syria and focused on Jacobs Ford and the Castle of Chastellet directly. He was fully aware *that any further bargaining or negotiations would only be in vain and that the more time he wasted, the more time Baldwin would have to complete his massive fortification. In 1179, only a few months after construction of Chastellet began, Saladin gathered a large army and marched southeast towards Jacobs Ford. The plan was simple...lay siege to the castle and its inhabitants before any reinforcements from Jerusalem or any of its neighbouring territories could arrive. Baldwin, on the other hand, was situated at Tiberias, situated on the Sea of Galilee, approximately a half day's march from Jacobs Ford. If any attack were to befall his project, reinforcements would be able to arrive relatively quickly. Moreover, the fortification at Jacobs Ford, at least what was completed of it, was relatively strong and was likely able to hold out until relief could arrive in the case of siege. Basically it all boiled down to the siege being, in effect, a race...could Saladin crack the stronghold's defences before the Latin forces arrived? And so it was that on the twenty-third of August 1179, Saladin arrived at Jacobs Ford and ordered his troops to shoot arrows at the castle, thus initiating the siege. While the archers distracted the men inside the fortification, miners dug a tunnel to breach the stone and iron walls at the northeast corner of the Chastellet. Once the tunnel was dug, Saladin's forces placed large pieces of wood into the tunnel and set them alight to sap the foundations," the old man explained.* [48]

"Sap the foundations...what does that mean?" Sarah asked.

"It is called sapping!" the Templar interrupted. "It is a method in which the tunnel's supports are burnt away forcing the walls to eventually collapse under their own weight," he explained.

"Thank you," the old man said and continued. "Sapping initially failed for Saladin and his troops. So, they were forced to put out the fire with buckets of water and were paid one gold piece per bucket to do so."

"They were paid to do so?" Simon asked pulling an exaggerated confused face.

"Yes, for it was almost suicidal to do it...not all of Saladin's men are eager for death as some may claim," the old man explained "Anyway, after the fire was extinguished, the miners were instructed to relight the fire. At the same time, Baldwin, having learned of this attack, called for reinforcements from Jerusalem. However, communications between Baldwin and Chastellet were slow and, by this time, the siege had been underway for several days. Baldwin's forces began to reinforce the main gates around the castle. Shortly after, the Muslims relit the fire in the tunnel, and the walls collapsed. As a result, the Crusaders' attempts to refortify the castle were in vain and, approximately six days after the siege began, Saladin and his troops entered Chastellet. By the thirtieth of August 1179, Saladin had pillaged the castle and killed most of its residents. On the same day, less than one week after reinforcements were called, Baldwin and his supporting army set out from Tiberias, only to discover smoke rising on the horizon directly above Chastellet. Obviously, too late to save the seven hundred knights, architects, and construction workers who were killed and the other eight hundred who were taken captive. Baldwin and his reinforcements turned back towards Tiberias and Saladin ordered the remains of the fortification to be torn down. Although Saladin claimed a military victory at Chastellet, his troops fell victim to another enemy. Directly after the siege, the bodies of the seven hundred Crusaders killed at Jacobs Ford were placed into a pit. The corpses in the pit began to decay in the August heat and, as a result, a plague ensued, killing approximately ten of Saladin's officers. But this setback did not diminish Saladin's military prowess. As a result of Saladin's victory at Jacobs Ford, Jerusalem was extremely vulnerable to capture because the entry into the kingdom by way of the Jordan crossing immediately south of Lake Tiberias...was now virtually undefended."

"You have mentioned this before...and it was not then that Gerard became the Grand Master of the Templars was it?" Peter asked.

"No it was not. Arnold of Tarroja was the next Grand Master after Odo...," the Templar answered in response to his question.

"So how come Gerard was not at Jacobs Ford if was so strategically vital?" Gabirol asked.

"He knew Odo would never agree to being ransomed...and he knew that Arnold de Tarroja was elderly...and he also knew with Reynald's support and influence, he would be next in line to become the Templars' Grand Master. So for whatever reason, Gerard and Reynald busied themselves around Antioch and Tortosa during that period. But just why it took so long for messages to get from Jacobs Ford to Jerusalem and Tiberias...well, let us just say that Reynald had many effective tried and proven means of getting messages transmitted across vast distances with his network of agents and using heliographs...so it beggars the question why was it not used effectively then?" the old man explained.

"Because he made sure no messages would get through in time so Jacobs Ford would fall I bet," the Hospitaller said through pursed lips clearly angered.

"And that Nicholas Templar...was he captured or killed then for I bet Alisha would have been concerned," Sarah asked.

"No for he was still stationed at that time at Castle Blanc...though not for much longer due to the losses incurred at Jacobs Ford. And Alisha did ask and find out from Brother Teric later...discreetly of course," the old man answered.

"You said things were about to get a whole lot worse for everyone...how so?" Ayleth asked hesitantly.

"Well, the candle for the end of Christian domination over Jerusalem had been lit with the fall of Jacobs Ford...and Princess Stephanie, feeling more alone and isolated than ever before, made for the city following closely behind Alisha. She brought Sister Lucy with her as well as Brother Matthew...," the old man sighed and shook his head.

Part VII

Chapter 37
Turansha

Jerusalem, Kingdom of Jerusalem, August 1179

Paul hugged Alisha as Tenno kept on rocking Arri gently in his arms. With just the three of them remaining in the room, it was quiet. Paul smiled seeing Tenno with Arri and he was glad that he was with them. Alisha turned her head and followed his gaze to Tenno.

"You have competition, for Arri seems to like him more than any of us," she said quietly and smiled. Tenno heard her comments and almost smiled back but just nodded.

"I have no problem with that," Paul replied wearily. He raised his left hand and felt behind his left ear. He could still feel the swollen lump there, but at least the pain from it had gone completely. He then ran his finger down the faint scar upon his cheek.

"How did you manage to get that healed so well?" Alisha asked as she sat up and ran her finger down his cheek looking intently at the barely visible scar.

"I am not totally sure...I shall need to speak with Percival, for he was with me and saw the woman touch me...just touch me, then that is all I can remember," Paul explained. Alisha looked at him quizzically. "I shall explain all that I know and what happened...what I can remember that is."

"From what I hear, it was indeed a good job Percival was with you. I shall afford him a little more respect for his actions," Tenno suddenly stated.

Paul relaxed back against the pillows still holding Alisha as he recalled hearing the woman saying that Percival lies and hides things...but his heart was pure of intent. He shook his head, puzzled at those remarks. He thought about Thomas and his men, that Thomas had explained previously that the Bull's Head Bandit had in fact once been one of them. But more confusingly and important was how had he and Percival been away for five days? Had they simply passed out and been asleep, temporarily poisoned somehow? As many thoughts filled his mind, he fell asleep still holding Alisha. After a few minutes, she lifted herself away from him and just stared at his face as he slept. She had no idea of where he had been or what had made him so ill, but it was certainly not just a simple case of heat exhaustion. Only now as he slept did she let her emotions out and she started to cry with relief softly. Tenno approached and placed his large hand upon her shoulder reassuringly whilst holding Arri in his left arm securely.

ℴℴ

Paul woke up but the room was now dark. He sat up slowly trying to focus and adjust his eyes to see. Alisha was beside him in her night gown fast asleep. Arri was beside her in a small crib she had obviously brought in. 'It must be late' he thought as looked around the darkened room. Movement in the far corner of the room drew his attention instantly. Alarmed he stood up out of the bed but he could not feel the floor beneath his feet. This puzzled him and he looked down quickly. The tall figure in the corner of the room started to walk towards him slowly. It must be Tenno he figured, but just as he thought that, his heart jumped as he saw the tall figure was wearing a large horned helmet. As the tall figure stepped near to the window, moonlight lit up the side of his face. Instantly Paul turned to alert Alisha and grab his sword, but his sword was nowhere in sight. Paul went to shout, but as he called out her name, she did not respond or move. He became aware that everything was incredibly silent around him. ''Tis a dream' he quickly told himself and turned to face the tall figure now standing just a few feet away. The figure stood perfectly still saying nothing.

"This is a dream right?" Paul said aloud.

"You tell me," the tall figure replied in a strong but soft voice, his face shrouded in darkness. He then leaned forwards slightly into the full light of the moon revealing his features fully. His face was middle aged, rough, but clean shaven and he was wearing the very same large Bull's Head helmet of the man he had killed defending Alisha.

"'Tis you...the Bull's Head bandit...how is this so, have you come to haunt me?" Paul asked, his throat now dry.

"You do not fear me?" the Bull's Head bandit asked and smiled.

"No...for this is surely a dream...or you are a ghost...," Paul replied then quickly looked back at Alisha and over at Arri.

"Fear not, Paul, for I am not here to scare or harm you or your family. In fact I am glad that you stopped me from harming these two."

"What...now I know this is a dream."

"Perhaps it is...but some dreams can be real in what they are."

"And just what is this then? Am I now cursed to have you follow me everywhere for killing you?"

The Bull's Head bandit laughed lightly and then stepped closer. Slowly he lifted off his helmet and lowered it to his right side, all the while smiling at Paul. He let go of the helmet and as it was about to hit the floor, it simply vanished.

"No, not at all. Sometimes when a person kills another, they become inextricably linked and connected. Like a stain upon each other's souls...but I am here to thank you."

"Thank me! Why...and how is this possible and is this normal?" Paul asked confused.

"In this location, in this city, I believe it is, for the forces that operate here allow it to be so...and that is why I am here to thank you for releasing me from the hell I was living in."

"How...how did I do that?"

"My physical body was suffering a multitude of ailments that afflicted my physical brain. Turned me insane...Lord I wish Thomas had finished me off when had the chance...but out of past respect, he did not, but he should have for I was not the same person. You killing me released me of that purgatory."

"This is a dream...'tis just a dream," Paul said aloud to himself and checked Alisha and Arri again.

"Perhaps...but know also that I represent the old ways, the days of Taurus...and in time you will understand that too...but understand now, I committed sins yet I am not in hell...for my physical intentions and actions were that of a diseased mind and body...that stripped away all reasoning and humanity...and that is why I stand before you now...'Tis intention of the heart and the soul that counts. I tell you this so you do not condemn yourself for killing either me or the Templar, for our Lord and his angels do indeed see all. But I must also caution you. Do not stain your soul with the death of the one known as Turansha...for if you do, his soul will linger around you in this life and the next...be warned...and thank you. Thank you," the Bull's Head bandit said and immediately started to fade before Paul's very eyes.

"No...come back. Please, what do you mean?" Paul called out. This time Alisha heard his call and sat up fast, alarmed. She looked at him, concerned, as he stood in his night robe looking confused. "Ali...I saw...I," he started to say but then thought better of trying to explain what he had just experienced or dreamt. Alisha beckoned him back into bed. 'Intention...'tis what Tenno said too,' he thought to himself as he climbed back into bed, Alisha looking worried as she helped pull the covers up over him.

∞ ∞

Paul could hear Arri making noises and sucking his fist. He opened his eyes to see Alisha shaking his toy horse Clip clop in front of his face playfully making him laugh. Long thin sunbeams shone through the slatted shutters on the window. Paul's mind immediately went over the previous night's events. Had he simply dreamt the whole thing up? As he was thinking this, a rap at the door drew their attention.

"Can I come in?" Sister Lucy called out.

Paul watched as Alisha stood and quickly moved across the room and opened the door to reveal both Sister Lucy and Princess Stephanie stood at the doorway. Alisha wrapped her arms around Sister Lucy excitedly and hugged her before standing back and beckoning them both in. Paul felt embarrassed lying in the bed as they entered the room, Princess Stephanie looking at Paul concerned. She immediately stood at the end of the bed. She looked elegant and cool dressed in a full length cream patterned dress and sun hat tied in place with silk ribbons, the small pearl head pendant positioned so it hung in the middle of her forehead.

"Sorry, but when Alisha took off, we had to follow," she explained looking embarrassed.

"Yes young lady...please do not be doing that again in a hurry," Sister Lucy commented as she picked Arri up and kissed him on his cheek. "And just wait until I get my hands on Theo for not looking after you as he promised."

"Wild horses would not have kept me away," Alisha replied and sat upon the bed again.

Brother Matthew appeared at the doorway and looked in. Princess Stephanie turned to look at him. She simply nodded at him and he slowly backed away and out of sight. Sister Lucy closed the door shaking her head disapprovingly at Brother Matthew.

343

"Yes, Alisha, but you left before we could give you details about meeting up with Turansha to get you to Alexandria safely," Stephanie explained quietly as Paul tried to sit up and she approached him. "I had this made for you...but you left before I could pass it on," she explained and handed Paul a small piece of embroidered cloth. As Paul gently unfurled it, Alisha looked across at the cloth. "It is for both of you."

Paul looked at the embroidered image of a unicorn and lion. The lion had a thorn in its paw and immediately reminded him of the mural image in the room of the Templars' headquarters and other depictions he had seen of it. The unicorn puzzled him as he started to read the embroidered words between the two images.

"What does it say?" Alisha asked.

"I shall never forget thee, for thee and I have ridden seahorses and galloped the plains of Heaven on unicorns in times past, and shall again," Paul read out and looked up at Princess Stephanie.

She blushed, her face reddening fast. She looked at Alisha very briefly, who was looking at her in surprise, suspicious almost. Alisha shook her head and looked at Paul. Sister Lucy could see and sense the awkwardness that had suddenly entered the room, the atmosphere tense even. Princess Stephanie smiled at Paul then looked at Alisha.

"'Twas done for both of you...so please do not take it out of context...or see it as something more than it is, as I can see how this must look," she said, her voice uncharacteristically shaky. "The images are powerful symbols Theodoric and your father taught me many years ago...well, not that many years as I am not that old."

"No harm done and it is a wonderful keepsake," Sister Lucy interrupted and handed Arri to Alisha quickly then moved to gently usher Princess Stephanie away from Paul.

Paul looked at Princess Stephanie. Their eyes met briefly and he knew the words were meant for him and him alone. He feigned a polite smile and quickly averted his eyes back to Alisha and stretched out his hand to offer her the cloth.

"Sorry...if my gift causes offence. 'Twas not meant to," Stephanie said quietly and walked back to the doorway. She hesitated on the threshold and looked at Alisha, who just continued to look at Arri. "I bid you a very long and happy life together. I pray your journey onward is safe. Turansha will meet you and escort you the remainder of the way. He has given me his word on that. Brother Matthew will let you know how and when, and at which of the gates he will meet you. I believe it will be the east gate...David's Gate. It also known as the Jaffa Gate so if you get lost, just ask for directions to that one," Stephanie explained. She fought to control her emotions and tears clearly began to well in her eyes. This would be the last time she would ever see either of them again she thought. She looked at Alisha. She liked her enormously and respected her, but she could not quell the feelings of envy that flooded her veins. She gulped and looked once more at Paul. He simply nodded at her and smiled. He could sense what she was feeling and thinking. Every part of her wanted to shout out her feelings for Paul, but she knew that was selfish and cruel. "'Tis just the pregnancy,' she told herself and placed her hand across her tummy. She looked up once more at Paul as he turned to look at Alisha. "Goodbye...my dear dear friends...goodbye," she whispered and turned around and left the room.

Sister Lucy looked at Paul and he acknowledged her with a raised eyebrow as she too shook her head. Alisha simply continued to look at Arri and play with his little fingers.

Port of La Rochelle, France, Melissae Inn, spring 1191

"Oh dear how terribly awkward...and sad," Ayleth said shaking her head.

"Twas indeed," the old man replied.

"Did Alisha accept the gift as genuine?" Peter asked.

"She's a woman...we women know when another is after their man...thankfully I do not have that problem," Sarah remarked and then laughed as she looked at Stephan.

"Alisha knew. She had always suspected Princess Stephanie liked Paul more than perhaps she should," the old man answered.

"Well I think it is very sad. And she did act gracefully and in accordance with her position as a countess," Ayleth commented and looked at the old man intently before he replied.

"Alisha knew that too...but the sudden awkwardness of that moment threw her. That is why she just sat and looked at Arri. It was her way of dealing with it for she too liked the princess a lot, yet still felt betrayed. But Princess Stephanie had the emotional maturity to understand her feelings and position...and Alisha could not remain angry as who would not love Paul she thought. She was grateful that Paul loved her as much as she loved him."

"Over one single little piece of embroidered cloth?" Simon asked loudly.

"Simon, yes. Sometimes that is all it requires. Just one little thing to change everything. But Princess Stephanie, her mind torn between her feelings for Paul and Alisha, and their imminent departure for good, felt she just had to do something. Rightly or wrongly, but love can be so self serving and selfish and make the very best of us do things we would not believe possible," the old man explained and sighed.

"I can vouch for that," Gabirol remarked and nodded his head in agreement.

"So what did Princess 'not so nice' do after that?" Sarah asked flippantly.

"Princess Stephanie you mean?" the old man said almost chastising in manner. "She gave Brother Matthew his orders, paid some fees due in Jerusalem for the forthcoming tournament her knights were due to compete in and, with a very heavy heart, left for Kerak almost immediately."

"Was she upset?" the farrier asked.

"Who, Alisha or the Princess?" Gabirol quickly asked back.

"Both were," the old man answered. "Alisha was not stupid and her instincts had always been aware, right from their first meeting, that Princess Stephanie felt attracted towards Paul. But her concern was whether Paul felt it back. As for the Princess," the old man paused, laughed to himself briefly then continued. "She felt a connection with Paul far deeper than anything she had ever felt before, despite their age gap. She returned to Crac de Moab feeling lower than she could ever recall. She vowed she would dedicate the rest of her life to her children. She knew there would come a time when Reynald would get himself either killed or imprisoned again. She would never have cause to visit Alexandria so knew she would never see Paul again...and so, alone in her caravan, for nearly two days, she cried all the way back to Kerak."

"That is so sad," Ayleth said softly as Miriam agreed with her.

"No it is not. She should be ashamed of herself," Sarah stated bombastically and folded her arms.

"How so? She is married to an animal of a man...is pregnant and Paul is a gorgeous and charismatic man...who would not fall for him?" Ayleth asked.

"I think we could argue this one for many an hour, so let me just say that Paul had to spend quite some time that evening reassuring Alisha, supported and backed up by Sister

Lucy, despite her knowing the truth of the matter. Alisha wanted to rip the cloth up and throw it away, but Sister Lucy explained that the actual embroidery was in part a code as Princess Stephanie had said...the lion and unicorn aspects...but also to be used in the future should they ever need her assistance. Alisha was not convinced of course, but agreed they should keep it."

"And Mr shifty, Brother Matthew...did he organise for them to meet Turansha near the border?" Simon asked.

"He did...Count Henry and brother Jakelin bade their farewells the following morning as they had to assist with troop deployments to reinforce Reynald and Gerard's forces as well as arrange the tournament that was still going ahead as planned. 'Twas the biggest event of the year and no one wanted to postpone or cancel it...too many wagers had been placed already despite hostilities having started with Saladin."

"But surely it would be madness to leave whilst hostilities were raging?" Peter asked.

"You would be surprised. Besides, Count Henry knew of Princess Stephanie's arrangement to have Paul met and safely escorted on. Besides, within Jerusalem, life went as normal with Jews and Muslims still going about their daily business assured of safe protection despite their armies being in conflict many miles away," the old man explained.

"I thought the Muslims would have left by then," Simon remarked.

"Why and where would they go? It was their home also. And besides, truces broken and conflict were part and parcel of events in Outremer...so despite their respective armies often being in direct conflict, the local populace would often as much just carry on as normal," the old man explained.

"So they headed for Alexandria after all?" Ayleth asked.

"Yes...yes they did indeed," the old man replied softly.

David's Gate (Bab al Khalil), Jerusalem, Kingdom of Jerusalem, August 1179

As Paul steered Adrastos out through the right angled gatehouse and onto the road to Jaffa, pilgrims were passing to his right as they entered in droves along with many Confrere Knights and their attendant squires coming into the city to register for the tournament. After the main tournament, most would move on to Kerak and the big event being planned there. Paul's mind drifted to thoughts of Princess Stephanie. He felt guilty that he had deliberately looked away from her pretending to concentrate on Alisha and Arri. He secretly wished he had been able to say good-bye properly. Alisha had already placed the small embroidered cloth away at the bottom of one of the drawers in the caravan.

"Where are Tenno and Theo? Are they not supposed to meet us here by now?" Alisha asked as she sat beside Paul, Arri strapped against her chest asleep.

Paul stopped the caravan a short distance outside the main gate entrance and looked around. The sun was already high and fierce. He had been told by Brother Matthew to wait outside David's Gate for the rest of the group, including Percival, Thomas and his men as well as a small contingent of Hospitallers who would part escort them. After waiting for nearly an hour in the full sun, a small group of mounted Hospitallers drew up beside their caravan just as Thomas walked through on foot escorting a Muslim knight on horseback who was clearly exhausted and looked injured the way he was slumped in the saddle. Several other Confrere Knights on horseback were following and arguing with Thomas, shouting down at him.

"Ah, Paul...we shall be with you as soon as we can. I just have to see this man upon his way," Thomas called up to Paul, seeing him waiting.

As soon as he said that, the other knights started shouting at him louder and protesting about letting the Muslim knight leave. Paul sensing the antagonism stepped down and rushed to stand beside Thomas.

 2 – 43

"Where is Tenno and the others?" Paul asked and placed his hand over his sword pommel.

The Muslim knight looked down wearily at Paul. His lip was swollen and he had a cut above his eye as well as a scar upon his cheek. The knight smiled painfully and pointed to his scar then the faint one upon Paul's face at which point a large Frankish knight, whom Paul immediately recognised as being the same one he had seen on his first night in Jerusalem trying to eject Muslims from prayers, tried to pull the Muslim knight down. Quickly Paul steadied the man on his horse as Thomas withdrew his sword and pointed it at the large Frankish knight and raised his eyebrows.

"They are just packing away their things...they shall be here shortly," Thomas replied whilst still pointing his sword at the Frankish knight. "You, sire, you should learn when you are beaten fairly and yield with grace. 'Twas but a tourney, and you lost fairly," he said directly at him.

"Fairly! He is a Faris knight...and a prisoner," the knight shouted back angrily as a crowd began to gather.

Paul caught a glimpse out of the corner of his eye of a column of Templars arriving from the north. Paul immediately recalled the conversation he had with Firgany and that he was once a Faris knight and how Taqi had wanted to be one before discovering the Ashashin.

"That he is indeed, and worthy of our respect. He beat not only you but also all twelve of us...therefore he is free to go," Thomas explained as the Templar column drew nearer.

"Really, then let us see what our Templar friends say about that shall we," the Frankish knight bellowed loudly so the crowd could all hear.

The Faris knight looked wearily at Paul, his gaze fixed. His eyes were green and he could have easily passed as a Christian knight but for his Faris uniform and armour. He was clearly exhausted. Thomas had also placed several satchels of fine clothes and gifts as well as plenty of water and supplies upon his horse.

"Paul?" a familiar voice suddenly called out from the lead Templars as the column pulled up.

Paul looked up and saw Nicholas looking down at him, the sun dazzling him as it sat behind Nicholas.

"Nicholas. What are you doing here?" he asked as the Frankish knight looked on bemused.

"I was tasked with leading these knights to attend the week's tourney. Gerard busies himself with other matters and preparing to accept his nomination as Grand Master in Master Odo's stead...no surprises there eh? But how come you are here... and is Alisha with you?" he asked and immediately started to look around with a large smile. Suddenly his eyes caught sight of her sitting cradling Arri sat upon the caravan driver's seat. Alisha gave a slight wave and smiled. The grin on Nicholas's face grew larger and Paul had to smile himself it was so obvious.

"Young Templar," the Frankish knight bellowed loudly drawing Nicholas attention back. "These men wish to let this Faris knight depart...and with much treasure."

"And the problem is?" Nicholas asked as he leant forwards feigning puzzlement.

"He is a prisoner. He cannot go."

"Thomas...'tis good to meet you again. Pray tell, is this man a prisoner?" Nicholas asked.

"Nope. We made a promise that if he could beat all of us in fair combat tourney, we would let him go free," Thomas replied.

"And did he?"

"Oh yes...I shall be walking and not riding for some days I suspect," Thomas joked.

The Faris knight leaned forwards and grabbed Paul's upper arm. He looked intently into Paul's eyes.

"I know you...," he whispered in pain, coughed, then pulled himself up straight in the saddle and looked at Nicholas. He took a deep breath ready for whatever Nicholas would say.

Nicholas looked at the man carefully for several minutes, then at Thomas and then Paul. He could sense Alisha was looking at him. He was so pleased he had got here in time to see her, he thought.

"Well!" shouted the Frankish knight.

"Then the word of Thomas as a knight must be kept...as must yours...if indeed you are a true knight and not one of the many false knights we have frequent these tourneys in search of fame and fleeting glory?" Nicholas finally answered.

Shocked, the Frankish knight threw his arms up in a melodramatic fashion. He shook his head several times in disgust, looked at Thomas, who pulled a massive grin face at him, and then barged his way through the gathered crowd.

"Thank you," the Faris knight whispered to Paul and Thomas.

"Let him pass," Nicholas ordered.

The crowd slowly parted and the other Templars formed a clear path toward the main western road. Slowly the Faris knight began to steer his horse through the crowd and along the cleared route. When he reached the main eastern road, he stopped and looked back briefly, nodded his head appreciatively and then set off at a gentle canter, dust kicking up behind him as he went. As the image of him and his horse vanished into a shimmering heat haze, the crowd all went back to their business.

"Paul, 'tis wonderful to see you again," Nicholas said.

"And you too," Paul replied but looked across at Alisha knowing he really meant her.

"Are you leaving or coming?"

"We are just leaving I am afraid."

"With escort I trust?"

"Yes…though I think they have been somewhat delayed," Paul answered looking at Thomas.

"We shall not be long. Tenno and Theo are just sorting Tenno's bows and replacement arrows as well as haggling over the cost of taking the blacksmith's old cart…but as soon as we are sorted, we shall be back so you may as well rest a while," Thomas explained.

"Ah good. That will give me at least a short time in your company if that is acceptable?" Nicholas asked Paul and immediately looked toward Alisha.

"Do you not have other duties to report for first?" Paul asked then realised how blunt that had sounded. "As it would of course be great to spend some time with you before we must leave," he rapidly added.

"I shall report our arrival and stable our horses first, but I shall be right back so please do not leave before we have said goodbye," Nicholas asked.

"I shall hurry the rest up and drag this excuse of a knight back shortly," Thomas joked and beckoned for Nicholas to follow him.

Paul smiled and raised his hand as they headed into the city passing beneath the main gate. Paul looked back at Alisha as she sat with Arri. Quickly he walked back to her and climbed up beside them. The sun was beating down even fiercer.

"Perhaps we should wait inside in the shade for them all to return," he said whilst a part of him did not want Nicholas to come back. He shook his head annoyed at himself for being so jealous and fully understood why Alisha had gotten so upset with Princess Stephanie's embroidered cloth gift.

He helped Alisha down from the driver's seat and got into the rear of the caravan with her. It was hot inside but at least the sun was not burning down directly upon them. He made Alisha comfortable as she prepared to feed Arri and was just pouring some rose water, when he heard someone jump up into the driver's seat and release the main brake. Thinking it must be Tenno, he moved to the rear door, opened it, looked up and saw what was undoubtedly the ugliest and most deformed dark skinned and very large face he had ever seen. Surprised, he blinked as his eyes focused upon the small dark, almost black eyes of the huge man now stood outside the door. A flash of something just registered in his mind as it came towards his own head…a high pitched ring in his ears and darkness enveloped him instantly as he was knocked out.

℘ ℭ

Paul felt as if he was buried underground, his head full of pain and he was rocking from side to side. In the distance he could hear Alisha calling his name. As he slowly began to regain consciousness, he realised he was lying upon the side bench of the caravan. Slowly he opened his eyes. In the dim gloom of the closed caravan he could just make out Alisha sitting on the opposite bench holding Arri. Confused, he went to sit up but realised his hands and feet were bound. Alisha indicated with his head he look to his left. She looked very calm but clearly worried. Paul's eyesight was blurred as he looked and saw the huge frame and grinning head of the man who had knocked him out. As his eyes began to focus, the pain intensifying on his forehead where he had been hit, he began to see clearly the deranged looking man sat beside Alisha.

349

Fig. 38:

As Paul struggled to sit up, he became aware of another far older and dirty man sat beside him. He had long dirty grey hair and was unshaven and unkempt. He also stank, a lot! The old man grinned at him. It was only then that Paul realised that he too was also tied and bound. Paul's mind ran as he tried to work out what was happening. They were clearly travelling as he could hear Adrastos repeatedly snorting with the driver struggling to control and steer him effectively. Paul looked at the large ugly man again. His head was distorted and deformed. Brother Matthew had told him to be at David's Gate, set within the west wall, yet clearly way too early for he would have surely known that the rest of the escort would have been finishing their tournament events. What was going on? Paul wondered. Was this Turansha's way of making sure they were not followed or betrayed etc. as he knew Reynald and Gerard were hell bent upon seizing him earlier? Alisha had not been harmed nor tied up so perhaps that is what was happening? The large ugly man certainly looked stupid and deformed so perhaps he had overstepped the mark and been a bit too zealous. Paul's head felt hot which made him feel sick and dizzy. He shook his head as he fought to keep his mind clear.

"Do not worry, young man...'tis but a mild concussive feeling...it shall pass," the old man suddenly said in perfect English.

"You speak English," Paul remarked surprised.

"Yes...and French or Arabic if you so prefer?"

"And what do you speak?" Paul asked the large ugly man.

The large ugly man just kept on grinning then stared at Arri in silence.

"Maybe he is deaf and dumb," Alisha whispered as the man kept his gaze fixed upon Arri.

"He is neither deaf nor dumb...far from it," the old man stated but the ugly man did not respond or show any hint of understanding.

"I see you are watched over," the old man suddenly said to Alisha. She looked at him puzzled. "Your mother...she is with you."

"What?" Alisha asked, more alarmed than puzzled, as Paul stared at him hard.

"'Tis true. You were with her when she passed into the next realm, yes?" the old man asked if it was a known fact.

"No...no. I did not know my mother at all. You are mistaken," Alisha replied, hugging Arri tighter, and shuddered.

The old man looked at Alisha and around her as if looking at someone else too. The ugly man noticed this and looked around Alisha also. The old man sighed, shook his head slowly no.

"My dear young child...I am not mistaken," he stated politely but assuredly.

Alisha looked at Paul as tears instantly welled in her eyes, the old man's comments touching an emotional nerve deep within her as she recalled it was Raja.

"'Twas my aunt, who was like a mother to me, whom I was with when she died," Alisha replied, her voice shaking with emotion.

The ugly man looked at Alisha then back at the old man and raised his eyebrow clearly showing that he did indeed understand them.

"Perhaps that is it then. Whoever she said she was, she is with you now," the old man replied insinuating he was still not wrong. He then looked across at Paul. "Do you know what this is all about and where we are going?"

Paul shrugged his shoulders no.

"Ask him," he replied and looked at the ugly man.

The old man looked at the ugly man in silence for several minutes as the caravan bumped across several rough sections of road.

"You were not always like this were you?" he asked him. The ugly man did not answer but simply stared back at him with his fixed grin. "You have a son...long since passed over," the old man explained further but still no reaction from the ugly man. "He sits with you now," he continued to say then closed his eyes and drew in a long deep breath as Alisha and Paul looked at him puzzled. "He says...you did not have to jump in after me and ruin your life too...and nor do you have to do what is demanded of you now," he continued slowly, breathed out and then opened his eyes again.

The ugly man just sat in total silence and stared at him with no hint of any emotion. Paul's mind was running fast. Who were these people? Surely Tenno and Theodoric would be on their way to meet them once they realised they had gone as they could not have travelled that far already. And what had happened to the Hospitaller escort? Arri started to wake and stretched out his arms pushing his hands up and out of the muslin wrappings and his shawl. Alisha shook his toy horse Clip clop in front of his face playfully as they continued to journey onwards...west towards Abrahams Oak, far from where the others expected them to be heading.

Abrahams Oak, 1.2 miles southwest of Mamre near Hebron, Kingdom of Jerusalem

Alisha was able to feed Arri by covering herself with his shawl. The ugly man looked away when she started to get Arri ready which in Paul's mind meant he had some scruples at least. The old man sat beside Paul remained very calm throughout the journey. Paul protested he needed to go to the toilet but the ugly man just stared at him grinning. They had heard people and children playing outside the caravan as they passed through several small villages. Eventually when they did stop having travelled some eighteen miles nonstop, it was darkening outside as a man opened the small rear door, his face covered in a black face mask and hood, just his dark eyes visible. For a moment Paul thought it was one of Al Rashid's men but then the man spoke in a deep and aggressive tone demanding that Paul and the old man stand up. The ugly man stood up but still had to stoop as he was so tall and grabbed the old man and physically lifted him to his feet with one arm and shoved him across to the small door. The black clad man outside pulled him out forcibly. Paul shot a look at Alisha as alarm registered across her face. Suddenly the ugly man grabbed Paul's left arm with a vice like grip and pulled him towards the door. He manhandled Paul down the small steps as two other men clad in black grabbed his arms. Paul looked back at Alisha holding Arri as the ugly man slammed the door shut, stood up straight and folded his arms as if now guarding the door.

"My young friend. Do not resist, trust me on this matter," the old man being near to him whispered but was silenced when one of the men holding him put a black curved dagger to his exposed neck and stared at him hard for several moments.

Paul looked at the ugly man and his mind was flooded with panic almost as he feared what they would do to Alisha. She did not scream inside or call out so at least she was remaining calm. Perhaps this was Turansha's way of ensuring security, he thought again, even if it was somewhat extreme. He looked around. They were clearly on a high plateau, with several small buildings a short distance away and a few trees. The sun was setting fast but he could make out a small church structure as well as what appeared to be an old tree trunk surrounded by a small stone wall. Near to it, several horses were tied up and similarly dressed men in black sat near a fire. As the man holding the knife to the old man's throat slowly lowered the knife, Paul recognised it as being identical to the one Brother Teric had given him to check up and find out about in Jerusalem, but he had forgotten all about it. Adrastos started to snort and kick wildly making the caravan jerk slightly. As Adrastos kicked out and other men tried to hold him steady, another caravan pulled up. Within moments a well dressed merchant trader along with his young female daughter and a Knight Templar were dragged from the rear of it, the Templar clearly having taken a severe beating as he had dried blood all down the side of his face and all over his white mantle. His hair was fair and for a minute Paul thought it was Nicholas, but he soon saw that it was not as he was thrown to the ground near to him, his hands tied behind his back. The wealthy merchant was pleading with the men holding him as they threw him to the floor. The young woman looked terrified as two men in black holding her looked her up and down. Her full length dress had been torn at the sides. Her eyes locked with Paul's. She had defiance blazing in her light blue eyes. She was terrified but also angry.

"Where is Turansha?" Paul asked.

"That way," one of the men stated and pushed Paul hard so he faced the group of seated men a short distance away.

As Paul began to walk awkwardly with his legs tied just below the knee towards the men, the Templar was kicked hard and pushed as he tried to stand and follow. The old man followed behind Paul shuffling along just as awkwardly as the merchant and young female also followed being held tightly by men on either arm. Paul saw a large caravan of assorted wagons, horses and camels situated just over the brow of the hill as he drew nearer the seated men. Paul could see that the seated men were eating, their backs to him. When Paul was pulled back to stand still, the middle man raised his right hand and motioned with his fingers for them to be brought around to stand in front of him. Quickly the group were dragged around to face the seated men. As Paul looked down at the man in the middle, he immediately saw that it was not Turansha. His heart beat faster and the realisation hit him that they were in dire trouble. Suddenly he felt a severe pain in his left leg as one of the men holding him kicked his leg hard and forced him to his knees. The other black clad men did likewise with the other captives, for captives was clearly what they now were. With his hands tied behind his back, his sword missing, he had no way out of his predicament. He felt totally helpless. The large ugly man stood directly behind Paul and grabbed his hair and pulled it forcing Paul to look up.

"You are not Turansha," Paul blurted out straining as his hair was being pulled hard.

The man sat in the middle of the group stopped eating some lamb on the end of a small skewer and wiped his mouth. His features were hard, his skin almost ashen white and pock marked but his beard trimmed short and neat. His eyes looked almost black in the dim light of sunset. Wearing all black and a black turban, he finished the mouthful of food slowly then placed his hands upon his knees and looked at Paul for several minutes.

"I am Turansha...though perhaps not the one you were expecting," he finally said in a calm and relaxed voice, then smiled as the others around him all laughed. They stopped laughing the instant he raised his hand. "And you...you are indeed Paul...Paul Plantavalu no?" he asked, but more as a statement of fact. "And in there," he continued and pointed towards Paul's caravan, "in there, is the famous woman of the oak...yes?"

Paul looked toward the caravan now surrounded by more men all dressed in black. 'Woman of the oak...what is that all about? And that is not Turansha,' he thought, his heart pounding and feeling sick.

"Please...please, whoever you are," the wealthy merchant interrupted holding his hands together in prayer fashion and tried to move nearer on his knees. "Please...I have many other carts all full of silks and fine gifts...I can have them all delivered to you if you just let us go," he pleaded.

353

Turansha looked at the merchant then whispered something to the man beside him. They exchanged a few words in Arabic. The man motioned with his forefinger for the young woman to be brought closer so he could see her properly. She flounced as she was pulled nearer and stamped her feet hard. The merchant saw the way he was eyeing her up.

"I understand that you and your daughter were taken in error this day for my men suspected you and she were in fact this man...and his young wife," Turansha explained and pointed the food skewer at Paul. The Templar started to cough up some blood as he knelt, his face near to the ground. One of the black clad men behind him kicked him hard to the floor again. As he coughed more, he made eye contact with Paul. He blinked and feigned a brave defiant smile. "I am afraid we have spent many years and killed quite a fair few in order to get that man and his evil spawn to stop a great evil...our quarrel is not with you," he explained to the merchant.

As the merchant smiled and sighed, he looked back at Paul. Paul's heart nearly stopped when he heard the man's comments. The merchant let out a nervous laugh.

"I have no idea of what we have done," Paul exclaimed as his mind rushed to try and comprehend what was happening.

"Nothing yet...but it is what you can do in the future that concerns me. I tried to end your line with your father, but alas he proved far too difficult a man to eradicate. Besides, the scrolls revealed that it was not him that would pose the greatest threat," he explained, paused and stood up slowly and approached Paul. He knelt down just in front of Paul and looked him in the eyes intently. "As handsome as your father too," he remarked and some of his men laughed until he raised his hand again to stop. "You see, we know your secrets. We know what you intend to do. And I too am known as Turansha."

"Then pray tell, let me know for I have no idea of what you speak," Paul replied.

"Do not insult my intelligence," Turansha snapped and swiped his right hand across Paul's face hard.

"Then do not insult mine and tell me of things I know not of," Paul shot back defiantly as anger started to rise within him.

"See, you have your father's courage and I suspect your mother's brains. A pity we must snuff it out," Turansha replied calmly and stood up.

"If I am to die, then at least let me know for what reason," Paul demanded loudly and spat some blood from his mouth as his gums swelled from the hard hit. "If you knew my father, then you would know that I am no threat to you, whoever you are!"

"Perhaps you are not...but your woman and child most certainly will be," Turansha replied and stepped back. "Bring her to me!"

Paul looked in alarm back to the caravan. His head felt as if it was about to explode with the overwhelming surge of panic that engulfed him totally. He tried to stand up, but the man nearest him, kicked him down again hard. Paul raised his head from the dirt and watched as two men entered the caravan. Moments later Alisha appeared carrying Arri in her arms. She looked around bemused. The large ugly man pushed her in the back to walk. As she approached, she saw Paul on the floor and she part ran toward him. Paul sat up upon his heels and shook his head no. Alisha stopped just short as she looked at all the black dressed men. She took a step backwards but straight into the large ugly man who just looked down at her grinning. He ushered her forwards to Turansha.

"We are all dead this hour my friend. Just pray for a quick death," the Templar whispered to Paul just as one of the men in black kicked him in the face hard, the Templar falling face down in the sandy soil nearly unconscious, his eyes rolling as he fought to remain alert.

Turansha looked Alisha up and down. He moved closer and stooped to look at Arri. Arri outstretched his little arm and Turansha smiled. Gently he let Arri wrap his little fingers around his large forefinger. He studied Arri for what seemed an age before looking up directly at Alisha. A cold chill ran down her back as his smile vanished and his eyes narrowed.

"You, I shall keep...but kill the rest," he coldly said and turned away just as two men grabbed hold of Alisha and another snatched Arri from her arms.

The merchant started to beg on his knees as one of Turansha's men approached him wielding a large curved sabre sword just as two more held him down forcing his head forwards. As he shook his head, tears falling from his face sobbing, he wet himself, his urine making a large pool around his knees. His daughter wept silently biting her lips as she was held up by two men. She shook her head no.

"Shame upon you, Umar...for this stain will go with you in this life and the next," the old man said calmly as he knelt the other side of Paul.

"NO!" Alisha shouted as she shook herself out of her stunned disbelief and started to lash out with her arms and kick, the two men struggling to hold her still. They forced her to her knees as she began to scream hysterically.

"No one has called me that in many years," Turansha said as he approached the old man. He studied him for several minutes as he tried to recognise who he was. Alisha stopped screaming and lowered her head and sobbed uncontrollably as the men held her beneath her arms.

"Ali...look at me. Do not let these excuses of men beat you. Live, do you hear me," Paul called out before he was hit hard across the back of his head. His head filled with pain and his ears rang but he refused to go down. He took a deep breath and looked up at the man who had hit him.

"Enough!" Turansha said with a raised hand. "I think I am beginning to remember this one. But the years have not been kind to you...have they?" he said as he knelt in front of the old man. He clicked his fingers and the man with the large sabre sword came over and stood beside the old man. "I should have done this all those years ago."

"Yes, you should have," the old man said, smiled broadly and outstretched his neck. "Now let's finish this shall we...if you dare!"

The Templar let out a laugh and coughed up more blood before laughing again.

"Good one, old man," he called out.

Turansha looked at the old man again, rubbed his fingers down his beard as he pondered what to do with him.

"I always did admire your bravery. Perhaps you are eager to die," he said to the old man and motioned with his hand for the swordsman to go to the Templar.

"Umar...you have no idea. You were wrong back then, and you are wrong about these people now," the old man explained calmly.

"How so for I have the parchments that prove who they are…and what that child could do."

"You spare them, and I shall lead you to the sealed Halls of Amenti as you always desired…and you will need him for it is written so," the old man answered indicating with his head towards Paul.

Paul looked at them, puzzled, then across to Alisha, who was looking at him, her face ashen white and her mouth open in shock. Turansha clicked his fingers again. Instantly the two men holding the Templar down raised him to his knees and forced his head forwards. The Templar struggled and shook his head until a third man approached and grabbed his hair and pulled it towards him. The Templar looked across at Paul beside him.

"Do not watch my friend…do not give these bastards the satisfaction," he said through gritted teeth as he took in short sharp breaths and then closed his eyes shut tightly, sweat pouring from his face.

Paul looked on as the man nearest him pulled the Templar's chain mail coif backwards to expose his neck more and ripped his white mantel. The Templar started to breathe fast and heavy in anticipation, spit beginning to come through his gritted teeth. Paul looked up as the man with the sabre sword raised it high, the setting sun glinting off the sharpened cold blade with a flash as it then came down hard. The blade sparked as it caught the metal links of the coif and deflected sideways into the base of the Templar's skull with a sickening squelch. The Templar dropped lower, opened his eyes looking sideways directly at Paul. Paul's stomach churned and he had to gulp to stop himself being sick.

"You fucking useless inbred arses!" the Templar snarled, his face contorted in agony, blood pouring from the wound across his skull.

The sword wielding man pushed his foot against the Templar's shoulder and pulled the sword up but had to yank it hard to remove it from his head. As the blade came away, white bone was exposed and brain matter oozed out. The Templar's gaze was fixed upon Paul as the sword was raised for a second attempt. He winked briefly. As the blade came down, it cut straight through the exposed skin of his neck, through muscle and the neck bones. The Templar's eyes rolled upwards turning white just as the weight of his head made it fall forwards, the pure brilliant white of his spinal column bones now protruding upwards clearly visible. But his head was still attached by muscle and skin around the front of his throat the sword having only cut half the way through. Quickly the swordsman threw his main sword to the ground and pulled out a large knife, knelt beside the Templar, grabbed a tuft of hair from the man in front, pulled his head back up, placed the knife against his throat and started to cut into his flesh. As his blade sank into the side of his neck, it severed the main artery, blood immediately spurting out in bursts. Paul knew that meant the Templar's heart was still beating. Gurgling sounds came from the Templar's throat when his head started to separate from his body being pulled upwards as the man continued to cut, then vomit coughed out of the throat area, the Templar's arms shaking violently in a convulsive death throe. The swordsman lifted the Templar's severed head up completely and kicked his body over. It fell beside Paul. The smell of iron from his blood and vomit filled Paul's nostrils and he gagged as he fought not to be sick himself. He looked away and up to see Alisha on her knees just staring in absolute horror, her eyes wide, her jaw dropped. The merchant was lying in the dirt crying, his daughter just looking down at him, her gaze fixed so as not to see the horror before her. She was visibly shaking uncontrollably. Turansha then stepped closer to Paul as the men holding him forced him forwards on his knees and a third man pulled his hair and head forwards just as Turansha pushed Paul's cope back slightly to expose his neck. Alisha's eyes widened further in terror, her throat dry, she could not even scream as the swordsman picked up the large curved sword and readied it near to Paul.

"No chain mail to mess up your stroke this time," Turansha said calmly.

"Do not watch, Ali!" Paul shouted, his voice deep sounding, his heart beating so fast and hard he could feel it pounding and pulsing up his neck.

"The sacred chambers!" the old man said calmly and quietly whilst looking at the ground.

Turansha flicked his fingers and beckoned one of his men to come over from where they had all been seated eating. The man ran over carrying a reinforced leather parchment tube. Quickly Turansha uncapped it and removed several parchments. Two were very old and one was clearly very recent. He unfurled the new one and opened it fully upon the floor in front of the old man.

"Look, old man. See for yourself why they must die. 'Tis written is it not…and the child from these two…look what it leads to," Turansha said and pointed to various symbols upon the parchment.

Paul struggled to see the parchment through his sweat filled eyes and grit from the ground all over his face, his hair being pulled ever tighter. In the fast fading light, Paul's eyes fell upon the familiar signature of Niccolas signed in the bottom corner.

"Umar, you have this all wrong. You will be making the gravest of mistakes if you kill them…and if you do, how do you know the woman will not go on to have another child?" the old man said and looked across at Paul.

"I do not…so thank you for pointing that out. I shall have to kill her myself… after I have had some pleasure with her of course for she is such a beauty," Turansha replied smiling menacingly.

Paul exploded with fury inside and jumped up fully, the force of doing so knocking the two men holding him, the third man holding his hair falling backwards pulling out a chunk of his hair as he went. The swordsman went to raise his sword but Paul head-butted him squarely in the face, the man's nose breaking loudly, blood pouring down his face instantly. With his hands tied behind his back, and his legs restricted by bindings, Paul turned and lunged at Turansha. He simply stepped aside and Paul landed heavily in the dirt. As he rolled over to try and stand up again, four of Turansha's men jumped upon him holding him down.

"He does indeed have his father's courage…and strength too," Turansha said smirking.

"If you know my father, then you will know he will hunt you down to the ends of the earth for this," Paul growled back still kicking out his legs and struggling against the men holding him.

"I know your father only too well…that is why we tried several times to get you and eradicate your line…and hers. Many have died in your place and in your stupid ignorant bliss you never even realised it did you?" Turansha explained and paused as he looked back at Alisha. "It took us a while to discover him in France and longer still the great Firgany, but we did. 'Tis a pity we were not successful then for it would have saved me so much time and inconvenience."

"Then tell us what great wrong we have done to you, so that perhaps we can put right whatever it was," Paul said almost pleadingly.

"'Tis not what you have done yet...but what you intend to do," Turansha answered and looked at the old man.

"What?" Paul demanded, utterly perplexed.

"Tell me, old man. We took these from your recently departed friend Niccolas... even though he tried to destroy them with fire...does it not show what the union between these two will cause?" Turansha asked as he knelt beside him and pointed to several lines and symbols upon the parchment. "We knew it left France with a wealthy woman and Philip's son. We just did not know what they looked like. We also knew of two other couples with the same charts, should one line fail. Sadly we had to erase them also. We would have perhaps done that sooner but for that abomination of a woman, Abi," he explained with a proud boastful look.

Paul's mind raced as pieces of the puzzle suddenly started to drop into place. The realisation that it was Turansha, or at least his men, who had taken the parchments, the same ones Gerard had been after from Niccolas when he had been killed. It was Niccolas himself who had set the crypt library on fire to protect them. The attack by bandits in France on Alisha's caravan when large arrows had been found...Abi's arrows no less. The caravan that had been massacred with the wealthy female killed along with her knights defending her. But why?

"Kill these and you will never recover the secrets of the chambers of creation... ever," the old man stated staring at Turansha. "I do not have the wisdom to unlock the mystery," he paused then looked at Paul again. "Only he does!"

Paul had absolutely no idea what the old man was talking about. Confused and his head full of pain, he struggled to think, but he knew if the old man was some-how bluffing or biding their time, he would have to play along for as long as nec-essary and pray for help to arrive. Several of Turansha's men started to light some torches and placed them in the ground nearby. Paul could hear drips as blood slowly drained from the neck of the severed Templar's head being held near to him. Tur-ansha looked at Paul for several minutes.

"Hmmm! Perhaps. But I have a simple test that will establish if what you say is true or false," he said, grinned and nodded at the tall ugly man. "Ishmael...if you would?"

Quickly Ishmael walked over to where the horses were tied up and removed two large 'two handed' swords and returned, stopping next to Turansha. He nodded at one of his men, who drew a small knife and quickly cut the ropes around Paul's wrists and legs, freeing him. Turansha motioned with his eyes for Paul to take one of the swords from Ishmael. Paul stood up slowly and looked down at the old man, who nodded he should take it.

Alisha struggled to free her arms but could not and saw Paul take the two handed sword. Her heart raced and for a moment she thought that perhaps all was not lost if he could fight. But it was not his own sword and he had never used a heavy two handed sword before. 'Put it through the evil man' she thought to herself then quickly looked around to see where Arri was. Her head felt light and dizzy and her stomach knotted so tightly it hurt causing her to bend forwards in pain, the men holding her forcing her back up to stand and watch. She caught sight of three elderly women near the horses. One was holding Arri and rocking him in her arms. Alisha's eyes narrowed as the anger rose within her. Ishmael banged his sword against Paul's sounding out a metallic clang which drew her attention back to them. Paul felt the sword shudder from the hit as Ishmael stood back a few paces and wielded the sword about his own body and head with one hand like it was a twig, the whooshing sounds as it cut through the air clear to hear by all. Turansha approached Paul. Paul raised his sword. He could easily lunge the sword into him he thought just as Turansha raised and waved a single finger no at him and smiled broadly. The urge to thrust the sword into him was overwhelming, but with all the other men around, he knew it would seal their own immediate deaths. As he thought this, he recalled the words the Bull's Head bandit had said during the dream in Jerusalem. Now it made sense why he said he should not kill Turansha. Paul felt the weight of the two handed sword and looked at Ishmael just as Turansha clicked his fingers. Immediately the two men holding Alisha forced her to her knees, pulled her hair back hard and one of them placed a small black blade against her throat. Paul felt like his very soul dropped within him. Alisha took in short sharp deep breaths through gritted teeth, the knife pushed hard against her throat causing it to bleed very slightly. She froze her movements. Could she grab her three pronged dagger out and stab one? she thought...'but what would then happen to Arri and Paul?' she realised instantly.

"So...Paul Plantavalu...I have waited a long time to meet you, and now I do. As my good Sufi mystic friend here will testify, I am a man of my word," Turansha started to explain, when the old man shook his head with disdain. "I am...and to prove it, I will promise you that if you beat my champion, then it proves you are the one who can open the Halls of Amenti...and I shall spare you all...for as long as it takes for you to lead us to the location. But, if he defeats you, then we know you are not the one."

"And then what?" Paul asked through gritted teeth, his voice low.

"Then we kill the infant and your wife will become one of my many brides... such a great honour for her...don't you agree?"

Paul raised the sword high ready to swing at Turansha but he just stood perfectly still and did not move, but simply smiled at him. Paul hesitated, confused, his gaze being drawn to Alisha as the two men holding her pulled her head back further revealing the knife pushing ever deeper into her white skin, a trickle of blood beginning to run down her throat. Her eyes were wide and she gently shook her head no.

"And if I refuse to fight?"

"Then you lose your head, so does the infant. Makes no difference either way... but if what our Sufi friend claims is true, then the spirit of our gods and ancestors runs through you and you should win. You take me to the Halls of Amenti and it is a win win all round...yes?" Turansha explained waving his finger around in the air.

Paul's mind raced as he tried to think what he should do. He looked at the Templar's head still held by the swordsman. He did not have a fighting chance at all. He looked at Ishmael. who was still grinning at him menacingly. If he could fight him long enough then hopefully Tenno would show up, or Abi. 'Where is she when we need her the most?' he thought. He shook his head, confused, as he had never heard of the sacred chambers of creation and just a brief mention of the Halls of Amenti once by Theodoric. By now the sun was sitting upon the far horizon, a blood red circle shimmering behind the black silhouettes of trees and a few buildings. Shadows danced all around them cast by the few flaming torches that had been placed in the ground. The old man, whom Paul now knew to be some kind of Sufi mystic, simply nodded slightly indicating he should take up the challenge. Paul got the sense from Turansha that he was somehow playing with him, one minute saying kill them and the next making him fight. If Paul and Alisha had been so important to send men to France to hunt them down, then what was he up to now and who were the other two couples already killed? After everything they had been through, was it all indeed just to end here and now, he thought just as a shooting star streaked across the darkening evening sky.

"My friend...your father has clearly failed to teach you enough in time...for if he had, then you would know that what lays hidden cannot be revealed and shared with mere mortal men, with all their corrupt base desires and perversions...so you see, I cannot allow for you to reveal it to the world, unless of course you reveal it to someone like me first of course," Turansha explained then laughed. "If you cannot beat Ishmael, my undefeated champion, then I know the gods and ancestors do not want either of us to find it...and you will all die," he said and walked back to sit near to Alisha where he had been eating earlier. "Now fight and entertain us," he said and clicked his fingers for more food to be brought to him. He looked at Alisha and grinned and licked his lips and winked. "Hatred...I see it in your pretty eyes," he commented and laughed more as he sat back and made himself comfortable.

Alisha wondered if she could get her dagger in time and thrust it in his throat beneath his thin beard. Arri let out a small cry which alerted her and Paul to his whereabouts with the three women now hidden from view behind some camels.

"You must not do this," the Sufi master said toward Turansha loudly then looked directly at Ishmael.

"Look, is his father not Philip de Gisors and of the Merovingian and Sicambrian lines...and his mother from the Keys family? You see, we know he is the one, the key holder...unlike his inept stupid elder brother...'Tis why we required your presence to confirm such," Turansha replied and paused as he looked from the Sufi master back to Alisha again, his words burning into her mind. "Hey...three angels once appeared here...so maybe they shall appear again this eve to save him," he mocked and pointed toward the black silhouette of the oak tree of Abraham and waved the scroll taken from Niccolas's crypt.

Port of La Rochelle, France, Melissae Inn, spring 1191

"Oh my Lord I think I am going to be sick," Miriam said, holding her hand to her mouth, and coughed.

The Templar pulled her close and rubbed her back gently.

"Me too," Ayleth remarked shaking her head and looking pale.

"I am sorry. Perhaps I should not be so graphic in what I explain and tell," the old man said as he looked at the faces all looking at one and other.

Gabirol shook his head no, wrote some more lines then looked up at the old man.

"No...you must tell it all as it was and happened, please," he said quietly then coughed to clear his dry throat.

All were shocked to hear what the old man had just explained. Simon pushed away his plate of cheese, no longer feeling hungry.

"Please, I wish you to continue. Beheadings are nothing new to my brother and I...unfortunately. But can you first explain why this Umar man, why he is also called Turansha...if you know...and the scroll, what was written upon it?" the Hospitaller asked.

"Yes do not stop now," the Genoese sailor said as he pulled the jar of mead nearer and began to pour himself another drink.

"Turansha...He started his career as a Saracen Commander, one of Saladin's spy masters in fact, but he was cruel and sadistic. He hated all Franks and non-Muslims and was a fanatical tyrant. He often worked hand in glove with the Ashashin when it suited his cause. Rashid knew this of course. Turansha had previously had many dealings...actually, run ins...with Philip and Theodoric many years before. Turansha had taken on the name after once being mistaken for Saladin's brother, which opened many doors for him. It helped him develop his contacts and spies all across Outremer and further afield. But he also knew that everything he had built was threatened by the knowledge that Philip or his descendants were privy to a great secret from antiquity, but also prophecies relating to a child born of an apparent Muslim woman and a non Muslim man...He also used his new name to establish contacts that eventually led to him being one of the major suppliers to Gokbori's troops as well as dealing in slaves. He was also despised and feared by his own men who were mainly nothing short of renegades...but trained very well. He also knew that somewhere in Egypt, a great treasure and source of unimaginable power was hidden...and that Philip and Firgany were guardians of its secrets. So Paul was correct when he thought that Turansha was just playing with him." The old man sighed heavily.

"I do not think I can listen to any more. 'Tis truly gruesome...that poor knight. Turansha is evil. Just pure evil!" Ayleth remarked looking pale.

"I am afraid to say that he was indeed a possessor of an evil and cruel soul. He was an individual who could not empathise with other people. He delighted in wielding power over others and he knew how to manipulate people," the old man explained.

"But why did he want Alisha and Paul dead...and their son? Why had he sent his men to France to do so?" Gabirol asked.

"It all goes back a very long way to when Philip and Theodoric knew Turansha, but as Umar...But Philip and later Firgany thought they had agreed upon a truce and to leave each other alone. Turansha was aware of a sealed secret vault in Egypt that supposedly contained all the knowledge and wisdom, as well as tools and weapons of unimaginable power...and initially worked with Theodoric and the Sufi master himself to try and find it...but they were deliberately held back by other forces. Turansha became firm friends with Saladin's personal poet and scribe...but he turned him and used him. He was sentenced to death and executed when Turansha double crossed him to further his own position," the old man paused. "But he also knew of the sacred Crimson Thread and how people born of that bloodline would be granted access to the sealed vaults...'Tis one of the reasons why Templars seal a lock of hair away, but that I shall explain later. When Turansha discovered that Philip, and even Firgany, were connected to it, he sought them out, at first befriending them. He is truly a cunning and devious man. But then he discovered that people like him, with evil intent and service to self, would one day have to answer for their evil wrong doings...

though if he had studied things properly, he would have learnt that no matter how low he had gone, there is always a way back up and for redemption, but he became blinded with his own lustful desire and material greed and power. He believed if he could wipe out any such line of people, then the powers would never be revealed and humanity would continue much the same way as it has, instead of the way it should go. That is why when he went to Niccolas's crypt, well, his agents did, they did not find the parchments and maps they wished but they did find the one he had recently done of Alisha and Paul...and Arri. He also knew that there were two other couples with almost identical destinies....sadly for them, he and his men found them, the results of which Paul witnessed with the massacre of the caravan on the route to Crac de l'Ospital..."

"Why though for what did the parchments show?" Ayleth asked, confused.

"Understand that Turansha had many older parchments and prophecies...and he was aware of a hidden secret family line that had blood and physical properties that could one day access and use the ancient tools...some say left by our forefathers who evolved to escape the physical bounds of this earthly realm, or just people far more evolved than us who mysteriously vanished. He wanted that knowledge and he believed that his own family tree was indeed part of that hidden line..."

"So he was doing away with the competition in effect?" Peter stated matter of factly.

"Yes...but he was not totally certain. But he trusted as the will of Allah that signs were given to him, so if Paul beat Ishmael, then he would see that as a sign that Paul must obviously be helpful to his ultimate aim..."

    3 – 13

"Sounds like a truly screwed up individual. Deluded or just plain mad!" Simon said.

"All three I suspect," the Templar remarked, still gently rubbing Miriam's back.

"So what happened? Did he win then or did an angel appear from that oak tree you mentioned?" Simon asked.

"Well I could tell you that an angel did make an appearance," the old man replied.

"No, I do not believe that," Simon shot back.

"Look, they were nearly two miles away from the city of Sidon at the place of Abrahams Oak next to the small village of Mamre. Turansha believed it held special powers and was drawn to the location. He also had parchments that showed a woman planting the sacred oaks, which is why he called Alisha the woman of the oak. He believed that one day, he too like Abraham would be visited by three angels there. This was something he had told Philip and Theodoric many years previous," the old man explained.

"What is so special about the oak tree then? I recall you mentioned it briefly before," Sarah asked.

"I want to know what happened with Paul," the Genoese sailor demanded.

"So do we all, but let him explain the oak tree first...please," Gabirol interjected.

"I shall keep this brief then. You see Abrahams Oak or the 'Oak of Mamre' or 'Oak of Sibta', located at Hirbet es-Sibte, is just 1.2 miles southwest of Mamre near Hebron, or as we call it, 'The Oak of Abraham'. It is an ancient tree which tradition says marks the place where Abraham entertained three angels after pitching his tent for the night. It is said the oak is nearly five thousand years old and has been venerated by Jews and Christians alike for hundreds of years...that was until Constantine stopped the practice by building a church there in the fourth century AD. Now there is a long-standing tradition that prophesises that the Oak of Abraham will die just before the appearance of the Antichrist. If the trunk remains dead, then the forces of evil and darkness would have prevailed...but if it re-grows, even if from its off shoots, then love and light will win," the old man explained.

"Ah...I get it now...so that is why that dagger had three acorns in it, or did until Ali planted one...I bet they came from that tree," Simon interrupted excitedly.

Gabirol smiled at Simon's enthusiasm and wrote down what he said as the old man nodded yes in agreement before continuing.

"Let me explain, for it will have relevance later. There is a phrase in the opening verse of Genesis 18:1 about God appearing to Abraham by 'the terebinths of Mamre'. Although the word 'terebinth' is an awkward word to say, it does however sound important...In Hebrew, the phrase is elonei mamrei, elonei being the plural of elon. Yet elon, not terebinth, actually means oak. Terebinth stands for a tree or bush from which turpentine is made. The word turpentine actually derives from terebinth. Also, there is a lot of confusion about where it was that God appeared to Abraham, with so many places making a claim on it. Confusion arose because the Hebrew word alon, which means oak, and elah, which means terebinth, sound the same when spoken. The word elon in Genesis, which has the initial vowel of elah and the final syllable of alon, looks like a mixing of the two that allows one to choose either meaning. But the Hebrew text of the Bible was originally written without vowel signs so the original pronunciation would have been alonei and not elonei. In any case, this is how the first translations were made of the Bible, and the second-century BC Greek Septuagint interpreted the word, that gave us 'pros te drui te Mambre', that is, 'by the oak of Mamre'. Yet, the next translation we know of, the first-century AD Aramaic version of Onkelos, a standard Jewish text to this day, has 'b'meishri Mamre', which can mean either 'in the plains of Mamre' or 'in the encampment of Mamre'. Since the verse in Genesis continues, 'And he Abraham was sitting in the entrance to his tent or ohel'. However when Jerome produced his fourth-century AD translation of the Bible into Latin, which was adopted by the Catholic Church, he followed Onkelos by choosing not 'in the tents' but 'in the plains of Mamre'. So which is it, the plains, encampments, oaks or terebinths? I say oaks because in the first place, while 'oaks' is the oldest translation we have of elonei, 'terebinths' is the most recent. The Septuagint rendition represents a genuine tradition passed down from the time the Book of Genesis was composed. Moreover, terebinths, whose small leaves indeed smell a bit like turpentine when crushed, may have an impressive-sounding name, but they are not very impressive in appearance. The terebinth is an evergreen shrub that rarely grows to more than seven or eight feet and is found all over Outremer, where it is one of the most frequent plants in the hillsides. Terebinths grow wild and can spread like weeds if you do not keep them in check. The common Palestinian oak, on the other hand, develops into a tall, stately tree. A whole forest or grove of such trees, now seen in only a few places but less rare in Abraham's time, is an impressive sight indeed. Would the Bible have bothered to point out that Abraham was sitting by some perfectly ordinary shrubs? And why single out 'the terebinths of Mamre' when terebinths were everywhere? But if Mamre had a well-developed oak grove, that would have been a landmark worth referring to."

"But what has that all to do with Abraham exactly?" the wealthy tailor asked.

"Well, the oak is surrounded by a wall over which it projects. According to tradition, it was opposite this oak that Abraham's tent was pitched at the time the angels came to him and promised him a son and heir and also when he was negotiating with Ephron the Hittite for the cave of Machpelah (Gen. xviii. and xxiii.). Some have connected the oak with an earlier stage of tree-worship as explained previously about the Druids. In Jerome's time, fairs were *held under it. It is still frequently visited by pilgrims and it has become customary to hold the Feast of the Trinity under its shadow, connecting the subject of the feast with the three angels of the biblical narrative. Near the oak in former times, on its north side, stood a terebinth, which, according to Josephus, had existed since the beginning of the world. It was under this tree that, in Hadrian's time, the great sale of Jewish slaves, numbering, it is said, no less than 135,000, took place."* [49]

"Oh, so a good place for Turansha to continue the practice," Peter remarked.

The old man looked at Ayleth as she looked saddened by all she had heard, the mood in the room having turned sombre.

"Ayleth...let me continue this tale...and then we can break for the evening and hopefully you shall sleep safe and soundly," he said softly.

"That poor Templar," she sighed heavily, clearly upset.

Sarah reached across and placed her hand upon Ayleth gently and smiled at her. Ayleth nodded and mouthed silently she was okay. Sarah looked back across the table at the old man and gave a slight nod.

"I shall continue then."

Chapter 38
Ishmael – The fight!

Abrahams Oak, 1.2 miles southwest of Mamre near Hebron, Kingdom of Jerusalem

Paul grasped the sword with both hands and stood up straight. Unlike his own two handed sword, this one was heavy, nearly six feet long and one of the rare two handed swords that was only just beginning to come into fashion. Few knights used them but Ishmael threw his around with such skill and ease like it was a long dagger. His heart beat faster and he was aware that everything now hung on what he did in the next few minutes. He closed his eyes and took a deep breath. The words of his father entered his mind as if to remind him that he should always tire out a bigger opponent before trying to engage directly in combat and then beat them. A man who is bigger and with more muscle to fuel will tire quicker than a leaner opponent. He also recalled how he had promised Alisha all would be well when he had held her in the caravan when travelling toward Kizkalesi. He wondered where Thomas was, recalling his statement that where they were going, he would need all the swords and good men he could find. If ever he needed them, it was now. And Theodoric's promise that all would be okay, and that he never promised anything lightly, was also looking like being incorrect.

Alisha looked on part terrified but also angry and she constantly struggled against the two men holding her. Turansha clicked his fingers as one of his men handed him Paul's sword. He placed it across his knees and looked at it. The man next to him whispered something to him and Turansha shook his head no at whatever it was he had said. He looked up at Alisha then toward Paul.

"Whatever you think...I am a man of my word. I take great care and go to great lengths to make it known that what I say and what I promise, I do. If," he paused as he looked at the old Sufi mystic briefly. "If you can beat my champion, I will know it is a sign and I shall honour my bargain to release you on the understanding you will lead me to the Halls of Amenti. I shall also return this to you for it is no good to me," he explained and held out Paul's sword high. He then grinned, his face looking twisted in the flickering light cast from the burning torches as the evening sky darkened, the sun now almost completely set on the horizon.

"I too am a man of my word," the silk trader said aloud and rushed forwards and knelt before Turansha. "I beg thee, keep my daughter, but let me go free and I shall return with more silks and gold than you can imagine," he pleaded.

"Really...I can imagine a lot. Besides, I have your daughter already no?" Turansha replied smirking. "And I have enough silks and gold."

The silk merchant's daughter flounced her arm free and walked up to her father,

her fists clenched and looking angry. Slowly her father stood up and looked at her. Suddenly and with no warning, she slapped him hard across the face as tears welled in her eyes angry at his comments. He rubbed his face, looked at her and then down ashamed at the realisation of his remarks. Turansha let out a laugh and waved the merchant to move out of his way as two of his men grabbed him and dragged him to the side.

Paul looked to his left to see where Ishmael had gone when suddenly an almighty thud shuddered and vibrated down his arms as his sword was hit by Ishmael's, the clash of steel echoing out loudly across the landscape. The force was so mighty it threw Paul's sword clear out of his hands landing in the sandy soil several feet away. Alisha let out a gasp as Paul managed to duck and step back a pace as Ishmael's second swipe just missed him hitting the ground near his feet with such a force, it kicked up a cloud as well as sent a spark from a stone as it smashed through it. Paul dived to his right rolling towards his sword as Ishmael jumped towards him, raising his sword high ready to thrust down upon Paul's back. As he swung the sword down hard, Paul dived to his left grabbing the handle of the sword on the floor as he rolled over it with his left hand. As he rolled onto his back, he instinctively raised his left arm with the sword in time to block Ishmael's sword blow as it struck hard. The clang rang out loudly and Alisha gasped again as both sword blades bounced against Paul's chest. Paul's eyes met Ishmael's as he leaned down pushing his sword harder against Paul's chest, his sword stuck beneath the sheer weight of Ishmael.

"You cannot win this fight...yield and I shall make your end swift and clean... this is not what I desire," he whispered.

Paul scowled partly confused.

"Then do not do this...for I shall not yield," Paul replied through gritted teeth, pulled up his legs so his knees were to his chest near the swords, then pushed his feet up hard into Ishmael's stomach and thrust up as hard as he could pushing him up and away.

Ishmael staggered backwards momentarily caught off guard as Paul jumped to his feet and held his sword with both hands pointing the blade directly at Ishmael just as he lunged toward him with a wide swinging arch of his sword. As he swung it down sideways at Paul, Paul knew he could not deflect the force of the blade and without hesitation, he jumped upwards and flipped himself backwards doing a summersault. He landed awkwardly upon his shoulders but Ishmael's sword whooshed past him narrowly missing his legs. Ishmael spun rapidly despite his immense size continuing the momentum behind the sword and raising it higher in one smooth movement, turning completely ready to bring the sword down upon Paul. Paul pulled his knees up to his chest into a squat position, looked up at him then sprung forwards directly at Ishmael's stomach causing his sword to thrust down beyond Paul's back, the quillon bar catching his spine hard, the pain not even registering as Paul pushed against him with all his strength. Ishmael fell backwards stunned with Paul lying upon him. They hit the ground hard in a cloud of dust. Turansha looked on impassively it seemed as Alisha stared in silence no longer struggling, her gaze fixed upon Paul. Instantly Ishmael wrapped his arms around Paul tightly and started to squeeze him. With his arms stuck by his side, Paul could only move his head up as the vice like grip of Ishmael increased. He could hardly breathe as he squeezed ever tighter. Paul looked down into Ishmael's eyes. He did not want to fight this man but Ishmael was trying, and if he continued, would succeed in killing him. Paul struggled to look up and saw Alisha. She and Arri depended upon him...nothing else mattered. He looked back down at Ishmael and stared hard into his eyes. Ishmael hesitated just for a fraction of a second at the look in Paul's eyes. Paul reared his head backwards as hard as he could then thrust his forehead straight into Ishmael's nose, his nose breaking instantly and blood shooting downwards. Stunned, Ishmael blinked his eyes but did not release his grip. He snarled and let out a loud groan as he wrapped his legs around Paul and began to squeeze even harder. Paul could feel the crushing strength against him and he could not draw breath as Ishmael's grip was so fierce. Paul began to feel dizzy and could not breathe as Ishmael, his eyes closed tightly, used all of his strength to squeeze yelling out a roar. Alisha sank her head sobbing not wanting to look any more. Paul knew he was about to die. His vision was beginning to blur when he recalled a conversation he had with Tenno about close quarter combat. 'You do whatever is necessary to survive...no matter what and only concern yourself with the ethics and morals afterwards. The dead do not have that luxury.' As Ishmael roared louder burning away his energy squeezing, Paul felt several of his lower ribs break. Ishmael's neck was exposed, the veins in his neck appearing as if about to burst under the strain. Paul sank his teeth directly into Ishmael's throat and around his Adam's apple. Paul's mouth was instantly filled with the taste of iron from his blood, his teeth sinking deeper into Ishmael's throat. Ishmael instantly released his grip but then grabbed Paul's head hard. As he pushed Paul's head up, so too Ishmael's throat bulged outward still firmly held between Paul's teeth. Paul bit deeper daring not to release his grip. If Ishmael pushed his head upwards, he would tear his own Adam's apple out. Ishmael froze as Paul bit his teeth even deeper. Ishmael completely lay his arms outstretched upon the floor and released the grip of his legs too. Both lay in silence as Turansha looked on. Alisha fearing Paul now dead just sobbed face down supported between the two men holding her up, her cries the only sound. Paul could rip Ishmael's throat out there and then and both knew it.

"I yield," Ishmael whispered struggling to say the words and not moving a muscle.

Paul felt around with his right hand for his sword lying in the dirt nearby. He grabbed it. Once firmly in his grip, he released his bite and jumped upwards and away from Ishmael but quickly turned the sword and placed the tip of the blade against Ishmael's throat. Paul's heart was beating so fast it was making a ticking sound he could hear. Ishmael moved his hands just a fraction and instantly Paul pushed the sword against his skin puncturing it slightly. Paul knew that Ishmael could kick out or roll or any manner of moves, but if he did, he would thrust the sword with all his might. They locked eyes.

"Do you yield?" Paul said loudly in a deep voice, Ishmael's blood dripping from his mouth. Alisha looked up instantly and blinked to clear the tears in her eyes.

Ishmael moved his head very slowly enough so that he could look towards Turansha, who was shaking his head no. Turansha clicked his fingers and eight of his men ran and surrounded Paul and Ishmael. As two went to grab Paul, he swung the two handed sword away from Ishmael and in a wide arch causing the two men to jump back out of range. Paul raised the sword at the others as they closed in. Ishmael stood up slowly and picked up his sword. He looked at it then to Paul, then slowly at Turansha.

"I beat him...fair and square, he yielded," Paul snarled as the other men stepped ever closer all around him.

"I did not hear him say so. You have not beaten him, so continue. I am enjoying this spectacle," Turansha replied and gave a slight wave of his hand to continue.

Ishmael looked at Paul and stepped closer as Alisha shook her head pleadingly no. Ishmael's eyes met hers. He clenched the two handed sword with both hands and looked up and down the blade and then at Paul. Paul held out his sword towards Ishmael but had to then swing it wildly towards the men encircling him to keep them at a distance.

"Please...I beg of you!" Alisha called out just as Arri started to cry in the distance. Alisha sighed, her lips quivering with emotion as she tried to speak again but could not.

Ishmael looked at Turansha, who was now busy choosing some food from a plate in front of him as he shifted to make himself more comfortable upon his seat. Ishmael raised his sword above his head and started to swing it about in the air in ever increasing speed as he approached Paul. Paul raised his sword ready. But just as Ishmael took his hardest and last swing through the air, as it swung in the direction of Turansha, he released his grip with a grunt of energy, making the sword fly through the air directly toward him. Paul followed the flight of the sword as it spun through the air almost in slow motion it appeared, its blade making a chop chop whoosh sound. Turansha sat back, looked at the sword coming towards him and calmly ducked low just as it passed above him narrowly missing his head. The sword impaled itself into one of his men standing behind him with a squelch of blood and shattering of armour and bone. The man staggered backwards under the force of the blow and then fell down dead, the sword blade having gone right through him, only stopping at the quillons of the handle. Turansha looked behind him and then slowly back at Ishmael and Paul. Alisha was shaking uncontrollably barely able to stand. Turansha clicked his fingers and more of his men rushed to form a larger circle all round Ishmael and Paul. Paul looked at Ishmael in total surprise at his actions. Ishmael stood up straight, felt his throat for a moment, then smiled at Paul. Paul shook his head puzzled.

"I have killed enough innocents for that excuse of a man. No more," Ishmael said loudly for all to hear and moved to stand beside Paul as Turansha's men all closed in around them. Paul held his sword up defensively as Ishmael moved to stand back to back with him. Turansha stood up, looked back down at the dead man behind him then back at Paul and Ishmael.

"You missed...silly man. Such a mistake," he stated with a grin and wiped his mouth of food crumbs and then stroked his neat beard as he slowly walked towards them.

"You cannot control fate," the old Sufi said loud enough for Turansha to hear.

"Shall we put that theory to the test?" he replied.

"You promised. You said you were a man of your word," Paul called out whilst keeping an eye on the ever approaching men as the circle got smaller around them.

"Well...I could say, I lied...changed my mind even. Besides, you did not win as Ishmael has changed sides. Not what was agreed. One of you should have died...but as you seem to have changed the rules, then both of you will die," Turansha replied calmly whilst grinning.

"Kill them, and you will never realise your ambition," the old Sufi man said.

"Oh please, old man, will you ever shut up?" Turansha asked feigning irritation but still grinning. He stood still for several moments thinking, many of his men now totally surrounding Paul and Ishmael standing back to back. "Funny how enemies can become friends so quickly is it not?" he commented then started to pace up and down as he thought.

Paul looked towards the horizon. The very last vestiges of the red sun shimmered briefly before vanishing completely. His mind raced. Could he and Ishmael together beat off these men around them?

"I am sorry if I hurt you...," Ishmael whispered.

"Likewise...'twas nothing personal," Paul replied.

"Very touching. Fools ruled by irrational emotion," Turansha said as he moved nearer.

"What is the matter with you? Did your mother not show you enough love as a baby?" Paul called out.

"Mother...very perceptive...as I was...how do you people call it...a bastard!" Turansha answered and laughed. "But your hearts rule your heads...that is why you are so weak and controllable," he then stated and flicked his fingers again. Two men snatched Arri from the woman holding him near the camels and rapidly walked back to Turansha.

Paul and Alisha looked on in alarm as the man uncovered Arri's face. Turansha nodded at the man who immediately pulled out his small black knife, identical to the one Brother Teric had found and put in Paul's satchel. Alisha shook her head utterly helpless and speechless. Paul's stomach churned as the man placed the blade near to Arri's throat. Turansha smiled broadly, clearly visible in the flickering light cast from the nearby flaming torches. He nodded at the two men holding Alisha forced her down to her knees hard as one instantly withdraw a large curved sabre and pulled it up under her chin.

"Never let it be said that I am not a fair man...you changed the rules of this game, so I shall change them further," Turansha grinned. "You have a choice to make. Ishmael has defied me openly, so he must be punished...and I know how much he already suffers from the loss of his family so I cannot inflict that upon him again as much as I would wish to...and death is an escape I will not grant him...but I shall deal with him later," Turansha explained and looked at Paul, his eyes narrowing. "But I shall give you a choice...which of the two people you love the most in this world do wish to save this eve?" he explained and motioned with his open hands toward Arri being held and Alisha in turn.

"NO!" Alisha screamed and struggled, the blade nicking her neck again causing another cut.

Paul looked in anger at Turansha, his mind fighting to comprehend exactly what he was saying.

"'Tis but a simple mathematical problem. I hear you are good at such matters. Which one would you like to live and which would you send to the other realms?" Turansha asked raising his hands and eyebrows in an exaggerated fashion.

Paul gripped the two handed longsword and faced toward Turansha. As he did, several of his men aimed crossbows at him directly as Turansha laughed and shrugged his shoulders.

"Spare them and I will gladly yield and submit to your swords willingly...just do not hurt either of them I beg you," Paul exclaimed, his throat dry and full of emotion as he fought to hide the tears that were welling in his eyes, a sense of total panic beginning to sweep over him at his utterly helpless position.

✳ 4 – 11

"NO Paul...kill me! KILL ME!" Alisha screamed hysterically as the man holding Arri held him higher for all to see, the blade held closer to his throat.

Paul hesitated. He could see and sense the pleasure Turansha was having acting out his cruel methods with such joy and relish. Paul looked at the sword in his hands. Turansha winked at Paul as if to say 'go on, try it' as if goading him.

"I will not dance to your tune or play your cruel games to satisfy your sick twisted power hungry ego, you pathetic man," Paul stated through gritted teeth and threw the sword to the ground in the direction of Turansha. "I would rather you kill us all. Be done with it and may your soul be damned."

"Brave words...but I am beyond damned ha ha!" Turansha laughed maniacally. "Like I said...you let emotions rule your head, and that will be your downfall. You Franks, you pathetic Christian idealists...you all cling to life too affectionately for you fear your god and doubt life after departing this world. But I will not kill you this day, young navigator...I shall let you suffer the pain of seeing your loved ones die. Ha, 'tis feeble of you all. Now choose or I shall," Turansha explained still smiling. He paused for several very long minutes. "Hmmm. Kill the woman, the baby can grow and follow what was written in the charts...but kill the baby and that will not happen. But then the woman may have another child so it starts again. Hmmm. You can see how difficult my position is can't you. Such an uneasy burden I must confess," Turansha explained and laughed again.

"I do not fear death," Paul snapped.

"Clearly. That is why you will not taste death this eve...until you have seen the life of one of your most beloved extinguished before your very eyes," Turansha replied as he paced back and forth behind the line of men surrounding Paul and Ishmael.

"No...Please, kill me if you must...me," Alisha sobbed pleadingly.

Paul knew there and then if either of them was hurt, he would make for Turansha no matter how many arrows or bolts and no matter that it would be his last action on earth. He could not live without either Alisha or Arri. He could feel the tension and energy rising within him as he drew deep breaths, Ishmael doing the same against his back. Turansha then nodded at the man holding Arri. He knelt down, holding Arri across his knee, pulled his little head back slightly and placed the knife near to his ear to start slicing across his throat.

"Noooo!" Alisha screamed loudly, her scream echoing out across the surrounding area.

Suddenly an almighty explosion of noise and white light lit up near to Turansha's animals causing the camels and horses to panic and bolt. The Oak of Abraham became silhouetted against the intense bright light beaming out from behind it. The man holding Arri paused and looked towards the display as the other men shielded their eyes from its intensity. Paul tried to see what was happening and

370

shielded his eyes too. Alisha gasped in surprise and shock at the same time. Several of Turansha's men started to back away until he pushed them back into place. But then he tried to see what was happening.

"'Tis true…the angels, they come this night," Ishmael said loud enough for all to hear as the outline of a person started to appear walking towards them as if floating just above the ground, the white light stretching shadows out across the ground all around it.

The light sparked and shone out from behind the figure as it approached slowly. Paul quickly looked at Turansha, and even he looked puzzled for a moment slowly running his thumb and forefinger down his beard. The man holding Arri looked at Turansha, confused.

"Kill it, now!" Turansha shouted.

The man quickly steadied Arri, and placed the knife against his throat again. Paul's eyes widened seeing this and he started to run towards the man. He had taken just one step, when the whoosh of an arrow zipped past his right ear so close, the flechettes brushed his temple. Paul's eyes followed the large arrow, illuminated from the light of the approaching being as it twisted its way toward the man holding Arri, who looked up. The man's eyes widened momentarily, his mouth opening in shock, but too late just as the arrow smashed through his top front teeth and careered onwards through his head. Stunned the man just remained perfectly still for a moment before rolling sideways dead, Arri rolling onto the floor beside him. Whoosh, as another large arrow struck another of Turansha's men, the being shrouded in bright white light moving ever closer. Alisha's head was pulled back hard by the guard behind her as the man on her left was about to slice her throat. She gulped in anticipation and confusion just as another loud bang exploded behind the oak tree. The being shrouded with light, streams of burning light arching out from its back looking like large fiery wings, stopped and stood still. Its body was completely black and difficult to see due to all the light behind it. It had a long thin white neck and a small face, but the face had no mouth, its eyes huge and black and what looked like a bird's beak almost for a nose and mouth. Some of Turansha's men began to walk away backwards terrified. Paul looked at Turansha, who was carefully studying the being of light. Paul saw his sword placed next to the seat he had been sitting at. If he could get to that he could get Turansha he thought.

"Quickly…kill the woman," Turansha shouted out clicking his fingers frantically over his shoulders.

Paul immediately made a run toward Alisha as the men holding her struggled to keep her down, the third man behind her pulling her hair hard. Suddenly the man was pulled backwards into the darkness. Paul hesitated for a moment and blinked when the two men holding Alisha had their heads pulled backwards and with a flash of movement, had their throats cut. As they clutched at their throats, blood gushing out, they fell forwards when pushed by unseen hands from behind. Alisha froze on her knees shaking, her eyes darting from left to right in shock. Turansha's other men aimed their crossbows at Paul, Turansha stood with his right hand held high. Arri made a squealing noise upon the floor as a very tall and large figure approached as if out of nowhere somehow missed in all the noise and confusion. Alisha jumped as she felt a strong hand grasp her right shoulder.

"'Tis okay, Ali...'tis I," Nicholas whispered, his other hand wrapping around her waist protectively and pulling her against him.

She spun her head to see Nicholas's face. Dressed all in black, he smiled broadly just as Brother Baldwin raised his hand beside him. Quickly she turned and flung her arms around Nicholas and buried her face in his chest and sobbed. Brother Baldwin raised an eyebrow as Nicholas winked back and held her tightly as he helped her to stand. Paul could see Alisha standing and that she was being held by someone but he could not make out whom. At that moment, the area went dark as the bright light from the being faded out and stopped. The Sufi mystic looked up and motioned with his head for Paul to look. Within moments many more figures appeared walking to positions partly surrounding the encampment. The very tall figure stopped near to Turansha, knelt down briefly and lifted up Arri, who was crying loudly. The tall man gently started to rock him and within seconds he stopped crying. Alisha suddenly aware that he had stopped crying turned around and broke away from Nicholas. As she ran towards the tall man, she hesitated as she looked at Turansha. It was only then that she realised the tall man was in fact Tenno. All of Turansha's men pointed their crossbows at Paul. A silence fell across the area until Ishmael grabbed two men near to him and banged their heads together hard knocking them out. As they fell, he caught one of their crossbows and pointed it at Turansha. He just looked across at him and laughed. Paul felt the sudden anger toward Turansha swell inside him. He ran over to where his sword was, grabbed hold of it and pulled it free, swinging it up and immediately ran for Turansha, one of his men firing off a bolt at him, but it missed him. Quickly Turansha's men formed a protective circle around him as Tenno moved further away to protect Arri. Alisha ran around the back of Ishmael and headed for Tenno and Arri. Just as she reached him, several more Templars appeared on foot around them all. Turansha laughed again at Paul as he stood just feet away, several of his men aiming directly at his head.

"Well...this is a surprising standoff, would you not agree?" Turansha said, grinning, and looked across at the being stood some distance off, its pure white face clearly visible in stark contrast to the darkness and flickering torches. "Seems my actions did indeed force an action from the angels..."

The being started to move slowly towards the group, several of Turansha's men clearly terrified but holding their ground. Turansha folded his arms and shook his head. Alisha placed her hand upon Arri as Tenno placed his other arm around her. Nicholas and Brother Baldwin moved and stood beside Paul, who quickly acknowledged them both with a silent nod. The being stopped just feet away from the group surrounding Turansha. Both Paul and Turansha looked on, puzzled, as the being's long white neck appeared to open in the middle as it coughed.

"I am no angel, you delusional arrogant fool...'tis I, Theodoric."

Paul let out a gasp of surprise. Turansha just raised his hand to his beard and stroked it with his thumb and fingers again shaking his head slightly. He then smiled broadly.

"And I thought you dead all these long years past...as ever the great deceiver and illusionist...Theodoric!" he stated and laughed arrogantly again.

The old Sufi mystic looked up at Theodoric, shaking his head in surprise.

"You took your damn time...and what have you done to yourself?" he asked relieved as Ishmael went over to help him stand up and mouthed sorry at him.

"Yes...we got slightly delayed...Abi had a little run in with the rest of Turansha's little empire...which no longer exists by the way," Theodoric replied and stepped closer. Just as he said it, Abi walked into view with her large composite bow, armed with an arrow. But she was clearly injured and covered in blood herself. She feigned a brave smile as she moved around the men to stand with Tenno and Alisha. Alisha smiled and placed her hand upon Abi's forearm.

"You are hurt?" Tenno said seeing the blood down her side. Her lip was also split and swollen.

"A little...and I have but one single arrow left I am afraid," she replied grimacing clearly fighting to hide the real pain she was in.

"How did you know we were here?" Paul asked.

"We got word from him, to him...somehow, so Theo says," Nicholas began to explain pointing to the Sufi mystic then Theodoric. "As soon as we came out with Thomas and his men in Jerusalem and realised you had gone, we knew something was wrong. Brother Matthew had sent the Hospitaller escort away too for we would be escorting you as ordered by Princess Stephanie...but they were not to leave until we had arrived. Also, Theo said he could see the oak tree in his mind."

"Yes...plus several pilgrims pointed which way you went...but do not ask...I shall explain later...if I am allowed," Theodoric said and stepped even closer.

Only then did Paul see that he had painted his neck and face with black and white makeup to make his neck appear long and the lower half of his face also black with his nose made to look like the beak of a bird. It was almost terrifying to behold, but the trick had worked for it had distracted Turansha and his men long enough.

"Well this is all nice and cosy...is it not? Any suggestions what we should all do now eh?" Turansha asked sarcastically, his men still all aiming at Paul.

As he said that, a column of men on horseback rode up fast. In the darkness it was hard to see who they were until the man at the front rode nearer. As he came into the light of the burning torches, Theodoric raised his arms and shook his head almost exasperated. Turansha laughed as he saw that the man was in fact Gokbori, one of Saladin's most trusted military officers. A tall charismatic man, he looked far younger than his real age, his face clean shaven, his skin deeply tanned.

"What strange happenings occur this hour? For we saw the light and heard the explosions," Gokbori asked as he studied the encampment before him.

"Oh just the usual," Theodoric said loudly. "One megalomaniac trying to make himself feel big and powerful by cutting the heads off defenceless people...you know how it is," he continued, his tone laced with sarcasm now.

Gokbori edged his horse closer trying to work out exactly what was going on. Turansha, surrounded by many of his own men, all aiming crossbows at Paul, stood just in front of them with his sword at the ready, Tenno stood back a short distance with Alisha and Arri. Nicholas and Brother Baldwin moved to form a new defensive line with several other Templars.

"I recognise your voice...you, whatever you are," Gokbori said, pointing at Theodoric.

"Good, you should do I taught you enough times how to fight," Theodoric replied.

Gokbori raised his hand and ordered his column of men to move forwards to form up behind him and to his side.

"Surely, it cannot be...Theodoric. You are dead...or have you somehow come back...as this. Is that what this is?" Gokbori asked, puzzled.

"No...he is just a man still, with trickery played out. We were just entertaining ourselves this eve with our captives, as is the right of those captured in fair combat," Turansha explained.

"Fair combat...I think not. Kidnapping us to execute us because of some mad idea you have about us," Paul shot back.

"A mad idea you say. You are a Christian and she is a Muslim yet you married. 'Tis forbidden for a Muslim woman to marry a Christian man. She should be stoned. She is an abomination to Allah...as was her entire line before," Turansha explained calmly.

Abi stepped forwards aiming her last arrow directly toward Turansha through his men. She gritted her teeth and pulled the arrow back, the tension in the string creaking.

"I let loose this arrow and it will simply pass through whichever of you fools happens to be in its path...," she said and winced in agony. She blinked to clear her vision as Tenno moved to stand just behind her. "She is no Muslim you stupid fool... you would have known that if you had checked the parchments properly. You only see what you wish to see in order to satisfy your sick blood lust."

Alisha looked at her, confused, just as Paul looked at Alisha and frowned. Perhaps Abi was lying to save any further confrontation, he thought.

"I think this matter has been concluded," Nicholas interrupted and stepped forwards.

"A Templar...and pray tell how many of you are there for we are numbered many here against you?" Gokbori said and sat back in his saddle, puzzled.

"That would not be the first time such odds were stacked against us now though would it?" Nicholas replied.

"Brave words for a man so outnumbered...but possibly true for you all fight as devils," Gokbori answered, his gaze falling upon Alisha.

"You woman...tell me what has happened here this eve...and what were the lights we saw?" he demanded.

Alisha looked up at Tenno briefly. Quickly she kissed Arri on his forehead, then walked towards Gokbori, moving around the outside of Turansha's men, Paul on the opposite side of them. She stopped when she reached Gokbori and looked up at him.

"Murder is what happened here this eve...by that evil man," she explained and pointed at Turansha. He just laughed out loud.

"Young woman, I know this man. He is a valuable asset to me and my commander. And here I find myself with a situation where my enemy stands before me threatening him and his men. And now you are likewise my prisoners."

"No we are not...for you do not know the men and woman you stand against...so do not challenge them...just let us be on our way," Alisha replied.

"Woman, you have no option but to do as I say and you are in no position to bargain or tell me what to do. Do you know who I am?"

Alisha stepped closer to Gokbori and looked up at him intently.

"Yes I do. You are a man of honour...or so I am told by Princess Stephanie...but he is not," she simply stated and turned away and started to slowly walk towards

Turansha. She tried to walk between two of Turansha's men but they blocked her way. Turansha clicked his fingers and gestured with his hand to let her through. Quickly and forcibly, she pushed her way through the men and approached him.

"Ali, no!" Abi called out and staggered forwards holding her side in pain.

Alisha stopped just short of Turansha and stared at him hard. He grinned at her and rubbed his beard. She felt for her dagger tucked in her waistband. He shrugged his shoulders and laughed as Gokbori looked on bemused and intrigued.

"You ever come near me or my family again...and I swear I will gouge out your eyes and feed them to the birds," she said calmly.

"Ha...such spirit and blind courage...and I bet you are great in bed...oh such pleasures," Turansha replied loudly and laughed.

"Then I will cut your balls off...if you have any, and stuff them in your mouth then put your head upon a stake for all to piss on...," Alisha said leaning in closer to him.

Gokbori laughed amazed at her words as Paul shook his head surprised.

"You see...that's what I am talking about," Nicholas whispered to Brother Baldwin.

Turansha stood still staring back at her, her eyes fixed upon his, not moving.

"I do not think with Gokbori and his men present, you are in any position to make such threats...and come the day when I am nestled between your thighs, you will remember this day with regret and feel the size of my balls as I empty my seed within you," he whispered back and winked.

Before Turansha could blink, Alisha pulled out her dagger and thrust it upwards, just stopping beneath his chin, the prongs of the three blades just nicking into his skin under his beard. All she had to do was push a little harder and it would dig into his throat where his jaw met his neck. As he tried to back away, she pushed it harder, one of the prongs piercing his skin making it bleed. He moved his hand to grab her arm but she raised her eyebrows and pushed it even harder again her eyes blazing with hatred and anger into his.

"I keep my promises and my word...you ever cross my path again, you will die... that I do swear...and look again, behind you," she finished, lowered the dagger quickly and stepped back.

Turansha wiped the blood from his neck near his jaw and slowly turned his head in time to see many men and knights on horseback slowly appear as silhouettes near the oak tree. It was Thomas, his knights and a mixed contingent of Hospitallers and Templars appearing as they moved closer. Gokbori smiled and shook his head as he saw them approach.

"Theodoric...This would count as a stalemate...especially with the bad light, would you not agree?" he asked as Theodoric approached him.

Theodoric lowered the black hood covering his head, placed his hands upon his waist and looked around at everyone in their various positions. He looked at the severed Templar's head in the dirt and shook his head disapprovingly. As he spun around to look at Paul, Gokbori saw a large square shield attached to Theodoric's back by straps. It was covered by scorch marks and various copper tubes. Part of his tunic had also been burnt away.

"Yes...yes I would have to agree with you," he finally answered as Alisha stood back next to Tenno and Abi. Nicholas smiled at her, proud. Brother Baldwin shook his head at him.

"What say you, we shall withdraw taking our mutual friend Turansha with us, far enough away of course, and you and your...your whatever they are, friends away in the other direction and be gone by first light taking with you whatever trickery you used this eve," Gokbori said leaning forwards on his horse.

"May I suggest something," Saladin's brother Turansha interrupted as he approached on horse from the middle of Gokbori's column of men and stopped beside him. Gokbori nodded yes. "I was supposed to meet with this young man and woman and guarantee them safe passage to Alexandria...as approved and authorised by my brother himself...Let them come with me and my men whilst you take that Turansha, Umar...or whatever he calls himself elsewhere you see fit. And let it be known that if any persons ever conspire or assist him in harming or threatening these people again, they will likewise be put to the sword. And further, if you... Umar, ever make plans, commission or cause harm upon these people, you will pay heavily no matter how important you consider yourself to my brother's plans," he stated and stared down at Turansha, who raised an eyebrow and smirked back at him.

"I think that at some point, you will have to explain fully what occurred here and these people," Gokbori replied looking at Paul then across to Alisha just as Abi nearly collapsed, Tenno quickly grabbing her to steady her.

"Oh...I am happy to agree to that, and leave with you as requested. But this is far from over. I tested the theory...for I knew no harm would come to these two... it proves they are indeed the ones," Turansha exclaimed, grinning, and ordered his men to lower their crossbows.

Theodoric helped the old Sufi mystic to his feet properly and began to untie his rope bindings. Thomas dismounted and quickly walked over to Paul.

"Sorry, my good friend...we got deceived and waylaid...but we had to bring reinforcements courtesy of Lord Sidon on yonder horse," Thomas explained as he checked Paul over. "You okay?" he asked.

"Is Percival with you?"

"Yes. 'Twas he who set off the light show for Theodoric. I think we better go and check he has not blown himself to Kingdom come with that powder Tenno makes," Thomas said nodding with his head towards the oak tree. "Please...do not be getting yourself into such scrapes again for we would all be but lost, my friend."

Paul looked at him bemused and not a little confused. Lord Sidon rode closer making his presence obvious as he came into the light of the burning torches and raised his hand then nodded at Gokbori, who nodded back in acknowledgment.

"Are we in agreement then?" Gokbori asked aloud again.

Theodoric looked at all in turn finally stopping at Turansha, who clicked his fingers and immediately his men started to move as one surrounding him as he moved through the Templars and Lord Sidon's men toward what remained of their horses and camels. Turansha looked back over his shoulder at Saladin's brother and part bowed his head then stopped to look at Alisha.

"'Til we meet again eh?" he said, bowed his head and continued walking away with his men.

Gokbori motioned for his column to follow Turansha. As the men filed past on horseback, many of the men looked down at Paul. When all of his men had disappeared over the brow of the hill with Turansha, he approached Paul.

"Young man, you clearly solicit great admiration and respect. I know not of many men who command such. I have heard of you...you have a great friend in Saladin's brother Turansha. He told me what you did for him. But I fear you have truly made an enemy out of the other Turansha."

※ 3 – 40

"No...I think he has made an enemy out of Alisha," Paul replied feeling sick, his body aching, not quite believing all that had happened within just a few short hours.

"You have my word, we shall take him and his men to the northeastern regions where his skills are better suited to serve us...and we shall not intercept Lord Sidon's men neither. And perhaps we shall meet again ourselves."

"Thank you...and yes, I hope so," Paul replied and lowered his sword and looked at Alisha.

Gokbori could see Paul was exhausted both physically and emotionally. Silently he pulled his horse away, bowed at Theodoric and the old Sufi mystic.

"I am glad to hear that you finally mastered our language," Theodoric said to Gokbori.

"Well I had to...as you lot are all so stupid you cannot learn ours," Gokbori replied, joking, smiled at him and with a slight wave rode off after his men. Saladin's brother Turansha shook his head disbelievingly almost as his own men pulled up behind him. Paul stood still for several minutes until Alisha looked his way. They both just stared at each other in silence before the realisation overwhelmed them. Alisha let go of Tenno and ran toward Paul. As she reached him, he fell to his knees. She knelt down fast and flung her arms around his waist as he wrapped his arms around her tightly and squeezed her. As she squeezed him, he felt the pain from his broken ribs shoot through his side, but he just held her tighter himself as both burst into tears with relief. Brother Baldwin looked at Nicholas and nudged him in the side.

"I am sorry, Ali, for I swore to you on the way to Kizkalesi that all would be well...and it has not been so," Paul whispered emotionally.

"Paul...you just got us through that...you can get us through anything," she replied and pulled him even tighter.

"Bet you wish that was you eh?" Brother Baldwin whispered close to Nicholas's ear.

Nicholas scowled at him mockingly as Tenno looked at both of them. Abi slowly walked over to Paul and Alisha still knelt on their knees just holding each other.

"I swear, I am never going to shed another tear...ever," Alisha whispered as she held Paul and kissed the side of his neck just as Abi knelt down beside them, covered in blood herself and injured in her side. Alisha looked at her and put her other arm around her. Abi was clearly in pain. "And thank you for saving Arri...again."

"And I swear, I shall learn every skill and trick there is in combat so we never find ourselves in this position again...I swear it," Paul commented.

"I, I very nearly did not get here in time...I was delayed shall we say...and no, do not ask me yet," Abi replied and sighed with a half grimace and laugh. She then wrapped her arms around both of them.

"And what did you mean...that I am not Muslim?" Alisha asked.

"Later child...later I shall explain," Abi answered then let out a sigh in pain but fighting to keep it under control.

Nicholas looked at Tenno staring at the three of them all huddled together as he gently rocked Arri. Ishmael just stood alone looking at the ground, his future totally uncertain now.

Port of La Rochelle, France, Melissae Inn, spring 1191

"Oh my Lord...just when I think they will be okay, something else happens to them. Do they ever get to Alexandria then...and what in the name of the Lord did Theodoric do and have upon his back?" Sarah asked shaking her head.

"Yes, and did that Brother Matthew set them up?" Gabirol asked.

"And who is Gokbori?" Simon asked.

"What happens to Ishmael?" Ayleth asked.

"Please, slow down and let me answer those questions in order," the old man laughed lightly. "Yes, they do eventually get to Alexandria and, true to his word, Gokbori led his men away taking Turansha and his men with him. Lord Sidon and his men stayed the night alongside Saladin's brother Turansha and his men...and quite happily so in each other's close company. They had frequently traded and worked together over the years so were more than acquainted with each other. Theodoric and the Sufi mystic treated Abi for she had quite a severe sword injury to her side," the old man began to explain.

"How did she get that?" Peter asked.

"Let me just say for now, otherwise I run the risk of never finishing this tale and only serve to confuse you, that she had other charges she had to look after...and one such other charge shall we say was not as lucky as Paul and Alisha...and Abi was more than a little lucky to escape with her own life and get to the Oak of Abraham in time."

"Yes, that is a point...how did Theodoric know via the old Sufi man?" the Genoese sailor asked. "And how come that evil shit Turansha called Paul a navigator...did he know about the Prior de Sion stuff also then?"

"Some could argue that the Sufi mystic told Theodoric using the power of his mind... though some would argue that it was simply Theodoric trusting his own instincts and following them just as he had done so many times in the past and been proved correct. As I shall explain later, Theodoric and the Sufi mystic had shared many experiences a long time ago...and he would also maintain that once connected, so to speak, each could impress upon the other's mind. Veterans of combat know this feeling...to trust that inner sixth sense but also of being able to work so closely with someone that you instinctively know what the other is thinking or about to do, especially when fighting back to back. 'Tis one of the reasons such close unbreakable bonds are made between brothers in arms... something that most other people will never understand...and, yes, Turansha was sadly aware of the many secrets and teachings of the Templars, the Ashashin and Prior de Sion," the old man explained.

"And Brother Matthew?" Ayleth quizzed.

"He maintained he told Paul to wait, as he did, and swore he had no idea of how they were then kidnapped right from under his nose or who told the Hospitaller escort to leave before the Templars arrived...there was much confusion in the city that day, what with the

tournament, but also with many of the Templars in debate over who to vote in as the next Grand Master, with Gerard's name being pushed the hardest."

"Really. Well I do not trust him. So tell us, how did Theodoric make himself look like an angel and why did he do that?" Sarah asked.

"Because Theodoric knew Turansha had many of his very well trained men with him. Men who are not afraid to die...with some even welcoming it. So along with Thomas they planned how best to distract, confuse and cause a big enough diversion that would allow Nicholas and Upside...I mean Brother Baldwin...to sneak in close enough to effect the safe rescue of Alisha...and then Arri. So he used some of Tenno's fire sticks and explosive concoctions that he had been teaching Thomas and his men how to make, attached to his back, and with clever stage make up, managed to present himself as an angel of light with all the burning lights shooting from his back coupled with several larger pots of flaming bright lights Tenno had fashioned on the ground behind the Oak of Abraham. That is what Percival set off. Some claim they saw him float down...but that I am afraid I cannot confirm...but it did the trick and even had Turansha worried for a moment. Though in the process Theodoric did burn his shoulder, but he could not flinch or call out or put the fire out as it would have given away the illusion."

"Wow...the power of suggestion eh?" Simon commented.

"You have no idea, Simon...no idea," the old man smiled.

"I have heard of this Gokbori. Is he not one of Saladin's most trusted and fiercest commanders?" the farrier asked.

"Yes, he is indeed...fierce but fair, and honourable. And he was certainly more than a little impressed with Alisha that evening. She left a mark upon him he would not forget in a hurry."

"I know this Gokbori. 'Twas his behaviour and attitude that swayed many a Christian knight to convert to Islam and his ranks...," the Templar said, his voice low.

"Please, tell us more of this man, for it seems we are all too oft fed a totally different story about these men," Peter asked.

"If you wish," the old man replied and faced Peter. "Gokbori, or as he is correctly named Muzaffar al Din Gokbori, was in fact at the time of his encounter with Alisha and Paul, one of Saladin's leading Amirs, that is a military commander. Gokbori meant 'Blue Wolf' in Turkish. He was the son of the governor of Irbil who had been a loyal supporter of the Great Zanghi whose conquest of the county of Edessa had been the first step in recapturing lands from the Christians in 1144. He even led the right wing against Saladin at Aleppo at the battle of the Horns of Hamma but changed side to Saladin's...which had profound effects, which led to Saladin's success. Consequently, Saladin gave him the cities of Edessa (Urfa) and Samsat but more importantly his own sister in marriage Al Sitt Rabia Khatun. Gokbori as Blue Wolf has gone on to set up colleges, almshouses and hospitals and is responsible for patronising officially the unofficial birthday of Muhammad so he is by no means a man of little influence...quite the opposite," the old man explained. "And later, there were those who prophesied that a day would come when the Blue Wolf would engage in mortal combat with the Red Wolf of Kerak...as in Reynald...and only the victor's religion would survive."

"And Ishmael...the ugly...what of him?" Simon asked mockingly.

"He may have been ugly outwardly, and due to no fault of his own, but he had a good heart," the old man started to explain but paused, closing his eyes. He sighed and took a deep breath before continuing. "You see, like the Bull's Head knight, whose mind had been diseased through sexual pleasures with too many different women...that is all it takes sometimes, and

then the madness and sickness of the mind takes over...and leads to wrong things. Doing wrong and being evil are two different things. Likewise with Ishmael...he was a good man but whose circumstances in life led him to where he found himself."

"What...as an executioner?" Ayleth asked.

"He was no executioner...not like the man who hacked off the Templar's head. No, Ishmael had previously been a man of good character and background. Tall, handsome, respected and wealthy. 'Twas the arrival of Christian knights, led by Reynald himself no less, that changed his world for ever...but not who he was inside."

"I knew Reynald would have something to do with it," Simon interrupted.

"It was shortly after Reynald had been released from captivity when he raided a small seaport held by Muslims. They totally wiped the village clear off the face of the earth killing everyone in it. Ishmael was in the hills with his eldest, fifteen year old, son when they saw smoke rising from their village. They rushed down headlong into the knights who were butchering men, women and children alike. The brutality that Reynald showed was merciless. One house was aflame with its occupants screaming from inside. A small child no older than a year and a half crawled out from a gap smashed in the wall by its parents. It crawled to a clear part of the path just as Ishmael was fighting his way through the knights with no weapons except his bare hands. When he was finally brought to his knees, one of Reynald's men asked what to do with the small child. 'Kill it' he ordered and turned his back. The man simply picked the child up under its arms, looked it in the face for a moment, then simply threw it up over the collapsing wall into the inferno that now engulfed the entire building, the screams of agony echoing across the area as people were burnt alive," the old man sighed.

"No, please do not tell any more...'tis truly sick," Ayleth commented, upset.

"If you insist," the old man answered.

"No...we need to hear this, please continue, and if Ayleth cannot stomach this, perhaps she should retire whilst you continue, please," Gabirol stated.

Ayleth took a deep breath then closed her eyes for a few moments.

"No...Gabirol is correct. You must continue. After all, it is why I left England to learn of the real world...sorry," Ayleth said emotionally and nodded at the old man to continue.

"Okay...then let me briefly explain that whilst Reynald's men held Ishmael down forcing him to watch the destruction of his village, his son was dragged before Reynald. Ishmael begged and pleaded with Reynald not to kill his only son. Ishmael's wife had died giving birth to his youngest daughter. Somewhere in the burning village his two daughters already lay dead. Reynald listened to Ishmael but demanded from him the location of the gold the village was known to possess and hold. Ishmael denied any knowledge of any such gold. Reynald's solution was to march them to the edge of the cliff overlooking the sea nearly a hundred feet below and threaten to throw Ishmael's son over unless he told him where the gold was. It was gold set aside to pay the Muslim Jizya tax. As the sun was setting, Reynald grew tired and ordered his men to throw the boy over. Ishmael broke down and pleaded more that he did not know where the gold was...but Reynald's men just pushed the boy off. Reynald told Ishmael if he did not remember fast, he would be following him. What Reynald did not expect however was for Ishmael to stand up, and lunge forwards, grabbing the man who had so easily just pushed his son off to his death, and wrapped his arms around the man and dived forwards off of the cliff, preferring to die along with his son."

"Ayleth, come on," Sarah said as Ayleth sobbed trying to wipe her eyes dry.

"I am okay so please just tell it fast, please," Ayleth blurted out.

"Reynald, he just looked over the edge of the cliff to the rocks and crashing sea below, shrugged his shoulders and simply looked back at his second in command and commented 'how annoying and inconvenient of the man to jump like that'," the old man explained, taking care to look at Ayleth and how upset she appeared. "But Ishmael did not die. A curse he claimed that somehow Allah had imposed upon him, for by rights he should have died from that height and with all the injuries he sustained. His face and head had been smashed against the rocks, the bones being shattered as well as his arm and lower leg broken, his shoulder shattered also, his teeth almost all knocked out and his nose compressed...but survive he did, by the fury that raged within him he claimed. He found his son's body and despite the agony from his injuries, the freezing cold winter sea at that time of the year, which alone should have killed him, he lifted his son's body out of the water and stood waist deep in the sea all night pleading to his god to either revive his son or let him die too...but he did not die...not only that, but he now had to live severely disfigured."

"If that happened to me, I would kill myself," the wealthy tailor remarked shaking his head disbelievingly.

"He wanted to, many times, but something inside stopped him. He was found the following morning still holding his son's lifeless body by men from Turansha's group. That is how he ended up serving him...his hate for Christians burnt deep into his soul."

"Why then did he take pity on Paul and not just kill him?" Gabirol asked.

"Ishmael had long since burnt out the anger and rage of revenge, for he knew it would only darken his own soul. He had always preached forgiveness and cooperation before Reynald's troops attacked. He also learnt that there are people just as bad and capable of inflicting evil from any religion," the old man explained and paused for a moment. "And when he saw Paul and Alisha pleading for their son's life...that was the final moment, when Ishmael knew he could no longer do what he was doing. Simple humanity is all he wanted to see."

"What happened to the wealthy silk trader and his daughter?" Gabirol asked, looking over his notes.

"The young woman refused to speak with her father or travel any further onwards to Alexandria. She demanded to go back to Jerusalem with Nicholas. The following morning she did indeed leave with him and the Templars, her father, ashamed and begging forgiveness, went back with her. Up until that moment in her life, she had idolised her father...and that one single event, when he gave in to his worst fears, changed everything. That is why she slapped him."

"My Lord. We hear so little of what really happens in Outremer. The truth, the real truth, seems so hard to find or know," Peter said, shaking his head.

"Truth! My friend, as I was once told, a very long time ago...Don't believe everything you hear or see. There are always three sides to every story. Yours, theirs and the truth..."

"You mentioned that many of the Templars were debating about who would be the next Grand Master as Odo was now captive. Is that when Gerard became the master then?" Gabirol asked as he checked his notes again.

"No...much to his utter disgust and Reynald offering payments discreetly to swing the vote in his friend's favour, Arnold de Tarroja was elected. Gerard was furious, especially as Arnold was many years older, frail almost. With Saladin in the area with raiding parties, the selection was a swift one. Brother Matthew argued that it was the importance of the vote that led to Paul and Alisha being overlooked as Gerard took priority...at least the vote for him, which even despite Reynald's attempts at bribery, was very close indeed, very close."

"And Ishmael?" Ayleth asked with a nervous, hesitant look.

"I shall come to him in a moment when I explain the journey to Alexandria. Suffering brings endurance, wisdom and a humble heart...that is what he told Paul that evening. You see, no matter what the circumstances or places we find ourselves in, we all, each and every one of us, have choices. You can't change reality in your own mind, or truth, but real truth can change you. Our egos constantly try to control life in one way or another, which makes it impossible to see our true selves, our passive selves...our selves beyond our minds. But Ishmael had seen what he was and he made a decision to choose a way that is good. He made his choice and it was one that ultimately saved Alisha and Paul."

"Are you telling me that he had forgiven Reynald then?" the wealthy tailor asked.

"Not quite for it was something he would never get over. But he adopted the attitude of 'when you forgive, you do not change the past or what has happened, but you do change the future and what will be,'" the old man explained and then slowly wrapped his hands around the sword in front of him. "And this...this Paul would never again let out of his sight. He picked it up from the ground and made himself a solemn vow."

"Can I ask a question please...perhaps a silly one?" Simon asked. The old man smiled and nodded yes. "Can you explain what Abi meant when she said Alisha was not a Muslim woman...for I do not believe it was merely to protect her from Gokbori nor Turansha."

Chapter 39
Between Worlds

As Saladin's brother Turansha and his men set up camp alongside Nicholas and the other Templars, Thomas's men formed a tight protective circle around Alisha and Paul's caravan. Tenno helped Abi up into it as Theodoric and the Sufi mystic discussed how best they would treat her wounds. Alisha and Paul together held Arri as Ishmael stood beside them somewhat bewildered himself. Paul studied the men all setting camp, some talking and laughing together despite being from opposing sides. It confused him why things were this way. But both he and Alisha were even more confused by Abi's earlier statement that Alisha was not a Muslim. Adrastos started kicking his front legs and snorting trying get Paul's attention. Eventually Paul walked painfully over to him and patted him several times then held his head close, which calmed him down. Ishmael still just stood alone. Alisha gently placed her hand upon his arm and smiled at him and nodded gently. Ishmael's change of mind and actions had without doubt saved their lives.

"Thank you," she said quietly. She could see the pain in Ishmael's eyes as he simply nodded back.

Paul looked at Alisha standing with Ishmael. What a day this had proved to be. He looked around at all the men, whom, if they were to run into each other again after tomorrow, would in all probability be fighting each other. He looked up at the stars that arched across the night sky shining more brightly than he had ever seen. Adrastos was hungry and kept snorting but Paul had not even considered that was the reason for his unease. A beautiful scent wafted across Paul's senses but he knew not from where. It reminded him of roses but was far sweeter and fragrant. Adrastos stopped snorting and settled almost at once with the arrival of the scented smell. Paul heard Upside laugh a short distance away. He felt incredibly grateful and humbled that all these men had put their lives on the line for him and Alisha. He closed his eyes and rested against Adrastos. He could feel emotions rising inside him as if he was a jug of water filling up fast. He fought to control the feelings for he was certain that if he started to cry again, he would never stop. How cold and callous Turansha had been. Had he been testing the will of God or just saying that after all the men had arrived. He shuddered as he thought how close Arri and Alisha had come to being killed. He sensed someone stand beside him and quickly stood up straight. It was Alisha.

"Paul...are you okay?" she asked softly.

He looked at her, unable to speak. He placed his hand upon his sword checking it was still there even though he could feel its weight. His ribs hurt but not as much as the pain in his back from Ishmael's sword where the quillon hand guard had caught him. Alisha's eyes were wide and seemed to sparkle and reflect both the flickering torches and stars. Adrastos snorted briefly, the moon appearing to sit on gathering clouds on the far horizon.

"I think he gets jealous of you," Paul finally managed to speak.

Alisha smiled and tucked herself gently against Paul and placed her arms around his waist. She rested her head upon his chest.

"Never again will I allow us to be in that position again…that I swear on all that is most precious to me in this world…," she whispered.

"And the next," Paul replied and hugged her then wondered how Abi was doing. In his mind he saw the look of the beheaded Templar as he told him not to watch. Such bravery and raw courage he thought. His eyes caught the sudden flash of lightning a long way off on the horizon as dark rolling clouds loomed like new mountains. The night blanketed the land in darkness, but soon the moon would play with the clouds as they rolled and thunder started, the deep rumblings strangely calming reminding him of home, the few raindrops arriving, creating soft rhythmic music as they splashed upon the caravan, horses and men alike. The air became fresh, the night rejuvenated almost. As the rain fell and the storm continued, Paul held Alisha closer and patted Adrastos to reassure him as flashes of lightning un-eased him. The rain was gentle, cool and welcoming, and it felt as if it was cleansing them almost. Paul looked up; the beauty of the thunderstorm playing with the moon-light shining over the low hanging clouds as they just as quickly began to roll away taking the thunder and rain with them to another land. Both stood holding each other relieved to be alive and grateful…very grateful.

஘௧

Brother Baldwin pulled over his proofed leather foul weather covering so it covered him completely but allowed him to look forwards. He nudged Nicholas in his side sat next to him to draw his attention away from staring at Paul and Alisha. Nicholas feigned a smile barely visible in the moonlight but kept looking at them holding each other beside Adrastos and the caravan. Smells of cooking started to fill the air and the muffled chatter from amongst the men. Abi let out an uncharacteristic moan in agony from inside the caravan, Theodoric and the Sufi mystic talking as they treated her. Alisha and Paul looked toward the caravan, but knew there was nothing they could do, but wait and pray she would be okay. Tenno appeared cradling Arri and approached Alisha offering for her to take him. Gently she took Arri in her arms. Paul acknowledged his thanks and Tenno simply bowed his head in his usual polite manner. All the while Nicholas watched, part fascinated and part envious. His heart ached so much for Alisha and he felt both foolish and ashamed for how he was feeling as his mind dreamt up a thousand ways that perhaps one day…one day he would be able to hold her in his arms. He sighed and shook his head. Just the momentary touch when he had held her as he pulled her up earlier had touched him deeply. He had not wanted to let her go. But she was not his and he knew that and the physical ache in his heart just would not go away. He lowered his head not to look any more, a deep and dull sadness filling his very soul he felt. Brother Baldwin rubbed Nicholas's shoulder reassuringly knowing his friend was suffering…the loneliness of unrequited love that fate so cruelly cuts through our hearts with no remorse nor respite.

Paul stepped up into the caravan, his hair still wet from the rain. Abi was just being covered with a heavy blanket by the Sufi mystic as Theodoric washed his hands still covered in Abi's blood. The floor was awash with blood and blood soaked rags and even some of Paul and Taqi's shirts that had been used. Alisha pushed past Paul to climb in holding Arri in her left arm, her face looking concerned. Two candles flickered away to show Abi asleep, her face a very pale white. Theodoric looked sinister almost as he still had all the makeup on. Alisha nearly slipped in the blood but Paul managed to steady her as he himself stepped inside fully. Abi lay perfectly still, her feet stretched over the end of the bench seat.

"Will she be okay?" Alisha whispered just as Arri let out a small cry.

Both Theodoric and the Sufi mystic looked at each other briefly before looking down at Abi. Tenno appeared at the door and looked in eager to hear.

"I shall not lie to you," the Sufi mystic started to say and rubbed his hands dry. "She is between worlds."

"What…what does that mean?" Alisha asked fearfully in a whisper.

"He means…she is very close to death. She may not last the night for she has lost far too much blood. It is an un-survivable loss," Theodoric explained and paused. "You need not whisper, she cannot hear you."

      1 – 3

"Where is your god now?" Tenno demanded, his voice full of anger as he banged his fist against the door frame making Alisha jump. "I am sorry…she must not die… must not," he stated and quickly turned and walked away out of sight.

Theodoric raised an eyebrow at Paul surprised at Tenno's little outburst just as Alisha sat nearer to Abi, placed Arri beside her and started to stroke her blonde hair gently. Abi looked serene in the dim candlelight as if simply sleeping.

"We are responsible for this…all of this, just like Sister Lucy and Niccolas warned us…as our fathers also warned. We were told there were those who would wish us harm," Alisha said and sighed deeply looking at Abi intently. "Are we cursed or just foolish. Do we deserve this for going against our fathers' wishes?" she asked Abi.

"Ali, she cannot hear you nor answer. You must prepare yourself for the worst this night," Theodoric explained as he continued to try and wash the blood from his hands.

"Theo, are her wounds truly that severe?" Paul asked quietly.

"Yes, my boy, that they are. 'Tis a miracle she ever got here," Theodoric replied and shook his head in sadness. "'Tis a pity Lucy is not here this hour to say her goodbyes…she would have wished to be."

"Do not speak as such…she is not dead yet," Alisha snapped emotionally and lifted Arri even closer beside Abi. "Abi…you listen to me and you hear me. You cannot…you must not die, we need you. Do you hear me?" she demanded "I will not shed another tear, that I swore, so do not make me break it already…do you hear me?"

Alisha looked at Abi for several moments but she did not move or reply. Paul stepped closer to be by her side. He knelt next to Alisha and held her hand and placed his other hand upon Abi's large hand. He closed his eyes and squeezed both their hands. He grimaced momentarily as pain shot through his broken ribs and his bruised back. He clenched their hands tighter and took in a deep breath.

"Abi...I know you can indeed hear this," Paul whispered as Theodoric and the Sufi mystic watched him. He then placed Alisha's hand upon Abi's chest and put his hand above hers. He paused as if struggling to think. His face was still covered in blood from Ishmael and he looked a fearsome sight. Gently he pushed Alisha's hand down until she could feel Abi's heart beating. After a few more minutes Paul opened his eyes and looked at Alisha. She studied his features, confused and hurting inside herself. Arri made a little yelping noise and gurgled happily. "Ali...can you feel that?" Paul asked. Alisha just nodded yes. "Well...that is called purpose! That continues to beat for a reason...that reason is you and Arri...she knows that, and with every beat, that purpose grows. She will not give up," Paul explained confidently and assuredly as if he was stating a certain fact. He leaned nearer to Abi and looked at her closely then gently kissed her on her forehead. "Hear me Abi Shaddana of Sardinia...you have a purpose, you are alive for a reason...that is why this still beats," he continued and pushed Alisha's hand firmly against Abi's chest, her beating heart pulsing into her hand it felt. "Do not give up." Paul kissed her forehead again, stood up and moved away.

The Sufi mystic and Theodoric looked at him briefly before looking back at Abi, Alisha and Arri.

Port of La Rochelle, France, Melissae Inn, spring 1191

"I think I need to make a vow to stop crying," Ayleth remarked and wiped her eyes again as tears rolled down her cheeks.

"I want to know why that evil Turansha did not use or take Paul's sword. He clearly knew what it was...," Simon interrupted.

"I should have explained that better" The old man coughed. "Many years previously, Turansha had access to the sword...and he tried to wield it...and when he did, it nearly crippled him. So yes he knew full well its power."

"Pity it did not. So why did it not?" Gabirol asked.

"Philip...Paul's father. He took it from him just in time before it could kill him," the old man answered and shook his head.

"What...why? I mean why did he not let it kill him?" Simon asked, puzzled.

The old man looked at the sword then up at Simon slowly.

"That, my young Simon, is a question he would ask himself a thousand times...but at the time, he believed he saw a spark of decency within Turansha and that he was worth saving."

"Clearly not...but can you explain how Theodoric knew Gokbori so well? You mention that he taught him." Gabirol asked, a little perplexed.

"Let me just say that Theodoric was instrumental in getting Gokbori to side with Saladin...in order to stop a greater...far greater...evil...," the old man explained and sat in silence for several moments.

"This Paul...'tis not easy to wield a sword at the best of times even when fully trained. He must have a natural ability to have wielded a two handed sword for they are indeed rare

and nor best suited to close combat," the Templar remarked trying to reengage the old man, who seemed to be deep in thought elsewhere.

"Then why are they made?" Peter asked.

"They are brilliant for stopping a horse by cutting its front legs with a single blow...but one on one combat, that takes sheer brutal strength," the Hospitaller explained as his brother nodded in agreement.

"But that sword, that is a two handed one," Simon remarked pointing at the sword on the table.

"Yes...but it is also unique and far lighter than a normal sword. That is why Ayleth was able to lift it so easily," the old man finally spoke in reply and all looked at the sword.

"If the caravan was full of blood and Abi, where did Alisha and Paul stay the night?" Sarah asked.

"They stayed with Abi as their own bunk was still free of blood. The Sufi mystic kept watch over Abi all night whilst Theodoric went to make sure Tenno was okay. He found Tenno meditating in silence beside Abrahams Oak so did not disturb him. It was only that evening they all realised how much Tenno obviously secretly felt toward Abi. Arri threw his Clip clop horse aside during the night and it fell upon Abi's blood leaving a small spot upon the toy," the old man explained wearily. "Huh, that spot Alisha would tell Arri was to mark Clip clop's heart where a very special woman had placed part of her soul inside him to make him alive..."

"Oh dear...does that mean Abi does indeed die?" Sarah asked hesitantly.

The old man looked up at her. He looked very tired and drained from what little of his face he did reveal. He looked down and with a deep sigh, rested his hands upon the sword and closed his eyes. He did not speak for what seemed ages. Eventually Stephan stood up and moved beside him placing a reassuring hand upon his shoulder.

"Please...I think it time we retire this eve," Stephan said quietly.

"But I want to know if Abi dies or not!" Simon replied loudly sounding impatient.

"So do we...but it can wait," Sarah said quietly and frowned at Simon hard and indicated with her head they should all get up and leave.

Gabirol looked at the old man sat in silence and not moving. He could sense the anguish and pain as if it was a tangible force he could feel. He looked at the others in turn. The Templar nodded back at him and started to stand up, his brother following suit.

"Your rooms are as you left them should you wish to stay the night," Stephan remarked quietly as they all began to stand, the old man still just looking down. "We can resume this in the morning for those of you who wish to hear the rest."

"Only if...if he is willing to of course," Ayleth replied as she stood looking at the old man sadly.

"I am sure he will," Stephan said as the old man nodded yes.

"Your hospitality is more than generous...and most welcome," the Templar said as he clasped Miriam's hand.

The old man finally looked up.

"I am sorry but I am weary. In the morning I shall continue...and I shall explain what happened to Abi I promise," he said softly.

"And about her remark that Alisha was not a Muslim?" Gabirol asked quickly.

The old man nodded yes silently. Within minutes Stephan and Sarah had seen them all to their rooms leaving the old man alone in the big chair, the dying embers of the fire behind him casting a warm glow. He sat in total silence for over an hour resting his hands upon the sword before finally looking up and around the large room. A single tear rolled down his white cheek. He placed his face in his hands as his elbows rested upon the table and he began to sob silently, his body shaking. Stephan watched him from the doorway of the main corridor. He shook his head, sad for the old man. Sarah came and stood beside him and looked in at the old man sobbing silently. Gently she pulled Stephan back and away to give the old man some privacy.

℘ ℭ

The sun was just rising over La Rochelle and the sky was a cloudless pale blue when a loud clang rang out from the kitchen where Sarah had dropped a large cooking pot upon the stone floor. As Stephan entered the main room, he was surprised to see the old man still sat silently at the table, his hands placed upon the unsheathed sword. His eyes were closed as if he was asleep sitting up. He approached the old man just as the Templar and Hospitaller entered the room yawning, both dressed in just their under suit clothing without any chain mail or mantles. Gabirol followed them and they all looked at the old man sat in total silence.

"Is he okay?" Ayleth asked as she stepped into the room behind them wrapping a shawl around her shoulders.

"Fear not, I am not dead...yet," the old man said aloud and opened his eyes. "Come, please sit for I am rested well enough."

"I shall sort some breakfast food and beverages," Stephan said as he ushered them all in as Simon appeared looking like he had slept in a hay stack, his hair sticking up.

"So did Abi die?" Simon asked impatiently as he sat down pulling his chair up with a loud screech across the floor.

"Give the man a chance," the Templar remarked as Miriam entered the room and smiled at him broadly.

"Sit, eat and I shall continue this tale," the old man said and nodded acknowledgement at all in turn as they began to take up their seats, the wealthy tailor struggling to button up his tunic.

Abrahams Oak, 1.2 miles southwest of Mamre near Hebron, Kingdom of Jerusalem

The morning air was crisp and cool as Paul stepped down from the caravan. After a fretful and sleepless night he looked around at the various brightly coloured little tents Turansha's men had set up. Two Templars stood guard a short distance away and acknowledged him as he moved to see where Tenno was. Thomas was sat preparing some food with Percival sat opposite. Paul had not even thanked them or Nicholas for coming to their aid. Percival saw him and raised his hand smiling. As he approached them he noticed Ishmael lying asleep on the dirt just a few feet away, his hands tucked up under his face. Both of the two handed swords were tucked beneath his arms. Paul looked behind him as Theodoric followed him down from the caravan steps and walked over to him fast.

"She has lasted one night...I honestly did not think it possible. I shall find Tenno yonder and inform him," Theodoric said as he looked toward the oak tree, Tenno still visible sat upright next to it. He had not moved all night. "Paul...I shall need to look closely at the small injuries on Alisha's neck lest they get infected so please make sure she lets me."

"Injuries?" Nicholas remarked as he suddenly appeared from behind them with Brother Baldwin.

"Yes...her neck was nicked by the blades of Turansha's men," Theodoric replied and quickly started to walk away toward Tenno.

"Nicholas...and you also, in fact all of you...I failed to thank you last eve," Paul started to explain, when Nicholas raised his right hand and shook his head no it was not necessary. "But I...," he tried to say again but Nicholas shook his head more and raised his eyebrows. "Thank you," Paul simply said quietly.

"You did very well yesterday," Thomas said aloud as he continued to stir his meal.

"If I had done well, Alisha would never have been placed in the position she was. I shall never make that mistake again...and I wish to be taught all there is to know about combat...everything," Paul replied and looked around at all the knights and soldiers, both Christian and Muslim all mixed together.

His gaze was drawn to movement from the nearby white tent as Turansha flung open the entrance flap, looked at him and smiled as he began to walk toward him. He waved briefly, his helmet carried beneath his left arm. Thomas looked up over his shoulder at Paul.

"I believe you could probably teach us a thing or two...but if it is the craft you wish to learn, then both I and my men will gladly train you," he replied and smiled again broadly.

"This, this, my friend, is how it should be, no?" Turansha interrupted as he stood by Paul and looked at all the men and horses camped together.

"Yes it should be," Paul replied as he looked across to see Theodoric reach Tenno.

"We shall have no further problems on our journey to Alexandria, that I can assure you," Turansha remarked. "When we stand together, we can stand against tyrants and evil doers like Turansha, though it sickens me he uses my name...but united...imagine it?"

"Yes...a wonderful but unrealistic dream," Thomas shot back as he looked at Turansha.

"Thomas. As ever the cynic my friend," Turansha replied and feigned a look of disapproval.

"Well, you know me," Thomas laughed back.

"Yes I do, only too well," Turansha replied smiling. "Paul, you should always listen to this one, for despite his rough appearance, he does actually have insight and wisdom in that head of his."

Ishmael woke and began to sit up. He pulled the two swords beside him closer and looked around himself. All looked on as the wealthy silk merchant's daughter walked past fast closely followed by her father. She stopped, thought for a moment then walked back to Nicholas.

"You there, you are returning to Jerusalem yes?" she asked pointedly in tone.

Nicholas looked at Brother Baldwin briefly before nodding yes.

"But," he said before the woman interrupted him.

"Good, then you shall escort me," she stated and quickly flounced around and walked back towards her own caravan.

Her father stood still, his shoulders low. He looked tired and embarrassed as the men all stared at him. After his daughter stepped up into their caravan, he lowered his head, slowly turned around and walked away toward one of the old brick houses nearby.

"Another strong willed woman," Brother Baldwin commented and nudged Nicholas.

Paul heard his comment and looked at him and both smiled at each other as Nicholas gave Brother Baldwin a glare.

"Do not worry, I am not offended for Ali is indeed a strong willed woman," Paul remarked. "And thanks to you, I still have her. I, in fact we, are honoured to know you. We shall never forget you," Paul continued and outstretched his hand to shake Nicholas's hand.

Just as Paul and Nicholas shook hands, Alisha stepped down from the caravan carrying Arri. She squinted due to the bright morning sun rising rapidly. She looked across and saw Paul and Nicholas and immediately headed for them. She was almost upon them when the wealthy silk merchant's daughter stepped down from her caravan carrying a large leather bag over her shoulder. She walked rapidly toward Nicholas and Paul arriving at the same time as Alisha. The merchant's daughter dumped her bag beside Nicholas and folded her arms.

"I am ready to leave," she stated in a demanding fashion.

Nicholas laughed briefly as Brother Baldwin shook his head bemused. Turansha stepped closer and looked at the young woman. He bowed slightly to acknowledge her.

"Looks like the big noise upstairs has answered your prayers," Brother Baldwin whispered to Nicholas but was overheard by Alisha.

Alisha looked at the young woman. She was tall and beautiful and well dressed. Her skin was flawless it appeared. Alisha rubbed her fingers over the cuts to her neck and then felt the spots upon her face that had come out. She suddenly felt very self conscious standing near to Nicholas as he turned and looked at her. She blushed and looked down. Paul noticed this and moved to stand by her.

"If she does not wish to go with you, she is more than welcome to come with us," Turansha said politely. The woman looking at him hard. "Though I am sensing not!"

"We shall guarantee her safe escort back to Jerusalem," Nicholas said and smiled at her before looking back at Alisha. His heart missed a beat as he realised that as soon as he said that, this would indeed be the very last time he would in all likelihood see Alisha.

Both Nicholas and Alisha looked into each other's eyes for several long moments. Paul could sense the emotion between them, but he knew also that ultimately Alisha was leaving with him. Plus he knew how easy it was to still like another just as he did with Princess Stephanie, not that it made him feel reassured as his own heart sank a little. He felt jealous of Nicholas as he stood looking at Alisha, standing upright, his broad shoulders, cheeky smile and looking confident, strong and every inch what a knight should be. Brother Baldwin eventually coughed loudly. Alisha stepped closer to Nicholas, looked back at Paul as if to ask permission, and then whilst holding Arri in her left arm, placed her right arm around Nicholas's waist, placed her head against his chest and hugged him. She closed her eyes as he placed his arms around her. He looked at Paul as if to apologise but he simply nodded it was okay. He would not deny them a farewell hug. He had saved her life twice now.

"May your god always be with you," Nicholas finally said then kissed Alisha on the top of her head and pushed her away gently.

Tears welled in her eyes but she quickly rubbed them away determined not to cry as Nicholas bowed to her and Paul. Nicholas felt sick knowing this was the last time he would see her but he fought to remain calm.

"Are we all ready then to break camp and leave?" Theodoric interrupted the awkward silence as he walked up behind them all accompanied by Tenno.

"I am!" the young woman exclaimed, instantly eager to be on her way.

Alisha looked at her just as Nicholas looked at her. Quietly he ushered her away smiling as he went and started to talk to her immediately. Alisha felt a tug at her heart as she watched him walk away. Paul watched her. He could see she was deeply upset.

"Come along...we must make sure we keep a very careful eye upon Abi as we travel," Theodoric said as he gently pulled Alisha around to face him.

Brother Baldwin looked at Paul for a few moments, then smiled and offered his hand. Paul shook hands with him.

"Look after him for us please," Paul found himself saying as he looked across at Nicholas and the young woman walking away.

"Oh I shall. 'Tis what I do," Brother Baldwin replied and paused as his eyes followed Alisha. "And you look after her," he said nodding toward her as she then started to step up into the caravan. "And I would wash your face," he remarked and gestured with his fingers around Paul's face that still had dried blood all over it.

Brother Baldwin gave him a quick wave and hurried off after Nicholas just as Lord Sidon walked toward Paul lacing his riding gloves in place. At the age of forty-nine he was short, stocky, and almost bald and his chain mail hung very low and loose as if not fitted properly. Paul immediately recalled all that he had learnt of Sidon and the myths surrounding it and the skull of Sidon. That all seemed so very long ago.

"Paul...I and my men must leave with haste but I just wanted to shake your hand and bid you a safe journey onward," he said with a large smile. "My good friend Balian has told me much of you. The great Bull's Head Slayer no less. 'Tis truly a pleasure and honour to meet your acquaintance, young sire," he said effusively and offered his hand to shake.

Paul looked at him, bemused. He shook his hand.

"My Lord, the honour is mine...and thank you for your timely attendance," Paul replied.

"Less of the Lord crap, laddy. My name is Reginald. Reynald some call me but I prefer Reginald lest I am mistaken for that other fool, Reynald de Chatillon."

"Reginald it is then...thank you," Paul replied and looked back toward his caravan.

Tenno was standing beside the caravan looking uncharacteristically anxious as he waited patiently for Theodoric and the Sufi mystic to check on Abi. Ishmael stepped closer to Tenno and they exchanged an acknowledgment as if some unspoken agreement had been made. They were both large in size and character and made for a fearsome sight Paul thought to himself. Pain shot through his side again as he moved, the broken ribs reminding him of the previous evening's events. Theodoric had burnt his shoulder, Ishmael had a bloodied nose and a Templar had been executed. Paul did not even consider the deaths of Turansha's men but did wonder how Abi had been so badly injured before her timely arrival.

ဆာ ርᲜ

Within thirty minutes, Nicholas and his men along with Reginald's were packed away, mounted and ready to leave. Turansha spoke for several minutes with him before they shook hands. Reginald moved his men off, bowed briefly at Paul and rode off toward Sidon closely followed by Nicholas and his Templars, who would head for Jerusalem further along the road. They did not even look back.

"My friend, 'tis such a great pity our people so love to fight and massacre each other," Turansha said softly as he came and stood beside Paul. Both looked at the small wooden cross set above the fresh grave of the executed Templar. "Now come. It falls upon me to complete my obligations and promise to get you to Alexandria. An obligation I must stress I am honoured to carry out," he said and paused as he looked at Paul. "We have much we can learn from each other. I hope we shall become firm friends."

 6 – 15

Paul looked back at him. Turansha reminded him a lot of Taqi. It was hard to imagine that he was the brother of Saladin himself.

Port of La Rochelle, France, Melissae Inn, spring 1191

"I knew the Lord of Sidon, Reginald. Truly short and ugly, but he more than made up for that on the field of combat. He was a restless character always on the go. Fine company too and not puffed up by his position," the Templar commented as he looked at the bowl of breakfast food set in front of him.

"Was he really that ugly as we have been told then?" Peter asked.

"No not really. But he was not handsome neither by any stretch of the imagination. Though he has recently married Balian's daughter I believe," the Templar explained and smiled as he looked at Miriam.

"How is that so?" Ayleth asked.

"Let me explain," the old man said and put his eating spoon down. "He was a close and good friend of Balian's. Reginald was present at the Battle of Montgisard in 1177 and fought beside Nicholas, but he was not at the Battle of Jacobs Ford in 1179 as he arrived too late with his forces. William of Tyre was very condemning of him for not getting there in time saying he could have saved many of the refugees from the battle if he had continued on his way. Sadly and consequently as he returned to Sidon, many refugees were killed in ambushes," the old man explained and paused briefly. "As stated, Reginald was indeed described as 'extremely ugly but also very wise'. He was one of the few native barons of the kingdom who spoke Arabic and was knowledgeable about Arabic literature. He was on good terms with

Saladin's other brother, Al-Adil. Humphrey of Toron once saw him hunting with Al-Adil, which did not endear him to those who would later support Guy of Lusignan. He was even accused of having secretly converted to Islam. You may recall all that I explained about the secret skull of Sidon and its connections to the Templars. I can tell you now that much of that was written by the author Walter Map, although the story at this time is not connected with the Templar Knights but has since been woven into it somehow," the old man explained and laughed to himself.

"I just want to know if Abi survives. Can you please tell me that?" Ayleth asked pleadingly almost.

"I met that Lord of Sidon too once," the Genoese sailor interrupted. "We used to pick up huge shipments of seashell stuff to dye things purple."

"That does not surprise me for Sidon's most important enterprise, especially in the Phoenician era, was the production of purple dye from the small shell of the Murex trunculus which was broken in order to extract the pigment. It was so rare it became the mark of royalty," the old man explained." As well as from another far more ancient source and reason."

"And Abi?" Ayleth asked, feigning exasperation, and raised her hands.

"Then let me explain fully what happened to Abi. For true to his word, Turansha and his men did escort Alisha and Paul, along with Thomas and his knights, toward Alexandria. And for three days they travelled undisturbed on good roads. All the while Abi lay unconscious. It was a deep sleep the like of which neither the Sufi mystic nor Theodoric had any experience with."

"Well can't that light woman heal her like she did Paul's face...surely if she was connected with that lot?" Sarah asked.

"No. What happened to Paul was something totally different and could only happen and take place in Jerusalem where he was. It was not something that could happen where Abi was...it was also a time that revealed Tenno's deep affection for Abi. It was on the third evening when Turansha ordered his men to set camp at one of the many Muslim staging posts situated just off the main road that ran parallel to the Mediterranean Sea that Tenno finally went inside the caravan and sat beside Abi and held her hand. Alisha and Theodoric sat with them whilst Paul helped the Sufi mystic outside prepare a potion he claimed would help her."

El Arish beach, Egypt, 1179

Paul wiped his face of sweat. The sun was setting yet the sea breeze was still warm and the air humid. He held the small box the Sufi mystic had given him and he waited patiently as he mixed some spices and leaves into a paste he had started to grind in a small stone bowl. Turansha's men were already setting their tents for the night amongst the many tall palm trees that gently swayed in the breeze. Several Bedouin tents were already set up and their camels tied up securely. A single story mud brick building sat alone at the very edge of the beach that ran parallel to the palm trees. Several of its bricks were however painted a bright orange and some bright blue. Behind them in the distance Paul could see Gebal Maghara. He only knew this as Turansha had told him as they travelled near. Paul looked around at Turansha's men. Technically they were his enemy, yet he did not feel threatened in any way, quite the opposite. He placed his hand over his sword just to check it was there even though he could feel its weight. He was developing a habit of constantly checking it was there yet knowing full well it was. He stepped forward a few paces so he could see past the caravan and looked at the sea that was gently rolling ashore in rhythmic harmony, its sound soothing almost. The evening sun was a brilliant crimson with gold hues reflecting off the few clouds on the horizon. He had never seen such an intensely coloured sunset. The Sufi mystic looked up at him and smiled.

"Paul!" Theodoric shouted loudly from inside the caravan, his voice laced with alarm and shattering the tranquillity of the area in an instant.

Paul's heart exploded in a rush of fear and panic and he instantly ran to the steps and jumped into the caravan dropping the Sufi mystic's box. Inside it was dark except for one small oil lamp, but it gave off enough light for Paul to see Tenno reaching across to take Arri from Theodoric, Abi still motionless on the side bench and Alisha on the floor near to Theodoric's feet. Her arms were down by her side, her tongue was stuck out between her teeth as white bubbling saliva was forced through them, her eyes wide but a pure white. Paul rushed to her side and knelt as she shook uncontrollably in spasms, her legs kicking out. He grabbed her hand but she was shaking so violently he could not restrain her. Frantic, he looked at Theodoric as he stepped over her and immediately turned her upon her side. He felt her forehead. She was burning up. Quickly and without word he ripped the top of her dress open and then pulled her entire dress down over her shoulders to her waist, her upper breast band covering sliding down with it. Paul looked at him in shock as the Sufi mystic looked in concerned. Theodoric leaned over Paul, grabbed the bowl of water used for cleaning Arri and promptly threw it all over her head and face and started to wipe the water over her. Theodoric looked down her body and could see she was still wearing silk trousers beneath her dress. Quickly he raised her feet and pulled them off forcibly and ripping them in the process. He threw them in the corner just as Alisha gasped out for breath, coughed and then started to breathe in short sharp pants. She tried to move as her body kept shaking.

"Talk to her," Theodoric ordered as he started to wipe her back down with a soaked cloth.

Confused and concerned Paul looked at Alisha as her eyes rolled back, her pupils wide. She was dazed as she tried to focus her eyes. Her body kept on shaking.

"Ali, 'tis me Paul...you are okay," he said reassuringly and rubbed her hands but looked at Theodoric.

As Theodoric wiped her down, he looked at her neck. Three areas where the knives had been at her throat and nicked the skin were raised and red. He turned and looked at the Sufi mystic.

"'Tis inflamed. Her wounds must be infected," he exclaimed before looking back to Paul.

"No...no...please, dear God, no," Paul said with fear evident in his voice.

Theodoric stood up and pulled off the mattress from the main bunk bed and threw it on top of the central table. As soon as he had positioned it, he leant down and started to lift Alisha. He motioned with his eyes for Paul to grab her feet, and within moments they managed to lift her and place her on the mattress. She was naked except for the crumpled dress around her waist which Theodoric immediately started to remove. He repositioned her breast band undergarment to protect her modesty, Tenno only then looking up fully at her. Eventually she lay still with just her undergarment covers on. Theodoric felt her forehead again, placed his two fingers over her wrist to check her pulse then looked back at the Sufi mystic.

"Looks like I shall need to make double," the Sufi mystic calmly stated and pulled away from the doorway.

"Look," Tenno said looking at Abi.

Very slowly Abi raised her left arm from where she was lying. She weakly grabbed the side of the table, felt the mattress and slowly moved her hand higher until it met Alisha's fingers. She placed her large hand over Alisha's hand and held it, sighed and just remained in that position. Tenno shook his head whilst gently rocking Arri in his arms and his mouth tuned up very slightly at the corners, the nearest thing to a smile Tenno had ever shown.

"This will be another long night, my friends," Theodoric remarked.

"Where is Lucy?" Abi suddenly asked in a very low whisper, her voice dry.

Tenno sat down and let out a noise that sounded like a laugh of relief.

"Abi…she is away to Kerak to stay with Stephanie…but only until the birth of her baby," Theodoric answered quietly and wiped her forehead again.

Abi clearly smiled, her eyes still closed and then squeezed Alisha's hand before falling into a deep sleep again.

"Theo…," Paul said.

"Alisha has a fever, the worst type for I fear it is from the metal that caused the wounds to her neck. Such fever can destroy the organs…so pray, Paul…pray," Theodoric stated too bluntly for Paul's liking but Theodoric did not believe in dressing it up or making the very real threat appear less.

Paul sat back upon his heels utterly confused and scared for Alisha. After all they had been through. He knew from overhearing his father's many discussions with his Hospitaller friends the slow and at times agonising death that poisoning of the blood can cause. His mind raced as he remembered the charts Niccolas had drawn up where it had shown a skull and cross bones symbol where a great change would occur in his life. He recalled how at the time his heart had missed a beat fearing it would be Alisha whom he would lose. Was this the profound change the chart was showing? He felt sick and looked at Arri in Tenno's arms. He was sleeping soundly. If Alisha died how would he feed him…how would he cope? He shuddered and a knot twisted in his stomach tightly and a sense of dread overwhelmed him at just the mere thought of her dying. Only now did he appreciate the massive enormity and responsibility that lay upon his shoulders and how his father must have felt all those years ago after his birth and death of his mother. He sighed heavily.

ℰᏉᏉ

Alisha thought she was floating as she felt weightless. Slowly she opened her eyes but all she could see was white, a white filled with what looked like textured silky pinpricks of gold. She tried to turn her head and move her hands but she was paralysed. 'Am I dead?' she thought. 'Arri!' she suddenly called out, alarmed. Everything was quiet. She could not tell if she was lying down or standing upright as she had no physical senses. A beautiful scent began to filter through her nose similar to roses and lavender. She suddenly saw her right hand being raised by another person's hand but she could not feel any sensation of being touched. She tried to force her eyes further to the right to try and see who the other person was but she could not...just whiteness. Her attention was drawn to the gold spots of light that began to swirl around above, or in front of her, she was not sure as she could still not work out which way up or down she was.

"Alisha," Firgany's voice said softly, barely audible.

In shock, Alisha tried harder to move but she simply could not move. She sensed her hand being squeezed gently as feeling started to register in her fingers only.

"Fear not, Ali, I am with you," Abi's voice said clearly.

'I am indeed dead,' Alisha told herself and panic for Arri started to flood her mind.

"No, you are not dead, child. Now look at me, look at me for I have someone here to see you," Firgany said comfortingly.

As his words filtered in, a bright image, barely visible at first, of Firgany began to form before her eyes. She gulped emotionally, her bottom lip quivering.

"Father," she called out.

"Yes, my child. Try not to fight this, for you are between worlds. The cord has not been severed," he explained, his eyes looking into her very soul she felt. "You must listen and try to understand what we tell you next...and accept it for what it is."

As soon as he had finished his words, Raja began to visually appear before her. She smiled and looked to her left and outstretched her arm for another person stood nearby. Slowly a man appeared. He clasped Raja's hand and turned to look at Alisha. Both stepped forwards slowly smiling broadly as Firgany stepped aside, all three now almost completely visible. But everything was still a brilliant white with the gold mini starburst everywhere. Alisha gasped in shock, the sense of disbelief overwhelming. She shook her head at Raja both pleased to see her but so very confused.

"Ailia...my beautiful daughter. It has been a long time," the other man said, his face kind and serene.

'Daughter. What is he talking about?' Alisha thought, confused.

"Yes, daughter," Raja answered as if she could read her mind.

"Yes, Ailia...and Raja, she is your mother," Firgany stated and smiled disarmingly despite the revelation shooting through Alisha like a bolt.

Alisha stared at all three of the figures before her. Were they a trick, was she hallucinating, was she dead for surely if this was real and the people genuine, then both Firgany and Raja would know she is not her mother. The realisation suddenly hit her recalling what the Sufi mystic had stated about her being present at her mother's death.

"Ali," Abi said softly as she squeezed her hand. "Do not be alarmed but it is true. You must get Theodoric to explain fully, but yes, Raja is indeed your birth mother and this is your true birth father."

"No, this cannot be...Father," Alisha replied emotionally and looked at Firgany.

He placed his hands together across his stomach and smiled at her. 'Deny it!' Alisha demanded in her mind as she looked at him. He shook his head no slowly.

"Alisha. It has been my greatest privilege to have been your father in your world.

You have been, are, and always will be my daughter...but I was not your natural birth father." He paused, seeing tears well in her eyes. "He was," he finished and indicated toward the man holding Raja's hand. He released his hold of her hand and stepped closer. Alisha could not deny the overpowering sense of knowing the man. A deep recognition that was almost tangible to feel.

"And Raja was my wife...your mother," the man said softly.

Alisha shook her head in total confusion. She looked across to Firgany looking for reassurance but he just nodded yes in agreement with the man.

"I am your birth uncle...let Theodoric explain," he simply said and smiled again.

"Ali...they speak the truth," Abi said beside her. "Your father died shortly after you were born, and Raja was taken prisoner. You were taken in by Firgany to be raised as his own."

Despite her vow to never cry again, tears began to stream down her face uncontrollably and she did not care. This was some terrible dream she told herself. But then she looked into the eyes of the man introduced as her father. The look of love and warmth that exuded from him told her all she needed to know that it was true. Then another man appeared. He was taller and looked very wise and gentle. Without being told she knew it was the tall white haired man Paul had described so many times from his dreams and who had saved him in La Rochelle. He tilted his head sideways and winked with a very broad smile.

"Remember me? It has been a very long time since last we met, my dear little sister," he said without speaking but she could hear him clearly in her mind.

"Sister...Then where are we truly?" Alisha asked as Raja moved closer to her, smiling.

"My dearest daughter. How I have so longed to be able to tell you that...but have not been able to for your own safety. But now you know of the intentions by men such as Umar...Turansha as he calls himself now, then now you must know all. But your time here is restricted so it falls to Theodoric to tell you. Keep Thomas and his men close, they are all from a Viking bloodline that will protect you. And you will need that protection...especially when your daughter arrives," Raja explained softly just as Niccolas appeared by her side and bowed.

"What of Abi? Abi...I need you with us," Alisha said, alarmed, and tried to look at her.

"Ali...I am trying to remain...but you must go back now and tell Theodoric he must tell you all...and to check Thomas and his knights' swords...that he must make the three fold water for both of us. He will know what that is...," Abi replied in a faint whisper.

Firgany, Raja, Alisha's birth father and Niccolas stood shoulder to shoulder looking at Alisha with apparent pride. The tall white haired man simply stood back a short pace and rested his hands upon his staff that seemed to appear from nowhere. As they all smiled, they raised their right hands together until they met except the tall white haired man who looked on. A brighter light shone and the image of a golden x appeared with what looked like a smaller x attached to the top right of the bigger cross. It grew in intensity and size obscuring their faces until all was just pure brilliant light all around her again, then silence.

છ૭ લ૭

Alisha let out a gasp as she reached up with her arms frantic with alarm. She kicked out her legs and struggled to sit. Paul instantly held her hands and pulled her arms together as she opened her eyes, her forehead covered in sweat. Her pupils were wide and she looked terrified as she tried to focus on Paul. She ached and hurt all over, the inside of the caravan being dark only adding to her sense of dread and panic. 'Arri' she mouth silently and Paul motioned with his head towards Tenno sat in the corner holding him. Alisha turned her head to see Abi lying almost beside her on the bench, her hand placed next to Alisha's thigh. Quickly Alisha grabbed her hand. Theodoric stepped into view and looked down at them both.

"Theo...I...I...met my real father and Raja," she paused as she fought to control her emotions. "She said she was my mother...and...and you must make the," she paused again as she tried to catch her breath as she struggled to breathe. "The three fold water...," she managed to gasp out before passing out again on her side, her hand placed upon Abi's.

Paul looked at Theodoric, concerned, and shook his head and shrugged his shoulders as if gesturing for an answer. Theodoric stood still for several minutes looking at Alisha and Abi. He nodded as if understanding what Alisha had said, raised his finger briefly before turning to leave the caravan.

"I shall be back shortly with what she asks for," he stated as he stepped out of the caravan and was gone.

Tenno and Paul looked at each other, puzzled.

℘ ℂ℞

Outside the caravan as the crimson sky turned an inky black as night enveloped the area, Thomas and his men set up their camp as Turansha's men did the same. Ishmael sat down beside the caravan's rear wheel next to where Adrastos had been tied for the night. The sand was still warm as well as soft. He sat with the two swords across his knees and closed his eyes. Inside, Paul started to light a new candle as the oil lamp was nearly out. Tenno had sat holding Arri for nearly two hours straight and he had not moved. Soon Arri would wake for a feed but Paul had nothing he could give him. Abi and Alisha lay perfectly still, Alisha holding her hand over Abi's. Every now and then Alisha would try to turn her head, but all Paul could do was wipe the sweat from her brow and try to keep her cool. Feeling tired, his ribs painful and his back aching, he lit the candle just as Theodoric opened the door and quickly entered followed by the Sufi mystic. They were both carrying a small blown glass type of cup.

"Thank our brave Templar who lost his head, for without him, we would not have had the items and tools to prepare this," Theodoric said as he pushed past Paul and immediately raised Alisha's head and placed the cup next to her lips. "She must drink all of this."

"What is it?" Paul asked, concerned, as the Sufi mystic did likewise to Abi.

"We call it 'three fold water' but I shall have to explain what it is later," the Sufi mystic explained as he started to tip the water gently into Abi's mouth. At first her lips were dry and would not part, but as the liquid moistened them, he was able to part them and slowly drip it inside her.

Theodoric did the same to Alisha, but she coughed several times involuntarily

398

spitting some back out across Theodoric's face and Paul sat close to her. It took several minutes before they had managed to get all the fluids inside them. Theodoric sat back heavily against the caravan's bench seat next to Paul and took in a deep breath.

"And now we wait...," he exclaimed, exhausted.

"And pray?" Paul said looking at him.

"No...just wait will do," Theodoric replied and closed his eyes.

Tenno looked on in total silence. He was praying for Abi and he made no attempt to hide that fact as the Sufi mystic pushed up alongside him and offered him a small leather water bottle with a covered leather teat. Tenno looked at it quizzically as the Sufi proffered it again for him to take.

"'Tis the same water with some goat's milk added. It will feed him enough and keep him settled until Alisha can feed him again," he explained.

Paul felt instantly light headed and shaky inside upon hearing that, as it meant that Alisha would recover surely, to feed him again...but he checked his emotions just as quickly.

Tenno took the bottle, looked at Paul and without even arguing or asking why it had been given to him, simply accepted and held it steady ready for when Arri awoke. Paul could have cried looking at him. A gentle rap on the door drew all their attention. Tenno leaned over and opened the door to reveal Percival looking in anxious and concerned alongside Turansha and his sister Sitt al-Sham Zumurrud from Damascus. Her caravan had just joined theirs for the onward journey to Alexandria. Her long silk dress and head scarf reflected the light from the candles shimmering like slow waves, the gold thread and ornate patterning sparkling in places. She bowed slightly and proffered up a small bowl containing rosehip oil. Without a word Theodoric accepted it and sat back down allowing her to see through to Alisha and Abi laid out both unconscious. They all just stared at them lying still, each with their own fears and concerns. The next few hours would be critical as to whether they would live or die...and it was now all out of their hands. There was now nothing anyone could do except wait...and pray as Paul did constantly.

Port of La Rochelle, France, Melissae Inn, Spring 1191.

"'Tis too early on a Sunday for tears...so I shall try not to," Ayleth said quietly.

"'Tis that but if we wish to hear the end of this tale, I fear we shall hear much more that may make us shed tears," Sarah remarked and feigned a smile at Ayleth before looking back at the old man.

 2 – 17

"I think you just may indeed," the old man replied and shook his head.

"Then please do continue, my friend, for I shall not leave this place until I have heard all, and I am most curious on what the three fold water is," Gabirol stated.

"Yes, me too," the wealthy merchant said rubbing his hands together.

"Three fold water...," the old man began to explain but paused as he looked at them all.

"Philip and Theodoric during their early travels came across certain documents housed in Alexandria. They were copies of even more ancient parchments. They detailed how to use crystals, certain stones, similar to what the Vikings used to navigate with and as used in the mechanical devices Niccolas had designed and made to always point north, and a pump system where water was forced through it at great speed and spun and twisted all once." The old man sighed and stopped for a few moments. *"Hmmm, now trust you I must, having told you all so far...but the secret of the water, as per the ancient plans, states that it changes the actual composition of the water. Instead of being two fold, as in made up of two elements, it is changed to be made up from three distinct parts. We have no way of seeing or understanding what happens for we simply do not have the tools to see, but in time we shall. Only then will we understand the meaning of three fold water. But it was taught, especially to the highest adepts and alchemists, as handed down by Thoth or Hermes to the Greeks, which all of us, all animated things, contain and are built upon water. Every part of our bodies is mainly water. But in some people, their physical body is able to produce and hold the three fold water, which is why they can heal others, see and know things others cannot. But all of us can take this three fold water and physically change to a healthier more balanced being."*

"You mean like the elixir of life itself. True holy water? Is that it?" Peter asked intrigued.

"Almost," the old man replied.

"Is water made from two elements?" the Genoese sailor asked, puzzled.

"The ancient documents tell us it is made of two elements yes. One part of one and two parts of another," the old man answered.

"But that is three...," Ayleth remarked.

"Yes, but still two elements, of which we are not permitted to understand at this time," the old man replied and smiled.

"But how did Theodoric get the crystal and materials to make this water?" Gabirol asked, puzzled.

"That is what the poor Templar who was beheaded brought with him. As I said, he was an incredible man. He was also the closest thing to a brother and family member Abi had...apart from the old white haired tall man of Malta...whose name by the way is Kratos."

"Ah...that was his name. You only mentioned it once before and I missed it," Gabirol interrupted and immediately wrote it down.

"Sorry, I thought I had given his name properly. In Greek, it means 'strength', which he certainly had. Well, the Templar had been raised himself by Kratos. He was like an adopted son to him. He was also of a great age...older than most shall I say for now...and along with the Sufi mystic, they knew the danger Alisha was in and what was coming. 'Tis why the Templar, who by the way came from Sardinia too, tried to warn Alisha and Paul...but he arrived in Jerusalem too late. He was being followed by Turansha's spies. When he looked inside the wealthy merchant's caravan that is when they struck and also kidnapped them for they believed them to be Alisha and Paul. They soon realised the man was too old to be Paul, but the Templar...they had wanted him for many years...," the old man explained and almost smiled as if remembering better times.

Gabirol noticed the way the old man looked as he spoke of the Templar, clearly with fond memories.

"You knew this Templar well yes? And you say Sardinia. You said just once, that Abi came from there," Gabirol asked.

"Yes, yes I did. And you miss very little for I did indeed say so just the once that Abi came

from Sardinia in this tale. It is where she was born. Her parents being the last of her line. She was just four of our years old when she went to stay with Kratos."

"This three fold water...did it work though?" Sarah interrupted.

"By the grace of God and with the materials the Templar had brought, Theodoric and the Sufi mystic were able to make the water...and yes...yes indeed it did work," he answered with a broad smile.

Ayleth cupped her mouth emotionally as Sarah smiled and patted her thigh she was so pleased. Stephan smiled at her show of obvious joy at hearing the water had worked.

"So...so what of this dream Alisha had whilst ill. Was that real? Did she really meet her father...and Raja? And how come that Kratos man was in her dream or other realm or had he died from his injury from the falling masonry back in La Rochelle...is that how he was there in the dream...thing?" Peter asked, confused, and waving his hands erratically.

"If it was no dream, but somehow real and happening within another realm, then Kratos must also be dead to this world. And why could they not tell Alisha about Raja being her real birth mother? Why was that left to Theodoric for it does not make sense?" Gabirol asked.

"I could say that Kratos was able to travel between realms, but I shall leave it at that for now. But if Alisha awoke and Theodoric did not explain it to her, she would forever think it was just that...a dream, but if Theodoric was able to tell her, it would confirm it in her mind that the experience was a real one, however it manifested itself."

"Oh my dear...if this is all real, I think I may have to make some small changes in my life," the Genoese sailor interrupted and smiled mischievously.

"Why?" Ayleth asked in all innocence.

"Well, from all that I have heard these past days, everything I have ever done, and not just in this life apparently, but everything, is watched and recorded. If I lie, they will know," he answered, pointing upwards with his fingers. "And...," he paused "...And just imagine if people like that Kratos really do exist and can travel between realms. Anyone who commits a crime, he would know about it. Murderers could never hide..."

"You murdered anyone recently?" the Templar asked.

"No...not ever. Well certainly not in this life time," he replied and laughed.

"That is why the veil is placed over us when we are born so all previous actions are not remembered. It gives us all the chance to do what is right without the guilt or influence of what we may have done previously. And some, who are pure of heart and spirit, volunteer to return to this realm of existence to help others," the old man explained.

"Is that what that Percival knight is...or Alisha even for did not Paul see her with Kratos in his dreams?" Gabirol asked.

"I shall answer that in the course of this tale," the old man replied with a smile.

"How can we believe these other realms of existence are true?" Simon asked.

"The best analogy I can give," the old man started to reply, when Simon raised his finger to pose a question.

"What does analogy mean?" he interrupted sheepishly.

"It means an example that demonstrates or illustrates a particular point so you may understand another matter that is similar," the old man answered.

"Well...that still does not help, but please carry on," Simon replied, smiling.

Sarah shook her head slowly as she looked at him.

"I shall use the analogy of a whale," the old man began."

"Oh good, like Jonah and the whale in the Bible," Simon said excitedly.

Sarah looked at him harder.

"We all know what a whale is...yet it swims within the seas and oceans oblivious to what happens on the land even though it is the same part of its world. Sometimes it breaks the waves and sees the clouds and sky above both in the day and at night, but it has no understanding of what it is for it cannot reach the heavens, yet the land, that is still part of its physical world yet even there, it cannot reach. If it did, it would feel the weight of its own physical body that is too cumbersome and not suited to the land...even though it breathes the same air as we do, it cannot survive long out of water and it will die. But sometimes, it can look upon the land and see things that are happening. Sometimes things upon the land enter the sea and affect the world the whale lives in. But we as physical beings are in exactly the same boat for we sometimes glimpse what is on the other shores and sometimes we have things from the shores thrown to us. But the main thing to remember is that just because we who live upon land, and though the whale cannot leave its physical world of water, does not mean that the land is none the less real does it?" the old man explained.

"Ah...so I am guessing that this Kratos man...he is not dead but can travel to the other shores briefly...but you mentioned the silver cord not being severed yet...and the executed Templar as being very old, like Abi. Can you explain that more?" Simon asked and looked at Sarah quickly.

"I can," the old man answered emphatically.

"And about the big cross with a smaller cross upon it...that also?" Gabirol asked.

"Yes...but those crosses are not the Christian crosses, but the written cross as in an x," the old man replied and put his hands together. "I have already explained about the silver cord as mentioned in the Bible...the term being derived from Ecclesiastes 12: 6–7 in the Old Testament, but about age I have not except having mentioned that Abi was far older than her physical appearance would make you think."

El Arish beach, Egypt, 1179

Paul had managed to feed Arri from the bottle Theodoric had provided. He seemed to have taken it very well, which to Paul felt like a minor miracle and godsend. Tenno sat beside Abi holding her hand tightly. Theodoric was talking outside the caravan with the Sufi mystic and Turansha and Thomas. One of Thomas's men had been taken suddenly ill but Paul was too preoccupied with Alisha and Arri to even take note. Paul winded Arri and he let out a loud burp and he smiled. As Paul reached for his toy horse Clip clop, Abi very slowly opened her eyes, her first image being that of Tenno looking at her. Tenno quickly let go of her hand and sat upright. She smiled and licked her dry lips. Quickly Tenno grabbed the small ceramic cup with rose water in and placed it gently against her lips as he supported her head with his other hand. She sipped some then rested back. As she focused on him, her gaze turned to Alisha. She outstretched her hand and held hers as she still lay unconscious.

"She...she knows all...but Theo must confirm it," she whispered as she looked at Alisha then turned to look at Paul and Arri. "He has much he must explain to you both...and Ali...she will be fine," she said then closed her eyes again. She sighed, reached out her other hand for Tenno's and pulled his hand to her chest and held it there as she drifted back to sleep.

The small caravan door opened as Theodoric looked in. Paul and Tenno both shot him a look and he raised his eyebrows and stepped up inside.

"Was that Abi speaking?" he asked as he sat himself down near to Tenno and looked at his hand holding hers.

Tenno nodded yes as Paul moved Arri to get comfortable.

"She said Ali knows all and you must confirm it. What does she mean?" Paul asked.

"Did she now? Hmmm! About what exactly?" he replied.

"My parents," Alisha suddenly answered in a very low dry whisper, her eyes still closed.

"Oh...that!" Theodoric replied and smiled as he checked her over. He felt her forehead and quickly smiled at Paul. "Her fever has broken."

As soon as Paul heard him say that, he relaxed and slumped. He had been unaware of just how tense and rigid he had been. The pain from his broken ribs making him jump momentarily. But he could not hide the huge smile that ran across his face. He kissed Arri, who was smiling and pulling Clip clop.

"She is going to be okay. Do you hear that my, little man. Mummy will be well again," Paul said emotionally and kissed him again and turned him to face Alisha.

"Paul, they will both be very weak for days...perhaps weeks. They will need both of you...," Theodoric explained and looked at Paul then Tenno, who simply nodded back in acknowledgement. "But now, now I must go and help treat one of Thomas's men, Mark, for he has fallen ill also."

As Theodoric stood up to leave, Tenno grabbed his forearm hard and looked at him. Puzzled, Theodoric shook his head.

"Thank you," Tenno blurted out, his voice clearly emotional as he gulped.

Theodoric looked at him for several moments in silence before answering.

"'Tis not I you need to thank, but the mystic and the Templar. 'Twas their effort and ultimate sacrifice that enabled us to do what we have achieved here."

಄ Ⓡ

Paul gently rocked Arri in his arms as he stood beside Turansha and his sister. Theodoric and Thomas approached them, the sun rising into a clear blue sky, the palm trees swaying gently in the sea breeze, Tenno remaining inside the caravan keeping an eye on Alisha and Abi.

"I am more than happy to move them both to one of my larger caravans for the remainder of the journey to Alexandria," Turansha's sister remarked kindly.

"That is generous of you. For this one's sake I may have to accept your offer," Paul replied lifting Arri up slightly.

"Ah...sorry for the delay. We may have a further one, I am afraid," Theodoric interrupted as he came and stood close. "'Tis Mark...he has had what I believe is a brain seizure."

"What. Are you certain?" Turansha asked, concerned.

"Yes. His face has dropped considerably on one side and he is paralysed. He does not respond to any questions and can only dribble in response to anything we do. He has also messed himself several times already," Theodoric answered as Thomas nodded in agreement.

"What are you to do?" Turansha asked.

Percival came walking up fast, bowed briefly and looked at them all in turn before speaking.

"Sorry to interrupt. 'Tis Mark," he started to say then hesitated until Turansha nodded he continue. "He just prodded me with his finger and wrote in the sand 'End me!'."

Theodoric looked at Paul before Turansha and then Thomas.

"He actually wrote that?" Thomas asked and took a deep breath. Percival nodded yes to confirm so again. "My lord. Today shall be yet another sad day."

"Why?" Paul asked puzzled.

"Because Mark is asking them to finish him. End him...kill him," Theodoric explained bluntly.

Paul looked at him then Thomas, surprised. Thomas nodded in agreement, his face full of sadness unlike Paul had seen him before. Thomas placed his hand upon Percival's shoulder and looked at him.

"Young man...this day there will be an empty space at our table...I know Mark would feel honoured if you were to take his place instead...," Thomas said sadly.

"What...I cannot take his place. He still lives...I cannot," Percival replied hesitantly.

"You cannot kill him...!" Paul interjected, alarmed.

"Paul," Thomas said quietly as he lowered his hand from Percival and looked across at him. "Mark knows he is damaged...and there is no potion Theodoric or the mystic can make in time that will heal him...Mark is asking us, as his friends and family, to end his misery and give him some dignity...if not, he could linger for months, even years, being spoon fed, his arse wiped by us...and for what?" Thomas sighed heavily. "'Tis a curse that befalls some...'tis God's will and Mark's wish we help him cross over."

"Cross over. You sound more like Theo and Niccolas than a knight," Paul replied, confused. He felt shocked that they could even consider killing their own friend.

"Paul...I shall explain later, but my men, my knights...we do not follow any king nor serve any master not of our choosing and those we do, we do so to serve, to protect and defend. We do not serve for glory, for gold or position. We serve to help others...and we will not be helping Mark by prolonging his suffering as it will only get worse," Thomas explained and looked back at Percival. "And I know he would want you to take his stead."

"And I agree with him," Abi suddenly said from behind Paul.

Quickly Paul swung around to see Abi stood before him being supported by Tenno on one side and Alisha on the other side. Alisha smiled but looking exhausted and a ghostly white still. She had pulled on Paul's long night shawl, whereas Abi was wrapped in blankets held close by Tenno. Alisha let go of Abi and moved closer to Paul and looked into his confused eyes.

"We are well enough...well enough now," Alisha said and smiled. She gently leaned forward and kissed Arri in Paul's arms then sighed at them both.

"It is settled. Percival, this day, we lose a member of our family...but we also gain another if you accept," Thomas said, drawing their attention. "And Mark...we have ways of putting him to sleep peacefully and with dignity."

"'Tis the right thing to do," Theodoric commented.

"And later, later we shall celebrate his life…and that of my great and noble Templar Knight brother already so dearly missed," Abi stated and sighed as Tenno looked at her intently still supporting her up.

"Theo…I have questions I needs must ask of thee…and sooner rather than later…," Alisha said as she looked at Theodoric, her eyes sunken and heavy, but alive.

"That I am sure you do," he replied and feigned a brave smile as Thomas turned Percival and ushered him away.

80 03

Alisha, Paul, Tenno and Abi sat around the small table, the caravan having been cleaned and put back to as near as what it was before. Arri was asleep wrapped up tightly and placed upon the main bunk. They all sat in silence, Tenno with his hand openly placed upon Abi's right hand. She looked tired and weary but smiled at him constantly. Alisha sat beside Paul holding his hand beneath the table resting upon her thigh. She looked very pale still but she smiled at Paul and sighed. Sunlight streamed through the small open side windows and despite the heat both Abi and Alisha had a heavy blanket wrapped around their shoulders. Eventually Theodoric appeared at the doorway, looked in and quickly stepped up inside sitting himself down at the corner of the middle table near to Paul.

"Mark…is it done?" Paul asked awkwardly.

"Aye…'tis done. Thomas and his men all bade him farewell, then our Sufi friend administered him with a warm drink. Mark smiled, nodded briefly, closed his eyes…and that was it," Theodoric explained and took a deep breath. "But now to you my dear child. You have some questions for me, I hear…questions I knew would one day come."

Alisha nodded and tried to sit up straight, but was simply too exhausted to move so stayed as she was leaning against the side of the main bunk.

"The Sufi…he knew, for he said I was with my mother when she died…'twas Raja. And Abi, she said I am not a Muslim…So please, I must know everything for they said I must ask you and you would explain," Alisha asked quietly just as Abi nodded at her then looked at Theodoric. She simply nodded at him to confirm what she had said.

405

Chapter 40
A Journey of Study

Theodoric coughed and cleared his throat. He sipped some of the rosehip water still positioned on the table. He was just about to speak when Turansha knocked on the open door and peered in.

"I am so sorry to disturb you, but I wished to inform you that we shall wait here another day. It will give Thomas and his men time to bury and honour their friend. Plus give my sister some time to relax after her journey here this far. Is that acceptable to you?" he politely asked and flicked the long white silk scarf from around his neck. Theodoric looked around the table and all nodded in agreement. "I see this is a personal matter. Please accept my apology for the intrusion," he said and bowed as he backed away.

"No...please, it is no intrusion. Thank you," Paul remarked as Tenno frowned at him.

Ishmael appeared beside Turansha and as they both looked at each other, Abi tried to sit up straighter.

"I think perhaps we would all benefit from what Theo could tell us," she said quietly and looked at Theodoric.

"Well...only if Alisha does not mind," he replied, looking over at Alisha intently.

She shook her head, confused, before looking to Abi, who nodded it would be okay. Not sure why and feeling slightly embarrassed, she was hesitant in case Theodoric would reveal too much about her. But as Abi had nodded she should, then trusting her, she agreed and indicated yes with a slight nod. Turansha stepped up inside the caravan and squeezed himself next to Tenno as Ishmael stepped up and managed to sit on the inside step next to the door. When he had made himself comfortable, he folded his arms and looked up to see everyone was looking at him waiting patiently. He had not been invited in, yet had made himself present. He shrugged his shoulders and as no one said anything, he stayed where he was.

"Ready," he then simply stated.

"Your mother...," Theodoric began and looked at Turansha then back at Alisha. "Our Sufi mystic friend was correct in saying he sensed your mother and that you were with her when she passed over...for you were. Raja was indeed your birth mother."

Paul clasped Alisha's hand. It felt cold and clammy despite the heat of the day. Alisha shook her head, puzzled, but after the experience with Abi, dream or otherwise, she wanted to know the truth.

"Are you sure you wish to hear this?" Paul asked, concerned. She simply shook her head yes.

"Your mother was Raja? That is why she gave you the piece of embroidered cloth with your birth name upon. She knew that when you gave it to Philip, he would know what Raja wanted for you...that you were her daughter and that you were not of Muslim birth," Theodoric explained gently.

"But...but Raja was a Muslim as was Firgany and my brother," Alisha replied then trailed off of her comment with the realisation that what she was being told meant that Taqi was not in fact her brother after all.

"Ali, when you were born, you were in great peril. There were many who sought you...to kill you. Your father, your birth father...he died protecting you and your mother. But in so doing, he managed to get you away but your mother was captured. Those seeking you out believed you dead and so your mother...Raja...she remained as a prisoner until Philip managed to break her out of captivity. That was nearly four years after she had last seen you. During that time, Firgany had taken you in claiming you as his own daughter. To protect you he changed your name from Ailia to Alisha. For your own protection you were told that your mother had died in labour."

"But why did she not tell me this when she did come back?" Alisha asked, fighting to remain calm.

"For your continued safety. Only Firgany, Philip and I knew the truth. And whilst in Mosul, that is when your mother converted to Islam. It afforded her more rights and protection."

"From who?" Alisha demanded.

"People like Turansha...but also those from within the church herself," Theodoric explained and sighed seeing the confusion and anguish in Alisha's face.

"So both sides want to harm her?" Paul interjected.

"Yes, Paul...and you also...and consequently Arri," Theodoric continued as Alisha and Paul looked at each other, alarmed.

"Please if I may speak," Ishmael said and sat up straighter. "You know nothing of me...but I have no life any longer. You have allowed me here this day despite who I am and what I look like. I know good people when I see them, and you are good people," he explained and looked at them all in the caravan. "So if you will grant me a great honour, I shall dedicate what is left of my miserable existence to the protection of all three of you...that I swear upon my life."

Alisha looked at him and could have cried seeing the sentiment within his eyes. Tenno looked him up and down before looking at Alisha and Paul and raised his eyebrows.

"That makes two of us," he stated bluntly and nodded a dipped and quick bow.

"And with Thomas and his men of a like mind, I believe we have the ability to look after you all well enough," Theodoric said trying to sound reassuring.

Alisha cupped her face in her hands and shook her head utterly confused and tired.

"In Alexandria, I will be more than happy to station some of my best men at your disposal," Turansha said and smiled. "Or at least contribute towards Thomas and his men."

"I do not understand any of this...," Alisha sighed and shook her head again looking down.

"I have spent time with Thomas and his men. They are not your average knights. Nothing happens by coincidence," Theodoric said as Abi nodded in agreement as Alisha looked up again.

"How so?" she asked.

"Ask him about the cross and smaller cross you saw," Abi said gently.

Paul looked out of the window opposite as several of Turansha's men surrounded the caravan and took up protective positions guarding it as his sister saw him and acknowledged him with a slight bow of her head. He felt for his sword. Quickly he untied the makeshift belt and scabbard and placed it upon the table for all to see.

"'Tis this they all desire isn't it?" he asked and sat back and folded his arms.

"If only that was the simple case," Theodoric replied and shook his head no. "Did Raja, your mother, tell you about any more children you would have?"

Alisha looked at Paul briefly then at Abi.

"In that dream I...we had, yes. They said I would fall with another child. A girl... why?"

"It is written upon both of your charts that is why. A daughter indeed. And people like Gerard and Umar, the other Turansha, also have seen those charts... that is why you must never trust them," Theodoric explained. "Never!"

"But why us...what have we done?" Alisha asked sadly as tiredness only served to confuse her more and she rubbed her hands over her face exasperated.

"'Tis your lineage...your birth right...both of you," Theodoric answered and looked at Paul and frowned as he spoke. "Your family trees stretch way back in antiquity. Paul already knows some of this, but you too, Alisha, so too does yours. One family line comes from what some call the stick of Ephraim, whilst yours comes from what is known as the stick of Judah. Now some believe that this represents just the family lines, whilst others see it as representing the actual lines of two religions within Judaism whilst others again see it as representing two religions of a common origin...as in Islam and Christianity and being rejoined. That is the danger of prophecy and miss-interpretation."

"Yes...I too am aware of this belief," Turansha interjected. "Some see it as the Old Testament representing one stick whilst the other represents the New Testament... yet others do indeed see it as being that of the New Testament joined with the Qur'an as the other stick."

"But what does that have to do with us?" Alisha asked, a sense of desperation in her voice. "And Thomas and his men...in the dream, they said I must ask about their swords. Why...why?"

"Their swords. Hmmm, I can answer that shortly, but for now, the main priority of all of us is to keep you safe," Theodoric said looking at Alisha. "Paul, your father must have known it was becoming unsafe to keep you in La Rochelle, especially after Alisha's caravan was attacked as it travelled to the port. He must have been made aware of the large arrows from Abi's bow that dealt with the problem."

Abi nodded in agreement.

"I cannot answer that for he did not say...not that it was obvious to me anyway. And I certainly do not understand this stick of Ephraim," Paul remarked, puzzled.

"It concerns a prophecy by Ezekiel, 37:15–25, in the Old Testament for he saw in a vision the coming together of the stick of Judah, and the stick of Joseph, signifying the Bible and another book...Ezekiel says 'The word of the Lord came again unto me, saying, Moreover, thou son of man, take thee one stick, and write upon it, For Judah, and for the children of Israel his companions: then take another stick, and write upon it, For Joseph, the stick of Ephraim, and for all the house of Israel his companions: And join them one to another into one stick; and they shall become one in thine hand. But many claim the second book refers to the Qur'an...but most are not aware that the ancient custom of making books was that of writing on long strips of parchment and rolling the same on rods or sticks, the use of the word 'stick' is therefore equivalent to 'book' in the passage as becomes apparent. At the time of this utterance, the Israelites had divided into two nations known as the kingdom of Judah and that of Israel, or Ephraim. Plainly the separate records of Judah and Joseph are here referred to. The Nephite nation comprised the descendants of Lehi who belonged to the tribe of Manasseh, of Ishmael who was an Ephraimite, and of Zoram, whose tribal relation is not definitely stated. The Nephites were then of the tribes of Joseph; and their record or 'stick' is as truly represented by an as yet unknown book or 'stick' of Judah by the Bible. Some argue that Islam and its holy book is the other stick," he explained and paused as everyone looked at him quizzically. "In the Peshitta, the Aramaic Old Testament, many words were mistranslated just as many have likewise been done within the Masoretic Tanakh, Samaritan Torah and Greek Septuagint, but the mathematical codes that are inherent within them have remained complete. But one stick cannot be fully read and understood without the other...and that is something many have tried to do."

"I do not profess to understand anything of what you say, but what of the cross symbol with a smaller cross attached to it. (Fig. 39: Cross with smaller cross upon.) That was made very clear in the dream." Alisha asked and turned to Paul.

"Was no dream, Alisha," Abi said quietly and smiled.

Fig. 39:

"If it is the cross I think they were showing you...then it is the x with small hook x That represents Jesus and his family...that of Mary and their daughter. My family were originally guardians of their secret and where they actually went after leaving the Holy Land...but that secret died with my eldest brother," Theodoric explained and took a deep breath before continuing. "And as it was written upon your parchments, the cross with the smaller hook cross, there are some who believe you to be another Mary and will have a daughter likewise. Your family tree comes from one ancient line as does Paul's...the joining of your families will lead to the birth of a true and pure bloodline. One that will even stand upon the shoulders of even the secret lines and remnants of the Merovingian Fisher Kings...," Theodoric explained and paused. "And that is why so many wish your line eradicated, forever!"

"But you told us that Thomas and his men were, or are, somehow connected with those bloodlines, so can we truly trust them?" Paul asked, concerned.

"Yes, as, Paul, your line is directly linked and part of the Merovingian line too. As for Thomas...Let me tell you this. In my many travels, and with your fathers, we often came across stories...almost legendary, of a band of seventy-two knights from the north, deeply connected with the Berserkers but also adherents and followers of ancient teachings and guardians in their own right of sacred knowledge and wisdom. 'Twas why I was more than a little interested in Thomas and his knights when we first met them. I suspected they were the very same knights we had heard of, but I was not sure as their numbers had been decimated. They follow no master, swear no allegiance but serve, and I do mean truly serve, only to protect the innocent and fight injustice wherever they see it. They fight for humanity, for its very own sake...not for kings, not for fame or gain as I have already said. They are possessors of great knowledge and have swords similar to what Paul has there," Theodoric explained and looked at Paul's sword upon the table. "They had all but given up on their quest...their endeavours...until they overheard us talking. It was only when Thomas unsheathed his sword."

"Yes...their swords, you must tell me more about those," Alisha interrupted abruptly.

"Their swords...and if you were told to ask me that, then you must believe that what you experienced was no mere dream, my child," Theodoric replied and winked. "Thomas and his men...well, you said it yourself once before, Paul. Can you imagine a whole army of noble knights armed with such weapons? Well...Thomas and his men have swords of a similar make having been made by almost identical means."

"How so?" Tenno asked bluntly as Ishmael nodded in agreement with his question.

"Many legends speak of the sacred swords, such as Damocles's sword and Excalibur to name just two...but Thomas and his men, they all carry small stone squares inscribed with ancient symbols. They detail lands to the far west...lands you travelled across," Theodoric said as he looked at Tenno. "They also have values and materials to enable them to make from the earth swords such as they carry."

"That explains in part why they said I must keep his men close," Alisha commented and looked down and bit her right thumb nail.

"If they said that...then I think we have indeed found you an army of kings," Theodoric remarked and half laughed. "Oh if only your father could be with us now," he said looking at Paul. "Alisha...did it never occur to you to ask how it was possible that you and Paul were granted special dispensation to marry and had it signed off as valid?"

"I certainly did," Turansha interjected and smiled broadly at Alisha as she looked up.

"No...I just trusted what my father told me...though he was not my father," Alisha replied and buried her face in her hands as she started to sob. Quickly she shook her head and opened her eyes. "No...I will not damn well cry again," she sniffed and looked defiant just as Abi frowned at her.

410

"Ali...," Abi said softly. "Firgany was far more than just your father. A father is not just the man who made you physically...he is the man that stood by you every step of your life. Who taught and guided you in all that you have become and ever will be. He is the man who loved you more than life itself...and that man was Firgany," Abi stated and forced herself to sit up straighter.

Tenno bowed his head sadly hearing this as he immediately thought of his own daughter. Abi instantly placed her hand over his.

"Thomas and his knights...what are we to do about them?" Paul asked hesitantly, trying to steer the conversation away from Firgany as it was obviously upsetting Alisha.

"Thomas and his men...they all come from Viking bloodlines that were also mixed with Merovingian and Carolingian bloodlines. So they are closer to you two than you could have realised. Almost family," Theodoric laughed. "And I would not be surprised if at some point we will learn of Percival's line being of similar lineage."

"You mentioned their swords. Please, can you continue?" Turansha asked.

"Yes...well, as for their swords. We must all understand that there is something truly magical about pulling material out of the ground and with knowledge, especially ancient sacred knowledge, fashioning it with other elements of fire and water into a sword is indeed...magical. Would you not agree?" Theodoric asked, smiling broadly. He let them all think about his words for a few minutes. "Thomas and his men each hold a small rune stone each encoded with maps of a place they have named Nova Scotia...for New Scotland. They also maintain a spoken secret between them of a single acorn on their rune stones representing a golden oak hidden in Scotland that reveals the coordinates and details of that land in the west they call Oak Island. You may have heard them laughing and joking about how a mighty oak is formed from a little nut that refused to budge. I believe they even nicknamed Percival 'the little nut'."

"And they each wield a sword such as this?" Turansha asked again as he looked at Paul's sword.

"Not exactly the same. But as said, he and his men are in part related to Viking Berserkers. They were truly fearsome warriors who would work themselves up into such a furious frenzy before battle that when they charged, they hacked their way through all and anything that got in their way. It is where we get our word for going berserk. But their swords...if you check them you will see they have all been marked and etched with the name of Ulfberht. It is not the name of the man who wields it, for how can one man use so many at the same time? No, it is the name of the Viking blacksmith who made the swords. Their metal is so pure it baffles utterly other blacksmiths, who cannot replicate its production."

"I bet I could," Tenno stated and raised a single eyebrow.

"Probably...No one else understands the methods and technology to forge such metal as the temperatures involved are so high. The fires that forge those swords are triple, if not greater than that even, of a normal blacksmith's furnace. Tenno, as you know, in the process of forging iron, the ore must be heated to liquefy it, allowing the blacksmith to remove the impurities called slag. All blacksmiths I know of add other elements to make the brittle iron stronger. But furnaces today do not allow iron to be heated to such a high temperature, thus the slag is removed by pounding it out, which is a far less effective method. The Ulfberht swords, however, are over three times stronger and more flexible than any others available. They are without doubt truly the most complicated swords ever to make, which makes them even more special...and that is why so many regarded the maker of the Ulfberht swords as possessing magical powers. To make a weapon from dirt is a pretty powerful thing, but, to make a weapon that could bend without breaking, stay so sharp, and weigh so little would be regarded as supernatural."

"For the first time, I think I can see and understand why the sword has been used symbolically to represent knowledge and wisdom. I had never looked at it like that before," Paul remarked and pulled his sword closer.

"Even the tiniest flaw or mistake could have turned the sword into a piece of scrap metal, yet Thomas and his men all possess one," Theodoric continued.

"Remind me not to fall out or have to face Thomas and his knights will you," Turansha joked.

"But where did they get their knowledge from then?" Tenno asked. "For we have similar swords...check mine for it too sounds remarkably similar." Tenno then removed his main Katana sword and placed it beside Paul's on the table.

"Probably the same sources," Theodoric replied and looked at the gleaming patterned blade of Tenno's sword.

"You mention that Thomas has stones with runes marked upon them. They do not show them to just anyone then?" Paul asked.

"No they do not. But he showed me. They measure about six by eleven inches. One stone features a rough map on one side and inscriptions on the other. A second stone bore a dozen letters on one side, and a third contained a long message of sixteen lines neatly inscribed on both sides. But like the message in Alisha's dream, they all have a crisscrossed character inscription, referred to as the 'Hooked X' or 'Stung A' because it represents the 'a' sound. But note this...the same symbol can be found on many runic carvings etched by Cistercian monks travelling alongside Knights Templar."

"You said the x represents Mary and a child...how so?" Alisha asked tired.

"The hooked x combines the upside-down V representing the male gender, the right-side-up V representing the female gender, and a small V on the top right arm representing a small female offspring. Together, that's Jesus, Mary Magdalene and their daughter...does that answer your question?" Theodoric replied and asked back.

"Yes...clearly. Are you therefore saying that Paul and I are somehow identical to this...that we are to be yet another holy family," she asked emotionally and sat back shaking her head no. "Because if you are, then no way. Sorry...sorry, Paul, for you will never come near me again if that is the case...to protect Arri. No, no way. I will not allow it," she protested.

"Ali...there are some things that are too far out of your control. The decision is not yours to make. Sorry to be so blunt and frank with you," Abi explained.

"No...and why would Cistercian monks use ancient rune symbols...'tis all just folly. Utter folly," Alisha snapped back. "I will never be put up so high, especially my children."

"Alisha...the symbols are but a few of many used by the knights and their monk supporters as part of their secret language to communicate with one another without giving away their true meanings. Thomas and his knights likewise are clearly privy to the same teachings," Theodoric explained softly, seeing the clear fear and panic in Alisha's tired eyes. "I think we have spoken enough. You should rest...both of you," he stated and stood up as he looked at Alisha and Abi in turn.

Abi nodded she agreed with him and indicated at Alisha she should rest.

Port of La Rochelle, France, Melissae Inn, spring 1191

"So Alisha is not a Muslim?" Sarah asked, perplexed.

"I want to know if the tall white haired old man who saved Paul and Taqi before is dead and up there or alive and down here. Would like to meet him," Simon interrupted loudly.

"Those stones you mention...if real, that means that the many claims we hear from the Vikings and Norsemen about their travels west are true. If yes, then how do they guide themselves?" Gabirol asked and quickly checked his notes again.

"In answer to Sarah's question...no...Alisha was indeed not a Muslim all along. 'Tis why she never attended services at any mosques...but that was not much different from many other Muslims in certain areas so it never really occurred to her...why would it?" the old man replied.

"But such a shock to learn and hear about," Ayleth remarked.

"Perhaps...but Alisha was stronger than she realised. She was exhausted and very weary from her illness, yet she accepted all that Theodoric had explained. And the more she learnt from him about Thomas and his men, the more reassured she felt...though Paul still had a hundred questions he wanted answers to."

"I know the Vikings are unbelievable sailors. We hear they have magical tools to navigate with," the Genoese sailor commented as if talking to himself aloud.

"Yes," the old man replied and paused briefly. "The Vikings are indeed remarkable sea-farers who confidently head into unexplored waters. Many Norse warriors managed to fearlessly navigate their way through unknown oceans to invade unsuspecting communities along the North Sea and Atlantic Sea coasts of Europe...and it was through the combined use of the power of a sun-compass with that of a sunstone that they navigated their ships after dark even. Some of you may know the well-known ancient Norse myth that describes a magical gem which could reveal the position of the sun when hidden behind clouds or even after sunset. 'Tis not magic but the application and use of certain crystals made of calcite that works as a remarkably precise navigational aid. It enabled Viking navigators to detect the position of the sun from the twilight glow on the horizon passing through two calcite sunstones. When used in combination, the dial and the sunstones could find the position of the sun even after it had passed below the twilight horizon. This means they could navigate their ships well after sunset, since the twilight glow can last all night long at high latitudes in summer. 'Sunstones' are mentioned in many written sources and are said to have helped the great Norse mariners to navigate far further than most believe...as Philip and Firgany discovered."

"This Abi female...I am intrigued by her. Is she not of a holy type bloodline then?" Peter asked.

"You like tall women do you then?" Simon asked, which solicited immediate looks from the others. "Oh...sorry. Inappropriate question is it?"

"Abi. What can I tell you about her?" the old man replied and paused as he thought

for a while. "*Her lineage is, in simple terms, different again. Many of her ancestors still lay buried in the Caucuses region...in places no one will recover for many centuries yet. And strange as it may seem, both hers and Tenno's family tree were in the great past, linked.*"

"*That explains why he fancies her,*" Simon interrupted. Sarah shot him a look of utter contempt and shrugged her shoulders, disappointed in him. "*Well 'tis true. Is it not?*" he asked defensively.

"*There was no denying the obvious attraction, for Abi felt it too. From their very first meeting they connected. 'Tis that perhaps they knew each other previously,*" the old man answered.

"*You mean as in previous lives?*" Ayleth remarked questioningly.

"*Yes perhaps...or even before that as I have explained before.*"

"*So where exactly did Abi come from? We know she was born in Sardinia and went to Malta...with that Kratos man, but why were they the last of their kind?*" Gabirol asked.

"*Their kind was almost completely wiped out by the Roman Empire when it expanded into their regions beyond the Black Sea. In time, man will again recover much of what they hid and left behind. I am sure many of you have heard of the many legends of the Valley of the Giants and many different giants in the holy books. Well, all myth is based upon fact the further back you trace it. Where Abi's ancestors came from is littered with many megalithic and ancient stone structures, most in inaccessible regions, that are almost identical in design and build as those of the Great Stonehenge in Britain and structures on Malta and in Baalbek. Cyclopean castles and menhirs dating back to the second and first millennium BC extend for many miles, as Philip, Firgany and Theodoric could testify having visited so many. Some of the huge fortresses sit at altitudes in excess of many thousands of feet making breathing difficult. Near the village of Tejisi, hah,*" the old man explained and laughed briefly before continuing. "*There is a sixteen foot high menhir, but now incorporated into a new church complex. Theodoric...such a character for he carved a large cross upon that one.*" The old man paused in total silence for several minutes. "*You know...there are more dolmens in that region than the whole of France. A legacy from a far more ancient civilisation than the one who placed the newer ones across Europe.*"

"*Why...I mean how come? Why the need to replace them or set new ones up?*" Gabirol asked.

"*You may not believe this, but the earth...it can move upon its own axis, and when that happens, that natural earth energy, that grid I have explained, the paths of the dragons, it too changes and must be remapped and brought back into harmony.*"

"*So how does Abi fit onto all of that?*" the wealthy tailor asked.

"*Because her kind were the main builders of such things. But understand this. Just because her physical body was far larger than most, like Tenno and even Ishmael, their souls could just have easily been born into a smaller frame. That is why it is foolish and ignorant to judge a person by their size and skin colour.*"

"*You mean I volunteered for this body?*" Simon asked looking down himself.

"*No, I think you were made to take that one for some previous wrong doing,*" Sarah shot back, making them all laugh.

"*But Abi, she has clearly dedicated her life to protecting Alisha...and I am assuming Paul also, but why?*" Gabirol asked.

 2 – 4

"Because she knows that it is through people like them, that one day, what was hidden long ago will again be recovered for all of our benefits. And it just may be that when that time comes, it will be of benefit to her in whatever physical body she is reborn into, if she so chooses to return to this world, our realm of existence," the old man explained. "If the line is destroyed that can access the secrets of antiquity, then we are all doomed to repeat the mistakes of the past and to never reach our true potential, none of us."

"But I saw a line in Paul's journal, near the end, where he wrote something about they would never leave us, whoever they are or were," Peter remarked.

The old man looked at Peter for some time before smiling.

"Peter...there was much Paul wrote, and much that was removed or destroyed from both that and many other journals he wrote. For his own safety and that of his family. But I know the line you refer to," he explained and took a sip of rosehip water before continuing. "He wrote what he recalled from a conversation he had with another being of light...which as yet I have not covered, but yes, he wrote that there are those of a higher realm who have stated that they have been with us from the beginning, and no matter what we do, they shall remain with us until the very end...whatever that end may prove to be." Peter nodded that was indeed what he was referring to and had read. "But Abi's bloodline can still be traced for she was related on her father's side to Queen Tamar, one of the most famous historic persons of Georgia, who lived during the period that was called the 'Golden Age' of Georgia. She even had the title of 'king'. She was of the Bagrationi dynasty, the ruling family. According to a family legend, taken down by the eleventh century Georgian chronicler Sumbat Davi-tis-Dze, and supplied with chronological data, the ancestors of the dynasty can trace their descent to the biblical king David and came from Palestine around AD 530. Yes, the same David who killed the giant Goliath with a stone from his sling! David was himself tall as evidenced when the bronze helmet they tried to put on the youngster's head before the fight did not fit! It was too small, not too big as most assume," the old man smiled as he explained this. "Ethnic Georgians call themselves Kartvelebi, and their land Sakartvelo, which means 'a place for Kartvelians'. According to the ancient Georgian Chronicles, the founding ances-tor of the Kartvelian people was named Kartlos, the great grandson of the biblical Japheth... Noah's son. Kartlos was son of Togarmah, son of Gomer, the eldest son of Japeth. Kartlos was known as 'a brave, gigantic man', 'the legendary giant'. And remember this fact, the land's flag is white with a red cross upon it, the same as England's. They also have a patron saint, Saint George, who also slays a dragon...identical legends no less.

"I do not think I am able to retain much of what you tell us for there is so much to learn and understand as you say," Ayleth remarked and looked sad as she spoke.

"Believe me, it will stay with you even if you think it has not," the old man replied softly.

"Good, because I cannot even remember what you said an hour ago," Simon commented, smiling broadly and glancing sideways at Sarah.

"And the dream that both Alisha and Abi had jointly...was that real or just a dream?" Sarah asked.

"Well, some dreams appear to foretell the future, whilst others are meaningless. The Greeks have much to say on dreams. But just as when Alisha and Paul shared a dream like experience inside the ruined cathedral, likewise Alisha and Abi shared an experience. I shall have more to say on dreams later," the old man answered.

"At least they survived," Ayleth sighed.

"Yes, yes they did. And so onward they would travel together for Alexandria," the old man stated and nodded.

El Arish beach, Egypt, 1179

As Theodoric continued to explain what he knew, Paul's mind raced back to Niccolas and his underground study crypt and the many gemstones, crystals, maps and strange tools, especially the one that had the spinning directional arrow that always pointed north. How he wished he had paid more attention back then. Also to the many stories his father had told him about his adventures with Firgany. He had always supposed his father had exaggerated to make the tales seem more exciting. Now he realised that perhaps all that his father had told him was indeed all true and that he had in fact downplayed them. With the details of Alisha and Abi's shared dream like experience, plus recalling his own, he only now began to accept and realise the importance of what his father had been trying to tell him so many years ago about people needing to see the truth that is hidden from them. He tried to recall his father's comments, and slowly they came back to his mind. He could almost hear his father's voice as if he was with him again. He closed his eyes. 'Paul... people are waking up all over the world for we all need to reclaim the power we were born with. Enforced religion destroys people's will and their god given right of free agency. We do not need a third party to act as an intermediary for we are all Spiritual Beings. We have the God given power we were born with...so do not ever give it up to just any man to make you feel guilty for their own self gratification of their ego or for profit! We are all spiritual beings having a physical experience. 'Tis not the other way! And, my son...always, always remember that a compassionate heart is far more effective against evil, more than any army. A compassionate heart can engage evil directly and it can bring light where there is only darkness.' A lump swelled in his throat as he remembered his father's words.

"Paul...Paul, are you all right?" Abi asked, seeing Paul looking sad and confused. Alisha gently nudged Paul as he seemed so far off in his mind.

"Yes," he suddenly replied sitting himself upright fast. "Abi, lest I forget to say it... thank you. For all that you have done, both noticed and unnoticed...even when you nearly took my head off."

"Only because you moved once I had loosed my arrow," Abi replied, forcing a smile despite her exhaustion and pain.

Tenno noticed her wince and looked across at Theodoric.

"'Tis time she rests," he stated, almost ordered in tone, as he stood up and gestured for Ishmael to stand.

Ishmael opened the small door and opened it to reveal Percival and Thomas along with all of his knights stood outside in silence waiting patiently for them. Abi leaned up so she could see and also Turansha's men standing behind them. She smiled before resting back down.

"Yes please. I think that I may rest now most assuredly, and Alisha must too," she commented just as Tenno kissed her hand gently and nodded at her. "And later, later we must honour my brother's parting properly and acknowledge a great loss to this world."

৪৩ ৫৪

Theodoric slowly followed Ishmael out of the caravan and stepped down onto the soft white sand. Many of Turansha's men surrounded the caravan in a protective cordon as Thomas and his men stood in an arrow formation so they could all look forwards. They looked dirty, tired and full of concern. As Paul stepped onto the stairs he immediately noticed this very real and tangible fact.

"Will they both live?" Thomas asked immediately.

"Yes, my friend, yes they shall," Theodoric answered with a large grin.

Thomas turned to face his men and immediately withdrew his sword and raised it high in the air. Not ones for making any great shows of emotion, Paul was surprised to see this.

"They live...and we continue!" he shouted exuberantly with a happy pitch to his voice.

Instantly they all drew their swords and raised them high and began cheering. Paul stepped down from the caravan utterly bemused at their outburst. Percival's eyes met with his as he nodded at him also smiling broadly. Paul looked at their brilliant shining swords and recalled what Theodoric had explained about them. 'An army of kings indeed' he thought to himself and he began to relax. He could feel the tension in his shoulders start to ease at once. For the first time in a long time, he actually felt safe and that things would now improve. He took a deep breath and felt the emotion and immense pride he felt toward the men before him. He looked across at Ishmael standing with his two swords...his only possessions in the world. He could sense the deep sadness that ran through him, yet Ishmael smiled at him and bowed. Suddenly Theodoric grabbed his arm.

"Come on, you, whilst they rest you have much to learn, so it may as well start now," he said aloud and started to pull him away from the caravan. "Vesica Pisces and the Emerald Tablets for starters!"

Thomas and his knights were still cheering as Theodoric half dragged Paul past him. Paul leaned towards Thomas.

"Thomas, I meant what I said. I wish to be taught all there is about combat, mounted and dismounted, hand to hand...all of it," he shouted above the noise of the men.

"That, my boy, we can do...that we can!" Thomas shouted even more exuberantly and lowered his sword. "You give us hope, lad...all of us."

Turansha stepped down from the caravan in time to see Paul being led away by Theodoric. He flung his scarf around his neck and looked at Thomas as he faced his men all still cheering. He could not help but smile at their obvious enthusiasm. He shook his head as he reminded himself that these men before him were potentially still his enemy. They were not Muslims, but he reconciled himself with the knowledge of what he had just heard about them. They served no master other than those they chose. So perhaps, and hopefully, together in Alexandria they would never become his enemy. His mind drifted to thoughts of his other Frankish Christian friends Lord of Sidon Reginald and Balian. ''Tis my fate to be born a Muslim...'tis theirs to be born Christian,' he thought then turned to look back at the caravan. At least Theodoric had explained how Alisha had been granted permission to marry Paul. But as he turned to look back at Thomas, his eyes met with Percival's and he immediately wondered what part he played in all that was happening.

"Percival...will you join me for a meal?" he asked and beckoned him over.

Surprised, Percival pointed at himself, frowned briefly but then smiled and started to walk over toward Turansha.

Port of La Rochelle, France, Melissae Inn, spring 1191

"True to his word, Turansha did indeed escort Alisha and Paul all of the way to Alexandria, though taking somewhat longer than planned travelling slowly in order for both Alisha and Abi to recover. And Theodoric...well he did not waste any time and immediately set about teaching Paul all he knew about past secrets, such as the Vesica Pisces as he said he would, the symbol of the fish, its Templar knowledge connections, as well as those of the Great Pyramid in Egypt and how it was the early symbol of the Christian Church. He also began to teach Paul all about mathematics, Gematria, and why Jesus changed Simon's name to Peter, in order to use a mathematical code. He detailed the hidden mysteries behind the significance of the number seven as a mystical number, like the seven candles on the Jewish candelabra and seven stars of Orion as well as how symbolism is so important. He started off by explaining the acts of John 102 to 104, where the importance of symbolism is actually stated. The first line reads, 'The Lord contrived all things symbolically'. He also briefly introduced him to the teachings about Rostau, which he would later discover was the Giza plateau and further related to the constellation of Orion and the constellation of Leo with many deeper connections to the symbolism of the Lion and the Sphinx. You see, all the details are connected to one of the Templars' most guarded secrets as depicted upon their paintings and secret parchments that show a Templar Knight pulling a thorn from a lion's right paw. It actually represents the Sphinx in Cairo with its right paw having a thorn removed, as in symbolically representing a rose, the thorn that is, for knowledge."

"Ah I see...withdrawing knowledge from the Sphinx...pulling the thorn from the lion's paw?" Peter commented.

"Yes exactly that," the old man replied, smiling broadly. "You see, Theodoric had been to Egypt many times to study the mysteries of Thoth, Hermes to the Greeks, and he actually went inside the Great Pyramid where he had a vision of the end of times...a time set way off in the future on or shortly after the beginning of the twenty-first century, not the five hundred years after the birth of Muhammad as so many Christians believe now in our time. But as he learnt, it was the end of the present way of thinking and world order as we enter a new spiritual phase, not the actual physical end of the world. This was something he so desperately wanted to share and for the world to know. In his naivety he believed it would help stop all the mindless bloodshed and violence that seemed to be spiralling in ever increasing brutality. He also explained briefly, if only to convince Paul that he, nor Arri nor any other child of his would be the prophesied Messiah as Alisha feared. He detailed how Christians know him as the Christ, and expect his imminent return. Jews still await him as the Messiah and Hindus look for the coming of Krishna. Buddhists expect him as Maitreya Buddha and Muslims anticipate the Imam Mahdi or Messiah. The names may be different, but many believe they all refer to the same individual. A World Teacher, whose name is Maitreya (My-'tray-ah). Preferring to be known simply as the Teacher, Maitreya will not come as a religious leader, or to found a new religion, but as a teacher and guide for people of every religion and those of no religion. He will come to inspire humanity to see itself as one family, and create a civilisation based on sharing, economic and social justice, and cooperation. He

will launch a call to action to save the millions of people who starve to death every year in a world of plenty. He will be pivotal in shifting people's consciences and to reevaluate their priorities so that adequate food, housing, clothing, education, and medical care become universal rights to all. A saner and more just world for all." [50]

"And you believe that?" the Templar asked incredulously almost.

"Yes...yes I do. And when that time comes, that individual, that guide, that navigator of enlightenment will have at his disposal the very ancient tools our forefathers placed, hidden from all others, that will demonstrate and prove beyond doubt, any doubt, our true origins and our true potential. But that very fact alone is what drives those darker forces to act against him and his believers," the old man replied with a seriousness of tone he had not displayed before.

"But if we all know this, I know that many would still not believe it, no matter what you prove to them. I also know that many would simply say it does not matter then what they do now, for it is all so far off in the future, by which time they may have been reborn many times over," the Hospitaller explained.

"I have heard that argument many times before, my friend. Yes indeed, and that is mainly why the Church suppresses such knowledge for it would lose its power and hold over people. But there will come a time when people become more enlightened and educated. Then they will be able to decide for themselves as well as understand better that they are ultimately responsible for their own souls. They cannot pass that responsibility to others under the guise of religion."

"But, but the Catholic Church claims that Muslims are 'summa culpablis' meaning the most blame worthy in order to keep enthusiasm and maintain fanaticism against them. If it knows all this that you speak of, then surely they know that they will have to answer for it in time," Gabirol asked, checking he had pronounced summa culpabis correctly.

"Some within the Church do...but many do not. They simply follow, almost blindly, that which is told to them. And those that do know it, most again simply do not fully believe it themselves only seeing the physical world we exist in and use the Church to further their own selfish desires and gains...that, my friends, is a reality that all religions suffer from I am afraid to say," the old man explained and sighed, shaking his head. "I have seen people burned alive by fanatical mobs after being whipped into a frenzy by overzealous priests, monks and so-called preachers of holy books simply due to ignorance, but mainly fear instilled into them of the threat of internal damnation by their own god that is supposed to have created them and love them. For it is not what we understand as god that causes all the evil and killing in his name... it is man, more correctly, a few men. Men who are opportunists who seize power and use and abuse it to serve themselves, not the god nor the people they claim to serve. But there will come a time, and it will come, when ordinary people will stop listening to them. They will see with their own eyes and hear with their own ears, the evil they commit in the name and defence of their religion, and they will put their hands up...and they will say, stop...enough, enough is enough...not in my name!"

"And you really believe that?" the Templar asked bluntly.

"Yes. Yes I do. It may not be, in fact I know it shall not be in our life time...but when the truth of our origins and mankind's potential is revealed, then yes, for most people are in fact inherently good, even when not directed by a belief in a god of faith, for that is how we were made from the outset. Theodoric and Philip themselves were once nearly burnt alive after Theodoric demonstrated how to make a rainbow. He simply spat out water as vapour against the backdrop of the setting sun that made a mini rainbow. One of the Cistercian monks condemned them immediately claiming it was evil sorcery. Theodoric argued it was scientific basis and symbolism behind the multi coloured coat of Joseph in the Bible."

"Yet was not Theodoric originally a Cistercian monk himself?" Peter asked.

"Originally yes. But despite his commitment to the Order, and because of his own family's background and history, his mind constantly questioned everything. He explained to Paul in quite some detail all about his former Order, the austere monks of Cistercian origin and how they saw the end times prophesied according to St John the Divine in the Book of Revelation, as they believed 666 meant 666 years since the birth of the Antichrist, whom they saw as being Muhammad and the religion of Islam. Muhammad was born in AD 570 so the end would be AD 1236 but he argued this was not the case and to stop all the hostile machinations against Islam...and he even tried the same argument on Muslim leaders, that is how and why he knew so many of them. He did however also explain to Paul the real esoteric and mathematical meanings behind it all including details about the Merica connection with the myths of Jason and the Argonauts being connected with stellar constellations, the star Sirius and Jewish mystical wisdom contained within the Kabala. In it, it is stated that the earth turned on its own axis. 'The entire earth spins, turning as a sphere. When one part is down, the other part is up. When it is light for one part, it is dark for the other part; when it is day for that, it is night for the other.' Paul learnt fast as Theodoric taught him as they travelled to Alexandria and began to realise how misled and uneducated the Christian world was. Theodoric even quoted the ancient Indian 'Surya Siddhanta' describing the earth 'As a globe in space' as well as about Pythagoras, who taught his students that the earth was a sphere, and the fifth century BC philosopher Anaxagoras, who taught that the moon darkened the sun during an eclipse, and that during a lunar eclipse the earth's shadow fell upon the moon. He also started to relate details about the fifth flight of the Phoenix and that it was years away, the world being round as his Arabic contemporaries agreed at the time whilst many Franks still believed it was flat. In the Qur'an, Chapter 21:30, it has direct parallels to the Enuma Elish of earlier Babylonian myth and the Gilgamesh epics which have identical Creation and Flood stories as adopted by the Jews whilst in captivity into the biblical accounts, complete with the hidden esoteric symbolism and mathematical codes for it says, 'Are the disbelievers unaware that the heavens and the earth were one solid mass which we tore asunder, and that we made every living thing out of water?' Theodoric quoted from many ancient texts in his attempts to show that they knew and understood the concepts behind our very own make up, how we are made. 'Tis why he was able to understand and know how to make the three fold water. He also explained Hinduism and its own creation myths as well...and that Hinduism appeared to be free of many of the dogmas of other religions due to its most fundamental belief of Tat tvam asi, which is Sanskrit for 'That thou art' as in the belief that the individual soul, Atman, is identical with the essence of God, Brahman. In Christianity 'The Kingdom of God is within you' is looked upon as meaning the same. The very basic tenets and core of Hinduism is Vedantism, the philosophy of Hinduism itself. The Hindu equivalent to the Book of Genesis is known as the Vedic hymns. It is thought that these hymns are some of the oldest surviving literary works in the world and Theodoric had access to copies when he studied in the East years prior. The commentary on the Vedas, the Bhagavata Purana, is emphatic that humans have existed on earth for four cycles of time, called Yugas, lasting several thousand years of the Demigods. Each Demigod year being equal to 360 earth years. The total cycle of four reigns of Yugas totals 4,320,000 years. Theodoric scared many in his early years when he stated as fact that mankind had already had four periods of existence, each ending in cataclysmic upheavals. Accordingly he pointed out that the end of the fourth period was not now, as so many believe, but nearly another thousand years in the future when the earth enters the processional cycle of Aquarius and enters the fifth time of man. This is referred to as the fifth flight of the Phoenix by the Egyptians and details the earth shifting on its axis every 12,200 years preceded by climate changes and energy paths of the dragons being reversed and changed in its direction caused by the sun, hence in Gematria the sun is equal to 666."

"How was Theodoric able to teach Paul all of this without books?" Gabirol asked.

"Theodoric had an amazing and brilliant mind. He remembered everything, always. And as they travelled, Abi and Alisha rested, Tenno keeping a close eye upon them at all times. He even took it in turns to feed Arri, who had certainly developed a liking for the mixture Theodoric had made up. The Sufi mystic often sat in during his teachings and backed him up in information where he lacked any."

"You mentioned 666. We all know that is the number of the Devil...the Beast. Why would he teach Paul anything about that?" Ayleth asked.

"Ayleth, if you can understand and believe me when I say that all the numbers in the Bible have great relevance and demonstrate a code of great antiquity that reveals a high understanding of the very earth we live upon, then you will perhaps be encouraged to learn that despite all its apparent failings, the holy books do actually support the reality that there is a greater plan being carried out. If you let me explain about the numbers, I can show to you that 666 is nothing to be afraid of," the old man said softly.

"Please...if you would for everything about the book of Revelation, I am afraid, scares me as you know," she replied.

"Then understand this...that there is a value of 216 regarded by Pythagoras as a magic number as it is the same as six to the power of three, or 6 x 6 x 6; 666 being the so-called celebrated Number of the Beast in Revelations. If we add a zero to 216, we get 2,160, which happens to equal the diameter of the moon in miles. Theodoric explained how he knew these measurements from ancient texts copied from a pre-deluge race in part recovered by the Templars. This measurement is also exact as calculated by some of the very best minds in Alexandria, though many still ridicule it, but true facts cannot remain hidden forever, just as the reality of the world being a sphere and not flat as so many still believe. When viewed from earth, the moon's apparent circumference is identical to that of the sun's apparent circumference. 2,160 years is also the processional period of each zodiacal cycle through the heavens. That our present astrologers do all agree upon. 2,160 x 12 equals the total complete processional cycle of all twelve signs of the zodiac at 25,920 years. 2,160 divided by 6 equals the 360 degrees in a circle. When divided by 24 hours it equals 90 degrees, a right angle. When divided by 12, it equals 180 degrees. When Theodoric detailed these facts and mentioned the Devil's number, 666, many years previously, that was when he was again almost crucified but for the timely intervention of Philip and Firgany. So you can see the perils inherent when trying to tell people the truth against the backdrop of religious belief and entrenched dogma."

"But that is what you are doing now is it not?" the wealthy tailor commented.

"Yes, but as I said from the start...I can read people very well. Theodoric never could for he was far too trusting and believed everyone would think and behave as he did. It took him a while before he finally realised and learnt that was not the case. That is in part one of the reasons why he took himself away into his own self imposed reclusive retreat and let everyone close to him believe him dead."

"These numbers from Revelation. Can you tell us more?" Gabirol asked.

"Yes I can, much more if you wish," the old man answered. He looked around the table at each of them and as they all seemed to indicate yes, he continued. "The early Christians and people of Qumran (where the Dead Sea scrolls were later uncovered) lived in small areas that used identical architectural designs that were four squares with three gates on each side, twelve in total, that represented the twelve tribes of Israel. In Revelations, the New Jerusalem is represented with twelve gates. Also the pillars that were raised in Solomon's temple were 18 cubits high with another four cubits high chapiters of capitals as we call them now on top, spaced apart by exactly seven cubits, which is 22 by 7. The ratio of 22 by 7 was evidently very important to them. And we know why as 22 over 7 is the standard engineering working formulae for calculating pi, without which, none of the huge cathedrals and churches being built now could have been designed and constructed. The actual Book of Revelations in the New Testament just also happens to be 22 chapters long. Within it are many mathematical details. In Revelations, the New Jerusalem is 12,000 furlongs square. 12,000 furlongs square is equal to 220 yards, as there are 220 yards in a furlong, multiplied by 12,000 is equal to 2,640,000 yards. There are three feet to a yard. So 2,640,000 multiplied by 3 equals 7,920,000. The earth's diameter is equal to 7,920 miles as the ancient parchments and sacred texts told us all along. It will be a long time in the future before these values and dimensions are again confirmed, but they are nevertheless absolutely correct, and very near to what some have calculated already," the old man explained and looked at each person again in turn. No one said anything. "As the New Jerusalem is a square, we can multiply our 7,920,000 by 4 which then equals 31,680,000. Also 7,920 miles multiplied by 4 equals 31,680 miles. 31,680 divided by our number 1,440 equals 22. In Revelations the number 144,000 is stated as an important figure. The number 31,680 is important especially within the numerical codes of Gematria, as certain phrases and words as spoken by Jesus total in value 31,680."

"Sorry, what do you mean by that?" Ayleth interrupted.

1 – 11

"It means that whole sentences and words within the Bible, when you change the individual letters into mathematical values as done in Gematria, you end up with certain values... values that constantly appear and repeat within its pages. Let me explain further. Note that 31,680 divided by 220 equals 144. Also if we were to draw a square box around the earth touching the equator, if you accept that the earth is of course round, the perimeter of the square would equal 31,680 miles. Pliny the Elder, in his 'Natural History', stated that 3,168,000 miles was the measure round the whole earth. Just two zeros incorrect! In the tarot cards, the major Arcana cards total 22. Again Theodoric explained all of these facts to Paul as they journeyed. The importance of the esoteric and super secret value of 1746 he also started to reveal connected to the Vesica Pisces and other sayings within the Bible, but he did not have the tools to hand to explain it properly."

"Why not?" Simon asked.

"Because he needed to be able to draw out certain aspects of what he was trying to explain. He did detail the many myths relating to the 'Green Man' symbolism in both Celtic myths and all the ancient religions, especially the Egyptian Osiris myths where he was likewise depicted as a green god. How they were all connected to solar and stellar constellations, especially in relation to the Dog Star, Sirius. In the Osiris myths where he is symbolically represented by Orion, the important numbers are 360, 72, 30 and 12. The value of 1,080 being a very important value also. 30 x 72 equals 2,160, which equals one complete Zodiacal *procession of 30 degrees along the ecliptic. 2,160 x 12 equals 25,920 just as 360 x 72 equals 25,920 which equals the number of years taken to complete the procession of all twelve signs of the zodiac. This is known as 'the great year'. The most prominent number in the Osiris Orion myth is undoubtedly the number 72."*

"Hang on...Thomas. Did not he and his men originally number seventy-two?" Simon asked interrupting and raised his finger.

"Yes they did," the old man answered and smiled at Simon. "Now 72 and 720 were frequently added to 36 and 360 making 108 and 1,080 respectively. 1,080 miles is the radius of the moon. As explained previously, in both Greek and Hebrew, each letter in the alphabet has a mathematical value attached to it. This is what is known as 'Gematria'. Theodoric used mainly Greek values as an example for easier cross-referencing as more information from those sources was and still is available and more up to date, but the same can be achieved using Hebrew. Used with magic squares it is also known as Numerology, which Theodoric also used frequently. These methods were used in Greek, Arabic and Hebrew languages and were regarded as the most sacred of all principles. It was also related to music, which was governed by the same numerical canon using harmonics, the second truly universal language. It may surprise you to learn that senior Templars were more than familiar with these practices and codes. The ancient Hebrew Cabalists were very much aware of these facts. Likewise the unknown and mysterious founders of early Christianity had their works and ideas thoroughly suppressed by their surplanters, the fathers of the Christian Church as we now have it, that they deliberately framed their sacred writings in the number code to guarantee its message across time. Because of this, many passages and whole books of the New Testament are full of numerical codes. Two of the most prominent numbers in the numerical cannon were, and still are, 666 and 1,080. 666 was the celebrated 'Number of the Beast' in Revelation 13 as you pointed out, Ayleth. It esoterically signified the positive and active charge of solar energy, whilst 1,080 represented the opposite and complementary principle in nature, its negative and receptive side associated with the mystic moon and its influence on the waters, both within the earth and human imagination, and thus with prophecy and intuition as opposed to the solar principle of rational intellect. The moon has a radius of 1,080 miles and a diameter of 2,160 miles as explained. Christianity was founded upon the inspirational word of Christ and the Holy Ghost. Well...Holy Ghost equals the Holy Spirit, which is written in Greek as," the old man explained and quickly wrote down some Greek letters and pushed it across the table to Gabirol first – το αγιον πνευμα – "in total they equal a value of 1,080 in Gematria and is the composed representation of the male and female elements of the terrestrial spirit. In Gematria, Jesus, spelt in Greek as," quickly he wrote another phrase in Greek – Inσουζ – "equals 888. Mary – spelt in Greek as – Μαριαμ – equals 192. When both are added together, 888 + 192, the total equals 1,080. Now as Ayleth pointed out, 666 features prominently and the early Christians came to associate it with an influence exclusively evil, mainly in part due to the Roman Emperor Nero having the numerical value of 666. Many have sought and still seek to exclude the number 666 as it represents to them the Beast, the Devil and some absolute principle of evil. Yet a structure such as the beautiful Glastonbury Abbey has built within its very proportions the measurements of 666 prominently. Glastonbury is very closely linked with Arthurian myth and Joseph of Arimathea. It is absurd to associate any number solely with evil forces. No number is exclusively representative of a particular moral quality whether negative or positive, and in any case, it is inconsistent to relate moral principles to numbers, for numerical relationships are precise and unalterable while morals are neither, morals being simply

adopted by consent in response to prevailing circumstances, time and place, Theodoric often argued that it would therefore appear that we today have chosen to ignore what a far wiser, more realistic generation had once found acceptable, who understood that a true cosmology must encompass every created element."

"Bit of a genius as well as an idealistic dreamer by the sound of him," the Templar remarked.

"Oh yes. He was that...and so much more and very proud of the fact," the old man smiled. *"If you pull out the drawings from Paul's folder, you will find the images he drew immediately after his experience with Percival beneath Jerusalem. The New Jerusalem, as detailed in the New Testament in Revelations, is clearly not designed or planned by your average human architect or builder as its elements are not selective, for they comprehend a universal scheme that when viewed by our thinking makes no sense at all, but when viewed in its true mathematical structure and codes, makes total sense. One enigma that has puzzled scholars for centuries is the meaning behind the twelve gates of precious stone that surround the New Jerusalem. These actually relate to the twelve essential mineral salts that all living organisms require to live. With Gematria, if we were to add the numerical values of Jesus, 888, Mary, 192, and the Beast, 666, we are in fact symbolically joining as one, fusing so to speak, the rejoining of the physical with the spiritual, the terrestrial with the celestial. The total value equals 1,746. Perhaps the most sacred number ever! By the way, the earth is tilted on its axis of 23.4 degrees giving us an angle of obliquity of 66.6 degrees and the earth travels around the sun at a mean average speed of 66,600 miles per hour so we complete one complete circuit of the sun every 365 days...and a quarter day the ancients tell us."*

"Oh dear, so if you believe in anything connected with 666 as being evil, you better jump off now," Simon joked.

"That is if what you claim is indeed correct...about the earth tilting upon its axis as you say and the speed you quote," the Templar remarked.

"I can only but go by...and rely upon...what facts I know and have learnt as recovered from our forefathers...that will one day be proven correct. That in itself should alert and tell many in the future the cyclic nature of man as they rediscover these facts and look back and realise our great ancestors already knew them ...but I fear even then, if we have not done what is expected of us now to safeguard and guarantee that message reaches them, it will not prove anything at all," the old man sighed.

"Are there many of these sacred phrases that are encoded?" Gabirol asked and wrote some words quickly.

"Yes, for all the great holy books contain them. All of them...every last word. That is why in the Bible it threatens anyone who dares to change the order and content contained within. Theodoric taught Paul this fact and he started with the value of 1,080. That number could best be learnt by studying just a few of the sacred phrases of which the letters in Greek add up to that number. They include: Holy Spirit – το αγιον πνευμα – that equals 1,080. The Spirit of the Earth – το γαιουμα – that equals 1,080, The Fountain of Wisdom, – πηγη σοφιας – that equals 1,080, Tartaros, the Abyss– η Ταρταρος – that equals 1,080, and Cocytos, a God of the Abyss – Κοκυτος – that also equals 1,080. Other correspondences that relate to the value 1,080 include the radius of the moon at 1,080 miles, the number of breaths drawn in one hour for the average human, the number of stanzas in the Rigveda, 10,800. The numbers of bricks in an Indian fire altar totals 10,800 and the number of beads on the Hindu or Buddhist rosary equals 108. Throughout the entire world in every tradition,

code of architectural proportion, computation of time and wherever else mathematics is used, the number 1,080 is always prominent and is usually referred to as the Yin side of nature, in contrast to the Yang, or solar significance of the number 666."

"And that most sacred number you said, 17 something...," Gabirol remarked, looking through his notes to see if he had written it down.

"1,746...well those two prominent numbers just mentioned when added together equal 1,746. This number helps to reveal the hidden secret esoteric meaning of Jesus's phrase of 'A grain of mustard seed' and written in Greek as Κοκκος στναπεως, which equals a total sum value of all the letters as 1,746. This figure is also given by many other sacred phrases such as the Spirit of the world – το πνευμα κοσμου – that equals 1,746 and the Glory of the God of Israel – η δοζα του Ισραηλ – that equals 1,746. The figure 1,746 is of paramount importance relating to the Great Pyramid in Egypt. It represents a symbolic fusion of Heaven and earth taking place between the terrestrial current accumulated in its rocky mass, and the divine spark of celestial fire, distilled from the atmosphere at its original gold tipped apex, from which was born the life essence; also known as the 'Spirit of the world'. The full wording of the Christian title of 'Lord Jesus Christ', written in Greek as 'Κυριος Ιησους Χριστος', has by Gematria the value 3,168. In addition, the very value of 1,746 not only related to the Great Pyramid but also had direct relevance to the distance of one of the alignments, which converge, on the projected site of a great secret that Paul would in time learn about...the Halls of Amenti...or the Chambers of Creation as the ancient Egyptians preferred to call it," the old man said and looked down and closed his eyes.

"Hmm. You mentioned earlier that you would tell us about Jesus and his parable about faith and a grain of mustard seed. Does that likewise adhere to this code you speak of?" Gabirol asked, having checked his earlier notes.

"Yes, yes it does. Jesus used a parable concerning faith as likened to a grain of mustard seed by which mountains may be moved. Plato wrote 'That solid which has taken the form of a pyramid shall be the element and seed of fire'. The root word pyr in pyramid means fire. In the vegetable kingdom, the seed of the mustard plant because of its colour and hot flavour represented the seed of fire. Jesus is quoted in Mark IV:31–32 where it says 'It is like a grain of mustard seed which when sown in the Earth is less than all the seeds that be in the Earth, but when it is sown, it groweth up and becometh greater than all herbs, and shooteth out great branches so that the fowls of the air may lodge under the shadow of it'. You see, Jesus gave all of his parables in relation to his disciples who were fishermen, in fish related symbolism. The early Christian Church used a symbol of a fish as its identifying mark. Jesus was born as the earth was finishing its processional cycle through the zodiacal constellation of Aries the ram with all previous parables being related to goats and rams and hence the shepherds watching their flocks by night on the eve of his birth and the sacrificing of rams. At the same time as Jesus was born, the earth passed into the next zodiacal processional cycle of Pisces, the fish. When this period ends, the earth will pass into the Aquarian period, the so-called spiritual age. It is for that time that the secrets and codes must be protected and carried over to," the old man said and paused as he checked to see if they had taken in what he had explained. Gabirol wrote as fast as he could. When he stopped, the old man continued. "The early Christian symbol of a fish denoted their Church. The geometric and esoteric symbol and illustration of the Great Pyramid is known as the 'Vesica Pisces' meaning the vessel of the fish."

Fig. 40:

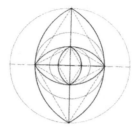

"The illustration of the Vesica Pisces is formed by the intersection of two equal circles, the circumference of each of which passes through the centre of the other. The Pyramid profile is placed within its geometric makeup by joining up the points that cross each other. It is not merely an abstract illustration for it occurs frequently in nature and represents perfect equilibrium between two equal forces. In the words of the ancient geomancers, it was an image of the inter-penetrating worlds of Heaven and earth, of spirit and matter. The dimensions and geometry of the Great Pyramid relate directly to the Vesica Pisces and symbolically to the number of fusion, 1,746. The Great Pyramid's height, not counting the base platform, is 481 feet and forms the longer axis of a Vesica Pisces when made from two intersecting circles of equal circumference of 1,746 feet. The perimeter of the rhombus contained within the Vesica Pisces is 1,110 feet, and the area of the rhombus equals 66,600 square feet. The height of the Vesica Pisces, when formed from circles with a circumference of 1,746 feet, is the same as that of the Great Pyramid's 481 feet."

"And...and this is all true, yes?" Gabirol asked quietly, almost disbelievingly.

"Yes, all true and provable," the old man answered and smiled. "The diameter of each of the two circles forming it is equal to that number divided by half the square root of 3, or 555.5 feet, giving the circumference of each circle as 1,746 feet. When the two circles are enclosed in a greater Vesica Pisces, the base angle of the Great Pyramid can be formed accurately to scale of its 51' 51" slope. The two inner circles that intersect at the Pyramid's tip and centre of its base accurately illustrates the form of an as yet unknown force field, as the ancients tell us exists within its structure. A known feature of the Great Pyramid is its strange peculiarities as supported by both traditional myths and modern experimentation. The numbers and values obtained from the Vesica Pisces are again also found within the New Testament in Revelations. The volume of the Vesica Pisces is 144,000,square feet which is the same as the number of souls in Revelations. The rhombus, as just previously mentioned, equals 66,600 square feet. In Revelation we know that the mark of the Beast is 666. The importance of the value 144,000 is important in its own right as detailed in the Bible, Revelations VII 3:4. And Theodoric explained in precise detail these facts and figures to Paul as their caravan made slow progress to Alexandria." [51]

"So all the self proclaimed prophets and priests shouting the end is nigh, are in error yes?" the farrier asked, puzzled.

"Yes, for they only see and make the teachings they read fit into their own present limited world view. That is why education is key. Knowledge properly understood. I have experienced many people who rant and shout as if on some personal crusade or commission direct from God, the wondrous good work Crusaders are doing...and they often quote the

Bible where it best suits their own argument. Such as Chapter 24, verse 14 of St Matthew's Gospel, where it states, 'and this gospel of the kingdom will be preached throughout the whole world, as a testimony to the nations; and then the end will come', and I have seen many a knight and pilgrim alike worked up into an almost frenzied state. This verse actually comes immediately prior to a chilling account of the final tribulations and too many so-called enlightened and wise clergy place this gospel firmly on the shoulders of the end of times. It implies that by spreading this gospel, the Christian is actually helping to herald in the end of times with all its terrifying tribulations. They call this task the 'Great Commission'. This also encompasses the area of self-fulfilling prophecies. Even in the Qur'an it is declared, that in the end times, a great eagle from the West would cast its shadow across the world of Islam and a great war would result. Only afterwards would peace reign, so they too actively seek the prophesied confrontation and some attach the eagle symbolism to that of the Holy Roman Catholic Church and its former eagle symbol of the Roman Empire...but could equally be applied to the eagle on Saladin's banners."

"You mentioned that before," Simon stated.

"Probably...but did I also explain the different types of prophesy and that the last and worst type is that of the self-fulfilling prophesy. That the war of Christianity against Islam would be a long drawn out one and why the Templars, Sufi and Isma'ilis wish to avert this self-fulfilling prophesy by fusing their beliefs into a single unified movement; especially as the symbolism of the eagle's shadow falling across all of Islam did not state, or indicate, who of the two sides would be the victor from which peace would then ensue. It is my greatest fear that this so-called prophecy will be the one that will cause the gravest of issues, misunderstandings and conflict...for there will come those people who will make the prophecy fit whatever circumstances prevail in the future. It will only serve to continue the bloodshed."

"Is that why you say education and knowledge must be taught?" Ayleth asked softly.

"Yes."

"Is, is that why we are here now...why you tell us this great tale with all these amazing facts?" Gabirol asked and looked at the old man intently, trying to gauge his every reaction.

"Yes...and the fact that the Sufi mystic, he claimed he saw in his visions great wars, wars unlike anything ever seen since the dawn of history...of another great country in the West that would also have its own banners carry both the sacred five pointed star and also the eagle. He also foresees a great calamity fall upon Southern France within a hundred years where Christian will fight against Christian and massacre each other in great numbers."

"Oh marvellous. Just what we need to hear," the wealthy tailor remarked and folded his arms.

"Forewarned is forearmed...so perhaps knowing this, many people can be saved...and perhaps, just perhaps, a disaster avoided. But knowing these events may come, and I do stress may as we all have the right of free agency to change things, for we are all ultimately masters of own destiny, at least the secrets of our ancient forefathers can be hidden and protected...rather than eradicated by ill informed peoples..."

"You mentioned about the fifth flight if the Phoenix, that is an Egyptian mythical creature you said, and something about the four ages of man. Can you explain that better, please?" Gabirol asked.

"The four past ages of man...that is something Theodoric knew much about. He certainly made sure that Paul would know all about it too. I can tell you but a small portion if you wish?" the old man replied.

"Anything, please," Gabirol answered quickly.

"Okay then let me explain that to the ancient Sumerians, the first age of man was around 11,000 to 10,000 BC, and was when the earth was passing through the zodiac sign and period of Leo, 'The Lion', and known to them as Ur.Gula. This sign symbolically represented their god, Enki, and the god of the African lands. In ancient Egypt, Enki was known as Ptah whose goddess wife, Sekhmet, was represented with the face of a lioness. So you see, they did not actually worship a being with a lion or crocodile's head. It was symbolic as a time marker. The Sphinx, which is a lion's body with a human head, though the head was carved that way many years after it was originally built, represented the time period of Leo, which would have been around the Sumerian's first time period. If what was learnt from the ancients is true and as discovered by the Templars, then the Sphinx was actually constructed in at least 10,000 BC...which clearly does not fit with the accepted teachings of the Church. After Leo, came the age of Cancer, which followed around 8,700 BC. This was depicted as a crab, which the Sumerians called Dub, meaning 'Pincers'. The later ancient Egyptians depicted Cancer as the Scarab beetle with its huge pincers. Cancer is followed by the age of Gemini, which the Sumerians called Mash.Tab.Ba meaning 'The Twins'. Note the Egyptian depiction showed two twins of both male and female. This tied in with the Sumerian belief that this sign is associated with one of their gods, called Enlil, whose first-born son Nannar or Sin had twins, Inanna and Utu, who were apparently born shortly after his arrival to earth having come from the heavens. Taurus follows Gemini and was known as Gu.Anna by the Sumerians, meaning 'Heavenly Bull'. The Egyptian zodiac represented the Bull with a disc on its back. This symbolism also represented the tenth planet, Nibiru, as this period coincided with an apparent passing of earth by Nibiru, another planet within our solar system with a 3,200-year orbit, as well as a visit of the god Anu to earth."

"Nibiru...tenth planet. What do you mean?" Gabirol interrupted.

"Ah...'Tis known as Wormwood in the Bible, and by many other names. The Templars have knowledge as did the Sumerians that showed that our planet is but one of ten planets. Nibiru being the furthest out. 'Tis referred to by them as planet X for ten and it just so happens that it is also known as the planet of crossing. Much about the return of this celestial body along with its dark star, our sun's own companion star is actually revealed within the ancient writings and even our own Bible, but I shall cover that later. Our earth circles the sun every 365 days...but the outer planet takes a staggering 3,200 years, but that I shall have to cover later if we have time also," the old man explained and paused until all had nodded in agreement. "The sign of Aries follows next symbolised by the Ram known to the Sumerians as Ku.Mal, meaning 'Field dweller'. The preceding age to the birth of Jesus Christ and the Piscean age was Aries, hence why all of the stories connected with Moses relate to rams, goats and shepherds. It is why we have shepherds watching their flocks by night on the eve of Jesus Christ's birth." [52]

"I can see that makes sense," Peter remarked and looked at Gabirol, who nodded in agreement with him.

"The early Christian Church symbol was the Vesica Pisces or Vessel of the Fish as stated earlier. The Vesica Pisces is linked to the Great Pyramid and sacred alignments in England. Jesus used the symbol of the fish throughout his ministry as well as most of his disciples being fishermen. Later Arthurian myths recount the same symbolism in the Fisher King. It is also stated in the Bible, that a thousand years after the return of the Messiah, the Devil will again be let loose to tempt mankind one further time. This equates to the Aquarian age when the Messiah is due to return and to the age of Capricorn, which follows it. Capricorn was often depicted as a half man, half fish or half man and half goat. The half man and half goat is immediately *recognisable as the image of the Devil as portrayed during the past thousand years. As said, after Aries, we have Pisces, known to the Sumerians as Sim.Mah, which meant 'Fishes'. This is represented by two fishes spanning a watery stream. Water is symbolic for spirit so we can see that this sign also represented a stepping-stone towards a spiritual age to follow, as in the Age of Aquarius. Aquarius is depicted as the 'Water Bearer' and known as Gu to the Sumerians. Capricorn was known to them as Suhur.Mash, meaning 'The Goat Fish'. It has been associated as a symbolic representation of the Mother Goddess, Ninharsag, who was nicknamed Nin. Mah, meaning 'Lady Fish'. In ancient Egypt, she was known as Hathor, who was depicted as a cow and bearing some similarity to the goat fish image. Egyptian artists occasionally linked Capricorn with an umbilical cutter, which was also a symbol for Ninharsag as she was the Mother Goddess. But aqua is also another word for spirit, 'tis why water is used for baptism as well as holy water being blessed, and remember, we know that our bodies are made up of at least two-thirds water. Our ancient forefathers actually state we are made up from seventy-two parts water to actual physical material."*

"This is all so very new and difficult to accept and believe," the wealthy tailor commented, his arms still folded. "I thought the Crusades, our men...and woman I now know, was a great and noble quest...but now, now I am just confused."

"I think it was the Italian St Anselm, Archbishop of Canterbury, who argued that the whole Crusade venture is nothing more than yielding to evil. That Jerusalem is not peace but a byword for tribulation and he was most certainly outspoken against monks of all Orders, including Cistercian monks, who continued to rant about killing Muslims as acceptable as God wills it," the old man sighed but then shook his head and smiled. "But despite all the conflict, reach Alexandria they all eventually did, Turansha stopping just short of the city."

Eastern approach road to Alexandria, Egypt, 1179

It was early evening as Theodoric sat beside Paul when the caravan drew to a halt. Abi was sound asleep still outstretched on the bench. Alisha stirred slightly upon the main bunk sensing the caravan had stopped. Arri gently stretched his arms and kicked out his legs whilst pulling the legs on Clip clop. The main braking lever creaked loudly as Tenno applied it fully. Paul moved several of the parchments on the table Theodoric had been showing him.

"So knowing all of this, this vast wealth of knowledge and information, why have you not continued with your obvious quest?" Paul asked, puzzled.

"My dear boy...I have never stopped my quest. But I did remove myself for a while. The pain and sorrow I caused people, not least amongst them being your father. I am not sure he would be best pleased knowing I am with you," Theodoric answered.

"He will be when he finds out how you were instrumental in saving us," Paul replied with a large smile. "But tell me, after all is said and done...do you have any regrets for the path you have walked?"

"In the main, no. But there are a few things I would do differently. You know, all I ever really wanted to do was to have a life like Robert the monk. He chronicled the First Crusade you know. But I would have loved to emulate, up to a point, Peter the hermit, who put the kernel of the idea of a crusade into Pope Urban's mind in the first place...but I would have done it with a more sympathetic approach of cooperation and respect towards Muslims and Islam. Hermits were originally mystical Gnostic type characters who took their name from the god Hermes," Theodoric answered and paused as he looked at Arri pull Clip clop. He smiled before continuing. "Paul, I have tried to teach you and explain much in just a few days...you learn fast, but there is still so much more to learn and understand if you wish."

"I do...so long as Alisha is in agreement."

"I am," Alisha said, her eyes still shut as she turned over and placed her hand upon Arri. "Do you think I have not heard all of what you have said these past days as I lay here?" she said and smiled and opened her eyes slightly.

"That is good to hear. All will make better sense then when I tell you more, especially about the Irish," Theodoric replied, pleased to see Alisha looking much better.

"Such as?" Paul asked immediately.

"Let me just say for now, that St Patrick of Ireland insisted that Jesus was born of normal means, and that once, just briefly, I was once married to an Irish priestess as part of the Celtic Church not ruled by Rome. I was lucky to be taught the rules and beliefs of the Celtic Church and also taught the secrets of their ancient bards and... and I learnt that the Celtic Church brought love whilst the Roman Church brings the law. I learnt that David and Solomon were Messiahs just as Jesus was who tried to remove the Maccabeans, who had usurped the Davidic line. I also learnt about the so-called end times and how it would bring in a sense of spiritual loss, disillusionment with religion, politics etcetera and an increase in revolutionary behaviour and conflict, just as nowadays, but far worse. Sadly that is one of those self fulfilling prophecies I tried so hard to stop. But alas, as the codes gave a long-term prophetic view on this as happening again in the future, I became utterly disheartened. But as the codes also predicted, a great man would appear who would be called 'The Guide', or more correctly, a 'Nautonier', which means 'helmsman', who would guide and who would start a new quest with the fusion between Muslim, Judaic and Christian religions who understood the need for a meaning in life. He would be all wise, all gentle; the Navigator! I once stupidly thought that man to be Reynald."

"Reynald! How?" Alisha asked, surprised, and sat up rubbing her hand through her matted hair.

Paul looked at her. She looked wild almost, but he was more than pleased to see her speaking and sitting up.

"Yes, Reynald. Can you believe that? But he was a very different man back then."

"Perhaps you should inform them more about their own backgrounds," Abi suddenly interrupted, her first full sentence in days.

"Paul, all I shall say this day on the matter, for I fear now is not the time nor place, but suffice it to say that your direct bloodline can be traced back all the way to Jean de Gisors, the obscure knight who led to the Merovingian dynasty. I will be able to show you confirmation once settled in Alexandria for we have much hidden there," Theodoric explained as Abi nodded her head in agreement still with her eyes shut.

"You have mentioned him before...or my father certainly has if I recall correctly," Paul replied as Tenno opened the small door and looked in. Ishmael appeared by his side.

"Then you may know, or perhaps not, that Jean de Gisors was related to Hugues de Payens, the first Grand Master of the Knights Templar after the Prieure de Sion had actually founded it in 1099 in Jerusalem. It is no coincidence that three of the founding Knights Templar just all happened to be connected or related in some way and how the town of Troyes became the Templars' strategic centre for their Order. It was from there the first major Grail romances come from. Peter the hermit was the personal tutor to Godfrei de Bouillon and main protagonist for calling Pope Urban II to instigate the First Crusade as I have said already. You may recall that monks from Calabria in southern Italy went to Orval in Belgium, set up camp there and established a monastery. Peter the hermit came from this group, who then went to set up the Abbey of Notre Dame du Mont de Sion. Chartres Cathedral is to have twelve circles about its rose window, which I believe you said your father took you to see the plans of once?" Theodoric asked Paul. "Do you know though that Hugues de Payens and those knights were all 'Johannite' initiates and they were all more than aware of the sacred hidden symbolism and significance behind the rose and twelve circles set around a larger circle."

"I am not sure, for I have been taught and told so many things these past two years. 'Tis all rather confusing to be honest," Paul answered.

"That is no problem for we shall have some time to teach you and ground you in all that is important," Theodoric explained and smiled broadly.

Alisha looked at both of them and felt uneasy about Theodoric's comment. She just wanted a peaceful life now and to concentrate upon Arri and being both a mother and a wife. She was still struggling to come to terms with all that she had recently discovered about Firgany and her real mother being Raja.

"We must continue this conversation later when we shall cover the many hidden meanings behind the 'twin riders on a horse' symbolism the Templars use but also its symbolic representation to the staff of John the Evangelist and the staff of John the Baptist, plus much more on the 'rose' emblems on church doors and cathedral windows...plus the not so minor aspects surrounding the fact that Jesus himself after the crucifixion wrote the book of John in the Bible, and as explained to you before whilst in Jerusalem that the key that opens all hermetic secrets is sex magic, the supposed secret of the Templars, that I feel we should discuss further for I am not sure I explained that properly."

Abi opened her eyes upon hearing Theodoric's last remark.

"Oh I think you did," Paul replied as Alisha looked at him quizzically.

"I did explain about the order of Tau, and its origins and connections to James the Just, brother of Jesus and teacher, as well as being connected to the hidden secret that the Jerusalem Church was the Qumran Community of which very few initiates and adepts know about as the knowledge is for future generations' benefits; not our time...did I not?" Theodoric asked.

3 – 35

"No...not that I can recall," Paul answered, shaking his head no as Tenno and Ishmael looked at each other, puzzled.

"Hmmm. I thought I had. Well, in short, the Qumran Community consisted of twelve perfect holy men who were the pillars of the community. But the two main principal pillars were purely highly symbolic representing both the 'Kingly' and 'Priestly' aspects of creating and maintaining the 'Kingdom of Heaven'. These pillars were descendants of the pillars of the united Upper and Lower Egypt. They had come down to the Qumran Community via the Boaz and Jachin pillars that made up the eastern gate of Solomon's Temple."

"Theo...I think you should indeed leave that until we are all settled...please," Abi said, her throat dry but with a smile across her face.

"I can see you are getting better," Theodoric joked. "But you are correct, as always. I can go on a bit can't I?" he smiled as Tenno nodded yes in agreement in an exaggerated manner.

"Well...it has certainly been a journey of study. That is for sure," Paul commented and smiled.

"That journey is now complete...look...for there is the great city of Alexandria," Tenno stated and stood aside and gestured with his open hand palm upwards toward the city a short distance away.

Paul moved nearer to the small doorway and looked down the slight incline toward the city, the brilliant blue of the Mediterranean Sea shimmering to the right, the famous tall lighthouse clearly visible in the distance towering above the buildings and harbour beside it. Turansha was sat upon his horse looking back at Paul. He smiled and raised his hand before looking back down toward Alexandria. Paul sighed heavily and the hairs stood up on end down his back. 'Finally, Alexandria,' he thought to himself and sighed. 'Finally.'

Chapter 41
Alexandria & the Emerald Tablet

Paul sat back down beside Alisha and looked at Abi and Alisha in turn.

"Well 'tis great news you both seem to be recovering. And Abi, I hope you shall live for many more years," Paul remarked as the caravan started to move again.

"Paul...I hope so, for I fear these injuries may have taken more than blood from me, for something feels different this time. You know, there are times when I just wish I could be held and told everything will be okay," Abi replied quietly and sighed. "But I shall stay as long as I am always able."

"Tenno...," Paul remarked and raised an eyebrow.

"Tenno...have you any idea of the age difference between us?" Abi replied and let out a laugh, shaking her head slowly. "But Tenno...he certainly makes me feel different."

"Abi, how is it that you look so young despite your age?" Alisha asked hesitantly as Abi adjusted the bandage across her side.

"Ali...that is something best left to another day, but all can say is that I simply age slower. That is all," she replied and winced at the pain in her side.

Paul leaned over, kissed Alisha on the side of her cheek.

"I shall go and keep Tenno company up front," he said and smiled.

Port of La Rochelle, France, Melissae Inn, spring 1191

"I must confess I find it hard to believe in the age of Abi and Kratos," the wealthy tailor remarked.

"Why...Abi was living proof of the longevity of her kind. It isn't only biblical figures who lived to well-seasoned ages of nine hundred years or more," the old man replied and nodded.

"What...is Abi nine hundred years old?" Ayleth asked, surprised.

"No, she was not that old, for she was just a little girl when she first met Kratos on the shores of Malta...beneath an ancient Holm Oak tree. She was just a few years old then and could not speak a word of Kratos's language...I thought I explained that at the start," the old man answered and sighed, trying to recall if he had actually mentioned it previously.

"Ah...I was not present at the start of this tale," Ayleth replied.

"Well I cannot believe it. Maybe in ancient times as stated in the Bible," the wealthy tailor replied immediately.

"Why, if it could happen back then, can it not be so now? There are countless ancient texts from many cultures that document life spans that we, people like you," the old man said and nodded toward the wealthy tailor, "find utterly and literally unbelievable. I know

many who argue that the ages are due to misunderstandings in the translation process, or that the numbers have symbolic meaning only, which yes, in some cases they do, but there is far more evidence that suggests our human life span has actually decreased significantly over thousands of years."

"I was taught that in some places, a year is understood as a different period, which has led to much confusion," Gabirol remarked.

"There is that too. In the ancient Near East understanding of a year could be different from our concept of a year today. In some instances a year meant an orbit of the moon, so just a month instead of an orbit of the sun of twelve months. But if we make the changes accordingly, while it brings the age of the biblical figure Adam down from 930 to a more reasonable 77 at the time of his death, it also means he would have fathered his son Enoch at the age of eleven. And Enoch would have only been five years old when he fathered Methuselah. Similar inconsistencies arise when we adjust the year figures to represent seasons instead of solar orbits. Numbers in Genesis could have both real numerical and sacred numerological or symbolic meaning, just as they do within the Book of Revelations as I have explained."

"How so?" Simon asked, pulling a face of exaggerated confusion and smiling.

"In both Genesis and the four thousand-year-old Sumerian King List that details the reigns of single kings in Sumer exceeds a staggering thirty thousand years in some cases. Much like the Bible, the King List shows a steady decline in life spans. The list differentiates between pre-Flood and post-Flood reigns. The pre-Flood reigns are significantly longer than the post-Flood, though even post-Flood life spans are shown to be several hundred years or more than a thousand years. In the Bible, we see a progressive decline over the generations from Adam's 930-year life, to Noah's 500 years, to Abraham's 175." [53]

"Why is that?" Ayleth asked quietly.

"According to what the Templars learnt, it is down to the very earth we live upon and our environments and diet. It is all somehow connected to long phases of the sun too as well as what is known as the ring of light that our entire world passes through and then departs from. There will come a time in the future when mankind will again rediscover the secret of our physical bodies...how they are made and what influences affect them. But there is a danger that comes with that knowledge, for then...man will be like the gods themselves."

"What, by playing and interfering with nature?" Gabirol asked.

"To a degree, yes. But just as sacred dances and fertility rites upon the land had real effects upon the whole landscape, so too our very thoughts have an effect upon the very land we stand on...especially water, the rivers, the lakes and seas. When we become disharmon-ised, so too does the very environment we live in. That is why the ancients all used water to symbolise spirit."

"So we have to go back to making sacrifices do we?" the Genoese sailor asked.

"No...not at all. Those practices took place due to a total misunderstanding of those very principles of how we are directly interconnected with our world. Much became lost in truly understanding our earth. Again that is a demonstration of the dangers of misunderstanding and misinterpreting ancient teachings," the old man explained and paused briefly. He looked at them, expecting a response but as no other questions came, he continued. "Post-Flood life spans in the Sumerian King List are questioned as the largeness of ages appears artificial. Etana's was 1,560 years, to cite the longest, and is also the sum of the two preceding reigns whilst certain other documented life spans seem simply to have arisen as multiples of 60. Other large numbers can be clearly seen as squares, such as 900 being the square of 30, 625, the square of 25, 400, the square of 20 and so on. But even among the smaller figures, the square of six appears far too frequently."

"Does this also fit in with other places in the world not mentioned within the Bible...such as the place where Tenno came from? All of those lands?" Peter asked.

"Yes. In ancient China, life spans of over a hundred years were commonplace. According to many Chinese medical records, a doctor named Cuie Wenze of the Qin dynasty lived to be 300 years old. Gee Yule of the later Han dynasty lived to be 280 years old. A high ranking Taoist master monk, Hui Zhao, lived to be 290 years old and Lo Zichange lived to be 180 years old. As recorded in the Chinese Encyclopaedia of Materia Medica, He Nengci of the Tang dynasty lived to be 168 years old. A Taoist master, Li Qingyuan, lived to be 250 years old."

"So how did they do that, as I could do with some of whatever it is they were taking?" Sarah asked jokingly and flicked her hair.

"If what the ancients tell us in correct, then in the main longevity can be maintained by nourishing life, including not only physical nourishment, but also mental and spiritual nourishment. By means of a healthy diet and meditation."

"Is that why Templars meditate?" Gabirol asked and looked over at the Templar.

"If that was the case, it certainly did not work with me," the Templar replied and laughed as he clasped Miriam's hand tighter.

"In Persia, the Shahnameh or Shahnama, which means 'The Book of Kings', is an epic poem written by Ferdowsi around the end of the tenth century AD It tells of kings reigning for a thousand years, several hundred years, down to a hundred and fifty years, and so on. Even today, people report life spans of some hundred and fifty or more years. Abi would most certainly fall into that category as per her kind easily. Yet there are many of our kind who live in the region where her ancestors came from who still claim ages reaching over a hundred and seventy years."

"So what do I need to do to live long?" Simon asked.

"Start by not asking so many questions," Sarah interjected.

The old man laughed at her comment and Simon shook his head, laughing too.

"From what I have seen and learnt over my many years, it is that exceptionally long-lived people have invariably led humble lives, doing hard physical work or exercise, often outdoors, from youth well into old age. Their diet is simple, as is their social life involving families."

"Well that is you most definitely guaranteed a short life," Sarah joked looking at Simon.

"Let me just say on this matter that longevity in ancient times has long been connected to practices of internal alchemy, or mind-body cultivation, especially in China. Here, longevity was connected with virtue. Likewise it is intertwined with Western spiritual beliefs as part of the Bible. Some mystics claim that God simply afforded those as mentioned in the Bible a longer time of life on account of their virtue, and the good use they made of it. And remember, Abraham was said to have lived to a hundred and seventy-five."

"All the old age stuff aside then for a moment, once in Alexandria, did things settle down for them...what was their home like, did she have another child and what happened between Tenno and Abi?" Sarah asked fast.

The old man laughed at her eagerness then looked at her intently.

"Many questions...so many questions," the old man said, still smiling. "Turansha led his men and sister into the city with Thomas and his knights following behind Alisha and Paul's caravan. He did try to convince Paul to stay at his very large residence, but both he *and Alisha were keen to see where they were to live. Turansha did insist that once settled, they must call upon him and be introduced to his friend Husam al Din Lu'lu, a great man of religion known as Shaykh...Fortunately Theodoric knew exactly where their home was for he had been instrumental in securing its possession with Philip many years before," the old man sighed. "And Abi and Tenno. Well...Abi was so weak that any thoughts of any kind of romance as such were certainly curtailed. But Tenno remained by her side constantly, even to the exclusion of Paul and Alisha. That is when Ishmael I think began to step up as their main protector. They thought Tenno had been silent in his manner, but Ishmael...huh, he became ever present and was a man of even less words."*

"Are we not to have a history lesson on Alexandria then?" Simon interrupted.

"Why, what do you mean?" the old man asked as Sarah looked at Simon and scowled.

"Well, so far you have always told us all about the places. You seem to have cut straight through this one...and I like the history parts. It is as if we walk in their footsteps when you tell us. And I really want to know about the lighthouse. It's the last remaining wonder of the ancient word isn't it...apart from the big pyramids, at Giza?" Simon replied enthusiastically.

"I too would enjoy learning of the city...if it has value?" Gabirol asked and winked at Simon.

"I am touched you ask it of me. I feared I may bore you with all that detail," the old man answered.

"No...puts me right in there with them," Simon replied and smiled as he folded his arms and rocked backwards upon his chair.

"Well in that case I can run through a brief history of Alexandria if you all wish," the old man asked and waited for their responses. The wealthy tailor shrugged his shoulders not sure but the rest all agreed they wanted to know more. "Then let me start by saying that Alexandria is truly a remarkable city and harbour. Did you know that it was designed and laid out by Alexander the Great's personal architect, Dinocrates? It incorporated the best in Hellenic planning and architecture. Within just a century of its founding, its splendours rivalled anything known in the ancient world. And of course," the old man started to explain and looked at Simon, "the pride of Alexandria was the great lighthouse, the Pharos of Alexandria, which stood on the eastern tip of the small island of Pharos. As Simon said, it was and still is one of the Seven Wonders of the World. It was the first thing that Paul had seen standing tall as he looked out of the caravan. Despite damage over the years, it still stood nearly 350 feet high. The city had certainly come a long way since Alexander the Great decided that the small Egyptian port of Rhacotis, being a natural harbour, would make for an excellent base for future operations in the eastern Mediterranean. It is close to the delta of the Nile, but far enough removed to avoid silting up and had the protective island, Pharos, guarding its entrance. It is also very well placed for trade, or warfare. So he commissioned his architect to build a new suburb beside the old town which had already been inhabited for over a thousand years, after which the whole city, both old and new, now joined, were named after him. But it was not until under Ptolemy, Alexander's successor in Egypt, that the new city began to grow and become a centre of tolerance and rapid learning and advancement in all manner of teachings...both political and religious tolerance as well as historical studies and alchemy...." the old man explained and paused.

"I know of this Ptolemy. Much is written about him," Gabirol remarked.

"Yes there is. He actually added legitimacy to his rule in Egypt by acquiring Alexander's body."

"What...how disgusting," Ayleth commented, feigning a look of disgust.

"Well, that may sound strange to us, but it is no different from our Church claiming the bodies, or body parts, of our saints is it?" the old man replied and laughed. "Ptolemy intercepted the embalmed corpse on its way to burial and took it to Egypt, placing it in a golden coffin in Alexandria. It remained one of the most famous sights of the town for many years, until supposedly destroyed in riots in the third century AD. Though I have seen parchments that show it was hidden, and still remains hidden."

"Ah...does Paul find his tomb then?" the Genoese sailor asked with a large grin.

"No, no he did not...for he would be led along another path toward a far greater discovery," the old man answered and paused as he thought for a moment. "But let me continue for I shall cover that later." He coughed and cleared his throat. "Alexandria was a capital city from about 320 BC and Ptolemy transformed it into one of the greatest centres of learning in the Greek world and founded what we would call it, a 'museum', home of the Muses. Great mathematicians such as Euclid, Archimedes and Eratosthenes are all connected with this academy and as most of you already know, its library became the greatest in the ancient world and it soon became a truly cosmopolitan centre. It was there that the Jews began to demonstrate the ability of a Jewish community to flourish in a new context without losing its identity. They integrated so fully with the secular life of the city that their own first language became Greek. It is they who first used the word diaspora, Greek for 'dispersion', to describe Jewish communities living outside Israel. Soon many of them no longer understood Hebrew at all. But they refused to let this diminish their strong sense of a shared identity as God's special people, according to the covenant revealed in a book which they now cannot read. They commissioned, with Ptolemy's support and approval, the first translation of the Bible, the famous Greek version known as the Septuagint. In addition to the library, Ptolemy planned the great lighthouse on the island of Pharos at the entrance to the harbour but it was only completed around 280 BC, under his successor Ptolemy the Second."
[54]

"I heard it is the biggest tower since Babel?" Simon interrupted.

"Yes it is big and by far the most impressive lighthouse of antiquity, and hence why it became famous as one of the Seven Wonders of the World," the old man explained. "The lighthouse consists of a three-tier stone tower, which has within it a broad spiral ramp leading up to the platform where fires burn at night. They are reflected out to sea by metal mirrors. Above the fires is a huge statue, of either Alexander or Ptolemy in the guise of the sun god, Helios."

"I do know from my own studies that Classical Greece has produced brilliant theorists, the dreamers of science. But were they not more inclined to simply study the intellectual appeal of good theories only and never actually tried to test them?" Gabirol asked.

"That was true for a time as they were disinclined to engage in the manual labour of testing their theories, mainly because so many were esoteric in nature anyway, but Alexandria changed all of that as it became a melting pot of their ideas and theories with those of the skilled Egyptian practices and traditions, especially in regard to their work in precious metals where people became interested in making practical use of Greek scientific theory. If Aristotle said that the difference in material substances is a matter of balance, then that balance might be changed. Copper might become gold. And so was born one of the greatest quests in alchemy...turning a base metal into gold...the philosopher's stone... but that was just the physical perception, for the true meaning was to transform us... people...from base physical beings into enlightened pure spiritual beings. But I guess I can save that aspect until later," the old man answered and looked at the wealthy tailor, whose ears had pricked up at the mention of gold. "Among the practical scientists of Alexandria are men who can be seen as the first alchemists and the first experimental chemists. Their trade, as workers in precious metals, involved melting gold and silver, mixing alloys, changing the colour of metals by mysterious process. These are the activities of chemistry. The root word for chemistry, chem, comes from the Arabic word Al-chem, alchemy. Anyone, so perhaps you know of this person, who studies architecture, mathematics and geometry will know of Euclid, who taught in Alexandria during the reign of Ptolemy. He demonstrated in the Elements, his thirteen books on geometrical theorems, many of which he derived from his predecessors, in particular Eudoxus, but he presents them with a clarity which ensured the success of his work and is why it has become Europe's standard textbook in geometry."

"Yes I know of his teachings," Gabirol said as the Genoese sailor looked at him.

"Archimedes was a student in Alexandria and I think many of us here have heard him too?" the old man said.

"Not I," Simon said aloud as the wealthy tailor shook his head no also.

"Well, let us simply say that he eventually exceeded what his teachers taught him. But it was in Alexandria in the third century BC that surgeons such a, Herophilus and Erasistratus started to make their first studies on the workings of human anatomy. Paul would later learn this when he studied much of what the Hospitallers teach."

"I have visited Alexandria many times...'tis truly a busy and open city. And the music you can hear there. Truly amazing," the Genoese sailor remarked.

"That is another side of the city. A scientist in Alexandria, by the name of Ctesibius, is credited with being the first to invent an organ with a hand-operated pump sending air through a set of large pipes. Each pipe is played by pressing a note on a board. This was the beginning of keyboard instruments. By the time of the Roman Empire, a few centuries later, the organ was a familiar and popular instrument playing a prominent part in public games and circuses as well as private banquets. The emperor Nero, an enthusiastic performer, is proud of his talents on the organ."

"We always picked up the latest maps from Alexandria. Always new ones coming out of there," the Genoese sailor remarked and sat back in his chair and chuckled to himself remembering so long ago personal events in the city.

"That is not surprising. As I had said earlier, maps, and the many map making cartographers in the city, was one of the main arguments Philip used to convince Paul that it was a great and wonderful place to go and live. They also used inks that were not acidic so did not destroy parchments. Most do not know that the circumference of the earth was calculated there as far back as 220 BC. Tenno would actually use his knowledge of his travels and the details taken from Thomas's rune inscribed stones to sell to cartographers. Huh...many people did wonder why there was a sudden explosion of new maps at that time, especially the ones with reference to Vinland south west of Greenland...Vinlanda Insula," the old man said smiling broadly as he recounted the details.

"You mentioned the circumference of the earth being calculated there," Gabirol reminded the old man.

"Ah yes. It was done by Eratosthenes, the librarian of the museum at Alexandria. He had heard that at noon on midsummer's day the sun shone straight down a well at Aswan, in the south of Egypt. He found that on the same day of the year in Alexandria it cast a shadow 7.2 degrees from the vertical. Note that number again 72? Anyway, he calculated the distance between Aswan and Alexandria, and applied it against the 360 degrees instead of 7.2 degrees, or fifty times greater. He discovered that camels take fifty days to make the journey from Aswan, and he measured an average day's walk by this fairly predictable beast of burden. It gave him a figure of about 26,000 miles. That is only a thousand more miles roughly larger than what our Templars discovered to be the case."

"I heard a rumour that the cup of the Last Supper and the Holy Grail came from Alexandria. Is that true?" Peter asked.

1 – 6

"The cup...or more correctly the Chalice of the Abbot Suger of Saint-Denis. But that was a first century BC cup that was later added to its mounting base between 1137 and 1140."

"Was that not the cup of the Last Supper then?" Peter asked.

"No. It was a totally different cup made out of sardonyx to hold wine for Mass, and was acquired by Abbot Suger for the French royal abbey of Saint-Denis, near Paris. The stone cup was set in gold and used in the consecration ceremony for the new altar chapels of the church on 11 June 1144. Suger, abbot of Saint-Denis from 1122 to 1151, was not only a Benedictine monk but also a brilliant administrator who served as regent of France during the Second Crusade. I met him...several times. With objects such as this chalice and the abbey's new Gothic architecture, he aimed to create a vision of paradise on earth that would awe beholders. He equated Divine Light with the real light shimmering through stained glass and glistening from gems. Abbot Suger's chalice was carved in Alexandria, but it was his goldsmiths who mounted the cup in a gold and silver setting with delicate gold-wire filigree set with stones, pearls, glass insets, and opaque white glass pearls. On the foot, a medallion depicts the haloed Christ, flanked by the Greek letters signifying: 'I am the Alpha and Omega, the Beginning and the End'. It served the abbey well that many people thought it connected to the Last Supper."

"Sorry to change the subject slightly. You said Pharos Island but when I went there, it was connected to the mainland," the Genoese sailor interrupted.

"You are not mistaken, for Alexander the Great ordered the island to be united to the coast by a three-quarters of a mile long causeway, the east side of which became the Great Harbour, and on an open bay on the west side lay the port of Eunostos, with its inner basin Kibotos. The lighthouse was truly a marvel as you have probably seen, with statues of Poseidon stood atop and masonry blocks interlocked and sealed together using molten lead, to withstand the pounding of the waves. 'Tis truly a great work," the old man explained. "You know, there are those who claim that the Pharos lighthouse is a vertical yardstick used in the first precise measurement of the size of the earth. After its foundation, Alexandria became the seat of the Ptolemaic rulers of Egypt, and quickly grew to be one of the greatest cities of the Hellenistic world second only to Rome in size and wealth. It fell to the Arabs in AD 641, and a new capital of Egypt, Fustat, was founded on the Nile. What is sad is that just a few months after the foundation, Alexander left Egypt for the East and never returned to his city. After Alexander departed, his viceroy, Cleomenes, continued the expansion of the city. You may recall I detailed how Alisha and Paul passed through the gates of Tarsus where Antony met Cleopatra. Well, it was in Alexandria that Julius Caesar had his affair with Cleopatra in 47 BC and was besieged in the city by Cleopatra's brother and rival. His example was followed by Mark Antony, for whose favour the city paid dearly to Octavian. Following Antony's defeat at Alexandria at the Battle of Actium, Octavian took Egypt for his own, appointing a prefect who reported personally to him rather than to the Roman Senate. There still stands a great Roman Theatre in Alexandria but in AD 115 Alexandria was destroyed during the Jewish–Greek civil wars which gave Hadrian and his architect, Decriannus, an opportunity to rebuild it. But Alexandria was not without its bloodshed such as when in AD 215 the emperor Caracalla visited the city and, because of some insulting satires that the inhabitants had directed at him, abruptly commanded his troops to put to death all youths capable of bearing arms. This brutal order seems to have been carried out even beyond the letter, for a general massacre ensued. According to historian Cassius Dio, over twenty thousand people were killed. In the third century AD, Alexander's tomb was closed to the public, and now its location has been forgotten. But not by all," the old man stated with a wry smile that Gabirol noted and wrote a comment on. "Despite Alexandria's historical importance having sprung from pagan learning, it now acquired new importance as a centre of Christian theology and Church government. There Arianism came to prominence and there also Athanasius opposed both Arianism and pagan reaction against Christianity, experiencing success against both and continuing the Patriarch of Alexandria's major influence on Christianity into the next two centuries. As native influences began to reassert themselves in the Nile valley, Alexandria gradually became an alien city, more and more detached from Egypt and losing much of its commerce as the peace of the empire broke up during the third century, followed by a fast decline in population and splendour. In AD 365, a massive tidal wave hit Alexandria causing extensive damage but by the late fourth century, persecution of pagans by newly Christian Romans had reached new levels of intensity. Temples and statues were destroyed throughout the Roman Empire...pagan rituals became forbidden under punishment of death, and libraries were closed. In AD 391, Emperor Theodosius the First ordered the destruction of all pagan temples, and the Patriarch Theophilus complied with his request. Some argue it was then that the great Library of Alexandria and the Serapeum were destroyed by fire, but as Paul was taught, there were several libraries by this time, and much was in fact secreted away. Others deny this and claim that the library was destroyed much earlier, in the third century, due to civil war in the time of the Roman Emperor Aurelian. The Brucheum and Jewish quarters were desolate in the fifth century, and the central monuments, the Soma and Museum, fell into ruin. On the mainland, life seemed to have centred on the vicinity of the Serapeum and Caesareum, both which became Christian churches. The Pharos and Heptastadium quarters, however, remained populous and were left intact. But then in AD 616 the city was taken by Khosrau the Second, King of Persia. Although the Byzantine Emperor Heraclius recovered it a few years later, in AD 641 the Arabs, under general Amr ibn al-As during the Muslim conquest of Egypt, captured it decisively after a siege that lasted fourteen months. The city received no aid from Constantinople during that time; Heraclius was dead and the new Emperor Constantine the Third was barely twelve years old. Notwithstanding the losses that the city had sustained, Amr was able to write to the Caliph Omar, that he had taken a city containing 4,000 palaces, 4,000 baths, 12,000 dealers in fresh oil, 12,000 gardeners, 40,000 Jews who pay tribute, 400 theatres or places of amusement."

"Oh yes...I must confess I have visited many there," the Genoese sailor joked and raised his eyebrows.

"In AD 645 a Byzantine fleet recaptured the city, but it fell for good the following year. Thus ended a period of 975 years of the Greco-Roman control over the city. Nearly two centuries later, between the years AD 811 and AD 827, Alexandria came under the control of pirates of Andalusia but it very soon fell again to Arab hands. In the year AD 828, the alleged body of Mark the Evangelist was stolen by Venetian merchants, which led to the Basilica of Saint Mark and their depoistaram for the body. Years later, the city suffered many earthquakes. After a long decline, Alexandria emerged as a major metropolis again at the time *of the First Crusade for both Christians and Muslims and lived a flourishing period due to trade agreements with the Aragonese, Genoese,"*

"Told you...that's why I went so many times," the Genoese sailor interrupted boastfully in tone. Simon pointed at him, looked at Sarah and then pointed to himself. Sarah just shook her head at him.

"I am most interested in those aspects related to alchemy. Can you tell us more on that for I believe it is of great importance with my studies?" Gabirol asked.

"If you wish," the old man acknowledged. "The tradition of alchemy being developed here in Europe can be traced back to the transmission of Islamic alchemical traditions. Like it or not, that is a fact, especially so during the past century alone. If you do not believe that then please understand that the term 'alchemy' is used, without the need for any comment or explanation, in three twelfth-century Latin translations of astrological works, one of which can even be dated to the first half of this century, which shows the author assumes readers will already be aware of alchemy. There is also another manuscript of an anonymous book entitled 'Alchamia', which is concerned with practical experiments in organic chemistry taken from al-Rāzī and with recipes of a somewhat magical nature. The interesting thing about this book is that it is definitely based on Arabic originals, showing that Islamic alchemy was being welcomed into Western Europe, although this book had no spiritual message."

"I can see why the Church is so vehemently against such books and teachings then," Peter remarked.

"Sadly yes, for we would all do well to read and understand them as we would learn much," the old man replied. "Alchemical imagery can be found in many books now being produced including Chrétien de Troyes' curious French romance of Cligés that mixes the heroic exploits of Arthurian knights with contemporary political, diplomatic and military stories from Greece, Germany and England, to bolster a love story which is clearly designed as a 'corrective' to the popular, but adulterous, story of Tristan. I can tell you this book is still undergoing changes," the old man smiled. Gabirol was quick to notice this and made a note to ask him about his comment later.

"I read that a great many books, especially of Muslim origin, on alchemy were lost when they were destroyed in a fire in 1180 in the library at Saint Pierre in Beauvais. Is that true?" Gabirol asked.

"Yes a great many books were destroyed in that fire. A fire started deliberately no less. But to return to the book of Cligés, its alchemical imagery comes at the climax of the main narrative. It is the part where the heroine is about to suffer grievously, before her life is transformed in a secret marriage of true love. Chrétien de Troyes thought that the Christian imagery of resurrection and the alchemical imagery of rebirth could give his story an added dimension. The heroine, who was been obliged to feign death, is severely flayed, and nearly roasted alive, by the doctors of Salerno, this is the stage of dissolution of the mineral, or mortification for the person. She is then taken into a ready-made tomb, like Christ's, sealed and guarded, from which she will rise again, the vessel of transmutation is often referred to as a grave or tomb. After that, she and Cligés, her husband, are hidden in a safe place, so that they can enjoy a true marriage, in a tower which seems to have no entrance, this is the hermetically sealed athanor, which provides a constant heat and which, because of its shape, is often referred to in alchemy as the 'tower' in which Sol and Luna, the sun and moon, male and female principles, are held captive for the uniting of the contraries, which must precede the new creation."

"Ah, I think I know where this leads us...and why you explain this all to us now, for

the heroine's name is Fenice isn't it?" Gabirol interjected, looking pleased with himself for remembering her name.

"Yes indeed," the old man answered.

"And what is the significance of that then?" the Hospitaller asked, bemused.

"Her name is Fenice. She is the Phoenix, the mythical bird that is reborn in the fire, a symbol for the reborn Christ, the bird that in alchemical symbolism stands for the final red stage of resurrection and perfection. 'Tis why some alchemists offer a red rose, with all of its symbolic and esoteric connotations to represent this final stage," the old man explained. "In his previous romance, 'Erec et Enide', Chrétien dealt with moral questions of integrity, responsibility, love and marriage, by using the Arthurian characters, story-lines and imagery, that were actually based upon ancient Celtic myths, which are hugely popular at the moment, thanks to the encouragement of Henry the Second of England and his new Angevin (Plantagenet) empire, which dominates the western coasts of Europe. In Cligés, Chrétien was writing a story about similar themes; but this time he also used the new imagery and symbolism of alchemy as it had come in from returning Crusaders...mainly Templars!"

"I was given a book titled 'The Book of the Composition of Alchemy'. But I must confess, I do not understand it," Gabirol explained.

"Well, that book is, as far as I am aware, the first Latin alchemical translation from Arabic. Its full title being 'Liber de Compositione Alchymiae', otherwise known as The Testament of Morienus Romanus. It is perhaps the first book in Latin which combines the spiritual and the practical teaching of alchemy. There are plenty of difficulties with this text, not least the fact that there are two versions, a shortened, more primitive, version and a longer version which is a later revision. The shortened version lacks an introduction and a beginning. It is only interested in the alchemical teaching itself, the dialogue between the adept, Morienus, and the seeker, Khālid. It just wants the meat, without the pastry, as it were; it cuts out the preamble to get straight to the science. Its provenance can be proved and its claim validated as another book called 'The Six Principles' (De VI Rerum Principiis). This mentions an important book on alchemy composed by the great philosopher Morienus and even copies part of its introduction, thus demonstrating that the alchemical Testament of Morienus Romanus as being written earlier."

"But what is so important about such books?" Simon asked and looked at Sarah expecting a comment or look from her, but she nodded in agreement with his question.

"The introduction, in the longer version, explains that the book is being published because the Latin world is ignorant of what alchemy really is. No clear definition is given, but it is hinted that it has to do with the transformation of natures and their conversion to a better state, that it is based on the assumption of the underlying unity of all things, and that it works by the mingling of basic contraries. The introduction claims that this is a book of divinity, which harmonises the two testaments and shows forth the truth. Now this is where these details connect back to Paul, and the sword ultimately and why I explain it now, because the story begins with a brief chain of transmission of teaching from Hermes, known as Thoth to the ancient Egyptians, the God of knowledge and wisdom, through Adfar of Alexandria and Morienus Romanus, to Khālid ibn Yazīd, who, in this story, is King of Egypt. He seeks wisdom from the Christian hermit Morienus, who comes, performs the great work, and departs before he can be detained. Khālid sends his servant, Ghalib, to find him. This is where the shorter version starts, with a single sentence of introduction...I shall read it as I have a copy," the old man said and leant down and removed a hard leather covered book from the satchel beside his feet. Slowly he placed the book upon the table and opened it.

"You have a copy?" Gabirol asked.

"That I do," the old man answered as he turned to the first page. "Here it is. It reads as follows. 'In the name of the Lord, holy and compassionate: this is the story of how Khālid ibn Yazīd ibn Mu'āwiyya (Calid filium Iezid filii Macoim) came into possession of the spiritual riches handed down from Stephanos (Adfar) of Alexandria to Morienus, the aged recluse, as is written in the book of Ghalib, bondsman of Yazīd ibn Mu'āwiyya.' Now in both versions, Morienus is found, living a self-sacrificing life as a hermit near Jerusalem. He is brought back to Egypt and questioned by the king. The rest of the book is in the form of a dialogue between master and pupil. Morienus begins by emphasising the underlying unity of all things, and he talks of the four elements, of sulphur and mercury, of the many names for the one path etcetera and he ends with useful tips on particular techniques involving such things as eudica, a kind of glaze, blood, the green lion or green vitriol, red ochre. There is, in other words, plenty of experimental chemistry in this little book. Nevertheless, there is a constant emphasis on the parallels between chemical and human development. There must be coition, pregnancy, birth and growth: the creation that they are engaged in must be organic generation, not mechanical construction. Some of the statements could refer to both chemical and personal states, such as that there is no growth without purification, putrefaction and a change of appearance. Some are deliberately arcane: there must be a double composition but the second composition is not the work of the hand. It is a mingling, in the correct proportions, of hot and cold, fire and water, wet and dry, earth and air. Cleansing the 'earth' or 'body' of darkness, whitening it, and infusing it with spirit or fire could refer to a personal purification and illumination, as well as a chemical one. As Morienus warns Khālid early on: 'No one will be able to perform or accomplish this thing, which you have so long sought, or attain it by means of any knowledge, unless it be through affection and gentle humility, a perfect and true love.' Then the dialogue turns to matters concerning the philosopher's stone, the spiritual dimension of alchemy seems to become more evident. The stone is given several enigmatic descriptions. It is delicate to touch but: 'there is more mildness in its touch than in its substance. In mass it is very weighty, but of a sweet taste, and its proper nature is aerial.' Its odour is at first very foul, that of death and decomposition, but later very fine. There should be no financial expense: it cannot be bought. On this point, Zosimos said: 'I enjoin you to spend nothing for this operation, particularly for the Golden Work'. Khālid presses Morienus to tell him where he can find it: 'King Khālid said: "Tell me where the sources of this thing are, whence it may be gathered as there is need of it." But Morienus fell silent and, casting his gaze downward, reflected deeply for some time. Then he raised his head and spoke: "Truly, this matter is that created by God, which is firmly captive within you yourself, inseparable from you, wherever you be; any creature of God deprived of it will die." No -one created by God can be without it. The secret is partially revealed: look within'. This revelation comes at about the mid-point of the dialogue. Having admitted so much, the teacher clarifies his statement: 'For this matter comes from you, you are yourself its source, where it is found, and whence it is taken; and when you see this, your zeal for it will increase. Consider this and you will find that it is true.' The philosopher's stone, like the spirit of humanity, is found within the soul. Khālid's own self is the mine, from which to extract that mineral. It does seem that this early Latin work is in the usual tradition of alchemy, working towards both a spiritual and a mineral transmutation. It ends with a statement that: 'The whole key to accomplishment of this operation is in the fire, with which the minerals are prepared and the bad spirits held back, and with which the spirit and body are joined. Fire is the true test of this entire matter.' There would be little possibility *of chemical change without a fiery furnace to provide the necessary heat; similarly, there would be few personal transformations without what may be symbolised as the purging and creative fires of the spiritual forge. The book ends, as might be expected of a religious work: 'Here ends the book of Morienus. Thanks be to God. Amen.' And this is where we come to the other great alchemical work...the Emerald Tablets. Its translation into Latin can definitely be assigned as the most famous of all Hermetic works, the Emerald Table or Tabula Smaragdina. It is found in a manuscript, from St Germain-des-Prés in Paris, in which it forms the end of the 'Book of the Secrets of Nature' (Liber de Secretis Naturae), attributed to Apollonius of Tyana. This Latin translation, accomplished (in Spain) by Hugo Sanctallensis, is very close to an Arabic version, although Hugo may have been translating, at least in part, from a Hebrew version of it. To give a date to Hugo's work, it is known that he did most of his work under the patronage of Michaelis Tirassonis, Bishop of Tarazona from 1119 to 1151."*

"I also know of this...my Lord how mightily strange that of all the places I could have stayed, I should find myself here," Gabirol commented and looked surprised for the first time as if some great revelation had just registered in his mind.

"The Emerald Table has been translated twice so far, once by Plato Tibertinus, responsible for 'The Book of Hermes on Alchemy' (Liber Hermetis de Alchimia), which also contains the Emerald Table. The narrator in this case is given as Galen (Galienus); but that is probably owing to confusion caused by the Arabic name for Apollonius, Balīnūs. All versions are equally cryptic, and all are no doubt susceptible of multiple interpretations."

"So this Emerald Tablet stuff...is it a religious book then?" Peter asked as both the Templar and Hospitaller nodded their heads.

"We both know of this Emerald Tablet," the Templar remarked.

"Yes...and no," the old man answered. "The original table was supposed to have been a tablet of green stone, not necessarily emerald, inscribed in Phoenician characters, which had either been discovered in Hermes's tomb by Alexander the Great, or had been taken from between the hands of the dead Hermes in a cave near Hebron. In the preamble to its appearance at the end of the 'Book of the Secrets of Nature', the reader is not promised a certain technique with which to master chemistry; he is promised the whole of philosophy. Then the table begins enigmatically: 'Things above come from below; things below come from above.' The correspondence between what is above and what is below underlies much Hermetic science. It can be interpreted astrologically, as the heavens figuring what is to happen on earth; metaphysically, as the correspondence between the universe and humanity; philosophically, as the relation between agent and patient; psychologically, as that between mind and body, and so on. I can tell you that it is but one of the reasons behind the construction and setting of all the recent cathedrals and churches across Europe where they are, as many reflect star constellations, especially Virgo."

"Sounds to me very similar to the biblical words 'As above, so below," Simon remarked.

"It is...and there are many more similar such as 'Everything portentous comes from one source, just as all things have their origin in one and the same principle'. And 'Everything proceeds from the One. There is a unity behind the multiplicity, which is the unity of being.' And 'Its father is the sun and its mother the moon.' The sun and the moon are alchemical symbols for gold and silver, or for sulphur and mercury; but more importantly, they symbolise the universal polarity of masculine and feminine, active and passive, fire and water. On a religious plane, they stand for the active spirit of morality and illumination, the Holy Spirit, and the passive state of unity and being God. These are the 'father and mother' of the magistery, that is, the mastery of the arts necessary for regeneration. Humans must be *filled with both before they can be transformed. 'The wind carries it in itself; it is softened by the earth.' If the spirit and the soul, fire and water, sun and moon, play an essential part in the 'great work', the mind and the body, figured by air and earth, the other two of the four elements and the four parts of the person, are not to be forgotten. We only know about our possibilities for improvement by using our brains; similarly we need the body to look after, nourish and nurse us. Indeed, the other version of the table in 'The Book of Hermes on Alchemy' says: 'Earth is the nurse thereof.' The next few lines are very corrupt in Hugo's version. The corresponding lines in 'The Book of Hermes on Alchemy' are: 'It is the father of all works of wonder throughout the whole world. The power thereof is perfect. If it be cast on to the earth, it will separate the element of earth from that of fire, The Gross.' This is a reference to the work of putrefaction and purification, the death of the body, the gross, to release the spirit, the subtle, the renunciation of material things to become aware of the spiritual. 'It mounts from the earth to the heaven. From heaven, it will flow back down to earth, because it contains the strength and power of what is above and what is below. By the same principle, all darkness is lit up.' The separation of gross matter, or body, and volatile matter, or spirit, is only a preliminary to the integration of the two in the perfected creation, or the divinised person. The spirit is embodied and the body is spiritualised in the creation of a new, spiritual person, one who could be said to incarnate the spirit of God. This is the illumination of the light of God within. The table ends with three statements. Firstly, 'it' is infused in every part of creation, is this a reference to the Agent Intelligence, the world-soul, the philosopher's stone, or all of them at once? Secondly, the microcosm, humanity, mirrors the macrocosm, the universe. Thirdly, all this is what Hermes calls his triple science or his three fold wisdom. Hermes combined the jobs of at least three gods, and was always called Trismegistus, thrice greatest. Sometimes in the Islamic alchemical tradition, there were three separate figures all called Hermes. Early Latin alchemy, like its Islamic progenitor, taught an experimental method, potentially applicable to metals and to men. It based its philosophy on a more or less pantheist view of the unity of the world. Most importantly, it believed in the indwelling of the philosopher's stone, the spirit of God within every individual, making it possible for him, after the right training, discipline and purification, to be united with God, to be reborn as a new spiritual man, to become like gold, embodied light. The origins of Western alchemy can be traced back to Hellenistic Egypt, in particular to the city of Alexandria. One of the most important characters in the mythology of alchemy is Hermes Trismegistus, Hermes the Thrice-Great. The name of this figure is derived from the Egyptian god of wisdom, Thoth, and his Greek counterpart, Hermes. The Hermetica, which is said to be written by Hermes Trismegistus, is generally regarded as the basis of Western alchemical philosophy and practice. In addition, Hermes Trismegistus is also believed to be the author of the Emerald Tablet. The Emerald Tablet is said to be a tablet of emerald or green stone inscribed with the secrets of the universe. The source of the original Emerald Tablet is unclear, hence it is surrounded by legends. The most common legend claims that the tablet was found in a caved tomb under the statue of Hermes in Tyana, clutched in the hands of the corpse of Hermes Trismegistus himself. Another legend suggests that it was the third son of Adam and Eve, Seth, who originally wrote it. Others believed that the tablet was once held within the Ark of the Covenant. Some even claim that the original source of the Emerald Tablet is none other than the fabled city of Atlantis."[55]*

"Atlantis...now I know this to be just a tale for Atlantis is indeed myth," the wealthy tailor retorted and shook his head disapprovingly.

"As I have said before...all myth is based upon fact the further back you trace it. But before you are so quick to make a judgement, let me continue and when you have heard all of the facts, then by all means make an 'informed' decision. Please," the old man asked.

The wealthy tailor hesitated and was about to speak when he caught the eyes of both the Templar and Hospitaller looking at him.

"Fine...I shall listen and reserve my final judgement...," he said awkwardly and his face flushed a bright red with embarrassment as everyone looked at him.

"I want to know about Alisha and Paul's house...was it big, small, horrid or lavish?" Sarah asked enthusiastically.

"Their home. Hmmm, let me detail that for you, for although it was theirs, they obviously had to share it with their somewhat now rather more extended family.

Port of Alexandria, Egypt, 1179

As Tenno steered Adrastos pulling the caravan through the wide eastern gate into the city, Paul marvelled at Alexandria's wide streets, copious use of marble, beautiful and intricate pillars, water cisterns, palaces, luxurious temples and its two harbours. He could see all around him very visible antiquities and authentic monuments from its ancient inhabitants, impressive heritage of royalty and power, and its show of former domination over other countries, its greatness, and its glorious superiority. It was ancient history alive. People were everywhere. At the main entrance gate through the city wall, Turansha spoke with the gate commander, pointed at Paul and Tenno sat in the driver's seat of the caravan and Theodoric on Paul's spare horse, Thomas and his men formed up behind. After a few brief moments, Turansha waved them to follow. After passing through the first gate, Turansha gave a quick wave and headed toward his own accommodation. Theodoric led the way riding slightly ahead as they travelled along the 'Canopic Way'. It was the principal thoroughfare of the city, running east and west through its centre. Ptolemaic and Roman monuments stood nearby. The road was intersected at its western end by the Street of the Soma, along which was reputed to be the legendary site of Alexander's tomb. Close to this intersection was the Mouseion (museum), an academy of arts and sciences, which once included the great Library of Alexandria. Paul remembered all that his father had told him about the academy. Somewhere in his trunk were letters of introduction from his father to members of the academy. He felt exhilarated at the prospect of learning and he could not hide the smile on his face. At the seaward end of the Street of the Soma were two obelisks known as Cleopatra's Needles toward the western end of the city, but before they reached them, Theodoric led them off the main thoroughfare toward several detached buildings each surrounded by their own walled gardens. Just visible in the distance was part of the inner city walls and beyond, the lake of Mareotis that shimmered in the brilliant sun. A canal seemed to snake its way past the city walls and then straightened as it headed toward the River Nile. Tenno steered Adrastos pulling the caravan up at the entrance. Theodoric smiled and motioned his head toward the large building that had a very pale pinkish whitewash covering on its walls. Paul stood down just as

Alisha appeared beside him, her face beaming with joy and a glow of happiness he had not seen in ages as she cradled Arri and took in the sights of the area. Paul could almost feel the history of this place in all its evidence and splendour. His mind raced wondering what their home would be like inside. It certainly looked too big to be theirs so perhaps they shared it, he thought.

✳   3 – 29

"Well, here it is. Your very own Fandaq," Theodoric said outstretching his hands toward the tall three storey high building before them set back from the road, several palm trees lining the entranceway.

"What is a Fandaq?" Paul asked, bemused, as he looked up at the building.

"'Tis like a…a hostel almost. Plenty of rooms, plenty of storage and places for your animals too. Your fathers used to rent it out to wealthy merchants, but I am pleased to see it has been vacated in time for our arrival as they obviously planned. I only hope they have not left it too messy for us," Theodoric replied and dismounted as Thomas pulled up alongside with Percival.

"My Lord…'tis truly a grand abode. I am glad for it means, if you are in agreement of course, that we should never get too much under your feet. Your father has done well," Thomas explained as he looked upon the big house.

Tenno applied the caravan's main brake as Alisha just looked on bemused and utterly surprised convinced there must be some mistake. 'Theodoric must have the wrong place,' she thought. Theodoric could see the look upon her face.

"Alisha, last time I was here was to hand the very deeds over to your father…so please…rest assured this is your new home. So come," he said and beckoned her to follow him.

৯৩ ৫৪

Theodoric unhinged the ornate securing latch and pushed the two large heavy wooden doors open and stepped inside closely followed by Paul and Alisha carrying Arri. Thomas and Percival stood behind them with Ishmael towering behind them. As Theodoric stepped forwards, his feet echoed on the beautiful pink coloured marble floor, a large curved stairway directly ahead of them that split into two going left and right greeted them. Columns spaced around what looked like an inner courtyard sparkled from the sunlight that shone down through a large opening above that was part covered by ornate wooden supports and coverings that could be pulled across for cover in the winter months. Several doors led to other rooms on the ground floor.

"All the downstairs rooms are for storage, food, books…lots of books, but your living accommodation is all on the upper floors. I would suggest you take the south facing main room overlooking the lake as it remains the coolest during the summer," Theodoric explained as he stepped further inside and aside.

Paul placed his arm around Alisha as they walked in both utterly amazed.

"I think I am just beginning to realise why my father suggested this as a good place to come and live," Paul exclaimed, feeling emotional.

"It has been a very long time since I was last here. You know, your fathers have

447

another just like this in Cairo, should you ever wish to move," Theodoric stated as Alisha stepped forwards slowly.

Percival and Thomas followed Paul into the inner entrance area, more of a courtyard it felt. Alisha walked over to the main stairway and looked up and around as sun beams shone down making Arri fidget briefly as he was dazzled. Alisha let out a gasp as her eyes met Paul's. He suddenly felt overwhelmed with a thousand emotions as everything that had happened during their journey registered. Tears welled in his eyes and he could not speak as he fought to control his feelings. He felt embarrassed but also filled with immense pride for his father. Alisha seeing the emotion on his face quickly walked toward him and grabbed his hand. A tear fell from his eye and she quickly wiped it away and laughed at him.

"Oh my dearest wonderful man...I love you, you kind and gentle soul, I love you," she said softly, leaned up and kissed him on the lips tenderly and then laughed again.

Paul just looked at her, the happiness in her face and little Arri in her arms. He found he could not speak.

"Well this is a right royal little palace you have here. We shall try not to destroy it," Thomas joked and patted Paul on the back as he stood beside him.

"It has two separate large baths, its own library, a chapel and a Muslim prayer room, so you can cater for all and any visitors," Theodoric explained as Alisha hugged Paul.

Ishmael came in and looked around almost as if in awe, his two swords now affixed to his back in a makeshift double shoulder mounted scabbard. He reminded Theodoric of images he had seen of Hercules. Tenno appeared carrying Abi in his arms as she rested asleep against his chest. He looked around, saw Theodoric and simply nodded. They both knew they had achieved their goal. They had gotten Alisha, Paul and Arri to Alexandria. Perhaps now, now Alisha and Paul could start to relax and enjoy their lives. Tenno looked down at Abi then back at Theodoric and the Sufi mystic as he walked in and stood beside them. The Sufi looked at Abi, checked her wrist for her pulse, then nodded at Tenno and smiled at him. Tenno closed his eyes and took a deep breath and then sighed with relief.

Within minutes, Theodoric ushered them up the stairs where they found a note from the previous tenants. They had left a lot of eggs and reeds of sugar cane, had cleaned the property and even made up several of the beds with the linen that had originally been stored there. Theodoric checked through the inventory and signatures of the property agent who had acted on behalf of Philip and Firgany. Thomas checked over the details with him and noted that Theodoric himself was listed as part owner with them. When he tapped the area with his finger quizzically, Theodoric shook his head and whispered no putting his finger to his lips asking he remain quiet on that matter. Thomas nodded in acknowledgement understanding him.

"You are a good man Theo...a good man," Thomas remarked quietly.

"That is gracious of you, Thomas, but I fear I have a great deal to make up for," Theodoric replied and sighed and then looked across the upper landing at Alisha and Paul as they checked in on one of the rooms. "An awful lot!"

ℬℭ

Paul pushed the ornately decorated wooden door open. He had been drawn to it by the large Celtic tree image carved upon it. He sensed that this room had been used by his father. As it swung open, Alisha stepped in carrying Arri. She kissed his forehead as she entered to keep him calm and moved into the middle of the room. Paul stood behind her and took in the room's simple beauty. The walls were plastered and whitewashed, the ceiling a light brown of natural wood and beams. A large window opened to the south overlooking a wall with a field beyond and the lake. Another window was situated on the west wall at an angle. It looked out across the western sector of the city. Trees gently blew in the breeze outside with a soft rustle. Both noted a baby's crib set next to the main bed. Alisha and Paul looked at each other. Their fathers had clearly sent word ahead that a baby would be arriving. The master bed was wide and covered in sheets and rolled down blankets. It had no posts and just a large headboard with a recessed shelf above it. The floor was tiled and felt cool. Alisha moved over to the main window and felt the curtains that had been tied back. She smiled and looked back at Paul.

"We are truly blessed...this is our room," she said clearly emotional. "Our room in our home."

Port of La Rochelle, France, Melissae Inn, spring 1191.

"I wish to know all about Alexandria for it sounds wonderful, wonderful," Ayleth said and clasped her hands together. "Please..."

"What more can I tell you of Alexandria? Perhaps our Genoese friend could tell us more?" the old man said and gestured toward the Genoese sailor.

"Hey, we sailed in, unloaded goods and then loaded up with more and returned. Sometimes we would stay a day extra and visit the fun places," the Genoese sailor replied and winked at Ayleth. She shot him a look of disapproval.

"Well, as Alisha, Paul and anyone else who would listen soon discovered, Theodoric spoke enthusiastically about the city, especially its history regarding Mark Antony, Cleopatra, Julius Caesar and the woman mathematician Hypatia, who all, for part of their lives at least, contributed to Alexandria's development to the backdrop of magnificent palaces, temples and public edifices decorated with luxuries from Europe, Africa and the East. Islam's conquest profoundly impacted Alexandria and port cities elsewhere in the Mediterranean. Within eighty years of the death of the Prophet Muhammad, Islam extended from western Turkistan to the Atlantic Ocean. Christianity, which had embraced the entire Mediterranean coast, was confined to its northern shores. Three-quarters of the coastlands of this sea, once the focal point of Roman culture for the whole of Europe, now belonged to Islam. The fact that Alexandria, so long Egypt's principal city, was vulnerable to attack by the Byzantine fleet, however, persuaded the reigning caliph 'Umar ibn al-Khattab, to order his generals to relocate to a more protected position. Misr al-Fustat, located some 140 miles to the south, became the seat of power. Shielded by a vast and unforgiving desert and served by the Nile, it developed into Egypt's new trading centre. Alexandria could only watch as the focus of power turned from the Mediterranean shore to the interior. The result was staggering.

In just a few hundred years Fustat and later its successor city, Cairo, a few miles away, became one of the wealthiest cities in the world. Trade was reoriented, primarily toward Asia, with commodities passing through harbours on the Red Sea and the Indian Ocean. Under the Fatimid Dynasty (969–1171), Fustat's markets burst with goods from Jiddah and the Hijaz, Sana'a, Aden and Muscat, and India and China. These included spices, pearls, precious stones, silk, porcelain, teak, linen, perfumes and paper, the latter unknown in Europe at that time. But in spite of the long shadow cast by Fustat and then Cairo, Alexandria did not become a backwater. The city continued to capitalise on her prime location, maintaining herself as an important Mediterranean port and providing a highly prosperous link between East and West and among Muslims, Christians and Jews for without the city of Alexandria, Cairo with the whole of Egypt could not survive. Alexandria was a lively melting pot of cultures where different creeds and religions mixed in the name of commerce. The twin harbours that the Pharos marked ensured that it remained an important, if vulnerable, player in what was at times a politically volatile climate.

"But in no way did Muslim rule inhibit commerce with Christian merchants. Indeed, trade was an important and valued activity in Muslim lands. Mecca was a trading city and the Prophet Muhammad had himself engaged in trade there in his early life. Across the Mediterranean, particularly in Italy, city-states lined up their galleys, keen to exploit Alexandria's favourable location and diverse goods. Not even Europe's religious wars could stop the pursuit of profit. Merchants from such cities as Pisa, Genoa, Marseille and Barcelona, in addition to ports in the Levant, docked in Alexandria, bringing an exotic array of goods. In Alexandria's harbours, a startling array of commodities are sold from bright silks from Spain and Sicily; pungent spices such as pepper, ginger, cinnamon and cloves from the East; slaves from southern Caucasus; Mediterranean coral, olive oil, timber, aromatics, perfumes and gums; and metals including iron, copper, lead and tin. Great quantities of local Egyptian produce, lemons, oranges, sugar, dates, capers and raisins would also have been stacked on the docks to be loaded and shipped to European markets. Flax is piled there for export, too. Such was the extent of trade that special rest houses called funduqs or Fandaqs were established to accommodate visiting traders and encourage business. While Muslim traders were free to find accommodation wherever they pleased in Alexandria, foreigners were forced to take rooms in funduqs designated for their country or city. Built around a central courtyard with storerooms and living quarters, these buildings or compounds provided secure locations in which to transact business and store merchandise. Some trading states are afforded privileges beyond their funduq; the Venetians, for example, have a church, bathhouse and bakery in Alexandria and are allowed to import cheese, among other goods, tax free. Theodoric counted no less than 28 European nations or city-states with formal representation in Alexandria, including non-Mediterranean countries such as Denmark, Ireland, Norway, Scotland and England, not to mention representatives from the East, so even Tenno no longer looked out of place. It is why Philip and Firgany...and Theodoric...had purchased an entire Fandaq complete with its own blacksmiths, dye factory and stables. Produce unknown to Egypt arrives by sea to Alexandria from all regions of the world and is always in abundance.... Also, the people of the Orient and those of the Occident meet continuously in this city, which is like the great market of the two worlds. Nevertheless, suspicion of foreign merchants still remains. The Crusades have devastated inter-religious relations. On more than one occasion, the Pope himself had imposed a total embargo on trade with Muslims. As a result, foreign visitors to the city were kept under close observation. Arriving non-Muslims were forbidden to enter the western harbour, and some markets in the city were restricted to merchants of a specific nationality or ethnic origin. One event during the Crusades was Reynald de Chatillon's attempt to attack Mecca from the Red Sea in 1183, which had particular repercussions in Alexandria and consequently why Saladin banned non-Muslim traders from entering Egypt's interior in an attempt not only to protect the holy sites in the Levant and Arabia, but also to safeguard Egypt's valuable commercial links with the East. The result was a concentration of European traders within Alexandria's walls. Alexandria was also an important harbour from which to visit the region's holy sites, whether in Egypt, Mecca or Jerusalem. Even pilgrims from as far away as Ireland.

"Christian pilgrims would visit several well-known churches and monasteries in and around Alexandria, as well as locations in the Nile Valley where Jesus and his family were believed to have sought refuge during their stay in Egypt. Alexandria's position was ideal as a transit point for travellers en route to Mecca and Madinah."

"Can always rely on Reynald to ruin everything...what did he do exactly?" the farrier asked.

"I shall come to that shortly."

"I know textiles form a large part of the industry in Alexandria as it was well positioned to take advantage of the dyes that passed through the town. Is that why Philip and Firgany bought the home there?" Gabirol asked.

"Yes, and do not forget that it was also Theodoric who had helped in that purchase. One of their new neighbours was a soap merchant as well as glass-worker and another was a Jewish jeweller to the north. Opposite their house was a Muslim swordsmith. A dye merchant lived a little further down the road toward the Green Gate or Crescent Gate as it was once known but also as the Moon Gate of the city. You see, Alexandria was not as sharply divided with delineated quarters defined by the religions of their inhabitants, like in Jerusalem, but consisted rather of a mix of peoples living throughout the town. The Templars owned a great many qas ʿāb, that is sugar cane farms, and they actively exported out through Alexandria. The main road runs from the Rosetta Gate at the east end of Alexandria to the Green Gate at the west end and the western harbour which most Muslims used. Many Venetians, Genoese, and Catalans had similar houses...Fandiqs...like Alisha and Paul's with large central spaces and courtyards with a cloister-like structure. Theodoric took Paul and Percival to an area in the southwestern extremity of the ancient city to the Kawm al-Shuqāfah burial grounds, with their remarkable Hadrianic catacombs dating from the second century AD. Nearby, on the site of the ancient fort of Rhakotis, is one of the few Classical monuments still standing, the 88-foot high marble column known as Pompey's Pillar but actually dedicated to Diocletian soon after AD 297. Paul spent many hours in the Catacombs of Kon el Shoqafa. If you look through his folder of drawings, you will see one he did. It cost him a lot to hire some helpers to light the tomb," the old man explained and laughed to himself. "Alisha was not best pleased I can tell you. Not only because of the cost, but also the fact that it was a hundred feet underground and not stable, but Paul loved the sense of adventure it gave him."

Fig. 41:

"I would have thought after his experience beneath Jerusalem he would have kept out of such places," Ayleth remarked.

"Not at all, if anything it inspired him more...and Paul learnt from Theodoric that, deep in the Kom el Shoqafa catacombs, the intellectual blend of those times is still obvious. The catacombs are not the only ones that were constructed in ancient Alexandria. Such structures were part of a Necropolis or 'city of the dead' that was built according to Egyptian tradition on the western edge of the town. Kom el Shoqafa was started as a tomb for a single, wealthy family, but was expanded into a larger burial site for unknown reasons. The name of the site, Kom el Shoqafa, means 'Mound of Shards'. The name comes from heaps of broken pottery in the area. Archaeologists believe that these were left in ancient times by relatives who would visit the tomb bringing food and drink with them. The visitors, not wanting to bring vessels that had been used at a gravesite back to their homes, would shatter them and leave them behind in piles. The main tomb at the middle level is covered with the sculpture and art that makes this catacomb unique. For example, in the room behind the temple pronaos are statues of a man and woman, perhaps representing the original occupants of the tomb.

Both of the statues' bodies have been carved into the stiff hieratic poses found in ancient Egyptian art. The man's head, however, has been chiselled into the lifelike style favoured by the Greeks. In the same way the woman's head has been carved with a Roman hairstyle. On either side of the doorway of the temple's facade there are two serpents carved in relief. These are meant to guard the tomb. They represent a Greek Agathodaimon, which is a good spirit. The Greek serpents are wearing traditional Egyptian double crowns, however, and in their coils they carry both a kerkeion, a winged staff, which is a Roman insignia and a Greek thyrus, a staff topped by a pinecone. Above the serpents' heads are Greek shields carrying the image of the legendary Greek monster Medusa, whose use here is meant to ward off unfriendly intruders. It is this mix of art and culture, Egyptian, Greek and Roman that is not found in any other catacomb in the ancient world that makes Kom el Shoqafa special. From the rotunda it is possible to enter a separate set of tombs through a hole in the wall. This section, known as the Hall of Caracalla, contains the bones of horses and men. The name comes from an incident in AD 215 when the Emperor Caracalla massacred a group of young Christians. While we do know that such a massacre did occur, there is no actual evidence that the remains in the hall are related to that incident. Why the men and horses are buried together in the hall continues to be a mystery. The tomb has many sarcophagi for the placement of mummies in the Egyptian tradition, but also numerous niches meant to hold the remains of those who chose to be cremated in the Greek and Roman style. As one writer put it, the catacomb is visible evidence of an age when three cultures, three arts, and three religions were superimposed upon Egyptian soil." [56]

"So as Philip and Firgany said all along, Alexandria was indeed a great cosmopolitan city in which to live," Simon stated simply.

"Yes, I guess I could have just said that from the start," the old man replied and shrugged his shoulders.

"No, I am glad you tell us these facts for I thirst for such knowledge," Gabirol interjected.

"So is that it? They get to Alexandria and live happily ever after?" Simon asked.

Sarah leant over and slapped his arm.

"Idiot...of course not or how else would the sword be here," she exclaimed, annoyed at his blunt remark.

"So what did they do then?" Simon shot back defensively and rubbed his arm.

"Took a bath first...a very long bath. They both discovered that Arri loved the water. Turansha sent one of his men over to liaise with Paul and Thomas and true to his word arranged a regular supply of food and other assorted goods for Thomas and his men's upkeep. In return Thomas and his men, including Percival, actively participated in training exercises with Turansha's men and carried out escort duties along the main roads. It kept them busy and focused...Tenno spent the first weeks nursing Abi morning, noon and night whilst Paul familiarised himself with the city. I think the only upset during those first few weeks was the loss of Clip clop as Arri would not settle without it. The Sufi mystic found it thankfully so disaster averted," the old man explained calmly.

"Tenno sounds like a real softy doesn't he?" Sarah commented.

"He was that indeed," the old man replied and looked at her. "But he was a man of adventure with an insatiable thirst for knowledge. When Abi slept, he kept himself busy instructing Paul in martial arts...that is, how to fight with all manner of weapons, and how to fight using just your body and an opponent's weight against themselves. Ha, Paul I am afraid to say walked away from many a session with Tenno with more than a few aches and pains... and bruises...much to the anger of Alisha. But Paul had vowed he would never let himself nor Arri and Alisha go through what they had on their journey...and eventually Alisha even joined in and started to learn the art," the old man explained and paused for a few moments. "Theodoric spent much of his time checking his astrological charts and parchments with the Sufi mystic...and there was much merriment when news came through that Gerard had not been made the Grand Master of the Templars."

"How did they find that out?" Ayleth asked.

"They received a letter from Stewart. Was just a simple one page letter, but you know, it meant the world to Paul, for despite everything, he still loved his brother."

"What did it say?" Sarah asked impatiently.

"That Gerard had not been voted in as the Grand Master but Arnold de Tarroja had indeed been sworn in, that he wished Alisha and Paul a long and happy future together and to not forget him."

"But no apology!" Peter remarked.

"No apology was expected or required in Paul's eyes. The letter spoke for itself as far as he was concerned."

"What about Sister Lucy then. Is she out of the story now?" Ayleth asked.

"She had promised Princess Stephanie she would stay as her midwife and remain a while until after her baby was born and that is what she did. But no, it was not the end of her part in this tale, for remember I said it was down to Princess Stephanie that this sword is here with us this day?"

"What about Ishmael? What did he do then?" Gabirol asked politely.

"He taught Paul those subtle little things about weapons so often overlooked. Together with Tenno, and using the blacksmith's furnace beside the house, they made a joint gift for Paul...a compound composite bow complete with a shaft that fired high velocity darts called nawak or majra arrows just like Tenno's. Paul went to bed on more than one occasion with sore fingers and aching arms as he tried to master it. Alisha did argue with him several times that he should take care of his fingers for they were essential for his trade as a potential map maker. Tenno gave him one of his jade wrist protectors. Paul learnt fast how swords and bows etcetera were made and even how weather affected them, such as the strings on bows, how when in transit you must unstring them or risk losing the tension in both the string and bow itself. How dampness and rain can cause swords to stick within their scabbards...the little tricks that make a difference."

"Ha, yes I can vouch for that aspect...but I learnt the hard way. 'Tis why my leg still carries a great scar almost its entire length," the Templar commented and rubbed his left leg. Miriam looked at him, concerned. "I was ambushed in the hills near the Sea of Galilee, it was misty, and my sword stuck...but it is amazing how hard you can hit someone with a sheathed sword," he smiled.

"Both Tenno and Theodoric noticed how Percival watched and learnt alongside Paul a little suspicious as to why, but they put it down to his enthusiasm. Plus as any good professional soldier will admit, you never stop learning."

"Why did Tenno give him a jade wrist protector?" Simon asked.

"Simon...you have never fired a bow before have you?" the Hospitaller asked.

"No!" he replied and shrugged his shoulders.

"Sometimes when you shoot an arrow, the string rubs down your forearm...and it can hurt as well as cause abrasions. A wrist protector stops that...and a jade one lets the string slip smoothly over," the old man explained. "Tenno also taught Paul much about blacksmith skills. They made friends with the blacksmith who lived two houses further along. He had learnt his skills in Aleppo. He showed why many Muslim swords are characterised with a beautiful pattern called Firind, what we call watering marks, and that their swords were made from a more flexible Asiatic blade of Fuladh steel from soft female iron treated and forged in various ways not like the pattern-welded, hard but brittle male iron of European made swords. But he was at a loss to explain the construction of Paul's sword."

"And what did Alisha do then...just look after Arri?" Sarah asked.

"No, she cooked, cleaned, of course looked after Arri and helped Tenno care for Abi as she slowly recovered. She also developed a love of music and poetry, and a powerful punch too. You know, she could throw Paul over her shoulders in one move...Tenno taught her well."

3 – 17

"Poetry? You mention the Sufi mystic naming him as just that...but does he not have a name?" Gabirol asked.

"A name...yes, yes he has a name," the old man replied. "His name is Attar of Nishapur... and also a great poet."

Chapter 42
Kratos, Staffs & Bees

It was early morning, the sun only just cresting on the horizon over Alexandria when Attar crawled beneath Alisha's and Paul's caravan. He started to rummage around beneath it trying to unhinge two secure bolts hidden from view. After a few minutes' struggling, a panel opened and several sealed tube containers fell out and upon Attar's chest along with a lot of dust and grit, some falling into his eyes. As he coughed and spat out the dirt, he blinked to clear his eyes.

"Attar!" a deep authoritative yet gentle voice said aloud.

Attar raised his head fast, the man's voice having startled him. He banged his forehead on the axle hard. Quickly he rubbed his head then looked to his side to see two large white booted feet, a long white cape reaching to the individual's ankles. The boots were a white, almost a pale cream leather type colour and well made. Attar knew exactly whose feet they were. Surprised, he slowly edged himself out shuffling on his back until he was clear of the caravan. He stood up and brushed himself down, his green clothes looking more a sandy colour covered in the dust. As he stood up straight, he looked at the tall white haired man stood before him who was smiling broadly, his hands resting upon his staff. The sun broke over the main house perimeter wall causing an almost halo like glow around his head.

"Kratos...," Attar said, bemused, and surprised to see him and shook his head.

"My dear friend, it has been a while," Kratos replied politely and part bowed at Attar.

"Why are you here?"

"To take those back to where they belong," Kratos replied and nodded at the tubes in Attar's hands. "Plus Abi..."

"Ah...these. I was hoping to copy them."

"You may still," Kratos smiled.

Suddenly Percival, Thomas and several of his men ran into the small conclave the caravan had been parked in as Adrastos and the other horses started to snort and neigh as the early hour disturbance alarmed them. Thomas looked at Attar then Kratos, his sword drawn and pointing toward him.

"'Tis okay Thomas. I know this man. He is here to help," Attar explained.

"How did you get in?" Thomas demanded to know.

"Put your sword away and I shall tell you," Kratos replied and winked at Attar, which made him laugh.

ဆဌ

Abi lay with her arms outstretched beside her. Her room was still darkened from the heavy curtains drawn across her window. Tenno was asleep sat in the chair beside her. A click on the door latch immediately awoke him. His eyes focused upon the door latch as it was raised slowly, and light began to seep into the room as the door opened slowly. Tenno swiftly pulled his sword up and edged it out ready to draw. The door opened fully to reveal the silhouette of Kratos. Tenno stood up fast. Kratos had to bend down in order to step silently into the room.

"Tenno...you have no need to fear me," Kratos said quietly and took a step forwards.

"I fear no man," Tenno shot back and unsheathed his sword and stepped forward to block Kratos. Kratos stood aside so the light from outside streaming into the main corridor from the open roof area shone upon him revealing his white hair and blue eyes. He looked down at Tenno. Tenno had never seen a man so large before. His eyes darted to the doorway as Attar and Thomas stepped into view. "Who are you?"

"Tenno...this is Kratos...whom I have spoken of many times," Abi said quietly, her voice dry. She coughed as she tried to sit herself up. She looked at Kratos as he smiled at her and stepped towards her. Tenno stepped aside, bemused. "I...I thought I would never see you again," she said emotionally.

Kratos knelt down beside her bed and with his left hand clasped her right hand whilst placing his staff beside Abi.

"My child...I came as soon as I could."

Thomas nodded at Tenno and his sword. Tenno immediately re-sheathed his sword as Kratos looked around at him.

"How do you know my name?" Tenno asked, his tone clipped.

"I know more about you than you can imagine," Kratos replied with a smile.

"I can imagine a lot," Tenno replied.

Abi let out a slight laugh.

"I can see why Abi trusts and admires you much," Kratos remarked and looked back at Abi.

"Aldin, he did not make it," Abi said, her tone changing to one of sadness.

"I know...I know," Kratos replied and moved his staff to rest upon Abi's legs and stomach. "Now we must sort you out properly."

Alisha and Paul appeared at the doorway still dressed in their night garments and gowns. Kratos turned his head slowly to look around at them. As his eyes met Alisha's, she gasped and held her hand to her mouth. Kratos smiled and stood up fully as Paul looked on bemused as Percival shrugged his shoulders. Ishmael appeared behind Paul looking in puzzled. Alisha saw the bee like necklace around Kratos's neck. Instinctively she grasped her bee pendant in her left hand. For several long moments Alisha stood and stared in silence at Kratos.

"You...you were the man who saved Taqi and I," Paul remarked and stepped forwards.

"Well this is most certainly a lovely reunion," Attar stated and looked at all in the room.

"Is Abi okay? What is happening here?" Theodoric said loudly as he gently pushed past Ishmael and moved to stand beside Paul. He froze like a statue as he looked up at Kratos. He looked utterly stunned.

Alisha placed her hand upon Theodoric's arm seeing the look of surprise and shock upon his face.

"Theo...'tis truly great to see you again, my friend," Kratos said and bowed politely at him.

Theodoric remained perfectly still just staring at him for several moments.

"Theo...are you okay?" Alisha asked.

Theodoric waved his hand from side to side and shook his head in silence. He blinked as he stared at Kratos. Kratos smiled and bowed his head again at him as all just looked on. Without a word, Theodoric turned around and walked out of the room clearly stunned at Kratos's appearance. Alisha looked at Kratos concerned for Theodoric.

"Do not worry for he will be fine. Probably a little shocked to see me again," Kratos explained, smiling. "And you...you my dear sister, we have much to talk about," he commented as he stepped closer to Alisha.

"Sister...that is impossible," Paul remarked with alarm in his voice.

Instantly Alisha recalled her shared dream with Abi when Kratos had said sister to her then.

"Nothing is impossible...when you know the truth. So come. The day is just beginning and there is much to do," Kratos replied, then looked back at Abi as she feigned a smile still in pain from her injuries. "We shall start by sorting you out."

Port of La Rochelle, France, Melissae Inn, spring 1191

"Sister. That's it...I am totally and without any doubt confused," Simon remarked shaking his head, perplexed.

"But Simon...that is not hard for you is it?" Sarah joked.

"How can she be Kratos's sister? That would mean Raja would be his mother too and far older than you have let us believe," Peter asked.

"He did not say sister in the manner we understand sister. Remember Paul's earliest dreams where he saw the tall man with the beautiful young woman?" the old man asked and looked around the table at them as they nodded in agreement except Ayleth. "Well, as Paul realised later at Kizkalesi, that woman was Alisha. The white haired man was also Kratos... and in that time, he was indeed her brother. As I explained before, souls are eternal and some souls always gravitate back toward each other. That is another reason why killing someone is like a stain upon your soul, for if the killing was deliberate with evil intent or wrong doing, that other soul could very well affect you in later lives...," the old man explained.

"Is that why they wear the same bee pendant necklace?" Ayleth asked.

The old man simply nodded in reply.

"You mentioned bees before. Will you tell us more that we may learn the mystery that surrounds the bees, for I know it features much within esoteric teachings?" Gabirol asked.

"It would be my pleasure," the old man answered.

"Do we have the time?" the Hospitaller asked and looked at his brother.

"I think so...in fact I am pretty sure already that we shall have more than enough time," the Templar answered and waved the unopened letter still in his possession.

"The choice will be yours," the old man smiled.

"The Templar who lost his head. What was his name again?" the Templar asked.

"'Twas Aldin Angelus, but called Elek Aldin mostly. Indeed much could be written about him alone but time does not allow that here," the old man answered.

"Why not?" the farrier asked.

"All I can say is that his tale is as complex and as vast as the one I now tell. But know this, he was actually eighty-four years old the day he submitted his life."

"What...eighty-four. No way!" Peter remarked.

"Peter, I have already explained the longevity of certain peoples. Elek was the same."

"But you said Abi and Kratos were the last of their kind," Gabirol exclaimed, puzzled.

"And so they were...but Elek was not of their kind," the old man replied and nodded.

"What...you mean there are other kinds?" Simon asked loudly.

"Yes, yes there are. There are five base types of mankind who inhabit this world," the old man replied.

"This world. Are there others?" the wealthy tailor asked.

"I can tell you that yes there are...many many more worlds."

"That is nonsense surely?" the farrier commented.

"Why for even our holy books tell us there are many worlds without number that the Lord has created...and many inhabitants thereon, but only the inhabitants of this world need concern you."

"Then why do these other people not come here and make themselves known?" the wealthy tailor argued.

"How do you know they have not already? What do you think the many strange beings that descend from the heavens are...and ask yourselves this...if you were looking down upon mankind with all its hatred, violence, greed and lustful ways...would you want to come and live amongst us, or would you wait until we were all spiritually awake and more peaceful?"

"If I was them, I would force mankind to behave," Ayleth remarked.

"Ayleth, that is exactly what some tried to do, a very long time ago. But that takes away our own individual right to free choice and free agency. That negates the whole plan of this world and how we live," the old man answered.

"That is what the Devil tries to do is it not?" Gabirol asked.

"The Devil as portrayed within the Bible, yes."

"So when will God return...or the other peoples whoever they are?" Sarah asked.

"What if I said that they have never actually left us...just keep a discreet distance for now?" the old man smiled in reply.

"So like Sarah said, when will they return openly then?" the wealthy tailor asked.

"When? When mankind again remembers the past, accepts the past and recovers the teachings of our forefathers. Then, and only then, and after we have sent a clear signal that we do indeed remember, only then will the messengers of God reveal themselves openly."

"How do we let them know we have remembered?" Ayleth asked.

"'Tis so simple really. So simple...and I shall reveal how by the close of this tale," the old man smiled.

"So getting back to this tale, how did that Sufi mystic Attar know to look beneath Paul's caravan and how come Kratos just turned up like that?" Gabirol asked.

"I want to know about his staff," Simon remarked.

"I bet you do!" Sarah shot back and laughed as she punched his arm playfully.

"I can explain some details about his staff, but I can also promise that you will not fully grasp what it is or how it works," the old man replied.

"Ah...so it is just like a woman then," the Genoese sailor remarked and laughed.

Sarah threw an empty plate at him. He ducked as it flew over his head. Simon smirked and pointed at the Genoese sailor.

"I am also interested to hear if Paul managed to gain access to what remained of the great library of Alexandria, before it was destroyed by Christians," Gabirol commented.

"Gabirol...'tis a great misunderstanding...the claim that Christians destroyed the library," the old man replied.

"Really? Pray tell you explain," Gabirol replied, puzzled.

"I shall as I explain Kratos and his conversations with Paul and Theodoric. And his later conversations with Philip when he arrived in Alexandria."

"When did he turn up then?" the wealthy tailor asked.

"Paul had sent written word to his father on several of the ships that sailed directly from Marseilles to Alexandria and back as soon as they had arrived safely. He also wrote that Theodoric was with them."

"Even though Philip believed him long dead?" Gabirol remarked and frowned.

"Yes...so you can imagine Philip's reaction when he learnt of this fact," the old man said and raised an eyebrow.

"No I can't, so please explain," Peter stated.

"I shall, so let me explain further."

Alexandria, Egypt, 1179

Alisha stepped closer toward Kratos and looked up into his crystal clear blue eyes with flecks of pale green and what looked like gold sparkles. He smiled down at her reassuringly as he towered over her. Tenno watched his every move. Abi reached out her hand for Tenno to take and pulled him nearer to her as Kratos knelt down. Only then was he able to look up slightly into Alisha's eyes. He took her hands and held them in his enormous hands. She looked like a small child compared with him. Paul looked on bemused but sensing the great exchange of emotion between the two of them. Alisha felt momentarily dizzy and Kratos steadied her just as Arri cried out a slight wail from his crib in the other room.

"I have him!" Theodoric was heard calling out.

Alisha felt a rush of feelings and emotions envelope her like someone wrapping a heavy blanket around her as Kratos looked more intently into her eyes.

"Do you remember me yet?" he asked quietly. Paul immediately recalled his dreams where he could clearly see Kratos looking at him and telling him to remember him. He stepped closer toward Alisha as Kratos looked at him. "And you too?"

"I do now," Paul heard himself blurt out.

Alisha shook her head no, a little confused.

"Only from dreams...I think," she answered as Theodoric appeared back at the door carrying Arri in his arms restless and wriggling both hungry and unsettled.

Kratos stood up, let go of Alisha's hands and stepped toward Theodoric. He looked down at him, winked and then looked at Arri, who cried and kicked out his legs and arms. Kratos smiled at him and leaned closer. Very slowly and gently he placed his right hand forefinger upon Arri's forehead and held it there for a few seconds. Arri stopped crying almost at once, blinked a few times and started to smile.

"I see you have not lost that little trick," Theodoric remarked quietly.

"Theo, you of all people know it is no trick," Kratos replied and looked back at Alisha and Paul. He clasped his necklace, which made Alisha clasp hers. "Please, you deal with Arri and I shall start the process with Abi," he remarked. Tenno stood closer to Abi and held her hand close to his side. "And you, my friend Tenno, you may assist if Abi is in agreement."

Tenno looked at Abi. She smiled and nodded yes at him. Tenno looked back at Kratos, raised a single questioning eyebrow then frowned but nodded okay.

₧ Ѻ

As Alisha fed Arri, Thomas and Percival helped Theodoric boil water for the main bath of the house. Theodoric was clearly perplexed at the arrival of Kratos and kept shaking his head and muttering to himself. Kratos placed several scented candles around the ornately decorated tiled bath. The walls were a pale orange colour, the bath and steps down into it sunk into the floor taking up most of the square room. The outer door to the room was open but the light coloured lace divider curtains hung loosely across it blowing in now and again in the breeze. Two small wicker-work chairs and a reclining single bed were set against the far wall. It was a tranquil place. Paul busied himself making everyone breakfast but was keen to speak with Kratos in person. No sooner had the bath been filled when Kratos entered the room with Tenno behind him carrying Abi. She was only wearing her night shawl. As Tenno gently placed her down on the reclined bed, he looked at her not sure what was expected of him next. Abi looked up at Kratos.

"Please...I wish for Tenno to help me and do this," she said softly.

"As you wish," Kratos replied quietly and looked at Tenno, who shook his head a little confused. "Here, Abi will show you what to do," he said and handed Tenno the staff.

As soon as Tenno held the staff, he felt a sudden pulse shoot through his arm instantly and then throughout his entire body. He swayed momentarily and Paul was concerned he would fall. Abi grabbed Tenno's arm pulling him straight.

"Please Tenno, just you," she whispered.

"What do I have to do?" he asked as he steadied himself.

"Abi will show you, if you are willing. But it is part ritual that will involve both of you giving and receiving of each other. Something I cannot do...but you can if you accept. But if you cannot nor wish too, that is fine but it will take longer to heal Abi," Kratos explained.

Tenno looked at Abi. She smiled and nodded at him.

"Whatever it takes, I shall willingly do it for you, Abi," Tenno answered then looked across at Paul just as Theodoric and Percival walked in holding two more large ceramic bowls of hot water.

"They will require total privacy...so I say we eat and discuss matters in hand," Kratos remarked and beckoned everyone else to leave. "And Abi...remember, the staff must stay within the water. We shall afford you both the privacy required."

Abi nodded in reply as Kratos ushered Paul towards Theodoric and Percival.

461

Once they had all left the room, Abi looked at Tenno.

"I owe you much for you have helped me in ways you cannot imagine. And you do not have to do what I ask next of you," she said softly as Tenno knelt beside her.

"Abi...whatever it is you ask of me, I freely give it...my life even," Tenno replied and held her hands to his chest.

⁂   2 – 10

"Fear not, my warrior friend...'tis not your life I shall take or need," she said and sat herself up. She paused as she looked at him intently. "Just your love."

"That, that, my warrior queen, I can most certainly give as you have it already. You had it the very first day I saw you," Tenno replied.

Abi smiled broadly, placed her hand on Tenno's face, reached up and kissed him. She held the kiss as she gently pressed her lips against his. Tenno gripped the staff in his left hand tighter as her tender kiss rippled sensations throughout his body. The sphere at the end of the staff began to glow a pale bluish green only diminishing as she broke away from the kiss. Tenno looked at her overwhelmed with emotions he found difficult to keep in check. She laughed softly.

෨ ෬

Having fed and changed Arri, Alisha carried him down the wide staircase. She stopped halfway and just took in the whole house, the lower floor looking more like a lavishly decorated cloister. She looked upward at the open roof. It would prove fun closing the covers in winter she thought. She took a deep breath as she looked around grateful and pleased to be there. She had expected a small house at best but this was far more than she could ever have dreamt. She heard laughter from Thomas and his men off in the distance. It was reassuring to know they were about. She wondered where the others had all gone. She had taken Arri from Theodoric to feed and left them all in Abi's room on the top floor but the room was now empty. Slowly she continued down the stairs feeling so proud of her new home but tinged with a little sadness as she thought of Firgany. He was and always would be her father in her mind and loved deeply within her heart.

As she walked past the main bathing room, she heard water lapping the sides of the bath. She went through the joining doorway, stepped inside the changing area cubicle and pulled the dividing curtain. Just as she did she stopped from pulling it across fully as she immediately saw Tenno and Abi in the large bath. Her eyes widened in surprise seeing both of them naked, just their top halves visible, Abi sat astride Tenno facing him and tenderly kissing him, her back toward Alisha. They were oblivious to her and Arri's presence. At first shocked, Alisha pulled the divider curtain back on its ringed rails slowly and as quietly as she could, but fascination got the better of her and she sneaked a peek through the curtain again. As she peered in, she sighed seeing the gentleness and tenderness between them as they kissed softly. It was the first time she had ever seen Tenno without his armour on. She laughed to herself. He was powerfully built, the muscles in his arms reflecting the light flickering from the scented candles upon the water droplets as they ran over him. Beside them in the water was Kratos's staff. It was making a

462

humming sound and emitting a pale bluish light. Abi held it tightly within her left hand, her right hand placed on Tenno's face as she kissed him. The intense intimacy from them was tangible and Alisha pulled back feeling that she was invading their privacy far more than just spying on them. Two such powerfully built people displaying such tenderness made Alisha shake her head. Feeling almost compelled to look again, she stole one more peek. Abi, her back still toward Alisha moved very slowly, her forehead now resting upon Tenno's forehead as he held her with his hands upon her hips just below the water. They had their eyes shut saying nothing. A large scar down Abi's left side glistened like a crimson and silver snake with the reflecting candle light and water. Daylight was streaming in through the gaps in the main double doorway as the curtains blew in and out gently. Tenno ran his right hand gently down the scar and it appeared to shine, just as the staff in Abi's left hand glowed more intensely. Slowly Alisha began to back away and gently rocking Arri so he would not wake. Back outside in the main foyer area, she leant back against the wall and smiled.

ഇരു

Alisha walked into the main cooking room of the split level kitchen to be greeted by the faces of Kratos, Theodoric, Percival and Attar sat around a large kitchen table. Ishmael stood bolt upright near the back door as if guarding it just as Paul was scraping plates from breakfast into a small wooden bucket near the back door itself. Thomas entered the room via the other door and Percival immediately moved along the bench so Alisha could sit down.

"Alisha...," Kratos said and placed his hands together as if about to pray. "Come and sit," he said and beckoned she sit near to him with a slight nod at the empty space to his right. "You have many questions I am sure, so I would suggest as my time here is limited that we waste no time at all."

"I agree with that," Paul remarked as he wiped his hands clean and moved to sit beside Theodoric opposite where Alisha was sitting herself down. "And we need to thank you."

"What for?" Kratos asked, looking at him.

"For saving my life in La Rochelle for a start," Paul replied instantly.

"It was something that had to be done. Nothing more and nothing less."

"I think it was a bit more than that," Alisha stated. "So thank you."

"I am here and you are all here. I am at your disposal. I am sure Theodoric will help me to answer any questions you may have," Kratos said and looked at Theodoric.

Theodoric took a deep breath and shook his head.

"I think I may have just as many questions as they have...starting with how come you are still alive...for the last time I saw you, you had more arrows stuck in you than a pin cushion, were on fire and you jumped off a cliff with your arms wrapped around that thing...whatever it was," Theodoric asked and looked uncomfortable.

Kratos smiled at him and just stared for a few moments in silence. Paul looked at Alisha and then Percival and Thomas wondering what thing Kratos had been holding.

"Theo...you have no idea how good it is to see you alive and well. I knew you had

463

gone back to the mountains of the Hindu Kush...and it did surprise me when you returned to Rochefort," Kratos began to say.

"What. You knew I had gone back there?" Theodoric interrupted.

"Of course. I promised you I would always watch out for you, and despite your 'self imposed' exile, I have never left you, my friend," Kratos smiled in answer.

"But...even though I faked my demise....I saw you die."

"No you did not. You only saw me fall off a cliff with arrows stuck in me and on fire holding that entity...but as you can see, I am not dead."

"No one could survive those injuries and that fall. No one, not even you," Theodoric shot back, almost argumentative in tone.

"Theo...you know so much, yet you still lack that absolute faith that all and everything is possible, if you believe it enough. And look at Ishmael there. Proof if any were needed the impossible can happen. And yes, I know you too, Ishmael, before you ask."

They all looked at Ishmael briefly then back at Kratos.

"But I also saw you with a large wooden stake that went right through you," Paul interjected.

"Yes you did...and that hurt, I will have you know," Kratos laughed. "That injury took more years from me than I thought it would....but no matter. I did what had to be done and you all sit here now, as does Arri," Kratos replied and looked at Arri asleep in Alisha's arms.

"'Tis that staff of yours isn't it? That is what heals," Thomas stated as he settled himself at the opposite end of the table.

"That is but a tool. It only increases the power and energy of what it receives... that is all," Kratos explained.

"Oh I think it is far more than that," Theodoric replied, shaking his head.

"I think whilst you are here, you should acquaint yourselves with what this city is about...for it may serve you well later," Kratos said and smiled. "And Arri...now our work can truly continue with new life," he sighed and looked at Arri and simply nodded.

"What?" Paul asked.

Alisha could not keep her eyes off of Kratos. His whole presence fascinated her. He was tall and broad and despite his age, he exuded a strength and calmness with a countenance she had never seen before. But his last comment flashed through her mind like a loud warning shout. She looked at Paul, alarmed. 'What did he mean?' she thought as her instincts screamed at her. Kratos immediately sensed her reaction and he placed his hand over her forearm and looked deeply into her eyes.

"Fear not...you will remember in time. All of it...and that once before you were correct, though some did not listen," Kratos said softly and turned to look at Paul. "But I suspect that he shall this time," he finished and looked back at Alisha.

Paul shook his head, puzzled at his remark. As Alisha looked into Kratos's eyes, she felt in herself that she knew this stranger sat beside her. Not just from her dreams and from what Paul had shared with her, but a deeper sense of knowing.

"How long will you be staying with us?" Paul asked.

"Just the one night if that is okay with you, then I must depart...and sorry, Attar, but I must take the scrolls," Kratos replied and looked at Attar as he frowned and feigned an exaggerated grimace and pushed the two tubes across the table.

Thomas leaned over and picked up one of the tubes.

"And did you not know that these were hidden on your caravan?" he asked, looking at Paul.

"Not at all. If I had, I think I would have been a lot more careful with the caravan," Paul answered.

"What are they?" Alisha asked hesitantly.

"Oh just something that was put together a long time ago. Which Niccolas was entrusted to keep and protect," Kratos answered.

"You knew Niccolas?" Paul asked quickly.

"Yes...a good man. He knew Elek Aldin too. A truly great man...and yet as he had his head removed, you had no idea did you?" Kratos asked bluntly.

Pauls mind immediately flashed back to that moment as Elek told him not to look. No he had not known the man but that did not stop the images or experience being any the less horrific.

"'Twas Niccolas who gave Elek Aldin his new name when he became a Templar...it means in old English 'wise protector' and he was certainly that," Kratos explained. "Paul, you are in this great city, but do not believe all that you hear...and let Theodoric show you around. Keep your mind open always, but I am sure your father has already taught you that?"

Paul looked at Theodoric and simply smiled in acknowledgement.

Port of La Rochelle, France, Melissae Inn, spring 1191

"Why did he say not to believe all that he heard there?" Gabirol asked.

"Why indeed," the old man answered. "Because there is so much that is told in error about Alexandria...especially about its founder and the great library."

"How so?" Simon asked.

"Remember earlier I explained that the so-called great fire of Alexandria supposedly resulted in the destruction of all its books and that I said only a part of the collection was destroyed? Well, despite all the myths, for myth is what it is, there was no actual great fire of the library of Alexandria that resulted in the loss of priceless knowledge...for the truly important works were not even in the library."

"Then please explain to us how this myth is still taught as fact," Gabirol said and charged his quill with more ink and placed a new sheet of parchment ready to write upon.

"Let me start by telling you that Alexander himself died after he was accidentally poisoned by wine. I shall explain in a moment. Many claim that a large number of great and wondrous, even magical, books were taken from Alexandria and held within the Vatican to this day in a secret library."

"Why?" Ayleth asked.

"Because the myth goes that there were great secrets within the Alexandrian library. But as I explained earlier, there were in fact several libraries there. But I can tell you that most of what was actually in the libraries was copied from other sources. You see, when the library was founded during third century BC by the Ptolemies, it was part of their taxation strategy, or more precisely a 'toll road' practice. Everyone passing through Alexandria had to hand over everything written on board caravans or ships for copying by Alexandrian

scholars and writers. Maps, logs, literature, diaries and so on, and everything was gathered in several locations within Alexandria. Most were actually log books from merchant ships and maps. You can still go and check the indexes of what was gathered, which shows it's a straightforward boring read. All the truly sacred and mystical books were located elsewhere as Attar and Kratos explained to Paul and Alisha that day."

"I have heard many stories of Alexandria, such as that of Hypatia. Is that all just myth too? Gabirol asked.

"Hypatia...the female philosopher...oh she was real enough. But again myth has taken over the story. The myths surrounding her purport to be historical accounts of her murder by a Christian mob in the early fifth century AD, and of the destruction of the great library of Alexandria, and of the alleged conflict that raged in the ancient world between Greek science and Christian faith. But let me tell you the truth about these events. The story repeats itself, even by respected historians, that Christians were then just a brutish horde of super-stitious louts, who despised science and philosophy, and frequently acted to suppress both, and who also had a particularly low opinion of women. Thus, supposedly, one tragic day in AD 391, the Christians of Alexandria destroyed the city's great library, burning its scrolls, annihilating the accumulated learning of centuries, and effectively inaugurating the 'Dark Ages'. Then in AD 415, a group of Christians murdered Hypatia, who was young and beau-tiful, of course, as well as brilliant, not only because of her wicked dedication to profane intellectual culture, but also because of the forwardness with which she had forgotten her proper place as a woman. Well, that is the standard myth as promulgated as fact, but it is all nonsense."

"Are you saying the great fire of Alexandria never happened?" Gabirol asked surprised.

"Yes, that is exactly what I am saying. You see, the fable of a Christian destruction of the great library is a tale about something that never happened. By this, I do not mean that there is some confusion or misunderstanding of learned opinion on the issue, or that the original sources leave us in some doubt as to the nature of the event. I mean that nothing of the sort ever occurred."

"I find this hard to believe...for I have dreamt of the great library of Alexandria all of my life. I have even planned to go there myself. 'Tis why I am on this journey," Gabirol replied agitated.

"Then I am sorry, Gabirol. But would you rather follow a dream based upon falsehood or the truth?"

"I...cannot answer that yet," he replied and sighed. "So please, explain what you say."

"The original library that was actually there, and it was a great library, as confirmed within Roman journals and Roman-era chronicles, tell us that at least part of the library was destroyed when Julius Caesar invaded Egypt in 48 BC and that Christians were responsible only for the damage done in Hypatia's time to a secondary 'daughter library', which had also been attacked by Muslim conquerors in the seventh century AD. There is absolutely no truth nor evidence, ever, that Christians were responsible for either collections destruction, and no one before now ever suggested they were. It is a modern fallacy, but one I fear will one day gain ground as a fact," the old man explained. He paused for a few moments as Gabirol wrote some notes. "The great library of Alexandria was already legendary even in the time of Strabo, who died around AD 23, and even he knew of it only as a tale from the past. We know the original library was built as an adjunct to the great museum in the Brucheium, the royal quarter, in the first half of the third century BC. Its size, however, is impossible to establish. Whatever the case, as various sources report the library was destroyed, either in whole or in part, during Julius Caesar's Alexandrian campaign against Pompey in 48 BC or 47 BC. If any part of it remained in the Brucheium, it would probably have perished when the museum was destroyed in AD 272, during Aurelian's wars of imperial reunification. It was certainly no longer in existence in AD 391."

"So what is left now that Paul was so eager to see?" Peter asked.

"Just a fraction of what there once was...just a few thousand scrolls, collected within a single building. The remaining part of what was once known as the 'daughter' library, located in the grounds of the Serapeum, the large temple of the Ptolemies' hybrid Greco-Egyptian god, Serapis. The Serapeum was destroyed in AD 391. After a series of riots between the pagan and Christian communities of Alexandria, riots were something of a revered civic tradition almost. A number of Christian hostages were murdered inside the Serapeum, which led the Emperor Theodosius to order the complex demolished and so a detachment of Roman soldiers, with the assistance of an eager crowd of Christians, dismantled the complex, or, at any rate, the temple within it. We have really good accounts of that day, Christian and pagan, and absolutely none of them so much as hints at the destruction of any large collection of books. Not even Eunapius of Sardis, a pagan scholar who despised Christians and who would have wept over the loss of precious texts, suggests such a thing. This is not surprising, since there were no books there to be destroyed. The pagan historian Ammianus Marcellinus, describing the Serapeum not long before its demolition, clearly spoke of its libraries as something no longer in existence. The truth of the matter is that the entire legend is just that...legend. For nowhere does it appear in any historical documentation."

"And does that also apply to Hypatia then?" Gabirol asked.

"Hypatia...she was real enough as I said. She was a brilliant lecturer in Platonic thought, a trained scientist, and the author of a few mathematical commentaries. Despite the extravagant claims often made on her behalf, however, there is no reason to believe she made any particularly significant contribution to any of her fields of expertise. She was not, for instance as she has often been said to have been, the inventor of either the astrolabe or the hydrometer. It is true that the first extant mention of a hydrometer appears in a letter written to Hypatia by her devoted friend, Synesius of Cyrene, the Christian Platonist and bishop of Ptolemais; but that is because Synesius, in that letter, is explaining to her how the device is made, so that she can arrange to have one assembled for him. At the time of her death, she was not even the beautiful young woman of lore...she was in all likelihood over sixty. She was, however, brutally murdered and then dismembered by a gang of Christian parabalani, a fraternity originally founded to care for the city's poor...that much is true. This was not, however, because she was a woman as female intellectuals were not at all uncommon in the Eastern Empire, among either pagans or Christians, or because she was a scientist and philosopher, the scientific and philosophical class of Alexandria comprised pagans, Jews, and Christians, and there was no popular Christian prejudice against science or philosophy. And it was certainly not because she was perceived as an enemy of the Christian faith; she got on quite well with the educated Christians of Alexandria, numbered many among her friends and students, and was intellectually far closer to them than to the temple cultists of the lower city...and the frankest account of her murder was written by the Christian historian Socrates, who obviously admired her immensely. It seems that she died simply because she became inadvertently involved in a vicious political squabble between the city's imperial prefect and the city's patriarch, and some of the savages of the lower city decided to take matters into their own hands. It may seem unimaginable to us now that Christians *from the lower classes in Alexandria could have conspired in the horrific assassination of an unarmed woman and a respected scholar, but, as it happens, that was how Alexandria was often governed at street level, by every sect and persuasion. In the royal quarter, pagans, Christians, and Jews generally studied together, shared a common intellectual culture, collaborated in scientific endeavour, and attended one another's lectures. In the lower city, however, religious allegiance was often no more than a matter of tribal identity, and the various tribes often slaughtered one another with gay abandon. The chasm between the two worlds could scarcely have been vaster. Hypatia was a victim of what might fashionably be called a social contradiction, one that none of the science, philosophy, or religion of the time had ever done anything to resolve," the old man detailed.* [57]

"And is it like that still?" Gabirol asked quietly.

"It shall always be like it for that is the manner of man unfortunately," he answered and shook his head disapprovingly, clearly thinking back upon past events.

"Why do you tell us these details for surely it has no relevance upon the story of the sword...surely?" the Templar asked.

"It has relevance, certainly to Gabirol I suspect," the old man answered and looked at Gabirol as he nodded in agreement. "But to also demonstrate that so much of what we are told and accept as fact is not always the case..."

"So what of the Sufi mystic...and Tenno and Abi getting it together...in a bath!" the Genoese sailor remarked and smirked.

Ayleth cringed at his remark.

"Did I not mention the importance and benefits of what Brother Jakelin referred to as sex magic, though magic is perhaps the wrong word to use?" the old man asked. Ayleth looked down as Sarah just laughed. "As for Attar, he knew what Kratos was doing for Abi. He knew only too well how his staff was made and how it worked, but also how Tenno was helping her."

"More like helping himself," Simon joked, trying to be funny.

"Tenno gave of himself...energy from his very being that helped Abi...'twas not just the act of coitious sex. It was even beyond love making...and perhaps if we have time, I may be able to explain that better," the old man said as he looked at Simon. "But Attar, he too was what some call a Medicine Man. He was a man who was a role model of what it is like to live in harmony and balance with the Creator and this world. It takes a long time, a lot of sacrifice and discipline to become a Sufi mystic and a Medicine Man. He was humble and never crass about anything," the old man detailed and looked directly at Simon. Sarah smirked at him. "He knew he had to strive daily to live within the will of the Great Spirit, God, whatever term you wish to use and to help people. Service to others...not service to self. He lived a very low key lifestyle. Many people sought him out. The more one serves the people and is quiet about it, the more one is sought out. The quieter one is, the more powerful is his medicine. The same as with Kratos. That is why I say to you all, praying to seek a vision, to seek truth is always right. Truth builds upon itself as the true mark of a warrior who conducts himself, or herself accordingly so that its beauty may shine in the faces of our children. You must understand that we all both individually and collectively become what we think...we move toward and become like that which we think about the most."

"Oh Lord, that means I shall become a great...," Simon started to say when the Templar interrupted him.

"That's enough, Simon!" he called out and raised his hand at him.

Simon laughed before the old man continued.

"What we think about creates our vision. If our thoughts are wise and good, then our vision becomes strong and truthful. If our thoughts are bad and self serving only, then our vision becomes tainted and distorted...that is why it is important to be aware of what we are thinking about. As we live our vision, our children watch and they learn to live their lives the same way. We need to live the walk of the true warrior. We need to walk in beauty and respect."

"To live and walk like a true warrior. How do we do that for we are not soldiers?" the farrier asked. *"Well, they are, but we most certainly are not,"* he continued, looking at the Templar and Hospitaller.

"As Tenno once said and would tell you, a true warrior...a master, is the person who no longer needs the sword having mastered true control. You will never hear me speak of Kratos carrying a sword...," the old man answered and looked at the sword upon the table.

"So how come Kratos just turned up when he did?" the Genoese sailor asked.

"He knew Abi was badly hurt. But he was a great distance away when he first sensed her pain. He also had information for Paul...but more importantly, he needed to check the parchments hidden upon Paul's caravan, pass on certain details from them to him, help heal Abi and then leave."

"I fear that Kratos and even Theodoric to an extant were using both Alisha and Paul for some great scheme of their own," Gabirol remarked.

"Of course they were...but that scheme was one that affects all of us...for the greater benefit of all...if not in our time them certainly for future generations' benefits. Besides...if you can believe what I tell you, then Alisha and Paul had previously agreed and volunteered to follow the very path they were now on," the old man explained and paused. *"Kratos also had more sacred books to pass on to Paul in person. Sacred books recovered from Timbuktu."*

"Sacred books...," Gabirol said, puzzled.

"Yes. The ancient texts of Timbuktu Kratos had recovered were an impressive sight, bundled in camel skin, goat skin, and some in calf leather and inscribed in gold, red, and jet-black ink, their pages were filled with words in striking calligraphy from Arabic and African languages, and contained an intriguing array of geometric designs. Timbuktu is one of the cities of Africa whose name is the most heavily charged with history. Founded in the fifth century, it became an intellectual and spiritual capital and located at the gateway to the Sahara desert within the confines of the fertile zone of the Sudan. Despite trade in all manner of goods from gold to slaves, more was made from selling books there. Kratos had made sure that a copy of the Book of John, like the one Theodoric gave Paul, was deposited in Timbuktu where it could be copied and shared."

"Sorry, is that the Book of John in the Bible or that other book you said was written by one of the original Templars?" Ayleth asked.

"'Twas the Book of John with prophecies as indeed written by one of the founding knights. He is known as John of Jerusalem, his real name being Jean de Vézelay or Jean de Mareuil, a Crusader who originally participated in the conquest of Jerusalem in 1099. Born in Burgundy in AD 1042, he was raised on the Camino de Santiago by monks. He became a monk and knight himself and went to the Holy Land during the First Crusade to regain Jerusalem from the Turks, who had seized it twenty years earlier. He knew Hugues de Payens, with whom he had founded the Order of the Temple. He was also one of the knights who had entered the very vault that first time and removed items he perhaps should not have taken, for he took one of the sets of glass eyewear, breast plate and a helmet he also found. It was that which he claimed let him see the visions of things to come...He died in Jerusalem around

469

AD 1120, and I strongly suspect after over use of them, though he was in his eighties by that time," the old man explained. "You see, shortly before his death, John of Jerusalem wrote seven copies of his book of prophecies. He gave three to Bernard of Clairvaux, who donated one of them to the monastery of Vézelay, the other four remaining examples were sent to various people. One being Kratos himself no less. He also sent the copies with details relating to massive crescent structures hidden around Stonehenge in Britain plus a large crescent structure in the Kingdom of Jerusalem."

"I must learn more of those prophecies," Gabirol remarked.

"And you shall, for it will fall to people such as you to copy them and make sure they are carried forwards...," the old man said and smiled at Gabirol. "Kratos was instrumental in making sure certain things were carried over or passed on successfully. Both Theodoric and Philip saw at firsthand how when they helped him educate King Louis and Queen Eleanor."

"Really...with what and how so?" Gabirol asked immediately.

"Oh...let me simply remind you of what I told you earlier regarding King Louis and Queen Eleanor when they travelled from France to the Crusades in 1147. Recall how they were accompanied by a contingent of Knights Templar and how the 'fleur de lys' became the royal coat of arms of France? Well Philip had the honour of saving King Louis of France and Queen Eleanor, en route to the Holy Land. But that story is not required here and now suffice it to say that he, with the guidance of Kratos, imparted much knowledge to the king regarding the hidden and sacred symbolism behind the fleur de lys and its ultimate connection to the Merovingian line all along."

 2 – 1

Alexandria, Egypt, 1179

Alisha looked at Kratos intently until he turned to face her.

"You have questions?" he commented.

"Yes...just a few," she replied. "Such as what does all of what has happened to Paul and I have to do with anything that threatens people like that evil Turansha that they feel they have to kill us...and my son? For I certainly wish no part of any of it."

"As I have said to you before, you chose this path. You volunteered for it...both of you," Kratos replied softly. "But as is the way with free agency, you have the right to abandon that path at any time. To live out your lives as you see fit."

"Alisha," Theodoric interrupted gently. "Each individual has to essentially work with their personal soul development in order to connect to a new consciousness that is coming. Many expect a new kind of mankind...a new race, a new root race as some call it, but what are you doing to prepare for it? You must prepare food for your bodies as well as your minds and your spiritual development...and although Kratos says you have free choice and can walk away from the path you have followed so far...is it really what you want for yourself and Arri?...For it is his future that you must decide how best your life will help him."

"Theo...I do not understand what you are saying. But I can tell you this, I shall do all and everything within my power to protect Arri, to the death," Alisha replied and pulled Arri closer.

Kratos frowned at Theodoric.

"Alisha, Paul. You both have it within you to put in place measures that will help your fellow man...in the future, but that choice is purely yours and yours alone. We can only help and guide you, but that is all...isn't it Theo?" Kratos explained and looked at Theodoric.

Theodoric sighed and eventually nodded his head in agreement.

"And this, this pendant. What is it for and what does it mean? "Alisha asked and raised the stylised bee pendant away from her neck.

"And the dreams...the shared dreams we have had and when alone," Paul stated rather than asked.

"Dreams...," Kratos said in response and paused as he looked at Theodoric first, then Attar and then back to Alisha and Paul. "I can tell you about dreams if you wish and then bees, and perhaps more on what you know and call Druids...bards and ovates."

"Please, for the dreams we have had have been both beautiful but also worrying at times," Alisha said.

"And that staff of yours. Will you explain that?" Thomas asked.

"I can explain that...but I strongly suspect you will not understand it still, and that is no reflection upon your intelligence," Kratos answered. He paused for a few moments as he looked around the table at each of them in turn. "Let me start by saying the world of the unconscious was, and still is, travelled at will by the Druids and magicians of old. The dream world is marked out with a pattern of lines and sacred centres representing both the form in which a vision occurred and which expressed the most sublime cosmic schemes...the cabalistic tree of life. So trusted were they in their wisdom and inspiration of their prophets that a world of piety and splendour existed where the whole world was shaped to its ideal archetype of a new Jerusalem built upon the earth patterns and numbers that originated from divine revelation as found at Giza, Stonehenge, and even now Glastonbury Abbey...and great monuments across the earth...even great monuments that lay hidden beneath the waves and within jungles in lands you have yet to discover, but they were all connected. Ancient Greek writers distinguished two categories of dreams, those that are insignificant, caused by hopes, fears, digestion, and other influences of the day, and those that are significant. The significant dreams come in three varieties. Some were literal visions of what will occur, some required symbolic interpretation, and others were visitations by gods, ghosts, or friends as they understood them. The Greek historian Herodotus of the fifth century BC is credited as the father of history, though his stories sometimes cross into myth territory. In Book 1 of his Histories, the Lydian King Croesus dreamt that his son would die from a wound caused by a spearhead. Croesus does everything in his power to keep his son away from weapons, but allows him to go on a hunt, where he is killed accidentally by the spear of the very man hired to be his bodyguard. Not only did Croesus's dream correctly predict the future, but also set into motion a series of events that led to its fulfilment."

As Kratos recounted these details, Alisha and Paul looked at each other. Paul's mind raced as he recalled his recurring dream of hearing whom he presumed was Arri calling out for his father. He and Alisha had shared the dream once and both agreed that they would make sure any son of theirs would never call Paul Father.

471

But now, as Kratos explained about dreams, he had to rethink that fact. Kratos sat in silence looking at Paul as his mind wondered. Eventually Paul realised he was looking at him.

"I am sorry. Please continue," he remarked apologetically.

"'Tis not a problem, Paul, and if you have questions, you must ask them," Kratos replied. "Now common in ancient literature were dreams with symbols that must be interpreted. For example, there is Penelope's dream in Homer's Odyssey. Penelope is waiting for her husband Odysseus to return home from war, and in the meantime has to endure fifty suitors living in her house and eating up her husband's wealth. In her dream, fifty geese are killed by an eagle that reveals itself to be her husband Odysseus. The geese symbolise the suitors. This was not only prophetic, since Odysseus does kill the suitors, but also a symbolic wish-fulfilment dream. In this same passage, Penelope distinguishes between significant and insignificant dreams. Dreams with no greater meaning come to the dreamer by passing through a gate made of ivory, she says, while significant dreams pass through a gate of horn. Ancient literature often features parents dreaming of destruction caused by their offspring. Herodotus gives an example of this, when the Median King Astyages dreamt of his daughter Mandane urinating until all of Asia is flooded. He then dreamt that she births a vine that overshadows all of Asia. Remember how vines are symbolic of bloodlines. Well the Persian sorcerers known as the Magi interpret his dreams to mean that Mandane's child will depose him. This indeed came to pass when Mandane's son Cyrus the Great dethroned his grandfather and became king of the Persians in the sixth century BC. When Hecuba, the Queen of Troy, is pregnant with her son Paris, she dreams she gave birth to a burning torch. A seer tells Hecuba her son will cause the downfall of Troy, which indeed happened when Paris's actions prompt the Trojan War. Similarly, the Spartan Queen Clytemnestra dreams that she births and breast-feeds a snake, shortly before she is killed by her son Orestes. This sort of symbolic dream became a common literary motif, but also reflects a reality where people believed in the prophetic properties of dreams. Artemidorus of the second century AD left us a book on dream interpretation, where he explained the meaning of dreaming such symbols as snakes, crocodiles, hunting, farming, and war. He even explained what it meant for a man to dream of having sex with his own mother. The third type of prophetic dream involves a visitation from a friend, family member, or god, who speaks with the dreamer," Kratos explained and looked at Alisha as she slowly looked up at him. [58]

"Like the shared dream I had with Abi...when I saw my parents...and you!" Alisha remarked quietly.

"Yes. This visitor dream is sometimes a dream-messenger in disguise, sent by a god. This dream-messenger can take any form, depending on what the god requires. In Homer's Iliad, Zeus instructs a dream-figure to appear to King Agamemnon, disguised as the king's friend Nestor. The image of Nestor tells Agamemnon to take his troops into battle against the Trojans. Zeus's purpose was to sabotage the Greek army. In the Odyssey, Athena sends a dream-figure to Penelope, which appears as her sister. The phantom sister comforts Penelope that her son will return from his journey. Nestor begins to talk, convincing Agamemnon and the rest of the army to fight. Many centuries after these stories were written, the Roman poet Ovid continued the tradition of dream-figures in his depiction of Ceyx and Alcyone. In his poem, Alcyone does not know that her beloved husband Ceyx has died in war, so Juno sends Morpheus, who can change form at will, to visit her in her sleep. Morpheus disguised himself as Ceyx and tells Alcyone that her husband has died. According to ancient literature, the visitor in the dream may also be a ghost. For instance, Achilles dreams of a visit by his dead companion Patroclus, who asks him to complete his burial rites so he can pass on to the underworld. When Achilles tries to grasp Patroclus, he touches only smoke."

"So what is the difference between a ghost or spirit or dream image? How can we tell?" Thomas asked.

"A ghost is a spirit or entity that still remains within these earth realms. It is still life...whereas an apparition is but a play back of an event or person, or persons, that has imprinted itself onto the environment...like a picture basically, but it is not life. A dream image can be a real life spirit that manifests itself to impart a message in the realms between this world and the next. But a dream where you see images of the future is your higher consciousness seeing across the wheel of time...for the past is the future and the future is the past," Kratos explained and smiled.

"Oh great. That really helps me understand that part," Thomas laughed.

"Exclusive to the realm of myth are 'apports', objects which one obtains in a dream and possesses upon waking. In a poem by the Greek poet Pindar, the hero Perseus is said to have acquired a golden bridle in a dream. Though these examples all come from myths, it seems people really dreamed about visitations from gods. Asclepius was a divinity with great healing powers. He was thought to visit his worshippers in dreams and give them medical advice, diagnoses, and even cures. Inscriptions at his sites of worship detail such dreams. Religious devotees hoping to have a significant dream would practise incubation, or ritual sleep in a sanctuary. Some sanctuaries had rooms just for this purpose."

Paul realised that this was similar to what he did when he deliberately tried to exhaust himself in order to dream deeply and learn things. Always trying to push his dreams to reveal more about maps and images he had seen. Kratos could see Paul's mind was running and he waited until he looked up again, then continued.

"In this cult and others, certain objects might encourage the hoped for communication with a god, such as ritual bathing, animal sacrifice, or sleeping on animal skin. Prophetic dreams appear frequently in Greek literature, from myth to history to ancient inscriptions. Greek religious culture allowed people to believe in the truth of these apparent dreams from the gods. Among religious Greeks, this belief was so strong that people bought dream books and practised rituals to induce prophetic dreams."

"But do you believe that dreams can foretell the future?" Paul asked.

"As I just said, sometimes a dream can see across the circle of time. Like standing in a stadium and looking across to the opposite side. You can see it clearly, but the only way to get there, is to travel around the sides," Kratos replied.

"Or jump down and cross the arena," Thomas remarked and smiled.

"Yes...you could do that, but then you miss out on the journey and all the people you would have met and passed as you went around...plus the arena may be filled with lions, fighters and other dangers," Kratos smiled back.

"What Kratos explains about time being a circle is over simplifying the matter, but is still a good analogy," Attar interrupted and sat up, resting his elbows upon the table.

"The divination of dreams, or oneiromancy as it is also called, has its roots in great antiquity," Kratos resumed his explanation. "For instance, if I use the Old Testament as an example, in the Book of Genesis, Joseph, the son of the Jewish Patriarch, Jacob, had the ability to divine the future based on dreams. This ability allowed him to interpret the Pharaoh's dream, which foretold a seven-year famine. This enabled Egypt to avoid disaster and contributed to Joseph's meteoric rise in the Egyptian hierarchy. The Bible is not the only ancient literary source that records the interpretation of dreams. The Egyptians had a 'Dream Book' which set out the meaning of many different types of dreams which is preserved in the form of a papyrus with a hieratic script. This papyrus was written up during the early reign of Rameses the Second (1279–1213 BC). Each page of the papyrus began with a vertical column of hieratic signs which translated as 'If a man sees himself in a dream'. In each horizontal line that follows, a dream is described, and the diagnosis 'good' or 'bad', as well as the interpretation is provided. Thus, as an example: 'If a man sees himself in a dream looking out of a window, good; it means the hearing of his cry'. The good dreams are listed first, followed by the bad ones, written in red, as it is the colour of bad omens. Around a hundred and eight dreams, which described seventy-eight activities and emotions, were recorded in the 'Dream Book'."

"Paul," Attar said, his tone serious as he looked at him. "As Kratos will confirm...I was blessed...more correctly, cursed I feel at times...with the ability to foresee events. But even though I can see them and I am forewarned, it does not mean that I am able to change what is to happen. Aldrin...I foresaw what was to happen to him...and even though I warned him, he still went ahead regardless."

"Why?" Alisha asked, surprised.

"Why...because he totally believed in his soul being eternal...and that his ultimate sacrifice would buy enough time to save you...you three," Attar replied seriously.

Alisha looked at Paul in alarm. Paul sat up straight and sighed before looking at Kratos.

"But we did not even know this man. Why would he do that?" he asked.

"But he knew you!" Kratos replied and raised his eyebrows.

"Then what other portents of the future do you know of and see?" Alisha asked bluntly and kissed Arri on his forehead and held him closer.

"I do not always choose what I see or learn...but I can tell you this...you will in time learn a great secret. A secret so powerful that it is a destroyer of worlds if used badly or it falls into the wrong hands," Attar answered and paused for a minute. "And not just this world you see."

"Destroyer of worlds?" Thomas remarked and laughed disbelievingly.

"Thomas...'Tis the responsibility of people like Kratos here to act as guardians of truly ancient sacred secrets...secrets that must be guarded and protected until the time when mankind can again be entrusted with them...and not before. And that, my dear friend, is where you come into this tale and why you sit there this day with us," Attar replied looking deadly serious. Thomas frowned at him hard and puzzled. "I have seen your destiny and path..."

"And...what does it show?" Thomas asked and ran his hand through his blonde hair, looking apprehensive.

"That I will not reveal...but I can say that all you have sought is not in vain for you will find your answers...and I have seen what is to befall France," Attar replied and sat up straight.

"Really?" Thomas commented and folded his arms.

"What of France?" Paul asked.

"As your father also saw...and why he felt it wise you move here...," Attar started to explain when Kratos looked at him sternly. "In the early part of the next century a great and terrible tempest and whirlwind made up from of its own knights of Christ will descend upon the Languedoc region in France and start a purge... killing many thousands in the name of God...and all to wipe out and eradicate the Cathars...and there is nothing...nothing you can do to stop it," Attar finished and shook his head.

"Why cannot it be stopped?" Paul asked confused.

"If you know these things, how can you live with yourselves knowing it?" Alisha asked quietly and looking sad.

"With great difficulty and a lot of meditation...believe me," Kratos replied softly. "You see, if we intervene, we negate the whole purpose of existence and learning. The whole world is connected and must all come together again...and only then... will the veil be lifted, but not before," Kratos explained.

"So you...you are what...just a guardian?" Thomas asked bluntly.

"Yes...yes that is exactly what I am. I am the protector of the lines...and it is my job to safeguard the bloodlines that will one day gain access to the ancient Halls of Amenti, chambers of creation, Hall of Records or whatever name they will be known as in the future...but not in our times now."

"Why not in our times?" Thomas pushed the question.

"Why...because like my staff and even swords such as Paul carries, if they fall into unscrupulous hands now, they will be abused. But also, most of the items of your ancient forefathers cannot be made to work at this time as your physical minds simply do not work properly nor are tuned to operate them. To do so now would cause you great danger, even death. Only when the entire world we walk upon enters a new phase of higher vibration of light again will mankind's full faculties be open to you and accessible again. To do so now, would be most dangerous. It would be like putting a small child in charge of a great 18 hands high thoroughbred horse and letting him out to ride it at full speed. Or to play with a sword..."

"So you are saying that we are like children still?" Thomas shot back.

"Do not take it as an offence...but yes," Kratos replied and smiled. "Can you imagine someone like Reynald being in possession of a great tool of power that can destroy entire cities in a single flash...that can control the minds of people hundreds of miles away stripping them if their own free will...can you?"

"And you have been doing this for how long?" Percival suddenly asked.

"Too long...far too long," Kratos answered and looked at him.

"But if what I have learnt is true, then you must have been doing this since the very dawn of our age...how so?" Paul asked bemused.

"You know about the longevity of the ancients yes?" Kratos asked. Theodoric looked at Paul and nodded at him yes he did. Paul nodded confirming he did. "Then know this...I was asleep for a great deal of time...hidden. 'Tis what I volunteered to do a very long time ago. 'Twas what you saw in your dreams. A time when you walked this earth also, and knew Alisha as she was in that lifetime...but to open the doors of your physical mind to that time and experiences would cause you great harm in this world now. That is why the veil is placed upon all souls who incarnate in this realm," Kratos explained slowly and looked at Alisha and Paul in turn, then at Thomas. "And you...you are exactly where you need to be at this time." Thomas sat back and frowned perplexed at his comments. "And you," he said then looking at Percival. "You...you must continue with what you do and dispel all doubts of your past and previous actions. 'Tis what you do now and who you are now that counts... so remove the burden of shame and guilt you hide for it is not necessary. 'Tis your intention that counts...and that is noble."

Percival shook his head, surprised, his face flushing a bright red with embarrassment as everyone around the table looked at him in silence.

"Intention!" Tenno suddenly said aloud as he entered the room through the main door supporting Abi stood beside him. He was wearing a long silk robe which made him look totally different, especially as his hair, usually tied back, hung down loose.

Kratos smiled and sat back and looked at them as they entered. Abi was still holding the staff as she slowly walked around the table towards him, Tenno gently holding her arm. Slowly she passed the staff to Kratos to take.

"It is done...I am much better for it and will be okay now," Abi explained and smiled.

Alisha smiled seeing Abi looking much better already even though still very pale.

"Good...then tomorrow we shall depart," Kratos stated.

Alisha looked at Abi, alarmed.

"Do not worry Ali...you shall see me again. Tenno knows why...as my injuries should have killed me but for the three fold water Theo and Attar managed to make in time...but the scar upon my very soul is deep and needs attention," Abi explained and moved to sit near to Alisha just as Paul moved along the bench seat the other way.

Tenno helped Abi to sit down and nodded at Alisha that he understood what Abi was saying. Paul looked at Kratos, confused.

"Normally, if the physical body receives injuries that are un-survivable, the spirit departs...and either goes up to the next realm or returns to this realm in a new body. Of course there is a middle ground between the realms. 'Tis called paradise by most cultures...but that is just a temporary area where the soul can adjust, reflect and then decide where it is going next. All the physical pain of whatever incident that caused death is also released...but in Abi's case, she did not do this, so the memory of the physical cause still touches her. Sometimes people who do not wait long enough before returning, bring with them a soul memory of the previous life's trauma. 'Tis why some people fear drowning, or other irrational fears and mysterious aches and pains in this life," Kratos explained as Abi made herself comfortable.

"But Abi...I have so much I need to learn from you. I need you here," Alisha blurted out, her voice full of emotion.

"I know...but I must go with Kratos to heal properly. I have promised Tenno I shall return, and I shall, I swear it," Abi replied and held Alisha's hand.

"Then what of that staff? You said you would explain that," Thomas asked.

Kratos looked at the staff. He picked it up slowly and started to unscrew the horseshoe shaped top. As it came away, he placed it gently upon the table. He then started to unscrew the ball section. The top half slowly unwound and then popped up as if under pressure. Within moments the entire staff was in pieces laid out upon the table. There was a small copper looking tube, a tetrahedron shaped crystal, three half spheres of different materials that fitted inside each other, a copper pyramid, what looked like a glass lens, three copper balls connected seamlessly by a coiled copper rod forming a circle, a circle of copper wires threaded about each other to form a round ring. Kratos sat back and looked at the pieces.

"There you have it. 'Tis but a simple mechanism but when put together, it accumulates and increases those natural forces that surround all of us and everything," Kratos stated.

"And how does it work then?" Thomas asked as he studied the parts.

"That is where it becomes complicated. The prophet you know as Moses... he had one of these. The one you know as Jesus likewise had a similar tool, but that I shall leave for another time to explain. 'Twas the only item Moses was allowed to keep that he recovered with his brother Arran in Egypt. Only one other person so far in this period of man has fully grasped and understood how it works. An Indian sage and philosopher...he understood the invisible spheres that make up everything we see in this physical world and the energy that holds it all together with invisible bonds. He was known as Acharya Kanad, born in 600 BC in Prabhas Kshetra, near Dwarka in Gujarat, India. His real name was Kashyap. Whilst on a pilgrimage to Prayag he saw thousands of pilgrims litter the streets with flowers and rice grains offered at the temple. Fascinated by small particles, he began collecting the grains of rice. A crowd gathered around him and they asked why was he collecting the grains that even a beggar wouldn't touch. He told them that individual grains in themselves may seem worthless, but a collection of some hundred grains make up a person's meal, the collection of many meals would feed an entire family and ultimately all of mankind, which is made of many families, thus even a single grain of rice was as important as all the valuable riches in this world. People then called him 'Kanad', as 'Kan' in Sanskrit means 'the smallest particle'. Kanad pursued his fascination with the unseen world and with conceptualising the idea of the smallest particle and wrote down his ideas and taught them to others. People then began to call him 'Acharya' 'the teacher', hence the name Acharya Kanad 'the teacher of small particles'. Kanad, whilst walking with food in his hand, was breaking it into small pieces when he realised he was unable to divide the food into any further parts, it was too small. From that moment, he conceptualised the idea of a particle that could not be divided any further. He called that indivisible matter Parmanu, or anu, atom. He proposed that this indivisible matter could not be sensed through any human organ or seen by the naked eye, and that an inherent urge made one Parmanu combine with another. When two Parmanu belonging to one class of substance combined, a dwinuka (binary molecule) was the result. This dwinuka had properties similar to the two parent Parmanu. He suggested that it was the different combinations of Parmanu which produced different types of substances. So you can see why this knowledge is considered important to alchemists. He also put forward the idea that atoms could be combined in various ways to produce chemical changes in the presence of other factors such as heat. He gave the blackening of earthen pots and ripening of fruit as examples of this phenomenon. He went on to found the Vaisheshika School of philosophy where he taught his ideas about the atom and the nature of the universe. He wrote a book on his research, *Vaisheshik Darshan*, and became known as 'The Father of Atomic Theory'. In the West, atomism emerged in the fifth century BC with the ancient Greeks Leucippus and Democritus. Whether Indian culture influenced Greek or vice versa or whether both evolved independently is a matter of dispute. Kanad is reporting to have said, 'Every object of creation is made of atoms which in turn connect with each other to form molecules.' His theory of the atom was abstract and enmeshed in philosophy as they were based on logic and not on personal experience or experimentation." Kratos smiled as he answered. "Like mist, or steam, when it cools, the tiny parts that come together become too heavy and so stick together and form water again, that is how our entire realm is likewise made but on a greater scale... and held together by that energy that runs throughout the world...the paths of the dragons as some call them, the very paths the Druids knew how to use and fly upon as well as heal with," Kratos explained and looked at Tenno as he said that. [59]

"Fly!" Thomas asked incredulously.

"Yes, fly. I am sure you must have heard all the stories and legends too, surely," Attar remarked as he looked at Thomas.

"'Tis why people like your fathers designed and have started a building programme that will re-establish the ancient paths of energy to keep this world in balance," Kratos said looking at Alisha and Paul directly.

"I do not understand what you mean," Paul replied.

"Did you not inform him?" Kratos asked Theodoric.

"Er...no not quite. We did not exactly have the full time required to explain it all. I was hoping to do so once settled here," Theodoric answered and shrugged his shoulders. "Besides, you could probably explain it better as you are here."

"Paul, you may recall your father was involved in the design of Chartres Cathedral yes?" Kratos asked. Paul nodded yes in answer. "Did you know it was the former capital of the Carnutes and the original site of the great Druid College and centre of inspiration?" Paul shook his head no. "Chartres is built upon a very ancient mound over a buried chamber and a natural meeting place of several powerful streams of natural earth current...paths of the dragon energy known as woivres or mercurial serpents. Here, geomancers hidden within Catholicism, like your father, built Chartres to accumulate a fusion of energy to send it out for the benefit of the local area. The natural forces that concentrate at such centres are so powerful that their misuse or unbalanced use can prove catastrophic. The myths of Atlantis claim the misuse of such power resulted in its destruction, but that is but part of the reason, for it vanished due to other factors too. Cyclical events that occur at regular intervals. Perhaps Theo will educate you on that in good time?" Kratos remarked and frowned at Theodoric, who raised his arms in mock protest. "You can see why initiation into the secrets is allowed only to those who have undergone many years of training, and usually at least twenty years minimum of oral teaching so secrets could not fall into the wrong hands. The main school for Druids was based at Chartres. But from all over Europe, the sons of important families went to Britain, the mystic isle of the north, to spend years in a Celtic Druid college. This memory is still preserved almost intact in Britain long after it has vanished elsewhere. The Greeks of this city, Alexandria, still afford great respect for the wisdom of the Druids and their skills in the civilised arts and magic."

21 – 14

"Are you a Druid?" Alisha asked as she rocked Arri gently as he began to stir.

"Me...oh no...I am from a time long before they walked upon this earth," Kratos answered and winked. He paused briefly as he looked at Alisha before continuing. "The Celts honour them as prophets and seers because they foretell matters using ciphers and numbers according to Pythagorean skill and practised magic arts. But as it became more diluted and distant from its original source, so too has it become more base and lost. But truth remains in the Emerald Isles and Malta where I often stay. But know this, the secret of the Druids is the same as that preserved by the Egyptians, the Persians, Indian Brahmins and the Chaldeans of Assyria. The Pythagoreans took their philosophy from the Gauls. There are countless place names in Britain which are of Egyptian and Assyrian origin yet people there do not even realise it. It is a mistake to assume that all the ancient stone sites, such as Stonehenge, were built by Druids and used by them, for in the main they sought out sacred woods and oak tree groves. A symbol of a sacred serpent spiralling upwards around a stone pillar is what they would often produce symbolising the fusion of earth energies and the cosmos. However, everywhere in the world you go, standing stones are associated with Druids. The hidden plan of Stonehenge is likewise encoded within the Book of Revelation in the New Jerusalem plan as well as many cathedrals. Especially evident at Glastonbury Abbey."

Paul immediately thought of the drawings he had made of what he saw and dreamt after his underground adventure beneath Jerusalem. Kratos saw that he was thinking and waited until he looked up again and then carried on.

"Covertly known and repeated by Christian geomancers, again such as your father, they have deliberately laid out cathedrals and abbeys to repeat the values and numbers, as well as the sign of Virgo, across France. The alignment of sacred stones, pathways of the dragon...the further back you trace their tradition, the higher and more universal the knowledge was. But in short, the Druids held secrets of a former world order fragmented into smaller groups of survivors. It was a golden age."

"And you are one of those survivors," Thomas stated.

"I guess I am," Kratos smiled as he answered.

Tenno looked at him and moved to sit opposite Abi and next to Kratos. He kept his eye upon him as Percival moved along the bench so he could sit down.

"So do you have all the magical powers Druids have...supposedly?" Thomas asked.

"Supposedly you say," Kratos smiled. "It is claimed that Druids inherited certain extraordinary powers from the ancients having the ability to fly as I just said, to raising the dead, to being able to control the weather, to travel in a state of invisibility, spirit or astral projection as some call it, and to pass through the barrier of time. 'Tis exactly what John did, the knight who wrote the John prophecies. Druids taught astronomy, astrology, geometry, music and mathematics. Those who mastered and understood these subjects knew the physical dimensions of the earth, the heavenly bodies and nature of the subtle unseen forces of nature. The prolonged course in oral tradition was done to exclude those whose minds would prove unequal to the responsibility of that knowledge. Initiation involved an experience of inducing the deepest form of terror. Paul, you have experienced that. Your father knew you would have to suffer that in order to set your mind on the correct path...as did Theo here," Kratos remarked and looked at Theodoric.

"Hey...if I had told you what was coming, would you have ever left home?" Theodoric replied and raised his hands then shrugged his shoulders.

"Probably not," Paul conceded and then held Alisha's hand.

"Your fathers knew you had to do it...and they trusted the parchments, what they detailed, but also what your mothers had both said," Kratos explained. Alisha and Paul looked at each other, perplexed at his last comment. "Both of your mothers knew you would have to experience the darkest of evils and endure the worst that life can throw at you...to make you become what you will be," Kratos continued.

"Well I think we have suffered and experienced enough," Paul replied and put his arm around Alisha reassuringly.

"Look, when I was beginning to learn things, I suffered too, as well as enter underground chambers and have the life literally scared out of me," Theodoric started to explain. "You ask your father about the massive underground chambers, especially in northwest France and the Emerald Isles, we had to endure when you see him next."

"Why...I mean why should I ask about them specifically? For believe me, I have many other questions I now wish to ask him," Paul replied.

"Let me explain then," Kratos interrupted and placed his hand upon Paul's left arm briefly. "Northwest France and Britain have many catacombs beneath woodlands with subterranean halls and galleries, and all with entrances found near earthworks. There are also many secret tunnels between old churches following ancient paths above ground. Many Roman roads simply followed the straight ancient paths. All are connected or related in some way to legends of a war between two races, where afterwards they agreed to accept equal share of the land divided horizontally. The victors took the surface whilst the rivals were banished beneath ground. But that is just legend...Spirits are believed to follow the sacred paths, paths of the dragons and mysterious lights are frequently seen on them...that is because they are connected to a very real energy force...the same force that powers that," Kratos remarked and nodded toward the disassembled staff upon the table. "It is the same force that makes a needle point northwards in the new navigation aids such as the one Niccolas had, though a simple Celtic cross works just as well to navigate...which

Theodoric can teach you all. Countless churches were deliberately built over ancient sites chosen by means of divination, dowsing, which are centres of intensified energy. Many ancient mounds are reputed in folklore as the homes of fairies, leprechauns and ghosts. Druids as well as other trained sages and mystics can free their senses from the physical body and travel to other realms as well as other locations upon this earth. Druids were able to do this at will... but most nowadays require other methods to induce this state, such as some herbs and mushrooms. But doing so is incredibly dangerous. All people have the ability to induce such states, but they have lost the knowledge how. But as for actual real physical flight...'tis just a skill and application of tools again. It may sound like magic, but one day man will again rediscover the sacred arts of flight...when they start to remember the past. Even the Greeks and ancient Egyptians made small versions of vehicles that could fly. Druids and shamans of Asia have accomplished flight, often from these mounds and hill tops where great heroes of mythology achieved apotheosis. Legends speak of the Druids' power of flight. Abaris, a British magician, travelled through the air to Greece with the aid of an instrument described as a golden arrow. Bladud, the Druid father of King Lear, crashed his vessel on Ludgate Hill in London, the site of an ancient church...on the highest point in the city, but that will one day be the site for a great cathedral to honour Paul the Apostle (St Paul's Cathedral. Consecrated 1697.) Remember Simon Magus who demonstrated flight but was cut down by St Peter during his demonstration in Rome?...Well he had a Druid pupil named Mog Ruith who possessed a flying machine and was said to have fought in aerial combat over the Emerald Isles with a rival Druid. But his craft was built of stone and a part of it still stands in Cnamchoill near Tipperary after his daughter erected it as a standing stone."

"Is this why we hear tales of flying carpets?" Thomas asked, interested.

"Partly. Many ancient texts, especially ancient Sanskrit, speak of great flying vessels...how to make them and fly them. But many strong traditions across the ancient world talk of flight. Traditions that people of a previous age knew how to levitate and move stone through the air. The degree of accuracy of the cutting and laying of stone in the Great Pyramid in Egypt is without equal and not repeated, nor will be. The use of sound is reported how the ancients moved stone. Stone levitated through sound could be used as a chariot moving along ley lines of energy, raised causeways and earthworks. But dangerous effects can reduce the force such as the moon or sunset etcetera. An eclipse would prove catastrophic so had to be known in advance. Chaldean astronomers were leaders and their skill not repeated until now. Chinese astrologers admit they had degenerated in calculating eclipses from a time five hundred years BC."

"You said you had to enter great underground caves and labyrinths...why?" Thomas asked Theodoric.

"Why indeed," Theodoric replied and shuffled on the bench briefly. "Sealed caves were...in fact still are...where great initiations take place. How many legends and myths have you heard that recount where people have found themselves stumbling into a fairy hill and enter another world, sometimes returning for a while before deciding to return to that other world? Also of lost time, sometimes hundreds of years. Just like the martyrs we discussed at our first meeting in Tarsus. True knowledge of the past can be gained by mystical means as all history is recorded forever written on the astral plain or akashic plains as some call it, and the only way I...and Philip...could gain any access to any of it, was by entering certain places. Now stone circles are places of natural energy and were used as beacons by ancient fliers. They also act as receiving stations from celestial stars, especially during certain parts of the year...and hence Chartres and the layout of Virgo across France."

"Theo, I think you reveal too much too soon," Kratos interrupted.

"I think not enough to be honest," Theodoric replied instantly. "With all respect to you," he finished and nodded at Kratos.

"Paul...you have a natural ability, as do you, Alisha, due to your very blood, of being able to tap into the energy, hidden knowledge and wisdom as well as travel to the other realms...and one day, if you learn, you will be able to do it at will," Kratos explained.

"Yes, not like me. I had to use the Cauldron of Keridwen," Theodoric laughed. "With a brew of herbs, fruits, fungi, henbane, belladonna, aconite, thorn apple, spotted skin of red birchwood mushroom just to name a few to induce the trance I needed to travel."

Tenno rubbed his chin both surprised and puzzled at Theodoric's statement. He looked at Abi as she smiled back at him. Kratos coughed and leaned forward and started to reassemble his staff.

"Stone circles were undoubtedly used for astronomy, but also as markers, beacons as explained, but also to carry a message across time for future generations' benefits as well as keep in balance the natural forces of energy that flow around this world. Their purpose was not just some superstitious powerless ritual, but for the worship of light....to draw down rays of sunshine and other celestial bodies into the earth and their own bodies. If you tap a standing stone, the sound the stone makes spirals upwards. Sometimes that energy becomes unbalanced and results in massive discharges. 'Tis why there are vitrified towers in Alba...Scotland....myth claims it to be the action of dragons. Some ancient towers and ruins are still illuminated at night by mysterious lights from within. And the energy that runs around our world is often depicted and known as a net stretched over the earth carrying the current."

"Niccolas and Theo there have explained certain aspects about the Druids... about knots, roses, apples etcetera, but I fear I still know so very little," Paul remarked as Arri started to fidget more in Alisha's arms.

"Then start by learning the basics...the seven virtues. Then Theo, and I am sure Attar, can start your education properly," Kratos commented as he affixed the final horseshoe shaped part to the top of his staff and locked it tight. He saw Percival and Thomas were looking at him intently. "And you two also if you have a mind for it."

"Most definitely...if I am worthy," Percival shot back excitedly.

"All born of this world are worthy of it," Kratos replied and placed the staff beside him.

"What are the virtues then? For I fear I have probably broken many," Thomas asked.

"It is what you do from here onwards that counts, and your previous intentions, which I know to have been good," Kratos answered and looked at Thomas intently. He then looked at Theodoric. "Theo, do you still recall the seven virtues?"

"You insult my intelligence," Theodoric replied but smiling broadly as he shuffled again upon the bench. "Of course I do. The Virtues of the Druidic Circle are the seven star points of Honour, Truth, Justice, Faith, Hope, Love, and Benevolence."

"Sounds just like the vows of a knight?" Thomas remarked.

"Then you are already there," Kratos smiled.

"So what of these...and the acorns and the black and yellow cords?" Alisha asked as she pulled out from her dress the stylised bee pendant that hung around her neck by a black and yellow cord, identical to the one worn by Kratos.

"Abi...are you all right with this or do you require rest?" Kratos asked before continuing.

"I am much improved. Honestly," Abi replied and held Tenno's hand tightly. Theodoric noticed this and that Tenno did not try to hide the fact.

"Good. Then I must ask Paul, do you understand the meaning behind the Dara Celtic knot?"

"Yes...both Niccolas and Theo explained it," Paul answered.

"I don't," Percival interrupted quickly. "Sorry."

"No need to apologise. I shall quickly refresh Paul's mind and for your benefits too. You see the Dara Celtic knot has many meanings. But the actual meaning of the word 'Dara' is from an Irish word, doire, which meant 'oak tree'. It is, pardon the pun, the root word for door and the Dara Celtic knot is associated with the root system of oak trees. The Celts and, especially, Druids considered the oak tree as sacred. One reason being that it can actually hold energy and even memories, just like stone. They used to derive meaningful messages applicable in day-to-day life through the language of trees. The oak tree is the symbol of destiny, power, strength, wisdom, leadership and endurance. All these attributes therefore got associated with the Dara Celtic knot. Roots of the oak tree represented in the form of Dara Celtic knot are symbolic of the great source of inner strength or divine resources we all possess."

"Is that why I have acorns in my dagger's sheath?" Alisha asked and moved her right arm about until she was able to remove her dagger from her waistband beneath her dress. She gently placed it upon the table and whilst holding Arri in her left arm, opened the side pouch and removed two acorns. "The third one I planted in France. I did not know they were special."

"Alisha, you did the right thing," Kratos said and picked up the two acorns from Alisha's open palm. "These, these came from Abraham's tree believe it not. The prophecy connected to that tree states that when it dies, then what you all know as the Antichrist shall appear. If we, as guardians of the sacred ways, succeed, then the tree of Abraham will again grow and the pure light of love, knowledge and wisdom will prevail. 'Tis why three acorns were taken from the tree...to guarantee its line would continue," Kratos said and smiled as he studied the two acorns held between his fingers. "These are specially created acorns...they will not perish."

"Are we to teach them how to use the black and white divining sticks alongside the ancient alphabet?" Theodoric asked.

Kratos looked up at Theodoric, then at Paul, Thomas and Percival in turn.

"Of course, you must," Kratos answered and began to replace the acorns in the dagger's sheath.

"And what of the Halls of Amenti?" Theodoric asked again, his tone more serious.

"Only that they exist...and the codes so that they may bring them up to date, but that is all," Kratos replied softly.

"Halls of Amenti. I have heard this several times before. What is it?" Paul asked immediately.

"'Tis a great secret from antiquity. One best left alone for now as your father realised," Kratos answered.

"Yes, though almost nearly too late," Theodoric said aloud and shrugged his shoulders.

Paul frowned and looked at both Kratos and Theodoric, puzzled.

"Let me explain in the briefest way I can...and mark my words, what is spoken of now, stays amongst you only. Is that understood?" Kratos asked and looked at them all in turn. All agreed with silent nods. Percival's eyes were wide in anticipation, which made Abi smile as she looked at him. "Then know that for untold centuries both historical and esoteric sources have passed down stories of a forgotten time-capsule of ancient wisdom, far greater in importance than any golden treasures. The various accounts speak of chambers located beneath the Great Pyramid and Sphinx at Giza and leading off from them, filled with a legacy left by a lost advanced civilisation far older than Egypt itself. Before recorded time even...but along with the stories are also preserved a number of prophecies foretelling whom, when and how the vanished time-capsule will be opened," Kratos started to explain and looked directly at Paul and Alisha. Paul pulled his shoulders back as a chill ran down his back, his hairs standing on end. Alisha looked at him, her eyes wide and glistening with sparkles. "A mathematical and astronomical code exists within ancient myths and legends that testify to a highly advanced civilisation that flourished on a global scale thousands of years ago. When decoded, this information pinpoints the location of a series of carefully concealed Halls of Records, for that is a better description of them, that contain artefacts and documents revealing the full extent of knowledge available at that time. The evidence leading to the Egyptian location has been obvious for thousands of years but only now that our own technology is advanced sufficiently are we in a position to recognise, and de-code it. We only need look above us to the brightest star visible, Sirius (the Dog Star), which holds the key to a legacy from a forgotten race. But that is all I can reveal now as it must remain hidden until that time when mankind can also be counted upon to use the items responsibly. Plus if found now, they simply will not work as the harmonics of the world are not yet set," Kratos explained.

"Harmonics?" Percival said loudly, looking confused.

"Yes, harmonics. Sound...music, it is the second universal language, but that is something Theodoric will have to teach you for time does not permit so this day," Kratos answered.

"Then why tell us these things if we are not to open and recover them?" Paul asked.

"Because you are but guardians who must guarantee the codes that will lead men of the future to their locations remain intact...as well as your very physical bloodlines, that you must protect and maintain at all costs, for without the correct physical beings, all the tools will be utterly useless. Do you understand that?" Kratos asked, his tone almost clipped but very serious.

Alisha looked at Paul, concerned, then at Arri.

"I can swear, we seek nothing but a peaceful life and to raise Arri in safety," Alisha said emotionally.

"Good...then I can return to my home secure in that knowledge...," Kratos replied and smiled.

"Can I just ask why the ancients, whoever they were, hid these halls? What happened to them?" Percival asked.

"Again you have much to learn...but in short, this world we exist upon is forever changing. When the Bible speaks of the heavens and stars falling from the sky, the sun not shining for three days etcetera, they recount real events from the past when the very earth we stand upon shifted its position in relation to the sun. Major catastrophes on a global scale have affected our earth and entire solar system and any civilisations that may have been present at the time. Mankind once reached a highly advanced stage of existence, far far in excess of anything you can possibly imagine. Most of the people had also reached a highly advanced stage of physical and spiritual growth and many left this realm of existence as we perceive it now. But those that still remained, those souls that had not grown or refused to evolve...they remained for ever trapped in a repeating cycle of death and rebirth. But before our ancient forefathers left, they buried, securely, time-capsules containing details and items of all of their history, wisdom and knowledge so it would benefit mankind again."

"And they used the only two universal languages guaranteed to span the vast expanse of time intact. A language that remains constant no matter how you present it...and that is mathematics and sound...harmonics," Theodoric interjected.

"So...you see, you all have responsibilities far beyond what you perhaps understood when you started this. So if you wish, you may leave now and follow a path that will prove far less complicated, frustrating and probably less dangerous too," Kratos remarked.

"I am here for as long as it takes and wherever it takes me," Tenno replied first.

"I am assuming Arri and I have no such choice?" Alisha asked.

"That, my dear girl, I am afraid to confirm is correct," Kratos replied.

"But you have my knights and me for as long as we are needed," Thomas said reassuringly.

Theodoric looked at Kratos and winked.

"And me...though I have no idea what I can contribute," Percival said and shrugged his shoulders.

"Look," Kratos began to say but paused for a moment as Arri started to cry a little. Quickly he reached over, placed his finger upon Arri's forehead and he immediately settled and lay awake looking up at Alisha, smiling. "Other prophets will come and go, and many will predict world-wide catastrophes and the advent of portentous signs indicating biblical scale destruction and death that are repeated many times, but in the last days as they shall be known, when people believe that all hope is lost and the world is heading for annihilation, then the Halls of Amenti will be revealed and uncovered which will remove any confusion about mankind's true origins and future potential. It will also reveal that all religions have carried across time the secrets that will lead to the recovery of man's true purpose. They will prove irrefutably, using mathematics, geometry and harmonics, all of which deal with specifics that are incontrovertible with no margin for error, that our understanding of our past history is seriously flawed and inaccurate. The ramifications of the evidence for mankind may be truly enormous with unparalleled consequences on how we view our origins, our past history, our future and, ultimately, ourselves. It proves that there is a choice and how to effect those choices available to mankind as it approaches a new millennium. Our ancient forefathers who buried the Hall of Records were very much aware of the fallibility of human nature and so in turn ensured that we would again find the answers to what appear to be unanswerable questions and paradigms...and as Theo has already explained, they used the one universal language that was guaranteed to span the millennium of time intact as it would remain constant and specific no matter how it would be expressed...mathematics."

"I am no good at mathematics," Percival commented and sighed.

"You do not need to be any good at mathematics. Perhaps your skill will lie in understanding other aspects, such as the Celtic Ogham alphabet," Kratos remarked.

"And what pray tell is that?" Percival asked, bemused.

"The Celtic Ogham alphabet, 'tis something you should all learn. It dates from the fourth century and is named after Ogmos, the Celtic god of knowledge and communication. Ogmos was associated with the Gaulish Ogmios and the Greek Hermes. The alphabet consists of twenty letters, each named for a different tree believed sacred to the Druids. Each letter is made up of one to five straight or angled lines incised on a straight base line. Because of the number of letters, and the number of lines that make up each letter, some argue it originated as a system of hand signs. But either way, using the black and white sticks, some call them wands, some have confused them with Druid staffs, but as you have seen, the staff is a totally different thing, you can meditate and ask questions and then throw the sticks down. Examples of Ogham writing have been found all over the British Isles, and parts of Europe. Many surviving examples exist as stone carvings, usually on tombstones and road markers. By simply throwing the sticks, you can make letters in the alphabet...but it is how you interpret them that really counts and understanding the meanings and symbolism of what each tree stands for and represents. 'Tis similar to interpreting rune stones, like you are familiar with," Kratos explained and looked at Thomas. [60]

Fig. 42:

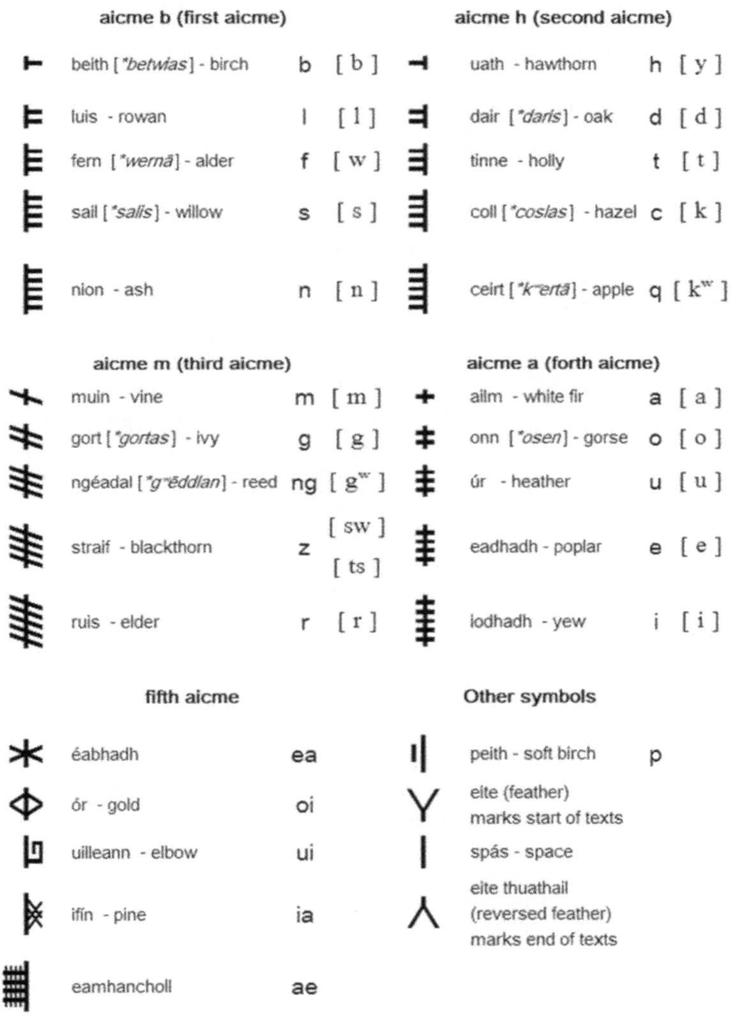

aicme b (first aicme)				aicme h (second aicme)		
beith [*'betwías*] - birch	b	[b]		uath - hawthorn	h	[y]
luis - rowan	l	[l]		dair [*'darís*] - oak	d	[d]
fern [*'wernā*] - alder	f	[w]		tinne - holly	t	[t]
sail [*'salís*] - willow	s	[s]		coll [*'coslas*] - hazel	c	[k]
nion - ash	n	[n]		ceirt [*'kʷertā*] - apple	q	[kʷ]

aicme m (third aicme)				aicme a (forth aicme)		
muin - vine	m	[m]		ailm - white fir	a	[a]
gort [*'gortas*] - ivy	g	[g]		onn [*'osen*] - gorse	o	[o]
ngéadal [*'gʷēddlan*] - reed	ng	[gʷ]		úr - heather	u	[u]
straif - blackthorn	z	[sw] [ts]		eadhadh - poplar	e	[e]
ruis - elder	r	[r]		iodhadh - yew	i	[i]

fifth aicme			Other symbols	
éabhadh	ea		peith - soft birch	p
ór - gold	oi		eite (feather) marks start of texts	
uilleann - elbow	ui		spás - space	
ifín - pine	ia		eite thuathail (reversed feather) marks end of texts	
eamhancholl	ae			

"But if all we shall do is worry about our safety, is it all worth it?" Alisha asked.

"You had to travel, to suffer and to learn. And why worry when you can pray? He, as in God, Allah whatever you chose to call him, is the Whole, and you are a part. Coordinate your abilities with the Whole and all will be well," Attar said and smiled.

Tenno feigned an almost pained look not understanding what he meant.

"You must learn that you are going to be responsible for bringing in a new age of man, the fifth root race. An evolutionary occurrence that will mark a New Age and a new understanding of humanity's relationship to what you all understand as God. You two," Kratos said as he looked at Alisha and Paul. "You are the seeds of the fifth root race...in the future when the earth passes through the ring of light... all of your offspring seed will be awakened and help guide and lead all others to the same potential."

"But why us? This is not what I want," Alisha said looking at Kratos with a frown, concerned.

1 – 4

"But Alisha...or should I say Ailia...this is what you asked for and volunteered to do," Kratos replied and leaned toward her.

"Well I do not remember it. And why are there no others who can do this?"

"Ali...there were...but I failed them. They are now all dead," Abi said softly and moved to face Alisha. "But I swear it, I shall not fail again." She paused as she looked into Alisha's eyes. "'Tis how I was injured, but my skill was not enough against overwhelming odds, but I did make it to you in time...," she sighed, still clearly weak.

Alisha lowered her head and sighed with her as she recalled the events, Abi having arrived just in time despite being severely injured.

"When you came to us, when we were unconscious...was that truly you, under your own will?" she asked Kratos, looking up at him.

"Yes, my little sister, yes it was," Kratos replied and placed his large hand over her left forearm as she held Arri.

"So if Alisha is your soul sister...then that makes Paul your brother in law," Percival stated and smiled, amused.

All looked at him for a moment then at Kratos. He simply shrugged his shoulders and smiled back and then winked at Paul.

"And this...you said you would explain this," Alisha said raising her bee pendant.

Abi reached inside her long tunic and pulled out an identical pendant and raised it next to Alisha's pendant. Both smiled at each other.

"The bee symbolism is a long one. Are you sure you wish to hear it for I shall have to tell you of my home too so that you fully understand it," Kratos remarked.

"Please, if you would," Paul answered as Thomas, Percival and Tenno nodded in agreement. Paul turned to look at Ishmael. "Ishmael?"

"Me! You are asking me?" Ishmael replied, surprised.

"Yes of course," Paul answered, even more surprised.

"Of course then...I just did not expect my opinion to be considered."

"Why would it not be? You are not a slave here. You are free to go as well as speak as you see fit," Paul explained.

Ishmael went red in the face and gulped trying to keep his emotions in check. It had been so long since anyone had considered his views and wishes that he had become accustomed to remaining silent and doing as ordered. Kratos looked at Ishmael and smiled. Ishmael smiled as best he could and simply nodded yes. His eyes met Paul's, who could clearly the see the pain that still sat behind them.

"Ishmael...you are part of the guardianship already," Kratos remarked. He sat back and looked at all in the room in turn as if studying them intently for several minutes.

Port of La Rochelle, France, Melissae Inn, spring 1191

"What...you cannot stop there. You must tell us all that he explained," Sarah interrupted the old man loudly.

"Sarah...I was not going to stop. I was just resting for a moment," the old man explained.

"Then please continue and explain all that he was about to tell," Peter asked impatiently in tone.

"Yes please, for this tale just gets stranger and stranger," Simon asked.

"Can you answer me how this Kratos character slept for...well, how many years?" Gabirol asked, puzzled.

"I cannot tell you exactly. But I can tell you, just like the Christians who slept in a cave and returned, what in their minds was just a night, several hundred years had in fact elapsed...likewise the same principle with Kratos. He had gone to sleep in some kind of see through sarcophagus, hidden deep below ground, and then many many, perhaps thousands if what we know is true, years later, he awoke to continue his work. Even after he awoke, he has since lived a great many years, more than we would consider normal," the old man explained.

"So please, tell us all he would explain, so that we may know, for if Alisha and Paul have not survived this tale, then we here must make sure that what they knew and were supposed to do is done!" Simon stated and sat up fast.

"Is that what this is all about...for us to continue what they could not?" the Templar asked as Miriam looked at him in agreement.

"As I said...at the end of this tale, I shall ask but one thing of you all, that is all. And yes, I shall tell you all that Kratos told them if you wish," the old man said softly.

"Please, for I feel there is a greater part of this story that we shall all be a part of," Gabirol said as he rolled his quill through his fingers.

"Good...you are all beginning to see where this is all going. Thank you," the old man replied and paused as he took a few deep breaths before continuing. "This tale started when a tall white haired man stood on the shores of Malta beneath an ancient Holm Oak tree and sensed something immediately after the original nine Templars opened the sealed chamber in Jerusalem. Well that man was Kratos himself. That is when Abi joined him. He was standing within the megalithic temple of Hal Saflieni, where men and women with extraordinary cranial volume and size were buried. These ancient people were linked to ancient Mesopotamian and Egyptian cultures and a race of men identified with the snake. The ancient megalithic temple was dedicated to the Mother Goddess on the island. 'Tis why the symbolic pendant Alisha, Abi and Kratos all wore looked like a woman, as well as a stylised bee. All the skulls within the complex were of a large size...but more interestingly, they were different to ours for they had but two parts to their skulls with inexistent cranial knitting lines, abnormally developed temporal partitions, drilled and swollen occiputs, but above all, had strange, lengthened skulls, lacking median knitting like ours. They are almost identical to similar skulls found in Egypt. The skulls were all found in the Hal Saflieni hypogeum, where a sacred well was dedicated to the Mother Goddess. When Kratos left the hypogeum

for the last time, he left a small statue of a sleeping goddess," the old man explained when Simon raised his hand.

"Sorry to ask but what is cranial knitting?" he asked sheepishly.

"'Tis the lines, known as 'Sagitta', where the skull sections fuse together. The skulls in the tomb have been considered 'impossible' by anatomists as their size and elongation is not the result of natural lengthening or of the cranium in the occipital area being due to bandaging or boards...Now the priests of the goddess of Malta operated out of very important centres known since pre-historic times...places where medical cures were conducted, and where oracles and ritual encounters with the priests of the goddess took place. There existed many sanctuaries and thaumaturgy centres, where priests surrounded the healing goddess in a direct expression of her divinity. In antiquity, the serpent was associated with the goddess and with healing capacities. The snake also belongs to the subterranean world. Therefore, a hypogeum dedicated to the goddess and the water cult was the right place for a sacerdotal group that was defined, in all the most ancient cultures, as the 'serpent priests'. Some have argued that those buried were a totally unique and separate race altogether. Some of the people buried there were artificially deformed, but most were not. These mysterious people erected gigantic temples to the Mother Goddess many thousands of years before Christ and in the main only bred within their own kind...eventually dying out altogether."

"But they did not as Kratos and Abi are still about," Sarah interrupted.

The old man shook his head no.

"No, Sarah...both Kratos and Abi were not from that kind, but a far older group. Remember, Kratos came from a time long before that and Abi's line came from the east of the Caucasus region, though she spent her first few years in Sardinia before joining Kratos in Malta. When Kratos first arrived in Malta, from a land far to the south past the Pillars of Hercules, it was still mainly uninhabited as the previous race had long since gone. That race was closely related to Kratos but he would remain alone for many years until the arrival of the Phoenicians on Malta for use as their Mediterranean outpost. The Phoenicians also erected temples to the Mother Goddess calling her Astarte, the snake-faced goddess. Here we find the representation of a goddess who is associated with the snake and healing powers, almost as if the Phoenicians wanted to continue an interrupted tradition."

"You mentioned Egypt...is that where other large skulls were found then?" Gabirol asked.

"Yes, just like the massive skulls recovered in Jerusalem by the Templars, skulls in Egypt, larger than that of the local ethnic group, and with fair hair and taller, with a heavier build were indeed found. This race kept its distance from the common people, blending only with the aristocratic classes and they were associated with the Shemsu Hor, or the 'disciples of Horus'. The Shemsu Hor was recognised as the dominant caste in pre-dynastic Egypt until approximately 3000 BC, being mentioned in various papyruses and the list of the kings of Abydos. Understand that towards the end of the fourth millennium BC the people known as the Disciples of Horus appeared as a highly dominant aristocracy that governed all of Egypt. The intermingling of this larger race with the indigenous population only started after the unification of Upper and Lower Egypt. What occurred in Malta was also reflected in Egypt."

"But what has that got to do with bees as Alisha asked?" Ayleth asked.

"I am coming to that," the old man replied and smiled. "In Lower Egypt, the Pharaoh's symbol is a bee named 'Bit'. It isn't coincidental that Malta's ancient name is 'Melita', which derives from the Latin word for honey. Malta's symbol was also a bee and its hexagonal cells. Melita has its origin in 'Mel' or 'Mer', which in ancient Egypt was the name attributed to the pyramids. Besides, the English term 'honey' is strictly related to the original name of

Heliopolis, which is 'On'. Paul's father owned a property there by the way. It is an interesting point that in Egypt, the Shemsu Hor guaranteed the respect of a solar religion and even today in Malta the sun is called 'Shem-shi'. 'Shem' is a word of Accadic origin, not Egyptian, deriving from the Babylonian term for the sun, which is 'Shamash'. This proves that the Shemsu Hor came from the fertile half-moon area. Another point is the fact that this long-skulled caste disappeared in Egypt, as in Malta during the same period between 3000 and 2500 BC. But there was another, third, caste who were present in the Euphrates zone, becoming part of the Arian stock known as Mithans, who the Egyptians called 'Naharin', meaning literally 'Those of the Snake' from Nahash, snak. The Mithans, who occupied a part of the Kurdistan area, were Abraham's people, whose description corresponds to that of the Shemsu Hor of fair hair and robust build. The 'serpent priest' tradition originated in the Middle East, with its foremost centre right in Kurdistan, where at about 5000 BC the matriarchal culture of Jarmo represented the mother goddesses as divinities with faces of vipers and lengthened heads. These divinities successively became associated as 'fallen angels' or 'Nephelims', that are most explicitly cited in the 'Testament of Amran' in the Qumran scrolls in which it is written... 'One of them was of terrifying aspect, like a snake and his mantle was multicoloured' and also 'his face was that of a viper and he wore all his eyes'. It concerns, in our opinion, not divinities in the strict sense, but individuals in a shaman expression, belonging to a highly developed and profoundly wise culture that had relationships with lesser organised societies of the period. Its members were considered as half-gods for the knowledge they possessed, just like in Egypt with the Shemsu Hor. Viper-faced statues of mother goddesses are found in the land of the Nile, dating back exactly from the archaic period of the Shemsu Hor. It can be argued that these serpent-priests were the most ancient race that first occupied the fertile half-moon area, particularly Anatolia and Kurdistan and Egypt, following migrations dating back 6000-4000 BC until reaching Malta to disappear around 2500 BC but this culture survived in the Middle East and probably included one of the most famous and yet mysterious Pharaohs of Egypt. It concerns the Mithans and the Pharaoh Akhenaton, the one who changed his name and led his people to a new city specially built to follow just one god."

"Ah...him. He is the one you mentioned previously as being one and the same as Moses of Biblical history yes?" Gabirol asked.

"Yes the very same. The reason why Akhenaton was linked to the Mithans is too long to say here but the way he was portrayed in his statues and bas-reliefs and with him, the whole royal family, is indeed that of an individual of lengthened head and human face but with serpent-likeness, characteristics found in the pre-dynastic Egyptian stock being the exact representation of the features of the Nephelims and the long-skulled individuals of Malta who are one and the same race as that in Egypt who ultimately led to the creation of the religious and spiritual sub-strata that characterised the greatest civilisations of the Old World. This group continued in the Middle East and somehow returned in Egypt around 1351 BC giving birth, through the heretic Pharaoh Akhenaton, to a religious reform that aimed to restore the ancient order...that order being the birth of a monotheistic god."

"So what of the myth of Atlantis then as that was mentioned?" the wealthy tailor asked.

"Well, some argued that Malta itself was Atlantis...but as Plato stated in his work, Atlantis was situated beyond the Pillars of Hercules, as in past the Mediterranean Sea and out into the Atlantic and beyond. Besides that, Kratos was specific in his original homeland being a continent sized island far off to the south surrounded by all the oceans of the world. If it was Malta, then that could not be the case. Also, an Egyptian document composed around 2000

BC, dating back to the twelfth dynasty, states that a serpent populace was destroyed by a 'star falling from the heavens'. Only one survived on an island destined to be completely submerged. What is this strange fable? Was it the record of a catastrophe that destroyed a particular Mediterranean region? The myth also connects the serpents to the figures of Mother Goddesses such as Tanit, Innanna, Isis and Eve. They are feminine divinities that carry the baton of a culture to which the snake brings wisdom, medical, scientific and esoteric knowledge. But a doubt arises...couldn't these serpents rather be human beings of strange physical form? Mythology is full of weird beings that often seem more likely physical differences rather than true divinities. For example, Cecrops, the mythical founder and first king of Athens, according to tradition, was born from the soil and his appearance was half human and half serpent. According to others, he came to Attica from Egypt and built the Acropolis, diffusing the cult of Zeus and Athena. Pythia or Python was a priestess of Delphi, taken by Apollo, who pronounced oracles. She took her name from Python the snake, killed by Apollo and believed to be buried under her temple. The woman enunciated the verdicts sitting on a sacred tripod set on the mouth of a natural gorge, from which vapours exhaled and communicated them to an assistant priest, whom in turn transmitted them to the postulant. But let's go back to Malta. Even Saint Paul, shipwrecked in the Maltese bay that still bears his name, dealt with a snake that bit his foot. In reality, in the days of Saint Paul, the first century AD, snakes didn't exist in Malta. So it's strange that such a reptile bit this holy man. This legend may well be interpreted in a different, simpler manner. The serpent was the last priest of the Great Goddess left on the island, whose total power was threatened by that of Paul, obliged to dismantle what was left of the last pagan bastion of the great Healing Goddess."

"Bees!" Sarah said bluntly almost sarcastically.

The old man laughed slightly and looked at her for a moment before continuing.

"Okay...the bee reminds us to take the honey of life and make our own lives meaningful and fertile. In other words, the bee tells us to enjoy what we do, whatever it may be. The bee is also very much associated with the feminine, fertility, growth, and motherhood. The queen bee is often the sole survivor when winter arrives, and she is the one who must build a new hive in the spring. The queen is the reason for most of these associations, if not all, since she is responsible for taking care of the hive. Bees' pollination leads to fertility of the land and without bees, the majority of pollination would not happen. The mythology of the bee is spread all over the world. In Egypt, the bee represented the energy of the sun and the bringer of the sweetness of life. The bee was the royal symbol for Lower Egypt and the emblem of the United Kingdoms of Egypt. Bees were associated with other Egyptian deities as well, like Neith, Amun, and Min. Greece also honoured the bee and they were symbolic of work and obedience. There was even a legend that the second temple at Delphi, site of the famous Oracle, was built by bees. This is clearly the beginning of how we see bees today, as busy workers. Early Christians picked up on these ancient traditions, and in Judges XIV: 8, bees are even praised for their industry, wealth, and creativity. Amazingly, we still see bees in this light, though it is thousands of years old! Bees continue to be seen as industrious, hard-working characters, creating wonderful, meticulous, hexagonal hives. Even now there are some scholars who believe bees are ruled by kings." [61]

"No!" Simon interrupted.

"Yes honestly there are," the old man replied. "From the earliest times the bee was used as an image to represent Mother Goddess and the hive was likened to the womb of the Great Mother. The most famous icon, depicting the goddess with the head of a bee and the feet of a bird, can be found in caves even today from great antiquity. It is known that bees existed in *their present form long before humankind. In many cultures they were a symbol of immortality and in an ancient Hindu custom that has survived today, a father will feed a child honey while asking Parvati, the gentle Mother Goddess, that the child might live to see a hundred autumns. In Ancient Greece the dead were embalmed in honey in the foetal position in huge urns, waiting for their restoration to a future life. In Celtic myth, bees were regarded as sources of great wisdom and messengers between the dimensions and in Christianity as emissaries of the Virgin Mary. Make a special note of that fact please even if you should forget all else that I explain about bees," the old man said.*

Gabirol wrote a note about the bees being emissaries of the Virgin Mary and underlined it.

"I think I am beginning to understand why my mother always considered it unlucky to kill any bees that came into our house as she said it was bringing blessings to the home," Simon commented.

"You had a mother?" Sarah asked jokingly.

Simon frowned at her with a mocking serious face, but then smiled.

"Yes that is why and very true," the old man replied to Simon. "Now over the millennia, bees have been adopted as the icon of Rhea, the Greek Earth Mother, Demeter the Grain Mother, Cybele, originally an Anatolian Earth and Mountain Goddess whose worship spread throughout the Ancient Greek world and Roman Empire, Artemis and her Roman counterpart Diana. Bees, like butterflies, another early Mother Goddess representation, are often etched or painted on protective amulets especially for children, babies, pregnant women, mothers, very old or sick people and to guard against loss, rejection, loneliness and grief."

"Is that why Abi gave Alisha the pendant then?" Ayleth asked.

"In part...but the power and ferocity of the bee should not be underestimated. The potency resides in the queen bee and the female virgin worker bees who gather the pollen," the old man continued.

"See, even in the bee world it is the females who do all the hard work," Sarah joked and laughed out. Stephan shook his head at her, smiling.

"The queen bee in myth symbolised the Goddess or her High Priestess and the worker bees her priestesses. Priests would become eunuchs to serve the Bee Goddesses, for example at the temple of Artemis, the Greek Huntress and Moon Goddess at Ephesus where her statues were adorned with bees. These priests were called Essenes, which means drones, the name given to the male bee."

"Is that where the Essenes of Jesus's time take their name from?" Gabirol asked.

"I could argue that was the case indeed, but I cannot prove that, but the Essenes themselves certainly behaved like a bee colony if you look at them close enough," the old man answered then paused briefly. "The bee, found in the ancient Near East and Aegean cultures, is believed to be the sacred insect that bridged the natural world to the underworld. They appear in tomb decorations. Mycenaean Tholos tombs were even shaped as beehives. The Goddess was also depicted as a queen bee in Minoan culture and this image was closely tied to the early bull worship that originally was dedicated to the Mother Goddess. The bee represented the soul and rebirth in Minoan civilisation, partly because it was believed bees were created from dead bulls, especially if the carcass was buried up to the horns in Mother Earth. This idea pervaded other European cultures and is still being recorded in England as such," the old man laughed to himself. "The bee was an emblem of Potnia, the Minoan-Mycenaean 'Mistress', also referred to as 'The Pure Mother Bee'. Her priestesses received the name of 'Melissa' for 'bee'. In addition, priestesses worshipping Artemis and Demeter were called* 'bees'. The Delphi Priestess is often referred to as a bee, and she remained 'the Delphic bee' long after Apollo had usurped the ancient oracle and shrine. In Greek mythology Melissa is the name of one of the nymphs that helped save Zeus from his father, Cronus. She hid him in the hills and fed him milk from Amalthea and honey. When Cronus discovered this, he turned her into a worm, but Zeus, in gratitude, changed her into a queen bee."

"Hang on...hang on, I have just got it," Simon interrupted and sat up straight and smiled broadly. "This inn...'tis it not named the Melissae Inn?"

"Well done, Simon...and yes it is."

"So this...this tale you tell us, it even relates to this very inn yes?" Simon asked excitedly.

The old man smiled and nodded as Gabirol looked around the inn checking to see if he had somehow missed something obvious. Stephan sat up straight and smiled as Sarah looked at him, puzzled.

"You know something we don't...don't you?" she said looking at Stephan intently.

"I am saying nothing...until this tale is finished," Stephan replied and folded his arms.

All looked back at the old man as he smiled too then continued.

"The Homeric Hymn to Apollo acknowledged that Apollo's gift of prophecy first came to him from three bee-maidens, usually identified with the Thriae. The Thriae was a trinity of pre-Hellenic bee-goddesses in the Aegean. Because bees were divine messengers, honey made into sacred mead, wine created from fermented honey, has traditionally endowed prophetic powers on the favoured. However, for two thousand years after Knossos fell the classical Greek tongue preserved 'honey-intoxicated' as the phrase for the drunken."

"There you go, we should call you honey," Simon laughed out loud whilst looking at the wealthy tailor. He just shook his head disapprovingly without replying.

"The prophetic Thriae, three maiden seers at Delphi, were the daughters of Zeus and demanded payment in honey. They drank mead brewed from a secret formula from the nectar of sacred bees that lived in the grove. This recipe was handed down to their successors who continued to prophecy at Delphi. The High Priestess, the Oracle of Delphi herself, assumed the name of Queen Bee and the bee symbol was engraved on coins at Delphi. But the most famous mead was that brewed by the Viking Giantess Gonlod who is called the mother of poetry. She owned the 'Cauldron of Inspiration' that the Father god Odin stole from her so that he might possess the gift of inspired utterance. But know this also, the sacred Omphalos stone at Delphi just happens to marry up with a stellar projection of the Argonaut or Magan Boat, but I shall explain that later if we have time," the old man explained and waited as Gabirol quickly made a note of his comment. "The bee is also seen in a number of Aegean and Near Eastern names and the Jewish historian Josephus noted that the name of one of the few Old Testament poets and prophetesses, Deborah, meant bee and she has been linked with the Mycenae Bee Goddess. Bees were a source of great fascination to the Greeks, and their mysterious origins inspired the legend of Aristæus. He was the son of the god Apollo, and had a beehive. But he tried to seduce Eurydice, Orpheus's wife, who subsequently died from a snake bite because she had refused Aristæus's advances. In revenge, Orpheus destroyed Aristæus's hive. To appease the wrath of the gods, Aristæus sacrificed four bulls and four heifers. From their entrails, new swarms suddenly appeared, so Aristæus was able to rebuild his hive and teach beekeeping to men. This legend is told by Virgil, the great Latin poet, in his famous 'Georgics'. Like the ancient Greeks, he believed that bees were born spontaneously from animal corpses. According to one Egyptian myth, honey bees were the tears of the sun god Ra. When the tears fell onto the soil, they were transformed into bees that built honeycombs and produced honey. Their religious significance extended to an association with the goddess Neith, whose temple in the delta town of Sais in Lower Egypt was known as per-bit – meaning 'the house of the bee'. Honey was regarded as a symbol of resurrection and also thought to give protection against evil spirits. Throughout ancient Egyptian history the bee has been strongly associated with royal titles. In Pre-dynastic and early Dynastic times, before the union of Upper and Lower Egypt, the rulers of Lower Egypt used the title 'bit', meaning 'he of the bee', usually translated as 'King of Lower Egypt' or 'King of the North', whereas the rulers of Upper Egypt were called 'news', meaning 'he of the sedge', translated as 'King of Upper Egypt' or 'King of the South'. In later times, after the union of Upper and Lower Egypt, the Pharaoh rulers used the title 'news-bit', meaning 'he of the sedge and the bee', which is conventionally translated as 'King of Upper and Lower Egypt' or 'King of the South and North'. The bee hieroglyph was used to represent the word 'bit', meaning 'bee' or 'honey', or the royal title 'King of Lower Egypt' or 'King of the North'. The Minoan, Merope, is connected with the bee-mask. Cretan bee-masked priestesses appear on Minoan seals. Before the Hellenes came to the Aegean, Bee of the mythographers recalled the tradition 'Merope', the 'bee-eater', in the old Minoan tongue. Orion, a suitor of Merope, was born in Hyrai in Boeotia, an ancient place mentioned in Homer's catalogue. According to Hesychius, the Cretan word hyron meant 'swarm of bees' or 'beehive'. Like some other archaic names of Greek cities, such as Athens or Mycenae, Hyrai is plural, a name that once had evoked the place of 'the sisters of the beehive'. This name Merope figures in too many isolated tales for Merope to be an individual. Instead Merope must denote a position as priestess of the Goddess. But surely Merope the 'bee-eater' is unlikely to be always a bee herself. This bee-eater is most likely to have been a she-bear, a representative of Artemis. The goddess was pictured primitively with a she-bear's head herself, and the bear remained sacred to Artemis into classical times. At a festival called the Brauronia, pre-pubescent girls were dressed in honey-coloured yellow robes and taught to perform a bear dance. Once they had briefly served Artemis in this way, they would be ready to be married. They were called Brownies. In later times, a Syriac Book of Medicine recommended that the eye of a bear, placed in a hive, would make the bees prosper. The bear's spirit apparently watched over the hive, and this was precisely the Merope's role among the Hyrai at Chios. The name 'Merope' also meant 'honey-faced' in Greek, thus 'eloquent' in Classical times. Now Aphrodite, Greek Goddess of Love, was worshipped at a honeycomb-shaped shrine at Mount Eryx. Her High Priestess was called Melissa, meaning bee, and the other virgin priestesses melissae."

"Hey, does that mean we have virgins here?" Simon joked. Only the Genoese sailor laughed at his comment, Sarah shaking her head feigning disgust. Ayleth blushed.

"Simon," the old man remarked and shook his head before continuing. "By virgin this meant that they belonged to no man, but practised a form of sacred prostitution that celebrated the fertility aspect of Aphrodite, the queen bee and the sacred marriage between earth and sky. the hexagonal shape of the honeycomb, six, was believed to be the number of Aphrodite and later Venus, as well as the sacred geometric shape of harmony. Bees, which were considered in Greece to be the souls of dead priestesses, were creators of this perfect form and thus greatly revered. Indeed the mathematician Pythagoras believed that the honeycomb form suggested a symmetry that was reflected in the cosmos itself. Bees are symbols of the Virgin Mary throughout the western world and especially in Eastern Europe. In the Slavonic folk tradition the bee is linked with the Immaculate Conception. July the twenty-sixth, being the feast of St Anna, mother of Mary, whose birth also resulted from an immaculate conception, is the time when beekeepers pray for the conception of new healthy bees. Note, if you did not know already, Alisha was born on the twenty-sixth of July. Coincidence *perhaps...,"* the old man said as he smiled. *"In the lands east of Italy, on the shores of the Black Sea, bees are considered to be the symbolic tears of Our Lady and the queen bee of any hive is called Queen Tsarina, a name associated with Mary, Queen of Heaven. Throughout Eastern Europe, Mary is the protectress of bees and beekeepers and consecrated honey is offered on altars on the Feast of the Assumption of the Virgin Mary on August the fifteenth, the date linked with her ascension into heaven. In Hinduism, the bee relates to Vishnu, Krishna or Kama, the God of Love. Did you know that beekeeping, also known as apiculture, was a Minoan craft, and the fermented honey-drink was an old Cretan intoxicant, older than wine? The proto-Greek invaders, by contrast, did not bring the art of beekeeping with them. Bee-keeping is depicted in Egyptian temple reliefs as early as 2445–2441 BC. Bees were certainly of great importance in providing honey, which was used both as the principal sweetener in the Egyptian diet and as a base for medicinal ointments. The Egyptians also collected beeswax for use as a mould-former in metal castings and also for use as a paint-varnish. As Kratos explained at length, and they did all stay awake, the wisdom of bees included a connection to the Goddess and to understanding female warrior energy."*

"Oh yes, Tenno certainly learnt that understanding," Simon laughed out loud.

"Trust you to lower it," Sarah said looking at him with a look of disgust again, though Stephan laughed and quickly tried to stop himself when she looked at him instead.

"Thank you, Simon, for that insight," the old man remarked and continued. *"Bee wisdom included reincarnation, communication with the dead, helping earth-bound spirits move on to their proper place, concentration, prosperity, industriousness, cooperation and fertility. The Royal Queen Bee possessed the virtues of being able to send and receive messages from higher planes and consciousness, to prophetic dreams and visions, wealth, industriousness, diligence, cooperation, productive hard work, sexual attraction, the power of giving back when taking, the ability to turn something unassuming into a wonderful creation, ability to enjoy and savour the sweetness of life, a connection with the earth and living things, divine messages, focus, sensitivity, and realising the fruit of one's labour. Even in the Qur'an, bees symbolise wisdom, harmlessness, and the faithful. And in Celtic cultures, bees were said to have a secret wisdom that came directly from the otherworlds. Many cultures believe that bees originated in Paradise and they are traditionally known as the 'little servants of God'. And because of its honey and its sting, the bee is considered to be an emblem of Christ: it represents his mildness and mercy on one side and his justice on the other."*

"Ah...does all this mean that Alisha and her bloodline then are indeed of the line of Jesus, as symbolised by the bee pendant?" Gabirol asked.

"But by that token, that means that Kratos and Abi are also related to his bloodline," Peter commented and looked at Gabirol.

"I shall come to that point in time, but as for bee symbolism, well, as workers of the hive, bees are a symbol of an industrious and prosperous community governed by the queen bee. They have therefore symbolised all that is royal and imperial in Europe, especially now France and in ancient Egypt. Three hundred gold bees were discovered in the tomb of Childeric the First (in the year AD 481), which showed that the hive was the model of an absolute monarchy. As organisers of the universe between earth and sky, bees symbolise all vital principles and embody the soul. The bee and the hive have long been symbols of industry and regeneration, wisdom and obedience, with a place in Egyptian, Roman and Christian symbolism. Honey is used to illustrate moral teachings. A man is exhorted to eat honey and the honeycomb, but warned against surfeit. It was a simile for moral sweetness, and for the excellence of the law, of pleasant words, and of the lips, and as a figure of love. 'Go to the bee,

and learn how diligent she is, and what a noble work she produces; whose labour kings and private men use for their health. She is desired and honoured by all, and, though weak in strength, yet since she values wisdom she prevails.' This quote exists in an Arabic text and is quoted by ancient writers."

"I learnt that the newly converted Clovis used a bee as his symbol, is that true?" Gabirol asked.

"Yes that is true. The beehive is an emblem of industry, and recommends the practice of that virtue of all created beings, from the highest sereph in heaven, to the lowest reptile of the dust. It teaches us that as we came into the world rational and intelligent beings, so we should ever be industrious ones, never sitting down contented while our fellow-creatures around us are in want, when it is in our power to relieve them, without inconvenience to ourselves. When we look at nature, we view man, in his infancy, more helpless and indigent than the brutal creation. He lies languishing for days, months, and years, totally incapable of providing sustenance for himself, of guarding against the attack of the wild beasts of the field, or sheltering himself from the weather. It might have pleased the Great Creator of heaven and earth to have made man independent of all other beings, but, as dependence is one of the strongest bonds of society, mankind were made dependent on each other for protection and security, as they thereby enjoy better opportunities of fulfilling the duties of reciprocal love and friendship. Thus was man formed for social and active life, the noblest part of the work of God; and he that will so demean himself, as not to be endeavouring to add to the common stock of knowledge and understanding may be deemed a drone in the hive of nature, a useless member of society, and unworthy of protection by the rest. The bee is a wasp, only gentler, and both have had a long relationship with humankind as friend and foe. The earliest recorded death from a wasp sting was that of the Egyptian Pharaoh, Menes, more than two thousand years BC. Back then, bees were the symbol of the soul, and their honey was placed in tombs as sacred offerings to the dead. The hornet found itself featured on the imperial crest of the Pharaohs. Meanwhile, the ancient Greeks called the bee 'Melitta', meaning 'Goddess Honey Mother'. Because the bee appears to die in the winter and return in the spring (they actually hibernate in the hive) it also became the symbol of death and rebirth. Remember I originally informed you that Malta is also known as Melitta... Early beliefs claimed bees were heaven-sent. Because of their ability to find their way home over great distances, the bee came to represent the soul. It stood for sexuality and chastity, as well as fertility and care, and there are many stories of small children being protected by bees. Killing a bee was believed to bring bad luck. In Ireland, honey-wine was thought to be the drink of immortality, and consequently bees were protected by law. It's no surprise that the bee has been held up as a symbol of social order, diligence and cleanliness. We've all seen how they work incessantly among the flowers, pollinating and gathering honey. For many, the bee became the symbol of good, and because of its untiring work, Christians adopted it as the symbol of hope. In France, it is recognised as the regal symbol. In short, the bee is more honoured than others, not because she labours, but because she labours for others...service to others, not to self."

"I thought only Paul's father could explain the symbolism and meanings about the bees? So how come Kratos did?" Gabirol asked, checking back through his notes.

"I did say that yes...well, as Niccolas told him of course, but as it was Kratos who taught Philip originally, and time was not on their side, it was appropriate and fitting that Kratos explained it. He could also answer with Theodoric why both Alisha and Paul had bee symbols upon their parchment birth charts. And remember how I explained that even Samson *in the Bible had many symbolic connections in regard to Orion and the Knights Templar, traditions of two twin pillars, just as Samson is connected to two pillars and where he slays the Philistines with the jawbone of an ass. That story was purely symbolic of astronomical information. Samson is the strong man constellation of Orion and the jawbone is the V shaped star group above him, which we today call the Hyades. This cannot be doubted especially when you learn that one of the first tasks of Samson is the slaying of a lion. Later Samson finds bees and a honeycomb in the dead corpse, which gives him an idea of a riddle. You may now see how bee symbolism is an important aspect of this tale. Samson posed the riddle 'Out of the strong came something sweet'. The hidden esoteric meaning behind this is to be found in the stars. The lion is of course the constellation of Leo, and next to it in the constellation of Cancer is Praesepe, the Beehive!"*

"Star connections again. It seems that everything, every time, always ends up relating and going, or pointing to stars...am I correct?" Gabirol asked.

"You have no real idea just how correct, my learned friend," the old man smiled.

"And Kratos explained all of this to Alisha and Paul?" the farrier asked.

The old man simply nodded yes.

"Well I wish to know what was in the parchment tubes hidden beneath Alisha and Paul's caravan. Can you tell us that please?" Ayleth asked politely.

All around the table looked at the old man waiting for an answer.

"Of course I shall, as soon as I have had a drink," he replied and poured himself a drink of rosehip water. "Now...where were we?"

PART VIII

Chapter 43
Dark Sun & the Celtic Cross

Alexandria, Egypt, 1179

All sat around the table in silence having listened intently to all that Kratos had explained about the staff and bees. Tenno rubbed Abi's shoulders as she sat with her eyes closed. Alisha finally faced Theodoric and broke the silence.

"Theodoric, you once said and explained to me, that Merovingian blood flows through both our families. That is why the symbols of the rose, the fleur de lys, apples and bees are connected strongly to us. And in the future, when the world is ready, and as long as the Crimson Thread has not been severed, then through a family with its connection to apples and bees, will the navigator of those times be revealed. Is that via Arri then?" Alisha asked.

"I am glad to see that you listened to me back then…and yes, that is correct is it not?" Theodoric answered then looked at Kratos for confirmation.

"Then what is in the parchment rolls that were hidden beneath our caravan?" Alisha demanded almost as Theodoric looked back at her then again at Kratos.

"They are family tree details…of both of you. They show who your parents are as well as your grandparents and further back, all the way to Merovingian lines and beyond. As far back as the Davidic lines," Kratos answered. "But also maps… of great antiquity…and how to navigate with them simply by using just a cross, a Celtic style cross, and symbolic nets."

"And if you look close enough, you will see Reynald's line is connected to your lines also…his mother is from your side, Alisha, and his father being from yours, Paul…," Theodoric explained quietly. "That is why he was able to marry supposedly above his known official status."

Alisha and Paul looked at each other, surprised. Alisha shook her head no slowly.

"Is that why Gerard was so keen to recover parchments from us?" Paul asked.

"Yes, as ordered by Reynald himself. But Niccolas hid them well…plus other copies your father is at this very moment in time having copied and also hidden elsewhere," Kratos answered with a smile. "And, Alisha…it does show Raja as being your mother as well as your blood father's line. But always remember, these physical bodies we inhabit are but temporary. Like a coat you put on and take off. Firgany, in this life, was without doubt your father though, so honour him by remembering and never doubting that."

"It makes me feel very uncomfortable…but I do not know who my blood father was and Firgany is and always shall remain so my father in my heart, always," Alisha said, her eyes welling with tears, but she quickly shook her head and composed herself despite the clear pain in her expression. She held Arri closer as he smiled away at her. "And maps of what?"

"You mean of where?" Theodoric remarked.

"The whole world, as a sphere and why the need to understand the net," Kratos answered.

"Well I am most interested to learn more," Paul said and folded his arms.

"Good, for that is why Attar will help you copy the maps and understand the net secrets and how to use the cross to navigate...without the need of any other device," Kratos answered. Attar smiled and nodded at Paul. "Much of what you shall learn is related to sacred knots and nets. The yellow and black bands we wear, and the Templars, well, again it is all related and connected to Egyptian symbology that has been carried directly over into Christian symbology. In Egyptian magic, and don't be afraid or put off by the word magic as it comes from the root word 'Magi', the three wise men, one of the most important symbols is that of the net."

"It has already been explained about the Magi," Theodoric interrupted.

"Good, then at the risk of repeating the information, the net represents many different things to Templars and mystics on several levels; from the net of lines that encircle our world, the paths of the dragon that flow within the earth as the ancients saw it, but are natural energy lines, to representing the nets cast by the Goddess of Love who weaved her web with the lives of man. Even to the colour, being yellow and black, representing the bee. All Merovingian kings were buried with many symbolic bees by the way as you know. In Greek traditions, this same net is represented by the net of Hephaestus with which the vengeful Olympian god ensnared his beautiful wife Aphrodite and her lover Ares. Always in net symbology, two deities or persons are linked to it, as are special knots for undoing it. In Egyptian myths, these two deities are Neith, known as Net, and Thoth. Thoth is called 'Great God in Het Abtit' or the 'Temple of Abtit', which was one of the chief sanctuaries of the god at Hermopolis. Thoth is in Greek, Hermes, the God of wisdom and knowledge who sealed away items in sealed vaults so that one day mankind would be able to recover hidden artefacts intact. It is where we get our root word for hermetically sealed. The hieroglyphs with which the name 'Het Abtit' is written actually mean 'House of the Net', or more precisely 'A temple wherein a net was preserved and venerated'. Now according to the Egyptian *Book of the Dead*, a dreaded net was thought to exist in the underworld, which was greatly feared by the dead. The departed dead or dying were required to know the name of every single part of it, including ropes, weights, cords, hooks and so forth. In the mythical battle between Marduk and Tiamat in the Babylonian epic, Marduk also ensnared Taimat with his net before cutting her open. Marduk and Taimat by the way are actually symbolic representations of our mother planet, and another planet that passes us every 3,600 years." [62]

All around the table looked at each other puzzled by his last comment except Attar who smiled broadly.

"You failed to mention that the symbol for Hermes is also the 'triple Tau' and in Gematria, Hermes equals 153," Theodoric stated and raised his eyebrows at Kratos.

"I am sure you have read in the Bible where Jesus informs his disciples to cast their fishing nets to the right and they will catch 153 fish. The number is very specific. That whole account is just a symbolic and allegorical continuation of ancient esoteric wisdom that connects the Great Pyramid with Jesus, including important mathematical values. Peter written in Greek has a Gematria value of 755, but

Peter was also known as the Rock, which equals 153 as does the actual word 'rock'. Peter was to become the rock and foundation of the Christian Church. The King's Chamber in the Great Pyramid is exactly 153 courses above its base line and its Grand Gallery rises exactly 153 feet. The ordinary twelve disciples didn't know or understand Jesus's hidden messages, as they were not supposed to as the information is meant for later generations' benefit," Kratos explained.

"Sorry you have lost me. That's twice now you have mentioned mathematical values and numbers without explaining what that's all about," Thomas pointed out.

"I thought I had. Sorry," Kratos replied. "The ancients had a science known today as Gematria whereby every sound, letter or syllable had an equivalent mathematical value associated with it as well as harmonic sound. Whole sentences within sacred holy books all carry this code, so that one day, they will again be seen for what they are and lead to the hidden locations of mankind's true past and origins... as well as help him through a transitional period of great trials and tribulations."

"I was told of these things whilst in Jerusalem by Theodoric, Brother Jakelin and Count Henry, but only the basics," Paul explained.

"Good, that is a start. But let me place just a hint of what you must learn about for I shall tell you now that the Great Pyramid had a Merkaba star on top, which cast shadows that formed the shape of the cross as employed by Templars, Hospitallers and the Knights of Lazarus. Also that its original cap stone of gold was never fitted, the stone that the builders rejected, and it is symbolic of a head missing. Like John losing his head. The hidden cap stone, a pyramidian, is surrounded by twelve chambers that each contain ancient artefacts and proofs of man's origins and pre-history, but should you discover its location, just as Moses and Aaron did, it must be left alone. 'Tis just the codes that mark its location that you are guardians of, nothing more," Kratos explained simply and to the point.

"Theodoric detailed much about the Merkaba star, so I am already aware of that," Paul said and looked at Theodoric as he spoke.

"Thank goodness for that means I do not have to repeat it all again," Kratos laughed. "The parchments also depict how to make and use a cross...a cross that can be used to navigate this world. That too must be guarded and handed down as, one day, if all goes wrong, man will again need to know how to map the stars and this planet...but that I can explain later this evening when we are a bit more relaxed... as well as show. Or perhaps Theodoric may care to do so?"

"Of course, I think I must have taught him as much as I could in the short period of time we have already had," Theodoric replied and raised his hands.

"Have you taught him about his father's work and Chartres Cathedral?" Kratos asked then looked at Paul.

 1 – 35

"He has," Paul interjected and sat up. "He has taught me so far that the new Chartres Cathedral is to have twelve circles about its rose window, just like the drawings my father showed me years ago when we visited the present cathedral there... twelve disciples, twelve months of the year, twelve knights of the round table, and Mary Magdalene's feast day is the twenty-second of July. Twenty-second day and seventh month. That's another reason why the Templars and the Prieure de Sion accord so much unusual reverence to her and the obvious significance of the twenty-second of July date? Both he and Niccolas have also taught me about its connection with the twin columns of Joachim and Boaz Pillars in Solomon's temple but also the height being twenty-two feet separated by seven feet etcetera and all the other stuff relating to pi being twenty-two over seven," Paul replied.

"Well in regard to the reverence shown towards the Magdalene, that is only part of the reason as initiates in the higher circles of both Orders understood that the symbolism and allegorical information is what was important. They were aware that in the future, the names were likely to change again but the story would always be the same, as would the colours and numerical values. Mary Magdalene is revered by Templars and the Prieure de Sion members and it must be understood that she is the only woman mentioned in all Canonical Gospels. She is also always listed first, which in Jewish traditions indicates her seniority over those named after her. She also had the unusual title the 'first apostle', apostola apostolorum, and acknowledged as second only to Jesus in Gnostic Gospels of Egypt."

Abi moved to stand, Tenno immediately helping her.

"I am sorry, but I feel weary. I hope you will excuse me for I need to rest," she said quietly.

"Of course, of course. We can resume this conversation later. It will give Attar time to copy the parchments too," Kratos said and stood up. "Rest well, Abi, rest well."

"Before you leave, one question that has always bothered me is the biblical account of creation in Genesis. Did the Lord really make the world in seven days?" Thomas asked.

Kratos looked at him then at Abi as she feigned a pained smile and left the room supported by Tenno. He sat back down holding his staff in his left hand and smiled as he looked at Thomas.

"My friend...that question has been asked of me more times that I can recall, but in short, let me explain," Kratos replied and paused as he made himself comfortable again. "Is Genesis mythical, many ask...well it is based upon fact though somewhat badly mistranslated over the years. All things were contrived symbolically and Genesis is no different and is but a simplified representation of real events. All the ancient myths of creation and the origins of man show a remarkable similarity. As an example, the Genesis account, by God, is almost identical to that of the Babylonian Enuma Elish, by their God Marduk. One day when the Babylonian and Sumerian languages are again deciphered and read, these facts will be proved, but for now I am afraid you will have to accept that what I tell you is the truth. Remember that the Babylonian accounts are based on the even earlier Sumerian accounts, which in turn are based upon even earlier sources...sources I have had access to," Kratos explained and winked at Alisha. "They even record details of our entire world as well as the planets and stars...information that is also written upon the parchments hidden in your caravan all along."

"And we had no idea," Paul remarked.

"They also contain a wealth of information about the earliest history of mankind and our solar system. But it is the many similarities between the biblical myths of the Old Testament and those of the ancient Babylonian epic known as the Enuma Elish that you should learn if you are able. The early Hebrews spent many years in captivity in Babylon and were certainly influenced by the Enuma Elish, which had been the Babylonians most sacred text for over a thousand years. Many of their clay tablets make reference to many gods, just as the plural meaning as per Genesis when God talks about creating man in 'our' image, and 'our' likeness, who directly intervened in man's physical creation and history. The biblical account of creation has many direct parallels with other ancient religious sources, including ancient Egyptian. This is why I tell you that all of the ancient religious doctrines, myths and legends are in fact based upon a common source. One Mesopotamian text describes instructions given to a god in charge of creation as follows: 'Mix to a core the clay, from the basement of Earth, just above the Abzu, and shape it into the form of a core. I shall provide good, knowing young Gods who will bring that clay to the right condition'. The Bible makes the same allusions to using the dust of the earth to create mankind. This is where I shall introduce you to the first of many meanings attached to ancient words and symbols; and as you shall see, a clearer picture begins to emerge. To claim that mankind was made out of the dust or clay is quite clearly absurd I am sure you would agree, but what was really inferred by the meaning of dust and clay? you should ask yourselves The actual Hebrew word used in Genesis is 'tit'. This is derived from the earliest known language of the Sumerians where TI.IT meant 'That which is life'. This indicates that the ancient chroniclers of the Bible were stating that Adam, which just happens to mean 'first man', as well as several other meanings, was created from already existing living matter. In Genesis we are told that after man had been created, God then created woman. 'And the lord God caused a deep sleep to fall upon Adam, and he slept; and he took one of his ribs, and closed up the flesh instead thereof; and the rib, which the Lord God had taken from man, made he a woman, and brought her unto the man'. (Genesis 2:vvs.21–22) Even in Islam and in their Qur'an, it speaks of the first woman being made from the rib. Allah Says in the Holy Qur'an Chapter 4 Surah Nisaa verse 1: 'O mankind! Reverence your Guardian-Lord Who created you all from a single 'nafs', and from it created his mate Hawwa, and from them twain scattered countless men and women'. The term used by Allah Subhanah in the Qur'an is 'nafs', which has been translated by some 'soul', and some as a 'person'. Regardless of whatever meaning of the term 'nafs' is taken, it clearly means that Allah created the first woman, Hadrat Hawwa, from the 'nafs' of Hadrat Adam. A later Hadith states 'Whoever believes in Allah and the Last Day should not hurt, or trouble, his neighbour. And I advise you to take care of the women, for they are created from a rib and the most crooked portion of the rib is its upper part; if you try to straighten it, it will break, and if you leave it, it will remain crooked, so I urge you to take care of the women.' In the above Hadith, the Messenger of Allah guided mankind that the women are created from a rib. The parable implied is that just as the rib has a natural turn or bend in its nature, the nature of woman is distinct and different from the man's. Just as the rib would break if one tried to change or bend it, the woman too should be accepted, appreciated, and honoured with her distinct nature; for if one tries to change or distort the natural nature of the woman she was created in, she too would break."

"You mean we would end broken," Theodoric joked.

"'Tis true what is said of woman…hell hath no fury," Kratos replied and smiled with a wink. "Now in ancient Sumerian the word TI stood for both 'rib' and 'life'.

In the Atra-Hasis, the name of the hero, written upon the tablet are over a hundred lines devoted to creation. These tablets were written way before Moses even appeared upon the world stage. Though in fairness there were in fact two characters that history has woven into just one identity...much like the fabled King Arthur," Kratos explained then paused. "That is another story for another time....
In the tablet I speak of now, we hear of many gods of which one is known as Enki who gave instructions to a goddess named Ninti, which means 'Lady of the Rib' in Sumerian, on how to create life. Some of the lines are un-readable but I'll quote it: 'Ninti nipped off fourteen pieces of clay; seven she deposited on the right, seven she deposited on the left. Between them she placed the mould...then she...the cutter of the umbilical cord. The wise and learned. Double seven birth Goddesses had assembled; seven brought fourth males, seven brought fourth females. The birth Goddess brought forth the wind of the breath of life. In pairs were they completed in her presence. The creatures were people, the creature of the Mother Goddess'."

"Those values again," Paul interrupted.

"Yes, you will always find them," Kratos remarked before continuing. "The number seven figures prominently and fourteen. Some argue that what is being described is clearly the production of people by artificial processes or some kind of hybridisation process. Like the Bible states, God made man in his image, though it actually states 'We made man in our image'. The new creature was called in Sumerian LU.LU which meant 'The mixed one'."

"But why would a god or gods make us in the first place?" Percival asked.

"The Bible states that man was created as 'there was no man to work the ground'. The Atra Hasis states, 'When the Gods, as men, bore the work and suffered the toil, the toil of the Gods was great. The work was heavy, the distress was much'. The Atra Hasis described that the rank and file gods rebelled against their leader known as Enlil. The father of the gods, Anu, had to be called down from heaven to resolve the problem. It was a god named Enki, also known as Ea, who provided the solution. 'Whilst the Birth Goddess is present, let her create a primitive worker, let him bare the yoke, let him carry the toil of the Gods!'"

"Oh great...so we were simply created to be slaves of burden," Thomas interrupted, almost aghast at what he was hearing.

"No...not at all. If that was or had been the case, we would still all be slaves now," Kratos replied and paused as Thomas shook his head, bemused. "And remember, the ancient clay tablets and scripts that detail these facts are more than six thousand years old based upon even older accounts...a long time before the two thousand year old Genesis story which so many believe as absolute fact now." All sat in silence for a few moments thinking upon his words. "I shall leave you to consider what I have explained," Kratos said and stood up slowly and then smiled at them. Theodoric and Attar were both grinning knowing the effect such information can have a person, having long ago learnt it themselves. "Woman was made from the rib of man. She was not created from his head to be above him, nor from his feet to be stepped upon. She was made from his side to be close and equal to him, from beneath his arm to be protected by him, and near his heart to be loved by him! Always remember that."

෫ ෬

Bemused and more than a little confused as well as concerned, Alisha and Paul took themselves off for a walk alone. As Attar busied himself copying the parchments, Theodoric and Kratos took Arri to look after him as well as talk and catch up. Theodoric was keen to learn how Kratos had survived his injuries and fall when last they had met and told Paul he would press him on the matter when alone. Alisha had been reluctant to leave Arri at first but as Kratos took him in his arms, Arri smiled and seemed more than content. He would not require another feed for a couple of hours and so Paul led Alisha to a part of the city his father had mentioned many times before, the obelisk set for Queen Cleopatra. It took them less than ten minutes to walk the route passing relatively few people as they were away from the main hustle and bustle of the city centre. Paul frequently checked he had his sword and held Alisha close, constantly watching out for trouble. Eventually they arrived at a raised mound that overlooked an open area facing toward the sea. Paul stood behind Alisha and wrapped his arms around her waist and pulled her close. She rested her face against the side of his and placed her hands over his and just looked out across the clearing, the dusty hues of light brown contrasting sharply with the brilliant white of the old defensive curtain wall and a large white block house, the blue of the sky reflected in the deep blue of the sea. The large obelisk Philip and Theodoric had mentioned stood defiant against the elements and time just a short distance away. A second obelisk lay in front of it where it had fallen at some remote time no one quite knew when. Three people who stood at the base of the standing obelisk looked tiny in comparison with it. It appeared a delicate rose pink in colour as the sun began its gradual path to the horizon. Paul smelt Alisha's scented hair. Their fathers had done more for them than they could ever thank them enough for, he thought. Their home was far more than the mere smallholding Philip had told them it would be.

"Shall we go and see if our fathers' initials are indeed carved in the obelisk?" Paul asked and kissed Alisha on the side of her face. He looked down at her as she pulled her face away to look up at him. He could see the three little scars upon her neck. A constant reminder how close he had come to losing her, his stomach knotting instantly. He shuddered.

"No...I like the view from here and I know it is there," Alisha replied and turned to face him fully. She clasped his hands and looked into his eyes. "Paul...do you believe we are somehow different...that we have a destiny?" she asked quietly and bit her bottom lip in her usual manner she always did when thinking. "I want nothing more than to raise our children in peace and safety. I do not want anything else."

"Children eh? So we shall have more," Paul joked and smiled.

"You know we shall," Alisha replied and playfully hit his chest. "But if we are somehow special...destined for something, then swear to me that you will simply act as guardian of the codes, whatever they prove to be as Kratos says...nothing more, swear to me," she demanded looking serious.

"You are most certainly special...and different, Ali...but as for destiny, my father said constantly that we are all ultimately masters of our own destiny. The parchments are just guides, to help. But our lives, they are here. This feels like home, does it not?" Paul replied and pulled her close. He ran his fingers through her hair and she closed her eyes momentarily. Gently he kissed her and he felt her shiver in his arms. He leaned lower and gently kissed her neck where the three scars were. Instantly she shied away and pushed him back, alarm in her eyes.

"No...," she said and looked fearful. "I am sorry, Paul...I did not mean to push you away. It just feels uncomfortable...I am not sure how to explain it...it just reminds me of how I felt when they were going to slice my throat, 'tis not you I swear," she explained emotionally.

"Ali, 'tis I who should apologise for I did not think. I only meant to kiss them better. Silly eh?" Paul replied looking into her eyes trying to search out every emotion in her.

"Please...I will soon be ready to show you my love again...when you kiss me, it still sends shivers right through me, and I do want you...so much, but my body still feels not ready. But it will not be long, and no, it is not silly. I must learn to trust you kissing me there for I know you would never hurt me...and you too must learn to stop being so tense and agitated as I have seen you of late. That sword I note you check constantly," she smiled.

"Ali, I am trying to relax...there is no rush for you to show physical love for me. As for the scars upon your neck...as Theodoric explained, some scars we cannot see. The hidden ones that may never heal. I must accept that and I promise I shall not try and kiss you there again. We have been through much and I also know what having a baby can do to a woman in normal circumstances."

"Oh you do. And how do you know this?" Alisha asked smiling as her eyes widened.

"Sister Lucy...she never stopped telling me," Paul answered and laughed.

"When we do, do you believe we shall have a daughter as I was told in that dream and as the parchments show...or another boy?"

"Well...I hope not straight away as I want to be totally selfish and have you all to myself to love and kiss and caress, but not on your neck," Paul half joked but at the same time feeling fearful almost. Alisha having a second child was a risk. And with Arri, he could not think of loving another child so much. "Ali, we have a truly wonderful home, surrounded by men who have vowed to protect us in a wonderful open city. Let us enjoy life as we have it for we alone cannot change the world. My father told me that was the mistake he and Theodoric made, though I did not know it was Theo he was referring to at the time."

Alisha turned around pulling Paul's arms around her and leaned back into him. She looked at the tall obelisk and then toward the main city itself shimmering in the heat haze. She knew the obelisk was called Cleopatra's Needle and she was aware of the story behind it as Theodoric had explained as well as the Pharos lighthouse that towered in the distance. A gentle warm breeze danced across her face bringing with it the sweet fragrant smell of a multitude of flowers and aromas. Paul held her tighter and looked down at her neck as she rested her head against his chest. Her hair hung loose, which suited her, he thought. He could just see the edge of the first scar upon her neck. Thoughts ran through his head that if he could one day take her to Jerusalem and beneath the temple, perhaps the woman of light would appear and she could reduce if not make the scars vanish as she had almost done to the deep scar on Paul's face. He ran his finger down his face where the scar still faintly remained, though barely visible now. If he grew a beard, you would never notice it. He smiled as he thought about growing a beard, but then his heart sank as he recalled how he received the scar. His mind wandered to Stewart and what was he doing. Was he okay and safe and how was Taqi with all the troubles in his region? He sighed and kissed Alisha on the side of her face again and just held her tightly.

ഇ യ

Paul led Alisha through the main outer wall entrance way of their home to be greeted by the sight of two large caravans and several mounted guards from Turansha's escort. Alisha looked at Paul, concerned, as the fully armed and brightly attired guards looked their way. As Paul approached the ornate main entrance doorway, he immediately saw Turansha speaking with Theodoric holding Arri showing him to Turansha and another taller man. Quickly Alisha and Paul approached.

"Ah, here you are. We did not expect you back so soon," Theodoric remarked, smiling broadly, rocking Arri.

"Paul, Alisha. It is good to see you again and that you have settled in well. Please, I hope you do not mind this intrusion but I have brought a very good friend of mine along to meet you," Turansha explained politely and motioned with his right hand toward the tall man stood beside him. "You two have much in common...maps and ships!"

Paul stepped forwards just as Alisha took Arri from Theodoric and looked at the tall man quizzically.

"Where is Kratos?" Alisha asked Theodoric as he handed her Arri carefully.

"Who?" Theodoric replied and winked.

"Assalamu Allakham. Paul...I have heard much about you. It is my honour to be acquainted to you. I am Husam al Din Lu'lu," the tall man smiled and part bowed his head.

"Wa Allakham Assalam," Paul replied and looked at the tall man immaculately dressed in a long cream coloured robe with long sleeves that hung low and cinched with an ornamental belt. Paul noted his sandals, or na'l as they were known. Made from palm fibre and smooth leather, he knew these fine sandals were the mark of a person of high rank, usually royalty. His robe part covered a wide embroidered collared shirt that had embroidered borders and he also wore a high conical hat, the qalansuwa, which consisted of a frame of reed covered with silk. Paul knew this man was of high standing just by the way he was dressed and his bearing. Two men immaculately dressed in white clothing with wide waistbands appeared beside him holding several layers of different materials and silks. They proffered them toward Alisha, who looked at them and then Turansha, confused.

"They are gifts from Husam," Turansha smiled.

"If you will accept them of course?" Husam asked and smiled again.

Paul's mind raced. Here stood before him, bearing gifts for no apparent reason, was a man of clear affluent means.

"Forgive us," Alisha started to say and looked at Husam. "We are new here and not yet accustomed to the ways so please forgive us our ignorance."

"I see no ignorance here...and you are indeed as Turansha speaks more beautiful than words can convey. It is my great pleasure to meet you both. I have heard much about you both," Husam explained politely and smiled.

Alisha smiled and blushed as Turansha laughed and shook his head and looked upwards briefly feigning embarrassment.

"Then I think we should ask you in," Paul said looking at Turansha first and hesitantly motioned with his hand toward the main doors.

"We shall not stay long as we have a delegation from the Templars arriving tomorrow that we must prepare for. Count John along with Brother Thierry and Lord Conrad of Montferrat," Turansha explained as he ushered Husam to follow Paul.

"Templars and who?" Paul asked puzzled.

"Ah yes, you know him of course as Brother Terricus from Tyre...or Brother Teric. He arrives by ship to discuss some matters of diplomacy. Perhaps you would join us? See if we can all resolve the continued madness that seems to be growing between our faiths," Turansha explained as he ushered Husam to walk before him.

Port of La Rochelle, France, Melissae Inn, spring 1191

"Sorry but how come Brother Teric was going to be in Alexandria? I thought they were at war?" Simon asked, confused.

"They were, but he was travelling to Alexandria with a contingent of Templars as well as Count Raymond and his wife, Princess Eschiva, to try and resolve differences and try to work out a peace plan that they could stick to. Count Henry was also attending to meet with both Gokbori but also Saladin's private secretary, but Turansha called him the name John," the old man explained.

"So the rumours were true after all. Raymond was indeed a traitor who thought more of Muslims than his own kind," the Hospitaller interrupted, shaking his head disapprovingly.

"No he was not that at all. Too many are not aware of the facts nor the lengths that Raymond went to to spare the whole kingdom from bloodshed, but I hope you will let me explain that?" the old man replied instantly.

"Please do explain for there are many rumours that still need to be addressed and answered," the Templar commented and sat up straight.

"It may be many years before people know the truth, but as long as just one person knows it, then it will be revealed," the old man began to explain.

"Excuse me, but who is this Raymond?" Ayleth asked with a raised finger.

"Ayleth, I shall explain for your benefit as you were not here when I first mentioned him," the old man replied and nodded with a slight smile. "Nicholas of Blancofort also attended as part of the Templar escort."

"No surprise there then...bet he only came to see Alisha?" Sarah interrupted.

"Perhaps." The old man smiled and continued. "But he was smart and brave and understood Muslims very well including the politics behind much of what was unravelling between Christianity and Islam. Upside...Brother Baldwin...attended alongside Raulfus Bructus and Laudoicus de Tabaria."

"I know them for I served with them...before they betrayed our Order and went over to the Muslims," the Templar interjected, looking saddened as he spoke.

"Please, I ask you not to condemn them for they were good men too. 'Tis easy to judge so let me at least give you all the facts," the old man replied and looked at the Templar directly.

"Do not be an apologist for them and their actions," the Templar stated abruptly.

"That I do not need to do as their actions are theirs and theirs alone," the old man explained

and smiled disarmingly. "But understand that all three knights developed a grudging respect and admiration for the Muslim commanders whilst growing increasingly disgusted with the actions and attitude of the likes of Reynald and Gerard," the old man remarked and paused waiting for a response from the Templar, but he just nodded. "Now Husam al Din Lu'lu was a man of religion known as Shaykh and he was respected by friend and foe alike for his bravery, prudence and good humour. He was an energetic naval and military man full of useful initiatives...very charismatic and engaging. He was also the commander of Saladin's entire naval fleet and had previous dealings with Paul's father, Philip."

"And what about Count Henry and Raymond?" Ayleth asked and frowned.

"Count Henry of Champagne, who as you know went by his esoteric name of John. He was the Grand Master of the Prieure de Sion as its political and administrative leader, the main force behind the formation and control of the Knights Templar. He was a driven man seeking peace before war. He often cut a lonely figure but that was his way of dealing with his unrequited love for Isabella, the sister of Queen Sibylla."

2 – 11

"Unrequited...why, did she not feel the same for him?" Sarah asked.

"Oh she loved him too, for many years, but she was married. But that is another story," the old man answered and smiled to himself. "But as I explained previously, Count Raymond the Third of Tripoli...he became a count at just twelve when his father was killed by Isma'ilis, the Assassins. Hence he did not fully trust them nor Al Rashid, the Old Man of the Mountains. However, he was the most intelligent of the Latin leaders and sought a peaceful coexistence with Muslims. And as our Templar friend has pointed out, he has been branded a traitor and responsible for the Christian defeat by Saladin's forces. But I shall cover that in greater detail later but know that he was an experienced and capable natural choice of leader to be regent who ruled the Kingdom of Jerusalem in the name of the dying young Leper King Baldwin the Fourth. As regent, Raymond showed he was patient, careful and ingenious in dealing with factions. Calculating also, he was capable of adapting to changing situations. An adaptability his hidebound contemporaries in Jerusalem rarely displayed if ever. He spent eight years as a prisoner in Aleppo where he learnt to speak fluent Arabic and gained a considerable knowledge of Islam...plus an admiration for his captors not hate. Unlike newcomers and crusaders, he saw Muslims as neighbours not enemies. Muslims saw Raymond as shrewd and the bravest of Latin leaders who also concentrated on joint harvests and rain collection etcetera. When the time came however to face Saladin, he fought as hard as the rest of the Franks but if Guy had listened to his advice, they may have avoided or even won Hattin," the old man explained and sighed and shook his head. He closed his eyes briefly then continued. "His wife was the beautiful Countess Eschiva, who was incredibly elegant and intelligent...Theodoric certainly warmed to her...more than perhaps he should but with her dark hair and eyes she was admired by all who met her. Surprisingly, Roger des Moulins, the Grand Master of the Knights Hospitaller, also attended the meeting in Alexandria. He was viewed as a kind and insightful knight who also wished to work and live alongside Muslims. He had many Muslim friends and learnt much from them including Gokbori himself," the old man explained and laughed to himself briefly. "Muzaffar al Din Gokbori as I have explained previously was one of Saladin's leading Amirs...military commanders. Gokbori meant 'Blue Wolf' in Turkish. He was the son of the governor of Irbil who had been a loyal supporter of the Great Zanghi whose conquest of the county of Eddesa had been the *first step in recapturing lands from the crusaders in 1144. He led the right wing against Saladin at Aleppo at the battle of the Horns of Hamma but changed side to Saladin's, which had profound effects, which led to Saladin's success. Consequently, Saladin gave him the cities of Eddesa (Urfa) and Samsat but more importantly his own sister in marriage, Al Sitt Rabia Khatun. He was very well versed in the mysteries surrounding the bloodlines of Jesus and that one had remained intact which became the 'House of Eddesa'. They were and still are known as the 'Master's people' or the 'desposyni', surviving members of whom journeyed to see the Pope requesting the revocation of the Pauline Church bishops in the Kingdom of Jerusalem and to be returned to them. But that was something he could not get involved with. But also present, and much to the surprise of Paul, was Al Isfahani, Saladin's secretary. It would prove to be a very beneficial meeting as it would ultimately lead to Paul following a path that changed his life." [63]*

"Oh please do not tell me that Paul becomes a Muslim," the Genoese sailor interrupted, shaking his head disapprovingly.

"Let me continue then so I can explain this better, but after I have detailed Paul's conversation with Kratos that evening," the old man replied.

Alexandria, Egypt, 1179

Alisha carried Arri toward the exit of the main dining area and stepped into the kitchen as Ishmael lit a lanthorn. The night was drawing in fast and the light fading as the sun disappeared behind the buildings. Several of the fine linens that Husam had given Alisha and Paul as a welcoming gift lay spread out upon the main table. Paul looked at Attar and Theodoric sat opposite him as Kratos walked back into the room and part bowed his head at them.

"Finally they have left. I hope you will excuse my absence whilst they were here. They are good men but I have spoken all I can with them," he explained and sat down at the head of the wooden table. "I see Tenno has not returned to join us?"

"I think he is still with Abi," Paul answered.

"Well I never saw that union coming," Theodoric said smiling.

"You must be losing your touch then," Kratos joked.

"I have been known to get things wrong...as you well know," Theodoric replied and winked in an exaggerated fashion. "Speaking of which and now that we have you here, perhaps you will explain to me just exactly how you survived that incident when last we met as you still refuse to tell me?"

Paul and Attar looked at Kratos as Theodoric folded his arms and raised an eyebrow.

"It was a surprise for you to see me, clearly! Perhaps now you can appreciate fully just how Lucy felt when seeing you again after believing you dead these past years," Kratos answered.

Theodoric sighed briefly and shook his head as Paul and Attar looked at him. Ishmael sat himself down hesitantly and looked at Paul as if to ask was it okay to do so. Paul opened his hand and gestured he take a seat near to him.

"Well, I walked into that one didn't I?" Theodoric coughed. "I intend to make up for that act...but I still wish...no, I need to know how you survived."

"As I taught you a long time ago, the body is capable of far greater things than most suspect. Mind over matter…and belief. Ishmael there is living proof of that as is Abi. I cannot explain to you in ways that you would understand, but I shall say that through meditation, the use of three fold water, much healing and some other tools of great antiquity, I was brought back from death's doors to continue in this present physical form before you."

"Tenno, he meditates, as do Templars. Is it something we can all learn?" Paul asked.

"Of course it is," Attar interrupted in answer.

"Then I hope you will teach me," Paul replied and looked at Kratos first.

"My dear boy, I must leave on the morrow's tide with Abi so I cannot, but between them, Attar, Theodoric and Tenno are more than capable of teaching you. You have Thomas who along with Tenno can teach you all the martial skills you may find useful," Kratos explained and smiled.

"But I thought you taught only peace and to never use a sword," Paul remarked, a little puzzled.

Kratos smiled again and looked at Theodoric briefly before returning his gaze to Paul.

"As Tenno can teach you, the true way of the warrior and true master is the one who can set aside the sword for good….but, and this is a big but, you presently exist within a violent and troubled world."

"But you do not have a sword," Paul commented.

"No, but I did once…and besides, I now have this," Kratos answered and lifted his staff and placed it upon the table. "'Tis far more powerful than any sword for both healing and destruction."

"And where did you get that from?" Paul asked as he studied the staff.

"That is a long story I am sure Theodoric can explain later. But its full potential can only be accessed and used by me for it is linked to me only," Kratos explained.

"Are there more of these for if there are, surely they could be used for healing a great many people?" Paul asked as he pulled the staff closer.

"There are indeed many more, but hidden. Hopefully sealed away until man can again be trusted to use them for they are capable of great destruction as I said."

"I have struggled with decisions on what career I should take. I would love to design and build ships and travel, but I cannot for I have a family now, and then I wish to study medicine and heal people…for what Roger, Roger des Moulins of the Hospitallers did for me…do you know of him?" Paul asked and Kratos nodded yes. "What he once told me sits heavy in my heart and I feel drawn to helping the injured and the sick, but I simply do not know what path to follow. A large part of me wishes to be a knight to serve and protect, but then I doubt myself and my abilities…for fighting is not what I consider myself good at."

"Paul," Tenno suddenly said as he re-entered the room. "No sane person likes fighting for it is a dirty, brutal and disgusting thing to do. But if it must be done, then do it so you can win. 'Tis not always noble to fight and kill, but sometimes necessary and it is your intention on why and how that matters," he explained as he sat opposite Ishmael.

Paul looked at Kratos to see if he agreed.

"Tenno speaks wisely. For in this world, sometimes you have to do bad things in order to create or safeguard a greater good. I would urge you to remember that. Even the Jesus figure you know of understood this as stated quite clearly in the New Testament. But I am not here to philosophise with you this eve," Kratos explained and sat back in his chair.

"Then will you at least answer me some questions...please?" Paul asked.

"Of course," Kratos replied.

"I wish to know what exactly the parchments are that Niccolas hid upon our caravan. I wish to know how come you are able to travel so freely, I wish to know why we cannot access the tools and teachings of the ancient forefathers, I wish to know why Abi gave Alisha her dagger, I wish to know what the Crimson Thread is really about and mine and Alisha's bloodlines, I wish to know who or what the woman of light was who healed my scar, I wish to know how Percival and I were missing for five days yet it was but a day for us, I wish to know what the black sun is all about and why it is depicted upon the wall mural in Jerusalem...I wish...," Paul explained hurriedly until Kratos raised his right hand.

"Paul. A lot of questions there...so let me start by saying that the whole problem with the world is that fools and fanatics are always so certain of themselves, and wiser people so full of doubts. You are wise beyond your years yet you do not realise it yet. You must learn to trust your own judgement and instincts and cast out the many doubts you harbour," Kratos said and raised his eyebrows as he looked at Paul intently. "But let me answer some of your questions starting with Abi. I must take her back to Hal Saflieni to heal her further. There is a room there that strengthens and increases natural rhythms within us. She will need to use it to fully recover. As for the dagger...'tis not just a dagger but also a map. Look closely at the three blades and the markings upon it as well as upon the base of the handle. That is all I shall tell you of it."

"What about the acorns that came with it?" Paul asked immediately.

"As I believe I explained before, the three acorns were symbolic but also taken from the great oak of Abraham...where you so nearly came to harm. Oak holds memories, natural memories like some stones. Oaks all hold the memory of the natural lines of energy that run across this world. 'Tis why the ancient true Druids revered them. Not only do they hold the soil and grasses at bay, but they also store and release energy throughout the surrounding area keeping it fertile. Kill the trees and the bees and you kill Mother Earth herself," Kratos explained.

"The tattoo across my shoulders is of two oaks...check out the leaf patterns," Theodoric said and winked. Tenno shook his head.

"The acorns contain all the stored memories too. It will be a very long time before humankind again learns of this simple truth...And the prophecies that surround the tree state that when it dies, it will mark the arrival of what most people call the Antichrist...and if the tree dies out totally, then the Antichrist will have dominion over the entire earth. Alisha by planting the acorns has ensured the line still grows."

Thomas and Percival entered the kitchen room and stopped at the doorway conscious that they had interrupted. Kratos motioned for them to sit down. Quickly they sat down, Thomas at the opposite end to Kratos and Percival the other side of Ishmael. Tenno acknowledged them with one of his slight nods.

"But I am still confused as to what I am supposed to do with the rest of my life...

Am I supposed to fight to defend?...Well, I am not sure what it is to defend other than my family. Am I supposed to learn healing or make maps?" Paul remarked puzzled.

"As Niccolas told you and Taqi, you will always have three paths open to you in this life. But if it comes to fighting, then as I said, sometimes you must fight in order to preserve all that is good. Those that you love the most, and the world that is good will not be destroyed by bad and evil men...but by good men who simply stand back, watch, and do nothing. Remember that. And what most evil men do not understand is that for every single act of evil committed, it unleashes a million acts of kindness. That is why despite so much violence and anger in the world, it will never win...even if at times it appears so for as you have heard countless times before I am sure, the dark shadows of evil will never win as long as there is but a single pinprick of light that still shines."

"But there has always been evil and war in the world," Thomas remarked.

"No...that is not so. There was a time when peace and harmony ruled this world. As Attar and Theodoric may explain to you, this world is like a school where you learn...to grow spiritually. One cannot appreciate the warmth if one has never endured the cold. Appreciate laughter having never known sorrow...and the hidden secrets of those past times, when recovered and used again, will ensure a new time of enlightenment and growth," Kratos explained.

"But what and how am I supposed to be a guardian of a secret that I do not even know?" Paul asked, puzzled. "And all this religious....stuff! Who is correct?"

"Religion. Ha!" Tenno interjected dismissively as Kratos and Paul looked at him. "Look, your religions here preach much, and maybe they do carry some code, but all I see is a lot of talk to explain things people cannot understand."

"That is true," Kratos replied quietly. "But there will come a time when people of all faiths from across the entire world will understand. Learning is one thing, but understanding is another thing altogether."

"My father once said that religion was only followed to the word by people too afraid to ask questions and terrified of going to Hell, whereas being spiritual was done by people who have been there...I think I am only just beginning to understand his comments," Paul explained.

"My people and those in China were writing thousands of years before your holy books were even written...," Tenno stated directly at Kratos.

"Tenno, they are not my holy books," he replied.

"You are a holy man yes?" Tenno asked.

"Some have called me that, but I follow no religion as such other than the principle of love and light. 'Tis a simple practice."

"You must forgive my bluntness, but I have studied this Jesus, and perhaps I do not know what hidden messages therein lay, I cannot see past the obvious facts of what is taught that contradict themselves," Tenno remarked.

"Such as?" Theodoric asked and rubbed his chin, intrigued.

"Salvation for a start. Unless I have heard it wrong your holy books proclaim an all knowing all seeing omnipotent God, yet he chooses not to forgive humankind that he made in his image, but instead instigates a system whereby he makes a virgin fall with child, in order to give birth to himself, so he can have himself crucified, slaughtered as a sacrifice, to save humankind from a

Hell that he himself created in the first place. This story of so-called historical fact is then communicated via conflicting written and verbal accounts decades after the events by anonymous authors, which are then subjectively passed on by flawed translators, most of whom cannot even agree on the meaning and interpretation of the word 'virgin'. So Paul, I would advise you do not waste your time being a guardian to something that is flawed," Tenno stated and looked at Paul intently.

"Tenno, you surprise me for you have clearly learnt much," Kratos commented and sat forwards as Theodoric looked at Tenno, bemused almost. "You speak wisely yet you answer your own question. For in truth, what you say is obvious...but what is not openly obvious is indeed the hidden codes that are carried within the books. That is why the true authors behind them placed within their structure allegorically, symbolically and mathematically codes that cannot be misunderstood or misinterpreted."

"It is better to walk alone than in a crowd that walks in the wrong direction," Tenno replied.

Theodoric started to laugh as Percival, Thomas and Ishmael listened on intently but all confused. Paul shook his head, just as puzzled at Tenno's comments.

"Paul, when Theodoric teaches you the very codes, please will you ensure that Tenno is taught likewise just as he will teach you all you must learn to defend yourself...and with the help of Thomas there and Ishmael," Kratos said softly and looked up at all of them in turn.

Theodoric looked at Tenno as he looked at him and frowned.

"Now as the night approaches, I shall answer your other questions briefly," Kratos said and pulled his staff closer on the table. "Firstly, I will not, repeat not, tell you how I travel freely, for I can promise...you will not understand it. In a thousand years from now they will only just start to learn of it. But I can answer that the Crimson Thread you speak of is but the bloodlines that run through both your family and Alisha's family, but it is hidden for good reason. When all other royal lines demand proofs of their lineage and histories and proclaim them loudly...let them for that acts as a shield that will protect the true lines such as yours. If you follow what is required of you, your lines will remain safe until the time they can be revealed...for the benefit of all humankind. Theodoric can tell you more and I am surprised he has not explained it already," Kratos remarked and looked at Theodoric.

"I have...briefly," he answered and shrugged his shoulders as Tenno stared at him.

"You frequently say humankind. Are there other kinds?" Percival asked.

"Very perceptive, young Percy," Kratos replied as he looked at him. "And yes, there are indeed others, but you all have enough problems with your own kind on this world to put right first," he explained and paused. "Only when you have done that, will you be welcomed back into a greater family."

"So the Crimson Thread simply represents a family tree?" Thomas asked.

"Not just a family tree. 'Tis so much more for the Crimson Thread can be traced back many hundreds of generations. Those details are written and displayed upon many parchments, such as those hidden upon Paul's caravan, but also within various vaults and crypts as placed by your father, Philip and Firgany. They also detail the family tree of Jesus and Mary Magdalene from their time after they stayed in La Rochelle," Kratos began to explain.

"La Rochelle! When...I mean where?" Paul asked, confused, as he looked at Kratos and Theodoric in turn.

Kratos smiled and looked at Theodoric and nodded at him to explain.

"Paul...you know that it was my family that was once charged with guarding secrets relating to the family of Jesus and where they landed in France. Well, they landed as you know at Roussillon where I come from...but they moved to La Rochelle, and there, hidden, are clues and proofs, some in plain and obvious sight. Mary Magdalene is reputed to have travelled to France in a rudderless boat named the 'Stella Maris'. Do you think it but a mere coincidence that the very road your father's house is situated upon is called just that, 'Rue Stella Maris'?" Theodoric explained and asked.

Both Thomas and Percival looked at each other in surprise and sat up alert. Ishmael just listened without saying or doing anything. Paul looked at Kratos as he simply nodded to confirm Theodoric's words. Paul's mind raced back to La Rochelle and his and Taqi's first meeting with Niccolas when he had told them there was a great secret he would share with them.

"Paul, at present in La Rochelle there are hidden the bodies of not only several of Jesus's immediate family, but also subsequent members. Also the remains of the original Templars. Your father as we speak is arranging movement and relocation of them because of the likes of Reynald and Gerard no less. He is also removing sealed boxes that contain the actual hair taken from both the physical real Jesus and Mary."

"Hair...why hair? What is so important about hair?" Paul asked, bemused.

"Like the acorns that have memories of Mother Earth contained within them, so too does our hair. A single strand contains everything there is to know about you. I do not expect you to understand or know what I mean, but there will, I promise you, come a time when man will be able to unravel its secrets and see what a person was simply from his hair. 'Tis why the Templars shave the sides and collect the hair of all new initiates."

"Why?" Tenno asked bluntly, his curiosity aroused.

"Because in the distant future, when man understands these secrets, he can access the information from hair that will enable him to again use tools from antiquity that would otherwise not work," Kratos explained but he could see the confusion on all of their faces except Theodoric's. "If, heaven forbid, the Crimson Thread is eradicated from history, then the tools that our ancient forefathers left a long time ago will simply not work. Like this staff. It only works for people of my kind, which presently stands at just Abi and I...but if you hold my hair in your palm and wrap it around the staff, it will work...not as efficiently but enough to start it working and adjust itself to a new strand, a new Crimson Thread."

"By the lords we were indeed wise to follow you here," Thomas commented with a large sigh and shook his head in disbelief. He looked uncharacteristically emotional. "Unbelievable for I never truly thought this day would come. Our purpose revealed fully," he remarked and looked at Paul just as Alisha entered the kitchen having settled Arri for the night.

"Well that explains the ridiculous haircuts the Templars insist upon," Percival said and folded his arms.

"The parchments beneath your caravan also held maps on velum and goats' skins that detail the route to a new world across the great seas. To a place marked out and named 'Oak Island' but they also show how it can be accessed, for there is a great treasure of knowledge and wisdom secreted away there. But again, no matter what man may do to access it should its location be discovered too early, then like the hidden Halls of Amenti in Egypt, it will not yield up its secrets until the earth has passed into the ring of light...and after the heavens have changed their course and the stars moved and the great destroyer of worlds has passed us by...again," Kratos explained and sat back.

Theodoric smiled seeing the look of confusion upon Tenno's face.

"I take it from your look that you know what he speaks of?" Tenno asked.

"Well I do not," Alisha said as she sat down beside Paul, clasping his hand gently. "Arri sleeps soundly," she said softly close to him.

"I know some of what he refers to...but I am sworn never to reveal it openly," Theodoric answered and looked at Kratos and waited for him to comment.

"'Tis not fate nor coincidence that brings us all here this eve, believe me. And Theo, I believe it is about time others were made aware of certain details, and not just as entrusted into the hands of Count Henry and Philip alone. Do you not agree?"

"Hey, 'tis what I have been arguing for years," Theodoric replied and smiled broadly. "Can I also tell them about Lazarus then?"

Kratos smiled and then his face turned serious.

"As Theo has already explained, Mary Magdalene, as you know her, landed in France at Roussillon, though many claim it was in Marseilles, along with Martha, her sister, as well as Joseph of Arimathea, but Lazarus also accompanied them. Joseph of Arimathea went on to Glastonbury in Britain, but Lazarus and Mary stayed in France in La Rochelle...Lazarus was the favoured confidant of Jesus Christ and was Mary's brother hence why other disciples were envious of him. Now understand that the Gospel of John never actually mentions who actually wrote it. Not once is the name John mentioned. But the author claimed he was the beloved whom Jesus referred to as the 'beloved disciple'. Only Lazarus was called this."

"Why do you tell us this?" Tenno asked, bemused.

 1 – 1

"Because it will have relevance connected with a later secret and the use of what I think you term the Atbash cipher," Kratos explained and looked at Theodoric, who acknowledged his remark with a slight nod. "You asked the meaning behind the dark sun...then let me explain a secret that is only shared within the highest initiates of the upper Templar, Hospitaller and Prior de Sion ranks. But even then, very few of them actually understand its true meaning."

"Should I be allowed to know these details for I have not undergone any training or study in these matters?" Ishmael asked hesitantly.

"Of course. But for you we would not all be sat here this eve," Kratos answered just as Alisha smiled at Ishmael and nodded yes. "There is a story about the mythical battle between Marduk and Tiamat in a Babylonian epic, where a god named Marduk ensnared another god, Tiamat, with his net before cutting her open. That story I can tell you actually relates to our very physical world we live upon, that being Tiamat. It is all symbolic but based upon real events from great antiquity, a very long time ago before man walked the earth and only great beasts of immense sized dominated what was once a planet almost twice the size it now is. It is also recounted within the Old Testament whereby Marduk is simply known as 'Wormwood' or 'The Destroyer of Worlds' but I shall explain this further later. Also the secret that the Magdalene was the wife of Jesus and bore his offspring to southern France where she is still revered as a medium of occult revelation and many prophecies that she will again return in France," Kratos explained then looked at Alisha directly.

"Well, 'tis not I that I can assure you," she remarked instantly.

"Why do you think the villagers at that dolmen stone place thought you were her? Or a returning Mary at least," Kratos asked as Thomas and Percival looked at Alisha, making her face flush red. "Mary Magdalene is often symbolised as a black or a dark blue. The Virgin Mary and Magdalene are often shown wearing blue as is Sophia. So know this, the star that represents Isis is Sirius. It appears blue to the naked eye as it sparkles. 'Tis also the star that regularly rises and sets with a pattern of seventy-two days. The seventy-two Dog Days as the Egyptians called that period. And Osiris was depicted by the stars of Orion with its three belt stars and smaller stars that represent the sword of Damocles or, as is being changed to now, Excalibur. From a region far beyond Orion, the constellation symbolised here as a lion, as in Leo, souls are born, and I do mean literally and physically. One day man will discover this fact that it is the womb from which all souls come. But, as the heavens constantly move in relation to us because of massive upheavals caused by another celestial body known as Marduk, or Wormwood...or as the Babylonians named part of it, Nibiru, the stars seem to change their positions. But an even greater celestial object passes us every 3,600 years. 'Tis a sun, but a dark sun. The companion to our visible bright sun," Kratos stated and waited for a response.

Paul thought back on his father's comments when he had told him that the constellation of Orion holds a truly great secret. Why hadn't his father simply told him all he knew? he wondered.

"A dark sun...is it evil?" Thomas asked, breaking the silence.

Alisha held Paul's hand tighter as he looked at Theodoric, who smiled and winked.

"Did tell you there is much to learn," he said and nodded, his grin growing larger.

"'Tis the dark sun that is depicted upon the wall mural you see at the Templars' headquarters in Jerusalem, even though most of them do not comprehend or understand its meaning, and no it is not evil in the sense that you ask. Everything in life has an equal and an opposite, a light and dark, and our sun is no different. But when that dark sun passes near to us along with all its attendant celestial bodies, such as Nibiru, it causes much damage upon this world that we walk upon," Kratos explained further.

"And...and when is this due to happen again?" Alisha asked hesitantly.

"Fear not, my dear sister of old," Kratos answered and winked. "Not until the age of Pisces passes into the age of Aquarius. But by then, man will...or should have, advanced beyond anything you can imagine."

"I can imagine a lot," Tenno interrupted bluntly.

"Yes, that you can," Kratos smiled. "The time of the return of the dark sun will not be until the earth enters the ring of light, and the age of Aquarius as I have said...not until the years starting from AD 2000 onwards."

"Then what have we got to worry about or protect?" Alisha asked confused.

"If you believe that we shall all live again...then everything, for you may find yourselves walking this very earth again at that time. And...and this is the important point to remember. In those times, there will be much fear, disasters and wars unlike any ever seen in this fourth age of man. But when they recover what was hidden by the last age and race of man, it will help guide them through the events that will unfold. They will learn and understand that it is all part of a naturally occurring regular cycle. Forewarned is forearmed. But...if the secret to locating and using the items as left by our ancient forefathers is lost, then instead of a new fifth age of man starting...all will revert backwards...," Kratos explained in all seriousness.

"Fifth age of man. Fifth root race...fifth flight of the Phoenix. They are all connected then to this dark sun event?" Paul asked.

"Yes...but as I have said, if what is hidden is revealed too soon, it will without doubt lead to man's utter destruction. But likewise, those souls who carry the knowledge and the physical bloodlines that can access and use what was hidden... if they are lost, then again all will revert backwards instead of forwards. Man will not evolve any further," Kratos answered.

"'Tis as Theodoric explained to me. Like the tattoo across his shoulders and back. Two women arched backwards opposite each other, their arms stretching into branches of a tree, with more branches spreading out, and strong roots set within mother earth herself. Theo, you explained how trees would help shield Mother Earth herself when the dark sun returned. So you knew of these things already?" Paul asked. Theodoric nodded yes and put his hands together and rested his elbows upon the table as Tenno stared at him quizzically. "If the earth was not protected then there would be no rebirth like the symbolic Phoenix rising from the ashes, representing the rebirth of mankind after each and every cataclysm that has happened, but this time, there would be no rebirth, no fifth age of man, the spiritual age that would finally allow us to escape the mortal bonds of this world and travel out into other realms of existence as promised to us by our most ancient forefathers as you explained!"

"Yes, I did explain very much like that. That is why you must protect your bloodlines and preserve the knowledge, for the future, not ours," Theodoric replied.

"You say mention is made in the Bible about this earth we walk being turned upside down and great cataclysms...can you show me where?" Thomas asked.

Kratos looked at Theodoric as if waiting for him to answer Thomas. Theodoric fumbled about beneath his tunic and pulled out his small leather bound Bible and flicked through its pages.

"Here...here you go. Just a few look. In the Book of Enoch 64:1, 3, you can read 'In those days Noah saw that the earth became inclined, and that destruction approached...And he said, tell me what is transacting upon earth; for the earth labours, and is violently shaken.' And here look...'Behold, the Lord maketh the earth empty, and maketh it waste, and turneth it upside down, and scattereth abroad the inhabitants thereof...The earth shall reel to and fro like a drunkard'...and again here in Isaiah 24:1, 20, 'Immediately after the tribulation of those days', and that is prior to the Second Coming by the way, 'shall the sun be darkened, and the moon shall not give her light, and the stars shall fall from heaven, and the powers of the heavens shall be shaken.' Well you know full well the actual stars do not fall, but they appear to do so as our planet moves violently. Oh and here look," Theodoric explained and flicked the pages quickly. "In Matthew 24:29 'The earth shook, the heavens also dropped at the presence of God: even Sinai itself was moved at the presence of God'...perhaps Kratos could give better examples?"

"What you have just quoted actually details the very real change in declination of the stars, as results from a shift in our planet's axis," Kratos replied as Alisha and Thomas looked at each other and shook their heads, not fully grasping what was being explained.

"Do you understand this?" Alisha asked Paul.

"Yes, but I have had instruction already by both Theo and Niccolas previously," Paul answered.

"Across the world, in all religions and myths, you will find references to a time when the stars fell or changed their places. In Ovid's account of the Deluge catastrophe, the chariot of the sun, driven by Phaeton, changed direction, the horses pulling it broke loose from their course and rushed aimlessly, knocking against the stars, and the constellations of the Cold Bears tried to plunge into the ocean. In the Timaeus Plato says that this 'signifies a declination of the bodies moving around the earth and the heavens'. In the same work he describes a cataclysm in which the earth moves 'forwards and backwards, and again to the right and left, and upwards and downwards, wandering every way in all six directions'. The paradisiacal Eden, Asgard, Meru, or Airyana Vaejo are said to have enjoyed a perennial spring-like climate, despite their traditional northern or polar location indicating that the axis must have been more or less upright. I am sure your dreams depict vividly scenes like this Paul...yes?" Kratos asked, looking at Paul directly.

"Yes," he whispered in reply.

"Then why do I not have these dreams...if as you say I was once your sister and experienced the same thing?" Alisha asked.

"Because the veil is strong on you, to protect you as you exist in this realm now...that is why," Kratos answered as Percival shrugged his shoulders, confused. Thomas feigned a confused smile at him. "Even the Greek astronomer Anaxagoras taught that during the Golden Age the stars revolved in a tholiform manner, as in a horizontal plane, a belief shared by another Greek astronomer, Anaximenes. Diogenes Laertius added that at first the polestar always appeared in the zenith, but afterwards acquired a certain declination. Similar references can also be found in ancient Japanese cosmogony and Chinese traditions. Perhaps Tenno knows of them?" Kratos said and looked at Tenno. He shook his head no briefly. "Never mind then," Kratos paused then continued. "For the Egyptians, a large fiery circle symbolised the cosmos, and a serpent with a hawk's head represented the pole, the central line our earth spins around upon. When the latter was placed across the diameter of the circle, it symbolised the pole of the earth lying in the plane of the ecliptic. A Magical Papyrus speaks of a cosmic upheaval of fire and water when 'the south becomes north, and the earth turns over'. Others speak of three days of darkness, whilst at the same time in China, they speak of three days of daylight. Many myths, especially from the lands that Tenno has walked across already, speak of the creation of four worlds, three of which were destroyed in succession. The first world was destroyed by fire and volcanoes. In the creation of the second world, land was put where water was, and water where the land was. When the time came for its destruction, the 'pole twins' left their posts at the north and south ends of the world's axis, where they were stationed to keep the earth properly rotating. The world teetered off balance, spun around crazily, then rolled over twice. Mountains plunged into seas, the land was inundated, and the earth froze into solid ice. Eventually the pole twins were ordered back to their stations at the poles. With a great shudder and a splintering of ice the planet began rotating again. As the ice melted, the world began to warm to life, and the third world was created. It was destroyed by waves higher than mountains which rolled in upon the land. Continents broke asunder and sank beneath the seas. That period is what you dreamt of Paul. 'Tis what you saw and experienced once before in another time and physical body. The present fourth world will be destroyed by a great shift and flooding caused again by the passing dark sun, unless we change our nature sufficiently to prevent it and use what our forefathers left for us to help guide us through it...," Kratos explained, his tone serious. "Even the Norse Edda refers to shifts in the position of the Midgard serpent, Midgard being our planet, and the serpent denoting the Equator, ecliptic, or Milky Way. According to a Norse legend, the wolf Fenrir, who had been chained up by the gods, managed to break his bonds and escape. He shook himself and the world trembled. The ash tree Yggdrasil, which represents symbolically the earth's axis, was shaken from its roots to its topmost branches. Mountains crumbled or split from top to bottom, and the stars came adrift in the sky. And Tenno, I am surprised you do not know this, but one ancient Chinese work, consisting of 4320 volumes, details the consequences that followed when mankind rebelled against the gods and the universe fell into disorder: 'The planets altered their courses. The sky sank lower towards the north. The sun, moon, and stars changed their motions. The earth fell to pieces and the waters in its bosom rushed upwards with violence and overflowed the earth.' Many legends refer to long periods of darkness when the light of the sun vanished from the sky, while others speak of the sun not setting for long periods of time. This time refers to the 'age of horror', when the earth's axis is tilted at ninety degrees, and consequently there was continuous darkness during the winter months and continuous daylight during the summer months. Norse mythology teaches that before the present order of things, the sun rose in the south, and it places the frigid zone in the east, whereas now it is in the north." [64]

"Truly there is much we do not know," Thomas commented and bit his thumb nail, puzzled.

"Perhaps too much for one man...but not so for a man with a good woman," Kratos replied and looked at Alisha. "But let me say that all the references to gods were in fact dealing with the planets. The Enuma Elish epic began by listing the gods which were begotten by Ap Su, which was the name for the sun. Ap Su literally means 'one who exists from the beginning'. Marduk, the chief deity of the Babylonians, battles against another god, named Tiamat, as I have already mentioned stands for our mother planet earth. The role of Marduk parallels that of the

Sumerian planet Nibiru. Marduk is a wandering planet on a collision course with the watery planet named Tiamat, earth. Marduk entered the solar system via Neptune and Uranus indicating a clockwise direction as opposed to the other planets' counter clockwise direction. 'Tiamat and Marduk, the wisest of the Gods, advanced against one another, they passed on to single combat, they approached for battle.' It continues that having acquired a 'blazing flame' and various 'winds', which are in fact other planets and moons, 'Marduk towards the raging Tiamat set his face. The Lord spread out his net to enfold her; the evil wind, the rearmost, he unleashed at her face. As she opened her mouth, Tiamat, to devour him he drove in the evil wind so that she closed not her lips. The fierce storm winds then charged her belly; her body became distended; her mouth had opened wide. He shot there through an arrow, it tore her belly; it cut through her insides, tore into her womb. Having thus subdued her, her life-breath he extinguished. After he had slain Tiamat, the leader, her band was shattered, her host broken up. The Gods, her helpers who marched at her side, trembling with fear, turned their backs about so as to save and preserve their lives. Thrown into the net, they found themselves ensnared. The whole band of demons that had marched on her side he cast into fetters, their hands he bound. Tightly encircled, they could not escape'."

"My Lord...I can see just how that fits my dreams almost," Paul exclaimed.

"The point I am making by quoting the ancient texts, which I fear will not again be revealed until they are rediscovered to confirm these details, is that all the myths actually relate to celestial phenomena and have direct biblical relations. It is apparent from the epic, Tiamat was extinguished. Marduk then became caught in the orbit of our sun. The comment 'charging her belly' and 'He shot there through an arrow, it tore her belly' is detailing the massive exchanges of energy between the two celestial bodies."

"Yes, yes for that is exactly what I saw," Paul said shaking his head with surprise. Alisha looked at him.

"Paul, you dreamt of a similar but later event. The original tale is of a time before man walked this earth...a time when the planet was almost twice its size before a large part was ripped open during that first encounter. 'Tis after that event that our earth obtained its stabilising moon. But during Marduk's second passing orbit, Marduk actually collides head on with Tiamat. That is when a large portion of our world was removed and all the landmasses had to move. 'Tis why they drifted apart and continue to do so...but those details need not really concern us, but so long as you are aware of them."

"So this Marduk...Nibiru in the older Sumerian version...is the dark sun?" Thomas asked.

"No...Marduk, or Nibiru, is a large planet that orbits the dark sun just as we orbit our sun," Kratos replied.

"So what became of this dark sun and Marduk...and the part ripped from us?" Thomas asked.

"The tale recounts that the Lord paused to view her lifeless body. To divide the monster he then artfully planned. Then, as a mussel, he split her into two parts. The Lord trod upon Tiamat's hinder part; with his weapon the connected skull he cut loose; he severed the channels of her blood; and caused the north wind to bear it to places that have been unknown. The other half of her he set up as a screen for the skies, locking them together, as watchmen he stationed them. He bent Tiamat's tail to form the Great Band as a bracelet. The bracelet is the asteroid belt."

"Asteroid belt. What is that?" Paul asked puzzled.

"Sorry for I give details that many are not aware of still. Forgive me," Kratos said as he looked at Paul and Thomas in turn. "The asteroid belt is a band that surrounds the sun where a planet should be, but is only the remnants of one. The tale continues to explain that the watery Tiamat, now broken in half, is shunted by one of Marduk's moons into a new orbit along with Tiamat's previous largest satellite, Kingu, which means 'Great Emissary', which is the moon we all see each month. The Babylonian Marduk is one and the same as the Sumerian planet known as Nibiru as explained, but the asteroid belt is the remains of a single planet totally destroyed by Marduk. It also pushed Mars nearer to us, which almost collided with us during the time of the exodus of the Moses figure. Its close encounter with us caused massive discharges of energy between the two bodies that resulted in our entire plane being covered in red dust from Mars. 'Tis but part a reason why the Nile ran red with blood, or so it appeared, as well as the massive geophysical events that occurred at that time. And please note this fact...the solar system is laid out to a set mathematical formula that allows for the existence of a tenth planet, a twelfth body that includes our moon which are also directly related to Pythagorean triangles."

"But there are not even eleven bodies in our solar system," Thomas stated.

"Thomas...there is indeed, my friend. You just have not found them yet," Kratos replied with a smile. "Let me continue briefly before I retire this night. In simple terms, the ancients had an advanced knowledge of the creation of the solar system, but expressed it in simplified terms, just note that the account points out that Marduk/Nibiru created the earth and the heavens as outlined in the Day one and Day two accounts of the Biblical Genesis. Also, in the Marduk epic, the term usually translated as 'winds' is considered as satellites because the actual meaning is 'Those that are by his side'. Also the Muslim's holy book, the Qur'an, Chapter 21:30, has direct parallels to the Enuma Elish where it states 'Are the disbelievers unaware that the heavens and the Earth were one solid mass which we tore asunder, and that we made every living thing out of water?', which proves they at least understand advanced biology too."

"Biology, what is that? And that is surely wrong for we are made from the earth, not water," Thomas commented as Percival nodded in agreement with him.

"No, my friend. Again, the ancients are correct for as we shall all learn, we are in fact two thirds made up from water...believe me on this fact for it is so," Kratos explained. "Like the very planet we live upon is also two thirds covered in water. And there is a vast ocean that covers the scar where Marduk ripped away a portion of the planet. If you were to take all the water away, the earth would look like an apple but with a chunk bitten out from that part. 'Tis why the bulk of the landmasses are all on one side but now pulling apart to re-stabilise and re-distribute its mass equally. 'Tis also why we have seasons as the planet spins to and fro as it travels around the sun. Our earth is the surviving half of a larger planet as alluded to in the Enuma Elish epic and it is worth noting that the Sumerians called earth KI, which literally means to cut off, to sever, to hollow out. Also Marduk, the Sumerian Nibiru, caused Venus to have a retrograde rotation different to all the other solar bodies. It just happens that the ancient Sumerian texts described Nibiru as watery and as glowing and brilliant with a shining crown. This would infer an internal source of heat allowing a temperate and even climate even when far out away from the sun. By reasonable logic, it would not therefore be unrealistic to assume that Nibiru would thus be able to support the development of life. If it did in fact collide head on with earth, due to the massive discharges that would have inevitably been exchanged between them, massive amounts of surface debris would have also been exchanged including any life forms present. Also Marduk, Nibiru, has a large orbit that brings it close to earth on a regular basis, every 3,600 years to be precise, and that is why regular catastrophic events have occurred at its passing. The biblical account of the archangel Michael and his angels who fought a great and terrible battle in the heavens is just another version of the Sumerian and Babylonian epic or at least a direct representation of some kind of cosmic cataclysm."

"Theodoric has explained some of those details already as we travelled here," Paul remarked and looked at Theodoric.

"I try my best," he replied and shrugged his shoulders as he looked at Kratos.

"I think I would rather remain ignorant of these facts for they send fear into me, for Arri," Alisha commented and bit her bottom lip as Paul clasped both of his hands over hers.

"Then I think I have explained enough this past hour," Kratos remarked and went to stand. "And here...you may view these until the morning," he said and removed a small rolled sheet of velum and gently rolled it open upon the table to reveal a detailed map of the entire planet including the hidden lands to the west. Beside it were two smaller illustrations depicting a large sun and planets in order with another dark sun with several other planets beside that. Another image depicted a sphere cutting across the path of another with a section missing.

Fig. 43:

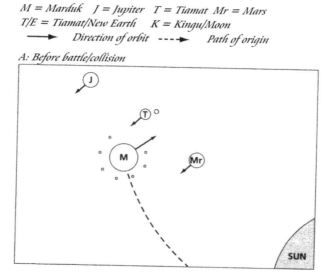

M = Marduk   J = Jupiter   T = Tiamat   Mr = Mars
T/E = Tiamat/New Earth   K = Kingu/Moon
⟶   *Direction of orbit*   ‑‑‑►   *Path of origin*

A: Before battle/collision

B

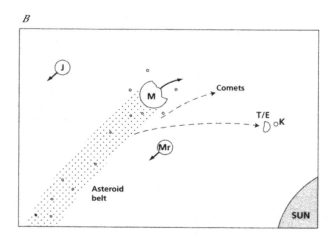

Tenno stood up also looking directly at Kratos.

"I think you have not said enough for clearly there is much more," he said bluntly.

"Yes, Tenno, there is…much more. But our time is limited," Kratos answered.

"Then stay longer. Do not leave tomorrow."

"I wish we could…but Abi, she must return with me to heal fully as I have already explained. Come with us," Kratos explained then asked. Tenno's eyes narrowed instantly as he looked hard at Kratos and his offer. "Oh and before I forget," Kratos said as he reached beneath his long white over tunic and pulled out what looked like a large Celtic cross. He leaned toward Theodoric and proffered he take it. "You left this with me last time we were together. Perhaps you would be so good and show these people how it works…if of course you can remember," Kratos joked as Theodoric took the cross from him and looked at it and smiled broadly. "Now, gentlemen, I would bid you good night…and ask that Alisha come with me for I have some words I would like to speak with her in private. Is that okay with you, Paul?"

Paul looked at Alisha as she began to stand. She looked at him and frowned as he kept hold of her hand. Quickly he kissed her hand and stood up too.

"Of course. If Alisha is happy to do so," Paul replied.

"More than happy to," Alisha said and playfully slapped Paul's arm and then walked toward Kratos.

ॐ ॐ

As Kratos led Alisha from the kitchen, his size made her look like a small child in comparison. Tenno followed them with his gaze as they left only turning to look at Paul once they had left. Paul looked at Theodoric as he fiddled with the circular section on the front of the Celtic looking cross.

"I thought you said the cross was a relatively new symbol…so why have you got that?" Paul asked as Thomas and Percival shuffled along the bench to see. Ishmael remained perfectly still where he sat. Tenno walked and stood behind Theodoric.

"It is, but this is far older than the cross symbolism believe you me," Theodoric replied.

Fig. 44: Celtic Cross Astrolabe

"Then why did Kratos have a cross belonging to you?" Percival asked as he looked at the cross in Theodoric's hand as he spun the circle section.

"He took it from me a long time ago. Ha…see, it still works after all this time," Theodoric laughed.

"What does it do?" Tenno asked bluntly.

"'Tis a simple but very effective navigation device…sit and I shall explain its workings if you wish."

"Looks like a cross to me," Thomas remarked.

"Ever wondered why the Celtic cross became important?" Theodoric asked and handed Tenno the cross.

 1 – 5

"Because our Lord was crucified upon one," Percival answered.

"Nope. That is the misconception unfortunately now forever linked to the cross symbol. But sit, and I shall explain."

"Please make it quick so I may visit Abi for she sleeps," Tenno asked and sat beside Theodoric closely looking at the cross. He handed it back to Theodoric.

"This," Theodoric said as he waved the cross, "is very much like a Celtic cross…

but the actual Celtic cross is in fact a very early symbol for a mechanical and working instrument that determines one's position of longitude...therefore enabling navigation on a journey, whether over the sea or not. It is a piece of pure genius by our ancestors which pre-dates anything we presently have by many thousands of years. This tool needs no external power to make it work, just the push of your fingers...no winding or tensioning. This actual cross was recovered from a site north of Alba by myself and your father," he explained and smiled at Paul. "Our ancestors had a lot more ingenuity and intelligence than we give them credit for."

"'Tis just a cross. How does it help navigate?" Tenno asked bluntly again.

"'Tis not just a cross. You see the circular part...it rotates and has markings upon it. This clever invention was so profound that it evolved into a symbol of navigation through even into the next journey after physical death and was placed over the deceased's grave to facilitate their passage. The Egyptians turned it into the looped cross, the ankh, but this...this is how they all originally looked. It has been subsequently re-created in stone and placed over graves across Europe..."

"I saw one on the shores of the new lands I walked across," Tenno stated. Theodoric looked at him briefly. "I did, I can swear it."

"I believe you, especially as parchments I have seen show this symbol drawn upon lands far off to the west," Theodoric said and paused. He looked at the cross for several minutes then continued. "The original working instrument was hand held, by the long lower half of the cross. The cross arm was pointed to a fixed star. The centre round piece mimicked the rotation of the earth against the fixed position of the stars, the wheel rotated on this central pin," he explained as he pointed to it. "At one of the points where each of the arms cross the wheel, there is a hole in the circle allowing a spy hole to view the etched degree markings on the rear showing the degrees of longitude. A plumb line is attached to the centre pin of the instrument to align the held arm parallel with the ground of the instrument reader. If I go on any further and explain this device, I fear I shall send you all to sleep; suffice it to say that it works."

"So you are saying that a Celtic cross is in fact an instrument as well as a sacred symbol?" Thomas asked.

"Yes that is exactly what I am saying. And more, much more for it also helped in the designs of ancient buildings, it helped shape philosophy and led to geometry. It was the actual secret instrument of the geomancers and the power of rulers as well as measurer of time. Look, the interweaving serpentine sine waves represent the cycles of order and chaos and the four arms represent the four seasons as well as mark the twelve signs of the zodiac so that one could navigate by the stars. As a consequence, and Kratos will back me up on this if you ask him, this cross also led to the use and understanding of nature's astrological mathematical values to design sacred buildings as I said...such as the Great Pyramid in Egypt and Stonehenge as well as countless others."

"But if that is the case, then why does the Church place so much emphasis upon the zodiac as being inherently bad and that we must shy away from all forms and practices connected to it?" Percival asked.

Theodoric lifted his Bible up and flicked through its pages before stopping at a point and started to read from it.

"Look and listen to what the Bible says...'And God said; Let there be lights in the expanse of the heavens to separate the day from the night and let them be for signs and for seasons and for days and years. And let them be for lights in the expanse of the heavens to give light on the earth.' Genesis 1 verse 14. Here the Bible is talking expressly about astrology when it mentions signs and their association with stars to keep time and the calendar required for hunter gatherers and for husbandry. And here look, 'Yea, though I walk through the valley of the shadow of death, I will fear no evil: for thou art with me; thy rod and thy staff they comfort me.' Psalm 23.4. Here the Bible talks clearly of a rod which is the old name for a measuring instrument. Now know this if you do not already, but the ancient methods of time keeping employed direct measurement of the rotation and orbits of the earth, the moon and the sun against the fixed stars and was known as astrology which simply means logic of the stars. It was not the astrology as used by so-called sooth sayers and fortune tellers...though the positions of the planets does have a very real physical effect upon a person depending upon when and where they were born. Although separated by time and oceans, Egyptian and other pyramids, mounds and henges when properly understood along with their legends and cultures all point back to that one universal source of original knowledge that was shared and understood by all using geometrical and astrological principles. So powerful were these ancient techniques that religions and governments clearly embraced them in the last millennium to measure and conquer the world while hiding them directly in the face of the public."

"Do you really believe that to be the case, that the information is deliberately hidden from us?" Paul asked.

"Yes and not only do I believe it...but I know that to be the case," Theodoric answered.

"But why would they?" Percival asked.

"Why...because if it was free for all to know and understand, then just like our ancestors, people would again ask the more important questions using mathematical measurement of the macro-cosmos and start to question what is the purpose of consciousness and how does the cycle of life and death work since it is obviously governed by time? And what then is time? Spiritually and scientifically, the real cross helps uncover hidden truths about a worldwide system lost in the mists of time...a time that does not sit with what the Churches proclaim is the truth. The ancient cultures spoke in a different language, one of images and symbols rather than written words, not easily understood by the modern mind. They left messages and warnings that have not been understood or heeded. It is true to say that those who master time are those who measure, and consequently rule! Therefore they have hidden the knowledge from the masses so as to maintain their power by creating a culture of deception. But as some of us know, the answers are not hidden, they are in full view and they are simple in concept and wisdom," Theodoric explained and paused as he placed the cross down. He sighed momentarily. "If we cannot see this simple cross for what it is, then what else can we not see that might bring hope for a better world for all of humanity and all of the children of the earth and its creatures? For what better joy can there be to walk with your loved ones on the face of the earth, in golden fields brushed by the winds and warmed by the life giving sun...and ask yourself why did ancient people revere the sun? Why is there a symbol of the sun on every Christian Church? And understand that even the Egyptians built pyramids, where Pyr Mid actually means 'fire in the middle' in its honour. Time keeping and prediction resulted from the correct use of this cross but the deep understanding of spiritual values has all been but forgotten in our world. Misinterpretation and deliberate obscurity and ignorance by religious and so-called academic authorities have led to a distorted view in the historical perspective of our ancient past. To measure is to rule just like the instrument you used at school. And remember this, that Stonehenge and the pyramids were part of a universal time-keeping network as well as part of a greater mystery that helps protect the very earth we live upon, but over time the echoes of the lost ancient knowledge begat religious systems. Religious symbols such as Christian and Celtic crosses look remarkably like our own mariner's astrolabes and astronomer's cross-staff. In other words, studying the stars led to worshipping the heavens. And remember that 'temple' means 'place of time'. 'Tis funny but this actual cross originated from this very city though the history of the real cross vanished during the many upheavals that fell upon Alexandria..." [65]

"Then how pray tell did you acquire that cross?" Thomas asked.

"This very cross was recovered by the first Knights Templar, in Jerusalem... It has helped in the design and construction of many of the new cathedrals and churches now being built, and your father...he would smile to see this now...but it is just one of many that the Roman Catholic Church demands destroyed or hidden," Theodoric explained and sighed as he looked at the cross carefully. "But your father hid this one in Alba, which is where I got it from."

"Why would the Church do that?" Thomas asked.

"Why...put simply, because when the seal of the past is broken and is no longer lost in the thread of time, then through the dust of ages the secrets will emerge and the ancient forgotten knowledge, historical and spiritual, will be rediscovered... then those in power who no longer have control over our understanding and perception of the past will lose that very power."

"How?" Tenno asked.

"Because," Theodoric paused as he turned to look directly at him, "who controls the past, controls the future!"

Chapter 44
Emissaries and Final Farewells

Port of La Rochelle, France, Melissae Inn, spring 1191

"What did Kratos want to speak to Alisha about alone?" the Genoese sailor asked.

"That I cannot say just yet, but I shall reveal it," the old man answered as he pushed the same velum sheet with images on that he had mentioned Kratos had shown.

Gabirol immediately leaned over and pulled the velum sheet toward himself, looked at it and then up at the old man with a look of pleasant surprise. He looked back down at the images and shook his head, delighted.

"I do not understand the phrase, who controls the past, controls the future," Simon said, puzzled.

"Simon, let me give you an example. What if you lived in a valley that was barren and where you have to struggle to survive, to make shelter out of materials that are flimsy and food is very scarce. Where water is limited and you endure mainly droughts...and what if your father told you that another family in the distant valley had been responsible for killing most of your ancestors and that you must not listen to anything that anyone from that family ever tells you as it is all lies...so you never venture to their valley and refuse to believe what they tell you despite the fact that your father was told by his father the same thing...and the truth is that one controlling power hungry individual from your family had started the lie to keep his own power and influence over you, the truth being that in the other valley, the family were loving, tolerant, generous and lived in a warm climate with plentiful food and fresh running rivers. So the family member who knows the true past but does not tell the remainder for his own control and power maintains that control and power and subsequently that family's future."

"Oh...I think I get your point," Simon remarked, still looking puzzled.

"You did have a father?" Sarah asked jokingly.

"Sarah!" Stephan whispered and shook his head no at her.

"Like the Celtic cross Theodoric demonstrated. By having it, an item from the past, though hidden from the majority of man, if given out freely then man can advance his future rapidly. Like the hidden records from antiquity that Kratos mentioned, by controlling to who and when they are revealed, controls what happens in the future," the old man explained.

"So can I just check that I have understood correctly what has been explained by this Kratos person," Gabirol said and looked down at his notes then at the old man, who simply nodded for him to continue. "So, the earth is indeed a sphere, there are twelve celestial bodies in our solar system, nine of which we know but others are still hidden, Venus spins on its axis in a retrograde opposite fashion to all the others, Marduk is a Babylonian name for a planet that is also called Nibiru in Sumerian which orbits a twin dark sun...but the planet is self illuminating."

"Yes, that is correct and when it passes close to our Mother Earth, it appears like a burning cross in the heavens. I forgot to mention that," the old man said and clasped his hands together. "It is also where the ancient civiliser gods known as the Annunaki, the shining ones, supposedly came from originally."

"The what?" Peter asked.

"Annunaki. They were described as tall beings who taught mankind all the arts and sciences we now have," the old man answered.

"And where is this written?" the wealthy tailor asked.

"Upon many ancient copper scrolls and clay tablets. Most of the copper scrolls, some of which were recovered by the original Templars, have been moved and hidden for safe keeping...as there are those within the Church who wish to see them destroyed."

"Why?" Ayleth asked.

"Because it details a history of man that stretches far back in time that, as said before, does not sit well with the doctrine as taught and promulgated by the Church. It threatens to undermine the entire authority of the Church and word of the Papacy," the old man explained.

"But if it is not the truth, that is unforgivable," Peter commented.

"Yes...and the longer it continues, the harder it becomes to reveal the truth," the old man sighed.

"So let me see if I understand this correctly," Gabirol remarked as he quickly flicked back through his notes. "Getting back to Jesus...before I forget. Some say that Jesus was just a man, but we should believe in a 'great omnipotent God' who was the architect of the heavens and not believe in the crucifixion. That Templars, well the higher inner circle at least, are apparently initiates of latter-day Nazarenes taught on the basis of the messages from the Jerusalem Church of James as found in the Temple scrolls," he detailed and looked at the old man first then at the Templar, "and they are the true teachings of Jesus that pre-date the crucifixion cult of Paul that was later adopted by the Romans. All Templars do not reject Jesus at all, they simply reinforce, if not remind people, that there is only one God, i.e. one Supreme Being."

"I think you have pretty much covered it, yes. But understand that in James's Church, the teachings of Jesus were certainly revered, but the crucifixion was considered to be a powerful symbol of 'faithfulness unto death'. This was then closely associated with the murder of Solomon's Temple architect, Hiram Abif, whom we shall discuss a little later, plus the Annunaki."

"I am so glad Gabi is keeping notes to ask later...I have lost count of all the things you intend to tell us later," Simon said, smiling broadly, then looked at Sarah and frowned as she scowled at him.

"Also note that the cross for the Templars was a mark of Martyrdom only...and not the source of magic that the crucifixion cult of Paul later believed it to be. Plus the cross was originally a Sumerian and Babylonian symbol that represented the all-important 'Planet of Crossing', Marduk or Nibiru, and also linked to the astrolabe Celtic cross...for remember, the early Christian Church symbol was in fact the 'Vesica Pisces', the 'Symbol of the Fish'."

"I cannot see how the Church will ever reveal truths if they have been so instrumental in suppressing them. They would lose all credibility and authority," Gabirol remarked and sat back.

"Not necessarily...for despite the apparent and obvious withholding of the truth, they still act as guardians of the hidden codes and knowledge that will be needed in the last days...or as Kratos would oft say and prefer, the days of changing," the old man replied and paused *for a moment.* "But when the Church does start to reveal truths, it will be the first vital step in the long process of releasing the Christian world from the prevailing principle of intellectual castration, exercised by the Vatican, and allowing it to build a civilisation driven by a desire for knowledge and a recognition of the worth of the individual. This drive from autocracy to democracy in government and aristocracy to meritocracy in social structure... within a framework of theological tolerance...will eventually prevail...just as it shall for Islam and all the great religions."

"And this map. Do the Templars have that too?" Gabirol asked as he studied the map again, closer.

"Yes, though I doubt our colleague here ever saw anything like it. But they also know that if the Templar mariners headed exactly due west on the forty-second parallel in search of a land marked by the star that they knew from Nazarean scrolls was called 'Merica', they would find it. The French Knights referred to this land as 'La Merica'."

"Hey, you are wrong for I have heard that name mentioned before...just the once when I was guarding a closed meeting in Paris," the Templar interrupted abruptly.

"And this map, it is how old?" Gabirol asked as the Genoese sailor leaned closer to view it.

"Many thousands...and copied from far older sources...," the old man answered.

"But if such things clearly exist, why in the Lord's name does the Church not come clean and simply say so?" Ayleth asked outstretching her hands towards the map, looking frustrated.

"Because as I have explained, it contradicts the teachings of what is written in the Bible... which claims that the world is just a few thousand years old when in fact the ancient writings stretch man's history back through many thousands of years and through three prior ages of man. So to control the present, as well as the future, those records of the past are likewise controlled, as in hidden and in most cases eradicated."

"But that is so wrong. It means we are being deceived," Ayleth exclaimed.

"That is why the higher initiates of such Orders as the Templars vowed to safeguard that past so when the day comes in the future when control over what is taught as our past can be openly questioned, then they would be able to reveal it back to the world," the old man replied.

"But to continue in what you have said, you stated that a large portion of our planet was ripped away and where now is a great ocean," Gabirol asked and looked at the old man. He nodded yes. "Okay...and places like Stonehenge in Britain and others across the world were built to stabilise the world as well as harness and increase natural energy...and act as astronomical and astrological markers...is my understanding correct?"

"Yes," the old man smiled in reply.

"Could you not have simply stated those facts as Gabirol just did?" the farrier asked.

"Yes I could have...but then it would make no sense. It would be like me introducing you to the Celtic cross Theodoric has and you simply accepting it just as a cross, nothing more. But by explaining its background and how it works, a greater understanding and revelation occurs," the old man explained.

"Okay, and," Gabirol said and looked at his notes again. "And the network of stone temples helps, or will help, our world to repel or resist any influence the next time this dark sun enters close with its attendant planets, the main one being Marduk, Nibiru. And the translation of rib actually means spirit."

"I am sooo glad you are taking notes and repeating it simply," Simon laughed as the Genoese sailor nodded in agreement with him.

"Yes Gabirol, well put. But also know that the ancients called Marduk...Nibiru...'the planet of crossing' as I mentioned a short while ago, but also 'the tenth planet' as denoted secretly as an X, which just happens to be the Roman letter for ten."

"So how will we know when the dark sun returns?" Ayleth asked, looking concerned.

"It has an orbit of 3,600 years...so at a rough estimate that means sometime between 2003 and 2018, during the first stages of the Aquarian, spiritual, age...and Marduk, Nibiru, will be seen as a fiery cross in the heavens during its last passing phase...but its dark sun will not be visibly seen until it swings past and away, but its effects will be felt years prior."

"Such as?" Simon asked, now also looking concerned.

"Such as the seasons will fall out of sequence, and as it tells us in the Bible, the seasons shall not be distinguished except by the leaves on the trees...there will be earthquakes and floods and great storms in diverse places where previously none had been. Fish will die in their thousand in the oceans and rivers...all the signs are carried over into the New Testament symbolically if you care to check, in the Book of Revelation...but one aspect that is not revealed, is the very simple fact that we, all of us, also have a direct bearing upon how our world reacts. We are all connected with the energy of the world...and if we are all afraid and negative, so too the world becomes affected. But if we remain positive and not afraid, that reinvigorates and positively charges our very world. This concept some have tried to convey esoterically within some of the tales being told today."

"Really...such as?" Peter asked.

"Such as the King Arthur and Holy Grail legends, where the land dies and becomes barren when King Arthur is weak and ill. As he remains weak, disheartened, afraid and negative, so too the land becomes. But when he is reinvigorated, so too does the land become the same. You see, we are all part of the one whole scheme," the old man explained then sipped some rosehip water.

"My Lord there is so much we are kept in the dark about...'tis a tragedy for sure," Ayleth remarked, looking sad. "Please, can you tell us all you know?"

The old man laughed briefly and sat himself upright.

"My dear child, if only I could...but it has taken me a life time to learn and, more importantly, understand, what little I do know. But if you will permit me, I shall tell you more of the story about this sword for it will impart some small measure of knowledge...and some wisdom I hope," he said and smiled at Ayleth.

She blinked and simply nodded yes. Gabirol and the Genoese sailor looked intently at the detailed map in front of them confirming parts they recognised.

"I want to know if Tenno left with Abi," Simon stated and raised his eyebrows questioningly.

Alexandria, Egypt 1179

Paul drew the heavy curtains aside letting the early morning sun shine through into the bedroom. Alisha was sat upon the edge of the bed feeding Arri and the room was already beginning to warm. Her night shawl hung down loose exposing her naked shoulders down to the middle of her back. Paul had retired to bed shortly after Alisha had left with Kratos. He had waited up nearly an hour before she entered the room and quietly slipped beneath the covers. He had asked if she was all right but she had simply replied she was fine but tired. During the night when Arri awoke, she had quietly seen to him before going back to sleep herself without speaking to Paul at all knowing he was awake. Paul's mind wondered what Kratos had spoken to her about that required the conversation to be a private one. Normally when they had retired to bed, they would always talk and Alisha would cuddle up close beside him before falling asleep but last night had been the first time she had not. At one point Paul was convinced he sensed her crying quietly. What had Kratos said to her? he kept on asking himself. He moved around the bed and sat beside her but she kept on feeding Arri and would not look at Paul, letting her long hair fall forwards hiding her face. He placed his hand on her back. Alisha looked up and took a deep breath.

"Ali...are you okay...what did Kratos say to you last eve?"

⚹　　1 – 5

Alisha took in another deep breath and looked up high. She sighed heavily as she held Arri to her breast as he fed. She shook her head then turned to look at Paul. Immediately he saw her eyes were wide and full of tears. As she went to speak, a tear rolled down her cheek.

"Nothing to worry yourself about...nothing," she said emotionally.

"Ali, you are crying. It must have been something."

Alisha looked at Paul intently. Another large tear rolled down her face as another hung in the other eye. Alisha wanted to tell Paul exactly what Kratos had told her but she had sworn an oath she would not, yet the sense of not being able to confide in him overwhelmed her senses. Her heart beat faster and she looked at the pained expression on his face. The scar upon his face was almost invisible she thought. That gave her hope and strength knowing how it had been healed and she knew they were watched over. She let out a nervous laugh which confused Paul even more.

"My dearest man, 'tis just a woman thing. Surely Sister Lucy must have told you how our moods swing and that we cry for nothing after having a child," she explained as both eyes dropped their tears.

Paul looked at her quizzically. In his heart he knew something was upsetting her more than just the physical after effects of having a baby. He knew her too well and he sensed the hurt she was hiding. Quickly he wiped away her tears and put his arm around her and helped support Arri as he suckled away oblivious to his parents' emotions. Alisha stared into Paul's eyes and he felt as though she was looking directly into his very soul. The tears in her eyes added to their beauty in a way that felt like her heart was wrapping around his and they were as one. Gently he kissed her on the lips. Alisha felt as if she was about to fall apart into a sobbing wreck and as he kissed her, it took all of her strength not to break down totally and hold onto him and never let him go. She buried her face into his shoulder and just rested her head there for a few minutes until Arri had finished. Only then did she look up.

"You know you can tell me anything...anything," Paul said as Alisha sat Arri upright and started to wind him.

"I know. And I do. 'Tis honestly just a woman thing," she replied softly.

Paul looked at her as she stared at him. There was an almost pleading look in her eyes and he knew absolutely that Kratos had said something to her and he had not exactly been discreet about it neither. He would have words with him later he told himself if he got the chance to speak alone with him at the dockside. Abi would be leaving on the morning tide with Kratos and possibly Tenno. Paul reflected back upon his time with Tenno and it felt as if he had known him all of his life. He would feel incredibly sad if he did leave but understood that if he loved Abi anywhere as much as he loved Alisha, then he would accept his decision to go and wish them both well. He would offer him Adrastos as a parting gift he told himself as he knew he would need a good horse.

Eastern Harbour, Port of Alexandria, Egypt, 1179

Paul led Adrastos following Theodoric as he hurried Alisha, who was carrying Arri tightly, and Ishmael along the dockside toward several ships berthed stern end on, in order to dock more vessels. As they walked nearer, Paul saw Tenno and Abi already stood at the far end of the dock holding each other. Alisha lowered the blue shawl from around her neck as the warmth of the sun shone down directly upon them and used a corner of it to shield Arri. Tenno and Abi had left nearly an hour prior to Alisha and Paul having told Theodoric to pass on their farewells to avoid any emotional departures. As soon as Theodoric had passed on the message, Paul had literally dragged Alisha and Arri out of the house, getting Adrastos as they went. Ishmael immediately followed them.

The Eastern Harbour was relatively quite compared with the more busy Western Harbour and only a few sailors and traders were present. In the distance just entering the outer harbour walls, a large Hospitaller galley steered its way gracefully into view. Just as Paul saw this, Turansha and Husam appeared riding up from his right leading a column of Faris Knights and white clothed Mamluk personal escort guards. Quickly Turansha dismounted and walked his horse the last few paces toward Tenno and Abi. Slowly Tenno opened his eyes and turned his head to look at him as Abi rested her head against his shoulders still hugging him tightly, her eyes shut in silence. Turansha looked toward Paul directly and smiled with a slight bow of his head.

"You should not have come," Tenno said abruptly to Paul as Theodoric threw out his arms in protest at his comment. Alisha walked straight up to Tenno and Abi as Paul acknowledged Turansha.

"We could hardly let you go without saying goodbye," Paul replied instantly as Adrastos snorted and raised his head. "Besides, you will need a horse and I can think of no finer gift we can give by way of thanks than Adrastos."

Turansha stepped closer smiling and untied his riding gloves as Husam dismounted and handed his reins to one of several foot guards that ran up beside him.

"Paul, 'tis not necessary," Tenno exclaimed as he held Abi closer. "And goodbyes are for funerals remember. I cannot accept your gift."

Adrastos snorted and neighed more and Paul had to pull his reins hard to settle him. Alisha stepped closer to Abi and placed her hand upon her forearm. Tenno looked down at her then Arri's little face just visible in his wrapped shawl.

"Abi...I had to say farewell and...and," Alisha started to say but her voice went dry with emotion.

Abi opened her eyes. She looked incredibly tired still and very pale and cold despite the rising heat of the morning sun. Several sea gulls squawked loudly above as the large Hospitaller ship started to pull around to berth. Abi looked at Alisha in silence for several moments then smiled.

"Ali, I shall see you again, I promise," she said quietly then turned her gaze towards a small odd looking boat berthed between two larger vessels hardly noticeable. "My ship awaits," she joked.

Alisha looked at the small vessel and noticed its name plate at the rear, which spelt out 'Stella Cougnes'. It was Kratos's boat. Paul looked at the vessel, puzzled. Neither he nor Alisha had seen such a strange vessel before.

"Is Kratos on board already?" Paul asked. Both Abi and Tenno nodded yes together. "Turansha, please forgive my ignorance," Paul said and bowed his head.

"'Tis not a problem for I see you have more pressing issues. I am here to greet the emissaries from the Templars and Hospitallers so worry not about our presence," Turansha explained and started to walk away toward the Hospitaller ship just as its stern was being secured against the dockside.

Quickly Paul handed the reins of Adrastos to Theodoric and walked toward Kratos's vessel as he waved back at Turansha. The clear turquoise waters of the harbour's calm sea lapped gently against the large dockside stones as Paul looked down upon Kratos's vessel. Puzzled he looked at it not sure what was stern and what was bow. The whole vessel looked almost like an elongated floating egg, with no mast nor sails or windows. No decks. Suddenly the nearest section against the dockside dropped away like a trapdoor opening downwards to reveal a set of steps. Then a larger section above the entrance opened upwards like a drawbridge being raised. As Paul leaned forwards to look inside, Kratos suddenly appeared making him jump, startled. Kratos laughed at the look of shock on his face and beckoned him to step down inside. Paul looked back at Alisha still talking with Abi and Tenno as Theodoric struggled to hold Adrastos steady.

"Don't dawdle...quickly come aboard," Kratos demanded, beckoning him down with his large hand waving him in.

Hesitantly Paul stepped off of the dockside and onto the floating wooden gangway then onto the vessel itself. It looked like a burnished silver coloured bronze. He could not match the colour in his mind. Oak wooden sections like recessed beams ran around its outer rim. Slowly he stepped down into the vessel and was amazed at the interior.

"What manner of vessel is this?" he asked almost in awe as he took in the beautiful oak panelling and smooth contours of the light coloured walls, deck and roof that seemed to have no visible joins.

"'Tis a very old vessel. Come, sit for I know you have questions," Kratos stated and sat himself down beside a built in table that appeared moulded to a central round column.

"Yes, I wish to know what you said to Alisha last eve that has unsettled her...," he replied and looked around the interior. Two bluish lights illuminated the interior. He ran his finger along one of them and felt the warmth coming from it. Kratos smiled broadly at Paul's obvious fascination. "I must have one of these one day," he remarked and laughed to himself amazed at the quality and build. "Such fine craftsmanship....pray tell who built this?"

"That, my dear Paul, I cannot tell you and I am afraid you will never have a vessel such as this in your life time. Not this life time anyway," Kratos answered and winked.

"I saw no sails...how does it move?"

"Oh it has sails as you shall see when we leave."

"I...I shall be sad to see you leave as there is so much I wish to ask and know from you," Paul sighed.

"Then let me start by saying that I explained some things to Alisha...of things past, of things happening now and of things to come. And I made her swear an oath of silence not to reveal what I explained," Kratos explained bluntly, but his voice calm and surprisingly reassuring. "But do not fear. 'Tis nothing untoward I promise. I also removed a part of the veil that shrouds most people from the knowledge of their past."

"Okay...and why is the past veiled? For I do not understand that still."

"As I explained before, because you have another chance every time you live to do what is right and correct mistakes of previous times and learn. To open your higher self that does remember all of what and who you are and without going against what you...and some of us...volunteer for. Alisha now knows what it was she...and you...agreed to do, but you can choose not to."

"Correct me if I am wrong, but is that not what happened to Jonas?...He did not want to follow what the Lord had commanded him and he got eaten by a whale and subsequently did what he was told?"

"No, Paul...he just needed a little reminder," Kratos answered and laughed lightly. "And seriously, Paul...do you think a man could be eaten by a whale and survive?"

"So it is just allegorical...symbolic then?"

"No...it was a real enough event. But try explaining a vessel such as this you now sit in...for it was one just the same, but black. That was all," Kratos replied and smiled with a knowing nod.

Paul sat back not sure whether to believe him or not, but then as he looked around the vessel, it was completely new to him. He had never seen anything like it before. He looked at the glowing light again and raised his hand about to ask a question but Kratos shook his head no indicating not to even ask how it worked.

"And Tenno...he will accompany you then?"

"Tenno. No...he is to stay with you as he vowed."

"What, I mean why? He loves Abi."

"That is exactly why he will remain. It has been her charge to watch over you and Alisha and protect you. As well as others. The others I am afraid," he paused briefly. "Both Abi and I failed in our duties is all I shall say. But fortunately, and so far, we have not failed you and Alisha...nor Arri. But Abi is not fit nor well enough to continue with her charge, so Tenno has sworn to her that he will whilst she recovers."

"And how long will that take?"

"I shall take her to the Hypogeum of Hal Saflieni...But it is her mind that needs healing the most right now as it weighs heavy upon her that she was unable to protect the others..."

"Who were the others?"

"Paul, you need not know that...but look, items they had and protected with their very lives as guardians, I am now having to entrust to you," Kratos explained and pressed a slightly raised boss on the table. Instantly the table seemed to part and revealed a deep drawer full of parchments, rolled up scrolls and many maps all tied together securely by crimson cords. He removed them gently, lifted them just above the table then placed them down as the table closed again. He pushed them toward Paul. "You must guard these well."

"But…but what if we had not come down in time to see you off? I would not have had these."

"I had no doubt you would be here in time. Now listen to me carefully, these are but a very small fraction of what you must learn. Take them home and study them…even if you think you do not understand them, for you will."

"But why me now? Surely you should be taking them?"

"I have many other copies. It will all make sense as you learn, trust me."

Paul looked at Kratos, his large presence exuding a calmness, kindness and authority that solicited not only respect but absolute trust.

"Is Kratos really your name?" Paul asked looking directly into his eyes. Kratos simply raised his eyebrows very slightly. His blue eyes with the flecks of green and gold were strangely beautiful Paul thought. 'Hope he can't read my mind too' Paul thought and quickly changed the question as Kratos raised his eyebrows even higher and smiled. "And Tenno has agreed willingly to put his own wishes aside for us?"

"Tenno is what we would call a true warrior. You can learn much from him. Like you, he is not only a protector of his family, which is now you, Alisha and Arri, but also all those in need. He is also an example and guardian of the ways of honour and courage for he will not put his own desires above what is right and he is motivated solely by what is his utmost duty…and no, Kratos is just one of many names I am known by. 'Twas one given to me whilst in Greece," Kratos replied and winked then smiled broadly.

"I think I already knew that."

"Tenno will see Abi again and she is far happier knowing he is with you."

"But you will not tell me what you told Ali?"

"No," Kratos replied bluntly then smiled again. "Now go, you must leave me and let Tenno bring Abi to me," Kratos said as he stood up.

Paul stood up, pulled the bundle towards himself and picked it up properly.

"Shall I see you again?"

"I am most certain of it," Kratos answered with a broader smile and tilted his head at him.

≈ ∞ ≈

Alisha hugged Abi tightly for several moments before stepping away to look at her. Tenno gently handed Arri back to her.

"'Tis time. I must now leave," Abi remarked as she indicated toward several men wearing white mantles approach down the gangplank of the Hospitaller ship. "I think there is one amongst them whom you know. Be careful, my little sister, for the heart can cause havoc," she explained and kissed Alisha on the forehead, winked at her then turned to face Kratos's vessel. "I am ready."

Tenno took her arm and began to walk her towards the dockside. Alisha felt sad as she watched them. Alarm registered as she suddenly realised she had not said farewell to Tenno. She went to call out when one of the approaching men raised his hand and waved smiling broadly. She took a second look as the image of Nicholas's smiling face registered. Beside him was Brother Baldwin, Upside being his nickname, she recalled immediately. Turansha and Husam waited patiently as Brother Roger and several Hospitallers along with several other knights approached them. Alisha watched as pleasantries were exchanged between both parties, Nicholas still smiling and looking directly at Alisha. Her mouth went dry and her heart raced at seeing Nicholas and she blushed. She suddenly felt very underdressed. As Turansha introduced the other men, Nicholas walked toward her. He was not wearing his usual suit and chain mail, just a single full length white robe, sandals and his sword only. Quickly she looked toward Abi and Tenno and saw them holding a long kiss as they embraced.

"Well this is truly a delightful surprise. I had no idea you would be waiting for my arrival," Nicholas joked and bowed. Upside slapped his arm hard.

"Behave, Brother," he said as he looked around the harbour checking for any threats.

Alisha blinked and smiled nervously.

"I...I had no idea you would be here today...I...I, oh it is good to see you," she blurted out, embarrassed, and leaned nearer and greeted him with a quick kiss on the side of his face. "Pray tell how you are here. Why are you here? For I thought I should never see you again," she asked and placed her left hand upon his forearm. She looked into his eyes without moving her gaze. His cheeky grin made her smile.

"You see, the Lord wishes us to see each other."

"Inappropriate, Brother," Upside stated and coughed and kicked Nicholas's leg hard.

Both Alisha and Nicholas laughed.

Paul stepped off of the vessel, nearly slipping upon the wet wooden floating platform against the dock stone wall. He steadied himself and looked up to see Alisha talking with several men dressed in cotton mantles with the emblem of the Templars. They wore no chain mail or their usual mantles, which surprised him. Tenno who was stood nearby still holding Abi looked down and acknowledged him as he stepped up onto the harbour side. To his left he could see Turansha formally greeting several other Templars and Hospitallers. He immediately recognised Brother Teric and Count Raymond stood at the front of the group. They were all smiling as they met Husam. Abi whispered something which drew Tenno's attention then she faced Paul.

"Paul, this is not goodbye for I shall return," she said and looked behind her at Alisha. "Now go and stand by your wife, or you may just lose her for she is perhaps the most beautiful woman these men will ever see," she smiled.

"I shall. And look after yourself and I pray it is not long before we meet again," Paul replied, kissed her on the side of her face. He looked at Tenno briefly as he nodded at him and without any further words Paul simply smiled at Abi then walked away toward Alisha and Arri.

"Keep an eye upon that Nicholas for despite his promise, you know what men are like," she said softly to Tenno.

"I shall," Tenno replied and looked toward Nicholas, his eyes narrowing, which made Abi smile.

"But do not hurt him," she laughed then gently kissed him once more and pulled away. Carefully and slowly she stepped down onto the floating wooden dock then on to Kratos's vessel as Tenno stood silently watching her. She looked back up at him as she stepped into the vessel's open hatchway. "I wish you enough always... enough," she said softly.

"I wish you enough too," Tenno replied his voice dry. Abi smiled at him then descended into the vessel, the last image of her in Tenno's mind seeing her golden blonde hair, plaited and tied into place upon her head, her broad shoulders and neck exposed to the sun. All of her armour and equipment Kratos had already stowed away so there was nothing more for Tenno to do but watch as the upper cover slowly closed down as if by magical unseen hands. Then the lower trap door type hatch moved upwards and slid silently across the steps and locked shut. That was it, she was gone from sight, but not from his heart, which felt heavy. A large part of him wished to jump aboard the vessel and steal whatever future he could have with Abi...but he had sworn to her he would watch over her charge. He turned his head slowly and looked toward Alisha just as Paul reached her.

"Ali," Paul said as he placed his hand upon hers still resting upon Nicholas's arm. She jumped and instantly pulled her hand away. "Nicholas!" Paul exclaimed as he immediately recognised him. "So soon we meet again."

"Paul...'tis indeed a wonderful day," Nicholas replied, which upon hearing, Upside raised his eyebrows and spun around and walked off towards the other men, shaking his head. "Upside. Hates the water," Nicholas joked.

Paul looked at Alisha, her face turning red as she blushed.

"I was asked by Brother Teric to accompany the emissaries for protection in the hope that we may somehow sort out some kind of working and lasting truce," Nicholas explained.

"But is it not dangerous to be here?" Alisha asked and rocked Arri as Tenno came and stood beside her and looked at Nicholas hard.

"I...do not think so," he answered, looking at Tenno suspiciously.

Alisha looked around at Tenno quickly then back at Nicholas.

"Tenno will not hurt you," she remarked and looked back at Tenno, "Why should he....will you?" she asked him.

"Exactly," Tenno replied coldly. "Why would I?"

"Paul!" Roger des Moulins suddenly called out, interrupting them.

Paul looked past Nicholas to see Brother Roger approach, his hand outstretched already to greet him. Paul shook his hand.

"Master Roger, 'tis indeed good to see you again," Paul remarked.

"Aye and you. I see your scar has healed well...incredibly well in fact," he remarked and leaned closer to see the almost invisible scar.

"I had the best physician sort it," Paul replied politely.

"Hmm. I am good but not that good," Brother Roger replied and rubbed his chin as he studied Paul's face.

"Where is all your armour?" Paul asked trying to change the subject and quickly noting that Alisha and Nicholas were looking at each other. Brother Roger slapped Nicholas on the back hard.

"Oh I am sorry," Nicholas laughed. "No...you can't wear full armour on a ship...

in case it sinks or you fall overboard. You would sink like a stone and drown," he explained.

Paul looked down at the bundle in his hands as he almost dropped it. He then noticed a note Kratos had secured beneath the crimson cords. Quickly he pulled it around to read. 'Remember, you will always have three choices open to you!' Kratos had written in French. Suddenly the sound of rapidly unfurling sails drew everyone's attention towards Kratos's vessel. It had pulled away from the dockside. They all looked on bemused at the strange sight of the vessel as it steered its way rapidly toward the harbour mouth, the whole front section appearing to rise like some gigantic fin, the sides suddenly folding outwards and down with sails rigged between them. The whole system seemed to pitch to catch the light breeze and instantly the sails bellowed out in full display. The whole vessel looked as though the top half and front had completely lifted up and forwards deploying the strange shaped sails. Abi and Kratos could just be seen at what looked like an aft deck. They waved.

 4 – 15

Fig. 45:

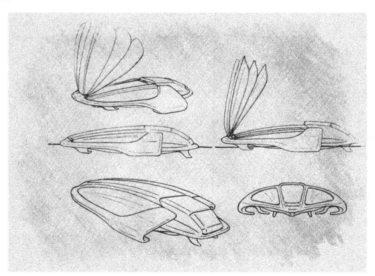

"Tenno...you have missed the boat!" Alisha exclaimed, alarmed, and looked at him.

He stared at the vessel as it left the mouth of the harbour at twice the speed of another ship in full sail that was also leaving despite virtually no wind to fill its sails.

"No...I did not miss it," Tenno stated, still staring at the fast disappearing vessel. "My place is here...with you," he remarked, looked down at Alisha, her eyes instantly filling with emotion as she registered the enormity of what he had just said. "Here," he said and reached to take Arri. Gently he took him in his arms and moved Arri's little face closer to his. Paul, Brother Roger and Nicholas looked on bemused. "You...you my little warrior, I shall teach you all that I know," he simply stated as Arri opened his eyes and smiled.

"Yes and me," Theodoric called out as he rapidly approached still trying to keep Adrastos under control.

Tenno looked at Theodoric briefly, raised his left eyebrow as if to disagree, turned away from the group and walked away slowly talking quietly to Arri as he went.

"Bit weird...but hey, that's Tenno for you," Theodoric remarked as Adrastos shook his head up and down. He noted the puzzled look upon Brother Roger's and Nicholas's faces.

Paul clasped Alisha's hand tightly and kissed it. As he watched Tenno, he recalled what his father had initially told him about Tenno. 'Don't ever mistake his silence for ignorance or arrogance, his calmness for acceptance and his kindness for weakness.' Paul gulped and felt very emotional inside all of a sudden. He glanced back in time to see Kratos's vessel as it sailed out of view becoming obscured by the outer harbour wall. Paul caught sight of two Hospitallers approaching carrying several sets of chain mail and armour. One of the men stopped in his tracks as he saw Alisha. As the other man handed Brother Roger his uniform, Nicholas went to take his from the man now stood rooted to the spot. Quickly the man dropped Nicholas's uniform, the chain mail landing with a heavy thud on the dockside stone at the feet of Nicholas. The man stretched himself as if he had injured his back, sweat beading from his head. As Alisha turned around, his eyes widened in pleasant surprise as he recognised her from their journey upon the Tarida.

"By the Holy Lord I thought I would never see you again," he said excitedly and stepped towards her fast and knelt at her feet. He grasped her left hand, Paul still holding her right hand. "'Tis an honour and a privilege to see you again. If I can be of any service, my sword is yours," he explained and looked up at her.

Nicholas looked at the Hospitaller, confused.

"Wrong, Brother, your sword is still very much ours," Brother Roger remarked and laughed. "Now stand and stop embarrassing the poor woman."

"But Master, do you not know who this woman is?" the Hospitaller said and stood up still holding Alisha's hand. After a brief pause, the Hospitaller let go of her hand and stepped backwards.

"You were on the Tarida. I remember you now," Alisha said softly.

"I hope someone will let me in on what occurs here," Nicholas commented as Brother Teric turned from Turansha and waved for Nicholas to come over. "Please, wait. I shall be right back," Nicholas said and quickly ran across to Brother Teric.

Alisha looked at his pile of chain mail, white mantle and assorted leather pads near her feet. She knelt down and tried to lift the chain mail but it was too heavy. Quickly she stood over the entire set and with both arms lifted it from the ground. She felt its weight then dropped it back to the stone floor.

"That is unbelievably heavy...and they wear that all the time?" she asked and looked at Paul.

Paul looked at Nicholas's armour then at Alisha. He was not sure how he felt with her reactions to Nicholas. As he looked over toward him near to Turansha, he saw

Count Raymond and who he assumed was his wife, Princess Eschiva, approaching them.

Suddenly the dockside erupted with the noise of a squadron of light cavalry. Paul instantly recognised the lead rider as Gokbori, still attired just as Paul had last seen him. As they drew up near to Turansha and Husam's men, Paul expected all the Christian knights to stand to and be on their guard, yet they were totally relaxed obviously not feeling in the least bit threatened by his arrival. Gokbori dismounted and Paul watched bemused as the group went through the greeting routine. Brother Teric broke away from the group and headed straight for Paul.

"Ah, Alisha and Paul. 'Tis good to see you so settled in already," he said aloud as he walked closer.

"And you also, Brother Teric. What is happening?" Paul asked as he looked past him at the group.

"Oh just a slight delay. Gokbori was held up outside the city by pilgrims blocking the road. He is just making his apologies and then we should all be off to Turansha's palace. Are you attending?"

"I do not think so," Paul answered

"Well we are invited," Theodoric interjected as he stepped closer, Adrastos pulling his right foreleg backwards on the stone slabs.

"Is Gerard accompanying you?" Alisha asked as she shielded her eyes to look in the direction of the Hospitaller ship.

"Do not be silly...'tis a hopeful peace delegation we bring. If he were here it would be for one thing only...to sack the city and all in it. No, he is not privy to this embassy," Brother Teric explained as Nicholas and Upside headed back toward them.

"But I thought he would be confirmed as the Order's Grand Master...," Paul remarked.

"No...It will in all likelihood be Arnold de Tarroja...God help all of us if Gerard becomes the overall Grand Master...I may have to consider resigning if he ever did," Brother Teric remarked just as Nicholas and Upside arrived.

"So how did Gerard ever become a Templar?" Alisha asked.

"Gerard...He was seriously ill and about to die when he took his vows and became a Templar...but he made a miraculous recovery and saw that as a direct sign from God that he had work for him to do," Brother Teric answered.

"But there is no denying he is a fearless knight despite always going against the orders given to him by Count Henry over there," Nicholas interjected.

"He is still a bully," Alisha stated.

"I do think he will ever forget meeting you in a hurry," Nicholas remarked with a broad smile.

Turansha approached, his long white tunic flowing as he walked rapidly.

"Please...please, my friends, we shall remove ourselves to my palace and I would beg your attendance...please," he asked looking at Paul first then bowing his head at Alisha. "Princess Eschiva is also keen to meet with you for she has heard much about you," he explained, looking at Alisha.

"Me? Why?" she asked, pointing to herself.

Turansha nodded toward Theodoric.

"Hey...I just mentioned you...in passing when I visited her recently. That is all," Theodoric replied and feigned a mock grimace.

"'Tis agreed then. You will come with us," Turansha said, smiled and turned away.

Alisha slapped Theodoric with the back of her hand playfully and scowled at him.

"Theo!" she laughed.

Palace of Turansha, Eastern Quarter, Alexandria, 1179

Paul, wearing his new fine silk robe as given by Turansha as a gift, stood beside Nicholas, now fully dressed in his full Templar uniform. Brother Baldwin stood behind him. They stood beneath an arch away from the rest of the delegation that were all stood in the centre of the marbled hall surrounded by columns and a large dome above. Theodoric was introducing Alisha to Princess Eschiva as Count Raymond introduced his delegation to Turansha's many guests. The fact that so many people were looking at Alisha did not escape Paul or Nicholas. Paul looked to his right to see Ishmael and Tenno sat almost out of sight in an alcove. He laughed seeing Tenno holding Arri close to his face almost rubbing his nose on his. He had insisted that he look after Arri so Alisha and Paul could mix at ease.

"She is truly captivating isn't she?" Nicholas said quietly then buckled slightly as Upside kneed the back of his leg hard. He looked at him and he raised his eyebrows disapprovingly.

"She is...yes," Paul replied and laughed at Brother Baldwin for kicking Nicholas.

"Sorry. I do not mean to be inappropriate, but Alisha has them all eating out of her hand. Turansha is no fool and he knows that. She will greatly influence many here this day, trust me," Nicholas said as he looked toward her.

Paul could see the clear admiration he had for Alisha. Upside shook his head and raised his eyes mockingly and as if by way of apology to Paul. Paul smiled at him then looked at Alisha. She was laughing as she talked with one of Husam's entourage completely at ease. Princess Eschiva looked across at Paul and she raised the small glass she was holding toward him and nodded as if to approve of Alisha. She touched the forearm of Count Henry and whispered something in his ear, nodded toward Paul, which made Count Raymond look at him and smile, and then she approached. She walked confidently and straight whilst smiling, her eyes fixed upon Paul.

"Watch out!" Nicholas joked.

"Ah...so you must be Paul whom I hear so much about," Princess Eschiva said and raised her right hand toward Paul. Paul just looked at her hand, bemused.

"Countess," Nicholas interrupted and quickly stepped forward and kissed her hand then looked at Paul to do the same.

"Oh...sorry," Paul said and gently took her fingers in his hand and kissed the top of her hand. He immediately smelt the sweet scented aroma from the oils she had rubbed into her silk smooth hands. As he went to let go, she quickly grasped his hand tightly and would not let go as she looked at him.

"Stephanie was wrong," she remarked as she looked at him smiling. "You are far more handsome than she explained."

"Thank you," Paul replied awkwardly as both Nicholas and Upside laughed.

"Do not blush. I speak as I see," she continued then looked back towards Alisha briefly. "And your wife...she is truly mesmerising. She serves us all well this day," she commented then let go of Paul's hand. She studied him for several moments. "Alexandria is known as 'The Pearl of the Mediterranean', the atmosphere here being more Mediterranean than Middle Eastern would you not agree?" she suddenly asked and sipped her drink.

"I...I could not answer that for I am not too aware of what exactly Middle Eastern is," Paul answered.

"Trust me...it is," she stated and smiled at him again. She stared directly into his eyes and he did not know whether he should hold his stare back or look away. Her full length cream and purple dress, laced at the sides and down her slender arms, showed off her slim figure. Her long black hair looked full at the sides but plaited at the rear and went half way down her back. She was elegant and her eyes a sharp blue. She then looked at Nicholas, who was staring at Alisha almost oblivious to anyone else's presence. "People are like candles. At any moment a breeze can blow it out, so enjoy the light while you have it...and tell your wife that you love her every day. And be sure to ask her, 'have I told you that I love you lately?'," she said quietly.

Paul looked at Nicholas, who made no attempt to hide the clear admiration he had for Alisha, yet his instincts told him that despite his obvious affection for her, he would never actually try anything. But his head told him he should be cautious none the less. He felt almost annoyed at himself that despite Nicholas clearly loving Alisha as he had freely admitted back at Castle Blanc, he could not help but admire and like him.

"So what am I missing here?" Count Henry suddenly said, interrupting, as he walked into view from the side.

"Just discussing Alisha making an impression," Princess Eschiva said and smiled as she turned to look at her.

"That she is indeed," Count Henry replied. "Paul...may I steal you away for a few minutes?"

"No you cannot, for I have not been formally introduced yet," Princess Eschiva said and raised her eyebrows in mock protest.

"'Tis remiss of me, My Lady," Nicholas said. "Paul, please meet Princess Eschiva," he said motioning with his hand toward her. Paul smiled and part bowed not sure exactly what he was supposed to do. "My Lady, I introduce Paul, the Bull's Head Slayer himself."

Paul frowned at Nicholas's last statement. Instantly he recalled the dream like meeting he had with the Bull's Head in his bedroom. Nicholas's comments felt wrong.

"I know who he is. But etiquette dictates lest anyone should accuse us of any improper conduct. Court protocol!" she explained, shaking her head mockingly. "You, my young man, and your beautiful wife," Princess Eschiva started to say when she looked at Nicholas briefly then back at Paul, "your wife," she emphasised as Upside poked Nicholas in the side again hard, "are well known. You are all the maids seem to gossip about, so I am at last pleased to formally meet you," she smiled.

"Paul," Count Henry interrupted and placed his arm behind him to usher him aside.

"We shall speak more later," Princess Eschiva said and raised her glass.

℘℘

Paul followed Count Henry a short distance to an open balcony that looked out across the eastern part of the city and harbour beyond. The Pathos lighthouse reflected intermittent flashes of fire and the sun's rays off of large mirrors and polished sheets of silver, a small pall of smoke rising from a fluted pipe on the side half way up the structure.

"Sorry to drag you away but I needed a private conversation with you," Count Henry started. Paul stepped back to look at several Mamluk guards as they entered the main hall area. Fully armed, resplendent in all their uniforms, shields and spears, Paul felt a rush of unease. "Relax, Paul. They are here as much for our protection as for Turansha and his men. Relax."

"Relax. I do not feel I shall ever be able to relax again, especially when people keep commenting upon me being the Bull's Head Slayer."

"I am afraid your actions have inspired many. It also gives all the hopeless romantics and poets something to feed upon."

"Like vultures."

"No...like hungry children desperate to hear something wonderful," Count Henry replied and raised his eyebrows.

"Forgive my cynicism but I have seen much already...and there is much to worry and concern oneself about."

"Have you made any decisions on what career you shall pursue?"

"No...I have tried but I have been a little preoccupied in just getting here," Paul answered and leaned against the ornate stone balustrade that ran around the balcony and looked toward the sea.

"A sailor's heart you have, that is for sure."

"That dream I am afraid I cannot follow. My place is here with Alisha and Arri now and always."

"You may be surprised what life throws your way. Within just a heartbeat, everything can change instantly and forever. I know Brother Roger intends to quiz you about joining his Order but based here in Alexandria. You would make a fine physician he says."

"Here! How so?" Paul asked, puzzled, and turned to face him.

"'Tis but one of the reasons we are here now. We must find a way of living in harmony again, for all our sakes. We are good personal friends here this day and we aim to secure treaties that will ensure we can remain so."

"I noted that Saladin's secretary attends. Why did not Saladin himself if this meeting is so important?"

"I am afraid he has other priorities dealing not only with Reynald and Gerard but also rival factions within his own faith in Syria...as we speak. 'Tis why he has sent both his secretary but also his deputy. And you must meet them. No matter what develops between our faiths and armies, you will be safe if you stay here."

"That is reassuring to hear," Paul replied but puzzled how he could make such a claim.

"Know this, Paul...Saladin, when he was a general, was known as 'the Lion' and he was Nureddin's deputy in Egypt. Upon Nureddin's death...I think it was on April 12, 1174, he took the title Sultan himself. Damascus, rather than Cairo, is the major city of the empire. Nevertheless he has fortified Cairo, which is rapidly becoming his political centre of Egypt but he still spends much of his time in Syria and Egypt is largely governed by his deputy, Karaksh."

"Why do I need to know this?" Paul asked, sensing there was more to come.

"Because," Count Henry paused and looked around to make sure no one was nearby who could overhear him. "Because you still have much to learn...and it is only in Cairo that you will be able to do so. Theodoric will, as he has agreed, teach you the basics that you must master and more importantly...understand. That is why I have pulled you aside now to ask that when Theodoric requests you go with him to Cairo that you go...please for it is truly important."

Paul looked at the serious expression in his face. Arri could be heard making a noise in the distance. Paul looked to see where he was. Alisha was still talking and laughing with the rest of the guests in the middle of the hall and wasn't even aware Arri was getting fractious. Tenno approached carrying Arri trying to calm him.

"I am sorry to interrupt. He tires and needs his comfort toy. Do you have it?" Tenno asked bluntly as he continued to rock Arri, who was punching out his arms.

"Here, let me take him," Paul said and went to take him.

"No! 'Tis fine. He just requires his comfort toy. You have business to discuss... yes?" Tenno replied as he pulled Arri back slightly from Paul.

Tenno's reaction surprised Paul for a moment. Quickly he felt around inside his small belt pouch and pulled out Arri's comfort toy Clip clop. He waved it in front of Arri, his eyes instantly focusing upon it. He outstretched his hands for it. Tenno nodded at Paul quickly. Gently Paul placed Clip clop against Arri's chest and he immediately pulled it close under his little chin, smiled and closed his eyes. Tenno looked at Paul.

"You are correct. 'Tis all he required," Paul remarked.

"I shall sit with him," Tenno stated and stepped backwards, bowed his head toward Paul then Count Henry and then walked away.

"I think your son has his own personal bodyguard," Count Henry joked.

"Looks like that. Perhaps I am no longer required all round," Paul said as he looked toward Alisha just as Nicholas moved to stand beside her as she placed her arm through his and continued to talk to the others as she held his arm.

"You have nothing to fear there. He is one of the most accomplished and honour-able knights I know," Count Henry said quietly and reassuringly.

"I am not so sure...'tis not self pity I feel either, but I made a promise to Ali as we docked on the Island of Halki that I would forever protect her and our baby...but I have nearly failed already with Turansha...the other one of course!"

"The operative word there being 'nearly'. They would not be here this day but for your actions, nor Princess Stephanie. You also now have Tenno and Thomas to teach you all you should ever need to know about swordsmanship and combat. Lord willing ye shall never require it...and it is self pity as your heart is aching over an imagined and wrongly perceived state that will not happen," Count Henry replied and looked toward Alisha and Nicholas. "Now come, I wish you to meet Gokbori properly and Saladin's secretary and Karaksh. You never know when you may have to call upon them for their help."

Paul looked at the assembled group all talking politely and laughing together. The Mamluk guards looked incredibly smart and fierce Paul thought.

Port of La Rochelle, France, Melissae Inn, spring 1191

"Fierce...we can certainly vouch for that can't we, brother?" the Templar remarked interrupting the old man.

"Most certainly can," the Hospitaller acknowledged.

"I thought the Faris knights were the fiercest?" Simon asked.

"They are...but the Mamluk forces. What can I tell you about them?" the Templar replied.

"I have never heard of these men. Who are they?" the wealthy tailor asked.

The Templar looked at the old man.

"Please, feel free to explain," he said gesturing at the Templar with his hands.

"Mamluks. The actual name means 'property'," the Templar began to explain.

"Or 'owned slave'," the Hospitaller interjected and smiled as Ayleth then smiled at him.

"Mamaluke or marmeluke is the Arabic designation for slaves. But nowadays, as they have progressed considerably since their early years, there are even noble Mamluks. They are all armed with three daggers, a sabre sword, its length depending on whether they are infantry or cavalry, but all carry a lance as well. Usually attired with a red upper surcoat or robe and blue chausses. They wear either a large turban or metal helmet and chain mail... and they are truly fierce fighters."

⁕⁂⁕   5 – 13

"If they are slaves, why do they fight so fiercely then?" Ayleth asked puzzled.

"Because they are now an established military caste in their own right, especially in Egypt. They originally rose from the ranks of slave soldiers, mainly of Kipchak and other Turkic tribes...including of Georgian and Circassian origin," the old man explained.

"Yes...and they are of great political importance as well as a powerful military force, particularly in Egypt, but also in the Levant, Mesopotamia, and India where they hold high political and military power. It is my mere humble opinion that it will be the Mamluks who will ultimately succeed in beating back our forces if we do not address and resolve our issues with the Muslims...," the Templar explained.

"That, my friend, is why you have that letter," the old man stated and smiled. "For it has been noted, your perceptive nature and political astuteness."

"Really...and I thought I was being sent to graze," he joked back.

"So how do slaves become an elite caste?" Gabirol asked.

"Because although Mamluks are purchased, their status is above ordinary slaves, who are not allowed to carry weapons or perform certain tasks. In places such as Egypt Mamluks are even considered to be 'true lords', with their social status above freeborn Muslims," the old man explained.

"How come?" Peter asked.

"The Mamluks in Islamic societies began with the Abbasid caliphs of the ninth century in Baghdad. They were known as Ghilman," the old man explained.

"Yes but why?" Simon then asked.

"Because using Mamluk soldiers gives rulers well trained troops who have no link to any established power structure whereas local non-Mamluk warriors are all too frequently more loyal to their tribal sheikhs, families, or nobles than to the sultan or caliph," the Templar further explained as the old man agreed with him. "Mamluk slave troops started out as foreigners of the lowest possible status who could not conspire against their rulers and who could easily be punished if they caused trouble, making them a great military asset. Under Saladin and the Ayyubids of Egypt, the power of the Mamluks has increased ten fold...unless I am mistaken?"

"No, you are correct on that matter," the old man remarked.

"How do they still recruit then?" Sarah asked and shrugged her shoulders.

"Mamluks are purchased while young and are raised in the barracks of the Citadel of Cairo. Because of their particular status and with no social ties or political affiliations, plus their austere military training, they are often trusted. Their training consists of strict religious and military education to help them become 'good Muslim horsemen and fighters'. Only when their training is complete are they discharged, but still attached to the patron who had purchased them. Mamluks rely on the help of their patron for career advancements and likewise the patron's reputation and power depends on his recruits. A Mamluk is also bound by a strong sense of belonging and attachment as well as having the honour and prestige of being part of an elite force. Mamluks are proud of their origin as slaves and only those who were purchased are eligible to attain the highest positions. The privileges associated with being a Mamluk are so desirable that many free Egyptians arrange to be sold in order to gain access to this privileged society."

"That is mad!" Sarah said and shook her head.

"Mamluks speak Arabic and cultivate their identity by retaining an Egyptian name. However, despite humble origins and an exclusive attitude, Mamluks are respected by their Arab subjects and they have earned considerable admiration and prestige as the 'true guardians of Islam' by repelling the Crusaders on many an occasion so many people now view them as a blessing from Allah to the Muslims. Many are trained as cavalry soldiers and, like a Faris knight, they also have to follow the dictates of furusiyya, the code that includes values such as courage and generosity, and also cavalry tactics, horsemanship, archery and treatment of wounds," the Templar continued to explain.

"You sound as though you admire these men," Gabirol remarked.

"Make no mistake...and I make no apology, I do. They are a worthy opponent," the Templar answered immediately. "Even when they relax or play sport, it is all centred on combat skills in one manner or another. Their training is rigorous and intensive."

"Just as an aside...," the old man said, raising his finger briefly. "Georgian Mamluks in Egypt are allowed to retain their native language, be informed and keep aware of the politics of the Caucasus region, receive frequent visits from their parents or other relatives, and are able to send gifts to family members or give money to build useful structures such as defensive towers, or even a church in their native villages in Georgia. These were gifts Reynald had his eyes upon..." The old man paused. "The beginnings of a Mamluk Sultanate of Egypt already lie in the Ayyubid dynasty that Saladin founded in 1174 with his uncle Shirkuh when he conquered Egypt for the Zengid King Nur ad-Din of Damascus in 1169."

"Not sure why we needed to know all that?" Simon said and sighed and picked at the bread crumbs upon his empty plate.

"That is because you don't listen. Everything we are told has relevance...does it not?" Sarah said to Simon then looked across the table at the old man.

"It does...so thank you," the old man replied and bowed his head slightly at Sarah.

She smiled, folded her arms and sat back against her chair looking rather smug, which made the old man laugh.

"I am concerned that something developed between Alisha and Nicholas...does it?" Ayleth asked quietly.

All looked at the old man at once, which made him laugh again at their expressions.

"You are all far too suspicious and cynical," the old man said as he chuckled. *"But let me explain that during that meeting, Paul noted many surprising things. Firstly he learnt all about the Mamluks as our friend here has detailed...but he also learnt and saw at first hand the mutual respect, and trust...yes trust...which they all had for each other. Turansha and Gokbori could have easily seized and held them all captive for ransom just as Brother Odo was being held by Saladin's forces. Neither side was forced to surrender their weapons and all spoke freely and openly. Paul spent over an hour alone with Karaksh, Saladin's deputy, Husam and Gokbori discussing maps and ships. Husam made Paul promise that he would visit Cairo and see the ships he was having designed and built there and that he must come sailing with him,"* the old man explained and paused for several long moments. *"Oh the opportunities that were opening up for them...and Alisha, much to her surprise felt comfortable and at ease with all she spoke to and her confidence grew considerably as a consequence. Yes, Brother Nicholas I am afraid to say did stand by her side most of that day."*

"And Paul did nothing?" Sarah asked loudly and leant forward.

"No...he just knew Nicholas, despite his feelings, would do nothing and he also knew that he would be leaving on the following day's early tide."

"This Paul sounds very emotionally mature for his age," Gabirol remarked.

"He was indeed...he was indeed, as well as displaying great emotional intelligence," the old man sighed. *"He was offered the opportunity to work and study at the main medical hospice in Alexandria, with both Turansha and Brother Roger as his joint sponsors and patrons. That only added to Paul's confusion as to what career he should pursue."*

"Where was Arri all this time?" Peter asked.

"With Tenno and Ishmael...until he required feeding. But even after Alisha had done that, with Princess Eschiva accompanying her to a private room, Tenno insisted on looking after Arri again," the old man answered.

"Bit weird if you ask me...that behaviour. 'Tis not right for a man, especially a warrior type, babysitting...," the Genoese sailor commented and laughed.

"Have you ever had children?" the old man asked, his tone clipped. The Genoese sailor immediately shrank back in his chair and shook his head no.

"I thought not."

"Did they stay all night then at this meeting...and what was the outcome?" Gabirol asked.

"Well...Paul was sat next to Conrad of Montferrat for a grand evening meal, and found him a little too boastful and loud. Alisha had both Nicholas and the Hospitaller knight who had bowed to her on the Tarida sat on either side of her facing Paul directly. She laughed often and Paul was happy to see her like that. Most of the discussion relating to politics was done at the furthest end of the table...a point Conrad was quick to point out and moan about

claiming he was being deliberately left out of whatever agreements and arrangements were being made," the old man explained then laughed to himself.

"What, what is so funny?" the farrier asked as the old man laughed for several minutes.

"I apologise. I was just recalling that Theodoric sat beside Paul and Tenno opposite him. Theodoric informed the table that he and Tenno had got off on the wrong foot when they had first met, but were now firm friends. Tenno looked at him with a deadly serious look, despite holding Arri in his arms, who was fast asleep, and said 'nothing has changed'." The old man laughed again. *"Tenno never smiled so it was impossible to know if he was joking or being serious..."*

"Why didn't Alisha or Paul have Arri?" Ayleth asked.

"Tenno insisted they enjoy the evening and that looking after Arri gave him something to do and an excuse not to have to talk to anyone."

"Okay I can see why he would do that. But the meeting was all very informal then?" Gabirol remarked and flicked back through some of his notes.

"Very informal. They were all good friends and they were there to try and carve out a way forward that would bring peace to the whole region," the old man answered.

"And how would they achieve that, short of killing off Reynald and all converting?" Peter exclaimed.

"By concentrating and focusing upon what they all had in common. And by implementing ideas as suggested by Count Henry of joint harvests, water collection and distribution as well as more trade and commerce so they would become more integrated and inter-dependent. They also discussed how best they could communicate more freely and quickly so any mistakes or misunderstandings could be resolved sooner, rather than later when it was too late and which all too often resulted in blood being spilt."

"Can I ask a different question please?" Ayleth said almost in a whisper.

"Of course," the old man replied.

"You seem to have forgotten that you said you would answer how Kratos could ignore pain...," she said and squinted and grimaced as if the question had pained her.

"I have indeed. 'Tis my age obviously," the old man said and smiled at her.

"Yes and what about Abi's comment that 'I wish you enough'. Enough what?" Sarah asked.

"Kratos used his mind...'tis as simple as that. This was something Tenno was well acquainted with for he had spent many years learning to meditate as I have explained already. The physical body is in fact controlled by the mind...not the other way as so many of you believe. 'Tis how some can walk through fire and not be burnt...'tis how some can receive impossible injuries, yet survive. Just take Ishmael as an example," the old man said then looked directly at Sarah. *"As for Abi's words...'twas a simple statement but meant she wished Tenno enough...I wish you enough sun to keep your attitude bright. I wish you enough rain to appreciate the sun more. I wish you enough happiness to keep your spirit alive. I wish you enough pain so that the smallest joys in life appear much bigger. I wish you enough gain to satisfy your wanting. I wish you enough loss to appreciate all that you possess. I wish enough Hellos to get you through the final Goodbye..."*

"I think I shall try and remember that," Gabirol said and started to write it down.

"'Twas a saying she had picked up on her travels," the old man explained further.

"And the ship Kratos had. What manner of a vessel was that?" the Genoese sailor asked.

"Did I not say...that I cannot answer...will not answer," the old man replied adamantly.

"So then what happened?" Simon asked.

"After much talk, quite some considerable laughter, most retired to sleeping quarters.

Turansha showed Alisha and Paul to a large guest room. Theodoric and Tenno were given an adjoining room to share which drew a look of disgust from Tenno when Theodoric prom-ised he would try and not belch or pass wind all night long. Ishmael asked to be allowed to sit outside in the corridor all night in a chair as he found it hard to sleep in a bed."

"Ah that is really sad," Ayleth remarked.

"He could really. But he saw it as his job now to protect Alisha and Arri," the old man explained.

"And Paul?" Simon asked.

"Of course...but Paul could not settle so when Alisha had given Arri his last feed of the night, he left them and returned to the balcony near the upper hall."

Palace of Turansha, Eastern Quarter, Alexandria, 1179

It was late when Paul placed his hands upon the cool feeling balustrades of the bal-cony and looked out across the roof tops below of the eastern sector of the city, the Pharos lighthouse shining brightly as its ten thousand candles blazed away inside being reflected out to sea. Paul wondered if it was needed as a full moon shone brightly high in the night sky illuminating the entire sea in a bluish light that cast sharp shadows. Lights still flickered in various windows and doorways and the night air was filled with sweet smelling scents Paul had never smelt before. A dog barked off in the distance. The sea was a calm flat surface and he was just able to pick up the scent of the salty sea air as he breathed in fully. His mind wondered about being at sea, in a boat he would design. He would love to know what kind of vessel Kratos and Abi had left in. The unique swivelling booms and self righting sails as the main mast section rose was intriguing. Then it dawned upon him that he had not actually seen a mast as such. He looked up as stars twinkled brightly directly overhead. Turansha and Brother Roger's offer to sponsor him was kind he thought...and helping people was as Brother Roger had said back in La Rochelle, just one way of following in Christ's footsteps. He certainly had no stomach for killing he knew that much about himself already...but he would learn all he could so as never to be in the position he and Alisha had found themselves in. He shud-dered as he recalled the events. 'To heal...to heal' he told himself. He felt the side of his face where the scar had been. 'What wonderful joy it would bring to this world if I could find and use whatever it is that the lady of light used upon me,' he thought and smiled to himself. And if Alisha were to have another child, how much would a device like Kratos's help and ensure her safety? He sighed heavily and looked across to the horizon. Instantly he recognised the constellation of Orion as it rose slowly, its three middle belt stars appearing to sit almost on the faint horizon line. He watched for many minutes as it slowly rose until eventually it was completely high in the night sky. A blue flickering on the actual horizon caught his eye just as the star Sirius breached the skyline revealing itself as a bright blue flickering ball of radiance. He had never seen Sirius look so blue or bright before even when the moon was not shining. He marvelled as it slowly edged its way higher. He then recalled Theodoric's comments when they were on the Tarida about the three cha-pels he had helped site...to reflect three important stars. So Theo has known all along…the three belt stars of Orion. He smiled and promised himself the first thing he would ask Theodoric in the morning would be about them…and Sirius.

"'Tis a beautiful city is it not?" Count Henry suddenly said quietly, making Paul jump.

Quickly Paul turned around to see Count Henry sat on the right of the balcony on a stone bench resting his head back against the wall almost hidden from sight.

"My Lord…how long have you been there? You gave me heart failure," Paul asked part laughing but holding his chest as his heart pounded.

"Long enough to see Orion rise and Sirius crest as you have," he replied and sat forwards a little. "Please, join me and sit for the air is warm. Too hot for sleeping."

Paul sat beside him and looked upwards where Count Henry was also looking.

"We came from out there you know…and it is where we shall return," he matter of factly stated. Paul looked at the stars then at Count Henry and back up at the stars again. "I note and see that Tenno has taken Arri under his wing…literally and physically…and you appear to have a new shadow…Ishmael."

"What…yes Tenno seems taken with Arri and he has a way with him. It greatly helps Ali and I…which is a godsend to be honest," Paul replied quietly.

"Does it not bother you…his closeness to Arri?"

"No, not the slightest. Should it?"

"Not at all, but I know many men who would feel threatened, jealous even. But it shows your maturity beyond your years…and Ishmael, you may as well come out now," Count Henry said and looked toward the doorway.

Paul looked at him, puzzled, then toward the large wooden shutter door hinged back against the wall as Ishmael slowly stepped into view. He raised his right hand slightly.

"Apologies. I just wished to make sure Paul was okay," he explained politely.

"Ishmael, there is no need to apologise or worry," Paul said and beckoned he come and sit on the opposite stone bench.

"Paul, you can never be too sure. I heard that…Conrad man speak much of Turansha to people today…and I do not believe he was referring to the Turansha who is presently here, but the other one…so I shall not rest if it is all the same to you," Ishmael explained quietly. "But I will not let this fact be known to Alisha."

"No, please do not," Paul replied, concerned.

"I am afraid that Turansha, the evil one as I shall call him, has unfinished business with you, Paul, so you should be on your guard always with that one."

"But you told me earlier to relax," Paul replied instantly.

"I did…and you must. But that does not mean you should not be on your guard always. Turansha used his name and similar connections to Saladin's brother to expand his own power, wealth and influence…and once, when he was nearly caught arranging to have Saladin assassinated, he managed to manipulate the facts and evidence and turn it all against Saladin's brother, Turansha's own secretary."

"Really. So what happened to him?"

"The secretary…he was immediately executed."

"And you say he still has unfinished business with me. Why?"

"Because he knows you are important. He knows from his many spies and connections that there are secrets that follow you. And know this, he has had prior entanglements with both your father and Alisha's...he knew what he was doing when he set up the scene for you and Alisha to be executed, which I do not believe was his intention."

"You mean we went through all of that for nothing?" Paul asked, exasperated.

"No, Paul. You suffered that so Turansha could prove something to himself and prove you would have protection arrive...even if that form very nearly did not get to you in time."

"You mean Abi?"

"Yes. So, Paul, always remain on your guard for that man to turn up one day on your doorstep," Count Henry stated bluntly and looked across at Paul intently. "I am not saying this lightly or to scare you...but there is bad blood between him and your respective families."

"My Lord..." Paul sighed heavily.

"Paul...I shall be your eyes and ears behind you always," Ishmael said and nodded at him.

In the brilliant moonlight, the stark shadows cast across Ishmael's features only enhanced and accentuated his physical injuries making him look like a mystical beast almost. But Paul placed his hand upon Ishmael's thick forearm.

"Thank you," he said quietly, almost whispering. He then turned toward Count Henry again. "Please, tell me all that I need to know to understand this land, these people and how I can help bring peace...if that is at all possible for it seems that peace has never existed in this world since Cain and Abel," Paul asked.

"Paul...Cain and Abel is but a simplified story of mankind as a whole...but you have met Kratos have you not?"

"You know of him then for I thought none of you did and why he did not present himself at the harbour," Paul asked bemused.

"I know Kratos only too well," Count Henry replied and smiled. "And he would be the first to tell you that a long time ago...there was indeed only peace upon this world. So never believe it when you are told that violence is the way of this world."

"Then tell me of this world now. Why is it such a violent intolerant mess?"

"Where can I start?" Count Henry said quietly. "Look, there was a time when Armenians settled in Palestine and the warlike Maronite Christians lived in the mountains, away from the power, influence and the control of kings, but Syriac-Christians remained deeply suspicious of the Latins when they arrived, especially after their arrogant attitudes and the slaughter they committed in Jerusalem when seizing it. I have to say that even today, the adoption of many local ways by Latins, such as dress and cleanliness, are sadly all superficial as the cultural gulf is just too big to be bridged I fear. Relations between Latin and Muslim states remain rooted in war and people like Reynald and Gerard only increase that fact and actively encourage it as I think you already know. I strongly suspect...and fear...that lasting peace is viewed as probably impossible as both sides cling to their own ideologies that will not accept each other's existence. Far too many Latins' and Christians' attitude is based upon the First Crusade's easy victories, which only serves to make them overconfident as personified by Reynald so the military elite have very high morale but an overconfidence that will lead to many military disasters unless we can avert it in the first place. And that is why we are here this day, this night...for here, we are all close friends despite coming from different backgrounds and religions," Count Henry explained with an impassioned tone Paul had not seen or heard before

"Then, please, teach me as much as you are able and I shall do whatever I can to make sure that people like the Reynalds and Turanshas of this world do not succeed," Paul replied and sat up.

"Then you must speak with Brother Jakelin de Mailly, for he knows more than I about the region. He has developed a critical overview of the geopolitical world we now find ourselves in."

⚹   2 – 45

"Geopolitical...what does that mean?" Paul asked, puzzled, as Ishmael looked at him and shook his head also.

"It means the land and its political make up. Such as the Eastern Kingdom of Jerusalem consisting of sectors. North, the Litani Valley with its many impressive castles, the Central sector from Mount Hermon (Jabal al Shaykh) along the Golan Heights to the Yarmuk valley, supposedly shared with the rulers of Damascus. But some of our Muslim friends want their lands to extend as far as the Balqa Hills around Amman where we dominate the fertile plateau between the River Yarmuk and Ajlun Hills. Southward lays the Latin territory of Oultrajordain where you have already been as it is controlled by Reynald and his forces. Crac de Moab, Princess Stephanie's home, lays between the River Jordan, Dead Sea and Wadi Araba in the west, and the strategic road from Amman to Aqabah. From Oultrajordain Latin forces, by order of Reynald no less, levy heavy tolls on Muslims between Syria and Egypt, even on Muslim Haj or pilgrim caravans travelling south to Mecca and Medina. In the early 1170s Saladin's re-conquest of territory south of Montreal (Shawbak) had a profound psychological impact liberating the Haj Road so that pilgrims from Egypt at least no longer paid humiliating tolls to the infidels. It is why he is so respected...and Reynald so despised by Muslims. But the biggest and most worrying major development that threatens all of Christendom is Saladin's unification of Islamic territories. Only in the far north do we have a neighbour not of a Muslim state, that being the Christian Cilician Armenia. But more importantly the long dormant concept of Jihad against us 'infidels' is being rapidly revived by Sunni scholars. Jihads have become organised campaigns to recover Islamic Holy Lands just as our Crusades have done likewise before. It is not to convert the Crusaders by force as that is not the true way of Islam. The Sunni Muslim revival is also directed against the Shi'a Muslim minority. The loss of Jerusalem to the Crusaders only increased its importance to Muslims being followed by an outpouring of Fada'il or Praise Literature about the city. So, Paul, if you wish to understand all that unfolds, you have much to learn and I fear not much time to do so," Count Henry explained. [66]

Port of La Rochelle, France, Melissae Inn, spring 1191

"'Tis a great pity that friendship between all the emissaries could not be translated into actual good deeds, for it would have saved many thousands of lives," the Templar remarked sadly.

"'Tis indeed. But there were people like Reynald, Gerard, Turansha...the evil one...and many within Saladin's own ranks who hungered for war," the old man replied and looked at the Templar.

"So I am assuming their meeting achieved nothing for war certainly still arrived at our doorsteps," the Templar remarked.

"It meant Paul met some influential people...and perhaps helped save some of their lives when all out war finally broke across Outremer...but unbeknown to Paul that night, whilst he spoke with Count Henry, neither of them had sensed or seen that Alisha had come to find Paul," the old man explained and paused.

"And she heard everything they spoke of...about the evil Turansha too?" Gabirol said.

"Yes, she heard all of it. To say her heart sank and felt heavy would be an understatement. But she made a promise to herself not to let any threats, perceived or real, spoil her life. She took herself away to bed and Paul never knew she had listened to all they spoke of."

"So what did Paul choose to do...for work?" Gabirol asked.

"Paul wished to learn and understand all about jihad he kept hearing about so Turansha, the good one, lent him many books translated into Latin from Arabic about jihad which stated the best jihad was still against evil in one's own heart...fighting the unbeliever came a close second. He read the famous military Latin treatise, the 'de reimilitaris' by the theorist Flavius Vegetius Renatus and he started to understand the Muslim way and Islam as a whole. He discussed the whole matter at length with Theodoric and three knights who rapidly became his close friends, Baldwin de Fotina whom you are already aware of, and Raulfus Bructus and Laudoicus de Tabaria."

"How come...did they stay in Alexandria then?" Simon asked, confused.

"At the request of Turansha...and likewise three knights from Gokbori's forces went away with Count Henry."

"Is that not risky...for the knights?" Ayleth asked.

"How come Nicholas did not stay behind as surely he would have been the first to volunteer?" Sarah asked.

"Why do you think/" Gabirol answered for the old man and raised his eyebrows.

"Count Henry made sure Nicholas was already aboard the Hospitaller ship early. He was not even given the chance to say goodbye to Alisha...but," the old man said and paused.

"But what?" Sarah asked impatiently.

"He gave Brother Baldwin, Upside, a note to pass on to her..."

"Oooh the...the rascal!" Sarah remarked and clenched her fists together.

"Please do not be so hard upon him and his actions," the old man said in his defence.

"And don't forget, Paul was given a letter by Stephanie," Peter pointed out.

"What good could three Muslim knights do for Count Henry?" the Hospitaller asked.

"Teach Latin knights how to lead...by example."

"Really...how so?" the Templar asked.

"Because unfortunately for our forces, and it is a weakness that Count Henry recognised and aimed to correct, was the simple fact that Christian knights all too often looked down upon their own infantry and were prejudice against them whereas Muslims saw both as important and believed and recognised that individual merit counted regardless of background believing in the luck of divine favour that enabled a man to win fame, fortune or power. Arabs were referred to as 'those peoples' from Bedouin tribes not those from the Fertile Crescent peoples. Saladin's army consisted of many Kurdish swordsman and cavalry. Turcomans lived outside the cities in regions across Celicia and Byzantine and many volunteered to fight against us freely. They have excellent eyesight and are known as devils in war and angels in peace. But the most successful small army to emerge after the fall of the Saljuq Empire was that of Zanghi and his son Nur al Din under whom Firgany had served. Leadership was Turkish and Kurdish and the troops were mainly Turcoman horse archers and Kurdish close combat cavalry. Most professional Tawashi cavalry were backed by Bedouin close combat Arab auxiliaries. Most Muslim officers were older, more experienced and wiser than their Christian counterparts and they read training books including the 'Siyasat Nama'. And Count Henry knew that ultimately Christian forces would have to adapt and become like them if we were to stand any chance of defeating them or negotiating a long and lasting truce based on equal and mutual respect," the old man explained and shook his head.

"This has never been passed down to us," the Templar commented.

"Sadly no...thanks to Gerard. If he had listened to advice rather than his own self proclaimed mission from God belief, things would certainly be different now."

"So what of the Mamluk lot you mentioned earlier?" the farrier asked.

"You know...It takes eight years to train a Mamluk soldier, first on foot, then on horse then archery. The 'Murda al Tarsusi' is a military manual specifically written for Saladin. Muslim officers and as many soldiers are literate unlike most Latins and swimming came second only to literacy. Muslims viewed overcoming natural cowardice as more admirable than feeling no fear, which they saw as being stupid."

"Gerard all over then...stupid!" the Templar said and laughed.

"When faced with an educated, fit, healthy and determined enemy, you need to match it like for like. But our forces, in the main, except our Templars and Hospitallers, are illiterate, uneducated and of poor health. And for Muslim knights and soldiers, protection of the weak by the strong was a powerful ideal of romantic honour remarkably similar to our chivalric codes. Faris knights were taught to shoot horses from under knights. Paul actually learned this when he attended some training sessions and demonstrations along with Brother Baldwin and the other two knights. He also learnt that the Turks believed they were destined to rule the world even after becoming Muslims. They continued to see themselves as a chosen people who had saved Islam in its hour of need. Muslim stories focused more on love and emotion of battle and the often-fraught relationship between men and women. Men wore perfumes which many Latins see as being effeminate. 'Siyar' meant 'rules of war' and Paul studied these carefully and learnt that according to all that he had read and understood, most battles were lost or won in the minds of the combatants. Muslim officers also showed great concern for their men and not as reckless as Crusaders, especially like Reynald," the old man said solemnly.

"You make it all sound too in favour of Muslims," the wealthy tailor said, his tone suspicious.

"Not at all. There are good men in our ranks too...but sadly their common sense, courage and foresight were and are all too often crushed beneath the weight of the more loud, aggressive and manipulative self serving nobility that ultimately has the last word in such matters...especially in matters of faith and propaganda," the old man said and looked at the wealthy tailor straight in the eyes.

"How did it all get to this stage?" Ayleth asked and looked down at her hands sadly.

"This last century has seen massive fortifications built by both sides. The Syrian city of Aleppo in the north has a long history of practical expertise in siege warfare whilst the Arab Bedouin have lost all political dominance to invading Turks and generally prefer to be left alone and now Islamic naval dominance is falling to increased superiority of naval *fleets from Pisa, Genoa and Venice. That is why Gokbori and Husam were so keen to build further ships to counter this."*

"Yes I can tell you we have dockyards full to capacity with new, bigger and better galleys being built every day," the Genoese sailor chipped in excitedly.

"To further answer how we have arrived at this present state, Ayleth, let me explain that many Latins watched and still watch in alarm as Saladin's position grows. Many from the kingdoms within Outremer have sent and still send ambassadors to Europe. King Henry the Second of England would not commit troops but sent much money. Thirty thousand Marks in total, a major amount, but under the protection and authority to use of Gerard de Ridefort. 'Tis what he was bringing back from Paris when he met Alisha and Paul that time on the northern Road outside La Rochelle."

"That seems so long ago since you told us that...I had almost forgotten that part," Simon interrupted.

"That money, as I believe I have previously explained, would prove to play a crucial role in the lead up to the battle of Hattin. King Henry the Second had levied heavy taxes in 1172 as part of his penance for the murder of Thomas a'Becket, as explained earlier when you asked, Ayleth," the old man said and looked at her. She nodded and smiled. *"He had promised to support by payment two hundred knights for a year. An emergency census was carried out throughout the kingdoms of Outremer to determine their military strength and many castles were strengthened. Taxes were raised again and the importance of Oultrajordain increased once Saladin controlled both Egypt and Syria. But Reynald ran an effective intelligence service among the Bedouin and planned to smash the Muslim ring that surrounded the Latin states and maybe even break into the Indian Ocean regions capturing all their inherent major trade routes. The support Reynald received from the Bedouin at the time seriously worried Saladin. It was during this period that Count Raymond the Third advised a passive strategy which was adopted, and it was for that position that many now condemn and blame him for missing any chance of destroying Saladin. But that was not the case as I shall explain as this story concludes,"* the old man explained and stared at the sword upon the table.

"Can I just ask quickly...you did say that Paul met Saladin's secretary then?" Peter asked.

"Yes I did, as well as Saladin's deputy, Karaksh. And he would meet them again..."

"I wish to know of the note Nicholas gave Upside...did he pass it on to Alisha?" Sarah asked.

"Reluctantly, yes he did pass it on...and she read it."

"What did it say?" Sarah asked impatiently.

"Oh...it started off simple enough stating that she was his Catherine Wheel around which his entire life revolved," the old man explained.

"That is totally unacceptable and inappropriate," Peter remarked, shaking his head disapprovingly.

"Here...decide for yourself," the old man said and removed a very small sheet of parchment from Paul's leather bound folder and gently pushed it toward Peter.

As Peter pulled it nearer and focused upon the small neat letters, Sarah stood up and rushed around to look over his shoulder as he began to read it.

"Well...what does it say?" Simon asked impatiently.

Peter looked up at him then at the old man before returning his gaze to the small parchment.

"It reads...Dearest Alisha, My very own once, only and ever truest Grail Queen. My

Alexandrian St Catherine, the wheel of my life and my world that I revolve around. Paul will know of what I write here for I have already told him, so do not feel that you must hide this for it would cast a sense of wrong doing upon you for which I alone would be guilty of causing. But know this, both of you. As you move through this life together...laugh often, even the silly little laughs to the loudest embarrassing laughs that hurt, and let each be foolish in each other's company...but cry too in front of each other. Hide nothing. Have passion for each other and respect, for then you will know true love that can endure pain and despair when it shows itself, for it will come as it does to all of us at some stage. Never dilute that love especially when the waters become deep and dark. When I am gone from you as I now must depart, I shall cry... that deep down silent cry that nobody shall ever hear. The cry you feel in your throat where you hold your breath and have to grab your stomach to silence the pain as you fight to stop yourself from screaming out loud when you know all hope is gone and the person who means the most to you is lost forever. When it would be a lesser evil to die than to part and still live... for therein lies a greater unbearable torment! Your Knight, at your service always, Nicholas x."

Peter placed the sheet down and looked up slowly. Sarah and Ayleth looked as though they were about to burst into tears as did Simon, who wiped his face and looked up at the ceiling pretending to study something seen.

"And...and when exactly did that Brother Baldwin, Upside whatever it was they called him, pass this on to Alisha...if he did?" the wealthy tailor asked.

"He only handed it over the day he left Alexandria as he was about to board the vessel that would return him to the port of Jaffa and on to Jerusalem," the old man answered.

"Why did he not give it to her earlier?" Ayleth asked.

"Because he felt it was wrong in the first place...but also that Alisha would then in all probability write a reply and consequently ask that he pass it on. He had come to admire and like Paul a lot over the last month of his stay. So just as he boarded, he slipped her the note. When she returned home, only then did she open and read it," the old man sighed as his words trailed off into a whisper. "'Twas a final farewell from Brother Nicholas and she knew it."

"Emissaries and final farewells it would appear?" Gabirol stated and looked up.

Chapter 45
Twin Churches, Meditation
and the Atbash Cipher

Alexandria, Egypt, October 1179

Alisha sat alone upon the wooden bench pushed hard against the wall of her balcony. Arri was just inside the bedroom soundly asleep with Paul downstairs talking with Theodoric. The sun was just touching the horizon where the sea joined the clear evening sky. With her hands shaking, she finished reading Nicholas's note and clenched it tightly against her stomach and closed her eyes. She took a few deep breaths then rested her head against the wall. A single tear rolled down her cheek and she quickly wiped it away determined not to cry again. She felt overwhelmed with a mix of emotions. Partly pleased, partly guilty, partly excited and partly annoyed at Nicholas for writing her such a heartfelt letter. He was right of course, she must not hide the letter and hoped that Paul would not be upset. She recalled the words Kratos had spoken to her alone and opened her eyes. She took a deep breath and stood up quickly. She would show the letter to Paul immediately for she knew if she did not, she never would.

Port of La Rochelle, France, Melissae Inn, spring 1191

"And...please tell me, what was it that Kratos had told her?" Sarah pleaded and feigned a look of pained desperation at the old man, her hands clasped together in prayer. "Please!"

"Why is she his Catherine Wheel?" the farrier asked, bemused.

"I cannot tell you what Kratos told her...not yet anyway" the old man answered quietly. "But I can explain what Nicholas meant about her being his 'Catherine Wheel', for you see Saint Catherine, who most of you must have heard of," he said and looked at them all in turn as they nodded they had, "supposedly came from Alexandria itself and was also known as 'Saint Catherine of the Wheel' and 'The Great Martyr Saint Catherine'. According to Christian tradition she was a saint and virgin who was martyred in the early fourth century at the hands of the pagan emperor Maxentius. She was both a princess and a noted scholar who became a Christian and converted hundreds of people to Christianity. In the Catholic Church she is revered as one of the Fourteen Holy Helpers. According to tradition, she was the beautiful daughter of the pagan King Costus and Queen Sabinella, who governed Alexandria. Being intelligent and studious left her well-versed in all the arts, sciences, and in philosophy, and having decided to remain a virgin all her life, she announced she would only marry someone who surpassed her in beauty, intelligence, wealth, and dignity. Raised a pagan, she became a Christian in her teenage years, having received a vision in which

561

the Blessed Virgin Mary gave her to Christ in a mystical marriage. As a young adult, she visited her contemporary, the Roman Emperor Maxentius, and attempted to convince him of the moral error in persecuting Christians for not worshipping idols. The emperor arranged for the best pagan philosophers and orators to disprove her, hoping they would refute her pro-Christian arguments, but she won the debate. Several of her adversaries, conquered by her eloquence, declared themselves Christians and were at once put to death. Catherine was then scourged and imprisoned, during which time over two hundred people came to see her, including Maxentius's wife, the Empress. All converted to Christianity and were subsequently martyred. Upon the failure of Maxentius to make Catherine yield by way of torture, he tried to win her over by proposing marriage. The saint refused, declaring that her spouse was Jesus Christ, to whom she had consecrated her virginity. The furious emperor condemned Catherine to death on the spiked breaking wheel, but, at her touch, this instrument of torture was miraculously destroyed. Maxentius finally had her beheaded. A tradition dating to about AD 800 stated that angels carried her corpse to Mount Sinai, where, in the sixth century, the Eastern Emperor Justinian established what is now Saint Catherine's Monastery in Egypt, which is in fact dedicated to the Transfiguration. But," the old man paused, "but there is no positive evidence that she ever existed outside the mind of some Greek writer who first composed what he intended to be simply an edifying romance. Catherine was an invention inspired to provide a counterpart to the story of the slightly later pagan philosopher Hypatia of Alexandria whom we have already discussed. Another inspiration for Saint Catherine comes from the writer Eusebius, who wrote around the year AD 320 that the Emperor had ordered a young Christian woman, Dorothea of Alexandria, to come to his palace to become his mistress, and when she refused, he had her punished, by having her banished and her estates confiscated. The earliest surviving account of the so-called Saint Catherine came over five hundred years after the traditional date of her martyrdom, in the 'Monologium' attributed to Emperor Basil the First (AD 866), although the rediscovery of her relics at Saint Catherine's Monastery at the foot of Mount Sinai was about AD 800 and implies an existing cult at that date. The common name of the monastery developed after the discovery. The monastery was built by order of Emperor Justinian the First who reigned around AD 527–565 enclosing the Chapel of the Burning Bush ordered to be built by Helena, the mother of Constantine the First, at the site where Moses is supposed to have seen the burning bush...the living bush on the grounds is purportedly the original. It is also referred to as 'Saint Helen's Chapel'. The site is sacred to Christianity and Islam."

"So you mean the whole Saint Catherine story is just a lie?" Sarah asked, almost shocked.

"Not a lie...for it could be argued that the cult of Saint Catherine of Alexandria originated in oral traditions from the fourth-century Diocletianic Persecutions of Christians in Alexandria. But there is no evidence that Catherine herself was an historical figure and she may well have been a composite drawn from memories of women persecuted for their faith. Saint Catherine is one of the most important saints in the religious culture of our times and considered the most important of the virgin martyrs, a group that includes Saint Agnes, Margaret of Antioch, Saint Barbara, Saint Lucy, Valerie of Limoges and many others. Much like the Moses story, but I shall come to that shortly," the old man said and cleared his throat.

"Make another note of that, Gabi," Simon said and nudged Gabirol hard. He shook his head at him before the old man continued.

"The development of Catherine's cult was spurred on by the reported rediscovery of her body around the year AD 800 at Mount Sinai, with hair still growing and a constant stream of healing oil issuing from her body. There are several pilgrimage stories that chronicle the journey to Mount Sinai, however, the monastery is the best-known site of Catherine pilgrimage, but is also the most difficult to reach. The most prominent Western shrine is the monastery in Rouen that claims to house Catherine's fingers. It is not alone in the West, however, accompanied by many, scattered shrines and altars dedicated to Catherine which exist throughout France and England. Some are better known sites, such as Canterbury and Westminster, which claim to have a phial of her oil, brought back from Mount Sinai by Edward the Confessor. Other shrines, such as Saint Catherine's Hill, in Hampshire in Britain, are the focus of generally local pilgrimage, many of which are only identified by brief mentions to them in various texts, rather than by physical evidence. Her principal symbol is the spiked wheel, which has become known as the Catherine Wheel, and her feast day is celebrated on the twenty-fifth of November by most Christian Churches. She also often carries either a martyr's palm or the sword with which she was actually executed. She often has long unbound blonde or reddish hair, unbound as she was unmarried. The vision of Saint Catherine of Alexandria usually shows the infant Christ, held by the Virgin, placing a ring on her finger. She is very frequently shown attending on the Virgin and Child, and is usually prominent in scenes of the Master of the Virgo inter Virgines, showing a group of virgin saints surrounding the Virgin and Child." [67]

"And you say the Moses we know of is likewise just a composite or made up?" the Templar asked, puzzled.

"In a fashion...as I have already intimated when discussing Moses, he is not the straightforward character we all read of in the Bible, just like the accounts of the Ark of Covenant, but as promised, I shall explain as we reach the end of this tale," the old man replied and smiled at the Templar.

✳ 2 – 44

"Sorry if I am changing the direction of this tale, but you mentioned earlier," Gabirol said as he quickly looked back through his notes. "Ah, here it is. You said that Moses was in fact some Egyptian...but I am interested in the comments you made about the Virgin Mary and Mary Magdalene arriving in France and staying here in La Rochelle. Can you quickly explain that further for I thought you said she landed where Theodoric came from in Roussillon?"

"I can confirm quickly what I said and meant," the old man answered as all looked at him expectantly, which made him smile. "Both the Virgin Mary, the mother of Jesus, and Mary Magdalene along with Joseph of Arimathea and Lazarus physically landed on the shores of Roussillon. They stayed there for a while...travelled to many places along the southern coast line before finally moving here...to La Rochelle," he explained and paused as they all looked at each other, Simon with his mouth hanging open as if in shock.

"So...the great secret that Niccolas told both Taqi and Paul is about them, Mary and her family. Are they buried here in La Rochelle?" Gabirol asked appearing excited, his eyes searching the old man's every facial movement and expression.

"As Kratos and Theodoric confirmed to Paul, her family was here...and perhaps some of it still remains. Niccolas spoke a great truth," the old man answered, expressionless, giving nothing away.

"How come we never realised it before. Of course, all the legends that speak and claim that the Virgin Mary walked around this point, hence why it is named Allee Stella Maris. 'Tis

563

obvious really," Peter exclaimed and laughed as he shook himself and then pondered on the old man's comments as they all sat in silence.

"Paul's father, Philip,...as I have explained...wrote many poems and stories, under different names to protect himself and family, but they all contained elements familiar to us through the many Grail quest tales and King Arthur myths, whom just like Moses and Saint Catherine are yet more examples of a combination of events and people. Many of Philip's romantic poems and stories are based upon the 'The Marias Poitevin' area...that mysterious, misty and secluded landscape east of La Rochelle. He hid much within his tales symbolically, just like the multi faceted and multi symbolic meanings behind the Templars' 'twin riders' upon a single horse," the old man said softly as he looked at Ayleth, who looked troubled as she bit her thumbnail just as Alisha always did.

"I am keen to learn and know of the many meanings for I believe I am not privy to any of them apart from the standard one being about the Order being so poor that two knights shared a single horse," the Templar commented.

"It would be nice to know," Miriam said as she sat closer to the Templar.

"In its briefest sense, I can tell you that it represents many things...from Christianity and Islam coming together and riding as one in the same direction, to representing the duality of life, black and white, to light and darkness, our visible sun to the approaching dark sun, to Jesus and his so-called twin brother Thomas, to the coming together of the twin Churches of Christ...the Church of Peter and the Church of John," the old man explained and clasped his hands together and waited for their response.

"I have heard many times my Masters within the Order speak of a twin Church, but I was never allowed to hear complete conversations about it, so I know what you speak of is based on truth," the Templar said looking serious.

Sarah reached over and closed Simon's mouth, which was still wide open.

"The Holy Family...it is here isn't it...in that Church of Niccolas's...we should go and find it, now," Simon suddenly said aloud and stood up fast, excited.

"No...you cannot, so please sit, Simon...please," the old man asked and indicated with his hand for Simon to retake his seat.

Sarah pulled Simon's arm for him to sit.

"Please just explain the twin Church if you would be so kind to?" the Templar asked.

"Then understand that there are those who transmit the doctrine of the so-called 'twin Churches', that of the 'Church of Peter' and the 'Church of John', or of two 'epochs', the epoch of Peter and the epoch of John. But the hidden knowledge, now being spoken of more openly in the hope that the truth will be revealed eventually, claims that the end is almost at hand... but it is not yet...of the Church of Peter, and that the Church of John will replace it completely. It is claimed that the more 'exoteric' Church of Peter will make way for the 'esoteric' hidden and truer Church of John, which will be that of perfect freedom. People like Theodoric and even Philip tried to make that happen now, rather than when the time is correct...which is most certainly not now," the old man sighed.

"I do not understand," Simon remarked.

"Now there is a surprise...," Sarah shot back and frowned at him.

"Let me explain. There is the obvious physical Church of St Peter as led by the Pope...then there is the hidden Church of St John...but those with this knowledge wrongly assume that the Church of St John will take over the Church of St Peter...but that is not what is supposed to happen. That is why some within the Church of St Peter so vigorously wish to see the hidden esoteric Church of St John destroyed or utterly subjugated and controlled."

"I still do not understand...what do you mean there are two Churches?" Ayleth asked, confused.

"That makes two of us for I have not heard of this...and you have?" the Hospitaller remarked then asked his brother.

"Let me try and explain this simply then for in the Gospels it is the apostle Peter who openly denied Christ Jesus, whilst it was the 'beloved disciple' John, to whom the dying Jesus commended his mother Mary, whom as you now know is also a symbol of wisdom, for safe keeping and protection. It is the Gospel of John that speaks more about the Holy Spirit than the other Gospels. Gnostic Christians invoke the mystical and apocalyptic St John as the source of their authority. You see, all the initiates in the past, the purest, most learned men, were all disciples of St John. They were also all persecuted by the official Church of St Peter because of their superiority. But the Church of St John, obliged as it always has been to exist and work in secret, continues to produce sons and daughters of God, and the time is coming when it will manifest itself in the world and show how far above the other Churches it is... but not in an arrogant controlling way, but in one of love and compassion. When it does, the Church of St Peter, having changed so much, and learnt so much, will have to reform and make many changes, whether it likes to or not."

Ayleth and the Hospitaller looked at each still just as puzzled.

"And the Templar symbolism of two riders...it also means this yes?" Gabirol asked.

"Just one of many interpretations...yes," the old man answered and paused briefly before continuing. *"You see, unlike the Church of Peter, which is the Church of Empire, the exoteric, involved with law and power, the Church of John is an underground Church of the esoteric, concerned with transcendence. It is the 'Secret Johannite Church' whose only law is love. It is decentralised, shamanistic, free and eternal, whereas the Church of Rome is centralised, hierarchical, complex, and worldly. The battle between the two Churches is identical in symbolism and reality to the Old Testament battle of the prophets with the priests. Mystic vision versus organised religion. The Church of John is the affirmation of spiritual brotherhood and rejection of the alienation of a worldly material civilisation. You will find signs of this universal Church of John in the different Gnostic communities that have and still appear throughout the ages. It echoes across time clear for those who wish to see it,"* the old man explained.

"I think I like this idea of a Church of love...for much of our Church scares me," Ayleth said softly.

"Then I am vindicated already in my decision to tell you this entire tale," the old man smiled. *"You see France plays a prominent role in the spread of the Gnostic tradition. Mary Magdalene, as you know and as the Gnostics totally believed, fled for safety to the South of France with Lazarus and his sister, Martha. Her feast day, July twenty-second, is still a major celebration here in France as already explained."*

"Why are the Gnostics frowned upon so badly?" Ayleth asked.

"Because," the old man said and sat up straight. *"Because in Lyon, the place from where in the second century the virulently anti-Gnostic bishop Irenaeus penned his writings which have helped forever define 'orthodox' Christianity and opinion against the Gnostics' as their fiercest critic. Know also that Southern France is the main area where the 'Good Christians' or Cathars, the name deriving from the Greek word katharos, meaning 'the pure' emerged this century. The Cathars received their Gnostic teachings from the Bogomils, meaning 'beloved of God', a Gnostic community active in the Balkans since the tenth century. At the heart of Cathar doctrine is the notion that true Christianity, which they claimed to have*

received in a secret line of apostolic succession from St John, is a life lived, not simply a doctrine believed. For them the life of Jesus was a model the 'Good Christian' must strive to emulate, not a vicarious sacrifice to be blindly accepted on trust. The existence of the Cathars challenges the legitimacy of the Roman Church. 'Tis why the Church wishes the Order eradicated." The old man paused and took a long slow breath. "And that is why knowing the machinations that the Church is orchestrating against them, that the upper initiates of the Templars, Hospitallers and Prieure de Sion push their teachings ever further away from view and keep them secret...for the Church of St Peter will turn upon them...if not now, then eventually," the old man said as he looked at the Templar and Hospitaller. Miriam clasping the Templar's hand looking alarmed. "Do not worry, Miriam...if he accepts what is written in his letter, the evils that may befall the Order will not fall at his feet."

"But...but what of my brothers within the Order?" the Templar asked, concerned.

"That, my dear knight, is one battle you and the Order cannot win. 'Tis why you are required to continue a greater service...if you choose to accept it," the old man said. Immediately the Templar took out the letter and started to break the seal. "NO!" the old man shouted, which made everyone jump. "No...do not be eager to read its content until I have finished this tale, please, for you will not get benefit from its content otherwise."

The Templar froze, his fingers having already forced the wax seal, cracking it, but not fully breaking it. He looked at his brother, who shook his head no and gently placed his hand upon his to lower the envelope. Miriam placed her hand on his other hand and did the same.

"If there is an evil plot against my Order then I must make it known," the Templar remarked.

"My dear Templar...there are and always will be plots against the Order. There has been from its very inception and it will continue beyond our life times. But the secrets...they are what are important. So please hear me...and know that the Cathars declare themselves the heirs of a tradition that is far older than that held by the Church of Rome and, by implication, both less contaminated and near in spirit to the Apostolic tradition. They claim to be the only persons who have kept and cherished the Holy Spirit which Christ had bestowed upon his Church...and it is through the Templars alone that great secrets and wisdom will be protected...for future generations' benefits."

"How can the Cathars make such a claim?" Gabirol asked.

"How...After the manner of the Bogomils and the followers of the Eastern Gnostic Prophet Mani, whom you will recall I mentioned earlier in this tale, which you Simon, queried why...the Cathars believe in a cosmic battle between the principles of Light and Darkness on whose meetings and encounters everything in the universe is based. Darkness was for them dark matter, the unperfected, the transient. They identify all clerical and secular rulers, principally the Roman Church, as the personification of the Darkness. The Cathars follow a tradition more ancient than that of the Roman Church herself. It is with some genuine confidence that they claim Rome is the party guilty of 'heresy' through her falling out from the original purity which had characterised the Church of the Apostles. As with the ancient Gnostics, Rome sees the Cathars as a threat for it spreads with alarming speed in Southern France. It is a religion of the pure spirit which takes possession of men's souls, and it therefore seriously endangers the materialistic Church of the Pope. Dangerous words, you may say...but I have already explained the basic beliefs of the Cathars again about the symbolism of twin riders upon a horse...the Cathars have a sacred book, 'The Book of the Two Principles', and also 'The Questions of John', which relates a discussion between Jesus and the apostle John, that the Cathars believe they are true Christians faithful to a secret tradition *stretching back to St John. Rejecting most of the Old Testament, whose deity they identified with Satan...the Cathars hold the Gospel of John in the highest esteem and make use of it in their rituals. The Cathars claim they are the legitimate heirs of the early Gnostic Christians and through them of the first apostles. The central tenets of the Cathars, particularly the prominence they ascribe to Mary Magdalene and St John, confirm they are a manifestation of an underground stream of secret teachings called by the prophet Mani, the universal 'Religion of Light' and as I have explained before, they have a manuscript written in Greek called the Levitikon, containing a version of the Gospel of John."*

"I think I missed that part of the story," Ayleth said shyly.

"Then to explain again briefly...it is an ancient text revealing the truth about the Church of John and the secret history of true Christianity. In the Levitikon the orthodox presentation of Christ has been excised in favour of a version which eliminated the miracles and the Resurrection, and presented Christ as an initiate of the higher mysteries, trained in Egypt. God is understood as existence, action, and mind, and morality as rational and benevolent conduct. The cosmos, in the ancient Gnostic tradition, is viewed as a hierarchy of intelligences. The part played by privileged initiation in the transmission of divine knowledge is central. Christ conferred the essential knowledge of this Gospel on John as the best-loved apostle, and it was transmitted thence through the Patriarchs of Jerusalem until the arrival of the Templars in 1118, after which the secret teaching is now kept by the Templar Grand Masters." [68]

"Oh great...I think I now see why it would be a disaster for someone like Gerard to inherit that secret," Peter remarked as Gabirol and the Genoese sailor both nodded in agreement.

"Quite...but from the Levitikon and Cathars, we have our Johannite Church of love... but it is one that shall remain in secret for some while yet. But Gerard was too selfish to comprehend or practise the sacred secret rites, for they are sacrificial in nature, and they enable those who perform them to receive the merits of 'redemption', and to participate in the preparation for the coming of the Paraclete. I did mention and explain the Paraclete earlier didn't I?" the old man asked, checking he had. "The belief in the efficacy of a specific rite in freeing man from the materialistic world and bringing him nearer to the spiritual redemption which will announce the Third Reign is very near to that of most Gnostic sects, for whom the method of redemption consisted not so much in the profession of certain opinions or virtues as in the practice of certain rites. The Gnostics include both men and women in the priesthood. Women are permitted into the priesthood of the rite...in fact they hold a very important place, for it is through women that salvation is to come. And in the attitude towards the Virgin Mary we find a conception of her as 'Created Wisdom', the invariable reflection of 'Uncreated Wisdom'. This can be seen to be very close to one form of Valentinianism, a Gnostic belief in which Sophia, or Wisdom, a divine principle which had fallen from the realm of light into the realm of matter, is conceived as being a double figure. So again we have twin symbolism. The higher Sophia remains in the sphere of light, the lower Sophia has sunk into darkness. Through this duality Sophia became the fallen divinity through whom the mingling of light and dark, of spirit and matter, in the world, had been achieved. She is also seen as the intermediary between the lower and higher worlds and an instrument of redemption."

"And do you believe that this rival...this twin opposing Church of John will take over the Church of Peter?" Gabirol asked.

"My friend. You misunderstand me. 'Tis not the intention of the Church of John to take over the Church of Peter...for they are part of the same whole. But the day will one day come

when a religious evolution of which we are all part shows us that a new religion is necessary. The combining of the two Churches offering both structure and the laws alongside one of freedom and love...with a complete and definitive synthesis of all beliefs and all ideas of which humanity has need to realise its origin, its past, its end, its nature, the contradictions of existence and the problems of life...the very essence of Christianity. But, by Christianity, I do not only mean the doctrine taught since the arrival of the Jesus you all know, but also the one taught before Jesus's arrival, in the old temples, the doctrine of Eternal Truth. The Church of Peter is one of force, the Church of John is one of love. The Church of Rome has as its Sovereign Patriarch, Peter, the impulsive, who denied three times his master and took up the sword, but John, the Saviour's friend, the apostle who relied on his heart and in it knew best the immortal sentiment, the oracle of light, the author of the Eternal Gospel, took up only speech and love. When these two reconcile and join as one, that will be but one sign that man is again ready to evolve spiritually. Then...and only then will humanity be unchained from its present limitations and shackles of religious dogma."

"How will we, us, mere mortal uneducated types, ever be able to distinguish what religion is right?" Simon asked, looking confused, his face red.

"Simon...All of you. There is a difference between being religious and being spiritual. But I will simply say this to you. I make no claim that I alone am right or that my teaching is the only one required or necessary for salvation. No one should ever accept the statements of anyone else on blind faith, but insist that everyone should prove these things for yourselves.

"Sorry, for again I do not understand you," Ayleth said quietly, embarrassed.

"Let me explain, and do not be embarrassed. Too many people feel afraid to ask questions that should be asked. The first followers of Jesus the Christ did not see his teachings as merely intellectual fodder meant for endless debate, nor as a mere set of humanitarian principles and moral pronouncements. The 'Secret Church' still exists in this world where spiritual awakening is experiential. It is about transformation, about a higher consciousness, not about dry words or external forms. Theologies and commandments are the formulations of men. No matter how sublime or noble, rational or logical, they are all man-made. Gnosis is the experience of the divine. Words along with all theological and philosophical discourses are insufficient to explain it. You must taste it, as the Psalmist declares, 'O taste and see that the Lord is good'. Psalm 34:8. And it is a very sad fact, a fact that many Christians choose to ignore or simply do not see, that throughout its entire history, Christendom has been and is a protest against the words of Jesus the Christ as Theodoric explained to Paul you may recall?" the old man explained solemnly.

"I understand all of that, but I fear I find it difficult to grasp fully what you have said about a Church being of love and light, especially in respect to the sacred sex magic rites you mentioned before, for how does this Church of John look upon that?" Gabirol asked.

"Even in most of the civilised world, at least as far back as five thousand years, there were female shamans or priestesses who represented the godhead in sacred sex rites and, in ancient Greece. They were known as hierodules. A hierodule would have skills similar to the shaman in that she could journey, in trance, into other dimensions, and merge with her spirit lover there. Part of the hierodule's role was to spend the night with a newly crowned king or queen, and while embodying her spirit lover, she would transfer the Sovereignty of the Land to the royal personage in sexual initiation. The Sovereignty of the Land could only be passed on through this sort of inter-dimensional intercourse, and it was a sacred contract that most civilisations honoured until relatively recently. This is especially evident within the ancient Egyptian Osiris rituals. You will find it referred to in alchemical texts as the

Divine Marriage, the Alchemical Marriage or the Hieros Gamos as Paul had it explained to him whilst in Jerusalem if you recall?"

"I do recall and that is why I ask about it now," Gabirol replied with a smile.

Both Simon and the Genoese sailor sat themselves up eager to hear more at the mention of sex.

"Let me say that with all 'Lesser Mysteries' the teachings are given in the form of allegorical stories in which the true meanings are hidden. All of this was to prepare those few who were going forward to the 'Greater Mysteries', where the inner meanings of the stories would be revealed and the fire initiation would take place. In other words, it is only at the Greater Mysteries level that initiates are shown allegories which have a dual purpose as both spiritual and astronomical or astrological teaching within stories that are a precursor to spiritual initiation. But the students of the Greater Mysteries are also under pain of death never to reveal anything of what they have been taught or seen. The whole purpose of the mysteries is to attain fellowship or unity with the Divine here and in the hereafter. This is not achieved by mere doctrine, but by the exercise of the 'Higher Magic' as in higher knowledge and wisdom. The outward form of this magic is expressed by ritual, in actual allegory. It was emblematic, symbolical, for the reason that in emblems and symbolism as well as dramatic rites, reside the only available human means for outwardly expressing the inward desire for at-one-ment, atonement, with what we know as our Lord, our all knowing and all seeing deity. These are after all merely the natural impulses of inward thought and belief. The ancient people who established these rites were well aware that a striking and dramatic rehearsal of the process of achieving unity, a material and symbolic representation of what is actually a psychical process, could not but assist it by bringing the mental and bodily parts of man into magical and rhythmic response with this psychic part and thus with the upward movement as a whole. Much of this is done through stories and plays...one of which features a sun god who dies and then rises again from the dead three days later, just as the sun 'dies', or reaches the nadir of its course on its yearly cycle during the winter solstice, and then begins its journey north again three days later. But because only those few that are deemed ready are chosen from the crowds of the 'Lesser Mysteries' for the 'Greater Mysteries', many left the Lesser Mysteries thinking they had been revealed the full teachings and that there had been a real person who died and rose again three days later."

"I am losing what you are telling us," Simon said quietly.

"All Lesser rites teachings, such as those given by Jesus, were allegories for a much deeper spiritual teaching which led to an initiation. The Greater rites not only taught men and women how to live, but also how to die. Have you ever wondered why some of the French call the orgasm la petit mort? The small death! Sex and death are very close together in that they are both initiations into another portal. What men are not receiving through sacred sex magic they seek for in promiscuity, rape, violence and war...due to a yearning for that portal...and the masters of evil and war know it."

"What? That is...is...I do not know how to answer that!" Ayleth exclaimed.

"So it is not simply just some animalistic urge forced upon us all to ensure we procreate... as in we go forth and multiply as ordered by God?" Peter asked frankly.

"No...'tis not the case. For those who have known and experienced true love and true love making, words simply fail to convey the wondrous feelings it brings...," the old man replied and looked at the Templar and Miriam. Miriam immediately lowered her face embarrassed as the Templar squeezed her hand tightly and smiled. "The Christian Church now only gives

the water initiation to the masses, in the form of the baptism, as if their congregations were attendees of the Lesser Mysteries. If the Church ever gave a fire initiation, the rank and file never got to hear about it. But shreds of what once was practised are visible in the New Testament, if you know what to look for. In Luke 3:16, we find John the Baptist talking about the water and fire initiation," the old man explained and quickly removed his small Bible from his leather satchel, opened it and began to read. "...I indeed baptise you with water; but one mightier than I cometh, the latchet of whose shoes I am not worthy to unloose: he shall baptise you with the Holy Ghost and with fire. There is also the anecdote about Saul known as Paul of Tarsus being hit by a blaze of the Holy Ghost's fire, causing him to fall off his horse. Then there's the story about the disciples all being gathered in the Upper Room ...And suddenly there came a sound from heaven as of a rushing mighty wind, and it filled the entire house where they were sitting. And there appeared unto them cloven tongues like as of fire, and it sat upon each of them. Acts 2:2–3. But the sacred sex rites finally fell out of favour after the Mystery Groves and libraries were destroyed on the orders of the fourth century Roman Emperor Theodosius. The violent domination and warring of all three Abrahamic religions, that is Jewish, Christian and Islam, has not been best served ever since, by mass ignorance, about the existence of the portal of sex and death."

"Please just answer me one simple thing...is sex bad or good?" the Genoese sailor asked bluntly.

"When done with love, 'tis truly a good thing," the old man answered as Ayleth looked away embarrassed.

Sarah looked at Stephan as he winked and smiled at her.

"So we have two Churches in Christianity...the exoteric obvious Church of St Peter and the esoteric hidden church of St John that is one of love?" Gabirol said as he checked his notes.

The old man nodded yes.

"You could have just said that from the start," the farrier remarked.

"Can we get back to the story of the sword then?" Ayleth asked and pointed toward the sword.

   2 – 3

"Of course, but it was you who asked in the first place for which I commend you. Now, where were we with the story? Ah yes, Alexandria..." The old man smiled and continued.

Alexandria, Egypt, October 1179

Paul sat alone in a secluded room of the upper floor of his home reading the letter Nicholas had given Alisha. She had simply handed it to him, said he should read it and do with it as he saw fit afterwards. He sighed and looked up. The room was the smallest on the upper floor and with just a single bed, a bench and large window it somehow felt more comforting than the other larger rooms. He read the letter again. He was not angry with Nicholas and actually felt a little sorry for him...to love someone so much and know it would never be. He told himself that should anything bad ever happen to him, he knew there was at least one man he could trust upon to love and look after Alisha and Arri. He asked himself if he was supposed to get angry but he just did not feel that way. A light tap on the door drew his attention.

"Come in," he called out.

Slowly the door opened and Tenno, dressed again in his usual black armour, peered around the door looking serious.

"Paul...Alisha has asked I check upon you. She fears you are angry with her. May I?" he asked and indicated he should enter.

"Please, come in. And no I am not angry at all...," Paul replied as Tenno raised his eyebrows quizzically. "Honestly, I am not."

"Good, for Alisha informs me of the letter's content. 'Twas very wrong of him and inappropriate."

"I have to admire the man for his boldness and honesty. But I also pity him for his love for Ali. I would hate to be in such a place."

"Then be on your guard for men like him will make advances upon her and should you lose her...it will be you in Nicholas's shoes...I think that is how you say it?" Tenno said and frowned.

"Thank you, Tenno. I appreciate your concern and advice. Tell me, how do you keep your mind sharp and free from such worries?"

"Who said I am free from such worries? My heart beats and my heart breaks just as easily as yours...plus, like Ishmael I have already lost all. No worse can ever be done to me...but I do meditate."

"My father spoke of meditation often but I never really listened to him. What exactly is it, so that I may learn as I am told it greatly helps both physically and mentally," Paul asked and proffered for Tenno to sit on the bench opposite.

"'Tis not as simple as explaining it...you have to practise it and master it."

"Then how long will it take me to master?"

"That I have no way of knowing as some people can learn and master it very quickly...whilst others take years and still never master even the basics."

"Then please, will you begin by teaching me. Kratos said I should and he explained that was how he was able to survive his injuries, as was Abi," Paul asked. "Sorry, I did not mean to mention Abi."

"Do not apologise for her absence...for she is still here," Tenno replied and placed his clenched fist across his chest.

"So please tell me and teach me. What is it that you do to meditate? What are the benefits? Will it make me stronger, fitter, smarter?"

"Slow down, Paul, for too many questions...please." Tenno said and paused. "Smarter, I doubt. Wiser, perhaps. Fitter, definitely. And I study what is known as Zen and the Way of the Warrior. It is recognised, in my lands, for its physical and mental training. The daily practice of zazen and breathing exercises remarkably improves one's physical condition. This is a fact you will discover if you listen, learn and practise."

"I shall, I promise. I must learn all that I can from you and Thomas as well as Theodoric," Paul replied, excited, almost forgetting the letter from Nicholas screwed up in his hand.

"Then know that most Zen masters enjoy a long life in spite of their extremely simple mode of living. Its mental discipline, however, is by far more fruitful, and keeps one's mind in equipoise, making one neither passionate nor dispassionate, neither sentimental nor unintelligent, neither nervous nor senseless. It is well known as a cure to all sorts of mental disease, occasioned by nervous disturbance, as nourishment to the fatigued brain, and also as a stimulus to torpor and sloth. It is self-control, as it is the subduing of such pernicious passions as anger, jealousy, hatred, and the like, and the awakening of noble emotions such as sympathy, mercy, generosity, and what not. It is a mode of Enlightenment, as it is the dispelling of materialistic ignorance," Tenno stated rather than explained. Tenno looked at Paul, puzzled, as he smiled at him.

"Please...'tis not often we get to speak at any length."

"That is true, for usually Theodoric makes an appearance," Tenno said and looked at the door as if to check. "Zen Buddhism came to China in the sixth century AD. It grew through the Sui (AD 598–617) and the Tang dynasties (AD 618–906) and enjoyed greater popularity than any other sect of Buddhism during the whole period of the Sung (AD 976–1126) and the present Southern Sung dynasty from 1127. Its commanding influence became so irresistible that Confucianism, assimilating the Buddhist teachings, especially those of Zen, into itself and changing its entire aspect, brought forth the so-called Speculative philosophy. Zen exercises profound influences on Chinese and Japanese men of letters, statesmen, and soldiers. In my lands it was first introduced into the island as the faith first for the Samurai or the military class as you would understand them, and moulded the characters of many distinguished soldiers whose lives adorn the pages of my land's history. It has gradually found its way to palaces as well as to cottages through literature and art, and permeates through every fibre of the national life," Tenno explained then went silent for a few moments as he clearly thought back upon his home...and family.

"And how do I start to learn this Zen?"

"Sorry, my mind wandered. Not a good example to start with," Tenno replied and sat up straight. "If a wise man holds his body with its three parts, that is his chest, neck, and head, erect, and he turns his senses with the mind towards the heart, he will then, in the boat of Brahman, cross all the torrents which cause fear. Compressing his breathings lets him, who has subdued all motions, breathe forth through the nose with the gentle breath. Let the wise man without fail restrain his mind, that chariot yoked with vicious horses. Let him perform his exercises in a place level, pure, free from pebbles, fire, and dust, delightful by its sounds, its water, and bowers...not painful to the eye, and full of shelters and eaves. When Yoga is being performed, the forms which come first, producing apparitions in Brahman, are those of misty smoke, sun, fire, wind, fire-flies, lightnings, and a crystal moon. When, as earth, water, light, heat, and ether arises, the five fold quality of Yoga takes place, then there is no longer illness, old age, or pain for him who has obtained a body produced by the fire of Yoga. The first results of Yoga they call lightness, healthiness, steadiness, a good complexion, an easy pronunciation, a sweet odour, and slight excretions."

"Sorry to ask, but what is Yoga?"

"That, my young Paul, is something I shall delight in teaching you. For it is a way of physically channelling that energy that runs through all things, and balancing it in perfect harmony by means and ways of simple exercises, both physical and mental. When the five instruments of knowledge stand still together with the mind, and when the intellect does not move, that is called the highest state. This, the firm holding back of the senses, is what is called Yoga. You must be free from thoughtlessness then, for Yoga comes and goes. This is the rule for achieving it, the concentration of the mind on the object of meditation…restraint of the breath, restraint of the senses, meditation, fixed attention, investigation, absorption. These are called the six fold Yoga. When beholding by this Yoga, you behold the gold-coloured maker, the lord, the person, Brahman, the cause, then the sage, leaving behind good and evil, makes everything breathe, organs of sense, body, to be one in the Highest Indestructible. And thus it has been elsewhere. There is the superior fixed attention, dharana, such as if you press the tip of the tongue down the palate, and restrain the voice, mind, and breath, you see Brahman by discrimination, taraka. And when, after the cessation of mind, you see your own self, smaller than small, and shining as the Highest Self, then, having seen your Self as the Self, you become Self-less, and because you are Self-less, you are without limit, without cause, absorbed in thought. This is the highest mystery…the final liberation."

"I must confess I have no understanding of what you explain," Paul said awkwardly.

"Good…then your mind is an empty slate that we can work upon. No bad habits already learnt. You will learn all the correct ways of sitting first."

"Sitting?" Paul asked, bemused.

"Yes, sitting. Even sitting must be learnt for there are three modes of sitting, namely, the Lotus-seat, Padmasana, the sitting with legs bent underneath…the mystic diagram seat Svastika, and the auspicious-seat Bhadrasana, while Yogaçikha directs the choice of the Lotus-posture, with attention concentrated on the tip of the nose, hands and feet closely joined."

"Who taught you?" Paul interrupted.

"At first, my father along with another great master and his son, Ei-sai, my friend. A man of bold, energetic nature he crossed the sea for China at the age of twenty-eight in 1168, and it was he who beckoned I come and study in China. And as I was commanded to go on Naval matters, that is how I now find myself here… My father took his teachings from a long line of descendants of the Do-sho line. I then studied Zen further in China under Fuh Hai, or sais as Buk-kai, who belonged to the Yang Ki, or Yo-gi school. I learnt a lot there."

"Such as?" Paul asked bluntly.

"Such as the first step in mental training is to become the master of external things. One who is addicted to worldly pleasures, however learned or ignorant he may be, however high or low his social position may be, is a servant to mere things. He cannot adapt the external world to his own end, but he adapts himself to it. He is constantly employed, ordered, driven by sensual objects. Instead of taking possession of wealth, he is possessed by wealth. Instead of drinking liquors, he is swallowed up by his liquors. Balls and music bid him to run mad. Games and shows order him not to stay at home. Houses, furniture, pictures, chains, hats, bonnets, rings, bracelets, shoes…in short, everything has a word to command him. How can such a person be the master of things? I was taught that there is a great jail, not a jail for criminals that contains the world in it…but fame, gain, pride, and bigotry form its four walls. Those who are confined in it fall prey to sorrow and sigh forever."

"So how do I learn not to be imprisoned by those four walls you speak of?"

"To be the ruler of things we have to first shut up all our senses, and turn the currents of thoughts inward, and see ourselves as the centre of the world, and meditate that we are the beings of highest intelligence...that Buddha, or your Lord God, never puts us at the mercy of natural forces, that the earth is in our possession, that everything on earth is to be made use of for our noble ends. That fire, water, air, grass, trees, rivers, hills, thunder, cloud, stars, the moon, the sun, are at our command and that we are the law-givers of natural phenomena. That we are the makers of the phenomenal world...that it is we that appoint a mission through life, and determine the fate of man...all of mankind."

"So you also believe as Kratos and Theodoric claim that we all ultimately can determine our fates and influence the very world we live upon?"

"Of course. That is why it is also so important to strive to be the master of our own bodies first. With most of the unenlightened, the body holds absolute control over Self. Every order of the former has to be faithfully obeyed by the latter. Even if Self revolts against the tyranny of the body, it is easily trampled down under the brutal hoofs of bodily passion. For example, Self wants to be temperate for the sake of health, and would fain pass by the resort for drinking, but body would force Self into it. Self at times lays down a strict dietetic rule for himself, but body would threaten Self to act against both the letter and spirit of the rule. Now Self aspires to get on a higher place among sages, but body pulls Self down to the pavement of masses. Now Self proposes to give some money to the poor, but body closes the purse tightly. Now Self admires divine beauty, but body compels him to prefer sensuality. Again, Self likes spiritual liberty, but body confines him in its dungeons. Therefore, to get enlightened, we must establish the authority of Self over the whole body. We must use our bodies as we use our clothes in order to accomplish our noble purposes. Let us command body not to shudder under a cold shower in inclement weather, not to be nervous from sleepless nights, not to be sick with any sort of food, not to groan under a physician or opponent's knife, not to succumb even if we stand a whole day in the midsummer sun, not to break down under any form of disease, not to be excited in the thick of the battlefield...in brief, we have to control our body as we will."

"And how exactly do I start to learn how to do that?"

"Start off by sitting in a quiet place and meditate in imagination that your body is no more bondage to you, that it is your machine for your work of life, that you are not flesh, that you are the lord of it, that you can use it at pleasure, and that it will always obey your order faithfully. Imagine your body as separated from you. When it cries out, stop it instantly, as a mother does her baby. When it disobeys you, correct it by discipline, as a master does his pupil. When it is wanton, tame it down, as a horse-breaker does his wild horse. When it is sick, prescribe to it, as a physician does to his patient. Imagine that you are not a bit injured, even if it streams blood, that you are entirely safe, even if it is drowned in water or burned by fire. To achieve this you must master the calmness of the mind. The Yogi breathing I mentioned briefly is fit rather for physical exercise than for mental balance, and it will be beneficial if you take that exercise before or after meditation. If you feel your mind distracted, look at the tip of the nose and never lose sight of it for some time, or look at your own palm, and let not your mind go out of it, or gaze at one spot before you. This will greatly help you in restoring the equilibrium of your mind. Calmness of the mind is essential to sages, and as I was taught, the stillness of the sages does not belong to them as a consequence of their skilful ability for all things are not able to disturb their minds; it is on this account that they are still. When water is still, its clearness shows the beard and eyebrows of him or her who looks into it. It is a perfect level, and the greatest artificer takes his rule from it. Such is the clearness of still water, and how much greater is that of the human spirit? The still mind of the sage is the mirror of heaven and earth, the glass of all things."

"You surprise me with your elegance and grasp of my language to express clearly what you mean to say," Paul remarked as he looked at Tenno.

"I do not seem to find adequate words to explain to Theodoric what I truly think of him," Tenno said and raised an eyebrow.

Paul was not sure if he was joking or being serious as his face was his usual emotionless stare. But he detected a glint in his eyes that made him think he was joking.

"He is a good man, I am certain of that," Paul replied and looked again at Nicholas's note.

"Good, bad...'tis difficult sometimes to determine a man's actions and his nature. Where, then, does the error lie in the four possible propositions respecting a man's nature? It lies not in their subject, but in the predicate, that is to say, in the use of the terms 'good' and 'bad'. For how does good differ from bad? A good action ever promotes interests in a sphere far wider than a bad action. Both are the same in their conducing to human interests, but differ in the extent in which they achieve their end. In other words, both good and bad actions are performed for one end and the same purpose of promoting human interests, but they differ from each other as to the extent of interests. For instance, burglary is evidently a bad action, and is condemned everywhere; but the capturing of an enemy's property for the sake of one's own tribe or clan or nation is praised as a meritorious conduct. Both acts are exactly the same in their promoting interests but the former relates to the interests of a single individual or of a single family, while the latter to those of a tribe or a nation. If the former be bad on account of its ignoring others' interests, the latter must be also bad on account of its ignoring the enemy's interests. Murder is considered bad everywhere, but the killing of thousands of men in battle is praised and honoured, because the former is perpetrated to promote the private interests, while the latter those of the public. If the former be bad, because of its cruelty, the latter must also be bad, because of its inhumanity. The idea of good and bad, generally accepted by common sense, may be seen as when an action is good when it promotes the interests of an individual or a family...better when it promotes those of a district or a country. Best when it promotes those of the whole world. An action is bad when it inflicts injury on another individual or another family...worse when it is prejudicial to a district or a country...worse again when it brings harm on the whole world. Strictly speaking, an action is good when it promotes interests, material or spiritual, as intended by the actor in his motive; and it is bad when it injures interests, material or spiritual, as intended by the actor in his motive." [69]

"Tenno, you would make a great teacher. You know that don't you?"

"No...I would not for despite my years of training, I still find my patience tested greatly by those that irritate me," Tenno replied. "In short, what I have learned is that we must not spend our whole lives in pursuit of those mirage-like objects which gratify our sensual desires. When we gratify one desire, we are silly enough to fancy that we have realised true happiness. But one desire gratified begets another stronger and more insatiable. Thirst allayed with salt water becomes more intense than ever.

A knock on the door drew their attention as it opened fast to reveal Theodoric peering in smiling broadly. Tenno shook his head disapprovingly.

"As I said...always present," Tenno remarked as Theodoric stepped into the room.

"Hiding away are we?" Theodoric asked.

"Yes," Paul replied as Theodoric entered the room and sat beside Tenno on the bench.

"Are you okay...with that?" Theodoric asked looking at Nicholas's letter in Paul's hands.

"This...yes. I actually feel a little sorry for him."

"My concern is that it plants a seed within Alisha...and seeds have a habit of growing," Theodoric said and looked at Tenno, who was looking back at him with a frown. "You need to go and reassure Alisha, for she is downstairs with Ishmael and she is biting her nails...whilst making supper...so go."

Paul looked at the letter again and tried to flatten it out. As he rubbed it flat, he noticed a barely visible set of crosses along the bottom. As he focused upon the images, Theodoric noticed his puzzlement and moved to sit beside him. Paul handed him the letter and pointed to the faint images. Theodoric held the note up against the window. As the light shone through, it revealed that Nicholas had drawn in lemon juice, several Templar crosses, but with sections missing.

"Atbash cipher," Theodoric smiled. "The heat from your hands has warmed the lemon juice. 'Tis but a crude method of concealment, but it would seem our friend Nicholas has left you a cryptic message."

"Or for Alisha!" Tenno stated and frowned disapprovingly.

"How do I read it?" Paul asked.

"Simple. Just gently wave it above a candle and the crosses will reveal themselves fully," Theodoric explained and handed the letter back. "But then you will need to decipher the code on the crosses."

"Great...and how do I do that?" Paul asked as he looked closer at the images.

"I can do it for you. 'Tis time you learnt about the code anyway," Theodoric replied and stood up. "Now go, see Alisha and put her mind at rest...whatever the code says."

80 CR

Theodoric sat at the small wooden table pushed against the wall of his small room, the single lanthorn illuminating his face as he read through some of his old notes in a small leather bound booklet. The edges of the stitched spine were frayed and coming apart. Gently he folded open a section just as a light tap on the door sounded out.

"Enter," he said without looking up from the pages.

Paul entered the room and closed the door behind him. He was still holding Nicholas's letter.

"She wishes me to destroy it...but I shan't. I wish to keep it until a day comes when I know she can read this again and feel nothing," Paul said as he stood over Theodoric then drew in a sharp intake of breath as he smelt stale body odour rise from Theodoric.

"Sorry...I am in dire need of some bathing...'tis the heat here...but please, sit" Theodoric said quietly as he continued to study his booklet. "So you think she feels something for Nicholas?"

"Yes...that I do know...but, but is that not normal for I am not that blind to see how good looking and charismatic he is."

"You feel no jealousy?"

"No...actually, yes I do in some small measure. But I must be insane for I love Alisha that much, that if she felt more for him, I would let them be together."

Theodoric placed his booklet down slowly and looked up and at Paul.

"You are indeed your father all over."

"What...why do you say that?" Paul asked and pulled up the spare chair and sat down beside Theodoric placing Nicholas's letter on the table in front of him.

"He once said exactly the same to me...a long time ago. But my advice to you now, just as I gave it to him...is if you love her, then be prepared to fight for her... and I do not mean just your enemies."

"But if she loves him more, then who am I to stand it their way?" Paul asked and sat back into the chair. As he folded his arms Theodoric suddenly, and without warning, slapped him hard across the face and glared at him. Shocked, Paul sat up holding his hand to his face. "What was that for?" he asked, confused, his face stinging as it turned red. Paul was surprised at the force and strength of the slap.

"Did you feel that?" Theodoric rasped back, his voice deep and almost menacing in tone.

"Yes!"

"Good. Now do not be a bloody fool and ever say such shit again in my presence. I made that mistake with your father," Theodoric explained and just looked back at Nicholas's note. Paul sat in shock rubbing his face not knowing what to say or do. Eventually Theodoric looked up at him. "I will not apologise for hitting you...but perhaps it will reinforce just how stupid your remark was. Alisha's heart is vulnerable and presently open to flattery and praise, no matter how well intentioned it was given. She is also fearful about many things...and now, now of all times is the time when you must remain steadfast, resolute and faithful to her, no matter what she says or does...and never give up on her. Do you hear me?"

Paul tried to understand what he was being told but he was still getting over the sudden shock of Theodoric's slap. If he had done so as a lesson, it had certainly worked in making sure he did not forget it. Both sat in silence as Theodoric waved Nicholas's letter just above a single candle he had lit from the lanthorn. After a few moments, the lemon juice images began to appear more visible as brown symbols.

"Theo...I am not sure," Paul started to say when Theodoric raised his hand he be silent.

"Ssssh! Know this...your father and I made a mistake thinking exactly as you do now. Alisha will not be better off with anyone else...only you. Do not adopt the holier than thou mentality and think you are doing what God wills as being noble...do not become a martyr of your own self."

"I sense much emotion behind what you say..."

"I did not mean to slap you so hard!" Theodoric said his face creasing as he smiled, the more familiar smile Paul was used too. "Come, let us see what this says shall we?"

Paul watched as Theodoric looked closely at the brown symbols and wrote down letters for each one as he worked his way across the line of little crosses. Eventually after a few minutes, a set of letters presented itself. Theodoric looked at it for several more moments.

"What does it say?" Paul asked eager but also nervous to learn what the coded message would reveal.

   1 – 2

"Hmmm. It says, 'Paul, you know you really love someone when you don't hate them for breaking your heart. You never lose by loving, but you always lose by holding back.' 'Tis what it reads," Theodoric said and looked at Paul. "So he knew you would read this."

"But how...for I do not even understand the code?"

"He knew you would one day...and that you would keep this," Theodoric said and waved the letter. "A smart man indeed."

"Then please, teach me how to understand the code he used."

"'Tis quite simple really. Look closer. He wrote it in lemon juice that remains unseen until aged or exposed to sunlight or heat for any length of time. And here look," Theodoric said and held the note up to Paul. "The small cross symbol is the Templar Cross...note that one part is darker than the rest. That denotes a letter from our Latin alphabet. That means we must take that letter as representing A and then run the letters after that by the same count. Let me show you," Theodoric explained and immediately started to draw a Templar Cross, highlighting just one part of it, then writing out the alphabet. "But of course that presupposes you understand the Atbash cipher and how to read letters from the cross in the first place."

Paul leaned closer and watched as Theodoric drew more crosses and letters. He then drew the entire alphabet alongside each symbol. He then demonstrated how the letter represented within the first cross stood for G, so G meant an A. The first letter revealed in Nicholas's letter was X, that meant it was really P.

"Please, you must teach me this," Paul almost pleaded, fascinated by it.

"Well, I can do that. It also has other meanings. When Templars are accused of standing upon the cross, as they recreate, more correctly enact by standing upon the cross during their initiation ceremonies, 'tis but symbolic of this code. For when Templars enter the Octagon, that shape that surrounds the Templar Cross, when using this code, they then tread upon the cross to make letters, then simply use it against the Atbash cipher. 'Tis really quite simple. 'Tis known as 'Passing through the Octagon' and 'Standing upon the Cross'."

Fig. 46: Atbash Cipher.

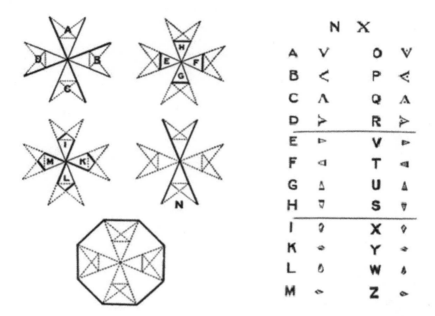

"So all the letters are made up from sections within the cross. Though I can see that the letters X and N are the same, yes?" Paul remarked, intrigued.

"Yes...but that is for a reason too, which we shall have to cover later for I fear you should be with Alisha and Arri," Theodoric said and looked at Paul intently for several moments. "Paul...If I appear hard, then for that I will apologise. But please learn, before it is too late, that true love such as you have with Alisha must be fought for...because once found, it can never be replaced...not even in the arms of another, no matter how beautiful, like the Princess Stephanie."

Paul recoiled back in his chair as Theodoric's words touched him as if he knew his deepest secrets and desires all at once. Did he know the thoughts and feelings he had felt when with Princess Stephanie? Paul wondered, his face reddening as if he had been exposed.

"How does Tenno cope and deal with his loss then?" Paul asked almost by way of deflecting Theodoric's words.

The door suddenly opened as Tenno leaned in and looked at them.

"I cope by using the old Zen proverb...let it go, or be dragged!" he said bluntly. "Now come. Alisha has cooked and she grows impatient waiting to serve," Tenno said, then closed the door as he left.

Theodoric looked at Paul, then laughed briefly and patted Paul on his arm. Paul smiled back and looked at Nicholas's letter.

"Paul, remember this, for perhaps my lesson this eve seems harsh. Having a soft heart in a cruel world, and keeping it so, shows great courage...not weakness. And as Tenno argues, and I have to agree with him, the stronger you become, the gentler you will be."

Chapter 46
The Holy Grail & The
Keepers of the Faith

A dog barked off in the distance but all was quiet in the house as Paul lay next to Alisha looking at her. Arri was asleep in his crib and though Paul valued these moments the most, he could not help but feel a sadness creep into his heart. He placed his hand upon Alisha's hip and gently stroked her. The silk nightgown was smooth to touch. He moved closer to her and put his arm around her waist. She placed her hand upon his and held it tightly.

"Sorry...I thought you were asleep," Paul whispered.

"No...I cannot sleep," she replied softly and pushed herself back and into Paul pulling his arm tighter around her.

With her body pushed against his, he could not help but feel aroused. It was a full moon outside and the room was gently lit by its cool glow, enough for Paul to see the side of her neck, her hair hanging down on her pillow. The temptation to kiss her was overwhelming.

"What troubles you?" Paul asked.

"Paul...," she started to answer but hesitated. Quickly she turned over to face him and clasped his hands together with hers. "Paul...that letter..."

"Ali...'tis fine. I am not blind to your beauty and neither is Nicholas. You are here with me now and hopefully I still have your heart."

"Oh my dear Paul...you have always had that and always shall," Alisha said and leaned over and kissed him on the lips, her touch sending shivers throughout his body. "In La Rochelle I told you I had always loved you...and even from before if what Theodoric and Kratos tell us...so please, my dearest man, know that I love you and only you," she explained and placed her hand upon his face. "And I can feel you want me, and I want you inside of me again...," she said and gently thrust her thighs against him.

"Ali, I only wish to love you and hold you when you are truly ready. And please, I know you feel much for Nicholas. I am not stupid."

Alisha pulled herself away slightly and sighed but kept her hand upon his face. Paul's heart raced as he wondered what her response would be.

"Yes, I like him very much. He is like another brother to me...and," she said softly then hesitated. "I cannot lie to you. That was but one of the things Kratos explained to me privately...so know this when I say Nicholas has touched me in a way, not physically I must stress, but inside in a way that confused me. But only briefly I swear it," Alisha explained, pained.

"Ssssh Ali. You need not explain to me...honestly," Paul replied and placed his finger over her lips. He desperately wanted to make love to her that instant, but a deeper sense inside him told him he must not. He felt that Alisha would respond but only from a sense of guilt, which was not what he wanted. "I do not wish to appear sanctimonious or holier than thou believe me, Ali...but, but I do understand. And as much as I would love to be as one with you, now is not the right time. I love you and that is all you need to know of me tonight."

Alisha lay in silence for several moments. She lowered her hand from his face and held his hands. Paul waited for her reply but she said nothing. He struggled not to gulp loudly as his throat was so dry. 'Say something' he thought but she just lay still looking at him. Eventually she turned over, pulling his arm around her as she moved. She tucked herself closely into him and squeezed his arm and kissed his hand before holding it against her chest. He could feel her heart beating against his hand. He sensed the heartache and confusion inside her and though he felt a gut wrenching sickness knot in his stomach, he could not help but love her even more. Gently he kissed her on the side of her face and lay his head back on the pillow and just watched her as she breathed. She was hurting inside and he understood this having felt similar thoughts about Princess Stephanie. Alisha had been honest with him, which is more than he had been able to be with her. He pulled his right arm away from Alisha's grip and then behind him to check his sword was still hung over the bed post beside him. It was, even though he knew it was all along. He placed his arm back around Alisha as his mind drifted back to when she had first told him she loved him in his small study room after reading his part finished poem. As clear as if it was happening again he could see her in his mind. 'I have always loved you, Paul. I always have and I always shall,' he recalled her saying softly as emotions filled her eyes with tears and she raised her hand covering the gauze bandage affixed to his face. That seemed so long ago already. He thought upon the parchments and all the symbols upon them. He wished in part that he had never seen them. Looking at Alisha, he sighed sadly and closed his weary eyes.

ɛɔ ଓ

Paul was standing on a hillside looking across a beautiful green valley with a lake shimmering in the afternoon Sun. People dressed in loose fitting cream coloured robes were out walking enjoying the view and picking flowers. Trees grew all around the lake and half way up the soft undulating hillsides. A castle sat on top of the nearest hilltop. Purple thistles were in full bloom near to him as a sudden yellow brightness lit up the entire valley, the walls of the castle beginning to almost glow as the bright sunlight lit it up from above. Stark shadows stretched away behind it and the trees, rapidly as the bright light, seemed to move overhead too fast for it to be the sun. Alarmed and curious Paul looked up as clouds seemed to vanish instantly as a large brilliantly bright ball of flame and white light streaked across the sky. People started to scream in terror. Bemused, Paul looked at them as they all began to run in panic, a father picking up his young daughter and running toward him. All of the trees suddenly bent sideways in an instant as if pushed down by some great unseen power before bending back and rocking sideways. A massive force slammed into Paul but he remained upright, unlike the man who fell with his daughter almost at his feet. In terror the man looked behind him as the ball of light above them exploded in a massive blast of intense blinding white light. A pop sound echoed out overwhelming all other noise; just the one single pop sound as the report was too loud to register. The man jumped to his feet, lifted his daughter and started to run directly at Paul. As he rushed forward, he opened his mouth as if to scream when the intense heat hit him and his daughter. Before the air could escape from his lungs to form a scream, he was vaporised in an instant. Paul flinched backwards, his eyes open wide in shock. He could sense a great heat rush past him and he could see the castle appear to melt downwards in the intense white heat, the trees being blasted flat, their leaves shredded in an instant, but the trees immediately below the blast remained upright like blackened poles of defiance. Paul blinked his eyes, trying to focus upon what he was seeing. As he blinked, he opened his eyes again to see many people in a street of beautiful houses. He instinctively knew this was another place. He watched as if from a roof top as the people walking in the street, part of an extravagant looking city, looked up at a similar ball of fire as it streaked across the sky. As it went pop, the blast wave hitting the people instantly, knocking many down, they looked in terror as an ever increasing ball of expanding white light and heat hurtled towards them. Mothers covered their children as others staggered, some falling and others trying to run for cover. A man leant against the wall to balance himself as he stared at the approaching death. In a flash, he burnt away completely. Paul gulped in shock as he watched the entire area before him simply blow away. When the whiteness cleared, he found himself walking on the street. It was covered in a white fine ash. The blast had been so intense it had sucked all the oxygen away putting out any fires at the same time. But the devastation was utter and complete. A few walls remained with the outlines of people burnt into them like ghostly shadows. Some bodies lay together in a final embrace of death, just their pure white bones left as if stripped and cleaned. Everything was white and a pale grey. Paul looked around as all was eerily quiet. He was dreaming again he told himself as he looked at his feet in the thick white pasty ash and dust.

"Remember me?" he suddenly heard Kratos's voice behind him. Paul swung around just as another fireball streaked across the sky and over the horizon before exploding in another brilliant flash of light. "Paul...do you still not fully remember me?" Kratos asked.

"Where are you...where am I?" Paul called out as he spun around.

"I am here, there and everywhere with you. I am with you now. Fear not that you cannot see me. But understand and learn from what you see," Kratos explained.

"Learn what?" Paul asked exasperated.

"What you see. You are seeing what happened when people did not keep the sacred sites in balance. When Mother Earth was not able to defend her own and deflect what comes every 3,600 years. These things you see now happened in this age of man. You have witnessed but a glimpse of what happened in what you call Alba, part of Britain, and also in Mohenjo-Daro, what you now call India."

"What! Why do you invade my mind like this and show me these terrible things?" Paul asked, more exasperated.

"So that you never forget it...what can happen again if the secrets of our forefathers are not protected and carried over. No matter what happens in this life of yours now, you cannot ever reveal the secrets...no matter what...ever."

"Why could you not explain this when you were with me in person?"

"Why...because you would not be able to see what you clearly can now."

"Is your name even Kratos?...for I am sure you have told me different before.

And can you not show yourself?" Paul asked aloud as he looked at the absolute destruction all around him.

"If you wish," Kratos answered and instantly appeared before him making him jump back. "Paul...this is your dream after all."

"'Tis no ordinary dream...just like the one Alisha and I shared in that ruined cathedral," Paul replied.

"At least you recognise this fact," Kratos replied with a smile and leant against his staff and looked around the destroyed street. "As for my name...I have used many names. Kratos was simply my last one. 'Tis Greek of course," he smiled.

"How can you smile whilst surrounded by all this?" Paul asked, confused at his calmness.

"'Tis but a long since gone event. All those who perished here have since moved on many times."

"Then what other names have you been known by...and what was the cathedral dream I shared with Ali all about? For I fear I am losing her."

"Too many names to mention...and you shall not lose her love...," Kratos replied and looked at him intently. As he spoke, images of both his and Alisha's parchments seemed to scroll across his vision momentarily. "The cathedral was showing you the present state of the Church, ruinous and decayed. But it also showed you how people like you and Alisha can rebuild it as a church of love and light. I am surprised you did not know this already."

"I know so very little, I fear. And I do fear I am losing Alisha for she feels for Nicholas."

"Yes, that she does," Kratos answered and smiled.

"'Tis nothing to smile about."

"In time, you will see it is indeed something to smile about. As I have said, you will never lose her love. Never!" Kratos replied and then vanished.

"Kratos!" Paul called out loudly, but after several minutes it became clear that he would not reappear. He looked around and waited to wake up but he could not. He wondered what else he was supposed to see or learn. White ash dropped all around him like gently falling snow. It was still eerily quiet. After what seemed hours he fell to his knees and held his hands against his stomach. Was he trapped in some other world? he feared as this dream seemed to go on and on. He closed his eyes and sighed heavily, confused. Suddenly three tall women all dressed in white appeared before him. He sensed their presence first then heard the crunch of ash beneath their feet. 'Trust in dreams, for in them is hidden the gateway to all that has been, is and will be' he heard a gentle and soft female voice say in his mind. Slowly he opened his eyes and looked up. The three women smiled at him. They looked identical. Paul went to stand when the woman in the middle raised her hand. Immediately Paul felt a force push against him and he fell backwards into the ash. He leaned up on his hands.

"Do not fear us...but hear us. We are not who you see with your eyes or within this state, but this is how we appear so you can comprehend us," the woman in the middle said without actually speaking through her mouth.

"Why are you here...and what do you want with me?" Paul asked.

"Nothing."

"Then who are you?" Paul asked and tried to sit up but he could not move.

"We are three from the womb of creation. We are known by many names, and perhaps you would know us as Gwenhwyfars! But sleep, old soul, and return to your present realm of flesh blood and bone," the woman said and leant towards him, her white hair appearing to shimmer and change to pale shades of purple and blue. She touched Paul's forehead with her finger and he fell backwards asleep.

ಬ ಛ

Paul felt heavy and could not move his arms and legs. He could feel the bed sheets upon him but he could not open his eyes. He felt utterly paralysed. Images of the parchments flashed across his vision with various symbols being highlighted appearing to glow gold almost. He saw Reynald's face as if he was standing beside him as he laughed loudly at Princess Stephanie as she sat at the edge of her bed sobbing uncontrollably. She looked at Reynald. "My father told me to always act like a queen and a king would find me...act like a bitch and a dog would bite me," she said, which Paul heard clearly. Reynald roared with laughter. "Well I am known as the Red Wolf of Kerak so, my dear, what does that make you then...a bitch no less!" Reynald replied. Paul felt anger towards him. Was this an event from the past or still to come? he thought. Princess Stephanie turned away and sobbed more. He could see she was still pregnant. His heart jumped to think this was in the present. He moved to comfort her when he then saw Alisha, her face filled with rage shouting at him though he could not hear her words as she threw the set of parchments at him. She looked angry and her eyes filled with hate, he thought. His mind raced as he tried to make sense of what he was seeing as this was not what Kratos had just told him. The look in her face was pure hatred towards him. He tried to move towards her as she kept shouting at him. As he went to touch her, she hit out at him. Stunned, he stood backwards as tears streamed down Alisha's face. "Father" he suddenly heard a young child calling out. Frantic and filled with alarm he tried to look around. Instantly he was surrounded by white snow, at first thinking he was back with the three women, but he was knee deep in cold snow, the wind blowing ever harder against him. Abi was calling out behind him. As he looked back, he could see Tenno forcing his way through the snow, the darkness of the night trying to envelope him almost. Suddenly Paul saw himself throwing his sword at a nearby tree, his face filled with rage! His vision focused upon the sword as it stuck into the trunk of the tree. He could hear Alisha screaming out loudly but he could not see her. He twitched and fought to shake himself out of the dream. 'Ali!' he called out desperately. His heart felt like it was about to burst from his chest and he could feel the anger and frustration of the dream as Alisha screamed a low empty scream that made his blood run cold.

"ALISHA!" he screamed aloud, his eyes opening wide in terror.

"Paul, 'tis okay. You are home and in your bed," Alisha said softly and wiped his brow with a damp cloth.

Paul started to shake all over as he looked around the chamber. He was in his bed, it was daytime, Theodoric and Tenno stood nearby with Percival and Thomas behind them all looking concerned. Paul went to sit up, but Alisha gently pushed him to remain lying down. He was soaked in sweat as were the bed sheets. Confused, he looked at Alisha as she smiled at him.

"What has happened to me?" Paul asked perplexed, his voice dry.

"'Twas a fever. You have been asleep these past three days straight," Theodoric explained.

"Alisha...Stephanie...she is in trouble with Reynald," Paul tried to say.

"We know...you have been calling out her name," Alisha said softly, looking at him filled with concern.

"Three days?" Paul said quizzically.

"Three days, my dearest Paul," Alisha said and wiped his head again. "We shall send word to her and check all is well...I promise."

Paul relaxed into the pillows but utterly confused. How could he have possibly been asleep for three whole days?

"I believe it is a reaction to all you have been through of late. 'Tis normal. You will recover," Tenno said.

Alisha leant over and kissed him on the forehead then looked at him.

"I did not say it properly the other night when I should have. I love you, Paul...I love you, do you understand me?" she said softly. He nodded he did as her eyes searched his. "I love you," she said again and smiled. "Now sleep..."

Reluctantly Paul closed his eyes, feeling weary and exhausted. Percival smiled at him, looking over Theodoric's shoulder.

SO CR

It was several hours later when Paul eased himself up and swung his legs out of the bed then wrapped the night gown around himself and started to tie the waist cord. The bed chamber room was empty as he stood up. He sniffed himself. 'I smell worse than Theo did,' he told himself as he walked toward the window. He looked down into the main rear court yard area to see Thomas and Tenno instructing Percival how to block with a sword. Several of Thomas's men were laughing as Percival kept letting Thomas's thrust through knocking him to the floor, but every time Percival got back up and tried again. Paul laughed to himself.

"Finally you are awake fully," Theodoric said from behind Paul, making him jump.

"Theo...I did not see you there," Paul remarked as he turned to see Theodoric sat on a chair in the corner of the room holding open Paul's parchment.

"Alisha was here until Arri needed his afternoon feed. You slept well this time. I do hope this does not become a habit as you had us all worried for a moment," Theodoric said as he placed the parchment down beside him upon a small table. "And look...you must have made an impression on Saladin's secretary for he has written to you," he continued and waved a small sealed envelope.

"Was she here all the time for I had some very strange dreams I can tell you," Paul said as he sat down opposite Theodoric on a small bench pushed up beside the wall.

"She has sat with you these past three days and nights, only leaving to feed Arri and change him."

"So who has been looking after Arri?"

"Who do you think?...Tenno of course" Theodoric laughed.

"My father and Firgany told me once of you. How they did not trust your judge-ment when they should have. They explained how your charts were even greater than those drawn up by Niccolas...though I did not know it was you at the time. They explained, similar charts led to the three wise men, the Magi, to find Jesus so I know 'tis not just fanciful nonsense...and that is why I must pay attention and heed what my parchments reveal and to trust in the work," Paul explained and looked at Theodoric, who appeared uncomfortable with what he was saying. "They also said you were once a good friend who understood how the charts really work. A brilliant man...a friend they let down to their eternal shame as they did not understand you nor pay heed to what you showed them. They swore they would not make that same mistake again...so I am asking you to explain them to me and to teach me everything," Paul said looking at Theodoric, who was clearly taken aback by his comments.

Theodoric rubbed his chin for several moments and struggled to find the words to respond to Paul's remarks. Hearing him explain what his father, Philip, and Fir-gany had said touched him deeply. It surprised him how deeply.

"Then I shall attempt to teach you all I know...or have learnt, I should say. And if you heed my advice on one thing only, then make it your priority to keep Reynald appeased and befriend Saladin...if the opportunity arises. It will help safeguard your futures believe me."

"How...how does someone like me keep a person like Reynald appeased and how do I even begin to even meet a person such as Saladin let alone befriend him?" Paul asked, puzzled.

Theodoric leaned forwards and handed Paul the sealed letter from Saladin's sec-retary.

"I strongly suspect herein lays your answer," he remarked as he handed it to Paul. "Your father was closely acquainted with him...for a time along with Princess Stephanie...he will know of you if you present yourself."

"But why should I? I mean, I do not even know what kind of a man he is...Rey-nald I do already...but Saladin," Paul replied looking at the envelope. He was just able to read the name 'Isfahani' written in Arabic and pressed into the wax seal.

"Why...Reynald I fear is a lost cause who will bring much bloodshed to this world far beyond his reach and time...but Saladin, or to give him his full title, Salah al Din Yusif ibn Ayyub, and known to his Muslim contemporaries as Nasi, but to us simply as Saladin...his family came from the Ayyubids of Kurdish origin as you probably already know. He served under Nur al Din, the Turkish ruler of Syria and northern Iraq, and he was educated and given military training in the cultivated surroundings of a Turkish court in Arabian Syria. But it is in Egypt that he has risen to power. He will gain more power I am sure as he listens to advice, particularly on political mat-ters, and makes use of existing military structures and tactics as well as new ideas. With a humane forgiving nature, piety, love of justice, generous and courageous, he has made a profound impact on those around him already. Even Christians trust his honour, such as Balian, Raymond and Master Roger, but he is no military innocent thrust into warfare against his will as some argue. He gained considerable experience as a staff officer under Nur al Din and fought in several battles before taking over as Vizier, the Chief Minister of Egypt, in 1169. He did not become the official ruler until 1171 but even then theoretically remained part of Nur al Din's realm until his death in 1173. Saladin is willing to take major risks as a commander and has a clear understanding of broad strategy, something Reynald seems to lack unfortunately. His greatness is such that many Latins simply do not accept that he is a mere Saracen... and as you have experienced with the Bull's Head bandit, legends grow claiming he is the grandson of a beautiful French Princess forced to marry a valiant Turk named Malakin, whom it is said lived long and tenderly with his wife, who was called the 'Fair Captive', from whom was born the mother of that courteous Turk, the Sultan Saladin, an honourable, wise and a conquering hero," Theodoric explained and waved his hands in a mocking fashion. [70]

Paul broke the wax seal and opened the letter. As he unfolded it, he was struck by the elegant and beautifully written letter, in Arabic.

"Ah...I think you may have to read this for my Arabic is not so good," Paul said as he studied the words then handed it to Theodoric.

Theodoric took the opened envelope and read its contents.

"Well, young sir, it appears you and Alisha made an excellent impression upon Isfahani for you have been invited to Cairo at a time that is convenient to you...a summons no less. It looks as though you will indeed meet the man himself."

"You must come with us...as my translator or something," Paul replied quickly. He paused as he looked down. Theodoric had mentioned 'Fair Captive' and it reminded him of the dream of the three tall white and fair women he had seen. He tried to remember the name the woman gave him.

"You look suddenly troubled. What is it?" Theodoric asked.

"I, I recall seeing three fair women in my dreams. One gave me a name saying they were all known as it...but I cannot recall fully. It was after a great devastation of parts in Alba and India...and their hair, though almost white, shimmered blue and purple at times," Paul answered as he struggled to recall the name she had given. "Gwenyfar...I think that is the name."

"Gwenhwyfar you mean?" Theodoric stated and raised his eyebrows.

"Yes, yes that is it. You have heard of them then?" Paul asked excitedly.

Theodoric sat up straight.

"Aye that I have...," he replied with a heavy sigh.

"Is there something wrong then? Please pray tell me what you know and if I was just dreaming...please."

"Did they say that your dreams are a gateway?"

"Yes, yes they did," Paul answered and sat forwards, intrigued.

"Hmm," Theodoric sighed loudly and paused for several long minutes. "The Welsh form Gwenhwyfar is cognate with the Irish name Findabair, which can be translated as 'The White Enchantress' or 'The White Fay', or 'Ghost', from earlier Celtic 'Uindo' for white, fair, or holy, and when coupled with the word 'seibara' means 'magical being' cognate with the Old Irish 'síabair' meaning a spectre, phantom or supernatural being. Geoffrey of Monmouth rendered her name as Guanhumara in Latin though there are many spelling variations found in the various manuscripts of his 'Historia Regum Britanniae'. The name is given as Guennuuar in Caradoc's 'Vita Gildae', while Gerald of Wales refers to her as Wenneuereia. Some pronounce the name as Gwynnever, or as you most likely know of it from the Holy Grail myths presently being propounded as Guinevere, as in King Arthur's bride."

"What...but I saw three women all claiming the name and saying they were from the womb of creation itself," Paul replied looking confused and tired.

"Look Paul, in one of the Welsh Triads, 'Trioedd Ynys Prydein', number 56 to be precise, there are three Gwenhwyfars married to King Arthur. The first is the daughter of Cywryd of Gwent, the second of Gwythyr ap Greidawl, and the third of Gogrfan Gawr, 'the Giant'. In a variant of another Welsh Triad, 'Trioedd Ynys Prydein', number 54, only the daughter of Gogfran Gawr is mentioned. Two other Triads, 'Trioedd Ynys Prydein', numbers 53, 84 mention Gwenhwyfar's contention with her sister Gwenhwyfach, which was believed to be the cause of the Battle of Camlann. In the Welsh romance Culhwch ac Olwen, she is mentioned alongside her sister Gwenhwyfach. In Geoffrey of Monmouth's 'Historia Regum Britanniae', she is described as one of the great beauties of Britain, descended from a noble Roman family and educated under Duke Cador of Cornwall." [71]

"Why then are the stories now being told speaking of only one? And why would three appear to me in my dreams...if indeed it was a dream?" Paul asked.

"Who appeared to you?" Alisha suddenly asked as she entered the room carrying Arri. She smiled at Paul seeing him sat up and out of bed. She walked across the room and knelt beside him and raised Arri closer to him to see. "Here...see your son he sleeps too. I thought you would like to see him," Alisha smiled and gently handed Arri over to him. "Now who did you see?" she asked again as she looked into his tired eyes.

"Just three women I dreamt of," Paul answered as he looked at Arri's little face as he slept. "He has gained weight, or is it that I am weak?"

"Do not try and change the subject...three women now is it?" Alisha joked as she stood up. She smiled at him then leant down and kissed the side of his face before whispering in his ears. "I have something that means we can again be intimate without the risk of falling with child again so soon. Princess Eschiva gave it to me. 'Tis next to my pillow. When you are ready, we can try." She kissed him again then stood up smiling at him. "Sorry to whisper Theo, 'tis rude of me."

"Do not mind me, young girl...after all am I not sat in your bed chambers... totally inappropriate in polite circles," Theodoric laughed back. "And I have already averted my eyes from the bottle of Silphium root you were given," he joked, Alisha immediately blushing.

"We have shared a caravan with you so I think it not inappropriate as we are past that, but Theo, you embarrass me if you know what it is I have," Alisha said, her face reddening.

"I am teasing you, and of course I know what it is. But be warned, it takes a couple of days to take effect. Take too much and you could harm your chances of conceiving ever again permanently...though it is all natural."

"I have absolutely no idea of what you speak of," Paul remarked as he gently rocked Arri.

"I shall let Alisha show you then...in good time," Theodoric laughed and winked at Alisha.

Port of La Rochelle, France, Melissae Inn, spring 1191

"What has she got then?" Sarah asked instantly eager to learn.

"Sarah, Ayleth, Miriam...it may also embarrass you all if I explain what," the old man replied, smiling.

"Please, you have to tell us now you have mentioned it," Miriam said and clenched the Templar's hand in hers tightly.

"'Tis nothing serious nor major, but just a simple herb that not only calms a woman's temper when it is that dreaded time of the month, but when taken properly, it can also stop the onset of pregnancy," the old man explained.

"Quick, I will order a barrelful now," Stephan joked.

"You will not need that for you shan't come anywhere near me for saying that," Sarah shot back feigning indignation but smiled.

"Is that allowed...for I have heard it said that it is viewed as murder by the Church?" the wealthy tailor asked.

"Some do argue that it is a sin to stop the natural process...but if God has given us the intelligence and wherewithal to make a drink that naturally stalls, not stops, the process, then is that not a good thing?" the old man explained. "What Princess Eschiva gave Alisha was not cheap. It was very expensive and rare...getting rarer all the time by over harvesting."

"'Tis Silphium isn't it?" Gabirol asked.

"You know of this too. Good...then you will also know that it is a herb now almost extinct. It is also where we get our symbol for a heart from," the old man explained.

"Heart...how so?" Simon asked.

"The typical rendering of a heart looks nothing like a real heart does it. Have you never wondered where the present image comes from?" the old man asked him and quickly drew out the shape of a love heart and pushed it across the table to Simon.

Fig. 47:

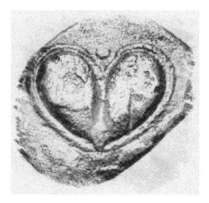

"'Tis a heart symbol yes," Simon remarked as he looked at the small drawing.

"No it is not...that is the shape of the Silphium seed. Papal condemnation of birth control is one of the Church's longest standing decrees. Famous names in the history of the Catholic Church, such as Clement of Alexandria, Hippolytus of Rome, and Augustine of Hippo, have

made strong condemnations of the use of any method that artificially blocks conception. But this wasn't always the case. While it is true the Church and its Fathers have been opposed to the idea of using methods and potions to stop conception since Saint Peter was given the burden of building Jesus's church, prior to that, contraception was widely used, especially in Rome, and it was in fact the Romans who are ultimately responsible for causing the extinction of what was the most effective herbal contraceptive ever to exist, through over-use. It didn't start with the Romans though. The herb is known as Silphium and is a plant possibly related to parsley, or more accurately a type of giant fennel plant cultivated for its resin known commonly as laser, laserpicium or lasarpicium, which was used as a culinary additive, a topical ointment or salve, and a medication for several ailments, and a form of birth control. It was cultivated in the oldest Greek city in North Africa, called Cyrene (now Libya). Legend claims that the Greek Battus and his men were led to a place called 'Apollo's Fountain' beyond the fertile grounds of Israsa, for the Libyans said the place had a hole in the sky, likely because the area received an unusual amount of rainfall. Battus settled there and named the city Cyrene in 630 BC. Silphium became so important to the Cyrenian economy that the plant appeared on almost all of their currency, identical in shape to the love heart we all know so well. It was and still is possibly the most popular and effective herbal contraceptive ever produced though now almost gone...just a few plants secretly cultivated by monks, and that included Theodoric. The plant was a highly prized item in the toolkits of physicians and mystics across the Mediterranean for at least seven hundred years. The plant even appears in historical records dating from seventh century BC Egypt, where it was part of medicinal recipes for stopping pregnancy and for inducing miscarriage to get rid of unwanted babies if already pregnant, as well as remedies for anything from coughs and sore throats, to leprosy treatments and wart remover. In fact, the Egyptians and the Knossos Minoans each developed specific glyphs to represent the plant, which clearly illustrates the importance it enjoyed in these early cultures. It was a versatile commodity too, as nearly every part of the plant was used, from the stalk, to the resin, to the tuber like roots. So versatile and sought-after, in fact, that it was over-cultivated and sold almost into extinction by the first century BC, though as Alisha discovered, there were still limited supplies available to a few. Pliny the Elder claims, in his 'Natural History', that the very last stalk of Silphium ever harvested was given to the Roman Emperor Nero as an 'oddity', which, according to some accounts, he promptly ate. The rampant over use of Silphium by Roman pagans is but one of the reasons it contributed to the early Christian idea that in any way blocking conception was and is a most evil thing. The double-tear shaped heart symbol first appeared in the historical record on the currency of Cyrene with its undeniable shape, which is a reproduction of the visual appearance of the Silphium seed, which as we now know and see is our modern symbol for romance and love...so it is in fact quite a bit older than most people realise," the old man explained. [72]

"Changing the subject a little...I do not understand why, if people like Kratos exist, and the beings of light, whatever they are...why do they not simply reveal themselves openly to all of us? I mean, would that not make us all sit up and take notice and behave?" Peter asked.

"Peter, as I have explained previously, if that was to happen, then most would only change out of fear, not by choice...," the old man replied.

"Perhaps...but if it was done with love, then surely we would all change for the better," Peter replied.

"But that would negate the entire point of being born...learning by experience and evolving by our own free will and choice," the old man explained then paused. "Look Peter, the *only way I can explain this without insulting anyone's intelligence, is to liken it to when I young boy finds a litter of new born puppies...all cuddly and soft and innocent. He feeds them, keeps them safe and helps them to grow. Then he leaves as his life takes another direction...then upon his return he finds those same puppies have turned into a wild ravenous pack of vicious hunters left fending for themselves. If he was to enter their pack now, what do you think would happen?"*

"They would rip him apart probably," Peter answered.

"Exactly...and the same would happen with any higher life form that came down amongst us...as we presently are. 'Tis why we must change, by our own free will and choice, because we wish to," the old man said and sat back.

"So all of these secrets and hidden things...is it just the higher initiates of the Templars then who are the guardians of the sacred secrets, the keepers of the ancient wisdom?" Gabirol asked.

"Well, as Paul recovered from his strange bout of illness, it was Theodoric who best explained much about such matters. I can explain that too if you so wish?" the old man said.

"Aye most definitely, please do," the Templar said enthusiastically.

"Good, then listen carefully as I explain," the old man smiled. "This may take a while."

Alexandria, Egypt, October 1179

Alisha had her arms wrapped around Paul's shoulders as she stood behind him. He sat at the main dining table with Theodoric opposite sitting patiently, his arms folded. Alisha kissed the side of Paul's face and stood up placing her hands upon his shoulders.

"Please, do not overwork his mind. I shall be back later and I do not want to see you still both sat here. He needs his rest," she said looking at Theodoric and raised her eyebrows.

Tenno entered the room carrying Arri.

"We are all ready. I worry Percival seems too keen to go shopping," Tenno said and feigned a mock grimace.

Paul looked at him with Arri.

"I promise I shall not spend too much," Alisha said and moved to take Arri from Tenno.

"Are you sure you would not rather stay and discuss matters?" Theodoric asked Tenno.

"No...you discuss a book that has supposedly been translated from older sources, of which there are no proofs, taken from manuscripts written down hundreds of years after the events claimed, and there are what, over eight thousand of which no two are the same and from which just a selected view were chosen to be included within the New Testament you speak of. Ones that a select few chose to create a version that would appeal to their then masters of Rome. Is that not correct?" Tenno asked in his usual blunt manner.

"Almost...but you fail to see that it is the hidden information contained within them that is important," Theodoric answered back.

"Then explain it to Paul and he can tell me later," Tenno replied and paused for a moment. "I do not wish to offend...but I fail to understand how you can believe that the word of your god is contained within a book edited by scholars of mixed ability, who in turn took them from earlier edited accounts of those eight thousand or so contradictory manuscript copies of fourth century scrolls that claim to be copies of even older long lost scrolls written in the first century. That is not faith, that is insanity," Tenno commented as Alisha began to usher him toward the door.

"That is why 'tis even more remarkable and proof that there is a guiding force behind what is contained within it then," Theodoric shot back defensively.

"Come on, Tenno, we have to get going," Alisha said and then smiled back at Paul as she walked to the door holding Tenno's arm. "We shall see you later."

Paul waved and laughed as Tenno looked back briefly following Alisha out of the room.

"He surprises me at times," Theodoric remarked as he moved several scrolls and parchments around in front of him upon the table.

"Why?"

"Because he of all people should understand the need to have faith...and how information contained within such books as the Bible will be held so dearly and close that they will not be lost, and consequently are almost guaranteed to be carried across time almost intact."

"Perhaps he simply does not believe such codes exist or are real," Paul remarked and looked at Theodoric. "I myself have many questions."

"Then let us see if we can answer them. So please, ask of me any question and I shall try and answer them if I know the answer."

"Okay, where do I start as I have so many," Paul replied and leant forwards placing his elbows upon the table. "For a start, who were, or are, the real keepers of the wisdom and sacred secrets for all these years? Is it the Knights Templar, the so-called guardians of the truth and keepers of the faith? Do they have the Ark of the Covenant that Moses had? Is the Holy Grail really the bloodline of Jesus Christ and are the Knights Templar also now the guardians of that bloodline? Why does the Church feel threatened by them? Is it because of the knowledge they have, even to this day? Is there a direct descendant of Jesus alive today, if so who is he or she? Would such a bloodline be powerful?" Paul asked.

"Paul, how many questions...," Theodoric laughed and waved his hand for him to stop. "I can answer them all if you wish, but certain aspects I cannot prove or show you unless we travel to Cairo, so perhaps Isfahani's invite should be accepted."

"I know that knowledge is power...supposedly, and I was told that I should and must trust your knowledge and learn from you. I have already learnt much from you but I feel it is just the tip of a sword I have yet to see."

"Indeed just the tip. So let me begin before Ali returns," Theodoric smiled and shuffled upon his chair as he made himself comfortable. "Our story really comes to us via The Knights Templar out of Egypt, through 'The Magi', which directly derived its knowledge from the Temples of Egypt. Whilst names and even languages have changed throughout history the common beliefs are fundamentally the same. It is from Akhenaten's monotheistic religion, as in the belief in 'one God' who created the Mer-Ka-Ba symbol, that the original Knights Templar symbol is taken from as I explained to you in Jerusalem remember?" Theodoric started to explain.

"Yes, how can I forget what you and Count Henry told me?"

"Good, then recall the strange Pharaoh, Akhenaten, was the first to believe that all men are equal in the love of 'one God'. Templars, like Akhenaten, believed in the true name of God as being 'RA' the God of Light and Creation and in the pure Energy Spirit of Jesus. Templars believe in the Love of the Creator, the most powerful energy in the universe. And to refresh your memory, Jesus did not die on the cross, but was released through a deal after three days on the cross, as it was believed that your spirit was dead or broken after three days of crucifixion. That is why on the fourth day the Romans would break your legs to bring on real physical death by suffocating. This was not done to Jesus, who eventually went to live in France with his wife, Mary Magdalene, and three children."

"Three children? You never mentioned that before!" Paul exclaimed, surprised.

"Oh...did I not? Well, he did have. And there lays to this day in a tomb in the Languedoc region of France, near Rennes Le Chateaux, bodies of this line. But both Firgany and your father were, and perhaps your father still is, working upon secreting away those remains to a more secure and safer region?" Theodoric explained and raised his eyebrows at Paul.

"If he was or is, then he has never even hinted that to me," Paul replied, seeing that Theodoric was expecting him to respond.

"Perhaps I should refresh your memory on certain aspects we covered in Jerusalem...such as the Merkaba star. Recall how I explained that when viewed in specific light conditions the Merkaba star produces a series of shadows that clearly form a 'cross' very similar to the Templar Cross and remember how the Atbash cipher works? The angle of view needed in order to see this cross is exactly the same as the angle that would be visible when looking up if the Merkaba star was situated on top of the pyramids at Giza. Mer means 'ascending place', Ka means 'true spirit' and Ba means 'soul' in ancient Egypt. Merkaba therefore means 'Ascending Place of True Spiritual Souls' also known as 'The Ark of the Covenant' the communication device with God or 'Temple'. If the Merkaba symbol was on top of the pyramids, are the pyramids the 'The Ark of the Covenant'? Moses is said to possess the Ark, so if Moses and Akhen-Aten were the same person, only then does this make a lot of sense. Also the Ark that Moses is said to have possessed had the Merkaba symbol on the sides. Some argue that this is the doorway that leads from our world to the spiritual world, the Ark of the Covenant's doorway to Heaven." Theodoric paused as he looked at Paul's reaction.

"Yes I recall all of what you have told me before," Paul replied.

"Good for the fact is that every known Temple in Egypt always had such a doorway to Heaven. These doorways were called 'false doors', how could such a doorway have any use, unless they become operational in another dimension, a 'spirit dimension' accessed according to many Egyptian rituals through meditation. Meditation is said to lead to higher consciousness as used by Buddhists, just like Tenno! Christianity does not mention meditation, yet the Knights Templar Order clearly use it daily, so one can only deduce that the Knights Templar religious traditions came from a different source other than Roman Catholicism. I can simply state that the Order's traditions come from the Nazarenes, who also practised meditation. This is but one more reason the Church plots to destroy the Order in time."

"Does Stewart know this?" Paul asked, concerned.

"Of course not. Not even Gerard knows this. But fear not, Paul, I believe the machinations are nowhere near ready or in place to carry out," Theodoric stated and paused briefly. "Know that there are numerous examples of Templar crosses on temples in Egypt along with ankh symbols on Templar tombs. The evidence is overwhelming. The 'Apparatus' referred to in the Knights Templar rule is the communication devise with God and is one and the same as the 'Apparatus' as depicted on all Egyptian Pharaohs' tombs still seen to this day."

"Yes I recall you explained all this, or Brother Jakelin did in Jerusalem," Paul remarked.

"Good...it shows you were listening then and it never hurts to refresh your mind as I said. And so to answer part of your question, Mary Magdalene, after the apparent death of Jesus, went to Europe and formed her own Church, not based on Christianity, but the old religion of Egypt 'Isis and Osiris', the same beliefs of the Magi. Mary Magdalene was a High Priestess of the Magi. She was accompanied by disciples of the faith known as 'Keepers of the Faith', which is an identical allusion to the Knights Templar, to guard her. It is this early form of an 'Order of Knights' that took the true faith from the Magi of Egypt, the same faith that Jesus practised. These were the same 'Keepers of the Faith' as the 'Keepers of the Holy Grail', the Knights Templar."

"What you say will greatly offend a great many people, especially within the Church," Paul remarked.

"Good. In time they will have no option other than to embrace the truth. Just as they will have to accept the very real fact that this very world we live upon is a sphere...not flat!" Theodoric smiled.

"Then what of the sacred pillars of Boaz and Jachin you once mentioned? How does that have anything to do with us today?"

"The sacred pillars of Boaz and Jachin as described within the Bible?" Theodoric repeated and paused as he rubbed his chin. "There is an ancient tradition in Egypt that in the city of Annu, called On in the Bible and Heliopolis by the Greeks, that there was a great sacred pillar. This was believed to be the Great Pillar of Lower Egypt with its counterpart in Upper Egypt in the city of Nekheb, which later became known as Thebes. Thebes was important in direct relation to the Omphalos sites and celestial projections across the whole of the Mediterranean."

"What...I mean what celestial projections and what are Omphalos sites?" Paul interrupted.

"Ahh, have I not explained them either? In ancient Egyptian myth and religious teachings, they had a celestial boat called the Magan boat...it was later copied by the Greeks and incorporated into their Jason and the Argonauts myths. The sacred sites across the Mediterranean that have Omphalos stones, which just happen to have sacred nets carved upon most of them, all marry up and align with the stars of the constellation of the Argo. This is just another example that proves our ancestors had an understanding of the world being a sphere and able to project across vast distances."

"I would like to learn more on those details," Paul replied.

"Then you shall. But getting back to the two pillars. In Egypt they became the 'Pillars of Thoth', or Hermes as the Greeks named them. The two pillars of Upper and Lower Egypt symbolically united the nation as one. It was stated that Thoth, Hermes possessed all his secret knowledge upon 36,535 scrolls that were hidden under the heavenly vault, the sky, and that they could only be found by the worthy, who would use such knowledge for the benefit of mankind. Manetho, an ancient Egyptian historian, apparently uncovered sacred pillars that detailed Egypt's earliest history...and it stretches back thousands of years. All across the ancient world, it was common practice to flank the entrance to a temple with two independent pillars. It is argued by orthodox academics that the Egyptians did not know the value of pi even though later Greeks maintained they actually learnt pi from them. Without the understanding of pi, there is no way the pyramids of Egypt could have been built. Without it, we could not build the great cathedrals now being constructed. We know that Moses was directly linked with the pyramids and Egypt having been brought up in the Pharaoh's palace, even by standard orthodox accounts, though as I have argued he was none other than Akhenaten himself anyway. Plus an earlier Moses figure became fused into the one character we now all claim to know so well...but I digress. Moses as we know figures prominently within the Old Testament where we find mathematical details concerning the two pillars that flanked Solomon's temple. It states that at the gates of Solomon's temple were two pillars made of brass, each eighteen cubits high, erected and known as Jachin and Boaz. Here listen," Theodoric said as he pulled out his old leather bound Bible and turned the pages rapidly. "Here...it reads, 'And King Solomon sent and fetched Hiram out of Tyre. He was a widow's son out of the tribe of Napthtali, and his father was a man of Tyre, a worker in brass. For he cast two pillars of brass, of eighteen cubits high apiece; and a line of twelve cubits did compass either of them about'. See, 'tis written down so despite what Tenno may believe, certain facts are still carried over. Now then, placed on top of these pillars were two capitals known as chapiters or decorative tops that were each four cubits high. So therefore the total height equals eighteen plus four, which equals twenty-two. In referring to Hiram of Tyre it states the following...'He cast about two bronze pillars, each eighteen cubits high and twelve cubits around. He also made two capitals of cast bronze to set on the tops of the pillars; each capital was five cubits high. A network of interwoven chains festooned the capitals on top of the pillars, seven for each capital. He made pomegranates in two rows encircling each network to decorate the capitals on top of the pillars. He did the same for each capital. The capitals on top of the pillars in the portico were in the shape of lilies, four cubits high. On the capitals of both pillars, above the bowl shaped part next to the network, were the two hundred pomegranates in rows all around. He erected the pillars at the portico of the Temple. The pillar to the south he named Jachin, which actually means 'He establishes' or 'He sets up', and the one to the north, Boaz, which means, 'In him is strength' or with different vowels, 'With strength'. The capitals on top were in the shape of lilies. And so the work on the pillars was completed.' 1 Kings 7:15–22. Note the lilies," Theodoric explained and pointed out.

"But there appears there are two values for the height of the capitals as it is given twice. Once at five cubits and once at four cubits. Why is that?" Paul asked, puzzled.

"It is my belief that the importance of the passages is in relation to the numerical values. Therefore we can have a pillar eighteen cubits high plus a capital of five cubits high equalling twenty-three, or we can have a pillar eighteen cubits high plus a capital of four cubits high equalling twenty-two. The actual reference to the pillars of the portico of the temple have capitals of four cubits high. Eighteen plus four equalling twenty-two. The two pillars are linked together with netting wound around the top of the pillars twice. The length of the netting between the pillars equals seven cubits on either side. Here we have the all-important numerical values of the pi ratio of twenty-two over seven. The main trilithon stones at Stonehenge in Britain are likewise centrally set at twenty-two feet and spaced with their centres being seven feet."

"Twenty-two over seven...hmm" Paul pondered and shook his head.

"Paul, please note as I have said many times before...the only truly universal language that can span the millennia of time intact is mathematics as no matter how it is written or expressed the values will always be the same. We can see important numbers within the passages I quoted, as in 18 x 4 equals 72. In ancient Egypt the seasons were calculated using the 72 Dog Days which were directly linked to the days of the Dog Star, which is Sirius. Sirius as you will discover has direct symbolic links to Mary Magdalene and Jesus and the five pointed star if you are not already familiar with that aspect? There were 72 Anunnaki in the Babylonian and Sumerian legends and the value figures predominantly throughout all religions. Seventy-two divided by the capital height of five is 72/5 equals 14.4. One hundred and forty-four and its multiples by the power of 10 is an important number that also constantly crops up in religious texts all too frequently...an example being the 144,000 souls as detailed within the Bible in Revelation. 18 x 5 equals 90, 90 degrees being an essential ratio for all Pythagorean triangles and angles. 18 x 200 taken from the Pomegranates, equals 3,600. 18, the pillars' height x 5, the first capital's height x 4, the second capital's height, equals 360. Two pillars at 18 cubits high are equal to a total of 36. 36 x 4 equals 144. 36 x 5 equals 180. Also if we take the 18 cubits high pillars and multiply it by the pillar's twelve cubits circumference we get 18 x 12 equals 216. 216 was regarded by Pythagoras as a magic number as it is the same as 6 to the power of 3, or 6 x 6 x 6. 666 is the celebrated Number of the Beast in Revelations in the Bible. Add a zero to 216 and we have 2,160, which happens to equal the diameter of the moon in miles if the details recovered and as being calculated now confirm. When viewed from earth, the moon's apparent circumference is identical to that of the sun's apparent circumference. 2,160 years is also the processional period of each zodiacal cycle through the heavens. 2,160 x 12 equals the total complete processional cycle of all twelve signs of the Zodiac at 25,920 years. 2,160 divide by 6 equals the 360 degrees in a circle. When divided by 24 hours it equals 90 degrees, a perfect right angle. When divided by 12, it equals 180 degrees. Are you following me so far?" Theodoric asked.

"Yes...and I shall keep on at you and ask you over and over again until I know all of this off by heart," Paul replied, eager to learn more.

"Good," Theodoric replied and smiled before continuing. "Then know that in between the capitals were nets and wreaths of chain work that were 7 cubits long for one capital and 7 cubits for the other, totalling 14 cubits. Why indicate this unless the total value of 14 was significant? The value 14 is very significant in relation to the Giza pyramids. 14 x 360 equals 504. 1 x 2 x 3 x 4 x 5 x 6 x 7 equals 5,040. Boaz was the great-grandfather of King David and represented 'strength' or 'it is in strength'. Jachin was the high priest who assisted the dedication of Solomon's Temple that represented 'to establish' and united 'stability'. Boaz, the left hand pillar, stood to the south representing the Land of Judah and signified 'strength', whereas Jachin, the right hand pillar, stood in the north and represented the land of Israel signifying 'establishment'. When united by the lintel of Yahweh, the two pillars provided 'stability'. Just as in ancient Egypt, whose country was united by two pillars in the two lands of Upper and Lower Egypt. As long as they remained joined, strength and stability would endure. In the 'old ritual' of the higher circle of Templar initiates, of which your father was...perhaps still is...one, the two great pillars are hollowed out to conceal hidden ancient records and valuable writings pertaining to the past of the Jewish people. Amongst these records there was the secret of the magical 'Shamir' and the history of its properties. The two pillars were bound to become important as they conveniently spell out the properties of pi in the sacred cubit measurements of the Bible itself. The message could not be clearer. Right in the middle of the Bible, in big letters, sacred measurements of pi expressed in the ratio of 22 cubits high pillars and 7 cubits distance between the pillars, 22 over 7. This shows that Solomon knew pi a long time before the Greeks. As we know, Solomon inherited his system of measures and ratios as handed down since the time of Moses, who we know came out of Egypt. This shows a definite link and that the same information from a single original source is being carried over."

"You have mentioned this before, but how did it survive to our present day... before the Templars recovered whatever it was they did that confirmed much of what was already believed?" Paul asked.

"In part, much was carried over via and through the community of Qumran. Now most people think of the Essenes, a group who it is argued Jesus came from, also known as Qumranians, as just another group of early Christians amongst many that existed in the Holy Land. The Qumran Community were the distillation of everything that was important to the Jews as a nation, the guardians of the covenant with their God and the embodiment of all the aspirations of a people. But one of the main areas of debate in relation to the Qumran Community has been the identity of the first 'Teacher of Righteousness'. The debate often focuses on whether it refers to Jesus, the Messiah, or his brother, James the Just, who was also referred to as Messiah, or even John the Baptist. I can tell you, and I am afraid you will have to simply accept, or not, when I tell you that there were actually two individuals given the title 'Teacher of Righteousness'. 'Tis yet another esoteric meaning of the twin riders' symbolism on the Knights Templar seal. But I can tell you, the 'Teacher of Righteousness' was none other than the brother of Jesus, James, who was the leader of the Jerusalem Church, which was in fact the actual Qumran Community, who had a scroll, known as the 'Manual of Discipline', which stated that the Community consisted of twelve perfect holy men who were the pillars of the community. If you ever wondered where the expression came from, now you know. The two main principal pillars were highly symbolic representing both the 'kingly' and 'priestly' aspects of creating and maintaining the 'Kingdom of Heaven'. These pillars were of course descendants of the pillars of the united Upper and Lower Egypt as I have already said. These had come down to the Qumran Community via the Boaz and Jachin pillars that made up the Eastern gate of Solomon's Temple. To the Jews, these pillars represent the kingly power of 'Mishpat' and priestly power of 'Tsedeq'. When united, they supported the great archway of Heaven, the keystone of the third most important word of Hebrew desire 'Shalom'."

"I think I shall need to write down much of what you say," Paul said as he sat up.

"No...that you must not do. Not yet anyway. You must train your mind to memorise all of it, and you can." Theodoric answered immediately. "Just remember this if you can, that the right hand pillar was known as Jachin, who was the first high priest of the Temple. To the Qumranians, this was the priestly pillar, Tsedeq, which embodied all that was Holy. Tsedeq is often translated as meaning righteousness though some have argued that it can equally mean rightness. This principle is identical to the ancient Egyptian concept of Ma'at, which we shall cover later. The left pillar of Solomon's Temple was known as Boaz. For the Qumranians this was the kingly pillar and stood for the house of David. Boaz was the great-grandfather of David, the king of Israel. To Qumranians therefore, Boaz represented Mishpat, which is often translated as meaning judgement. It also signified the law and rule of Yahweh himself hence why the dispensing of justice was always connected with this pillar. The Biblical Jacob erected his first pillar at Mizpah, which is simply another spelling of Mishpat. Saul was declared the first king of Israel at Mizpah. When these two pillars are in place with the Teacher of Righteousness, Tsedeq on the left hand of God, and the earthly Davidic King, Mishpat, on his right hand, the archway of Yahweh's rule is in place with the keystone of Shalom locking everything together at its centre. Shalom is understood the world over as a form of greeting that means peace. For the Jews of the Biblical era, it had far more complex meanings. In short it meant establishing the rule of Yahweh with a moral order of government supported by both the kingly and priestly pillars. The whole order of the community of Qumran insured that the symbolic image of two pillars held together by a supporting cross member were carried on into the next millennium as it has done so. I have explained how the mathematical values inherent within the pillars of Boaz and Jachin are 22 over 7. But what I have not explained before is the connection with Samson and the constellation of Orion. Do you wish to hear now or later?" Theodoric asked, seeing Paul yawn.

"Absolutely I do...so please excuse me yawning. I am just a little weary still that is all but my mind is fine," Paul replied.

"Good. Then know that other Biblical reference to twin pillars is stated where Samson stands between two pillars and pulls them down. There are too many symbolic meanings behind the Samson and Delilah story to explain now in one afternoon; suffice to point out that it does have connections with the later Knights Templar, a consequence of which being that the Knights Templar never cut their hair at the back just like Samson. It does not take a genius to note that the actual symbolic representation of two upright pillars joined across the top is identical to that of pi. Π or smaller case π. Note also that the ancient Egyptian Djed pillars are depicted with five rings at the top of the column with a further four extended rings above giving us the same numerical representation of the pillars of Jachin and Boaz."

"I thought they shaved the sides of their heads to seal away their hair, so it could be used later if necessary," Paul interrupted.

"Aye that is but one reason. But look again at them when you see your brother or Nicholas next time. The backs of their heads, their hair remains long. And after their initiation ceremonies, they grow their hair back on the sides...well, most of them do."

"I vaguely recall my father mentioning the skull and crossbones and a value of 58. Are you able to explain that to me?" Paul asked, changing the direction of the conversation as he momentarily thought of both Nicholas and Stewart.

"Of course. There is presently, along with many similar heads in the Templars' possession, large skulls that are wrapped in the cloth of white linen, with another red cloth around it. A label is attached, on which was written the legend CAPUT L VIIIm. Some are gilded in silver. Now Caput LVIIIm means 'Head 58m'. It is an enigma for all but the upper inner circle initiates of the Templars."

"Can you tell me what it means then or are you under oath not to reveal it?" Paul asked.

"You of all people have a right to know and understand what it means...so I see no reason why I cannot tell you," Theodoric replied with a big smile and winked. "I can tell you that the M is in fact the astronomical symbol of Virgo. It is worth noting that an important ancient Egyptian number that has many symbolic meanings, has the value five. It is the number of the Pentagram and the five-pointed star image that represented Sirius and eight is associated with Isis, who was also represented by Sirius in the heavens. The numbers five and eight are also present in the 'Brothers of the Ross Cross' but that is a separate order your father and I tried to form as a safety net in case the Templars are ever removed by the Church. 'Tis part of the reason I walked away when we could not agree upon its path. But who knows...perhaps one day it will surface again," Theodoric sighed as he thought back upon past events. "Huh, funny. We had an image made of a rose constructed with a centre of five petals surrounded by eight petals."

"I sense this pains you to talk about the matter. What happened?" Paul asked.

"Well let me just say that our Order was supposed to be formed as an inner worlds Order, consisting of great Adepts. When compared to normal human beings, the consciousness of these Adepts was to be like that of demi-gods. This 'College of Invisibles' would influence the development of great truths to the average man... bit arrogant really as I look back upon it. We hoped the new Order would prove to be the genesis of better operative and functional societies. We even had our own secret greeting drawn up," Theodoric sighed.

"Really? Please tell me. Who knows, perhaps one day your Order may still happen," Paul said and smiled.

"No...not in my life time that I can guarantee. Though I believe your father and Firgany secreted away enough secret information that, in the future, it may be resurrected so to speak."

"And the greeting?"

"You are your father's son for sure," Theodoric remarked and his smile returned. "It went, erm...May the Roses bloom upon your Cross."

"And?"

"And that is it," Theodoric laughed. "'Tis similar enough to the Templars' other saying as inscribed upon many of their chalices."

"What other saying?" Paul asked, eager to hear.

"It also relates to the value fifty-eight funnily enough. It is of a feminine origin and nature known as Mete, the Baphomet or mother of breath, the formula of faith, inscribed on all chalices belonging to the Templars. It reads as 'Let Mete be exalted who causes all things to bud and blossom, it is our root, it is one (1) and seven (7), it is octinimous, the eight fold name'. As you shall learn, Jesus is also associated with the number eight for everything is connected...everything."

"I sense we shall be going to Cairo sooner rather than later to learn these things," Paul commented.

Theodoric laughed and shuffled upon his chair.

"Aye most certainly...but before then, another valuable number that crops up again and again is 64, which you should learn about. It is connected to the Chinese I Ching and has something to do with the very building blocks of man...but that I am afraid we shall not be privy to until the time of Aquarius. As everything appears to be intrinsically linked by our universal mathematical pattern, it should not surprise you to learn that the Giza complex is actually set out on an 8 x 8 grid square system, which equals 64. Not only do we find the important 64 value but also note that the Golden Mean proportion of the grid is based on a ratio of 5.8 hence the Head 58 connection with the Knights Templar. It just so happens that each side of the Giza 8 x 8 square equals half a minute of equatorial latitude as in 921.44 ancient sacred yards, or royal cubits, 64 x 1440 equals 921.60. A difference of .16 no less if what the ancients have handed down to us is correct of course. It is the 921 value we are interested in. Jesus is also linked directly with this number as his recorded ministry as detailed in the New Testament lasted exactly 921 days. Why bother including such a time scale for no apparent reason? Note that if you take a bearing from the Great Pyramid's apex of 26 degrees, which all the passages within it are angled at, leaving 64 degrees to make 90 and then travel in a northeasterly direction the bearing points towards for exactly 365 miles, 365 days in the year, you end up at Bethlehem. Note also that the Great Pyramid sits in the northeastern corner of the grid on just four squares, or more correctly, 1/16th. That number 16 again. There is a clue there to a great secret you must work out yourself. I shall also show you how the Golden Mean radius drawn from the northeastern corner of the Great Pyramid passes directly through the Sphinx. 'Tis yet another clue."

"A clue to what?" Paul asked, puzzled.

"That, my dear Paul, is one you and you alone must work out. You will understand why if the time ever comes you do," Theodoric smiled. "But let me explain some other aspects that will helpfully guide you," he said and paused. "If you look closely at the Gospels, it is worth looking at one of Jesus's teachings in Matthew 13:47."

"Yes I do recall Count Henry actually mentioning that very passage," Paul interrupted.

"Good again as it shows you can remember things. Well in that passage Jesus likens the coming Kingdom of God to the lowering of a net into the sea, after which the good fish are put into pails and the net thrown away. You are aware of all the net symbolism by now I trust?" he asked as Paul nodded yes. "Good...for there are many parables from Jesus that are symbolic relating to nets and fish as his ministry occurred during the Piscean age. Note that the fish are placed into pails. Pails were only used for carrying water so here we have a direct link with both the Piscean symbolism and Aquarian symbolism. Aquarius is pictured as a man carrying a pitcher of water, a deliberate symbol since water carrying was strictly women's work. Jesus was fully aware of the symbolism, as indicated in John 13:5, where Jesus carries a pitcher of water to wash the feet of his disciple. He does so by pouring out the water and this is designed expressly as part of a baptismal rebirth-ritual involving the Aquarian pouring of water rather than the Piscean total immersion. This incident occurred during the Last Supper just twenty-four hours before Jesus's apparent crucifixion. Jesus declares to his disciples that their continued fellowship with him must somehow be a function of their participation in this strange Aquarian initiation ceremony, even though they cannot understand its full significance yet. In short, Jesus is saying that if their association is to be continued with him after his death, then that association must become an Aquarian one. They would all have to be physically reborn together again to experience the Golden Age of Aquarius, which Jesus, as the ceremonial and symbolic 'water carrier', would personally inaugurate. Only then would their fellowship be resumed, whether symbolised by the breaking of bread or the sharing of wine, in Jesus's own words 'Never again will I drink from the fruit of the vine until I drink it new with you in the Kingdom of my Father.' Matthew 26:29. This also has major symbolic implications for the latter Arthurian myths and Knights Templar...now referring back to the fish being separated into pails with only the good being kept, and the net being thrown away. This is symbolic of the men and women of the Piscean age, who will all be subjected to scrutiny with the coming Aquarian, or spiritual, age. As predicted in the Book of Revelations and other religions, the Aquarian age will be a time of peace, a Golden Age, after which the Devil will again be let loose to test once more mankind's resolve to be spiritual and to let only the elect escape from the physical world. The next age after Aquarius is that of Capricorn, the goat...a half fish, half goat but also portrayed as half man and half goat as typified by the folklore image of the Devil. Many ancient myths and legends state that their great civiliser gods walked on water...Jesus did likewise. The legends continue by stating that in every case, the god, or great civiliser, was conspired against, attacked and either killed, and later resurrected or departed on a boat or vessel across water. King Arthur did likewise also remember for he was taken on board a vessel and departed across the sea attended by fair maidens? One notable character, who was a great civiliser, was the Egyptian god Osiris, represented in the heavens by the constellation of Orion. He was conspired against just like Jesus, he was struck down, was sealed inside a container or vessel of some kind and cast into the water then drifted away on a river, eventually reaching the sea. Those who have studied Arthurian legend will immediately see identical similarities for remember, King Arthur was born of two fathers, and was expressly linked to the Fisher King, born of water, as in spirit, the other a mortal man. He was also referred to as the 'Once and Future King' just as Jesus was and also as Osiris as Orion was. All the legends state that King Arthur was a direct descendant of Jesus Christ himself, hence 'Holy Grail', which comes from the words 'Sangraal', which when correctly translated from 'Sang Raal' means 'holy blood' or 'royal Blood'. But as you also know, much of the King Arthur legends are in fact based upon two characters of historical reality, merged to continue the codes from antiquity, but also their bloodlines of genuine pedigree and genealogy."

"Yes, my father told me that much already...but also that the King Arthur myths now also carry the same symbolism and mathematical codes. Is that true?" Paul asked.

"Aye 'tis true...your father speaks truth. In Gematria, where a sound, letter or vowel is replaced by a mathematical value, Excalibur, King Arthur's mystical sword that came from the Lady of the Lake, water again, is equal to 773," Theodoric said and paused looking at the pommel of Paul's sword just visible as he recalled when he was given the sword by a lady from within a lake. "Jesus likewise spoke of a two edged long sword that he had brought with him as stated within the New Testament. Well, in Gematria this equals 772. By the convention of Gematria, these are both symbolically identical. Also the constellation of Orion has a few faint stars that point downwards from the three main belt stars and are known as the 'Sword of Orion'. Yet another symbolic connection! Excalibur in its original spelling equals 755. 755 is the average mean distance in feet along each face of the perimeter base of the Great Pyramid. Excalibur remember was drawn from the stone, as in sword in the stone. So anyone drawing knowledge and wisdom from what is hidden within the Great Pyramid is not only symbolically drawing the sword of knowledge and wisdom from the stone, but actual real knowledge and wisdom...The pyramid as we know it is the greatest stone monument on earth. King Arthur also had twelve Knights of the Round Table, just as Jesus had twelve disciples. Remember there are twelve signs of the zodiac, twelve months in a year, twelve essential mineral salts, twelve precious stone gates in the New Jerusalem and twelve hides at Glastonbury that deal directly with the numbers and figures quoted in Revelations. Glastonbury is heaped in Arthurian myths and legends, far too many to explain here with such limited time," Theodoric explained, his tone passionate as he revealed details enthusiastically.

"I do know that my father said the Moses figure, the Akhenaton one, is connected with the Great Pyramid. How so exactly?" Paul asked.

2 – 12

"How so? For starters Moses's name is written Mosheh, as shown in Exodus 2:10 and 15 and is derived from the verb masha, which, means 'I drew him from water'. Again the water element. The myth of Moses states that he was found in a reed basket and then grew up in the Pharaoh's household. He was known to be an initiate of the mysteries of the Great Pyramid. Now it is from Moses that we have the events of the Old Testament, the Ten Commandments and other laws, so in effect, what we know of the Great Pyramid came first. One of the most intriguing elements from the Old Testament is the name of the unspeakable Lord God Almighty 'Jehovah', which means, 'I am that I am'. The true sacred vowels of Jehovah are unknown for we only have the consonants YHWH of which Jehovah is the most widely used. The same applies to the name KHUFU, after Pharaoh Khufu who supposedly built it, which some have translated as 'The Lord protects me'. Here again the vowels are absent, we only have HWFW. It is well known, and the Hebrew texts are quite explicit on this point, that the name YHWH derives from the Hebrew verb HAVA (h) meaning 'I am', and from HWFW (Khufu) to HAVA (h) is linguistically an extremely short step, shorter in fact than the northern English pronunciation of brother is from its southern pronunciation of brother. The ancient Egyptian form HWFU is historically the older of the two and in YHWH we appear to have a Hebrew version of the name HWFW. Another fact in support of this is that the name Jehovah is above all the God of the Exodus and the name appears to have been in free use only during the few weeks between the beginning of the

Exodus and the Israelites' arrival at Mount Horeb where Moses promptly imposes a strict taboo on the name he had himself revealed only a short time before."

"You must have spent a lot of time studying all of this," Paul remarked.

"Aye that I did as well as your father also. But we were fortunate to be privy to sacred texts, scrolls and met people that will not be revealed again until nearer the Age of Aquarius. I think your father came to see it as more of a curse though, whereas I did not...but that is another story for another time," Theodoric replied and paused before continuing. "There are many links with the name Jehovah and the Great Pyramid. The Great Pyramid was known as the building of light and also the way, the same words and meanings are also related to Hermes and the Great Pyramid by way of Gematria. How many times does the saying 'I am the way and the Light' also the Life, occur in the Bible? In Isaiah 26, a reference to Jehovah is very suggestive of the pyramid and its symbolism. Remember the angle of 26 degrees within the Great Pyramid is repeated several times. Is it a coincidence that the following appears in Isaiah 26? The text states 'We have a strong city where walls and ramparts are our deliverance, open the gates, an identical allusion to the Egyptian Osirion, Orion, ritual of the chamber of the open tomb, to let a righteous nation in, a nation that keeps faith'. Jehovah then states that the text is an ever-lasting rock, the paths of the righteous is level and thou markest out the right way for the upright...as clear reference a to the pyramid's passages and symbolism as one can get and not referring to some imagined spiritual wall. Jesus likewise, knowing full well the symbolism of the pyramid, also spoke about it, in particular in Matthew 21:42. 'The stone which the builders rejected has become the chief corner stone.' Jesus declared that Simon, whom he changed his name to Peter to fit the mathematical code, was to become the chief corner stone of his Church. Peter in Gematria equals 755, the perimeter base length in feet of each face of the Great Pyramid is also 755 ft. As Simon, his name did not fit the mathematical code and explains why Jesus changed it to Peter. A nickname for Peter just happens to be Rocky! It is worth pointing out that the Jews brought the sacred cubit from Egypt. The English inch is identical in length to the sacred inch. (Up until the reign of Queen Elizabeth the First.) Moses was the most powerful man in Egypt at the time and if there were many secret measurements, he would certainly have been privy to them. From Moses these measurements percolated down through the priesthood of the Israelites, to Jerusalem and the Jewish nation. To add weight to the theory that Moses was in fact a pharaoh himself, though some in time will confuse these details and perhaps claim that Moses was not a pharaoh but certainly lived during the time of Akhenaten instead. But I am telling you now, he was one and the same...," Theodoric stated confidently.

"Why do you say that some will confuse the details?"

"Because even the name Akhenaten and the language of the ancient Egyptians is being eradicated as we speak, young Paul...to hide the truths of our greater past that is why. But your father took measures to ensure the language would again be understood." Theodoric smiled knowingly. "He and Firgany commissioned many stone carvings with Greek and hieroglyph sentences inscribed upon them. It would not take long to work out how to again read the language of the ancients should all other traces be eradicated."

"And where are they now?"

"That I have no idea," Theodoric laughed. "Understand that even the Egyptians themselves referred to the Pharaoh Akhenaten as the Heretic King. When he left, or died, the priesthood tried to erase all reference to his reign from history. All hieroglyphs detailing his life and reign were defaced. Akhenaten's successors attempted to destroy all record of his existence. Even his name was obliterated from statues and carvings all over Egypt. Akhenaten had been proclaimed a heretic after his death, as a consequence he is now popularly referred to as 'The Heretic King'. Remember that Akhenaten was responsible for the design and use of the Merkaba star as I explained earlier."

"So how exactly is it that you know all of this?"

"Because of copper scrolls and details the founding Templars recovered."

"And where are they now?"

"Most are hidden...but some are with the Pope...and they detail how Akhenaten ruled for seventeen years during the first half of the fourteenth century BC. In the fifth year of his reign, he became inspired by a new monotheistic religion which caused him to leave his capital at Thebes to establish a religious centre at Armana two hundred miles to the north. His new religion was completely revolutionary as he denounced the pantheon of ancient Egyptian gods, chief of whom was Amon, and began to preach the philosophy of a single and only one god, the Aten. Aten was an invisible and omnipresent deity who was pictorially illustrated as the rays of the sun. This sounds very similar to the same all omnipresent single god Jehovah as proclaimed by Moses doesn't it? Not just another one of history's coincidences? It must be remembered that until Moses appeared on the scene, early Hebrews worshiped a variety of gods themselves, only converting to the single deity Jehovah during the Exodus. Likewise, monotheism, a single god religion, was totally unknown in Egypt before this time. Akhenaten's new religion created resentment amongst the priesthood and ruling elite of his day. This fact alone however would not account for the overwhelming paranoia generated after Akhenaten's death and justify the obsessive lengths to which his successors went to eradicate not only his teachings, but also his memory completely. This suggests that Akhenaten was feared even after death. To go to these extreme lengths, the priesthood must have had good reason. They must have held him personally responsible for some huge wrongdoing of an unprecedented scale. Akhenaten was the actual Pharaoh of the Exodus and as Egypt suffered as a direct result of the Pharaoh's apparent actions against the God of Israel, they consequently suffered on a scale never before experienced, and so held him personally responsible."

"So why was he so feared?"

"Because he had gained access to sealed sacred chambers near Giza that revealed man's true past and belief in a single deity...but he was forced to reseal the chamber he had accessed, just like Moses and Aaron...though he was allowed to keep a staff...a staff identical to the one Kratos carries to this day...as well as how to construct the mobile Arks we now all call the Ark of the Covenant. It cannot be argued that he was a religious fanatic responsible for the savage persecution of his opponents as all the limited available evidence is very much to the contrary as it appears that he was totally the opposite to a tyrant. Hieroglyphics that have survived record his decrees ordering the mass release of slaves and banning blood sports. Hymns and writings by Akhenaten himself preach the sanctity of life. It also appears that he was a dreamer, a romantic and possibly an inefficient ruler yet there is nothing to account for the anti-Akhenaten purge that followed his death and swept the entire land of Egypt. Even his new religion, Atenism, was not forced upon his people as most citizens continued to worship as they pleased, and outside Akhenaten's religious city of Armana, religion seems to have been largely ignored. Yet no other Pharaoh is ever known to have aroused such posthumous hostility even towards those who did instigate new religions, persecute opposition or commit acts of heinous cruelty, there was no attempt to obliterate their memory. Their policies were simply annulled and their followers executed. So again we have to ask ourselves, what was so different about the mild mannered Akhenaten?"

"I think I know where this is going. His reign...it coincided with the last passing of the dark sun didn't it?" Paul remarked.

"My word...you are well ahead of me already for I thought it would be a while before we got to that stage...but yes, yes it did. Egypt suffered socially and politically during Akhenaten's reign but it must be noted that his nephew, Smenkhkare, had been made co-ruler and continued to rule after Akhenaten's death. As a co-ruler, why wasn't Smenkhkare also blamed and held jointly responsible alongside Akhenaten? one should ask. Akhenaten it seems was held singularly responsible for the plight of Egypt. Now Akhenaten is thought to have ruled sometime between 1400 and 1350 BC and the dynastic records indicate that he reigned for seventeen years. It is not known exactly how long Smenkhkare ruled alone, for much of it was shared with Akhenaten. Paintings of Akhenaten during his early reign show him alone whereas later depictions show him enthroned alongside his co-ruler Smenkhkare. It would therefore seem that at some time after Akhenaten's move to Armana, the co-regency began. If this co-regency began immediately, Akhenaten's reign would have ended in around 1353 BC. It is more likely that Smenkhkare was appointed co-regent toward the end of Akhenaten's life in a political manoeuvre to avoid civil war. It is therefore assumed that Smenkhkare ruled alone for most of his fifteen years thus dating Akhenaten's rule to around 1382 to 1365 BC. This just happens to tie in with the date for the eruption of Thera, a massive volcano that erupted due to the impact and influence from Marduk as explained to you before."

"So the biblical accounts of the disasters during the exodus were in fact real physical events...yes?"

"Yes they were. Again we have to come back to the question of why Akhenaten was so feared. When he came to power, Egypt was one of the most effective, if not the most effective, military force on earth. Yet by the time he died, Egypt had lost control of half its empire and was in turmoil. It had been believed that this turmoil was caused by civil war and political upheaval, however it was in fact a series of natural catastrophes that were ultimately responsible. Around 1380 BC, intensive flooding destroyed crops and left the nation on the brink of starvation. The natural disasters that befell Egypt at the same time affected the entire globe, was the direct result of the near passing of the tenth planet Marduk, or as also known, Nibiru, which in turn shunted both Mars and the earth dangerously close to each other's orbits thus causing huge energy discharges to be exchanged between the two planets, which in turn momentarily affected their rotations, hence why the eastern hemisphere was in total darkness whilst the western hemisphere was in constant daylight for the same period of time. I would further argue that Akhenaten is one and the same person as Moses hence why the fear of him even after his death. Remember that nobody knows where Moses is actually buried. And as Mars nearly collided with us, a lot of its red soil was deposited across our world. 'Tis why the Nile appeared to run red with blood."

"I have seen that very event in my dreams...from my earliest dreams...I have seen this and...and it is not the first time either...it has happened," Paul exclaimed, looking concerned as the realisation hit him.

"And it shall not be the last time either...hence why our descendants must be made aware so they can prepare in time," Theodoric replied, his tone now quiet and serious. "It must be realised that biblical chronology is very prone to gross numerical exaggeration, symbolic in meaning, and can vary from one version of the Old Testament to another...so Tenno was not that far wrong in his earlier statement. But we are informed as if it was an absolute fact that Rameses the Second was the pharaoh of the oppression who ruled 1290 BC to 1224 BC yet there is however no firm evidence whatsoever to back up this bold assertion. I cannot get into the full debate on this as it would take many hours to explain, suffice to say that all the information provided in the Old Testament indicates that the Exodus, and the Israelites' subsequent forty years in the wilderness, which was more for symbolic reasons with the value forty, occurred sometime between 1450 BC and the middle years of Rameses the Second's sixty-seven year reign. However, the evidence proves, not suggests, I might add, that all these events were in some way connected with the tumultuous period of Egyptian history known as the Amarna age. This period was marked by the succession to the throne in around 1367 BC of the enigmatic king named Amenhotep the Fourth. In the last years of the reign of Amenhotep the Third, Amenhotep the Fourth, his son, became pharaoh and proceeded to take unprecedented steps at introducing a form of monotheistic worship. Amenhotep the Fourth not only transferred his seat of power from the old city of Thebes to a new site nearly two hundred miles downriver to the east bank of the Nile known today as Tell el Amarna, but he also changed his name from Amenhotep, which honoured the god Amun, to the very one and only Akhenaten himself, which means 'glory' or 'spirit'. That is why there is so much confusion over him...this is identical to the one God view of Moses. Now if Moses was a contemporary of this period, surely he would not have opposed such a like minded pharaoh. Being highly intelligent I am sure he would have been foresighted enough to see the value of actually embracing such a concept jointly, not entering into a confrontation. The long-term benefits for all, all striving for the same goal, would be enormous. This is why I can state confidently that Moses is one and the same person as Akhenaten, but as you have been taught...question everything always," Theodoric said and paused as Paul took in all of what he was saying. "Akhenaten was a great artist, poet, mystic and philosopher and was totally unlike any other pharaoh before or since. Akhenaten ruled for just seventeen years with fewer than thirteen of those years based at Tell el Amarna. After this, he simply disappeared completely from the pages of history. Some scholars have argued that he died from the plague that was thought to have swept the entire country and Near East in his later reign. He was, as we saw earlier, briefly replaced by the mysterious figure named Smenkhkare, who was his co-regent. Smenkhkare met an untimely death at a young age to be followed by the boy-king Tutankhaten. After succeeding to the throne, the priests of Amun at Thebes quickly changed his name to Tutankhamun, which is a name that honoured their god. Tutankhamun only reigned for nine years, when he died in mysterious circumstances at the age of just eighteen. Egypt's throne then fell to Akhenaten's old vizier, Aye, and then to Tutankhamun's military commander, Horemheb, who immediately set about erasing all trace of not only Akhenaten's reign, but also every other Amarna king, as in Smenkhkare, Tutankhamun and Aye. He even outlawed their names and Akhenaten's years on the throne became known as the time of the 'Rebel' or 'Rebellion'. Horemheb attacked everything connected with Amarna and the now reviled faith of Aten. He destroyed their temples, defaced their reliefs and chiselled out their inscriptions. All of Akhenaten's family tombs were looted and their mummies desecrated and cast out to disintegrate in the desert. Horemheb even went as far as destroying Akhenaten's gleaming white citadel carting off the material for other building projects. Why weren't Akhenaten's remains treated in the same manner as the rest of his family and his courtiers and thrown into the desert? I can tell you why…because they still feared Akhenaten above and beyond simple fear or hatred. This means that whatever he did must have been absolutely extraordinary. If he had been held responsible for the biblical scale disaster that befell Egypt during the Exodus, they would have simply stated so and, as just mentioned, simply thrown his remains to the ravages of the scorching desert. The anger and fear felt towards Akhenaten would certainly have been felt towards Moses with his all powerful God who had caused such destruction for that is very easy to understand. That is because they are both one and the same person. It also explains why they did not desecrate Akhenaten's body for fear of a reprisal from his God. It is worth noting that the hymn to Aten bore distinct parallels to the verses of Psalm 104, which was first recorded in Solomonic times 980 BC. And remember, all our Christian prayers end with 'Amen', a purely Egyptian word. Know that the Jewish word for 'Lord', Adonai, becomes 'Aten' when its letters are transformed into Egyptian. Also circumcision, a requirement of Hebrew law for every newborn child, was first practised by the ancient Egyptians yet not by any other Asiatic or Middle Eastern culture. In other words, the Jews had clearly inherited the tradition via Moses from the Egyptians. Stating that Moses and Akhenaten are in fact one and the same individual outraged many Muslim leaders your father I dealt with, as Moses is an important prophet in the Qur'an and to say anything that questions it is considered blasphemous…so you must be guarded about whom you discuss these facts with. But also note this, another meaning for Moses simply means 'born of'. The name usually required another name to be added or prefixed to it such as Thothmoses, which meant 'born of Thoth'. Rameses means 'born of Ra' or Amenmosis, 'born of Amen'. Whilst the Moses element is spelt slightly different when rendered into English, they all mean the same. Because of this fact it is very likely that either Moses himself or some later scribe dropped the name of an Egyptian god from his full name. Another similar story to Moses is the birth narrative of Sargon the First, who ruled over Babylon and Sumer hundreds of years prior to Moses, where it states that Sargon's mother set him in a basket of rushes. With bitumen she sealed the lid and cast him into the river, which rose not over his head. How very similar to the birth narrative of Moses can you get? The birth story is almost undoubtedly a fiction created in the later sixth century BC for the birth of the Jewish nation, the ancient theme of creation emerging from the waters. Again this indicates that these events were all symbolically designed to carry the same information and any inherent codes, but simply adopted to a new era, place and peoples."

"I fear I shall never fully learn and understand what you tell me," Paul sighed.

"You look tired. Do you wish for me to stop...and rest?"

"No...I wish to learn as much as possible whilst I can...and before Alisha returns for this all worries her greatly," Paul answered.

"Okay, I shall continue," Theodoric replied and coughed to clear his throat. "It is worth noting that Moses was a skilled performer of magical rituals and was deeply learned in the knowledge of the accompanying spells, incarnations and magical formulas of every description. The miracles that Moses wrought suggest that he was not only a priest, but a magician of the highest order, and perhaps even a Ker Heh, an Egyptian High Priest. In the Bible, Acts 7:22, it states the following," Theodoric explained and quickly flicked through his Bible again. "Ah, here...'And Moses became learned in all the wisdom of the Egyptians, and was mighty in words and in deeds'. The Egyptian third century High Priest Manetho stated that Moses, a son of the tribe of Levi, educated in Egypt and initiated at Heliopolis, became a High Priest of the Brotherhood under the reign of Pharaoh Amenhotep otherwise known as Akhenaten. This at least shows they agree on the same time period. He was elected by the Hebrews as their chief and he adapted to the ideas of his people the science and philosophy which he had obtained from the Egyptian mysteries, proofs of this are to be found in the symbols, in the initiations, and in his precepts and commandments. The dogma of an 'Only God' which he taught was the Egyptian Brotherhood interpretation and teaching of the pharaoh who established the first monotheistic religion known to man. So this is Manetho's account and version as passed down to him. It is highly unlikely that he would have been privy to information that would connect Moses as one and the same. At the end of the day, it is really quite irrelevant exactly who was Moses, the facts are that the ideal of Moses, his laws and his teachings and all the inherent codes within them have survived down through the millennia of time to us now so that we can use that information to recover the lost wisdom of the ancients so we are all ready and prepared for the next time the dark sun passes us."

"But that passing is not for another few hundred years...the time of the Age of Aquarius yes?" Paul asked.

"Yes...but safeguarding that knowledge...that is the almost impossible task when faced with such opposition as established religion..."

"Yes I am beginning to see that."

"Moses also understood that matter consisted of atoms just like the Persian I explained about before, and that these atoms were hard, solid and immutable and that gravity accrued to both atoms and to the bodies they composed. Gravity was proportional to the quantity of matter in every body. The Egyptians concealed mysteries that were above the capacity of the common man under the veil of religious rites and hieroglyphic symbols. It was the most ancient opinion that the planets revolved around the sun, that the earth, as one of the planets, described an annual course about the sun, while by a diurnal motion, it turned on its axis, and that the sun remained at rest. If there are indeed codes stemming from ancient Egypt via Moses and Jesus, how were those codes then carried on until the present? Well you and I both know the answer to that."

"The Knights Templar...or at least the upper inner circle of initiates, the guardians of the Holy Grail," Paul answered.

"And the Prieure de Sion."

"But many people are aware that they supposedly guard the Holy Grail," Paul remarked.

"Many people are indeed aware of that and that King Arthur is connected to the Holy Grail, especially in light of all the new romances being sent out stating as much. But what people are not usually aware of however is that the actual Grail myths are themselves mainly symbolic having been written and constructed years after similar factual events. The reasons why being the new myths carry on the encoded mathematical information and will ensure they continue. It is through the Grail romances connected with King Arthur that many of the sacred details, especially in regard to measurements, were brought out of Egypt via King Solomon's Temple and then back to England. The first transmission of the information which is shrouded in myth and mystery is via the biblical character Joseph of Arimathea who is often associated with the legendary King Arthur and the knights of his round table. They are inextricably linked despite the apparent separation of nearly six hundred years. The Grail myths state that Joseph of Arimathea was a disciple of Jesus Christ and that he fled to England just prior to the Jewish uprising of AD 70 which led to the eventual sacking of Jerusalem by the Romans. The first part of the myth comes directly from the Apocryphal Testament of Nicodimus, the publican who befriended Jesus and arranged for his supposed burial. After Jesus's crucifixion, Mary, his mother, is reported to have gone to live with Joseph for some fifteen years until her death. Later Joseph heads a delegation sent by the Apostle Phillip, consisting of twelve saints according to William of Malmsbury. They escorted with them the Holy Grail, which was at that time manifest in Mary Magdalene and also Josephenes, the son of Jesus, though he is often referred to as being the Son of Joseph. They sailed in the small ship called the 'Mari Stella' the 'Stella Maris' or 'Sea Star' and are reported as landing initially in Southern France with the British delegation, including Josephenes, travelling onwards and arriving at Glastonbury on Easter Eve thirty-one years after Jesus's crucifixion. You are already aware that they all stayed in La Rochelle so I need not repeat all of that," Theodoric stated as Paul nodded yes. "The myth continues that on arrival in Britain, the local king, Arviragus, gave the foreign refugees some land in 'Ynys-Wytrin' a location that also became known as Avalon and is traditionally ascribed to Glastonbury in Somerset, England. Though physically it was identical to the marshlands around Cougnes north of La Rochelle. It was here that Joseph thrust his staff into the ground whereupon it started to grow as a Hawthorn tree, a tree that blossoms in January. A later evangelical mission to North Wales by Joseph and many of his followers saw them imprisoned by a local king. Josephenes appeals personally to another king called Mordrayous to free them. The Welsh king is beaten in battle by Mordrayous, who then takes his land and his daughter Labell. Joseph is released and founds a monastery at Glastonbury where he was to be eventually buried. Later kings such as Marius and Coillus give the monastery further tracts of land, which became famous as the twelve hides of Glastonbury. Now the famous round table linked to King Arthur was first mentioned in Wace of Jersey's 'Roman de Brut' back in 1155 and then again in Robert de Baron's poem 'Joseph d'Arimathie ou le Roman de l'estoire dou Graal et Merlin'. In this poem Joseph was commanded to make a table in commemoration of the Last Supper, with one empty place for that of Judas. This seat was a seat of great peril to be occupied by only the true searcher of the Grail. It has been argued that Joseph of Arimathea was in fact the great-grand-father of Queen Boudicea from Colchester. Note that Colchester's original name was taken from Colchis in Turkey from the Jason and the Argonaut myth and that wild saffron from there was brought to Colchester, called Camuludinum and later Camulod by the Romans. Saffron gave its name to several locations around East Anglia. Camulod with the T and D being interchangeable at the time so that it could just as rightly be spelt as Camulot, the mythical seat of power for King Arthur. It is feasible that Joseph of Arimathea brought with him sacred units of measure from Jerusalem from where the sacred measurements were introduced by Moses who in turn was from Egypt as you know. Also at Glastonbury, there are two small enigmatic tombs...they are both small pyramids. A strange choice of style for a Christian Abbey to incorporate, especially as it would have been anathema to the early Church of Saul. This indicates that the early Church that founded the Abbey at Glastonbury was in fact the Church of James, the brother of Jesus. It appears that Moses brought many Egyptian religious influences with him on his flight from Egypt. We can see direct evidence of many of those influences even to this day. For instance, Christians all around the world still finish their prayers with an intonement to the Egyptian god Amen as I just explained, but Thoth who was known as 'three times great' is identical to the Holy Trinity. So as an initiate and disciple of Jesus, who was in turn a direct descendent of Moses, it is more than probable that Joseph of Arimathea was well educated in the ancient secret rites and sacred measurements. According to various accounts regarding the Holy Grail, it was reputed to be the cup that Jesus used during the Last Supper which eventually became seen as the cup which caught his blood when he was crucified and it then became the vessel containing his blood. It is argued that the Holy Grail is in fact a bloodline from Jesus Christ himself with the inference that when Mary fled to France with Joseph of Arimathea with the Holy Grail, this in actual fact stood for her being with child, Jesus's child. From this bloodline, a long line of heirs was to flow resulting in what became known as the Merovingian bloodline. The cup of the Holy Grail was then brought to England by Joseph of Arimathea and was believed to have miraculous properties. Its subsequent loss by the British was deemed to have disastrous consequences for King Arthur's kingdom. We have already seen earlier the connection of King Arthur's sword Excalibur and its connection to the Great Pyramid. Excalibur is returned to the Lady in the Lake at the end of Arthur's reign. The sword represents wisdom, knowledge, spiritual awareness and compassion as it could only be drawn from the stone by the truly worthy. It could be seen then that this refers to only the truly worthy and enlightened being able to draw it from the stone, as in the Great Pyramid, its secrets and knowledge only to be applied for good and the benefit of others. In the Bible, Jesus speaks of the two edged long sword, which as I demonstrated earlier is numerically identical to Excalibur. The true meanings behind the Grail legends and its hidden wisdom and knowledge had very little to do with the actual historical King Arthur of Britain yet the quest for the Holy Grail is perhaps one of the most haunting themes in Christian history. As already mentioned, the Grail has been viewed as a cup used by Christ at the Last Supper which was recovered from Pontius Pilot by Jesus's uncle Joseph of Arimathea and brought to Britain as a sacred talisman. It was apparently either buried or lost in Britain and became the object of search that lasted many centuries. Legend has it that King Arthur's knights found the Grail by which time it was not only viewed as a holy relic but also as a magical vessel that contained secret wisdom and knowledge. The Grail legends are set apart from other Christian relics or doctrines due to its blend of mysticism, occult and religious connections all at once. Also there are accounts of Joseph of Arimathea's journey from the Holy Land, through Europe to Britain that forms the basis for the belief and validity of the Grail as a physical reality. Hard historical facts recorded in the Gospels state that Joseph and Nicodemus received the body of Christ and buried it, apparently! If Mary Magdalene arrived in Southern France carrying the vessel of the Holy Grail, as symbolised by the cup with Joseph, it is highly probable that in actual reality she was indeed carrying a child, which would in a very real physical sense mean that she was carrying the Holy Blood, the Holy Grail. Eventually from this bloodline, a descendant of Christ would return to Jerusalem unopposed by the Vatican to reclaim his legitimate throne, as indeed was the case, as I shall cover later."

"What do you mean indeed was the case?" Paul asked, puzzled and very curious.

"Survivors of one branch of the bloodline actually went to Rome and had an audience with the Pope to claim back that which was theirs...but the claim was rejected and they were sent away."

"Oh...I do recall some mention of this previously."

"The fact is that Joseph was Jesus's uncle or at least related in some way as he was able to recover Jesus's body. Jesus had been sentenced and crucified as a common criminal, which would have meant that his body would in normal circumstances be buried in a reserved area for criminals only. Under Jewish and Roman law only a relative could claim the body and dispose of it accordingly. Saint Matthew also tells us that Joseph was in fact a wealthy man. He must have been, to provide Jesus with a tomb. He apparently made his fortune from dealing in the tin trade. The traditional journey route of Joseph with his delegates, Mary and the Holy Grail just happens to follow the trade routes for tin as described in detail by the Greek writer Diodorus Siculus shortly before the birth of Jesus. He states that tin was transported at low tide to the island of Ictis, thought to be Saint Michael's Mount in a bay off southern Cornwall, hence the merchants transport the tin on to Gaul where it then takes thirty days of journeying to carry it in sacks upon horses to the mouth of the river Rhone. Traditions in France, western Ireland, Gloucester, North London and the Cornish tin mining region all tell of Joseph's involvement in the tin trade. A Cornish tradition is emphatic in stating that Joseph made voyages to Cornwall in his own ships and that he once brought the young Jesus with him and his mother when they landed at Saint Michael's Mount. Jesus visiting Britain is historically very feasible and backed up by many local legends. Very little is known of Jesus's early life from the age of twelve to thirty when his ministry started. It is certainly widely believed that he travelled extensively abroad. There is even a 'Jesus Well' at the mouth of the river Camel in Cornwall en route to Glastonbury. Eight miles north of Glastonbury there is a prevailing legend that states that Jesus once stayed there. There is a church there that has a story relating to a strange energy emanating from a cave beneath the church itself. A common saying in the area is: 'as sure as our Lord was at Priddy'. We can be quite certain of the early links between the Holy Land and Britain that are supported by historical evidence and that the Christian religion was practised in Britain very shortly after Jesus's death. The sixth century writer Gildas states that it began in the last year of the reign of Tiberius, which was only four years after Jesus's crucifixion. Also Glastonbury, known by its ancient name of Glastonia, is specifically mentioned in religious texts as already having a church even before Christian missionaries of the Catholic Church arrived in the sixth century AD. All the evidence suggests that Joseph was indeed Jesus's uncle and that after the crucifixion he did in fact bring the Holy Grail to England...and your family from your mother's side come from Britain...," Theodoric explained and paused as he looked at Paul.

"Please continue," Paul remarked and blinked his tired eyes and clasped his hands together.

"Okay, but stop me if this becomes boring or you tire...Now Christian legends of the Holy Grail claim the original Grail legends were of a pre-Christian Celtic symbolism simply disguised to keep it alive in the trappings of Christianity itself. The Celtic traditions were taken from an even earlier ancient source of wisdom and knowledge that was directly connected with ancient Egypt, including connections of the Uffington white horse, which is in fact a Celtic representation of a feline animal symbolically identical to the Sphinx...not a horse. But according to some, the real bearer of the Grail was not Joseph, but a powerful pagan god named Bran. In ancient Celtic myth, he was the possessor of a magical cauldron capable of bringing people back to life. This does not necessarily mean bringing back to life physically from the dead, but back into a spiritual life just as the later Qumranians referred to those outside of their community as being dead. This was a symbolic death and newly baptised members could be raised from the dead symbolically when they became full members within the community. There is a lot of confusion and mystery surrounding the actual Grail itself as it is presented in many different formats. Early Christian documents generally depict the Grail as a large dish containing the host for some unnamed person and were thought to contain mystical secrets. King Arthur's knight, Sir Percival, underwent many spiritual trials in order to penetrate the mysteries. This indicates that the actual quest for the Holy Grail is indeed linked to spiritualism and that the individual who seeks it must be pure of heart as testified by various accounts. The legends surrounding the ancient Egyptian 'Chambers of Creation' state that it would only be found by those individuals deemed worthy and pure of heart as well. This was a supposedly a pre-Deluge temple set out with a small pyramidian at its centre surrounded by a further twelve circular chambers that contained artefacts and proofs of mankind's true origins and past. Sealed away hermetically by the god Thoth, in Greek Hermes, where we get the root for the words hermetically sealed. It was this chamber of creation, as also mentioned in other holy books where Moses commands Aaron to return some artefacts prior to leaving on their Exodus as the details are meant for later generations' benefits to help guide them in the last days, as the Knights Templar are aware of. The Grail only became associated as a dish much later in the Grail legends. Earlier it had been more common to associate it with the vessels and cups of Celtic myths. It must be noted that the Celtic Bran apparently was in possession of one of which it was said 'the virtue of the cauldron is this. A man slain today if, cast into the cauldron, by tomorrow he will be as well as he was at best, save that he will not have the power of speech.' It was reported that this cauldron could also determine the weak from the brave with the following statement. 'If meat for a coward were put in it to boil, it would never boil, but if meat for a brave man were put in it, it would boil quickly.' There are several other Celtic myths relating to dishes, including one that belonged to the King of Rhydderch in which whatever food was asked for, it was instantly obtained. Another legend is that of the horn of Bran, the Niggard from the North, and the Crock and dish of Rhygenydd the Celtic, which all claim the same miraculous powers. They all have direct parallels with so many descriptions of the knights watching the entrance of the Grail at Arthur's court, after which every knight had whatever meat and drink he most desired. From all the mass of information relating to the Grail romances, one thing is very clear, they have in the main been composed within our century by roving clerics and conteurs known as Bards, who have used Celtic source material and disguised it within Christian doctrines. The question that begs to be answered is just what was it they wanted to preserve? What is the message they are trying to carry across the millennia of time and why hide it within symbolism and esoterica?" [73]

"I do not know yet...but I intend to," Paul answered.

"Good man. That is the spirit. 'Tis blindingly obvious they are trying to guarantee that ancient knowledge pertaining to some great secret is being woven into a new palatable story suited to our time thus ensuring its continued survival up until a time on the future. The fact that it has to be carried across to a later time indicates that the original composers are aware that whatever the secret is that was to be revealed, now is certainly not the correct time. Clearly then it is being preserved for a much later generation."

"That I can understand quite easily," Paul commented and thought for a few moments.

"There is a Druidic revival in Wales at this very time where the Grail legends are being developed further. It is too simplistic to state that they are just resuscitating old pagan religious ideas that had defied earlier Roman attempts to suppress them and also the early Christian missionaries, as they were in fact maintaining the flow of the esoteric wisdom of the ancients. It is no coincidence that Bran, the magical cauldron and the story of a miraculous child who possessed a secret doctrine are all part of the same revival. This revival has almost identical symbolism to both Jesus as a child and also the Egyptian God Horus, the son of Isis and Orion. I know that Thomas has taken a great interest in these Grail stories and I think you will find that is one of his main reasons for volunteering to stay with us. He writes notes often. He has told me that he believes you and Alisha are connected to the Grail legends and that one day he will return to his homelands near Germany and compile his own story..."

"Really...is that allowed? I mean should he be allowed to?" Paul asked, puzzled at Theodoric's revelation.

"Hey, you know these Germanic types. Very efficient and smart. I believe he would do well in writing such things. Far better than I for sure."

"I know he is particularly fond of Percival, though he keeps calling him Parzifal as he cannot quite pronounce his name properly," Paul said and smiled.

"Well if he does, I have certainly given him some early pointers," Theodoric laughed and winked.

"Such as?" Paul asked.

"Oh such as explaining that the true Grail quest is one of a spiritual quest to provide a key to enlightenment, details of a chaste order of knights who reside in the Munsalvaesche, the Grail castle, and are sustained 'by virtue of a stone most pure'. I did strongly hint that such a chaste order was in fact his men but he roared with laughter when I said that."

"Why did he laugh?"

"Because his men are far from chaste...I think the local whore house here has never had such regular customers who pay so well...," Theodoric explained and laughed.

"What...really? Do they honestly go there?" Paul asked, bemused.

"Yes...except Percival...well not yet anyway," Theodoric explained smiling broadly.

"I see," Paul replied and thought for a few moments before continuing the conversation. "You mentioned something about a stone most pure...is that the Kabba Stone in Mecca?"

"Hah...no...well actually it is part of the same...let me explain. The Great Pyramid itself was known as a building of stone most pure and undefiled in an idolatrous land as outlined in Isaiah in the Bible. As I explained to Thomas about that chaste order of knights, 'that never is a man so ill but that, if he sees the Grail on any day, he is immune from death during the week that follows. Besides, his looks never change...he retains the same appearance as on the day he saw the stone. Whether it be maid or man, even if he beholds the stone two hundred years, he keeps the appearance of his prime, except that his hair turns grey...The stone is called the Grail'. Identical allusions to these have been made by mystics and occultists across the millennia of time regarding the magical properties within the Great Pyramid itself so that is why I explained as such. In view of all the many other mathematical connections from Gematria relating to the Great Pyramid, I can confidently state the Grail legends certainly indicate and point towards a connection between the two."

"Is that not wrong to say such things for Thomas will believe every word of it?" Paul said and shook his head.

"Good, I hope he does believe every word of it for it is in fact true, young Paul. I can also tell you now quite categorically that the Templars were not formed in 1118, 1119 nor 1120 as so many claim. And certainly not to protect pilgrim routes to Jerusalem. I have documents that prove that the last Count Henry of Champagne, prior to the one you know, was actually setting out for Jerusalem to meet with members from the Knights Templar as early as 1114 before the Bishop of Chartres called him back. There is overwhelming evidence that proves that the nine original Templars never actually defended the pilgrim routes as to do so with just nine of them would have been an impossible task. It is also known that they spent many years carrying out excavations under the temple in Jerusalem itself looking for something. Huh and you have experienced yourself what occurs there...All the Knights Templar took the same vows as monks of poverty, chastity, obedience and were religious as well as a military force hence why they are frequently termed as warrior monks. They called themselves the 'Poor Knights of Christ', who adopted two knights riding on one horse as their symbol. The nine original knights stayed in Jerusalem for nine years and Baldwin the Second, who had succeeded the earlier Baldwin the First, who accepted the crown of Jerusalem but died in 1118, granted the Templars the use of the Al Aqsa Mosque on the temple Mount of Jerusalem as their headquarters. Though it is not really a mosque! You already know how secretive and very mysterious the chivalric order is...They now hold the deeds and titles to many tracts of land both in Europe and England. The order was founded by French knights led by a man named Hugues de Payens, meaning 'of the pagans', after being inspired by Saint Bernard of Clairvaux, who was also the founder of the Cistercians. After the knights had taken residence near to the Church of the Holy Sepulchre, which was built on the site of the Temple of Solomon, they immediately started searching for some kind of buried arte-fact or treasure and, as said, they did not actually ever protect the pilgrims as origi-nally claimed at all. These original knights went on to found the military Order that has become one of the most powerful forces in the Christian world owing allegiance to the Pope alone. Many nobles and wealthy landowners join the Order handing over their own deeds to their lands. Due to the Templars' international connections, they soon became the first bankers, who have introduced the system of bonds and cheques that can be exchanged for goods and services in parts of the Christian world. This only serves to further increase their wealth." [74]

"But you too were once a Templar...a fact you hid from me," Paul interrupted.

"Yes I was. And yes I hid that fact...though not very well you have to agree, eh?" Theodoric laughed in response.

"Well your surcoat did give it away," Paul smiled back.

"Look, the Templars, although swearing sole allegiance to the Pope, are none the less strangely independent from his authority and are in real terms led by their Grand Master. The Grand Master of the Prior de Sion, or Prieure de Sion, which is the political arm of the Templar organisation, is often referred to as the 'Nau-tonnier', which is an old French word meaning 'Navigator' or 'Helmsman'. Count Henry of Champagne was one of the Order's Grand Masters as was your father."

"What? I thought he rejected that position?" Paul asked, confused.

"Then you thought wrong. 'Tis why he was also named John," Theodoric replied and sat back and folded his arms.

"But you said the name was symbolic and out of respect and memory of Saint John...so why did you not tell me this in Jerusalem when Count Henry was explain-ing it all to me then?"

"'Twas considered too soon to tell you...then!"

"Too soon, but now is okay?"

"Yes. Now you know and understand far more, and nor will you be so quick to speak of or reveal it for you know at first hand the dangers it brings. Also, it means that perhaps now if Count Henry steps down or falls in battle, you would actually consider taking back on the mantle your father walked away from...continue the line as it should have been."

"No. My father must have had good reason to walk away, and I must confess that much of what I hear and learn concerns me, especially the deceit and hidden truths I am constantly being made aware of."

"That may appear as such, but it is sadly a necessary evil to protect a greater good. You cannot always remain so pure in a filth ridden world."

"Perhaps not...but I can try," Paul replied feeling awkward.

"Would you rather I end this conversation now and never speak of such matters again?" Theodoric asked and leaned forward looking at Paul intently.

"You know full well I do not wish that..."

"Good, you had me worried there...just for a moment," Theodoric smiled. "And you do remember then how the Order was originally founded...?"

"Yes, from that monastery set up in Jerusalem founded by members from the 'Order of the Sword', also known as the 'Order of the Tau', but who can be traced back to Altopascio in Italy, who then moved to Orval in Belgium...the one founded by mysterious monks in 1070 from Calabria in Southern Italy. They were the ones who went on to Jerusalem finally becoming the Order of Sion, or as you say Prieure de Sion, the hidden political and administrative wing that set the wheels in motion for the formation of the Knights Templar and of which Count Henry is presently its Grand Master," Paul detailed.

"Impressive. Could not have said it better myself," Theodoric remarked. "Of course you do know the 'Order of the Sword', is an allegorical allusion to the two edged long sword that Jesus proclaimed in the New Testament and again recounted and updated a thousand years later into the Grail romances as Excalibur?" he asked.

"Yes, with that sword representing knowledge and wisdom being drawn from the stone. The group was also known as the 'Order of the Triple Tau' based in Calabria, Southern Italy but originally from earlier origins in Palestine having fled after the fall of Acre. This became known more publicly during the ninth and tenth centuries as 'The Order of St James of Altopascio'. This group stretches back to the Essenes and further back into antiquity. From this group however knowledge regarding hidden secrets eventually resulted in Godfrei de Bouillon relinquishing all his rights in France, and heading for Jerusalem and ultimately the first crusade. Pope Urban the Second and Saint Bernard of Clairvaux were instrumental in this...," Paul recounted in detail. [75]

"Now you are just showing off," Theodoric commented and laughed and looked at Paul proudly. He shook his head, impressed. "The Templars wield great power for they are constantly involved in high level and international politics dealing with nobles and monarchs throughout the lands. In Britain, the Master of the Temple regularly attends the king's parliament and is viewed and recognised as the head of all religious orders, even taking precedence over all priors and abbots in the country. And as you have witnessed here in Alexandria, the Templars' political influence even extends to the Muslim world. Imagine the great you could do if you entered that sphere of power and influence but remained grounded as you are now."

"No thank you for I have seen what that power does to people. Count Henry aside perhaps...but no, 'tis not for me, I know that now," Paul answered.

"Look, Paul, as you are now acutely aware, Jesus survived the ordeal of crucifixion and Mary Magdalene gave birth to his child who, as already mentioned previously, led to the family tree which finally culminated in the Merovingian bloodline of which noble households all across Europe now try to marry into in order to claim legitimacy and claim a royal blood descent. But your family tree also comes from that line...on both yours and Alisha's sides. Of all the claimants ever, you, and especially Arri, have more rightful claim and legitimacy than all the others. Imagine what you could do if you ruled. The peace you could bring."

"Theo, you are making me feel uncomfortable. 'Tis not what I wish for or desire, especially for Arri."

"Paul...that is precisely why you would make a great noble and humble leader," Theodoric began to say then paused for several long minutes as he looked down. "I am sorry. Of course you are correct. 'Tis a mistake I made with your father. I shall not mention such a stupid notion again...I am sorry," Theodoric said and looked up at Paul and sighed.

"I do not wish to offend you, Theo, but my father must have had good reason to walk away for I am certain it was not through lack of courage," Paul said softly, seeing the pained expression upon Theodoric's usually happy face.

"No, Paul, the error is mine. Your father sought a better way of safeguarding the line...the Crimson Thread, as well as a better way of carrying the sacred hidden knowledge across time."

"How...how did he propose to do that?" Paul asked, intrigued.

"He sought to hide your family tree away completely...to let all the other nobles and royals fight between themselves if necessary, whilst your line remained anonymous...hidden. But also to use artists, poets, story tellers and architects to encode the secrets from our past. To have them carry it across time within a brotherhood of love and mutual respect whatever your race, colour or religious background."

"Such as people like Firgany?"

"Yes exactly so. Your father accepts the need for a political wing as such and a military arm to help guarantee and act as guardians of the sacred knowledge, but he also saw the need for a new kind of Order based upon peace, for he senses a time when the Church and other Orders will turn upon the Templars and try to utterly eliminate them from the pages of history and all that they stand for...just like what happened to the Moses, Akhenaten, you now know all about," Theodoric explained, looking sad. "Your father and Firgany both knew and became aware of hidden powers and messages within the landscape that invoke energies through rituals and that also their esoteric knowledge could be incorporated into the hidden geometry you will now find within the proportions of the cathedrals and churches the Order now builds. He hides the very secrets in plain sight...a genius!"

"I always knew that of him," Paul sighed and wondered where he was and what he was doing at that very moment.

 1 – 21

"Before we end this conversation, I need to explain more about the word Baphomet, which is revered to such an extent that it borders on idolatry by some Templars. Just in case you ever find yourself being accused of devil or idol worshipping. You see Baphomet is associated with an apparition of a bearded head. Some will tell you it is in fact a corrupted form of the name of Muhammad. But it is more like the Arabic 'Abufihamet', which is pronounced in Moorish Spanish as

'Bufihimat', which literally means 'Father of Understanding' or 'Father of Wisdom'. These are identical allusions to the ancient Egyptian God Thoth known as Hermes to the Greeks as I keep saying! Father in Arabic also implies 'source'. Here we have a definite connection of the Templars with the ancient Egyptian myths. And sorry to repeat this but I must so you remember it, that the Templar head is known as 'Caput LVIIIM' meaning 'Head 58m'. The Giza pyramid's layout as connected to an 8 x 8 grid square layout which has a Golden Mean proportion on a ratio of 5:8. The M is actually the zodiac sign for Virgo. I can tell you now that many cathedrals now standing and others yet to be built as planned, are all positioned exactly to mirror the constellation of Virgo. Also the very significance of the value of 58 relates to the Star Sirius in 10,500 BC and the Great Pyramid."

"How can you state such a date of great antiquity?" Paul asked quizzically.

"Easy, for the ancients tell us so in their own words as recovered in their many writings and teachings...of which I shall teach you all about."

"I look forward to that. But I would so very much like to learn more about my ancestral family, for I truly know nothing and that which I thought I did, I now know to be wrong...much is hidden from me."

"Okay," Theodoric said and sighed. "Let me tell you that during the First and Second Crusades, the Merovingian kings wore the crown of the Kingdom of Jerusalem and were protected by the Order of the Temple and the Prieure de Sion. Also the Merovingian kings were referred to as the 'long haired monarchs' as they did not cut their hair just like Samson in the Old Testament where his strength came from. I have already pointed out Samson's connection to the constellation of Orion and similar biblical connections. Their hair supposedly contained their virtue, the essence and secret of their power. Well you know why hair is important. The Merovingians took this belief very serious, and in AD 754 when Childeric the Third was deposed and imprisoned, his hair was ritually shaved off at the express command of the Pope. It is important to realise that the Merovingian kings were not regarded as kings in the modern sense of the word, but were regarded as priest-kings...the embodiment of the Divine which is identical to the status of the ancient Egyptian Pharaohs and the Judaic Messiah. They were also viewed and accepted as rightful and duly acknowledged kings without any prior upheavals, turmoil, usurpation or extinction of an earlier regime as typified by other bloodlines across Europe. The Merovingian line takes its name from a unique and elusive member of its historical bloodline who was known as Merovech or Meroveus. He was apparently a semi-supernatural figure worthy of any classical myth. His name even bears witness to his miraculous origin and character as it echoes the French word for 'mother' as well as both the French and Latin words for 'sea'. Again here we have a connection with water and water as you know represents spirit. Not only that but according to tradition, Merovee was born of two fathers. When pregnant by her husband King Clodio, Merovee's mother supposedly went swimming in the ocean where it is said she was seduced, or raped, by an unidentified creature known as a Quinotaur, whatever one of those was. It was apparently some form of beast of Neptune from beyond the sea. This beast impregnated the lady a second time. When Merovee was born there allegedly flowed in his veins a comingling of two different bloods, as in the blood of a Frankish king and the blood of a mysterious aquatic, spiritual creature. This is almost identical to the accounts of King Arthur and his connection with the Fisher King. This type of legend was quite common in the ancient world as well as across Europe as they were symbolically or allegorically masking some concrete historical fact. It clearly indicates some form of intermarriage of two bloodlines, one of which is special as it is related to aqua, water, which as we know is symbolic for spiritual. A pedigree has been deliberately transmitted through the mother, as in Judaism for instance where dynastic lines were mingled through marriage. The Franks became allied by blood with a special bloodline that originated from beyond the sea...the bloodline that Mary brought with her accompanied by Joseph of Arimathea from the Holy Land. The historical facts of this union became symbolised in the subsequent fable of the sea creature designed to be esoteric and only understood by those initiated into its secret meanings."

"And both my bloodline and Alisha's are connected to these Merovingians?"

"Yes...an absolute simple and emphatic yes!"

Paul raised his sword and untied it and placed it upon the table.

"Then please explain, if we have the time what the triple Tau is all about?" Paul asked and pushed the sword toward Theodoric. "You covered it briefly in Jerusalem but I know there is more."

"To fully understand the meaning of the triple Tau, we must look at what is called the Star of David. David did not invent it but Jesus used it and positioned himself to be the 'Star of David' as prophesied of old, which held many esoteric meanings. It is also formed by overlaying two pyramids. I have already detailed the Merkaba star connections so it should come as no surprise to learn that this symbol does not appear in any ancient Hebrew books on religious life, and is only in use in the very distant past of Judaism as an occasional decorative motif along with Middle Eastern images, including the Swastika. It is now becoming popular in a large number of Christian churches, especially those erected by the Knights Templar. It is very rarely, if ever, used within synagogues at this present time. But notice that if the two lateral lines of the Star of David are removed, leaving the upward and downward pointing arrows of priest and king, the result is the stonemason's square and compasses. The priestly or heavenly pyramid becomes the stonemason's square, an instrument used to measure and ascertain the trueness and uprightness of buildings, and figuratively, human goodness, the quality that the Egyptians called 'Ma'at'. The kingly or earthly pyramid is depicted as the compass, which marks the centre of the circle from which no Master Mason can materially err...that is the extent of the power of the king or ruler. This can be associated with the circles of the Vesica Pisces and the circles involved in sacred geometry, which the Templars are certainly familiar with. The Great Pyramid is directly linked with this symbolism, one in the sense of the compass and square representing the pyramid shape, and secondly, in the sense that the Star of David is made up from two pyramids. It would be logical therefore that the symbol of the unified Messiah ship of Jesus should be the mark of Christianity itself, as in the Star of David, which of course it was for a short while and the symbol for Judaism was the cross.

Not the four pointed cross of later Christian design, but the cross known as the 'Tau', which is the shape of the cross upon which Jesus was crucified. For this 'Tau' was the acknowledged and accepted cross and mark of Yahweh, God and which the Kenites bore on their foreheads long before Moses came across them in the wilderness of the Sinai. It looks identical to a capital T. It was also the magical mark painted on the doors during the Passover. The actual later Christian crucifix style cross is in fact derived from an ancient Egyptian hieroglyph. This hieroglyph had the very precise meaning of 'Saviour'. This is translated into Hebrew as 'Joshua', which in turn translates into Greek as 'Jesus'. So here you can see that the shape of the crucifix is not a symbol of Jesus, it is his name itself! The other main symbol from early Christianity is the sign of the fish, the Vesica Pisces. This symbol is in fact a very ancient badge of priestliness and was the symbol of the Nazarean party. It was used by Christians to identify their holy places in Jerusalem at the end of the first century AD. This was the only symbol open to them at the time. Also, if Jesus were indeed an initiate of the Great Pyramid's symbolism, he would have been more than aware of the Vesica Pisces's importance to it. Also John the Baptist was an initiate of the Great Pyramid and it has been argued that he was the one who adopted the symbol. Coincidentally, the name 'Nazarean' is a form of the word 'Nazrani', which means both 'little fishes' and 'Christians' in modern Arabic exactly as it did in Aramaic two thousand years ago. Now it is well known that James the Just became the first bishop, in Hebrew 'Mebakker', and that he took to wearing a mitre as a badge of office. All bishops now wear this. Its origin is without doubt attributed to have come out of Egypt with Moses."

"Mebakker...my Lord that is the very name Kratos called himself in my dreams many times," Paul interrupted excitedly.

"Well I guess we could call Kratos a bishop I suppose...but mark my earlier arguments that Moses and Akhenaten were one and the same as they take on more credibility when it is realised that the mitre, with its split front and rear sections and its tail, is identical to a modern bishop's head-dress and known to have come via the Nazareans from Egypt. Not only that, but the actual hieroglyph image of a mitre stood for 'Amen', the creator god of Thebes that was later merged with the Lower Egyptian Sun God Re, as in Amen-Re. I must also tell you that the ancient Egyptian fabled chambers of creation were linked to Thoth, Hermes, and that he had hidden sacred books away, an almost identical symbolic enactment by Moses. You see, apart from the known books attributed to Moses that have survived, it is known that a far larger collection originally existed as Tenno so kindly pointed out. One such book that has survived is the 'Assumption of Moses' which is known to be an Essene work. It details instructions given by Moses to Joshua."

"I never knew there were other books about Moses...I did know that many books were discarded at the council of Nicea in AD 325, or there about," Paul remarked.

"'Tis one of the few paragraphs I can actually spout from memory...I think," Theodoric joked and coughed briefly. "It went like this...Receive thou this writing that thou mayest know how to preserve the books which I shall deliver unto thee and thou shalt set them in order and anoint them with oil of Cedar and put them away from the beginning of the creation of the world, until the day of repentance in the visitation wherewith the Lord shall visit thee in consummation of the end of the days."

"So it speaks of secret books being given to Joshua by Moses to keep hidden," Paul remarked.

"Exactly! This is clearly a symbolic reference to sacred hidden books of antiquity as it states, quite contradictory and impossible to have been the case, that he had made them from the beginning of the creation of the world. Moses being privy to all the secrets of the ancient Egyptians would have been well aware of the sacred books hidden away by Thoth, Hermes. As he had clearly used many other symbolic stories of Egyptian origin, we can immediately see here his intention of carrying over the sacred buried books myth into his new monotheistic religion. It is important to note that the character of 'Hiram Abif', who was the builder of Solomon's Temple, was murdered by three of his own men. He was an Egyptian murdered because he refused to reveal his secret king making rituals that were used to anoint and validate a pharaoh's position to the throne, and also enabled the pharaoh to become a star and join Osiris in the heavens after death. Hiram Abif was none other than the Egyptian King Seqenenre Tao the Second. However, the actual story of Hiram Abif is also a symbolic amalgamation of two important stories that were deliberately linked to form a basis of a moral code. The Hiram of biblical origin is of Israelite blood by his mother's side and Tyrian on his father's side. He therefore symbolised the union of two peoples who were both antagonistic towards each other and opposed in religion, yet now united in one man. 'Hiram' is short in Hebrew for 'Ahiram' meaning 'my brother is exalted'. In addition, Hiram Abif is described as being 'most wise' and imbued with prudence and understanding. Hiram Abif also denotes from the Hebrew 'Av' meaning 'father' or 'leader' that was the Chief Builder of the Temple of Jerusalem. All these are historical facts. The biblical scriptures are very quiet in relation to Hiram Abif's death and hint at his mysterious demise. A man so important in his position as to have been called the favourite of two kings, of Israel and Tyre, would hardly have passed into oblivion when his labours were complete without so much as a mention, unless his death had taken place in such a manner as to render a public account of it improper. As a consequence it was kept secret within a society and later adopted as a symbolic vehicle for moral conduct and rituals. Even if the all-important account of Hiram Abif proved utterly to be just a myth from two amalgamated sources, it would not in the slightest way affect the validity of its message. The legend relating to him, just like the myths and legends surrounding King Arthur, are of no real narrative value, but are of immense importance to a symbolic point of view illustrating one of the most vital philosophical and religious truths, namely the dogma of the immortality of the soul. If the soul is in fact immortal, then this would give us yet another very good reason why the ancients went to such lengths to preserve their wisdom and knowledge for future generations, for they would be those very later generations themselves."

"So I keep hearing. That worries me for Kratos spoke with Alisha in private and swore her to secrecy, even though my father said there should never be secrets between a husband and wife."

"Why does it worry you then?"

"Because he said that I would never lose Alisha's love...that does not mean I will not lose her though does it...in this life time?"

"Sometimes it does not pay to think too much...and in theory, keeping no secrets is preferable and wise...but not realistic in this world."

"How do you mean?"

"You love Alisha yes...yet you have a place in your heart for Stephanie...am I correct?"

"Oh my Lord...was it that obvious?" Paul asked shocked and immediately looked around the room to check no one else was able to hear.

"To me, yes!" Theodoric smiled. "Your secret is safe with me."

"I feel ashamed for how I felt...and humbled that Alisha has the honesty and integrity to be able to tell me of her feelings toward Nicholas. That makes her a better person than I."

"Rubbish. Women act and think differently. Trust me on that. Tell her by all means if it makes you feel better...but it certainly will not make her feel better," Theodoric explained and looked at Paul for several minutes in silence. "Now come on, we have much else to discuss whilst they are away."

"Please do continue," Paul replied and feigned a brave smile.

"Fact and imagination, the real ideal, may be closely united when the goal permits. The Hiram Abif story, put simply, ensures that key elements of a code are carried across the millennia of time as they have been. We know from the story that the morning star in the east is of importance and that the direction or position relating to a northeasterly direction is of major importance as it is all covered within the story. You should acquaint yourself with it thoroughly if you can. Symbolism within the order that carries the story also relates and keeps pointing back to Egypt and the Giza plateau and certainly pyramids in one form or another. The Second Book of Chronicles states that three distinct categories of workmen were involved in the construction of Solomon's Temple. They were the bearers, the hewers of stones and the overseers. The actual sacred codes of antiquity were encoded within the dimensions of ancient temples across the world, and now cathedrals of England and Europe, that all connect them to a single source and theme...that theme being primarily celestial in its symbolism and relating to a sacred hidden treasure..."

"So an understanding of geometry and the land is essential?"

"Yes, and an understanding of maps is truly important...an interest you already have."

"Great! So as Kratos told me, I volunteered for all of this. It perhaps explains my interest in maps," Paul mused and shook his head.

"Yes...and it is all connected to sacred geometry, cathedrals and sacred sites as I keep telling you. Would you like me to start you on a path of discovery about it all?" Theodoric asked and poured himself some clear water.

"Yes...as it appears I am destined to learn these matters," Paul replied.

"Paul...sarcasm does not suit you...we can leave it of you wish, for you are master of your own destiny whatever you think ultimately as are we all."

"Sorry Theo. It just feels like I am being pushed," he started to explain but paused. "No, not pushed, guided I guess."

"Good, at least you realise that," Theodoric said and smiled broadly and sipped some of his drink. "I will start then by getting you to look at certain numerical figures encoded in the Book of Revelation in the New Testament in regard to measurements of our planet, showing that the mysterious authors of the text were fully aware of the earth's dimensions. Yes?"

"Yes, please do."

"Okay, then know that in Revelation, we are told that the New Jerusalem is constructed in the form of a large square with the perimeter being 12,000 furlongs. Twelve thousand furlongs is equal to 31,680 feet. Well it just so happens that if we draw a square around the earth's circumference to fit exactly around its equator, the distance is equal to 31,680 miles...but it will be many hundreds of years before the rest of the world catches up on these facts! At Stonehenge in England, the width of each of its lintels, the top sections that form a circle on top of the sarsen stones, is equal to 31.680 inches with the circumference of its lintel ring equalling 316.8 feet, the diameter being 50.4 feet. This figure, with an added zero, can also be obtained from 1 x 2 x 3 x 4 x 5 x 6 x 7, which equals 5040; 7 x 8 x 9 x 10 equals 5040 and 5040 is also the exact measurement of the ancient Greek mile. As you shall learn, these details have direct relevance to the ancient Egyptian Edfu building texts, which detail the layout of the 'Chambers of Creation' in identical layout to the above. You see, the measurement of 3,168, 316.8 and 31,680 are all prominent in the construction and layout of Glastonbury Abbey, Glastonbury being known as an ancient and prehistoric site for religious worship and Celtic Druidism. It was also the site of the first Christian church anywhere in the world. Saint Joseph of Arimathea, as I explained earlier, after the crucifixion journeyed to Britain, arriving at Glastonbury. On Wearyall Hill on the Isle of Avalon, Glastonbury, he struck his pilgrim's staff into the ground where it took root and blossomed into the Holy Thorn, the descendants of which still grow there to this day. On a site below this, Saint Joseph built a church on a plot of land consisting of twelve hides or 1,440 acres. One hide equals 120 acres. Here the early Christians founded their first church and dedicated it to the Virgin Mary. In the Doomsday Book, the twelve hides of Glaston were to be forever exempt from taxes. The king's writ does not run within its boundaries. Glastonbury has always been held in special regard and is unique amongst sanctuaries in Britain. To this day it is still a place of constant pilgrimage. Glastonbury is shrouded in mysteries and legends dealing with the Holy Grail and King Arthur and is often called the English Jerusalem. The original Saint Mary Chapel was laid out to incorporate the dimensions of the Vesica Pisces and the twelve hides overlaid with a grid of 74 one-foot squares were later incorporated into the Abbey itself. The ground plan of the New Jerusalem as given in the New Testament Book of Revelations is identical almost to that given by Plato of his allegorical city Atlantis, the twelve hides of Glaston, and the ground plan of Stonehenge. The following are the dimensions to the ground plan of the first Christian settlement at Glastonbury."

Fig. 48:

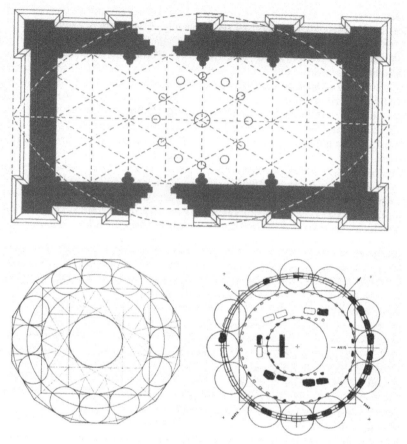

"I recall my father had many drawings of Glastonbury Abbey."

"I bet he did! There are twelve small circles arranged in groups of three that represent, in an astronomical context, the seasons of the moon, 1,080 is important in Gematria and also equals the radius of the moon giving a diameter of 2,160 miles in case you are not aware, and the months of the Great Year, each of whose months consisted of 2,160 years. There are 2,160 miles in the moon's diameter, as also equals one complete zodiacal procession of thirty degrees. Each of the twelve circular cells measures 21.60 feet. The circle that passes through the middle of the cells measures 316.8 feet in circumference, or a hundredth part of six miles. The circle through the centre of the small circles has a diameter of 100.8 feet. The circle within the square has a diameter of 79.20 feet. As a scheme of cosmology, the diagram can be measured in units of 100 miles instead of feet. The diameter of the circle within the square then becomes 7,920 miles, the diameter of the earth, and the diameter of the small circles equals 2,160 miles, which equals the moon's diameter as said. The circle with a diameter of 79.20 feet within the square, when multiplied by 4, 4 being the four sides of the square, we get 316.8 feet, which, as just mentioned earlier, is the circumference of the circle that runs through the centres of the twelve cell circles. The area of the square containing the circle with a diameter of 79.20 feet is equal to 0.144 acres, which means that the side of the square is equal to a hundredth part of the side of a square containing an area of twelve hides, which equals 7,920 feet, and 7,920 thousand feet equals 12,000 furlongs, which, as we know, equals the length of the side of the New Jerusalem as given in Revelation xxi. Four times 7,920 equals 31,680 feet, which equals the perimeter of New Jerusalem; 31,680 feet equals the perimeter of the twelve hides of Glaston; 31,680 miles equals the perimeter of the square containing the earth. Pliny, in his 'Natural History' stated that 3,168,000 miles was the measure round the whole earth. Just two zeroes incorrect! It is also worth noting that the entire geometric image of cosmology can be projected, in feet, over the site of Stonehenge with amazing accuracy. This clearly points to a universal understanding in antiquity of advanced mathematical science that all points to a common source. The circles of the New Jerusalem diagram are projected with the exact and correct dimensions as at Glastonbury and define the measurements of the concentric stone rings at the Stonehenge site. A circle with a diameter of 79.20 feet can be shown contained within a square, the western side of which coincides with the inside of the Saint Mary Chapel wall, which also measures 79.20 feet. The diagram that can be produced would be proportioned so that its perimeter of 4 x 79.20 feet equals 316.8 feet, the same as the circumference of the circle which runs through the middle of the ring of cells as already mentioned earlier, however its significance here in relation to Glastonbury Abbey itself is that the area of the square is 0.144 acres. This is a microcosm of the twelve hides of Glaston, which cover 1440 acres. In other words, the side of the square in the diagram of 79.20 feet is equal to a hundredth part of the side of a square containing an area of twelve hides, which is 7,920 feet. The earth's diameter is 7,920 miles. Also 7,920 thousand feet equals 12,000 furlongs, which is the length of the side of the New Jerusalem as given in Revelations xxi. I have repeated this to get the message across."

"I think you will have to repeat all of that again so I may write it all down," Paul commented and sat up.

"I shall…but as I have said already, you need to be able to memorise all of these details."

"That is a tall order," Paul laughed.

"Paul, if I can do it, you with your brilliant mind most certainly can!"

"I hope so."

"Good…"

"As for Glastonbury itself, I must point out that from a personal view, I feel that there is something very special about the place. It stands on a small mound that makes it a virtual island that rises from the low marshy countryside that surrounds it. This area was once an island. Here then we have an image of a sacred place on a mount isolated and surrounded by water exactly as the ancient Egyptian myths recount when describing their primordial mound of creation, the same mound that the Great Pyramid was built upon. If we get to Cairo I shall show you. The mystical Avalon of Arthurian myth is described in the same manner. Silbury Hill was also known to have been surrounded by a large moat of over thirty feet in depth and width. Glastonbury Tor itself, set to the east...note the east connection again... rises as a great conical hill. Between the Tor and the town itself, is the moon shaped dome of Chalice Hill, which is closely associated with the Holy Grail. At its foot are the springs and holy well. A protective lid which has the Vesica Pisces engraved upon it covers this well. This is one of the reasons why Glastonbury is still a place of constant pilgrimage. Glastonbury with its earlier names of Avalon and the Crystal Isle reflect the ancients' belief that this area was indeed a most sacred site and a place of mystical visions. It was reputed to be a form of a gateway to another world. The king of that world was known as 'Gwyn ap Nudd' and had his palace beneath the Tor. Here we have an almost identical tradition to the ancient Egyptian belief of an underworld. Glastonbury became the site of the first Christian church anywhere in the world after Joseph of Arimathea arrived with twelve disciples. I can tell you that there is a treasure at Glastonbury...but not one in the physical sense of gold and jewels etcetera, but knowledge encoded within the Abbey's geometric dimensions. Many legends talk of underground vaults beneath the site and surrounding it. These are identical allusions to treasure as related to the Temple of Jerusalem and the Great Pyramid. None have as yet revealed any treasure in the physical sense. The reason being, as I have just stated, because the treasure is not of a physical nature at these sites. The treasure lies in what they state and where they all point...the Great Pyramid!"

"Then we shall indeed take up Ishfahani's invitation to visit Cairo and see the pyramids myself."

0 – 0

"That is most encouraging," Theodoric smiled and continued his lesson. "Glastonbury has been referred to as 'The Holiest Earth' and 'The English Jerusalem' by many researchers of Grail romances and mystics alike. Many ancient prophecies identify Glastonbury as a place of regeneration, just as the Giza pyramids are referred to. One preserved prophecy that was recounted from a sixth century book, known as the 'Book of Melchin', states that the tomb of Saint Joseph together with a Grail talisman will one day be discovered and that 'Thenceforth nor water nor dew of heaven shall fail the dwellers on that ancient isle.' This prophecy is remarkably similar to the Holy Grail legend of the lame Fisher King, who has also been associated with the surrounding marshes of Glastonbury, that when he is healed, his barren kingdom will also flourish again and restore the primeval golden age. This same prophecy has been proffered in regard to the Great Pyramid's missing capstone, with identical symbology, and that its eventual restoration will likewise herald the dawn of a new golden age. Another peculiar connection between Glastonbury Abbey and pyramids comes from the highly unusual presence of two pyramids on the site and a rather enigmatic pillar. Pyramidal shaped tombs are unheard of on Christian sites, especially ones of such antiquity. Yet if Joseph was indeed the originator of the site, it makes plausible sense why we find two pyramid shaped tombs on the site, as he was very much aware of the symbolic importance of this shape. The two pyramids and pillar are clearly marked on any map or site survey. Also a line can be drawn between the centres of the two monuments outside the chapel that cuts the central axis of the chapel at the midpoint of the Glastonbury scheme. The monuments and two corners of the chapel mark angles of an octagon within a circle of a radius of 50.4 feet. Jesus it must be noted was often referred to by the Gnostics as 'The Ogdoad', the eight fold. In Gematria Jesus equals 888. Also note that the 12-fold symmetry of a New Jerusalem diagram, when laid over the plan of the chapel, defines its proportions and the positions of the original twelve cells and central church. The full wording of the Christian title of 'Lord Jesus Christ', written in Greek as *'Κυριος Ιησους Χριστος'*, has by Gematria the value 3,168."

"Theo, I am sure you explained most of that already when we journeyed in the caravan," Paul interrupted.

"Have I? Hmmm. Well, it never hurts to be reminded as I said," Theodoric laughed. "Well so long as you keep in mind that all the ancient sacred sites and new ones being designed and built by the Templars are all set out to a precise geometrical plan to mirror celestial constellations as well as follow ancient paths of energy, then you will be on your way."

"I shall always keep that in mind, I promise," Paul replied.

"Good. For the sacred sites relate to stars and constellations and when viewed together show the cathedrals in France make up the image of the main body of stars that form the constellation of Virgo. Reims Cathedral will represent the star 'Spica', the one that seems to be symbolised both as a sheaf of wheat and a lily flower. Owing to its royal connections, it is Reims, not Chartres, that will become the most important cathedral in France where kings will be crowned for many centuries no doubt. Reims represents the place of the 'fleur de lys' and it signifies the Annunciation, the selection of a woman to bear the future prophesied Messiah. The Virgo figure spread out across Northern France indicates that the next Messiah would be French and of royal blood, from the Merovingian bloodline...'tis why the French Royal House adopted the 'fleur de lys' as their personal symbol and insignia. In Egypt the actual symbol of Osiris was the 'fleur de lys' but you probably already know that?" [76]

"I am sure I vaguely recall being told by my father...but I cannot remember exactly when. But you say a new Messiah figure will be French. Good, for I am actually English...," Paul remarked and smiled.

"But what is Arri for he was registered in France?" Theodoric quipped back and raised his eyebrows.

"No...I will not allow him to become something that will undoubtedly put him in harm's way."

"Paul...that is exactly what your father tried to do with you and Stewart. 'Tis why your names were changed and your identities shrouded in a cloak of mystery... not that it worked for look what happened with Turansha?"

"But I have this...and I know how to use it," Paul said and stood up and lifted up his sword from the table and began to tie it around his waist. "I shall learn all there is to learn if you will help me...but so that I am informed and therefore forearmed."

"It will be both my pleasure and my honour," Theodoric replied and stood up. "We are all Keepers of the Faith, Paul, whether we like it or not."

Chapter 47
Darkest of Ages & the Solace
of Stewart & Taqi

Port of La Rochelle, France, Melissae Inn, spring 1191

"You detailed Paul's dream about a great explosion over Alba and melting the forts...which many attribute to dragons' fire. 'Tis clearly not the case then?" Gabirol remarked.

"No, not dragons, but you can see how the legends attributing it to them began. But even as recently as the sixth century, the same things have happened. We are already calling that period the Dark Ages...and for good reason," the old man replied.

"Please, 'enlighten' us then if you will pardon the pun," Peter said and gestured with his hands in exaggerated manner and laughed.

"There are writings from that period which state there was a sign from the sun, the like of which had never been seen and reported before. The sun became dark and its darkness lasted for eighteen months. Each day, it shone for about four hours, and still this light was only a feeble shadow. Everyone declared that the sun would never recover its full light again."

"Where is that written?" Gabirol asked as he charged his quill with more ink.

"In the sixth century 'Historiae Ecclesiasticae' written by the historian and church leader John of Ephesus, where he states that between the years AD 535 and 536, a series of major cataclysmic climatic events took place with catastrophic consequences. Procopius, who lived between AD 500 and 565, who was a late antiquities scholar and one of the main historians of the sixth century, also referred to the strange behaviour of the sun and believed that it was a bad sign and the beginning of other events. He actually said that during this year a most dread portent took place. For the sun gave forth its light without brightness...and it seemed exceedingly like the sun in eclipse, for the beams it shed were not clear."

"And where was that written?" Gabirol asked as he started to write down more notes.

"'Tis written in the 'History of the Wars, the Vandalic War' but there is yet another reference from the sixth century writer Zacharias of Mytilene, who authored a chronicle that contains a section referring to the 'dark sun' for the period of AD 535 to 536. He basically stated that the sun began to be darkened by day and the moon by night, while the ocean was tumultuous with spray from the 24th of March in that year till the 24th of June in the following year...And, as the winter was a severe one, so much so that from the large and unwonted quantity of snow the birds perished...there was distress...among men...from the evil things. And that was from his Chronicle, 9.19, 10.1 before you ask," the old man joked looking at Gabirol.

"Why are we not told these things?" the farrier asked, looking concerned. "If it happened then, it can happen again now can it not?"

"Yes it could and most probably will," the old man replied as Ayleth raised her hand to her mouth, alarmed. "Worry not, Ayleth, it will not happen in your life time...of that I am most convinced. But know this, the three I have mentioned are but an example from among many

accounts from all over the known world, written in the same period of time. In all, the sun was described as getting dimmer and losing its light and described as having a bluish colour. The effects were also observed with the moon for it wasn't as bright any more. The reduction of the light resulted in the reduction of heat, no rain and a very long winter that resulted in crop failures and for birds and other wildlife to perish. Famine and plagues struck many areas and there were a huge number of deaths. And as Tenno confirmed during his time spent with Philip, even in China and Japan, the event was also recorded in great detail. Massive droughts and thousands of deaths. In the Beishi chronicles, the official history of the Northern Dynasties, it mentions that in AD 536, in the province of Xi'an, eighty per cent of the population died and the survivors ate corpses to survive."

"That is disgusting!" Ayleth remarked, shaking her head.

"Well Tenno confirms this as true from the many books he had read. AD 536 was without doubt a terrible year for everyone, everywhere."

"So what caused this great tragedy...the fireballs in the sky?" the wealthy tailor asked.

"Well if it had been a falling star, though star is not really correct, but a falling rock that travels at such great speed that it smashes into our ground with such a force, it does explode very like the descriptions given...but no holes, craters, are to be found that can confirm this. Besides, as Paul saw in his dreams, the balls of light exploded up in the air...not on the ground," the old man explained.

"So what was it?" the wealthy tailor asked again, looking worried.

"We know that great volcanic eruptions cause the sun to be blotted out, but again, we know that many legends speak of balls of flame streaking across the heavens and exploding with the brilliance of the sun...but much of the period in question is shrouded in darkness, pardon the pun, for few records remain, and why so many now refer to it as the Dark Ages... literally and physically. It certainly acts to remind us of our fragility as human beings and the fact that no matter how powerful and 'advanced' mankind becomes, we are still at the mercy of nature. 'Tis why the ancients sealed so much of their knowledge and wisdom away, so it could be recovered one day...but as I have already said, only when we again are capable of understanding what we find and can use it properly and safely," the old man explained and sighed before continuing. "I can tell you that a comet also passed over Britain in AD 652, and impacted somewhere in the west. Britain experienced a mass exodus at this time because nothing grew for over a decade. This was truly the real Darkest of Ages for Britain. Gildas chronicled these events, and it also explains why the ancient British language is found in parts of Brittany, where the British fled to. Gildas is also buried at a monastery in Brittany."

"Well that partly explains in my mind why we have dragons mentioned so frequently in Britain...especially Wales," Ayleth remarked, looking a little more relaxed.

"Sorry, but who is Gildas?" Simon asked and looked at Sarah.

"Hey, don't look at me as I don't know either," she shot back and looked across at the old man.

"Gildas...or Saint Gildas as some call him. I can tell you there are two stories about his life. His real documented life but also the more esoteric and mystical one that connects him with King Arthur and the Grail legends," the old man explained.

"It would wouldn't it," the wealthy tailor said, his tone dismissive.

"It would not be the first time esoteric attributes have been added to a genuinely historical figure now would it?" the old man replied and smiled disarmingly before continuing. "Now Gildas lived between AD 500 and 570 and was also known as 'Gildas the Wise', or 'Gildas Sapiens', and he was a sixth century British monk, best known for his scathing religious

polemic 'De Excidio et Conquestu Britanniae', which recounts the history of the Britons before and during the coming of the Saxons. He is one of the best-documented figures of the Christian Church in the British Isles during the sub-Roman period, and was renowned for his biblical knowledge and literary style. Of course the Gildas as handed down to us differs between the two versions, but both agree he was born in what is now Alba, or Scotia on the banks of the River Clyde, and was the son of a royal family. In his own work, he claimed to have been born the same year as the Battle of Mount Badon. Educated at a monastic centre, under Saint Illtud, he chose to forsake his royal heritage and embrace monasticism and became a renowned teacher, converting many to Christianity, and founding numerous churches and monasteries throughout Britain and the Emerald Isle. He is thought to have made a pilgrimage to Rome before immigrating to Brittany, where he took on the life of a hermit. However, his life of solitude was short-lived, and pupils soon sought him out and begged him to teach them so he founded a monastery for these students at Rhuys, where he wrote De Excidio et Conquestu Britanniae, criticising British rulers and exhorting them to put off their sins and embrace true Christian faith. He is thought to have died at Rhuys, and was buried there."

"But you said there are two different versions?" Gabirol quizzed.

"There are...the first being written by an anonymous monk in the ninth century, and the other written by Caradoc of Llancarfan, in the middle of this century. You can probably guess which one has connections to King Arthur?" the old man smiled.

"The latter," Gabirol smiled back.

"Yes...Now some scholars attempt to explain the differences in the versions by saying there were two saints named Gildas, but there was just the one. The discrepancies between versions can be accounted for by the fact that they were written in different countries, and several centuries apart. The first 'Life of St Gildas' was written by an unnamed monk at the monastery Gildas founded in Rhuys, Brittany, in the ninth century and according to this tradition, Gildas is the son of Caunus, king of Alt Clut in the Hen Ogledd, the Brythonic-speaking region of northern Britain. He had four brothers...one brother, Cuillum, ascended to the throne on the death of his father, but the rest became monks in their own right. Gildas was sent as a child to the College of Theodosius (Cor Tewdws) in Glamorgan, under the care of Saint Illtud, and was a companion of Saint Sampson and Saint Paul of Léon. His master, Saint Illtud, loved him tenderly, and taught him with especial zeal. He was supposed to be educated in liberal arts and divine scripture, but elected to study only holy doctrine, and to forsake his noble birth in favour of a religious life. After completing his studies he went to the Emerald Isles, where he was ordained as a priest. He returned to his native Britain, where he acted as a missionary, preaching to the pagan people and converting many of them to Christianity. He was then asked by Ainmericus, high king of the Emerald Isles, Ainmuire mac Sétnai, to restore order to the Church in his lands, which had altogether lost the Christian faith. Gildas obeyed the king's summons, and travelled all over the island, converting the inhabitants, building churches, and establishing monasteries. Saint Gildas then travelled to Rome and Ravenna, where he performed many miracles, including the apparent slaying of a dragon while in Rome. Intending to return to Britain, he instead settled on the Isle of Houat, off Brittany, where he led a solitary, austere life. At around this time, he also preached to Nonnita, the mother of Saint David, while she was pregnant with the saint. He was eventually sought out by those who wished to study under him, and was entreated to establish a monastery in Brittany. He built an oratory on the bank of the River Blavetum, today known as Saint Gildas de Rhuys. Fragments of letters he wrote reveal that he composed a rule for monastic life that was somewhat less austere than the rule written by Saint David. Ten years after leaving Britain, he wrote an epistolary book, in which he reproved five of the British kings. He died at Rhuys on the twenty-ninth of January AD 570, and his body, according to his wishes, was placed on a boat and allowed to drift. Three months later, on the eleventh of May, men from Rhuys found the ship in a creek with the body of Gildas still intact. They took the body back to Rhuys and buried it there," the old man detailed as Gabirol wrote quickly.

"Sounds identical to the send off King Arthur got?" Peter interrupted.

"It does indeed and that is where the second version of Gildas really differs. The second 'Life of St Gildas' was written by Caradoc of Llancarfan, a friend of Geoffrey of Monmouth and his Norman patrons. It was written in this century, and includes many elements of what have come to be known as mythical and esoteric histories, involving King Arthur, Guinevere, and Glastonbury Abbey, leading to the general opinion that this version is less historically accurate than the earlier version. For example, according to the dates in the Annales Cambriae, Gildas would have been a contemporary of King Arthur, however, Gildas's work never mentions Arthur by name, even though he gives a history of the Britons, and states that he was born in the same year as the Battle of Badon Hill, in which Arthur is supposed to have vanquished the Saxons. In the Llancarfan version, Saint Gildas was the son of Nau, king of Scotia. Nau had twenty-four sons, all victorious warriors. Gildas studied literature as a youth, before leaving his homeland for Gaul, where he studied for seven years. When he returned, he brought back an extensive library with him, and was sought after as a master teacher. He became the most renowned teacher in all of the three kingdoms of Britain. Gildas was a subject of the mythical King Arthur, whom he loved and desired to obey. However, his twenty-three brothers were always rising up against their rightful king, and his eldest brother, Hueil, would submit to no rightful high king, not even Arthur. Hueil would often swoop down from Scotia to fight battles and carry off spoils, and during one of these raids, Hueil was pursued and killed by King Arthur. When news of his brother's murder reached Gildas in the Emerald Isles, he was greatly grieved, but was able to forgive Arthur, and pray for the salvation of his soul. Gildas then travelled to Britain, where he met Arthur face to face, and kissed him as he prayed for forgiveness, and Arthur accepted penance for murdering Gildas's brother. After this, Gildas taught at the school of Saint Cadoc, before retiring to a secret island for seven years. Pirates from the Orkney Islands came and sacked his island, carrying off goods and his friends as slaves. In distress, he left the island, and came to Glastonbury, then ruled by Melvas, King of the 'Summer Country' (Gwlad yr Haf, Somerset). Gildas intervened between King Arthur and Melvas, who had abducted and raped Arthur's wife, Guinevere, and brought her to his stronghold at Glastonbury. Arthur soon arrived to besiege him, but, the peacemaking saint persuaded Melvas to release Guinevere and the two kings made peace. Then desiring to live a hermit's life, Gildas built a hermitage devoted to the Trinity on the banks of the river at Glastonbury. He died, and was buried at Glastonbury Abbey, in the floor of Saint Mary's Church."

"I never knew Guinevere was kidnapped or raped...," Ayleth exclaimed, looking shocked.

"Well the Llancarfan version does detail the earliest surviving appearance of the abduction of Guinevere episode, common in later Arthurian literature. Huail's enmity with Arthur is also a popular subject in Britain at this time. He is mentioned as an enemy of Arthur's in the Welsh prose tale Culhwch and Olwen, written around AD 1100. A strongly held tradition in North Wales places the beheading of Gildas's brother Huail at Ruthin, where what is believed to be the execution stone has been preserved in the town square. Another brother of

Gildas, Celyn ap Caw, lived in the northeast corner of Anglesey. 'Twas Gildas who describes the doings of the Romans and the Groans of the Britons, in which the Britons make one last request for military aid from the departed Roman military. He excoriates his fellow Britons for their sins, while at the same time lauding heroes such as Ambrosius Aurelianus, whom he is the first to describe as a leader of the resistance to the Saxons. He mentions the victory at the Battle of Mons Badonicus, a feat attributed to King Arthur in later texts. So you see there is much that leads to confusion and why sometimes it is far easier to explain the tales in a simpler fashion, of course including the codes within them. Did you note the twenty-four, twenty-three and seven specifically mentioned? 'Tis why it is also easier to explain the phenomenon of exploding fireballs in the sky as dragons rather than even attempt to explain exactly what they really are on a population that still mainly believes the world is flat," the old man explained and stopped for a few minutes before continuing. "The explosions from the air cause devastating carnage for they melt stone, turn deserts to glass and hurl great building stones of many tons hundreds of feet...'tis why we must protect our Mother Earth so that she can defend against such intrusive and destructive objects that enter from the heavens," the old man said and paused again. "Just visit Caermead in South Wales to see just a small example of the power of the fireballs. 'Tis perhaps a greater irony that it is through war that man may learn the secrets of how to defeat such things as I was once told by a very wise man." [77]

"I learnt a long time ago that what we learned in school, was just what we were intended to know, and accept as fact. There is a great variation between what we learned and the enormous amount of evidence that was just ignored, or perhaps more correctly, deliberately concealed from us...'tis why I am on this journey now," Gabirol commented.

"You are lucky for some of us never got any schooling," Simon remarked.

"Yes...it shows!" Sarah commented and pulled a large false smile at him.

"Our father used to scare us as children about fire coming from the sky. He would oft use that as his excuse for drinking...," the Templar remarked.

"And that he held us responsible for our mother's death giving birth to us do not forget, brother," the Hospitaller interjected with a look of repugnance.

"Yes...and that," the Templar replied with a shrug.

"You mention fire in the sky. 'Tis the description given of 'The Welsh Dragon' which is called or known as 'Maen Mellt' in Welsh. That translates to 'stone lightning' no less," the old man explained.

"Now why does that not surprise me?" Peter said aloud.

"And Paul, he learnt all about this too?" Gabirol asked.

"Of course, and much more besides," the old man answered.

"And what of his brother, Stewart, all this time?" Ayleth asked curiously.

"And Taqi, wherever he has gone?" Simon chipped in loudly.

"Stewart...?" the old man said quietly and paused for several moments sat in total silence. "Stewart!"

Principality of Galilee, Kingdom of Jerusalem, mid November 1179

Stewart stood alone beside the outer wall of St Peter's Church looking down and out across the Sea of Galilee to his left, the sun reflecting brightly off the almost flat water surface visible beyond the outer city walls. To his right he viewed the main castle, its drawbridge lowered across the water filled moat as several knights walked their horses across and through the main large vaulted entrance. In the distance he caught a glimpse of three sets of sails just visible above the fortress wall that ran from the main castle and parallel with the shore line, the moat passing beneath it and joining the main city defensive wall. He rolled up the black and white Beauseant banner flag around its pole and gently rested it against the wall safely. Behind him some distance off, his troop of Templars were removing their saddles from their horses and unloading them. It was late afternoon but the sun was still burning away fiercely above them. Two Templars roared with delight as two sergeants poured wooden buckets full of cold water directly over them. Stewart's mind wandered as he pondered why this beautiful city was classed as one of the 'four cities of hell' in an Islamic Hadith recorded by Ibn Asakir of Damascus. He had been discussing that fact with Gerard as they approached the town after another long patrol. Stewart was learning fast that Gerard certainly knew his history and facts on a great number of things. 'It could have been the fact that the town had a notable non-Muslim population' he thought. It had a Jewish community and he recalled his father telling him stories about the time he had visited the area and about a large mosaic depicting the twelve signs of the zodiac in one of their synagogues. He would see if he could visit it he told himself. He knew that the city, though only the size of a town really, was long and narrow in its layout. There were some seventeen natural hot salt springs and he welcomed the chance of finally being able to soak in one that evening after vespers. Gerard had insisted he try it. He looked down at himself. His light beige field-mantel was a grimy sand colour with patches of red dirt. His chain mail was caked in even more dirt and the exposed sections filled with sand and grit only added to its heavy weight. His feet ached, his under garments felt damp from several days of sweat, which just as quickly evaporated leaving stain lines, and the inside of his helmet stank. It would be good to get himself and all his equipment cleaned. The leather stitching on his sword handle had started to work loose at the top near the pommel where it had rubbed constantly as he rode. As he held it, he thought back to the sword his father had offered him at the bridge crossing back in France. He closed his eyes as he tried to shake the image of Firgany from his mind as he lay dying. He had always admired and respected Firgany. He sighed heavily, feeling the weight of guilt upon him almost like a tangible force pressing down on his shoulders. The look upon Alisha's face as she stared up at him haunted his dreams almost every night. How could he ever apologise or make amends for such an event. He opened his eyes and looked upwards as he fought to stop them from filling with tears as he recalled his own father and the last images he had of him. Gently he rolled up his right sleeve and pushed the chain mail up his wrist enough to reveal the scar upon his forearm. The night Paul inflicted the wound seemed such a long time ago. He shook his head feeling stupid and ashamed of that night's activity not quite believing he had actually done it. Horses suddenly riding into the open area beside him drew his attention. As he stood up straight and squinted to see, he immediately recognised the two front riders approaching with a squadron of knights following behind them escorting two caravans. It was Count Raymond and Balian de I'belin with all their glorious colourful banners, horse covers and various coats of arms fluttering wildly on their standards.

"Ah Brother Stewart...you have not yet set your standard. Are you coming or going?" Count Raymond asked as he pulled his horse up near to him.

Stewart immediately grabbed hold of the rolled up banner and held it close.

"My Lord, Sire, 'tis good to see you all return safe and well from Jaffa. And no, I have not set the standard for we have only just arrived also," Stewart replied and bowed his head slightly.

"Where are Gerard and Lord Reynald?" Count Raymond asked. "Though I use the term Lord loosely," he then whispered to Balian but still loud enough for Stewart to hear.

"They are away to the armoury and vaults already to secure items seized, My Lord," Stewart answered and motioned toward the castle entrance.

"Great...you mean more ill gotten gains stolen from pilgrims no less," Count Raymond said, shaking his head with disapproval, and immediately rode forwards toward the drawbridge.

"Brother Stewart, do not take his words personally. 'Tis neither you nor your Order he has a problem with," Balian said and quickly followed after Count Raymond.

Stewart stood back a pace as the remainder of the squadron filed past. Princess Eschiva looked out of her side window as her ornate but rugged heavily built caravan passed him. She smiled and acknowledged him as he bowed his head out of respect. He watched as the column disappeared across the drawbridge into the castle, then picked up his helmet from off the stone blockwork nearby but immediately dropped it as it was so hot having sat exposed to the direct sunlight. His riding gloves fell out and as he picked them up, his helmet rolled across a large flagstone engraved with a basket with a fish on either side. He looked at it momentarily then collected up his gloves and helmet by the straps and stood up straight. 'Why am I here, Lord?' he asked himself as he looked around and shook his head tired, filthy and confused.

Port of La Rochelle, France, Melissae Inn, spring 1191

"Ah bless him," Ayleth said softly.

"Bless him you say? He was an ass. A short tempered arrogant ass," the Genoese sailor said crudely.

"People change...and in Outremer they can change very fast," the Templar remarked as he looked at the Genoese sailor.

"Well he can't bring back Firgany can he? He should have done something when it mattered," the Genoese sailor shot back defensively.

"Hindsight is the only clear vision any of us will ever have...," the old man said softly and looked at the Genoese sailor and Templar in turn. "The high ideals and beliefs Stewart had did not match the reality of what he was witnessing, experiencing and doing alongside Gerard."

"So Raymond let Stewart believe they had been to Jaffa only, yes?" Gabirol asked.

"Yes at that point in time he did. As I said earlier, if Gerard knew they were going to Alexandria, he would have either insisted on going, in force, or tried to block the whole embassy. 'Twas a necessary lie," the old man answered.

"Problem is, there are always too many necessary lies being told," the Hospitaller stated, sounding disgruntled at the old man's words.

"That I am afraid is also true," the old man acknowledged.

"Where was Nicholas?" Ayleth asked.

"He stayed on in Jerusalem with Count Henry and Brother Baldwin."

"Why do they call Brother Baldwin Upside?" Gabirol asked.

"Apparently he had a mouth that appeared to be upside down. When he smiled he looked as though he was grimacing badly...," the old man answered and laughed to himself briefly.

"Thanks, that has just ruined my image of him," Sarah joked and huffed with an exaggerated sigh.

"I have heard much about Tiberias as it figures much in the Bible, does it not?" Peter asked.

"It does along with its shoreline. But our Templar friend here can tell you more I am sure as he was garrisoned there," the old man explained and nodded toward the Templar.

"Aye that I was," he paused. "But only briefly before it fell," he replied and sat up looking awkward.

"You were there when it fell?" Gabirol asked, interested.

"I was. But if I tell you, then perhaps I may ruin our friend's tale here," the Templar explained and raised his eyebrows quizzically as he looked at the old man.

"It may...so let me explain about Tiberias for you and I shall reveal your part in this tale as it nears its conclusion, yes?" the old man asked. The Templar nodded his head silently as Miriam smiled at him adoringly and held his hand tighter. "Then let me tell you that the substantial fortress of Tiberias was laid out inside the city walls, on the shore of the Sea of Galilee, in the vicinity of the old Jewish Quarter. A water filled moat connected to the sea enclosed and protected the fortress from the south. Its design was almost identical to the building style and plan of the fortress located at Belvoir, the only difference being that in the latter case the moat was not filled with water."

"You said was. Does that mean it no longer stands?" Simon interrupted. The Templar looked across at him. "Well he did say 'was'," Simon protested.

"I shall explain, Simon, in full I promise," the old man smiled. "Now the fortress of Tiberias was the heart and seat of the Principality of Galilee and governed by Count Raymond and Princess Eschiva as well as being an important Templar base of operations in the area. It had massive ten feet thick walls, oriented east to west perpendicular to the shoreline. The façade of the wall was built of large ashlar stones that were carefully fitted and bonded together, some of which have drafted margins with diagonal stone dressing across the surface of several of the stones in the jambs of the gate. The fortress also made good use of ancient construction items. It also had a very strong iron portcullis on the main gate entrance. The broad moat was kept full of water that protected the fortress from the north and also a moat on the western side so that the entire fortress was surrounded entirely by water, a kind of island cut off from the other parts of the city, which was joined to them by way of wooden bridges that could be raised."

"You said they made good use of ancient construction. What was that then?" Peter asked.

"Recovered lintels and columns of the previous buildings that once stood upon the site. 'Tis why so many carvings were set upon stones such as a basalt ashlar slab decorated with a crude relief of a five-branch candelabrum, cornice stones and capitals, column drums, fragments of Italian marble and other limestone and basalt elements. They came from an ancient and magnificent structure that was probably a synagogue from the Roman or Byzantine period," the old man detailed and paused briefly. "But whilst in the city, Stewart took the opportunity of climbing to the summit of Mount Berenice, high above Old Tiberias, rumoured to be the site of Queen Berenice's palace but I can tell you it was never there. Mount Berenice rises to a height of 650 feet above the Sea of Galilee, Tiberias being just south of it. The hill is in the form of a pyramid, with its base parallel to the shoreline of the lake. The eastern side of the hill is just wild cliffs and caves. The western side, by contrast, slopes gently, and is, in effect, a direct continuation of the Poriah ridge which looms above it. Stewart had to ascend the hill from the east, by way of a path that sloped up the cliff face from the city below. The pinnacle-like nature of the site, soaring up sheer from the Sea of Galilee, provided Stewart with breath-taking views of the lake and the sites around it, perhaps the finest and most interesting panorama in the region as the city of Tiberias lay in the palm of his hand beneath him. Across the lake, are the remains of the ancient city of Susita (Hippios), in its day the most important on the eastern shore. To the north, he could make out the sites of the ancient fishing villages of Capernaum, Heptapegon (Tabgha) and Migdal-Tarichaeae. Beyond them in the distance are the two highest peaks in the country, Mount Hermon to the north, and Mount Meron to the northwest," the old man detailed fondly.

"You mentioned hot springs. What are they?" Ayleth asked.

"My dear, the seventeen springs of Hamat Tiberias have been known since antiquity for their curative properties. According to the sages of the Talmud, the springs were constantly hot as they stream past the entrance of Hell. As Stewart knew, there was an ancient Greek inscription on the Hellenistic mosaic floor belonging to the synagogue in Hamat Tiberias, which is an ancient synagogue on the outskirts of Tiberias, located near the hot springs just south of the city. The synagogue dates to 286 and 337 BC, when Tiberias was the seat of the Sanhedrin. The mosaic floor is made up of three panels featuring the zodiac and with Helios sitting in his chariot holding the celestial sphere and whip. There are images of women symbolising the four seasons in each corner and the twelve signs of the zodiac encircle the entire mosaic. Another panel shows a Torah ark flanked by two seven-branched menorahs and other Jewish ritual objects."

"Sounds like a lovely place, not a hellish one," Sarah stated.

"It was indeed," the old man replied.

"So who was Queen Berenice? Never heard of her before," Simon asked.

"She was the beautiful daughter of King Herod Agrippa," the old man answered. "Agrippa being the grandson of Herod the Great and Mariamne the Hasmonean. She lived in the first century BC and the Roman general Titus, who was later to become Emperor of Rome, could resist neither her charms nor her beauty. He fell in love with her and took her to Rome with him. When he became emperor, however, he was obliged to send her back to Judea, as the Roman people would not tolerate a Jewish queen. Titus sacrificed his love to the glory of ruling an empire, and Berenice returned to the land of her birth. This fascinating sequence of events is no way connected with the hill that towers over Tiberias though as Berenice spent the remainder of her life in far-off Banyas, but this did not discourage the local people from bestowing her name upon the hill. In Arabic the site is known as Qasr Bint al-Malik, which means 'Palace of the King's Daughter'."

"And why do you tell us these facts?" the farrier asked, his tone almost curt.

"Because it was there, upon that hill, that Stewart would sit in silence. 'Twas the only place where he could feel comfortable. It gave him solace in a mad confusing world. He contemplated many times about leaving the Order and seeking out Alisha and Paul to try and put

right all the wrong doings he had done and what he perceived as all being his fault alone,"
the old man explained sadly.

"In my mind that shows he has a good heart," Ayleth remarked and immediately bit her
thumb nail.

"He had that for sure. He also knew, from Gerard ironically, the history behind Tiberias
as Gerard delighted in passing the hours of journey talking about all things historical and
biblical, and Tiberias was certainly connected with Jesus. Remember, Gerard saw it his holy
mission to do God's work."

"How so?" Simon asked and looked at Sarah quickly.

"How." The old man replied smiling and paused momentarily. "Let me briefly explain
that according to the Gospels, many people from Tiberias sailed to Capharnaum to meet
Jesus. Christian tradition shows the presence of a large Judeo-Christian community that
concentrated the memory of many evangelical episodes in Tiberias. Tiberias is the most
important city on the shores of the Sea of Galilee and it could already have been so in the
time of Christ, as it was the residence of the tetrarch Herod Antipas. It was he who founded
it and had given it the name of his protector and friend, the emperor Tiberius Caesar. In
the Gospel according to John, boats that came from the city of Tiberias to the place of the
multiplication of the loaves in John 6.23 are mentioned. The increased importance of the
city is shown by the fact that the lake is called 'Sea of Tiberias'. According to Epiphanius,
Christianity became established in Tiberias in the fourth century, when a convert from
Judaism, Count Joseph, obtained permission from the emperor Constantine to build a church
where the pagan temple of Adrian had stood. From him, we also know that in Tiberias, as
in Nazareth and Capharnaum, there were Jews who believed in Christ and kept and spread
the books of the New Testament translated into Hebrew and so Gerard viewed the entire area
as especially holy and important."

"I never knew that. Never thought of Jews believing in Jesus before," Peter commented,
looking surprised.

"In the seventh century, Saint Willibald saw many churches as well as synagogues of the
Jews. At that time, talk began of the presence of Jesus in that city. Many Gospel stories became
connected to Tiberias such as the healing of a leper, the house of Peter's mother-in-law, the
episode of the woman, a sinner, who washed Jesus's feet with her tears and dried them with
her hair, the healing of the crippled woman, the episode of the centurion, the paralytic who
was lowered from the roof and even the Canaanite woman being granted fulfilment, which
actually took place near Tyre and Sidon but was nevertheless superimposed upon Tiberias
too. This information was collected by an authoritative witness, one being the Russian abbot
Daniel, who personally visited Tiberias in AD 1106, and confirmed by other visitors, who
added the miraculous catch of fish, the house of James and John, sons of Zebedee, the vocation
of Matthew and other episodes taken from the apocryphal Gospels on the childhood of Jesus.
It was Herod who brought his love of amusements and magnificent buildings to Tiberias. It
had a forum, a stadium, and public baths. For the Jews he convinced to live there, Herod built
a synagogue. For himself, he built a grand palace adorned with representations of animals,
contrary to Jewish custom, and around AD 61, Tiberias became the Capital of Galilee, usurp-
ing the place Sepphoris once held. There are four towers to the north of the city. Bastions that
faced the sea from the north and south of the city still stand."

"And what was the name of the church Stewart stood beside when you started?" Gabirol
asked.

"'Tis the Church of Saint Peter. It was on the shores nearby, where Stewart saw twelve large

white stones placed to represent the twelve apostles that Jesus was said to have instructed and where he told Peter to cast his nets and catch 153 fish. In Gematria by the way, soul equals 153," the old man explained.

"Truly?" Ayleth asked.

"Yes, truly. And yes it was as described within the Gospel narrative of the 'First Miraculous Catch of Fish' along with the Calling of Peter and Andrew as Apostles as written in Matthew 4: 18–22 and Luke 5: 1–11 that took place where Stewart stood. The very form of the Saint Peter's Church was built to commemorate this Gospel event with its one nave and narrow windows similar to portholes. It represented the hull of an overturned boat, whose bow was visible on the outside of the apse. The Bark of Peter! A traditional symbol of the Church, whose head, the Roman Pontiff, heard the command of Christ saying 'push out to the deep waters.' And Stewart never found any trace of the so-called Palace of Berenice but he did find the romantic and aged ruins of an older sixth century church on Mount Berenice. 'Twas there, as I said, that he would oft sit and seek solace for his perceived wrong doings. One evening as the sun was setting, he sat alone and thought about Alisha, Paul and Taqi. He looked to the northern horizon in the direction he knew the Ashashin Masyaf castle lay and wondered what Taqi must be doing at that same moment. There was a heaviness in Stewart's soul and he did not know how to deal with it, which frustrated him even more," the old man said and gently lifted his drink and sipped a small mouthful. [78]

"I am interested to know what Taqi got up to," Simon interjected with a loud voice and large smile. "He seems to have vanished from this tale!"

"Okay, if you wish...if you wish," the old man said and placed his drink down. "Taqi had been at the Castle of Masyaf, situated in the Orontes Valley, approximately eighteen miles to the west of Hama, for several months when Stewart had wondered about him. It served to protect the trade routes to cities further inland such as Banyas. The castle itself stands upon a natural high platform of solid rock, which makes for an impressive and imposing castle to behold that is for sure."

Masyaf Castle, Ashashin headquarters, Syria, mid November 1179

Taqi fought to catch his breath as he stood bent over, his hands resting upon his knees, his lungs feeling like they were burning and about to burst. The sun was setting fast behind the mountains to the west causing the castle and sandy path he was stood on fall into shadow. Al Rashid stood bolt upright, his arms folded and looking at him raising his eyebrows questioningly. He was dressed in his usual black clothing looking just as menacing as always whilst Taqi wore a simple black shirt and loose fitting black chausses. He looked behind him at the rest of his training group rapidly approaching as they struggled to run up the sandy path.

"You wish to remain top of your class, you need to get moving again and fast," Al Rashid said and his face creased into a smile.

Taqi tried to stand up straight, his lungs still burning. He felt sick but forced himself to look up at the path that ran steeply to the eastern side of the main castle outer wall. All he had to do now was get to the rope secured around the far side and climb the sheer 200 feet high wall to the top to win the challenge. He forced his legs to move, his feet immediately sinking into the soft sand of the path. He glanced briefly at Al Rashid and quickly set off up the path. By the time he reached the main wall, his legs were also burning and his toes were feeling numb in his tight fitting black leather boots, though Taqi did not think them anything like boots, more like socks. Further down the path several other team members were closing on him. He looked up the sheer face of the high wall that seemed impossible to climb. The wall slightly inclined away from him, but the large stonework gave very little to hold onto. Two ropes hung down from the top just reaching the bottom. A small flame flickered on the battlements above where one of the trainers was waiting with a lanthorn, the night creeping in ever faster. He had until the sun totally vanished behind the western hill to his left. If he did not make it, then he would fail the day's task and have to repeat it all again the following day. He pulled on the rope taking up the slack in it. As he tensioned the rope, his arms hurt instantly from his earlier endurance test, carrying two heavy sacks, one in each hand, over a course of nearly ten miles. The others were approaching fast. He spat upon his bare hands, rubbed them together then pulled the rope away from the wall. He placed his right foot against the wall, leaned backwards and despite the pain in his arms and the blisters upon his feet, he started to walk himself up the wall. A single bead of sweat trickled down the temple on the side of his face. He was hot, exhausted and very thirsty. He had sweated so much, his body no longer produced any except that one rivulet...he was dehydrating fast. Half way up the rope, some 90 feet, he had to stop as his arm muscles felt as though they were about to rip. He wrapped the rope around his back and under his armpit and held the rope out so he could rest back into it taking the tension off of his legs and upper arms for a minute. His mouth was dry and he felt dizzy though he was not sure if that was due to the sheer height he was now at or the fatigue overwhelming his senses. He looked down to see the others arrive at the ropes. One grabbed the rope he was on, the tension immediately pulling it down and consequently across his back then across his thigh causing a friction burn. He swung around holding the rope with just his arms, his back bouncing off the wall. As another climber started to ascend, his added body weight pulled the rope hard against Taqi. He struggled to push away from the wall but eventually managed to roll to the side, his knuckles scuffing between the stonework and rope. With the weight of the other climber on the rope, he could not now push out and half walk up the wall. He locked his feet around the rope and started to pull himself up just as one of the trainers below pulled one of the others away from the second rope clearly too exhausted to attempt the climb despite wanting to. Taqi looked up, the sun almost gone from view, gritted his teeth and gave it all he had to climb. The climber below caused the rope to hang tight, which only added to the ordeal. As Taqi slowly reached the battlements and the small opening, he could see the trainer with the lanthorn leaning over and offering his outstretched hand for him to grab. Taqi thought that if he let go of the rope to reach out, he would fall, so kept climbing upwards in very small pushes with his feet locking the rope and pulls with his arms. As he flung his left arm over the battlement, the trainer grabbed him by his cord belt around his chausses and pulled him hard, hauling him over the wall completely landing hard upon the solid stone walkway. As he lay on his back, the trainer immediately looked back over the battlements and waved the following climber on. Taqi was exhausted as he lay in pain on his back, his arms and legs pulled up in agony as his muscles contracted in spasm and cramps. He started to laugh with relief, then thought he would cry with pain but laughed louder instead before realising Al Rashid was stood over him. He blinked his eyes as he focused on him, his tall frame appearing like some giant stood over him. Slowly and painfully Taqi rolled over and forced himself up against the wall.

"How...Master...how did you get up here so fast?" he asked Al Rashid, who was smiling at him, his face lit up by a dark orange glow from the last rays of the sun.

"There are more ways in and out of this castle than you know," Al Rashid replied and looked over at the trainer as he helped haul over the next climber. "Looks as though just two of you succeeded today...," he remarked and rubbed his beard just as the sun finally vanished behind the western hillside. "Taqi, next time a brother offers you help, take it. That was not part of the test to refuse it to complete it alone...you had made it to the top, that was all that was required."

Just as Al Rashid had finished speaking, the other climber rolled around the floor moaning in agony trying to remain quiet as cramp overwhelmed his muscles in both his legs and arms. Al Rashid and the trainer both laughed, their arms folded as they looked pitifully at him and Taqi.

"You think today was hard...wait until the morning," the trainer exclaimed and patted Taqi on his shoulder. "You did well today, very well."

"Indeed, young Taqi. First again in your group. Your father would be proud of you," Al Rashid said and looked down at him and nodded a form of acknowledgement.

"I hope so...Master," Taqi replied.

Taqi forced himself to stand and get his muscles moving again as he had been taught. He had come a long way, he thought to himself as he recalled back to the day when had first met Al Rashid when he saved not only his life, but also his father's and Alisha's. What he would give to be able to spend just one more minute with his father, he thought. A shiver ran down his back and he looked to his right and southward across the plain. How was Alisha? he wondered. Al Rashid watched him as he just stared out across the battlements. As Taqi sighed, Al Rashid knew he was thinking of his family.

"It is only right that you miss your family and father...but carry on the way you are and you will have a family that will never let you down...and we shall not throw your life away on some reckless hopeless cause or mission. That is not our way as I hope you are learning?"

"I cannot hide the fact that I worry for my sister...that is all. I know my father rests...and here I am beginning to learn that there are no limits to what we can do," Taqi replied and leaned forward to look down the high wall. "That I would have said once was impossible after all we have done this day...Master," Taqi explained.

"Good. I understand your sister is in very good company and protected...we do have our spies you know," Rashid said quietly as the trainer helped the other man to his feet. "And as I tell our English recruits, it is all about how you look at things. Impossible becomes I'm Possible," he said with a large grin and winked. "'Tis very appropriate, perhaps silly, but they seem to like that word play. Now come, you two have an early start tomorrow."

As Al Rashid led the way towards a set of stairs that spiralled down, Taqi took one more look south. He felt as if he could sense people thinking of him. He was in Alisha's prayers and he knew it, felt it in a way that was too strong to be dismissed.

It gave him some solace as his exhausted mind fought to stay awake. It was at that exact same time that Stewart had been looking in his direction wondering what he was doing.

Principality of Galilee, Kingdom of Jerusalem, mid November 1179

Stewart lay awake in his bed staring at the small candle that flickered away in the northeast corner of the room. The other eleven men in the dormitory were all asleep. One of them passed wind in a loud and long drawn out fashion as another snorted briefly then turned onto his side. Outside the window the silhouettes of the two Templars on guard were clearly visible. As he turned over on his side pulling the single cotton sheet with him, his wooden bed creaked noisily nearly waking the knight on his right. He could not sleep despite feeling tired. Compared with some of the places he had slept in recently, this castle overlooking the Sea of Galilee came as a most welcome change. He could sense the history in the area. Over the past few months he had come to value, respect and love his fellow Brothers, whom he learnt to rely on and trust with his life. They had shared much and endured much together and La Rochelle seemed so far off and so long ago, but the events that led to Firgany's death tarnished everything. It felt like a stain upon his soul and again he wondered how Alisha and Taqi were and feeling. If it had been his own father killed, he would not bear it. They must hate me, he thought. He had chosen this path and he would stay upon it, besides, what else would he do? He was not talented like Paul, he could not draw...being a Templar was all he had ever thought of being or seen himself doing. His father's words drifted into his mind reminding him that everyone always had three choices. He could almost see his father in his mind, which for a brief moment made him smile. He heard the words his father spoke the day he left to become a Templar squire as if it was only yesterday. 'Stewart, my boy, there are always three paths in life as well as three things in life that once gone, you can never get back. Time, words and opportunity...but know also the three things in life that can destroy a person...anger, pride and not forgiving. And there are three things in life that are never certain...fortune, success and dreams. Plus three things that make a person...commitment, sincerity and hard work. But the three things in life that are the most valuable are...love, family and kindness. If you do not have those three, then you may as well have nothing...but if you lose all of that for whatever reason or circumstance, then keep in mind the three things in life you should never give up on...hope, peace and honesty...and the three things that are constant, Father, Son and Holy Spirit...' Stewart rolled onto his back again as his father's words echoed in his mind. Stewart jumped as he saw a tall figure stood beside his bed looming over him.

"Fear not, Brother Stewart, I have not come to bugger you as your fellow brothers oft joke," Gerard whispered and pulled Stewart's sheet off from him. "You have a visitor who demands your presence now," he explained and walked away.

Bemused, Stewart got up, pulled on his surcoat and quickly tied his sword around his waist, then put on his barrack wear sandals and hurried after Gerard into the corridor.

Stewart followed Gerard along the corridor, Gerard's boots and spurs echoing out with every step. 'Should I have dressed properly?' Stewart asked himself, seeing Gerard was still dressed in full armour despite the late hour. His mind raced as he wondered who could be visiting him. As Gerard turned right into the main reception area, two lanthorns flickering away, Stewart immediately saw the back of a tall woman, her hood pulled up, waiting patiently. 'Alisha' he thought as she turned slowly to face him, but as she looked up and the light from the lanthorns fell across her features, he instantly realised it was Princess Eschiva.

"Brother Stewart. I am so sorry to disturb you this late hour but I was asked to pass on a message to you should I see you," she explained quietly.

"My Lady, 'tis no problem I assure you," Stewart replied and bowed his head slightly.

"I bet it's not," Gerard joked as another Templar entered the room and stood beside her.

"May I speak with you in private?" Princess Eschiva asked Stewart then looked at Gerard.

"You may...but this is not usual practice...be advised young Stewart, no exceptions made here so make this quick," Gerard stated and winked as he ushered the other Templar away to stand with him near the large arched doorway.

"Stewart, I am sorry but I could not tell what message I have to pass on for it is from your brother...Paul," she whispered and leant closer to him. "Raymond knows I am here so there is no impropriety on my part."

"My Lady, but how? For my brother is, or should be, in Alexandria," Stewart answered, confused.

"He is...," she whispered and searched his eyes for any hint of shock.

"Then pray tell how you have a message from him and why is it so important you pass on a message now that could not wait until the morrow?" Stewart asked, puzzled, and frowned. "Are they in trouble?"

"Sssh, not so loud. I cannot tell you the details but I promised that if I saw you, which I did not think I would until I passed you earlier holding the standard so I knew 'twas you. Now here, take this quickly and read it when you are in private surroundings," she explained and looked back toward Gerard and the other Templar stood in the doorway. She handed Stewart a small rolled up parchment sheet and quickly stepped away from him. "All you need know is that he and Alisha and your nephew are very well...that is all."

Stewart looked at the small scroll then quickly hid it away beneath his surcoat as Gerard looked back at him.

"Thank you," he said quietly as Gerard started to walk back toward them.

"Just tell him I was passing on a message from Brother Nicholas."

"What message do I say?" Stewart asked in a panic.

"Just say that Nicholas wishes you to ask Gerard to have him moved to join your troop. I don't know, you think up something," she quipped back quietly.

"Sorry Brother Stewart, 'tis late and you know the rules regarding visitors... especially beautiful ones," Gerard remarked as he stood beside Princess Eschiva. "Your personal guard shall escort you back to your chambers."

The other Templar stood forward and motioned with his hand for Princess Eschiva to leave.

"You will ask for him, yes?" Princess Eschiva asked and began to follow the other Templar.

"Ask what?" Gerard asked and smiled broadly with his hands behind his back and stood up on his heels briefly.

"Erm...'tis, 'tis," Stewart mumbled his words awkwardly.

"Dear oh dear. Sometimes I do despair," Princess Eschiva said as if chastising Stewart. "Master Gerard, you have other knights of your Order whom, knowing of your increasing reputation and courage, and knowing Stewart is your Gonfanier, have asked for him to put in a good word so that they may join your squadron... My Lord...I should have just asked you myself," she exclaimed and shook her head feigning disapproval as she frowned at Stewart.

"Really. I am most surprised and eager to hear whom as most seem desirous to leave my troop as I train them so hard and work them even harder...so who are we talking about? Not your brother surely?" Gerard asked Stewart, partly amused but not at all suspicious of Princess Eschiva's real motives.

"Brothers Nicholas and Upside, I mean Baldwin...Master," Stewart blurted out to confirm her story.

"Ah really. Both very good men...but I am not sure Brother Teric will agree to such a transfer as they are two of his best knights...but as I am the senior Master in the Kingdom at the moment as the Grand Master is...on his travels, I think we can arrange it," Gerard smiled. "Courageous you say they claim?" he asked with a large grin.

"Yes, Master Gerard, that is correct. Your fame spreads," Princess Eschiva replied and put her arm through his and turned him away from Stewart and started to walk him toward the doorway.

The other Templar looked at Stewart and frowned suspiciously, Stewart just shrugging his shoulders at him. As he followed after Gerard and Princess Eschiva still looking back at him suspiciously, Stewart felt the scroll beneath his surcoat.

Port of La Rochelle, France, Melissae Inn, spring 1191

"Well that is not fair on Brother Nicholas. Could they not think of a better excuse?" Sarah interrupted loudly. "Now the poor bugger will probably get saddled with Gerard...the very last place he would want to be I bet?"

"You are so correct there, so very correct," the Templar stated and sighed, rubbing his forehead as if pained.

Miriam looked at him, concerned, seeing the look upon his face. As he lowered his hand, he looked at the old man intently.

"You know don't you?" the Templar asked the old man.

"Yes," he replied and smiled.

"Know what?" Miriam asked, concerned, looking at each in turn.

The Templar sat for several long minutes in silence staring at the old man, who simply looked back at him.

"For heaven's sake, one of you speak and tell us what!" the farrier demanded.

"My brother here," the Hospitaller started to say and leaned forward. *"He was Princess Eschiva's designated personal bodyguard for quite some time on secondment to Count Raymond's forces from Gerard,"* he explained.

All looked at the Templar in surprise.

"So, if you were, then you are the other Templar Knight that eve...yes?" Gabirol asked.

The Templar paused for several moments as he looked at his brother then Miriam before turning to face Gabirol.

"Yes...that was indeed me," the Templar finally said, his voice dry.

"Then...then that means this tale you recount is indeed true!" the wealthy tailor exclaimed in surprise, shaking his head.

"I can but only confirm that the details as the old man recounts did indeed happen, though I know not what the actual conversation was...but I recall very well the occasion and the Gonfanier being woken as detailed," the Templar explained.

"Did you go to Alexandria then?" Miriam asked softly.

"No...I had that very week only been made her personal guard and escort after they had landed back in Jaffa."

"But what about Nicholas then?" Sarah asked impatiently.

"Nicholas...huh, Gerard was not going to let the chance of having two of the best knights in the kingdom slip through his fingers if they wished to join his troop...," the Templar explained. *"Even if they did not actually wish it but was the error of a covered lie!"*

"So poor Nicholas and Upside ended up with Gerard?" Ayleth asked.

"Unfortunately, and much against their wishes, they did indeed," the old man confirmed.

"But that was because of a lie," Ayleth protested.

"Yes it was, but as good knights they followed their orders as handed to them...and that is how they found themselves serving in Gerard's troop alongside Stewart always at the vanguard," the Templar explained.

"And you were there?" Miriam said proudly and clenched his hand tightly.

"I am surprised Princess Eschiva could not have simply got the message to him another way, more discreetly, as her actions nearly compromised them all if you ask me," Gabirol said.

"She had no other way as she was due to leave for Antioch the next day...to discuss matters of state alongside her husband and a delegation from Saladin direct from Aleppo...and I went with them," the Templar explained.

"Can I ask a question...?" Simon asked sheepishly.

"Of course," the old man replied.

"You said that Al Rashid, the old man of the mountains...told Taqi he had English recruits...how is that so?" Simon asked.

"The Ashashin were open to all and any who wished to join their ranks. Whether Muslim or not...'tis another reason why the Templars sought a fusion with them for they shared much in common," the old man explained.

"Well, changing things slightly, and now we know we are in the company of greatness," Simon started to explain and nodded toward the Templar, *"can I ask...talking about Taqi now...if it was so easy to climb the walls of the Ashashin castle, how come Saladin did not manage it when he laid siege to it? Sorry to change the course of the conversation but I had to ask before I forget."*

"My friend, I am glad you ask as I feel uncomfortable talking about matters concerning

me...but I cannot answer that question. Perhaps our more esteemed guest can enlighten us all more?" the Templar remarked and looked back at the old man.

"You should learn to take credit when and where it is due. Modesty is one thing, but to hide it completely to the point of almost denying it only but insults your past. Be proud of what you did and achieved," the old man said, looking at the Templar.

"'Tis exactly what I tell him," the Hospitaller said and smiled broadly at his brother.

"The castle?" Simon interjected, turning his hands over impatiently.

"Simon, in answer let me explain that the Ashashin inherited the castle after they seized it in 1141. The foundations and lower layers of the castle are of Byzantine origin but the upper levels were added by the Nizari Ismailis, whom you know as the Ashashin," the old man started to explain. "Al Rashid knew his castle was built badly...but through deception he made people such as Saladin believe it to be impregnable, plus they greatly feared him."

"Then why stay at a site that is not really a stronghold?" Peter asked.

"Make no mistake, Al Rashid did increase its defences...but importantly, Masyaf Castle and the surrounding countryside functioned as the capital of a Nizari Emirate. As I have already explained, Saladin besieged it in May 1176 but he ended it with a truce after Al Rashid himself had infiltrated Saladin's tent and left him a personal message..."

"I cannot recall you telling us that," Simon commented.

"He did. Just proves you don't listen or cannot remember," Sarah said.

"I did, Simon, but no problem. As I explained, it was not just a simple death threat made against him that caused Saladin to lift the siege...it was one of mutual respect, for Al Rashid could have easily slit his throat as he slept. But also, they had a common goal in seeking a working peace with the Christians and agreed that if called upon, then alongside the likes of Count Raymond, they would all join forces should the time ever arise," the old man explained further.

"What...Saladin working with Raymond?" Peter said, bemused. "So the rumours he was a traitor were true?"

"Well, let me explain the rest of the story before you make a judgement on him and his actions," the old man said. "But as for the castle itself, it was perched on a rock overlooking a boulder-strewn plain with a curtain of mountains directly behind it on its western, northern and eastern flanks and it could be argued that its defence system was really quite poor. But what the Ashashin lacked in might, they made up for in stealth. Plus it had many secret passages and cisterns. Any assault would most certainly breach the walls...but the close hand to hand fighting that would follow would be incredibly costly to any attacking force...," the old man explained.

"I am sorry but I think I must have missed when you explained about the Ashashin for I do not understand what they are exactly other than Taqi joined them," Ayleth said quietly.

"In brief, Ayleth, during the last century, an order of Nizari Isma'ilis was formed in Persia and Syria by a man called Hassan-i Sabbah. These were called the Hashashin, who captured many mountain fortresses and posed a threat to Sunni Seljuk authority in Persia. Hashashin, or Ashashin, but known to us as 'assassins' are most famous and feared for the way they get rid of their opponents...through highly-skilled assassinations. As Al Rashid explained to Taqi many times, is it not better to take out and kill one despot ruler who would lead an army to war, that could potentially kill many thousands?" the old man said.

"But what happens when another ruler takes over who they again simply do not like? Do they kill him also?" Gabirol asked.

"It did not work that way. Taking the decision to assassinate a person was not done *lightly. And remember, the Ashashin, or more correctly Al Rashid, went to great lengths to seek a peaceful existence based upon mutual trust and respect between all sides. Remember, he could have easily killed Saladin and others at any time."*

"Why, were they that good?" Simon asked.

"Yes they most certainly were," the Templar replied instantly.

"I do not see how sneaking into someone's bed chamber whilst they are asleep and slicing their throat is at all honourable," the farrier remarked.

"It takes a rare form of courage to sneak through your enemy's position, to get past well trained guards and then get yourself back our alive...and besides, slicing a man in half on the battlefield is not exactly any more honourable or noble...," the Templar explained.

"If I was to be killed, I think I would rather be killed in my bed, comfortable and asleep rather than wetting myself on the battlefield and seeing what is coming," Simon remarked.

"It can be arranged," Sarah joked looking at him with a mocking look of menace.

"So what did the letter from Paul say to Stewart?" Gabirol asked.

"Well here, read it yourself," the old man said as he pulled out a small flattened scroll parchment and gently handed it across to him.

Gabirol took the parchment and laid it flat upon the table and began to read it.

"Read it aloud please," the Templar asked.

"It reads...'Dear Stewart. We have arrived safely in Alexandria, but not after some considerable experiences with a certain Turansha, the merchant, slave trader and spy. He wished us all dead and did his utmost to do so. As it is our entire family that he takes issue with, I thought it only prudent and wise to inform you. Be on your guard always. If you have cause to run into him, do not be fooled by his words or actions and I pray you instantly slay him where he stands for he will most certainly you. The courier of this message has explained that there is more than a fair chance of meeting you and why we have entrusted this message to be passed on to you via them. We pray it reaches you in time and finds you well. We also wish to tell you that we have given our son a second name of Stewart in honour of you. We hope you will find it in your heart to forgive us for all and any distress and dishonour we have brought upon you. It was never our intention to ever do that. You will always have a welcome in our home and remain always in our thoughts and hearts. Your loving brother, Paul."

 0 – 0

"He asks for that fool's forgiveness. It should be the other way or have I missed something?" the Genoese sailor remarked, surprised, as Gabirol looked up.

"This Paul...he truly has a good heart," he said quietly.

"Yes...as is the case with Stewart also," the old man replied.

"So what happened after he got that then?" the wealthy tailor asked, looking at the parchment.

"A period of relative peace I suppose. Poor Brothers Nicholas and Upside were duly summoned to join Gerard as explained, very much to their disgust, though more so Upside's, and Nicholas actually became firm friends with Stewart despite Stewart's often distant and unapproachable manner at times," the old man explained as he looked at the sword in front of him.

"And what did Stewart make of the letter from Paul?" Ayleth asked.

"The letter...," the old man said and paused. "He took himself away to his favourite spot

overlooking the Sea of Galilee up on the mount, sat amid the old ruined sixth century church, opened the scroll and read it several times...then cried openly and unashamedly."

"Oh bless him," Ayleth remarked sadly and sighed. "Bless him."

Chapter 48
The Halls of Amenti

All in the inn sat in silence looking at the old man as he appeared to drift off in deep thought until Simon coughed loudly.

"Bless Stewart indeed," the old man said softly.

"So what happened next then?" Simon asked impatiently.

"Next? To be honest, the following months simply flew by very fast compared to the chaos and turmoil of the previous two years, and it was a welcome time of just relaxing into a new way of life. Arri grew so fast it was almost unbelievable," the old man laughed. "Tenno tended to spend much of his time with him whilst Paul spent a lot of time with Turansha accompanied by Theodoric."

"What did Percival, Thomas and all his men do during that time then?" Peter asked.

"They trained, trained again then trained some more, every day."

"And visited the whore house!" the Genoese sailor remarked, smiling broadly.

"Yes, yes they did that. Alisha warned them all, she did not care for their activities outside but under no circumstances were any of them to bring a prostitute home to the house. And one thing that both Alisha and Paul did do regularly together, was train in hand to hand combat as taught by Tenno. Even Thomas and his men all began to join in and learn Tenno's ways," the old man explained.

"Alisha did as well?" Sarah asked, bemused.

"Yes. It was a way of keeping fit as well as learning to defend herself. Both Alisha and Paul meant it when they swore never again would they allow themselves to be placed in the position they had found themselves enduring with Turansha, the evil one of course."

"And what about Abi and Sister Lucy all this time?" the farrier asked.

"Lucy was forced to stay longer at Kerak with Princess Stephanie due to hostilities between Reynald and Saladin constantly battling against each other. Princess Stephanie of course welcomed the fact that she stayed as she was a godsend when her baby was born. But Abi, she did as Kratos had advised and spent her time in Malta recovering."

"So does she come back, Sister Lucy that is?" Ayleth asked.

"Yes. 'Twas upon the death of Master Odo whilst still in captivity that she finally managed to arrange a passage to Alexandria. Saladin had been trying to arrange for the exchange of Master Odo for one of his own relatives, his niece, but alas Master Odo succumbed to illness and died in chains before the exchange could take place. I am sure Master Odo was happy about that fact as he refused to be ransomed for it is against the Order's Rule. But at the arranged hand over, Sister Lucy went along with Balian. When the exchange did not go through, it was Turansha who agreed to take Sister Lucy back to Alexandria as well as an embassy consisting of Conrad de Montferrat."

"Why, I mean how come he would go with Turansha?" Gabirol asked, a little perplexed.

"With the death of Master Odo, the acting Grand Master of the Order, Arnold de Tarroja

immediately became the actual elected ninth Grand Master, despite his age of over seventy, and he wished to resolve the conflicts with Saladin as speedily as possible so dispatched Conrad to seek a truce," the old man started to explain.

"He may have been old, but he was certainly brilliant," the Templar interrupted. "But I thought he did not take over as Grand Master until 1181?"

"No...it was earlier, but it took time for the official papers to be authorised and approved, which did take up until 1181. He was as you say a brilliant man. He was a Catalan knight who had served in the Order for many years and was the Templar Master in both the Crown of Aragon and Provence where he had spent most of his time fighting Muslims as well as for Portugal. In reality he was only appointed as the overall Grand Master because he was viewed as an outsider whose power base was outside the Holy Land...a fact that appealed to the Order's political arm, as Grand Master Odo had become embroiled too much in Jerusalem's politics. It was Torroja's influence that greatly reshaped the fractious rivalry between the Templars and Hospitallers. Alongside Master Rogers they agreed the factionalism in the face of renewed Muslim pressure was unacceptable. Later the two Grand Masters met for mediation with Pope Lucius the Third and King Baldwin the Fourth and the problems were resolved for, as it is recorded, Torroja was a skilled diplomat acting as a mediator between several political groups in the East. He also conducted successful peace negotiations with Saladin after raids by Reynald of Châtillon in Transjordan but I shall cover that later. If he had survived, so much would be different," the old man sighed. "But as for Sister Lucy... in no way was she going to miss Arri's first birthday so that was it, and so at the end of April, she found herself being escorted into Alexandria by Turansha alongside Conrad and Brother Teric."

"The peace plan and truce...it obviously did not work that time?" the Templar remarked.

"Not that time it did not due to Reynald's continued actions, but Sister Lucy got to Alexandria. Princess Stephanie pleaded with her to stay and help with her newborn son, named Reynald too, but she was adamant she wished to leave. The first Alisha and Paul knew she was coming was when Turansha arrived at their home with her."

Alexandria, Egypt, late April 1180

In the dusty rear walled courtyard, Paul was trying to punch out at Alisha, as Tenno stood behind her holding her forearms. Every time Paul thrust forwards, Tenno moved Alisha's arms to deflect or block his move. Wearing loose fitting shirts and chausses, Alisha had to keep re-buttoning her top. Theodoric sat in the shade half asleep gently rocking Arri in a small crib as he had his afternoon sleep. Percival, Thomas and two of his men watched Tenno carefully as he instructed Alisha and Paul and tried to copy what he was demonstrating.

"Now do as I have taught you," Tenno whispered in Alisha's ear then stood away from her.

"Paul...if you dare!" Alisha said looking at Paul directly and smiled as she took up a defensive posture.

Paul looked at Tenno briefly then back at Alisha.

"This may hurt you if this goes wrong," Paul laughed as he looked at Alisha, her hair loose and all ruffled.

Quickly Paul lunged for her just as she instantly stepped sideways a little to her left and with her right arm blocked and deflected Paul's right arm away and down, the momentum behind Paul's swing forcing him to fall forwards. Alisha hooked up his right leg, spun around and kicked his left leg up as she went backwards to the ground. Paul fell face first into the dirt as Alisha jumped to her feet and stood over Paul instantly grabbing his hair and pulling it hard.

"Who gets hurt?" she laughed as Thomas and his men laughed loudly seeing her stand over Paul.

"He is fine...fine!" Theodoric called out, confused, still half asleep, saw what was happening then checked Arri quickly. "Yes...still fine," he coughed.

Alisha let go of Paul's hair, and he instantly spun over onto his back, locked his legs around hers and pulled her down and onto her back, immediately rolling on top of her and straddling her holding her down by her arms.

"That's not fair," she called out spitting some sand from her mouth and tried to wriggle.

"Submit?" Paul asked laughing.

"I'll hurt you where it counts," she said through gritted teeth as Paul's eyes fell to her cleavage revealed as her top had unbuttoned again. She scowled at Paul and indicated she was nearly exposing more that she wished.

"If I let go, don't try anything," Paul said and let go of her wrists.

Quickly she raised both her arms up and placed her hands together beneath Paul's left armpit, pushed sideways to her left and sat up fast causing Paul to fall to her side in the dust. Just as quickly Paul grabbed her arms and by so doing pulled her over and on top of him. Paul stuck his fingers in her ribs and made her yelp playfully, Paul's eyes immediately looking down her top again. She saw the look in his eyes and smiled and stopped wriggling as she lay on top of him. For a moment they became oblivious to everything else around them. She laughed softly as Paul put his arms around her and pulled her closer. With her hair hanging down loose, as she leant nearer to him smiling, her hair hid her face as she kissed him. Her soft lips pressed against his, her sweet taste sending a pulse through him. As she broke the kiss, she opened her eyes and looked at him in silence. He could feel the love from her and he felt incredibly lucky to have her.

"Oh for pity's sake, get a room you two. I leave you for a few months and you lose all morals!" Sister Lucy called out as she walked across the courtyard dressed in a full length dress that looked more like a man's habit and wearing a large wide brimmed hat. "Now where is that little man of mine?" she asked smiling at Tenno as she walked past him.

Alisha and Paul sat up bemused but pleased to see her as she rapidly walked towards Theodoric. He was asleep, his foot still resting upon Arri's crib. She kicked his foot hard. He jumped and sat up fast, alarmed, and blinked as the sun silhouetted Sister Lucy so all he could see was a dark figure before him. Alisha and Paul stood up and dusted themselves down as they walked over to them. Sister Lucy huffed and placed her hands upon her hips. As soon as she did that, Theodoric knew exactly who it was and stood up fast. He grabbed her hands and held them tightly.

"My beautiful Luce...am I dead?" Theodoric asked excitedly and shook her hands and kissed them.

Tenno approached with Thomas and Percival, intrigued how she was there.

"Clearly still as blind as a bat...," she replied as Theodoric pulled her close and hugged her tightly, clearly pleased to see her.

Alisha and Paul laughed at the very obvious show of emotion from Theodoric and the stern look Sister Lucy was trying to maintain, but then she too laughed and hugged him back as he lifted her off of her feet and spun her around, her feet knocking the crib. It immediately woke Arri and he cried briefly. Tenno leaned in and gently lifted Arri from his crib and passed him to Alisha as Sister Lucy patted Theodoric, kissed him on the lips, which made Thomas and Percival both pull a face of mock disgust, then pulled back so she could see Arri. As Alisha stepped nearer, Sister Lucy's eyes welled with tears as she looked at him.

"My Lord he has grown," she said as she clasped his little hand, his face red as he sniffed and caught his breath. "And you, you wake him with alarm," she said and playfully hit Theodoric.

"He is fine. He cries very little does this one," Theodoric explained and held Sister Lucy close as she looked at Arri. "Now explain how come you are here...in Alexandria. How did you get here?"

"I came with Turansha," Sister Lucy replied and looked toward the rear court-yard double doors as Turansha stood there, bowed his head politely and entered closely followed by two Mamluk guards and Brother Teric.

As Turansha approached alone, Paul was immediately struck by the gaunt and thin look of his face. He looked unwell and Alisha noted this too. He was carrying a thick reinforced leather parchment tube sealed at both ends. Before he reached them, Conrad de Montferrat followed in behind him and stood with Brother Teric.

"Assalamu Allakham," Turansha said, his voice lower than usual.

"Wa Allakham Assalam," Paul replied and bowed. "Are you okay, for you look a little unwell?" Paul asked.

"A little travel weary...the past months journey has been fraught and...a little difficult. 'Tis why I have come with Sister Lucy now...for I have a gift I wish to bestow and entrust to you...but please, open it later in private," he explained and looked behind him suspiciously at Conrad as he approached with Brother Teric.

"Are they your prisoners?...I do not understand," Paul asked, puzzled how they were there with all the ongoing hostilities and tense situation.

"They are under my protection. Conrad is here as an ambassador...hopefully to speak truce terms...a drought is foretold, a blessing in disguise I think, and we must stop the madness of conflict," he said just as Conrad reached them.

Conrad bowed briefly, looked at Alisha, his eyes immediately gazing upon her open top revealing her cleavage. Awkwardly she started to re-button it as Tenno stepped closer looking at Conrad hard. Thomas laughed seeing his stern reaction. Brother Teric bowed at Paul and he bowed back pleased to see him.

"Come on...today we celebrate. I want to hear all about your journey," Theodoric said excitedly on purpose to break the awkward silence. "And you must tell us how Princess Stephanie is. We hear she has had a son also?"

As Theodoric ushered Sister Lucy into the main house, Tenno gestured for Conrad to follow as he towered over his small frame. Alisha laughed and had to stop herself from being too loud as Conrad followed Theodoric with Sister Lucy constantly looking back up at Tenno. Thomas winked at Paul as he led Brother Teric and they all entered the house.

Alisha handed Arri to Sister Lucy, Theodoric still smiling and clearly very pleased to see her. He looked unusually emotional, which surprised Paul but it was nice to see. Tenno stood at the end of the table just staring at Conrad as Percival sorted them all a drink. Thomas and his two men stood near the main door into the dining area with the two Mamluk guards talking amongst themselves as Turansha pulled Paul aside and to the end of the room. Brother Teric stood silently observing everyone and looking around the large open dining hall.

"I am sorry Conrad invites himself in. As I have warned before, Paul, watch him closely and do not trust him," Turansha said quietly as he placed the parchment tube on the work top beside Paul. "I do not say this lightly nor out of malice or to divide you, but he serves only himself. Please try and remember that."

"Why do you say that?" Paul asked, puzzled, and tried to not look at Conrad too obviously.

"He is supposed to be here to discuss a truce, but all he will talk about is his belief and claim to the throne of the Kingdom of Jerusalem and that we should join with him and help overthrow your king. But you could never prove that so it is pointless revealing such to your lords for they will not believe you. And as I have learnt from bitter experience, it will be you who finds yourself charged with treason."

"How can he make such a claim?"

"Oh he has legitimacy, but he is blinded by greed, wealth and power. I fear he could be as bad as Reynald."

"How so?"

"Because Conrad is smarter than Reynald and he is in contact with that evil piece of work Turansha..."

Paul looked at Conrad, alarmed. Just the very fact that he was in his house was now a major concern. Turansha quickly pulled him around to look at him and away from Conrad fearing his look would give away what he had just been told.

"I have my best and most trusted men watch him. Unfortunately we need him at present to counter concerns of Reynald's continued threats to attack Mecca. I do not understand his zeal to attack us constantly, but I know Conrad there would love to see Reynald removed...so perhaps we can use that to gain support from Conrad's circle for a truce," Turansha explained quietly and paused wincing in pain and holding his stomach. "Though I fear any truce will only be temporary."

"You are in pain. What is the matter?" Paul asked concerned.

"'Tis a bad stomach that is all. It has laid me low these past few days. But here, I wish for you to take this and keep it safe...always," Turansha said and pushed the parchment tube towards Paul. "They are things your father, Theodoric and I put together in Aleppo years ago. You must now take them."

"Why? Why now?"

"Because...because I fear that whatever troubles my stomach is going to kill me," Turansha explained and looked at Paul directly.

Paul could see the intensity in his eyes that he was deadly serious. Turansha placed his hand upon Paul's forearm and squeezed it tightly just as Alisha came over smiling broadly, her hands behind her back, and stood beside them.

"And what plans are you concocting?" she asked raising her eyebrows in mock suspicion.

Turansha grasped Paul's arm tighter then let go and smiled at Alisha.

"Just a gift I wish for Paul to have and accept," he said and looked at the parchment tube.

"Oh really. What is it...or is it secret?" she replied and laughed.

"A secret of sorts yes. Just something Paul's father and I did together."

"Then I must see," Alisha said and went to pick up the tube.

"No! Not here, please," Turansha said and raised his arm in front of her.

She stopped and looked at him quizzically but then placed her hand upon his forehead.

"You are fevered!" she exclaimed, concerned.

"Just a little...nothing anyone can catch I assure you," Turansha replied reassuringly.

"Then you must let Theo make you some threefold water. It will help you," Alisha said and held his hand.

As she held his hand, she felt a strange sensation she had never felt before run up her arm. She momentarily shuddered and looked into his eyes, which displayed an almost helpless look. He knew he was dying and that she could sense it.

"'Tis too late for that, Alisha," he remarked calmly.

Without thinking, Alisha put her arms around him and hugged him. He feigned a brave smile at Paul as Tenno and Conrad both looked over.

"Let us know if there is anything at all we can do," Paul said quietly.

"Look after those. That is all," Turansha replied and nodded at the parchment tube.

Port of La Rochelle, France, Melissae Inn, spring 1191

"So what was in the tube that was so important and why was he dying?" Sarah asked.

"Details about ancient Egyptian Coffin texts and what are known as the Edfu texts. They all relate to the sacred layout and location...though not actual location really, of the so-called Halls of Amenti...or Chambers of Creation. The very sealed vaults that were hidden containing all the previous knowledge, wisdom and ancient artefacts of a former global worldwide civilisation," the old man explained.

"And Turansha. Why was he dying?" Ayleth asked.

"We all must die in all manner of ways, but with Turansha, it was ahead of his time. To this day I shall believe poisoned," the old man explained.

"Poisoned...by whom?" Peter asked.

"The other Turansha I bet!" Gabirol remarked.

The old man simply nodded in agreement.

"Why would he poison him?" Simon asked.

"Because he knew he possessed secrets and he wanted them. He had tried this once before to remove Saladin's brother by arranging for various documents to be found that would implicate him in a conspiracy against Saladin...but Turansha, Saladin's brother, managed to deflect the blame and onto one of the evil Turansha's spies," the old man explained.

"Who was that then?" the farrier asked.

"None other than the good Turansha's own friend, secretary and poet."

"Some friend!" the Hospitaller remarked.

"Yes indeed...but let me explain some more about Turansha for I fear history will not remember him in the way it should," the old man started to explain but checked all were okay for him to continue. "Shams ad-Din Turanshah ibn Ayyub al-Malik al-Mu'azzam Shams ad-Dawla Fakhr ad-Din was his full name but known simply as Turansha. He, like his brother Saladin, was a Kurdish ruler, being the Ayyubid prince or emir as they prefer, of Yemen as well as Baalbek and Damascus from 1176 to 1179 and finally Alexandria. He is known and acknowledged for strengthening the position of his younger brother, Saladin, in Egypt and playing the leading role in the Ayyubid conquests of both Nubia and Yemen. Like many of the Ayyubids, little is known of his early life before his arrival in Egypt and just as well for much of it was spent with people like Philip, Theodoric and Firgany."

"Saladin was his younger brother?" Simon asked, surprised.

"Yes. Turansha had no real desire for power and Saladin only really took it for what good he thought he could do with it. You see, Saladin was vizier to the Fatimid caliph and in 1171, Nur ad-Din Zangi, the Sultan of Syria, allowed Turansha to travel to Egypt to join his younger brother, at a time of rising tensions between Nur ad-Din and Saladin. Nur al-Din empowered Turansha to supervise Saladin, hoping to provoke dissension between the brothers. However, this attempt failed as Saladin granted Turansha an immense amount of lands. Saladin was in the process of rebuilding the power structure of the Fatimid state around himself and his relatives. The iqta' or 'fief' given to Turansha composed of the major cities of Qus and Aswan in Upper Egypt as well as the Red Sea port of Aidab. Turansha was the main force behind the suppression of a revolt staged in 1171 by the Black African garrisons of the Fatimid army so he was certainly a capable individual. He developed a close relationship with the poet courtier 'Umara, who had been a power player in Fatimid politics before Saladin's ascendancy to the vizierate in 1169. On September the eleventh, 1171, the last Fatimid caliph al-Adid died and the Ayyubid dynasty gained official control of Egypt. A number of accusations of murder against Turansha arose following the caliph's death. According to a eunuch in the service of al-Adid's widow, al-Adid died after hearing that Turansha was in the palace looking for him. In another version, Turansha is said to have killed al-Adid himself after the latter refused to reveal the location of state treasures that were hidden in the palace. Those treasures by the way just happened to be the very parchments now given to Paul. After the caliph's death, Turansha settled in Cairo in a quarter formerly occupied by Fatimid emirs. The Nubians and Egyptians had long been engaged in a series of skirmishes along the border region of the two countries in Upper Egypt. After the Fatimids were deposed, tensions rose as Nubian raids against Egyptian border towns grew bolder ultimately leading to the siege of the valuable city of Aswan by former Black Fatimid soldiers in late 1172–early 1173. The governor of Aswan, a former Fatimid loyalist, requested help from Saladin, who immediately dispatched Turansha with a force of Kurdish troops to relieve Aswan, but the Nubian soldiers had already departed. None the less, Turansha conquered the Nubian town of Ibrim and began to conduct a series of raids against the Nubians. His attacks appear to have been highly successful, resulting in the Nubian king based in Dongola requesting an armistice with Turansha. Apparently eager for conquest, he was unwilling to accept the offer until his own emissary had visited the King of Nubia and reported that the entire country was poor and not worth occupying. Although the Ayyubids would be forced to take future actions against the Nubians, Turansha set his sights on more

lucrative territories and he managed to acquire considerable wealth in Egypt after his campaign against Nubia, bringing back with him many Nubian and Christian slaves."

"Slaves?" Ayleth asked.

"Yes...slaves and yes some were Christians. That was the way it was and still is unfortunately. Though Turansha began to change his attitude to this practice the more he learnt,
especially from people like Firgany. Turansha sought to establish a personal holding for
himself while Saladin was facing an ever increasing amount of pressure from Nur al-Din,
who seemed to be attempting to invade Egypt. Baha ad-Din ibn Shaddad, Saladin's aide, suggested that there was a heretical leader in Yemen who was claiming to be the Messiah, and
that this was the principal reason that Saladin dispatched Turansha to conquer the region.
Also, 'Umara, Turansha's poet friend, had considerable influence on his desire to conquer
Yemen and was the one who pushed him to gain Saladin's approval to use such a large part
of the military forces in Egypt when the showdown with Nur al-Din seemed to be so near.
Turansha's departure from Egypt did not bode well for his adviser, 'Umara, however as the
poet found himself caught up in the conspiracy against Saladin when the evil Turansha
tried to implicate Saladin's brother. Consequently 'Umara was executed but it was a close call
Turansha would not forget. In 1174 he quickly conquered the town of Zabid in May and the
strategic port city of Aden, a crucial link in trade with India, the Middle East, and North
Africa later that year. In 1175, he drove out the Hamdanid emir, Ali ibn Hakim al-Wahid,
from Sana'a after the latter's army was weakened by continuous raids from the Zaidi tribes
of Sa'dah. He then devoted much of his time to securing the whole of southern Yemen and
bringing it firmly under the control of the Ayyubids. Although al-Wahid managed to escape
Yemen through its northern highlands, Yasir, the head of the Shia Banu Karam tribe that
had ruled Aden, was arrested and executed on Turansha's orders. The Kharijite rulers of
Zabid, Mahdi Abd al-Nabi and his two brothers shared the same fate. Turansha's conquest
held great significance for Yemen, which was previously divided into three states of Sana'a,
Zabid, and Aden but became united by the Ayyubid occupation."

"So quite a significant figure, and with some considerable political clout," Gabirol noted.

"Yes indeed he was. But although he had succeeded in acquiring his own territory in
Yemen, he had done so at the expense of his power in Cairo. Saladin rewarded him with rich
estates in Yemen as his personal property but he never felt comfortable there and repeatedly
asked his brother to transfer him. In 1176, he obtained a transfer to Syria, which he governed
from Damascus. In addition, he was given large fiefs in Baalbek that used to belong to his
father Najm ad-Din Ayyub. Upon leaving Yemen, the administrator of his estates there was
unable to promptly transfer the revenue from his properties to Turansha. Instead, he left
Turansha behind roughly 200,000 dinars in debt, but this was paid off by Saladin. In 1179, he
was transferred to govern Alexandria and that is when, whilst en route, he came into this
story and met Alisha and Paul." [79]

"So to confirm, Turansha was poisoned by the evil Turansha because he wanted secrets as
written upon the parchments he gave Paul?" Gabirol asked for clarification.

"Yes, that is correct," the old man answered.

"My Lord, Paul was certainly mixing in the highest of circles wasn't he?" Simon remarked.

"And what exactly did the parchments reveal?" Gabirol asked, eager to know.

"That I can answer if you wish," the old man answered.

"Aye please do...," the wealthy tailor said as the rest all nodded in agreement.

Alexandria, Egypt, late April 1180

Paul, Theodoric and Tenno stood around the wooden table positioned in the centre of what was becoming Paul's new study. As Tenno placed a large lanthorn down, Theodoric spread open the parchments as Paul placed the tube down on a chair beside him. It was dark outside and Alisha and Sister Lucy could be heard talking in the bedroom next to them as they sorted Arri out for the night.

"My word...It has been a very long time since last I saw these," Theodoric said as he almost lovingly flattened the expensive velum parchments out.

"Are these the ones you and Father worked upon with Turansha then as he claims?" Paul asked.

"Aye...'twas in Egypt that your father and I first secured these parchments and translations...from Sufi mystics who gave a great account of details taken from what are known as the Edfu texts. It was Turansha who helped us translate them into both Latin and English, for it is the English language that reveals a truer meaning strangely enough," Theodoric explained as Tenno listened intently.

"So what is so important in them?" he asked in his usual blunt manner.

"They start off by explaining the emergence out of the Nun, the primeval waters of creation, of a sacred island. This is identical symbolically to the primeval mound of Heliopolis, a place near to both Cairo and Giza, but also with the island of Glastonbury surrounded by water, and as the Giza pyramids once looked when also surrounded by water. They speak of a 'first occasion', which is identical to the Zep Tepi, the First Time as I and Count Henry explained to you before," Theodoric said and briefly looked up at Paul, "in Jerusalem remember. This original island was known as the 'Island of the Egg' and surrounded by a circle or channel of water, an almost identical description of Atlantis as given by Plato. At the edge of this water was a field of reeds and a sacred area known as 'Wetjeset-Neter'. Glastonbury Tor was surrounded by water full of reeds it should be remembered. Sacred pillars, known as Djed pillars, were erected at the Wetjeset-Neter sites that served as perches for the first divine beings to inhabit the area. Numbering just sixty, they were led by a group known as the 'Drty' the Falcons or Sages who in turn were ruled by a strange figure known as 'Pn' or God."

"A what?" Tenno asked.

"A 'Pn' Just say Pun...Now various other groups were present, but what is of interest here is that these enigmatic beings preceded the highly revered later gods of the Greater and Lesser Ennead of Heliopolitan tradition."

"What is Heliopolitan?" Tenno interrupted.

"They were a group who lived and worshipped in an area of Cairo known as Heliopolis. Sacred processions of the pharaohs were always taken through the area in a northeasterly direction. Anyway, on the original Island of the Egg, a violent conflict broke out caused when a serpent known as the 'Great Leaping One' opposed the sacred domain's divine beings. As a consequence of the battle that followed, all the inhabitants were killed and darkness descended upon the earth again. Alternative names are recorded for the island such as 'The Island of Combat', 'The Island of Trampling' and 'The Island of Peace'. The only thing to survive from this period is a single Djed pillar. In view of all the symbolic connections with pillars from the pillar that Manetho found inscriptions upon, to the pillars of Solomon's Temple, it appears apparent that pillars are of some kind of important symbolic meaning. Eventually a second generation of beings was created known as the 'Shebtiu'. The new leaders are known as Wa and Aa known as the 'Lords of the Island of Tramplings'. Eight members of the Shebtiu were given special names yet for no apparent reason, the significance being the value of eight itself. The Wetjeset are joined by other divine beings as well as a figure known as the Falcon. He is known as the 'Lord of the Perch' and 'The Winged One'. He commands a group of individuals known as 'The Crew of the Falcon'. They are also known as the Senior Ones, Elders or the Elder Culture to denote Egypt's divinity. This second generation of divine beings was known as the Netjeru who became the new rulers of Wetjeset-Neter. Eventually they built a temple known as the 'Mansion of Wetjeset-Neter'. The Edfu Temple texts state that this building stood in a vast enclosure which surrounded an inner enclosure which held the real temple. Exact details are given as to its measurements of thirty cubits west to east and twenty cubits from south to north. This temple eventually became damaged or destroyed and the Shebtiu Wa and Aa were ordered by the god of the temple to enter a place named 'Place in which the things of the earth were filed with power'. This is yet another name for the water encircled island. Inside magic spells caused the water to recede by using mysterious power objects known as 'iht', pronounced 'icked', that had been stored within the temple. After all this, the Shebtiu simply sailed away to whom knows where. After a period of time, the world began to evolve again and the Wetjeset-Neters were succeeded by the Shemsu-hor, who were the ancestors to the pre-dynastic Egyptian race led by Horus of Behdet. He led to the first Horus kings that led up to the foundation of the first Dynasty of a united Egypt in 3,100 BC. The Edfu texts preserve the memory of a long forgotten culture that built Egypt's first temples way before the first pharaohs. It is worth noting that after the Island of the Egg re-surfaced from beneath the primeval waters after the period of conflict, it became a tomb for the ghosts of the first divine beings. After its emergence it also became known as 'Underworld of the Soul' and became the first resting place of the body of Osiris, the God of the Underworld. The important point to note here being that the term Underworld is that as used in the Heliopolitan texts to describe the Duat Underworld, whilst the resting place of Osiris is being linked with the fourth hour, which forms part of the House of Sokar. I shall explain the hours shortly," Theodoric explained enthusiastically and coughed. "Now Orion is positively linked to the Giza plateau known as Rostau. Osiris can be linked with both Giza as Rostau and with the House of Sokar, the region in the Duat that is also linked to the apparent subterranean chambers and passages thought to exist beneath the Giza plateau. In turn, as we discovered, the original first sacred mound of the Wetjeset-Neter, with its field of reeds, water encircled island and temple complex, was indeed the Giza complex. Now what may surprise you, if the ancient maps of the world are correct, is that the Giza site geographically marks the centre of the entire earth's landmass, and the three main pyramids are constructed upon a raised mound of stone. When they were originally constructed, the entire Giza plateau was indeed a fertile and lush green area with an abundance of water. Not only that but a broad trench was cut into the rock to channel water from the Nile to the Giza site. The Osireion Temple at Abydos was also linked to the Island of Creation as outlined in the Edfu texts. Its cyclopean structure differentiated it from all the other temples in Egypt. This temple is in fact far older than believed and was constructed by the same people who were behind the construction of the Giza and Dashur sites...Not the Egyptians! What is so intriguing about the Osireion Temple though, is the fact that it has a water channel all around its inner walled enclosure that is fed by a well thus mimicking in stone a representation of the Island of Creation. The very fact that the ancients placed so much importance upon the water element is not surprising as we are mainly made up from it and totally dependent upon it. The prehistoric Creation Myths of Edfu recall specific individuals, events, locations and building projects from the epoch of the Elder Gods. Yet encoded in these ancient textual accounts is much more than this...clues that, if interpreted properly, will reveal the nature, appearance and meaning of what has remained in darkness beneath the bedrock of the Giza plateau for the past 11,500 years. The Underworld of the Soul can be considered to be the main source behind the legends of the Duat Underworld. The Edfu texts state that this area can have an alternative title of 'Bw-hnm', which means that the place is a physical reality as the prefix 'Bw' actually translates as 'place' and the suffix 'hnm' has several meanings. It can mean 'kingship' as in coronation, a 'coming together' as in royal jubilee festival, or it can mean a 'consecrated well'...or simply 'place of the well'. However it can also be translated Bw hnm as 'a deep underground place that is constructed', which the translations strongly hint at being the correct interpretation. The Edfu texts inform us that the iht relics as mentioned earlier were in fact stored in the Bw hnm with Shebtiu guardians being able to enter and conduct magical spells that continued the act of creation outside. Accordingly at the bottom of the Bw hnm, the underground structure, there could well be the so-called Halls of Amenti or as they named it, the Chambers of Creation or Hall of Records containing the lost legacy of a forgotten race of great antiquity. As I mentioned earlier the earliest form of name for the primeval mound in the Edfu texts is the Island of the Egg. The egg, swht, is never fully explained as to what exactly it is. It is described as a creative force used for the formation of the earth. As with all Egyptian names, this egg was known by many different names such as bnnt, meaning, 'embryo' or 'seed'. This was seen as the nucleus of the iht power objects as used in the Underworld. The egg has also been associated as being one and the same as the so-called 'great lotus' or 'throne'. So perhaps here we can see the origins of the symbol of the lotus, which was eventually symbolised in France by the fleur de lys!"

"Ah I did wonder where all of this was going," Tenno interrupted.

"Then let me draw your attention to the word bnnt translated as 'embryo' as this is in fact a female rendering of the masculine root bnn, which means 'to copulate, to beget, to be begotten, virile, phallus'. It is derived from the same root as bnbn, or benben, the name given to the stone, obelisk or pyramidian, which were all associated with the primeval hill. This particular benben stone was none other than the 'builder's stone that was rejected', the chief corner stone, as in the Great Pyramid's missing capstone pyramidian. All records show that the Great Pyramid always had its capstone missing and a Merkaba star set on top of it."

"So if I understand you correctly, my father, Firgany, Turansha and you had these parchments that detail all of this as being translations taken from ancient Egyptian texts...the Edfu texts, that state or claim that the underground complex located beneath the original primeval mound of Giza or Rostau is actually a physical representation of a benben stone. And that beneath Giza there are passages represented by the various hours of the Duat, the Underworld?" Paul asked.

"Yes, Paul. The Edfu texts in simple terms tell us that what we are dealing with here is some kind of enormous stone, buried underground at the heart of, or at least central to, the Giza complex. From a symbolic perspective, if we view the Giza complex in its celestial representation of Orion, the central and most important star to the constellation is in fact Orion's heel star, Sirius. Yet at Giza and the surrounding area, where Sirius would be projected in relation to the three main Giza pyramids, there is nothing on the ground, not even a very slight raised mound. The very obvious omission of Sirius being represented on the ground in the first place should scream at us to ask why."

"I do not understand this meaning projection of Orion over Giza...do you?" Tenno asked looking at Paul.

"No neither do I for it has not been explained to me," Paul remarked.

"What. I am certain I did...Did I not?" Theodoric asked, surprised. "Well, in that case I shall have to show you one of my own parchments...No, wait," he said as he flicked through the many parchments and pulled out one and placed it on top of the others. "No need for here is one of the same."

Fig. 49:

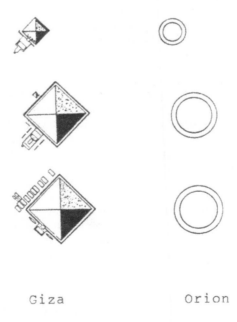

Giza   Orion

"Look, 'tis the constellation of Orion when projected over the three main pyramids of Giza. They match...and all the other stars of the constellation also match up with pyramids upon the ground."

"How do you know this? For that cannot be measured," Tenno asked.

"Because the ancient parchments recovered in Jerusalem tell us so...and they have so far been proved correct in every other aspect. And there will come a day in the future when man will again be able to confirm these details as true. Also, there is an ancient Egyptian coffin text, in particular the spell numbered 1,080, which reads 'This is the sealed thing, which is in darkness, with fire about it, which contains the efflux of Osiris, and it is put in Rostau. It has been hidden since it fell from him, and it is what came down from him onto the desert of sand.' This indicates a benben stone laying buried at the heart of the Giza Rostau's subterranean complex. The fact that it has fire about it means it has a pyramid as the root word for pyramid is Pyr, which means, 'Fire'. Also all the texts speak of the twelve hours of the Underworld and the Duat. We all know the importance of the value of the twelve....both for its numerical value and symbolic value. Now we have seen the value of twelve and also seven throughout the Bible and Holy Grail legends so I would like to bring to your attention, in regard to all I have explained, the story of Enoch when he found himself taken on a visit to the seven heavens. Once in the seventh heaven, he found that he was alongside a house built of crystals and surrounded by strange tongues of fire. The floor had the appearance of crystal with a ceiling like the path of the stars and lightning. Inside the room there were moving wheels as bright as the shining sun and beneath it came streams of flaming fire. Enoch is stating the same thing as the Egyptian Coffin texts: 'the sealed thing with fire about it'. It is possible that the fire being referred to in both cases was merely light shimmering and refracted through transparent crystal like surfaces. Philip and Firgany both believed that the power iht relics were hand held, identical to the staff that Kratos carries and a lingam style crystal resonating the natural energy contained within the nucleus located at the heart of the complex. The Babylonian god Oannes was portrayed as carrying in his hand a device of power and also the curious legends that feature Enoch that claim some kind of sacred stone was placed beneath the Giza pyramids."

"Sorry...what is this god Oannes? "Tenno asked, puzzled.

"Oannes. He was a Babylonian god. He is depicted as half man and half fish, but if you look closely at his images, you will see he is a man who resided in the sea by night for protection, but came out of the water by day to teach mankind. He wears a fish suit over his head and down his body. When the Babylonians spoke of him, they said he had two faces, an outer face of a fish which he could remove and reveal his human like face," Theodoric explained.

"Like a waterproof suit of some kind then?" Paul remarked.

"Absolutely...but to a primitive race it would seem magical and that he had two faces, one just being some kind of mask. But also symbolically it can represent a being that is both physical and spiritual as coming from water, which is aqua, which stands for spirit. And remember the Merovingians how their founder king was supposedly born of two fathers, one a being from the water, and hence why they are still called the Fisher Kings! But back to Enoch...for the Jews of Alexandria during the Ptolemaic period viewed the Great Pyramid as having been made by Enoch himself, who was also equated with Thoth or Hermes. Enoch was said to have been the inventor of the twelve fold division of the starry canopy which is reflected within the astrological sections of the pseudepigraphal books accredited to the patriarch. Enoch then went on to become confused with later stories circulated among the Copts of old Cairo that featured the legendary King Saurid Ibn Salhouk, who, being warned of the coming deluge, built the pyramids of Giza and then constructed secret chambers in which all the arts and sciences of his race were preserved."

"All...I mean everything I am hearing from you seems to come from great antiquity and pre-dates all that is stated within the Bible...Does that mean our Bible is wrong?" Paul asked.

"No not at all. If anything it reinforces its validity, even if it is taken from older sources of great antiquity," Theodoric replied. "According to one lost tradition, Enoch constructed vaults, in which he sealed away items that included tablets inscribed with strange words that angels had given to him. The vaults were sealed and then Enoch constructed two indestructible columns, one made of marble so that it might never burn, and the other made of Laterus, a form of floating brick, so that it might not sink in water. It is worth noting that on the brick column, the seven sciences of mankind were inscribed. On the second column he placed an inscription stating that a short distance away, a priceless treasure would be found in a subterranean vault. Now we can of course simply choose to ignore these stories as pure fable, but as they all seem to be saying the same thing and using the same symbology, especially as these legends bare no connection at all with Enoch's few brief mentions in the Book of Genesis, nor does he appear in any other Hebrew sources. We can even gain some idea of the actual layout of the complex from the account of the Duat Underworld as outlined in Heliopolitan cosmological tradition when it speaks of the first division or hour consisting of an 'arrit', which means a hall or anti-chamber of the Duat. Once past this entrance, there were twelve more divisions or hours to pass through. This symbolically indicates twelve further chambers or rooms. As the symbolic journey involves moving from one division into the next, this suggests that the rooms are connected, and as they are related to the sun passing in a circular motion it is tempting to think of the chambers being formed in a circle. Further support for this idea comes from the fact that we know that the twin Aker lions, which were set as guardians at the gates to the entrance and exit of the Duat Underworld, can be seen as representative of the equinoctical horizon during the processional cycle of Leo represented by the Sphinx. There were two at one time but the second one now lays broken and buried. The chambers also represented the twelve fold division of the ecliptic. Even more substance to the suggestion that the actual chambers of the Duat were formed in a circle comes from the fact that the Duat was itself conceived as being round like the path of the sun. Also the Sun God Ra, in the 19th and 20th Dynasty wall inscriptions, is referred to as 'Ra, exalted Sekhem, Lord of the hidden circles, bringer of forms, thou restest in secret places and makest they creations in the form of the God Tamt'. The Duat was often described as being composed of circles."

"But that is identical to the layout you spoke of depicting the New Jerusalem and as overlaid on Stonehenge and Glastonbury Abbey," Paul stated.

"I know...exactly, and even the layout of the Kabba stone in Mecca," Theodoric replied and smiled. "Exciting isn't it? Now as the egg of creation was in the middle of the Duat, then it becomes clear that it is in actual fact situated in the centre of a circle formed from twelve smaller circles as you have already made the connection. So the actual pyramidian, benben stone, that stone that the builders rejected and mentioned in the Edfu texts, is situated at the centre of a complex surrounded by twelve chambers and buried in the Duat Underworld. 'Tis indeed an exact geometrical illustration of the New Jerusalem. It would therefore appear that a design pattern of twelve chambers, all connected to myths of buried sacred books of wisdom and knowledge and mathematical codes, have indeed been passed down through the millennia of time intact from the darkest depths of antiquity." [80]

"So where is this final location? Why has no one recovered it yet?" Tenno asked eagerly.

"How do you know it hasn't been already?" Theodoric asked, looking at him. "But I tease for as I have mentioned previously...the contents of what lays hidden must remain so as it is not for our times, just as Moses, Akhenaten whatever name you give him, realised and was forced to reseal the one chamber he did manage to access."

"And you say that all myths, legends and even our own Bible all contain these same codes and clues that clearly spell out...or point to, its location?" Paul asked more intrigued.

"Yes, yes they all do with all their inherent obvious mathematical codes and symbolism. It is all there...but we simply cannot work it out yet, and even if we did, we would be denied access for we are but the guardians who must make sure the codes remain until the future generation that can understand them needs what is hidden...and only then."

"And safeguard the bloodlines of those who can actually use the tools, of course?" Tenno remarked just as Thomas entered the room.

"Conrad has finally left. Brother Teric along with Percival, John and Peter are escorting him to Turansha's. Pity Turansha had to leave early...he does not look well," he remarked. "Sorry...please continue what you were saying."

Paul acknowledged Thomas and continued.

"So you do not actually know the location of any of these halls?" he asked, surprised.

"No...how mad is that?" Theodoric laughed and looked up at him as Thomas closed the door behind him.

"No more mad than people living in fear of two omnipresent beings that don't really exist as they are told. Or the mad people who usually spend their time finding ways to judge others in the name of their god even though their own holy book forbids them to do so," Tenno stated.

"Were you born a cynic?" Theodoric asked.

"No...my cynicism is sadly backed up by hard reality and experience...'tis a skill I have perfected over many years dealing with ignorant fools," Tenno replied.

Thomas looked at Paul not sure if Tenno and Theodoric were joking with each other or not.

"Well it is those ignorant fools who will guarantee they carry faithfully the messages which contain the concealed codes...now here look at this image," Theodoric said and pulled another parchment and laid it out on the table. "This is a scaled image of the planets Mercury, Venus and our earth. Notice how they marry up perfectly with the sizes of the three Giza pyramids. We know the measurements of the Great Pyramid refer to earth and its actual size, as well as distance from the sun, so we are pretty certain the others likewise relate to the size and dimensions of Mercury and Venus."

Fig. 50:

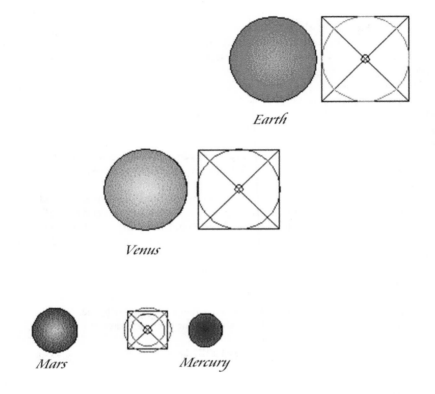

Earth

Venus

Mars   *Mercury*

"Is this genuine?" Thomas asked as he looked at the images laid out upon the table.

"Yes...and Turansha has entrusted them to us...for safe keeping," Theodoric explained. "Well, to Paul at any rate."

"I cannot do it alone," Paul replied instantly.

"You do not have to," Thomas remarked and stood up.

"All that we have learned will be either hidden or destroyed by the Church. The language of the Egyptian symbols will vanish unless we protect it. It has already all but gone and very few can now read it," Theodoric explained as he studied the parchments then looked at Paul intently.

Port of La Rochelle, France, Melissae Inn, spring 1191

"'Tis my understanding that the language of the ancients is forever lost. No one can now read or understand what the symbols mean," Gabirol remarked, looking at the old man.

"That I am afraid is true. Though I can confidently say there are still a few who know

how to...but for their own safety, they cannot reveal themselves. And many translations as Paul had do survive," the old man replied.

"So am I correct in understanding then that the Giza pyramids are not tombs nor built by the Egyptians or have I misunderstood you?" Peter asked.

"You have heard correctly, Peter. Egyptian tombs, from across their vast history, are adorned with symbols and pictures, but the Giza pyramids are totally devoid of any inscriptions of any sort. Besides, even the ancient Egyptians themselves tell us quite categorically that they did not make them," the old man explained.

"Really...where?" Gabirol asked.

"They have an ancient book, fortunately already copied into Greek, called the 'Virgin of the World' where it details how Queen Egyptus, pregnant with the child of a god was expelled into the desert. She saw on the horizon three gleaming stars of light, which turned out to be the three Giza pyramids reflecting the sun brilliantly. She arrived at the pyramids and that is where she stayed and it is from her we get the name Egypt from."

"But we are told they are tombs," Ayleth remarked, looking confused.

"No. No pharaoh, in fact no bodies, have ever been recovered from within any of the Giza pyramids."

"But it has a stone coffin, a sarcophagus, inside the main pyramid," Gabirol said.

"'Tis no coffin, my friend. It never had a lid and its dimensions are identical in proportion to form that sacred item all of you are familiar with," the old man smiled.

"The Ark of the Covenant!" the Templar said quietly.

"Yes," the old man nodded.

"Then what in the Lord's name are they for and who built them?" the wealthy tailor asked.

"That I shall explain later in more detail as that part of the story will reveal why and by who, but for now, please believe me when I say they are not tombs. They are thousands of years older than you can imagine, and they also contain vast knowledge and wisdom and they once created a most powerful and limitless free energy that fed a worldwide grid."

"So what happened to the parchments Paul was entrusted with?" the Templar asked.

"Stephan...would you?" the old man said softly.

Stephan stood up and quickly left the room. All around the table looked at each other puzzled as the old man smiled. After a few minutes they had sat in silence, Stephan reappeared carrying a large reinforced leather tube. Sarah looked at him in shock almost as he placed it on the table directly in front of the Templar.

"Where did that come from?" Sarah asked, surprised.

"Oh...it has been above our bed," Stephan smiled.

"And you are telling me the same parchments you speak of are in there?" the Templar asked as he looked at the tube before him.

"Yes I am indeed. And if you accept the charge and commission contained within your letter, then we shall be entrusting their continued safe keeping to you," the old man answered.

The Templar opened his eyes wide and shook his head in surprise as his brother looked at him also puzzled. Miriam smiled proudly.

"You...you know far more about me than you have let on don't you?" the Templar said, his voice dry.

"That, my good knight, I do. 'Tis not deception I play upon you, but a necessary measure for my own peace of mind that you are indeed the best man suited to do this...if you choose," the old man replied solemnly.

"So you knew all along that I and my brother were to be here when you first sat beside us?" the Templar asked, bemused, still looking at the tube.

"Yes, my friend, yes. Did you not question or wonder why your respective Grand Masters sent you back here to La Rochelle and to this inn specifically to dine?" the old man asked and looked at the Templar then the Hospitaller.

"I did...," the Hospitaller replied instantly.

"We were told we could dine well here first before reporting to our ships prior to leaving for Outremer to be part of King Richard's Crusade," the Templar explained and sat up straight. "Pray tell, have we been played?"

"No, not played, my friends. I would like to see it as guided. Would you not both agree you are tired and weary of war?" the old man asked.

The Templar looked up at his brother as he clasped his hands together looking nervous all of a sudden. Emotion began to register across the Hospitaller's face and he nodded his head nervously and embarrassed. The Templar reached across and placed his hand upon his brother's hands reassuringly.

"I think the expression upon my brother's face answers that question," the Templar replied as the Hospitaller fought to control the sudden surge of overwhelming emotions that seemed to well up uncontrollably as soon as the old man had said his last remark.

"Phew...I think you have touched a nerve there, old man," the Hospitaller blurted out as tears welled in his eyes.

"Good, for it tells me all I needed to know," the old man replied and paused for a moment as he looked at the Hospitaller as he struggled to contain his emotions, embarrassed. "Let me tell you both...you will not be going on any Crusade. You have more than done your fair share of war...and any more would just break you."

"I am afraid you are wrong there, for whatever is written in the letters you have given us, our ships leave soon and we have orders from our masters we cannot break," the Templar explained as Miriam sighed sadly.

"My dear knights...Check the seals on the back of your envelopes again carefully for they are the seals of your own Grand Masters. I will not reveal what the contents are as that is private to both of you, and you will have a choice to make, but the one choice you no longer have is that you will not be returning to Outremer," the old man explained.

As he finished his words, the Hospitaller screwed his eyes up tightly and gritted his teeth as he desperately fought to control his emotions as he started to cry upon hearing that news. He shook as the Templar squeezed his hands reassuringly again. All looked at the Hospitaller, Ayleth covering her mouth in shock having never seen a man cry before. The release of tension and realisation that he would not be returning to war, war that he was so thoroughly exhausted and weary from, was just too much for the Hospitaller and he could not stop the tears. Miriam stood up and placed her arms around his shoulders as he sobbed. The Templar with tears welling in his own eyes looked across the table at the old man in silence.

"Thank you," the Templar said in a whisper.

The old man bowed his head as Simon wiped away a tear quickly hoping that no one had seen him, Gabirol shook his head and smiled as the Genoese sailor looked on a little confused. Peter and the farrier smiled, more to hide their emotions they felt for the Hospitaller.

As the Hospitaller sat upright, his fists clenched, all the years of pressure seemed to flow from him in great waves of sobbing tears. He kept his eyes shut. The Templar stood up and beside him and put his arm around him as Miriam moved aside.

"Is it true, our service is finished and our ships already gone?" the Templar asked, looking at the old man then toward the windows.

The old man nodded yes in silence, but as the Hospitaller had his eye shut, he did not see. He forced his eyes open, his lips quivering unable to speak for a moment.

"Truly?" he finally managed to blurt out. The old man nodded yes again. "Thank God," the Hospitaller said quietly, closed his eyes again and just sobbed. As he shook, Ayleth wiped a tear from her eye.

"How is it that you have the ability, the authority to raise such orders and bring them here? How is it you already knew of these two before they even arrived?" Gabirol asked.

The Hospitaller upon hearing his question opened his eyes and fought to stop his tears. All looked at the old man.

"That I shall reveal at the end of this story...and as promised, then you can open your sealed letters that will reveal exactly why," the old man replied.

The Templar sat back down and patted his brother's shoulder as he did.

"Then I pray tell you get on with it, please," the Templar said and beckoned for Miriam to come and sit beside him.

"Does this mean you will be staying?" she asked quietly as she sat down.

"Looks like it, my woman," the Templar replied and held her hands.

Immediately she clasped her hands to her mouth and the tears instantly ran down her cheeks in silence. He kissed the side of her face and pulled her close as she closed her eyes crying with happiness.

"Oh my Lord, please continue this tale before we all end up crying," Simon said aloud.

Sarah leaned across and thumped his arm, looked at him hard before suddenly breaking into a nervous laugh and nearly crying herself. 'Sorry' she mouthed at him silently.

"I think I had better," the old man laughed and pulled himself nearer to the table.

Alexandria, Egypt, late April 1180

Theodoric and Paul remained in his study room after Alisha had quietly called the others down for a light evening meal. It had been a long day and certainly emotional for Theodoric with the arrival of Sister Lucy.

"Let them sort the others out first eh? Besides I wanted to explain to you that, as your father and I discovered, there are in fact twelve pyramids on the Giza complex, though just eleven remain...one was destroyed. But where that pyramid once stood, you can still gain access to a massive underground complex of tunnels. But I strongly advise you never enter...for you may not come out again," Theodoric explained as he rolled the parchments up carefully.

"And my father knows all of this?"

"Yes...and much more besides. What a great time we would have if he was with us now eh?"

"Yes that I do not doubt. I have not shown you my drawings that I did from my dreams have I?"

"No, Paul, you have not. But I would caution you who you show," Theodoric said as he inserted the rolled parchments into the tube.

"Why?"

"Because, because you reveal things that some people will recognise...But the way you draw...you execute your images in such a realistic fashion...'tis truly remarkable."

"What is wrong with that?"

"Paul, the Church takes issue with the Celtic Church over how it draws images, especially holy images of saints and depictions of events. They argue that as God created the world, only he can create images that look real. 'Tis why images I have remain hidden, for what people do not understand, they will condemn and persecute you."

"But why, that is insane. My father draws beautiful images with the drafts he produces for his building plans...and what about my ship designs?"

"They are not viewed in the same manner or way. But the pictures you drew of Alisha...I can tell you now, they will be looked upon as being wrong. I knew a man who could draw and make the image look real...," Theodoric explained and placed the end cap on the tube and sealed it.

"And what happened to him?"

"He was burnt at the stake accused of being a sorcerer trying to capture the souls of people in his pictures. In league with the Devil to compete against God..."

Paul looked at Theodoric, surprised.

"That is truly insane!" Paul remarked as Theodoric opened the door and motioned for Paul to pick up the lanthorn.

"Yes it was. Now tomorrow, I shall show you on the maps some places of hidden wisdom...structures, some obvious and some still buried. If Alisha allows it."

"You mean if Sister Lucy allows you," Paul said as he followed Theodoric out of the room and closed the door behind him.

Theodoric smiled at Paul but inside his stomach knotted. 'If those who watch over you allow it more like' he thought to himself and questioned if what he was about to set in motion was the correct course of action and whether he was actually steering both Paul and Alisha in the right direction and ultimately safety...or mortal danger!

ꕤ

A single candle cast its light across two parchments held open by the leather clad hands of a knight, the chain mail on his forearms glinting in the darkness of the room. As the parchments were spread fully, identical symbols were pointed out by a single black covered hand tapping a finger upon them.

"Our Templar informant copied these well from Gerard's originals...now we know for certain," the knight whispered, his hands moving the parchments until Pauls name was positioned beneath Alisha's name. A black bladed knife stabbed down upon Alisha's name, and then cut downward across Pauls name. "Their lines must be eradicated...forever!"

Bibliography – Book 2

27: After – Extracts from Livius.org. Alaturka.com. Tarsus-Mersin Wikipedia (Contains full listings of sources).

28: Ater – 'Studies in Ancient Judaism and Early Christianity', by Pieter W. van der Horst.

29: After – 'New Researches on the Quran: Why and How Two Versions of Islam Entered the history of mankind', by Dr. Seyed Mostafa Azmayesh

30: After – Emmanuel Le Roy Ladurie (1975) Montaillou, 'The Promised Land of Error', Random House/editions. Gilmard, Lambert, Malcolm (1998), 'The Cathars', Oxford: Blackwell. 'Confessions of an Illuminati, Volume III'. 'Espionage, Templars and Satanism', by Leo Lyon Zagami.

31: After – 'Christianity Revealed – Christianity and the Essenes', by Dr M D Magee. Michael Walsh (2003). 'Warriors of the Lord: The Military Orders of Christendom. Grand Rapids', by William B. Eerdmans Publishing,

32: After – Smail R. C. 'Crusading Warfare 1097–1193', New York, Barnes & Noble Books, (1956) 1995. & 'Crusaders Castles of the Twelfth Century', Cambridge Historical Journal 10, no. 2 (1951).

33: After – 'The Great Tale of Prophet Adam & Prophet Jesus In Islam', by Muham Sakura Dragon. Sobhani, Ja'far; Shah-Kazemi, Reza (2001). 'The Doctrines of Shi'ism: A Compendium of Imami Beliefs and Practices'. I.B.Tauris. 'Five Pillars of faith' by Arthur Goldschmidt Jr. & Lawrence Davidson (2005). 'A Concise History of the Middle East', (8th ed.). Westview Press.

34: After – 'RASHID AL-DIN SINAN', by Dr. Naseeh Ahmed Mirza. Melbourne (Australia) Alamut.com

35: bible-history.com

36: After- Nun, Mendel 'Gergesa (Kursi) Kibbutz Ein Gev', 1989. Nun, Mendel 'Ports of Galilee Biblical Archaeology Review 25/4: 18, 1999'. Holm-Nielson, Svend Gadarenes in 'Anchor Bible Dictionary vol. 2, ed', D.N. Freedman. New York: Doubleday, 1992. Weber, Thomas Umm Qais, 'Gadara of the Decapolis Amman', Economic Press Co, 1989. M G Easton. Illustrated Bible Dictionary. 1897.

37: After – Bernard Hamilton, 'The Leper King and His Heirs: Baldwin IV and the Crusader Kingdom of Jerusalem', Cambridge University Press, 2000. Steven Runciman, 'A

History of the Crusades, vol. II: The Kingdom of Jerusalem', Cambridge University Press, 1952.

38: Raynald of Châtillon – Wikipedia. (Contains full listing of all sources).

39: gotquestions.org

40: Selected Poems By Suhrāb Sipihrī.

41: After – 'The Templar Revelation: Secret Guardians of the True Identity of Christ', By Lynn Picknett, Clive Prince.

42: After – Campbell, Duncan B. (1988). 'Dating the Siege of Masada'. Zeitschrift für Papyrologie und Epigraphik. 73 (1988): Cotton, Hannah M. (1989). 'The Date of the Fall of Masada: The Evidence of the Masada Papyri'. Zeitschrift für Papyrologie und Epigraphik. 78 (1989): Richmond, I. A. (1962). 'The Roman Siege-Works of Masada, Israel'. The Journal of Roman Studies. Washington College. Lib. Chestertown, MD.: Society for the Promotion of Roman Studies. Zeitlin, Solomon (1965). 'Masada and the Sicarii'. The Jewish Quarterly Review. Washington College. Lib. Chestertown, MD: University of Pennsylvania Press.

43: After – 'Jerusalem's Mysterious Well of Souls May Hold Ancient Secrets', by Mati Milstein. National Geographic.

44: After – 'What is Beneath the Temple Mount?' By Joshua Hammer. Smithsonian Magazine. April 2011.

45: After – Jeremiah 20:21.2 Kings 24:25. Daniel 1:1. to Daniel 3:25. Ezekiel 41-42. Barbara G. Walker. 'The Woman's Encyclopedia of Myths and Secrets'. New York, HarperCollins, 1983. Revelation 1:18. G.R.S. Mead. 'Pistis Sophia' Kila, MT, Kessinger Publishing. Ephesians 6:11-13. Matthew 13:49-50.

46: After – 'The Conference of the Birds' by Farid al-Din Attar. 'Animal Symbolism in Celtic Mythology', by Lars Noodén 1992. Davidson, H.R. Ellis. 'Myths and Symbols in Pagan Europe: Early Scandinavian and Celtic Religions', Syracuse University Press: Syracuse, NY, USA, 1988. René Guénon, 'The Language of the Birds', Australia's Sufi Magazine. 'The Treasure' 2 1998. Ormsby-Lennon, Hugh 'Rosicrucian Linguistics: Twilight of a Renaissance Tradition,' passim. Ed. Ingrid Merkel, 'Hermeticism and the Renaissance: Intellectual History and the Occult in Early Modern Europe', 1988.

47: After – bahaistudies.net. Mead, G.R.S. 1921. 'Pistis Sophia', London: & 1892. Simon Magus. & 1900. 'Fragments of a Faith Forgotten', London: The Theosophical Publishing Society. Legge, Francis (1964) [1914]. 'Forerunners and Rivals of Christianity, From 330 B.C. to 330 A.D'. (Two volumes bound as one ed.). New York: University Books. (Original Cambridge University Press edition, 1915.)Harris, J.R.; Mingana, A. (eds.). 'The Odes and Psalms of Solomon', Manchester. Text 1916; Translation and Notes 1920. Hurtak, James and D.E. Hurtak, 'Pistis Sophia Text and Commentary'. Los Gatos: Academy For Future Science, 1999. J. M. Watkins. 1st edition (1896): Masseiana Revised 2nd edition (1921): Charlesworth, James H. (1973). 'The Odes of Solomon',

Brock, Ann Graham. 'Setting the Record Straight – The Politics of Identification: Mary Magdalene and Mary the Mother in Pistis Sophia', Jones, F. Stanley, ed. (2002). 'Which Mary? The Marys of Early Christian Tradition', Leiden. Pearson, Birger Albert (2004). 'Gnosticism and Christianity: In Roman and Coptic Egypt', New York & London: Continuum International Publishing Group. Horton Jr., Fred L. (2005). 'The Melchizedek Tradition: A Critical Examination of the Sources to the Fifth Century A.D. and in the Epistle to the Hebrews'. Cambridge University Press. Williams, Frank (2009). 'The Panarion of Epiphanius of Salamis', Book I (Sects 1-46) (Second ed.). Leiden; New York.

48: After – Battle of Jacob's Ford. From Wikipedia. (Full sources listed).

49: After – 'Oaks or Terebinths?', by Philologos. Bill Morris.

50: After – Benjamin Creme – Share International. share-international.org.

51: 'The New View over Atlantis', Paperback – 17 Feb 1986 by John Michell. Astrological age & from Wikipedia. (Full sources listed).

52: 'Gods of the New Millennium', Alan Alford. Hodder Headline. 'Gods New Millennium', free open source.

53: After – 'Did Ancient People Really Have Lifespans Longer Than 200 Years?' By Tara MacIsaac , Epoch Times.

54: 'Dinocrates. GREEK ARCHITECT', by: The Editors of Encyclopædia Britannica.

55: After – 'The Legendary Emerald Tablet'. Ancient Origins. 'Mysticism and Heresy: Studies in Radical Religion in the Central Middle Ages', (c.850-1210) by Angus J Braid.

56: After – Lee Krystek – unmuseum.org/7wonders/catacomb.

57: After – First Things – 'The Perniciously Persistent Myths Of Hypatia And The Great Library', by David Bentley Hart & Atheist Delusions: 'The Christian Revolution and Its Fashionable Enemies'.

58: After – Miriam Kamil, 'Ancient Origins. Dreams and Prophecy in Ancient Greece'.

59: After- April Holloway, 'The Indian Sage who developed Atomic Theory 2,600 years ago'. Ancient Origins.

60: After – Ancientscripts.com – chapter Auraicept na n-Éces in the 15th-century work 'The Book of Ballymote (Leabhar Bhaile an Mhóta)', by Prof Curtis Clark of Cal Poly Pomona – Ogham font.

61: After – 'Pure Spirit, Bee Symbolism', by Ted Andrews's, 'Animal-Speak', by Jessica Dawn Palmer's, plus 'Animal Wisdom', and Steven D. Farmer's 'Power Animals'.

62: After – 'Egyptian Gods I' by Sir Ernest A Wallis Budge.

63: After – 'Gods Warriors – Crusaders, Saracens and the battle for Jerusalem', by Dr Helen Nicholson & Dr David Nicolle.

64: After – G Hancock. 'Imprint of the Gods', Pygmalion 1995. 'Yggdrasil And The Cosmic Chaos', Xavier Séguin.

65: After – 'The Golden Thread of Time: A Quest for the Truth and Hidden Knowledge of the Ancients', by Crichton E M Miller

66: Hamilton, Bernard (1978). 'The Elephant of Christ: Reynald of Châtillon'. Studies in Church History.

67: After – 'The Cult of St Katherine of Alexandria in Early Medieval Europe', by Christine Walsh, Ashgate 2007. wikipedia.org/wiki/Catherine_of_Alexandria. (All sources fully listed).

68: After – 'The Hidden History of the Secret Church, An Introduction', by Zaidpub in Catholicism, Christianity, Gnosticism.

69: After – 'The Religion of the Samurai: A Study of Zen Philosophy And Discipline in China and Japan', by Kaiten Nukariya. Cosmio Classics, New York.

70: After – 'Saladin and the Saracens', MEN-AT-ARMS 171, Osprey Publishing, by Dr David Nicolle.

71: After – 'Trioedd ynys Prydein: the Welsh triads', by Rachel Bromwich, University of Wales Press, 1978.

72: After – 'Ancient Origins. 'Silphium, the ancient contraceptive herb driven to extinction', by Martin Clemens.

73: After – 'Holy Blood, Holy Grail', by Michael Baigent, Richard Leigh and Henry Lincoln. 'A Critical Commentary and Paraphrase on the Old and New Testament …, Volume 2', by Simon Patrick, William Lowth, Richard Arnald, Moses Lowman, Daniel Whitby. 'Secrets of the Code', by Dan Burstein. 'The New View over Atlantis', by Jean Michelle. 'The Hiram Key', by Christopher Knight and Robert Lomas.

74: 1911 Encyclopædia Britannica, Volume 26. Templar's. knightstemplarorder.org (Full sources listed).

75: After – 'Holy Blood and the Holy Grail', by Michael Baigent, Richard Leigh and Henry Lincoln. 'Order of Saint James of Altopascio', Paperback – 1 Jan 2012 by Ronald Cohn Jesse Russell.

76: After – 'Bloodline of the Holy Grail' Paperback – 1 Sep 2004 by Laurence Gardner. 'Holy Blood and the Holy Grail', by Michael Baigent, Richard Leigh and Henry Lincoln. 'The Book of Secrets and Notes about the known history of the Royal Grail families of Europe', by William Walter Warwick IV. 'In Search of the Holy Grail and the Precious Blood: A Travellers' Guide', by Deike Begg, Ean Begg. 'The New View over Atlantis', by Jean Mitchell.

77: After – Gildas – Wikipedia. (Full sources listed.)

78: After – 'A Classical Dictionary: Containing an Account of the Principal Proper Names', by Charles Anthon. 'Tiberias – The four evangelists', by Minzar Terra Santa. Custodia.org.

79: After – Houtsma, Martijn Theodoor and Wensinck, A.J. E.J. Brill's 'First Encyclopaedia of Islam', 1913-1936. (1993). Sobernheim, Moritz (1913), 'Baalbek', Encyclopaedia of Islam: A Dictionary of the Geography, Ethnography, and Biography of the Muhammadan Peoples', 1st ed., Vol. I, Leiden: E.J. Brill, pp. 543–544. Mohring, Hannes. 'Saladin: the Sultan and His Times'. Baltimore, Maryland: The Johns Hopkins University Press, 2008. Maalouf, Amin. 'The Crusades Through Arab Eyes'. London: Saqi Books, 1984. Holt, P.M. 'The Age of the Crusades: the Near East from the eleventh century to 1517'. 1 ed. 'A History of the Near East. 2', 'The Age of the Crusades: the Near East from the eleventh century to 1517', by P.M. Holt. New York: Longman Group, 1986.

80: After – 'The Amduat papyrus of Panebmontu', by John H. Taylor. British Museum. 'When Time Began', by Zecharia Sitchin.

Lightning Source UK Ltd.
Milton Keynes UK
UKHW011219130119
335492UK00001B/66/P